Fri July 16-93

FROM SEA
TO SHINING SEA

FROM SEA TO SHINING SEA

James Alexander Thom

BALLANTINE BOOKS • NEW YORK

Library of Congress Catalog Card Number: 83-91168

ISBN 0-345-33451-5

Manufactured in the United States of America

First Trade Edition: July 1984
First Mass Market Edition: December 1986
Eighth Printing: December 1990

For my mother
DR. JULIA S. THOM
A pioneer in her own time

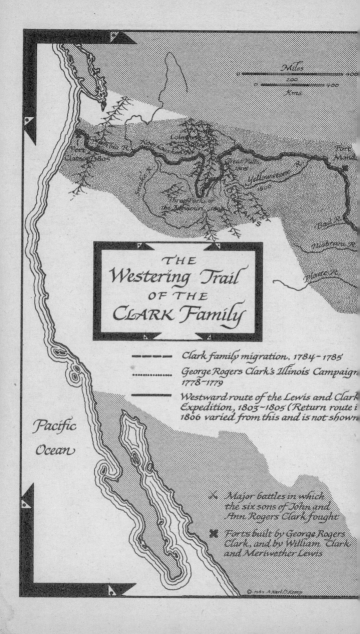

0 | Miles | 400
0 | 200 | 400
Kms

Pacific
Ocean

THE
Westering Trail
OF THE
CLARK Family

– – – – Clark family migration, 1784–1785

· · · · · · · · · · George Rogers Clark's Illinois Campaign
1778–1779

———— Westward route of the Lewis and Clark
Expedition, 1803–1805 (Return route in
1806 varied from this and is not shown)

✗ Major battles in which
the six sons of John and
Ann Rogers Clark fought

✗ Forts built by George Rogers
Clark, and by William Clark
and Meriwether Lewis

N

Battle of
Paulus Hook,
Battle of 1779
Monmouth, 1778

Battle of
Brandywine, 1777

Battle of
Germantown, 1777

Battle of
Fallen Timbers

Detroit

Fort
Pitt

CAROLINE COUNTY

Harmar's Defeat, 1790

ALBEMARLE
COUNTY, VA.

nse of St. Louis,
Kashaskia, 1778

Birthplace of
Jonathan and
George Rogers Clark
Thomas Jefferson and
Meriwether Lewis

Fort
Jefferson, 1780

Atlantic
Ocean

Sieges of
Charles Town,
1776 & 1780

Mississippi R.

Northwest Territory~Captured from
British by George Rogers Clark and
ceded to U.S. after the Revolution

Kentucky~Founded by George Rogers Clark

Lands first mapped by William Clark
in 1804–1806

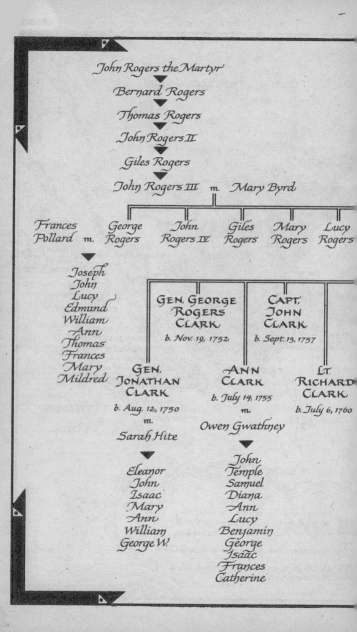

John Rogers the Martyr

Bernard Rogers

Thomas Rogers

John Rogers II

Giles Rogers

John Rogers III m. Mary Byrd

Frances Pollard m. George Rogers · John Rogers IV · Giles Rogers · Mary Rogers · Lucy Rogers

Joseph
John
Lucy
Edmund
William
Ann
Thomas
Frances
Mary
Mildred

GEN. GEORGE ROGERS CLARK
b. Nov. 19, 1752

CAPT. JOHN CLARK
b. Sept. 15, 1757

GEN. JONATHAN CLARK
b. Aug. 12, 1750
m.
Sarah Hite

Eleanor
John
Isaac
Mary
Ann
William
George W.

ANN CLARK
b. July 14, 1755
m.
Owen Gwathney

John
Temple
Samuel
Diana
Ann
Lucy
Benjamin
George
Isaac
Frances
Catherine

LT. RICHARD CLARK
b. July 6, 1760

The CLARK Family Tree

Elizabeth Wilson Clark m. Jonathan Clark

...ildred Rogers | Byrd Rogers | Rachel Rogers | ANN ROGERS m. JOHN CLARK

m.
Rev. Donald Robertson

...APT. ...MUND ...ARK ...25, 1762

ELIZABETH CLARK
b. Feb. 11, 1768
m.
Col. Richard Clough Anderson
▼
Richard C. Jr.
Elizabeth
Cecilia
Ann

LUCY CLARK
b. Sept. 15, 1765
m.
...j. William Croghan
▼
John
George
William
Charles
Charles
— TWINS —
Lucy
Elizabeth
Edmund (DIED IN INFANCY)
Nicholas

GEN. WILLIAM CLARK
b. Aug. 1, 1770
m. (1ST)
Julia Hancock
▼
Meriwether Lewis
William P.
George Rogers Hancock
m. (2ND)
Harriet Radford
▼
Jefferson

FRANCES ELEANOR CLARK
b. Jan. 20, 1773
m. (1ST)
Dr. James O'Fallon
▼
John
Benjamin
m. (2ND)
Capt. Charles Minn Thruston
▼
Charles William
m. (3RD)
Judge Dennis Fitzhugh

I am Ann Rogers Clark. My blood's flowed across this land like rivers, from sea to sea.

If ye know my name, tho' that's not likely, it's on account o' the deeds of my offspring, which were considerable. I mean the deeds were considerable. Aye, but the offspring were considerable, too. I bore ten, my first in 1750 and my last in 1773. Their father was John Clark, as solid and goodly a man as ever did eat bread.

Of my children, six were boys, and they all came up heroes, each in his own ways. There's kinds o' heroes, y' understand. There's conquering heroes, and exploring heroes, and thinking heroes, and then there's enduring heroes. My boys were all of those. Lord ha' mercy, what they did! That ye well know; it's in history books.

Most men would say the fame of her sons is fame enough for a woman. Most women would say likewise. Even I, oftimes, have said 'twas enough for me.

But what I've done, that's considerable, too. I bore them, and I reared them through all the croups and agues and festerations, and the putrid fevers and the tick-sicks—not a one o' mine died a child, as many did in those days—and I made them what they were, with a little help from menfolk and tutors. And then I watched them go out one by one to battlefields and frontiers they'd likely not come back from, all over the high and low and the hither and yon of this land, where they'd tend to risk their dear fool necks against every sort o' hazard that God, Devil, King, or Man could conjure.

That's no inconsiderable thing, what a mother o' heroes does.

Wherever they went, my young'uns, they went first, and showed the way, all across this continent. They took big chances and made big changes. And talkers! They could change the look o' the world by what they said about it, and harangue men into doin' what they'd never ha' thought they could do. A joke and a song and a dream o' glory, they'd say, will carry a man through the Doors o' Hell. Some of my sons had dreams o' glory that the others made to come true, you'll see as you hear their story. They were all of one heart, they were made o' flint and steel, and they were bold. Aye, it was boldness that put the name of Clark in all the history books and clear across the map o' this land, from sea to sea. No one family wrought more change on this country than did the Clarks o' Virginia, and they were my offspring, I'm proud to say.

What follows is the story of what we did, and how, and who we were, and why. I'll vow there's not a made-up yarn y've ever heard to compare with it.

BOOK ONE

1773–1784

1

MASTER BILLY CLARK, THE YOUNGEST OF THE SIX SONS, SAT in a bright, warm rectangle of September sunshine on the waxed wood floor of the nursery and played with the gray wooden horse with red saddle and wheels that his Papa had carved and painted and given to him on his third birthday. He rolled it a few inches on the floor by pulling its string, and thought about the real horses in the stable, about how they smelled and blew their noses. But most of his mind was on something far away and outside, and most often he was gazing at the sky outside the west window, seeming to listen for those songs or sounds that only a child can hear.

He saw the sunlit blur of his blond eyelashes, and heard, in the shadowy part of the room beyond his island of sunshine, the pleasant voices of his oldest sister, Annie, and his Mama, who had baby sister Frances Eleanor at her breast. The baby made wet sounds and said, "Ng, ng," in her throat, and the women's rocking chairs creaked.

They were talking again about that thing called Annie's wedding, which was to be soon. Annie talked about it all the time now, with joy and fear in her voice. The boy didn't understand much about it and was not very interested in it. But he liked the music of their voices in the room.

He was always enveloped in the voices of his family. Their voices were always around him like a comforter of many colors. Even when his Papa and his older brothers were out in the barns and fields and woods, and his sisters were elsewhere in the house, he could hear their voices, and the sounds of what they were doing, and know where they were. Right now he could hear his Papa's deep voice outside below the window, with the murmuring voice of Cupid the skinny slave man, and the *thunk, thunk* of a mallet striking wood. And . . .

He frowned, and listened hard again for that faraway some-

3

thing, trying to hear through the spinning shrill of the locusts His Mama would always say he was like a dog listening for summer thunder. Something not quite a sound, something in th sunny distance beyond the meadow gate, had at last softly troubled his inner ear, and his heartbeat sped up a little and h looked at the blue sky over the yellow-green treetops.

But he could not tell yet. He turned back to his little woode horse. He picked it up in his right hand and with his left h reached for a large ball, a ball made of a dried, inflated pig bladde painted blue and green. He put the wheels of the wooden hors on the surface of the ball and made it roll, as if the horse wer walking around the world. Then he put them down and listene hard again, now with his eyes shut so he could hear even better His Mama and sister were still talking, and the baby was stil groaning and sucking, and his Papa and the Negro were stil talking and hammering down in the driveway, and the locust were still shrilling, but now Billy knew something was coming something out beyond the meadow gate, though he could not ye really hear it, and he was growing excited, and behind the brigh orange of his sunny eyelids he began to see a remembered face, a pair of dark blue eyes like his own.

"Mama!" he said. His eyes were open wide.

Ann Rogers Clark turned to him. "Aye, son?"

"Jo jee common!"

"Say what? Georgie's comin'? Nay, Billy, I think not Georgie's far, far yonder,"—she nodded toward the west—"ou behind the mountains, where th' Indians are. Y'know that."

He shook his head and frowned. "Jo jee common," he insisted

"Mought be he's right?" black-haired Annie suggested. "H always knows where we all are. Uncanny-like."

"I know. But . . . No. George wouldn't come over the moun tains now. Not with harvest so close. Not if 'e grows twenty bushel o' corn to the acre out yonder, as he claims. Though tha sounds a tall tale to me."

"But," said Annie, "he'd come home for my wedding!"

"Sure and he might, if he knew of't. But he doesn't."

The boy had abandoned his ball and horse and was standing now at the window with his little hands gripping the sill, looking and listening out over the plantation.

The only people he could see outside were his Papa and Cupid. They were inserting poles lengthwise through two hogsheads of tobacco. These poles would be axles when the barrels were pulled to market by oxen along the rolling-road.

Mrs. Clark and Annie were talking of weddings again, but the woman, bemused, was watching the boy. It was strange how he always just knew where everyone was. Now and then it proved embarrassing, as when he'd turn up brother Johnny romancing some wench or other under a haymow or in the barn loft. It was strange, that special sense of Billy's, and it was strange about his dream

Mrs. Clark began rocking her chair again while the baby sucked. She saw how the pressure of the baby's mouth mottled and wrinkled the tired skin of her teat. Twenty-three years she'd been bearing and nursing her children, and now one of them, her own namesake, was about to marry and begin the same great, absorbing, demanding, body-and-soul-consuming occupation. For Mrs. Clark, this was a bittersweet time. Now she returned her gaze to Annie's flawless oval face, her wide-set brown eyes, her always-smiling mouth with its full underlip. Her beauty was ripe now. She would begin bearing within this year surely, and with the years those firm teats of hers would darken and wrinkle like these.

"Ye listen now, Annie, as I'm just about to give the very advice my own mother, rest her soul, gave me ere I married your Papa. She said to me, 'Ann girl, your man will have you with child all the time, if y' let him. I've had nine o' you,' she told me, 'and I love y'all as I love my life, but if I had it to do over, I'd rest a couple o' years between. Now, only way to keep your man off you,' she told me, 'is nurse your babies longer, like the Indian women do.'

"That's what she told me, Annie, and she spoke true. A man thinks that if ye have a babe at your teat, y're still too much in motherin' to lay with 'im yet. A man doesn't know much about such things, and so if he respects you at all, and I know Owen does, why, he'll not press ye. He mought go jump on a slave woman, but he'll leave y' be, remember that, Annie."

"But Mama, y've bore ten of us," Annie laughed. "Didn't ye remember her advice, or what?"

Mrs. Clark's blue eyes looked at a corner of the ceiling and she nodded and pursed her lips. "I remembered it. After I'd had Jonathan, and then Georgie right away after him, why, methought I'd nurse Georgie a long spell and get some respite from that man stuff. I mean, bearing children's a fine thing, most important thing a body can do, I suppose, and what our Dear Lord fit us out to do, but after two, why, the marvel of it'd wore off, and I remembered your Grandmama's advice, and I thought t' try it. But . . . Well, it would ha' worked, I reckon, 'cept I couldn't go through with it. I'd see your Papa was a-wantin', lusty man that he is, and I'd feel guilty like some sham dodger, not worthy o' good John Clark.

"And, too—Damnation, girl, I'll just out an' say it: When John wanted me, I wanted John. And so I weaned little Georgie."

Annie clapped her hands and laughed, red-faced. "Oh, Mama!"

"And so 'twas, by the very next year, '54 that was, you came along, my darlin', our first girl, and John honored me by naming you after me. And a blessing y've been every day o' those eighteen years since. So, I guess—"

A gunshot echoed out of the woods.

"KSH!" Billy imitated it, pointing a finger. "Eddie shoot tokey!" Then he turned his gaze back toward the road, down beyond the meadow.

"See?" said the girl. "He always knows."

"Aye. And indeed Edmund will have a turkey, by Heaven. He never misses."

"You were but fourteen when y' married Papa, weren't you?" said Annie, turning back to marriage talk, her heart's main concern.

Mrs. Clark put the baby girl on her shoulder and patted her back. "Fourteen. Aye, I've been raisin' children far longer than I ever was one myself. Yes, m' darlin', I'm tired and half broken down by children now. But what better could I ha' been doing, I always say, than bringin' you ten wonders into this world? If pride's a sin, then I'm a sinner. And, then, our Good Lord loads us only with such burdens as he created us fit to carry. I . . ."

She looked at Billy, who still gripped the windowsill, gripped it hard, his sturdy little body poised like a question mark, his copper-red hair ablaze with sunlight. What on earth has got ahold of him? she wondered.

"You're not a bit broke down!" Annie was protesting. "You're the most beauteous Mama in Caroline County, nay, in all Virginia, you are." That was an accepted truth, but one that always made Mrs. Clark snort. She snorted.

"If beauty's what keeps a man jumpin' on ye, I'd as soon have been homely as ham," she grumbled. But then her face diffused with a golden smile that meant she'd been jesting. "Y're a kind girl, Annie, and kindness is the best of all your beauty. Thankee for your loving words."

Billy now was flexing his knees and glancing frantically toward his mother, then back out the window. He gave a curious little hop of excitement and cried: "Jo jee common, Mama! He *is*!"

And then they heard it, faint, far down the Fredericksburg Road, a voice raised in an Indian yodel, and a moment later it came louder, and they rose a little in their chairs, feeling shivery around their necks and shoulders, and after a while they could hear hooves beating up the dirt road from the meadow gate, and Mrs. Clark's heartbeat quickened. Feet were thudding on the floors downstairs, all going outdoors, and girls' voices were exclaiming, and when Billy darted away from the nursery window and down the stairs, Mrs. Clark rose with the baby on her shoulder and looked out the window down the road between the rows of oaks. She saw her son Johnny in shirtsleeves and brown breeches sprinting down the driveway yelling, "Well, hey! Well, HEY!" and saw a drift of dust coming among the trees. And then a horse and rider burst into view at the end of the rail fence, the horse a sweat-stained roan, the rider dressed in pale deerskins, now howling the name of Johnny, who stood in the horse's way poised to spring, his left arm raised and crooked.

"By heavens, Annie, it is George!" He was dressed as usual like a red savage, and coming at full gallop now he leaned out and hooked his left arm in Johnny's as he rode past him, yanking him off the ground and swinging him up behind the saddle, that old daredevil trick of theirs. And now the lathered horse with both of them on its back came skidding to a rump-down halt below the nursery window in a billow of dust, as the family swarmed laughing and whooping to welcome George home from the frontier, their surveyor, their backwoods adventurer, their Seldom-Seen, as John Clark often called him. Every time he came back it was a surprise and a commotion. Every time. Mrs. Clark carried the baby girl and hurried down the staircase, smiling, tears in her eyes. He was her secret special lad, George was, the first one born with red hair and the look of her Rogers family about him, and she thanked God he was home safe once more after a long, fearful unknowing.

He looked ever more like an Indian as he strode in the front door with a rapturous, wild-eyed, squealing little Billy on his shoulders and all the rest reaching to touch him and crying greetings to him. She noticed that these were no crude rawhide garments he'd made himself, such as he'd worn on previous homecomings, but fine, neat doeskin things, tunic and loincloth and leggings, tanned soft as velvet and decorated with fringes and thrums, colored beads and quills. "Aha," his father was telling him, in a joshing tone but looking somewhat pained, "ye've got yourself a squaw out yonder." George just laughed at that, neither affirming nor denying it.

7

"Hey, Mama," he said in a deep and tender tone when he saw her in the hall, and he drew her close in his right arm to kiss her forehead and the red hair over her ear. He smelled of woodsmoke, horse sweat, and something like a wild animal musk. He looked down at the baby in her arms, at the swirl of thick, nearly black hair, at the dark brows and long lashes. "Now here's a Clark I've not met yet," George said. "She looks like you, Pa. A Clark and it rhymes with dark." Mr. Clark chuckled at that old litany of the family phenomenon; they had alternated like that with but one exception, the ten children: Jonathan the firstborn had been dark like his father, then George red-haired like his mother; then Annie dark, Johnny redheaded, Richard dark, Edmund a redhead. Then Lucy had broken the pattern for the moment, and was the only red-haired girl of the clan. Then Elizabeth, dark-tressed, and redheaded Billy, and now this black-haired lastborn. But even the dark-haired ones were tinged by the Rogers coloring; in sunlight their hair was highlighted copper-red. And their complexions were fair and lightly freckled. For there had been Rogers blood not far back in the Clark family, too. Ann Rogers Clark's husband John was in fact one of her cousins, which to her meant that the bold blood of the Rogerses had flowed two ways into her offspring.

This George, though! To her he was the quintessential Rogers, like her beloved father and brothers: an adventurer, a soul-swaying talker, a man born to stir up the world. She stood back now amid the clamor of her children and looked him in the face to see if the past year in the wilderness had changed him. There was still that imp's smile, the dimpled cheeks, the piercing dark blue eyes, the hawk-sharpness of his long nose, and that square chin. His face was brown as cordovan now, and his red hair and eyebrows, usually the color of an Irish setter's coat, were sunbleached light as straw. But there was something deeper in his merry eyes now, some new sad knowing, as if he had learned something important in this past year, his twentieth year. She'd know what it was ere long; he'd let it out as he talked.

And there astride his shoulders was Billy, who worshipped him and dreamed of him though he'd only seen him three or four days of his life, Billy who was a replica of the George of seventeen years ago.

"Well," she said at last, and her eyes traveled over his elegant leather garb, "if y' do have a squaw, bring her here to sew for your family, eh? For she plies a neater needle than any of us!"

"No squaw, you two! Ha, ha! Put that out o' your heads. But

isten, I've been with a Mingo family. No finer a people. Wait ill I tell you of Chief Logan. Hey! I've a thousand tales to tell nd but just a few days to tell 'em in! Now, say! Lookahere! What's this varmint a-crawlin' on my shoulders? Is it a coon, or catamount, or what?" Billy went into gales of tickled laughter s George hoisted him off his shoulders toward the ceiling and hen lowered him to the floor. The boy immediately grabbed his ndian belt and proceeded to climb back up.

"What sayee: just a few days?" exclaimed John Clark. "You're :oing right back out?"

"I'm comin' to the capital to plat out some lands I've sur- -eyed, is all. Got to get back to harvest."

"But Annie's bein' wed next month. Surely y'll stay."

"Is she now! Are ye now?" he cried, turning to find her in the nob and cupping her flushed cheeks in the palms of his hands. 'And who's the man? Is it Owen Gwathmey?"

"Aye," Annie said, her brown eyes overflowing anew at the vonder of her betrothal. "Owen," she gasped.

"Well, by my eyes! You're smart, Annie! A hundred rakehells nd dandies after you, but y' chose one sound man! He'll take :are o' you well, that one will! I admire Owen; he's a brick!" Now he turned to a tall youth beside him. "Dick! Hey, young- ter, you're horny-handed now. Is Pa workin' ye hard?"

"By heaven, he is! Like a field slave," Dickie laughed. He was hirteen, erect, big-footed and rawboned. His dark hair was lank vith sweat. He had run in from the fields.

"And where's Eddie? Hullo! Here he comes!" Edmund ran tomping through the front door, red forelock flying, a long rifle n one hand, a turkey slung over his shoulder dribbling blood, its ead shot off. Edmund was eleven. He flung down his bird and eaned his gun against the wainscot, then pressed in among his rothers and sisters to give George a shy hello and hug. "Hey, iow, Eddie, that's the *hard* way to shoot a turkey. I'll have to lave a match with you! Can't let you outdo me, now, can I? Aha! Lucy up there! How's my favorite redheaded sistereen, any- oo?" She had bounded halfway up the stairs to get up where she could look at George over the heads of the others. She was :ight, a blur of red curls and big freckles. She held a hand out ver the bannister and grinned, showing him a homemade rock ling and a gap where her front teeth had been. George recoiled n mock astonishment. "By Jove! What'd ye do, shoot yourself in he mouth?" They all roared with laughter, and she squirmed nd licked her mouth corners in delight and embarrassment.

They had been moving slowly along with him in the hallway

toward the sideboard where the decanters sat. Billy was back up on him now, sitting on his left arm, while grave, milky-skinned little Elizabeth, five years old and demure, held his right sleeve and trailed along, waist-high in the press of tall people.

John Clark bustled happily ahead of his brood, his body thick and hard as an oak trunk, grinning yellow-toothed, his dark hair grizzled at the temples and queued in back, his face handsome, kindly, etched with smile lines and rugged as a rock cliff. He reached for a decanter and set out five crystal glasses. "Brandy from Burk's peaches, remember?" he said, and poured for himself, George, Dickie, Johnny and Edmund. The five clinked their glasses together. It was their tradition that a son could join in toasts after his tenth birthday. Annie poured sherry for herself and her mother.

"To homecoming, our beloved son, with thanks to the Supreme Director of All Things for your safety."

"Homecoming and thanksgiving," George said, and they drained their drams. "Now," George said, turning to them with a brilliant smile, like an actor to his audience, "God love us all, let's eat and catch each other up on all the news o' the year! What's our new Royal Governor like, Pa? I hear he's locked horns already a few times with the House o' Burgesses."

"A King's man to the marrow, Dunmore is," growled John Clark. "Packed the Court with Tories, and no one's happy with 'im."

"Lucy," said Mrs. Clark, "run tell Rose to fetch Master George a roast, to hold him till supper." The girl leaped down the stairs with a flash of petticoats and ran out to the kitchen house bawling for the cook in a tomboyish voice.

"I hear talk of a patriot committee in the House," George was saying. "D'ye know much about it?"

"Aye. We'll talk of't after a bit, though," John Clark said. "Kings' politics and tyranny are no fit subjects for children's ears."

"Indeed not," said Mrs. Clark, drawing back the corner of her mouth in a rueful half-smile. "They'd rather hear you tell of scalpin' and flayin' Indians, and an explanation why y've still got your own hair on your head."

"Aye, George," Edmund exclaimed. "Ha' ye kilt any savages yet?"

"Oh, the contrary! I hate to disappoint ye, Brother, but of late, Indians been my best friends. Listen, I'll tell of a kinship a hundred times more interesting than fighting!" At these words, his mother's blue eyes looked deep into his. She did not smile, but there was a softening, an easing, of the fine careworn lines in her face.

The Clark house was large and the central hall was wide and long, but it was growing very crowded now. Black faces peered in through the family circle as servants edged closer to see this wild man back from the far fearsome places, this big-voiced wild man whom one or two of the older women could remember rocking to sleep or wetnursing, twenty years ago.

"Jo jee," young Billy had been imploring softly, over and over, as he sat on his brother's arm. "Jo jee?"

"Aye, Billy?" George answered when, for a moment, no one else was talking.

"Jo jee, I dream bout you wif Indians."

"Did y' now, Billy? When? Last night?"

Billy shook his head slowly, red mouth open, wide blue eyes full of wonder and love. "Ev'y time I go to sweep."

There was a murmur all around.

"It's true," Mrs. Clark said, gently rocking the baby girl in her arms and looking at Billy. "Every night he dreams, sometimes he calls out, and every morning he tells me what he dreamed of you. Y' mought be far away, George, but all th' same you're always here. That lad is, well, he's like a piece o' your soul that y' didn't take along when you left home. He's uncanny about you."

George looked into the eyes of the little brother on his arm, his little stranger about whom he'd just heard such a thing, looked at him thoughtfully, gravely. Then he jounced him up and down and grinned to make him grin. "Is that so?" he exclaimed. "Why, I'd ha' thought 'e was just a plain old catamount, but one that climbs people 'stead o' trees!"

And the happy uproar resumed.

TWENTY CANDLES BURNED IN THE DINING ROOM THAT EXtravagant evening. Their warm light gleamed on waxed-oak window casings and chair rails, and glinted off pewter serving dishes. A portrait of Queen Caroline, after whom the county was named, some mediocre colonial painter's copy of an elegant original, stared woodenly from above the sideboard toward the long dining table where all the Clarks, except Jonathan, the eldest son, sat together joking and laughing over the feast. John Clark was at the head of the table and George at the foot. Edmund's turkey was the main course; beside it sat a huge game pot pie with flaky crust, all its meats—squirrel, rabbit, venison, and boar—also furnished lately by Edmund's unerring rifle. Platters

11

of honeyed squash and glazed carrots, turnips and snap beans, steamed alongside, and heaps of popovers stood folded in napkins on the buffet. Rose the cook and her daughters kept coming in from the kitchen house with replenishments. Everyone had things to tell, except infant Frances Eleanor, who could not talk yet but laughed when others did. She had been brought down and propped in a mammy bench near the table so that even she, at eight months, would be here to enjoy the presence of her Seldom-Seen brother.

"Jonathan's risen in the world since last you were home," said John Clark. "He's moved to Woodstock, in Dunmore County, where he's Deputy Clerk o' County."

"Ah, is he now," said George. "I wrote to him at Spotsylvania Courthouse; hope they passed it along to him. Dunmore, eh? The Governor's already named a county after himself? Woodstock. Isn't that by Shenandoah? That's splendid country, by Heaven. Eh, well! Deputy Clerk! Old Jonathan's got a practical head on 'im, as we all know." He chewed a mouthful of rabbit and pointed his knife at the turkey. "Give me the little bubs o' meat off the back, Pa, if you can dig 'em out for me. That's the best part of a turkey, to my mind. Aye, Jonathan the Scholar! How clear I recollect those dreary days at Parson Robertson's school—how is old Uncle Donald, by th' bye? Well? Good— and how, once or twice every day, at the *least* once or twice, he'd remind me what a bad pupil I was, compared with Brother Jonathan. Ha, ha! Jonathan was a proper scholar, he was! He could memorize other men's dull words by th' mile, that's what Brother Jonathan could do so well, and that's what made a scholar, in Parson Robertson's view. I couldn't do it, but Jonathan could. No wonder he's a Deputy Clerk already. As for me, God be praised! I'm a legend at the Parson's school, isn't that what they say? Worst pupil ever? Ha, ha!"

"He refunded me your tuition, George. Said he couldn't take my money for such a lost cause as you."

"Ha, ha, ha! He's a legend too, isn't he? A Scotchman who refunded some money! Well, he sure made Jonathan bookish enough, anyhow. Ye got your tuition's worth on him, Pa."

"Indeed. Always in a book, he was. One day when he was a-readin', I told him to go hitch up the carriage, and I swear he did it without once taking his nose out o' that book! How can a body hitch up a horse and carriage without seeing either one, I ask?"

They all laughed. That was their favorite story about Jonathan.

"I know just what book that was, too," George said. "It was Montesquieu's *Spirit of Laws*. I recall a day when I sat in that classroom with that bedamned tome open on my desk. I read at blamed first page twenty times, and I couldn't tell Parson the hint o' what it said! O' course that earned me another lecture on what a good scholar Jonathan'd been. Ha, ha! But now look at us. Old Jonathan's sitting in his clerk's office, with pigeonholes full o' deeds an' all, and getting his wages for pokin' round in dusty paper, but me, no scholar at all, I'm a-layin' out land, and makin' farms out o' wilderness to sell to newcomers, and by Heaven, Pa, I'm worth twenty thousand pounds sterling in land if he's worth five in cash, that smart scholar! Did I tell ye, Pa, that Higgins sold me his share of our place out on Grave Creek, the one you came and saw? And already I've had three generous offers on it, from gents comin' down the Ohio. And hear this! I've engrossed land with a salt lick for ye. It'll make y' rich. Pa, I'll say it again, that you've got to come out, move out and stay. Our fortune's in Kaintuck. Virginia soil's exhausted from growin' tobacco, y' know that. I pray y'll bring the family out. We'll be that country's first and foremost family, I swear it. We'll be in Kaintuck what Jeffersons are in Albemarle!"

"Egod, George, how you can talk!" exclaimed John Clark, shaking his head. "I'm ready to mount up and ride!"

"Ye saw the land! You know how fine it is!"

John Clark groaned. "Must you tempt me by speakin' on't?"

Sisters and brothers were turning their heads back and forth from one end of the table to the other. It was hard for anyone else to get a word said when George and his father were talking about Kaintuck. John Clark went on: "Aye, it's fine. Never have I seen such soil. But son, things are all in question in this colony now, with King George and his acts, and a man dares not move till he knows what's to come next. By what Parliament says, anyone west o' the mountains is an outlaw, and what good's the land claim of an outlaw? Ye say you're worth twenty thousand quid in land out there? But the King forbids ye even *being* out there. How smart is that, I ask? My grant here's secure, I know. What sort o' father would I be, taking my family out to dubious land? And where the red Indian still prevails, I might add? Aye, son, I saw the land in that valley, and I can't get the picture of it out o' my head, nor forget the feel of it 'twixt my fingers, any more than you can. Someday we'll come. Not yet awhile. Here in the Old Dominion at least, I know where I stand. And a man with this size a family has to know where he stands."

"Let's talk about my wedding," Annie exclaimed. "If we're to

13

talk o' something important to this family, let's talk o' what happens next month, on the twentieth of October! Who cares about some forest, out on the Ohio River, I mean, except the Indians who live there?"

"Right!" cried George. "Your wedding! I want to know about it! Who comes? Who's the music, I'd like to know? By Heaven, I'd like to know about this shivaree!"

"No, huh uh," Billy exclaimed. "Talk bout Jo jee wif Indians Pwease!"

"After a bit, Billy," his mother said. "Hush now. The wedding's important, and Georgie wants to hear about it, don't ye, son?"

"You heard me say so. Billy, after a while I'll tell ye of the greatest Indian I ever saw, but first we hear of the wedding. Is that fair?"

Billy nodded. Anything George wanted was what should be.

"Fiddlers and pipers," John Clark said. "Mr. Henry's bringing 'em up from his father-in-law's public house. That's the music."

"Ah! Mister Henry'll be here? I wish I *could* stay. I'd like to talk to that gadfly!" Patrick Henry was the Clark family's lawyer. In the House of Burgesses he was a constant scold against King George's policies, and his name was known out on the frontier where disrespect for authority was esteemed.

"No, now," Annie interjected. "We're talking about my wedding, not about politics, remember?"

John Clark laughed heartily. He was relieved to be back on the topic of the upcoming event. He always got unsettled when George urged him to move the family west. Ever since George had taken him on a tour of that country two years ago, he had wanted to go to Kaintuck so badly he could taste it, but the day-by-day business of running a plantation had kept him tied down in Old Virginia, and he was comfortable here when he wasn't being prodded to uproot. Now the prospect of his daughter's marriage to a scion of an old family was comforting, like an anchor.

"Will Jonathan be down for the event?" George asked.

"Sure he will," said Mr. Clark. "I've writ to 'im, and I'll write again and tell him you're here."

"Ah, but y' heard, Pa, I told you I can't stay. I would fondly love to, but I can't. Sorry, Annie."

"Well, y're never here for anything else. So how should I hope y'd be here for the main time o' my life?" she accused.

"Annie," Mrs. Clark said sharply.

Sometimes the family felt that George had forsaken them.

With his energy, imposing looks, and golden tongue, he reasonably could have become a lion amidst the Tidewater gentry. He could have married into the Pendletons or Lees or Hancocks, gone into the legislature, grown fat and prosperous, and occupied himself, as most of the gentry did, in being English-like. Many a daughter of the plantation aristocracy had had a coy eye on him. But George had not deemed himself precious, and instead had chosen that dangerous and comfortless world out beyond the mountains of his boyhood dreams, leaving his peers to their balls and minuets, their cards and fox hunts and social rivalries, and their fine-horse breeding and their mating games, both of which they conducted in much the same way. He had gone to be a land finder, a phantom of the woods, and a consort of savages, and thus had deprived his neighbors and his family of himself, it sometimes seemed to them.

But in a way, distance had made him closer and more dear to them. Because of the hazards of the wilderness, real and imagined, he was always in their prayers. And whenever he came home, he found himself ever more of a prized curiosity, a story-teller, a voice of boundless optimism. For John and Ann Rogers Clark themselves knew and loved the frontier. They had in fact started their marriage as pioneer homesteaders, out in remote Albemarle County, in the shadow of the Blue Ridge. They had carved an estate out of the forest there, in seven happy, hard years, and their first four children had been born out there, in a log house that John Clark had built with his own hands and tools. Only the terrorism of the French and Indian War had finally driven them back to the Tidewater, in 1757, for the sake of their children's safety. John and Ann Rogers Clark still felt the pull of western horizons, tied though they were now to this lowland plantation. In a way, George was dwelling where their hearts dwelt, and they were still free and young through him.

"Reverend Archibald Dick will say the vows," Mrs. Clark said. "And we've sent word for the old Albemarle neighbors to come, those who'll think it worth the journey." She smiled a sly smile. "Meseems a few o' those earthy folk ought to leaven the spirit o' the occasion, mixed in with the gentility hereabouts."

George grinned and winked at her. "That, I wish I could see. Say, maybe I should send some of those ring-tailed river rats and bear-biters from Red Stone Fort back here as I go through. Give them a dram o' corn and they'll whump you up a wedding celebration fit for th' history books!"

"George," said Annie, drawing out his name, hardening her eyelids and pointing a threatening finger at him, "ye do any such

15

a thing and I'll disown you. My wedding's going to be good and proper, marked by good manners and politeness all 'round."

He leaned back and tilted his head. "In faith, girl! If it's that sort o' weddin' y' want, a *tame* one, well, why d'ye keep askin' *me* t'be here for it?"

"Jo jee! Jo jee!" Billy called through the laughter. "Tell me bout wiver wats an' bear-biters! Pwease!"

"Hey, yes! I promised you a yarn, didn't I, young man? I promised to tell you about the finest Indian chief of all. River rats and bear-biters some other time. This is a better story!"

Billy scooted low in his chair and put his hands between his thighs and scrunched his neck protectively down between his shoulders and shivered once, his mouth hanging open. He glanced once at his mother and father to reassure himself of their nearness and then waited to hear the wonders. The rest fell still and watched George's mouth as he paused to form the opening words to his tale. Edmund, Dick, and Johnny, though hunters and farmers on a man's scale, were now open-faced boys; Lucy was squirming, and Elizabeth silently slid down from her chair to go and stand by her mother's skirt. Even the parents were expressionless now. All faces were cleared of whatever had been in them, ready to receive. Beyond the doors of the bright room, dark shapes moved and yellow eyes gleamed; even the Negroes were listening. George raised a big, long-fingered hand and made his eyes look wild. Then he began, in a voice deep and dark as a cave.

"Oftimes, out there in that country, ye'll *think* you're alone, all, all, alone, but y're *not*! You're always bein' watched!"

Billy shivered and scooted so far down in his chair that only his eyes showed above the edge of the table.

"It was like that, the first day I met Tah-gah-JU-tay, the great MING-o." He put a deep resonance on the syllables of the strange Indian words, making them sound most savage and ominous. Mrs. Clark bit her lips to keep from smiling. She was hearing her own storytelling style, pauses and intonations. George had learned yarn-spinning from her bedtime stories of long ago.

"It was a perfect fall day," he went on, lightening his tone and making a panoramic sweep with both hands, his sleeve fringes swaying hypnotically. "Yellow meadows and fallen leaves all warm with a hazy sun. Ripe berries and wild grapes everywhere. Y' know the kind of a day.

"I was on a great, sunny meadow, overlooking a curve of the mighty O-HI-o, with my compass and chain and notebook, a-layin' out terrain. I didn't suspect there was a human soul inside hundred miles! It was so *still*! All I'd hear was that *rustle*, *rustle*, when a breeze goes through dry leaves. Or now and then, *ht*! *tht*! a walnut or acorn fell. Sometimes I'd hear squirrels' feet *rustlin'* in the leaves—leastways, I *thought* they were—and once in a while:

"FFFTHTHTHTHTHRRRRR!" He startled them almost out of their chairs, and in the pantry someone gasped and dropped something. ". . . I'd flush a quail."

"Oooey," breathed Edmund. "That sounded so real my trigger finger twitched." George barely managed not to laugh at Edmund's remark, biting inside his cheek to keep a serious face.

"Shhh!" said Annie, who seemed now to have forgotten even her wedding.

"So there I was," George continued, "in all that space and quiet, just workin', concentrating, as ye have to do when you're surveying. I'd poke that old maple Jacob's staff in the ground, and I'd put my brass compass atop it, tighten down th' thumb-screw. Y' know how brass'll shine in the sun. I love that. Then I'd sight along to a spot, then I'd pace out, payin' out those thirty-three feet o' chain, and stake down the end." They could see him doing it, all that complicated calculating and measuring. "And an interesting notion occurred to me just then," he went on, "that these brass and wood instruments o' mine were *tools*, *tools*, mind ye, for imposin' a humanly order onto th' wilderness! That was what I was doin' out there, all alone, all, all alone—or so I thought—there where no white man ever stood before, why, I was doin' the very, very first bit o' *civilizing* on that wild land." His mother looked at his father, and they nodded. They doubted that much of this notion was registering with the smaller children, but they knew their son George had a far deeper mind than Parson Robertson had ever suspected. "But all that while," George continued, raising a cautionary forefinger, "I was gettin' farther and farther away from my *rifle*. That rifle o' mine . . . Well, ye *live* by your rifle out yonder, y' understand. It leaned up against a tree trunk, where I'd put it, as you never lay your rifle on th' ground, eh, Eddie? And I was getting farther and farther from it, as y' can't help doin' when you pay out chain. Now and then I'd cast an eye back at that rifle, and I remember thinkin' once, it's shiny metal and maplewood, too, like my surveying instruments, and the thought hit me, why, it's *another* tool for putting order on the wilds."

Johnny, the family's poet, nodded at this apt phrase.

"Well, I had *just* been thinking that peculiar thought," George went on, "out there in that place where I thought me a hundred miles from any livin' soul, when *all of a sudden*—" He lowered his voice to a chilling whisper: "I felt a . . . *presence!*"

Billy emitted a shivery moan and Elizabeth curled her fist in her mother's skirt.

"Aye! Know how your back'll draw up and the hair'll raise on th' back o' your neck? When you feel . . . *eyes* on ye? Eh! I'll tell y' this, old family: Out yonder, y' have to be keen to that feelin', heed it and trust it quick, ere it's too late, elsewise it might be the very last thing y'll *ever* feel!

"And I, well, I was so far from my rifle by then, methought I'd felt the feelin' too late. *Too late!*" he hissed.

Annie now had her palm on her throat and was swallowing with terror. Dickie's mouth was hanging open. George went on:

"I turned, sloooowwwly, my eyeballs goin' like this. And I started edging as sly as I could toward that tree where my rifle stood. But *alas!* Before I was one pace toward it, I saw him in the corner of my eye! Lord, a jolt o' cold poured down me like I'd stepped under a waterfall in January! There, no more than six steps from me—somehow he'd got that close to me, stealthy as a sunbeam—stood this *huge, armed Indian!*"

Billy, seeing in his mind's eye an Indian with huge arms, was starting to pull the tablecloth toward his mouth. His mother reached and pried his clenched hand off the linen and held it in her own.

"Well, old family, was I ever in a pickle! That savage had a musket on his arm and could ha' shot me 'fore I'd got halfway to my gun! All's I could do was look at him over my left shoulder, and that's what I did, I looked at him over my left shoulder for a long spell, seemed like unto an hour, though I know it was four seconds or so. But *never* had I seen such an Indian! And he was starin' straight at me! Y' want to know what he looked like? Why, he was tall as me, at least, a hand over six feet, I'd say. His face looked as if 'twas cast bronze, and he was still as a statue. Eyes black and steady-blazin'. It was those eyes I'd felt on my back, and no wonder, either! Well, he had big chest muscles, and these braids of long, shiny black hair that hung down over his chest. And he had a band round his head with so many eagle feathers sticking up that his head looked like a shuttlecock. He had a red blanket over one shoulder, like those Roman senators y' see with their togas, in the history book. And he had a big necklace on, made o' bear claws, and panther teeth, and porkypine quills, and another made o' bangles o' pure beaten silver! But most of his decoration was knives and pistols and tomahawks, that stuck out all over 'im!

"And that, old family, that was the first I ever saw of Tah-gah-U-tay, great chief of the MING-oes!" George now sank back in his chair and stopped, hands on thighs and elbows akimbo, and looked around at his stricken audience. The servants had crept out of the shadows now and stood in the lighted doorways, some hugging each other, all looking at George's mouth.

"But, but," Lucy began stammering, "what happened?"

"What happened? You ask what happened! Why, what *does* a warlike savage chief do, when he's got a careless white man caught like that, cornered thirty yards from his gun? What *does* he do? You've heard all the tales; tell *me!*"

"Kills you an' cuts your hair off! And bites your eyes out," she said, adding one shocking embellishment from the horrors of her own imagination.

"Right you are, sister! And so that's what he did to me, then and there!"

"Aw, no," Dickie howled, clapping his hand on top of his head. "How dare y' make a joke out of a good story!"

"What! I'd never do that!" cried George. "He didn't kill me at all! What sayee, Betty?" The child had her hand up.

Elizabeth worked her rosebud of a mouth, then said in a tiny voice, "'Cause you came home."

"So I did! And here I am, little lassie, hardly dead at all. And what say you, Johnny?'

"Besides, you told us already that the Mingo chief was your best friend," this handsome lad reminded him smugly.

"That's so right, aye, Johnny! That's what comes o' good listenin'! You all hear that? Don't just listen to the yarn a man's tellin', listen to everything he says."

"That's mean, George," Annie said with saucy indignation. "It's bad to end a story with a catch trick."

"It would be, aye. But I'm not endin' the story yet. The best part's now. Listen:

"I knew, by the fact that I was still alive, that this mighty savage wasn't hostile. So I turned to face him straight on, and he looked me over good. And all at once he smiled, as bright a smile as your own, Annie, and he raised up his right palm like this, and he said in better King's English than Parson Robertson's even,"—George's parents chuckled; Donald Robertson's native Scotch brogue was so thick even after twenty years in the colony that he was sometimes nearly incomprehensible— "that chief said to me, 'You are a Virginian. You make a house on the creek by the graves.' And I showed him my hand, and I said, 'That's so.' Well, then he came over and took my hand just like

19

a gentleman would, and said, just as plain, 'I am Tah-gah-ju-tay. Your people call me Logan, and they know me as their friend.' Well, I'd heard aplenty about this Logan, back at Fort Pitt, and I was tickled it was Logan instead o' some unprincipled Shawnee that I'd have to watch out o' the back o' my head. So I told him my name, and we walked over to a tree and sat down in the sun to smoke together. I had some tobacco, and he mixed it with some dried leaves and bark and seeds he shook out of a decorated bag. They call that mixture *kinnickinnick*, boys, and when you smoke it the hands on your watch stop moving and your fingers feel fuzzy, and your head becomes one big eye so's you can see the whole world. Try some, if y' ever get the chance.

"Well, we talked that whole afternoon away, that Logan and I did, and I came to understand more in those hours than I ever did in a week at a school, or even more than Dr. Mason taught me at Gunston Hall. That Indian's mind is like, well, like ye said Peter Jefferson's was. Or like Grandpapa Rogers . . . aye, I was minded o' him. And I've learned a lot more since, going and staying at his camp. But here's what I remember best, and I swear I can remember it just about word for word, maybe because o' that kinnickinnick. Maybe if Parson Robertson had smoked that stuff with us, I'd ha' been able to memorize the way Jonathan could. Ha, ha! But here's what Logan said, anyways, and here's how he said it:

"He pointed at my survey tools there in the meadow, and he said, 'George Rogers Clark, you are drawing your unseen lines on the land. Such is the way of Virginians, and Logan is sad.' And he said, 'I, Logan, am the brother of all white men. Once I thought to go live among whites, and have my people in their schools. I tell my red brothers to keep peace with white men and learn their useful things. But my red brothers tell me now that they cannot do this if the Virginians keep coming to draw lines on the land and put families here. Your boats now go far down this river and take families to the Cain-tuck-ee. There they drive the game from the sacred hunting ground, where it is decreed that no tribe may live but all may hunt.'

"Then I told Logan that we need those places, because there are too many people east of the mountains, and they need to find new room to live in. And he said to me:

"'The red man too needs room to live in. But he does not come in with his tools to draw lines on it and take pieces of it from the Great Spirit who owns it. Logan is sad because the way of the white man and the way of the red man cannot be, in the same world.' So I pointed west and told him there was land

ithout measure, room for both peoples. But he said, no, there
s room for all the red people *or* all the white people, but the
uth is there is not room for both. He told me he was saying that
ot in anger but in sadness.

"Well, I thought then of something we've heard Tom Jefferson
ay: that someday the Indians could take up our ways and live
mongst us, and enjoy English thought and comfort. And I
ooked aside at that fine Mingo, and I saw him in my mind's eye
ll done up in a jackcoat and white breeches, pumps and a powered wig, counting coins and dancing minuets. And by God, it
as a notion so outrageous pitiful I was ashamed to ha' thought
t. I knew then why it was true what he said, and why it was so
ad. I could see, bright as brass in sunshine, that it's a problem
ithout a peaceable end. And that made me as sad as he was.

"So then I said to him, 'Tah-gah-ju-tay, all I can do then is
ray that when there is finally no more room, you and I at least
ill be too old to fight each other.' And he said he wished like-
ise, but had little hope, for he thought it would be soon."

"Oh, my," Mrs. Clark murmured. Her eyelids were glinting
ith tears. Now she knew what she had seen in George's eyes in
he hallway that afternoon. All the children looked at her, then
ack at George. He knew he was no child's storyteller for this
oment, and he wondered whether this could mean anything at
ll to the younger ones. Surely not to Billy, who was still wide-
yed and tense, as if he expected the Indian in George's story to
hrow down his pipe suddenly and leap up with a tomahawk in
is hand.

"And so that's what we had to say on that," George said.
Then after that, why, the chief smiled like as if to cheer us both
p, and said he wanted me to come to live awhile in his camp,
ecause he thought I was one of the good ones of my people. I
old him I would, and he said, 'While you live with me, you will
xplain how you reckon the unseen lines you draw on the land,
nd how they can have force even though they do not exist after
ou take your tools away.' Good question, isn't it, Pa? Makes a
ody ponder, eh? Then this Logan got a little mockery look, and
aid to me, he said, 'Wolves and dogs raise a leg to squirt on the
round, and they say, "This land is mine." But other creatures
o not care for those squirts. If that is what you do with your
ools there, the red man might be like the other creatures who do
ot mind the squirts of wolves and dogs.' That's what Logan
aid. That's no dumb savage, Pa, is it? I'd say that's a man who
ees even farther than a County Clerk."

John Clark nodded. He felt, strangely, almost jealous of h
son's admiration for the fatherly savage.

"Well," George went on, "it made me laugh, it was so ap
And Logan laughed too, and told me he'd take me someday
the mouth of the Ka-na-wha River and show me something tha
would prove what he said. So one day last spring we went, in
canoe. It's right far down the Ohio, took us days to reach it. A
this way we went, just so he could teach me something. Wel
there at the mouth of the Ka-na-wha, it's a fine spot there, goo
site for a town someday. Logan led me to a big boulder, ju
about hid in tree roots and bushes. There was a lead tablet fixe
on the rock, and there was writing on it. The language wa
French. I made out what I could of it, which was precious little
me being the kind of scholar I was. But Logan translated it fo
me. There was a date: 18 August, 1749, it was."

John and Ann Rogers Clark looked quickly at one another an
smiled. "The year we were wed," she said. John Clark nodded

"Aye," said George. "Well, it said on that plate that on tha
day a Captain de Celeron claimed for the French Crown all th
land drained by that river and its tributaries. When I looked up
Logan was a-grinnin' at me. And all he said of't was, 'There ar
your squirts of wolves and dogs.' Brought me all that way t
show me that tablet and say that, think of it! Some teacher, he
now? Not twenty years that tablet had been there, and that gran
diose claim meant no more than a dog-squirt. It's England
now, and whose next, I wonder?"

John Clark winked and pointed at George. "It bears out what
said about claims out there, the very thing I said. Here, I knov
my land is mine."

"So sure, eh? With King George sayin' you don't have thi
and ye can't have that? But forgive me. I'm off my story."

"Some story it is, too," Johnny said with one eyebrow cocked
"An Indian who reads French?"

"Ah, now, a skeptic!" George exclaimed. "Johnny, you d
have a sharp ear. But what you don't know, as I hadn't yet tol
it, is, Logan's mother was a Frenchwoman. So there y'are. Th
world's full o' wonders, but there's explanations for most of 'em.

"Did you just now make that up?" Johnny challenged.

"On my word it's true. He's a halfbreed. But as oftimes
happens, he's the best o' both peoples. And I'd reckon it migh
have something to do with his fondness for whites, now
mightn't it? Far as I know, there's but one living white man h
hates. A certain Indian fighter, named Cresap. Cresap's fathe
killed Logan's father. Logan and this Mike Cresap stay ou

f each other's paths like a hound and a bobcat."

The older Clark children and their parents were finding all
this quite interesting, but Lucy and Elizabeth were starting to
fidget. Billy listened on with rapt attention—or at least watched
his brother's face as if entranced.

"You said he had weapons all over him. Why, if he's so
peaceable?" Dickie asked.

"Mind you, Logan was a great warrior. He'd taken many a
scalp, in his younger days. The nations battle amongst themselves all the time, as y' know. He'd fought aplenty."

"Wif huge arms," interjected Billy. He made fists and waved
em in front of his face. The others smiled at this strange statement, then turned back to George, who said:

"I aim to bring Logan here someday. Have him stay in my
family as I have in his. I'd like Tom Jefferson to see him, hear
what he thinks. He'd learn something from Logan."

"Maybe y'ought to go fetch him here for Annie's wedding,"
said Dickie. "A good halfbreed livens things up, if y' give 'im
some barleycorn, like they do old Mattapony Daniel at Mister
Wright's cockfights."

"Don't you dare!" cried Annie.

"Dick, that's hardly very respectful, after all I've told you,"
George said. "But . . ." He put a finger to his lip. "Maybe not a
bad idea! Bring him *and* Cresap! Yee AH-ha!" He clapped his
hands. "What a night we'd have!"

"Yah-ha! Yah-ha!" Billy yelped, clapping, eyes squinting shut
in joyous release. All evening he had had an Indian cry pent up
in his throat, and now it could come out. "Yah-ha! Yah-ha!"

GEORGE WAS GONE BEFORE THE CHILDREN WERE UP THE
next morning, his saddlebags full of notebooks and maps, off to
Williamsburg to plat his lands. He had ridden off to the capital
in his best old frockcoat of forest-green wool, his best pair of
shiny boots, tricorn hat, and a riding cape borrowed from his
father, and thus, his mother told the children, he looked just
"bout as civilized as anybody. "He'll be back in three or four
days," she assured them, "the way he rides. Even allowing time
to do his lands and soak up some government gossip, he'll be
back 'fore there's time to miss 'im. And he hinted he might have
come to buy a few presents for family, too. Well, say! Where did
Billy get to? He was right here two winks ago."

The boy had gone up to the bedroom where George had slept,
and let himself in. And there on a clotheshorse hung what he had
come up to see: George's deerhide clothing. William looked at it for

a long time in the morning-lit room, dust motes drifting around
voices faint in far parts of the house. He looked at the Indian sur
design on the back of the tunic, a sun of white beadlike shells in th
center, and rays of red and blue quills radiating out from it, up
down, left, right. Then he reached to touch some of the lon
leather thrums that hung along the yoke, and along the seams of th
sleeves, and remembered those fringes swaying as George waved hi
arms and told his story of the Indian.

Billy ran a finger along the fringes and made them move. The
he put his nose against the deerhide and shut his eyes and inhale
deeply. And like a hunting dog sniffing its master's shoes, he wen
where the scents had come from: The campfires in dark forests a
night. The lodges where Indian tobacco had been smoked. Th
villages where meat was cured over fires. The rivers from which fis
were caught and cleaned. Far roads where horses ran, sweating wit
their speed. Fields where one lay down and crushed flowers an
wild herbs and autumn leaves. Springs and brooklets where one la
in moss and ferns to drink. Hunts where gunpowder flashed an
made sulfurous smoke. The butcherings, where buffalo blood an
bear grease stained the sleeves. The trading posts and frontier inn
where rum and whiskey were sloshed. But most clearly, the sunn
meadows where a surveyor sweated for hours over his compass an
chain with his gun leaning against a distant tree. Billy was far awa
in those places when he felt a *presence*. Eyes on his back. He felt
chill, and slooowwwly turned to look for a huge-armed India
chief. But it was his mother, standing in the doorway, looking a
him with her eyes full of tenderness. She came and stooped an
kissed him on the forehead.

"Come," she said. "Breakfast's on the board."

And then in four days George was home again, his saddlebag
even fuller. There were presents from Williamsburg's shops an
manufactories. For Elizabeth, a comb inlaid with mother-or
pearl. For Lucy, a long tin peashooter. "Blow, don't suck it," h
warned, "or y'll have beans in your lungs." For Frances Eleanor
a doll she could play with when she grew older. A dozen gunflint
for Edmund, an inkwell of crystal for Johnny the poet, a penkni
for Dick. And for Billy, his first compass, a small pewter one wit
a slit sight in its folding cover. He showed him how to line u
North and see where the other directions lay. "And one day whe
I'm home again," he said, "after y' learn to read Euclid, why, I'
teach ye how to survey, just like Grandpapa Rogers taught me.
They all sat stunned with delight, while George ran upstairs to h
room to fetch Annie's wedding gift. "Lord, he *must* be makin
money out there," John Clark mused.

Annie's present was from the frontier, not from Williamsburg.
was a beautiful tippet, a shoulder shawl made of mink skins dark
her hair, delicately sewn together by some Indian woman. She
s astonished. Her eyes swam in tears as she rubbed it on her
eek to feel its incredible softness. "You didn't know I was getting
rried," she said. "How did you know to bring me this? I
ught y'd pick me up some glinty bauble in the capital!"

"Why," he said, "it's true I didn't know it'd be a *wedding*
sent. But you're my beauteous sister, and when I saw that, I
ew it was made to be on your shoulders. I do love ye, Annie,
d I'd stay if I could for that great day o' yours. That great day
Owen Gwathmey, I should rather say!"

She was so overwhelmed she wrapped her arms around his
ist and pressed her cheek against his chest, and sniffled, and
ally said, "O, sometimes I just don't know what to make o'
u. Y' come threatenin' to turn my wedding into a vulgar hi-
ks, but really you're just as sweet and gentle as a, as a . . . I
n't know what!"

"I'll be at your weddin'," he said. "You won't be able to see
, but you'll know. Is that good enough?" He patted her gently
the back and then turned to face his parents, still holding
nie in the crook of his arm. "And you two, honored parents,"
announced, "listen here, it didn't escape my notice that her
dding's on the same day as *your* birthdays! October the twen-
th, isn't that so? I don't know whose doin' that is, but it sure
esn't sound like mere happychance!" They were smiling
adly, utterly astonished that he had remembered that date.
o I've got things for you two as well, and I'll just have to give
n to you right now."

For John Clark it was a matched set of flintlock pistols with
ony handles inlaid with silver filigree. They were costly pieces,
ich George really could scarcely have afforded to buy. He had
n them, with their velvet-lined carrying case, from a gaming
nt at the King's Inn, his first night in Williamsburg. He did
t explain this to his father, a devout Episcopalian who be-
ved that craps and cards were evils. Betting on cockfights and
rse races John Clark could condone, and sometimes did so
mself, rationalizing that it is natural for cocks to fight and
rses to run, but not for man to deal cards or throw dice. John
ark sat running his fingers over the elegant pistols, and George
rned to his mother.

"And now for you, Ma. This."

It was a beautiful little book bound in soft Morocco, with no
inting on the backing or cover. The edges of the pages were

25

gilded. "Now what in the world is it, a little Bible or something
It's so . . ." She slapped her cheek. The pages were all blank a
snow. "Well, how in the world am I supposed to read this? The
forgot to print it!"

"No, Ma," said George, laughing. "That book's for *you* t
write. You put down some o' those proverbs and maxims y'r
always givin' us for our moral and practical guidance. You ca
title it what y' like, y' see? *Ann Rogers Clark's Book of Proverb
and Cautions*, or something more flowery-like." He grinned a
her perplexity.

"What proverbs?" said she. "I don't say proverbs!"

"Maybe y' don't know it, but ye do. Like, um: 'A gentlema
will keep his fingers away from his face except when he eats
shaves, or prays.'"

"Oh fiddle," she retorted, "that's no proverb, that's advice.

"Well, that's what a proverb is, Ma: seemly advice, said in fe
words."

"Well," said she then, "when ye were littler, I said it in fewe
words yet. I said, 'Don't pick your nose.'"

They all laughed. Billy giggled, sitting on the edge of hi
chair, swinging his legs and pretending to excavate a nostril.

"Don't write *that* one down, please," George chuckled
"Here's one I remember: 'Red hair's no excuse for tantrums.' Y
don't know how often I have to recite that one to myself. I
works, too."

"Well, I don't know if I'll be able to write a Book of Proverbs
thanks all the same," she fussed, trying to hide her flattered feelings
"Huh! What am I supposed to do, follow myself around the hous
all day with a pen and this little book here, listening for proverbs t
fall from my lips? George, I'll vow, you're a caution, you are
Well . . . Maybe I'll write down dates in the lives o' my children
Start with Annie's wedding, maybe. And birthdays of her young
uns. If she's like I been, that'll fill up this little fancy book quic
enough! Hmp! I'll write down the days when you come and go
George, and stir us all up. Ye scoundrel. Come give me a kiss on m
face. I wish to Heaven ye wouldn't go away so soon to those places
Eh! When y're gone, what I know about your welfare is like thes
empty pages! But, it's not for me to try and stop ye, I who made yo
the sort that goes, for as the Lord knows, if there's an empty place
Rogerses'll rush into it. Just be careful, son. I didn't raise you al
those years for ye to go have a short life. Give your parents thei
care's worth, that's what I say!"

"Well, now, there y' are," he said, blinking. "That right ther
ought t' be the first proverb y' write down!"

* * *

AND THEN GEORGE HAD GONE, BACK TOWARD THE WILDER-
ss, as suddenly as he had come out of it, and Master Billy Clark,
youngest brother, was nearly inconsolable. He would go out
o the yard alone and put his compass on the grass and find West
it and then sit gazing in that direction and pining. He told his
other he wanted to learn to read at once, so George would come
ck and teach him to survey. He would go to sleep at night with his
mpass in his hand. He resumed dreaming about George, dreams
er more vivid now. One night when Annie and her mother were
ting up late in their nightdress planning their details about the
dding, they heard him yip in his sleep. Mrs. Clark went in with a
ndlestick and sat on the edge of his trundle bed. Eddie, Johnny,
d Dickie slept in the same room. They were snoring or mum-
ng in their covers. They slept like logs because of their hard work
the plantation and their long hours of study. Johnny moaned
en in his sleep, saying the names of girls. Johnny was perpetually
love, with someone or other, stunned with heartaches and
iting awful poems. One could never know who was this moon-
lf's object of love at any time. It would as likely be some bonds-
an's daughter he had tumbled in a haymow as some spoiled
anter's girl he had pranced with twice around a ballroom; to him
y miss was a princess; they were aristocrats by the color of their
ir or the shine in their eyes, or the shape of their lips or the curve
their hips, to use one of his own frequently repeated rhymes. All
s dreams were of love.

Billy's compass gleamed in the candlelight, and he rubbed it
d looked at it.

"Mama," he said, "tell me a story about Jo jee."

"Oh, my. There are so many stories about Georgie," she said
a voice she hoped was soft enough not to awaken the other
ys. "Say, darlin', I'll make you a trade deal. A favor o' mine
r one o' yours. I could tell you a story of 'im every night, if you
n promise me I'll see smiles on your old glummy face next
y."

"I can pwomise." He showed her how he could smile. It was a
stful, forced little grimace.

"Fair enough, then. Well, let's us see, now. What story
ould I tell ye first about that brother Georgie o' yours? Like I
id, he's been just one yarn after another. Well, there's the story
out Georgie and your Grandpapa Rogers out surveyin' on the
attapony. Then there's a story about George and Grandmama
gers and the whippoorwill call. Or, about when Mister Law-
nce's Indian boy made Georgie a bow and arrows. Or, there's

27

the story about when Georgie won *all* the medals at Dr. Mason
school, one medal for foot runnin', and one for wrestling, an
one for horse racing. Only boy who ever won all three. Or, th
story about when Georgie was, oh, just about your age, and wer
a-walkin' all by himself through the woods down to Mister Jeffe
son's mill with a bag o' corn to grind. Or, about the first time h
ever went up to the top o' the Blue Ridge and looked at th
western mountains." Billy was squirming, these all sounded s
good. "But," she said, "instead, why don't I just start at the be
ginning, and tell about the day Georgie was born, for that was
day I still shiver to remember, as there were Indians that day.

"Indians when 'e was *bo'n*?"

"Yes. Like omens, they came."

"Ooo!"

"And lightning. Lightning struck that day."

"Oooooh!" Already he was seeing pictures and she hadn't eve
begun.

"Then here's the tale, darlin'. It's seventeen years before yo
were born, in a place y've not yet seen, that this story began. Bu
first:

"Can ye remember how big my belly was just before France
was born? Well, that was the way I was that day, too, because
had Georgie in me then. So you have to remember I was lik
that the day these things happened, all right now? All righty
Now, y'know we lived out west in Albemarle County then, tha
was where the frontier was in those days. We were right by Blu
Ridge. And on past the Blue Ridge didn't *anybody* live, 'cep
wolves and bears and Indians, and a few hunters. Y've heard u
talk of Albemarle County."

"Uh-huh."

"November nineteenth was the date of it, in 1752. Your Papa
wasn't home that day, he was out a-huntin' deer on the moun
tain. That day, Billy, was raw and cold and gray as bullet lead
Been spittin' sleet all through the morning, it had. Your brothe
Jonathan, he was two then, was snug down in our big bed to na
so he'd stay warm, just like you are now, 'cause that day the col
wind just blew in through one wall o' that cabin and out th
other without pause for a how-d'ye-do or a fare-thee-well. Eve
with a big cookfire in the hearth, it was cold inside, and the
wind was moanin' and whistlin' round the house like demons.'
She glanced at him and saw him pull up the coverlet agains
cold, and knew that her storytelling was effective.

"Well, son, just then there came a ruckus from the henyard,
out back o' the cabin. There was an old scoundrel fox had al-

eady kilt two o' my hens that month, and I was sure he was in here. So you know what I did? I took your Papa's spare gun, that ld musket that's over the mantel in the kitchen house is the very ne, and I loaded it. I looked to be sure little Jonathan was sleep, and then I eased open the door and stepped out into the ind. I figured I had a good chance to surprise that old thievin' ox, as the henyard was out round back from the door, and I was ownwind to boot. Can't y' just see me, with a big belly and a ong gun, a-tippy-toein' round the corner of the cabin? He, he!"

"Yeah! He, he!"

"Thunder was a-crackin' over the Blue Ridge as I went reepin' round that house, gun muzzle first, aimin' to bring that ad fox to justice for his crimes.

"Well, Billy lad, listen now: If that *had* been the fox there, I ouldn't have surprised him a half as much as the surprise I got ust then! What I saw there in place of a fox made such a flash o' ear go through me, I couldn't ha' been hit harder by lightning! My heart like to stopped, and my guts clamped down so hard, I wear it started me having my baby. For you know what I saw in hat henyard instead of a fox?"

"A nindin?" he whispered.

"Not just one Indian but two. The one inside was just hand-ng a hen across the fence pickets to the one outside. And, Billy, ust then the one inside looked and *saw me!*"

"Oh, nooo!" he breathed.

"And then th' other one saw me too!"

Billy groaned.

"Fancy it, Son, the stew I was in! Me with one ball in my gun, and two full-grown braves in my henyard. And *just then*, I eard a voice off my side, and there was *another* Indian man here, and two squaws, and they were all lookin' at me too! And was a startin' to hurt so bad in my belly I could scarce stand still, 'cause Georgie was ready to come out!

"Well, I don't know how long we stood there like so many posts. Chickens were squawkin' and runnin' all over each other as only those stupid creatures can do so well. I don't know how I ooked to the Indians, but I could see they had the chicken-tealin' emotion writ all over their faces! They looked guilty as oxes!"

"You bettuh shoot 'em, Mama!"

"Well, before I could or couldn't, a lightning bolt cracked down, blinding white, and fired up a tree-top down by the spring, so close by I swear it budged me an inch in my shoes, and Lordy, I felt a real squeeze in my belly, and what I wanted most was to get indoors and get laid down, because y'll never know, Billy, praise be, how much it hurts when a baby starts a-comin'!

"But those Indians were standin' there thinkin' what to do, and I didn't have a plan myself, so there I stood with that cocked gun, pointin' it first at the two Indians, then the other bunch, dependin' on which way I was a-wobblin' at the moment. Son, I didn't have any idea whether I could shoot one and then run lock myself in the house with Jonathan 'fore the others could shoot an arrow in me. And if I did get in, why, I feared they could burn down the house with me and Jonathan in it! Y' still awake, son?"

The top of his head, all that was visible of him now, nodded rapidly.

"Thought y' were. Well, Billy my son, I'll never surely know why those Indians did what they did then, but I reckon they just got ashamed, like any ordinary people do. One older man said something, and the one put down the chicken, inside the fence, where it splayed out all feathers and cackles and finally ran under another hen. The Indian sprang over the fence then, and I nigh pulled th' trigger to shoot 'im in midair, as I feared he was comin' for me. But instead, they all herded together, still lookin' wary at me, and dignified as they could act, bein' chicken thieves, I mean, they all strolled away down past the spring into the woods, toward the river, there where that blasted tree-top still stood a-smokin' from the lightning. And it took all the guts I had, but I stood there lookin' after 'em with that cocked gun till they were out o' sight. There was more lightning, and I could hear Jonathan screamin' inside the house. I went in finally, all but carryin' my belly in my arms and draggin' that gun after me. I barred the door and laid out ball and powder on the table, shooshin' Jonathan till he piped down. Rest o' that afternoon I hulked and groaned round in that little room like a sick cow, peerin' out through chinks for a sight o' Indians, sittin' down on a stool now and then when the pain passed over. I wanted to yell for your Papa or scream prayers, but I knew if I scared Jonathan thataway, then he'd howl and scare me worse than I already was."

"Hurry up, Mama," said a voice out of the darkness, Edmund's voice, "what happened, anyway?"

She clapped a hand over her startled heart and swallowed. She turned and saw in the candlelight three pairs of eyes. Johnny, Edmund, and Dickie all were sitting up listening to her story. Billy had jerked bolt upright, eyes bugging.

"In Heaven's name," she gasped finally, "don't you ever give me a start like that again! I've scared myself half to death recallin' this tale as it is!"

"I'm sorry. But what happened?"

"What happened was that I set my jaw and decided I'd have to have that baby without any help whatsoever, and hope no Indians came to set th' house afire while I was busy. So I laid me down on the bed and commenced.

"Thank th' Lord, though, as it happened, that newborn just sort o' took over it all himself. It was just all *over* with, I don't remember much about it, though I did all the things I knew to do. But it was just as if his mother's womb was just 'where he'd been,' like, and he'd decided right then to move out on his own. He's always been like that, ever since, as ye know.

"So when your Pa came home next morning with a deer, he found me with a red-haired, blue-eyed baby, and little Jonathan sittin' there in bed beside us lookin' utterly hornswoggled. And we named that newborn after my brother, who's your dear Uncle George Rogers."

"Jo jee got bo'ned!" Billy cried suddenly, clapping his hands and bouncing in bed. "Jo jee got bo'ned! Wif wightning, an' Indians! Oooooo!"

"Just so!" she chuckled. "And with a start like that, why, he's a one to be watched, wouldn't ye say, boys?"

"Tell me how I was born," said Dickie's voice.

"No, me," Edmund and Johnny said at once.

"Some other time," she sighed. "One at a time's enough, enough!"

JOHN CLARK HAD HIS OWN NOTIONS ABOUT HOW TO GET Billy's mind off of George. "There's two ways to chirk up a little'un when 'e's got all downcast," he said. "Give 'im something, or teach 'im something. I aim to do both." And so at breakfast, he whispered aside to Rose the cook, and a few minutes later he got up from the table and went out to the pantry. When he came back in he was carrying a fat little black boy, purple-black as a plum, three years old, who was dressed in clean gray homespun pants and a patched but spotless shirt of indigo flannel. The chunky little fellow was looking around the room and half-smiling with wonderment at being brought into the dining room of the big house by the great master himself. John Clark stood at the head of the table while all the family looked at the child and smiled. One could not look at him without smiling; there was a droll, sly look about him that foretold the character of some great and funny rascal.

"Here we have Little York," John Clark said. They had all seen him around. He was the son of Nancy, one of the cooks, and his father was thought to be a field hand named Big York, who steadfastly denied that it was so. "York," said John Clark, "you know which one of these folks is my son Billy?" York licked his lips lavishly and rolled his gaze around the table, then grinned and pointed to him. Billy sat half-smiling, looking up in blue-eyed bemusement.

"That's right," said John Clark. "That's Master Billy. Now tell me, York, how would you like to be Master Billy's own particular man?" The child nodded vigorously and licked his red lips again, even though it was unlikely he had any notion what the words implied. It was plain that he liked the look of the little redheaded boy, and they had played together a few times in the summer, and so the words sounded good. "Well, then, you're Master Billy's man, from now on, York." The family laughed and exclaimed their approval. "You two get to know each other, and be good friends to each other, and someday when ye learn how to do a few things useful, why, y'll do 'em for Master Billy, eh? And does that sound all right to you, Son?"

Billy nodded, and said, "Thank 'ee, Papa." None of the other boys had ever had his own particular bodyservant, but they understood. When they had been Billy's age, the family had not yet become prosperous; there had been only one cook, and the few male slaves, except Cupid, had been field workers. Cupid had served as bodyservant for all the males of the family, and Cupid's wife Venus had administered to all the girls.

"Good enough," John Clark said, and lowered the black child to the floor. "Ooof," he said, "what a chunk of it you are! Now, York, you go round there and say hello to Master Billy." York waddled around behind the chairs and went to greet Billy in the only way he knew how: with a hug. Billy beamed and hugged him back, a little confused by what this gift meant, but very pleased. He liked the way Little York smiled and smelled. "Come get your boy, Nancy," John Clark said. "'Cause Master Billy's got some work to help me do, if I'm to get this daughter o' mine married and off my hands, isn't that so, family?"

"OUR FATHER, HAVE MERCY ON THIS POOR BEAST AND MAKE his pain be brief, as it is Thy supreme order of things to feed the dumb creatures to the smart ones," said John Clark, and, grunt-ng the word "Amen," he swung the maul with force and precision at the hog's face. *Chewk!* Bone crunched between the eyes. Dick and Johnny got the legs and yanked the animal aloft before he could fall. And while Billy was shuddering with the shock of what he had seen his father do, they hauled a rope that raised the stunned animal up to hang head down from an oak spar over the slaughter pen. Nearby was a hewn-log butcher table, and a large kettle of water steamed over a wood fire.

John Clark was the only man his sons had ever heard of who prayed as he slaughtered. This prayer was of his own wording, as were all his prayers; John Clark was a man whose prayers were not ritual, but talks with his God.

"Now put the catchment under 'im," he commanded, picking up the long butcher knife, old gray steel shiny only on the newly ground edge. "Come round here, Billy. Time ye learnt this." Edmund slid a trough under the hanging hog as Billy crept reluctantly closer, his head reeling, heart pounding, afraid, for the first time, of his father. "Stand right here now and watch this."

Holding the hog by a foreleg to keep it from swinging, John Clark thrust the blade into the animal's throat, clear up to the handle. "Right in that spot," he told Billy. "Then, ye move the blade thisaway to cut the big art'ry from 'is heart, y' see? There! There it comes now." A deluge of bright red blood gushed steaming into the trough in the chilly October morning air and Billy watched, terrified but spellbound. "Thing is, be quick," his father was saying. "Want t' get 'im bled ere his heart stops, y' see? Some folk hang their pig up awake and squealin' and stick 'im, but I never could do that. Besides, excitement taints the meat." The blood gushed and spurted and Billy watched, feeling faint. Then it slowed to a stream, then a trickle. Billy was aghast that his father could stand to keep the knife in there and let the horrible blood bathe his hand. "Now while th' knife's still in, I cut the gullet," John Clark explained, beginning to work the handle hard as if through something tough. "We're goin' to leave his head on, to put an apple in 'is mouth. There." He pulled the dripping knife out. "Reach in there, and ye'll feel what I've done. Come on, Billy my boy, don't be delicate!" He grabbed Billy's wrist and forced his little hand into the hot, wet, bloody opening.

It was too much. Billy screamed and began wailing. The older boys laughed, but they laughed weakly, because they could remember the first time they had had to learn this. John Clark did not relent. "Now ye feel that hard thing, like a tube? That's what

I just now cut. That's this," he said then, and with his free left hand he grasped Billy's and placed it at his own gagging, keening throat. "That's where it is in you," he said.

The thought of it all, the pig's gullet, his own, was just unbearable. Billy screeched and gasped and wailed and tried to escape.

His father's iron hand suddenly began shaking him, till his teeth all but rattled. Loudly, but not angrily, the deep voice drove through the howling turmoil of Billy's mind: "I'll not abide such caterwauling! Cease it, right now! There be things ye got to learn, and there's no nice, girlish way to learn 'em! Can y' hear me? STOP THAT SQUEALIN'! By th' Eternal! They'll think it's you I'm slaughterin'. D'ye think Georgie would be proud o' you now?"

That worked. Billy stopped struggling and his screams trailed off. Thinking of Georgie looking on had shamed him. He still sobbed, but he was no longer frantic.

"Now," John Clark was saying, releasing Billy, "that's better. Georgie learned this long before he could learn to survey land. Now, boys, scald 'im and scrape 'im." They swung the carcass down and, grunting, heaved it into the steaming kettle. Soon then they had it on the table and were adroitly scraping off the hair with wide iron blades.

"Did 'e cwy? Did Jo jee cwy?" Billy gasped out. His bloody hand felt hideous and sticky, and the greasy steam was nauseating.

"No, he didn't."

"I sowwy I cwied. Don' tell Jo jee I cwied, Papa, huh?"

"I won't tell 'im."

"Jo jee bwave, he di'n cwy," Billy said wistfully, feeling unworthy.

"That's right, he was brave, he didn't cry," John Clark said, then he chuckled. "But he surely heaved up his breakfast! Ha, ha!"

"Jo jee did? Jo jee puke up?"

"He did for sure, son. And *you* didn't. And believe me, vomit's a sight messier'n tears."

Billy suddenly felt a lot better about himself. The older boys were watching him and smiling sympathetically.

"I cried, too, Billy," Dick said.

"I," Johnny told him, "cried *and* puked." They talked as they roped the pink, hairless carcass back up onto the spar.

"So did I," Edmund admitted.

"Not to mention, y' also beshit your breeches," Dick snorted.

"I didn't either!" Edmund's face went as red as his hair.

"Aye, but ye did," his father reminded him.

"Well, just that first once. I butcher all the time now; everything I shoot I clean."

"No right man *likes* doin' this, Billy m' boy," said Mr. Clark. "But we have to know how, 'cause we have to provide for family. God knows how many animals you'll do this to as the years go by. But it's as God meant it. That's why He put meat-bearin' animals here in Creation. Only thing a sin about this would be to enjoy it. Now ye watch and listen close, because I'm about to show ye how we take the guts out without dirtyin' the meat. This beastie's going to be the feast at Annie's wedding, y' see! And he'll also be sausages, and lard, and puddings, and scrapple, bacon, and chitterlins, and soap, and brush bristles, and candles, and a blow-up ball toy, and all kinds o' good things for family, y' see? For as we say about a pig, Providence shows us how to use everything but the squeal—and we'd save *that* up for dancin' music, if we knew how to catch and presarv it. Waste is a sin, t' my mind, Billy, though somehow they don't harp on it in the Scriptures. Especially is wasted life, be it swine or man."

Thus he talked on, as he pulled the pig's short tail and carefully cut a circle around the anus, then sliced open the carcass from there to the throat and removed the varicolored guts all in a slimy, sliding piece, teaching precepts and morals as he worked, and the boys worked with him and listened, and it was as absorbing almost as a story, so interesting, though not entirely understandable, that even the gleaming guts didn't make Billy feel sick.

John Clark could not help talking about the meanings of all the things people did, because God's intents were plainly there within everything that lived and grew and moved and died. And his wife, good Ann, was likewise—though, being a Rogers, she could say these things better, in his opinion. The Rogerses were real talkers, and they were firm in their faith, and they believed in their own thinking. Ann's great-great-great-great-grandfather was John Rogers the Martyr, who had been locked in a dungeon of St. Andrews Castle back in Scotland two hundred years ago, and then burned at the stake, for being so bold as to believe in God in his own way. All the Rogerses took pride in that ancestor, and seemed to live as if they felt him looking over their shoulders. John Clark appreciated that in their family—after all, he had some of that Rogers blood in him, too—and he was profoundly content in having got Ann Rogers, the most beautiful Rogers daughter, as his bride those long years ago. Not one day, in almost a quarter of a century since, had he ever regretted that choice. Many of the marriages among the gentry that he knew had been marriages for advantage, for fortunes or connections o breeding lines, and if a husband and wife came to loving each other truly, so much the better. But John Clark had adored Ann Rogers from the moment he had seen that fresh, tall, pink-and rose thirteen-year-old squinting at him in the summer sun twenty-five years ago, and her good character had only deepened and broadened his adoration for her over the years, till now he could not even imagine being without her. "If something took ye away untimely," he had told her once when she was having trouble with a childbirth, "I shouldn't even want to live on." And he had meant that.

It had been true then and it was even more true now. He had worked like a titan all his life, and every effort he had made from topping tobacco plants to shaping horseshoes on a forge had been for the betterment of their life. He knew too that every effort she had made, from the labor of weed-hoeing to the labor of childbearing, had been for that same purpose. And raising their children to feel and understand all God's intents was also for the betterment of their life together, because it would not be a good thing in life to be ashamed of offspring.

And so now John Clark was saying, for the benefit of these offspring working near him: "Aye. The wasting o' lives is man' worst sin. *War!*" he snorted. "D'ye know how many precious lives are wasted in that abominable business? If one slayin' is a murder, what's a thousand a day? Lives wasted because men are too vainglorious to sit face to face and talk things out! My boys, I remember a day a thousand died! Back in '55, 'twas, when that war was on against the French and Indians. Some militia rode in one day, some bandaged, all thirsty and sooty, they rode up to our house in Albemarle, goin' home from a lost battle. They told us how the Frenchmen and savages had ambushed General Braddock's whole army in the woods near Fort Pitt, and killed a thousand of 'em. A *thousand*, boys! One thousand Christian Englishmen, all slain in one day! Think on *that* for the wastin' o' life! I swear that was the worst day I've ever had in all my days, when I heard that news. I got sicker than anyone ever got a-slaughterin' a pig, I'll tell ye so." His lips were tight, his eyes darkening with the memory. Then he went on:

"Now, hear me. Sometimes, like when Georgie comes home, and everybody wants t' know, 'have ye kilt any savages yet'"—he glanced up from his meat-trimming at Edmund, and Edmund's eyes dropped—"well, it doesn't please me to hear a question like that, though I know that's what everybody wants to hear of. And I know, too, someday it might be George or an Indian, who's ever quickest, and let us pray then that it's George who's quickest. But I'd rather hear him say what he said, that he's befriended an Indian, than that he's killed one. For an Indian's a far higher creature in Creation than is a hog like this, or even a calf, or a pet dog. Indians pray, did y' know that?" He looked at them one by one, then bent over his knife and went on. "Indians pray. George told me about that Logan's religion, told me after you all were a-bed. Said for all he knew, that savage's god was the same one as ours, but just by a different name. Now mind you, I allowed as how I thought that was probably not so, and I told George I thought that was pretty loose thinkin'. Nonetheless, that Indian prayed, and lived reverent, George said. So even an Indian, with his unredeemed and misguided soul, does *have* a soul. And so, to think it's sport to kill Indians, why, that's to condone the wasting o' life. And I'll have none of it in this family, hear me now, all of you." Edmund blinked his downcast eyes and worked harder over the pile of entrails before him.

One disapproving look from John Clarke was more effective than a whipping. He had never had to lay a switch on any of his sons, and only once had he had to knock one down—once when George had been having a red rage. John Clark did not believe in whipping. Once long ago on the way from Port Royal, seeing a sheriff administering a public whipping upon an adulteress, John Clark had got down from his wagon, snatched the whip out of the sheriff's hand and looped it around his neck, at the risk of being arrested and whipped himself. A person's body is the home of his sacred soul, John Clark believed, and not to be punished or damaged by another. Thus, war was an abomination before God. "In war," he said now, "all men red or white are but meat left to rot on the field where they fell. Man is offal, and only the buzzards are fed. Kings and soldiers call that 'glory,' to the disgrace of the very word!"

Now his sermon veered off onto another tack; he had reminded himself of something else. "Seducers of womanflesh are the same," he said, with one of those sad, accusing glances now at Johnny. "They violate the temple of a woman's soul, and make it but meat. And use the word love like soldiers use the word glory." Johnny's forehead reddened, both with shame and indignation. But he did not protest; after all, how could his father know that Johnny's loves were *real*? That he was passionately, totally in love with the mysterious soul inside each shapely body he caressed? But John Clark, who had loved the same woman all his life, only said now:

"Bear in mind, every girl is someone's precious daughter. Like my Annie. And likely she's also someone's sister. Would y' have *her* trifled with?"

There. Put in those terms, it struck Johnny hard. He put his head down and pondered as he worked, and hoped his father had had all his say about that.

John Clark would never have thought of giving so long a speech just standing up in front of people. Speeches were for natural talkers, like the Rogerses, or for burgesses, or for licensed rectors. But when John Clark was working he was thinking, and if the thoughts he had seemed likely important enough to help his sons be worthy, then he could talk as long as anyone.

"There," said he, "that about does our pig. Let's get all this up to the kitchen and smokehouse, for it's a long way from ready for our Annie's wedding feast, hey, boys? And that day's not afar off. How y' feelin' by now, Billy my boy?"

"I fee' bettuh, Papa."

"Aha. Fine. And y've learnt something, isn't it so?"

"Aye, Papa."

"So here's our pork, thank the Lord. I wonder if any venison will come our way." He cast a glance at Edmund, and a sly smile.

"Watch me," said Edmund, eager to please. "I'm out 'fore daybreak tomorrow."

EDMUND CLARK HAD SET HIS MIND TO WAKE HIM UP AT four, because he had a promise to keep.

He dressed in darkness while his brothers breathed and snored and muttered in their sleep. He did not put on shoes, because he could move through the woods more quietly without them. He reached up in the darkness and felt for his rifle, and with a soft grunt lifted it down, then his powder horn and bullet bag. He could see the rectangle of the dormer window, and bright stars. He went out of the room and down the hall and down the stairs, feeling his way with his bare feet. He lifted the latch of the back door and went out into the night air and closed the door behind him, trying to be stealthy as an Indian.

The grass was frosted underfoot. The air was crisp and cold and the night was silent. He could smell the smokehouse where the pork was hanging in hickory smoke, and the smell of it made him salivate. There was a patch of yellow light in the kitchen house door and he could smell pone baking. Old Rose was al-

eady up, as always before anyone else, getting the breakfasts
eady. Edmund knew he could go in the kitchen house and Rose
vould exclaim and wrap him in a musky hug and give him
omething hot to eat, but he went on past the kitchen house.
George had told him that it's better to hunt hungry.

Edmund walked on dirt road past the smells of stables and
pigpens and tobacco sheds. He came to the end of the road and
valked on grass for a way, then climbed over a stile and walked
on a long way through a meadow under the cold stars, toward a
larker line that was the edge of the woods. He entered the woods
nd walked with one hand before his face to fend off twigs. A few
eet away a slow, regular huffing sound began, and became faster
nd faster until it was a pulsating rush: a ruffed grouse drum-
ning. He noted where its nest was; he would come here in
laylight and get it. Deeper in the woods an owl was calling. *Hoo
too-hoo, hoo hoo-hoo, hoo hoo-hoo, hoo-aw!* Edmund went on,
eeling the ground slope gradually down as he crept toward the
Mattapony River. There were places where deer came to drink at
laybreak. George had begun bringing him down when Edmund
vas six, and he had learned all such places.

"EEEEEEYOW!" came an insane scream out of the darkness
lirectly in front of him. Edmund recoiled, heart thumping, but
ie knew the woods sounds too well to be afraid; it was merely the
vild preamble to a barred-owl's statement, which now came
100ting down from a high invisible limb as Edmund walked un-
ler, shaking his head. Those idiotic-sounding birds had used to
nake him think Indians were ready to leap on him, when he was
maller and hadn't yet got used to them.

The Indian legends in this region were old; it had been settled
or years. Grandpapa John Rogers had been one of the surveyors.
But the first white man to walk here had been Captain John
Smith of the Jamestown Colony, more than a hundred and fifty
ears ago, when he had been brought through as a prisoner of
he Youngtamund Indians. In Edmund's mind, Captain John
Smith looked like George, but in old-fashioned clothes, because
t was George who had always been with him in those woods and
old him all the old stories. And now George was out where the
ndians were still dangerous, and, like Capt. John Smith, walk-
ng in places where white men had never walked before. Ed-
nund thought that would be a strange and wonderful feeling,
and wondered if he would ever get a chance to feel it. George
had told him it made a man feel honored.

Edmund could hear a spring purling in the darkness off to his
eft and knew which one it was: the one that seemed to come

right out from between the roots of a big beech. He went to it and stretched out on the moss and drank, shivering, smelling the decaying leaves. Edmund never had to carry a water gourd when he went hunting because George had shown him where every good spring and brooklet lay for ten miles in every direction. George had learned every inch of the Mattapony and Pamunkey river land helping old Grandpapa Rogers survey. Edmund could just barely remember Grandpapa Rogers: a lean, long-legged man with a face dark as one big freckle, hair and eyebrows white as snow, and eyes like two dots of blue sky. There were as many stories in the family about Grandpapa Rogers as there were about Georgie, and Mrs. Clark often would say that the two had been cast in the same mold. Grandpapa Rogers had been a very bold man, and one of the proudest tales about him was about the way he had defied the powerful Colonel Byrd and eloped with his daughter—that story about the whippoorwill call, that Mrs. Clark could not tell without getting a quaver in her voice. It was one of Edmund's favorite stories, and it glowed in his imagination like a legend of knights and ladies.

The woods were thinner here, and Edmund could see a paleness ahead which he knew was the river, reflecting starlight and the first rose-gray of morning. The leaves under his feet gave way to grasses and reeds now, and he walked now and then in shallow, chilly water, his feet sinking in cold ooze, the smells of muck and decay rising. He was in the marshy place now, where frogs dinned in the springtime and all the kinds of web-foot fowl lived and where in the summer the air was so thick with mosquitoes that a body couldn't hear anything else.

Edmund walked through the cold water knowing he was leaving no spoor to frighten the deer, and he soon felt the land rise a few inches. He perceived a large tree he had had in mind, and stopped there, and stood with his back to it. There was a forked sapling in front of him and beyond it lay the river. A fish jumped in the river, then again, and again. There were no insects in this season and so the fish, Edmund reckoned, must be jumping for the sheer joy of it. The sky was paling downriver to the east and the trees on the banks began to separate from the gloomy background on the far shore and become distinct, one by one. The river steamed in the cold air.

Now it was almost light enough to see gunsights, so Edmund put the rifle butt on the ground and tilted the powder horn over the muzzle and poured a charge down the barrel. The weapon was about as long as he was tall. He felt in his bullet bag for a lead ball and patch. He put the ball in the oiled cloth, and shed them down the barrel and tamped them firmly in with e hickory ramrod. Then he slid the ramrod back into its groove d lifted the rifle, and opened the flash pan to trickle in the iming powder. He eased it shut, felt the flint to be sure it was ;ht, then rested the gun-butt on the ground again and began aiting, shivering. Cold is just one of those things that be, eorge had taught him, and you have to make yourself believe it)esn't feel any worse than warmth, or otherwise you couldn't and it. Edmund listened to the gurgle of the river and the other tle sounds: a muskrat in the reeds, the croak of a heron, an-her owl far off, the hush of a tiny breeze as the air stirred with e coming of morning. Edmund gazed downstream and ought of how this river ran into the York, some twenty leagues)wn, and thence into the mouth of Chesapeake Bay, where, e family stories said, the Rogerses and the Clarks had first nded in the Colony, some three or four generations ago. All at ancestral lore was vague in Edmund's eleven-year-old mind, it he was ever aware of it, and especially when he gazed down e Mattapony in the direction of the sea.

Edmund now heard his own empty stomach skitter and grum-le as he waited and shivered. The surface of the river was like lver now and the stars had faded out. It was true what George ad said: to be cold and hungry made one a keen hunter. And)w Edmund heard the faint sounds he had been listening for: te sound of steps in the frosty dead leaves.

He raised the rifle to rest the heavy barrel in the fork of the pling, and put his hand over the icy steel flintlock.

Then he saw the buck come out of the edge of the woods and alk gracefully through the reeds to the water's edge, raising its nees high, pausing, stepping again. When it was silhouetted gainst the surface of the river, Edmund pulled back on the flint-»ck and felt the strong spring compress, and kept pulling back ntil he felt it cock. The deer turned its head both ways, down-ver first and then upriver so that it was looking straight toward im, but if it saw him it mistook him for a part of the woods, nd lowered its muzzle to the water, its branched antlers now lhouetted against the silver stream.

Edmund snugged the gunstock against his shoulder. There as just enough light to see the gunsights by and he lined them p on a place just behind the deer's shoulder. He had been uivering but he put a control over it and the rifle was steady. 'hen he thought the words of his Papa's prayer. *Dear Father, ave mercy on this poor beast*.

He squeezed the trigger and saw the orange flash and then the

gun cracked open the silence of the morning, jolting his shoul
der. He smelled the powder and heard hundreds of waterfowl
and small birds squawk and splash and flutter and saw them
disperse against the predawn light beyond the drifting veil o
gunsmoke, and when the smoke thinned, he could see the buc
collapsing into the river's edge.

Edmund was sad in the way it always made him sad to kill
beautiful thing, but the buck had died quickly and suffered onl
a moment because of Edmund's skill, and Edmund had fulfille
his promise and this would be what he would add to Annie'
wedding feast.

JONATHAN CLARK, ELDEST OF THE SIX SONS, WAS FEELING TH
pull of home. From the next rise, he knew, he would be able t
see the roof of the house. The October afternoon sun was on hi
back and he rocked with the horse's easy canter. It had been fin
weather for riding and he was almost there. Down amidst the dr
grasses and reddening sumac of the roadside stood a zigzag fenc
of split rails that he and his father had built so long ago, whe
Jonathan was a boy of ten, to mark the corner of the family land
The wood of the fence was silver-gray now from thirteen years i
sun and rain, and the bottom rails were rotting, returning to earth
as wood must do, but Jonathan could remember the work of tha
long-ago day: the thud of the maul on the splitting wedges, th
tannic tang of the new-riven oak, the pale grain, the sweat, th
grunting, the swinging and lifting, and the cheerful voice of hi
father musing aloud on how a man should live. There was hardl
an acre of these hundreds upon which Jonathan had not poure
sweat, changing the look of the land, making things grow. Now h
was a man old enough at twenty-three to sense the cadence o
seasons, the accretion of labors, the erosions of time on the coun
tryside. For four years now he had lived away from here, but h
had not forgotten anything. Annie had been six when that fenc
was built, and tomorrow she would become a wife. Jonathan
sucked an eyetooth and shook his head.

The hooves beat rhythmically on the packed dirt, the horse'
muscular barrel breathed and rocked between Jonathan's thighs
He rode past a man he didn't know, an old man driving an ox
that pulled two rolling hogsheads of tobacco. The man waved,
and Jonathan touched the peak of his three-cornered hat in re
ply.

And now he was on the top of the rise, and there ahead in
flat, broad bottomland lay the Clark family seat: the stone house,
the outbuildings and barns, the short row of one-story dependen

es in which the servants and field hands dwelt, the pastures and
oodlots, the grainfields and tobacco plots and vegetable and
erb gardens, the stables and the paddock, the symmetrical
owns of the big, red-leaved oaks and yellow-leaved maples that
ied the drive and surrounded the house, all aglow in late sun-
ine.

There was his home, that solid, orderly piece of the world, to
hich he always returned with a sense of mellow longing, how-
er much he might grumble about having had to interrupt his
ork to go and visit as a dutiful son must do. Jonathan was an
mbitious man, who hoped to rise by law and public service up
and beyond the place his father held in life, and he aimed to
it without building fences and pulling stumps and raising and
lling livestock and crops for the rest of his days. It was his
tention to become a magistrate. But in Caroline County cer-
in royally favored families, such as Taliaferros, Taylors, and
uckners, always got those appointments, and so Jonathan had
oved to Spotsylvania and then Dunmore counties in search of
pportunities. This was the ambition of mind that Jonathan
lark carried upon his tall, square, brawny farmer's body, and it
d taken him away from this place he loved with a love that he
alized only when, as now, he was coming home.

Jonathan saw now that he was overtaking a couple of riders—
man astride and a woman on sidesaddle—who were moving
wn the road at a walking pace. Both wore dark riding clothes
at were very dusty. They obviously had come a considerable
stance. Jonathan presumed that they were on their way to the
edding. The man carried a long rifle across his saddle and
nathan could also discern a sword hanging at his left side. The
oman wore a cloak and a wide dark hat, but was so small she
ight have been a very young girl. Jonathan was twenty yards
hind them when first the woman and then the man turned
eir heads and saw him coming.

"Hallo," he cried as he overtook them, squinting to see if he
cognized them. He did not, though the man looked familiar.
They reined in and sat their horses across his path. The man
as of sharp features and had large, jutting ears, and he was
udying Jonathan keenly, as if trying to recognize him too.
good day, sir," said he, and then he smiled, and his severe
ld eyes warmed and sparkled. "You're one o' John Clark's, I'll
ager."

There was little hazard in that wager; Jonathan was a replica of
is father, strongly built, rugged-faced like Squire John Clark,
rikingly handsome with his dark brows and fair, freckled com-

plexion, but a head taller. Like his father he dressed in sombre and serviceable wool, almost like a minister. He wore a plain white stock at his throat, and a black riding cape. The ribbed stockings that encased his powerful and well-shaped calves were gray wool.

"I am, sir. Jonathan Clark is my name, and yours is?"

"William Lewis is who I am," said the man, extending a hand as thick and hard as Jonathan's own, "Bill Lewis, an old neighbor o' yours when you were a lad in Albemarle. Here is my wife Lucy, whom you might remember as Lucy Meriwether." Jonathan tipped his hat to her and she smiled and nodded. She was, though childishly short and petite, a very comely woman with high cheekbones, big, luminous blue eyes so heavy-lashed they looked almost sleepy, a squarish jaw that suggested strength and a most delicately shaped mouth.

"I know the names Lewis and Meriwether," Jonathan replied with a nod to her, "from my parents' talk. But forgive me not recalling if we've met. I was a young'un then, and can scarce remember Albemarle folk, save for a few like the Jeffersons whom we saw more frequent. Shall we ride on, Mister Lewis? We're almost there. D'ye know Tom Jefferson much?" he asked as they resumed their way along the road at a walk.

"Oh yes, quite well," chuckled Lewis. "I'm in his employ, in fact. I do the financials of his estate."

"Ah! Is he coming to the wedding, d'ye know?"

"I bear his regrets to your parents and the bride. He's busier than a dozen men, what with public office now, besides the estate and his science. Say, now, Jonathan, as for this bride Ann is the sister who was born in Albemarle, I presume?"

"Aye. Eighteen she is now."

"I remember well the day she was born. It was the day we brought the news of Braddock's disaster. Your mother was birthing 'er just whilst we rode in. Might y' remember that?"

"By heaven, I'm not sure," Jonathan chuckled. "I remember many a birthing, that's certain. The fact is, the very first thing I can recollect from my memory is my brother George being born. Rather, I should say, waking up one morning and seeing him there in the bed in my mother's arm." He smiled and shook his head, glancing at some cattle in a field that had used to be in barley.

Mrs. Lewis's voice rang out suddenly, in a mellifluous laugh. "Do you remember, Mister Clark, were your feelings something in the way of jealousy when you beheld that newcomer?"

"Jealousy? Why, I don't know, ma'am. But . . . P'r'aps they

were. I recall I wasn't especially pleased." It seemed an odd query.

"Mmm," she said, nodding and smiling. "*Our* firstborn was quite distressed to find an usurper when our second appeared. D'ye remember, Bill?"

"I do," he nodded, pursing his thin little mouth. This Lewis appeared to be some years older than his wife, and Jonathan had the passing notion that their children would be fortunate if they took their mother's traits of appearance rather than their father's. She was truly a fetching creature, with an aura of warm vitality about her that made Jonathan uncommonly aware of the loneliness of his bachelor life. He had always been too preoccupied with making his career to think forward much to marriage. His mind passed quickly over the several young women who seemed interested in him—some of them were very interested—but they all seemed either frivolous or half-alive when considered in comparison with this vibrant little equestrienne whom he had just now met. Jonathan Clark was not fool enough to become infatuated with the wife of a family friend, or anyone's wife, for that matter. But something in her nature had stirred in him a kind of longing, as if any woman worth considering henceforth would have to be something like this.

". . . from Albemarle are coming," Lewis was saying, and Jonathan came back as if from a reverie, strangely wistful and lonely. "Mister Lawrence rode with us a while, but hurried on ahead a while ago—at a gallop, actually—claiming that he was very, very thirsty. We offered him water, but apparently that wasn't what he was thirsty for. D'you remember Lawrence? 'Twas he who bought your father's farm in Albemarle."

"Aye. Him I remember. He owned an Indian boy, didn't he?" Jonathan could remember the boy, a sad-faced wretch who had befriended George and made him a bow and arrows. Those two had learned to converse in some strange, made-up tongue. Jonathan had not developed any such affinity for the little savage, but George . . . Well, sometimes George seemed to Jonathan more Indian than Virginian.

"I'm not sure anyone ever 'owns' an Indian," Lewis said. "Not enough to keep the little heathen from running off one day. Near broke old Lawrence's heart, it did, him having tried so hard to make him a proper Christian."

"Hm. Here, Mister Lewis, Ma'am, here we turn. This is the place, and let me be the first to bid you welcome to it. Ah, but I do love coming home!"

Children whom Jonathan didn't know were running, squealing, among the trees along the drive. In front of the house Cupid, in livery, was bowing and helping two feeble old gentlemen down from a chaise whose driver sat with upright whip and an air of importance. From the open front door of the house came a drone of many voices, talking, laughing voices, and now and then a loud guffaw or the excited squeal of a girl. He knew the family certainly must be busy with company; usually he was seen and hailed before he was halfway up the drive. Now Cupid saw him, and broke into an ivory grin, but said nothing and continued to hand the elderly passengers down from the chaise.

"There's Jonathan!" he heard Edmund's voice shout from somewhere in the house, and then, before he could dismount, he saw the family boiling out the door to meet him.

"Hullo! Hullo," he cried, dropping to the ground and taking hugs. "Ma, look, I've guided the Lewises in. Hey, Pa! And, say! How d'ye, Billy?" The little lad was looking critically at him, studying his plain, dark apparel. "Nothing t' say, eh? Ha, ha! Hey, Annie, y' look like you're about to have an apoplexy! Is Owen here yet, eh? Maybe there's time yet to talk 'im out o' this foolishness."

"Oh, you!"

"A cup! Quick, get this man a cup!" Dickie was exclaiming. He looked a bit cockeyed, and had apparently been greeting many guests with toasts at the sideboard.

"Lucy Meriwether! Heavens, you were but a child when last I saw ye."

"Nor've I grown much, Mrs. Clark, but I've two little 'uns, even littler'n me," laughed that thrilling voice, and Jonathan was aware of it even in the crush and babble. He saw her descend from the saddle onto the mounting block, a cascade of dusty skirts. And then Brother Johnny's handsome face appeared, and Jonathan hugged him and pounded him on the back, and Johnny too was redolent of peach brandy.

Then they were inside, moving through the hallway, through a gauntlet of half-remembered names, Cabells and Campbells, Redds and Putnams and Purdies and Todds, and of course Rogerses and more Rogerses, of faces familiar but older, of handshakes, callused or soft, of exclamations about how much or how little he had changed. And here was Parson Robertson, his beloved old teacher, thin and dry-skinned and wet-eyed with a long, fond look at his prize pupil. And then finally they were at the sideboard, and he was clinking glasses with his family in the usual toast to homecoming, and the delightful heat of the liquor was spreading down his gorge while the fruity fumes lingered in his head. He looked into the moist, crinkling eyes of his father, who sighed and rocked on his toes and said:

"Well, son, y're here! Here for the event!"

"Here I am! Your last letter told me in about eight ways that I'd better be. Ha, ha! And ye know who I am: your most dutiful son. Home for a wedding and birthdays! Aye!"

John Clark beamed with pleasure. Jonathan was his favorite son, if he would admit he had a favorite. "So, you remembered our birthdays too! Ah. Shame you missed George. He was here and gone so quick I wasn't sure I'd really seen—"

"Oh, but I didn't miss 'im."

"What sayee?"

"You saw George?" asked Mrs. Clark.

"He detoured up by Woodstock t' see me on his way back west. Didn't he say he would?" Jonathan was stroking his sister Lucy's red curls as she stood close and embraced his waist.

"Why, no! Why, that's a considerable detour," exclaimed John Clark.

"Aye. Showed up all a surprise as usual. Said 'e was goin' to cut up over and take the old Nemacolin Trace to Fort Pitt. Always has to try a new way, as y' know. Lookee what he brought me from Williamsburg. How could he afford a fine fob like this? I never figured him to make a shilling, that blamed hill-hopper!"

Jonathan did not mention that he had forgotten his parents' birthdays until George had reminded him.

"Well, well-a-well," said Mrs. Clark, looking at the fob as Jonathan slipped it back into his waistcoat. Smiling with a private satisfaction, she turned to the Lewises, to lead them up to the room where they'd be staying. She glanced down from the stairs at Jonathan and her husband, who still stood talking to each other in the crowded hallway.

Someday, she was thinking, someday they'll esteem my George as he deserves t' be. Someday. Perhaps.

2

CAROLINE COUNTY
October 20, 1773

"DO YOU, OWEN," SAID REVEREND ARCHIBALD DICK, RECTOR of the Parish of St. Margaret's, "take this woman, Ann, to be your lawful wedded wife, to love, honor, and cherish, so long as you both shall live?"

"I do." Owen's voice rumbled deep and gentle, and it was a reassuring voice.

To Ann Rogers Clark, it was the sound of reliability; it was the voice of a man of solidity, like her husband John Clark, whose broad back she was now watching through blurry eyes. She felt Billy stir beside her and she patted his arm to keep him from fidgeting. Around her hushed the breathing and snuffling and whispering of a hundred people or perhaps more, and near the back of the church there were the little knockings and scrapings made by latecomers creeping in, and outside she could hear horses and harness. People from distant Albemarle had kept coming in through the morning, many of them having been up before daylight to ride the last twenty or thirty miles from wherever they had slept along the roads. She had not thought so many of them would come, but they were there, in the pews behind her; she could smell horse and dust on them, and some reeked already of corn whiskey, which, she knew, they sometimes would start the day with if they had no fires for tea or coffee. She was profoundly touched that so many had come, so many of these rough and earthy people out of her family's distant past. It appealed to something in her to think of their muddy buckskins and homespuns intermingled with the satins and velvets and watered silks of the Caroline gentry. Some of the guests from Albemarle could remember when Annie the bride had been born, or professed they could, and probably believed it, but the real reason they were here was their old friendship for John Clark. Many of John Clark's friends had been his friends for thirty or forty years, and to his wife that was another proof that he was as good a man as she knew he was.

She kept looking at him as Reverend Dick's fluty voice led on through the ceremony. She looked at John's broad back in its black wool frock, and the black ribbon that bound the queue of his gray-flecked hair behind his collar, as he stood beside his—their—daughter.

"Do you, Ann, take this man Owen to be your lawful wedded husband, to love . . ."

That strong back of John's, and her own fruitful loins, had made their world, in the quarter of a century since she and John had said these same vows. Now for a moment, as she heard Annie's beloved voice quaver, "I do," her own body remembered what it had felt like to be a bride's body: elastic, resilient, vibrant with hopeful desires. And then the feelings of her age returned: of flesh stretched and collapsed, of twinges of pain deep in her organs, of bruised nipples and milk-heavy dugs, of back and legs

48

perpetually weary. Annie, that wan virgin in lace standing up there now with her head bowed toward big Owen's shoulder, that Annie would one day house in her body all such familiar infirmities, would be tough inside instead of tender.

Ann Rogers Clark sighed aloud, but no one heard the sigh because the people were suddenly all astir; it was over, and cloth was swishing and shoes were scuffing, voices were talking and sobbing and laughing, and she came out of her reverie and the first thing she saw was husband John turning to look at her, his eyes all shimmery, too, and his face engorged with the strain of not weeping aloud, and she was sure that he likewise had been thinking about themselves, about the flow of time.

And the second thing she saw was Annie's face, which was intent upon the ruddy, self-conscious face of Owen Gwathmey, her husband from this moment on. Billy's hand was tugging, and he was asking something about "awful wedded husband," but people were closing in now, cooing congratulations to her, and Jonathan's voice was trying to joke by her ear, ". . . get used to it, Ma, y've got nine more weddings to go."

While in the back of the church a huge uproar was building, with men's voices roaring and whooping, and the sounds of bodies thumping and doorjambs quaking as half the Albemarle men tried to squeeze through the door at once and get to their horses. She could hear Mr. Lawrence's voice bellowing, "RACE FOR TH' JUG! YEEEAH-HAH!"

"RACE FOR TH' JUG!" other voices howled, and the commotion moved outside to the hitchrails under the oaks. Horses were whinnying and quirts swishing and voices yodeling and then hooves were thundering off down the road toward the Chesterfield Tavern, where there awaited a jug of hard spirits previously bought and set aside in preparation for this traditional wedding-day race. The tavern was a league nearer the church than was the Clark house, and thus had been selected as a way station for any guests who feared they might perish of thirst on the way to the reception. Though the Race for the Jug was an old Albemarle tradition and appeared to have been arranged by that contingent of the guests, several of Caroline County's fancy young bucks caught on at once and sprinted to their horses. Caroline County was famous for its racing horses and riders, and these youths had no intention of being outrun on their own countryside by a company of frontier rustics. In a moment a troop of them, mostly friends and peers of the older Clark boys, were pounding away in pursuit, their elegant coattails flying. Knowing the county better, they veered off through a field to make a shortcut. Thus the race had all the look and spirit of a cavalry maneuver, and even before the two contingents were out of sight through the blazing reds and yellows of the autumn foliage, some of the older wedding guests were already on the church stoop, placing wagers. "They can't help it, Lord, forgive them," Reverend Dick said aloud. "It's in their blood." He was trying to look disapproving, but a smile kept flickering on his narrow young face.

In the meantime the bride and groom had been glad-handed and kissed all down the crowded aisle and onto the church lawn, where a carriage with driver waited to convey them to the Clark house. Behind it stood John Clark's own chaise. Owen and Annie were lifted bodily from the ground and placed in the carriage and the driver was ordered to make all haste to the Clark house, without stopping, or even slowing, at the tavern. The driver's whip swished, and the carriage darted forward so quickly that the couple's heads bobbed back, and they were off at a run with the crowd cheering behind them. John Clark within seconds had his wife and small children in his carriage, and they too were spanking along the road in that gleaming, fresh-painted vehicle, one of the lightest and best-made in the county. Ann Rogers Clark waved back at the mob outside the church, and saw them all making for their own horses or carriages, before they faded from sight in the road dust.

John Clark was no breakneck fool who would jeopardize his family for the sake of speed, but he was as much at home on or behind horses as on his own feet, and his horses were fine ones, and so his progress homeward was enough to fan the locks around his children's cheeks, and he was a long way down the road before sons Johnny, Dickie, and Edmund could catch up and gallop past on their own horses. They grinned at him as they pulled ahead, and Dickie shouted back: "A shilling, Pa, says I'll pass Owen!"

"A shilling it is!" cried John Clark.

Lucy was grinning into the wind, gap-toothed, Elizabeth sat in the crook of her mother's arm half-smiling and watching the roadside whiz by, and Billy stared after his brothers, his little freckled snub nose turned up in the breeze and his eyes half-closed. The carriage rumbled smoothly as John Clark steered past the dips and ruts of the road, and the two big geldings in the harness ran with manes and tails streaming, their powerful sleek rumps working. "Happy day, Mama!" Lucy cried from sheer exuberance.

"Oh, yes, it is indeed!" cried Ann Rogers Clark, feeling young again. Her husband laughed with his high spirits, and then called back:

"Lookee! Lawrence got the jug!"

"Heavens, already?"

The old Albermarle bachelor had come pelting back up the road whip-and-spur, waving the jug he had snatched up at the tavern, and met the bridal carriage head-on, yelling its driver to a halt. And when Squire John Clark drew his vehicle alongside, old Lawrence was leaning sideways off his prancing horse, passing the jug to Owen Gwathmey, crying, "Your first swig as a husband, poor fellow! The first o' many to lament your lost liberty!" Owen took it with a laugh and sucked long at its neck while Dickie and Johnny and Edmund raced around and around the stopped carriages, laughing and asking for their turn.

"What o' my shilling, Pa?" Dickie shouted.

"Aye, what of it? Ye didn't pass 'im, he stopped to drink!"

A few of the Albemarle racers had come back following Lawrence, as had some of the Caroline youths, humbled but merry. Most of the riders, apparently, had stayed at the tavern for a nip.

And so when the bride's entourage rode past the Chesterfield, there indeed were the many fine horses tethered outside; and now the sports came pouring out the door to get back in their saddles and race on to the Clark house for the rest of the wedding shivaree. Some of them in mounting took deliberate pratfalls off the other sides of their horses to create more hilarity. Some literally vaulted over their horses and landed laughing on their heads. If Annie was as perturbed by the rowdiness as she had said she would be, she was hiding it well. She was radiant as summer and laughing full-throated at the hijinks with the rest of them.

AROMAS OF ROAST MEAT AND BAKING BREAD MET THE WEDding entourage before they were halfway up the drive. They found awaiting them, on tables and sideboards and trestles, the kind of feast aristocrats might expect. Here was the pork John Clark had butchered, a huge cauldron of small-game stew, a pot of corn chowder, platters of cornbread cakes and muffins and Yorkshire popovers, cheese and buttermilk and squashes, mincemeat, wild nuts, suet puddings, fruit compotes, sugar of both the maple and cane varieties, and both kinds of cider, harmless and otherwise. A fat young buck deer, which Edmund had provided as promised, was turning whole on a spit over a firepit beside the kitchen house, where a sooty Negress in grease-stained clothes stood basting the flesh and slicing it off. The Clark farm

51

was known throughout the parish as a cornucopia, because of Mrs. Clark's well-tended vegetable and herb gardens, Mr. Clark's orchards and his industry as a farmer, and their sons' skills as hunters and gatherers. Many of Caroline County's freeholders planted all their acreage in tobacco, which they sold at Port Royal for currency or tobacco certificates, and then had to buy most of their foodstuffs. Theirs was a money economy and tobacco was their money. But John and Ann Rogers Clark had learned self-sufficiency up on the Albemarle frontier, and raised or hunted everything they needed, and thus had full larders and pantries no matter how the crop and pricing of tobacco were in any year. Most of the colonists had stopped using tea in protest of the Tea Tax and missed it sorely; Mrs. Clark, though, had several tonic and delicious brews blended from flowers and herbs.

And now the wedding guests fell on the famous Clark board as if they had been fasting for days. Ann Rogers Clark went about as if in a daze, her mind befuddled by her heart, but she oversaw the feeding of the horde so well by habit and instinct that, as she whispered to her husband once, "They can't tell that I'm non compos mentis today, can they, John?"

Annie, meanwhile, was so surrounded by her peers that her mother could scarcely get to her. Most of them were unmarried planters' daughters from around the county, giddy with sherry and lemonado, simpering and giggling with their hands over their mouths, rolling their eyes heavenward, and being gushingly envious of the bride's happy fortune. "But," a Buckner girl whispered to a Goodloe girl, "I certainly mean to marry someone more dashing than her Owen Gwathmey, when my day comes!"

"Well, I too!" exclaimed the other. Both these belles had already been involved flirtingly with George, before his departure, and lately with Johnny, proof that their tastes did indeed run to the dashing.

As for Johnny himself, the presence of so many young women this day under his own roof was both a delight and a perplexity. He would falter between the angelic sheen of one girl's pristine skin and the bawdy promise in another's laughter. Like the hungry guests at the tables, he had a problem of selection. And his ingenuity was taxed as he tried to home in on certain girls while avoiding others he had already won and cast off. At length, all his desire swung like a compass needle toward a certain magnetic, green-eyed creature named Betsy, daughter of a small freeholder up the road. Her swollen bosom reminded him of breast of pheasant, and her smile was sly and lewd, and at once Johnny was in love again. But even as he was trying to coax this succulent lass off to the privacy of a secluded corner or unoccupied room, his conscience was being prodded by the echo of his father's recent admonition: "Every girl is someone's precious daughter, and most likely she's also someone's sister." And Johnny could not pretend it wasn't so, because her father, Mister Freeman, a work-worn, hardy little man, and two loutish brothers were right here on the premises as invited guests, all keeping half an eye on her. Johnny would glance at them and would wonder what they would do to him if they knew the color of his desires. Common and laconic though they were, doubtless they had just as strong a sense of her honor as Johnny had of his own sister's. But this did not keep him from wanting to love her as quickly and completely as possible. *Ah, the sweet agony of desire!* These words repeated themselves in his soul, and he memorized them. Surely he would be writing another poem before this passed.

The benign Indian summer weather blessed the many children who had come with their families. The yard was covered with bright fallen leaves, and the air was warm and the ground was dry, so they could frolic outdoors without coats. There were two pony carts for them to ride, and a match of shuttlecock and battledore had been set up, and spirited games of whipcracker and hide-go-seek swirled around the grounds. Inevitably, games of Indian war were soon on, all over the estate, marked by long periods of silent sneaking suddenly broken by outbursts of ghastly screaming. Through energy and force of personality, Lucy Clark quickly rose to the rank of general in these affrays, but she grew discouraged as her foes conceived her to be General Braddock and kept defeating and killing her. Once her mother had to detain and disarm her after she ran upstairs and came down with both her rock sling and her new peashooter, with which she had hoped to turn the tides of war. Billy, meanwhile, lived and relived the role of master scout George Rogers Clark, creeping unseen and unnoticed along fencerows and under shrubs and around fodder shocks while ambushes and massacres raged nearby. On one of his patrols late in the afternoon he happened upon a gasping, moaning, breathless life-and-death struggle between two half-undressed people beside the herb-garden hedge. One of them was his brother Johnny; the other was a strange, strong young woman he was calling Betsy, who kept pulling him toward her while whispering desperately for him to go away. Billy watched this struggle, open-mouthed, for a while, then decided they were playing something and not really fighting, and with a shrug he crawled away to spy on General Lucy Braddock's army.

At dusk a stagecoach rumbled up the drive, bearing Patrick Henry from neighboring Hanover County and a raffish company of musicians rented from his father-in-law's ordinary. They were quickly fed and cidered and then stationed at one end of the large downstairs parlor, which had been rearranged as a ballroom and lit by many candles. Jonathan led the assembling dancers in a toast to the bride and groom, and then another: "To my esteemed parents, the lord and mistress of this manor, on their birthday! Long may they live!"

"Hear, hear!"

"Long live good friends and neighbors!"

"Long live the King!" someone shouted, perhaps from habit.

"And enlighten the bloody tyrant!" bawled a magnificent voice. Dubious laughter muttered through the room, as Mr. Henry paced forward to stand by his musicians. He swept up his glass of port in a grand gesture, scowled over his spectacles as if about to begin one of his ferocious speeches, but then broke into a smile and cried, "It's time for music!"

A fiddler tucked his instrument under his chin and sawed out two long, plaintive notes turned up at the ends like the baying of hounds. Lines of men and women began forming as if by magic. Squire John Clark bowed before his wife and took her hand, but she pulled back, protesting:

"Get on with you, John! I? Dance? I've done nought but raise children for twenty-odd years, and I can't remember . . ."

But she went with him, and remembered how to dance a reel. With a cheer the lines of men and women advanced on each other with wide eyes and prancing steps, and the ball was in motion, with Patrick Henry in twice as much motion as anyone else.

To most of the older guests, Henry was still that Hanover ne'er-do-well whose love of wine, dance, and debate had caused him to fail several times in both commerce and farming. He had married a pubkeeper's daughter and had shown signs that he would never have anything but frivolity and tavern gossip in his head. But then he had read law and become a lawyer, and had made a name for himself a decade ago in a celebrated Hanover County case challenging a decree of King George III. Soon he had got elected to the House of Burgesses, where he had boldly denounced the Stamp Act of '65 and made himself a popular champion of the common people in their efforts to gain more say over the governing of their own lives. Henry was one of the ew out-of-county lawyers who had been qualified to practice in Caroline, where there was always a brisk business in slander and assault and battery cases, bastardies and creditors' suits, and he was prospering. But he was still a man who loved loud words and music, and he maintained that the tavern is the best place for a lawyer or politician to educate himself about the leanings and meanings of men. It was said that when Patrick Henry replaced his spectacles from the bridge of his long nose to the top of his forehead and stood up to speak in the House of Burgesses, the conservatives would grip the edges of their seats and brace themselves for the worst. Nothing that King George III or Governor Lord Dunmore could do, it seemed, was agreeable to Patrick Henry. And the common people loved him, for at last they had a strong spokesman, in a colony whose courts and legislature had always been dominated by royal favorites.

John Clark had brought Mr. Henry to the wedding party mainly for the sake of the music, but of course the presence of the Great Gadfly added a special dimension to the event, and when, as the evening wore on and the talkers began to separate themselves from the dancers and migrate into the library, they tried to draw Mr. Henry in with them. "What?" he cried. "Talk government whilst the bride and groom are still dancing?" And he plunged back into the ballroom.

His musicians were a versatile lot, with two fiddles and a French horn, and a banjo in reserve for certain pieces, and they were able to perform with equal alacrity the jigs and reels the Albemarle folk liked and the minuets the Caroline gentry preferred. Dance, like everything else in Virginia society, from horse racing and wrestling to billiards, was competitive, and though scores were dancing, each man and woman was trying to out-caper or out-swoop all the others. It was said that courtship was the main concern of Virginians, and every swain and belle present was trying to cut an unforgettable figure.

John Clark had unbunged a keg of whisky and one of cider, and for the more delicate drinkers there were such elegant mixtures as mulled Madeira, Sangaree, and orchard punch, as well as Virginia brandies and rums of the Indies. By midnight, even those who were not dancing reels were reeling. The groom, whose first swig of the day had been given him on the road from the church, had toasted and been toasted without pause ever since, and was too amiable a fellow to refuse any cup or goblet offered, and so was by now very unsteady. He waved his arms to keep his balance, and when he walked he appeared to be swimming in slow motion.

Ann Rogers Clark watched her new son-in-law's deteriorating condition with mixed feeling. He was comical, pathetic, a bit more human than he had ever seemed to her before, with his red-faced expression of woozy bliss. If he's this agreeable a fellow drunk, she thought, he must indeed be as good a man as he seems. But Lord in Heaven, I'm afraid he's not going to do poor Annie a whit o' good on this night of nights. She watched Annie, happy Annie, with pity. Maybe I should have told her about a thing like this happening, she thought.

But I just never thought of Owen drunk, she thought. I just never foresaw this kind o' happenstance.

It could be such a hurtful thing for Annie if Owen get clumsy, or just falls asleep on 'er, she thought. Maybe I ought to get to her and forewarn her that suchlike might happen.

Nay, maybe I rather hadn't. It might make her afraid o' the conjugal bed.

But Annie solved the dilemma herself by coming to inquire. "Mama," said she, with a dubious glance toward her stupefied groom, "can, ah . . . can a . . . is a gent . . . I mean . . ."

"Darlin', I'm glad ye asked, though I don't know the answer, as your father has never got quite that unsteady. But whether he can or not, darlin', remember this, and don't forget it now: if he can't, it's not the end of th' world, for come tomorrow, or the day after, at least, he'll be sober."

"PA," SAID EDMUND, "I WANT TO SHOW COUSINS JOHNNY and Joe the pistols."

John Clark twisted the spigot of the cider cask and turned. There stood Edmund, all dressed up and wearing shoes for a change, and with him stood his cousins, Joseph and John Rogers. They were tall, handsome youngsters, aged eighteen and sixteen, both redhaired and freckle-faced like their father George Rogers.

"If't please, you, sir," said Joseph. "Eddie told us you wouldn't mind."

John Clark sipped from his cup of pungent cider and smacked his lips, and smiled. "I wouldn't mind at all. Come along here." He was proud of the pistols.

He led them away from the sideboard, through the crowded hallway, past the ballroom, toward the master bedroom in the rear of the house.

"Squire Clark," called someone from the door of the ballroom as they passed, "not through dancing, are you?"

"Not at all, Judge!" he called back. "Just cooling my shanks

56

and warming my cockles!" He raised his cup to the guest and opened the door to lead the three boys in. There was already a candle burning in the room, and a figure moved in the shadows near the dresser. "Ah! Pardon us, dear wife," he said. "What are—"

"Nay, come on in. But shut the door. I don't want the rest to see me doing this. They'd think I was gettin' old." She sat on a cushioned chair, her shoes off and her feet in a bowl of water. "You almost ruined my old feet, y' dancing fool. Hello, Joseph, John. Don't tell your father you saw me thisaway, promise?"

"Promise, Auntie Ann."

"I brought them in to see what our Seldom-Seen Son brought me. Here we are, lads." He set his cider cup on the dresser, pulled open a small top drawer, and lifted out a tiny brass key. He pulled the pistol case to the front of the dresser top, moved the candle up close to it, and unlocked the box. When he raised the lid the candlelight gleamed on the silver and steel, and the Rogers boys moved close. Their eyes were wide, and Joe's lips formed a silent whistle.

"Lord above," he said, "I'd give a pretty for a pair like them!"

"I guess they'd cost a pretty," John Clark said. "George is a pretty extravagant fellow. In every way," he added. He knew these two lads idolized George as much as his own brothers did, if not more. They were always begging their father to let them go west with him. "If my sons ever disappear," George Rogers would josh John Clark, "I'll know 'twas your son led 'em off." "That could well be," John Clark would retort, "but it'd be your Rogers blood that'd make 'em follow. They're three of a kind, as alike as the three tines o' the Devil's pitchfork." George Rogers would laugh and nod then, because he felt that was true, and he liked it. George Rogers Clark was his godson and namesake, and his favorite one of his many, many nephews.

"Uncle John, may I heft 'em?" asked Johnny Rogers.

He took up one in each hand, held them up in front of his shoulders and turned them in the light, looking from one to the other, caressing their flintlocks with his thumbs. He leveled first one, then the other, toward a far corner of the bedroom where a cloak hung on a coatrack looking like a man in the shadows. He clucked his tongue twice and jerked the guns upward as if they were recoiling. Edmund looked at his father, remembering the lecture in the slaughter pen. If John Clark was thinking those things now, he didn't show it. He was sipping his cider and watching Johnny Rogers hand the weapons to his brother Joe.

But then he began musing aloud, as he usually did only when he was working.

"Well, a pair o' pistols like those, they're a handsome possession, certainly. But they remind me somewhat o' jewelry, there in that velvet case like that. Pistols might be o' use to some kinds o' folk. Highwaymen. An officer of troops. I'd personally never bought pistols. Pistols are made to point at *people*, and I've no occasion to do such a thing. A long gun's useful, though, as we've all got to provide for our families, isn't that so, Eddie my boy? But pistols, well, like I say, they're pretty, and valuable, but somewhat useless, like jewelry."

Ann Rogers Clark sat behind them in the shadows, shaking her head slowly and half-smiling. She'd heard all this before, at least three times since George had brought the pistols. Her husband was a lieutenant of county militia, and had been for ten years, but fortunately those had been peaceful years, for John Clark was so imbued with the Sixth Commandment that surely he would never raise his sights on a man, enemy or no. And she thought now, too:

If't had been Jonathan gave him those pistols, not George, he'd have worked it out some way in his head that pistols are as useful as hammers and saws.

Joseph Rogers had taken his turn sighting on the cloak, and had handed the weapons back to John Clark, who now was locking them back in their case. "So there they are, boys," he said. "Pretty, aren't they? But extravagant. Well, now, dear wife," he said, turning, "are y' ready to put your dancin' shoes back on and take another tour o' the ball?"

"Thankee all the same, John," she replied, wiggling her toes in the tepid water, "but my feet were made to walk to and fro, bed to cradle, and they find dancing to be extravagant."

AT ABOUT ONE IN THE MORNING, WHILE THE MUSICIANS were resting, mopping their sweaty brows, and re-cidering themselves at the cider cask, the wedding guests decided it was time for the bride and groom to take to their nuptial bed, and set up a great merry rush and clamor about it. All the men and boys crowded in to try to kiss her goodnight as the ladies, giggling and cooing, propelled her through the ballroom and hallway and swept her up the stairs. Just before she disappeared beyond the upstairs balustrade, she cast one last desperate look over the laughing, shouting mob below. She found her mother's face and looked wildly into her teary blue eyes, her own face full of imploring. Ann Rogers Clark, her heart swollen painfully with are, raised her chin in that way which made her look regal as any queen, shut her eyes, and pursed her lips in a kiss, a kiss across the distance. When she opened her eyes Annie was being pulled into the bridal chamber, her head tossed back as if she were being abducted from the familiar life she had known. But he smiled for her mother. Then the door closed, and a great cheer went up from the mob downstairs. Now, they knew, the women up there would be undressing her, perfuming and caressing her, to make her ready to receive her groom.

The menfolk now turned to give Owen Gwathmey his finishing touches. They encircled him and poured him glass after glass of courage and passion, advising him, giving him specific instructions that caused him, even in his stunned condition, to blush livid. This was a moment of torment for John Clark, who for this moment almost hated his good friends for the words that were coming from their stinking, drooling mouths.

Finally, when poor Owen couldn't stand up anymore they declared that it must be time for him to lie down, and so they shouldered him and carried him upstairs to the bridal chamber, held him up swaying and sagging and stripped him, and dumped him into bed beside the cowering bride, jibing him to do his bounden duty. And then they roared back downstairs singing, leaving the pair alone at last. In the darkness Annie Clark lay stiff, almost sickened by the alcoholic vapors emanating from the big, gasping, naked man beside her, and she heard the fiddles downstairs strike up the rowdy old tune, "Hang On Till Morning."

NOW THAT THE BRIDE AND GROOM HAD RETIRED, PATRICK Henry got less musical and more political. He took over the library and started trying to make it sound like the floor of the House of Burgesses. He stalked about, waving his cup, his spectacles on the top of his head, and orated.

"Since Lord Dunmore repacked the Caroline Court, surely you all have noticed, at least half a dozen of your friends have been brought to trial on charge of making seditious remarks against the Crown! Remember John Penn? Remember . . . Why, damn my eyes, there's two people in this very house right now, dancing in that room, who have been indicted for criticizing King George! I, who've said three times as much, by some odd quirk have yet to be tried." One got the impression that Henry would like nothing better. "Our aristocrats," he went on, "believe those good people take their sauciness from my own intemperate mouth. Nonsense! I only echo the people's sentiments, I don't shape them!"

"Mister Henry," interjected John Clark, "you're being modest."

Laughter rippled around the room. Patrick Henry himself had to lick a smile off his lips before continuing, as ferociously as ever. "The only representation you've ever had has been your peer juries. Thank God for the juries, God bless the juries! Were't not for you, every man heard blowing his nose in the direction of London would be on the pillories." They all knew of the Penn case. The jury of common planters that had served in John Penn's trial had been instructed by the magistrates to find him guilty of sedition and fine him heavily. They had instead decreed a fine of one penny. Only by such means had the ordinary colonists mitigated the heavy-handed authority that filtered down from King George through his colonial governor to the magistrates he appointed. But even jurors could be intimidated. Most of the tobacco merchants were royalists, and they were not above warning a juror that they would grade his tobacco inferior if he dared to thwart the magistrates' intentions. Patrick Henry, after a lifetime of listening in taverns and courthouses, knew well all the royalists' methods, and hated them. Perhaps it was true, as he said, that he only echoed the common men's sentiments, but he made a point of echoing them and echoing them until the common people could never forget their grievances for a waking minute.

Jonathan sat on an upholstered chair across the room, listening to these things he felt were true, and earnestly studying the speaker's voice and mannerisms. Jonathan was trying to see what it was about Henry's demeanor that made him so convincing, so provocative. Jonathan had slowly come to understand that hard work and intelligence alone were not enough to make a public servant stand out and gain fame. There had to be a certain power of personality, an ability to excite people or cast a spell on them, as for instance brother George could do. George, like Henry, could catch people's fancy, make them yell in agreement. Jonathan felt that he was lacking in these qualities himself. He, like his father, earned confidence, but neither of them was an exciting man. Jonathan envied men who had that flair, that theatric quality; he thought they had an unfair advantage to advance in public life, almost the same sort of unmerited advantage as was held by those who had huge Crown patent grants of land and were thus marked for prominence. Sometimes Jonathan resigned himself to believe that one either was born with that flair or would never have it. Other times he hoped it could be learned and acquired, and so now he was using this chance to study one of the most stirring of them all, and was paying less attention to what Patrick Henry was saying than to the way he said it.

"Hear, hear!" someone cried, in response to something Henry had just said, and Jonathan realized he had no idea what the man had said even though he was engrossed in listening to him. He looked into the bottom of his empty glass and wondered if it was the brandy that was so diffusing his faculties.

At that moment a hand took his wrist, a big, rough, red, freckled hand, and held his arm steady while pouring a dram of brandy into his glass. He looked up, and there beside him was a big, rough, red, freckled face. It was his Uncle George. George Rogers was a mighty stonemason, carpenter, and engineer, who had made himself into Caroline County's most respected builder of bridges, churches, gristmills, dams, and public buildings. He was Ann Rogers Clark's closest brother, and George's namesake. As important and impressive as he had become, he was still a charmer, a Rogers. His blue eyes were merry and mischievous and his smile was elfin. "I saw ye gazin' all forlorn into your glass there," he said, "and figured you were too numbed by Mister Henry's harangue to go fetch the bottle."

Jonathan laughed. "Nay, just lost in the ponders, I guess."

"Aye, me too. It's somethin' about weddings. They make me ponder too. So! So, now my niece is a married woman! I am just obfuscated! It seems no time since she sat on my knee and took that Dutch doll I'd bought 'er!"

"She still has it. It sits on a chest in her room." They were speaking quietly. Mister Henry was still proclaiming about the rights of man, over by the hearth. Some of the men in the library were still raising their voices in response to his exhortations, others were talking among themselves in twos and threes, and some sat snoring with their chins on their chests, liquor and pipe ashes dribbling unheeded onto their vests. Beyond the doors and hallways, the fiddles and fifes were playing a jig.

Now George Rogers was saying, ". . . told your Mama today, 'Sister Ann,' said I, 'y've raised a fine brood. I cherish 'em every one, and couldn't more if they were my own.'"

"Thankee, Uncle." George Rogers had a large family of sons himself, and doted on them, but in his great avuncular heart there seemed to be room for unlimited nieces and nephews.

Another hand settled on Jonathan now, a light hand on his left shoulder, and he turned and looked up. It was another uncle, this one Parson Robertson, his old teacher. Here was the man Jonathan loved more than anyone outside the immediate family, the man who had taught him how to think. The old Scots schoolmaster, tall and somber, beamed down on him. He wore his usual black wool frock coat and waistcoat, believed to be his only ones, and although he had exchanged his brown farmer's breeches for a black pair for the occasion, these too were so bagged out at the knees that he looked as if perpetually ready to hop off a stile. His face was gray and long, as was his hair, but kindly and intelligent. "Ah," said Jonathan, patting the bony hand on his shoulder. "Come sit with us. We were talking of family, and how weddings make ye feel."

"Join us, Parson," said George Rogers, and he hopped up and fetched a chair for the old gent, placing it at Jonathan's other side. Parson Robertson was married to Jonathan's Aunt Rachel. He farmed, and Aunt Rachel sold eggs and sewed clothes to supplement his tutor's fees, and the pair were as frugal as bread pudding, but due to the Parson's scrupulous honesty and a philanthropism that belied his Scottish birth, they remained as poor as Uncle George was rich. The parson had got off the ship from Scotland more than twenty years ago, but still had such a burr in his speech that many Virginians could scarcely understand him. Still, he was known as one of the very best teachers, in a colony where good basic education was hard to find, and Jonathan Clark had been one of his best pupils, along with Jamie Madison and Harry Innes and Samuel Edmundson. Donald Robertson had fled Scotland to escape the strictures of religious doctrine there, and thus the undercurrent of all his teachings was intellectual liberty. There was a joke that he had married Rachel Rogers primarily to acquire John Rogers the Martyr as an ancestor. It was, in fact, George Rogers who had made up that joke. George Rogers was respected and liked his pedantic brother-in-law as much as anyone in the family did, but had always felt that anyone on such a high intellectual plane needed some down-to-earth teasing now and then, "to keep 'im from just floating away," as he put it. And one of his slyest ways of teasing the parson was bringing up the name of his worst pupil. So he said now:

"Have ye heard, Parson, that my nephew George has become a builder?"

The teacher pursed his lips, and raised his eyebrows skeptically. "A builder?"

"A builder?" Jonathan said.

"Aye. Seems he's about to erect the largest structure west of

'ort Pitt. He came visited me last month, to brush up on points
' joining and leverage and so on, that I'd taught 'im long
ince."

"I didn't know that," Jonathan said. "He told me nowt about a
uilding. What's it to be?"

"Why, a fort. A log fort. He has a contract to build it. He's
oing right well, that lad is. Smart. *Smart!*" He always added
hat emphasis when he was teasing the Parson about George.

"A fort wheerrr?" the parson inquired.

"Why, a settlement on the Ohio, named, ah, let me recollect.
believe Wheeling, he said."

Jonathan shook his head. "I've heard there's much Indian
larm lately thereabout. I didn't know he was to build the fort,
hough I'd heard the people wanted one, so they wouldn't have
 go all the way to Pitt if there's an outbreak."

"I tried to discourage him from going out," George Rogers
aid. "But y' know him."

"Aye," said Jonathan. "Advice runs off 'im like rain off a
oon."

"So did education," said the parson.

"But he's certainly smart," repeated George Rogers. "*Smart!*"

"How smart's a man who goes out there at a time like this?"
aid Jonathan. "There's bad unrest there, so I read and so I
ear."

"That gent by the doorr theerrr," said the parson, inclining his
ead. "That Captain Lewis, d' ye know'm? He asserts thot thrrr's
een Indian sign as farrr doon as Albemarrrle."

"It's spooky out along the mountains," Jonathan said. "Imag-
ne how it must be way out there past 'em."

"Well, I don't like the thought o' that lad bein' in an Indian
var," said George Rogers. "But he'll take care o' himself as well
s any man could, I'll say as much."

"From what Pa tells of 'im," Jonathan muttered, "he's gotten
o Indian 'imself, I'm not sure but what he'd be on their side." It
ad been a spiteful thing to say, and his Uncle George's expres-
ion made him regret it at once. Now and then Jonathan would
lurt out something like that and get an unexpected glimpse of
is own envy of George. He forced a chuckle. "I'm jesting,
hough, o' course. I pray for 'im every day, as we all do. Hey,
ookee here at the fob he brought me from the capital! He toured
vay up to Woodstock to say hey to me." Jonathan was proud to
e able to say that. One thing certain was that he loved and
dmired his younger brother far more than he envied him. And
he thought of him out there in the dark heart of the Indian

country was fearsome. "I spent two hours trying to talk him ou o' going. I told him about all the out-country families I'd see come back over the mountains scared for safety. I told him he' be foolhardy, and more fool than hardy, to go on out. Told hir to stay and come back down for the wedding. Make the famil happy. O' course I didn't know then that he had a fort to build But he just laughed, said his usual litany how he had that coun try in 'is blood. How he was goin' to make Clark a name ou there. Bet me I'd be out there myself someday, and the whol family likewise. There's no arguing with 'im."

"My argument," said George Rogers, "was with my boys Jo and John. He had 'em in such a buzzel they wanted to go wit 'im. I told 'em, 'Talk to me about it in five years, when y're bot weaned proper.'"

"The oonly argument I iver had wi' Master Georrrge," sai the parson, "tha' is, the oonly thing 'e iver said tha' I could no answer, was, when I'd caught 'im sky-gazing in the classroom, ' said, 'Sir, if ye truly believe in freedom o' thought, then wh does it botherrr ye if I sit heerrr having a guid time wi' m mind?' Heh! Fair said, eh?"

Jonathan looked in surprise at his old teacher. The parson ha never told that story before, nor had he ever spoken of Georg with a tone of fondness in his voice like that. It's almost, he thought with a shiver, the way folks start talking respectfull about a man who's dead.

And he remembered his last sight of George, George riding up the road, leading his packhorse, turning to wave back, the huge shadowy flank of Massanutten Mountain dwarfing him. An Jonathan remembered having had an awful premonition at th time that that would be his last vision of George. But of cours he had not told that to the family. And Jonathan didn't believ in omens anyway. Such things, Parson Robertson had taugh him, are not valid parts of an enlightened rationale. "I'll outliv ye, Jonathan," George had told him once, pointing westward "Open places are healthier."

"Hey, Jonathan." Dickie's voice laughed behind him. "Hullo Uncle George. Parson, sir." Dickie was presently a pupil of th parson and felt awkward calling him 'Uncle' as he always ha used to.

"Hullo, Dick," said George Rogers. "Thought you'd be abed by now."

Dickie laughed, and there was considerable aroma to hi breath. The parson's face stiffened when it billowed around him, but Dickie was having too fine a time to notice. "Listen to wha

appened up at Port Royal, that I just heard tell of. I think it's
unny as all get-out. D'you remember Roy's Warehouse, where
'a used to take our tobacco?" He was leaning on the back of
onathan's chair.

"Aye, o' course."

"D'ye know that when Mister Roy died, his business was sold
o Magistrate Miller?"

"No, I hadn't heard it. What's funny about that?" Thomas
Roy had been a popular man with the planters; James Miller was
a royalist, who probably would be high-handed and hard to deal
vith."

"Nothin's funny so far," Dickie went on. "But ol' Miller, he
moved the main entrance from th' street side around to the
vharf side. Ye remember that narrow gangplank up over the
Rappahannock, where we'd sit an' fish while we waited for Pa to
get th' tobacco weighed? Well, that was th' only way a body
could get to ol' Miller's office. So here's th' funny part: so many
planters would get drunk at Roy's Tavern and fall off that gangplank into the river tryin' to get to Miller's office that the Court
made him move it back around! Ha, ha, ha! And him a justice
himself!"

"Ha! ha! Ha, ha, ha!" Even the parson was laughing.

That was a story Jonathan liked. He could remember well that
high gangplank and the murky river flowing far below among the
pilings, and could imagine the drunks falling off. But he liked
best hearing about a judgment against a Tory.

Uncle George was roaring with laughter too, bending forward
and slapping his knee, and his Rogers laughter was so loud that it
overrode one of Patrick Henry's perorations. Henry pulled his
spectacles down from his forehead to the end of his nose and
stared over them.

"What d'you find so amusing, Squire Rogers?"

"Ha, ha! Hey, nothing you said, Burgess Henry, but a tale this
nephew o' mine just told. Dick, boy, would ye like to tell it to
the gentlemen present?"

And so the slightly tipsy thirteen-year-old had a large audience
of substantial gentlemen to tell his story to, and told it well, with
only a few slurred words. And although Mr. Henry and some of
the others had already heard the story, or read it in the *Gazette*,
Dickie's narration was a resounding success, and dispelled some
of the disgruntled gravity that Mister Henry had brought into the
room. Dickie staggered out to their applause, blushing with a
happy self-consciousness. He had actually stolen the floor from
Patrick Henry.

*   *   *

IN THE SMALL HOURS OF THE MORNING, JOHNNY LAY WITH his arms around Betsy Freeman's magnificent hips, mumbling into her superb bosom that if she would only yield the rest of her charms to him, he would straightaway go to her father and speak of marriage. He knew, deep in his rational mind, that it was a terribly rash promise to make, one that he had never made to anyone else before, but he was desperate with desire, and to possess her wholly at last after these twelve hours of hot pursuit seemed worth any risk. If he could have her now, if he could only penetrate that last few inches to the warm inner mystery of her, then tomorrow he could think about how to deal with the consequences.

It had to be soon. He was as exhausted and uncomfortable as he had ever been in his life. His groin ached unbearably, and though he and his temptress were burrowed deep in the hay of the stable mow, the chill of the October night air on his sweat-damp underdrawers and bare back made his teeth chatter as he poured forth his frantic vows. It was incredible that he could be burning like a charcoal kiln in his loins at the same time his nose rankled with cold and dripped on her chemise. Only that part of him that he held plastered against her was warm.

Egod, but she was a stubborn wench, he had thought twenty times this night. A dozen times he had been ready to give up the siege. But at those moments she had somehow sensed his weakening resolve and allowed him to untie one more ribbon, loosen one more lace, slip off one more shoe, pull out one more hairpin. And now she had drawn from him the promise of promises, and she murmured at last, "Ah, Johnny, Johnny! Oh yes, if ye must," and she took his hand in the pitch darkness and guided it to some warm, soft, smooth place, which he could not immediately identify because of the numbness of his cold fingers. She gasped and started, and he was afraid it was because of the shock of his cold hand. But she was pushing him away again, for the hundredth time, and she hissed with a chilling urgency:

"Someone's here!"

The hay rustled loudly as they sat upright, wisps of alfalfa cascading off them. Horses were nickering, stamping, thumping in the wooden stalls.

Voices, several voices, were muttering in the stables not ten feet away. Someone whispered and someone snorted and someone snickered. A sliver of lanternlight fell between the planks. Johnny and Betsy cringed, wanting to grab their discarded garments and dress themselves, but knew their rustlings in the hay would be heard. There was a moment of stillness then, in which he rapid squeaks of the violins far away in the house could be eard. Then one of the voices said ominously:

"Gi' me your knife. I'll get that filly first!"

The words struck a cold panic in Johnny's breast. He was stiff nd numb and aching and absurdly out of costume, but there as no honorable thing to do but take a stance to protect her. In he darkness she was making little gasping groans of terror, and hese piteous sounds galvanized Johnny. "No!" he shouted in a uavering croak, and leaped out of the hay into the stable cor- dor ready to fight to the death for his lady love.

The intruders recoiled, incredulous, at this apparition in hay- visps and drawers. The horses, whose tails they were cutting off, eared in their stalls and whinnied in stark terror. The lantern ell to the ground and went out. There was a frenetic banging of ooves and thudding of flesh. The commotion spread to the pad- ock outside the stables, where several score horses belonging to he wedding guests panicked and started running and neighing. he fiddle music in the house trailed off, and doors were bang- ng, voices were shouting. "What goes?" "What?" "Horse hieves!" "Indians!" The paddock fence rattled and threatened to reak under the force of lunging horseflesh. Candles and lan- erns came pouring out of the house. Someone fired a pistol in he air, doubling the confusion.

It was an old country trick, Johnny realized then, for ranksters to cut off the tails of the horses of wedding guests, and he had interrupted such a prank.

The lights and voices were coming closer. Johnny turned, eaped back into the haymow on top of his terrified paramour, lamped a hand over her mouth, and drew clothes and hay in ver them.

No evidence was ever found to determine who had managed o cut the tails off a filly and two geldings in the Clark stable that ight. Johnny had seen who two of them were—those two outish brothers of Betsy herself—but of course he was in no osition to reveal what he knew.

While the household and guests were out and about in the ftermath of this disruption, it was discovered that Master Billy Clark was missing from his trundle bed. For a long time the fear eigned that he had somehow been kidnaped by the interlopers, nd a rider was sent out to fetch the constable, and a boyhunt vas on that very nearly discovered Johnny Clark and Betsy Free- nan, who, though nearly naked deep in the hay, were too shiv- ery with cold and fright to consummate their union.

Before daylight Master Billy was finally found, asleep under discarded clothes in the bridal chamber. It was deduced that **▮** must have gotten up at one in the morning to follow the hilari▮ in there, then had got lullabyed back to sleep by the groom snoring.

At least that was the story of it that the Clark boys made up ▮ josh their brother-in-law for the rest of his life.

3

Ohio Valley
April, 1774

THE PALE GREEN LEAVES OF APRIL WERE A BLUR AS TH▮ horses galloped headlong down the slope into the ravine towar▮ Pipe Creek. George's heart was in his mouth; his blood was ra▮ ing toward the awful joy of first combat. Branches swished pa▮ his head and lashed his arms and thighs but he scarcely fe▮ them. A great scream was building in his throat, ready to bur▮ forth. Alongside him in the crackling, thudding onrush plunge▮ a bay stallion ridden by Captain Mike Cresap, the veteran India▮ fighter. In a sideward glance George saw Cresap grinning like ▮ running wolf. In this creek valley they had overtaken and co▮ nered a Shawnee war party and were flushing them into th▮ open. The Shawnees were running in the cane and reeds, tryin▮ to disperse and vanish. Cresap, cocking back his old razor-shar▮ broadsword, closed on a fleeing brown back and the killer ye▮ pulsated in his throat. The sword whistled as Cresap overtook ▮ sprinting warrior. In the corner of his eye George saw that war▮ rior pitch forward, and at that sight, the cry that had bee▮ gathering in his own throat tore out, quavering and thrilling▮ Before him, darting fleet as a deer, was another warrior. Whe▮ the Indian glanced back over his shoulder, George glimpsed h▮ ochre-painted cheekbone and raised his tomahawk to aim a blo▮ at it. Coming abreast of the running warrior, George swung th▮ tomahawk, but the brave dodged aside and the blow missed.

Not reining in for him, George spurred his horse harder and bor▮ down on another fleeing Indian. He was vaguely aware now of th▮ curdled war cries of the other men, of the noise of horseme▮

coming down the other creekbank to cut off the fugitives, and of the popping of gunfire somewhere to his right. A gun discharged close behind him and a musketball hummed past his ear, an exhilarating sound, making him feel almost unbearably vital.

Now the brave running before him in the high grass was almost within arm's length. George yodeled again and struck with a sidearm sweep that seemed to have in it all the power of God's wrath. It met something, with such a jolt that he thought his arm would tear off. His charge had carried him to the creek's edge, and here he wheeled and rode back into the cane, seeking the man he had just struck. He saw blood on his tomahawk and another whoop escaped from his throat.

The canefield was a melee of smoke and confused movement now. Cresap and his men were galloping back and forth, yelling, swinging sabers and tomahawks, or firing their rifles down into the waving tall cane. The smell of gunpowder rankled in the sun-heated, grassy-sweet air. George rode in among the others, crisscrossing the field, hungry for a glimpse of another human target. His eyes felt as if they would pop out and his whole body tingled in anticipation of quick steel or lead. His temples pounded with pulsebeats; he was pouring sweat.

There were no more Shawnees to be seen. They had vanished like rabbits in the tall growth. George could not find the one he had struck. Here was a trampled place in the cane, spotted with fresh bright blood; there lay a musket with a broken stock, butterflies tumbling over it.

He rode toward a place where several militiamen had dismounted and gathered. They stood in a circle around a dead Indian and watched one man make a circular knife-cut in the scalp and pull up on the hair. The Indian's neck was half-severed, spurting blood, and as the militiaman tugged at the black hair it looked as if the head might come off before the scalp did. But now the bloody topknot separated with an audible *pop*.

George knew this was not the Indian he had struck, nor was it the one Cresap had slashed with that first saber blow. The man scalping this Indian knew it was *his* Indian; that was the unwritten rule. But the others now were free to take souvenirs. One sliced off an ear; another took another ear. One flopped the corpse over and cut the breechclout away and was starting to cut away the genitals when George turned away. His throat suddenly felt clogged. The men butchering the Indian were chuckling and talking and he did not want to hear what they were saying or see what they were doing.

In the first moments after the skirmish, George had been disappointed that he had no scalp to claim; now he had seen a scalp-taking and he knew it was a thing he would never do. Now a great wave of weariness came through him, followed by burning thirst and a sense of disorientation. Suddenly he was almost sickened by the memory of the bloodlust he had felt. Cresap, who was reputed to have more than two dozen scalps to his name, was riding along the edge of the creek yelling angrily, trying to regroup his company. George realized at once that this letdown of discipline and vigor right after a fight could be a dangerous time. As for himself, he felt weak almost to the point of lethargy. He looked back at the group. One man, arms smeared with fresh blood, was standing waving a scarlet-dripping strip of skin a yard long. They were skinning the corpse now.

So this had been his first taste of mortal combat, his first real Indian fight. Four days ago near Wheeling, Shawnees had murdered two Virginian hunters, and these men had gathered under Cresap at the new fort to ride out and find the Shawnee party and take revenge. Now they had caught them here and run them down and scattered them; they had killed at least one, but it would take a long search in the cane to determine just how much revenge they had gotten.

By midafternoon they were sitting mounted before Cresap, ready to ride out of the creek bottom. One militiaman, who George knew was a boatwright by trade, sat slumped in his saddle, face white as paper and his shirtfront all bloodsoaked. George doubted that that one would make it back to the fort.

ONE OF CRESAP'S LIEUTENANTS HELD THE END OF A ROPE, the other end of which was tied in a slipknot around the neck of a slightly wounded young Shawnee brave, who had been found hiding among reeds in the creek. Probably he would not have been found if blood from his shoulder wound had not reddened the water around him. No one knew whose he was. He was not painted like the one George had struck; Cresap didn't claim him, probably because he was such a wretch and looked no more than fourteen or fifteen years old.

This boy was their only captive. Blood tracks in the tall cane had indicated that two or three other wounded Indians had escaped into the creek, maybe to bleed to death or drown there; the rest of the war party, about sixteen of them, had vanished with no further trace.

Some men of the company wanted to try to pick up the Shawnees' spoor and hound them on down the river and kill the rest of them.

"That'd be a fool's errand," Cresap snarled. "We've no surprise left. They'd ambush us till they had us all."

It had been a remarkable lesson to George. All that shooting and shouting and bloodlust and bewildering haste, though it had seemed a battle in the full sense of the word, had had hardly any more result than a boar hunt.

The men were not satisfied. With that democratic spirit of frontier militia, they now proposed that Cresap lead them on some more fruitful raid before their return to the Wheeling settlement. They wanted more scalps than this one; they wanted to frighten all the Indians of the region back into peaceful submission. They were not interested in any distinctions between tribes; they wanted simply to kill Indians until no more Indians would dare kill Virginians. They knew that Michael Cresap hated Indians and that he knew how to kill them.

"There's a big Indian got his camp up at the mouth o' Yeller Creek," said one of the men. "Wouldn't be out of our way t' go git him."

George's scalp prickled. *Yellow Creek.* He realized the "big Indian" the man was talking about was Chief Logan. He opened his mouth to protest, but Cresap spoke first.

"No, by God, not that one. Hurt him and ye'd start a war." George was surprised, and relieved. So there was more to Mike Cresap than just the blind-mad Indian killer.

"There already *is* a war, Cap'n," said one rifleman, a burly roughneck named Jake Greathouse, whose cabin and trading post were just across the river from Logan's camp. "Ye read what th' governor said."

"Where he sits in Williamsburg, His Ludship don't know much," Cresap said. He glanced around the semicircle of horsemen, the hunters, boatmen, carpenters, farmers and adventurers who were, for the moment, warriors. Two days before, in the fort at Wheeling, they had planted a war post, in imitation of the Indian manner, struck it with their tomahawks and performed a war dance around it. They had read Governor Dunmore's proclamation and danced around the war post. Such dancing seemed to have the same effect on white men as it had on Indians; they were still up on a mood of that and did not want to hear peaceable reasoning right now, especially not from Cresap. But he said, removing his hat and wiping his sleeve over his forehead:

"Listen to me, damn yeh! Y' came to me, 'member, and asked me to lead this company. While I'm a-doing it, we won't strike Logan. I don't like that uppity chief any more'n you do, but we won't strike a friendly camp and that's all I'll say on't." He glared around. His face was shiny with sweat and the oil of long-un-washed skin. His dark hair was matted and flecked with chaff. His hard jaw was stubbled and the pores of his nose were black. There was dried Indian blood on the right sleeve of his hunting shirt.

George wanted to speak up. He had no particular authority in the company, no rank. Most of them didn't even know he was the man who had built their fort. Nevertheless, he spoke now.

"I know the Mingoes in that camp. I'll tell ye this, there's some o' you and your families might be long dead but for Chief Logan."

"Who the hell are you?" someone muttered. George ignored that and pointed at Greathouse. "You," he said, "you know Logan's a friend. Tell 'em."

Greathouse looked around at the eyes on him, uncomfortable. Then he sneered. "I know he's *your* friend, Clark. But I ain't no Indian-lover."

A flash of fury reddened George's vision. But he clenched his jaw. *Red hair's no excuse for tantrums*, he thought, and kept still. He saw Logan's fine, thoughtful visage for a moment in his mind's eye and wanted to say more for him. But he knew he would do no good arguing for him against this belligerent lout, especially in the midst of these men's war-post sentiment.

"That's all, then, boys," Cresap said, giving George a curious, sidelong look, as if appraising him. "Got enough daylight to get halfway back to Wheeling. Let's ride."

Someone drew abreast of George as the column of horsemen twisted through the woods. George got a whiff of whiskey, which brought him out of his battle reverie. He looked aside and saw a barrel-chested man of perhaps fifty, with grizzled, unruly whis-kers and merry eyes and a brilliant grin. The man winked at George and proffered his flask. George thanked him and took a swig of the powerful stuff, which burned all the way down. "Thankee, Mister . . ."

"Helm," said the man. "Len Helm, that's who I am. Fauquier County. Y're a mean rider, son, and a smart head, too. Any time y're thirsty, why, just holler." He winked again and raised the flask in a salute, then dropped back. George grinned, feeling better, and repeated the name once in his mind. Len Helm. Then he thought back to Logan the Mingo and his family. It seemed a good idea to go and visit with him, to let him know he was in danger.

Chief Logan looked intently at George across the small fire that burned in the center of his lodge, and the lines around his mouth were deep and drawn. Logan had noticed his young friend's unusual solemnity all evening, and understood that it must have to do with the clashes between the Virginians and the Shawnees that had erupted so frequently this spring along the border. Logan dreaded the things they might have to say across the grain of their friendship. The piping of tree toads came in from the darkness and filled the silences. Logan's sister had fed the men a large platter of soft hominy flavored with wild mustard and wild onion and strips of smoky-flavored meat. One of Logan's brothers, a handsome, quiet chieftain who revealed neither the charm nor intensity of Logan, sat at the third place by the fire, his eyes shut so it was not clear whether he listened or dozed. Opposite him was Logan's brother-in-law, equally somnolent. George suspected that they found it easier to retreat into this sleepy attitude than to deal with the presence of a Virginian in the lodge in these times. Logan's sister, beautiful and serene, huge with child, now sat on a mat in a shadowy corner of the lodge, illuminated by an oil wick in a geode bowl, eating hominy with a horn spoon. The gathering was like so many George had spent in Logan's village the year before. But then they had talked about all manner of things in the world; now they said little and seemed to wait for each other to begin the discussion of unpleasant news. Logan lit and passed a pipe, and when they all had smoked, George said:

"The anger of our peoples puts shadows on our friendship." Logan nodded with a forlorn smile and George continued: "You know of the murder of the two Virginians last week near Wheeling?" Of course Logan knew. Everything came to his ears, as he was a bridge between the races. He nodded, but a narrowing of his eyes showed that he did not like George's choice of the word "murder." George went on. "You know that Captain Cresap caught the Shawnees at Pipe Creek two days ago and avenged them?" Logan knew this too. His eyes flashed at the name of Cresap. His brother and brother-in-law stiffened, and opened their eyes at the sound of the name. "Did you know," George went on, "that I was among the men who rode with Cresap that day?"

Logan's eyes widened with surprise and displeasure, but only for an instant. "I did not know." He looked down into the fire. "What I foresaw seems to come closer to us, the time when we will have to face each other over the fires of battle instead of the fire of the lodge."

"I hope never. But I had rather tell you I rode with Cresap than have you hear it from someone else."

Logan nodded, grim but assenting. "I pray that your heart will never chime with that of Cresap."

"I came to warn you that some of Cresap's men spoke of raiding you here. Whether you believe this, Cresap said no. In that, my heart did chime with his."

"It was not his heart but his head that said no. He would be glad to kill me, but he is no fool." Then Logan looked at George and sighed, and said, "I wish you were not a Virginian."

In the past year, Virginians had pushed as far down the Ohio as 350 miles below Fort Pitt. The tribes saw Virginians clearing land and killing game deep in the sacred hunting ground of Cain-tuck-ee. The chiefs were beginning to see too that this intrusion could drive a white wedge between the Algonquian peoples north of the Ohio and the Cherokee, Creek, and Choctaw nations of the south.

"I have listened to the talk of the chiefs," Logan said. "Some of them say that every Virginian found in the valley of the Beautiful River should be killed. Most of the nations would want to keep peace with you if you would stop coming to draw the lines on the land. But the Shawnee nation does not even pretend to care for peace anymore.

"You, my friend, came to warn me for my safety. I return the favor. I tell you that Virginians are in danger. Not from Logan, but from others. As your brother, I ask you to guard yourself."

They fell silent and gazed at the coals. They were heavy with resignation over the inevitable hostility between their peoples. It made it hard to talk of the lands and skies and spirits as they had used to. War was in the air. Militiamen had been ordered by Governor Lord Dunmore to garrison the forts, and the great runner Daniel Boone had been sent out among the settlements to summon all subjects of Virginia back across the mountains. George remembered what his father had said about the frontiersmen's land claims. An Indian war would be a good excuse for the Royal Governor to nullify all the holdings of his troublesome backwoods subjects. George could sense the craft of His Majesty's ministers at work. But that was all so vague and distant. And George was, after all, still a loyal subject.

He could feel himself being drawn into the role of a fighting man now. He had sold his farm at Grave Creek for a good profit, then had traveled farther down the river to survey in the Cain-tuck-ee, for the Ohio Company. But the call for militia had interrupted his career as a surveyor, and he could already foresee a pattern of attacks and counterattacks, eye for eye and tooth for tooth, stretching into an indefinite future. He knew he could void it only by retreating to seaboard Virginia, and that, he knew, he would never do. The frontier had its hold on him now. He had tasted the profound grandeur of virgin wilderness and had lived minute by minute in a world unprotected by law, where each man was his own king. He had idled in the buzzing, sunny hospitality of Indian villages, he had lain enwrapped in the musky embraces of chosen maidens, in cheerful liaisons sanctioned by villagers who liked him and wanted his blood in the tribes. First he had been enveloped by the Indians. But now an edge was forming between his race and this race he had come to love, and he could feel the edge now. He was becoming a part of the cutting edge of civilization. Any life behind that cutting edge would be insufferably tame and dull.

In her corner, Logan's sister had blown out her lamp flame and lain down heavily to sleep. Logan had put sticks on the coals, and started the tobacco pipe in circulation again, and he studied George in the pungent smoke for a while, then said:

"Tell me this: You have now fought in a blood fight; you are a new soldier. How was it for you, in your heart? How was it for you, in your head?" He looked like his old self now; he was inquiring into the soul of a man, about the matters of deepest importance to men.

George leaned closer to look into the fire, as if the answer were there, and rested his arms on his knees. He spread his long, strong fingers and looked through them at the flames, thinking. The vast woodland night outside the glow of the lodge chirruped and shrieked with insects and night birds, and breathed with the sounds of running creekwater and breezes in the foliage.

"Ye said it well," George began. "It was one thing in my heart and another thing in my head. A fire was in my heart, and I have never felt so strong. But then when it had ended and the fire left my heart, it was my head that was full of ashes."

He shrugged, out of words. "I'm not proud that I enjoyed it so much. I'd rather never do it again. I'll have to think on it each time it happens."

"Yes," said Logan. "You must think on it. A man is a wolf, but he is meant to be more than a wolf. The glory of my people is in war, and my heart often has burned with that glory. But I too grew sick and full of ashes. I put away the blade long ago, and since have always talked for peace. I do not want that blaze in my heart again; I no longer need it." He looked up from the fire, into which he, too, had been talking. "Did you take any life by your own hand when you rode with Cresap?"

"I don't know. But when I struck I had the feeling of it."

Logan nodded, again understanding. "Your God tells you not to kill. I hope you will always think of that. A warrior believes his courage is proven each time he makes blood flow. But there are some chiefs who understand further than that; they know greater courage sometime may be proven by preventing the flow of blood."

"But most chiefs were warriors first."

"Yes," said Logan. "And sometimes they are forced to be warriors again."

TWO WEEKS LATER, CHIEF LOGAN AND HIS BROTHER-IN-LAW rode down into the valley of Yellow Creek toward their camp leading a pack horse with two small deer strapped across its back. They had been gone two days and their hunting trip had been easy. Morning sunlight dappled the forest floor. Through the fresh spring foliage, still glistening with droplets from a pre-dawn shower, Logan could now see a glimpse of his lodge. He raised his voice in a pleasant call of homecoming.

No voice came back. That was curious. He did not hear the music of the voices of his sister's children. And there was no woodsmoke. The camp was deserted, except for two dogs. Under the kettle outside the lodge, the ashes were cold and wet. Logan sniffed the air. He scanned the ground. There were no new footprints since the rainshower, only those of the dogs. That meant his family had been gone overnight, or at least since before daybreak. He peered inside the lodge. It seemed undisturbed, but a string of cured peltries was gone from the roof-poles where they had hung. His father's and brother's muskets and powder horns and bullet bags were not in the lodge.

So the whole family had gone someplace. He could not imagine where, but he was not alarmed. The men had taken their weapons with them.

Then Logan saw something that made a needle of alarm prick at the base of his skull: in a patch of soft earth in the packed dirt at the center of the lodge there was a boot print; the heel and sole of a large white man's foot. *Cresap*, Logan thought.

Yesterday on the hunt Logan had seen Cresap and a dozen Virginians riding along a bluff, two hours' distance from here. Logan had recognized some of them. His friend Clark had not been with them. They had passed without seeing Logan.

Quickly now, Logan and his brother-in-law hung the deer carcasses from an oak limb, out of reach of dogs or wolves. Then they searched the ground more carefully.

Under the canopy of a dense maple they found the prints of

an iron-shod hoof heading toward the river. Walking, leading their horses, carrying primed guns, stooped low over the faint trail, peering ahead now and then into the foliage and listening intently, they followed the hoofprints. Logan came to a boggy place where the hoofprints were sunk deep and were full of water, and here they saw moccasin prints also. One was small, a woman's print, but deep. He thought of his sister with her burden of child. The needle of alarm in his spine was burning and shining now as he pointed this out to his brother-in-law.

The trail was faint as they went down a slope toward the Ohio's bank, but here was a piece of torn moss, there a broken may-apple stem. Logan was jolted by a strange noise, half cry, half gasp, behind him. He glanced back quickly at the awful sound, not realizing it was his brother-in-law's voice until he saw him stopped there in his tracks, hand at throat, mouth agape, bulging eyes fixed on some high point ahead. Logan shot his gaze in that direction.

A bloody baby hung in a tree, upside down. It was impaled on the sharp end of a lopped-off limb, its skin strangely wrinkled by dried slime. From its belly hung a cord and placental sac. Flies swarmed over it.

Beyond and below it was a hazel shrub draped with intestines. At the base of the shrub lay Logan's father, his abdomen cut open and alive with flies, his scalp gone, eyesockets shredded by buzzards. Something hung from another tree beyond the shrub.

It was Logan's sister, strung up by her thumbs, naked, scalped, slit open from her ribs to her genitalia, both breasts gone. Logan and her husband saw her at the same moment.

Teeth bared and clenched, panting and whimpering, the two Indians darted about in the glade until they had found them all. They found the children, and Logan's brother; all had been tomahawked and mutilated, partly skinned, and their carcasses had been gnawed by animals and pecked by buzzards. Under a bush there was an empty liquor jug. Fastened on a tree trunk nearby was a swatch of cloth with two bullet holes in it.

Ice-cold shivers had been racing from Logan's temples down to his knees as he searched the glade, and a bubble of grief grew bigger and bigger in his chest; now his entire body was quaking and the veins distended in his neck. Every blood relative of Tah-gah-ju-te, whom the whites had called Chief Logan, lay or hung butchered in this bright green glade, over blood-darkened ground. No family was left but this whimpering brother-in-law who knelt, chest heaving and eyes bloodshot, under the eviscerated carcass of his wife.

The bubble in Tah-gah-ju-te's chest was too big to contain. In the bright red whirlpool in his brain he saw the face of Cresap and then an endless line of Virginians. The bubble in Tah-gah-ju-te's bosom burst. A long, throbbing howl poured out of his throat, once, twice, again and again. The other's voice joined his.

Tah-gah-ju-te and his last of kin howled like wolves for a long time on the bank of the Beautiful River, and then became silent and began to collect the remains of their family. They took them back to the camp on the pack horse that had carried the deer from their hunt.

PANIC SWEPT THE VIRGINIA FRONTIER.

Tah-gah-ju-te, once peacemaker and friend of the white men, had renounced his English name of Logan. He had sent word to the white settlements that he had taken up his hatchet and would not put it down until he had killed ten whites for each slaughtered member of his family. He had called on other chiefs to help him avenge the massacre, and there were many in the mood to join him. Bands of painted warriors from many of the Algonquian tribes soon were flitting silently along their trails through the deep woods, going to the isolated cabins and the small settlements the Virginians had built in clearings beside creeks and springs and rivers throughout the Ohio Valley. There was much ground to cover; the cabins numbered in hundreds. But the Indians knew where each one was. Soon, white men were falling dead behind their plows, struck by arrows or musket-balls from the woods. Mothers and their children, working or playing in sunny clearings outside their cabins, would look up and see the last sight they were to see: painted, copper-skinned forms running toward them with hatchets and knives. Babies were sliced to death screaming in their cradles. Dirty smoke rose from burning cabins. Vultures circled through the smoke and slowly settled through it to pick at the flesh of disemboweled women or throat-cut cattle. Then the long files of warriors, bloody-fresh scalps of auburn or white or brown hair tied to their belts or gun muzzles, would vanish into the sun-flecked woods again, to lope over a hill or down a ravine to the next cabin. Sometimes a sobbing survivor from one farm would have outrun them to the next and warned its inhabitants, and here the Indians would have to besiege the fortified cabin and burn the defenders out into the open where they could be killed. Thirty Virginians—men, women, and children—looked up into the fury-crazed eyes of Tah-gah-ju-te himself as their life leaked out f them. He had thirty scalps by June, ten for his father's, ten for is brother's, and ten for his sister's, and then he put down his omahawk. But the war had started, and it went on.

All but the bravest or most foolhardy Virginians fled as the anic raced along the frontier. On one day, George Rogers Clark at in his saddle among Cresap's militiamen guarding a ford and ounted a thousand settlers crossing the Monongahela eastward vith their baggage and livestock. Cresap rode to and fro, bristling vith weapons, his hatchet face gray and sullen. He had just earned from a survivor that the mad Mingo was blaming him or the slaughter of his family. George, who now had in his ocket a militia captain's commission signed by Governor Lord Dunmore, rode alongside Cresap and put a hand on his arm.

"Look at it this way," he said. "You must be a big man around ere if the Indians palm everything that happens onto your houlders."

Cresap finally smiled, but it was a smile with a sneer in it. He aid, "By th' Eternal, if I could find Jake Greathouse, I'd cut his ver out and feed it to 'im on a plate!"

For it was Greathouse who had murdered Logan's family. The Mingoes had traded with Greathouse often, and had had no reaon to be wary of him, other than for his sharp trading practices. ut on the last day of April, with a gang of ruffians, he had lured Logan's relatives out with drink, proposed a target-shooting conest, and, after the Indian men had emptied their guns at a target f cloth on a tree, fallen upon them with knives and tomahawks. he story had been pieced together later when Cresap quesoned two of the accomplices. Greathouse had fled, no one new where. "Lord look th' other way if I ever find that reeky illain," Cresap muttered.

"Or if the Mingoes ever find him," George said.

A LONG RANK OF MILITIAMEN MOVED SLOWLY ON FOOT rough a beanfield toward the Shawnee town. Behind them rode another rank. George was riding slightly behind the secnd rank, looking over their heads toward the silent village. The y was overcast and the air was so close and sultry it was hard to reathe.

The rank kept moving forward, rifles at ready. George looked his right and could see another company advancing through ll corn toward the north side of the town. There was not a ice anywhere, just the whispering tread of the militiamen rough the field. Most were ragged, sweat-drenched, shirtless or a hunting shirts of gray homespun. The straps of their powder horns and gun bags crisscrossed their backs. Joe Bowman from Dunmore County, a sinewy, straw-blond lieutenant of George's age, his second in command of the company, looked up the line toward him, and their eyes met. George nodded. They had predicted this morning that this town, like all the others they had invaded, would prove abandoned, and it looked as if they had been right.

The column, under the command of Colonel Angus McDonald, had marched from Wheeling to the upper Muskingum River country, to carry the war into the heart of the Shawnees' lands. Most of the warriors had gone to join the great Shawnee chief Cornstalk and his army of a thousand somewhere down on the Ohio, thus leaving their towns undefended. The militia had seen Shawnee scouts everywhere along the way, but the populations of the towns had simply melted away before their advance, taking with them everything portable. In each case, the column had formed ranks and marched cautiously into the village just this way, finding no one to shoot and nothing to plunder.

In ten minutes, the Virginians occupied the town. The captains sent their men out in squads to cut down and burn the crops and set wigwams and lodges to the torch. Soon the air was dense with sharp-smelling smoke; fires crackled and rushed. This was the last town. Now they would return to Wheeling. Bowman came up to George and yawned, his eyes reddened by smoke. "Sure is an exciting war, hain't it?" he said.

"Surely is. Don't know if my poor heart can take it. But," he added, "I doubt we could be spendin' our time better." A council lodge nearby collapsed and its flames rushed higher, sending up ash. "They'll have to come in off the war path soon. They'll have a hard time getting ready for winter after what we've done." This campaign on the Muskingum had been a valuable lesson. Tedious and businesslike though it was, it proved that there is far more value in offensive war than in defensive. "And," he added with a wink at Bowman, "unless our boys die o' boredom, why, do prefer a war without casualties."

A few weeks of Lord Dunmore's War, as it had come to be called, had created a conviction in George's mind, a strange conviction for a soldier, one he seldom discussed with others: that bloodshed was useless and tragic, and that any strategy which accomplished an objective with the least bloodshed was the best strategy. It reminded him of something his mother had said once while bandaging him after he had cut himself with an ax: "Blood belongs *in* a body. To me, blood is an obscenity when it gets out of its veins." George had repeated those words often in his mind. He had thought a great deal about that bloodlust that had boiled in his heart that day at Pipe Creek, and had decided that bloodletting was not the glorious thing soldiers pretended it was. Pa is right, George thought. There was not much he could do to avoid being a soldier, the world being as it was, and there would always be fighting. But he'd be damned if he would ever have that sick weariness again that he had felt after his first battle. He would still have nightmares sometimes in which he rode howling through Indian hordes with a bloody broadsword and gore up to his elbows and a belt full of scalps, and then he would reach the bank of a creek and his mother and father would be standing there looking at him in dismay, and then they would turn their backs on him.

DUNMORE'S WAR ENDED WITH A BATTLE GEORGE ONLY heard about. He was among fifteen hundred officers and men who were moving down the Ohio from Fort Pitt under the direct command of Lord Dunmore when runners from downriver brought news that Colonel Andrew Lewis and a thousand mountain men had fought Cornstalk's warriors to a draw in a daylong battle at the mouth of the Ka-na-wha. It had occurred on October 10 and it had cost the lives of twenty-two officers and fifty-five privates, but Colonel Lewis had stood fast until the united tribes had broken off and withdrawn in the evening.

Now, with Lewis's force and Governor Dunmore's main army about to join together in the heart of their country, Cornstalk and the other chiefs sent runners to Dunmore, asking to talk peace.

Lord Dunmore's army encamped on the Piqua Plains, a grand array of tents dominated by Dunmore's spacious pavilion all aflutter with flags and banners, and the chiefs came to this camp to sue for peace.

Governor Dunmore was a haughty man, very aloof from all his troops and officers, even, it seemed, contemptuous of them. He insulted his colonial officers by excluding them from his negotiations with the Indian chiefs. He and his Indian agent, Dr. Connolly, took the great warrior chiefs—Cornstalk, Blue Jacket, Moluntha—into the pavilion and talked to them in secret. And when even Colonel Lewis, the hero of the conflict, was excluded from the negotiations, there was such an uproar of indignation that the whole army was on the verge of mutiny. George saw the hard-bitten veteran Lewis and rosy-cheeked Dunmore arguing violently with each other on the parade ground, and then, before the astonished gaze of half the army, Lord Dunmore actually drew his sword and threatened Lewis with it. The troops were roaring with anger.

Somehow, Lewis controlled himself, and kept his men from rising in mutiny against the Royal Governor. But from that moment on, Dunmore was the object of hatred and suspicion and rumor. George sat by a cookfire in the evenings and listened to Bowman and others talk. "Th' fancy fool's no friend o' Virginia, that's plain. He's a King's man, all out, and he's got to be watched." Some of the officers claimed to know that Dunmore had precipitated the war deliberately for the purpose of calling the Virginians back inside their frontiers. George remembered his own suspicions, those dubious thoughts he had had last spring in Logan's lodge. George sat gazing down at his red breeches and weskit, the officer's uniform of Dunmore's Royal Virginia Militia, and had the awful feeling that he was in the wrong uniform. He wished he had been with Lewis's division instead of Dunmore's.

The rumors grew uglier as the army sat in the field at Piqua Plains and watched the chiefs come and go. Some of Cresap's scouts gossiped that Jake Greathouse had murdered Chief Logan's family under secret orders from Dr. Connolly, to get Dunmore's War started for him.

Bowman and Helm were members of a society called the Sons of Liberty, and they were keenly suspicious of the governor. "What's he cookin' up with those redmen in that tent?" Bowman would whisper, his eyes narrowed. "I warn ye, it's for the advantage o' King George, not us. I tell ye, boys, he's a King's man, and he's slippin' the King's sceptre up our ass!"

There was no doubt anymore that Dunmore was a King's man. He had proven that earlier in the year. When the Virginia Assembly in Williamsburg had passed a resolution declaring sympathy with Massachusetts after the Boston Tea Party, Dunmore had dissolved the Assembly. Even out here on a golden plain in the Ohio territory, the stress between the Crown and the colonies could be felt. "I'll say this," Bowman murmured one chilly night. "Every man jack of us is goin' to have to take his stand 'fore long. As for me, I can't wait to get out o' these Goddamn red clothes. They itch on me like lice."

TAH-GAH-JU-TE, THE MAN WHOSE VENDETTA HAD PUT THE frontier in flames, would not come to Lord Dunmore's peace talks. The governor wanted him, and sent a special messenger to persuade him to come to the council.

The messenger returned without the Mingo chief. Tah-gah-u-te had refused to come. But he had dictated a reply. George read it, his heart squeezing with sadness.

I appeal to any white man to say if he ever entered Logan's cabin hungry and he gave him not meat; if he ever came cold and naked and he clothed him not. Logan remained quiet in his cabin, an advocate for peace. Such was my love for the whites that my countrymen as they passed said, 'Logan is the friend of white men.' I had even thought to live with you, but for the injuries of one man . . . who the last spring, in cold blood and unprovoked, murdered all the relations of Logan, not sparing even women and children.

There runs not a drop of my blood in any living creature. This called on me for revenge. I have sought it; I have killed many; I have fully glutted my vengeance. For my country, I rejoice at the beams of peace. But do not harbor a thought that mine is the joy of fear. Logan never felt fear. He will not turn on his heel to save his life.

Who is there to mourn for Logan? Not one.

George clenched his jaw and swallowed. He thought of the first time he had seen Logan, that sunny, idyllic fall day two years before, when he had materialized so silently, bringing a friendship and wisdom and nobility that had inspired George as almost nothing had before. He thought of Logan's fine clear eyes and benign features as he had seen them so often in the light of his hospitable fire. He remembered the rich sense of love and envelopment he had always felt in the midst of Logan's people, almost as great as that in his own family. He thought of the soft voices and the laughter and the warmth of embraces, and looked back at the words Logan had sent:

There runs not a drop of my blood in any living creature.

The war was over. Lord Dunmore had secured what seemed a good treaty. The Ohio River was designated the boundary between the Indians and the whites. The Indians agreed not to go south of the river into Virginia. They agreed to return all white prisoners and stolen horses, and to let some of their chiefs, including Cornstalk himself, stand as hostages until they were returned. Even the officers who were suspicious of Dunmore admitted that he had bargained well.

83

Now the nights were cold and the leaves were blowing off th
trees. George drank parting cups with men who would soon b
dispersing back to every part of Virginia, and many like himsel
who, in defiance of Dunmore's wishes, intended to go right bac
out to Kain-tuck, to make their own worlds and be their ow
kings. George drank with young Joe Bowman, pale-eyed an
straw-haired, who had been so close to him that they could al
most read each other's thoughts; with Benjamin Logan, a sol
emn, deliberate soldier whose one apparent passion was for th
land of Kain-tuck; Simon Butler, an auburn-haired wildernes
scout of gigantic size, infinite endurance, and mysterious pas
John Montgomery, a lean, dark lieutenant who followed ordei
to the letter but could think like a general himself when ther
were no orders; John Gabriel Jones, a bespectacled, thoughtfu
youth from down in the Holston Valley country; Daniel Boone
a cool-tempered, serene Quaker already widely known as a path
finder and surveyor; Jim Harrod, a burly, impatient town-builde
who had a half-finished town far up the distant Kain-tuck-e
River; and Leonard Helm, gray-whiskered, strong, and droll as
dancing bear, of whom it was said he must have found a whis
key-spring in the wilderness because he always had a flaskful t
drink or share. George felt a bond with these men, an unex
plainable notion that some of them, somehow, would be in
volved in his own destiny. These were all durable men, an
bold. They all had boundless dreams and found honor in figh
ing, and were quick to adopt or quit causes. George remembere
his fellow militiamen mutilating an Indian corpse at Pipe Creek
and the fate of Logan's family, and was aware that these me
could be as savage as the Devil himself. What's going to happe
when the land is filled up with this new kind of Virginians
George wondered. Who's going to be able to govern them? Ho
could there ever be a *civilized* country made up of men lik
these? What's all this leading to? What does the Supreme Direc
tor of all Things have in mind for that country out there?

Leonard Helm said good-bye now with his old motto:
"Any time y're thirsty, Clark, why, just holler!"

THERE WAS ONE MORE FRIEND FOR GEORGE TO SEE BEFOR
heading downriver to the far Kain-tuck country to resume h
surveying. It would be an awkward visit, perhaps even a disaste
But no white comrade-in-arms had influenced his life as muc
in the past year as had Tah-gah-ju-te, both as friend and as foe
Not to go and see him, George thought, would be dishonorable

And so he rode to Yellow Creek.

At first George thought Logan had not recognized him, his look was so sullen and hostile.

But then Logan said simply, "Clark," and did not even extend his arm, and it was worse than not being recognized.

Logan's eyes were pouched and bloodshot and he stank of rum. He stood swaying slightly. His mouth corners were drawn down, and the skin of his cheeks was flaccid. George had never seen so drastic a change in a man in so short a time—except, of course, those on battlefields who changed from live men to dead.

It had cut him painfully when Logan had declined to reach for his hand. It hurt as badly now as Logan stood barring the door to his lodge and did not invite him to enter. George clenched his teeth to steady his spirit and tried to think of the right thing to say. He thought of speaking of friendship, but knew that would not do with Logan now. He thought about offering condolences, but knew that that, coming from a white man, would be even worse. He thought about saying something in praise of Logan's eloquent reply to Lord Dunmore, but he knew that Logan had said those words to get them out of his heart and would not want them back.

Finally, George said, "Do you remember the day when we first met, and I was making lines on the land, and we smoked and talked?"

Logan went back deep behind his red eyes, and seemed to be remembering, but he did not speak or even nod. George went on:

"You began to teach me then, of matters that I could not learn from anyone else. You told me that the whole land is too small for our two peoples to live on together. Then Greathouse made this come true. You know it was Greathouse, don't ye? Not Cresap. But if it had not been Greathouse it would have been someone else, someone of your people or mine.

"I came to tell you this, Logan: Whatever happens between our peoples, in my memory ye'll always be my greatest teacher. If we never meet again, I'll keep learning from you, just by remembering and thinking on what you've said. Listen:

"I'll never hate your people. And I'll never give them a cause to hate me. Probably someday we will have to fear and respect each other, but never hate. D'ye hear me? That's what you taught me."

Logan stood, still swaying and scowling, looking at George, saying nothing. George wanted to reach out and offer his arm again, but knew Logan would not take it. So he dipped his head, turned on his heel and leaped onto his horse, and started to ride out of the dismal camp. He had gone ten yards when Logan's voice came: "Clark!"

He halted the horse and turned in the saddle.

Logan had not moved or changed his expression. "No one can teach you how to act when you are betrayed," he said, raising a rum bottle. "But I choose this way."

He turned and stumbled into his lodge and George rode away toward Kain-tuck.

4

RICHMOND,
COLONY OF VIRGINIA
March 23, 1775

IT WAS A CLEAR, FRESH DAY AFTER A LONG SPELL OF RAINS, and Jonathan Clark reluctantly left the sunny Richmond Street and entered the musty old St. John's Church.

He took a pew midway back, sat down, yawned, and shut his eyes. He hated to be indoors on a day like this, but he had to be here. He was Dunmore County's delegate to the Second Revolutionary Convention. The delegates had been meeting here in Richmond since Governor Lord Dunmore had dissolved the House of Burgesses in Williamsburg.

Jonathan kept his eyes closed for a while, hoping that by pretending to snooze he might avoid conversation. He had many unsettling things in his mind. The Colonies and the lives of the Colonists seemed to be coming all apart. One could not proceed along one's chosen course because of all that was happening.

His father wanted him to take a leave and come home to help on the plantation. Extra grain would have to be planted this year, because all the counties had pledged to grow quotas of food for Boston, which the British fleet had blockaded in retaliation for the destruction of a shipment of British tea.

Tea, Jonathan thought. Tea! The world turned topsa-turva over *tea*! He sat and worried about all this, and about the effects on his career, eyes still shut, and listened to the noises of the arriving delegates.

He listened to the scuffing of shoes on the wooden floors, the scooting of chairs, the echoing knocks of canes on furniture, as he delegates wandered in and settled themselves. There were phlegmatic bursts of throat-clearing and coughing. It almost sounded like a hospital for the aged and infirm. That, he thought, might account for the plodding and cautious conduct of he Convention's business so far: all these old men.

He heard greetings and jokes and chuckles in voices familiar and unfamiliar. He heard the stertorous voice of Edmund Pendleton, Caroline County's conservative delegate. He heard Tom Jefferson's voice nearby, so soft it was barely audible; he heard George Washington and Benjamin Harrison talking close behind him. He heard several voices rise in greeting to Patrick Henry, and heard Henry's sonorous voice answer. Henry sounded grumpy—probably because the tone of the convention so far had been too calm, too careful, too conciliatory, for Henry's taste. So many of the important delegates seemed still to yearn back to those pleasant and comfortable times when connection to the motherland had been all benign and sunny. But was it ever? Jonathan thought. Well, maybe it had been for *them*, the old favored families, the magistrates, those who flattered the Royal Governors. But never for the rest.

He opened his eyes as the session came to order, closed them again for the invocation, opened them again.

The business opened this morning with a resolution concerning Jamaica's stance "in the unhappy contest between Great Britain and her colonies," followed by a wish that Virginia might soon "see a speedy return of those halcyon days, when we lived a free and happy people." Jonathan's eyes started to close again. This, combined with spring fever, was the kind of atmosphere to put a man to sleep.

Suddenly there was a general shuffling and stirring and a volley of coughs, as Patrick Henry asked for the floor. His brow was knit as he held a piece of paper and began to read:

"Resolved, that a well-regulated militia, composed of gentlemen and yeomen, is the natural strength and only security of a free government . . ." There were murmurs throughout the church. Henry read on: ". . . that such a militia in this colony would forever render it unnecessary for the mother-country to keep among us, for the purpose of our defense, any standing army of mercenary soldiers, always subversive of the quiet, and dangerous to the liberties of the people, and would obviate the pretext of taxing us for their support." The murmuring grew louder. Patrick Henry glanced around the room over his spectacles, then continued to read: ". . . that the establishment of such militia is, at this time, peculiarly necessary . . ." Now the voices were rising in volume, drowning out Henry until he raised his own voice, adding: ". . . to secure our inestimable rights and liberties from further violations."

"Resolved, therefore, that this colony be immediately put into a state of defense . . ." Again he was drowned out; again he raised his voice further:

". . . to prepare a plan for imbodying, arming, and disciplining such a number of men as may be sufficient for that purpose!"

Then Henry pushed his spectacles up onto his scalp and stepped down amid the hubbub that he had raised. Jonathan's heart was pounding. He had expected nothing more radical to be proposed at this convention than a few petitions, or at most a resolution to quit importing goods from Great Britain. But this hotspur was talking the language of rebellion.

"Gentlemen, gentlemen!" someone was shouting. It was Richard Bland. He was one of the warmest of the patriots, a Virginia delegate to the Continental Congress, and Jonathan half expected him to take up Henry's cry. But when the clamor died down, Bland said instead:

"Really, sir, those resolutions are not only rash, but harsh and, and, well-nigh *impious!*" There was a rumble of voices.

Benjamin Harrison then arose, stiff with age but elegant in satin and silk. "There are still friends of American liberty in Parliament," he exclaimed, "and as yet they've no cause to blush for our indiscretion! His Majesty himself appears to relent, and to look on our sufferings with an eye of pity. Is this a time to disgust our friends, extinguish their sympathies, turn their friendship into hatred, their pity into revenge?"

"Hear, hear!"

One by one, delegates got up and addressed the assembly, though in truth they were talking at Patrick Henry, who sat with his glasses on top of his head, sometimes laying a finger beside his long nose, and scowled.

They demanded to know how he could think the colony was ready for war. They wanted to know what military supplies there were, what arms, what generals, what money. "We're poor," cried one delegate. "If we had troops, they'd have to go naked. And yet you talk of assuming a warlike front against the most formidable nation in the world? A nation ready and armed at all points, her navies riding triumphant in every sea? Your measure, sir, sounds brave, but it's the bravery of madmen!"

Others got up and spoke of the security and luster and domes-

comforts the colony had derived from its connection with
great Britain, and of the ray of reconciliation that was beginning
to dawn on them from the east, and they contrasted this with the
horrors that would be raised by a call to arms. "And in such a
form the world would not even pity us," intoned a speaker, "for
we'd have rashly drawn it upon ourselves!"

"Hear, hear!"

Jonathan found himself sitting on the front edge of his bench.
He was on the verge of rising to speak himself, but wasn't sure
which side he would take if he did. The men opposing Henry's
call to arms were no less patriotic than Henry; Jonathan knew
that. They were just cautious; they, like Jonathan and Jonathan's
own father, felt themselves to be still Englishmen. But they had
all, at times, cursed the high-handedness of the British ministry.

At length, the orations against Patrick Henry's resolutions began to lose steam, every objection having been made several
times, and suddenly Henry gathered his legs under him and
stood up again. He kept his glasses on top of his head and strode
to the front, and stood there, no paper in his hand now, looking
from face to face until each man had grown still. He began in a
gentle but distinct voice.

"No man thinks more highly than I do of the patriotism and
the abilities of you worthy gentlemen.

"But different men often see the world in different lights.
Therefore I hope it won't seem disrespectful if I should speak
forth my very different sentiments freely."

There was considerable chair-scooting and throat-clearing as
they all settled to listen to him.

"The question before this house is one of awful moment to
the country. For my part, I find it no less than a question of
freedom or slavery. We have a responsibility, to God and our
country, to arrive at truth. If I should keep back my opinions
now for fear of giving offense, I would be guilty of treason toward
my country, and an act of disloyalty toward the Majesty of
Heaven—which I revere above all earthly kings."

Jonathan loved Henry's voice, and the pregnancy of his words.
Sometimes it was hard to believe that a man so eloquent had
failed at so many ordinary pursuits, that a man so solemn could
be such a make-merry as Jonathan knew him to be.

"Mr. President," Henry went on, "it is natural to man to indulge in the illusions of hope. But should wise men, engaged in
a great and arduous struggle for liberty, shut our eyes to painful
truth and listen to the siren song of hope? For my part, whatever
anguish of the spirit it might cost, I am willing to see the whole

89

truth, and to provide for it. I know of no way to judge the futur
but by the past. Judging by the past, what has there been in th
conduct of the British Ministry in the last ten years to justif
those hopes with which you have tried to solace yourselves? Is i
that insidious smile with which our petition has lately been re
ceived? Trust it not; it will prove a snare to your feet. Suffer no
yourselves to be betrayed with a kiss. Rather, ask yourselves hov
this gracious reception of our petition comports with those war
like preparations which darken our land. Are fleets and armie
necessary to a work of love and reconciliation?

"Let us not deceive ourselves. These are the implements o
war and subjugation—the last argument to which kings resort.
ask gentlemen: What means this martial array, if not to force u
to submission?" Now he put a keener edge on his voice, ane
continued: "Has Great Britain any enemy in this quarter of th
world, to call for all this accumulation of navies and armies? No
sir, she has none. They are meant for *us*. They are sent over t
rivet upon us those chains which the British Ministry have beer
so long a-forging!"

Then he dropped his voice again, and asked what the colon
had with which to oppose armies and navies. "Argument? W
have been trying that for the last ten years," he said. "Entreat
and humble supplication? We have already done this to exhaus
tion.

"Our petitions have been slighted. Our remonstrances have
produced more violence and insult. We have been spurned with
contempt from the foot of the throne. In vain, after this, may we
indulge the fond hope of peace and reconciliation."

He now took a deep breath and cried out in a tone that made
shivers run down Jonathan's cheeks:

"There is no longer any room for hope! If we wish to be free
if we wish to preserve those inestimable privileges for which we
have been so long contending, *we must fight*! I repeat it, sir, we
must FIGHT! An appeal to arms and to the God of Hosts is al
that is left us!"

Jonathan's pulse was throbbing in his temples. He saw that the
faces of many of the delegates had gone white.

Henry now lowered his voice again, but spoke with such pre
cise enunciation that his words were as forceful as when he hac
shouted.

"They tell us, sir, that we are weak, unable to cope with s
formidable an adversary. But when shall we be stronger? Will i
be the next week or the next year? Will it be when we are totally
disarmed? And when a British guard shall be stationed in every

use? Shall we acquire the means of effectual resistance by ing on our backs and hugging the delusive phantom of Hope, til our enemies have bound us hand and foot?

"Sir, we are *not* weak! Three millions of people armed in the ly cause of liberty, and in such a country as this, are invinci- e by any force our enemy could send against us!"

Jonathan noted his use of the word "enemy" and his mouth t dry. Henry was referring to fellow Englishmen as if they were other race. Now he went on, in the grave faces of his au- ence.

"The battle, sir, is not to the strong alone; it is to the vigilant, e active, the brave. Besides, sir, we have no choice. Even if we ere base enough to desire it, it is now too late to retire from the ntest. There is no retreat but to submission and slavery. Our ains are forged; their clanking may be heard on the plains of oston! The war is inevitable—and let it come! I repeat, sir, *let come!*"

Henry paused, and he paused at the risk of being shouted wn before he could finish. Or maybe he *had* finished. His last ree words hung like a bloody banner in the still air over the ads of the delegates, in the rafters of the church. But no one oke; no one even murmured.

"It is vain, sir," Henry said with a sarcastic edge on his voice, o extenuate the matter. Gentlemen may cry, Peace, Peace, but ere is no peace. The war is actually begun. The next gale that veeps from the north will bring to our ears the clash of arms! ur brethren are already in the field! Why stand we here idle? Vhat is it that gentlemen wish? What would they have?" Now e spoke as if from a tightened throat.

"Is life so dear or peace so sweet as to be purchased at the rice of chains and slavery? Forbid it, Almighty God," he now early bellowed. "I know not what course others may take, but for me—" He flung up his arms, his fists knotted as tight as is brows, and shouted: *"Give me liberty, or give me DEATH!"*

And in the reverberations of his words he stepped down and ok his seat. There was not a whisper of applause. Jonathan felt if his heart were as big and heavy as a mountain; his hands ere shaking, and realized that the transfixed, gaping, chalky- ced listeners were beginning to blur; he was looking at them rough tears. He jumped up, as if to dodge from under the great eight upon his heart, and raised an arm. Others were now sing all around, and somebody cried:

"To arms!"

Fists were being raised and shaken.

"To arms!"
"To arms!"

Richard Henry Lee, white-wigged, his fine features drawn, face going from chalk-pale to florid as he talked, took the floor in the midst of the uproar, and talked, scarcely heard, about the realities of the situation, and the odds against the success of arms, but finally, as the noise subsided, he said: ". . . admitting the probable calculations to be against us, we are assured in holy writ that 'the race is not to the swift, nor the battle to the strong,' and, if the language of genius may be added to inspiration, I will say with our immortal bard: 'Thrice is he armed, who hath his quarrel just!'" Lee droned on, but Henry's words "liberty or death" seemed to linger like echoes in the backs of all the delegates' minds. Jonathan had never seen a roomful of people remain so agitated for so long. And when Henry's resolution for militia was put to vote, it was swept through with little opposition, that mostly from older members, who had come to the convention expecting a mood of reconciliation with Britain. Most of these august ones were visibly shaken by the sudden turn of events Henry's speech had caused, but some of them were walking about with misty eyes and more youth in their step than anyone had seen for ages.

The next order of business was formation of a committee to prepare the plan for a militia. Patrick Henry and Thomas Jefferson were named to the committee, which included the few delegates with military experience. Among these were Colonel Washington, Colonel William Christian, and General Andrew Lewis, hero of the Battle of Point Pleasant last fall at the mouth of the Kanawha. These three were clustered near the door at the end of the day's proceedings, receiving blessings and advice from the departing delegates. Jonathan, waiting nearby to shake their hands, watched the veterans Washington and Lewis, who stood shoulder to shoulder surrounded by the powdered wigs and velvet coats of their well-wishers, and he fancied them standing just like this nearly twenty years ago amid the humming musketballs and the cries of the mortally wounded on that awful day of Braddock's defeat. They were fighting for the Crown then, he thought suddenly; how must they feel now, knowing they'll surely be fighting against it soon? Suddenly he became more aware than he had been all day of the audacity of what had been wrought here in this old Richmond church, by a group of responsible, propertied men swept along on the crest of a wave of idealistic words.

We're all likely to ruin ourselves by what we've done here today, he thought.

That, or we'll find out who we really are. Englishmen with the rights of Englishmen, or . . .

Or Americans, he thought.

A hand closed around his upper arm. "Jonathan," said a soft voice, and he turned to see Tom Jefferson's ruddy face. "How goes with you?"

"Right well. A big day, this, eh?"

"A great one. I expect a celebration tonight. A somber one withal. Join us?"

"I'm laying at Cap'n Gunn's, and they've planned a dinner. But thankee."

"Come." Jefferson kept his hold on Jonathan's arm and edged in among the delegates crowded around Washington and Lewis. "Colonel, you should meet this old neighbor of mine from Albemarle, Jonathan Clark."

Washington's handshake and proximity gave Jonathan a totally new impression of this grave, big-boned farmer-soldier, whom he had heretofore seen only across rooms, and it was an impression both attractive and forbidding. Washington's hand was enormous, strong, and warm. Jonathan was aware that he was standing before a man whose physical size and strength were at least the equal of his own, someone who, like him, was accustomed to looking over the heads of men; if from a distance Colonel Washington looked soft and wide-hipped, it was a delusion of skeletal structure; his two hundred and more pounds obviously were all hard muscle and big bone. His eyelids were heavy and he was slow to smile; his eyes, Jonathan now could see, were shrewd and somehow sad. His cheeks and cheekbones were deeply pitted, and the powder or flour he used to subdue the appearance of those scars gave a false pallor to what was really an outdoorsman's complection. Colonel Washington was known as a man of few and well-chosen words; he offered none now; he bowed slightly and then looked in Jonathan's dark eyes as if awaiting some pertinent information. Tom Jefferson filled the silence: "Jonathan's Clerk of Dunmore County," he said, then grinned, obviously amused by a sudden thought, and added, "Jonathan, maybe we ought to change the name o' your county, eh?" Washington started to smile, but his eyes looked sadder still. Apparently he was not taking lightly the changes of the day. Then he said:

"Clark, is it. Lately I heard of a Clark named to do my old duties—that is, surveying for the Ohio Company. George Clark. A relation?"

"Aye, sir. My younger brother, he is."

"And a born Westerner if ever there was one," said Jefferson.

Now Washington laid his hand on Jefferson's forearm; a thoughtful look had come over his face. "As for the West," he said, "this committee of ours mustn't ignore its defense. Mister Clark, a pleasure to know you."

"If I can ever be of service, Colonel."

"I expect you can, sir. I expect we'll all have a great need of each other ere we reap what we've sown today."

JONATHAN LAY THAT NIGHT IN A GUEST BEDROOM AT THE Gunns', so full of dinner and brandy that he almost dozed with the candle still lit. His emotions were drained. He sat up in bed, yawned, reached for his diary, a palm-sized notebook, and made the terse daily entry in pencil:

> Clear: at Richmond, the Convention continued: lay Capt Gunn's.

He blew out the candle, turned on his side and pulled the blanket up on his shoulder. He tried to imagine what an actual conflict with the mother country would cost him, and his family, and all these Virginians he had come to know. But the thought was too enormous. He could not think of it at all. A parade of faces passed through his head: Henry's, Washington's, Jefferson's, Parson Robertson's, George's, his father's and mother's—and he went to sleep with Patrick Henry's resonant voice rolling around him, distorted by its own echoes.

CAROLINE COUNTY,
April 29, 1775

"HEY! JOHNNY CLARK!"

The cry came with the hoofbeats of several horses. Everybody at the breakfast table scooted chairs back and started to rise. "That's Cousin Joe," Johnny exclaimed.

"This time o' morning?" said Ann Rogers Clark.

Johnny raised the window sash and leaned out, thinking perhaps Joe was bringing him a message relating to one or another of his sweethearts; many of the messages that came to the Clark house were of that nature. The sun was not yet above the horizon. Bands of cream-colored sky silhouetted the leaves of spring outside the window. Five young horsemen were controlling their excited mounts in the roadway. They were Joe and Johnny

Rogers, and three others, all in their hunting shirts and armed with rifles. They were fellow members of Johnny's militia company, so recently mobilized by the Revolutionary Assembly and just beginning to take training. Johnny saw by their weaponry that they had not come as messengers of love. "What's it about, fellows?" Johnny called. Most of his family was crowding at his back.

"Come on! Patrick Henry's marching an army on Williamsburg! We're mustering at the Bowling Green!"

"Mercy on us," murmured Mrs. Clark. "Give a man an army, and he'll use it."

"Henry? What for?" called Johnny.

"To give Lord Dunmore some proper hell!"

"You mean about the gunpowder!" For once Johnny Clark was growing excited about something besides romance.

"Aye! Proposes to make 'im put it back, or pay for it!"

"Stay a minute, boys, I'm with'ee!"

He started from the window, but his mother seized his arm and held him, searching his face with those drilling blue eyes. For the first time ever, he was aware of the little squint-lines beside her eyes and tiny wrinkles at the corners of her mouth.

"I wish you wouldn't go, Johnny. I mean, without your Pa knowing."

"You tell him, Ma, when he gets home. We can't wait." He started to pull free, then paused and gave her a peck on the cheek, and she released his arm, sighing.

"No," she said. "I guess ye can't."

Johnny bounded up the staircase to the boys' sleeping room, yelling for Cupid to go saddle up Atlas. Dickie stormed up the stairs after him, all elbows and big feet, followed by Lucy and Elizabeth, both exclaiming at once. Johnny pulled on his canvas hunting shirt, belted it, slung powder horn and shooting bag over his shoulders, hung a sheath knife on his belt, and lifted his rifle down from the wall. Dickie's arm reached up beside him and took another gun down. Johnny paused. "Ho, Dickie, what're you up to?"

"I'm goin'."

"You're not a minute man."

"Maybe not, but I can outshoot any durn fool in your company."

That was true. But Johnny said, "Ma won't let ye go. You're only fourteen."

"Nigh on fifteen. And Ma doesn't stop us when we're doin' right by conscience." That was true too. Dickie was slinging on his horn and bag. And now Edmund was pushing between them, getting his hunting rifle down. Both his brothers reminded him snortingly that he was only twelve. But he retorted with the truth that he could outshoot both of them put together. So all three trooped downstairs, Lucy and Elizabeth following them back down. At the foot of the stairs stood Billy, not yet five years old, bright red forelock hanging down over one blue eye, watching all this commotion with his mouth half open. Johnny, putting on his three-cornered hat, paused and looked down at him, and ruffled his hair.

"Billy, you stay here and protect the girls. That's the most important part."

Everybody laughed. Except Billy.

Johnny's company was supposed to be infantry, according to the militia plan. But most of the men in it had horses, and it was hours by foot to the Bowling Green, minutes by horse, and they did after all call themselves minute men. Johnny ran outdoors and vaulted into Atlas' saddle, while Dickie and Edmund ran to the stable to saddle Herk. They would have to double up on Herk, as their father had taken the only other good saddle horse. In a minute they rode around the house, Eddie behind Dickie. Their mother was coming from the kitchen house with a bag of provisions for Johnny. She saw Dickie and Edmund, looked astonished, then set her lips in a white line. She seemed ready to protest, but instead just called toward the kitchen house, "Rose, fetch another loaf and about a yard o' sausage! Johnny, you watch everybody keeps warm. I'm holding you responsible for your brothers."

"Stay warm, you two," Johnny commanded. Then he reached down and touched her hand, and, with a whoop, the Clark boys and the Rogers boys and the others all kicked off into a gallop. Johnny was a bit ashamed for having given his mother no more of a good-bye than that, but, after all, he was a soldier now, and his comrades-in-arms had been looking on; surely she'd understood that. And Dickie and Eddie, who were younger, had not even touched her hand in parting. Still, he was annoyed with himself, and if he had been alone he would have gone back to embrace her and give her a good-bye kiss.

Two miles up the road they began overtaking a lone rider cantering ahead of them, cape flying. The man and the horse looked very familiar.

"It's Pa," Dickie shouted. John Clark was supposed to be on his way home from the tobacco warehouse at Port Royal.

He turned and saw them coming. Everybody reined in, horses lowing. "Y're going the wrong way, aren't ye, Pa?" Johnny said. "I was coming home when I heard the governor's plundered he arsenal, then about Cap'n Henry, so I turned about." His oots and saddlebags were dusty. He had no rifle with him, but ately had taken to carrying in his saddlebags the set of pistols George had given him—the "useless" guns. "Dickie, Eddie, y're bit short in the' breeks to be along, say what? Did ye disobey our mother?"

"No, Pa, she didn't try to stay us."

"Well, then, come along, but stay by me. I'll not have you all ein' rash. Let's go, then!"

BY MAY 2, THE COLUMN OF VOLUNTEERS SEEMED TO tretch a mile along the road.

"Look at us!" Johnny exclaimed, his voice tight and shivery. "I ay, to hell with Dunmore and his bloody Royal Marines!" ohnny imagined that the Crusaders of old, clanking along the usty roads in their mail and armor, must have felt this same ierce, happy righteousness. He felt that he and these compatriots f his were crusaders, their holy cause being Liberty. Patrick Ienry's original force of seven hundred Hanover County riflemen ad been swollen to thousands, as armed men and boys from ounties along the route had poured into the column like creeks nto a river. Edmund Pendleton, and then Peyton Randolph, peaker of the House of Burgesses, had come to the Bowling Treen and tried to persuade the Caroline minute men not to ollow Henry, but they had pleaded in vain. Spirits were too high.

The Hanover drummer could be heard at the head of the line, is chattering cadence making the pulse beat a little faster. Back oward the rear, voices were singing a new patriot song: "Our each-brandy fellows can never be beat . . ."

Spirits were in concert. All were angry at Dandy Dunmore. ome now and then grew quiet in contemplation of the chance hat tomorrow might be the day when they'd die. The sight of anners fluttering, of muskets and rifles glinting in the comfort- ble spring sunlight, of dust rising from the trodden road, gave ohnny Clark that exquisite sense of vitality he usually felt only vhen he soared on the wings of new love.

He laughed at himself suddenly, at the way he was mixing all hese thoughts together—Crusades, Liberty, being in love, being nartial—into one heady feeling that was really, he realized, noth- ng more than the giddy recklessness of defying an old authority.

"Hey-o, Johnny Clark, how d'ye?"

He heard this just as a hand gripped his knee, and he looked down to his left to see the seamed, strong face of Isaiah Freeman, the poor neighbor farmer whose daughter Betsy had been Johnny's true love once—for a whole month after their close call in the haymow. Isaiah Freeman was marching alongside Johnny's horse, musket aslant over his left shoulder. He was not a young man, had not been a militiaman probably since the French and Indian War, and might well not have come. His face was a-gleam with sweat, his gray-shot eyebrows beaded with it.

"I do right well, Mister Freeman. How d'ye?"

Johnny had a momentary sense of irony, of pity; here holding his knee and smiling up at him was a man who likely would have wanted to shoot him had he known of Johnny's lustful liaisons with his dear daughter.

And now Isaiah Freeman said:

"A great day, what?"

"A great day."

Mister Freeman shook his head, grinning. He had few teeth left. The sound of thousands of shoes and hooves beating and shuffling on the dusty roadway was like an incessant, rushing whisper. "Cap'n Henry says 'twas but part of a great British plot," said Freeman.

"What was?"

"Dunmore takin' the gunpowder. All th' Royal Governors of all th' Colonies. To make us all helpless at once, like."

"Y' don't say so!"

"Aye, lad." Mister Freeman breathed hard as he paced alongside. "It's what they aimed to do up at Massychusetts. But th' folk got wind of it and fit 'em off at two towns. Lexington and uhm, Concord, 'twas. A real bloody affair, they say."

Johnny's scalp prickled. He had heard what had happened at Lexington and Concord, but only now did it strike him that this was, really, the very same sort of an occurrence. Trust Patrick Henry to see through an incident and recognize it as part of a whole plan! "Well a-well," Johnny said, "fair puts your hackle up, doesn't it? Reckon all their Royal lordships are as lowdown as our old Dunmore, then?"

"'Pears like," Freeman replied with a sure nod. He was still clinging to Johnny's knee, as if helping his weary self along. "By th' bye," he said, "Betsy wonders why y' ain't been around in so long." Johnny knew Mister Freeman wanted his daughter married into the Clark clan as badly as she wanted it herself. But Johnny's passion had cooled when he had begun to observe it

etsy Freeman all the earmarks of a classic scold, and a man-
ap as well, and he had never gone after all to speak to her
ther about marriage. Apparently she had spoken of it.

"Aye, and I'm sorry," Johnny said, thinking fast, "but tell 'er
ve been taken much lately with thoughts o' soldierin'."

That had not been true before, but it was now.

MESSENGERS HAD BEEN RIDING OUT TO MEET THE COLUMN,
essengers from the Common Council of Williamsburg, beg-
ng Captain Henry to stop his march. They were fearful of the
onsequences of an armed confrontation there. But Henry sim-
ly detained the messengers, to prevent them from carrying back
report of his numbers, and led on.

When the troops were within twenty miles of Williamsburg,
nother messenger came, bearing the news that a detachment of
oyal Marines had gone up to make a defense at the Governor's
alace. This word sped back along the column, and it increased
e martial spirit of the troops in general, while causing them to
flect more deeply, one by one, on their mortality. How many
Marines? some wondered. They were essentially farmers and
new nothing of warships and Marines and the like.

They marched four more miles under such apprehensions,
ntil sundown. It was the evening of May 3. They had reached
n inn and pub, called Doncastle's Ordinary, about sixteen miles
bove Williamsburg. And here they encamped for the night,
me of the officers taking lodgings in the Ordinary, the troops
uilding cookfires and laying out their blankets in the meadows
ll about. John Clark and his boys Dickie and Eddie camped by
ne fire; Johnny was off with his militia comrades in another
art of the field.

There was a great deal of visiting during the twilight hours,
en wandering from fire to fire in the great smoky campground.
Many found friends they had not seen for years.

"John Clark, is't not?"

He looked up and saw a powerfully built, gray-eyed man with
sword hanging at his side. John Clark rose and extended his
and.

"Bill Lewis, that's you?"

"It is. How d'ye? I'm still hung over from that wedding party
' yours back in seventy-three." He grinned, and nodded down
t Dickie and Eddie. "You two are growin' up fine."

"Are there many here from Albermarle?" John Clark asked.

"A company. I'm their first lieutenant. Mostly sprats, but

some o' your old neighbors. Ye might like to come over a[n]
see."

Lewis revealed as they strolled over that he had another ch[ild]
now, a son having been born the last summer. He was ve[ry]
proud to have a son, and had named him Meriwether Lew[is]
after his wife's family.

"Well, congratulations, a bit late," John Clark said. "Wi[th]
those two lustrous names, why, he ought to become quite som[e]
thing! As for me, my Annie's about to make me a grandfather,
I'm told!"

As a heavy dew settled that night, men sniffed t[he]
smoke of their fires and aromas of cooking meat, and talked [of]
weapons, of kings and governors, of Tories, of Royal Marines, [of]
liberty and death, and, of course, of sweethearts and wives a[nd]
children. Young Johnny Clark's throat often that evening f[elt]
clogged with the density of his emotions. It was past midnig[ht]
when, calmed at last by two gills of rum taffia, he managed [to]
grow drowsy under the springtime stars, looking long and lon[g]
ingly at them and wondering whether he would ever see the[m]
again. Somewhere in a nearby company, late revelers full [of]
nostalgia and taffia were softly singing the popular song, "Johnn[y]
Has Gone for A-Soldier," and it was the lullaby that put him [to]
sleep.

At sunrise, while the troops were breakfasting o[n]
whatever they had in their pouches, the Governor's Receive[r-]
General rode up to the Ordinary with a small guard of dragoon[s.]
Johnny trembled, cold with dew. A glowing mist hung kne[e]
deep over the campground. The Receiver-General went into t[he]
Ordinary and was with Captain Henry for a few minutes. Son[e]
of the militiamen drifted near the Redcoats and studied the[m]
insolently. But if the dragoons were intimidated by the hord[e]
they concealed it well, sitting at attention on their sleek wa[r]
horses and gazing over the heads of the mob. They're brave f[el]
lows, Johnny thought. But he could see the sheen of sweat o[n]
their faces.

When the Receiver-General had come out and ridden aw[ay]
with his guard, Patrick Henry emerged from the inn and mu[s]
tered the troops for an announcement.

Governor Dunmore had had a thoughtful night, he said. H[is]
Lordship had decided to abandon the Palace and take refu[ge]
aboard the schooner *Magdalen*. And he had sent Mr. Corbi[n,]
the Receiver-General, up to pay £330, which had been dete[r]

100

mined as the value of the confiscated powder from the Williamsburg arsenal. The money, Henry said, would be consigned to the Virginia Assembly and used to purchase a like quantity of fresh gunpowder to be used if needed for the colony's defense.

"In sum, gentlemen, with thanks to your patriot zeal, Virginia has saved her means of defense, and, I suspect," he added, breaking into a fierce grin and thrusting up his fist, "gone a long way toward ridding herself of a graceless overlord unsympathetic to her welfare.

"I thank you, brave gentlemen—and boys—and Virginia crowns you with her laurels. We've done what they did at Lexington and Concord, but not shed a drop of precious Virginia blood. *We've won, boys, we've won!*"

And anyone far back in the ranks who might not have heard his full peroration did hear that last triumphant bellow.

And young Johnny Clark, his chest swollen with joy and camaraderie, swore he saw two thousand hats in the air at once, floating above a deafening *huzzah* in the light of a rising sun.

5

KING WILLIAM COUNTY,
COLONY OF VIRGINIA
September, 1775

A BLACK HAND HOLDING A WHITE CLOTH REACHED UP OVER Annie's flushed face. She lay gasping from her last terrible squeeze, and the wet cloth cooled her brow. Two vague starlike shimmers of light in the room gradually grew smaller and brighter until they were candle flames again. The cool cloth came down gently into her eye sockets and wiped out the sweat and cooled her eyelids, and when it was lifted away she could see the yellow eyes of the old black midwife who stood over her. The midwife's face was wizened and her mouth protruded almost like a muzzle. But the little yellow eyes were kind, and the thin lips of the muzzle had a patient, gentle smile. Hannah Gwathmey, Owen's mother, had said this old woman long ago had brought Owen himself into the world, and that she knew everything and could cure anything. That was reassuring, because Annie felt that everything down inside her was being squeezed to a pulp. She thought of her own mother, who had suffered like this ten times, and she thought of her grandmother's advice that her mother had not taken, and she thought, Oh, Mama, I'm going to, I'm going to keep Owen off me long as I can, because I don't think I could stand this again. She lay in dread of the next great squeeze and wished her mother were here to hold her hand and talk her through it.

But her own mother was not here. The white woman who was hovering off there in the gloom beyond the foot of the bed was mother-in-law Hannah Gwathmey, and she was not much comfort.

Hannah Gwathmey was a good and caring mother-in-law, but she was being no help in this. She seemed to be afraid of what was happening here in this room, afraid to lend a hand to it. She seemed to want to leave everything up to the old Negress and the other servants who came and went, carrying things.

She's not a bit like my own Mama, Annie thought. Mama would be in charge of it all if she was here.

But her Mama was not here, here at the Gwathmey plantation, The Meadows. Her Mama was not here, though she would have been if she had been called in time.

Not even Annie's husband was here. At least, she had not seen him for what seemed like an eternity, though probably it had been only hours. Maybe he's here now, she thought. I wish he were.

"Owen," she panted. "Is Owen here? Is he?" She remembered that she had asked that question earlier, but time seemed as squeezed out of shape as her innards, and she didn't know whether she had asked it minutes ago or hours ago.

"Mast' Owen not heah, 'm," murmured the Negress. There was no gentleness in her voice when she said this. Annie blinked and looked at her and saw the old wrinkled lips compressed in a hard line. The woman said, "He out wi' d' radders."

Annie swallowed. It scared her that the midwife had said that: *Out with the riders.* She knew what that meant, and she could not now look at the old midwife's yellow eyes. Owen Gwathmey, whom this same old black angel had served up to the world from Hannah Gwathmey's womb twenty-two years ago, now was out leading a band of the Night Riders, galloping all over the parish as they did every night, stopping at every plantation and going through the slave quarters with lanterns and pistols, counting faces.

The night riders were a new and frightful thing in Virginia.

When Governor Lord Dunmore had fled from the minute men at Williamsburg last spring, he had taken refuge aboard a British warship in the York River, and from there he had sent word through the Colony that he would free every Negro servant who would rise up against his master.

No other words could have created such terror in the Colony, where a half the population was enslaved Negroes. Although there had not yet been any known instance of a slave responding to Dunmore's offer, the dread of an uprising had nearly petrified the Colony. Immediately the Committees of Safety had authorized vigilante patrols to keep the blacks from roaming or gathering at night.

And old family servants like this midwife could only tighten their lips and bear the nocturnal insults, and go on serving their white people. But Annie, her spirit already quailing from fear of pain of childbirth, wondered whether this strange old woman might try to do something to her, or to her child when it came, because of what her Owen and his night riders were doing. Annie was vulnerable and helpless, and her imagination was troubled.

And now the great, terrible squeeze was coming again. Sweat began to run off her forehead and down into her ears again, and she tried to arch her back to keep it from breaking, and she clenched her teeth and made little groaning sounds in the back of her throat, groans like the ones little Frances Eleanor had used to make when she pulled at her mother's nipple back in the sunny nursery of the Clark home in Caroline, back in those glowing, peaceful, happy days when they would sit talking of the joys of the coming wedding.

WHEN OWEN GWATHMEY RODE HOME FROM HIS PATROL after midnight through a cool mist, he was full of news. "They want me to place myself a candidate for the county's sheriff!" he cried to his parents as they met him in the vestibule. "What of that, Father? Your son's going to be sheriff of King William County, they say!"

"Well, fine! And more news: my son's already made me a grandfather!"

Owen's chin went down and his eyebrows went up. For a moment he seemed to falter between leaping up the stairs or pulling off his muddy boots in the vestibule as he had done all his life. His mother caught his arm in this moment of hesitation. "She wants to name him John, after her father," she said in a

103

low voice. "Don't you think he should be named Owen, after you or *your* father?"

"It's a boy, then!"

"Perhaps you should discuss with the poor thing on this matter of names," Mr. Gwathmey suggested.

Owen went upstairs with all the speed and noise of a war horse, and when he came down an hour later, eyes full of tenderness and enchantment, the question had been settled. The boy would be named John Gwathmey. "Annie," her mother had told her at least three or four times during those long talks about marriage, "I hope your firstborn boy you'll name in honor o' your father. Now they'll likely want you to weaken on that and name him Owen or suchlike, a name from *his* family. But it's *you* that creates that child, darlin', and it's right you should be let to name it for your own father. Mind ye now, I'm not trying to plant th' seeds o' trouble in your new family, but a girl ought to name her firstborn son after her own father."

"But Mama," Annie had replied, "your father was John and your husband was John, but you named your first one Jonathan. I don't think you always follow your own advice, Mama."

"Well, it was different. There was a tradition in your father's family, that each eldest son would be John or Jonathan, alternating like that, and it was time for a Jonathan."

"But then you gave in to *his* tradition, Mama! You really *don't* follow your own advice, ye know!"

And her mother had paused then, and had looked up at a corner of the ceiling, as she would always do when you'd caught her like that, as if she herself were cornered up there, and finally she had said:

"Annie, how d'you think a body learns advice worth giving, anyways? Why, by making mistakes herself long since, that's how! Now, if you have a boy and want to name him John, you stand your ground!"

And so now Annie had stood her ground, and she lay in the big bed upstairs at the Gwathmey house, in their plantation, a Clark girl all alone in the Gwathmey home, and she had convinced the future sheriff of King William County that she should have the say-so in this matter. And so the baby boy that lay cradled in her right arm against her swollen bare breast, this little scowling, livid, blotched creature that had caused her so much agony, would be *John* Gwathmey after all. Mama will be pleased, she thought. And sure Papa will be.

And the old midwife, humming to herself as she cleaned up the mess in the room, looked over at her once in a while and smiled.

104

That little old Clark girl there had sure had her way with that big bad night rider.

JOHN CLARK THOUGHT THE NIGHT RIDERS WERE AN UGLY necessity, and he did not like it when they came riding up at any hour of the night to unsettle his Negroes. But in one way they were good. Being out and around all over as they were, they were usually full of news, and these were times when the news seemed terribly urgent and important.

Tonight when John Clark first heard their hoofbeats out in the drive, he had been reading and rereading the *Virginia Gazette*. Copies of that journal's war issues went from hand to hand among neighbors until they fell apart at the folds. From these old second-hand and third-hand newspapers John Clark had learned the saddening but stirring stories of what the patriots were doing up north. He had read about a band of volunteers shooting down a thousand British Redcoats on two hills called Bunker Hill and Breed's Hill near Boston, almost stopping the British army before running out of ammunition and having to retreat. He had read about a merchant named Benedict Arnold and a Vermont militia commander named Ethan Allen, who had surprised the British garrison at old Fort Ticonderoga in New York, capturing half a hundred pieces of artillery to be used in the rebel cause. He had read about the planter George Washington, a Potomac aristocrat from up in Fairfax County, being selected to command the hungry, ill-clad rabble which was called the Grand Army of the United Colonies. This so-called Grand Army was a mob of fourteen thousand, without tents, living in everything from bark huts to sod houses, possessing not ten rounds of shot per man, and having extreme difficulty obtaining food because of a bad crop year throughout the colonies. Such was the dismal news one could read in the *Virginia Gazette* about this unpromising civil war with Mother England, and it was news already weeks old by the time written accounts of it had come down.

But the night riders always had fresh news about what was happening that very week in Virginia. These men would come trotting up the drive, mud-spattered or dusty, always thirsty, and while some of them were going through the slave quarters, their leader would stand in the hallway at the sideboard with John Clark and bolt down brandy while telling him the news of the Virginia Colony. It was in fact from a night rider that John Clark had learned that he had become the grandfather of a robust little Gwathmey named John in his honor; he learned it a whole day before a letter about it came from the Gwathmeys. The night rider, Mike Brown Roberts, had laughed over his dram, saying, "So, then, Mister Clark, meseems young Owen must ha' sobered up from that wedding party after all, eh?" Roberts had been a guest at the wedding.

"A boy, then," Ann Rogers Clark had breathed, squeezing her hands before her waist. "And she did get by with namin' him John. Well, now. Well-a-well, now! One's breath isn't always wasted on advice, is it?"

AND THEN IT WAS FROM THE NIGHT RIDERS TOO THAT THEY learned of the siege of Lord Dunmore at Great Bridge, down near Norfolk. War on Virginia's own soil!

His ex-Excellency the Royal Governor, as the people now liked to call him, had fortified a peninsula between Hampton Roads and Dismal Swamp, with his Redcoats and the Royal Marines from the sloop. There, with a few pieces of artillery, he apparently intended to hold out until reinforcements could arrive by sea. And during his wait, he was free to move up and down the coast in the warship, plundering the coast towns for food and trying to stir the blacks to insurrection.

John Clark sighed. The war news made him heavy at heart and clouded the bright calm view he had always had of his family's future. Already his own sons, despite all his lectures to them about the immorality of war, were being drawn by the distant glory-song of armed conflict. Johnny, the oldest one still at home, was most passionate about marching in the cause of Liberty, and this mystified and troubled his father, because Johnny was of so sensitive and loving a nature that it was impossible to imagine him actually doing harm to another man. But Johnny drilled enthusiastically with his company of minute men, and practiced his swordsmanship every spare moment on fodder shocks, slashing and jabbing them to fragments. And sweet Johnny had exulted almost like a fiend when an order had come to eject all Tories and English-born militiamen from the ranks; it was as if his poetic soul had learned to hate.

"So then what's being done about Dunmore?" John Clark asked the night rider. Sitting halfway up the stairs watching and listening was little Billy. On the step below him and almost pressed against him sat York. The little fat black fellow was desperately afraid of the men who came at night and shone their lanterns around in his mother's cabin, and he was able to stay this close to one of them now only because his friend Billy was next to him.

"Well, sir," said Roberts, "Colonel Woodford's regiment's

een sent down to Great Bridge, with an order to drive 'is udship out if he can."

"Woodford's and not Henry's, eh?" said John Clark. "That's ood, anyway." Patrick Henry, because of his popularity among e patriots, had been given command of one of the two colonial giments, but the Safety Committee had had the wisdom so far put only Woodford's regiment in the field. William Woodford as a veteran of the French and Indian War. Henry had never ldiered in his life, except to lead an excited mob last spring own the road toward Williamsburg.

"And so," the rider continued, smacking his lips after a sip of adies rum, "there sits Bill Woodford in Great Dismal Swamp, ith all them minute men and no cannon, watching Dunmore's rt, and probably prayin' he'll not get a chance to attack 'im. By hat I hear, all those boys want t' do is hunt boar in there. And ; I see it, all 'is Ludship needs do is wait till those fools've shot p all their powder, and then walk out with 'is Redcoats and tch 'em chawin' their bacon. Oh, by th' bye, did you hear yet e caught John Corbin for a spy?"

"Oooh," Billy whispered to York. "A spy!"

"Oooo," York whispered back. "Wha'sat, a spy?"

John Clark was shaking his head. "Ah, that's sad. Mind ye, ve no love for Corbin. But one's own neighbors! They'll not ang 'im, I hope." The Corbins were one of Caroline's most rominent Tory families.

"Hang a spy," Billy whispered to York, clutching his own roat and sticking his tongue out of the corner of his mouth. ork cringed, white eyes bulging in the shadows, wondering hether a spy was what he was.

"They've flung 'im in the guardhouse at Williamsburg. They ay he was carrying messages to Dunmore," said Roberts.

Boots clumped in the mud room at the rear of the hall as the st of the riders came in. They stood looking so longingly at the ecanters that John Clark told them to help themselves. Then he dded:

"If I was to run out of ardent spirits, I wonder me, Mike Rob-rts, whether your patrol would have such a keen interest in my oor, tame nigras."

The riders laughed, their big voices filling the hallway. Well," said one of them, "ye do have one missin' out o' quar-rs, Mister Clark."

"What?"

"But I found 'im. He's right up there a-spyin' on us."

And when York saw all these dreadful night men looking and

pointing up at him, he flung his fat little arms around Billy'
waist and began wailing. Billy was moved to action. He stoo
up, gripping the banister, and faced them defiantly.

"No," he proclaimed. "Yorkie's not a spy! He's my persona
own man!"

JONATHAN CLARK PACED ABOUT HIS OFFICE IN THE COUR
House, heels resounding on the plank floor. He could not si
still. He could not get the news of Great Bridge out of his mind
Colonel Woodford had defeated Dunmore's Redcoats there with
his regiment of half-trained Virginians! They had shot down
thirty or forty British Grenadiers on the wooden bridge, repelling
two waves of real Redcoat Regulars, and had driven Dunmor
off the peninsula and re-opened the road to Norfolk, without th
loss of one Virginian! The war was really on Virginia's soil now
and Jonathan was so stirred that he could not work.

He could hear shouts outdoors. He put on his hat and coa
and went out. It was a mild winter day, almost like spring, an
most of the townspeople of Woodstock were out in the streets
Abraham Bowman, a strapping young farmer of Jonathan's age
hailed him and fell in step beside him, grinning and sucking the
fresh air through his teeth. "Wright and Marshall are pittin
their best cocks up at Wright's shed. What sayee to a bet or two?'

"Lead the way. Ah, Lord! I couldn't stay in. Maybe a man'
not meant to sit on a chair all day."

"Sure not."

They walked up the dirt street between the hewn-log houses
Down a side street, a gang of young horsemen were whoopin
and charging in a gander-head-pulling contest. The white gande
hung by its legs from an oak limb, squawking and flapping a
each rider galloped by and tried to yank its head off. Jonatha
and Abe stopped to watch. Several unsuccessful passes wer
made. "Wisht I was horseback," Abe said. "Bet you I could d
'im the first try." Bowman was known as one who would bet or
anything, especially his own abilities. A horse was spurred,
hooves beat, and then a triumphant shout went up. A youn
man reined in, holding the gander's head high in his bloody fis
while the white body in the tree flopped and sprayed blood and
rained feathers. "That's th' way it's done," Abe Bowman said,
and they walked away. "Say, friend Clark, what d'you hear from
your brother George? Joe was askin' me t' other day." Abe'
cousin Joseph had been George's lieutenant in the Indian uprising. "Joe esteems him right high."

"Oh, last letter I got, he said he'd laid out a town, Leesbur

108

he called it, seventy miles up the Kaintuckee River. Said he looked for fifty families to be livin' in it by Christmas. O' course it was last July he wrote that, and I guess they'd not even heard o' Lexington and Concord by then. Medoubts they even know out there that a war's on."

"Oh, they know more out there than y'd reckon they would. Joe bet me that Dunmore's connivin' out there in '74'll mean a lot o' British-like Indians to bother with."

Jonathan remembered what Washington had said about the need to defend the West. But he shrugged. Worthless wilderness, he thought. They turned into the hubbub at Wright's tobacco shed, and stooped to look at the cages of the fighting cocks. "I like the looks o' Marshall's birds. I'll lay a pound on his the first go-round."

Abe doubled over and slapped his thigh in exaggerated hilarity. "Y'll never learn, Jonathan Clark! Now listen, no matter how someone else's birds look, never bet against Wright's!"

"I take that to mean you'll accept the wager?"

"I do! Oh, ye fool! It's a tradition! Wright's always wins!"

They leaned their elbows on the rail of the cockpit. Abe Bowman was still laughing and shaking his head. The air in the shed was close, and stank of tobacco and whiskey-breath. There were about thirty men around the pit, and most of them appeared to have been at the jug since morning. Many of them were speaking German. A large part of the populace of Shenandoah County was made up of German frontiersmen. The name had been changed recently to Shenandoah to obliterate Dunmore's name. Jonathan had had a lot to do with that. As the county's clerk and representative to the Revolutionary Assembly, he was becoming an ever more avid patriot, and that was one reason why Abe Bowman was so drawn to him.

"Here come the first cocks," said Bowman, nudging him in the ribs. "Poor Clark! Tradition, remember? He, he!"

The trainers threw in their roosters. Wright and Marshall were both squat, fat-faced, mean-eyed men, and it was said that the only way to tell them apart was by seeing which roosters they held. The bettors started shouting. Abe Bowman immediately began taunting Marshall's rooster, which was standing in one place, scraping the ground nervously with the claws of its right foot, bobbing its head like an ouzel, swelling and deflating, backing slightly as Wright's bird advanced. "Hey-o, Marshall bird," Bowman yelped at it, "don't just stand and wait! What are ye, a buzzard?" That brought on a wave of laughter and similar jibes, Bowman jabbed Jonathan again with his elbow, sure his point was being taken. Wright's bird kept advancing until the tailfeathers of Marshall's reluctant bird touched the pit wall.

Then the laughing taunts were suddenly drowned by an explosion of squawks, whiffing and flapping wings, and thudding bodies. The air in the cockpit was so full of dust, drifting feathers, and bloodspray that the whiskey-dazed spectators could not follow what was happening. The jeering stopped and now a dozen voices were shouting questions, in English and German. Both trainers stood with their mouths open, squinting into the turmoil.

It was over in seconds. Wright's bird lay in a tattered, twitching heap in the center of the pit, bleeding from both pecked-out eyes and from other wounds beneath its feathers. Its neck appeared to be broken. The ground under it darkened with blood as its movements grew feeble, then ceased. Marshall's cock stood arched, blinking and crowing over it, flapping its iridescent feathers back into place. Its beak and spurs were crimson.

"Well, Abraham," Jonathan said, extending his hand, palm up, to accept his winnings, "my bird took your advice. So much for traditions, eh?"

The men stood around later and drank from a demijohn of rum that Wright had paid up in losses. Marshall's cocks had overthrown a tradition of many years, defeating seven of Wright's ten best birds. "'Twas a true rebellion," Jonathan gloated, raising his cup to Marshall. "Worthy of Lexington, Breed's Hill, and Great Bridge."

Heads were turning. Hoofbeats were coming lickety-cut down the road from Massanutten Mountain, and a voice was crying to herald some great news. Jonathan couldn't make out the words at first; half the voices in the shed were still discussing the outcome of the cockfight, and the other half were demanding quiet to hear what news the rider was bringing.

And then he heard it:

"They've burnt Norfolk! The Redcoats burnt Norfolk!"

The courier was halted by the crowd outside Wright's and he blurted what he knew of it. In retaliation for Great Bridge, Dunmore's Redcoats had raided Norfolk from the sea and set the town afire. Hundreds of people were homeless and seeking refuge farther inland. The drunks from Wright's shed were roaring in anger.

"By God in Heaven!" Jonathan Clark bellowed, shaking a huge fist toward the East. "That does it for me!" He turned to Abraham Bowman and yanked him up by his lapel. "You're a Son o' Liberty," he yelled into his pale blue eyes, "are you with

110

me? I'm goin' soldierin', by God! Devil Dunmore will pay for Norfolk!"

"I'm with you!" Abe Bowman shouted. "And I'll bet a hundred quid we'll run the last Redcoat off this land before a year is out!"

6

KENTUCKY RIVER VALLEY
June 6, 1776

GEORGE LAY AS LOW AND STILL AS A SNAKE UNDER THE HIDden ledge of limestone and peered out through a sun-dappled screen of maple leaves at the Shawnee's dark, unblinking eye and the circle of vermillion war paint around it, and he thought:

He sees me.

George tightened his hand on the walnut handle of his knife, and his heart beat fast against the ground. The warrior was so close, kneeling down out there and looking in, that George could have put the knife right in his eye if his arm were ten inches longer.

But if he sees me why doesn't he do something?

Come on, Shawnee, he thought. If you're going to do something, do it and let's get this over with. You people have slowed me up enough today. Come a little closer and let's get it done. I've got a meeting to go to.

The eye did not look away, but it blinked once. The maple leaves were aglow with sunlight, brilliant green. They stirred a little, but it was a movement caused by a breeze; the Indian had not touched them. George could smell wet limestone and humus right under his nose. His clothes were soaked with sweat and creek water. He and his friend Jones had spent half the day running, hiding, swimming, and backtracking to elude these five or six Shawnees, but they were tenacious as bloodhounds. Now they were out there in the green woods combing this bluff, and if George and Jones were to get to Harrod's Town today, or ever, it looked as if they would have to kill a Shawnee, this one outside their cranny. At least one they'd have to kill; maybe they would have to kill all of them. But first there was this one to deal with, and this one would not move.

George hoped he would move this way. If he moved away, that probably would mean he was going to get some help to look into this cranny. If he came this way, George was pretty sure he could get a hand on him and a knife in him before he could make too much noise.

Come, George thought hard, as if he could will the Shawnee to come closer.

It would have to be with the knife. George's rifle was under his body where he could not extract it without moving noticeably. And he could not use the long gun in this tight place anyway, and besides that, its priming powder would be wet from his clothes. George lay willing the Indian to come closer.

It would be hard to do even with the knife. George could not move his lower body because John Gabriel Jones was lying across his legs. And Jones could not move off George's legs because he was wedged in under the limestone so tight that George could feel the pressure every time Jones inhaled. He didn't know whether Jones could see the Shawnee or whether he knew one was here. But Jones had not moved or whispered, even as cramped as he was, so probably he knew. George hoped he knew, because he did not want him to move or whisper just now.

Come, George thought to the Indian, who had just blinked again. *Move, damn ye!*

The painted face moved slightly down and to the side, so now George could see both eyes. A ruddy brown hand now came up stealthily beside the face, to push some maple leaves aside. It was the Indian's left hand, and there was no weapon in it, which would mean that he probably had his musket in his right hand, one of those nice new British muskets they were all carrying these days. George hoped that if the Shawnee did have a weapon in his other hand, it would be his musket instead of a knife or tomahawk.

The Shawnee's hand was pushing leaves aside and now George could see the green light from the sunny maple leaves gleaming on the Indian's oiled brown forearm and he could see the black dirt under the Indian's fingernails. The Indian was on his hands and knees, and George now could see part of his right shoulder with sun on it, as well as the face and the hand. It was bright out there and it well could be that the Shawnee really had not seen George's eyes in the shadows. The painted face was young, with square jaws. The face was no more than five feet from George's face and the eyes were probing.

Now, George thought, and, quick as a copperhead, he grabbed the Shawnee's wrist with his own left hand and pulled.

JIM HARROD LOOKED OUT THROUGH WHAT HE WAS SURE was the only glass windowpane in Kentucky. It was good to see so many people milling around in the compound; it gave Harrod's Town an air of special importance he thought it deserved. He and his thirty workmen undeniably had built the best and stoutest fortified town in all of Kentucky. The place still smelled of raw new wood, and the entire compound had been paved with sawdust and shavings and hewing chips and tanbark, which was far nicer to walk on than dust or mud, especially when you had a crowd in.

Harrod turned from the window and looked across the crowded room at what he was sure was the only Swiss mantel clock in all of Kentucky. It was four o'clock. He scowled and growled.

"I swear to God, that Clark boy's got this whole country bumfuzzled! He calls everybody here to my town, for some mysterious God-damned callathump. Then 'e gives us all th' bubble by not showin' up for his own meeting! I swear it makes less sense than tits on a boar hog!"

"Don't get your internals all in an uproar, Jim," said a soft, merry voice nearby. "He said he'd be here, and he will be. Meanwhile, let us poor folk wallow in the luxury of your great city." It was Daniel Boone, who so loved to play off against Harrod's beetle-browed bluster. Boone had brought most of his men down from Boonesboro for the meeting.

Harrod scowled at Boone's strong, serene face, then grumbled, "Well, there's not a whole lot o' day left, so I say we'd better start the meeting without him. We all got a good idea what it's about, now, don't we?"

They did know. That Clark redhead had talked to every soul in Kentucky, it seemed, in the last three months. He had talked to them and asked their views on the future of the territory. Even when most of them had been preoccupied with digging up the next stump, hewing the next log, shooting the next meal, or fighting the next Indian war party, he had forced them to look further ahead: You're making your house in Kentucky, he'd say. This is a sacred land to the Indians, and they sure don't mean to let you stay here. How do you intend to protect yourselves? By the Virginia militia? Do you intend, then, to be represented in the Virginia Assembly as a new county of Virginia? Or do you mean to establish an independent state and have your own militia? Or do you expect to be under the proprietorship of Henderson's Transylvania Colony? Or are you going to be British

113

subjects and appeal to the Crown for your safety? How much gunpowder have you? Not much, is it? Where do you propose to get more? He had made them all think on these questions and had told them they would not survive long without some sort of law and some sort of military protection. Since the start of the rebellion in the East, Indians had been coming down across the Ohio in larger and more frequent raiding bands, equipped with good British guns and plentiful English gunpowder, and with sharp new red-handled scalping knives of British steel, often even led by British army officers from the forts at Detroit and Vincennes and Kaskaskia. The British intend to drive us all back across the mountains, he had said, and it will be easy for them to do unless we have a means of defense. What will it be?

He had showed up everywhere, that intense and likable Clark lad from Virginia, full of news and interesting talk, and his disturbing questions. With him usually was his friend John Gabriel Jones from the Holston Valley, a tough, bespectacled young man with that same agreeable gift of gab and good sense. Sometimes they arrived in time to help raise a log cabin or budge out a stump; sometimes they showed up with a fresh-killed deer when there wasn't anything else to eat but flour and berries; sometimes they arrived in time to foil a theft of horses by some Indian band, or to escort some decimated family to the safety of one of the walled towns. The fact was, those two were as well known around the country as Boone or Harrod, and they had helped people and made them think; and so now that they had sent word of a public meeting at Harrod's Town, the people had come from miles all around. They all knew now what the needs and the problems were. And so, though Clark and Jones had not arrived, the settlers proceeded with their meeting.

And when the pair trotted in at twilight, blood-spattered and thorn-tattered and loaded down with shiny British muskets and scalping knives, they were greeted at the gate by Jim Harrod in a surprising manner. Tipping his hat and bowing slightly with all the grace of a trained bear, Harrod said, "Welcome to Virginia's spankin'-new county of Kentuck, Mister Assemblyman Clark and Mister Assemblyman Jones. Sorry you didn't get here in time to vote for yourselves, but it doesn't matter, as most everybody else did."

FOUR DAYS LATER, IN THE GREEN GLOOM OF THE FOREST, John Gabriel Jones sucked in a breath between clenched teeth, and stopped. He was trembling with pain. He took off his spectacles and wiped sweat off of them with the end of his neckerchief.

114

His narrow face was yellow-gray under his woodsman's tan. George turned in his saddle and looked back to where Jones stood in the path, leaning on his rifle. Jones tried to take a step forward; again he squinted and gasped.

Damnation, George thought. "Come, Mister Assemblyman Jones," he said, swinging his leg over to dismount. "You ride." George's own feet were hot and throbbing almost beyond endurance. When they touched the ground he groaned aloud. They felt as if he were standing in boiling water.

"No," Jones said, "you been letting me ride all morning. And e's your horse, anyways." Jones's horse had foundered two days earlier, and since then the two "assemblymen," as they jokingly called each other, had been sharing George's mount.

They were a hundred miles east of Harrod's Town, on their way to Williamsburg, carrying petitions from the Kentuck settlers. It had rained every day, but there had been so much fresh Indian sign that they had not dared light fires to dry their moccasins, and so now they were suffering the torment that hunters called scald feet, and had been limping along the steep trails, taking turns riding George's horse.

Even riding did not relieve the pain much. They could not bear to put their feet in the stirrups. And when their feet dangled, they felt as if they were engorged with boiling blood and might burst.

George helped Jones onto the horse, then hobbled on in advance, trying to concentrate on the woods ahead. The misery dulled his senses, and this was far too dangerous a trail to stumble along half-alert. The Indians knew all the trodden paths between the settlements, and watched them like buzzards.

After a few hundred excruciating steps, George stopped and stood listening to the dripping woods. Since morning he had been hearing distant gunshots, faint *thuds* on the eardrums, filtered through wet air and dripping water. Hunters from Martin's Station, he would think, more hoping than believing.

He heard nothing now. "Let's go," he ordered his feet in a whisper, then gritted his teeth and winced and limped. This matter of his feet was somehow disgraceful. They were not bonebroken, not cut; it was only pain, and he did not believe that mere pain should cripple a body.

"Godalmighty, man," Jones said after a few hundred more yards. He had ridden alongside to find George hitching along, face contorted in a gray and sweat-slick grimace. "George Clark, I prayee, let's hole up someplace and doctor these bedeviled

115

trailbeaters of our'n. I can't go any more, nor can you, if you admit it."

"All right, Mister Assemblyman Jones," George grinned an groaned. "Yonder's the Licking, and down it a league is Ma tin's. We'll put in there if we can make it, eh?"

"Thankee, Mister Assemblyman Clark. *Thankee!*"

The assemblyman thing was a joke between them. They coul not really be assemblymen until Kentuck was a county, an Kentuck could not be a county until the Virginia Assembly vote to admit it. The people voting at Harrod's Town had not know of that technicality, or had simply ignored it. "But look at thisaway," Jones had said. "If it does get to be a county, we' got a head start."

MARTIN'S STATION WAS DESERTED. ITS FOUR CABINS STOO empty and locked. A few pigs wandered grunting among th buildings. There were no boot or shoe prints in the damp eart But there were tracks of many Indian moccasins. "The folk must've packed out in the rain," George said. "Those India tracks are real fresh. Likely they followed out looking for th people. Be back any time, I'd wager, to burn the place down.

"What now for us, then?" Jones groaned. "We're not fit to g dodgin' Indians, like we had such fun at t'other day. We need fire. We need to make some foot salve."

"We'd better fort up, I reckon, or we'll be smellin' brimston through a nail hole before we're a day older. Let's use Mr. Ma tin's big cabin yonder." It stood on a rise in the middle of clearing, up from the river, away from the other structures. Any one approaching it from any direction would have to cross fift yards of open ground.

They went to it. It had no windows, just gun ports, and on thick, oaken door secured by an iron lock. Jones stood with hi teeth bared in pain, leaning against the door in a despairing pos ture. "What now?" he groaned. "Chop the door in?"

"Not if it's to be our fort." George took off the short swor that hung at his side. "Kindly take my hanger here and go stic us a pig, while I let us in."

At the expense of the worst pain yet, George climbed fingers and-toes to the top of the stick-and-daub chimney. He tore o chimney down to roof-ridge level until the opening was wid enough to admit him. He let his legs down into the sooty aper ture, and paused to watch Jones. Jones was mincing along like firewalker, cooing seductively to a sow he had cornered in th angle of a rail fence. George grinned. "Get 'er, Mister As

116

mblyman," he called softly. It would have been easier to shoot
er, but they dared not make the noise.

At that instant Jones flung himself on the sow and stabbed her
rough the heart before she could squeal. They fell in a heap
nd she died under him after a few twitches.

Now, wincing with agony, George braced feet and elbows
gainst the inside of the flue and eased himself down. He lost his
old and fell most of the way, yelping as his feet hit the hearth.
kettle rolled clunking on the floor and ash-dust swirled in the
arrow beams of light through the gun-ports.

The cabin was empty except for a large hewn table and a
ench in the center of the one big room. The occupants at least
ad had time to remove everything portable, even their bed-
eads.

The iron lock yielded at the lift of an inside latch, and he
pened the door to let in daylight, Assemblyman Jones, George's
orse, and the dead pig.

They forted up, pausing now and then to look and listen.
hey heard two faraway gunshots while butchering. They built a
re and rendered some pig fat. George went to the edge of the
learing for some oak bark. They limped about, fetching water
nd more wood, some green corn, grass for the horse, and a long
ole. They swept away their tracks with a bough, then locked
nemselves in about midafternoon with the glorious aroma of
oasting pork. George was sure by now that Indians controlled
ne whole countryside here in the Licking Valley. It seemed
nost likely to him that Kentucky's first two elected representatives
night die defending this log-walled room, their political careers
ess than a week old. But he did not say so. Instead he anointed
ones's feet with an ooze of pig fat and oak bark. Then Jones
nointed George's feet. The pain began to ease at once. Their
noccasins were drying near the fire.

They loaded their rifles and pistols, and laid them out on the
able with powder horns and rifle balls, ramrods, patches, and
xtra flints. The long pole would be used to knock the roof off if
ndians set it afire. The plan was that George would do the
hooting while Jones loaded. Jones, with his weak eyes, was an
ncommonly poor shot among frontiersmen.

"Now, Mister Assemblyman Jones. Set for a siege?"

"Aye," replied Jones with a nervous laugh, sitting on the
ench with his feet wrapped in oozy rags, arranging rifle balls in
neat row in a groove of the tabletop. "Aye, thou defender and
awmaker of Kain-tuck. Bring on the tribes."

"I'll eliminate the Shawnee nation first," George said. "Afte them, the rest'll go down easy."

While they were waiting and eating, doctoring their feet an watching at the portholes, they talked about what they should d if only one of them got to Williamsburg. Jones was astonished all the connections George had among leading Virginians. "Bu if nothing else comes to pass," George said, "I swear by my lif I'm going to get some ammunition transported back out here. think our jurisdiction's damn nigh overrun, by the looks o' this and hardly a man in Kaintuck's got enough gunpowder to blov his nose."

"LISTEN," GEORGE HISSED. IT WAS TWILIGHT NOW. THE had let the hearth fire die because it smoked too much with th chimney torn down. For light they had made a smoky littl lamp, using a broken cup, some pig fat, and a cloth wick George picked up both rifles and limped to one of the firin ports.

He could see nothing but the darkening clearing and th gloomy forest beyond it, and a stretch of pale river, but he coul hear something: a faint, metallic sound, repeating and repeating and a fragment of voice. He listened for a long time, hardl breathing, puzzled. He looked back once and saw John Gabrie Jones praying at the table with his eyes shut; he looked as if h were saying grace over a banquet of guns and ammunition.

George eased a rifle muzzle through the porthole, aiming to ward the noises outside. He could hear them talking in the edg of the woods now; they were about to come forth into the clear ing.

George snorted suddenly, pulled the rifle back in, and hob bled to the door. To Jones's astonishment, he unlatched it an swung it wide open and stepped out, and Jones heard him say

"About your chimney and pig, Mister Martin, I'll make goo on 'em, and thankee. You folks are a welcome sight."

Jones's sigh of relief blew out his little lamp.

SUNLIGHT FLASHED OFF THE BRASS SPEARHEAD ATOP TH regimental flag. The banner, salmon-colored silk with a lon fringe, flapped lazily above the cloud of road dust stirred up b the dragging feet of overheated, exhausted marchers.

Captain Jonathan Clark nudged his horse's flanks with hi heels and looked at the flag. In the center of the silken rectangle was depicted a white scroll, upon which was inscribed:

118

Jonathan looked often at the flag, trying to inspire his limp d sagging morale. He felt dust between his teeth, and his strils were clogged with dust-reddened snot. Sometimes he ought the troops in this regiment raised twice as much dust as y other body of men because they dragged their feet so much. They just shuffle along, he thought angrily, squinting against e dust and sunglare. The sun was just a few degrees above the arolina treetops, and already was drilling hot, and every morn-g for days it had been in their eyes as they trudged eastward ward Charles Town.

This German Regiment, as it was called, was not all he ished it could be. The privates were surly and stubborn, mut-red to each other in their incomprehensible tongue, and owered insolently at their officers, Abe Bowman and Bill elson, John Markham, Morgan Alexander, who were, like nathan himself, mostly of English stock. The regimental com-ander, General Peter Muhlenberg, was of their own kind, and ey liked him, and thus he had to tend to many details of disci-ine and dispute that should have been handled by the com-any officers. Most of the troops did actually know English fairly ell, but often acted as if they had not understood orders given English. And they would retreat into their own tongue when ey wished to mock their officers. General Muhlenberg was a ne and fair man, an old friend of Jonathan's, but he had been a ergyman and was too soft-hearted to be much of a disci-linarian. He usually would choose not to believe that his foot ldiers were capable of being crafty and disobedient; he did not elieve those were Germanic traits.

But the 8th Virginia was a troublesome unit, and already venty men had deserted during this long, stifling forced march om Georgia.

Jonathan could understand their discontent. They had left the lean, green mountains of the Virginia-Pennsylvania frontier far ehind, to march now in suffocating heat through eternal and onotonous plains and swamps and fields of poor red earth, atchy scrub and sparse, dusty pines, stung by no-see-ums and veat bees, and tormented by mosquitoes that came upon them ut of the marshes like whining clouds. They had been put in an rmy under the command of General Charles Lee, who was rever trying to anticipate where the British fleet might show up long the Southern coast. Thus the army had marched back and orth from place to place—in General Lee's own words, "as confused as a dog in a dancing school"—and now after a swelterin[g] disease-plagued encampment in Georgia they were hurrying u[p] to Charles Town, where a British fleet had hove to and l[ay] threateningly offshore. It seemed to Jonathan that the British ha[d] a great advantage. They could just show up anywhere, whi[te] sails off a coastal town, and the Continental Army would have [to] go there and try to arrive in time to keep them from doing wh[at] they had done to Norfolk.

Here in the South the sick list was long and the sick staye[d] sick. Dysentery was universal, everybody had rashes, and som[e] of the men were beginning to suffer the fevers and chills of m[a]laria.

Jonathan pulled a damp, filthy handkerchief, stained the col[or] of brick dust, out of his sleeve and mopped his face, and looke[d] ahead at the long column of dusty coats, black tricorns, kna[p]sacks, and shouldered muskets stretching out of sight on the inf[i]nite straight road, the forward companies obscured by their ow[n] dust, and wondered what sort of soldiers these Germans woul[d] prove to be in the face of fire and steel.

It was not their manliness or courage he doubted. They we[re] frontier people, after all, and most of them had been on the edg[e] of their lives more than once. They were accustomed to fightin[g] individually.

What he feared for was their obedience. The square, straigh[t] unthinking responses of drill were unnatural to them. He coul[d] see that already, in their resistance to training. They had learne[d] to obey only so far as to avoid punishment. Under fire, he ex[-] pected, they would fall to anarchy and, like Indians, preser[ve] their individual selves to fight another day. That was the be[st] way in wilderness fighting, of course. But now they were soldie[rs] of the Continental Line, trained according to Bland's an[d] Harvey's military texts, to fight other squared-up regiments in th[e] European manner, advancing in open fields with bayone[ts] against bayonets, instead of sniping from the cover of rocks an[d] trees.

When we get to Charles Town, Jonathan thought, spitting [a] gob of dust-red saliva onto the roadside and listening to the dis[-] mal shuffling of reluctant feet all around him, pray we shan[']t break and rout, and disgrace that pretty pink flag!

GEORGE PACED OUTSIDE THE DOOR OF GOVERNOR PATRIC[K] Henry's bedchamber. He could hear Henry inside, dictating cor[-] respondence to a secretary from his sickbed.

George's scald feet were cured, but they still felt prickly some[-]

120

imes when he had to stand still, so now he paced back and forth
n the gloomy hall.

Henry had been elected, a month before, the first governor
under Virginia's new constitution. He had been installed in the
Governor's Palace at Williamsburg, which Lord Dunmore had
so hastily vacated, but had retreated here to his private home in
Hanover County during a bout of ill health. The house was
quiet except for the governor's voice and, from some distant corner of the dwelling, the voices of children with their tutor. Mrs.
Henry had died the year before, after a long illness, leaving him
with six children. The house seemed oppressive and sad. George
wondered how a man could run affairs of state in such a depressing atmosphere, especially while ill himself. You'd think he'd
want to be carried out and set under a shade tree, George
thought. How can people stand so much indoors?

The bedchamber door opened and the secretary poked out his
head, a youthful, pallid face under a white-powdered wig. He
looked George up and down once, making evident his disap-
proval of the petitioner's wild appearance. George was still in his
smoke-tainted, fringed hunting shirt and buckskin leggings
stained with the blood of pig and Indian. Around his waist was
an Indian-bead belt, fastened in back by thongs and supporting
his hanger sword and a pistol. He had set his knapsack and hat
on a chair by the door and leaned his rifle on the wall.

"His Excellency will see you now," the secretary said, then
recoiled timidly as George shouldered through the door past
him.

The room was dim and hot. Heavy curtains had been drawn
against the daylight, and two bedside candles burned in air dense
with the smells of medicinal powders and stale bedclothes. One
might have thought a man was dying in here, but the voice that
greeted George from the pile of candlelit pillows was deep and
strong, though curdled with phlegm. "George Clark! What a
pleasure! Take this chair here and let me see you, lad!" George
took a hot, damp hand.

"Your Excellency. Thank you for receiving me. It is, as y'll
see, quite urgent."

"In good time. How is your father? Your mother?"

"Both well, to my knowledge. I've not been home yet."

"Must be urgent indeed, then." Henry had pushed his spectacles to the top of his high forehead, which seemed two inches
higher than it had been the last time George had seen him.
Henry looked considerably older than his forty years. His face
was fever-blotched, and his eyes, bushy eyebrows above and con-

centric pouches beneath, blazed with candle flame. "How come you to Hanover?"

"Well, sir, finding myself and my friend John Gabriel Jones elected Kentuck's delegates to the Virginia Assembly—" Henry's eyebrows lifted. George continued. "We went to Williamsburg and found the Assembly already adjourned. So I've brought straight to you what I was taking to them."

Henry shook his head and stretched out his hand. "Welcome to the governing business. Though I can't say you're a bona fide delegate, as Kentuck's no county of Virginia."

"Her people desire that she be. They've petitioned. I'd intended we should come just as deputies, to negotiate for admission to the state. But the people did things their own way while I was detained elsewhere. Withal, I have petitions praying Virginia's protection, and one disputing Colonel Henderson's claims on that country."

Henry regarded the ceiling for ten seconds, as if adding sums, then looked back to George and said, "There's many a faction, besides Henderson, who'd deny Virginia has any proper pretension to that country."

"That I well know. I've heard every side of it."

"The Assembly won't sit again till October."

"Aye," George sighed. "Meantime, Indians are swarming on the settlements, egged on by the British, and I doubt there's fifty pounds o' gunpowder in all o' Kentuck. That can't wait much longer. We need powder, and that's why I've come straight to you."

Again the governor studied the ceiling. "You put your mother state in a delicate spot, George. It would be a stretch of our power to arm Kentuck; some would say an intrusion on country not our own. That's serious."

"Kentuck's a part of Virginia under the old charter."

"True. But don't forget, we're shrugging off a king, and maybe with him our claim to some territory. There's northern states in the Continental Congress who say the West ought to be the common property of the united colonies. And don't forget, even Henderson's isn't the only land company claiming rights in it."

"Not to mention the Indians," grinned George, "if ye mean to name everybody who has a say-so." His grin vanished as quickly as it had come. "I know full damned well, sir, that I'm putting the state on a delicate spot. But without powder, we'll all be killed or driven out. If that happens, y've got no defense on your rear at all." He had deliberately put that in military terms, and now stared hard at Henry. He knew the governor fancied himself

military man at heart, and, as governor, he was commander-
in-chief of the Virginia state forces, and would be determined to
know good strategic sense.

"I don't know if you've read Virginia's new constitution,
George."

"In fact, sir, I have." His old mentor George Mason had
penned it.

"Then you know the limits on my powers in such matters as
domain. I'm no dictator, by any means. Whether Virginia asserts her claims to the western country, the Assembly will have
to decide, when they sit again in October. I'll see that it's a first
issue of business. But till then I guess you can't know whether
you're to be a true delegate or not."

"That's not important to me, sir. Defense is."

"You surely know my sentiments on Kentuck, George. I think
it's worth claiming."

"It would be Virginia's greatest wealth."

"Here is what I can do, George. I'll write a letter to my Council, favoring the gunpowder. You'll take the letter to them at
Williamsburg. Make as much persuasion to them as you've
made to me, and you'll likely get your ammunition with little
delay—probably as a loan to neighbors in distress, though, I
fear, not as a provision to Virginia citizens. How much powder
are you thinking of?"

"Five hundred pounds at least."

Henry pursed his lips. "Five hundred. Better ask for a thousand, then."

"And the expense of guards and transport," George added.
"That's all through hostile country, as y' know."

Henry touched his temple with two fingertips, put his glasses
down from his forehead onto his nose, peered over the glasses at
George, and then replaced them atop his head. "They're likely
to contest you soundly on that."

"They had better not," George said with heat. "Not if they
mean to have Kentuck."

Henry cleared his throat. Then he pulled a bell cord to summon his secretary. He smiled and relaxed. "Stay for supper,
George. It does me good to see you. You Westerners are like
fresh air to me. Where's your other delegate, your Mister . . . Jones, was it?"

"Gone home to the Holston, to fight Cherokees till the Assembly sits again."

"Hm. Active fellow; I'd like to have met him. You'll convey my
regards to your good family?" He seemed to have forgotten his

supper invitation, and George was glad, eager to go. Home was in the next county, and he hadn't been there in nearly three years. Home! He could feel it pulling on his heart; he could see his family around a candlelit table. "Five hundred pounds of powder!" Henry mused as the secretary entered. "That's a tall order, George. But we can't afford to leave any quarter unguarded."

THIS TIME, JOHNNY WAS NOT IN THE DRIVEWAY TO GREET him as he galloped up, but here came little Billy tearing down the middle of the road toward him, yelling, "Georgie! Georgie," and followed by a tubby little black boy, two barking bird dogs, and two sisters, Lucy and Elizabeth, their skirts flying. Billy looked as if he were determined to get run over, and in an instant George realized that the rascal expected to be snatched up and swung onto the horse's rump as Johnny had used to be.

I hope Ma isn't watching, he thought. He slowed the horse just slightly and headed him to Billy's left, and leaned far out and down as he swept past. His left arm caught Billy around the waist and snatched him off the ground. It almost knocked the breath out of the little fellow, but he was deliriously happy, hugging to George's side and yelling like an Indian. They trotted up to the front door trailed by the children and dogs. Billy was grinning triumphantly down at York between Indian yelps, and the little blue-black child came running along rolling and buffing, his eyes wide with amazement. George saw his mother in the door with a little girl who must be Frances Eleanor beside her, and his father was riding in from the tobacco fields. Edmund came sprinting after him, coming at an angle across the field, at every third step springing over a row of plants. George lowered Billy to the ground, where, still in a frenzy of rowdy exuberance, he pounced upon little York and the two tumbled and grappled and growled like a pair of bear cubs, the dogs leaping over and around them.

"God be praised," his mother said as he dismounted, "you're still amongst the livin'!" And she hugged him hard, and she saw the old bloodstains on his sleeves, and hoped it was from butchering meat.

And then the family swept, clamoring, into the great, cool hallway, where the old business of getting reacquainted could start all over again.

"I saw a lot of cattle in the north pasture, Pa."

"I'M RAISING BEEF FOR THE GRAND ARMY. TWO HUNDRED head I have now."

124

"Good. It'll take a hundred of 'em to feed Jonathan. Where is he?"

"Last letter said they were marching to Georgia. But that's been weeks."

"He's a captain," Edmund said. "Y'ought to see how grand 'e looks in a uniform!"

"I'll bet! A captain in the Regulars! Now, that *is* grand! And where's Johnny?"

"At drill, up at the Bowling Green," said Mrs. Clark. "If he's not home, he's either at drill, or up to his usual pursuits."

"Ha, ha, ha! Not over that yet, eh?"

"Indeed not. It's worse. He thinks he's got to get in a lifetime of sparkin' ere he goes to war. As if he doesn't expect to come back." Mrs. Clark's voice caught as she said this. "Well, ye know how he goes on about things." George saw the little glint of desperation in her eyes before she firmed herself. When Johnny went to war, that would be three she'd have to pray for.

George knelt and nuzzled Elizabeth. Her face was so perfect, with its little nose and halo of black curls, that it made George's heart ache. Then she blinked shyly and smiled at him, and he could see that it was she who was in the toothless stage now; the tip of her pink tongue showed in the gap between her eyeteeth. Lucy had teeth now, but she had reached the gangly phase and looked rather like a boy in a dress. Her nose was even longer, and had a scab on its bridge, among the great freckles. She looked as full of mischief as an imp of Satan. "Hey, sweetheart," he said to her. "You're still my favorite redheaded sister, I hope."

"I'm your *only* one," she said, a little impudent, it seemed.

"You are?" He acted shocked. "No, you must be mistaken. I have one with no front teeth." She smiled finally, at that.

"Georgie!" Billy cried. He was up on the stairs now, with York standing below him at the banister. "Georgie, can I wear your hat?"

"If you can find it. I don't know where it got to."

Billy held it up, smiling wide, and put it on. It came down over his eyes and he had to tilt his head far back to look down at them in the hallway. Everybody laughed at him, and George said:

"Later I'll show y' a few things about that hat. After I have another drink."

"And a story! About the great MING-o," Billy cried.

George paused as he was sniffing a glass of brandy, and a picture flickered in his memory, a sad spectre: Logan, as he had last seen him, a reeking ruin.

Edmund had been looking at the dark stains and slits that

125

looked like knife cuts on George's sleeves, but knew better than to ask the question with his father standing here. He was somehow sure they were Indian blood. He watched as George set down his glass and picked up the youngest daughter and held her on his arm, the arm with bloodstained sleeves.

The little girl looked at the stubble on George's face and blinked a little in the liquorish smell of his breath, and she looked a bit frightened, but she smiled a very timid smile. "Oh, but you're a beauty," he said, "and you don't really know me at all, do ye?"

She nodded. "You're Georgie," she said.

"Yes I am! And you're Frances Eleanor, and the last time I saw you, you were a suckling."

"I'm Fanny," she said. "That is the name they call me now."

"You're Fanny; and you know what? You talk a lot plainer than your brother Billy did when he was your age."

"Yes," she said with adult clarity and gravity. "I should say I do."

Laughing, George handed her to his father, saying. "Quick, Pa, send her to the school! She can teach the parson to speak English!"

"Oh, my, oh my!" Mrs. Clark exclaimed, "oh, I'm laughing so, I'll be gettin' all strawberry-blotchy the way I do! Oh, I'm glad you're home with us! Oh, I'm so happy! But *please*! Let me get my breath!"

"I haven't seen Dick," George said. "Where's he?"

"He's off to drill too," said John Clark. For a moment then there was no laughter. It was as if they all had become aware of the not-so-distant war, as if they had heard cannon on the horizon, like the grumble of summer thunder, but they had heard nothing. George took another sip of brandy. It had been a long time since he had savored anything so smooth, and this was like heaven to be here among family, warming his soul with this velvety, fruity stuff. The frontier corn whiskey burned like acid going down, and the trader's rum that reached those parts left him feeling the next morning as if he'd been scalped in his sleep.

"I heard on the road," he said, "that Owen's the sheriff o' King William now."

"That he is," said John Clark. "And did ye get my letter that he's a father?"

"Aye, I did. I'm an 'Uncle George.' That sounds good."

"And he's like t' be a father again this year, Annie tells us."

"Again? Isn't that wonderful!"

"Well, I don't know what's so wonderful about it. It happens

126

ll the time," said Mrs. Clark. "In this family, anyways. I told
hat girl . . ." She paused, glancing at her husband. "Well,
ever mind what I told her. But I'll say I'm glad we've got no
nore daughters of bearin' age yet. What with all these would-be
warrior sons to worry about, I don't have time to worry about but
ne daughter at a time."

"Well, it's a blessing you don't let yourself worry about other
people's daughters too, then," mused John Clark. "I do. I expect
very day to see some passing fancy o' Johnny's show up on the
oor stoop with a babe-in-arms and say, 'Tot, meet your
Grandpa.' Grrr!"

Here they were all talking about babies again, and Billy was
etting impatient, standing up there on the stairs looking down
is nose from under George's marvelously smelly hat.
Georgie," he cried, "come on! You said you'd show me about
ne hat!"

"I will! Soon as I have another sip here, I'll show you. And
ou and I got some surveying to talk on, too. Y' learned to read
uclid yet?"

"I can read *some* words!" He reached into the pocket of his
eskit, remembering something. "Lookee!" He held up the
ompass.

George's hat was a battered, sweat-stained, rakish thing, but
ppeared to be just a hat, at first glance, a floppy, very wide-
rimmed black felt hat with the right side of the brim turned up
nd fastened to the round crown. "Now look at this," George
aid, reaching up and taking it from Billy's head. "There's times
d ha' been in a pickle without this wondrous old hat." They
ood around him and watched. "Lookee here at this bone here,"
e said, pulling out the sliver that pinned up the brim. "That's
urkey-leg bone, and many's the time I use it to pick a raspberry
eed or some stringy bear meat from 'twixt my back teeth." He
ut it back. "Now this feather. Y' think that's just a decoration?
's sure not. Look at the point, all black with ink. That's th' very
en I write ye letters with. Now, lookee here, stuck in the brim.
ght here. Needles! One for leather, one for cloth. If I didn't
ave those, why, Billy, I'd have to go 'round sometimes with my
ind end shinin' out through a split in my breeches."

"Oh, Georgie, really!" Frances Eleanor admonished. It threw
im off for a minute, that prim little voice, and everyone was
ughing.

"Ha, ha! Well, now, this hatband. See how it's all a braid of
read and thong? Well, when I sit down to mend things, why, I
ull out however much I need. I'm a regular seamstress, y' see!

127

A man's got to be, out there where all the gels, what few there be, are somebody else's wives." He looked up and toward the door, listening for a moment, then went on: "So there y'are, family. Add that this wondrous hat is sometimes my water pail and forage basket, and the only roof over my head for a month at a stretch, and y' see why I'd be in a pickle without it. I wonder whether it's Johnny and Dickie comin'. I hear four horses, or is it five?"

They just now heard the hoofbeats, faint, far down the road, and they looked at him, wondering how he could have heard those hooves already, even while talking. It was uncanny, like a dog's hearing, or an Indian's, or . . .

Ann Rogers Clark remembered a long-ago day, remembered sitting in a rocking chair in the nursery, remembered Billy listening through the window, as if for summer thunder, and then George riding home.

The horsemen were Johnny and Dickie, and with them were cousins Joe and Johnny Rogers, all in their militia garb and armed to the teeth. They swarmed in through the front door and began pounding George and hugging him. Leaving the Bowling Green after muster, they said, they had been told by someone that George Rogers Clark was in the neighborhood. What was he up to, they wanted to know. Why was he here? Had he come back to join the army?

"No," he said. "I'm on business for Kaintuck, and I'll tell you what it is in a bit. Listen, I'm off for Williamsburg next week first thing, but I've got a lot o' stories to tell before I go, stories to make your back-hair rise up."

Ann Rogers Clark hugged her waist and looked at him, slowly shaking her head.

Nothing's changed, she thought. Nothing's changed.

7

CHARLES TOWN,
SOUTH CAROLINA
June 28, 1776

THE DAY WAS DAWNING TO BE BRIGHT AND HOT. THE SUN WAS scarcely out of the Atlantic, peeping over the scrub and hut around Fort Sullivan, just gleaming on the windows of the stately waterfront houses along The Battery of Charles Town across the harbor, but already Jonathan Clark could feel it blazing on his back where he sat under the awning of the officers' mess. Jonathan was sweaty and dizzy. He had hardly slept; he had been shivering all night and wishing for the warmth of morning; now it was morning and he knew the sun would be almost unbearable again today.

There were about two dozen officers on benches at the tables, among them this morning General Charles Lee himself, who had come over from his headquarters to discuss Fort Sullivan's powder supply with Colonel William Moultrie, the South Carolina militia officer in command of the fort. General Lee was giving the fort very little powder. General Lee had made it clear that he did not believe in Colonel Moultrie's squat, unimposing, unfinished little fort. General Lee expected the British fleet to sail right past it, demolish it with a few contemptuous passing shots, then sail on into the harbor to bombard Charles Town. Lee expected the main attack would be made by the 3,000 Redcoats that had been landed and encamped on Long Island, east of Fort Sullivan, and thus Lee had diverted most of the available powder to his Continental troops, which he had placed between the Redcoats and the city. General Lee wanted to give Moultrie only enough powder for twenty-eight shots from each of the fort's twenty-six eighteen-pounders. Lee had repeatedly called the unfinished fort a "slaughter pen" and every day since his arrival at Charles Town he had mocked Moultrie's belief that it could serve any purpose. Their quarrel over this was the current gossip of the American officers. Jonathan now heard Lee say, in that contemptuous tone of voice his officers had come to know so well:

"What is it you call that, that *stuff* your little fort's made of?"

"Palmetto, sir," sighed Colonel Moultrie for perhaps the fourth time, staring cold-eyed across the table at the slovenly General Lee, who, now that he had liberally spotted his waistcoat with pork grease, was feeding scraps to his "honest quadruped friends," as he called the dogs that were always around his feet. "As I've opined already," Colonel Moultrie said, "palmetto may prove better than oak, under fire. I've seen men ruined by oak splinters, but I sure don't reckon palmetto will splinter."

Jonathan wiped his face with a napkin. He was sweating to soak his clothes.

There was no more denying it: malaria had caught up with him.

But Jonathan wouldn't go on sick call with it. He was determined not to be sick abed on his first day of war, which, he was sure, would be any day now.

The city of Charles Town was as ready for siege as it could make itself. Men had sent their families into the country for safety, then had turned to, alongside soldiers and slaves, to build barricades in all the principal streets, and to tear down waterfront warehouses that might have obscured the defenders' view of the harbor. Citizens had even contributed their lead window-sash weights to be melted down for bullets.

Most of General Lee's army had been deployed to defend the city itself and the approaches to it. A large body of regular troops under General Armstrong stood by on the mainland, at Haddrell's Point, as the northern defense for the city. On the northeast end of Sullivan's Island were concealed 700 South Carolina sharpshooters, directly across Breach Inlet from the Redcoats encamped on Long Island. Thus the sharpshooters were outnumbered four to one, but that was of little concern; Moultrie knew the swift and tricky currents of Breach Inlet would keep Redcoats from fording it as well as bullets could. Apparently without knowing it, General Clinton had stranded his Redcoat army on a shadeless, mosquito-plagued sandbar where they could hardly bother anybody. And thus it was that Moultrie firmly believed that the defense of Charles Town ultimately would turn out to be a cannon duel: his fort against Admiral Sir Peter Parker's fleet. That was why he kept demanding more powder.

Lee, a British officer who had resigned his commission to fight on the rebel side, scorned militia, and thought Moultrie was too democratic with his men. There was talk that Lee wanted to replace him with a more authoritarian, less popular, officer. Just now Lee was scoffing.

"Your little fort's but half made! Only two walls. It's a slaughter pen, I say, and there's no retreat from it."

"I don't intend to retreat," Moultrie said.

"The fleet will knock your little fort down about your ears in half an hour."

"Then we'll fight from behind the ruins of 'my little fort.'"

"And after they've knocked it down they'll shoot right up your rump through that unfinished side, then turn round and bombard the town. Ha! Huh!"

"I say give me some powder, General, sir, and they'll never get past our muzzles."

Jonathan looked at the mild, persistent Carolinian with a rush of admiration. Then an onslaught of feverishness came over him, making sweat prickle on his face and causing his senses to extend and contract like a telescope.

"I think Moultrie's right," said Ensign Croghan's soft, deep voice. Jonathan mopped his brow and nodded to his friend across the table. William Croghan, dark-haired, with deep-set blue eyes and a jutting chin, was English-born. He had turned down an offer of high rank in the British army because he believed in the American cause. He had joined the 8th Virginia in April and had become Jonathan's closest friend. He pronounced his name "Crawn." Everybody was fond of Bill Croghan, for his candid irreverence and unfailing cheerfulness. Though his skin was fair and smooth as a child's, he was hard-muscled and manly. He was a grand raconteur. Being a great-nephew of George Croghan, Britain's deputy Indian agent under Sir William Johnson, Bill Croghan was full of wondrous Indian anecdotes—many of them about Sir William's legendary procreative powers that had increased the North American Indian population by an estimated thousand halfbreeds.

Now a stirring in another part of the pavilion signaled General Lee's brusque departure. Everybody was rising to attention. The general stalked out of the tent, wiping his chin with his coat sleeve, followed by his pack of canines and his staff officers, in that order. "I believe they like their master so well because he always reeks o' meat," an officer remarked.

"Who does," Croghan asked, "his dogs or his staff?"

Jonathan laughed despite his misery.

The atmosphere relaxed after Lee's departure, and there was familiar, easy talk, that casual after-breakfast hubbub that was one of the most pleasant parts of an officer's life, in Jonathan's estimation; it was so much like mornings at the Clark home. While most of the officers jabbered about the eternal politics of soldiering, Jonathan and Bill talked nostalgically about homes and families. If Jonathan was malaria-sick, he was twice as homesick. Bill Croghan had heard about every member of the Clark family, and had heard probably a hundred of Ann Rogers Clark's "Maxims to Live Decent By," as Jonathan liked to call them.

"Up! Up, gents!" someone was shouting. "Look! The fleet's on the move!" There was a lively turning of heads, scooting of benches, press of bodies. Jonathan rose, heart pounding, and looked out toward the Atlantic.

Offshore to the southeast, beyond low, scrubby Sullivan's Island with its squat fort, above the sun-silvered horizon, stood the topsails of the British men-o'-war. The vessels were under full sail, their tall canvas looking creamy and translucent against the backlight of the morning sun. Colonel Moultrie had risen, pausing to button his waist-length artillery jacket and don the glossy black-leather Romanesque helmet of his Corps. He squinted at the fleet, then limped rapidly toward the exit on his gouty foot.

"Wishing you a good shoot, sir," Bill Croghan called as he passed. Officers were pouring out of the pavilion, mounting their horses outside.

"Thank y' kindly," Moultrie answered without looking back. "That's what we aim to have."

THEY STOOD ON THE SWAMPY GROUND OF THE MAINLAND north of Sullivan's Island and watched with pounding hearts as the awful moment approached. Still full of breakfast, the Continentals stood like spectators in some enormous coliseum, voices murmuring with awe and dread.

The towering fleet glided ominously toward the channel, the ships' massive bows munching the blue water. There was a terrible sense of unstoppability in the moment now, no way to call it off, no way to prevent the impending destruction. In the fort on the beach of the island, off to the east, Moultrie's black-jacketed cannoneers were swarming like black ants over their huge iron guns. Their shouts came up as voice-wisps on the wind. Each cannon, longer than a man's body, squatted on its massive oaken carriage on four small wooden wheels, pyramids of the eighteen-pound black iron balls stacked behind it, and the tools of the trade were in the cannoneers' hands: the sponge-staffs, ramrods, shovels, sledgehammers, waterpails, powder barrels. The muzzles faced through apertures in the thick ramparts, faced that narrow channel of blue water through which the slow-moving ships would have to pass within a few moments. The ramparts were crudely made, but massive: ten feet thick, walls of shaggy-looking palmetto trunks laid horizontally, the spaces between the walls filled with tons of sand. The ramparts looked like flood dikes rather than walls. The fort seemed impregnable.

But then there were the ships, nine of them in a file, and each one of them was a fortress bigger than the one on the beach. Jonathan and Bill Croghan looked at each other, then looked back to the ships.

The ships, seen in the terrible clarity of fatal moment, were both monstrous and sublime. Their hulls were as big and heavy as courthouses; the canvas and intricate rigging that pulled them on looked fragile as spiderwebs and moth wings. Their sails were taut-full of the onshore wind, and the Union Jacks, blood-red with blue and white crosses, rippled from mastheads and fantails. Dozens of pennants and many-colored signal flags ran through the riggings. Flags. Flags in the wind. The flag of South Carolina stood out from its staff above the fort in the stiff, hot wind, a blue-black banner with a white crescent moon in its corner and the word LIBERTY in its center. And a few feet from where Jonathan stood, the little salmon-pink banner of the 8th Virginia Regiment crepitated atop its pole. Flags fluttered as the moment compressed. Jonathan could see men on the ships now, tiny as fleas; he could see cannon ports checkering the hulls; each of the warships carried more guns than Colonel Moultrie had in his whole fort. The size and the relentless, quiet progress of the fleet into the mouth of the gauntlet now for the first time made Jonathan doubt Moultrie's confidence, made him fear that the ships *would* drive right past the fort and into the harbor.

Jonathan drew out the gold watch his father had given him, attached to the fancy fob George had given him, and opened the cover. It was ten o'clock in the morning. He heard snatches of voice from the fort. His mouth was dry; his heart raced. The first ship was almost abreast of the fort now, in the neck of water between Sullivan's Island and James Island. "That's a frigate, right?" he asked Bill Croghan.

"Yes. The *Active*, I think." The defenders knew much about the enemy fleet that had lain at anchor so long outside; South Carolina fishermen were daring spies.

Farther down the line there was the towering canvas of the *Bristol*, Sir Peter Parker's fifty-gun flagship.

"Great God in Heaven," someone exclaimed in the ranks, "why don't somebody shoot them boats?"

And then Jonathan nearly jumped off the ground when the morning burst open with a crash of cannon. Four or five of the fort's big guns discharged at once, shaking the swampy earth underfoot. Seconds later, a sail of the *Active* caved in. A yell went up from the fort.

Now the sides of the *Active* spewed orange tongues of spark and fire, and blue smoke hid her hull. Jonathan had never heard such a peal of noise in his life, not even the great cracking, rumbling thunderstorms that rolled up the Shenandoah Valley on summer evenings, and his heart quailed.

"She's dropped anchor!" Bill shouted. "She's going to stand there and fight!" It was plain now. The *Active* was going to sit right in the face of the fort and pour broadsides into it while the other ships passed on her far side. The earth seemed to quake every time the concussion from the ship's guns rolled ashore. They were belching out their horrendous fire and noise with an amazing rapidity, and geysers of sand leaped up in and around the fort. Between the blasts and through the ringing in his ears

133

Jonathan could hear men's voices shouting and whooping in the fort. Sandspouts leaped, shrubs and trees behind the fort disappeared, an old fishing hut burst apart in a flash of splinters and spinning boards and roof thatch. Jonathan was surprised that anyone could still be alive in the fort, but apparently there were many, still quite alive. The troops of the 8th Virginia were still dumbstruck, overawed by the tumult and watching like an audience as the fiery panorama unfolded under the blue sky.

Now the *Bristol* flagship, the largest vessel ever to have entered this channel, her high oaken side checkered with twenty-five gun ports, drew abreast of the fort and erupted in such a storm of cannon fire that she disappeared in her own smoke. The rampart of the fort shuddered with the impact of at least a dozen simultaneous direct hits. Bright sand sprayed fifty feet into the air, and behind its windblown, drifting veil, Jonathan saw the South Carolina flag go down, its staff snapped off at the base by a cannonball.

But now came a still greater storm of noise: Colonel Moultrie's eighteen-pounders were answering with a booming salvo from the right, one gun per second. The *Active* and the *Bristol*, and now another fifty-gun giant, the *Experiment*, were all at anchor directly in the line of fire. Two other ships, the *Solebay* and the *Thunder*, a bombship, also were dropping anchor and discharging broadsides at the fort. Now the five gunships were anchored in a line less than 500 yards offshore, and at this close range, the Carolinian gunners could hardly miss. Through the blown smoke now Jonathan watched the warships take their punishment.

Sails twitched and turned to rags. Rigging snapped. Oak rails and bulkheads disintegrated and spun overboard in chunks and splinters to splash into the channel. Spars and booms shivered and dropped. Shrouds parted and hung flapping like rope ladders, masts crashed down like felled trees, cannon leaped up and fell, fires broke out on the decks, gaping holes appeared in the freeboards, sailors and marines were blown out of the rigging and off the decks like sparrows in a shotgun blast.

At the sight of this havoc, the gunners in the fort and the troops along the shore raised a resonating *hurrah!* Bill Croghan's hand gripped Jonathan's arm; he was grinning, but there were tears in his eyes; this was, after all, the navy of his native land.

Colonel Moultrie's appraisal of his fort was proving true. When a cannonball hit the ramparts, the wall would buck and sand would fly like the dust beaten out of a rug, but the spongy palmetto logs and their fillings of sand were simply swallowing the British lead.

His artillery was proving as sound as his fortification. His gunners were cool and deliberate, wasting no shot, and the decks and rigging of each ship in turn were being reduced to a shambles of rope, splinters, broken bodies, and blood. And, to the greater thrill of the onlookers, a tiny, dark-clad figure, some madly brave artilleryman, had picked up the fallen Carolina flag, attached to a sponge staff, and now stood as a human flagpole atop the rampart, in the hail of British shot, holding the riddled banner up in the wind while his comrades lashed it to the stump of the flagstaff. Jonathan gritted his teeth and prayed that the brave fool would not be blown apart.

Still, for all this heartening display, the guns of the fort were not sinking any ships. And now, covered by the fire of the anchored gunships, three more white-sailed frigates came plowing up the channel, going around the far side of the gunships, headed for the harbor. Apparently these fast vessels were going to avoid the fort's barrage almost entirely. Jonathan realized this suddenly, amid the thrilling spectacle of the gunnery, and his heart sank.

The first of the three frigates now emerged beyond the anchored ships. Unscathed, she had got north of the fort, past the line of its fire, and was coming about, as if to turn at the end of the island, lie offshore, and pour fire into the fort through its unfinished and unprotected side, thus making it the "slaughter pen" that General Lee had warned it would be.

"That one's the *Actaeon*," cried Bill Croghan, who was now watching the frigate through a spyglass. "God, I'm afraid she's going to enfilade the fort!"

"Damnation!" Jonathan yelled, "I wish they'd give us something to do! I didn't walk all the way to Charles Town to lay idle and watch!" The little rosy-silk regimental banner fluttered against the sky, now like a symbol of uselessness.

"Hey! What's this now?" Croghan yelled. There was an outburst of cheering from the fort; some of the officers of the infantry along the shore were capering and throwing their hats in the air. At first Jonathan could not determine what they were celebrating. They were pointing toward the *Actaeon*. There was something odd in the way she was standing.

Jonathan was a stranger to ships, but even to his eye, the frigate looked somehow crippled. She was listing slightly; her sails were empty and flapping uselessly in the wind . . . and she was not moving. "She's aground!" Croghan whooped. "She's fast stuck in the shallows o' that *love*-ly channel!"

"*Yaaaaahaaaaa!*" someone yodeled, and a ripple of derisive laughter went through the ranks. "Some sailors, them Royal swabs!" a voice yelled between the slamming, booming explosions from the fort.

Well, that was a small piece of good luck, Jonathan thought. But now going feverish again and feeling somehow vulnerable and doomed, he wondered what all this was coming to in the big scheme of things. There were still ships coming up the channel; the five gunships were still pouring cannonballs into the fort's ramparts; there were no orders for the Virginia troops; there was no intelligence from General Lee about whether the 3,000 Redcoats down on Long Island were on the march yet.

Suddenly Bill Croghan grabbed Jonathan's arm and pointed up toward the town.

Yes! The two other frigates seemed to be in trouble now. They had veered to pass the stranded *Actaeon*, and now they, too, seemed to be aground, sitting in the channel in awkward attitudes.

And now most of Sir Parker's fleet, which had looked so irresistible, was at a standstill, locked in a thunderous duel with the fort or blocked in the channel by its own grounded frigates. This juggernaut of a fleet, which had been plowing so resolutely up the channel an hour ago in a straight battle line, now was sprawled all over the narrow channel, running up signal flags, slowly disintegrating under Moultrie's methodical cannonade. It was a merry piece of mayhem.

Now there was nothing more pressing for the 8th Virginia to do than stand in the hammering midday sun with marsh water in their shoes and enjoy a great spectacle of the enemy's desperation, played out against the choppy blue waters of the channel, the shimmering beaches of James Island across the way, under a crystalline sky in a scouring hot wind.

IT WENT ON THROUGH THE AFTERNOON. WORD CAME THAT Moultrie had sent to Lee demanding more powder, and it seemed unlikely that Lee could refuse now. Moultrie's gunnery officers had been sparing of powder, sighting each big gun as if it were a hunting rifle, scarcely wasting a shot. They were aiming at the ships' waterlines now. Maybe they would sink some ships. It was certain the British were not going to sink the fort. The bombship *Thunder* was lofting bombshells one after another into the compound from her mortars. These would have killed everyone in the fort, but that the ground within the works was so soft and wet—a sandy morass—that they were swallowed and smothered on impact, and few exploded.

Jonathan's troops, waiting in the sun, were near collapsing

with heat, and he wondered how those artillerymen in the stifling, smoke-filled confines of the fort could still be moving. He
could see them through his spyglass, stripped to their drawers,
rags tied around their heads, shining with sweat and black with
powder, laboring like ants in the superheated gunpits to keep the
big cannons swabbed, loaded, and aimed. But they were happy
in their work, especially when the firebuckets full of grog would
be passed to them.

In midafternoon, when General Muhlenberg's Virginians at
last received orders to cross over to Sullivan's Island and reinforce the sharpshooters guarding Breach Inlet, the fusillade was
still on, undiminished. The fleet was expending ammunition as
if its supply were limitless, making a constant thunder across the
channel and a haze of acrid gunsmoke. Marching down past the
cove, the Virginians could look out across the water and watch
the British try to free their grounded ships. They were trying to
pull them off with lifeboats full of rowers attached by long lines
to the ships' sterns; they were trying to kedge, taking anchors out
astern in rowboats, dropping them to the bottom, then pulling
against the anchor ropes by shipboard windlasses. But all this was
futile, and dangerous in the extreme with the fort's cannonballs
plunging in all around. Finally all such efforts were abandoned,
and apparently the captains were just waiting for the tide to come
in.

In the light of sunset, a sunset blood-red through
the smoke of the cannonade, the tide at last floated two of the
frigates. But the *Actaeon* still sat hard aground; likely she was
taking water, perhaps from a shell hole in the hull. And she still
blocked the channel.

With the cool of evening, Jonathan's malarial chills had returned, so overwhelming him that he hardly knew what he was
doing. The regiment was encamped now on a sandy, scrubby
flat, without tents or mess, on half-watch, the off-duty troops
bedding down clothed and at the ready in case Clinton's Redcoats should try to cross Breach Inlet. It was not likely they
would try. They had made one effort early in the day, at low
tide, Jonathan learned. But the ranked Redcoats, weighted down
with weapons and packs, had sunk and fallen in the sandy-bot-
tomed watercourse, floundered into hidden potholes, been
tipped over by the ripping currents, or peppered by rifle balls
from the hidden Carolinian sharpshooters on the other side, and
had been called back. They were over there now, three thousand
of them, stranded until the fleet could come back down and take

them off with its lifeboats. It was not likely they would march down into the water again, especially now that the tide was rising. "Unless," Bill Croghan speculated, "it's to escape the mosquitoes." It was agreed that Clinton could not have made worse use of his army.

"Well, at least," Jonathan said, "they've been safer there on that sandbar than they would have been on the ships." The cannon were still thundering. Moultrie had gotten his powder.

The shooting was still going on after nightfall. Jonathan could read his timepiece by the flashes of bombardment. Now and then the clouds of smoke would glow red or orange as something burned. Jonathan sat wrapped in a blanket, shivering. It seemed there had never been a time when that infernal thundering had not existed.

At about ten o'clock the sky became yellow. Jonathan thought he had dozed, that morning was coming. But Bill Croghan came and knelt by him. "The *Actaeon*'s afire," he said, "and we can see it from the beach. Let's go have a look at that spectacle, my friend." They identified themselves to their sentries in the eerie glow and walked through scrub to the beach. They sat on the sand watching the ship burn in the distance. There were small boats all around it. They saw the yellow flames climb the masts and make a path of reflection on the water. Not far off, the roar and flicker of the cannonfight at the fort continued like a lightning storm.

Then the flames of the *Actaeon* suddenly blossomed, grew bigger and brighter, and a dull *boom*, deeper and more muffled than the cannonfire, rolled across the water. Above the hulk, flaming spars and timbers and sparks were arcing through the sky and a dense, yellow-red smoke cloud was climbing, seeming to turn inside out as it rose. The sparks and flames whirled down like burning straws and were extinguished in the harbor. The frigate was becoming shapeless now and was half-hidden in steam.

"There went her magazine, I'll bet," Bill said. And after a while he said, "What do you think will come o' this fray, Jonathan? Do you suppose Charles Town's really safe?"

"God willing. Listen, Bill. I should rather face Clinton's bayonets tomorrow than another day o' these shivers. Walk me back, Bill, ere I shake myself apart at the joints. I've got to get back in my blanket. That boat fire's just too far away to keep me warm."

"You're quite sick, aren't you?"

"Quite some." He slapped at his ear, where mosquitoes were

ironing. "I've seldom been sick. But this Southland, I'll vow, it's plague country."

"Maybe after this campaign I could take you home on a con-valescent leave. And meet that marvelous family o' yours."

"Might could be. That sounds good to my ears."

JONATHAN SAT UP IN HIS BLANKET, STARTLED AWAKE BY SUD-den silence. There were no more cannon. In the night wind and over the surf he thought he could hear wisps of voices yelling far away; then he heard the quizzical murmurs and mutterings of waking troops nearby. Jonathan got up, the night air making him shudder again as he left his blanket, and he staggered to the fishing shack that was serving as regimental headquarters. Gen-eral Muhlenberg was sitting in lamplight at a field table, his round German face sleepy-looking, several other officers stand-ing around him. They knew nothing yet.

A runner brought pathetic news half an hour later. The fort had run out of powder.

"But why've the British stopped shooting?" someone asked. No one knew. But the worst was to be expected. Likely the ships were being readied to sail on into the harbor and start bombard-ing Charles Town. And likely the Redcoats would try again to ford the inlet at next low tide.

The sleep-dulled troops were mustered and stood yawning, groaning, scratching in the waning smoke-glow, slapping at the clouds of marsh-mosquitoes that had discovered them outside their blankets. They stood and suffered while their officers awaited news and orders from General Lee.

At two in the morning the news came, and it was scarcely believable.

The battered fleet had come down with its boats and taken Clinton's troops back on board, then had cut cables and was slipping out to sea. They had abandoned their siege of Charles Town!

A mighty yowling and yodeling of triumph and relief rippled along the windswept shore. Lee's army, which had seen the en-emy only at a distance, was feeling victorious.

When dawn broke, they stood watching the half-junked Brit-ish fleet limping away up the coast.

THE VICTORY CELEBRATION IN CHARLES TOWN WAS SPICED by a delightful report, which came by way of deserters from the British fleet.

One of Colonel Moultrie's cannonballs, well aimed at the

Bristol, had ripped the breeches off Commodore Peter Parker, laying his backside bare. By the evening after the victory, there were already being sung, throughout all levels of Charles Town society, several hastily composed ballads about Sir Peter Parker's pants.

As the battle story was pieced together, Colonel Moultrie grew steadily in stature as its hero. Word from deserters and prisoners was that about seventy of his projectiles had struck the *Bristol* alone, killing forty of her crew and wounding perhaps twice that many more; not a man stationed on the flagship's quarterdeck had escaped injury. Casualties aboard the other ships had brought the fleet's death list up to at least seventy. "Our decks looked like a slaughterhouse," said a defector. "Never's the Royal Fleet had such a drubbin'!"

Ten Americans had died and about twenty had been wounded.

Colonel Moultrie insisted that if General Lee had allotted him enough powder from the beginning, "I could have sent the whole damned Armada to the bottom." No one doubted him.

Another popular hero was Sergeant William Jasper, the man who had stood on the ramparts raising the South Carolina flag. Jasper was offered an officer's commission for his bravery, but declined it because of his lack of education. So he was awarded a sword.

In the aftermath of the battle, many prominent Carolinians whose sentiments were still loyalist gave up all they had and fled from Charles Town. The rest of the population went into a sustained celebration of deliverance. For a week, Charles Town society held feasts and balls in their elegant homes for the defenders; gracious and beautiful ladies danced on the officer's arms and thanked them with glittering eyes; some eluded their husbands and chaperones and bestowed gratitude in closer and deeper ways. Everyone was happy and falling in love, and while this heady romance between soldiers and citizens was still in the air, a swift rider from Philadelphia thundered in with the news that the Continental Congress had declared independence from England. There was a thoughtful pause in the celebrations while the populace considered this stunning, hopeful, but frightening news. Then the celebration started again with increased gaiety.

It continued until the smallpox came.

THROUGH THE BEATING OF HIS HEADACHE, JONATHAN heard the voice of the physician. "Open your eyes, Captain. Talk to me."

He didn't want to open them. His eyelids were swollen and itchy and when the bright summer light hit his eyes it stabbed like needles into his headache, and it made him sneeze because his nose itched constantly and intolerably. And he was almost overpowered by sleepiness. He was always sleepy, yet he was kept from sleeping by the palpitations of his heart, and by dread of the night terrors that would come when he did sleep.

He opened his eyes and for an instant saw the silhouette of the physician's head and shoulders. Then the sneezing started, the great, racking sneezes that shook him from head to foot and made him gasp for breath and started the interminable dry coughing. He coughed until he was bathed in sweat, and the sweating made his skin prickle so intensely that he twitched all over. His throat was so parched that his voice rasped.

"Ye could be wrong, eh? I've been malarial for quite a spell, I know."

"In Charles Town," the doctor's voice rumbled, "we well know the small pocks." His voice drifted off; he was saying something to somebody nearby. Then his voice came back to say: "Regrets, Captain, but I'll have to put you with the rest."

With the rest. Jonathan's heart clenched. He knew that meant the quarantine hospital: the sorrowfully polite name for the old sheds at the end of the freight road, next to the swamp beyond the city. The doctors of Charles Town knew well how to quarantine the dreaded pocks. Often they had stopped ships outside the harbor to isolate the sick sailors aboard until their whole crews died or recovered. Charles Town would do anything to prevent another great epidemic like the one in 1718.

This time the small pocks had come to Charles Town by land, carried by the Continental Army, and so now it was necessary to isolate a large number of their recent heroes, to take the suffering heroes and stack them in the old rat-infested sheds where rice and hemp, tobacco and cotton, lumber and indigo had been stacked for the last hundred years.

"Eh, well," Jonathan groaned. "Then see that I'm put near my friend Ensign Croghan."

Bill Croghan had been taken away to the sheds three or four days earlier, Bill Croghan of the jovial nature and the baby-smooth complexion.

JONATHAN'S CONSCIOUSNESS WAS DARK ABOVE AND DARK BE-low, droning with a million flies and a dismal chorus of groans and sobs and screams; and between the darkness above and the darkness below was a yellow-white, shimmering glare: July sunlight on parched sand and scrub beyond the open-sided shed. It must be a hundred and ten degrees in here, he thought. His blood felt as if it were boiling in his veins.

When he was awake he could remember to keep his hands from scratching the maddeningly itching pustules. What was that his mother had used to say? "A gentleman should keep his fingers away from his face except when he eats, shaves, or prays." It was the ones on his face that itched worst. When he was awake he could remember not to scratch. When he was asleep they had to tie his hands to the sides of his cot with strips of cloth. Even then, he would work his itching wrists against those bindings, and writhe to scratch his back against the bedding under him, and this would break many of the bumps open and he would wake up lying on a slime of his own pus and sweat.

Now and then in the hellish cacophony of voices there would be a pulsating cackle or an outburst of incoherent words as some wretch would go crazy with the heat and the itching. Several times Jonathan had barely managed, by force of will or by talking to Bill Croghan in the next cot, to keep from slipping off the edge into that wonderful tempting madness. Sometimes he believed that if he could just let go and scream and cackle and wail like those others, it would cool him and make the itching stop.

Instead, he had clenched his teeth and prayed silently, or talked to Bill, and had been able to bring himself back from that awful, tempting edge.

And sometimes he had been able to control himself by concentrating on the disease itself. Sometimes he could not bear to think directly on it; other times it helped to consider the very essence of it. When he did this, he could explain his discomforts to himself and assure himself that it would last for only a certain number of days.

He and the other officers had been given a reading from Dr. Thatcher's old broadside, titled A Brief Rule To Guide the Common-People How to Order Themfelves and Theirs in the Small Pocks, or Meafels. Most of the Charles Town physicians used it; others departed from its suggestions according to their own notions. Jonathan understood from Dr. Thatcher's writings that the pocks was a disease in which "the blood is endeavoring to recover a new form and state," as the pamphlet said. In the first four feverish days, it said, the blood is trying to separate by boiling; in the second stage, that which he himself was entering now, the fever abates and the separated poison is expelled through the skin by the appearance of pustules. There would be

142

nearly a fortnight of this itching and mattering and soreness to be endured, he knew, and then, if he was to survive, there would be a spell of copious nosebleeding, and the pustules would dry up and he would recover.

I can stand anything for a fortnight, if I know it will end then, he told himself sometimes.

Other times he was not so sure he could. A minute in such torment could seem an hour; an hour could seem a day; a day could seem an eternity.

And sometimes he would think about the scarring he would have after it was over, and he would think: What's the use of enduring, anyway?

THE DOCTORS WOULD NOT PERMIT MIRRORS TO BE brought into the sheds. No man, they felt, should see his own face while he was poxed. This was both blessing and curse. Jonathan did not want to see his face. But in not seeing it, he was left at the mercy of his imagination. And his imagination was merciless. He could see what was happening to Bill Croghan's once-flawless countenance.

And then in his mind's eye he would see his own face as clearly as if he did have a mirror.

It was better to keep thinking about living than to bother with thinking about how one would look.

TWO AIDES WERE TRYING TO CHANGE THE BEDDING OF A lieutenant in a nearby cot. The lieutenant was groaning pathetically as they turned him. He was an extremely grave case.

Before the small pocks had struck, Jonathan had come to know every officer of the Virginians by face and name. He knew he must have known this officer once, but he could not recognize him now. Every inch of the man's skin was pebbled by furiously red vesicles topped with greenish and bluish heads of pus: his shoulders, arms, hands, even his ears and eyelids. On each cheek the pustules were coalescing into one great seeping sore. If the lieutenant survived, Jonathan knew, this would leave the worst sort of scarring. But it was doubtful that he would survive. He could neither eat nor drink, and the doctors had been saying that his kidneys and circulation would be damaged surely.

The lieutenant's groans built to a catlike moan now. He had been left lying on his back too long on his soiled bedding, as there were so few doctors or assistants; the seeping pus had dried to a hideous glue, and as his back was raised from the bedding,

143

the rotten skin came off in patches to reveal the striated muscle beneath. Farther down, blood was gushing from his anus. Jonathan swallowed a great surge of pity and nausea and turned his eyes away.

Now, in turning from the sight of the dying lieutenant, he found his friend Bill Croghan looking on in pity. Jonathan's eyes and Bill's eyes met, wavered, stared a moment in unutterable remorse, glanced apart, then returned and held. The whites of their eyes were barely visible through their swollen, glistening red eyelids.

It was hard for Bill and Jonathan to look at each other, but it grew less horrible each time.

"How are you, friend?" Croghan asked, managing what appeared to be a smile.

"Not one of my best days ever, but I get by. And you?"

"Better, I think. I'm breathing quite free now."

This, small as it was, was cheering. Suddenly Jonathan began to expect that Bill really would survive. "Oh, for a breeze," he said, trying to remember the nearly forgotten sensation of fresh, cool air on healthy skin.

"Aye. Hey, now, look at me," Bill said. "I'm going to sit up, I feel that good!"

Wincing and shuddering, he raised himself weakly onto an elbow and swung his red-pocked legs sideways till his feet were on the dirt of the floor. He wore only a wad of sheet around his loins, his doctor being one of those who believed dressings and ointments aggravated the pustules. Croghan sat now, flaming red and disfigured by swellings, but smiling proudly.

"Bravo," Jonathan said.

Croghan tried to laugh; it came as a raspy chortle. "Hey, now let me have a look at you up close, old fellow," he said. "I've learned enough from Dr. Thatcher I reckon I could prognose you." He leaned close and examined Jonathan's arm and gradually his gaze traveled up until he was looking at his face. Jonathan felt all squirmy as his friend looked so closely at him. "Looks to me like they're ripening up nice," he said cheerfully. "Nice and red and distinct, nice white tops on 'em. Not green or black, not hard, eh? Good signs, good signs, the good doctor says." He prattled on cheerfully. It was amazing. He sounded like anything but a victim of the dreaded pocks.

Now Croghan began examining his own arms and legs, looking at each with a careful detachment as if he were a healthy doctor and this diseased limb his patient. "Mine's a bit messier," he said, "but not so bad as some I've. . ." He went into a spasm

144

of coughing and sank back gingerly on his cot. "Pardon me. Must lie down a minute." He lay there coughing and pouring sweat. His tongue began a dry clicking against the back of his palate. Jonathan, alarmed, raised himself painfully up on his elbows and called for a water boy.

The water carrier came. Like most of the aides, he was someone who had had the pocks already and was not afraid to be among those sick with it. He was a private, perhaps nineteen or twenty, short, with a pit-scarred face. He was gentle. He raised Croghan's head and put a cup to his lips. "Thankee," Jonathan said for his friend.

"Aye, sir." The lad stood back and for a moment stayed and waved his hand back and forth over Bill Croghan, stirring up the flies, which immediately settled again. There was just nothing that could be done about the flies. Even if there had been a slave available to stand over each patient with a fly-whisk, the buzzing multitude would have prevailed. They droned through the shed, darkening the air by their numbers. They fringed the eyes, mouths, and sores of every man who was unconscious or too lethargic to raise a hand.

Croghan was sleeping now, it seemed. Jonathan looked at him for a while, then sat up painfully and waved a rag back and forth over him. He looked around the dolorous scene in the stinking, murmuring, suffocating gloom under the old shed roof. There might have been two or three hundred men in this shed. As an infantry officer Jonathan could make a fair guess of numbers of men standing or marching, just at a glance. But lying in rows on pallets, all inflamed limbs and putrid flesh in sweaty, wadded, bloody, or yellowing sheets, under the blurry gaze of his swollen eyes, they were uncountable.

And this was just one of the sheds.

It occurred to him after a while that he was sitting here, moving his arm, waving flies away from his friend. He would not have thought he could sit up and do anything.

But doing this for Bill Croghan, he realized, somehow made him less aware of his own torment.

GOVERNOR HENRY HAD PREDICTED EXACTLY HOW HIS PRIVY council would respond to George's request for gunpowder for Kentuck. It was well received—up to a point. Bedecked in a new scarlet coat he had bought for the occasion, George stood before the eight councilmen and argued vehemently. These men all knew his brother Jonathan and they knew of George's connections with Henry and Jefferson and George Mason, and so, despite his youthfulness and his somewhat overpowering frontier directness, they listened very respectfully to him, and without much quibbling agreed to write a requisition for five hundred pounds of gunpowder. But, they stressed, it was only a loan to needful friends, and George would become liable for it in case the Assembly should later refuse to receive Kentuck as a county of Virginia.

George agreed to that, and they wrote him an order for the gunpowder. Then he told the Council that it was out of his means to pay for safe transport of the powder, and asked them to authorize that it be sent at public expense. Here, as Henry had predicted, they balked. Just providing the powder, they said, was an act for which they might be faulted. "For us to ship it," Benjamin Harrison protested, "might be seen as an overt act of intrusion in a dubious place. Please, young sir, understand this. We'll say all we can for the admission of Kentuck when the whole Assembly meets in October. That country's of supreme interest to us. Whatever caution we have to exercise, don't think we undervalue the West. Please."

George looked around the elegant council room, at the sleek and august members of the Council, and saw by the regretful cast of their countenances that mere argument was not going to move them further; they were determined to play safe. But he knew, too, how Virginia coveted its old charter rights to the rich western country.

If they can't be talked into going out on a limb, he thought, I reckon they can be scared out onto it.

He set his jaw and, fixing a steely eye on them one by one, he stood up slowly. He remained, leaning with his knuckles on the table.

"Very well, then," he said in a flat, cold tone. "If Virginia can't give us protection, I'm sorry to have to say I'll need to seek it elsewhere. I have no doubt there's plenty of factions willing to give it. I'll say this," he declared, suddenly picking up the gunpowder requisition by one corner and flipping it toward them across the table, "if a country's not worth protecting, it's not worth claiming. Gentlemen of the Council, regrets—and good day, sirs."

HE WAS THIRTY MILES UP THE ROAD TOWARD CAROLINE County, Dickie riding alongside him, when galloping hoofbeats approached from behind.

He was not in the least surprised that it was a messenger from the Council. He had been expecting one.

The Council had reconsidered. The gunpowder would be sent at public expense. He could hire boats and guards and pick up the powder at Fort Pitt and take it down the Ohio to Kentuck; Virginia would bear the expense.

146

He had won. His mother state now was committed to the defense of Kentuck.

"And I'm damned relieved on it, too," he confessed to his family when he finally got home in August to visit. "Nobody but Virginia has the right to that country, and I'd have felt half a traitor going to anyone else for help."

BUT AUGUST COOLED INTO SEPTEMBER, AND SEPTEMBER yellowed into October, and when the Assembly convened in Williamsburg, George still had not been able to get the powder and leave for Kentuck. There had been delays and more delays. Gunpowder was the scarcest thing in the thirteen colonies, where everything was scarce because of the British blockade of the seacoast ports, and whenever a quantity of powder was earmarked for George's Kentuckians, it would somehow be diverted from Fort Pitt to the army in the East. While George was waiting, his fellow Assemblyman John Gabriel Jones came up from the Holston Valley and helped George try to recruit guards to transport the powder, if it ever became available.

They could have formed most of their squad from among George's brothers and cousins, if eagerness had been the only criterion. Dickie wanted to go, but his father refused to let him. Johnny was willing to go, though his strongest yearning was to join the regular army and serve under Washington; he had seen how well brother Jonathan had looked in uniform, and fancied what a figure he himself would make in all that brass and braid. Cousin John Rogers had already made up his mind to join Washington, and when the summer slipped by with George still detained in Virginia, he finally went away and enlisted. But the one most rabid about going west with George was Cousin Joe Rogers. He hung around the Clark home imploring George to take him along, and rode with him down to Williamsburg twice.

The Assembly was fighting a controversy that George had forced upon them through Patrick Henry: whether or not to give Kaintuck a county government and assume responsibility for its defense. Governor Henry and Thomas Jefferson wanted George to advance his argument to the whole Assembly, and to educate them on the present circumstances of the region. There were foes aplenty to the annexation, two chief ones being Colonel Henderson's Transylvania Land Company and Colonel Arthur Campbell, County Lieutenant of Virginia's westernmost county, who coveted the expanses of Kaintuck as a natural extension of his own domain, Fincastle County.

George seemed always to be on the road between home and

the capital, and though he was desperately anxious to get out over the mountains before winter, he made the most of the delays, and his family made the most of his unusual long visit. He had to tell at least one frontier story every night he was at home. He began teaching little Billy the basic elements of surveying. Ann Rogers Clark one day paused at her spinning wheel, where she was making cloth for army uniforms, and heard George coaching Billy in the yard below the window.

"Now let's hear that geometry again. A rectangle is what shape?"

"Like a dog standing up."

"And a triangle is?"

"Like a dog sitting down."

"And a circle is?"

"Like York's belly!"

And then the wonderful sound of their laughter together.

To Ann Rogers Clark, the spinning wheel had become like a prayer wheel. Before George had come home, she had prayed for him over it. Then she had prayed for Jonathan after she received his letter about Charles Town's preparations for attack. She had prayed thanks after his letter telling of the victory, then had begun praying for his life again when news came of the smallpox plague in Charles Town. And when his next letter came, saying he had had the pocks and gotten well, she had given thanks for his life but also had begun praying for herself, for the strength and wisdom she would need when he came home. No Clark or Rogers had ever had the pocks before, and she went around wondering how badly scarred he'd be, wondering whether she should say anything, whether she would be able not to stare at his face, whether she would cry. Yet for all her dread, she was always at windows, looking down the road, listening for the sound of hooves the way Billy had always used to listen for George's return.

Lucy and Elizabeth and Fanny were in the spinning room with her. It was the room that had been the nursery, but now it was full of the implements for the making of cloth. "We won't be a-needing a nursery any longer," she had told John one day, "so we'll use the room this way." She had noticed the quizzical little frown on his brow then, and had answered his unasked question: "Ten's enough, John. Ye heard what th' physician said last time. Another would kill me, as like as not. And there's too many here dependin' on me, yourself most of all, for me to go dyin' in labor."

With her three daughters cooped up with her in a room for hours every day with the monotony of carding, combing, skeining, and spinning, Ann Rogers Clark found herself more and more in her old role of storyteller. The girls did not actually ask er to tell stories, because they knew what her answer would be: Stories are for bedtime. Besides, Georgie said he's going to tell he story at supper of the man who found the whiskey spring. I'd hink y'd had enough stories." So they didn't ask her to tell stories. ut Elizabeth, especially, had developed the art of asking ques- ons that would lead her mother into telling a story before she ealized she was telling one. And so Elizabeth's sweet, shy voice sked now, through the hum and the hush of their industry:

"Mama, how comes it to be we're in Virginia, and not in ngland?"

"Oh. Well, it was because of your great-grandpapa, I suppose. ou know his name."

"Giles Rogers."

"That's correct. Now, ye remember who his great-great-grand- ather was?"

"He was the one they burned up."

"Yes, he was John Rogers the Martyr. He was also the one who ave the world the first complete English language Bible! Re- ember what a body did in his life, not just how he died. So, nyway, Giles Rogers, maybe because he was like John Rogers, he isagreed with the King about something, and so he got on a ship nd sailed over to Virginia, in 1680, it was, to put some distance etween himself and the King. Well, d'you know what happened ust when his ship was a-sailing up to Virginia's shore?"

"No, Mama," Elizabeth said.

"What happened, Mama?" asked little Fanny.

"I know," said Lucy, who had heard this many times. "He ad a baby in the bay."

"Better to say, his wife had a baby. Just as the ship sailed into hesapeake Bay, why, she had a baby boy. And they named him ohn Rogers, after the Martyr. And that John Rogers was my ather, who got us all started here in this country, and no finer a an ever walked, all will agree. He grew to be very old, eighty- ight years, but he was a strong and happy man almost to his ying hour, and it's a pity he didn't live just a few years longer, o's you'd all remember 'im."

"I remember him," said Lucy. "He had all white hair."

"You might remember him. You were three when he passed to eaven, as he surely did." She wasn't sure whether Lucy really emembered him, or had come to believe it from all the tales.

Lucy said, "He was the one who did the bird whistle for randmama, wasn't he?"

And so of course Elizabeth and Fanny wanted to hear about the ird whistle, and so their mother gazed up toward the ceiling,

through the myriad glowing filaments of lint floating in a late afternoon sunbeam from the window, and started telling another story.

"My father John Rogers, he became a surveyor. 'Twas he
taught it to your brother Georgie. Now this land along the Mattapony was wild land then, and he went all about and surveyed
and got a lot of it, just as Georgie does out west. He had a
passion for land. Well, one day he met a young woman named
Mary Byrd and fell in love with her, and that made him think it
was about time he got married and had a family. But listen! That
Mary Byrd's father, he was a very rich man, and he did not want
his daughter to marry John Rogers, as they had different feelings
about the King. So he forbade his daughter ever to see John
Rogers again. Well! Ye know how such words will set on a headstrong young woman, and she was headstrong, she was. So John
Rogers and Mary Byrd schemed how they might keep on seeing
each other, and here's the way they did:

"There was a great old willow tree where Colonel Byrd's land
sloped down to the James River. Well, John Rogers would paddle his canoe up to that willow tree, and take ahold of a branch
to hold himself there. He was too proud to set a foot on a plantation where he wasn't welcome. Then he would make a call like a
whippoorwill, and he'd keep makin' that call till Mary Byrd
would hear it, and she would come down the bank to the willow
tree and get in the canoe, and off they'd float to the other side of
the river where they could be together! They used to joke to me
that they were both birds then, she a Byrd bird and him a whippoorwill bird! She used to tell me that she'd run down to that
willow tree a thousand times when *real* whippoorwills called!"
The girls laughed, then waited for more. "Well, the upshot was
they ran off and got married by and by, and when Colonel Byrd
heard of it, why, he sputtered like spit on a griddle, and he
disowned her. And poor Mary Byrd never saw her family again,
which I reckon would ha' made her woeful sad, but she was so
happy with John Rogers that it never showed, if she was. They
lived on a plantation they called Worcester, in King and Queen
County, and there they had nine children, who are now all your
aunts and uncles, except me, and as ye well know, I'm your—"

"Our storyteller!" cried Fanny.

"Oh! Bless me! You tricked me into it again!"

"But that's not all about the whippoorwill call, Mama," said
Lucy. "Tell what Georgie did when Grandmama passed over."

"No, I shall not, not now. I've wondered why I'm so uncommon weary this evening, and I just now see it's because you
all've got me spinning two kinds o' yarn at once!"

THAT NIGHT AS THEY LAY IN BED, SHE TOLD JOHN ABOUT the yarn-spinning in the old nursery room, and he, warmed and mellowed by the brandies he had drunk with George and Johnny after supper, chuckled and began feeling tender. It was cool in the room and warm under the comforter, and he turned on his side facing her and began stroking her hip and squirming. Oh, oh, she thought. And she gently lifted his hand away.

"It's been so long, Annie darlin'," he murmured.

"Yes, it has," she said. It had in fact been some four years, since before Fanny was born. "Now, John," she said with her voice full of loving kindness, as this was not going to be an easy thing for him to hear, "I've come to a place in my mind that I guess you haven't yet. And I guess I must tell ye now.

"John, my good husband, you know my life's all yours, don't you? Of course you know. But it's what I was telling you about the nursery. We've had that body thing for twenty-five years, but we can't anymore, not lest ye want to kill me." He was lying very still now, tensing, as he realized she was saying something of great finality. She felt him bracing himself, and she went on: "I know a wife's to do her husband's will. And I have done and was my will, too. But now, no more, John, for if I carry another child, as I would the way you and I are, well, then you couldn't have me at all! Because I'd perish! You know what Dr. Tennant said. John, old darling, I adore ye, even more than when we had that, but . . . now I have to make a declaration of what ye surely know already, and that is, we've come past that.

"I prayee, John, don't turn from me and sigh, nor make me move to another room. I feel bad enough about it without that. I want to sleep at your side to the end of this mortal life—aye, even beyond it. Please, just hold me and go to sleep. Remember . . . remember the time we first saw the homestead in Albemarle together? Remember that glorious morning? On the meadow, when we knelt there and saw the place where you'd build our house? Remember how those flowers waved in the wind, and the sun was on us, and us so young?"

He was still for a while, and she didn't know whether he was sulking or remembering. But at length he said:

"Why d'ye ask me that just now?"

"Well," she said, and the tears were starting to course hot and wet down her temples, "Because . . . because I loved you more that moment than ever before or since, I always thought, but . . . I know I do more now than I di . . . than I did then."

And soon she felt him quaking in the darkness with his great,

151

suppressed sobs, and they held each other and wept silently unt[il]
they were exhausted, and she went to sleep remembering th[e]
flowery green meadow under the Blue Ridge.

AND IN THE MORNING AT BREAKFAST, WHILE THEY WER[E]
still feeling haunted and bewildered, glancing cautiously at eac[h]
other amid the lively talk of their children and the clatter [of]
plates and silver, George announced that he heard a rider turn[n-]
ing in, and that it must be a message about the powder, and h[e]
excused himself from the table and shot out into the hallway[.]
On his heels at once were Johnny, who always imagined mes[-]
sages were for him, Mrs. Clark herself, who had a sudden word[-]
less certainty that it was Jonathan home for his furlough, an[d]
Billy, who was just naturally always at George's heels.

"Well, I'll be a red-beaked ripsnort if it isn't the Grand Hig[h]
Sheriff o' King William County!" George cried from the fron[t]
door. "Owen! Welcome!"

Owen Gwathmey lumbered in the door, hearty, red-face[d]
from the October cold and, it transpired, from the flush of sel[f-]
conscious pride. "I was in the neighborhood on a matter of of[-]
fice," he said, "so thought I'd just come say in person instead [of]
the post, that your Annie just two days since has given me an[-]
other boy!"

Ann Rogers Clark clapped her hand to her chest and rolle[d]
her eyes. The infant wasn't due for weeks yet, they'd thought[.]
George poured a toast despite the morning hour. Owen said[,]
"We named him Temple, after my mother's family. We'll war[n]
all o' you who can to come to the christening."

"May your tribe increase," George toasted. "As it seems to b[e]
doing anyhow."

"See, Annie," John Clark said into his wife's ear, "it's all th[e]
same, we can keep havin' children *this* way!"

And his words surged into her heart with such an impact tha[t]
she felt a sensation like hot needle-pricks all over her skin, and[
]slamming of her heart, and a need to cry, out of tenderness, bu[t]
she contained all that because of the happy people present, an[d]
as usual when she contained such a thing, her fair skin went re[d]
and blotchy and broke out in a rash. She left the uproar to catc[h]
a look at herself in a mirror down the hall.

Wouldn't ye know it, she thought. It's one o' those that make[s]
me look like I've eat raspberries out of a trough!

And at that moment they heard Jonathan's voice hallooin[g]
from down the road, and when he saw her in the doorway, he[r]
blue eyes swimming in her livid face, if he had not known th[at]

as her old usual stirred-up-feelings rash, he might have thought
and Bill Croghan had come home to another epidemic.

No one was ready for Jonathan's arrival; they had been braced
for it for days, but now Owen's news had so disarmed them that
no one of them could recompose whatever front he or she had
intended to put up for Jonathan. Now they were caught with
their emotions in disarray, and Jonathan and the slender young
officer beside him were dismounting and moving among them.
Jonathan came to his mother first.

He had always greeted her by giving her his cheek to kiss, and
this time there was a momentary awkwardness when he didn't,
but she reached up and held him and kissed him there anyway,
just as she always had, on that poor, sallow, scarred cheek, on
the ruins of that skin she had bathed and soothed and pampered
and nuzzled so many thousands of times in his childhood, and
her eyes swam with tears and she was beginning to heave with
sobbing. "Now, now, there, Ma," he was saying in that deep-
chested gentle voice, patting her arm, "what kind o' soldier are
you?"

"I'm all right," she managed to say. "Just all weepy-happy
cause you're whole and home. And sorry your friend has
see . . . see me lookin' my worst."

It was easier for everybody after that, and in a moment a typ-
ical Clark family reunion was in full ferment in the hallway, and
gradually Jonathan got to seem as if he had never looked any
different.

IT WAS ONE OF THOSE RAREST OF TIMES, WHEN ALL THE
Clark boys were home at once, and the days flew.

It was a rare time in another way. There was romance in the
house, and for once Johnny was not involved in it.

There were two romances. Colonel Isaac Hite, a substantial
gentleman whom Jonathan had known during his clerking days,
a relative of the Bowmans, came through with his family from
Frederick County. Among them was his eighteen-year-old
daughter Sarah, whom Jonathan had not seen since she was
twelve. Sarah Hite had luminous, sleepy-looking blue eyes, high
cheekbones, cornsilk hair, a rosebud of a mouth set in a resolute
jaw, a lark's song of a laugh, and a vibrancy of manner that drew
Jonathan back to some old, vaguely remembered yearning. For
hours he regarded her, Cupid's arrow festering in his heart, and
tried to remember what it was that he was remembering, and it
was not until that evening at table, when someone mentioned
the name of Captain Bill Lewis, that Jonathan remembered,

153

with a start and a flood of warmth, Lucy Meriwether. He turne and studied Sarah Hite in this new light and he understood no what had been haunting him. She had not seemed to look any thing like Mrs. Lewis before, and still did not really *look* like her but she *was* like her.

Johnny, with his connoisseur's eye, had found nothing ex traordinary about her, and so was merely polite to her as to an family friend. Bill Croghan found her very fetching, but coul see enchantment written all over his friend's face and decide not to compete for her attention. And that was just as well, be cause someone in the Clark family was already watching Bil Croghan with lovesick eyes.

It was Lucy.

Twelve she was then, a freckled tomboy with knee-scabs hid den under her dress, and no romantic notion had ever befor entered her head. But somehow she had gotten the most sicken ing crush on this elegant Englishman in patriot's uniform. Sh laughed uproariously at his mildest witticism, tilted her head an rested her freckled cheek on the back of her hand in an absur pose of assumed femininity, and scarcely took her eyes off him She was transparent as a window pane. Bill Croghan becam aware of it at once. Being a wholesome and merry man, he like her immensely as a child, but knew he would have a case on hi hands if he didn't handle her right. And so he became like child when he had him in tow. He spent much time with he that October, walking and clowning with her in the yard, prac ticing the peashooter and sling with her, stooping and collectin pretty autumn leaves or studying woolly-bear worms with her under a blue fall sky. She was flirting, a travesty of coyness, an had about as much girl-guile as a polliwog.

And Bill Croghan kept it all under control by calling her "Lit tle Brother."

And now for a while George did not have to be the sole bar at the table, because Jonathan and Bill Croghan had a mos stupendous yarn to spin about Charles Town. Bill especially hac a mastery of description that enabled the whole family to see i all as if they had been there themselves: General Lee and hi food-stained vest and his dogs, the great ships plowing up the channel, the cannon blasts, the splintering ships, the water spouts, the brave sergeant with the Carolina flag, the grounded warship burning and exploding in the channel at night, and then all the aftermath, celebrations and feasts, the dancing and mu sic, the elegant Charles Town belles in all their finery. He tolc them how the South Carolina flag had been redesigned to in-

ude a palmetto tree, and he taught them two or three of the
ore acceptable songs about Sir Peter Parker's pants. George lis-
ned as if he were determined to absorb every detail, and even
terrupted now and then to ask about particulars. He explained
at the people of Kaintuck were always starved for news, and
is was how they liked to hear it: in such a way that they could
e it with their own eyes. George cheered for Colonel Moultrie
hen the tale was done, and proposed a toast to him. Then he
ked Jonathan:

"And you, y' saw all this from a grandstand, as it were, and
dn't have to shoot a bullet or dodge one?" He did not mean it
 deflate Jonathan, but Jonathan, as men do who have just
issed combat, took it that way. His eyes darkened and he stared
 George for a moment, then glanced at Sarah Hite down across
e table, as if to see whether she was smirking at him, then
oked indignantly back at George.

"Yes," he said coldly. And George caught the tone and under-
ood.

"I'm glad," he said. "Two reasons why. First, I'd shudder to
ink of you in such a danger. And second, if ye'd been down in
e midst of it someplace, you two, why, you'd not ha' seen it on
ich a scale, and so I wouldn't have near so grand a story to tell
m out yonder, would I!"

Johnny was intrigued by this notion. "What d'you mean about
ich a scale, George?"

"Well, probably you'll see what I mean, soon enough. But
hat I mean is, it's little and squalid when you're down in it."
e was remembering his own first combat, on Pipe Creek. "But
 you're a general, lookin' down on it from a hill, and making it
 like you were God himself, why, I'd reckon you'd see so
uch glory in it, it'd turn your head."

"*Amen!*" said John Clark.

And Bill Croghan tilted his head and gazed at George as if he
ad just discovered a new breed.

GEORGE ROGERS STOOD UP FROM THE BIG TABLE HE USED
 a drawing desk and laid his calipers down on a large square of
per covered with sketches of king posts and trusses. He came
rward, hand reaching and mouth twisted into a tight-lipped
nile, his eyes intense. His hair was almost as much white as red
ow, but his face was still ruddy and youthful, his body firm and
ect. "Well, George! You!"

"Uncle."

They gripped hands, then spontaneously put their arms

155

around each other's shoulders and hugged. Behind George inside the door of the study, Joe Rogers stood, anxious and half smiling, watching this reunion. And behind Joe in the hallway murmuring and staring, stood most of the rest of the Rogers clan.

Everything about this uncle's family reminded George of his own. There had been ten children born to George and Frances Pollard Rogers, the youngest a daughter about Fanny's age, and five of the Rogers children were named Johnny, Lucy, Edmund, William, and Frances. There was a joke that if any of the Clark and Rogers children somehow got exchanged at church, it would be next Saturday before anyone noticed.

"Well, Nephew, I know why you're here. Close the door, Joe, and wait outside. George, let's us sit by the fire."

They drank to health and talked briefly about the war and then got to the heart of the matter.

"Joe's determined to go with you, and he tells me you want him to. Is that so?"

"It was his idea, I hope he told you."

"Yes."

"In a way, Uncle, I prayed you'd be able to talk 'im out o' the notion."

"As I say, he's determined. All but declared independence. I reckon if I'd denied him, he'd have just gone off and joined Washington. In the same way, I prayed you'd just tell 'im you didn't want 'im along."

"I could've told 'im that, but it wouldn't ha' been true. I need people I can count on to help me take that powder out, and I wish I could find ten o' his caliber and spirit." He saw both pride and sadness in his uncle's eyes at these words. "But I had to hear you say, Uncle, that if anything happens to 'im, you'll not grudge me."

The expression in George Rogers' face was fear, now. He replied, "Well, sure and I'll *say* it. O' course one can't know how he's going to feel at a time like that. But no, I don't aim to grudge you. Y' know I care for you as I do for my own. By my eyes, George, you *are* my own. I don't want to lose either o' you. But you know it's not our way in this family to try to stop someone who believes what he's doing. I know ye can't guarantee anything, Nephew. All I ask is, keep 'im out of harm's way as well as ye can."

"I can swear this: Long as he's in my sight, my own life stands 'twixt him and any harm. That's as much guarantee as any man can give. As for Joe, I've already told him what he'll have to

156

guarantee me: he's to expect no coddlin' on account o' being my cousin."

"By God! I should say not! I'd switch you if ye coddled 'im! Now . . . Well . . . Let's bring him in. I'm set to say good-bye to my son. And to my best nephew."

8

ON THE OHIO RIVER
December 23, 1776

THE OHIO WAS GRAY AS LEAD, A MILE WIDE, RUNNING FAST, thick with floating ice chunks. The longboat speeding down midstream with five rowers straining at its oars was so heavy with armed men, lead, and powder that its gunwales were barely above water. It bothered George to have all the powder in one boat, but one boat was all that Fort Pitt had been able to spare.

Young Joseph Rogers, the rower nearest the stern, sat in the very center of his seat, erect, looking straight astern. Facing him, at the tiller, was his cousin George, wrapped to his chin in a cloak, looking intense, almost angry. The clouds were low and somber, spitting snow into the river. Both riverbanks were white with snow, the cliffs and denuded trees etched dark against them.

George suddenly broke into a grin, looking at his cousin, and Joe Rogers asked, between laboring breaths, "What's amusin'?" They had been rowing almost nonstop day and night since Fort Pitt and had come almost three hundred miles down this forbidding river, and every foot of the way, Joe had felt that he would perish of exhaustion—unless the overloaded boat capsized first and drowned him.

George replied, "Y' never look left nor right, Cousin. Scared you'll see Indians?"

"I'm scared if I roll my damn eyeballs one side or t' other I'll tip this damfool boat over."

George laughed voicelessly, breath steaming in the cold air. Then he craned his neck to look ahead downriver, put the helm over to his right to avoid an ice floe as big as a bowling green, and told the rowers, "Pull, boys, you're flaggin'."

Someone groaned, but they dug in harder.

"By th' Eternal," Joe Rogers gasped. Being a relative, he felt more free to complain or question than did the others. "What's th' hurry, anyways?"

George swept both banks with piercing eyes. "Mister Assemblyman," he called forward, "how's it look?"

John Gabriel Jones had been studying the river and the bluffs with the aid of a spyglass. He had a wool scarf tied over his three-cornered hat and under his chin to keep the hat on and his ears warm. Looking back, he said, "Clear."

Now George nodded and looked back to Joseph. "Y' recollect those Shawnees that were tradin' at Pitt? Well, they shoved off day before we did."

"Well, what of that?"

"Well, I'm chasin' 'em," George said, grinning.

"Say what? Y're joshin' me, George."

Everybody in the boat laughed.

"I am," George said. "Actually, they're chasin' us."

"Come on now."

"I mean it. I think we slipped by their camp at the Scioto last night, but I'm about nine-tenths sure they're tailing us now. Does that inspire you to lay on those oar-sticks, Cousin?"

Joseph strained his weary muscles to add speed. His eyes were bulging. "It do," he said.

The river gurgled around the hull. Oars dipped and swashed monotonously. George watched the river course all around as if his head were on a swivel, and now and then would look astern with a spyglass. "Make sure those kegs are chocked up," he said once. Snow was melting in the bilges and the rowers' feet were in icy water.

After another wordless, benumbing, breath-wracking hour, George studied the river astern and then turned around, lowering his spyglass. The intensity in his expression sent a bolt of dread down Joe's spine. "Mhm," George said. "Listen now, all. They're back there. Five canoes. We've got a two-mile lead, but I'd like to open that up by a mile or two. Here," he said to Joseph. "Swap ye seats. Mister Assemblyman, relieve Larkin up there if y' would."

Young Joseph crawled like a lizard to the stern seat, gripping both gunwales so hard his red-chapped hands were white-knuckled. He took the tiller, and it was obvious that he did not like sitting with his back to Indians.

158

With George and Jones now applying their rested muscles to the oars, the boat surged forward like a trout.

George rowed like a demon, looking past young Joe toward the dots that were the Shawnee canoes. He knew that five strong oarsmen might outrun Indian canoes for a while, but this boat was heavy and the rowers had been exerting themselves for a week. He thought of the river course. Ahead in the bends of the Ohio lay three long islands that divided the river into narrow channels, and beyond stood a set of limestone bluffs on the south side of the river.

"Mister Jones," he said. "What we'd best do is bury these kegs at Limestone Cliff, then set the boat adrift a little way on down, and light out afoot for Harrod's Town. There we'll get horses and help, and come back for the powder. How does that sound?"

That sounded all right to a boatload of men who hadn't a notion of what else to do. All they could do was try to wring a few hundred more oar-strokes out of their pain-wracked muscles and blistered hands.

THEY LANDED AT THE BLUFFS AND CACHED THE FIVE ONE-hundred-pound powder kegs at intervals along the limestone cliff base, covering them with stones and driftwood. It was frantic, strenuous work in the twilight. The men were exhausted and their cold-stiffened hands were painfully torn and stove by the work. They grunted and swore and panted in the half-dark, tumbling among snow-slick stones, always peering upriver for sight of the Shawnee canoes.

When the kegs were hidden, he hurried the panting men back into the boat. "Don't a one of you forget where these lay," he warned, "in case we get scattered." With that ominous warning, he shoved the lightened boat off from shore, hopping in and commanding them to work like the Devil. They rowed silently for several miles until George steered to the mouth of a creek he had been watching for. Here they piled ashore, slung their guns and provisions onto their aching shoulders, launched the empty boat back into the current, and set off on foot into the Kentuck interior toward Harrod's Town, a file of seven dark shapes lurching along through leafless woods, wading in an icy creek to leave no tracks on the snowy hillsides. Joseph Rogers winced and gasped and anticipated arrows in his back, and thought that perhaps he should have listened to those of his family who had implored him to stay home for Christmas.

* * *

Lucy Clark awoke long before daylight in need of her chamberpot, but as usual it would require fifteen minutes of struggling willpower before she could get up out of bed in the cold, dark room to use it. She squeezed her thighs together, snuggled closer to the body-warmth of her sister Elizabeth, and thought about two exciting things that for days had been inseparably linked in her mind: Bill Croghan and Christmas Day.

Bill Croghan had been on furlough here since October and now it was Christmas morning, and he had been the first thought in her mind, the moment she awakened, on every single morning. Oh, what a prince he was, and how desperately she adored him.

She squeezed her eyes shut and concentrated. Sometimes when she did this, remembering particular things he had said, she could hear the exact sound of his voice in her head: the depth of it, the tone, the lilt, just the way it had sounded in her ear. But it was hard to do. Any little sound in the dark bedroom could throw it off and she would have to start again: like that little snot-whistle noise in Elizabeth's nostril just now. Lordy, I could put a pillow on 'er face, Lucy thought with a flare of impatience. Or like little Sister Fanny over there on the far side of the bed: just at the moment when Lucy would have Bill's voice all ready to speak in her head, Fanny would snort in her sleep, or say "um" or "mum" or "giffle" or some child-sound like that, and Lucy would hiss an exasperated sigh and have to start all over again.

And sometimes even when there were no sounds at all in the room, Lucy still couldn't create Bill's voice in her head, because she would distract herself in some way. Like now, needing to get up for the chamberpot and having a shivering twinge at the mere thought of it. Mercy, she thought, I might as well get it over with.

And then back in bed a minute later, the warm pee-smell rankling in the cold air, her icy feet making Elizabeth's bed-warm legs jerk, Lucy would try again to create Bill Croghan's beloved voice. It was best if he had said something just the day before that she could remember word for word, because then it would be fresh in her mind just the way it had sounded. Yesterday he had said a very memorable thing to her in a very memorable way, and she concentrated on it now: "Lucy-luce, you silly goose, I'll give you a kissmus on Christmas!"

A kiss! Today!

She could remember and hear the voice exactly now.

Bill Croghan had kissed her once before. It had been on Thanksgiving Day, she remembered: He had come to the table

160

just as she was sitting down, and he had pushed her chair in under her as a true gentleman prince would do, and, as no one else had ever done that for her before, it had surprised her knees and she had plopped back onto the chair seat. Her mouth had dropped open and the family had laughed at her, and at that moment Bill had laughed behind her and said, "Ho, silly goose, your knees are loose!" and had kissed her right on top of her dust-bonnet. Then he had gone around to his side of the table, and while her father was saying the Thanksgiving Grace, she had sneaked a look across the table at Bill, and he had caught her looking at him and had wrinkled up his nose and made rabbit-nibble faces at her until she had almost laughed out loud—which would have been a serious crime during one of her father's prayers.

It was such things as these that Bill Croghan did that made Lucy feel sure that he loved her as she loved him; they were like codes. Of course he couldn't just come right forth and say he loved her, right here and now. He was twice her age now. But she had figured ahead by arithmetic and knew he wouldn't always be. She would probably have to wait until she was fifteen to get married, as her mother had. By then the war probably would be over and Bill Croghan would come back to Virginia to stay.

Oh, Dear Lord, she thought now with such a heart-clench that tears squeezed out of her eye corners, *may he be safe in the war!*

But it was Christmas morning now and everyone was safe at home here at the Clark house—except George, who was almost always gone—and Lucy lay now spooned against Elizabeth's back and thought about the present she had made for Bill. She wished it would hurry and be daylight so she could give Bill Croghan his gift. He would like it so much, that's when he would give her the kiss, she knew, and not on the top of her bonnet this time, either, she was sure, but instead probably right on her cheek.

Lordylord, I'm too excited, she thought; I'll never get back to sleep.

That was what she was thinking when she slipped off to sleep under the thick comforter in her sisters' body-heat, and she slept so deeply she was the last one up on Christmas morning.

JOHN CLARK WAS ESPECIALLY PROUD THIS CHRISTMAS BE-cause Parson Donald Robertson, the teacher of his sons, was here as guest for the holidays, and thus there would be a very proper and profound invocation before the giving of gifts.

Lucy Clark understood well enough what an honor this was,

161

as she had been told so often—half of the Revolutionary leaders of Virginia, it was said, had been pupils of his—but on any Christmas, and especially this one, she would have dispensed with the honor gladly because Parson Robertson's invocations were perhaps even longer than they were deep. His wife, Auntie Rachel, lately had developed the scandalous habit of dozing in the middle of them.

But today the parson's invocation was somewhat more interesting than usual, being, in effect, a lopsided history of the Revolutionary War to date, dwelling on the victories and ignoring the defeats, with about equal portions of credit for the victories being given to the Father, the Son, the Holy Ghost, and General Washington. He thanked them for having forced General Howe to evacuate Boston, for the deliverance of Charles Town, and for the wisdom and principles that had resulted in the Declaration of Independence—not forgetting to hint that some of his former pupils had had a hand in its adoption. In his invocation, the parson chose to omit the bad news of the autumn: Washington's loss of Long Island and his long, grim retreat, the losses of Fort Washington and Fort Lee, Arnold's defeat on Lake Champlain. After all, it was Christmas time, and Reverend Robertson would not want to depress spirits by admitting that the American Revolution was almost a lost cause, that the Grand Army of the United Colonies had dwindled to a couple of thousand men, through captures, desertions, casualties, diseases, and expired enlistments. No, this was a time of joyous and noble beginnings, the time of the Saviour's birth.

All through this, Lucy Clark stayed on her suffering knees and stole glances at Bill Croghan. And finally, when it was over, she scarcely noticed who was giving what to whom in the gift exchange, until Bill Croghan came over and gave her what he had made for her—a new leathern slingshot—and she gave him what she had made for him—a new leathern slingshot. They laughed at each other, and the rest of the family laughed at them. And Bill Croghan, wiping tears of hilarity from his cheeks, said, "Now, here's your Christmas kissmus," and gave her a peck on the forehead before she even had time to blush. "And," he laughed, "a happy Christmas to you, Little Brother!"

She leaped up.

"Oh, but you're an awful man!" she cried, fleeing the room in tears before the astonished family and guests. She stopped in the doorway and shouted back at him through sobs of mortification: "Here I am who's going to marry you, and y' still call me Little Brother!"

162

GEORGE WAS SLOGGING THROUGH MELTING SNOW IN A warming sunshine, two of his men panting at his heels. At this moment he had just remembered that this was Christmas Day, and was turning to say a greeting to them about it, when he was jolted to a halt by the crack of a gunshot nearby. It rolled in echoes through the hills. His scalp prickled and he was ready to drop behind cover, but then he saw the large brown form of a buck deer career out of a thicket and fall in the snow in a clearing a hundred yards ahead. It had been a hunter's gun; whether white man's or Indians he was not sure, though it had sounded like a long rifle. With a motion of his hand he bade his companions take cover. He stood behind a large beech tree and cocked his rifle and watched the place where the deer lay twitching, watched for the hunter to come claim his prey. He watched for a long time, searching in vain among the bare trees for the figure of a man. Whoever this hunter was, he was cautious and apparently knew how to hunt in Indian country without becoming sudden prey himself.

The man who eventually stepped out of the woods into the edge of the clearing and advanced on the deer was a huge man. His shoulders looked a yard wide; his rifle was aslant across his chest, carried at ready. For all his great size he moved lightly and silently as a wood spirit. There was no mistaking him. Grinning, George eased down the flintlock on his rifle, and called out:

"Butler!"

George stepped out from behind the beech and waved his hat. The big man's gun was on him at once. "Don't shoot, it's me, Clark!"

Simon Butler uttered a whoop and came sprinting across the snowy clearing. They met each other halfway and they hugged and lifted each other off the ground, pounding each other's backs with thumps that sounded as if they were beating oaken barrels, both laughing Christmas greetings into each other's ears. George's two men came out from cover and walked up hesitantly to see this scout who at twenty-three was already a legend.

Butler was two inches bigger in every dimension than even George. And he was handsome, though in a coarser way, with a jutting square chin, a long, bent-down nose that almost touched his lip, thick auburn hair, and skin so creased and permanently darkened by exposure that it looked like bootleather.

George introduced his men to Butler, then, while Butler was gutting the dead buck, explained the situation: the long-awaited gunpowder hidden at Limestone, the pursuing Shawnees. He

163

told Butler that four of his men, including his cousin Joe Rogers and Assemblyman Jones, had been too fatigued to keep up and had been left to rest at an abandoned blockhouse on the east fork of the Kentuck River while George and these two had continued on this way to get help from Harrod's Town.

"This meat's for Harrod's Town," Butler said, hoisting the eviscerated animal across his shoulders and tying its front and hind feet together in front of him. "I'll come with ye." He led them off in a southerly direction, and even though the buck he carried must have weighed nearly two hundred pounds, the other three men almost had to run to keep up with him.

JOSEPH ROGERS FELT HE WAS CAUGHT IN A WHIRLWIND IN the wilderness this Christmas Day. He was riding fast up the Licking River bank with eleven other armed horsemen. They were heading back up toward Limestone, with five pack horses to fetch the hidden gunpowder. Seven men had shown up at the blockhouse the day before, a hunting party led by the settler John Todd. Assemblyman Jones had talked them into going up for the cached powder. And now the band was thundering through the woods toward the Ohio, the cold wind making their eyes water, bare twigs whipping their frozen ears and cheeks as they plunged through thickets. Cousin George was going to be pleasantly surprised when this group showed up at Harrod's Town with the powder; George was probably just now down there trying to organize a pack train. They'd likely meet on the trail someplace, those going north for the powder and these already coming down with it. A great Christmas gift for Kaintuck, and Joe Rogers was delighted to think that he would be one of the bearers. Meanwhile, it was all he could do to stay on the galloping horse in these woods, hanging on its back like a burr, his heart in his throat. He had, after all, come for adventure, and it was adventure he was—

The gray woods ahead suddenly sputtered orange sparks and puffed smoke. The horses reared, whinnying, stumbling, falling. The last thing Joe Rogers saw before his horse fell sideways was John Gabriel Jones pitching out of his saddle, blood spurting through the smashed left lens of his spectacles.

Joe thrashed in the snow and dead leaves, trying to get his right leg out from under the weight of his horse. His rifle had fallen out of his reach. He unsheathed his knife. Ahead, howling Indians came running through the gunsmoke. Around him lay struggling horses and groaning white men; behind him, the rest of John Todd's men were galloping desperately back out of the ambush, shouting curses and confused commands. Joe slashed left and right with his knife as two painted Indians loomed over him. Ruthless strong arms pinioned him to the ground and tore the knife from his hand. Elbows and palms smashed against his nose and eyes. He was dragged from under the horse, yelping in pain and fury. Yelling and running sounds swirled around him. Hoofbeats were fading into the distance. More blows made his ears ring and his brain flash, and treetops tilted against the sky. His clothing was being cut and torn from him and then his wrists were being bound, cruelly tight, behind his back. He blinked a curtain of flowing blood out of his eyes and saw a kneeling warrior slicing the scalp off of Assemblyman Jones.

The next thing Joe Rogers was aware of was that he was very cold, naked, sitting backward astride a trotting horse, his feet tied under it to keep him from jumping or falling off. On the next horse he saw the white backside of another prisoner. The horses were being led swiftly through the snowy woods, by a file of what seemed to be about forty exuberant braves with painted faces.

Joe Rogers felt like the sorriest excuse for an adventurer who had ever lived. He thought of the promises Cousin George had had to make to his father.

It was Christmas Day and Joe Rogers was sure it would be his last day.

GEORGE, WITH SIMON BUTLER AND A LARGE MOUNTED party from Harrod's Town, rode up toward Limestone to get the hidden ammunition. On their way they met John Todd and the bandaged survivors of the Christmas Day ambush. Over a horse's back hung the mutilated bodies of John Gabriel Jones and one of Todd's men, named Graden. George sat listening to Todd's report of the ambush and the ensuing fight with knives and tomahawks and rifles used as clubs, and then the escape of these few.

"And my cousin Joe," he interrupted. "Where's he?"

"We couldn't find 'im. Just some of his clothes." Todd's gaze dropped.

George worked his jaw muscles mightily. He was seeing Joe's cheerful, round face and his fair Rogers hair. He remembered the guarantee he had given Uncle George. Then he made his eyelids hard, and said, "Pray those Shawnee haven't wrung out of 'em anything about that powder. Let's go look."

All the way up toward the Ohio he had to make himself stop seeing images of Joe being tortured in the ways he knew Shawnees did such things.

The powder was all there where they had buried it. They

loaded the precious kegs one by one onto the pack horses, while Simon Butler stood at the top of the cliff watching for Indians. Jim Harrod rode alongside George as the last keg was being loaded. He put a big hand on George's shoulder. Harrod's eyes were glinting. "Boy," Harrod said, "this stuff's the salvation o' Kentuck. Thankee." His hand tightened. "Thankee," he said again, and then rode off.

THERE WAS JUBILATION IN HARROD'S TOWN WHEN THE POW-der was brought in. Harrod made a speech and ordered a barrel of whiskey opened. George supervised the division of the powder supply among the few remaining settlements. Soon afterward, a courier came from Fort Pitt. Harrod assembled the townspeople for another meeting. He stood George up beside him and said:

"This word came today. The Assembly declared Mister Henderson's land company illegal. They made Kentuck a county." The crowd of red-nosed, muddy-footed listeners in the room began to grin and buzz. Harrod held up his hand. "That means," he went on, "we got power to have a government, and raise a militia for defense. And," he added, throwing a heavy arm over George's shoulders, "you folks all know Mister Clark here, our assemblyman. You'll be glad to know he's a major now as well, and he's in command of the Kentuck militia. And his headquarters will be right here in my town. I don't know about you folk, but that makes me feel god damned good!"

The room shook with yells and whistles and stomping, and the settlement that night consumed another barrel of whiskey. And George Rogers Clark, just lately turned twenty-four, came to be called not just Assemblyman Clark and Major Clark, but the Father of Kentucky.

> At a court martial of all the officers of the county: Pres^t, Geo. R. Clark, Danl Boone, Jas. Harrod, Jn Todd:
> Ordered that any perfon called into service by the Invaf-ion Law, as is the cafe with all now in this county, in cafe he leaves the service be looked upon as a deferter, & the Commanding Officer is defired to advertife all such throughout the colony, as deferters, in the moft public manner.
>
> G. R. CLARK, Pres^d.

That, George thought, looking at the handbill, won't apply to

166

many. Those who are still here aren't the deserting sort. But this hould discourage any who might.

There weren't many still in Kentuck. The settlements of Leesburg—which George had laid out, it seemed now, so long go—and Danville, and McClelland's and Hinkson's stations, ad been abandoned. Even brave Benjamin Logan had closed is little fort and had brought his folk—about twenty men and heir families—to Harrod's Town.

Now there were only two settlements still occupied in all of Kentuck: Harrod's Town and Boonesboro, fort towns within wenty miles of each other on the Kentuck River. Between them hey could muster barely a hundred fighting men, three-quarters f whom manned the bigger and stronger fort at Harrod's Town. The whole population of the new Virginia County of Kentuck ad been reduced to about three or four hundred stubborn souls. There were more women, children, sick, and wounded in the wo settlements than there were able-bodied men. All these had o be fed, but almost any venture outside the palisades for meat r corn resulted in more dead and wounded defenders. Cattle nd pigs the Indians had not yet killed or stolen were brought nside the walls, where they made filth and added to the crowding.

Thus the year 1777 had opened. Kentuck was overrun with arger bands of warriors, better led and equipped than they ever ad been. They had good English guns and plentiful English mmunition, warm blankets of English wool, and scalping nives of English steel. They left printed English handbills at the ites of their attacks: leaflets printed at Detroit, offering reconciliation and security to any who would abandon the Rebel eresy and come to live as good, loyal subjects in British Canda. The Indians were being paid handsomely for scalps and risoners taken west of the Alleghenies. It was terribly plain that Kentuck was now the Revolution's western front, and that the British meant to sweep all the settlers out of the western lands. In short time they had driven thousands back over the mountains nd forced the rest into these two little fortified settlements. The ew county was under siege, and Major George Rogers Clark ound himself in charge of the hopeless task of holding it. Simon Butler came in from a patrol one day with the news that he had een Black Fish, one of the most able of all Shawnee warrior hiefs, encamped near the Ohio with a very large body of braves. Now that the smaller bands had scoured the countryside of isoated families and small outposts, it was almost certain that they were being combined into a force of several hundred, which

Black Fish would throw upon these last two islands of defense Harrod's Town and Boonesboro.

To prepare for a siege, George led a heavily armed company of two dozen riders, with pack horses, on a week-long sweep through the abandoned settlements, to forage corn and anything else edible that might have been left behind, as well as flax and hemp. They rode hard and fast through the cold and rainy weather, and found that there was very little the Indians had not looted already. Indian signs were everywhere among the bleak and sodden hills and valleys.

The riders got back to Harrod's Town on the eighteenth of March. They were scarcely inside the gates before the Shawnee horde rushed the fort from all sides.

They came howling and yipping like wolves out of the woods and across the clearing, sprinting toward the palisades, diving behind stumps for cover, peppering the stockade walls with musketballs, sprinting and diving again. They were using covering fire in an intelligent way to get across the open ground and close to the fort, and were shooting as if they had unlimited ammunition. George barely had time to form a defense.

Inside the compound was pandemonium. Panicky livestock milled in the mud and manure, getting in the way of the riflemen. George, racing from one blockhouse to another, skidded on one steaming-fresh cowpat and almost fell, then was nearly bowled over by a squealing, zigzagging sow. "Harrod!" he bellowed. "Get these infernal animals penned up! I can't fight Indians and livestock too!" Harrod dispatched a herd of boys to herd the animals, and for a few more minutes, until they had accomplished the roundup, the commotion was twice as bad: the *whack-whack* of lead hitting the logs, the ceaseless yipping and gunfire from the Indians outside, the squealing and lowing and neighing of animals and shouting of riflemen and the yelping and wailing of women and children, the shrieking of terrified babies from inside the cabins, the whisper of Indian bullets overhead, the fluttering rush of fire arrows arcing toward the fort, the cracking *thud*s of the defenders' rifles, the dense, eye-stinging smoke of gunpowder and burning oak.

The defenders were shooting well, though; George had organized them into squads that took turns firing from the portholes and reloading, while women hurried from hearthside to gun ports, fetching hot lead in skillets, and the Shawnees were unable to reach the walls yet through such steady and accurate fire.

The battle had held this way for about an hour, under a fast-moving cover of darkening clouds, when a stinging, drenching

ownpour of cold rain suddenly came hissing across the clearing.
extinguished a stubborn roof fire. The Indians paused where
aey lay, and their firing slacked off. In the distance near the edge
f the woods, George saw a chief on a black horse riding the
eriphery, yelling in a voice powerful and clear even at this dis-
ance of two hundred rain-filtered yards, calling back his war-
ors. That, George was sure, was Black Fish—obviously a foe to
e reckoned with.

And after another five minutes there was not a live Indian
ithin sight of Harrod's Town. The Shawnees in withdrawing
ad gotten all their wounded away.

The only white casualty of the fray was a married man, Hugh
Vilson, who left the fort too soon after the battle. He was killed
nd scalped a half-mile from the stockade when he went out
efore nightfall to scrounge for Indian souvenirs.

THE BITTER RAIN THAT HAD CURTAILED BLACK FISH'S AT-
ack continued for ten days, becoming as much a curse as it had
een a blessing. The ground inside the palisades was a chilly,
inking, churned, knee-deep soup of mud and animal waste and
uman excrement. It was constantly being tracked into the build-
ags. There was a damp chill in every room, firewood being wet
nd scarce, and everyone was sniffling and shivering. Many of
le children lay all day wrapped in damp bedding, feverish and
hilling by turns, and everyone was weak from dysentery brought
n by bad drinking water, musty corn, and tainted, half-cooked
ork fat. Even such a crack hunter as Butler would come in
mpty-handed most days; Black Fish's braves, still roaming the
.cinity of Boonesboro and Harrod's Town, were killing whatever
ame had not been driven out by flooding rivers.

"What the hell's this?" Jim Harrod asked one morning as his
ook brought breakfast to him and George.

"Th' usual, sir," said the cook, setting down plates of some-
aing gray-brown, flat, and steaming, with grease congealing
ound the edges.

"Which 'usual' is it," Harrod grumbled, scowling at it,
scorched cow chips or fried starch?"

Killing time usefully during the rainy days, some of the men
ent around the outside of the stockage prying Indian musket-
alls out of the logs. They collected nearly two hundred pounds
f lead, which they melted down to make balls for their own
fles.

The rain stopped finally, and the temperatures dropped below
eezing. As the river fell and the ground hardened, George de-

tailed his riflemen into watches and had them gazing off the walls constantly for the return of the Shawnees.

It was the twenty-eighth of March when they came, and their arrival was so stealthy that they surprised several hunters outside the fort.

"They're here," gasped one of the survivors. "They scalped Pendergreet. I saw 'em carry Pete Flinn off still kickin'."

And now once again the disciplined warriors of Black Fish were advancing on Harrod's Town under a hail of musket fire. The defenders, now reduced by disease and wounds to sixty-four men and boys, were barely managing to keep them off the walls. Many of the riflemen, their vision and reflexes dulled by disease and fatigue and shakes, were not the shooters they had been ten days before. And Black Fish, now more familiar with the ground, had improved his tactics. One side of the fort would be sprayed by musketballs fired from good cover, and while the riflemen behind that wall were flinching against whistling lead and flying splinters, half a dozen braves would come at a crouching run to stumps or defilades a few feet closer to that wall. Then another quarter of the fort would absorb a fusillade and the warriors would advance there. This Black Fish was a good general indeed, and George studied him admiringly through a spyglass as he rode to and fro just a little beyond range of accurate fire. George was growing desperate. No new mode of defense came to mind. He shuddered. The temperature seemed to be dropping by the minute, and the riflemen's firing and loading was being hampered by numb fingers and shivering limbs. It seemed to be near zero.

George had an idea then, while watching Black Fish race from one distant quarter to another: it's *him* that's making 'em so damned effective; it's *him* we ought to put out of the fight. He remembered Jonathan's story about Charles Town, how the greatest part of the artillery had been concentrated on Admiral Parker's ship. If we can see that Indian, he thought, might be we could hit him. Like to blow *his* damned pants off. He called together five of his best marksmen.

"Boys, there's fifty quid out o' my own pocket for the man that shoots that Black Fish off that black horse yonder. And," he added, now pouring an extra long powder charge down the barrel of his own rifle, "if *I'm* the one gets 'im, y'each owe me ten. That fair?" He had kept his voice down, so that the rest of the shooters wouldn't get greedy and forget to keep shooting at the nearby attackers. His marksmen grinned and nodded—though he knew probably not a one of them had ten pounds to his

ame—and began setting themselves up to concentrate on the
eat Shawnee. George could outshoot anyone he knew of ex-
ept Simon Butler and maybe Boone, so he was fairly confident
at he had a chance to claim the prize himself, unless he blew
mself up with his overloaded rifle. Or unless Black Fish was
rotected by his Supreme Being.

He aimed about a degree over Black Fish's head and about a
orse's length ahead of him, and squeezed the trigger. The recoil
most threw his shoulder out of its socket. He saw immediately
at the shot was wasted; Black Fish at that instant had wheeled
is horse and was not at the place where George had sent his
ullet. While he reloaded with another long charge, three more
per-loud *bangs* crashed over the general din of shooting.

But Black Fish apparently was becoming aware that he was a
arked special target now; he bent low over his horse's neck and
egan maneuvering the animal through some of the smartest
odging and sidestepping George had ever seen. A lesser man,
e thought, would probably just ride back into the trees.

George and his sharpshooters got off about three more super-
narged shots apiece at the elusive chief, but missed, and George
as about to believe that Black Fish was indeed favored by Mon-
o.

But it seemed the fort was too. Once again the weather inter-
ened to save Harrod's Town. The Shawnees were not dressed to
ght in subzero temperatures, and after another hour Black Fish
alled them. The firing stopped. The frontiersmen stood shaking
nd stamping and flailing their arms for warmth, peering out
ver the frozen, deserted clearing, still not quite convinced that
e siege was really off. The ground was rock hard now, and the
old seared nostrils and made bones ache. Men stood with their
ands between their thighs or inside their coats, stood shaking,
reath crystallizing, and stared out at the frosty silence.

In the afternoon scouts went out. When they came back, they
rified that Black Fish was really gone from the vicinity.

That night Jim Harrod broke open a demijohn of rum and
ad hot grog made, allowed a pig to be killed for fresh meat,
nd, despite the cracking cold, made his people feel a warm
ratitude for another miracle.

FIRELIGHT HAD ALWAYS BEEN GEORGE'S SPECIAL CONFI-
ant. While other men slept, worn out by events, he would sit
p, as he did now, on a bench with a blanket over his shoulders,
nd look into the shifting orange coals, and ponder, with the
reglow, on what those events must mean in the larger picture.

171

It was too easy to let one's mind be hemmed in by the walls of stockade or the edge of a clearing or the end of a day. It was such a temptation to shut one's eyes and go to sleep thinking only of tomorrow's food and tomorrow's security. It was so natural, out here in the wilderness, to think nothing of that distant struggle in the East.

But by firelight George would piece together things that he had learned from others. Through Joe Bowman's angry words two years ago he had learned to suspect Lord Dunmore's treaty making. Through Bill Croghan's words he had come to understand the tenuous cohesion of interests shared by Britain with the Iroquois and Algonquian chiefs. And through the eyes and ears of such far-ranging hunters as Boone and Butler, he had received hundreds of minute bits of western information that must fit somewhere into a large picture of a general truth, out there beyond the visible horizons: a continental picture. These scouts would see or hear something on the trail, something that would hint at the origins and purposes of the warriors and the white agents who flitted across the long wild distances of the territory north and west of the Ohio, the Northwest Territory: that vastness Virginia believed to be Virginia's, but which England had since the end of the French and Indian War, considered an extension of British Canada.

And George, by listening to all talking men, had been gathering puzzle-pieces to fit together in his mind during these silent and solitary vigils over the coals of a hearth while other men slept.

Two large and general truths had become evident to him. The first was that the Colonies' western front was his own Kentuck and that it was more important to the British than most of the Revolutionary leaders dreamed it was. Kentuck extended like a wedge between the powerful Indian nations north of the Ohio—the Shawnees and Chippewas, the Delawares and Miamis—and those south of the Cumberland and Tennessee—the Cherokees, Chickasaws, and Creeks. As long as Kentuck was occupied by Virginians and defended by their little forts, it would be an obstacle to the designs of the British. It could guard those great water-roads, the Ohio and Mississippi. It could provide meat and grain and timber, as well as rear-guard protection, for the East.

If, on the other hand, the British and Indians could drive the Virginians out of this stronghold—as they had almost done already in these first grim months of 1777—then all the tribes, northern and southern, could be turned loose unhindered on the inner frontiers. Fort Pitt would fall. Wheeling. Point Pleasant.

Red Stone Fort. The Greenbrier settlements. It was plain that this was Britain's whole design on the West, and had been for a long time.

Little by little, he had been able to piece together a picture of Britain's western force. It centered at Detroit, where the British lieutenant-governor, a Scottish gentleman named General Henry Hamilton, maintained his headquarters and purveyed English gifts and weapons for his Indian allies. From Detroit it stretched northwestward to Michillimackinac, and southwestward to remote forts like Post Miami on the Maumee, Fort Sackville at Vincennes in the Wabash Valley, and Cahokia and Kaskaskia on the Mississippi. In all these places, Governor Hamilton had Indian agents at work supplying and arousing the Indians to attack the Colonies' western frontiers.

Evidence was that Governor Hamilton was treating with an ever-widening circle of tribes: Miamis, Weas, Piankeshaws, Pottawatomies, Sacs, Foxes, and even the Sioux beyond the Mississippi. Hamilton was responsible for an enormous extent of wilderness, but he was apparently a shrewd and far-seeing enemy, and was making the most of his responsibility by letting Indians do his fighting and terrorism for him.

I wonder, George thought suddenly, whether he's sitting up right now by his hearth fire in Detroit, thinking as I am about these causes, these lands, these tribes, these distances.

He suddenly felt an intense personal interest in a man who, heretofore, had been only a name. I wonder what he looks like, George thought. I wonder how he thinks. That man in particular is my one personal enemy.

Across these hundreds of miles of night and wilderness now George sensed that other brain, the brain of a British gentleman officer who was his own tactical opponent, and suddenly he had a strange and intriguing thought, unlike any thought he had ever entertained: that the Northwest Territory, that vast region of forest and prairie bounded by the Ohio, the Mississippi, and the Great Lakes, was a chessboard, and he was sitting on one side of it and Governor Hamilton was sitting on the other. The thought was so odd and exciting that he squirmed with restlessness, and got up to put another log on the dying fire. As it crackled to flame, he poured a cup of rum, wondering if Hamilton might just now be having a cup of rum in a firelit room three hundred miles to the north; he filled and lit a pipe, wondering if Hamilton might just now be having a pipe of tobacco . . . Virginia tobacco.

It was a good and amusing fantasy, and he thought:

I have an advantage: I know he exists and I know a bit of his plan. He's never heard of me. He doesn't know I sit here thinking of him and guessing what he'll do next. He doesn't know that there's a brain burning like an all-night lamp down here in a log fort in Kentuck.

And so he's not ready for me. He expects nothing to come from here but more scalps. He doesn't know of me at all. That may be my only advantage . . . but it is an advantage.

The rum warmed him and buzzed in his head, and it fueled these wonderful fancies like oil in a lamp. Lord but this is good at such a time as this, he thought, and poured another cup.

He was happy for a change, and full of hope. For weeks of sleepless nights he had been haunted by remorse over Cousin Joe, and that had been his cup-thinking. But now that old sense, that sense that his destiny was here this side of the mountains, was back, so strong it drove the gloom out, and he remembered one of his mother's proverbs, the one that said, *One can do whatever he doesn't know he can't do.*

Hamilton, he thought. Hamilton thinks he's got us boxed in. He's largely right. It's about all we can do to hold our place. But if this were a game of chess, I'd be thinking ahead of him. I'd figure . . . I'd figure on doing what he thinks we can't.

I'd figure on going after *him.*

He laughed voicelessly into the fire at the audacity of such a thought. It was absurd, he knew, it was rum-headed absurd, to be sitting here a virtual prisoner in this stinking, isolated fort, surrounded and outnumbered tenfold by enemies, and thinking about an *offensive.* But the thought had taken root.

In no way could Hamilton expect Kentuck to make an offensive, he thought. Likely he's a good rational British officer and figures only on rational possibilities, not absurd ones. He'd never be prepared for what I might dream up. That's another advantage I have, he thought.

We'll not last long, just defending, just waiting for them to descend on us. They'll not stop descending till we're bled dead. But if *I* was to descend on *them.* . .

Like the wolf on the fold, he thought: it's the wolf that has the day. Hamilton has been the wolf, and us the fold. But what if I was to be the wolf.

He thought of those campaigns in history that had always most excited his imagination: the bold surprises. He thought of Alexander. He thought of Hannibal, crossing the Alps. Of Spartacus, suddenly out of his chains. He thought of more recent bold strokes: Benedict Arnold showing up at Fort Ticonderoga, then

174

at Quebec. Washington stealing across an icy river to raid Trenton last Christmas Day, that astonishing, table-turning victory, the news of which had reached the frontier only days ago. *Surprises*.

From Kentuck, he thought, I could reach the enemy's posts on the Mississippi, the Wabash, with speed and ease, by water, and surprise him there.

By the Lord God! he thought, leaping up and throwing the blanket off his shoulders. He was too excited to remain sitting. His notions were swelling up; they were too grand to sit with now; he had to get up and walk them around the room. His absurd thought of an offensive was beginning to make all manner of sense now. Not only would such an offensive stop this shedding of innocents' blood in Kentuck, it could block off Detroit's western water route, it could capture cannon, with which Virginia could truly control the Western rivers; it would give him the power, perhaps, to neutralize the tribes by cutting off their pay and supplies. Aye, it might even solidify Virginia's charter claim to the great, rich Northwest Territory.

He thought of Jefferson now, and George Mason, and Patrick Henry, and Washington; he knew how they coveted these lands for Virginia. And suddenly, in thinking their names, he began to see a means toward such an audacious end:

Of course he could not launch an offensive with his own Kentuck County militia—a mere hundred men already clinging to survival by their fingernails—but if he could gain support among the leaders of his mother state, those leaders who were, after all, family friends, as well, then surely he could get enough men and supplies—and *authority* —to go and strike at the heart of General Hamilton's whole murderous web!

George never got to sleep that night. Dawn found him still up, drawing maps and making notes, sipping rum, frowning and smiling at once, walking around staring at the ceiling and pounding his fist into his palm.

It was undoubtedly the grandest single piece of thinking that had ever been done in Kentuck. And when he opened his door at daybreak and looked out, he could scarcely believe that he was still in this cramped and filthy fort, with two hundred wretched people and fifty starving animals, because in his mind he had just soared like an eagle over half a continent.

IT WAS HARD FOR GEORGE TO CONTAIN THE EXCITEMENT OF his plan, but he had to. He could not share it with anyone here in Kentuck; they would think he had gone stockade-crazy. Besides, it was the sort of thing that would depend on secrecy for its success, and so, for the time being, it had to remain his personal secret. Thus he kept it inside his own head and on his own note papers, day after day, and nurtured it and added to it as an oyster does its pearl. Sometimes he seemed moody and distracted to Harrod and the others, but that was easy to explain; the whole population of the fort was going around now with thousand-yard stares from the long confinement and the discomfort and the repulsive rations and the sickness and the constant danger.

He needed more specific information. He called in two shrewd young scouts. They were Benjamin Linn and Sam Moore. They were free spirits, and game for anything that would get them out of this squalid fort.

He showed them on a map where the towns of Kaskaskia and Cahokia were on the Mississippi, not far up from the mouth of the Ohio.

"Go there by way o' St. Louis, which is here, across from Cahokia," he said. "Pretend you're free-lance hunters just down from the Missouri, with no allegiance to the Rebel cause. Hire out to the commandant, if ye can, or at least get close to him some way. His name is Philip de Rocheblave. He's French, but close attached to the British, I've heard. Find out how deep he is in the business of sending Indians down on us. Get to know merchants, too; they always understand the underside of a place better than anybody. I need to know about the fort there, about cannon, about troops, about horses, population, food, farming, boats, everything that makes a place a place. I need to know what folks there think of our Revolution, how ready the local militia is, whether there are any British Regulars garrisoned there. I need to know all about factions and sympathies, who owes what to whom: I mean, boys, I want y' to come back with everything you can soak up, both facts and gossip. If ye have to get into somebody's bed to learn a thing, well, get in. Don't write anything down, and don't be too transparent with your curiosity.

"Now, aside from the fact that y'll probably be shot if you're found out, it ought to be mainly a heap o' fun. Get back here by summer if ye can, but not lest ye feel you know the place inside out by then. All right? And don't ask me why I want to know all this. I'm just a curious sort, about things in general. Very well, then, boys. Any questions? Guard y'r arses jealously, and God be with'ee."

And when these two spies had vanished—he could only hope they would someday return—he turned back to the defense of

176

Kentuck. Black Fish had returned with the mild weather of spring, with more warriors and more murderous energy than ever.

9

BRANDYWINE CREEK
September 10, 1777

IT WAS ALL SO BEAUTIFUL, SO IDYLLIC, BUT YET SO CLOSE TO the very border of life and death, that Johnny Clark felt driven to commit poetry.

He stooped into the luminous half-shade of his white tent, and opened the lid of his field trunk, upon which was carved:

John Clark IV
Lt. 8th Va. Regt.

He lifted his cherrywood letter-box out of the trunk, shut the lid, ducked out of the tent, and walked down through the camp in the lush meadow to his favorite place under a willow at the edge of Brandywine Creek. He sat on the moss with his back against the willow's trunk, opened the letter-box, uncorked the ink bottle, and then sat for a minute with the goose-quill pen between his thumb and forefinger, trying to recapture the mood he had been feeling. His sword hilt was pressing into his side, so he unbuckled his belt and laid the sword on the moss beside his thigh. He looked at it there, and the sight of it, brass and deadly steel and black scabbard lying on the cool, delicate, innocent green moss, stirred the sentiment he had been suffering. Or had he been enjoying the sentiment? Ah, both suffering and enjoying. The joy of sadness.

Nothing but his love of womanly beauty had ever made Johnny Clark want to write poetry before; he had written quite a lot of it under that influence, later destroying it bit by bit as, with the clear vision of cooled passions, he had seen how bad it was. What he felt now, with no woman in sight and not even any particular one in mind, was so similar somehow—so bittersweet, so tinged with that tragic sense of short-lived beauty—that it made his heart ache and sing at once, as only woman ever had done before.

He twiddled the goose-quill and looked about for inspiration. Beyond the drooping, silhouetted fringe of the willow branches, up the meadow to his right, the neat rows of little white officers' tents blazed against the dark green grass. Further to his right, stacked muskets stood in rows like sheaves in the field. At his left, under the very roots of his willow, flowed the clear, lazy green water of the Brandywine, whose name was poetry to him. He remembered his mother's old story about Grandpapa and Grandmama Rogers, and their willow tree by another river, and the whippoorwill calls. Oh, yes! he thought. And now they're dead.

Upstream near Chadd's Ford he could see the fieldstone walls and mossy roof of the house where the elegant Marquis de Lafayette, Washington's newly imported French major-general, made his headquarters. The Marquis was a romantic and graceful figure, whose soulful and idealistic eyes—Johnny had looked into them briefly once while the Marquis was inspecting the Regiment—gave him, too, that same tragical air: the vulnerability of a flower; green moss with a sword on it, Johnny thought now. From a few yards downstream came the murmurs, laughter, and splashings of dozens of soldiers bathing their whitenesses in the green creek.

Like a ritual cleansing as they prepare themselves to die, he thought, suddenly flooded again with that chivalric sense of pity and pride. Now again he almost touched the quill to paper . . . but paused again. Somewhere out of sight, caissons were trundling along a road; somewhere a horse whinnied; somewhere the round, deep voice of a sergeant was chanting drill commands; elsewhere axes rang with the building of fortifications. The grass and woods sloping up from the opposite shore of the Brandywine were hazed by the sunny smoke of cookfires.

Tomorrow it may be the smoke of gunpowder, he thought. Sir William Howe had landed a reported 16,000 British troops at Chesapeake Bay for a march against Philadelphia, the seat of Congress, and now, here, on the eastern bank of the Brandywine, the Continentals were digging in to lie in wait for him.

Washington's army was in high morale again, confident, its ranks swelled by thousands of enlistments since his desperate and brilliant invasion of New Jersey last Christmas, a triumph when he had been thought vanquished.

Johnny had come with Brother Jonathan and Bill Croghan

after their convalescent leave, and had received his lieutenant's commission in March. They had been in Maryland and Pennsylvania ever since. Johnny had seen no action yet, and he had suffered severely from the eternal lack of privacy and the absence of women. But the spring and summer bivouacs had been pleasant enough; there was something undeniably grand and heartening about the brotherhood of officers and soldiers in an army that felt it had God on its side of the question. This was enough to overbalance the boredom and the miseries of army life: the lice, the fleas, the flies, the rats, the mosquitoes, the irregular and sometimes repugnant rations, the sweaty marches, the long, unexplained waits for news or orders, the frightful rumors, the politicking of staff officers fighting each other for advantages like crayfish in a bucket.

No: the comradeship of brave men, the heartening but slightly scary novelty of being a people suddenly without a king, the thrilling sight of a brand-new thirteen-starred flag, that occasional glimpse of the bold, durable, solid, somber Virginian who was their beloved commander-in-chief—in all these sights and feelings was a poignant sense of unity, that same holy Crusader sense he had enjoyed two years ago on the road to Williamsburg as an eighteen-year-old militiaman in a hunting shirt. But now the sense of it was a hundred times more grand and holy, probably because death or defeat were so much more likely than they had been then.

Sixteen thousand enemy! And sure to be here tomorrow!

His heart was slamming. He looked down into the limpid, slow water of the creek and wondered if he would be as ready to die tomorrow as he was today. Then he put the quill-point in the ink bottle and wrote the line that was in his head:

"O green and peaceful Brandywine, within thy verdant banks"

What he wanted to speak of now was the blood that surely would color it tomorrow. But the only words he could think of to rhyme with "banks" were "thanks" and "ranks." And, with a sudden sense of embarrassment, he scratched out his opening line, crosshatching over it until it was definitely unreadable, and started anew an inch farther down:

Dear Fath^r:
We're laying in a nice valley eight leagues from Phil^a

where Gen^s Washington and Nathan^l Green are in hopes of
Blocking Gen Howe who comes with a large army
   I am well as were Jonathan and Bill when last I saw
them, yesterday, and expect we will do ourselves credit
when the Brit. come, P^rhaps tomoro'. . . .

The thought came to him that he might never write another line of verse.

The thought came to him that he might never see another girl.

It started out so grand and clean and orderly and glorious the next morning, everything Johnny had expected of it, the stuff of epic poetry.

THE FIRST GLIMPSE OF THE ENEMY'S NEAT BLOOD-RED AND snow-white ranks moving over lush green morning-fresh grass on a far ridge beyond the Brandywine, glint of sunlight on brass, the buzzing, hushing, hivelike sound of tens of thousands of men preparing to meet in battle. The distant chatter of drums, rumbling of caisson wheels, faraway pulsebeats of marching feet, road dust drifting among trees, one's own heartbeat. And just below and before him, waiting: the dark blue long-tailed coats crisscrossed with the white shoulder straps of gun bag and bayonet scabbard, the Continentals, his Virginians, in black three-cornered hats, little regimental flags hanging limp in the sultry morning air, waiting behind the raw earth and stacked logs of breastworks, thousands of soldiers all alike, waiting, unspeaking, only their faces different: here a prominent nose in profile, there a snub nose; here a bronzed face lined with wrinkles and shaded with dark whisker stubble, there a smooth pink one, rosy cheeks soft with unshaven blond down; here a hard thin mouth with clenching jaw muscles, there a wet-lipped red mouth hanging open; blue eyes and brown eyes all watching that far hill on the other side of the Brandywine, watching still another line of red come over the green height, listening to the throbbing sibilance growing louder, hearing now and then a fragment of human voice, the eerie, wheezy whine of a bagpipe; then rattles, clankings, hoofbeats, shouted commands among the trees.

Then the long wait: sun on the back, sweat inside the wool coat, the mist being burned out of the valley, a glance now and then down the line toward the pinkish-orange regimental flag, a glimpse of Jonathan a hundred yards away walking down-slope from a cluster of officers. Above and beyond, a column of American cavalry was cantering northward, behind it, in its dust, a bristle of bayonets, as if half the army were going away on the road among the trees toward the forks of the Brandywine. The very air was dense, as if compressed between the two armies. And the beautiful, sad inevitability of it! Johnny Clark felt as if the moment were itself a great wordless poem, the tension before the stroke, so grand and clean and orderly and glorious it was, more than he had dreamed, even.

But then when the British artillery erupted across the creek, blossoms of blue-white smoke, deafening waves of concussion, the ground shaking and bucking, the air full of clods and sod and splinters, then there was no more glory or order, and it was all very local and dirty and confused. His mouth was full of dirt. Someone's hand bounced on the ground and lay there, wrist-bones sticking out of the red flesh. A three-cornered hat fell from the sky, now a blazing-white sky raining bits of wood and dirt and metal and cloth and pieces of men.

Bleeding from the nose and spitting out dirt then, Johnny found himself moving among his men in the shambles behind the breastworks, thinking most of them were dead because they were curled up, face down, and then he saw that they were not dead but cringing, trembling, some with their breeches all beshit from fear, while the ground and the breastworks jerked and the gun-thunder pounded on and on. Then in a red-misted dream of shame and fury he found himself grabbing men by their collars and their pigtails and making them stand up and take their weapons, cursing them for snivelers and tuck-tail hounds, whacking some across their backs with the flat of his saber blade. One trembling, curled-up man just would not get up, and when Johnny yanked him up by sheer force the man stood staring with pain and hatred, his chin blown away, shattered teeth-roots and smashed jawbone jutting white through the blood-ooze of his mouth, and Johnny wanted to cry an apology, but did not.

They were all on their feet eventually, not cringing anymore, but standing and waiting for the attack, one and another now and then being decapitated by a ball or blinded by splinters or grapeshot, men dead and ruined who might have been all right yet, had it not been Lieutenant Johnny Clark's duty as an officer to make them stand ready.

And Johnny stood and clenched his teeth and wept tears of disillusionment, because that imagined epic poetry of battle did not exist after all. Now it seemed not a glorious and knightly art, but simply a sickening science of shredding flesh and blasting bone to smithereens, all in the name of some abstract notion

Patrick Henry yelled about in Assembly and Thomas Paine wrote about in pamphlets.

One hundred yards up the line, Major Jonathan Clark was smoking his clay pipe, watching the bombardment, and thinking he should trot down the front to see how young Brother Johnny was doing with his first day of war, when word came down the line to all the company commanders that General Greene would cross the Brandywine at Chadd's Ford and attack the British flank there. Light knapsacks and fixed bayonets. Orders for each regiment would be down momentarily.

Well, then. There'd be no time to visit Johnny. Jonathan dipped his head at the sound of a whistling shell, tapped the dottle out of his pipe while dirt and gravel rained on his hat, then moved down the line at a crouch getting his men ready to march. After Charles Town, he felt familiar with artillery; it had lost some of its terrors for him. Of course, one still had to respect it. A man would have to be a fool not to.

But there was a new and dreadful unknown right before him now; it was said to be the supreme test of any soldier's mettle:

A bayonet charge.

As he went down the line he looked at bayonets and thought. He looked at the long, grooved spikes of steel and thought what they were for. None of his men had ever used a bayonet for its intended purpose, as it had not been that kind of a war so far. It had instead been a marching, waiting war and now and then a shooting and sniping war. Most of the men had used their bayonets only as spits on which to cook meat over campfires—on those rare occasions when there had been meat.

But the British, he was thinking now as he looked at these lethal steel spikes. They're said to be the very masters of the bayonet. It was said that the British generals had such faith in cold steel that they often ordered their Redcoats to attack with unloaded muskets. Cold steel only. Generals who ordered such attacks were praised for their boldness of spirit—although the generals themselves did not do any charging with bayonets.

God have mercy on us all, Jonathan thought. Especially watch over dear Brother Johnny and my friend Bill.

IT WAS MIDDAY NOW AND A WHOLE DIVISION OF VIRGINIANS was running northward along a dusty road, gasping in the heat, stumbling. Johnny Clark was almost strangling in dust and his lungs were afire.

An hour before, they had been formed up on the east bank of the Brandywine, ready to cross at Chadd's Ford and go against he British with bayonets. But then a courier had arrived from General Washington, and the whole thing had changed.

A huge force of Redcoats and Hessians, under Lord Cornwallis's banner, had suddenly appeared on the Continentals' right flank, near the forks of the Brandywine four miles to the north; they had hit General Sullivan's troops and were rolling them backward.

And so now Greene's Virginians, instead of attacking across the river, were running up the zigzagging roads to reinforce Sullivan. And it was a run of four miles.

Gasping with exhaustion, sweat-soaked, they were at last led off the road and formed hastily into a long rank on a forested hilltop. Beyond the trees and below the hill, musketfire sputtered and cannon thundered. Off to the right, as the troops mopped their brows and regained their wind, Johnny could see General Greene holding a hasty council with the field officers. It all seemed so frantic, so desperate. Johnny felt a sense of doom.

GENERAL MUHLENBERG SALUTED GENERAL GREENE AND then spurred his horse down to a knot of officers near the flag of the 8th Virginia. He talked rapidly to them while pointing toward the roar of the invisible battle. Soon Jonathan came trotting along from company to company, stopping at each one and talking fast.

"Hey, old Johnny," he cried, running up and grabbing him by the bicep, grinning through the dust that was caked on his sweaty face. "Here's what. Sullivan's troops likely will fall back right through here. We open and let 'em through. Then when the lobsterbacks come up the hill, we meet 'em with massed volleys and bayonets. Got that, brother mine?"

"Plain as day."

"It'll be a tangle," Jonathan said in a tight voice with a hard squeeze on Johnny's arm. "Don't forget to pray for me, and I'll do likewise for you."

And then he was gone.

AND NOW SULLIVAN'S RETREATING TROOPS WERE APPEARING on the meadows below in a commotion of shouting and shooting and disorderly running. Officers were riding back and forth in haste and confusion, waving their swords and shouting unintelligible commands, which sounded more like pleas. Some of the retreating men were running pell-mell across the meadows, not even looking back; some were hesitating and looking for their leaders; some were stopping to kneel and fire their guns back

183

toward the woods before they came on. Some limped along, some were carrying wounded.

Johnny dressed his ranks and had his men look to their flint locks. Many swigged from their canteens as they waited. "All right, then, all right!" Johnny shouted, too nervous to be still. "When those Redcoats get here, they'll think they've stepped into hell by mistake, hey? Stand your ground!"

Now the retreating troops, straining for breath, came straggling into view over the brow of the hill, heads wobbling, and strange, poignant looks of surprise came onto the faces of some of them when they saw the long ranks of Virginians standing there waiting. They passed among the Virginians and went into the woods behind them. Down on the meadow now, tight, precise, rectangular companies of British infantry were coming, bayonets leveled, each company followed by its drummer; white leggings rose and fell in unison as they came over the bright grass, stepping over bodies, flowing around shattered gun wheels and dead horses, coming on inexorably.

Now a bugle sounded, and General Muhlenberg rode downward with his sword pointing toward the enemy. And the Virginians, still not recovered from their long run, moved forward in neat ranks over the brow of the hill and started down the slope. The first ranks of Redcoats now were a hundred yards down-slope, climbing steadily.

The command came down the line to halt and deliver fire. "First rank," Johnny shouted, "kneel and aim." They knelt. "Fire!" Their muskets sputtered and crashed, and he saw several Redcoats stagger and fall. "Reload! Second rank, stand and fire!" Another crackling volley, and more Englishmen sagged and fell and their comrades closed ranks around them and kept coming on. "Second rank, kneel and load, third rank stand and aim. Fire!" More Redcoats tumbled. But the companies came on and the distance was closing, and there were too many of them to kill with volleys of bullets. Now a bugle played the charge, and Johnny bellowed, as if these would be his last words, his voice breaking: "Let's go!" and led them at a run down the slope toward the advancing scarlet line. They ran with that untidy variety of noises running infantry make: bullet bags jouncing and rattling, breath wheezing, cloth swishing, muskets rattling, canteens clunking, shoes thumping, men grunting and farting. The air was hazy with powder smoke. Other companies were running ahead, to the right, the white Xs across their backs bobbing as they jogged downhill in the eye-blurring smoke. Men were straggling and stumbling, the lines in poor array; it was a sloppy charge. And now there was nothing between Johnny's company and the enemy; it was as if an icy hand had gripped his hot, pounding heart when he really began to see them, see their faces forty feet away. It was a veritable wall of grim-faced human beings, their glinting bayonets leveled at waist height, dense as fence pickets, their odd, erect black hats making them look tall as giants—but their faces were the faces of *people*: pugnacious, grim, half-scared, perhaps, but determined and angry.

Somehow it was not just a dreadful phalanx of marching mechanisms now, nor was it a league of granite Romans, but mortal *people*; and the Virginians, seeing vulnerable faces, began howling like wolves and Indians and hurled themselves the last few feet onto the enemy line.

The two fronts crashed together in a din of brutal noises: grunts, howls, and screams, steel clashing on steel, cloth ripping, metal crunching on bone and cartilage, metal whacking on wood. The Virginians were past the control of commands now; and that deep part of them that had always been Indian fighter, hunter, barnyard brawler and shivaree roughneck, took over their desperate souls. They bared their teeth, used their guns like spears and clubs and quarterstaffs, crouched and pounced, choked, gouged, and bit their way past the bayonets and into the red ranks. With a hum of tension in his throat, Johnny waded in, slashing and hacking with his saber at flesh, brass, wood, and steel. A bayonet punched through his clothes and scraped past his ribs; with his lower lip bitten between his teeth he hacked at the Englishman holding it until, bathing his hands and face in hot blood, the Englishman yielded and sank down and the bayonet fell out of Johnny's clothes. Then came another bayonet, jabbing toward his eyes; he caught the steel in his left hand, twisting it aside and down with all his might. This Englishman was strong, with a ruddy, heavy-jowled workingman's face and light blue, wide-open eyes, and he nearly lifted Johnny off the ground as he strained with both arms on the musket. Johnny stared into the light blue eyes, cocked his sword arm, and thrust the blade in under the Englishman's ribs.

Now it was a deadly Donnybrook Fair here in this corner of the battlefield. The sweeping designs of generals were forgotten; each man was simply striving at each moment to murder another man before that man could murder him. A Virginian lay on the bloody grass with a bayonet through his groin, trying to throttle the Redcoat who leaned over him. Another Virginian, eyes nearly popping out of his head, stood wrestling with a British lieutenant, twisting his sword away with one hand while thumb-gouging his eye out with the other. Another Virginian had produced a non-regulation tomahawk from an underarm sheath and was splitting British skulls with sickening wet *whacks*.

Johnny was too busy fighting to give any orders, and there were no orders anyway that would have had any effect, unless he had screamed, *Kill!* And that order would have been unnecessary.

THERE WERE SEVERAL SUCH BRAWLS BEING FOUGHT ALONG this sector now. Not all the American companies were fighting so fiercely. Some had been scattered and put to flight by the British charge; others had been simply overrun by it, stabbed and trampled to the last man.

One melee was going on under the flag of the 8th Virginia. Jonathan Clark chopped off the left hand of a British grenadier with a mighty swishing saber stroke, and the same stroke laid open the thigh of one of his own sergeants, who was fighting alongside him. The fighting quarters were too close. The ranks were coagulating into mobs: dense masses of contorted faces, straining limbs, jabbing steel, point-blank pistol shots, knife fights and fist fights. A six-foot British soldier jerked his bayonet out of the ribs of a Virginian, stepped over the body, and ran with his bloody spike aimed at the youth who carried the regimental banner. The boy saw him coming, lowered the pole, and impaled the Redcoat with the brass spear on its end. Blood spurted onto the pink silk as the Englishman fell, his weight snapping the slender pole. But while the young flag-bearer was trying to extricate the banner staff from the Englishman's writhing body, he was clubbed to death by another Redcoat.

YARD BY YARD NOW, THE AMERICANS WERE BEING FORCED back up the hill by wave upon wave of English companies. Some of the enemy ranks now trotting forward out of the woods wore blue coats, red breeches, and red, high-pointed hats. It was a moment before Jonathan realized that he was seeing Hessians. Cornwallis had German mercenaries, and these were coming now, it seemed, by the thousands, from some inexhaustible Germanic reserve in the depth of the woods. Some of the Germans in the 8th Virginia now were hearing the German commands coming from the enemy's side; their faces went strange, but they kept fighting as they had been. And the enemy kept materializing in the shadows of the trees, then emerging into the smoky, bright sunglow of the meadow battlefield, their drummers rattling away incessantly.

The Virginians, borne back and back, their clothes tattered, hands bloodied, were beginning to glance around in desperation for their officers now. Their murderous passions were growing exhausted, and they needed guidance now, some order that would recombine their individual desperations into a common will. Each had been alone in hell fighting those countless red demons for as long as he could stand it. Now they needed their comrades; they needed to feel their fellows shoulder to shoulder with them again, because there were too many red demons, too many bayonets poking at them like pitchforks.

Jonathan was shouting, trying to rally his companies. But always, just down the slope, was that oncoming wall of stolid, clean-shaven, well-fed British faces, that picket fence of bayonets, the massed crimson of uniforms.

B'God but they're brave, he thought, and with a rush of admiration he thought, even in this desperate and murderous moment, he thought how fine a thing it was to have been born an Englishman.

THE VIRGINIANS THUS FOUGHT AND FELL BACK, FOUGHT and fell back, delaying the British, allowing Sullivan's wounded and shattered force to retreat. Cornwallis's infantry kept coming, British and Hessians. The retreat was in the direction of the hamlet of Dilworth. Late in the afternoon the Virginians crossed through a draw near that village, regrouped still again, turned and set up another defensive line. Cannon came rolling up soon, pulled by lathered, wild-eyed horses nearly dead of overwork; the cannon were set up covering the defilade. Here, spewing grapeshot, they stalled the oncoming Redcoats for a bit, while General Greene conferred quickly with field officers in a farmhouse beside the Dilworth Road. Jonathan watched Greene limp to and fro on his bad knee. Greene was as good a Yankee as Jonathan had ever seen, a Rhode Island blacksmith's son, a private risen to general on his merits.

"My gentlemen," he began, "due to a great cleverness today on the part of General Howe, we're in an unfortunate situation. Cornwallis made a feint this morning that caused us to divide our forces in the face of a superior force. Due to that, our army is now in a general retreat, in the direction of Chester Town. We have the honor, sirs, of guarding the rear." He paused a moment and looked at their faces. "This is an honor fraught with hazard, certainly. But it's our opportunity to prevent defeat from becoming disaster. A very great honor, it is.

"Your boys have had quite a day already, I know well. But if

187

they keep Cornwallis delayed here for a while longer, they'll have allowed the army to withdraw in an orderly way, not in a rout, and will have done perhaps the best service of the day. Here, sirs, are the specifics, and here's what we'll be required to do."

DELAY A WHILE LONGER, JONATHAN THOUGHT AS HE RE-turned to the 8th Virginia. Retreat. Philadelphia's lost after to-day. He felt exhausted, heavy-hearted.

Cannonades were still crashing along this front, and miles to the southwest, where this hellish day had begun, an eternity ago, it seemed, artillery still rumbled like a thunderstorm.

He found Brother Johnny still alive, though limping and rag-ged. Johnny had no visible wound, but somehow had strained his thigh during the hand-to-hand fighting; he could not really remember where or how. Jonathan told Johnny what had come of the council in the farmhouse, and they parted once again. English cannonballs were whickering through the trees now, bringing down showers of splinters and bark, and the drums of the British brigades were coming closer and closer. The Virgin-ians braced themselves to try once again to slow down Corn-wallis's inexorable advance.

AND THUS THE SUN WENT DOWN OVER THE BEAUTIFUL Brandywine Valley, a sun dimmed to brick-red by the haze of powdersmoke and dust. At dark the shooting ceased, and Gen-eral Greene at last led his rear guard down the road toward Chester Town, their ears ringing in the silence.

THE ROAD OF RETREAT WAS CLOGGED WITH EXHAUSTED IN-fantrymen, with cannon, with pack horses, with wagons and lit-ters carrying wounded men. The troops slogged and limped along the Chester Road, dark shapes on the starlit roadway. Their bandages, the belted Xs across their backs, were ghostly pale in the dark. Shouts for a clear road would come from be-hind; soldiers would curse and groan and edge into the roadside weeds. Troops of cavalry or dragoons would trot past, leather creaking, spurs and weapons clinking and rattling, horses blow-ing, leaving the smell of horse sweat in the air and dung on the road. More shouts, more hoofbeats, and the jingle of harness and rumble of wooden carriages and iron-rimmed wheels, and artillery caissons would rumble by up the road, their drivers call-ing ahead for clear highway. And after all this had passed, the Virginians came along. Behind them the road was empty.

The refugee army crossed Chester Bridge long after nightfall in the flickering light of torches. The young Marquis de Lafayette was in command of the contingent guarding the bridge. His face was specter-pale in the torchlight as he sat on his warhorse and looked down at the passing troops. Johnny's gaze slid down from the aristocratic face and saw linen bandages from Lafayette's hip to calf, sopping crimson from a wound. It was no wonder he was pale. Johnny tipped his hat as he limped by, and the Marquis, his big feminine-looking eyes glinting, returned the gesture. It had been his first battle, too.

Beyond the Chester Bridge the defeated army halted to make a tentless camp under the stars, and Johnny sat with a group of officers by a small fire on a meadow slope. Bill Croghan had lain back on the ground with a coat over him and fallen into a profound sleep. One of the officers was a New Jersey man, a major who had fought at White Plains in the disastrous autumn of '76, and he was complaining about the commander-in-chief.

"A farmer, that's all he is. A damned Virginia farmer who thinks as slow as the seasons turn!"

"We're farmers, too," Jonathan said softly. "Virginia farmers, like him."

The major was quiet for a while, appraising Jonathan's tone. Then he resumed. "His Excellency has fine days now and then. Like at Trenton and the like. But then he makes blunders. Like today."

"Anyone makes blunders," Jonathan said.

"Perhaps so. But today our farmer-in-chief was monumentally stupid. He divides us, caught by a trick, so Cornwallis comes around on our rear with his six thousand or so. That's what undone us today. You saw it."

It seemed that what the major was saying was true. Johnny could remember seeing the cavalry and infantry going up the river that morning.

"And so, what's he cost us, our brilliant farmer-in-chief?" the major went on in his rankling tone. "We seem to muster up this evening about a thousand short, I hear, and it looks like to me that half the rest of us are leakin' blood. And Philadelphia's lost for certain, I'd say. Well, sirs, it's my feeling, the way to lose a war is, put a Virginia farmer in charge."

"Aye, well." Jonathan tapped out his pipe on his bootheel, and seemed to enlarge in the dim fireglow. "You're quite entitled to squawk about Virginia farmers, sir. But in Virginia we farmers have a sport with squawkers. First, we hang them up by their heels. Then we grease them up and yank their heads off."

The major from New Jersey, after a moment of silence, rose, excused himself, and went away muttering, and several officers of the 8th Virginia laughed him away.

"It's some'at true, though, isn't it?" Johnny asked confidentially when he was at last alone with Jonathan, "that there do be brighter generals?"

Jonathan's strong arm snaked across and settled on his shoulders. "I'll ask'ee to recollect somethin' Ma always would say. Remember," he went on in that deep, calming voice of his, "how she'd say, 'I'll vow I've never had a day I didn't make at least one mistake in bringin' you all up—but ye haven't thrown me out yet, so I must be doing fair in general.' Remember her saying that?"

Johnny grinned. He could remember how she'd sound when she said it: with a little upturned snap of pride at the end.

"Anyway," Jonathan said, "General Washington's made some mistakes. But I doubt there's another soul on this continent could keep this army together."

"No, I guess not," Johnny said after a while. "Less they'd make Ma commander-in-chief."

And they pounded each other on the back, these Clark boys, raising a sound that was most rare in the beaten American army that night:

Laughter.

"HOLY GODLY, WHAT FUN THAT SPYIN' BE!" BENJAMIN LINN slapped his thigh and set down the rum cup, nodding to it for a refill, and George poured, with a grin.

"Didn't I say it would be?"

"Aye, Mister Clark, ye did, and right y'were as usual. Heh!"

"That Sewer de Roachblob," brayed Sam Moore. That had become their contemptuous pronunciation of the name of Sieur de Rocheblave, commandant at Kaskaskia. "What a gull he was! He just swallered whole that bag o' malarkey we give 'im. He's not a half as shrewd as he says he is." Moore sipped from his cup and brushed some burrs from his leggings, then looked grinning up at George, who had opened a pocket-sized notebook on the table to a blank page and now was trimming a fresh nib on the quill he had taken from his old hat. Outside the open door, the curious of Harrod's Town were loitering, excited about the mysterious return of the long-gone pair. It was rare for people to be gone from Harrod's Town that long and come back alive.

"Just start from the beginning," George said, "and talk, and then I'll throw ye questions I've got. Ben?"

190

"Well, sir, we snuck up to St. Louis first, like ye said do, then we got on board a bateau headed down to Kaskasky, so that when we got off there they'd believe our story that we'd been up th' Missouri trappin'. We acted s'prised there was a rebellion goin' on. Perty soon we got in t' see Roachblob, got in by sayin' we didn't believe it and wanted to hear it from a 'thority. We got in, hired on as meat-hunters for th' town."

"What's he like?" George asked.

"Blowed up like a bullfrog with 'imself. A haughty man, eh, Sam? He's Frenchy, but got King George stamped all over 'im. No slouch, I'll say that. He runs a right elegant militia."

"But more for love o' parade than fear of attack," interrupted Moore.

"Aye. Medoubt they could fight their way 'crost a boo-dwahr, but they're pretty dressed and jolly," Linn said; then he gave George a description of their fort and quarters, their numbers and their armaments and the cannon at the fort, the times and customs of the guard. "Likable rascals," Linn went on. "They're perty lukewarm on Britain, spite of Roachblob's haranguin'. So's most of the population. They're a lazy-loosy sort o' folk. They find British reg'lations perty stiff. But Roachblob's got a grip on 'em. Tells 'em us rebels is anything from cannibals on down to baby-rapers, an' tells 'em only King George can perteck 'em from us. He, he!"

"Do they believe 'im?"

"About half-believe, I think. They're a somewhat fraidy people, right, Sam? And we make 'em a right handy bogey, as they've never saw many of us Virginians to know how genteel and harmless we be."

George laughed, then he touched the quill to paper and asked, "British in the garrison?"

"Usually been a company of 'em at Kaskasky, but's all been called back to Canady."

"For how long?"

The men shrugged. "Till who knows?"

George nodded, and made some marks on the notebook page. "I know you're trail-weary, boys, so forgive me for keepin' you overlong, but I've been waiting quite a spell with a thousand questions about that place."

"Ask away, Major Clark," said Sam Moore, gurgling some more rum into his cup and settling forward with his elbows on the table. "It's a rare day when we'uns know more'n you do about anything, and we're enj'yin' it whilst we can!"

By midnight George had pumped their memories dry, getting

information from them that they'd hardly realized they had, and in his notebook was a clear enough picture of the Illinois Country outposts to convince him that he could surprise and occupy that territory with as few as five hundred men.

Now, he thought. All I need do is go to Governor Henry and persuade him to let me do it. I guess I can stop up this bedamned Indian war right at its source!

He thought of General Henry Hamilton at Detroit, on the far side of the chessboard, and he thought:

My move, Mister Scalp-Buyer.

10

GERMANTOWN, PENNSYLVANIA

October, 1777

JOHNNY CLARK STOOD IN THE WOODS WITH COLD OCTOBER fog on his face and tried to see a road, a landmark of any kind, but trees ten yards away were invisible. I might as well be a fish in a milkpail, he thought.

We're lost. Just lost.

Near him in the murk he could see three or four of his soldiers with their guns and bayonets, and just beyond them the red clothes and white underwear of the British prisoners they guarded. Elsewhere nearby he could hear the invisible presences of other companies: the knock of a scabbard or canteen against a gunstock, a throat-clearing, a *sniffle, hawk, spit*, a murmured complaint, a query. But they were invisible. Off in the distance, in a direction he presumed was southward, though it did not feel southward, there was a muffled sputtering of gunfire, and cannon were booming.

How can they even see what they're shooting at? he wondered.

It had all sounded so clever in the orders; it had all looked so neat on the maps, a plan so intricate and well conceived and daring that no one would have dared call Washington a dumb Virginia farmer again: four divisions marching all night southward down Skippack Road, parallel with the Schuylkill River, toward Germantown. Dividing before daylight into four columns. Bits of white paper pinned to their black hats so they could identify their compatriots in the dark. Attack through and around Germantown with bayonets fixed and catch Howe's whole army in its blankets before reveille. Oh, it would have been diabolically clever, it would have been brilliant. But then the day had dawned like this: in a milky fog.

The 8th Virginia had practically walked over this unit of British Guards, had rousted them up half-dressed and herded them along like cattle, but to where? With no road to follow, creeping along over wet grass and among red-leafed autumn maples, over fences, around cribs, with no idea where the other columns were, unable even to find the town, General Greene's division was astray in a muffled blankness and now there was gunfire, which meant the surprise was lost.

After Brandywine, the British had occupied Philadelphia; Congress had fled to Lancaster. Washington had hoped, by surprising Howe here, to recover Philadelphia. And it might have worked, Johnny thought bitterly, but for this damnable unexpectable fog.

It might yet, though, he thought. The gunfire in the distance was increasing to a steady, crackling roar. Maybe, he thought, maybe this fog isn't everywhere, maybe the other columns found Howe's camp and surprised him enough.

A major materialized out of the fog. "This way," he said. "I've found a road."

"Come on, lads," Johnny said. "Herd those lobsterbacks along."

They moved off now, following the major, who picked his way along so hesitantly, stopping and veering and thinking, that he inspired more rueful headshakes than confidence.

They got onto the road within five minutes, and were walking it seemed from nowhere to nowhere on ten yards of packed dirt roadway with grass and brown weeds and fallen leaves at each side and then that confounding circumference of fog. As they moved along, the din of shouting and gunfire grew louder and louder before them. Off to the left front, a crash and a flare of yellow in the fog showed where a cannon was being fired. They could smell gunpowder smoke now; it seemed to diffuse everywhere in the fog; it stank in the nostrils and stung in the eyes.

"Wait," the major said, and strode off toward the cannon.

"Company, halt."

"Halt."

"Halt."

The command went back into the fog.

Johnny stood looking at his troops with weariness and pity. Half of the men were barefooted; some had wound their feet with strips of strouding. Some had footless stockings clinging to their calves. One tall boy wore a sleeveless uniform coat from which both long, bare arms protruded, and his hat perched atop a filthy mass of head bandages, brown with old blood. Many of the men had no coats or hats. The garments of some still showed the rips and rents that they had sustained weeks ago in the hand-to-hand battle at Brandywine. There seemed to be no such thing as a quartermaster in Washington's army this fall.

Someone had fashioned a new regimental flag from a piece of buff trouser cloth and inked the words VIII VIRGA. on it. It now hung on an ash pole, and he gazed at it. The original probably still was lying there in the battlefield at Brandywine, stained by British and American blood, and the thought haunted him like a poem of pathos.

The invisible commotion ahead went on unabated. Vaguely, through the fog and smoke, Johnny thought he could discern the rectangular form of a large building. So much shooting and shouting was coming from there that he presumed it must be a fortified house, under attack.

A musketball hummed past his nose, and a dozen shots flashed in the fog ten yards away. Before Johnny could move, a body of men came charging out of the fog from that direction with their bayonets leveled, bellowing murder, and the two companies were but twenty feet from clashing before the attackers saw that these were Americans like themselves, and hauled up.

"By heaven, forgive me," their lieutenant implored, coming ashen-faced toward Johnny. "I saw those red coats," he explained, nodding toward the prisoners.

This turned out to be a company of Marylanders, and was, like everybody else, it seemed, lost. "I saw a damned crow fly by upside down, he was so lost," the Marylander tried to joke. "I . . ." The lieutenant was looking over Johnny's shoulder. His eyes bulged. "Oh, thunder," he muttered. Johnny turned to look.

The entire fog bank behind him seemed to be turning pink, then deepening to scarlet. It was a line of advancing British infantry, looking as long as a regiment, treading out of the haze with bayonets at the ready. Johnny looked to the other side of the road, as a way to retreat; his men were babbling excitedly. From that side of the road came the sounds of horse, and a long line of British cavalry materialized, just then seeing the ragged Continentals and their prisoners in the road and turning guns on them. The prisoners cheered and laughed.

There was nowhere to go. A youthful British officer, handsome but for his sleep-puffy eyes, walked close to the two American lieutenants and stopped, clicking his heels once.

"I presume," he said, "you're discreet enough to give me your swords, gentlemen, and order your men to ground their arms?"

It was such a strange, absurd moment. Here Johnny Clark stood, in a hazy world no more than thirty yards around, while cannon and musketry roared unseen somewhere outside its misty horizons, and he was being addressed politely in cultivated English by a most agreeable young man who was his enemy. Somehow the whole matter of war seemed revealed as a game, and he was almost stupefied by a great sense of relief. Johnny had felt this way only once before: once when a young lady he'd loved, but disliked, had said she was tired of him. He told his men to lay down their muskets.

He turned his saber in his hand and presented it hilt-first to the smooth-cheeked Briton, who smiled.

"Thank you. And you." The Englishman took the Marylander's sword, too, bowed slightly, straightened up, and sighed, then rose on his toes two times. "Ehmm! I say. It's rather good to be alive, what?"

"So my mother always tells me," Johnny replied, "but then, 'twas she that put me into this lunatic world."

GOVERNOR'S PALACE,
WILLIAMSBURG, VIRGINIA

November, 1777

THE OTHER THREE AUGUST CONSPIRATORS WERE ALREADY IN Governor Henry's library when Thomas Jefferson arrived. In the years since George had seen him, Jefferson had acquired some markings of maturity: a few gray hairs among his crisp waves of red, and tired bluish swellings under his eyes. But at thirty-four he had not lost that vaguely distracted look of boyish wonderment. There's still a thousand things at once a-workin' in that head of his, George thought.

Jefferson walked to him, smiling, his woolen clothes as always a bit ill-fitting, his stride purposeful but a little ungainly, and George was so happy to see him that he had an impulse to give him a genuine frontier bear-hug. But not wanting to startle him out of his celestial wits, he instead just extended his hand.

"George. By Jove, you're fit. I've not felt so hard a hand sinc my father's."

"And I take the hand that penned our independence, and I'r honored, sir."

Governor Henry came close and took Jefferson's hand, an tilted his head toward George. "Our young friend here's bee doing some headwork on a scale reminds me o' yours, Tom He's about convinced me he can do what all the western com manders haven't been able to do: shut our back door on th British."

"He can," piped in George Mason from where he sat, gout ridden, in a hearthside chair.

"I'll not be surprised," Jefferson said. "I know this fellow."

"What I know," said Henry, "is that he traipses in from th hinterland every fall, all covered with burrs and bear sweat, witl a list of wondrous outrageous demands to embarrass the Assem bly and the Executive with. You can count on him, like th leaves turning red." George glanced aside at Henry from unde an arched eyebrow and was glad to see that he was smiling as h said this. "I really believe he can do it, the way he's worked i up," Henry went on. "I mean to say, it'll strike you as a strateg of the absurd on first hearing, but there's not a detail I can se he's left to chance. His biggest obstacle I reckon on is not th enemy at all, but getting it past the short thinkers in the Assem bly. It calls for a lot of authority granted on the sly, seems t me."

"I'm intrigued already," said Jefferson, going toward a chai and pulling George after him by a wrist. "Enlighten me, neigh bor." They sat down next to Dr. Mason, George's old mentor

George told him what his spies Linn and Moore had learned He quickly outlined the military stores and advantages existing a Kaskaskia, Cahokia, and Vincennes, and Rocheblave's role ii the incitement of Indian atrocities. And then he unveiled, in a tight, swift, positive narrative, his audacious proposal.

"I declare with no doubt," George began, jabbing a stiff fore finger into his palm, "that I can secure that whole territory nortl of the Ohio, stop the Indian raids coming from there, block u] the Western Rivers against British traffic, and, in fact, sir, foi the entire British design on our western frontier, inside of three months—with but one regiment of Virginians." Jefferson's rec eyebrows lifted and his eyes gleamed. George Mason nudged th governor with his elbow. "One regiment," George went on, stil jabbing with that long, hard forefinger, "and militia, I mean; I'n quite aware no Regular Army can be spared." He was headin;

off all possible objections, having heard them already in his long, private sessions with Governor Henry. "I would intend to float my regiment down the Ohio to Kentuck. Discipline 'em there. Boat on down to Illinois where Fort Massac used to be, and, to avoid patrols on the Mississip, go over the prairie to Kaskaskia. Surprise that place by night and get into the fort. They scarcely bother to guard it. Then gain Cahokia right after, the same way. Then . . . well, sir, then I should start to council with the savages—who would by then damn well listen to the Rebels, wouldn't they?—and get them neutral. Then I'd build a strong fort at the Ohio's mouth, and arm it with the cannon from Kaskaskia. D'you see a flaw thus far, Tom? Surprise! That's the trick! The advantage o' surprise is worth a regiment. D'ye see? A coup like this is a bargain! Not to do it will mean a fortune for western defense next season—*if* it could be defended at all, by then."

Jefferson was trying to frown, to pose any possible objection to this thousand-mile foray into the wilderness. "What if . . . what if something failed? It sounds workable—nay, bedazzling—but—"

"We could take refuge on the Spanish side of the Mississippi, if we got outnumbered or something. Spain's neutral, o' course, but not at all kindly disposed to the British. A main thing I'd do is gain the loyalty of the French who inhabit those places, once I'm among 'em. They're just plain galled by the British rule."

Jefferson sat sipping a glass of port and pondering, gazing into the fireplace, and George remembered that night by the firelight in Harrod's Town eight months ago when this plan had first blossomed in his own solitary head.

"Cost," Jefferson began. "The state's purse is flat."

"Such men as I'll use cost but a fraction of what regular troops cost. They bring their own clothes and weapons and can range for weeks with what they carry on their backs. Hunt off the land and fight in the Indian mode. As special pay for the special hazards, I recommend we'd offer 'em what Kentuck's got aplenty: land."

Jefferson nodded over these persuasions. But then he said, "There's something bothers the lawyer in me, and likewise would bother the other lawyers in the Assembly: taking state militia out of the state. And the county lieutenants where you recruit, they're not going to like that either."

"Aye. That's another reason for secrecy."

"Ah. What?"

"The governor suggests I'd have a public set of orders, authorizing me to recruit just 'for the defense of Kentuck County.' That would forestall such objections, and hide our aims as well."

"Very shrewd indeed. But how do you explain it to these rangers of yours when you lead 'em off the edge of the world?" He smiled with raised eyebrows, sitting back and steepling his hands.

"However best I can when the time comes. By that time I reckon we'll all be pretty much of one mind and they'll be willing."

Mason actually gasped aloud in admiration of that statement. "Lord," he said, "give us *generals* who think that way!"

George's plan was convincing them all; he could see that. Patrick Henry winked at him once or twice to assure him how well he was doing.

George and Governor Henry shared a secret that they had not yet revealed even to these other conspirators. It was a part of George's plan—the ultimate end of it—and it was so audacious that George had hesitated to reveal it even to Patrick Henry in their first few meetings. George had feared that the mere mention of it would have killed the whole scheme because Henry would have thought him deluded. But in their last previous conference, George had revealed it to him: after taking the Illinois and Wabash forts, winning the alliance of the French, and neutralizing the Indians, George intended to sweep on up the Wabash, down the Maumee to Lake Erie, and seize the British western headquarters at Detroit, with General Henry Hamilton in it. He was sure he could do it, with his five hundred men, although conventional military opinion was that it would require an army of thousands to do that.

So he had at last broken it gently to Governor Henry, who had come to believe it could be done—if done in the guerrilla mode George had in mind. But neither of them had mentioned it to the others. Because now both of them wanted not to be thought daft.

George Rogers' eyes were glimmering with tears, and his clenched jaw muscles worked. George could barely see this, because his own vision was blurred with tears too. He said:

"If Joe'd only been able to keep up. But . . . Aah, what-ifs don't do any good."

"Never mind. You only guaranteed for him while he was in your sight. And 'twas he who wanted to go. I promised you I wouldn't grudge you." His hands came up, palms upward, and he shrugged, out of words, raising his eyebrows and looking down aside at the rug. George could not bear to look at his face. After an excruciating silence—even the Rogers children outside the room were being still—George Rogers said, "Tell me frankly: Is there any use o' hoping?"

"Frankly, there isn't. We can pray, though, as I've done a-plenty."

"You know the savages. What likely might they do to my boy?"

"If ye really want to hear it . . ."

"Aye."

"They take prisoners for two reasons. One, to adopt. Two, lately, to take to Detroit for bounty. The British buy prisoners from 'em." He didn't mention that they were also buying scalps.

"I've heard of . . . They . . . torture . . ."

"Don't think o' that." George had already thought of that enough. "If a Shawnee family's had a son killed—it's a pity how many sons they lose, their lives being what they are—the tribe's chief will give 'em a prisoner to replace him. Usually he has to run the gauntlet first. If he makes it, then the family can either adopt him or put him at the stake to revenge their loss." He thought momentarily of another Rogers who had burned at the stake, and wondered if his uncle was thinking that too. "Most usually, they'll adopt him, if he's brave."

"In that case, they would Joe."

"Aye. They sure would Joe."

"Now," George Rogers said, firming himself up, and George knew they were coming to the other difficult part. "Now, about Johnny." He clenched his teeth and took a deep breath, and said, "This seems like that same day all over, to me, does't to you?"

"It does."

"He wants to go out with you now." Johnny Rogers' enlistment in the Continental Army was up. He had spent a year tramping up and down the coast of Virginia and sitting in wait for British fleets that never came, and had been disillusioned by the futility of it, and now he was inflamed by George's new mission.

"Even more than Joe, I hoped you'd refuse to let 'im," George said.

"And I'd hoped you would."

But both knew Johnny Rogers would be an asset. Though they did not say this, Johnny was wiser and more able than Joe had been; if the family of George Rogers had a shining star in it, Johnny was it. And now he wanted to follow his Cousin George into that same hazardous wilderness that had swallowed Joe up so swiftly.

"I'll refuse to take 'im only if you'll refuse to let him come, Uncle. Ye know how I am about that. I can only give you the same guarantee I . . . I gave you on Joe."

"Once again, George, that's good enough for me."

If George's love and admiration for his uncle could have increased from what it always had been, it did so with those words.

11

CAROLINE COUNTY,
VIRGINIA
Thanksgiving Day, 1777

THAT YEAR THE CONGRESS DECLARED A THANKSGIVING DAY— as some joked, to give thanks that there still was a Congress.

George was at home, and the family was thankful for his presence, though it was debatable just how present he was, he was so absorbed in his great scheme. Half his soul was a thousand miles off in the West, and the other half was at Williamsburg, where his influential friends were trying to sneak his plan through the Privy Council without exposing it to debate.

Richard, now eighteen, was trying to get his father's permission to go with George out west. "His cousins go with 'im, why can't his own brother?" he would implore. But John Clark needed Dick and Edmund to help him tend the place, because of all the extra farming he was doing for the army. Billy, now seven, could drive a team and butcher an animal and tend a tobacco field, or do just about any man's work, but only on a wee scale, so John Clark could not let another grown son go off to war yet. "Next year, Dick," he finally promised with a sigh.

Edmund was fifteen now, a big redhead, quiet, kindly, solitary, and he wasn't talking war yet, because he really could see how his father needed help. "It's a good thing for the British Eddie can't go," George told Johnny Rogers, "as that lad can fairly shoot the toenail off a sky-high buzzard, and call which toenail before he shoots. Not to exaggerate but just a little." It was Edmund, in fact, who put the fowl on the table that

Thanksgiving Day; as usual he had ignored the turkey's big body and shot it between the eyes.

"Why tear up th' body meat," he'd shrug with a smile, "when nobody eats turkey head anyways?"

Lucy was still preoccupied with Bill Croghan, though she had not seen him for almost a year and did not have a good word to say about him. She had never forgiven him for calling her "Little Brother" the last Christmas. But she still had it in a secret place in her head under her fire-red curls that she was going to marry him when her age caught up with his, and her way of going about it was just to work quietly and diligently to get over her natural tomboyish traits, so that whenever he might next see her, he would not call her "Little Brother." As her mother confided to daughter Annie: "Lucy's like a caterpillar that's made up its mind to hurry up and be a butterfly. Ye want to tell th' poor thing it's not somethin' you work at, it just happens."

As for Annie, whom the brothers now liked to call "Madam Sheriff," she had to tell her mother, with an abashed flush, that her most recent sanguinity hadn't happened and she was probably going to have a third child come next year.

"Lord a God," her mother breathed. "You've still got one toddlin' and another not weaned! Don't you remember at all that advice I gave you?"

"Aye," Annie said, now with that old wistful smile of hers. "But Owen asked Dr. Campbell about that o' the nursing, and he told 'im 'twas but an old wives' tale."

"Old wives! Hmph! Well, I like that!"

Jonathan and Bill Croghan were not at home for the holiday. Both were in winter quarters with Washington's army in a place called Valley Forge in Pennsylvania. When they would write to the family, both would put their letters on the same sheet, paper being so scarce—as everything was.

Money was nearly useless in the Colonies by now, and even the tobacco certificates were terribly inflated, as Britain had shut the ports to trade. A pound of tea, if anyone could have found it, would have cost £10. On the Clark's Thanksgiving table, the teapot steamed with sassafras and herbs, and there was a pot of dandelion coffee. The Clarks had, with their usual self-reliance, adjusted bit by bit to the shortages, and anything they could not produce on their own plantation, they just considered it didn't exist. One of the severest shortages was salt. Cider vinegar from John Clark's apple orchard served in its place.

It was cold and raw and spitting snow outdoors, but inside it was close and warm and happy. George said a frontier-style

Grace over the table that was so amusing that Ann Rogers Clark meant to write it down in her little blank book, but was too busy, and its wording had evaporated from her mind before she had a chance to sit down with pen in hand.

Because it was a day of thanks, they gave no asking prayers. But in the small hours after everyone was bedded down, John and Ann Rogers Clark knelt on the floor side by side at the foot of their bed and asked for the deliverance of their son Johnny and nephew Joe Rogers. Johnny's whole company had vanished in the Battle of Germantown, and Jonathan had written that more than likely they had all been captured in that awful confusion. John Clark prayed aloud for him, and then they remained on their knees to have their own private words with God.

May his captors be humane, she prayed, as they must be, as Thou are the God of all us English peoples.

She thought momentarily of the High Church that had burned her ancestor at the stake, but put that out of her head quickly.

He's all sweet and dreamy down inside, she prayed. Let him not have to make himself cold and hard against ill use. Amen.

She lay on the pillow later with John Clark snoring beside her and turned her soul up toward Pennsylvania; she listened to her heart to get a sense of whether Johnny was alive. She listened to her heart and to her womb, and finally got the sense that he was alive somewhere up there. But she had too a heavy feeling of dread.

If he's alive, though, she thought, whatever his distress, being alive's the thing to be thankful for.

She heard Annie get up in the bedroom across the hall and tend to her crying baby boy Temple, and heard Annie and Owen talking low for a while, then there was silence again and Ann Rogers Clark went to sleep listening to the cold wind around the eaves.

NEW YORK HARBOR

Thanksgiving Day, 1777

IT WAS THE GRIMMEST, DARKEST, MOST OMINOUS SIGHT Johnny Clark had ever seen, that prison ship, and his soul sank a little deeper with every stroke of the oars that pulled him toward it.

The hulk lay there in the choppy cold water ahead, without

he masts or spars or even the flag that give a ship the look of life; t lay like an enormous floating coffin, between a harbor and a ky as somber as death. From somewhere forward on its deck, lack smoke rose and was whipped away into the snow by the aw channel wind.

The oars of the cutter rose and fell, rose and fell, and the side f the prison ship slowly loomed closer and higher. Johnny was ne of twenty prisoners being rowed out to the ship. The rest vere enlisted men, sitting in their thin and tattered clothes, hug-;ing their knees, their leg-irons hanging between their ankles. The eight rowers, dirty Brooklyn waterfront wretches, looked as f they could be Charon's own oarsmen. Two middle-aged Brit-sh soldiers with pistols and muskets stood over the prisoners, :loaks wrapped about their faces. The chubby British ensign in :harge of the rowboat stood beside Johnny, an arm over the iller, constantly running his tongue over his chapped lips.

As they drew near the hulk, two dark figures appeared at the ail above, their heads and shoulders visible; they seemed to be :arrying something heavy between them. Then two more ap-)eared, also carrying a burden. They moved to the head of a ;angway ladder, which slanted down the ship's side to a floating)latform alongside. There was a rowboat tied to that platform, vith four men in it.

Now the figures started down the gangway, and Johnny saw vhat they were carrying: man-size bundles wrapped in canvas.)ne carrier at the head and one at the feet of each bundle, they abored down the gangway and put the corpses down on the edge)f the platform. The men in the boat then lifted the bodies down nto their vessel while the carriers went back up the gangway. The rowboat cast off then and its oars started moving.

"Well, there's shore leave for two more Yankee Doodles," the 3ritish ensign said with a sharp, barking laugh. He shook his ead. "Take off two and put on twenty. Keep that up and she'll ;et pretty crowded, what?"

Johnny looked at the ensign with distaste. "You're a sorry oker," he said.

"Hey! I'm not joking. That's the only way I've ever seen any Yankee Doodles get off the *Jersey*." He waved to the rowers of he dead-boat as it passed close by, going shoreward. Then the utter tied up at the platform. The ship stank of decay and filth. Even the north wind knifing down off New York Harbor failed to)low the stench of the grave off the *Jersey*'s sides.

Johnny followed the ensign up the gangway first. The enlisted nen came dragging their rattling chains up after him, the armed guards following. Through the boarded-up gun ports Johnny seemed to hear a mournful murmur of voices. Or was it just the wind in his ears? Or his imagination?

He passed between sentries at the head of the gangway and stepped onto the deck. He glanced forward and aft while the ensign handed a packet of papers to a thick-bodied, broad-faced naval officer. The main deck, all worn, weather-grayed teak-wood, was an expanse of perhaps two hundred feet in length, wisps of snow-dust blowing along it. The vast wooden surface was interrupted only by sealed hatches, a capstan, and three huge stumps where the masts had been. The dark smoke he had seen was pouring from one small hatch forward. The only rigging was a tall derrick on the starboard side, supported by guy ropes that vibrated in the howling wind.

The ensign had turned his mocking face and was contemplating Johnny. Johnny said to him, "So this is what the Royal Navy smells like." And as the two officers' faces began to lengthen and darken with indignation, he added, "I'd say the whole ship is a poop deck."

The stout officer glowered at him. "You're not going to last long." Then, after staring malevolently at him for five seconds, he returned to his papers. "Clark, is it?"

Astern, rising ten feet above the main deck, was the quarter-deck, like a small fort or castle, separated from the main deck by barricades with firing loopholes. Atop this stood a small guard tent, shaking in the cold wind.

"Stand here, Leftenant," said the naval officer, who then ordered guards to take the chained prisoners forward. They went, scraping and rattling, abjectly. They did not turn to look at Johnny. He was not one of their officers. He had been separated long since from the rest of the men of his company, during weeks of being shuffled from one bleak prison compound to another.

"Now, Clark," the stout officer growled. "Follow me." He led toward a door through the barricade into the quarterdeck. Johnny took one look back, and the ensign tipped his hat to him, still smiling mockery, and called: "A Happy Thanksgiving to you, Yankee Doodle. Ha, ha! A happy one!"

Johnny paused there and looked past him. There was only the windswept deck, below which he knew not how many American soldiers were confined, and, all around, the iron-gray, white-capped waves racing by, lapping their cold tongues against the rotting hull, waters too cold and swift and wide for anyone to think of swimming, and in the distance, the low, dark shores of British-held New York and Long Island.

Johnny had a notion, almost a certainty, as he stepped into the fetid gloom of the quarterdeck and started down a steep companionway, that he would never leave this foul hulk until he was carried down the gangplank in a canvas shroud.

VALLEY FORGE, PENNSYLVANIA
Thanksgiving Day, 1777

"OH, BUT I'M THANKFUL FOR IT!" A PRIVATE EXCLAIMED, LICKING his lips, rolling his eyes and rubbing his flat belly as he held his cup over the kettle. The mess-man flobbed a spoonful of overcooked gray-brown rice into the cup and the soldier moved a step along the plank table. He stopped and licked his lips comically again as another mess-man dribbled a teaspoon of vinegar over the rice. "A drop more?" he coaxed. The mess-man shook his head.

The Thanksgiving Day feast was a half a gill of rice and a spoonful of vinegar for each man and officer. Jonathan Clark watched the soldier move away. The soldier's bare feet tracked mud through the snow as he walked to a log and sat down with others to eat. Jonathan smiled at his soldiers' jests about the holiday feast, and looked piteously on those who were too torpid, tired, or sick even to joke. On this ration they were expected not just to keep their half-naked bodies and discouraged souls together, but also to labor like beavers building log huts for their winter quarters. It was only the hard labor that kept them from chilling from exposure. But how long, he wondered, can men do hard labor on a blob of rice or a fistful of fire-cake a day? The British had foraged the countryside clean in the autumn, taking virtually every last pig, cow, or goose and every bit of harvest, and all the wagons in the vicinity, before settling down for a fat and gala winter in Philadelphia. Thus, getting even a little of anything every day for his nine thousand soldiers, let alone *enough* of anything, was General Washington's most desperate problem. Shelter was being provided, but slowly. Nine hundred little ten-man huts were being built in the valley. Axes chunked and saws rasped all day every day. There were plenty of trees for the logs. And there certainly was plenty of mud to chink between the logs; after every chilly rainfall or meltoff of snow, there seemed to be enough mud in Valley Forge to chink the widest gap in the world—"except the ones between my ribs," Bill Croghan would joke. The snow was littered everywhere with bark and wood chips, and great, smoky bonfires of limbs and brush burned night and day, fed by half-clothed soldiers trying to keep warm as they worked on their huts. Everyone was soot-smudged and reeked of stale woodsmoke. General Washington, in one of those gestures of his that bewildered but touched his troops, was living in an unheated linen tent nearby, where he had vowed he would stay until every soldier was housed, even though a snug and roomy stone farmhouse stood awaiting his occupancy a short distance up the road.

From morning till night, Jonathan saw plights that would make his heart squeeze: a shoeless sentry at dawn, wrapped in a ragged blanket, shaking so hard he could not have raised his musket, so hoarse he could not have challenged a passerby. A soldier sleeping curled up on the frosty ground with his hands between his thighs and his bare feet buried in dead leaves because he had no blanket. A soldier gnawing a soot-blackened chunk of pumpkin shell. No, he would see not one but fifty soldiers like that. And there was nothing he could do about it, except pray, pray that the next morning would dawn dry and mild with enough sunlight for the soldiers to feel, or pray that Nathanael Greene, now Quartermaster General, would find a ton of boots or beef or blankets or brandy somewhere, or that good weather would permit the soldiers to finish their hut-building a few days sooner. That was all Major Jonathan Clark could do about it. Pray. He had just written a letter to Sarah Hite, asking her to pray also.

Jonathan watched another sticky glob of rice come out of the kettle and go into another soldier's cup. He remembered how his mother fixed rice on holidays. With turkey livers and bits of onion and butter and sage cooked in. Or as a pudding with currants and apple-pulp and black-walnut meats in it and a bit of maple-sugar cake crumbled on the top.

Well, there'll be a time for that some other day, he thought. Meanwhile, *Thank You our divine Providence for this plain and honest rice.*

And for this Thy vinegar.

12

Valley of the
Monongahela

January, 1778

Now RIDING AT THE HEAD OF A FILE OF FRONTIERSMEN muffled in fur hats and wool blankets, George crossed over the snowy Alleghenies and led the descent toward old Red Stone Fort, which was to be his recruiting station.

He drew a long breath at the sight of the flint-gray Monongahela, the lavender stain in the evening sky above the western ridges. He always felt as if he were leaving a close room and emerging outdoors when he crossed the divide from the seaboard into the western watershed. This time the sense of space and change was doubly thrilling, because he knew he had now committed himself to an enterprise that would demand every shred of his wit and nerve for months to come.

The men behind him, except for Cousin Johnny Rogers, were old comrades from Dunmore's War and the defense of Kentuck. Len Helm, the legendary "man with the whiskey spring," had signed on as a captain when told that the enterprise would be as bodacious as anything Benedict Arnold had done. Joe Bowman was there as second-in-command, his brother Isaac a lieutenant. John Montgomery was there as a company commander, and then there followed half a dozen men these officers had brought with them. Bill Harrod, brother of Jim Harrod the town-builder, was supposed to be already at Red Stone Fort, at work enlisting a company he would command. And William Bailey Smith had promised he would be waiting at the mouth of the Kentucky River in March with two hundred men from the Holston Valley country. Not a one of them knew what the destination or purpose was, but they had come with George simply because he had convinced them all that he was fixing up the liveliest doings west of the mountains. He had promised them parcels of Kentucky land, and an adventure they'd someday tell their grandchildren about. That was enough for them.

Johnny Rogers was riding alongside Leonard Helm, Johnny had been appointed a lieutenant in Helm's not-yet-existent company. Helm was saying to him:

"Now, lad, if I was to act on all the intelligence those Orders o' th' Governor tells me, I'd still be a-sitting in Floyd's Tavern where you found me. But I know your cousin's up to somethin' right glorious, because he told me so. And I believe what-all he tells me, because he is not only as good a fightin' man as I ever saw, and the longest thinker, but he can be trusted. Yes sir, it is known by all that George Rogers Clark is as honest as a cockstand." Johnny whooped a laugh in the cold air.

George knew, as his horse picked its way down the snowy trail into the valley, that it was not going to be as easy to recruit five hundred men as it had been to get these old compatriots of his. Most men fit for soldiering were already in the Continental army, or serving in their own state and county militias. But he had Henry's orders, telling all the county lieutenants to cooperate with him, and he had the authority to offer each rifleman 300 acres of land, and he had his own reputation, which, west of the mountains, was considerable. And he knew that among them, his captains knew personally just about every long hunter, sharpshooter, ridge-runner, desperado, and Indian fighter west of the Alleghenies.

And for the mission he had dreamed up that night last year by the hearth fire in Harrod's Town, those were exactly the kinds of men he needed.

JOHNNY CLARK SAT WRAPPED IN A BLANKET, BUT HE COULD not stop shivering.

Most of the American officers confined in this room, which was a converted gun room and thus without windows or portholes, simply remained in their bunks on days like this, when the dank harbor wind seemed to come straight through the uncaulked cracks. Johnny had had to get up for a while, unable to lie any longer on his aching joints and bedsores.

The only heated quarters on the *Jersey* were those of the British officers, just above. Johnny could hear them walking back and forth up there, so constantly that he had decided they must have a dart board on the wall to play with. The deck planks creaked above as they walked about. Sometimes one could hear their voices. Now there was a bit of laughter. Johnny scowled up at the massive oak beams overhead, and snarled, "Laugh, ye bloody furuncles! God, laughter is a sacrilege on this dungeon-ship!"

"Nay," said the Poet. It sounded like "Day," because the Poet's nose was, as always, stuffed. Like most, he had the grippe, and had it perpetually.

Johnny looked quizzically across the table at the Poet, whose real name was Captain Coffin. Before him on the table were sheets of paper and a quill in an ink bottle. He was not writing his poems at this moment; he was sitting with his hands between his thighs, trying to warm his fingers enough to write the next line. Captain Coffin had his blanket up over his head. He looked rather like a monk, a narrow-faced monk with a runny nose, Johnny fancied. Like those who copy Bibles by hand in their cells all their lives. Johnny admired the Poet, admired his patience, admired his ability to write verse under any circumstances and discomforts, however hopeless, and even admired what he had heard of his verse. But the Poet was hard to abide sometimes; he had too much forbearance; he was too much like a saint, like a martyr. It was uncomfortable to live with someone who never complained and always forgave. "What d'you mean, 'Nay'?" Johnny challenged. He was testy. His old sweet soul had soured.

"I mean," said Coffin, "laughter's always good to hear. It's music. Especially here, now. There's precious little of it aboard this sad vessel."

"True," said Johnny. "But I wish 'twas us had cause to laugh now and again, not *them*." He glowered at the ceiling again.

"It *would* be a sacrilege if *we* laughed," someone said from the gloom of a nearby bunk. The bunks were, in actuality, makeshift shelves, three high, allowing their occupants only about two feet of space in which to turn on their straw bedding. In the shadows of nearly every bunk there was a pallid face dimly visible. Other officers lay with their faces to the walls. The only light in the room was that of a candle lantern hanging from a beam over the center of the one table in the center of the room. This table was the place for what little activity there was in the cell; here they wrote, here they read if they had anything to read, here they sat if they wished to talk face to face, here they had, now and then, what they called their "Town Meetings" to draft petitions against the squalor and the slop of their daily lives, and here they sat to eat the slop their petitions never caused to improve. Some of the officers made a ritual of getting up and taking seats at the table once or twice every day so that they might still consider themselves civilized beings rather than mere burrowing animals. Johnny was one who did this. Some never came to the table, except to eat. Some had become too ill to do even that. The lantern burned day and night, a fuzzy light always in a pall of bad air and, now and then, tobacco smoke, when the sutler's store on the main deck had acquired a few twists of it, when some officer turned up some valuable to barter for a few shreds of it. The candle burned and was replaced, burned and was replaced. One could tell day from night only by the slits of daylight between the uncaulked planks and timbers.

Through those same planks and timbers came always a dismal murmur, the voices of the enlisted men, who were packed by the hundreds between decks in the holds forward. "You think we're close in here?" one Lieutenant Hoag had told Johnny one day long ago. "Down there, they're packed like mackerel in a barrel."

"An apt analogy," the Poet had said.

"It is, and that's why I used it," Hoag had replied. "They smell like mackerel down there."

"Aye," another officer had said. "Spoiled mackerel, at that."

"Like what our slop's made from," a Massachusetts lieutenant had said.

"They let 'em lie too long after they die," Hoag had said. "They ought to remove a man soon as they know he's dead."

"Turnkey tells me they do," said the Poet. "But sometimes there's so little difference between the poor mortals dead and those nearly so, that they don't know for quite a time."

It was during that discussion that Johnny had inquired about the British ensign's remark. "Is it true that no one's ever left this ship except in a canvas shroud?"

"Some few hardy fools have jumped and tried to swim—in fairer weather, o' course," Hoag had answered. "The result, about the same. Just saves the deadboat a trip out."

"I'd 'spect," Johnny had said after a pause, "that a stout swimmer might make it."

"Might," Hoag had replied, casting a speculative eye at Johnny. "Are you a stout swimmer, perchance?"

"All us Clarks have swum since we could crawl down to the water."

"Well, sir, Mister Clark," Coffin had intercalated then, "if you get the urge to swim—I mean, come fair weather—mind this: the guards aboard be picked marksmen, and they're always listening for a man-sized splash. A man in the water is fine practice for them."

"I see," Johnny had replied. "Then one would want to go over without a splash, would 'e not? I'll remember that, come fairer weather."

Those first few weeks, then, he had calculated plans for slipping silently over the side some fine spring day during above-decks exercise. Surely one could work his way like a spider down the hull and slip silently into the water; surely one could swim mostly underwater until out of musket range; surely one could tay afloat and get to shore, particularly with an incoming tide; ohnny knew a means of improvising a float by tying one's water- oaked breeches shut at the knees and catching air in them, and hen resting one's chin on them for bouyancy when exhausted. Ie had thought about it a lot, and in his mind's eye he had nade the escape time after time.

But spring was still weeks away, and already he felt so weak- ened by the constant cold, the fevers, the dysentery, the sheer nactivity, and the insipid diet, that the distant shores were be- ;inning to seem impossibly far away. He doubted now that he'd iave the strength to swim the ship's length.

Besides, his breeches now were full of holes from the splinters n the bunk.

Come spring, though, he would think sometimes, come pring we'll see how we feel about swimming.

VALLEY FORGE, PENNSYLVANIA

February, 1778

'WHY ARE YOU SHAKIN', SOLDIER? COLD OR AFRAID?"

"Cold, sir."

"Not afraid, eh? That's good," Jonathan Clark said.

The soldier didn't answer. He didn't need to. The look in his eyes was pure terror. He looked as if he might faint. So did half the other men in this company.

Oh, they were cold, too. They were standing in ranks in an inch of snow, and a third of them were barefooted. Some had no coats, others no hats.

But they had been cold all winter. Now they were afraid. So it was time for Jonathan's lecture. He had given it to about half the companies so far.

"Now, hear me," he began. "I know how ye feel. You'd be shaking in your boots, if y' had any boots to shake in."

That brought a chuckle from some of them, and it brought their attention a little way around toward him. They looked at this tall, broad-shouldered young officer with the dark but cheer- ful eyes, the pock-marked but handsome face, and his warm voice and good humor were somehow reassuring, as they faced this unthinkably dreadful thing that was about to be done to them. He had obviously had the dread pocks, but was a hale man withal. Now he went on.

211

"I'm Jonathan Clark, Major, 8th Virginia, and I give ye my word: You'd have more cause for fear if we were *not* doing this."

"As you've heard, there's small pocks in camp. We've done all we can to keep it isolated, but that malady has a way of getting about, wherever there are many souls crowded together.

"You've probably heard it said already—I'm sure y' have, a rumor gets around an army camp about five times as swift as orders do." Again, an appreciative chuckle. "You've likely heard already that what we're doing in this hospital,"—he pointed toward the hovel in front of them which went by the name of hospital— "is that we're deliberately infecting men with the pocks.

"Well, if that was all of the truth, I'd not blame ye for shakin' in those boots y' don't have. But let me tell you what a miracle it is that the good Doctor O'Fallon is doing in there." They were listening well to him, doing their best to believe, though it was against their instincts to believe such a thing.

"I have already had the pocks, as you can see. I came down with it in an epidemic after the siege o' Charles Town. Because I've had it, I have no fear of it anymore. I can go amid an epidemic of it without fear. Know why? Because a man can get the pocks but once—I mean, *this* pocks. The other kind we don't much need to worry about here, as there's not been a harlot in sight all winter." They laughed now. "It might be," he said, "that the British in Philadelphia are getting all that. See how lucky we are?" They were having a good time now, laughing at these thoughts.

"I can work with the good doctor," Jonathan said. "I can touch infected men and have no fear. D'ye wonder why it is a man has the small pocks but once?" He had them curious now. Their fear was in suspension. He knew that fear grows in unknowing, and he was giving them knowledge. "Blood," he went on, "has a property. I'm no doctor, so I can't put it in a doctor' language, but blood has a property that fights disease. I reckon it's like what happens when the Redcoats come to Lexington or such a place: all the patriots run to Lexington to drive 'em back. Well, that property in your blood is like a patriotism in your body: it's to stop the invasion of a foreign evil, if y' follow me." Some were nodding, others listening with mouths hanging open.

"What we're doing is like that. Well, we invade your arm with a speck o' pus from a poxed man. That pus is the foreign evil like the Redcoats I spoke of. Just a light scratch on your skin and a spot o' pus put on it. What happens then is that patriotic property of your blood rushes to that place, and it stops the invasion *right there*. And in so doing, your blood learns how to fight that particular evil. So. Instead of bein' generally invaded, like I was, you'll have but th' one spot of disease, one scar, there on your arm. And ever after, you'll be able to walk through an epidemic of the pocks without any fear of it. The rest of your natural life! Think what a gift o' God that is!"

They were seeming to believe him; their faces were beginning to show some hope where they had only shown fear. He concluded:

"General Washington, ye know it, is a man cares about his people. He doesn't want an epidemic here at Valley Forge. And I'll tell it true, he's the first general ever knew enough to do this for his army.

"Now, I've seen you walk into the face of bayonets and grape-shot when he needed y' to do it. So I reckon ye won't be afraid to walk in there and face a doctor who's like to save your life. Now s'pose I tell one more truth: that no man or woman ever died—nay, nor even *sickened*—from this little pinprick you're about to take. It's true! My word on it. And General Washington's. And if *that* isn't enough, maybe y'll take the word o' God on it. If you want that assurance, you have it from our chaplain, the Reverend Mister David Jones. Mister Jones," he said, turning to the slender, almost frail-looking, man who stood beside and behind him, "gentlemen may want to pray with ye, before they proceed in and be treated."

Jonathan left their souls in the care of the chaplain and stooped in through the low door of the hospital cabin. A young man in a white apron stood over a table, arranging small cups and pen-size iron lances. He looked up as Jonathan took off his cape and coat and hat and hung them on a wall peg. "Ready, Major Clark?"

"Ready, Dr. O'Fallon. Another set o' men getting their souls fortified right now." They could hear Reverend Davy Jones's voice droning in prayer outside.

"I think it's your talk fortifies 'em most," the physician said. "I'm not so certain mere prayers alone would prepare 'em."

"'Mere' prayers!" Jonathan mocked him. "In faith, Bones, one might guess you're an Unbeliever!" He rolled back his sleeves, picked up a lance and a cup, and pulled back a linen curtain that hung from poles in a corner of the hut. "Now, Corporal," he said to a young man lying inside on a cot, "are y' ready to give for this worthy cause?" He drew down a sheet to expose the man's chest and shoulders, which were covered with white-topped pustules of the readiest kind. The donor looked askance through his swollen eye-

213

lids at the lance in Jonathan's hand, coughed violently, then sighed and turned his face toward the wall.

"Aye," he said in a weak voice, "help yourself, Doctor."

Well, well, Jonathan thought, stooping close over the young soldier to cut the head off a pustule and press its matter out with the edge of the cup, wouldn't Ma be tickled to know she's now got a "doctor" amongst her sons?

"DONE," DR. O'FALLON SIGHED A FEW DAYS LATER. "AND may I never have to look into another pair of terror-struck eyes again, nor puncture another palsying arm, so long as I live. Now every man jack in this army who'd never had the pocks before has just a wee touch of it now, thanks be to us. It gives me shudders to think what we've been doing. Even though," he added quickly, "I do believe in it."

"You'd *better* believe in it!" Jonathan exclaimed. "I've been vouching for it for a week now, in the belief you believe in it."

Dr. O'Fallon and Jonathan were now cleaning instruments and vessels with hot water from a kettle. They had become very close while working together in this unprecedented project.

"Now, Dr. Clark," said the physician. "Something to celebrate the completion of that ordeal?" He had been calling Jonathan "Doctor" since the day the donor had done so. O'Fallon went to his medicine chest and drew out a half-full demijohn, measured out a double dram for each of them, and set them on the table.

"You're sure this isn't calomel, or some other of your Devil's potions?" Jonathan queried, looking into the cup.

"Calomel's colorless and tasteless," O'Fallon said, raising his cup to Jonathan and then sipping from it. "I assure you, this is neither. Ahhhhh! My word on't!"

"Ahhhh! Your word's as good as your brandy." He felt very good, very happy. He felt certain that he had helped spare many a man from the awful, deadly misery that he had suffered less than two years ago.

Boots crunched on the snow outside. The snow had half melted during the day, then had frozen over as temperatures plunged. The door opened inward on its leather hinges and Bill Croghan came in, huffing and shivering. At once Dr. O'Fallon poured him a brandy. "Health," Croghan said, winking and drinking.

"Health indeed!"

"I don't see the usual queue of doom-faced soldiery outside," Croghan said.

"We're done. Every man's infected good and proper. But only in his arm, I pray," Jonathan said.

"And so I pray. Listen. Much news from home!" Croghan now referred to the Clark house in Caroline County as his home. He had had to put his English home out of his mind entirely. "Your derring-do brother Colonel George Clark has gone over the mountains once again. Apparently his mysterious mission is under way at last."

"Mm. You mean Major," Jonathan said, his cup halfway to his lips.

"No. Colonel. That's what I came to tell you. I've a letter from your Little Brother Lucy today. The scallawag finally condescended to write to me, bless her heart. Anyway, she says he's a colonel now." He handed a paper to Jonathan. Jonathan perused it while, outside in the cold, the footsteps of marching soldiers crushed in the snow, and the incredibly strident voice of Baron Von Steuben, Washington's new Prussian drillmaster, screeched drill commands.

"'Little Brother Lucy'?" exclaimed Dr. O'Fallon, thumping the heel of his hand against his temple. "By all that's odd, I've got to meet the rest of this Clark clan!"

"Aye, you should!" Bill Croghan exclaimed. "Get Doctor Jonathan here to extend you an invitation, and you'll never regret it." He extended his cup for another dram, and tilted his head toward the frantic voice and the half-coherent ravings of the Prussian, whom General Washington had put in charge of retraining the Continental troops for the coming campaigns of spring. Von Steuben, with the ferocious energy of a mother bear and the muzzle-blast language of a master sergeant, was giving the ragged army no leisure to think about its itchy little spots of small pocks, or any of its other myriad miseries. "Listen to that voice!" Croghan laughed. "How'd you like to be married to a *woman* with a voice like that? Ha, ha! Have you heard what the troops have nicknamed him? 'Herr Schpittenschlobber.' Ha, ha!"

"By Jove!" Jonathan slapped Lucy's letter with his knuckles. "Brother George *is* a colonel! Well, though. It's only militia," he snorted, "so he'd better not try to bear rank over me, ever!" Then he shook his head and compressed his lips. "Lord help 'm, if he's set himself a hard task and has to depend on *militia* for it! Especially such lawless yayhoos as he'll be a-findin' out on the backside o' those mountains! Poor George! A colonel of bear-biters! Lord help 'im!"

* * *

GEORGE ROGERS CLARK SAT BEHIND THE LONG TABLE I[n]
the main room of the public house in Red Stone Fort and eye[d]
his latest recruit, who was about to be entered onto the muste[r]
roll by Cousin Johnny. The volunteer looked as if he had neve[r]
once stood up to full height in his life. He had leaned against th[e]
door jamb before coming in; now he was supporting himself o[n]
the table, both palms lying flat on it, his rangy body hangin[g]
between his shoulders, one long leg crossed loosely in front [of]
the other, as if his arms and the table were all that could kee[p]
him from collapsing on the floor and going to sleep.

He did not appear to be weak; there was sinew and long, rop[y]
muscle evident there. But he was either the laziest or tirede[st]
man George had ever seen. He was dressed more like an India[n]
than a white man. His face was weathered and bony and hollow[-]
cheeked. He looked as if he had not been under a roof or i[n]
bathwater for two years. He looked, in other words, like half [of]
the volunteers George had managed to sign up: rough, raw, flea[-]
bitten, half-civilized if that much.

"Your name?" asked John Rogers, holding the quill point i[n]
the ink pot and looking up at him.

The man muttered something that sounded like "Hom'[n]
Cawnsuluh." Johnny squinted. "What was that first name?"

The man licked his lips. "Hom'n."

"Uh, is that Harmon? Herman?"

"Mhm," the man said, nodding. Johnny wrote somethin[g]
down and then looked up again and said:

"And that last name again, it was what?"

"Cawnsuluh," the man replied, then wiped his teeth with h[is]
tongue.

"How d'you spell that?"

The man's eyes narrowed, then glanced about. He looked lik[e]
a trapped animal. But then he fell back on his natural indolenc[e]
and with a lazy leer of a smile, said:

"Hell, yew th' man with th' pen. *Yew* spell it."

Johnny sighed and shook his head and wrote something dow[n]
George stood up. "Keep," he called, "fetch me and this ma[n]
some grog."

Even this laconic newcomer seemed struck by the redheade[d]
deep-voiced officer who was extending his hand to him; he pulle[d]
himself into an almost upright posture and reached for the han[d]
shake. "Come and have a cup with me by the fire," George sai[d]
cheerfully, "and we'll get acquainted, and I'll tell ye what m[y]
expectations are. I'm George Clark, and this is my show."

"How d'ye?" The woodsman picked up his rifle from where

aned on the table and, mouth hanging open, followed George
ward the hearth. There the whopper-jawed, greasy-haired inn-
eper was setting down mugs for them.

"Well, now, Mister Consola," George began, "tell me what
untry y've seen lately."

They took time, these personal talks with new men. But
eorge never failed to learn something useful from them, and
usually was able to imprint the new recruits with some of his
wn confidence. By shrewd but easy-sounding conversation, he
as able to divine pretty well what a man's sentiments and loy-
ties were. He had turned away two or three, during the last few
eeks, whom he had suspected of being Tories sent to spy on
m.

But the recruiting so far had been a crushing disappointment.
stead of the three hundred men he had expected to have by
w, he had only one hundred. The county lieutenants were
ocking the efforts of George and his officers, discouraging en-
tments and even enticing recruits to desert.

The dilemma lay in the secrecy of the expedition. It could
cceed only if it remained a secret. But because he could not
veal his true purpose, he could not convince anyone of its
portance. The county lieutenants and other leading citizens
cused him of getting the countryside in an uproar, trying to
cruit their own scarce manpower away for the defense of a
stant region whose people were fools to be there anyway. The
orst trouble was with Colonel Arthur Campbell, leader of Fin-
stle County, who had so recently failed to block George's
ove to get Kentuck made a separate county. Now Campbell
emed determined to thwart anything George was doing, ex-
utive orders or no, and it had come to a point where George
d gone up and banged a fist on Campbell's desk and accused
m of sedition. It had done no good.

Spring was coming on and George had but a fraction of the
en he needed. Therefore he used all his power of persuasion
every man who came in. And so now he quizzed and listened
this rancid bushloper, gradually became convinced that he
as a much better man than he looked to be, and noted that he
ight be especially useful as a hunter or courier, as his drawling
story indicated he had been just about everywhere George had
er heard of. Apparently he sagged and slouched so much only
order to conserve energy for the times when he was on the
ove.

They finished their cups. George stood up. Console—or
hatever his name was—unfolded himself and rose, grinning a

217

grin that looked like an old churchyard full of crooked tom
stones. George swore him in and pumped his hand. "I'm glad
have a man like you," he said, meaning it. "Now if you'll
back to the pup over there who wrote your name, he'll see yo
get victuals and a berth."

"I'm sure glad I come, Mister Cunnel! Ah'd reckon this go
be a rail ramsquaddle hijink, ayup-ha!" And he shambled ba
to Johnny Rogers.

At that moment, Bill Harrod came in, looking like a whipp
dog. "Five more o' mine have gone over th' mountain," he mu
tered. "Crump says he saw 'em talking this mornin' to those tw
poop merchants from Fincastle, Long Jaw Campbell's boys. A
now they're gone."

"Damnation!" George ground his molars. "Get one and lo
five!"

"I'll send a squad out after 'em."

"No. I'm not going to do that anymore. They don't come ba
either!" He was clenching and opening his fists. "'Scuse m
Bill. I left something in my room."

The innkeeper watched George stalk through the door. F
had seen Colonel Clark in that state a lot of times now, and I
shook his head and sucked an eyetooth. He knew that somethin
would probably be broken in there before the colonel came ba
out.

"LEFTENANT JOHN CLARK!" SAID A VOICE AT THE GRATE.

"Here," he replied, startled and curious, rising stiffly from th
table. Hoag looked at him across the table and said:

"Here indeed. Where else could y' be?"

"You're wanted," said the voice. A key slid in iron and turne
The turnkey, with a pistol in his belt, walked him up
gloomy companionway to the door of the British officers' qua
ters, and rapped. A voice called, "Enter." The turnkey opene
the door a crack. "I have Clark, sir."

The door opened. The burly British naval officer studie
Johnny for a moment, then reached in and put on a hat. H
came out into the corridor, buttoning his tunic. "Follow me,
he said, leading him through the doors and barricades to th
maindeck.

"What's it about, if I may ask?" The officer did not bother
answer, and Johnny wanted to clout the back of his insole
head.

It was another cloudy, raw, bitter-cold day, but even th
much gray daylight was enough to make him squint. He took

218

ep, grateful breath of the fresh air, but it jolted his befouled ngs and threw him into a fit of coughing. Smart-looking sen- es turned and looked at him with disdain.

His buff breeches were dingy with the grease and old food bbed into the thighs, with the stains of rat-droppings. His tat- red hose hung loose on his wasting calves. The dark blue wool his coat was flecked all over with chaff and straw and lint. His hiskers felt all a-crawl suddenly, as if the lice in it were seeking eper refuge from the cold wind. He felt he was a disgrace to s uniform, but there had been nothing he could do, down in at waterless, airless dungeon, to keep himself looking smart.

He was led forward the length of the barren, gray deck, and it emed a mile, with the wind slicing through his clothes. Char- al smoke and rancid steam billowed over him as he passed the rward hatch.

At the forecastle, a thick-necked, brutal-eyed Tartar of a man, earing some sort of fleece-lined leather skullcap with earflaps, d apparently two or three American army coats, stood guard- g a door, not with a gun but with a two-foot-long cudgel.

"Here's Clark," the British officer said to this brute. "You have at Virginian wants to see him."

The squat doorkeeper nodded. He touched Johnny on the oulder with the end of his cudgel, as if to impress upon him its eight and hardness, then tilted his head toward the door. He nlocked the door with a huge iron key and pushed it inward. A nse, gagging odor emanated from the darkness inside. "Cla'k f' reeman," he called in, then prodded Johnny to enter.

Freeman? Johnny thought. He did know many Freemans.

Another troll, this one with a shaved skull, three folds of flesh 1 the back of his neck, and ape arms, beckoned him in with a ck of pig-eyes, and the door closed and the bolt slid behind m.

The stench here was so sharp it stung his nostrils and he had close his throat to keep from gagging. The troll led him down ladder into a dark well of murmurings and whisperings, then st the edge of what seemed to be a dark warehouse of stirring rms stacked on wooden shelves. Then they went down another dder to a deeper well, and, finally, down a third into a confine ith slimy floors and an atmosphere so dense and fetid that he as afraid to breathe more than tiny sips of it. Rats twittered in e gloom and moved boldly in dim pools of lantern-light be- reen rows of wooden racks. He was being led aft now, into the wels of the ship, and it was indeed like a trek through a bowel, nk with the smell of excrement and putridity. Here there was

219

an oppressive rush of pitiful noises: phlegmatic breathin, groans, explosive coughing, unintelligible talking, tuneless sin ing, frantic-sounding whispers, the rustle of turning bodie thump of bone against boards. Bare hands and feet hung into th aisle. It was true what Hoag had said: the prisoners were pack here like mackerel in a barrel.

How can they live? he wondered. He was sickened by th incredible disregard for comfort and dignity.

And what poor Freeman lies here? he wondered. What mockery that one so named would be locked deep in a stink-ho like this. As his eyes grew accustomed to the gloom he could s half-naked skeletons of men, white and close as maggots on th long racks; they seemed not even to have straw to soften th planks they lay on. Somewhere below and aside, invisible gloom, was an open space from which came a clammy, cave-li dankness, the chill of cold, wet stone, tricklings, drippings. W it the bilges and ballast? he wondered. An open latrine? Or bot

Now the troll stopped, and kicked a rack.

"Freeman," he growled, "'ere's your bloody officer."

A matted mass of dark hair turned in the shadow; Johnny heart quailed with dread.

A face—rather, a hollow-eyed skull with badly blemished sk stretched over it, protuberant brow, broad cheekbones and mouth prominent as a monkey's between sunken cheeks- turned into the feeble lamplight. The lower lip hung slack, r vealing gray teeth in rotting gums. Johnny did not recognize th half-living cadaver, though something about the bone structu of the face stirred his memory. Other faces were turning to lo at him, too, and he heard voices saying, "Look. It's an officer "An officer?" "I think it's an officer."

Now the specter named Freeman groped out into the ais with a scrawny, long hand. Overcoming revulsion, Johnny too it.

"Thank'ee for comin', Mister Clark." The voice was curdle

"Glad to, Mister Freeman." Saying this made Johnny brea loose in a wet, raking cough and he felt much of the matt loosening in his lungs and felt the point of sharp pain there. Th man in the shadows said:

"Y' know me, then?" The eyes looked radiant for a momen

"O' course," Johnny lied.

"I saw ye one day on deck," the voice rasped. asked . . . asked 'em weeks ago if I mought talk wi' ye."

"They just now fetched me. Took their time, didn't they?"

He still didn't know who this was; the face and voice we

ghastly. The way of speaking was plainly the Scotch-Irish of down home. Johnny was sorting in his mind among the many Virginians he'd known named Freeman.

"They know I'm not . . . I'm not long f'r this life," the face said. "So reckon they decided t'grant me one boon."

"You'll be fine," Johnny said feebly. Freeman was still holding onto his hand, as if onto life itself. Freeman's hand was like a fistful of rabbit bones. Johnny saw that the guard troll was standing off in the shadows, listening, digging in his nostril with a dirty digit.

"So I wanted t' ask'ee," Freeman went on. He paused, and a tremor vibrated his hand. "Ye do still mean t' marry Betsy, am I right?"

Betsy! Now Johnny knew. This, then, was one of the brothers of Betsy Freeman. Which brother he knew not; was it Micajah, the one who liked to be called Mike, or . . . He couldn't even remember the other one's name. Johnny had not seen Betsy since '75, nor had he intended to. He remembered the day he had ridden toward Williamsburg with Patrick Henry's militia, remembered Isaiah Freeman, this wretch's father, walking alongside his horse, asking virtually this same question. God, would they never get over it that a Clark had courted Betsy? He had all but forgotten her. Surely she wasn't still waiting about for him, not as lusty and comely a wench as she had been. Johnny felt a twinge of poignancy, and at the same moment a flash of bitter humor at the absurdity of it. Had that shrew actually kept up the fiction of this attachment in the minds of her menfolk all these years? Or was this young Freeman here, in his extremity, just out of touch with time, deluded by an echo of long ago?

The gaunt face was still intense, a spark of lanternlight burning in each eye.

"Betsy," Johnny said. "Why, ah, what does Betsy say on the matter?"

"Oh, sir, why, that y're betrothed. As it's so, ain't it?" Now Johnny fancied he saw a flash of insistence in those sockets: the brotherly protectiveness of a sister's honor. What was it his father had said? *A lass is likely someone's sister.*

Johnny flushed with indignation at the thought of her, and wanted to tell this wretch that his sister was a liar. It was all so remote, from a lost time and unreachable place, and seemed so utterly inconsequential anyway; how could the deceits of her heart intrude now on their present misery? And yet, despite all that, he was bemused, and had he not been steeped in war and horror and the sense of his own decay for so long, he might have been flattered.

Instead, he was indignant, and was about to say so. Another coughing fit racked him first, though, and it was a minute before he could turn back to those anxious eyes in that skull.

And he realized that the matter now was not one to do with his feelings, nor even Betsy's, really, but the burning question inside this dying young man: his need for one scrap of favorable and hopeful knowledge in his last days. Johnny glanced away from the ravaged face, and saw other faces peering at him, many faces, interested faces, though how much if anything of this they were comprehending he knew not. Some probably were looking at him only because he was a new sight on the edge of their muzzy, limited world. But others might be the brothers of sisters, pretty sisters of precarious reputation, and they might well be comprehending the gist of this conversation; maybe this Freeman lad had told them something of it already. Nobody in this sumphole of death needed to hear a harsh denial made to a dying peer, and Freeman himself least of all should have to hear it. And so Johnny said, in a rush of pity for all people in all hopeless plights:

"God willing, when all this is over, Betsy and I should be together."

The hand squeezed on his with its tiny bit of strength. "That's . . . on y'r word, Mister John Clark?"

Johnny's scalp prickled. He had not expected to be making promises to a dying man.

But, after all, he had said only "be together."

Still, as his mother had used to say: *What a body understands your promise to be is the promise you've made.*

But he could not deny this brother what he needed to hear.

"On my word, Mister Freeman."

"God bless ye, Mister John Clark."

"God bless y'rself, Mister Freeman."

The next week, Freeman—Johnny had learned from the ship's officer that it was Mike: Private Micajah Freeman of the Sixth Virginia—left the *Jersey* in a canvas shroud, one of five victims of putrid fever to go ashore that day to wherever it was the British took the hundreds of cadavers from the ship.

He took Johnny Clark's promise with him.

LIEUTENANT HOAG, OF COURSE, FOUND IT ALL DE-lightfully ironic, the best thing he had heard since he had been confined on the *Jersey*. "The sins and the false vows of your lusty youth return to haunt you!" he laughed. "Poet, you must do a verse, on the come-uppance justly due such careless swains as leave a trail of light promises and fluttering hearts behind them! Ha, ha!"

"Indeed," replied the Poet, smiling fondly at Johnny's gloom, "I am already composing!"

"Compose, please," chuckled Hoag. "I shall lie here meantime and continue to *de*compose."

Johnny would not have told them about the vow that Micajah Freeman had extracted from him, but they had caught him coming in, shaking his head and muttering and looking like one deeply damned, and by cajolery and kindness they had made him tell the tale of his visit down forward. Now their raillery made him wish he had kept it to himself.

"A scold, is she?" Hoag said, shaking his head slowly. "There's nothing worse than a scold! I suspect that Johnny Clark the Fourth, that erstwhile carefree swain and sower of wild seed in Caroline County, Virginia, may be the first inmate in the *Jersey*'s history ever to choose a permanent berth, rather than go home to the fate that awaits him there!" He lay in his bunk chuckling, asking others what they thought of such a thing, and wasn't it wonderful that there really is some justice in this unjust world after all, and so on, till some of the wretches were actually enjoying themselves, and looking at Johnny with fondness and archness in their expressions. The Poet sat over his paper and tapped his temple and scribbled.

"Wait," he would say every minute or so, raising his quill, "I nearly have it here."

And even Johnny was beginning to laugh at his own plight, at the absurd coincidence of it, by the time the Poet finished his verse and read it aloud.

> *The Day of Judgment falls most just*
> *Upon the fickle-hearted swain,*
> *Who left her pining, and now must*
> *Fulfill the love which he didst feign.*

Johnny laughed feebly, ruefully, at this, at all the attention, but his laughing brought on his coughing, terrible, wet, phlegm-moving coughs. Now the rag he used as a handkerchief was sodden and slimy with mucus, and there was blood in it. He saw blood in it now for the first time, and he sat and looked at it for a while.

Maybe that promise is nothing to worry myself on after all, he thought. Maybe I'll never get home to face Betsy Freeman at all.

13

VALLEY FORGE,
PENNSYLVANIA

May, 1778

SIX THOUSAND CONTINENTAL SOLDIERS PARADED DOWN THE long side of the sunny, May-green meadow, in perfect step to the beat of drums. From a distance, with their neat ranks and billowing banners, they looked like a perfect army as they tramped down toward the little hillock on which General Washington stood waiting to review them. From close by, where Jonathan Clark marched, there were pitiful details visible, traces of their poverty and the miseries of winter. Many were still shirtless and hatless and barefooted. The gentle May sun shone on bare shoulders and backs and scalps, healing the boils and ringworms and skin infections that had afflicted them during the long, wretched winter. Most were as skinny as whippets. But their eyes were bright and their steps were light, their muskets and bayonets were polished.

On the high ground with Washington were General Gates and General Greene, and the Marquis de Lafayette and Baron Von Steuben. The talk in the army was that this parade was not just an ordinary review for a commander-in-chief, but Von Steuben's personal gift to General Washington; he was as proud of this army as Washington himself was, and today he was demonstrating to His Excellency how much it was improved. All the men were aware of this, aware that it was Herr Schpittenschlobber's great day, as they tramped down the field toward the general officers, and so they fairly strutted in their eagerness to make it a big success for their beloved drillmaster.

For everyone agreed that Von Steuben was the best thing that had happened to the poor American Army since the victory at Saratoga. Steuben, with his cursing tantrums, his unintelligible profanities, and his ridiculous, jabbing little swagger stick, had, in months, turned General Washington's half-starved, half-naked, half-spirited mob of an army into an organization that could pivot and flank as smartly as Prussians, march without straggling, load and fire twice as many volleys per minute on voice commands as they had been able to before, and could make as orderly a bayonet charge as any line of Redcoats. The whole army loved the little brute-faced tyrant, because he made them feel smart as an honor guard, potent as a legion, but especially because of something he had said at an officers' dinner in General Washington's headquarters. "No European army," he had said, "could have held together through the hardships of this winter here!" That tribute had been overheard and carried back to camp, and had spread throughout the army.

And now they were on review, a new-spirited army ready to come out for the spring campaigns, and they were determined to repay his tribute. They were going to show General Washington what the Baron had made of them. They were aware of him on the hillock as they were of the commander-in-chief himself.

As the 8th Virginia neared the reviewing stand, the fifers joined the drummers, and they were playing that piece that always gave Jonathan the martial shivers.

It had been a British marching tune, before the Battle of Lexington, a merry song meant to make a mockery of the American yokels. But after chasing the Redcoats back to Boston, the "yokels" had adopted the song as their own, and now "Yankee Doodle" was their own, a song and a joke combined.

Now the 8th Virginia was abreast of the mounted officers, and there was Washington, big, monumentally dignified, sitting high on his great dappled gray warhorse, that fellow Virginian farmer with his stolid, kindly face; and there beside him was the Baron, intent, high-colored with whatever emotions of pride or anxiety he must be feeling, and Jonathan was so stirred by the sight of them that a silly grin broke out all over his face. He raised his sword hand in a salute and went by, his step in cadence with the tread of his regiment, and when Washington returned his salute and, it seemed, slightly nodded to him, Jonathan was so crowded with feelings of pride and affection that the spring-green trees blurred in a curtain of tears.

The six thousand stood at ease in their ranks after the parade, stood in the mild spring breeze, and listened to Washington's voice as he read the great news. Even those in the farthest corners of the field could hear him distinctly; it was a strong voice, though few had ever heard it raised before. The Marquis de Lafayette sat smiling handsomely at his side as he read the announcement, and it was therefore as great a day for Lafayette as for Von Steuben. The news was that King Louis of France had signed an alliance with the colonies. In the pauses, the calls of a cardinal and an oriole rang in the nearby woods, and Jonathan thought of this news and what it meant; it meant that this impoverished, lonely new country, fighting its former king, now had a rich and powerful ally that had declared war on England. America was no longer alone in the world.

A dense hush lay over the meadow when the announcement was concluded; then, at a signal from Von Steuben, the artillery began firing volleys. The birdsongs stopped. The guns thundered again and again, a volley for each of the thirteen colonies. The smell of gunpowder drifted over the field, and when the last echoes had rumbled away, Washington cried:

"Long live the King of France!"

And the army roared, as in one voice:

"LONG LIVE THE KING OF FRANCE!"

The chaplain gave an invocation then, in a straining, reedy voice, thanking God for moving King Louis' heart, thanking God for the friendship of Steuben, and for the faith and fortitude that had carried the army through the desperate winter, and for the holy cause of Liberty that it could now pursue with renewed strength.

The army remained hushed as Washington, his hat held against his chest, slowly raised his head from the prayer and, his face working with emotion, reined his warhorse around to ride away. They watched his broad back above the stallion's massive haunches, and they wondered at him.

Then they saw him rein the horse in, and bring it about. They watched him stand in his stirrups, his jaw muscles working; they watched him raise his cockaded black hat high over his head. And then they heard him yell out in a huge voice, for once casting away his usual reserve:

"Hurrah! Hurrah! Hurrah!"

Jonathan snatched off his own hat, flung it in the air, and cried, "Hurrah!" All along the lines now, hats were spinning in the air.

"HURRAH!" the army bellowed. "HURRAH! HURRAH!"

And General Washington rode off the field and into the woods.

THE POET AND LIEUTENANT HOAG HAD TO SUPPORT Johnny, one of them under each arm, to get him up the companionway and out on the deck where he could sit in the May sunlight. He was dizzy, and his lungs bubbled.

He sat on the deck on the port side of the ship with his blanket over his legs and his back against a bulkhead of the quarterdeck, and from here he was able to look over the sparkling blue water at that misty-blue stretch of land that was Long Island.

Johnny sat with the sun on his face and pretended that he could feel it baking the poisons out of him. He breathed the sun-charged air through his open mouth, as if he could actually inhale sunlight into his lungs where it would dry them and heal them. He sat this way for an unmeasured time, listening to the waves lapping on the hull, hearing the drone of many voices, the raspy coughings, out on the main deck where hundreds of enlisted prisoners were sitting and sprawling in the sun; he sat hearing above him the slow tread of pacing guards, hearing wisps of conversations that surfaced and submerged in his consciousness without beginnings or meanings or endings; he heard the raucous cries of gulls, and once looked up to see one gleaming white and incredibly graceful against the deep blue sky. It was holding itself against the wind, lazily soaring but going nowhere, staying there about twenty feet above the ship's rail. Johnny had time to study its remarkable beauty, even to the delicate bluish tips on its white wings, as it soared unmoving there.

Bird, if I were you, and I could do that, I'd turn away from this reeky putrid hulk and sail off over there to the clean land. Why don't you go there? he wondered.

He watched the hovering gull and remembered that day less than a year ago when he had sat just like this under a willow tree on the bank of the Brandywine, trying to write a poem that had turned instead into a letter to his father. He thought of that day and all that happened since to turn him into a dying man.

He watched the beautiful gull in the air and then realized that the reason it stayed here instead of going to a beautiful clean place was because it was waiting for slop to be thrown off the ship.

God, but it's a shame the way things are, he thought.

He decided that he probably would never be able to write a snip of poetry again, knowing as he did now how things really are in the world.

This was not like any other springtime. Every other springtime that Johnny could remember, he had been about the business of falling in love. Even if there had been no particular girl he had loved at the coming of a spring, he had fallen in love with the probability of being in love, and then every spring when he had been like that, some girl or another, or more than one, had entered into the sunny mist of love-feeling all around him, and she had become the specific object upon which all that feelin had come to bear. For a while. Till the next one.

And where's that got me? he thought. I've had to promise m soul to one I'd already escaped from. All because of a ridiculou coincidence.

He tried to remember what it had felt like to desire Betsy Free man. He could not remember her face now. He could r member the night of the wedding party when he had la making vows and caressing her, and his hands could even re member the caresses. But he could not remember her face, an his body was too sick to remember desire.

But he could remember the face of Micajah Freeman down i the odorous below-decks darkness, and the light that had com into his dying eyes when he had made that impossible promise t him. When he tried to remember Betsy Freeman's face h would instead see the death's-head of Micajah Freeman.

Hell's fire, he's dead, he thought. That promise doesn't mea anything now.

Nay, he thought. It means more.

I wonder if the family knows I'm alive, he thought. I wonde if the British actually ever send the letters we write.

He doubted that.

I ought to write to them again now and tell them I'm sti alive, he thought.

Or maybe I ought to wait and see if I die before I tell them I'n alive, he thought. That amused him a little. He felt his lips smile

The sun was making him sweat now and he could feel th sweat tickling down his neck and ribs, and along his groin h could not distinguish between the tickling itches caused by swea and those caused by lice. He reached down and turned th blanket away off his legs, and he could see the fleas jump on h dirty breeches. His legs were in the shade of the ship's rail, an when he took the blanket off, the harbor breeze was cold on h sweaty legs and he broke out in gooseflesh and shivered violent and was afraid he would start coughing, that terrible coughin so he put the blanket back over his legs.

Can't stay comfortable, he thought.

But it's better up here than down in that tomb of a roo where I've been so many months. Here there's sunlight and ai Got to get busy and inhale a lungful of sunlight. The effort tic led, made him burst into coughing, and he filled his rag wit bloody mucus. He looked at the crimson gobs of stuff and wa sad and angry. He remembered something his mother had sai Blood shouldn't be seen outside of a body.

228

Surely there's not a hope of getting well, he thought. It's a waste of life, that's what it is. And it's all coming to this over a lot of hot-headed words from looniacs like Patrick Henry and Samuel Adams and Thomas Paine. Before we got infected with those words, we were Englishmen. Just like that one up there.

A British guard passed above, musket on his shoulder, looking down from the sky at Johnny with human eyes, blue eyes with reddish eyebrows, in a ruddy, healthy face that could have been the face of one of his own brothers.

Johnny remembered looking into a pair of blue eyes and thinking something like this as he killed an Englishman at the Battle of Brandywine. He remembered what it had felt like to put the sword blade into the man's innards while looking into his blue eyes, and he wished with all his soul that he had never had to feel that.

Patriot words, he thought angrily.

Then the beautiful pure-white slop-eating seagull appeared above the red-clad blue-eyed British sentry, against that deep blue May sky, and hung there in the air again, its little feet tucked back along its smooth-feathered white body, hanging in the air, free to go where it liked and do what it would do, even if that was only to dive into the sea for garbage.

Nay, Johnny thought. Maybe I'll get well. Us Clarks been strong. Flint and steel. I'll breathe sunlight every day they let me up here and maybe I can get well.

Tomorrow, he thought, I shall try to come up here under my own power. If I can't do it tomorrow, maybe I can the next day. The more you try, the more you can do. As Ma always said.

All I know is, I'm going to stay in sunshine and clean air as much as I can. I don't know how much a body can recover itself thataway.

But maybe a body—even such as I am now—could recover itself enough by summer to jump ship and swim over to that land yonder.

The British sentry was passing again and looking down at him with his blue eyes, and Johnny smiled to himself.

Isn't it a grand thing, he thought, that an Englishman can't ever know what an American's thinking.

IN ALL HIS YEARS OF HUNTING, SURVEYING, AND SOLDIERING in the Ohio Valley, George Rogers Clark had never seen a place as much to his liking as this. He stood in a high meadow above the water-falls and gazed westward along the great bend of the

229

Ohio, and the valley had so much the look of a paradise to it that, for the first time in many months, he dreamed of something besides his mission.

This is the place for the Clark family seat, he thought. God's love! What a site for a city!

The valley was wide and fertile, and watered by crystalline springs and creeks. He stood with his back to a sun-dappled grove of mulberry trees. A clear spring gurgled from the earth near his feet. Beyond the meadow, giant, graceful elms and walnuts and oaks and maples towered, some of them five or six feet through the trunk, their spreading limbs casting pools of shade a hundred feet wide on the grass. Far down beyond them curved the mile-wide river, tumbling and spraying, with a constant rushing sound, through a long chute of rapids, descending twenty feet over a great limestone fault.

And just above the falls lay the oblong wooded island upon which his troops were building their stockade and learning to march. He could hear faintly over the water-rush the shouts of drill and the ring of axes.

Yes, here was his regiment now, more than five hundred miles downriver from Fort Pitt, building a camp in the heart of enemy country and preparing for the last long trek to his targets on the Mississippi, three or four hundred more miles to the west by water and trail through the wilderness. He was nearly ready now for the big thrust of his plan, and his Strategy of the Absurd had come to seem more and more absurd every step of the way. Any other strategist would have called it off by now, he knew; he had almost done so himself two or three times along its ill-starred route.

He had designated them the Illinois Regiment because of their destination, but they were little more than a company.

He had come away from Red Stone Fort early in the spring, discouraged and enraged, with only 130 men instead of 300. They had obtained boats and ammunition at Fort Pitt, and embarked down the Ohio's flood toward the Kentucky River where they were to be joined by Captain William Bailey Smith's promised 200 Holston Valley volunteers, and all the way down George had assured himself that with Smith's men he would have some 330—enough, perhaps, to succeed still. They had rowed 500 miles to the Kentucky without, as far as he could discern, even being seen by Indians.

He had found Smith waiting as promised—but not with 200 men. He had only 20. The Holston settlements had been too worried about Cherokees to let 200 fighting men be taken away, Smith had explained.

At that dismal moment George had almost quit his scheme. He had sat down with the forlorn Smith in a rain-soaked tent for a cup of rum to ease the agony of disappointment.

But then, inexplicably, George had been stirred by an outrageous, desperate, elated certainty that he could *still* do it. That there were only a third as many men meant only that it would be three times as hard, not that it would be impossible.

And so he had brought them on, to this remote and unpeopled island by the Falls of the Ohio, while his boat-weary troops grumbled and wondered why, if they had been recruited to defend Kentuck, they were proceeding a hundred miles beyond its last settlements.

At last, on that little island one night in the light of a huge bonfire, he had assembled his regiment, and had described to them all that he had learned about the British Governor General Hamilton the Hair-Buyer, and about his web of Indian agents and his line of forts on the Mississippi and Wabash. They had listened with keen interest, as there was hardly a man among them who had not lost at least one blood relative or loved one to the Hair-Buyer's hired savages. And then, after he had worked them into a state of boiling rage over Hamilton's atrocities, he had revealed to them the true nature of their secret mission.

For an awful moment they had sat in shocked silence, with the bonfire roaring before them and the falls rushing behind them, and George had had every reason to expect they would turn in mutiny against him.

But instead, almost to a man, they had risen around him, raised their fists and guns and knives and voices, and cheered him. He had almost keeled over with relief. And Leonard Helm, dazed with admiration for the audacious plan, had turned to Johnny Rogers, crying:

"What did I tell ye, boy? Oh, he always was a one to grab th' Devil by th' foreskin!"

That night a few had had second thoughts and deserted. And the next morning George had had to thrash one surly brute who had raised the complaint that they had been tricked. Since then there had been no more dissent. They were all for Colonel Clark now. They devoured his every word when he harangued them about the chance he was giving them to serve their country. They subjected their anarchic souls to the hard demands of military discipline.

During their training, George had joked to Johnny Rogers that he felt as if he were domesticating a wolf pack. They had come to admire him, and tried to please him. He had swelled their heads with praise whenever they did something right, but raised swellings on their heads if they deliberately did things badly.

Until by now he had convinced them that they were a special breed of men with a special opportunity to do more good than all the huge armies marching up and down the seaboard. He knew they had frolic in their blood, and he had persuaded them that the upcoming adventure was going to be the greatest frolic this territory had ever seen. And so by now he had them in the palm of his hand, and he was shaping them into something greater than a mere guerrilla band.

It was the most ruffscuff lot of chawbacons that had ever gone by the name of a regiment. Almost every man in it had been living like a wolf in that dangerous realm between the white frontier and Indian territory, and their weather-cured hides bore scars to tell their hazardous histories: here a puckered bullet scar on a freckled shoulder, there a row of bear-claw scars down a flank, here a thin knife scar across a neck, there the gnarled vestige of a bitten-off ear. There was a noseless man, and a sergeant with a whitish tonsure shining through his greasy brown hair: one who had been scalped and had survived.

But they had qualities. He had watched them row like galley slaves day after day on the way down from Fort Pitt; he had watched them dance and cavort and brawl around their camp fires. They were durable, quick, and rowdy. Most men avoid danger; these liked it and looked for it. They were cunning, but had their own kinds of honor, and they were Spartan, and they had spirit. What they lacked in numbers and cannon, they would have to make up for in spirit. They were, as Leonard Helm liked to phrase it, a people fit to goose bears.

But a major element of their spirit now, that which George knew would most suit them for the particular task, was that they were vengeful—seethingly, bitterly, murderously vengeful. Almost every man in the Illinois Regiment now considered himself to have a blood feud with the notorious Hair-Buyer. Almost every one of them had dreamed sometime of taking that British officer's own scalp. And now here was this Lieutenant Colonel Clark, who seemed to have worked out the only way in the world for them to do it.

George strolled down from the mulberry grove now and moved into a meadow that gave him a wide view of the dark high hills of the north bank. There, just above the falls on that side of the river, was a rock bluff from which one could see the whole great southwesterly curve of the Ohio for miles and miles. It was a grand, high, lonely place, with a steep stream falling to the river nearby, a perfect place for a mill. Up on yon bluff, he thought now, daydreaming beyond the war, up there I'd build me a mill, and a fine house with a white-pillared porch, and here I'd sit with an elegant wife at my side, and watch the city grow here where I stand, and see the sun go down over the falls every evening.

What wife? he thought then. He could envision a woman in a billowy dress, but in his mind's eye he could not put a face on her. But there would be someone. Someday when this task was done, and he had time for his own life, there would be someone who would be as good for him as Ann Rogers had been for John Clark.

He thought of them. He had never seen a place that his parents would like better.

Aye, he thought. This place is it. I'll survey and engross it soon as I have the leisure. This mulberry grove on a hill. This is where my family will come to. After this war they'll come here. I can just feel it.

But first there's this game o' chess to finish with the Hairbuyer.

ON THE TWENTY-FOURTH OF JUNE, A BRIGHT, CLEAR DAY with the river running high from a recent rainfall, George loaded his regiment into the rowboats with their guns and ammunition and enough jerky and parched corn for a week, and shoved off the upper end of the island. Left behind to garrison the outpost were seven sick militiamen deemed unfit for the rigors of the trek. They all went around to the north side of the island to watch their comrades shoot the rapids.

The boats were rowed upstream a mile, then swung about into the main channel and aimed down toward the rapids. As the current sped them toward the roaring, milky-white water, the men grew wide-eyed. "George," Bowman gasped, "y'sure this is safe?"

George beamed at him. "Long as th' boys don't stand up and dance, we should stay right side up and bob right through like corks!"

Now the water was falling away before them, and the boats dithered and jounced down a gurgling, glassy-green waterchute between two boulders and then bucked through a churning pool of foam and headed into the next chute. "OooooHOW!" Bowman howled. "There goes m' gizzard, right into my hat!"

The boats were soaring and dipping down the rushing staircase of water when the bright midmorning sunlight took on an eerie

yellowish pall. There were odd, blurry edges on every shadow
double gleams on every highlight. Those who dared look up saw
the sun darkening in a cloudless sky, saw its light slowly winkin
out as if a giant eyelid were closing over it.

"An eclipse!" George yelled as soon as he understood. "
blessed omen to send us on our way!" But he wondered for
moment if Chief Logan's Great Spirit were trying to scare him
out of his purpose.

And then after a while they were in the frothy but gentle cur
rent below the falls, the men chattering like children in the
relief, squinting to watch the black disk of the moon release th
sun, and then their world was normal again. They gazed aroun
with mouths agape, looking back at the white water in the ord
nary glare of June sunshine, looking at the high, forested bluff
at each other, at their own hands on their oars or rifles.

Joseph Bowman was looking strangely at George now, an
finally asked with feeble levity, as if unsure whether to joke o
not:

"Now, c'mon, George. How'd y' arrange a thing like that?"

THE OARS WERE DOUBLE-MANNED. MEN NOT ROWING o
scanning the shore slept in the bilges. There were some thre
hundred miles more to go by river, deeper into enemy country
before they would hide the boats and set out overland. Georg
sat in the prow of the leading boat, like the tip of an arrowhead
with nothing in front of him but the little green-and-yellow
striped Virginia flag flapping on its standard, and the great river
He leaned back against the gunwale and contemplated the pearl
sky, the undulating green bluffs etched with gray cottonwood
and greenish-white sycamores, the wildfowl always soaring in th
sky or skimming the water. And he contemplated the river. H
listened to the regular *pash pash pash pash* against the boat hul
underneath him. The French called this one *La Belle Rivière*
and most Indian tribes' names for it meant the same: the Beau
tiful River. And rightly. It was majestically beautiful, curvin
through a thousand miles of primeval forest and virgin mead
owland from Fort Pitt to the Mississippi, so wide most of its wa
that a boat in midstream was out of accurate musket-range from
either shore; deep enough in most seasons even for large boat
with a current gentle enough to permit fairly easy travel up
stream by oar, paddle, and sometimes even sail. To the practica
traveler, trader or soldier, its beauty was enhanced by it
usefulness as a road through an almost impenetrable wilderness
George saw rivers in both those ways, as beautiful and useful

234

it he had also, long since, begun to understand rivers as earth-
apers. He had seen how rivers force their ways through and
ound mountains to descend to the sea; he had seen how they
e down valleys and carried dirt and trees down. When he was
or on a river, he seemed to feel, through its tug on his flesh or
a the hull of his boat, the very tilt of the continent. With a
nd in the Potomac or the James or the York or the Rappahan-
ck, he seemed to touch the Atlantic through watery extensions
'his fingertips. Here in the Ohio, or on such of its tributaries as
e Monongahela, the Muskingum, the Kanawha, he was sensi-
e of the vast westering drainage.

He hung an arm over the side of this heavily laden war boat
w and felt the cool, green water of the Ohio on his hand. But
e could imagine that he felt as well the Mississippi's yellow
aters beyond that—though he had never seen it yet, only heard
' it—and beyond that great muddy current, he imagined his
ger-nerves like antennae touched the warm brine of the Gulf
Mexico.

George and Tom Jefferson had talked much about rivers. Into
e Mississippi above the village of St. Louis on the Spanish
de, the Missouri poured from westward, and rumor had it that
was even wider and longer than the Ohio, and that it drained a
atershed far bigger than all the lands on this side of the Mis-
ssippi. His own spies, Moore and Linn, had seen that won-
ous Missouri. The theory was that the Missouri started in a
eat range of western mountains which Indians called the Shin-
g Mountains, and that on the farther slope of those mountains
ere was a river that ran westward down to the Pacific Ocean.
That would mean, George thought, that the main lowland of
is whole continent lies betwixt two mountain ranges, maybe
ree thousand miles apart but parallel to each other. What runs
st off the Alleghenies goes to the Atlantic, as we know, and
hat runs west off them goes to the Mississippi and down to the
ulf, as we know, and what drains east off the Shining Moun-
ins does the same. And what runs west off the Shining Moun-
ins goes to the Pacific.

With his hand trailing over the side of the boat in the limpid
een Ohio, he thought of these immense distances and the long
vers and the great tilting slabs of land they ran off of, and he
ondered, as Thomas Jefferson had mused aloud to him,
hether there could be a water route all the way from here to the
acific. Legend had it that there was. Explorers for ages had
een seeking a Northwest Passage from sea to sea, but to no
vail. In Jefferson's opinion, if there really was a passage to the

Western Sea, it was by these very rivers. The Ohio, the Mi
sissippi, the Missouri.

By the Maker! George thought. It's almost too much to stretc
your mind over!

I wonder if I'll ever see that, he thought, now wiggling h
fingers in the current of the Ohio.

When I get to the Mississippi, when I get to St. Louis, h
thought, then I'll see that Missouri, and I'll put my hand in
and feel its water, and feel where it's been.

By the Eternal, he almost prayed now: Let me find the tim
and the strength, someday, when this war's over with, to go u
that Missouri and over, and go on down to the land's end!

His scalp was prickling, as it had that long-ago night when h
had dreamed this big scheme that he was on now. He was thinl
ing that way again now, but farther on.

To the land's end! he thought. By my God! May I live to g
there!

14

MONMOUTH, NEW JERSEY

June 28, 1778

MAJOR JONATHAN CLARK DREW HIS COAT SLEEVE ACROSS H
brow to try to stop the sweat off his forehead from pouring int
his eyes and blurring his sight. He desperately sucked air with h
mouth open, trying to get enough breath to take him a littl
farther up the slope. Never in his life had he been so hot, neve
had he endured such sultriness, not even at Charles Town.

He gasped for another chestful of the oven-hot air. Some c
his slogging troops were wavering, staggering, eyes rolling, pan
ing through open lips, their blazing feet often tripped by the sof
sandy soil.

It was the hottest day in anyone's memory, and they had bee
marching all day in it toward Monmouth, pursuing Genera
Clinton's retreating army toward the New Jersey coast. They ha
marched, waited in the shadeless roads, marched more, waite
more, all day long; already today, dozens of soldiers had co

lapsed on the road; several had died; and now, now that their smart Steuben-style marching had been worn and baked down to a weaving trudge, now they were close upon the enemy and would have to try to fight a battle.

Led by General Greene, the Virginians had left the road a few minutes ago, passed through a sparse wood, through a swampy ravine, and now were trying to climb a rise of ground, an abandoned field overgrown with raspberry brambles. The men were so spent that the brambles that snagged their clothes nearly pulled them off balance. Beyond the top of the hill they were climbing, powder smoke and battle dust arose, a smudgy yellow that dimmed the descending sun. Artillery was so close now that the concussion of each report could be felt passing through the stifling air like ripples in water. Musket fire was sputtering continuously there, and shouts sometimes rose over the din. The regiment halted and waited while sappers tore down a rail fence. Jonathan plucked a red berry. It was not quite ripe, and its tang was more refreshing than the hot water in his canteen.

The smell of gunpowder was choking-sharp here. Jonathan watched the sappers work on the fence and wondered what the great sway of the battle was like now. One never really knew, it seemed, unless one happened to be the general, and maybe not even then. One saw only his own little approaches to the battlefield, then his own little immediate circle of mayhem and suffering for a few minutes or a few hours, but the whole context of it was always beyond, always a great, mysterious confusion. Only at Charles Town had he been able to see the great panorama of it. At Germantown he had seen nothing but fog and then a few yards of shooting, running, dying. He had not known for two days afterward that Brother Johnny's unit had been captured. Probably not more than two or three hundred yards away from Jonathan himself that had happened, but in that battle it might as well have been on another continent.

And now there was this. The battle of Monmouth, New Jersey. All he knew about it was what he had heard from couriers coming back to report to General Greene. When Clinton had evacuated Philadelphia with his huge army on June 18, heading across New Jersey to the sea, General Washington had vacated Valley Forge to chase him. Clinton's army, slowed by its enormous, twelve-mile-long baggage train, had moved barely five miles a day; the Continentals, being threadbare and lacking everything, had made nearly ten miles a day and now had overtaken Clinton's army. General Charles Lee had been sent ahead with an advance force to attack Clinton's rear while Washington brought up the main army. But then the surprises had started happening. Lee, on being counterattacked, had ordered a retreat instead of holding till Washington's arrival. Washington, astonished to see Lee's force coming pell-mell toward the rear, had met Lee on the road, demanded an explanation, and, as a courier had said it, "cursed him till the leaves shook in the trees." Washington then had taken after Lee's retreating troops himself, riding like the great Virginia horseman he was, and almost singlehandedly had slowed the retreat, stopped it, and begun rallying Lee's force to begin making a stand. The couriers, reporting all this, had been beside themselves with amazement. "Called General Lee a poltroon, he did! Lord, that's Lee's last battle, sure!" And another had reported, "His Excellency rode till his horse died, then hopped on another!"

And now Washington was busy forming a line of battle on the edge of a marsh. General Greene's division, including the Virginians, was to form its right wing, and that was where they were going now as they clambered, faint with heat, up this rise to take their position.

That poor, sorry Lee, Jonathan thought. There had been rumors lately, in the officers' circles, that Lee was trying to discredit General Washington, to betray him. The air was always full of such intrigue and speculation. Jonathan chose not to believe that Lee was a traitor. An overrated tactician, perhaps, but surely no traitor. At any rate, he had retreated, and had brought the battle to this state of affairs, and now the Virginians were climbing up one side of a rise, on the other side of which the battle seemed to be raging full force, and now they would be in battle in this inferno of a summer day, and Jonathan once again would be responsible for that one little corner of battle he could see and understand.

Now the fence was down and the ranks began moving forward again, still further thinned by heat-strokes. Jonathan looked down the line at his men. Most were so heat-flushed and gaping-mouthed that if they had fear, it could not show through their physical misery.

Close on the left now a tremendous artillery barrage was under way. Smoke and dust hung over the field like a choking fog.

"Fix bayonets!" was the first order to come down the line. And as Steuben had taught them to do, they all at once slipped the steel spikes out of their scabbards and locked them with twisting wrists onto their sunhot musket muzzles.

"Music!" The drums started rapping their ominous, blood-stirring cadences.

"Arms at port, march!" And with their weapons aslant across their chests the Virginians toiled obediently through the sand and heat into the drifting banks of smoke. Jonathan's eyes watered and the membranes of his nostrils stung. Every breath was an assault on his lungs. In the pall of smoke he could see only the sere, sparse grass and the limp weeds before his feet; the shape of a dark bush or scrub tree would materialize in front of him, and he would expect it to be a Redcoat or a dragoon.

But the enemy did not appear yet in the choking yellow smoke, and soon Greene's brigades were on line in control of this high ground. By now the sun was low in the west, glowing a sullen orange.

The heaviest action, judging by the noise of it, seemed to be down toward the left. Most of the smoke seemed to be drifting from there. Now and then through a rent in that curtain, Jonathan could see rows of scarlet uniforms, or winking yellow muzzleblasts. A staff officer galloped along the Virginians' front, pointing down that way and exulting: "What luck! We've got the buggers enfiladed!" And he rode through the ranks back down the hill, shouting for artillery.

In a minute, caissons came rattling up the slope behind the Virginians, the horses surging to pull their loads up through the sandy ground. The pieces were unlimbered and chocked and aimed straight down along the enemy's ranks. The British down there were not advancing; they had been fought to a standstill by the troops and cannon of the left wing. And now the artillery here on the hill opened up on the exposed flanks of those Redcoats, cutting them down in swatches. It was like a nightmare, all outlines blurred by a smoke as thick and sour as Hell's brimstone. The cannon crashed repeatedly here on the high ground, while the artillery of the left wing thumped down there, and the British ranks at the bottom of the slope were trapped in the bombardment from two angles. The ground down there was strewn with fallen Englishmen, lying inert or crawling, while the ranks of them kept wavering, re-forming, trying to advance. Once again Jonathan was stirred by amazement at what those British Regulars could endure.

And now he saw that a wide front of the Redcoats—perhaps a battalion of them, though he could see only fragments of the picture through the haze—was wheeling left and coming toward this high ground, led by a saber-swinging officer. They were apparently coming this way to outflank the force in front of them, or were simply charging straight against this artillery that was devastating them. It was a brave mad move if they were coming

239

here; they had a long way to come, in the open, in the breathless furnace-heat of the slope, hidden by nothing but drifts of smoke. Jonathan turned to his captains. "Stand this ground!" he yelled. "Prepare to fire in volley! But don't shoot till you can see the pimples on their chins!"

Some of the men grinned at the sound of this command. Jonathan had thought it up at Germantown: words chosen to make the oncoming juggernaut ranks of scarlet seem less formidable. At times like these it was hard to remember that Redcoats were vulnerable flesh and blood, as well as guts and steel.

A slight, hot breeze was stirring the smoke as the sun descended, and now much of the main front could be seen; it was more than a half-mile long, stretching away across the main road, in and out of copses of brushy growth, tall trees, morasses, orchards. A bridge across the low ground was packed with British infantry and light-horse. Now and then the smoke clouds would part and Jonathan could see a jutting structure among the trees that apparently was Monmouth Court House, more than a mile away. The masses of British units did not seem to be advancing anywhere, except the grenadiers tramping resolutely up the slope toward the Virginians. Coming up to meet the hail of lead, which now was poised to fall upon them.

But now a quicker motion down the slope, off to the right, caught Jonathan's eye. It was a squadron of British light cavalry coming around the marching grenadiers to lead the charge up the hill. Jonathan's heartbeat quickened. Cavalry was always a fearsome and stunning sight, sweeping across a field: the great horses, blacks and bays and sorrels and grays, racing forward under the spur, too dumb and disciplined to fear bullets, ridden stirrup-to-stirrup by reckless young men whose own courage was magnified by the speed and power they had at their command; Jonathan himself was enough of a rider and horse-racer and foxhunter to know the precipitous kind of power they must feel. In battle he and his men had never yet faced a charge of horse, and it frightened him. They came so fast there was hardly time for firing and reloading. And every man, from childhood, had known to get out of the way of a running horse. Jonathan was afraid his men would flee before this; already they were looking confused and irresolute.

So he ran a few paces out past the front rank toward the oncoming cavalry, pointed his sword toward the plunging, thundering wall of horseflesh, bellowing:

"Ready and aim! And no man o' mine dast miss anything so big as a horse!"

They came on. Jonathan's heart was slamming. They were a hundred yards away; their hoof-falls were strangely soft in the deep sand, but now he could hear the snorts and their slumping breath and the jingle of metal as they came through the smoke. The riders were swishing sabers around their heads. At seventy yards their commander began a deep-throated war cry that was taken up in chorus by the rest:

"Yoooooooooooo!"

Jonathan responded, unthinking, with the wild, high-pitched, half-Indian yodel of the frontiersman, and the Virginians all joined in with the blood-curdling ululation, heartened by it, purging their own fears by it:

"Eeeeyiyiyiyiyiyiyi!"

To his astonishment, the horses shied at the shrill sound; they flung their heads, wild-eyed; some reared, breaking the impetus of the rush. Those behind virtually ran up the backs of those in front; and at that moment, so thrilled by their own shrieking that they forgot to wait for the command to fire, the Virginians in the front ranks began discharging their muskets. They may have been resisting a cavalry charge, in tactical terms, but in their own quickened minds, they were simply stopping a runaway herd. The animals, first terrified by the hideous wail and now stung and punctured by musketballs, were stumbling, rearing, crumbling back on their cruppers, going every way but forward; their riders thus were transformed suddenly from bellowing demons into mere riders out of control of their mounts, helpless, frightened, and vulnerable. It was like mayhem at a horsefair now: lunging bodies, grunts, whinnying, spraying sand and roiling dust, flailing hooves, ears back, teeth bared, the thud of great bodies falling, legbones and ribs snapping, lost swords twirling through the air, brown beast-eyes wild with pain and terror.

"Second ranks, FIRE!" Jonathan thought to yell in the face of this appalling spectacle. They delivered a second volley, and more horses wheeled and fell. Cavalrymen in their short red coats groaned and sobbed and tried to disentangle themselves from the crush and surge of their tumbling beasts, or were shot down as they tried to rise from the ground and use their pistols. Some were dragged away, caught in their stirrups, others were galloping away, in or out of control of their mounts.

Lord God, Jonathan thought, eyes bugging with disbelief, we broke a cavalry charge!

That done, the rest was easy. Infantry seemed like a shooting practice now. The 8th Regiment fired volley after volley and reloaded with the Prussian precision Von Steuben had taught them, even though every breath was a scorching torture and their vision was blurred with sweat and the tears of smarting eyes; and soon the slope in front of the Virginians was a carrion heap of wounded, twitching, uncomprehending horses, some struggling to rise on their forelegs, and of dying men lying supine on hot sand with their forearms flung over their shattered faces, leaking good English blood into the New Jersey sands.

And after the assault was repulsed, Jonathan as usual was sunk almost unbearably in remorse and pity, exhausted, miserable as a child, smoke-choked and fatigued almost to the point of collapse.

The Battle of Monmouth was ending. Washington tried to form a counterattack with his spent forces. But he simply ran out of daylight. In the dusk the armies disengaged and gathered up those who had fallen victim to wounds and heat. Sometime in the middle of the night Clinton's army crept away. It reminded Jonathan of Charles Town, when this same General Clinton had taken his soldiers off the island and the fleet had cut its cables and sailed off in darkness.

In the morning when the Americans awoke, sleeping with their muskets on the sandy ground, there was no British army.

The day after the battle, a woman camp-follower named Mary Hayes, smeared with mud and blood, was brought before General Washington and her story was told. She had been a water carrier for her husband's crew of cannoneers. When her husband was shot down before her eyes, she had taken his place as loader for the duration of the battle. Washington named the sturdy Irishwoman a sergeant on the spot; the cannoneers nicknamed her Moll Pitcher and spread her fame throughout the army.

And thus on that day Jonathan saw a widow in triumph and a general in disgrace. General Charles Lee was relieved of command and returned to the dumb companionship of his trusted hounds. He had fought his last battle. Rumor was that he would be court-martialed for cowardice—or even treason.

July 4, 1778

LUCY BOUNDED INTO THE HOUSE FROM THE YARD, YELLING, "Mama! Papa! Come see!" Then, as if remembering suddenly the new ladylike demeanor she was trying to attain, she slowed to a walk in the hallway, straightened her posture, and carried herself quietly into the study looking, except for a slight swagger in the attitude of the shoulders, quite feminine. All the windows were open to admit some breeze into the high-ceilinged room where her parents sat. John Clark was at his writing desk and Mrs. Clark was on a settee with a letter-box on her knees. They were looking up at Lucy and starting to set aside their papers. "Come see," she said in a quiet voice now. "Edmund's done something for the Fourth of July. Come, please."

They followed her out across the driveway and into the shade of the big trees in the yard. Edmund and Billy were standing at attention under a huge oak. Behind them stood Elizabeth and Fanny, squirming with excitement. York stood behind a tree behind the girls. Edmund held a sword, his father's old militia saber, upright against his right shoulder. Billy stood holding up Edmund's flintlock long rifle, which was gleaming in the sun-dappled light. It was several inches taller than he was. In front of Billy, stuck in the ground, was a forked stick. "Stand there, please," Edmund told them, turning his head stiffly. Then he looked severely at Billy and said, "Load."

Billy, his heels together and back stiff, lifted the powder horn that hung around his neck and poured a charge down the barrel. Swiftly, then, as if he had been doing this all his life, he pulled a ball and patch from his shot bag, reached high to push them into the muzzle with his thumb, and then whisked the ramrod out from under the rifle barrel and slid it down the muzzle in one sure, straight motion, then tamped twice, whisked it out, and replaced it. Then he lifted the rifle to his waist and poured prim-ing powder into the pan. All this had taken but twenty seconds and he had not left his posture of attention. His parents looked at the two boys with some wonderment, and apprehension, as Billy had never used a loaded firearm before, to their knowledge.

"Now, ready and aim," Edmund commanded, and as Billy strained with a contorted mouth to swing the heavy gun up and settle it in the fork of the stick, Edmund pointed the sword to-ward a distant elm. Upon its trunk, some twenty-five yards away, they now saw a pinkish speck: a tiny square of paper fixed to the tree trunk. John Clark's mouth dropped open and he started to say something, because beyond that tree lay a fenced pasture full of his precious army beef cattle. York, behind his own tree, had his hands over his ears. But Edmund was saying now as Billy cocked the gun with his small hand and squinted down the long barrel:

"In celebration of the second anniversary of our indepen-dence, and in the honor of our brothers Jonathan and George and John Clark: *Fire!*"

The powder flared and puffed, then the rifle crashed and it recoil shoved Billy's upper body back five inches.

Immediately, then, Dickie stepped out from behind the dis tant elm and came around it to look at the little target pinned to it. And even as the acrid smoke drifted away from the rifle, they heard Dickie yelp:

"Great Haunt! You won't believe your eyes!" And he came running to them. His mother rolled her eyes and touched he throat, gasping:

"He was right behind that tree . . . He . . ."

"Lookahere!" Dickie cried, and thrust his hand under thei noses. In his palm lay the paper, a rectangle of about four by five inches, with the Union Jack of Great Britain drawn on it with red and blue paints.

And in the very center, at the junction of the crosses, gaped a ragged-edged bullet hole.

The girls had come close to look. York had crept out from behind his tree, and was coming forth with his face full of curi osity. Edmund and Billy still stood by their posts, beaming, and the parents looked at them aghast.

"I been teachin' him in the woods," Edmund said. "Give him a few years till he can lift that thing without busting his guts, and he'll be good as me."

BEHIND JOHNNY'S CLOSED EYELIDS BLAZED AN ORANGE glow, swimming with white specks. The sun baked his chest. His breeches were soaked with sweat. The planks of the *Jersey*'s deck were hard under his bony rump and elbows. His chin was sunk on his chest and he breathed through his mouth, both to shut out the stink of decay and disease and to inhale as much sunny air as possible into his lungs.

Johnny believed his lungs were improving because of these sunny days on deck; he believed it even though one damp night of cold harbor air would make his lungs tickle and hurt and fill up with bloody mucus again. This summer, he thought, I will become well in the lungs. I have to do that or the next winter will kill me.

The deck of the prison ship was like an anvil and the sun was like a hammer, and he lay between them, suffering the full weight of the sun instead of seeking shade, because sunlight, he believed, was his only cure. It'll cure me or kill me, that's all right either way, he thought. I had rather be dead o' parching right now than drown in my own snot come winter.

He would think like that for a while, then he would find himself beside the Brandywine with his soul full of bittersweetness, the sunlight through willow-leaves dappling and dancing on his thighs, while a thousand voices droned like bumblebees. Then he would open his eyes to the glare of the sun again and there would be the gray, splitting, weathered wood of the old ship's oaken taffrail a few feet above; the murmur of voices would still be around his swimming head, and he would know where he was for a while, and would consciously gasp the hot air for a while longer until he would drowse again and the dream of Brandywine would come. It was as if he had been born at Brandywine and there were no dreams from any earlier time.

"Ahhhh," said a mournful voice nearby, "here they come, God rest their souls."

"Aye," said someone else with equal mournfulness. "God rest."

Johnny did not have to look; he knew they were talking about the corpses. In this July heat, the enlisted men in the holds were dying of a dozen diseases, or simply from heat and suffocation. The dead-boat was making three or four trips a day now. Even in the less crowded gun room, two Yankee officers had died in their bunks the last week.

Despite himself, Johnny opened his eyes and took a sidelong look forward to the gangway where prisoners, two by two, were carrying shrouded corpses to take them down the ladder to the docking raft off the starboard side. The soldiers were half-naked, bearded, their scrawny bodies so gray with filth and slick with sweat they looked like field slaves or coal diggers as they carried their pitiful burdens through the gangway and toiled down out of sight over the side with them.

Johnny was drifting in the river of heat behind his closed eyelids again when he was jerked into wakefulness by shouts coming from somewhere and clattering sounds like wood against wood. "*Guards!*" someone was shouting. "*Guards!*" There were footsteps thundering on the deck and Johnny opened his eyes to see a red blur go between himself and the taffrail: a running Redcoat with his musket. "To the gangway!" cried a voice. The thumping sounds continued and then, through his confused stupor, Johnny heard the *pam* of a pistol shot, more scuffling, and a strange, rising growl of savage voices, hundreds of voices. A British officer of guards ran by, sword in hand. "*He-hey! He-hey!*" came a distant voice, as if from down on the water. A musket banged then, followed by a louder mob-growl. Johnny was trying to get the strength to rise.

Then there were Redcoats running in the other direction,

clambering up ladders onto the quarterdeck. The ragged figure
of Yankee prisoners ran and shuffled and leaped among them
getting in their way, it seemed, deliberately, yelping and laugh
ing and cursing. Twice Johnny tried to rise, his heart thumping
twice he was tripped over by running legs and knocked flat on
the hot deck, while those who had tripped over him thumped to
the deck and were trampled and stumbled over by others. At last
Johnny got to all fours and climbed through limbs and torsos to
the taffrail, where he pulled himself up to look over the side.

At first it made no sense, what he saw: there was the dead-boat
being rowed away, as it was every day; it was about forty feet out
pulling steadily away on the sun-blazing blue-gray water.

And then, while the commotion continued around him on
the quarterdeck, Johnny began to comprehend.

The men in the boat, rowing, were not the dead-boat crew
they were prisoners—the same filthy scarecrows who, minute
earlier, had been carrying corpses down the gangplank. Johnny'
heart leaped. Somehow they had got the boat; they were escap
ing! Down forward on the docking raft at the foot of the gang
plank lay six or seven bodies, but only four of them were in
shrouds. The others were the crew of the boat, hurt or dead; one
was propped on an elbow with his hand over his eyes.

Escaping! A wave of joy surged in Johnny's breast—but then a
prickling of dread helplessness. The fugitives were still within
musket range, and so plain and vulnerable in the slow, open
boat. He expected any moment to hear gunfire, to see those
brave desperadoes crumple up, stopped by musketballs.

The rowers pulled with a dreamlike slowness; the boat seemed
to be almost standing still, holding them there as perfect targets
giving the Redcoat guards all the time in the world to take aim

But moment after moment went by, dip after dip of the oars
while the mob-shouting everywhere on the deck began to turn
more and more to cheering.

Johnny turned from the rail and looked up. And at last he saw
why the guards were not shooting at the boat.

They were surrounded by prisoners, by unarmed but jeering
cheering, taunting prisoners.

Some of the British guards and crew were hemmed in up on
the quarterdeck by Rebel officers; another group of Redcoat
stood at bay on the maindeck, bayonets leveled at the horde of
gaunt, dirty, grinning, furiously happy American prisoners of
war, who surrounded them, taunting and spitting.

It was obvious now why the guards dared not discharge their
guns at the escaping boat. If they emptied them, they would be

obbed and torn apart by a hundred bare hands before they ould reload.

The guards stood, sweating, back to back. Even their officers ere at a loss how to command them.

For a taut minute Johnny felt that anything might erupt—that he mob might rush the guards in a general mutiny, or that the uards, in their tense state, might shoot into the mob or charge hem with steel. It was a moment exactly like this, on King treet in Boston eight years ago, which had exploded into a racas killing five citizens and had come to be known as the Boston Massacre. It would be bloody pandemonium if either fac- ion moved first, Johnny realized. And now some voices up on he quarterdeck were beginning to debate the possibilities, to make suggestions.

"Kill the God-dang gaolers!" sang out a voice twangy with Virginian accent.

"Aye!" shouted another.

"That lieutenant there, with a face like a turd-pie! I want to ut his head in th' swill-pot!" There was a wave of jeers and whistling. Johnny balled his fists, his soul screaming for that ind of revenge. But his reason prayed nothing would happen. A lot would be a waste of blood, even if it succeeded. Even if the risoners killed their keepers and took over the ship, they would till be prisoners. The vessel could go nowhere. There were no mallboats to go ashore in. More likely the Royal Navy would ust sail a warship up alongside and sink us, Johnny thought. Or ust let us starve.

But the hubbub on deck was subsiding now. Johnny turned to ook after the fugitives, whom he'd almost forgotten in the ten- ion.

The boat was more than a hundred yards away now, and the scapees within it were going easy on the oars, gazing back ap- parently for a farewell look at the dungeon-ship. One of them tood up in the stern and waved. Many voices cheered from the hip, many arms were waved in reply, and there were more miles than Johnny had ever seen on the *Jersey*. It was obvious now that the mob on the ship was not going to riot, but had only been buying time for the men in the boat. Now the boat was safe out of musket range and the event was nearly over, and every American still aboard the *Jersey* was a bit more free, in his spirit, because of them.

The man standing in the boat was yelling something through cupped hands. His voice came faint into the wind, but Johnny heard the words:

"July the fourth! It is . . ."

Is it? Is it? Johnny thought. By heaven, it is! Two years sinc
independence!

And from the throats of the hundreds of prisoners holdin
their captors captive, three brave cheers burst forth; a seagul
soaring over veered off in fright.

THAT NIGHT THE OFFICERS IMPRISONED IN THE GUN ROON
could not keep from smiling at each other, laughing wistfully
Even though the air was so hot and dense that the lanter
scarcely burned, they were happy.

"Didn't I say so?" Lieutenant Hoag burbled. "The one way o
this *Jersey* is by way o' the dead-boat! Ha, ha!"

"Lord in Paradise," Johnny groaned, looking misty-eyed, "
wish I was with 'em! Independence! God Almighty! What
day!"

"Independence, you say?" Hoag snickered now. "Why, frien
Clark, if you escaped off this boat, you'd be married, by a death
bed promise, to a shrew you can't even abide! You'd call *tha*
independence? Ha, ha!"

"THERE SHE LAYS, JOE," GEORGE SAID. "KASKASKIA."

"Perty as a virgin," said Bowman. "And little does she know.

It was the evening of July fourth. The blood-red sunset on th
far side of the Mississippi Valley reddened their flushed faces
George was awestruck by his first sight of the great river.

The Illinois Regiment was lying, legs burning with exhaus
tion, stomachs gnawed by two days' marching without food, i
the waving meadow grass on a bluff overlooking the angle wher
the Kaskaskia River flowed into the gigantic Mississippi. In th
angle was the town, a cluster of gardens and streets and wel
built houses of stone, timbers, and plaster. Above the villag
were grainfields, pastures dotted with cattle and sheep, an India
village of dome-shaped huts, a quaint and massive Old Worl
Windmill, and the river road fading northward up the Mis
sissippi through the evening haze toward the smaller villages o
Prairie du Rocher and Cahokia. Across the Mississippi from Ka:
kaskia, on the Spanish side, barely visible at this distance, lay th
tiny village of St. Genevieve.

The whole valley was lavender, red, gold; the Mississippi wa
a broad brassy ribbon with a red path of sunflecks coming acros
it. And beyond were the low purple bluffs of Spanish Louisiana
"Imagine it, a pocket o' civilization out here 'twixt Noplace an
Nowhere," George said.

"Yup. And imagine: It's a-gonna be our'n, 'fore the day of independence is over." Joe Bowman was one of that brotherhood who called themselves the Sons of Liberty, and he was deeply stirred by the timeliness of their arrival. To him it was another of George's propitious arrangements, like the eclipse. It was useless for George to protest that he had expected to invade the place a month earlier; Joe was convinced that George had worked it out for the Fourth of July.

Leonard Helm lounged at George's left, and he was studying the village through a spyglass. The troops, mostly stripped to their breechclouts to catch any breath of evening air on their sweaty bodies, lay or sat in the grass along the brow of the bluff, kneading their leg muscles, tending their feet and their weapons, and looking down on Kaskaskia, light-headed, famished, rapacious, thinking their private thoughts of attack, plunder, revenge.

"I feel like th' wolf fixin' to swoop down on th' fold," Helm murmured with a mean grin, still squinting through the glass. "That there," he said, pointing to a large house fortified by a high stone wall, "so that's their fort, eh? Don't look like much of a fort t' me. And the Sewer de Roachblob, he lives in that big house inside, eh? What I'll do is I'll haul that mother-scalpin' skunk-fart of a French Tory whore's son outer that house and I'll nail his cock-bag to th' big elm tree thar, that's what I'll do."

George shook his head and clucked his tongue at Helm's language. This was the vengeful attitude he had nurtured in his men to get them down the Ohio and across the Illinois plains to his destination. You can get a lot of mileage out o' hate, he thought. They were in a simple raiding and plundering mood. But what they had to do now was not going to be quite that simple, and it was time to tell them so. "Now, fetch me all the officers. I need to talk to 'em before we go down there," he said.

They came and knelt around him on the slope. He pointed to a solitary farmhouse on the near bank of the Kaskaskia River, where, according to his spies, boats were available for ferrying the troops across the Kaskaskia to the town. They would sneak down the slope and capture the house as soon as darkness had fallen, he said. Then they would try to ferry all the troops across to the town before midnight. Bowman would take part of the force to surround the town, while George would lead the rest straight through the streets to the fort, which he expected he could seize by surprise. "If I do, I'll signal with a pistol shot and one hellacious yelp," he said. "If not, and ye hear battle, then you'll come in and help me storm the fort.

249

"Now," he said. "Here it is about Kaskasky, once we've got 'er, and listen damn good to this, my boys, 'cause we fly or we fall, on what I tell ye now:

"Make every man understand that I'll not tolerate one act of plunder or savagery of any kind. There'll be no scalping, there'll be no looting, there'll be no raping, or even an ungentle gesture at any woman, girl, sheep, or even bitch dog in that town. We'll use only what force we need to keep the civilians out of our way, and there'll be no intercourse of any kind with the inhabitants until I say so."

The captains were flabbergasted. "No looting?" exclaimed Helm. "Th' boys won't like that! Takes th' fun out of it. Not to mention th' profit."

"Fun enough later. And profit's for merchants, not soldiers," George said. "One other caution, most important: we'll take pains never to reveal how few we are. We must never bunch together where we could be counted. If we can, we must seem a thousand. We can negotiate only from a dominant posture—and that'll be no mean trick where we're outnumbered ten to one."

The officers looked at each other. They hadn't talked much about numbers, but they had thought vaguely about them.

"What d'ye mean, 'negotiate,' George?" Bowman asked.

"I mean, first, their surrender. Then, this."

He reached inside his pouch and drew out a handbill about the alliance with France. It had come by courier to the island last month.

"It means," he explained as they studied it with curiosity in the waning light, "we invade them as enemy. Then with the help of God, and that news there, and what wisdom and humanity we have, we turn their loyalty around. Then we won't be outnumbered by enemies, y' see? Simple: we just make friends of 'em."

They looked at him in the twilight, looked at him perplexed and astounded, squinting and scratching their jaw-stubble, digesting this new and complicated responsibility he had put upon them. This was no plain old raid; it was like some fancy diplomatic jiggery-pokey as well, as Helm put it.

This Clark was the damnedest thing, as they had been saying aside to each other all the way along this thousand-mile beeline. He always knew more than they did and he was always making things bigger and more interesting than anything they'd ever done before. It was confounding. But it gave them shivers, and for some strange reason it made them all feel more important than they had ever felt before.

"In about ten minutes we'll start moving down to the farm-
ouse," he said. "So tell your boys what I said, and warn 'em any
reach o' those orders is on pain o' death. And . . ." Now his voice
ent softer, vibrating with that warmth he could turn on at just the
ght times, like a smile you could hear in the dark. "Thankee,
nts. I sure picked my people right. Let's be about it, now."

BOWMAN'S MEN HAD ENCIRCLED THE TOWN AND WERE
rouched, mostly naked and still wet from the river crossing, in
e dark fields and along the roads, waiting in the dew-damp
idnight air, hearing the creaking and croaking of katydids and
ogs and the whine of the mosquitoes that were thick in the air
round them. They waited and wondered whether anything at
ll was happening. So far they had not heard even a dog bark.
Suddenly a pistol shot rang out from amid the dark silhouettes
f the village houses, followed by Colonel Clark's great voice
odeling:
"*Eeeeeeeeeyaaaaaa, hoooey! Rocheblave is ours! Come to town,
nd make some NOISE!*"

JOHNNY CLARK SAT WITH LIEUTENANT HOAG AND CAPTAIN
Coffin at the table under the smoky lamp, eyes cocked toward
e ceiling, sweating in the airless heat, listening to the angry
oices of the British officers in the quarters above. They could
ot make out the words through the thick planking, but they
ould hear in the inflections that much scolding was going on;
ey could hear in the tromp of boots and the creaking of boards
at many men were coming and going, and that a great deal of
oor-pacing was being done by the staff officers of the *Jersey*.
All this had gone on through the night of July 4 and into the
ree hours of the morning of the fifth, and now it was midmorn-
ng, and the activity had resumed. In the meantime, the mood
f the prisoners had been just the opposite. Almost all night
ong, songs of liberty had been heard coming from the enlisted
nen's confines. The prisoners had stayed awake most of the
ight singing, and telling and retelling the wonderful story of the
scape, each witness relating what he had seen and heard of it
rom where he had stood, until a detailed picture of the whole
ncident had been assembled, and then that whole story had
nade the rounds several times. It was that the men of the corpse
etail—a sergeant from a Maryland regiment, and the rest pri-
ates from various states—had been talking about the Day of
ndependence while carrying the corpses across the deck, and
vhen they had descended the ladder to the docking raft, their

251

heads still full of the word "Independence," they had found the dead-boat crew quite off guard. The privates, as if by some wordless mental message, had glanced at each other and at the crew, then at the sergeant. The sergeant, looking up and seeing that no sentries were watching, had given a nod, and at once the prisoners had grabbed the boat crew, choking them and taking their knives and cudgels and using these on them, then had leaped into the boat, taking the oars and shoving away. Two sentries on deck had heard the scuffle, and had called for help and aimed their weapons at the boat, only to find themselves pressed back from the rail by a mass of prisoners. A guard officer then had aimed his pistol down at the boat, but his shot was deflected when Americans on deck lurched against him. And then most of the prisoners had joined to create the diversion that had tied up the whole guard detail until the boat was out of range.

The question whether the fugitives had reached shore safely in their little boat had never been answered, but, said Johnny:

"Unless they're brought back aboard this stinkpot and seen by our own eyes, there's not a man aboard will believe they didn't make it. A man believes what he wants to believe, and by heaven, I choose to believe they're safe and happy right now in some patriot's kitchen, feeding for the first time in a year on something other than Royal swill an' shoddy!"

"That I choose to believe too," said Captain Coffin. "Hey! Liberty! Ha! By th' powers, my soul is free, going thither and yon with those spunky boys!"

"Well and good," said Hoag. "But I wish our Royal keepers upstairs there would finish puttin' blame, and get about the business o' running this jail. It's three hours since they should have let us on deck for air, and I for one am about to suffocate."

There followed a long, thoughtful pause. Johnny said at last: "Now, y' don't suppose they'd . . ."

"Don't even say it," warned Coffin. "*Absit nomen, absit omen.*"

But the word of it came down an hour later, in the form of a proclamation from the ship's captain: as punishment for yesterday's incident, and to maintain a better degree of security aboard H.M.S. *Jersey*, said the proclamation, all prisoners, officers and men, would be forbidden henceforth to go above decks. Johnny thought of the sunshine and the gulls against the blue sky, and felt as if a vise were closing on his chest. No more sunlight and fresh air to cure his lungs.

Hoag mopped his face with an already sodden rag and looked about at the sweat-slick faces around the table.

"It's July, gentlemen," he said. "After July comes August."

15

"HURRY, JOHN CLARK! *HURRY!*" THE RIDER WAS YELLING AT the top of his lungs before he was within a hundred yards of the house, scattering chickens and geese both ways out of the road. And as the family rushed out of the house from the breakfast table, the rider was telling the news even before he had reined down his frenzied horse. The story gushed from his mouth like beer from a stoven barrel, and it was such a tall tale they were sure he was making it up.

Their George had swept down on the enemy outposts in the west and captured them all without spilling a drop of blood, friend's or enemy's. That was about all he knew of it, and he repeated it three times for them.

"Not a bit o' bloodshed, praise be to God!" Ann Clark exclaimed.

"You can hear it all from gents who been there," panted the rider, "if y' hurry up to Fredericksburg!"

"Fredericksburg?"

"John Montgomery. Be through there today likely, on his way t' Williamsburg! He's got their commander, escortin' him to prison!"

"Their commander? George caught their commander?"

"Yeah! Aye, the uh, the one . . . a commander. Isn't that grand! Hey! I got to ride! I'm takin' the news on down the road. You should go to Fredericksburg, sir and madam! Oh, oh, y' should!"

"Eddie, fetch Mister Burrus here a stirrup cup. Cupid, water his horse." John Clark was all but turning in circles, looking dazed.

Billy was gaping like a fish, blinking, breathing hard as if he had raced a mile. From what he understood of it, his brother George had won the war or something. "Papa," he cried at last, "we have to go! I'm harnessing the chaise!" And he was out of sight around the house before John Clark could say do or don't.

"HURRY, PAPA," EXCLAIMED BILLY. THE ROUGH ROAD WAS nearly shaking the carriage to pieces. John Clark and Billy were on the driving seat. Mrs. Clark, Lucy, Elizabeth, and Fanny were jouncing in the back, crammed in shoulder to shoulder. Dickie and Edmund rode ahead. It was some seven leagues to Fredericksburg, and John Clark was bent on getting there to hear whether this wild genie's tale was true. Along the road, people waved their hats and yelled when they passed, as they had already heard the frantic courier.

IT WAS EASY TO FIND LIEUTENANT MONTGOMERY IN FREDericksburg. There on the shady road in front of the public house was a crowd yelling around a wagon, as sassy and bumptious as only a crowd of town Virginians can be. On the back of the wagon stood a man of about John Clark's age, in shackles and iron collar with a chain running down to leg-irons, dressed in what once had been an elegant, braid-trimmed white uniform, now besmirched by the bilgewater and mud and road dust of a thousand miles, staring out over the heads of the jeering crowd, trying to stay dignified while they galled him and cursed him and his ancestors. His iron-gray hair was kinked and matted with chaff and he had several weeks' gray stubble on his jaws, but he still looked haughty and defiant. This was the prisoner, and Lieutenant Montgomery, rangy and brown-faced, was standing on the wagon seat high over the crowd, announcing in a loud voice all the crimes this man had done on the frontiers.

". . . inciting red savages to murder the innocent! Putting British guns and scalping knives into their cruel hands! Buying the scalps of our own people!"

"Flog 'im!"

"Give 'im to us! We'll skin 'im from the heels up!"

"Hang 'im by his own guts, Lieutenant!"

Three bewhiskered guards in buckskins stood around the wagon to keep the townspeople a little way back from the prisoner.

John Clark flicked the reins and clucked his tongue to drive the chaise slowly up through the crowd. Dickie and Edmund rode alongside as the mob parted, and when the family was within ten feet, John Montgomery saw them, and broke out in a big grin and stopped talking for a moment. Billy was holding to the seat with his knuckles white, eyes fixed on the man in irons, mouth hanging open. John Clark reined in the carriage, stood up, and said, "John Mongtomery, good day."

"Good day to you, Mister Clark, Mrs. Clark," he replied, tipping his coon-fur hat. The crowd saw them then, and heard their names, and they raised a cheer of greeting, laughing and pointing to the prisoner. John Clark and his sons were well known in Fredericksburg. The crowd simmered down then to see what would come next. The prisoner had turned his proud, suffering stare in their direction, to see what this distraction was—or perhaps he had heard Montgomery say their name. The lieutenant said now:

"Hey, Mister Roachblob, just lookee here who's come up. Here's Squire John Clark, and his missus. That name has a sound on your ear, hey, ye scummy frog? This be th' father and mother o' Colonel Clark, who y' met of late. Say how d'ye, Roachblob, to your superiors."

Every emotion but happiness crossed Rocheblave's face in two seconds. He shut his eyes and went pale under his dirt, then opened his eyes and turned red, his eyebrows roofed up and his mouth corners went down, his eyes got shimmery, and his chin wrinkled like a currant. Then he hauled in a long breath and composed himself. And he bowed, a courtly bow, his chains rattling, and said:

"M'sieu, Madame, my compliments. Some, some, solace it is, to see that the Colonel Clack who deed to me thees, is well born."

John Clark dipped his head to him, and replied, "Aye, sir, who is born a Virginian is well born."

The crowd yelled its delight. John Montgomery leaned over and slapped his knee. Then John Clark raised his voice over all that. Quiet a man as he was, he could roll his voice like a senator.

"Welcome to the Commonwealth, sir. Whatever befalls you while you're here, I hope you'll ponder your crimes and grow to be a better man. May I present my good wife Ann—stand up and curtsy to 'is Lordship, Annie—and my sons Richard, Edmund, William. Get up, Billy, my boy. My daughters, Lucy, Elizabeth, Frances." One by one they stood up in the carriage and acknowledged the haughty wretch in the wagon, as strange an encounter as the townspeople ever had witnessed. And finally John said to him, "How did my son treat ye, sir?" The Frenchman set his mouth hard, and replied:

"Ungently, M'sieu. That is the word. Ungently."

John sighed. "Aye, th' lad was always forceful. Quick of temper. But . . . But . . . how did he hurt you, other than your pride, I mean?"

The Frenchman's eyes dropped. Montgomery laughed scornfully. "George woke 'im in his nightshirt and scared the bejeebers out of 'im, that's all the hurt he did! Hyeh! Wouldn't let no one lay a hand on 'im. Nor on anybody else." The crowd laughed at the thought of this haughty foreigner standing scared in his nightclothes. Billy looked up at his father, who now said:

"If it's true what you've done, sir, our son's even more gentleman than we esteem 'im. We're not barbarians, sir, I wanted you t' see that. Mister Montgomery, may I have the pleasure of standing treat for you and your boys, in the public house? Have'ee th' leisure? I'd like to hear how George is, and how his circumstances appear."

"Honored, Mister Clark, honored! And I've letters for ye from 'im. Yes, and a mile o' yarn t' tell!"

John Clark tipped his hat and started to sit back down in the carriage, but then paused, and said, "M'syoo, will ye join us? Surely y'd like to get out o' this sun." The Frenchman nodded, and looked as if he were about to cry.

"And so," John Clark roared, "come one and come all who'd like to drink a toast to my—" He saw Ann Rogers Clark in the corner of his eye. ". . . to our son, George Rogers Clark!"

And up went a shout that made the family blink back tears of pride.

"YE NEVER SAW THE LIKE," LIEUTENANT MONTGOMERY told the fascinated crowd in the pub. "Everything went just as 'e'd foreplanned it, but easier. We got us in and around that town without so much as rousin' a dog! George made a beeline up a street right for th' fort, broke one door latch, and caught this man right in 'is bed. With 'is own wife, to 'is credit. Then 'e turned the whole of us loose to hollo like demons and scare them people silly. We ran 'round that town all night like naked savages. With torches. Howlin'. But he wouldn't let us harm a soul, or even raid a pantry, even though we'd not eat for three days or so. By morning light those people were 'spectin' to be torn asunder by our teeth and claws and eat raw. This here Frenchman here'd told 'em all Rebels're cannibals, didn't you, ye . . .

"George let their imaginations reduce 'em to flop. And when morning come, they all creeped up a-hidin' behind their priest's skirts, beggin' us not to strip their families or burn their church. By then George had 'em where he wanted 'em. Well, they grov-

256

eled and whined and begged a while, and then he stopped 'em right there, and said, 'Hold on! Who d'ye think you're talkin' to, savages?' He said, 'Do we look like people who'd hurt innocents or make war on a church?' Heh, heh! Well, we looked just so, o' course, and he knew it. Then he said, 'I came here t' *stop* th' flow of innocent blood, and catch this murderin' Rocheblave! Rest of ye,' he said, 'can go on about your business, as free people under our flag!' Then 'e told 'em about the alliance, which o' course this polecat here'd never done." The listeners were smiling, murmuring, shaking their heads in wonderment.

"Well, Mister Clark, by this time they were beginnin' to get the drift, and I thought that priest was goin' to crawl up an' lick George's toes out o' gratitude. And by sunup, those people in that town were throwin' a festival o' deliverance! Why, their church bell was clangin' and whangin', and they were tyin' ribbands and flowers over everything, and kissin' us and puttin' wreaths round our necks, and whoopin' and singin'." Montgomery's eyes were damp as he recollected the scene, which apparently had moved him immensely, and he went on:

"Well, all, that's how we took Kaskasky, and got its cannon, and listen: by then those people was so stuck on us that Rocheblave's whole militia wanted to ride under our flag! I mean it! And that's what they did! That very mornin', they rode out with Joe Bowman and his company, up th' river road to th' other towns, and told 'em what had happened, and that celebration spread up there, and Joe set up a government in Cahokia in th' fort there. Then George sent that priest over to Vincennes, to win 'em over likewise. And, folks, that's how George Rogers Clark put Britain out o' business in th' West, with but a hundred and thirty men to his name."

"Is that *all*? A hundred and thirty?"

"Aye! And th' only blood shed was from our feet, he marched us so fast across that danged Illinois prairie to get there! Aye, by God! And this wilted cock of a Frenchman here's all that's left of that murtherin' web on th' Missip'. That's the story, friends, and it's true as the words o' the saints, and I'll say this." He paused and shook his head and blinked as if he had just stepped down off a whirlwind. "Am I ever tickled I got to have a hand in it!" He drained the rum out of his glass and sat shaking his head while the tavern buzzed with exclamations.

"Sir, sir," Billy Clark was saying. "Sir, what about the Indians?"

John Montgomery looked at him for a moment, then leaned toward him and smiled. "About the Indians, Master Clark?

Why, by time I and my boys left to bring this prisoner here, why, not one peep's been heard out of 'em. No sir, that brother o' yours, why, he knows redskins better'n about anybody. He figures they're gonna look at that little Virginia flag flying over those towns, and they're gonna hear those French traders talk about that redheaded war chief that suddenly came from nowhere and threw down the British flag, and, son, he reckons it won't be too long till they start askin' permission to come meet 'im. And when they do, why, he aims to talk some sense into 'em. Y' want to know what they're callin' your brother out there now, young man?"

"What, sir?"

Montgomery leaned still closer, and with narrowed eyes and an ominous tone said:

"The Chief Long Knife."

"The Chief Long Knife?"

"The Chief Long Knife."

Billy pursed his lips. His eyes were glazed with wild wonder. "Whhhhhhhwwwww!" he whistled low and long.

EVEN INTO THE DUNGEON-SHIP *JERSEY* NOW AND THEN seeped news of the war.

Word of the alliance with France set off a cheer which was deafening inside the hold—though merely a strange, muffled roar heard by fishing boats passing by—and inspired the Poet to pen an elegy on France. There was another cheer when a new prisoner brought word that the French admiral Count D'Estaing had sailed into the Delaware with eighteen ships and four thousand French soldiers. A dead, demoralizing silence reigned in the ship when word came that General Charles Lee had been court-martialed for treason after his retreat at Monmouth. And when news came that Tories and Indians had massacred more than two hundred American settlers at Fort Forty near Wilkes-Barre on Independence Day—that same day when the prisoners had escaped from the *Jersey*—the gloom was deep. Thus the war news came, always months late.

"We're like a man in his grave," Johnny Clark commented once to the Poet. "All's we know o' the world is what we overhear when living men pass into the churchyard."

"By Heaven," exclaimed the Poet. "What a verse could be writ on that conceit!"

And then on a September night Johnny was jolted out of a demon-crowded nightmare by a hand jerking at his wrist.

"Come, Johnny," wheezed Hoag's voice, "sit up and hear th' news!"

At the table sat a fresh, crisp new prisoner, an ensign of the Virginia Line, who had been brought aboard late in the afternoon. He was a round-faced, red-lipped, pimply little fellow who looked as if he should be on a stool in a countinghouse. "Tell him, Padgett," said Hoag to this newcomer, "what you just told us. Sit here, Johnny." The youth was trying now not to show his dismay at the sight of the cadaverous ruin of a redheaded officer who was easing himself painfully onto the bench across the table. He said:

"Well, it's this, sir. I was caught by British pickets, while carrying dispatches from Williamsburg to General Washington, sir."

"Y' needn't call me 'sir,' Mister Padgett, I'm nought but a corpse."

"Uh, yes, sir." The youth swallowed hard. "Anyway, the chief item of fact I had on me at the time was of a matter just learnt from away far off west—from the Mississippi River, believe that!—that a company o' Virginia irregulars on July Fourth last captured all the enemy's outposts in that valley, and blocked up the western supply route to British Canada. And all that, sir, without a man hurt."

Hoag prodded Padgett's shoulder with a sooty knuckle. "Go on, lad, tell 'im who done it."

"It was a Colonel Clark, militia."

Johnny felt a shiver start in his temples and race down between his shoulders. He swallowed a lump and started blinking tears. "That . . . that wouldn't ha' been a George . . . Rogers . . . Clark, would it, now?"

"The very one, sir. I remember the name."

Johnny's knobby-knuckled fingers were clutching the table's edge, and his head was turning on its scrawny, stubbly, sorespotted neck, the Adam's apple gulping up and down, the eyes spilling over, tears making pale tracks down the grime on the bags under his eyes, the eyes glinting fiercely, pitifully, as they darted to the Poet, then to Hoag. Strange little whimpers were catching in Johnny's throat and he fell into an awful fit of coughing, and when he finally got through it, Hoag's hand patting him on the back, Johnny took a painful deep breath and tilted his face back and pursed his lips, and he emitted a long, high, eerie wolf's howl that woke every British officer in the quarterdeck above.

16

MOUTH OF THE MISSOURI

October, 1778

THEY HAD RIDDEN THROUGH THE HIGH, RIPPLING TAN GRASS
of a rolling meadowland some four miles, northward from St.
Louis, and then veered toward the east, under a vast sky full of
towering sun-tinted cumulus clouds, past copses of yellowing
maples and scarlet oaks, and now suddenly the ground seemed to
drop out from under them and they were on the point of a bluff
looking down on a hazy, lush, wooded valley five or six miles
wide, full of broad waters and willow-covered sandbars and forested islands. The vista was so grand that it made George draw a
deep breath. The Spanish governor said beside him:

"There, my friend. The Missouri. You see it now."

George sat on his horse and looked down at the juncture of
the two great rivers. Beside him sat the elegant Don Fernando de
Leyba, lieutenant governor of Spanish Louisiana. Behind him
was Teresa de Leyba, the governor's sister and ward, sidesaddle
on her mare, the breeze whipping at her black dress and riding
cloak, her face a perfect pale oval in the sunlight. And around
them, a hundred yards off in every direction, sat George's bodyguards, hats pulled low to shade their eyes, gazing about with
their long rifles resting on the pommels of their saddles. It had
become necessary for him to have bodyguards, because in these
four incredible months he had become the preeminent figure in
the whole Mississippi watershed. Or so he was called by his new
friend and ally, the Spanish governor.

Here the Mississippi came yellow-brown down from the
north, the blue Illinois bluffs five miles beyond it; and curving
down into it from the northwest, flowing under the bluff on
which they sat, was the murky, gray-brown Missouri, itself two
miles wide here at its mouth: roiling, shallow, carrying large
trees as if they were bits of chaff. Its discharge made a wide
curving smear of muddy gray out into the slightly clearer water
of the Mississippi.

It was an awesome stream, the Missouri, as voluminous, it
seemed, as the Ohio. George gazed up it as far as he could see,
ten or twelve miles, he estimated, until its wide channel and
islands disappeared among woods and hazes, and then he
thought beyond that; he thought away to the Shining Moun-

tains, and over them, and down to the western sea.

"Our fur traders," the governor was saying, "believe it is a thousand miles to its source."

George turned to look at the governor's handsome, almost beautiful, face, beautiful because it was so much like his sister's: dark-eyed, delicate-featured, sensitive. "More than a thousand," George said, "more than that by far. Verendrye went up it as far as the Mandans, and his narrative placed their towns some fifteen hundred miles from here. And even at that place it was a big river, having come maybe another thousand, by what he could gather from the Indians."

De Leyba looked at George in wonder. "Verendrye?"

"Forty years ago, a French explorer."

"Don Jorge, my friend! I did not know of this person." He shrugged, a rueful smile on his lips. "I am embarrassed! I am governor of this territory and you tell me things I do not know of it! Ha, ha! Teresa, my sister, listen to this wizard of yours! This Cid!" He reached over and squeezed George's upper arm, his favorite gesture of affection.

De Leyba belied almost everything George had ever been led to believe about Spaniards. He was warm, gentle, naive, and humble. He was an aristocrat's orphaned son, who had suffered a plague of misfortunes in the Old World and at last had fled to New Spain with his sister and wife and two small daughters, to try to rebuild a life. Governor Galvez in New Orleans had assigned him to the remote post of St. Louis, where the previous administrator had died of fever. And just two months after his arrival here, this Virginian had arrived on the other side of the river, sweeping out the British presence and astonishing every living soul in the valley.

This invasion had made de Leyba and Colonel Clark natural allies—not because Spain harbored any love for American Rebels, who would rise up against a king, but because of her eternal hatred and suspicion of Britain. As governor, de Leyba was commandant of St. Louis's garrison, and he was in awe of George's conquest of the Illinois. Had he known how small and destitute George's so-called army was, he would have been more awe-struck—but perhaps a little less comforted by its presence, since he saw the Americans as a buffer between his territory and the British.

Still more astounding to the Spaniard were the Indian councils that his friend Don Jorge Clark had been holding for two months at Cahokia across the river. From his stone mansion above St. Louis, de Leyba could see the hundreds of Indian campfires twinkling at night, and, when the wind was right, hear drums. The trader Vigo came to St. Louis every week with amazing reports from Cahokia: Colonel Clark by now had made treaties with a dozen tribes who had been carrying the tomahawk for Britain. Indians had been coming from as far as 500 miles away to see and hear this Long Knife chief, and he had orated to them, threatened them, made promises to them, and made friends of them. Most often, Vigo related, Don Jorge would convince them that they were fools to fight Britain's war, that it was beneath the worth of true warriors to be used by white men. He did not want them to fight on the American side, but simply to stay neutral and keep out of his way as he drove the British from his country. The Indians, Vigo said, were amazed at such direct and forceful talk from a white man, and were spreading his fame even to the Great Lakes and into the plains of the Missouri.

As for himself, Don Fernando de Leyba considered himself fortunate to have stepped up alongside an extraordinary man, a man of destiny, at a most propitious time, and was excited at the prospect of helping him. Besides that, he *liked* this Don Jorge Clark better than he had ever liked any man, of any age or nationality. Here was a man who was as de Leyba imagined men should be: fair, cheerful, unafraid, tireless, and honest, and a patriot to his state. And almost unconsciously, then, when those first unexpected flickerings of passion between his sister Teresa and Don Jorge had become evident, Fernando de Leyba had begun to promote their affection. Rather than try to cloister his maiden sister against the attentions of a bold outsider, as a Spanish don would be expected to do, he had encouraged her to be kind to him, to play her *gitarra* for him in recitals and take his mind off the tension of the Indian councils across the river. Teresa had complied, and within weeks Don Jorge Clark had surprised and delighted de Leyba by asking him to permit their betrothal.

George turned now in his saddle and stretched his arm back toward Teresa. "Come up," he said. "I want to look at this with you by me."

She rode alongside and stopped, and they sat with the brisk fall breeze on their faces and looked into the valley.

This entrance of the demure Spanish beauty into his heart was one of the happy strokes of fortune that had befallen him since his arrival in the valley of the Mississippi. She seemed to him sometimes like a princess in a chivalric tale. His sway over the French people of the valley, their apparent devotion to him, his success in swinging the loyalties of those thousands of savages on the other side of the river—all these serendipities had bathed this whole region in an unreal light, and now finding himself in love with this almost ephemeral wraith of a virgin was like a part of the glowing legend he found himself living. He was so clothed in triumph and the admiration of the people around him that he might fairly have tingled with the sense of his own potency; yet Providence had played such a strong role in his successes that he had to feel as reverent as a crusader. There had come over the whole unlikely adventure a sense of magic, of enchantment; even his raw, rough frontiersmen seemed to feel it sometimes, the strangeness, the specialness.

Sometimes when George was standing in the shade of the great council elms at Cahokia, with the symbolic sword and war belts and peace belts in his hands, watching the fine, proud, handsome faces of his former brown enemies warm and soften in the smoke of peace pipes, he would look aside at Joe Bowman and Johnny Rogers and others of his officers and men, and he would see in their faces the same childish wonderment that he had used to see in the faces of his little brothers and sisters when he spun stories for them. These few soldiers of his knew they were in a perilous circumstance, of course; they knew that one wrong word or gesture under the council elms could cause the horde of savages to rise up and slaughter them on the spot. And yet they too, like the crusaders of antiquity, seemed to feel that they were safe within some holy spell, hardly able to believe what was happening to them and yet having faith that it would turn out well. It was a kind of spell George had to resist sometimes, with his own hardened frontier sense of reality. But the spell was on him this morning as he sat under the glowing clouds with a princess at his side, looking over a rich valley which he controlled as surely as might a king in armor. And Fernando de Leyba was aware of it, too; that was why he sometimes referred to his friend as the Cid.

And now, as if to add another dimension to the bright dream, George was here looking down upon a river whose name had always been mythical to him, and it was even more awesome than he had imagined it. He remembered a day only four months ago, though it seemed now to have been a day in another and a lesser era, when he had trailed his hand over the side of a boat and felt the waters of the westward-flowing Ohio with his fingers.

"Wait," he told his princess and her brother, and he spurred his horse and rode down the steep bluff, through brush and high grass, down and down through dry leaves and deadwood till he was at the foot of the bluff and galloping across the bottomland toward the river.

He dismounted in a copse of cottonwood saplings, looped his horse's reins, and strode out to the half-sandy, half-muddy river-bank. He waded out through the shoreside eddies to a place where a strong current ran between the shore and a parallel sandbar.

He stood there, in the cold water as deep as his thighs, and dipped that same hand in the current. He felt the water and looked upstream.

This water, he thought. Once it was snow on the Shining Mountains.

He looked up once and saw them all on the bluff almost a half a mile above him: Teresa and her brother, and the guards with their long rifles sticking up like the lances of knights.

He remembered the dream of the white-pillared house on a bluff above the river, and the lady in a billowing dress sitting beside him. He saw it again now, that vision, and now the woman had a face. A delicate, pale oval face.

He turned back to the river and looked down at his hand in it and thought of all the miles and of the land's end.

Someday, he thought. Somehow and someday.

BUT SOMETIMES WHEN HE WAS AWAY FROM TERESA, ALONE in his cot in a guarded room in Cahokia, with the murmur of a thousand encamped warriors nearby, the enchantment would dissolve like mist and show him the thin, hard lines of reality.

His army, never a fourth the size it pretended to be, was now reduced by expired enlistments to some seventy men and officers, and these were divided between Cahokia, Kaskaskia, and Vincennes. When George was not counciling, he was trying to run his newly conquered empire by pen.

The Illinois Regiment was suffering from want of clothing and shoes and supplies, and winter was nigh. So far there had been no word from Governor Henry in Williamsburg. George did not even know whether Montgomery's party had got east alive with Rocheblave. George had also sent a courier named Myers directly to Henry, bearing written reports of the conquest and a desperate plea for men and money and provisions. But he did not know whether Myers had gotten there, either.

As there was no money, everything had to be got on credit: cloth, blankets, leather, flour, salt, beef, rum, tobacco, and such services as blacksmiths, physicians, and even washerwomen, had to be got on the credit of the State of Virginia. The villagers and merchants in the valley were happy to provide all these for their new allies, but not free. They did not know the State of Virginia itself, but they had enough faith in its Colonel Clark to accept his personal signature on their bills. Soon, George hoped, Governor Henry would send money and troops to enable him to hold this vast territory which he had secured so handily. In the meantime, the Kaskaskia garrison would send bills up to Cahokia, and George would sign them for Virginia, and the bills would be sent back down to Kaskaskia so the purchases could be made. But with each authorization, George would admonish his officers: "Keep purchases at a minimum. We must live spare, being so far from the resources of the Mother State. Above all, keep a notation of every expenditure, however small."

He constantly reminded his officers wherever they were to keep the strictest discipline. "Every man is under scrutiny by French, Spaniards, and Indians. Challenge them to be a good emissary of our country," and not to reveal how few they were. "We play mockingbird, making so many sounds they'll guess we're hundreds."

And at Cahokia the councils continued, in the shadow of the great ancient Indian mounds, and the fame of the Long Knife spread through the vast Middle Ground, and George knew that the Hair-Buyer, the Englishman on the other side of the chessboard, surely was finding fewer and fewer Indians who would hire out to ravage the frontiers. For George, that sense of performing a sacred duty continued to grow, and to enchant the whole adventure.

And yet there were these moments of clarity, when he would lie awake in his lonely cot in Cahokia surrounded by the Hair-Buyer's former mercenaries, and the parade of Indian faces would fade, and through his satisfaction would penetrate the feeling that he was holding up his whole shaky empire with nothing but words: with nothing but the signature *G.R. Clark* on treaties and commissions and vouchers, and the breath of his speeches.

CAROLINE COUNTY, VIRGINIA

Thanksgiving Day, 1778

THE CLARK FAMILY TABLE HAD THREE EMPTY PLACES THIS SECond Thanksgiving Day, but there was much cause for thanks: everyone was surely safe for a while.

Johnny was alive. Word had come that he was a prisoner of war, and that, as late as last summer, he was still living. He was on a prison ship anchored off New York, which, to the family at home, seemed a fairly safe place during the war. Perhaps it was not a good and healthful place to be; Mister Freeman down the road had been informed that his son Mike had died on a prison ship, of putrid fever. But the Clarks could pray that Johnny was on a better-kept ship. Maybe he was well. Maybe.

Jonathan was absent again this Thanksgiving, but he and Bill Croghan were apparently in a state of relative security for the winter. Both armies were settled in for the season. Jonathan was now second in command of a regiment commanded by Colonel Light Horse Harry Lee, encamped somewhere in New Jersey near Washington's headquarters. Bill Croghan had become a regimental adjutant.

As for George, he too probably was safe from harm. Judging by all the news about him that had trickled east over the mountains, he was very much in control of everything in that remote region, and had made treaties with most of the tribes that before would have threatened his garrison. And so, for the first time in many years, the family thought it did not have to worry so much about George.

Another blessing to be thankful for, in Ann Rogers Clark's mind, was that daughter Annie for a change was not with child. Shortly after baby Samuel's birth, Owen had gone away to serve in the Continental Army, and so Annie was having a respite. She was here at home with her family; her two toddlers and the baby were here with her, but at least she was not pregnant, and probably would not be for a while—unless Owen should manage somehow to get a winter furlough.

The fowl on the table this year was the yield of Billy's rifle instead of Edmund's. Edmund had shot four turkeys in the week before Thanksgiving, but they had been served in other ways on other days, and Billy's first kill had the place of honor in the middle of the table. He was very proud of it, and referred to it several times during the meal as "my turkey," and with a benevolent smile kept watching everybody eat. They all were aware of his eyes on them and had the tact to eat it with apparent relish, and say "yum," and smile back at him, although it was in actuality rather a tough and scrawny old bird that probably would not have lived through the winter even if it had not caught Billy's bullet.

Edmund knew his own turkeys had been fatter and more tender, but he was so proud of what he had taught Billy about hunting and shooting that he really was as pleased as Billy that this one was on the table, and he grinned as he chewed and chewed and chewed.

Billy Clark in his eighth year had been doing men's work on the plantation, and now he had also begun to put game on the table, so he not only felt worthy, he also was happy in the knowledge that, for another year at least, he was not going to be sent to Parson Robertson's school. This pleased him. His brother George, he knew now from all the family stories, had been a misfit in that school, and so Billy knew quite well that he would have been likewise if he had had to go there.

Thus the family was happy and content this Thanksgiving Day, and the only foreshadowing was Dickie's enlistment. He had, with his father's reluctant permission, signed to go with Lieutenant John Montgomery when and if Montgomery could raise a company of reinforcements to take back out West to George. Governor Henry had gotten the Assembly to authorize such a company after the news had come of George's success in the Illinois. But recruitments had been slow because manpower was scarce, and so Dickie was here for one more holiday, waiting. One thing John Clark could be thankful for was that delay; with the rivers freezing now and the mountain passes filling with snow, it appeared that Montgomery would not be able to set out until spring thaws. And so son Dickie too was safe for a while to come.

They talked long after dinner about George in the West. Each member of the family had images of what his life must be like now that he was a conqueror.

"He lives in a palace," said Fanny. "He sits on a throne, and servants bring him meat and bread to eat. And when he's full, he gives the rest to the Conquered, who eat it all up greedily. And the Conquered love him because he doesn't make them starve."

The family always sat bewildered when this doll-like five-year-old was giving one of her perfectly enunciated recitations like this, not just because her speech was so precise and certain, but also because her imagination was so vivid. In her mind, the Conquered were a people who crawled on all fours and fawned at the feet of her brother.

"He doesn't live in a palace," Elizabeth now tried to correct her. "Out in the West all they have to make houses with are grass and animal skin and strings." To Elizabeth, the main image of the West was the great prairie they had crossed in John Montgomery's account.

"It is *so* a palace," replied Fanny. "It's made of gold the Spanish gave him so he would be kind to them. The Spanish are afraid he will conquer *them* if they aren't polite. In his palace he has a waterfall with a statue in it. He also has a cage with a

whippoorwill bird in it to sing him to sleep at night, for he i
quite homesick, you may be sure."

"He doesn't need a whippoorwill to sing to him," Bill
scoffed. "He can sing whippoorwill songs better than the whip
poorwills can. Isn't that right, Mama?"

"As well," Mrs. Clark said. "I don't know about better, but h
sounds just like them."

"You promised to tell us ever so long ago about Georgie an
Grandmama Rogers and the whippoorwill song," Elizabeth re
minded her.

"So I did." Ann Rogers Clark could see that her little one
images of George were becoming fantastical, so she decided t
tell that story, in which George himself had been a child of th
family. "All right, then. Now, you remember I told you all ho
your Grandpapa Rogers would come to call on your goo
Grandmama before they were married?"

"In a canoe," said Elizabeth.

"And he'd whistle like a whippoorwill," said Billy.

"And she went a thousand times to the willow tree when a rea
bird sang, because she was in love," said Fanny.

"Aye. And she was in love all of her life, right up to the ver
last day," said Mrs. Clark, "and he with her just as much so
Well, you know that your Grandpapa taught Georgie a great par
of what he knows."

"To survey," Billy piped up. "Making lines on the land."

"And he also taught him to make that whippoorwill call. Tha
was one of the first things Georgie learned from his Grandpap
Rogers, and he did learn it well. I swear that Georgie would si
on the roof of the house outside his window at night, and carr
on a conversation with the whippoorwills out beyond the fence
Jonathan used to complain—remember this, John?—that h
couldn't study for all the bird calls outside his window?"

Annie laughed. "Fancy Jonathan not able to study, even if th
house had been on fire!"

"Hmhmhm! But. The happy life had to come to an end, as al
happy things do, and so Mama, your Grandmama, took ill an
began to pass away. But she said she wouldn't go till she'd see
all her nine children one more time. And so we were all sum
moned to their house in King and Queen County, and it was
good while before we got there, as some of us had to come som
distance, as far as Carolina, even. But by and by we were al
there at Worcester farm, your uncles George and Giles and Joh
and Byrd, and your aunts Rachel and Mary and Mildred an
Lucy. Most all of us brought our mates and children, so we wer

great in number, and the place was a-hum like a hive. Mama lay propped up on big pillows, and we'd go in one or two at a time and sit by her, with Papa, your Grandpapa, always by the far side o' the bed watchin' her. Oh, he was a constant old sentinel! He'd sit there by th' bed, deep in rememberin', I suppose.

"Well, after all, they were such lovebirds, and tho' white-haired by then, why, I 'spect they were the same two in their bosoms as had courted on th' sly with their whippoorwill calls, and she who'd given up her birthright for him. Not a soul came from the Byrds to see her."

Ann Rogers Clark looked at her own family around the table, and had to clear her throat before going on.

"Well, once she'd counted us all, and knew we were all there, why, she decided I guess that she could go then. I. . . I suppose that's th' way I'll want it when my time comes, too, t' see you all. There in a big bright room, with your Papa beside me."

"Ann," said John Clark. "Come now."

"Well, once she knew we were all there, why, Papa shooed the last of us downstairs, and then no one was called up for, oh, an hour or two. Then Papa came halfway down the staircase and asked me to go fetch my Georgie. I asked him why and he said, just do. So I went out, found Georgie under a big tree, a-tryin' to teach that half-Indian language o' his to a clutch o' cousins, and I brought 'im inside and sent 'im up. And I stayed down-stairs with brothers and sisters, all of us wonderin' why he'd sum-moned this particular grandson at such a time—until we heard the saddest and loveliest sound:

"There in the upstairs hall of that big house, we heard so clear and loud, once and then twice and many times, th' call of a whippoorwill!"

She looked around the table. All her children were absolutely still, watching her, seeming to understand. She cleared her throat again and blinked, because the points of candleflame were blurred and shimmering with rays.

"Papa couldn't do th' whippoorwill call anymore, for he'd lost his teeth, but Georgie could do it to perfection, and that's why he'd sent for 'im, so your Grandmama could hear those notes once more and maybe remember their willow tree.

"Half an hour later a door opened and shut upstairs, and the whippoorwill stopped calling. Georgie came slow down the stairs with Papa's arm across his shoulder. And we knew she was gone."

*   *   *

WINTER TIGHTENED ITS ICY RING AROUND THE MISSISSIPPI Valley towns. Snows fell and melted, then fell and stayed. George had finished his Indian councils at Cahokia and returned to his base in Kaskaskia. Here he kept bargaining for flour and meat, leather, cloth, and rum for the little regiment of men, and waited with dwindling hope for a messenger to come from Virginia before the rivers froze and the trails drifted shut.

It had been six months since he had sent Montgomery to Virginia with the prisoner Rocheblave and the report of the victories; it had been four months since he had sent Myers, his best courier, with more recent news of the occupation, the Indian councils, and the desperate problems of pay and supply. If those messengers had got there, surely some acknowledgement would have come back from Patrick Henry by now.

Of course, they might not have got there. They had gone as far as the Falls of Ohio, he knew that. Word had come from the little outpost on the island of their passing through.

But something could have happened to them beyond the Falls. The Shawnees, among other tribes along the upper Ohio, had not come to his councils, and were still active. News was that a large body of them had besieged Boonesboro for two weeks before Boone's sharpshooters and bad weather had forced them off. And Simon Butler, George's best scout, had failed to return from a reconnaissance in the Ohio country early in September. There were still hazards aplenty between here and Virginia, and maybe neither Montgomery nor Myers had made it through to Williamsburg. Or, if they had, maybe the returning messenger from Governor Henry had perished. That was just as likely. George and his invaders were too remote from their government to rely on the hope of messages getting through one way, let alone being answered.

And so the ice locked the rivers, and no more boats came from anywhere. Now and then some hardy courier would arrive from the Falls by way of the Buffalo Trace, or down from Bowman's outpost at Cahokia, or across the windswept prairie from Helm at Vincennes, but finally even these stopped traveling, and every settlement closed itself off from the frigid wilderness and began living close to the hearth, neither sending out anyone—except hunters— to other places nor expecting anyone to come.

Very well, George thought as Christmas came and went and the year turned. Here we'll sit till spring, and that's good enough, I reckon, as the Indians and the British likewise will sit where they be, as no bear gains ground from another when they're all hibernating.

And come next spring we'll get more troops from Virginia, and then we'll cross to Vincennes and pick up Len Helm and the militia there, and then up the Wabash we'll go and down the Maumee, and with most of the tribes in our way laying neutral, by heaven, we can own Detroit by June next, and that's the end of Britain in the West.

It was a pleasant enough winter, here in Kaskaskia. The French were vivacious and hospitable. They had snug houses, and imported wines and brandies and chocolates, and real silver and crystal glinting on their tables. They had fiddles and zithers and flutes, and Monsieur Cerré, the leading merchant, even had in his home a harpsichord, upon which his wife could play tolerably well, and a billiard table, upon which he himself could play tolerably well. The belles of Kaskaskia were flirtatious and charming, and on many a cold night George and his officers were kept warm with dancing. Some of the American soldiers had found wenches in the town to keep them company in their off-duty hours, and many a young Virginian found himself unofficially adopted by some warm-hearted family or other. Grandmères knitted woolen socks for them; grandpères played backgammon and chess with them and cracked walnuts and hickory nuts with them by the fire and taught them a little of the French language. All in all, it was a more luxurious winter season than most of them would have had in their own frontier settlements, and so the morale stayed high. The troops had little to worry about except living up to Colonel Clark's expectations of them as soldiers, and that, for the most part, they were eager to do.

George spent a good portion of his time alone in his quarters in Rocheblave's old house. He had set up a comfortable bed in a small downstairs room off the study which served as his headquarters. Madame Rocheblave and her servants had removed to the home of a friend in the town, and her upstairs rooms now housed the duty sergeant and guard detail. George's solitude mystified several of Kaskaskia's young ladies. He liked to dance with them and talk with them, drink tea with them, accept their kindnesses and let them tutor him in their tongue. But he let them know that his heart was already given. Two or three tried to test the strength of his vows and quickly found that he was faithful and could not be misled.

George had to keep negotiating for food and services, and calculated like a countinghouse clerk to keep his accountings straight. He had signed his name to a thousand vouchers by now;

he had expended more in Virginia's name than all his lands and belongings were worth. He sensed that this bulging packet of records might yet be all that could save him from personal ruin, and though he hated it, he guarded it as he guarded his own life.

A few days into the new year, George was laid low by an onslaught of intestinal cramps, chills, and fevers, worse than anything that had ever hit him. Old Dr. Laffont of Kaskaskia bled him and gave him barks, and, when he worsened, called in a younger colleague, Dr. Conard, for consultation. Conard was more modern, a believer in chemical medicines, the more the better, and between the two physicians they very nearly killed George in the next fortnight, until he came out of a delirium one evening with a healthy appetite for beef, the image of Teresa in his mind, and a conviction that he was going to live after all.

And it was then that the first awful rumors came:

That the Hair-Buyer General, Governor Henry Hamilton, was in the Illinois Country with an army of eight hundred soldiers and Indians, coming to recapture the Mississippi Valley.

George was aghast. Could Hamilton somehow have stolen such a move on him without the least warning? The old notion of the chess game came back to George, and he castigated himself for having got so complacent and distracted that Hamilton might have jumped him in his moment of triumph.

The people of Kaskaskia were petrified. They had gladly given their oath of allegiance to the Americans, but had never dreamed that the British would return in such force. They knew it would go badly with them when the British came, and they were voting to capitulate. They wanted George and his Americans to take asylum on the Spanish side of the river so there would be no war fought over their town. George snorted, ordered their spokesmen out of his headquarters, and sent for his officers and scouts to track down the source of the rumor.

At last it was traced to a French hunter and some Negro woodcutters who had stumbled upon a hidden Indian encampment beside the road to Cahokia. The Indians had told them they were part of General Hamilton's army of eight hundred, which was coming to attack the town. George's scouts then went out and found the abandoned encampment, and said that apparently no more than thirty Indians had been there. They had fled eastward since, along the main trace between Kaskaskia and Vincennes. The scouts had ridden long and hard, but had found no sign of an enemy army within thirty or forty miles of Kaskaskia.

So it had been a false alarm. But to George and his officers, it was as ominous now that the alarm was past as it had been before. It raised questions that he had to ponder long after the Kaskaskians had breathed their sighs of relief.

"They weren't friendly Indians," George told his officers. "They'd been hiding there for days. Any Indians I've treated with know they can come camp right in the shadow o' this town."

"If they really were enemy, though," Johnny Rogers queried, "why would they spoil Hamilton's surprise by explaining their presence all so handily like that?"

"A joke," said Dick Brashears, a lieutenant. "Just a prank by some mongrel band. I'll bet it is."

"No," George said. "We have to presume they're hostile. Why would they say those numbers, eight hundred? Well, like as not, to keep the Long Knives from swarming out and catching 'em. That's what I'd ha' said if I was them, caught prowlin' like them." He stalked around and around his desk, frowning at the floor, stroking his chin. He stopped in front of the hearth and kicked a log in the fireplace. It sent up sparks and began burning brighter. He gazed at the strengthening flame. "Get me a brandy, Johnny, and pour one for anyone else thirsty." He sipped and stared at the flames and thought. Then he turned to them. "Now let me tell ye what confounds me. When they skedaddled, they went toward Vincennes. Meseems they wouldn't go thataway, between two forts flying our flag, now would they?"

He was concentrating like a chess player now, tapping himself on the temple. "Some little things been botherin' me. Len Helm hasn't sent a word since early last month. I just blamed that on th' weather. But another thing. Mister Vigo started over there last month to trade. I gave him some news for Len, requiring replies. Vigo should ha' been back long since."

There followed a silence so complete that the officers could hear the soft flutter of the flames in the fireplace. Finally Johnny Rogers said, "What are y' thinking, Cousin?"

His answer chilled them.

"It would surprise me, but then it *wouldn't* surprise me, if the Hair-Buyer really *was* somewhere out there nearabouts, and has a ring around Vincennes. A net across the trail, maybe."

Another dreadful silence held until Captain Dick McCarty coughed and said, "What might y' mean by nearabouts, Colonel?"

"The upper Wabash, maybe. Ouiatanon, or Post Miami." It was an awful thought. Ouiatanon was but a hundred miles or so up the Wabash from Vincennes. Ouiatanon was an Indian town where Hamilton's agents had had a trading post before the Long

Knives came. George was calculating, counting weeks, trying to imagine whether Hamilton could possibly have raised and moved a large force from Detroit to there between late summer and December, when the rivers froze. It didn't seem likely. George had presumed Hamilton to be a rational and orthodox English officer, not one who would try a bold stroke like that. A Strategy of the Absurd.

At last he turned to them from the fire. "I sent some scouts on toward Vincennes, to take a careful look-see. We should know ere long whether there's a net out."

"I'll be eager t' know," said Brashears. "I can stand even bad news better'n my imagination."

"My boys," growled Lieutenant John Bailey, "came out here with'ee t' fight Redcoats an' Indians. I reckon they'd still like t' get a chance to."

ON THE TWENTY-NINTH OF JANUARY THE ANSWER CAME. The portly trader Francisco Vigo from St. Louis brought it. He rode in splattered with mud to his shoulders. His heavy dark eyebrows were peaked with worry and his red tongue kept licking his chapped lips.

"My colonel," he said, "is it known by you that the Governor General Hamilton occupies Vincennes since the last month?"

George swallowed. "Him in person? Good God! And what of Helm?"

"His prisoner, but well treated. Eh, then! Sit down, my colonel, and hear the news, for I've been there a long time and I have much that you must know. For weeks he would not let me to leave there, though I protest I am a Spanish citizen. He is afraid I would come tell you of his presence."

George was rubbing his forehead and trying to grasp the whole consequence of that staggering news. "Thanks be to God he let ye loose! I'm surprised 'e did!"

"Only after he make me promise I would not come and tell you on my way to home. Such a perplexion I had, for my word is my honor! So, I do honorably: I hasten to my home first. I touch my door. Then I turn and hasten here to tell you!"

17

TO GOVERNOR PATRICK HENRY
COMMONWEALTH OF VIRGINIA

D^r S^r

As it is now near twelve months since I have had the least Intelligence from you I almost despair of any Relief sent to me

A Late Menuv^r of The Famous Hair Buyer General, Henry Hamilton Esqr. Lieut. Governor of Detroit, hath allarmed us much; on the 17th of December last he, with a Body of Six Hundred Men Composed of Regulars, French Voluntier and Indians Took possession of St. Vincent on the Waubach, what few men that Composed the Garrison not being able to make the least Defense

He is influencing all the Indians he possibly Can to Join him: I learn that those that have Treated with me have as yet Refused his offers. I have for some time Expected an attack from him as he has Blocked up the Ohio R

I fortunately got every peace of Inteligence that I could wish for, by a Spanish Gent^l Mr. Vigo that made his Excape from M^r. Hamilton:

No attack to be made on our Garison at Kaskaskias until the Spring as passage is too difficult at present. Braves sent to war against different parts of the country Especially Kentucky. Both presents and Speaches sent to all the Nations South of the Ohio Amediately to meet at a great Council at the Mouth of the Tennessee R to lay the Best plans for Cuting off the Rebels at Illinois and Kentucky. the Grand Gate and his Nation living at Post St Vincent told Mr Hamilton that he and his people was Big Knives and would not give their hands any more to the English. Ninety Regulars in Garrison a few Voluntiers and about Fifty Tawaway Indians that is shortly to go to war they are very busy in Repairing the Fort which will Shortly be very Strong, One Brass Six-pounder two iron four pounders and two Swivels Mounted in the Bastians plenty of Amunition *and provitions and all kinds of warlike Stores, Making preparation for the Reduction of the Illinois & has no Suspition of a Visit from the Americans This was Mr Hamilton's Circumstance when Mr Vigo left him*

Being sensible that without a Reinforcement which at present I have hardly a right to Expect, I shall be obliged to give up this Countrey to Mr Hamilton without a turn of Fortune in my favour, I am Resolved to take the advantage of his present Situation·and Risque the whole on a Single Battle

I shall set out in a few Days with all the Force I can Raise of my own Troops and a few Militia that I can Depend on the whole to only one Hundred, rest goes on board a Small Galley Mounting two four pounders and four large Swivels one nine pounder on Board

This Boat is to make her way good if possible and take her Station Ten Leagues Below St Vincents until further orders

I shall March across by Land my self with the Rest of My Boys. the principal persons that follow me on this forlorn hope is Cap^{ns} Joseph Bowman John Williams Ed^{wd} Worthington Rich^d McCarty & Fran^s Charlovielle Lieut^s Richd Brashears Ab^m Kellar Ab^m Chaplin J^{no} Jerault And J^{no} Bayley and several other brave Subalterns. You must be Sensible of the Feeling that I have for those Brave officers and Soldiers that are Determined to Share my Fate let it be what it will. I know the Case is Desperate but S^r we must either Quit the Countrey or attack Mr Hamilton No time is to be lost

Was I sure of a Reinforcement I should not attempt it Who knows what fortune will do for us. Great things have been affected by a few Men well Conducted. perhaps we may be fortunate We have this Consolation that our Cause is Just and that our Countrey will be greatful and not Condemn our Conduct in Case we fall through if so this western countrey as well as Kentucky I believe is lost

Any Expresses you may have sent I expect has fallen into the hands of Governor Hamilton

I have the Honour to be Sr Your Very Humble Servt

G. R. CLARK

The Illinois Regiment came along in an arrow-shaped fil with its scouts forming the head of the arrow. and the long dral line of riflemen following, feet squishing in the cold mud, the drizzle hissing around them, the French militiamen following behind them and then the pack horses, and more flanking scouts bringing up the rear. Their panting breath condensed in clouds. The men were loaded with their long guns and ammunition pouches and their knapsacks and shoulder-hung pouches and their pistols and tomahawks, and their blanket rolls across their shoulders. Their deerskin outer clothes were rainsoaked and heavy. The land was flat as a tabletop, but walking was as strenuous as climbing because of the weight they carried and because every step brought up a foot clogged with mud like bread batter.

The ground had thawed on the surface but was still frozen under the sod, so the water from the drizzling rain and the melted snow did not seep down, and it was too flat to drain, and so some miles of the plain were like shallow ponds as far as they could be seen through the mist, water ankle deep and sometimes calf deep, and where the water lay like this the marching was not quite so fatiguing because the mud underfoot was more like soup than batter. On these stretches the feet were always soaked with cold water, but not weighted with anchors of mud, and it was a little less bad, in its way.

There were no horizons because of the mist. The men in the rear could see the men fading into the mist ahead of them. They could see now and then the vague shape of a brush thicket, and ghostly, pale patches of snow, and for fifty yards around they could see the matted gray and tan prairie grass and dark brown weed stalks, and the footprints ahead filling with muddy water, and the muddy channel they were churning across the unseen prairie in an easterly direction along the Kaskaskia-to-Vincennes trace.

They had been on the plain for ten days now, and it had been raining or sleeting or snowing all those days. They had at first covered twenty to thirty miles a day by slogging from daybreak to dusk. The officers had given up their horses to buffalo hunters, and now marched in the mud with the troops. Each evening they would seek a campground raised enough that they would not have to lie down in water. There were no tents, and so they slept in the rain, rolled into their blankets with hides over them. If they had not been so extremely fatigued by the marching, sleep would have been impossible in these conditions. As it was, the troops plummeted into sleep with their evening grog still warming their blood, and got up at half-light, sluggish as half-frozen reptiles but eager to march because it warmed them.

They had been lucky so far, finding buffalo herds every day.

Each evening the hunters had ridden in from the surrounding plains with great briskets and haunches and shoulder-humps of buffalo. Each evening, one of the companies would take its turn providing the roast and the entertainment. Each company tried to outdo the others, and so the long, painful misery of every marching day was made more bearable by anticipation of the evening frolic. Under conditions in which two hundred yards was an ordeal, George knew, the men must not be permitted to think in terms of two hundred miles. It was better to let them conquer a day at a time and then celebrate their triumph over that day.

And now in these last few days they had been coming through that part of the country where several tributaries of the Wabash lay across their path. These were mere creeks, ordinarily, but were so flooded now that every sort of ingenuity was needed to get across them. In water to their waists, the men felled trees upon which to float across the deep main channels. Whole days were spent, strenuous, chilling days under the perpetual rain and sleet, crossing these flooded valleys, swimming the horses across, rafting the barrels and bundles over to reload on the pack animals on the other side, still in waist-deep floodwater. Now, as they neared the Wabash Valley, they found themselves constantly in deep, cold, brown water adrift with stained sponge-ice and woodland debris. And George, who had to keep them believing that they would soon get to Vincennes and have their revenge on the Hair-Buyer, made it a point never to mention what the great Wabash itself would surely be like when they reached it. It'll be like a Mississippi, he thought, or a Missouri. Dear God let Cousin Johnny be there with the gunboat.

George had named the boat the *Willing*. Now he wondered if he should have christened her the *God Willing*.

ABOARD THE *WILLING*, LIEUTENANT JOHNNY ROGERS STOOD on the stern deck wrapped in a buffalo cape with sleet stinging his cheek, watching the rowers strain to move the vessel against the Ohio's fast current, and wondered whether it would be possible to get up the Wabash in time to meet Cousin George after all. Even with her squaresail up, full of a following wind, and two men on every oar, rowing from dawn to dusk, they had managed only about ten miles a day. There were a hundred or more miles to go up the Ohio and then up the Wabash to the rendezvous point, and the *Willing* was creeping. As if the current weren't enough problem, the river was over its banks in so many directions that even John Duff, their pilot, was sometimes dubious about whether they were still in the channel.

Well, all we can do is row like demons and get there when we can, he thought. And if George makes better time than we do, then he'll just have to sit and wait a day or two longer, because I sure as Satan don't think he can cross that Wabash without us or attack that dang fort without these cannon.

He watched the rowers: half French and half Americans. He had divided them that way according to George's advice, so that neither half would think the other was having it easy. George always thought out such things.

He can surely put a responsibility on your shoulders, he thought.

But never a half o' what he puts on his own.

Later, Johnny had his spyglass on the mouth of the creek where the regiment had hidden its boats last summer to start marching overland to Kaskaskia. It had been little more than a mosquito swamp then. Now it was full of water from bluff to bluff and looked like a river mouth.

He felt a sudden shiver and whipped the spyglass up to see if he had seen what he thought he had seen, along the north shore.

Nothing but more floating logs. He had thought he had seen a canoe.

Of course it was likely that the *Willing* would be seen by Indians somewhere along the way, and might well have to fight her way past them. Vigo's report had said Hamilton's Indians were posted on the Ohio. But where? There hadn't been a sign yet. Maybe at the mouth of the Tennessee? The *Willing* would be close upon it by nightfall.

At dusk, John Duff blew a cloud of condensed breath into the fleet and said in a low voice:

"I haven't seen a redskin yet, straight on, but there's somethin' just offside a mite in my eye-corners that's keepin' my head on a swivel."

"How long since this case o' the swivels came over you, Mister Duff?"

"Since about Massac Creek. It went away, 's why I've not spoke it. It's back now."

"I felt it there too."

Duff's eyes were shifting, poking into distant dark thickets and trees bristling atop the bluffs a mile away. "I've just got a real caution 'bout tyin' ashore tonight, Mister Rogers."

The boat shuddered as something bumped along under her keel. "You on the bow, look alive! We're running over things!" John Rogers barked, then he turned back to Duff. "Remember that island in the mouth o' the Tennessee? If it isn't washed

279

away, maybe it would do for tyin' up tonight." If you were tied to an island it was like having a moat around you.

They entered the Tennessee's mouth in last light and found the island. It was smaller in circumference because of the high water, and aswarm with raccoons and opossums and other small game getting crowded as the land shrank. Johnny moored the *Willing* in a screen of willow-brush tops on the downstream end of the island. One squad slept on the open deck hugging their rifles, and a sentry stood at bow and one at stern. The rest of the men slept close under the hinged panels along the gunwales, out of the sleet. By ten o' clock the *Willing* was still. Her low, dark shape hung among the willows while the Tennessee's current burbled and purled under her hull. The only sounds aboard were a snore, a cough, bone on plank as some achy sleeper turned over.

John Rogers was kept awake by the sounds on the island: splashings, squeaks, scurryings as its concentration of animals tried to find space or eat each other. John Rogers was full of anxieties about this floating arsenal. Cousin George had made him keenly aware how important it was to the chances of taking Vincennes, and how important the attack would be to the whole scheme of the war here in the West. George had lately taken to calling it "my war," and that was just about the whole truth. Virginia seemed to have forgotten her Illinois Regiment, and George really was doing the whole thing out here.

And it was plain that he didn't intend to fail at it, either. Anyone else in his situation would have probably just given it up when news came that the Hair-Buyer had Vincennes. An ordinary man would have packed up for the safety of the Spanish side. But Cousin George, no. Instead he lights out after Hamilton himself, saying, "Give me my druthers, and I'll be the wolf, not the sheep."

Well, he do put a load on a man's back, John Rogers thought. And by the Gods, I mean to carry mine. If this caper fails, I don't mean the blame to fall on me.

Now he was lying here in the dark in a gunboat's cabin with three dozen fighting men and a load of artillery and gunpowder around him, and he was nervous and sleepless and wanted very much to sit up and have a nice soothing pipeful of Virginia tobacco, but because of all the powder there was no smoking or fire allowed on the ship. Even any cooking had to be done ashore.

All this was keeping John Rogers edgy, and it was a long time before he let weariness swallow him.

HE EXPLODED OUT OF HIS DREAMS. GUNS WERE CRASHING, ootsteps on deck were resounding, men were yelling "Fire!" and :ursing, and he could smell smoke and see an orange glow round the hatch.

He fought his way out of his blanket, bumping into hard, wift-moving forms, his heart pounding in his ears, his pistol in is hand. *Fire!* And what else?

Emerging on deck, he saw a swirl of yellow smoke, men crambling and tumbling, some firing their rifles over the sides, wo or three with blankets trying to beat out flames and sparks all ver the deck. A ball hummed past his ear, and another whacked nto the oaken jamb of the hatchway.

Out on the river now he could see firelight and the shapes of wo canoes. And from one of the canoes, something aflame, railing sparks, arced through the air coming straight toward im. It went like a comet over the stern, hit some willow limbs, nd shattered into fiery fragments which fell hissing into the iver. Fire arrows. Another came bending through the dark, ame from out there on the water where muzzleblasts were flashng. The Indians were not on the island but in canoes. "Fire ails!" he yelled. "And raise those breastworks!" Some of the nen were already doing both. It was good that they knew what to lo, because he couldn't be heard over the shooting and all the abble of English and French words and the howling of the Indins on the river.

Men were stamping the fire, smothering it, all over the deck, ven scooping up flaming wads of oil-soaked bark fiber and vhole fire arrows with their bare hands and tossing them over he side.

Now and then some rifleman would utter a triumphant vhoop. They were hitting Indians and putting holes in canoes.

Soon no more fire arrows were coming. In the distance and lownstream a canoe seemed to be burning. Light from its blaze ame wavering over the moving water.

And the last spark on the *Willing*'s deck had been quenched.

There was no sign of Indians when dawn grayed. A fog blotted ip far shores. The gunboat stank of charred wood and wet, corched wool. Two or three of the men wore grease and gauze n their hands like medals, and were excused from rowing. No ne had been shot, though one man had got oak splinters in his lose when a musketball plowed into the gunwale right under his ace.

John Rogers praised the men for their bravery and quick action, particularly those who had doused the fire. "We'd have gone so high we'd been landing all over Illinois and Kentuck but for you," he said.

And then the *Willing* moved out into the fog, with muffled oars and no one talking, down the Tennessee's current and then up the Ohio. Lieutenant Rogers was thankful for the fog. As slow and lumbersome as this vessel was, it would be easy for Indians to follow her, both in canoes and along the bluffs, and it seemed quite possible that the gunboat might have to fight all the way to Post Vincennes, now that she'd been seen.

On the other hand, he thought, maybe they'll be a-lookin' for us up the Tennessee. It might've appeared we were headed up thataway. Or maybe they'll just think we're making for Fort Pitt and only watch for us on the Ohio. Hope this fog lasts.

Though if it does, how'll we even *find* the Wabash?

GEORGE LOOKED BACK AND SAW HIS MEN STILL COMING along. The land had disappeared behind them, and there was no land to be seen ahead. All the ground between the creeks was overflowed. The bottom was oozy and invisible under their benumbed feet, and there were roots to trip them and twist their ankles. Many had lost their moccasins and shoes. The water reached their thighs, their hips, their waists. They carried their rifles across their shoulders and their powder horns around their necks. A man would grasp a sapling branch with one hand and keep a hold on it until he could clutch the next with the other hand, because the current was strong. But there were stretches where nothing protruded above the water to support them. That precarious fear of falling, of slipping under, made a strain as exhausting as the effort itself. Or the hunger. In this drowned land amid the tributaries, there was no game, and they were now down to the crumbs and scraps in the bottoms of their pouches.

He would look back with pity and worry in his heart and a feigned smile of confidence and cheerfulness on his face and watch them come wading along under the eternally leaden sky, their leather clothes soaked black, rain dribbling off their hats, their stubbled faces drawn and fishy-white with exhaustion, the pouches under their eyes purple, their red eyes and leaky red noses the only warm color in this whole, dripping, hushing, slopping, gurgling, gray-brown infinity of floodwater, and he would be alarmed for them, and would wonder if they really could keep this up all the way to Vincennes, as he had convinced them they could.

Some of the short men toward the rear walked near the

orses, hanging onto their packsaddles and manes and tails.
very breath was a gasp between chattering teeth. They could
mell the raw, cold smell of the icy water and feel the slow,
eady tug of the current pressing them. Every time a man would
umble and thrash, the hands of a comrade would snatch the
eight of his rifle off of him and grab his collar or pigtail to
ipport him until he got his footing.

They were running on jokes and desperate laughter now.
'eorge made up all the happy banter he could as he led them
long. "By gum!" he'd say, laughing, "wouldn't the Hair-Buyer
e just all a-twitter if he knew we're this close, comin' to pay
im a call? Hey, Joe, wouldn't ye just looooove t' catch him in
ed in 'is nightgown, the way we did Roachblob? Ha, haaaa!"
.nd the laughter would ripple back along the line.

"I git 'is scalp, you can have 'is nightcap," someone would
ry, taking it up.

"You can have 'is merkin," someone else would yip, "I git 'is
odpiece!"

A dead muskrat floated by, and George snagged it with the
oint of his sword and held it up. "Lordy," he exclaimed.
When the *muskrats* drown . . ."

Laughter. Then somebody said, "Save that, Colonel! For
night's soup!" More laughter.

And later when the water was up to George's ribs, he heard a
urst of shivery laughter a few feet behind him, and shouts.

"Hey! Lookee at that leetle tadpole go!"

"Hey, Dickie! Got room fer me on that thang?"

George turned and saw what the gray-faced men were laugh-
ng at. The little drummer boy had hauled himself up onto his
loating drum and he was lying on his stomach on it, hanging
ith one hand onto the fringe of a big sergeant's coat and being
owed along. Responding to their laughter, he began showing
ff, splashing with his feet, even letting loose of the sergeant's
addle with his hands. George roared with a happy release of
aughter and turned to continue ahead, seeking the bottom with
is benumbed feet.

And when after a while that hilarity had died down and he
vas hearing nothing behind him but the dismal swash and
hlegmatic breathing and now and then a piteous groan, he
vould have to start up again.

"Hey, I feel some warm water, Abe. Is it springtime already,
r'd you just sneak a leak?" More laughter came from the trem-
ling wretches all around, and someone took up the joke.

"Don't add to it, Abe, I'm neck-deep already!"

*   *   *

"WHERE IN THE NAME O' GOD'S GREAT GEOGRAPHY IS TH
Wabash?" John Rogers muttered. John Duff was grimacing i
the rain. The Willing had just labored around the edge of an
other wooded, inundated point to find herself in still anothe
backwater cul-de-sac. Below on deck the men were pushing th
boat along slowly with setting poles. Along each gunwale the
walked toward the stern, each straining against a long pole h
had stuck into the river bottom. When each reached the afte
deck he would pull up his pole, carry it to the bow, then get i
line behind the last man, set his pole in the bottom, and walk
straining, toward the stern again. And the galley would slide
few more feet through the willows.

"Damn me if I know," Duff murmured, peering in all direc
tions through the maze of copses and reed-swamps and fals
channels.

"All hands, lay off and rest," Rogers called out. "Pagan, woul
ye please scamper up that mast and look us up a path back to th
river?" Pagan, an old, one-eyed ex-sailor, went like a monkey u
the shrouds to the masthead twenty feet above the deck, hooke
one leg over the spar, and perched there, taking in all the point
of the compass with a slow sweep of his one eye. Then he spok
down. "Onliest water I can see big enough for us, and I can
swear it's the main road o' the river, sir, is 'bout two hundre
yard off starb'd."

"Very well," said Rogers, squinting up into the spitting rain a
the little wind-flapping scarecrow silhouetted against the bruise
colored clouds. "Can ye see a way to get to it?" Johnny Roger
was getting an awful despairing choke in his voice. They ha
come early this morning to a point of bluff with large elms on i
which Duff had sworn marked the mouth of the Wabash. A
couple of Kaskaskian rivermen had confirmed Duff's landmark
And so the Willing had nosed toward that bluff through th
misty expanses of turbid water and headed into a wide stretc
that seemed to be the mouth of the Wabash. They had searche
the bluff with spyglasses for signs of Indian sentinels. They ha
seen none, but that did not mean none were there.

And so they had gotten into the Wabash Valley and as far a
they knew they had not been seen by any Indians since the fraca
in the Tennessee River. As far as they knew.

But now in the course of this long, rainy day they had thus fa
gone up three blind channels, and this was the third time the
had had to send Davy Pagan up the mast to have a look-see. Th
first time, they had been able to turn the boat around and ro

out. The second time, the *Willing* had run aground on some hidden hummock, and only by putting men out in the cold water with ropes and shovels had they been able to back her off. A day gone by and they still were surely no more than two miles up the Wabash, with more than a hundred miles to go to their rendezvous with the Illinois Regiment.

Now Davy Pagan had studied the maze and he called down:

"Sir, I'd say back 'er down the way we come, 'haps one quarter mile, and there's a bay-oo big enough to bring 'er about. Then we p'ceeds 'bout three hundred yard and there's a reed patch on th' larb'd, openin' through to open water. Might have to push 'er through, but through them reeds lies the way, I'd say, sir. I see no other."

"Very well, Mister Pagan. And can y' see what lies beyond that open water? Can y' see the bluff, the elms, any hills?"

"Sir, I see nowt but water, then mist, thick as on th' Firth o' Forth on a November morn."

"Eh, then, come down, Mist—"

"HOOP, HOOP! Avast, sir!" Pagan cried down suddenly, tightening his grip on the perch and leaning far out, peering till his eye popped. "Yonder comes a wee boat, sir, with but one soul in 'er, and comes a-flyin'!"

Now everyone was gaping aloft at him, as if trying to see through his eye what this might be. As they craned like this, they began to hear, faint in the dank air, yipping voices.

There was no mistaking it: Indians. Excited ones. "To arms, and stand ready," Johnny Rogers called. The men laid down their poles and scrambled for rifles. "What see now, Mister Pagan, eh? Sing out, damn it!"

"It's a canoe with a Christian in it, it is! But I make out a long canoe a half a mile ahind of 'im, up to her scuppers in heathens. They're after his skelp, sir, way I see it!"

"Hell's fire! All these guns but we're blind down here! How many Indians in that canoe, Pagan?"

"I make out eight. Our white man's 'bout tuckered, sir. If I had my gun up here, I'd sink me a heathen canoe!"

The Indian voices were distinct now. The riflemen on deck were tense with frustration.

"Can y' get his eye, Pagan?"

The little man put his thumb and forefinger in his mouth and emitted a shrill whistle, then waved his hand in a summoning motion. "He's seen me, sir, and's a-comin' thisaway!"

"Good! Now come down."

Two long, tense minutes passed. The Indian voices, urgent as the song of foxhounds Johnny Rogers remembered from Virginia, were loud and near now. Then the sounds of splashing, panting; a shape among the trees; then the prow of a canoe weaving among drowned shrubs. They could see the man in it now.

"Damn me if 'tain't Myers!" someone hissed.

"Get 'im aboard! Raise those shields and stand ready!"

The men reached strong arms down and yanked the gasping, astonished white man out of his canoe and swung him aboard. A dozen flintlocks cocked and were aimed over the oaken breastworks toward the sounds of splashing paddles and excited Indian voices out in the flooded woods. The prow of the big war canoe came into view, then a painted face, two, three . . .

And when the Indians suddenly discerned the long, low shape of the gunboat lying in their path, they stopped paddling to grab for their muskets, gasping queries to each other.

"Shoot 'em," said Johnny Rogers, and twelve guns cracked almost as one. The war canoe for a moment was full of jerking arms and twitching bodies, and then it turned over with a flurry of splashing. The sulphurous smell of gunpowder drifted through the dank air, and no one came up from the bloodstained water.

MYERS WAS GEORGE ROGERS CLARK'S CHIEF COURIER. HE had gone from Kaskaskia to Williamsburg in September, loaded with messages, and had had to wait for the fall session of the Assembly before starting back, as he explained now, slumped on a bench, sipping rum, in the cabin of the *Willing*, and he had a lot of letters from Governor Patrick Henry and congratulations from Benjamin Harrison, speaker of the House of Delegates, and messages from friends and families of the Illinois Regiment—"a good twenty pounds of mail," said he, lifting the precious bag with one hand and then letting it drop to the deck—and he was just skintight full of news of war and scandals and politics back East, but first, he wanted to know, what in the ding-dong, owl-hootin' blue-flame hell was Colonel Clark up to now and why was this scorched gunboat sitting here in a slough of muddy branchwater two miles off the Wabash River with that crazy one-eyed swab perched up on her at tree-top level, a-whistlin' and flapping his arms like a jaybird on a limetwig, anyhow?

"Well, Mister Myers, I'll try to explain it all to your satisfaction and wonderment by and by," replied John Rogers, "but first will y' kindly show me where in all this God damned water the Wabash River runs, because I got to get up it in a terrible hurry. Otherways, y'll never get to deliver your mail."

* * *

THE ILLINOIS REGIMENT WAS WITHIN SEVEN OR EIGHT miles of Vincennes now, but from the looks of the expanse of swift floodwater now in front of them, they might as well have been hoping to attack London.

George stood looking at it, and the men and officers were gathering behind him, dazed and numb and weak from hunger. They had not eaten for three days. They had been two weeks without shelter, and there had not been a day in those two weeks when it was not snowing, raining, or sleeting. They had waded countless swollen creeks and crossed three rivers. They had stopped at one place for two days to cut down a huge tree and build a dugout pirogue to ferry them across river chanels.

And now they were facing the biggest stretch of open water they had seen yet, and they no longer had the pirogue. It had been sent down to find the *Willing*, with orders for Lieutenant Rogers to bring her on day and night. Without the *Willing*, without her meat and flour and rum, without her broad hull to float them across the flooded Wabash, it seemed, the regiment must surely perish of exposure and starvation here in these wintry floodlands, within three leagues of its unreachable destination. To go back two hundred miles over the way they had come would be impossible. To the officers and men gathering behind Colonel Clark now, that was the way their situation looked as they stood in floodwater on the edge of the last major river before the Wabash, the Troublesome River, which the French called the Embarras. They looked at it, hearts sinking.

But now to their amazement George's voice rang out as cheerful as ever.

"All righty, then, boys, let's don't trouble ourselves with the Troublesome!" He pointed downstream. "We'll just follow the bank down to the mouth, two-three miles yonder, isn't she, Mister McCarty? And then we'll need only cross the Wabash herself. Damned if I've got time to play in every little creek, I'm after that Hair-Buyer!" He strode off southward now, waving his right arm in a sure, impatient summoning motion that utterly belied the wild desperation he really felt.

And the men, as usual, trusted his determination, and hoisted their guns and fought off their shivers and went limping along after him. "Master Lovell," he said, leaning down to the drummer boy, "tap out somethin' to strut by."

And so Dickie Lovell did, and soon the whole staggering, blue-lipped, hollow-eyed line was singing "Katy Cruel," their favorite marching song:

> *O, diddle lully day*
> *O, de little lie-o-day!*
> *O, diddle lully day*
> *De little lie-o-dum day!*

And down, down they went, on lower and lower ground, with their *O diddle lully day O de little lie-o-day*, the tune going round and round in their heads with its senseless but heartening monotony, and George led them on down, his eyes stinging with tears sometimes at the sound of their fine, manly voices, at the thought of this seemingly fatal trap he'd led them into, knowing they were as hungry and spent as he was but kept coming along because he didn't seem to mind it and because he seemed to know what to do next, and soon they were wading again, searching in the twilight for the Wabash. Somewhere along the way the drummer changed his cadence and the men picked it up and started singing a song old Leonard Helm had made up and taught them, about a homemade liquor so bad that only every other mouthful could be swallowed, so that you had to sip twice as much to do you the same amount of good, and each refrain ended with a *"glup, spit, patoooo!"* in imitation of spitting out the awful stuff. And the soldiers sang it and sang it and tried to outdo each other with the awful sounds of spewing and gagging and retching, with each new depth of revolting noise earning a laugh. It was the lowest and most hilarious form of humor, and a noisy march for one so deep in enemy country, but George did not try to hush them because it was keeping their minds happy. Anyway, he thought, this abominable weather surely was keeping everyone, Englishman and Indian alike, burrowed in at the fort. There had not been one sign of anyone across the entire Illinois in the two weeks since they had marched out of Kaskaskia. So they must have their singing now, he thought; it's all the nourishment they've got.

And now night was falling and there was not a spot of ground anywhere for a camp, and for the first time George was afraid that his determination had outreached his judgment, that for the first time since he had been leading men he had led them not just to the limits of their abilities but beyond them. The men could not lie down or even sit down to rest in this cold water; soon it would be too dark for them to walk in it, and if they tried to spend the night standing still in it waiting for morning light, they were bound to die of exposure. *Glup, spit, patoooo!*

Bowman came splashing up with the word that some of the weaker men were having to be hauled along by their stronger comrades, arms draped over their necks for support, while others were holding themselves up only by hanging onto the horses.

"Hard fortune, George," Bowman whispered.

"Come on, man, y're doubting," George hissed at him. "What did I tell you about that?" It gave George a little straighter spine himself, having to straighten up Bowman's. But ahead, the trees and bushes were losing their outlines in the deepening gloom, and no matter how promising a blurred patch or smear of darkness might look, when he reached it it would prove to be not solid ground but merely a willow thicket two feet deep in water, with nothing beyond it but more water, more reeds, more tree trunks. The evening was drizzly and the hush of water on his hat and the hiss of it in the trees and the *plurp plop plip* of it dripping into the water seemed eternal. He felt as if he had been born with this rain on his head and this icy ooze around his feet; he felt that it would always be like this and that it was his punishment for bringing his good and faithful people out on this mad errand of patriotism. Or is it patriotism? he wondered, wondering deep below the levels of words, is it patriotism or is it but a terrible ambition for glory?

That was an awful, unsettling thought, a thought he'd never had before. When he had started devoting himself to the defense of Kentuck there had been no ambition in it, he knew that. When he had planned the capture of the Mississippi posts, he had not felt ambition then, either—just a great, swelling eagerness to do a bold and useful service for his state.

Maybe something had happened when the Indians at Cahokia had started seeing him as a great white father. Maybe it was the adulation of the Spaniards and the French. Of Teresa. Of his own men.

Maybe you started believing your own legend, he thought; maybe that's why you thought you could make a madman's enterprise like this work.

His fingertips stung with wet cold, and twigs slapped his aching-cold face in the dark, and his heart was pumping as if it were ready to quit. His nose was running into the stubble on his upper lip, and he felt like a snot-nose boy and wanted to cry with remorse for what he had started and now doubted he could finish.

But then he remembered his own words to Bowman and he whispered them eagerly to himself.

"Stop doubtin', man! Get eager!" And he remembered and whispered: "I don't intend to let anything stop us!"

And then he could feel under his feet a slight rising of the ground. "Come on, boys," he shouted back toward the sounds of splashing, gasping and moaning, "come on, now, it's shallowin' up! Campground just ahead here!" He didn't know that was so. But it was as if he could make it so by sheer wishing.

And it came true. They were on a forested hillock of about two acres, surrounded by gurgling, whispering water, and there was a huge amount of dead wood drifted up on it. "Make fires," he shouted. "Big fires!" He didn't worry about fires being seen. It was nine o'clock at night and they were out in the middle of a flood where not even wolves would be on such a night. And it was a matter of life to get these hungry, exhausted men dried and warmed before they just went cold to the heart and died.

Soon the little camp was ablaze with a dozen strong bonfires, the hardwood smoke rankling in the rain, and the men crowded so close to the blazes that steam rose off their clothes. George went around the campfires as usual to dispense praise and good cheer. Then he lay down shivering in his damp blanket, his stomach growling and stuttering with emptiness, and thought troubled thoughts for a long time—thoughts about ambition, about overweening pride, about irresponsible rashness, about whether the pirogue had found the *Willing*, about whether it would be necessary to start killing and eating the horses. All this went around and around in his head and, with the shivering and hunger, and the endless watery sounds of this drowned world, made him more and more wakeful.

Then he heard somebody snoring nearby in the dark. He smiled. He picked up their *O diddle lully day o de little lie-o-day* and let it go around and around in his mind, and then older songs blended in, home songs from old Caroline, and then he remembered "The Quaker's Wooing," and *hum hum hi ho hum, fall liddle li dum diddle alla day* started going around and around, and then he heard the music of plucked strings, and a tune of Teresa's *gitarra* began repeating itself.

Thank Lord God for this spot of dry ground you left us, he thought, and then he felt such a swell of gratitude for this latest deliverance of his troops that he stopped shivering and went to sleep.

THE MEN AWOKE THE NEXT MORNING DULL WITH THE weakness of hunger and the aches of cold, and the sight of the brown, cold, dirty sea of water and flotsam surrounding their island camp demoralized them at once. George looked around at the flooded woods and then at the haggard company of scarecrows gazing sullenly about, and he could not imagine how he

as going to animate them this morning and make them willing
move off the one piece of solid ground in the world and go
rther into that awful water, toward horizons of still more water.
he French volunteers were huddling together in knots, casting
gly looks his way, and even his own boys did not seem to be
ppreciating their legendary leader very much this morning.

Suddenly a dull, muffled *boom* rolled across the waters; heads
rned quizzically. *What the devil.*

And at once he had it. He sprang to his feet.

"Hear that, boys?" he shouted. "It's the morning gun at
Iamilton's fort! We're that close, lads!" And now the men were
n their feet, cheering, shaking their fists in its direction, whoop-
g and frolicking, thumping each other on the back and shout-
g threats and profanities at the Hair-Buyer. And warmed by
at spark of cheerful fury, they allowed themselves to be led into
e water again and waded southward with their *de little lie-o-
um day* and their *glup, spit, patoooo.*

And in the afternoon, their heads and bodies again benumbed
y emptiness and suffering, they slopped ashore on a low bluff
at was the western bank of the Wabash. They had at last got
elow the mouth of the Troublesome River. They were now
bout three leagues downstream from Vincennes. Now they had
nly to cross the Wabash to its eastern shore and march those
st nine miles up that eastern bank, and they would be upon
eir prey. In those words, it sounded simple. But George gazed
cross the great river and he understood that what they had done
a the last two weeks had been mere practice for what lay ahead.

There was no other side of the Wabash to be seen.

The mighty river swept by, dirty yellow, dimpled and swirling,
arrying whole trees and floats of debris and misshapen pans of
oating ice. Beyond its wide channel as far eastward as he could
ee over the table-flat floodplain, there was nothing but yellow-
rown water, water, water, its expanse broken only by leafless
ark trees, white-limbed sycamores, snarls of drift, and the tops
f bushes. Beyond the broad channel of the Wabash, he could
ot see a foot of ground anywhere. Nor a sign of the *Willing*,
or even the pirogue he had sent to look for the *Willing*.

The dismal panorama hit him in the stomach like a cannon-
all. His vision blurred, the light dimmed, brightened, dimmed.
he woeful voices of the men seemed to be coming from inside
is own head. His whole brain and soul seemed to be muddling
nto a chaos of hopeless confusion, frustration, regret. I should
ave gone to de Leyba's house and never left Teresa's side, he

thought: a private man with no vainglory. It was vainglory brought me here, and we're doomed by it.

He had to keep his face toward the river because he could not let the officers or men see his face now. He felt like dropping to his knees and crying in despair.

But there was a presence beside him. Bowman was there on his left. Someone else was on his right now; it was Captain Worthington. They were waiting for him to say something. So he said it.

"At last, gents. The Wabash. The last barrier between us and Hamilton. We've done it, boys. We've crossed the Illinois in winter. A thing supposed to be impossible. Congratulations to us all."

They were looking at him through the sides of their eyes, unsure what to say to this. Finally Bowman cleared his throat. "Hamilton's a gone gosling, sure enough," he said, evidently still feigning eagerness, then he added, "What ought we t' do first, George?"

George took a deep, shuddering breath. It was obvious they weren't going to let him give up. It was still his show and they still believed he could do something and so, now without the inner fire of vainglory, he still had to do something and it still had to make sense. So he started talking.

"Put a detail to making a raft," he said. "Big enough for, say four men. We'll send it across yet today to reconnoitre the far side for a good landing place. If they find ground to walk on we'll have 'em sneak up to th' town and liberate some boats, just in case something's befell th' *Willing*. Ed, you divide your company up and have 'em cut ash and hickory and find bark to make canoes. Everyone else can go hunt, dig roots, find slippery elm bark, anything edible except our horses. I doubt there's much game on this shore, but there might be at least one deer stranded here—th' Good Lord usually arranges things like that for times like now. Keep everybody busy, gents. As my Ma says, 'Idle hands make evil thoughts.' If I've forgot anything, think of it yourselves. Hop to it, then, my friends."

They went away, and now they were not pretending eagerness; their voices were lively and full of authority. Soon every man was busy.

It was odd how that had worked out. *Their* needs had saved *him*. He remembered another one of his mother's sayings. It was back when she'd birthed Fanny, her tenth. Someone had said it was about time she gave up mothering and rested. "Nay," she had said. "I've started something, and now I wouldn't stop if I could, and I couldn't stop if I would."

It was funny how one always came to understand her sayings by and by.

BY THE NEXT MORNING, TWO SERIOUS TRUTHS WERE EVIdent: There was virtually no game in the area, and the *Willing* had not reached her appointed station on the Wabash below. Hunters combing the flooded woods for miles around had determined the first fact; the scouts in the pirogue had come up the river to tell him the other.

One of the privates had a theory about this, and his fellows egged him on until he came and told George about it. "The rain falls forty days and forty nights, as y'see, sir, and th' animals go two by two lookin' for an Ark, and thar sets th' *Willing*, so they just take 'er an' head for Ararat!" And the soldier turned away, prancing like a leprechaun, slapping his knee while George and the onlookers roared with laughter at his wit.

The starving troops now worked feebly but steadily making two canoe frames from peeled, split ash. There was no birch in the vicinity, so they peeled great limber slabs of bark off various kinds of trees and tried them. Inner bark of elm seemed to be about the best, and men with tomahawks, knives, awls, and leather thongs were sitting around in the rain working with numbed fingers, tailoring bark to cover the frames, while others experimented with candle tallow and pounded bark fiber to make a substitute for pitch to seal the seams. The canoes were shaping up rough-looking and flimsy, but apparently they would have to serve, along with the pirogue, to do the ferrying the *Willing* had been meant to do. George kept returning to the river to watch for the four scouts who had gone out the day before on their raft. At last the shout of a sentry upstream heralded their return. They were in a sorry condition. They came paddling ashore weakly on logs, their feet and arms in the cold river water, looking like half-drowned rats. They were brought staggering up to a bonfire, and as they warmed themselves and drank hot sassafras tea, they made their dreary report. Unable to find any land on the other side except a low hill surrounded by water, they had paddled farther up toward the town until, at dusk, the current had broken up their raft. They had spent the entire night awake, lying on old logs in the backwaters, half in and half out of the water, staying together only by holding each other's hands, keeping their souls together only by joking and praying and singing Len Helm's drinking song. George clamped his jaws and listened to this piteous account.

"By my eyes!" breathed a listener, taking his blanket off his shoulders and draping it over one of the scouts, "I thought *I* had a hard night!"

The smaller of the two bark canoes was finished, and put in the water, and with a few minutes' more caulking and plugging, floated without leaks. Immediately George sent Captain McCarty and three of his men up the river in it to make another attempt to steal boats. But they returned within an hour, reporting that they had been stopped by the sight of four large campfires on the shore a league upstream, and figures clad in red—whether Indian blankets or British uniforms they had not been able to tell at a safe distance.

"Well, then," George said with a sigh, "use what daylight's left to go on down and try to find the *Willing*. Tell Cousin Johnny that I'm mighty impatient for 'im." He sensed some troops standing nearby and knew he'd better lighten up his tone of voice. "Tell 'im," he said, "that the pair of elephants might be enough to feed the regiment."

The troops could still laugh a little. He was glad to hear that.

THE NEXT MORNING, FEBRUARY 20, WAS MISTY, AND THE air was close down to freezing. Even the dull report of the morning gun up at Fork Sackville caused little cheer. The men sat huddled in their blankets, their eyes hollow and haunted. There was much coughing, little talking.

But in the French company they were talking. Captain Charleville came with a worried expression and told George that the people in his company were having a democratic discussion about trying to return to Kaskaskia. George hopped to his feet. He strode into the French camp. Within two minutes of fast talking, he had reminded them that they had volunteered to come with him, laughed off their notion of retreating, and told them to go out and hunt food for their comrades if they were so eager to go walking. They were ashamed to meet his eyes, and were bewildered by his cheerful but forceful manner, and soon they had faded into the woods in every direction with their muskets. "Now," George said to Charleville. "My thinking is, democracy is a fine thing, in its place, but this isn't the place. So long as they're scattered out there in the woods, they won't be holding assemblies, if ye see what I mean. Good day, Cap'n."

Now there was nothing George could do yet but try once more to work up the spirits of his own men. He went around the camp talking up the certainty of success, boasting about the canoes, talking about the imminent arrival of the *Willing*, rubbing his stomach and assuring them that with so many hunters out there would soon be meat. He decided that if no turn of fortune had come by tomorrow, he would have the first of the horses butchered. But he kept this decision to himself.

At noon, things began happening. The sentry on the river bank decoyed ashore a passing boat carrying five French hunters from Vincennes. They were astonished to see the Americans here, and told George there was not the least suspicion of his presence. They said most of the inhabitants were chafing under Hamilton's hauteur and were still sympathetic toward the Americans. The repairs on the fort were nearly finished, they said. They also said they had seen two small boats adrift a little way up the river.

George detained the Frenchmen as politely as possible, in case they might have thought to go back to Hamilton and betray his presence. He gave them the opportunity to join his army and to contribute their boat and their provisions to his regiment, hinting that they would be much happier if they did. They shrugged, and, with wan smiles, they volunteered everything. George sent Captain Worthington up the river in the newly finished canoe to seek the drifting boats. At that moment a gunshot was heard somewhere to westward, and soon one of the Virginians staggered into camp with a small doe across his shoulder. The whole camp was suddenly alive and in the highest spirits. One small deer among a hundred and thirty starving men meant scarcely a couple of bites apiece, but, cut small, organs, brain, tongue, and all, and extended through a gruel of roots thickened by the flour and goose fat the Frenchmen had contributed, it was as welcome as a feast.

While it was cooking in a kettle, Worthington returned, having found one of the drifting boats.

Not much, a cup of slop and a found boat, George mused. But they're a change of fortune and the boys've got spirit again. Now we've got two boats, a pirogue, and a bark canoe on hand.

He called the captains in for a conference. They sat before him, hollow-eyed, hollow-cheeked, faces looking like skulls in the dim light of the sheltered campfire, their shoulders wet with rain. But they were smiling, feeling the miracle of digestion, and waiting to hear what he had to say.

"Get 'em ready," he said with that old cocky grin. "We'll start ferrying across the Wabash first thing in the morning."

18

WABASH VALLEY
February 23, 1779

A RED-TAILED HAWK SOARED IN THE COLD AIR A THOUSAND
feet above the river. In the east the sky was yellow and the horizon was blue-gray. In the west the sky was deep, clear blue and a
last star was fading. Far below the hawk there spread miles of
lowland covered with water on both sides of the river, and where
no currents ran there was white-edged ice. The ice held the tops
of bushes and reached in among the tree trunks of flooded forests. In the east the ice reflected the yellow of the sky and in the
west it was gray.

The hawk flew eastward over the river and then dipped its left
wing and began drifting northward in a wide arc, descending. It
passed high over a town that stood on a plain surrounded by
floodwater and dimpled with frozen ponds. A thin film of
chimney smoke hung in the still air over the town and over a
large Indian village north of the town. Near the town, on a low
bluff where the plain met the river, stood a fort with a blockhouse at each corner and a gate facing the town and an arrangement of log buildings inside its palisade. Smoke rose from the
chimneys of the buildings in the fort. As the hawk drifted silently over the fort and swung southwesterly out over the river,
men in red coats were walking across the frosty ground inside the
fort. A circle of Indian tents and a corral of horses filled a part of
the parade ground.

The hawk's wide circle back down above the river brought it
over a wide, flooded plain three or four miles wide, about a
league below the town. It was water unbroken by ground or even
by trees or shrubs. Huge stretches of it were covered by thin ice,
and a path had been broken through some of this ice. The hawk
veered east from the river and saw a long line of men below in
the water, moving slowly, slowly toward the town, breaking ice
as they went. Two boats and two canoes were moving alongside
the men. The hawk soared high over the line of men and then
tilted in the sky and sailed toward the southeast.

GEORGE'S VISION WAS GOING STRANGE, FROM THE HUNGER-
faintness and from the pain of his bones and flesh in the ice
water. Everything would go blinding bright, then dark, then

296

bright again. Sometimes the horizon would seem to slant. Once he looked up and saw a hawk high in the blue morning sky, then it divided and became two hawks, then one.

It was bad here that there were no bushes or trees to grab for support, and worse that there were none to be walked past to give a sense of progress. There was no way to conceive of distance or time, only the slow, disorderly splashing, gasping, coughing, blowing, moaning, and the intermittent racket of Dickie Lovell's drum behind him. The drummer rode on the shoulders of a big sergeant. The horizon, that thin, low, blue line of land they were struggling toward, stayed the same. There was no *diddle ully day*; no one had breath for singing.

The men had awakened this morning on a little island with their wet clothes frozen to the ground. Then he had given them a speech of praise that had brought tears to their eyes, and to his. He had pointed across this stretch of water and told them it was the last obstacle between them and the Hair-Buyer's fort, and then he had led them straight into the icy floodwater again to start this last three or four miles to Vincennes.

And now they were in the middle of this endless sheet of water and he was doubting that they would be able to make it across. For the first time, he was doubting whether *he* could make it across. It was the first time in his life that he had doubted that his body could do his will. It had always had the power to go where he would drive it, no matter how much it hurt, but now he could scarcely force it to move and he felt that at any moment it would simply seize up and stop here in the middle of this infinity of ice water.

He pulled out his pocket watch, and when he got it in focus he saw that they had been in the water for an hour. He looked back. Some of the men were now staggering two and three abreast, the weaker supporting themselves on the shoulders of the stronger. Some of the big men were carrying two knapsacks and two rifles now while their unburdened fellows concentrated on making themselves move. "Oh help me, I'm cramped up!" a voice would cry, and a boat would tilt as that man was dragged aboard like a water-soaked log.

The torturous stepping and quaking went on for another eternity and when George looked at his watch again only ten minutes had passed. He put the watch away, determined not to look at it again. The sun was coming up and it was the first sun he had seen in the nineteen days of the march, but it gave no warmth.

He glanced back again and now in the faces he could see

fear—the stark, strained fear of collapsing and going under. Now his concern for them was almost a panic. He could feel his own dependable body failing, his head whooshing, his heart fluttering, his spine stiffening into a shaft of ice, and was sure they must be closer to the end of it than he. There seemed to be a mile yet to go, and there would be hearts stopping before that mile was made.

"Boats!" he shouted. He jabbed his finger ahead toward the distant woods. "Quick! Make land! Unload! Come back for people! Fast, now! Master Lovell, lay on those sticks!" The pickaback drummer hammered away till he was red in the face. "You flankers! Here!" Two rugged riflemen, each six and a half feet tall, splashed toward him. "Go on ahead," he gasped. "Walk tiptoe, or walk on water, or something, but be ten feet tall and keep yellin' back that it's getting shallow."

"Aye, sir," said one. "But what if it ain't?"

"Say so anyway, man. They need to hear it. Off ye go!"

The boats were far ahead now. George was nearly frantic for his people; their sounds from behind him were so piteous and extreme now that he could not bear to look back. The two tall scouts kept calling back, "Gettin' shaller! Yahoo! Gettin' shaller!" But he could see the water was to their ribs now; it was getting deeper. There were a few little bandy fellows in this troop who didn't stand to the armpits of those two men; they'd be head-under by the time they got there. *Boats!* George thought. "BOATS!" he yelled.

And then he saw them coming back, oars and paddles flashing fast; they came by with water gurgling and broken ice gnashing around their bows, and voices back in the line were yelling for them. "Here! Git Isaac! He's a-foldin' double!" "Boat! Oh, God damn, hurry! Help this whoreson ol' Shad here! His eyes gone blank!" "Hey! Man here whose feet don't reach bottom! Go some room?" And then the boats, loaded hull-down with men stacked like cold fish in their bilges, sped past again, their panting rowers hurrying to get them ashore and come back for more. George wanted with all his soul to grab a boat and hang on and ride those last few hundred yards to shore, but he knew he couldn't do that and still look them in the eyes. No. There were still too many in the water still coming along because he was.

He could see the textures of the bark of the trees now; he was close enough to see that lovely gray-green mottle on the white sycamores and the old gray tatters of hickory shagbark and the smooth silver-gray of beech trunks, and oh, how he wanted to touch them once more, how he loved trees! But the water was to is chest now; it grew deeper as he strained against it and advanced with this nightmare slowness, holding his powder horn and gun above his head with excruciatingly sore arms and shoulders and prickling-cold fingers. The drum was still rattling back here somewhere, and there were encouraging shouts from those who had already been put ashore, and the boats were coming out again in a great hurry to get those who had had to stop back here because they were simply too short to keep their faces out of the water; but the sky was flickering now, from blue to black, back to white.

And at last there was a sapling at hand, and a floating log, and the column was thrashing and splashing in disarray into the flooded edge of the woods, breaking ice as they came. Some men had strength to climb ashore before they swayed and fell to their knees. Others clung to bushes and waited for the boats to come. Some waded into the shallows, gasping for breath, then found that without the water to buoy them they were too feeble to stand, and fell face-down amid the floating ice chips. With his own last bit of strength, George got one arm under a muttering, raying skeleton of a man and dragged him ashore. Then hands rubbed his arms as his knees started to buckle under him.

And now the boats were out there one last time, a hundred yards out, heaving aboard the last dozen men whose heads and shoulders and upraised rifles still dotted the sheet of water. And then the boats beached and put those last few ashore.

We did it, George thought. We'll never be the same, but we did it. Not a man failed me. Hot tears began running down his nose.

Dear God I never saw such a people. Thankee O Lord for giving me such as these.

THE RED-TAILED HAWK HAD RISEN TO A THOUSAND FEET again, flying over the ice-burnished flatland. It had veered miles eastward away from the big river, but now far below and ahead of it was another long, wide body of water, another flooded river. Down on that river, nosing slowly upstream among false channels and islands and thickets, moved a sixty-five-foot riverboat, her oars munching thin ice as she crawled slowly eastward.

The boat was the *Willing*. Yesterday afternoon Lieutenant Johnny Rogers, trying to keep to the channel of the Wabash in the boundless brown waters, had mistaken the current from the mouth of the White River for the current of the Wabash and had veered into the channel of the tributary. This morning the vessel was ten miles up the wrong river, creeping farther and farther

from Vincennes, and as yet neither he nor Duff, nor anyone els
aboard, knew that they were climbing the wrong river. But th
predominantly eastward progress was beginning to make Lieuten
ant Rogers uneasy. The only thing hereabouts on the map tha
tended so much eastward was the White River.

He stood on the afterdeck with his cloak drawn around hin
and squinted and watched the winter sun shimmer over ice an
frost and sparkle in his own frosting breath and heard the oars
crushing and the rattle of breaking ice along the hull.

Have we got off the cussed Wabash again? he wondered. H
looked up and saw a speck moving in the sky. A hawk.

I wish I could be up there, he thought. Just long enough t
look things over once, that's all.

NOW THEY HAD OVERCOME ALL THE OBSTACLES AND THE
were here, and the fort stood squat and solid as a castle, lit fron
behind by the descending sun and its glare off the floode
Wabash. But George knew that the odds ahead of them wer
probably greater than the ones they had overcome already. Tha
fort was well laid out and newly rebuilt, and could be expecte
to stand off a thousand attackers. Among its garrison was a com
pany of British Regular Infantry, among the world's best soldiers
Indians in the British pay came and went constantly, and rein
forcements from Detroit could be expected down the Wabash a
any time as the Hair-Buyer prepared his spring offensive. An
Hamilton himself, George knew, was no sloth. That he had de
scended by surprise from Detroit upon Vincennes was proof tha
he was both shrewd and bold. That he planned to build an In
dian force in the spring and drive all frontiersmen back over th
Alleghenies proved that he was ambitious—likely as ambitious a
George himself.

And here was George with this weakened force of guerrilla
who, except for the cold blue flame of their vengeance, coul
hardly stand up. Surely most of their gunpowder was deteriorate
by the weather. The gunboat, reinforcements, powder, food, an
artillery originally calculated into his invasion strategy were no
here, and God only knew where they were.

Orthodox strategy held that a fort could not be besieged with
out cannon and vastly superior numbers of troops. An orthodo
strategist right now might look over this situation and advis
George, since he could not retreat, to walk up to the fort an
surrender. He smiled grimly at this notion.

Sure is a good thing we're not orthodox, he thought.

* * *

So he stood with his spyglass resting in the fork of a dogwood tree and started remaking his strategy.

The only advantages we've got, he thought, are surprise and spirit. I know there's not one American here who'd quit short of dying.

So it seems we've got to play mockingbird again, he thought.

The evening gun of the fort boomed once, and its smoke and echo rolled over the flooded valley.

In the twilight the tattered regiment, lean and shaggy and hungry and silent and dark as a pack of wolves, ran through the deserted streets of Vincennes. They began moving fences and carts and barrels and everything portable out toward the edge of town nearest the fort, digging trenches and setting up a network of sniping positions, and getting on rooftops and behind chimneypots, almost without a sound.

There was no interference from the townspeople. George had sent a French-speaking aide into the town with a warning that he was here with a thousand men and would treat anyone found in the streets as an enemy, and that he would kill anyone who betrayed his presence to the fort. From the looks of the locked and shuttered houses, the townsfolk had taken him at his word.

But if anyone *had* slipped into the fort with a warning, then the commandant of the fort might believe there were a thousand Americans out here. George wanted him to believe that.

Fifteen minutes after the evening gun, a whippoorwill called. And a detachment of rooftop sharpshooters commanded by Lieutenant John Bailey started sniping at the sentries on the palisades of the fort. Their rifles cracked and flashed in the dusk, and soon the sentries were cringing behind the palisades, calling for their duty officer, so busy protecting their heads that they could not shoot back. While they were thus pinned down and distracted, a squad of Captain John Williams's men, pushing a load of logs and boards and shovels in a heavy cart, trundled out into the open ground between the town and the fort, and quickly dug and built a little sharpshooters' fortress a mere thirty yards in front of the fort's gate, so close that the cannons' muzzles could not be lowered far enough to fire on it. From down in that secure pit they could see silhouetted against the last rosy light of evening any head that moved above the palisades or at any firing port. In the meantime, also under cover of Bailey's sharpshooters, Joe Bowman led a squad of riflemen with picks and shovels and a powder keg around the fort to start tunneling in the riverbank. Their assignment was a dangerous and dirty one, but promised to be rewarding: they were to undermine the powder

301

magazine in the fort's west side—Vigo had shown in a sketch just where it was—and blow it up from below.

And so the battle—this final move in George's two-year chess game with General Hamilton—was engaged. He had told his men to do as much shooting and shouting as a thousand devils, and they were happy to oblige. They howled like Indians from the edge of the town and fired with deadly accuracy at the fort's apertures and yelled obscenities and insults at Henry Hamilton with their twangy, hog-calling voices.

"Hey, Guv'nor! Yer mama's teat was a carbuncle! That's how ye got so mean!"

"Hey, you Hair-Buyer! Yea, you, ye cross-eyed, skunk-bit, pus-suckin' felon! Your scalp, as pay for my daughter's!"

"Hamilton! If he gits your scalp, I got dibs on your eyebrows!"

"And I git your balls! And I don't mean *eye*balls! Hih, hih, hih!" Their laughter was as cold and hard as blades on whetstones.

These taunts were answered by a few blasts of cannon fire from the blockhouses, but the cannoneers could see no targets except muzzle flashes, and were reluctant to fire blindly at the town whose inhabitants were supposed to be under their protection.

And something else was making the artillerymen reluctant about using their big guns.

Every time a cannoneer moved near an embrasure to put a swab or a load down a muzzle, three or four uncannily aimed rifle balls would hum through the embrasure and whack through his hat or clothes or flesh.

After a short while the cannon ports were virtually buttoned up, and the cold moon rose on a hot duel of small arms and verbal abuse. To George's happy surprise, there was as much ammunition for the one as for the other.

Messieurs Busseron, LeGras, and Gibault, the only three men of Vincennes who had refused to sign a loyalty oath when Hamilton had captured the town, had joyously led George into a parlor, moved chairs and lifted a rug, raised floor planks, descended into a hidden cellar, and hoisted up kegs of powder and bars of lead. Busseron and LeGras, officers of the Vincennes militia, had hidden the ammunition in December, in anticipation of the Americans' return. "For," Busseron had explained, "Le Capitaine Helm he say to us how many time since, '*pas de rien*, that copperhead Clark would no let the Hair-Buyer keep thees fort!'" Gibault, a younger brother of the Kaskaskian priest, had suddenly spread his arms and tilted his head, eyes brimming with tears of happiness, and wrapped George in a garlicky Gallic hug.

And George had patted him on the back and laughed, feeling better than he had for a long time. Having given up on the *Willing*, he had presumed that his boys would have to skimp on powder and wait for sure shots and sound like no more than a firing squad. But with all this, they could pop off at that fort to their hearts' content and sound like a whole army after all!

SOMETIME AROUND MIDNIGHT, GEORGE HEARD BOWMAN calling him. "Colonel!" came Joe's voice from a little way down the line.

"Here, Joe!" he called back. Neither had shouted very loudly, but it was in a lull in the shooting and voices were carrying well in the clear, windless night, and their deep voices were distinctive; from within the fort suddenly they heard a familiar voice let out a twangy yelp of delight and bellow: "George! Joe! Heyah! Heyah! Heyah! I knowed it! I knowed it!" It was Leonard Helm's voice, said to be the loudest noise west of the Alleghenies, a voice that Helm boasted could loosen the bark on a beech tree at two hundred yards, and he had heard and recognized their voices out here, and now he was howling with joyous laughter from inside the palisade, a laugh to drown out all other voices. George and Joe listened and chuckled as they met in the moonlight. They heard a lot of the frontiersmen along the line hollering greetings to their old friend, and going, "Glup! Spit! Patoo!" and he was whooping back.

"Listen to 'im, George," Bowman said. "I swear he'll call every loon down from Canady! HI, LEN!"

"HI, JOE! HI, GEORGE! HI, Y'OLD COPPERHEAD!"

"HI, LEN!"

"HI, GEORGE! WANT ME T' CAPTURE THIS PLACE FROM INSIDE?"

George winked, elbowed Bowman's ribs, then cupped his hands around his mouth and answered: "NO! GET DOWN IN YOUR DUNGEON AND STAY LOW! WE'RE ABOUT TO START SOME SERIOUS SHOOTING!"

"HEE HEE! ALL RIGHT, Y' OL' LONG KNIFE! NIGHTY-NIGHT, NOW!" And they could hear gruff voices inside the fort, and Helm's voice fading away, exclaiming, "I be utterly God damned, Gov'nor! If that don't twiddle your codpiece! Th' old Long Knife hisself! Hey, I'll drink t' that!"

And then more laughter all along the lines, then some commands from inside the fort; another volley of musket fire crashed from the fort and musketballs whickered through the bushes and sang off rocks and slapped into the log wall of the church near George and Joe, but hitting nobody, and instantly the long rifles were crackling in reply, and again the shooting from the fort was silenced.

"Well, if the Hair-Buyer didn't know yet who was a-raidin' his fort, he does now," George remarked. "Old Len! B' God, captivity by his Lordship the Governor-General himself hasn't refined him much, has it? So, Joe. How goes your mine?"

"Mucky. We're like beetles in a fresh cow pie. We've got eight feet or so, but she keeps cavin' in. I know the Redcoats can hear us down there and it makes 'em narvous. But they dasn't get up on that parapet and fire down on us 'cause Bailey's boys up on the chimbleys can sweep it perty clean. So we just muck along, but she keeps a-fallin' in. What's new up here?"

"Just a lot o' prime shooting."

"Fine sport for Sons o' Liberty, it is."

"The ladies of the town are baking bread and making enough soup for a thousand. I've got to go over to Busseron's house now. They tell me the Piankeshaw chief's there wanting to meet Long Knife in person. He's like this with ol' Len, and he wants to join us against the fort with a hundred braves."

"That's interesting. Will ye take 'em?"

"No. We came to punish Hamilton for using red men, so we wouldn't be right using 'em ourselves, now would we? Morals, y' see."

"True," said Bowman. "Morals it is."

"Besides, mixing a hundred Indians with our boys in th' dark? Whew! Nope. Too confusing."

THE SUN ROSE. FROST GLITTERED ON YELLOW WINTER grass and frozen mud, and lightened the long blue morning shadows. The sun warmed the Americans' backs and shone blindingly in the eyes of the British defenders on the front wall of their fort. The frontiersmen, many of them barefoot, all in mudcaked and filthy clothing, eyes red from fatigue and gunsmoke, snot-streaks tracking their powder-begrimed faces, stood or crouched or lay behind barrels and carts and trees and woodpiles and their hastily built breastworks, and kept loading and firing at the fort those few yards away, poking their long rifles through knotholes and between wagon spokes and under logs, sighting on any minute sign of life or movement in the fort, squeezing the triggers, then drawing the long guns back, wiping their runny noses on their sleeves, then tilting their powder horns again.

They fired and loaded with a workmanlike concentration. They were not doing so much taunting and insulting now. After thirteen hours of the night cold and the powder fumes and the yelling and the coughing, most were painfully hoarse and some had lost their voices altogether. Squads kept moving back into the village to take breakfast and gulp hot coffee and tea while others went up and took their places. George talked to all of them he had time for, and he studied them and wondered how much longer they could keep it up. They had been on their feet for twenty-four hours now, ninety percent starved, and most of that time they had been either wading in ice water or building fortifications and sustaining a tense, busy gunfight. Most of them were lung-sick but just ignoring it. Most men would have been wanting to sleep or hide or just lie down and die by now. But almost every one who came past him this morning would ask, "When kin we tear down that 'ere fort and git that 'ere Hair-Buyer, suh?" He would wink and slap a shoulder and say, "In good time, man. Let's just grind 'em down a mite more and watch for our gunboat t' come up."

He had decided to wait till midmorning for a sign of the *Willing*. If she didn't arrive out there with a few rounds of cannon shot to strengthen his hand, he was going to have to start bluffing Hamilton down anyway, because these boys couldn't keep this going forever, and even if they thought they could, they probably could not storm that fort without at least a half of them dying. George was pretty sure all the cannon in those blockhouses were loaded with grapeshot, and even if they were silent now, they would poke out and belch death all over the place the moment he should attempt a charge.

By the middle of the morning George was so bone-weary and feverish that he was having to think everything through twice before giving an order or a permission, to avoid using bad judgment. Much longer, he felt, and he would be going blankheaded. Whatever he was going to do, he decided, he had better do it while he could still think. And the *Willing* still had not been seen.

So this seemed as good a time as any to send his first demand to Hamilton. Going into the little French chapel that he had made his headquarters, he sat down in a pew. He took his feather quill out of his old hat, and twirled it in an inkpot. Then he wrote, with strong, slashing pen-strokes:

Lt. Governor Henry Hamilton Esqr
Commanding Post St. Vincent

Sir

In order to save yourself from the Impending Storm that now Threatens you I order you to Imediately surrender yourself up with all your Garrison Stores &c. &c. for if I am obliged to storm, you may depend on such Treatment justly due to a Murderer   beware of destroying Stores of any kind or any papers or letters that is in your possession or hurting one house in the Town for by heavens if you do there shall be no Mercy shewn you.

Feby 24th 1779

G.R. CLARK

•The gunfire fell silent. A white flag was waved near the log church. When the fort gate was opened a few feet, a Captain Cardinal of the Vincennes militia, who could speak English, went from the church to the fort with the truce flag over his shoulder and Colonel Clark's letter in his hand. The gate closed after him.

Half an hour passed. The Americans rested in their shooting-places, cleaned their rifles, measured powder, replaced flints, bragged about fancy shots, gnawed French bread, coughed, blew their noses, or tried to doze in the winter sunlight under their tattered blankets.

Inside the fort then, a bugle called Assembly. Another half hour passed. Voices filtered out of the fort, and once there came a cheer of manly voices. Then the gate opened slightly, and Captain Cardinal returned down the road with his white flag.

It was not the answer George had wanted, but it was an answer that confirmed his first estimation of his enemy.

Govr Hamilton begs leave to acquaint Col. Clark that he and his Garrison are not disposed to be awed into any action unworthy of British subjects.

H. HAMILTON

Captain Cardinal related what had happened inside. Hamilton had read the surrender demand inside the gate. Then, red-faced, he had gone to his quarters, taking his officers with him. They had come out looking nervous but resolute, and then all the troops had been assembled on the parade ground. There Governor Hamilton had read Colonel Clark's letter to them and told them the officers had resolved not to surrender them into the ands of such barbarians. The Redcoats had cheered and vowed they would stick to Hamilton like the shirt on his back.

"Eh, well," George said. "And his French Canadians?"

"They," Cardinal replied, "did no cheer."

"So be it," George said to his captains. "Let's grind 'em some more. Tell the boys to shoot double-smart." Bowman passed the word down, adding his own emphasis: "Mister Clark wants them Redcoats in there to crawl up their own ass holes for a hidin' place!"

It resumed in the wan sunlight now, in the spirit of a turkey shoot. Within minutes the fort was buttoned up again. George was pleased with the shooting, but knew he would have to do something to exploit the advantage soon. The men were growing impatient to get into the fort and exact their revenge. And at this rate, powder might run so low it would have to be rationed, unless the *Willing* should show up, and George had learned not to count on that. Just as he was pondering his next move, a white flag appeared above the fort. George ordered a cease-fire and waited. A very nervous French Canadian came down.

The message was that General Hamilton proposed a three-day truce, during which neither side would work on fortifications. He wanted to hold a secret conference with Colonel Clark inside the fort—or at the gate, if Colonel Clark was reluctant to come in.

George scratched his whiskery chin while he read the lines, then between the lines. It was almost three weeks since he had left Kaskaskia to come on this forlorn adventure, an awful, painful three weeks worse than anything he had ever endured, with never a moment's ease. But now he seemed to have Hamilton ground down further than he could have dared to expect. All the suffering seemed not to have been in vain.

Bowman and other officers feared it was a ruse to get George close to the fort where he could be shot or seized.

"No," he said. "I think he's stalling for time till his reinforcements come down the river. Way our boys are shooting, he's afraid there won't be anybody left in there for 'em to reinforce. And that about the fortifications: your tunnel-bugs got him worried, Joe."

"Somethin's got t' change perty soon," said Captain McCarty. "My boys is fed, fat, and sassy, and's sayin' they'd like to get into that fort and get at the heart o' th' matter with that Hair-Buyer." And so George wrote an adamant reply:

Col. Clark will not agree to any other terms than that of Mr Hamilton's surrendering himself and Garrison, Pris-

oners at Discretion—If Mr Hamilton is desirous of a Conference with Col Clark he will meet him at the Church with Captn Helm
Feb 24th 1779

G.R. CLARK

The fort, battlefield, and town lay almost silent in the wintry midday sunlight as the messenger clambered gingerly through the barricade and went up the road and into the fort. But suddenly, from the commons beyond the town, faint yells and war whoops sounded, followed by a brief rattle of gunfire, then a few more sporadic shots. "Go see what that is," George snapped. If it was an attack on his rear right at this moment when he had gained some advantage. . .

But it was not. The word came in that Captain Williams and his boys had caught a band of Hamilton's Indians coming in from the warpath.

They trooped through the town soon, half-running, cursing, manhandling six war-painted savages, whom they yanked along by ropes tied around their necks. Williams's teeth were bared like a snarling wolf's, and his eyes were bulging. "There was twenty of 'em," he said, "comin' in with these." He swung up a heavy fistful of scalps—brown hair, white hair, blond hair, each with its patch of skin encrusted with brown dried blood—and snarled "Bringin' these in to sell to Mister Hamilton! They musta thought we was Hair-Buyer's agents a-comin' out to greet 'em Walked right up to us a-whoopin' and a-poundin' themself on their chest, jolly as ye please. Didn't realize their mistake til they was plumb amongst us. Tried t' light out. These here we caught. T' others . . . Show 'im, boys!" His men whooped and waved fourteen fresh scalps in the air: scalplocks of black Indian hair, still dripping red. George set his jaw. Williams's men were getting what they had come to Vincennes for, even if the rest hadn't yet. "I thought," Williams went on, "some o' the boys might like to have a go at these murderin' scuts. What sayuh George?"

"We'll see. None o' your boys hurt?"

"Not a one."

"Good! Good job, Mister Williams. But now stand by. I'm concentratin' on Hamilton himself right now. Meseems the Hair-Buyer's about to knuckle under."

"Begumpus! Ye don't say so!"

"Yonder comes his messenger down." George walked out onto the meadow to meet the messenger. They talked for a moment, then George came back to the church and his eyes were flashing and he was grinning big, but a bit dazed, as if he could not quite believe what he had heard.

"Well, boys, look smart now! Mister Hamilton's comin' right down to talk about givin' up. Bringing old Len Helm down with im!"

"Bejeezus!"

"Givin' up? Don't we git to kill 'im?"

"He's goan give up? Why, Gawd damn! He ought at least waited till our boat got here to cannon-shoot him a time or two!"

"Why, a fort like that'n, we'd 'a helt it a year!"

"Bo', I'm let down! Be good to see ol' Len, though."

"He gives up, that means we kin hang 'im sted o' shoot 'im, hat right, Cunnel?"

George held his hands up to hush their clamorings. "Keep our pants on, now! He hasn't surrendered yet, he's just comin' down to talk about it. Now listen, all of you." And there were a lot of them around now; having gotten wind of Williams's captives, many had taken advantage of the white flag to wander over. "Listen now! You all know I'm a talker and I don't like to be interrupted when I'm talkin'. So by God if any one o' you kills Henry Hamilton while I'm talkin' to 'im, I'm going to be mad."

Nasty laughter went through the crowd. George said:

"Now you can give him all the hateful looks y' want. They'll do him good. But keep your mouths shut and don't throw any knives or tomahawks at 'im, even by accident, because he is a bona fide representative of his Britannic Majesty. Ye hear me, now?" They were all leering happily. They loved it when he talked to them like this. They knew too that if he had not expressly forbidden it, someone among them actually might have used the Lieutenant Governor for mumbledy-peg practice, truce flag or no. There was nothing sacred or awesome to them about any British general, and this one in particular; to them he was simply the murderer of their kin. But Colonel Clark had his reasons for telling them not to kill him yet, and Colonel Clark was the only law they knew outside themselves. "All right," he said. "Cap'n, take those savages o' yours 'round that side of the church, out o' sight, and you may inquire of 'em about when they were sent out and who sent 'em, and where they got those scalps. That'll be nice intelligence to present Mister Hamilton with if he tries to act pious." The Indians were jerked and booted

309

around the corner. George had been glancing anxiously towar
the fort as he talked, and now he saw the gate swing wide an
two figures appeared, one in red, the other in a hunting shir
"Now move back and give me talkin' room," he said, "'caus
here comes Len Helm bringing His Lordship down."

Now, George thought, bracing himself for the confrontatio
that had brought him through so many months and so man
miles and so many miseries, now we're going to meet this Hai
Buyer and teach him th' fear o' God.

"He walks proud," Bowman mused as they came closer.

"Now he does, aye. He'll slink when I'm finished with 'im.

HAMILTON STOPPED FIVE FEET IN FRONT OF GEORGE AN
stuck out his hand. "So you are Colonel Clark." He was study
ing him keenly.

George kept his arms folded across his chest. "So you ar
General Hamilton."

Hamilton's gray-blue eyes hardened when his hand was ig
nored, but he did not blink or lower the drilling stare. The eye
were shrewd, hooded, under bristly reddish-black eyebrows. H
was long-jawed, with a sensual, somewhat sulky mouth. He wa
lightly freckled, and there were bluish hollows under his eye:
and George could see at once that he was what his mother use
to call one of those "starer-downers." Hamilton lowered his pro
fered hand as inconspicuously as he could and clasped it in hi
left behind his back and braced himself to stare down this Vir
ginian. George could see that was what he was doing, and al
though he was an unvanquished starer-downer himself, he wa
not going to bother with it. Instead, he grinned, crinkled hi
eyes, and winked at Leonard Helm, simply dismissin
Hamilton's challenge. He stepped past Hamilton and threw hi
arms around the grizzled stalwart, guffawing and pounding hir
on the back. "Godalmighty, Len," he exclaimed, "it's good
smell brandy again."

There were tears suddenly in Helm's eyes, and he hugge
hard. "Thankee, George. I didn't know if ye'd talk to me agin.

George dropped his voice almost to a whisper. "What's hi
chances in there?"

Helm was quick. "He's forlorn. His Canadians are mopey an
he doesn't trust 'em an' his Tawaways don't cotton t' bein' shot a
in a box. Troops boatin' down but he don't know when. But h
has guts."

Hamilton in the meantime had turned his glowering star
onto Bowman's ghostly pale eyes, but Bowman just looke

mused, then headed over to greet Helm too. And so Hamilton, clenching his jaw and grinding his right heel into the earth, found himself left staring at the most piratical, snaggle-toothed, scrawny, unshaven, stinking, menacing mob of beings he had ever seen, all lumpish as trolls in their rags and disintegrating deerskins and animal-pelt hats, all smirking at him with a happy malevolence, winking at him, leering at him, spitting tobacco juice at his feet, nudging each other in the ribs and making kissy-lips at him, and it was obvious at once that he was not going to be able to stare down a single one of these insolent louts with his gimlet-eyes; to them he was no more than a hog at the butcher's block. Every one of them felt superior to him. One gigantic and hideous specimen bowed his head to reveal a scalp-ing scar, the pale skullbone visible through a thin integument, and then looked up and leered at Hamilton's white wig while testing the edge of a hunting knife with his grimy thumb and saying softly, "Heighdy, Bub. Wanta see m' new purty?" And he held up a bloody hank of hair which Hamilton realized at once was the fresh scalp of an Indian.

Hamilton spun and stood scowling. "Colonel Clark," he rasped, "if you're quite done there, I've brought down a page of articles. I trust you will find these reasonable and honorable." George stepped over and took the sheet of paper, opened it, held it in his big hard hands, and read it while Hamilton stood clasp-ing a wrist behind his back, now trying not to meet anyone's eyes.

George hid his astonishment at Hamilton's proposed terms. The great Hair-Buyer, commandant of the whole British western theater, was actually offering to yield up Fort Sackville with ev-erything in it. He wanted his troops and officers to be allowed to keep thirty-six rounds of ammunition per man and enough provisions for a long march back to Detroit, and his wounded cared for "through the generosity of Colonel Clark." He wanted to surrender with the full honors of war.

It would be so easy to accept those terms and end this stren-uous campaign, George knew. But then Hamilton would go back to Detroit and resume his mischief. And Hamilton was not thinking yet, as George had determined he must. To George's mind this was not just a chess game now. He and his men had a more severe judgment of Hamilton.

George handed the document to Bowman and came to stand close in front of Hamilton. The general's uniform—scarlet coat and gold epaulets, white trousers and shining boots—was impec-cably clean and elegant, though the scarlet was faded and the

311

gold braid was frayed; he was, after all, a frontier commande with many years of service.

"Governor, hear me," George said in a forceful voice. "I de manded you surrender at my discretion. In my language tha means unconditionally. It's as vain of you to try to bargain wit me as it is to think of defending yon fort. My cannon will be u in a few hours, though I doubt I need 'em. The bankside of you post is already considerably undermined. I know to a man whic o' your Frenchmen ye can count on, and that's precious few Now, my boys been begging my permission to tear your fo down and get at you. If they do that, Governor, I doubt a soul o you will be spared. On the other hand, if y'll surrender at discre tion and trust my generosity, y'll have better treatment than you stand here and haggle for terms."

The muscles in Hamilton's jaw tightened. "Colonel Clark, I never take so disgraceful a step as long as I have ammunition an provision, and I have those in plenty. I can depend on my En glishmen!"

George nodded, but replied: "Well, goody. But you'll be ar swerable for their lives. The result of an enraged body o' me like these falling on you," he said, sweeping an arm toward th men crowding close, "must be obvious to you."

"Mister Clark, I perceive you're trying to *force* me to a fight i the last ditch!"

"Well you might suppose!" George shouted suddenly i Hamilton's face. "Every fiber in me cries to let these men aveng their massacred families! Aye, I'd relish any excuse to put you Indians and partisans to death, and you too!" His eyes were bla ing and his men were leaning forward and almost growling in a ominous chorus of assent. "No terms, Mister Hamilton."

Hamilton's eyes narrowed and he did not flinch. It was tru what Helm had said; he had guts. "Colonel," he said in a cris tone, "in December when your friend Captain Helm stood de fenseless and alone at the gate of that very fort, I gave him th full honors of war. Ask him if that's not so."

"And well ye should have," George replied. "But the big di ference between you and him is, Cap'n Helm's never bought woman's or a child's scalp."

Hamilton's nostrils flared and his lips suddenly looked thi and gray. He could control himself well, but George knew tha he had stuck him where it hurt. Soon Hamilton said in a lo voice, as if hoping the woodsmen might not overhear: "The nothing will do but fighting?"

"Nothing but that or, as I've said, surrendering without condi

312

ons. You're a murderer, Mister Hamilton, and you're caught. Only honorable men may demand honorable terms."

A tic had started under Hamilton's left eye, and George made point of staring at it, with a suggestion of a sneer. Hamilton now made a feeble attempt to explain something that seemed very important to him. "I always urged my Indians to bring me prisoners, not scalps; never encouraged barbarity. But you know how they . . ."

He stopped, because the Virginian seemed to be swelling up and tensing as if he were about to strike him dead on the spot, and Hamilton realized that no victims of Indian warfare would ever swallow such an excuse. So he said now: "Will you stay your hand, Colonel, till I return and consult with my officers?"

"Do that. Good day, Gov'nor."

MOST OF THE WAY BACK UP TO THE FORT, HAMILTON WAS so busy composing himself to say anything to Helm. Hamilton was a dutiful son of a noble Scottish family, and this was the first time in his long and effective career that he had ever been faced down or humiliated—and this by a man who, according to Helm, was but about twenty-five years old, about half Hamilton's own age. Helm had been prattling on exuberantly: "God dang, ol' George ain't changed nary a bit! He, hee! A regular, ring-tail, rum-suckin' fire eater, ain't he? Sure made you look 'bout big as a piss-ant, Gov'nor! Hee, hee."

"Captain Helm, shut up or I shall hang you from the flagpole, swear it."

"Wal, y' could, I reckon," Helm twanged on cheerfully, "since there won't be no Majesty's flag up there t' be in my way! Boy, ain't them some—"

"Stop calling me 'Boy,' damn you!"

"Boy, ain't them some fine-lookin' soldier-boys he got? Every one of 'em's dangerous as a den o' bobcats! Hee! Most 'mazing thang 'bout ol' George, t' me, is how he can keep a *thousand* such blood-guzzlin' runagates under control."

Helm glanced out of the corner of his eye at Hamilton's fine-cut profile as they walked up the slope toward the gate, and he could see that his seemingly harmless prattle was having its intended effect.

THE SIX CAPTIVE INDIANS WERE STANDING IN A CLUSTER with rope tethers around their necks, and their hands bound cruelly tight with thongs behind their backs. They were surrounded by the jeering, hissing frontiersmen, who were only awaiting

Colonel Clark's permission to execute them for their crimes George came around the church and stood looking at them. They stood there with that dignity that George had seldom seen in any men except Indian braves who expect to be killed and know that to be killed by an enemy is a high honor.

Captain Williams was determined that the savages should be killed. He had learned that the scalps they had been carrying had been taken from families down along the Kentucky River. "These here are murderers," he said, "and they come in waving all the bloody confession in their hands. They don't need a trial." George himself looked at them with rage and loathing. What they had been doing was exactly what he had exerted himself and his men so hard to stop. Still, he dreaded saying, "Kill them." To him that was something no one less than God had a right to say.

Williams went on. "My boys got scalps. I say anyone here who's ever lost a blood relative to such polecats as these is welcome to put 'em to the ax. If nobody else wants to, we'll be glad to finish up."

George looked at the captives and pondered. Their painted faces were Satanic and did not stir any pity. It was not a matter of pity.

Hamilton had gone back up to the fort an hour ago to talk with his officers and still had not returned a decision. George suspected that he had recovered some of his nerve after getting back inside his fort and among his Redcoats. Maybe his officers were urging him to hold out for honorable terms.

The *Willing* still had not been heard from. Bowman's diggers had a long way to go in the collapsing mud before they could get their powder-keg bomb placed under the magazine. The men had been firing at the fort some eighteen hours or so before the truce flag and were running on grit alone, and if they were forced to start shooting again they might have neither the powder nor the stamina to keep it up another night.

Hamilton seemed to be hesitating and apparently needed one more sign of the Americans' resolve. So George said it now.

"So be it, Cap'n. Take these murderers up to the gate road. I want His Lordship to get a good look at this."

The six Indians were put in a circle and forced to their knees. The Kentuckians milled around them and poked at them with knives and swords and hatchets. Thirty yards away, Redcoats, Tawaway Indians, and Canadian militiamen lined the palisade like spectators at a Coliseum and looked down with a horrified fascination.

314

"Any man who's had blood kin murdered by Hair-Buyer's savages, step up," George announced loudly enough for everyone in the fort to hear. But so many candidates came forward that it was necessary to draw lots. While that was being done, George kept scanning the palisade for a glimpse of Hamilton. So far, he was not there.

The defenders now were getting their first clear look at the legendary Long Knife, and their attention was divided between him and the ominous preparations. Whatever they had imagined of him, he was no disappointment. His queued red hair gleamed in the winter sunlight. His brow was broad and craggy, cheeks smeared with gunpowder. His eyes were so deep and terrible that their intensity could be seen from the fort, and his hard jaw was shadowed with red whiskers. He prowled like a lion around the site, the tattered, stained skirt of his long leather coat flapping around his thighs. When he turned his broad back to the fort, a circular Indian design of quills and beads could be faintly discerned on the stained and muddy leather.

Hamilton and Helm had just climbed a ramp to the parapet now and were looking down at the scene, and Hamilton seemed to prefer studying his adversary to watching the awful business of the savages. He said, maybe to Helm, maybe to himself, "Is he Scottish, do you suppose?"

"He's American, Gov'nor."

Now George turned, and his eyes fell on Hamilton and Helm. He stared at Hamilton for a half a minute, head tilted thoughtfully, then, still looking at him, said something Hamilton could not quite hear. At once, a frontiersman stepped aside from each Indian and held his rope tether while another man stepped up close with a tomahawk in his hand. The chieftain of the captive band straightened his spine, threw back his head, and began chanting his strange, quavering death song. The others joined with their voices. Hamilton's face went pale and the tic started by his eye.

The Kentuckian standing over the chieftain raised his tomahawk, and the chieftain was looking straight at him when he struck. The song stopped. The Kentuckian stepped back. While the watchers murmured, the Kentuckian delivered two more whiplike blows at the mangled forehead and the chieftain slumped to his side and lay twitching. Then the Kentuckian bent and scalped him. While the other doomed ones continued their songs, two frontiersmen dragged the chieftain, by the rope at his neck, around the fort and down to the river, and threw his body into the yellow flood.

George looked up and he saw that Hamilton was still watching, and noticed that he had involuntarily put a hand to his throat. He had bought many scalps, but likely this was the first scalping he had ever witnessed.

And now the Indians on the palisade were all looking at Hamilton and crying at him in scolding voices, for he had always said he was their white father who would protect them against the Long Knives, and he was standing here doing nothing.

The next Indian's song broke off and he tumbled forward with a cloven skull. Then the third. Each was scalped as soon as he fell; each was dragged down and thrown into the river, and the Long Knives were yipping with the bloodthirsty thrill of it. While the next tomahawk was being poised to strike, George looked up once more at the face of Governor Hamilton and then turned and strolled away from the executioners' circle, as if bored, and stood with his back to the scene, gazing over the bright yellow winter grass and into the clean blue hazy woods beyond the river, because he was not bored but too stirred and sickened to watch anymore. His blood surged with the joyous wrath of justice each time a tomahawk made its ghastly *chewk!* But at the same time his bowels would grip with the shame of murder, and nausea was backing up behind his throat.

This is the vengeance we all wanted, he thought in revulsion. There seemed to be a red mist whirling around him, and through it came the sound of the executions, faint, like the voices of children playing outside a house.

And thus the world was reeling and he was trying to see, through that red mist, the cool blue distant woods where, it seemed, the only preservation of the soul could lie, and he thought of Teresa, two hundred miles beyond those woods, thought he heard a handful of *gitarra* notes.

GEORGE SAT ALONE IN THE CHURCH LATER, HIS HEAD ROARing like a windstorm, a wooden letter-box on his knees, looking at a ray of afternoon sunlight slanting in through a chink in the log walls. He knew that he and his opponent of the chessboard both had been changed inside by the executions. Hamilton seemed to have little of his spine left, and his last message had been simply a plea, not a demand, for honorable terms of surrender.

Brave man, George thought. He's wrong and he's a murderer, but he's brave. He just wants a scrap of honor, as a brave man would.

316

But now I'm a murderer too, he thought. I can say I was an executioner, but the difference is only in the words.

So now I'm a murderer too. That must change how I judge murderers.

Or does it?

The light and shadow in the chapel were swimming, whirling. He sat with his pen and paper and thought hard to steady the world.

He had the blood of prisoners on his own hands now, and so he was able to see Hamilton for what he was: a brave, proud, dutiful, *wrong* man being crushed by circumstances out of his control, an evil man perhaps but now simply doing the good thing of trying to save his soldiers' lives and hold out for a scrap of dignity.

I'd try to save *my* boys. Lord God but I would! His throat tightened and he blinked, remembering coming out of the ice water yesterday. Was that only yesterday?

I can't have them dying just to deny Hamilton that scrap of dignity, he thought. Even though they'd be glad to.

In front of him was the crude wooden altar where Frère Gibault, the one priest of the region, did services, trying to save souls, far from the seat of his religion. Frère Gibault's face swam in the gloom, then Vigo's, de Leyba's, then Teresa's; all those benign and beloved faces moved and blended and faded. And then he was seeing his mother's and father's faces, those proud and steel-souled people who, though neither had ever taken a life, were as resolute as soldiers in their own ways.

All these faces and the voices that belonged to them milled and murmured around him, until he opened his eyes and shook himself and found himself sitting in a tiny, cold church with something needing to be written.

He had come all this way and had done the impossible but though he should have been exulting in triumph he was sunk instead in a profound bittersweet sentiment and had scarcely enough strength and concentration left to lift the quill to the inkpot and think of a word to start with.

Finally, with a sigh, he leaned over the paper and began.

1st -Lt. Gov. Hamilton engages to deliver up to Col. Clark Fort Sackville as it is at present with all the stores, ammunition, provisions, &c.
2nd -The Garrison will deliver themselves up Prisrs of War to march out with their arms, accoutrements, Knapsacks &c.

3rd -The Garrison to be delivered up tomorrow morning at 10 o'clock.

It was, more or less, the same set of terms Hamilton had wanted, except that he was not going to let Hamilton and his men march away.

He gave the paper to a messenger and watched him go up toward the silent fort, the white flag flapping over his shoulder. Then George went back into the church and stood alone, his back braced against the wall, eyes shut, feeling the greatest pain and weariness he had ever felt. Pinpoints of light sparkled and swam among billowing gray and yellow clouds behind his eyelids. He saw a tomahawk embedded between an Indian's eyes. He saw Hamilton's sharp eyes and pouty mouth. He saw oceans of muddy water and then he saw Hamilton's face again.

What will he do when it comes right down to signing it? George wondered. Will he change his mind and decide to fight to the end?

Now George desperately wanted Hamilton to sign it. If it proved necessary to resume the fight, he wondered if he could really win. Half the Americans were slumped in their coverts out there so sound asleep now that even gunfire probably wouldn't wake them. What if Hamilton sees how they are? What if he begins to suspect there's only a hundred of us instead of a thousand?

As it is, George thought, if he does give up, we'll have more prisoners to guard than men to guard them with.

That was why he had set the surrender ceremony off till the next morning: so he wouldn't have to try to guard them tonight.

What have we done here? he thought. He was alone in a room thinking, as he had been two years ago at the beginning of this outlandish venture, and now that he had done it, it seemed more impossible than it had when he had planned it.

What we've done is we've taken the whole Northwest Territory, if Hamilton signs that, and if we have, we'll have to hold it.

God help us, he thought.

He heard a voice calling outside.

It was Helm. Helm, with a carefully contained smile, handing him back the same piece of paper he had sent up to Hamilton.

George unfolded it. Under the terms in his own hand was a paragraph in Hamilton's hand:

Agreed to for the following reasons, remoteness from succours, the state and quantity of provisions &c. the unan-

imity of officers and men on its expediency, the Honble terms allow^d and lastly the confidence in a generous Enemy.

H. HAMILTON
Gov. & Superintend^t

Thank God, George thought. I don't think I could've performed another minute.

I'm just plumb out of everything.

LOOKING IN A MIRROR THE NEXT MORNING IN MAJOR BUSseron's house, George stropped an ebony-handled razor and began shaving away his lather-soaked red whiskers. It was the first time he had looked in a mirror since Kaskaskia, and he was astonished at the hollowness of his cheeks and eyesockets.

Likely I've lost a stone's-weight of flesh this month, he thought. Most all of us look like cadavers too busy to lie still.

But he felt better than he had felt for weeks; he had slept a sleep that had felt a thousand fathoms deep, on a cot in warm, dry blankets in the old church, waking only once in the night, to hear his officers and bodyguards snoring in their bedding around him. Then he had put himself back into his deep slumber with a prayer of thanks for their safety. This morning he had coughed up an awful amount of phlegm and corruption and it had been several minutes before he could walk without wincing and limping. Now he had had a breakfast of porridge and hot pork and had washed the gunpowder off his face and shaved off his itchy whiskers and would be going up to the fort within the hour to accept Hamilton's surrender. In his duffel he had found his last clean linen shirt and stock and a pair of clean blue garters with silver buckles with which to fasten up his mud-stained, fringed leather gaiters. With these little touches of cleanliness and color he was trying to make himself look genteel enough to accept on behalf of Virginia and Congress the sword of His Britannic Majesty's defeated general.

Bowman winked at him as he whacked mud-clots out of the fringe of his buckskins and draped his sword-belt over his shoulder.

"Some dandy, George, y' air, y' air. Did y' notice Hamilton didn't raise his flag this mornin'?"

"Mhm. To save himself the humiliation of having to haul it back down, I'd guess. I didn't hear 'im shoot his morning gun today either, did you?"

"Nup. Prob'ly scared we'd start shootin' back again. Heh, heh!"

George put on his old black hat, with its right brim pinned up with a turkey-bone toothpick and the writing-quill plume sticking out of the band. "Ready for this great day?"

"Wait." Bowman reached toward him and tilted the hat at a jauntier angle. "Now. Y' look like you're goin' to a victory 'stead of a church meetin'."

They stepped out into the cold morning sunlight, where the troops stood in company ranks in the street grinning like elves. Their faces all had been washed, and . . . He smiled at them and announced:

"I was proud to say we won this battle without shedding a drop of American blood. Then I had to spoil it all by orderin' you to shave." They laughed and howled, and his heart swelled with love for them. He pulled his watch out of his pocket and flipped open its gold cover, then shut it and asked, "What time is it? My watch is full o' water." They laughed again, and somebody told him it was ten minutes till ten.

"Let's march up a-lookin' smart, boys, and get what's ours. Master Lovell," he said to the drummer boy, "give us something to step to."

The drumbeats gave him gooseflesh. *Tut-tuttle-tut-tut pamp, tut-tuttle-tut-tut pamp, tut-tuttle-tut, tut-tuttle-tut, tut-tuttle-tut, pamp pamp!* The tracked mud of the road had frozen hard and there were feathers of frost in yesterday's footprints. The shadows of walls and tree trunks were shallow blue, dusted with frost. The column passed the barricade and went up the road toward the gate of the fort. Beside the road on the ground were the ruddy bloodstains where the Indians had been executed. Joe Bowman's company flanked right and halted to stand in ranks on that side of the road. McCarty's flanked left and took up the stand on the other side. Then the companies of Williams and Worthington marched up to halt behind George, and when the officers commanded, "Parade Rest!" the drum stopped with a loud *pamp-pamp!* Behind George stood a red-nosed soldier with the Stars and Stripes folded over his right arm and Virginia's red-and-green colors over his left. All across the meadow the people of Vincennes came, those of all ages, running, skipping, tottering, tradesmen in smocks and merchants in velvet coats, pregnant women heaving along, crones in wimples, *coureurs de bois* in buckskin and scarlet wool, slack-lipped children. They crowded into the sunny space along the front wall of the fort, flanking the gates, where the reflected sunlight was warm and where they could examine the bullet-pocked palisades or stare at Long Knife and his shabby, barefooted soldiers. *"Où sont tous les autres?"* George heard several voices query. Mostly the citizens kept their eyes on him, watched him standing there with his monumental stillness, his deep blue eyes fixed on the carved initials G.R.—*George Rex*—above the gate, jaw muscles working. He glanced up once at the bare flagstaff. Sun-tinged little clouds crawled across the cold blue sky above the fort and drifted eastward. Beyond the fort the muddy flood of the Wabash gurgled, carrying trees and forest debris and ice chunks. Somewhere in the ranks someone sneezed and someone else hacked up a wet cough.

Then drums rattled within the fort. Voices came through the palisade, a wooden bolt rumbled, and the twelve-foot gates swung open slowly to reveal the ranked Redcoats at attention inside, their Brown Bess muskets at shoulder arms. While the drums beat slowly, Governor-General Hamilton appeared in the gateway, followed by two other officers, and marched down the grade toward the American colonel. Hamilton's coat was brushed, his boots were black and shiny, and his powdered wig was silvery. He carried his hat in his left hand and squinted in the bright sunlight. The voices of sergeants bellowed behind him and the ranks of Redcoats paced forward a few steps, then halted with a stamp, at attention just within the gate.

Hamilton stopped and clicked his heels a yard in front of Colonel Clark. He grasped the hilt of his sword and unsheathed it and everyone could hear the rasping ring of the fine steel as it came out. Then with a flick of his wrist he tucked the blade under his right arm so that the hilt was within reach of the victor.

Without taking his eyes from Hamilton's, George reached out and closed his hand around the hilt, feeling the cold polished silver and the smooth leather of the grip. This was the moment. This was the end toward which he had been pressing since that solitary night of brooding and planning in Harrod's fort two years ago. He stared at Hamilton's fatigue-swollen eyes, eyes that looked as if they had been weeping, and seeing the defeat there he knew that beyond his boldest dreams he had turned the Hair-Buyer's world upside down. He had wrested from King George a wilderness territory nearly the size of the thirteen colonies combined, and had not spent the life of one American to do it.

He pulled the sword away from Hamilton. "Governor, you and your garrison are my prisoners."

"I grant you, sir."

Now Hamilton let his eyes wander toward the ragged ranks of American woodsmen. They stood, leaning on their rifles, indescribably gaunt and filthy, clothes drab as compost, their sunken cheeks and their chins nicked by razors. Some had put red bandannas around their necks to give themselves a bit of color for the ceremony: *panache* and bare feet. General Hamilton mentally added them up: the little band, scarcely more than two squads, on the left, an equal number on the right, and the reeky, weatherbeaten scarecrows lined up behind the colonel. Hamilton flicked his gaze over the meadow and toward the town, and finally he said:

"May I ask, Colonel Clark, where is your army?"

The Virginian's sudden smile was dazzling. He reached out and nudged Hamilton's elbow with a knuckle as if to share a delicious joke.

"This, sir," he replied, "is them."

Hamilton dropped his head forward and gave a strangled little whimper.

Man, George thought. I'd hate to be him. Then he turned his back on him and waved the English sword high. "BOYS! POST VINCENNES . . . *IS OURS!*"

With a deafening outburst of war whoops and cheers and yokelish yodels, they broke ranks and stampeded for the gate, snatching their Colonel Clark off the ground and bearing him laughing on their shoulders, jostling past the astonished Redcoats into the fort.

Hamilton stood by himself on the yellow dirt road among the tittering townspeople with his empty scabbard at his side, and tears ran down his long nose.

19

CAROLINE COUNTY,
VIRGINIA
June, 1779

THE MESSENGER WHO CAME HOWLING UP THE ROAD TO THE Clark house this time was seventeen-year-old Cousin Edmund Rogers. The handsome redhead was so frantic that the family at first thought he surely was bringing news of death or catastrophe.

His horse was lathered and wild-eyed, and Edmund was simply babbling till he got his tongue straightened out. "Johnny . . . George . . . Cousin . . . I mean . . . Cou . . . Joh . . . No. They're at my house! Johnny is—"

"What Johnny? Our Johnny?" cried Mrs. Clark, clapping her hand to her throat.

"No! *Our* Johnny! My brother Johnny's at our house! Y' must come! He's brought back . . . Oh, y'll never believe this! He's brought back another . . . He's brought a real British *general* this time! The Hair-Buyer one! George captured 'im, he did, and's sending 'im to Williamsburg, all chained up! And other officers. And the Grand Judge of Detroit, he caught him too! George did! He caught the whole murderin' pack of 'em! Oh my God, come hear Johnny tell it all! Come on! Come on!"

THE ROGERS HOUSE LOOKED LIKE AN ARMED CAMP. A guard troop commanded by Captain Williams was posted around a row of old brick slave quarters where the prisoners were being kept for the night. There was a crowd of neighbors, curious to see the notorious scalp-buyer and to hear the incredible news from the West.

Johnny Rogers looked strained and thin from the journey, but he was happy and bubbling with marvelous tales of the victory. When John and Ann Rogers Clark arrived, Johnny stood straight as a Prussian to greet them, his eyes shimmering with tears. And then they all, the Rogerses and the Clarks, sat in George Rogers' library and listened to Johnny try to tell the story, and it was apparent from his breathlessness and the tears that kept coming to his eyes that he was so moved by what had happened that it was hard for him to talk. He told them of George's plan for the attack on Vincennes, about the nearly impossible march he had undertaken, and about the role the *Willing* was to have played in it. He told of the grueling voyage of the gunboat, the Indian attack in the mouth of the Tennessee, the rescue of Myers the courier from Indians, the frustrating effort to keep the *Willing* on the right way. And then:

"When we got that bedamned boat in sight o' the fort at last, can you imagine what we felt seein' the American and Virginia flags a-flying over it 'stead of the Union Jack! I was so bumfuzzled for a time there I couldn't understand why those flags were up. I wondered if it was a trick, that the Hair-Buyer'd put 'em up to trap us! I didn't believe it could be Cousin George. I mean, after all, I'd just come a-rowin' up through that drowned land, and it was ice water as far as ye could see, I mean that, and

323

I still don't see how a mortal man could ha' got there, I swear to the Eternal God I don't, but there they were, they'd taken that blamed fort the day before, and there they sat guarding more prisoners o' war than they had men to guard 'em with! Redcoats, a whole company of 'em, and companies of French Canadian militia from Detroit, and all the principal agents in the scalp-buying business. O' course I was mortified I'd missed the whole fight, but so overjoyed they'd not lost a man.

"Ha, ha! Oh, listen, they had those British in a corral, and they were hanging nooses in the trees around 'em, and lookin' at 'em with wolf eyes, and twirling tomahawks careless around 'em. O' course, George had given orders no prisoner was t' be hurt, but *they* didn't know that, and they were so scared they looked like they were poopin' peach pits—Excuse me, ladies present, that's a saying Leonard Helm used about 'em, and it just slipped out there, careless-like.

"Speaking o' Helm, that old rascal, he was so pent up from being a prisoner all winter, he got George to let him take a force up the Wabash to hunt some British reinforcements that were due down from Detroit. And damn my eyes if Helm didn't surprise 'em and surround 'em, and without firing one shot! He captured forty more soldiers, and more Indian agents, and ten boats bearin' forty thousand pounds' worth o' military provisions and Indian trade goods, all stuff they were planning to use to hire Indians for their spring offensive. But, ha HAAA! There won't be a spring offensive now! And in one o' those boats was Philip DeJean, the Grand Judge of Detroit, who's about as important a scoundrel as Gov'nor Hamilton 'imself. Lord have mercy, people! I can't wait to see Patrick Henry's face when we ride in with this catch! Oh, what that Cousin George has done! Why, there's not been the like of it ever! I . . . I . . . What have I forgot? Have I told ye—Oh! That Myers we picked up. He had messages from the Assembly, congratulations to George for takin' Kaskaskia last summer. Late, it was, but George read it to th' troops in the fort there. And he asked 'em to think back to the start of it all, back at the Falls, and then he told 'em they'd probably done more good out there, just those few of 'em, than all the armies marching up and down the coast. And, listen, I wish ye could have seen their faces. They were just comin' to realize it, I guess. Then he told 'em they were a company of heroes, every man a hero, and his voice, you know, caught, like, and I looked and he was cryin'. And they threw their hats in the air for 'im. God, I still get shivers." Johnny's own voice broke now, and his eyes were brimming, and for a moment he couldn't speak, but just sat shaking his head at the wonder of it. All the Clarks were blinking rapidly and breathing deep breaths and shaking their heads slowly, envisioning their son and brother across the thousand miles. Billy looked as if he were in a trance, his eyes glazed, looking at Johnny Rogers' mouth as if he could will more of those wonderful words to come out of it.

"Johnny," said Mrs. Clark, in that rich, plangent voice of hers, "tell us how he is. Is he well?" She was thinking of how much he must have suffered in those three weeks. One day of that sort of exposure had put men in their deathbeds with pneumonia, she knew that all too well, and this was her son they were speaking of. "How does he look?"

The question caught Johnny off guard, and his eyes met hers, then fell away, then came back.

"Why, why, yes . . . Yes, he's well. He's th' happiest man I ever saw in all my days. He's . . ." He saw George's face in his mind's eye now, and saw it in the light of her question, and realized only now that George had looked more like a man of fifty than of twenty-six. But he did not say that. He said, as cheerfully as he could, "Well, it's no wonder, Auntie, he and all his boys were lookin' some'at scrawny last I saw of 'em." And hollow-eyed and stooped and trembly and coughing their lungs up, he did not tell her, adding instead: "It's nothing a few weeks o' that good English salt beef and brandy and chocolates they captured won't cure. Ha, ha! And th' summer sunshine, yea, by Heaven! I bet he looks as good as ever by now. When he gets back 'round to St. Louis and sees that sweetheart o'—"

He stopped himself. George had told him not to mention Teresa de Leyba to them, that he would do that himself someday, that they would likely take it wrong that he was betrothed to a Spanish Catholic. Damn, Johnny Rogers thought. It's what comes o' talking too fast.

"What?" Elizabeth exclaimed first. "Georgie found him a sweetheart out in the *prairie*? What is it, another squaw?"

"Betty," her mother said sharply. "Now what's this, Nephew?"

He looked around, half-smiling, waving his hands casually as if to dismiss it all. "Just a lady from one o' those towns. Ah . . . I've got letters from 'im for you all. Maybe he mentions 'er, I don't know. Say," he asked, to change the subject, "where's Dick?"

"Oh," said John Clark, "why, he's probably out there by now. He joined wi' John Montgomery and a company to go join George. I'm surprised if you didn't pass 'em on th' river, or someplace." His voice trailed off. He wondered why they *hadn't* passed somewhere along the way.

"Well," George Rogers said now, with a sigh. "Ann. John. That's what your son has done, and I suppose I'm as proud as you are. I'm proud o' my son Johnny here, too, I'll declare before God!" He crumpled his mouth in a teary smile, gazing at Johnny.

"Oh, Lordy," Johnny exclaimed. "Proud o' me? I thought when I showed up so late that George'd hate me out o' the family for failin' him! But y' know what he said to me? He said, 'Cousin, don't bother your head a minute about that. I floundered round in that bedamned river myself and I know it's a miracle ye got here at all. Only a Rogers could ha' done,' he said to me. And I reckon he meant it, for 'e made me a captain and put me in charge o' his Royal Excellency th' Scalp Buyer."

They were all still for a few moments, both families wrapped in their thoughts, all aware of a wide, deep oneness encompassing their two families, in which cousins became brothers by what they had undertaken together, by the trust they had invested in each other.

Billy sniffled. His eyes were overflowing and the tears ran down his nose and his nose was running onto his lip. Almost strangling, he said:

"I jus' love George."

Johnny Rogers made a little groaning sound in his throat. "Aye, Billy. I do too."

They all breathed hard for a while, then Fanny said, "He lives in a palace, doesn't he, Cousin Johnny?"

"A palace?"

"Yes, and the Conquered wait upon him hand and foot, don't they?"

Johnny looked at her for a moment and then smiled at her. "Well, Fanny, last time I saw him, he'd been living mostly out o' doors. But I . . . He just might be in a palace by now. Or a mansion, at least. If I had my say, he surely would. And, as for the Conquered—Well, they be right out yonder in the slave sheds, and they're bound hand and foot as they deserved to be. They're not very happy. A lot o' folk out beyond the mountains took the liberty o' spittin' on 'em as we passed through. Would you all care to go have a look at 'em, and maybe a spit?"

John Clark swallowed. "Well, I've never once spit on a man, though I've felt my mouth fill up a time or two. But I would like to have a look at this Hair-Buyer, yes, I would. A hair-buyer,' he murmured as he rose from his chair, his hands braced on his thighs to help himself up. He was shaking his head sadly. "God pity a world where an Englishman would do that!"

THE GUARD CAPTAIN THREW OPEN THE DOOR. "ON YOUR feet, Gov'nor," he yelled in. "Your betters are here!"

There was a rattle of chains and a voice growled, "God damn you, yokel bastard Williams! I'll have your head if you speak once more like—"

The officer was chained to the bedpost. He began to rise, confused, at the sight of this well-dressed family, of the regal woman and pretty girls. He had a pencil in his grimy hand, and some white cards fell to the floor as he moved. His face was dirty and haggard, long jaw dark with stubble, his red coat and white breeches were dark with filth, and his sandy hair was dishevelled and specked with bits of chaff.

Williams commented as they entered, "He still won't eat humble pie, Mr. Clark. He's as squawkin' arrogant as a gander."

The Englishman was standing now, looking hard at the family. The room was bright and bare. Its walls were whitewashed brick and its floor was packed dirt. The only piece of furniture in the room was the cot. "I beg your pardon, ladies," he said, bowing slightly, "for my language. I didn't expect . . ." Then he fastened his eyes on John Clark's face. "Your name is Clark?"

To John Clark it was so much like that moment last year at Fredericksburg. "Clark it is. And you're the Englishman who buys scalps? Good God, man!"

The prisoner flinched, but kept his head up and stared at John Clark's dark eyes. His own cold blue eyes were terrible, lined with pain and sunken with fatigue, and blazing with intensity. He was already quite certain who these people were before him. "I, I must presume you're Colonel Clark's family."

"I'm his father. This is his mother, Ann. And what children as aren't yet off to war."

Hamilton bowed slightly to Mrs. Clark, not wanting to meet her eyes. He let out a long, slow sigh. "Well, I don't know what to say to you. If it pleases you to stand there and look at me, the spectacle your son has made of me . . ."

"Believe me, sir, it's no pleasure," said John Clark.

"Colonel Clark brought the world down around my head. I could despise him. And you. But as I thought when I first laid eyes on him, I only wish he'd grown up a Loyalist instead of a Rebel."

"He did grow up a Loyalist," John Clark interrupted. "It was he likes o' you, sir, that changed him to a rebel."

Hamilton took a short, sharp breath. It was apparent that he was not going to get sympathy here. He said:

"If you have any influence in this Commonwealth, Mister Clark, I pray you will convey to your government my protest about the ill use I've had as a prisoner of war." He raised his arms to show his chains.

"Sir," said Mrs. Clark, "one of my sons is a prisoner of war on one of your prison ships these two years past. I wonder me how he's been used."

Billy had pressed between his parents and now stood with his head cocked, looking at Hamilton. In the silence he said:

"My brother George catchered you."

Hamilton compressed his lips and looked down at the gawky, freckled boy. He nodded, his eyes seeming to look a thousand miles.

"He told me he would," Billy said. "And 'e did, sure enough."

"That is correct, Master Clark. But the war is not done with yet. We shall see what becomes of your brother."

Billy set his own lips, then looked up at his father.

"May I spit on 'im, Papa?"

"No, you mayn't. Clarks don't spit. No matter who at."

"D' YOU SUPPOSE," JOHN CLARK SAID TO JOHNNY ROGERS later, "that if he was back at Detroit, he'd still pay scalp bounties? I mean, he doesn't seem a man repentant of his sins."

"I don't know, Uncle John. He was humble, oh, really humble, when he was with George. Stayed in his shadow every minute, I guess afraid he'd get killed by chance. But th' moment we put chains on 'im and started back, he's been a snot like this."

"Ah. I see. Then methinks 'e's acting his pride, and maybe he *has* learned something. What were those, those cards he had?"

"Why, those are his sketches. He's drawn scores of 'em in hi still hours, comin' over. It's like he takes a refuge in drawing Y'd be amazed how good they are. It'd been a better life for u all had 'e been an artist."

"What are they of?"

"Anything 'e sees. Trees. Countryside. People. He's got a whole gallery of his old Indian chiefs, all in pencil. If y'd like to see, I'll have Williams fetch 'em."

"No. No, don't take 'em from 'im." John Clark had a certain vague antipathy toward artists, stemming from what the Scriptures said about graven images. He had never allowed portraits to be done of his family. Billy had shown some budding talent as a

328

draughtsman which his father did not actually forbid, but did not encourage either. But this had provoked his thoughts, this of a captured killer retreating into the solitary concentration of drawing.

"Wait," Johnny was saying. "He drew sketches of most of us. Mine's over here." He went to a bureau and lifted a paper-wrapped packet out of a scuffed leather ditty bag. "He was kinder to my image than to Williams'," Johnny chuckled. "Made him look like a proper blood-suckin' devil. Ha, ha!" He showed the little cardboard sketch around to them. It was a true representation of the young officer, hatless, gazing off to the artist's right. "I guess that's how I looked at the tiller comin' up the Ohio. Watchin' the north shore for Shawnee. Hm, hm. They tried to raid us one evening, but we drove 'em off. Protected His Lordship from 'em. I was tempted to throw 'im to 'em. Wouldn't that a' been ironic, him scalped by them? Ha!" Then his face darkened. "They got Myers, did y' know?"

"Myers?"

"George's courier, the one we'd snatched from the Indians hardly two weeks before. George sent him and another man ahead by canoe with messages to Virginia and Congress about the victory at Vincennes. They got just a way past the Falls. There they were found scalped and all the papers scattered and gone. Otherwise you'd have heard of all this some time before. Poor Myers." Johnny shook his head. "Sometimes a man will look lucky. But 'e's just marked for later."

"Then it's not wholly safe out there even after all."

"Nay, and never will be, I reckon. The Shawnee never came and talked with George, and they're the strongest ones out there in th' Middle Ground. But it's a damn sight safer than it was. George holds sway out there now. You can't conceive o' how reputation works out yonder. Yon Hair-Buyer General was reputed the Great Father and protector of all the Algonquian tribes, but the Long Knife snared 'im and tied 'im up, without a man lost. Ye can't imagine what an impression that makes in the bosom of a savage. Such force and foxiness are the stuff their dreams are made on. I saw how they gazed on 'im at Cahokia last summer, and that was even *before* he'd caught Hamilton himself. Listen, Uncle John: out beyond the mountains now, there's no name's got a half the power o' his."

"Power in a name," John Clark mused. He shook his head.

"What'll he do now?" Ann Clark asked. "When will he come home?"

"Auntie, if I was you, I wouldn't look for 'im till after he's

329

occupied Detroit itself. That's his heart's desire, and when Montgomery gets there with a fresh regiment, why, I'd say Detroit's going t' have Virginia's flag over it inside a month."

"But *Detroit!*" John Clark exclaimed. "Whole armies of Regulars have failed even to *get* there!"

"I know. But they didn't do things the way George does things. And they had no reputation like his to blow 'em a clear path. Believe me, Uncle John. Give him Montgomery's troops—with Cousin Dickie amongst 'em, too!—and I say Detroit might as well not raise the Union Jack some morning, for they'll have to pull it right back down before noon!"

JOHN MONTGOMERY'S BOATS SWUNG TOWARD THE EAST bank of the Mississippi and started up the mouth of the Kaskaskia River. The water changed from muddy yellow to clear green as they rowed into the smaller stream. And then there on their left were the roofs of the town, and beyond and above the roofs stood the vanes of the old windmill. A cannon shot boomed in the town, and smoke rolled away from atop a long, low stone wall. Captain Montgomery, gaunt and sunbrowned, half-smiled, the first trace of a smile Dickie Clark had seen on him for two weeks, and pointed. "That's the fort," he said. "Rocheblave's old house is inside that wall, and that's where your brother is, if he's here."

A crowd had gathered on the shore, men, women, and children chattering in French, and a few hallooing Americans, rangy, ragged figures with rolled-up shirt sleeves, leather pants, and pistols and knives in their belts. "There's some of the old-timers," Montgomery said. "Hey! Davy! Hey, Abe! Herman! Aha! And look up the street there, Dick Clark, here comes down the ol' Long Knife 'isself! GEORGE! YA, HA! HERE WE BE AT LAST! WHAT THERE IS OF US!" A twinge of distress passed over Montgomery's face, and he said, "You watch 'im. He's goin' to be disappointed, but he won't show it."

George was on the little plank wharf when the first boat bumped up against it and Montgomery sprang off. Dickie watched as George and Montgomery hugged each other and whomped each other on the back. George was leaner now; his shirt hung looser on his wide shoulders, and all the muscles and sinews and veins in his brown forearms were defined as if his skin were thin as silk. But it was the change in the face that gave Dickie such a pang: Every bone was visible, his eyes were hollow and somehow wilder and more intense, his nose looked even more like a hawk's beak, and his jaw muscles were as distinct as drawn on the skin by some anatomist. There were many fine rinkles and pain-lines around his eyes and mouth; they were isible from ten feet away in the afternoon sunlight. "John, hn," he was saying. "I'm glad you're here and sorry ye missed e big event last winter. There's Dickie! Brother, stop gapin' nd get out o' that boat and gi' me a hug! God damn, but I'm lad t' see family! Hey, ye look a bit underfed. Hasn't Monty een a-feedin' you right?"

"You do too, George. God! Hallo! Oh, hallo, ye damn big ol' Conqueror!" In Dickie's arms, George was hard and spare as ristle, but still so strong it seemed he'd squeeze his guts out at oth ends. "Ooof! We've heard all th' story, brother. I'm so roud I could bust."

"Aye? Well, it's nothin' compared to what we'll do with anther Clark here." He released him, and Dickie could see his aze going over the boats, watching the emaciated, barefoot mitiamen climbing out. "Are there more comin', Monty, or hat?"

"This is all."

It was true what Montgomery had said; George wasn't showing is disappointment, not much. But Dickie could see the eyes ow a little wilder, the pain lines deepen, even as George kept niling and watching them haul themselves wearily out of the oats. "How come?" he said quietly. "Recruiting trouble like last me?"

"Not so much that. I'd raised three times this many. But th' sual powers—you know, the Short Eyes—just as we set out, ey took the liberty o' sending us long way round to chase herokees that was botherin' their butts. Well, George, you ow. Desertions. Sick. Wounded. I've a hundred thirty-five ere, and they need shoes and food 'fore they'll be much help."

George's jaw muscles were working. "If I'd foreseen this, I'd a' gone on to Detroit from Vincennes, while we were already in otion. Maybe we were too spent to've done it, but we all anted to. Now we've stopped and rested to wait for you, and y old boys been aging 'bout a year a day."

"I did my best, George."

"Y' don't need to tell me that. I know you did. Well." Sudnly he was grinning, getting taller and warming up, it seemed, d he said, "Well, let's muster 'em, and have a big hello. hey're part o' the Illinois Regiment now, and that makes 'em oice. How'd Dickie do, chasin' Cherokees?"

"He's a Clark, that's sure. Not afraid o' nothin'."

"Damn so. There's nothing to be afraid of, is there, Brother?"

331

"Not that I've seen," Dickie lied. He had been plenty afraid in the Cherokee country. But of course the brother of Long Knife had not dared show his fear.

As the men trudged up toward the fort, carrying their sacks and kettles and guns, George watched them carefully, and they watched him carefully, smiling half-afraid. They had heard much about the Long Knife and knew they were in for something. Montgomery was saying:

"What's this do to Detroit, d'ye think, George?"

"Why, I don't give up easy, you know. I've got a thing or two up my sleeve. I sent back to Kentuck for the county lieutenants to furnish me what men they could. And after them seein' the Hair-Buyer go through all dressed in chains, I think they might comply. What you've brought added to my old boys, we've got a couple hundred, and some Frenchmen from here, they served me well, and they like bein' heroes. And then if Kentuck sends a couple hundred more, why, I don't think Detroit would be all that impossible." They were walking up the street of Kaskaskia now, George with one arm over Montgomery's shoulders and one over Dickie's, and the civilians were running and gawking and cheering, and George said: "Y' know I've always had a peculiar notion about possible and impossible. And after what we did last winter, it's even more peculiar."

BUT WHEN THE KENTUCKY TROOPS DID COME, HE COULD no longer hide his disappointment. They were not two hundred, but only twenty. They came limping into Vincennes, where George's forces were to rendezvous for the march against Detroit. They were barefooted, exhausted, sick, and half-starved.

There had been two hundred of them at the start, but their officers had seen fit to take them on a detour up into the Shawnee country and raid the tribal town of Chillicothe. They had burned and looted the town, but the Shawnees, knowing of their coming, had melted away in front of them, giving them no one to fight. On the return march to Kentucky the warriors had followed the weary troops and sniped constantly at them, killing or wounding nearly a half of them, and when the demoralized force had recrossed the Ohio into Kentucky, most of them had disbanded. Only these twenty had come.

Dickie watched George get up from the table after this forlorn news and go into another room. He knew George was removing himself from the sight of the officers so he could work out his rage in private.

When he came back out, he was calm and quiet. He held a

conference with the officers. He wanted to go on to Detroit, now, even with this ragged little force of only two hundred. But he knew how foolish that would be. They were not enough to make a respectable showing going through the Lakes Indian country, or to haul the cannon they would need to attack Detroit. Though George believed he could take the city with two hundred, he was not sure how many of them could make it there. Many had been so weakened by the winter campaigns that they were sick all the time now, with malaria, with agues, with sore bones, and with mysterious fevers. But the deciding factor was the weather. The summer had been a drouth, and the rivers were so low that boats would not travel. The Wabash, which had been a roaring flood all winter, now was a stagnant, sluggish trickle in the muddy riverbed. "The most perverse river on the face of God's earth," growled Abe Chapline. "It's like she's just decided she's carried enough water for this year, and isn't going to carry no more."

"It took Hamilton seventy-two days last fall to come from Detroit because the rivers were low," George said, "and he had half a thousand Indians to help 'im. I'm afraid, boys, I'll have to say this, and I know I'd sure be the last to say it: we're going to have to forget Detroit for this year. We'll just have to dig in and concentrate on holding what we've won."

The officers nodded. They were relieved, in a way, but they were disappointed, too. "Well," said Bowman. "Maybe it's just th' Good Lord tellin' us we've already done enough for now."

"Nay, Joe," replied George. He glanced at Dickie. "As our Ma would used to say, 'While there's somethin' needing done, you haven't done enough.'" Dickie smiled, remembering that. "I'd bind myself seven years a slave to have five hundred men right now," George went on, through narrowed lips. "If we had 'em, by Heaven, we'd go, somehow, even if we had to put wheels on the boats and pull 'em there. But we don't have enough able-bodied, and that's all there is to it. I'm sorry, boys. Come next spring, maybe. Meantime, I've got a fort to build at the Falls, and one at the mouth of the Ohio. And while we're here, we've got to make the best use we can of these few people of ours, because we Long Knives've got one hellacious reputation to keep up, all over this hundred thousand square miles, and that's going to spread us thin as rock soup."

ON JULY 4, LIEUTENANT HOAG WAS LIFTED FROM HIS BUNK by four other officers and placed upon the table in the middle of the gun room of the *Jersey*, on a large rectangle of sail canvas.

This was wrapped and tied around him. The Poet, who was still able to stand, took his place at the head of the table, and five other officers stood or sat along the sides of the table, gasping and dripping sweat, and the Poet said words over the corpse. Johnny Clark could not get up to attend the funeral, but through the whooshings and buzzings in his head and the sounds of the gurgling in his lungs, he could hear some of it.

"Our compatriot at last has gained his full independence . . . freed by Divine Mercy from his sufferings. . . ."

A year now since the enlisted men had made their escape in the dead-boat. A year now since the Jersey's jailers had decreed that all prisoners would be kept below decks. A year now since Johnny Clark had lain in the sun on the deck to breathe fresh, sunny air into his consumptive lungs. A year now since he had looked up and seen a sea gull white against the blue sky.

The wonder of it was that the year had passed and any of them were still alive. Hoag had already been here when Johnny had first set foot on this floating dungeon, more than a year and a half ago. Thanksgiving Day of 1777, that had been, and now it was July Fourth of 1779. The wonder of it was that Lieutenant Hoag had lived so long. He had not seemed like the sort of man who particularly desired to live. All his humor had been mordant and bitter. But it had been humor.

Hoag had laughed aloud for some reason in the middle of last night. The laughter had started him coughing, and he had coughed for a long time, and this morning they had found him still and dead.

". . . has known already the feeling of the tomb. But now his mortal soul may leave this tomb and ascend, as did our beloved Saviour from His . . ."

Lieutenant Hoag was carried out sometime while Johnny Clark was delirious. Johnny had seen him there on the table and then he had been unconscious and when he had come back his old friend was no longer on the table, and some other prisoners were sitting around it looking at Johnny, and Captain Coffin was kneeling beside his bunk in the oven-heat, wiping his brow with a dirty wet rag, saying, "Y've been raving, old Johnny."

"Hoag's gone."

"He's gone."

"I want to go with 'im."

"No, not yet awhile, Johnny. What would I do here without you? You and I are the old sages in this place now, don't you know? Now that Mister Hoag's escaped, there's not a soul in this room's been here a half as long as either of us."

"If that's an honor, I'd as soon not have it."

"Well, Johnny my boy, here's more honor, and I should hope you'll want to rally yourself long enough to enjoy it a bit. Them that came to carry Mister Hoag away told it: D'you know who's presently in a dungeon in Williamsburg?"

"King George, I pray."

"Ha, ha! Nay, but a rather important one of his minions. That general they called the Hair-Buyer. Governor Hamilton of Detroit."

"Ah. Well . . . that's something."

"Yes. And d'you know who caught him and sent him there?"

Johnny stirred. Suddenly he wanted to sit up to hear what he was sure he was going to hear.

"Brother George did it? Got the Hair-Buyer himself?"

"That's what they said. And some grand Canadian judge as well, and a whole boatload of scalp-buyers." The Poet was smiling because he could see Johnny smiling. He said, "Do you want to give one of your famous wolf calls? If you do, give me time to plug up my ears."

"Ha . . . huh . . . ha, ha. No. It'd kill me sure."

"Oh! A moment ago, you said you wanted to go."

"Well . . ." He coughed ferociously for a while. Then he said. "I'd like to celebrate a while first."

"That's what I thought. So come then, Old Johnny, and sit at the table with me and those smiling gents, for we'd like to celebrate with you. It's been a long while since you've been to the table."

"Don't know . . . if I can . . . but . . ."

"But your brother would be pleased if you sat up and celebrated in his honor, wouldn't he? One day you can tell him you did so."

Johnny lay with his head back on the straw-covered planks of his bunk, and hot tears were running down his temples and into his ears. The Poet said: "Well? Coming?"

"Aye," Johnny groaned. "I'm just gatherin' the strength . . . to get up. Hey, you know what, Cap'n?"

"What, Old Johnny?"

"Brother George is . . . going t' put so many o' those . . . lords in jail . . . they'll run over, and . . . have to put the rest in here! Ha, ha!"

DICKIE SAT ACROSS THE TABLE FROM GEORGE AND WATCHED him pour another glass for each of them. It was the best brandy Dickie had ever tasted. It was some that Captain Helm had liberated when he had captured the British boats. George was saying, "It's satisfying to think that this was Henry Hamilton's private stock, and it's us sitting here drinking it instead o' him. Isn't that satisfying, Dick?"

"It's satisfying to me. And I reckon it must be a hundred times more so to you."

"I'm just glad I got some o' this before ol' Len had a chance to use it all. To the health of all Clarks, Dickie, wherever we be." They raised the glasses.

"To our health." They sipped and let the flavor drain over their tongues.

It was the first time George and Dickie had been able to sit down by themselves. Dickie was still a private, and George had been very busy with his officers. All plans for the winter had finally been worked out. The Virginians had been divided up among the posts at Kaskaskia, Cahokia, and Vincennes, and George would take a small party and go down and build a fort at the Falls. Settlers had been pouring back down the Ohio into Kentuck ever since the news of the Western conquests. A fort was needed there for their safety.

"I'm going to have to make you an officer, Dick, so I can sit and drink with'ee now and then."

"Well, ha, ha, I—"

"I'm not joking. I need you. Look here, now, brother. I want to show you something o' what we've got ahead of us." He got up from the table and went into a corner, and picked up a cherry-wood chest, and set it on the table. Carved in the lid was "GEO. R. CLARK." He opened it with a key and began lifting out rolls of paper, and what looked like bundles of scrap paper. He untied strings and unrolled the large sheets. The first was a large map, drawn in pencil. "This is the Northwest Territory," he said. "It's what we've come into control of. This up here is the Great Lakes. Here's the Mississippi. Here's the Ohio. Everything within there is ours now, but only if we can keep it. Do you know what we've got to hold it with?" Dickie shook his head. "Reputation," George said. "We've got a reputation, and it's one hellacious reputation, as y've heard me tell. But reputation, as someone said, maybe it was Shakespeare—I wish Jonathan was here, we could ask him who said it—said, 'Reputation is a bubble.' Listen and listen well, Dick: One blunder, one act o' cowardice, one oversight, one piece o' neglect that we might do in all this country, and *pop*! there goes our bubble. Listen: At Cahokia last summer, when I signed treaties with the tribes that live in this country, I warned 'em that if they broke their word, the Long Knives would feed them to the buzzards. Pretty cocky for a ragtag band o' sick, broke men like we've got, eh? But I mean to *keep* our reputation good, by Heaven!" He banged his palm on the table. "I've bluffed and strutted and waded to my neck in ice water to get it, and I'm jealous of it!" Dickie looked at George wide-eyed. "God, God *only* knows what we'll have to do yet to keep this country. But here are some of the things." He put another large sheet of paper on top of the map. "Here's my plan for the fort we'll build at the Falls of Ohio. Look. Earthwork ramparts. Log blockhouses. There's a spring here inside, so there's always fresh water, even in a siege." He pulled another sheet from underneath and put it on top. "Here's the fort we'll build next spring at the mouth of the Ohio. Much like it, but bigger." He put a finger on it. "This will stop all British traffic on the upper Mississippi. Then if we get any men and money from Virginia or Congress, we'll go clear up and get Detroit, and then Britain's done in these parts. Here's something else that would serve us well. This idea I got after Cousin Johnny brought that gunboat through hell and high water. It's a musketproof oar-ship, with cannon. A small fleet o' these, and you've got forts you can place wherever they're needed on the Ohio. Tom Jefferson's our new governor, and he's been behind me since the beginning, so I can count on his backing, maybe even better than I could on Henry. Is your head whirlin' yet, Dick? I hope you didn't aim to come out here and loaf. Ha, ha! Because that's not all." He put the map back on top. "All this space here, we've got to keep in an uproar. I intend for the British to expect me everyplace. Michillimackinac. Detroit. Natchez. Hamilton left Detroit in the charge of a Captain Lernoult, who's as fraidy as a chicken, they say. I intend to keep him in hot water and running in a hundred directions. That way he can't gather up and come at us. I've got a hundred French bushlopers who go everywhere and they'll spread those rumors. They love to lie and gossip as much as they love to tiddle squaws, and that's a lot." He paused, cocked his head and asked:

"Is this a little different from what you expected, brother? You look a little bit obflusticated."

"It sure is a lot more complicated. I didn't think I'd have to do anything out here more intelligent than shoot from behind a tree."

"Hm, hm, hm! Well, surprise. And it's even more complicated yet. Know why?"

"Why?"

"Because we're poorer than fleas on a skeleton. You may not

be old enough to've learned it yet, but anything is ten times as hard if y' have to figure out how to pay for it without any money."

"But Mr. Montgomery, I thought, was bringing money when we came. Something like ten thousand dollars."

"So he did have. But that didn't even cover the back pay for the boys I brought out here a year ago. Dick, when I started this caper, Patrick Henry gave me £1200. That was exhausted before we even left Fort Pitt, spent on boats, grain, shoes, and th' like. The money Monty brought is Continental currency. It's sunk to about a penny to the dollar in worth, as the traders hereabouts well know. Look at these." He held up the bundles of paper. "These scraps I guard with my life. They're vouchers for credit. I've written about fifteen thousand of these so far, to support the Illinois Regiment. They're promises that Virginia will pay these suppliers for what we've purchased. Now, these traders don't personally know anybody named Virginia, but they do know, and trust, somebody named George Rogers Clark. More of that 'Reputation' for you. That means they gave credit only on my signature. Here I've signed for supplies and services amounting to several times what my own lands are worth, though I was pretty land rich when I came out here. Sometime before winter I'm going to send all these bedamned vouchers to Williamsburg in care o' the auditor of state, and then when the state honors 'em, I'll start feeling about a hundred years younger. I wish to high Heaven I'd never seen these things, but I have to watch 'em all the time, for I'd be ruined if anything ever happened to 'em. I mean ruined for good. A signature on credit is a promise, as you know. And I have to keep my promises. Because the one thing'll prick the bubble of a reputation, Dick, is one broken promise. Especially a money promise. The way most people are in this world, sad to say, they'll forget most kinds o' promises—honor, oaths, vows of any kind—long before they'll forget a money promise.

"A lot of people hereabouts have helped me with this credit thing. There's people you've yet to meet. Vigo the trader. Cerré the merchant. Busseron. Even the Spanish governor across the river." He paused here, took a drink of brandy, and went on. "They've undersigned me with their own names. I'm as beholden to them as I am to any American. And they're ruined with me if Virginia doesn't honor these. So. So, there, Dick. You can see, I guess, we cover a lot of ground in a lot of ways.

"Now I'm good at getting around, but it's hard to be more than three or four places at once. That's why I need you as an emissary, Dick. Y'll stay a few more weeks yet in ranks, as ye've things to learn. But I do need a lieutenant I can trust for everything, so I can be in all these places at once. You're going to be probably the travelin'est lieutenant this side o' the mountains. Think you can handle that?"

Dickie swallowed. "You know me. Show me a way someplace once in daylight and I can get there in th' dark o' the moon."

"I know you, y' say." George looked at Dickie in a strange, dark way that gave him shivers. "How well does a man know family he never sees? You hardly know me, do you really, Dick? I mean other than what talking I've done?" George jolted down his brandy and poured another. "Dick, I'm glad you're here, because I can say things to you I can't say to anybody else because they all depend on me. I can't . . . I dasn't . . . ever let on when I've a doubt. Once on the way to Vincennes, I forgot to look cocksure, and they almost fell apart. Slow me down if I get talking too fast to make sense, Dick, for I've got a lot I haven't been able to say.

"Listen, and I'll tell something I learned, and it surprised me something awful: When you're surrounded by people who look to you for everything, you're more alone than if you were the only soul on earth. Because you can't let on that you're dubious or hangdog about anything. By God, they won't let you! Someone has to keep grinnin' in the gloom and givin' orders, and y'know who. Dick, I can trust ye never to tell a soul this, but when we'd crossed that Wabash last February, and the gunboat wasn't there, and I saw how weak and helpless we all were—no, now listen—why, I had the godawfulest notion there for a spell, that the only right thing I could do, the only thing I could do to save my poor people, was to walk up to the Hair-Buyer's fort and surrender, just so he'd feed us and shelter us 'fore we all died!"

"My God, George!"

"Aye. I'd got 'em in a situation that dang nigh killed 'em, and in spite of all th' tales you've heard about me knowin' what to do all the time, why, for that little while there I didn't know what else we *could* do. Now: can you imagine, brother, what would've happened if I'd told 'em any such a thing! Well, that's what I mean by alone. If I'd let that slip out to anybody, even Joe Bowman, bless his great and true heart, we'd ha' lost it all."

He poured another brandy for each of them, staring at Dick's astonished countenance over the bottle, and some spilled and ran over his fingers, making him look down. Then he raised his eyes again and said:

"Know what saved us when I was that addled?"

"What?"

"Providence."

"Providence?"

"Meseems when a man's alone like that, havin' to be God for a godforsaken people, then Providence steps in and takes over. I'll have to tell this story to Pa someday, as it upholds all he's always told us. But, yes, Dick, it was Providence."

"How so?"

"We'd just flopped ashore out o' the ice water onto that last shore. Scarce a man could stand up and stagger. Our heart-fires were about gone to ashes. And then guess what showed up. Going right past that place, on their way to the fort?"

"What?"

"Some squaws in a canoe. They had a kettle and some corn and a hunk o' buffalo. Now why would they come by that wayward place just then, I ask ye? But they did. And we bought that food from 'em, that manna from heaven, and made a chowder. Hot chowder. One mouthful apiece was about it all came to. But it gave us strength to get up and move on, and that evening we attacked the fort, and the next day it was Hamilton who gave up, not us. Does that sound like Providence to you?"

"It does."

"By then I'd already had about all th' vainglory wrung out o' me, Dick. I was wishin' I had double-hinged knees so's I could kick my own hindy-end for bringin' those trustin' good lads into such an extreme. Now I'm glad it happened, Dick, because"— he paused and swallowed, and gazed into his glass with wet, red-rimmed eyes—"because if somehow we'd won out anyway, without that gift o' Providence, then I might be sitting here right now like Caesar, believin' I maybe *was* God!"

For a long time Dickie could think of nothing worth saying. Finally he said, "From what I've heard here, there's folks just about believe you are."

"I know it. What counts is that *I* don't believe it. I wouldn't if I could. I wouldn't want to be a god if they offered it to me. Too damned lonely. Who would ye talk to, eh? You wouldn't even have a brother!"

He stared. Then he winked at Dickie. And then he began to laugh a little, and Dickie laughed, and it got bigger and bigger and more uproarious, and they grew helpless with laughing, and their howls went out the open windows into the summer night, over the fort and the town and out among the night-noises of the frogs and katydids, and sentries heard their Colonel Long Knife laughing, laughing as if he had needed to laugh forever, and the sentries shook their heads, at first, and then soon they were chuckling, at their posts in the dark perimeters of the town.

MAJOR JONATHAN CLARK STOOD WITH THE SUN BEATING ON his back, stood on a platform on the roof of the house that was Colonel Light Horse Harry Lee's command post. With his eye to the lens of a long telescope mounted on a tripod, he looked across the Hackensack River, over the heat-shimmering scrublands around the distant town of Hoboken, and beyond that lowland to the shimmering Hudson, and the island of Manhattan on the other side. He could make out a church steeple in the city of New York. New York. The British stronghold all during the war and apparently destined to be so forever.

He moved the glass slowly down the near shore of the Hudson and brought it to bear on a low, squat structure he had been studying with a growing interest for weeks:

The British fort on the spit of land called Paulus Hook.

The fort was an affront to General Washington, and it had become almost an obsession with Colonel Harry Lee. There it sat, on the New Jersey side of the Hudson, which Washington considered *his* side of the Hudson, and with its big guns it commanded this side of the Hudson's mouth. Where it sat the Hudson was about a mile wide, and were it not for that fort, American ships could probably come up the river hugging the New Jersey shore, relatively safe from the guns of New York's own battery.

It sat there, seemingly immune to attack. It was a strong welldesigned fort of thick earthen walls and covering redoubts, surrounded by a water-filled moat and garrisoned by two hundred Redcoat artillerymen and a whole battalion of infantry, all housed in stone buildings within the fort. The only road to the fort crossed the moat over a drawbridge, and inside the drawbridge was an iron-grill portcullis. The fort's view of the marshy countryside and of the straight, flat road was so complete that the defenders could have their drawbridge up and portcullis closed before any body of attackers could come within a half-hour's march of it. It was the kind of fort the British had the time and money and manpower and machinery to build. It was impregnable to any kind of direct assualt, and as Jonathan Clark stood studying its massive form in the August sunlight, he thought:

If the forts in the West had been like this one, Brother George couldn't have done what he did. Not even George, audacious as he is, would have dared besiege a place like that.

Yet . . .

Yet, it's but a work o' man. And there's no work o' man that a smarter man couldn't get into. He and Colonel Lee agreed on that. They had long been plotting how to get in.

He took out his watch. It was about time for something to happen that Jonathan had observed happening at that fort for several weeks.

The British military were a regular and methodical people. They did certain things at certain times. Jonathan had noticed that on certain days of the week, a large troop of British foragers would set out early in the afternoon, to range the New Jersey countryside plundering the farms and homes for fresh meat. And most interesting to Jonathan was that the drawbridge and portcullis would be left open for their return. The foragers had to range far, and usually, Jonathan had noticed, they still would not be back in by the time dusk obscured his view of the fort.

Now, as he watched, sure enough, the drawbridge came down, and a large procession of English troops moved out onto the road. They were tiny at this distance, even seen through the spyglass, and were so distorted by the shimmering heat waves that he could make them out only as a line of red and flashes of sunlight on metal, but it appeared to him that most of the fort's garrison must be in that foraging body—probably all the dragoons and most of the infantry, he guessed, except the current guard watch. They had to go out in strong force, of course, because Colonel Light Horse Harry's Virginians kept a watch over the countryside. As Lee had remarked once to Jonathan, "Thanks to us, it takes a British battalion to capture an American cow."

Jonathan took his eye from the telescope and straightened his back. He pulled a kerchief from his sleeve and wiped sweat from his face. He said to a lieutenant standing behind him, "Keep that glass on that foraging party, and keep me a record of where they go today, as far as you can follow 'em, all right, son?" Then he stepped off the platform, ducked in through a dormer window, and went down the stairs. There was a murmur of voices in the parlor where Colonel Lee kept his office, and some junior officers came out. Jonathan knocked, and was called in.

Young Light Horse Harry Lee was one of the most courtly and dashing members of that large clan of courtly and dashing Lees of Virginia. Even on a sweltering August day like this, billeted in a farmhouse doing the humdrum duties of an outpost commander in a static war, he looked as if he could be attending a glittering ball. The color in his finely sculptured face was always high and florid, and his eyes glittered with fun, and his silvery-white wig was always as tidy as the curling iron could make it. He wore rather more braid on his blue coat than regulations prescribed. But for all his prettiness and charm he was a resourceful and brave officer, always looking for clever ways to embarrass the British. Jonathan Clark now believed he had one that Harry Lee would like to try. "Sir," he said, "d' you suppose General Washington would permit you to capture or destroy yon British nest on Paulus Hook, if you convinced him it could be done handily?"

"Mister Clark, you devil! Sit down and tell me what's on your mind!"

Jonathan talked for a quarter of an hour. He brought out a notebook and recited dates and times and numbers he had been recording. He got up and showed the Colonel certain details on his wall map. Lee kept pursing his lips and rubbing the palms of his hands together as he listened, now and then interjecting some fact or opinion that he thought might be helpful. Finally Jonathan finished. Lee went back behind his desk and sat there for a minute, fingers steepled neatly under his chin, gazing thoughtfully at the map, and Jonathan could tell nothing of what he thought of the idea. But at last, Lee said, clapping his hands together once:

"Let's ride up to Dey House early tomorrow, and see what His Excellency thinks. It just tickles my fancy something fierce!"

GENERAL WASHINGTON SAT AND LISTENED TO THE WHOLE scheme, nodding, glancing down at the map on the table, his big hands lying still on the edge of the table. After Jonathan and Lee had made their presentation, Jonathan watched Washington.

He remembered the day he had met him, at St. John's Church in Richmond, and thought how far they all had come since that day, how much of their naiveté had been lost on so many bloody fields, yet how little had been achieved. General Washington's eyes were tired and marked with so many more little lines of worry and concentration. But there was still that massive, solid serenity in his whole demeanor. A clock ticked in a corner as Washington digested it all with that thoroughgoing caution of his, and for a long while it looked as if he were not going to approve of it. It was, after all, a rash plan, depending a lot on chance, and many a complex plan of His Excellency's had been wrecked by chance. The fog at Germantown, for instance. But at last Washington brought his blue eyes directly to bear on Jonathan's face, and his voice was warm as he said:

343

"One might imagine you'd been studying your brother."

Jonathan swallowed that with a smile. He knew it was meant well, and, too, he had grown used to hearing it. Jonathan knew that Washington had been very impressed and heartened by George's successes in the West. The victory at Vincennes had in fact been one of the few bright gleams in the war thus far this year, and Washington spoke often of it in the dinner parties he held for his officers. But damn it, Jonathan thought behind his smile, George isn't the only Clark in this world.

Washington turned to Lee now, and said: "It's really rather admirable, isn't it? I see no fault with it. I should say, yes, do it, but with one caution:

"As we have no general offensive just now that this would serve, lives shouldn't be wasted on it. If it functions as the complete surprise it would seem to, take Paulus Hook and I'll see that we arrange to hold it. But sirs, if you meet resistance or the plan somehow goes awry, and your men are in great danger, then please be satisfied just to disable their cannon and break off the engagement. We won't expend our good people except for great, great advantages."

ON AUGUST 19, JONATHAN CLARK AND COLONEL LEE stood among reeds in the swamp beside the road to Paulus Hook, and watched the evening light change. Half a mile up the road lay the fort; Jonathan could see the British colors hanging limp in the sultry air above the ramparts. He could still distinguish the red in the flag.

It was still too light. Only by deep dusk could one troop of men become indistinguishable from another.

"Patience," Colonel Lee said softly. "Another fifteen or twenty minutes."

Jonathan listened hard for hoofbeats or the tread of marching behind him down the road. If the British foragers should come up the road now, or in the next hour, returning to the fort, the whole plan would have to be abandoned. If they did return early, the Virginians were simply to melt into the swamp until they had passed, then regroup to march back and cross the Hackensack to their base, under cover of darkness, and nothing would have been lost.

Jonathan looked at the tense faces of the nearest men. There were three hundred of them back there among the reeds along the road levee.

This waiting was the worst part, waiting for something so slow and unhurriable as the fading of evening light. The march down

ad been something of a game. The Virginians had had to cross
lot of ground in the distant view of the fort. It was impossible
to get close to Paulus Hook without being seen, and so the Vir-
inians had had to give the impression of being an American
oraging party. They had zigzagged with a seeming aimlessness
rom farm to farm along the dirt roads all day, gradually working
heir way down into the swamps a few miles from the fort. And
.ere they had made themselves invisible to come the rest of the
vay. If the British in the fort had seen them, they apparently had
allen for the deception, or simply had paid them no heed, for
he drawbridge was still down and the portcullis was still open,
pen for the routine arrival of the British foragers. So far so
ood.

Jonathan watched the light change and listened to a catbird in
he reeds and saw a gull pass overhead, gray now in the dimming
ight. He saw a light of some kind, a torch or lantern, pass
eyond the iron gates within the fort. "If they're lighting up in
here," he said, "it must be about right now." He turned to look
gain at his troops. Their coats were dark, purple-looking now
nstead of blue, and he knew that red coats now would also look
urple. Lee nodded, and squeezed Jonathan's elbow.

"All right, lieutenant," Jonathan said, his heart beating
vildly, "pass the word to get up on the road." And he climbed
ıp the bank of the causeway and stood in the middle of the road,
.ee beside him. With rustlings and hushings the troops were
limbing up onto the road behind him now and forming four
iles. He kept his eye squinted and his ear cupped, but there was
to sign or sound that the British were closing the gate. He heard
 plaintive bugle call inside the fort, and saw the Union Jack
lide down.

He held up his right hand now, and then waved it forward and
egan striding up the road toward the gate, and he could hear his
roops coming behind him. He had not advised them to be
tealthy. He wanted them to clank and clunk and step heavy,
ınd sound for all the world like a British foraging party returning
iredly up the familiar road to their own fort. That was the key to
is whole plan: the Americans had to be mistaken for the return-
ng British party. If they were not, they might expect either or
oth of two things to happen in this next half mile: either there
vould be shouts and the clanking of iron gates and drawbridge
:hains, or there would be muzzleblasts of the fort's gate cannon
ınd a thousand pieces of grapeshot whistling down the road.
onathan walked on, thinking of these things, hearing the follow-
ng tread of his men.

345

It became the strangest, longest half-mile he had ever walked. In the cooling evening air, in the deepening dusk, under the full gaze of the British sentries high on their gate stations, he was trudging straight up an open road toward the yawning gate of an enemy castle, or so it seemed, with every intention of walking right in. He swallowed as the ramparts grew taller and taller; he swallowed though his dry mouth gave him nothing to swallow. And it occurred to him now that he was actually doing this that it was far more implausible even than it had seemed when he had started telling Harry Lee about it. It was more like a George thing than a Jonathan thing, as Washington had suggested; it was more like the bizarre hijinks of some reckless frontiersman than the careful plan of a scholarly, gentlemanly Clerk of County, engaged to be married to the very proper Miss Sarah Hite. He could hear Colonel Lee laughing voicelessly between his teeth.

Now the gate was a mere sixty yards away, fifty, forty . . . . Jonathan caught a whiff of cooking, an oniony, glutinous smell like fat stew, coming from the fort, and he could see the sentries' heads and shoulders and tall hats atop the walls, silhouetted against the lilac-gray sky. One of the sentries now raised his right hand. Jonathan felt a chill; he expected that sentry to yell out an alarm. Jonathan raised his own right arm now, and took a deep breath, ready to yell for his men to rush the gate before it could be shut. Twenty yards . . . fifteen . . . ten . . . . And then the sentry simply lowered his hand and called down:

"Good hunting, Sir?"

It was incredible! Hilariously incredible! The guard had only been waving a hello to the oncoming troop! He had no suspicion! Jonathan called back up, sounding as English as he could.

"Quoit! Quoit good!" And he heard Colonel Lee's whispery laugh again.

And then the great oaken planks of the drawbridge were resounding under his heels, and then the thick, dark gates were beside him and the *George Rex* escutcheon was above his head, then behind him, and he was inside the fort, in the compound, and there were British soldiers walking around in lamplight not thirty feet from him, going to and from their evening meal.

"Now, boys," Jonathan said to the special squad just behind him, and they darted out, six of them to either side, sprinted up the wooden steps to the sentries' posts and, before they could cry out, clubbed them unconscious. Jonathan now drew his saber and signaled frantically to right and left, and suddenly his men were rushing forward around him on both sides, fixing bayonets. Colonel Lee led a company onto the artillery parapets. A British fficer in short red jacket and powdered wig had been coming)ward Jonathan as if to greet him, and stopped, bewildered. As e opened his mouth to cry out, Jonathan grabbed him by the ont of his jacket, held his sword point under his chin, and said, Sir, you're my prisoner or you're a dead man. Which?"

The Englishman nodded. "Yes," was all he could say. His yes were wild as he watched the hundreds of blue-coated strang- rs streaming into the torchlit compound. Unarmed British sol- iers, some in work coveralls, were stopping stockstill and utting their hands up, or turning to run, some beginning to yell or help. A few pistol shots flared near a stone house in the enter of the compound, and several muskets discharged on the ring platforms around the walls. On the parade ground now, ne Americans with fixed bayonets were pressing knots of terrified narmed Redcoats backward into corners and against walls. A onfused babble of voices was rising. Jonathan jerked the officer)ward the mess hall. "I want you to step to the door there," he id, "and advise them all to stay where they are and offer no 2sistance. Understand?" He jabbed the officer's neck slightly 'ith the sword blade. When they stepped into the door of the 1ess hall, they found about fifty soldiers, some milling around, thers still seated, in the steamy, dim room.

"Attention, attention!" the officer cried, and it was fortunate 1at he had a loud, clear voice. The noise subsided, and he elled, "Be calm! Be calm! I'm afraid we're overrun! We're pris- ners! Please don't risk yourselves!"

"Very good," Jonathan said. Then he held the officer in the oorway and summoned one of his own lieutenants to place a quad on guard around the building. Fifty prisoners at once, he 1ought, very pleased with himself. His troops, well controlled y their lieutenants, were rounding up the little groups of pris- ners and herding them into the center of the parade ground. Vith those in the mess hall and these, it looked as if they had early a hundred captive already. It was thrilling how well it was 'orking! Up on the ramparts all around now, silhouetted against 1e twilight sky, figures were moving fast, and he could hear eep shouts and steel clashing, now and then a cry of pain. It)unded as if Lee's company were nearly all the way around the igh walls now.

"Come," Jonathan said to his captive officer, "let's go to the owder magazine, shall we? COME, HIGGINS! BRING YOUR OMBER BOYS!" A captain ran up, followed by a squad of eavy-footed soldiers clanking with metal. The British officer led)ward a low, stone structure with one massive door and pointed to it. "Is it locked?" Jonathan asked. The officer nodded. "Do you have a key?"

"No, sir. I'm dragoons."

"Break it in, boys," Jonathan said. And the squad set to work with the prybars and stone hammers they had lugged all over the countryside for this eventuality.

Chank, chank, went the tools, and Jonathan kept his head swiveling, watching every corner to see that his plan was going flawlessly. It seemed to be. He looked at the Redcoat officer. "What d'ye make of our little surprise?"

"Rahtheh duddie play," he replied.

"Oh! Is it! He says it's duddie play, Higgins."

Higgins laughed. *Chank, chunk, screech,* went the tools. If the plan continued to succeed, the powder magazine would be open and ready. If something went wrong, Jonathan intended to blow it up as he left. And Lee's men up on the parapets carried hammers and steel spikes to plug the cannon vents in case the fort could not be held. But so far it looked as if the fort would be held. Jonathan was just making this happy appraisal when he heard a heavy fusillade of gunfire in the deepest corner of the fort. Musketballs whistled and ricocheted through the compound; two whanged off the stone wall of the magazine, just missing the wreckers. The balls kept coming. They were kicking up gravel from the parade ground and thudding into the flesh of British prisoners and American guards alike. "Down, DOWN!" Jonathan cried to his men, and peered around the corner of the magazine, toward the source of the gunfire.

It was a large stone house, officers' quarters, he guessed. Apparently a large body of the enemy had dashed inside at the first alarm and now were firing from the windows, peppering the whole compound. Their shooting was haphazard, but there was so much of it, and so much was ricocheting, that it was hitting a lot of men. Many were falling, sagging to their knees, staggering.

Jonathan's first instinct was to get a company together to storm the house. One houseful of Redcoats should not be able to stop a clever coup like this. Jonathan left the magazine and sprinted to the center of the parade ground. He was about to call officers to get an attack company formed up when an ensign, Lee's aide, came running across the grounds calling for Major Clark. "Here!" he answered.

The ensign ran to him. "Colonel Lee's orders, sir. We're to withdraw!" He flinched as a musketball sang past.

No! Jonathan thought. No, we're almost done! We can silence that house in five—But the ensign went on:

"He said I should remind you of the general's cautions, sir. And assure you that he's destroying the cannon as he goes." Jonathan, clenching his teeth in frustration, looked around. Under the sounds of the shooting he could indeed hear the *tink, tink, tink* of hammers on spikes.

So he gave a long sigh and resigned himself to it. This was no time to be disobeying orders, even if those orders brought him up short. He said:

"Tell the colonel I'm complying. That I wish to take our prisoners back with us. And that I shall blow the magazine as a parting gesture."

COLONEL LEE LED THE VIRGINIANS AND THEIR WOUNDED and their 125 British prisoners a quarter of a mile down the dark road. Then he stepped out to the side to let them file past, and stood looking back at the dark fort.

Come on, Mister Clark, he thought.

Come on now. The plan was a brilliant one and it worked as well as it could have and there's no point in you lingering too long over your handiwork.

Come on.

Then a smile spread on his face. He could hear a heavy tread on the road, one trotting man. Soon on the night-dim surface of the dirt road he saw the big figure of the man coming.

And just as Jonathan pounded to a halt beside Colonel Lee, the inside of the fort turned bright yellow and five quick concussions shook the ground and the night roared. They watched a bright orange, smoky flash balloon over the fort and then, to the gleeful yells of the troops on down the road, watched flaming debris rain down on Paulus Hook. Lee looked at Jonathan in the light of the fireworks and saw a smile of satisfaction on his face. And Jonathan said:

"There."

They walked happily on down the road. Colonel Lee kept putting his hand on Jonathan's shoulder and chuckling. Jonathan was thinking:

George didn't have anyone to stop him, being on his own out there like that.

"Brilliant," Colonel Lee was saying. "Brilliant!"

"Really, I guess we did quite well. Enough to show that I could . . . that it could be done."

A FEW FEET FROM JOHNNY CLARK'S BUNK IN THE GUN ROOM of the *Jersey* a young officer was sitting with his face in the corner.

349

Here the newer prisoners had picked and clawed at the rotten planking of the hull until they had worried a fist-sized hole through to the outside, and here they would take turns sitting with their faces to the hole breathing the fresh air that came through. They called it The Window. "Don't make it too big," the Poet had warned them, "for it'll have to be plugged somehow when the winter winds come." But these newcomers had not spent a winter on the *Jersey* as yet, and so some of them, while sitting at the hole, would keep picking away at the punky oak to enlarge the hole. Some of them even plotted naively about how the hole might be enlarged enough, in time, to permit a man to squeeze through, drop into the water, and swim ashore. Sometimes Johnny would slump in that corner trying to get fresh air to his lungs and he would hear them talking that way. He would not even bother to tell them how hopeless that was. A breath of air was too precious to waste on advice to men who were as vainly hopeful as he himself had once been.

"What's that?" said the officer with his face at the hole.

"What?" asked the next one in line.

"It sounds like small arms. Way off. From over by New York. Shh!" He had his ear to the hole now. "Aye. Somebody's shooting up a lot over there, I'll swear it."

"Let me hear."

"D'ye suppose Washington's attacking New York?"

"Let me hear!"

"Shhh!"

"Mister Clark wants at th' Window." Johnny had hauled himself out of his bunk and was dragging himself over.

"Clark's not in line."

"Let 'im, damn your eyes! He's sick and he's been a long time here. Let 'im."

Johnny gasped his thanks and put his face to the hole. If the Americans were taking New York, maybe they would capture the *Jersey* soon and free everyone and the sick could get well. That was what he was thinking, and he wanted to see if he could tell whether that was happening or not.

He couldn't tell much. He could hear the shooting. It was coming from the west on a slight breeze across the water. It was very far away and hardly audible over the noise of wavelets lapping the hull below. It was very faint, faint as fingertips being drummed on a tabletop. It might be from the vicinity of New York Town but it did not sound anything like a full-scale battle, that was certain. He put his ear to the hole and listened a while. Sometimes the sporadic sounds would fade beneath the sea-sounds, then they would be audible again.

"What d'you make of it, John Clark?" someone said. He hook his head slowly, then turned his face and looked out into he darkness. Just the jagged, splintery hole with a darkening wilight sky outside and the bright spark of, Johnny thought, Venus, and a low, black silhouette of the far shoreline.

"Enough, Mister Clark. My turn," said the nearest man behind him. Johnny nodded. He was sometimes deferred to by the newer prisoners because of his extreme poor health and his older brother's recent fame, but he did not like to abuse the privilege.

He was arranging his bones to crawl away from The Window when suddenly he saw a yellow flare on the western horizon, then a glow, and five or six seconds later heard a short rumble like summer thunder.

"Something . . . something blew up . . ." he said, and then started coughing painfully. They helped him away and toward his bunk while the next man in line, and several others, all tried at once to get an eye to The Window, exclaiming, querying, cursing, and shoving each other.

When Johnny Clark was back in his bunk he was exhausted, and his heavy breathing precipitated more and more coughing, and that tired him more. It was a long time before he could rest, and he almost did not live through that night to learn a few weeks later that the noises across the water had been an American attack on the British fort at Paulus Hook on the Hudson.

And then for some reason he still did not die, and still did not die, and he was still alive weeks later when a new Yankee captain came aboard prisoner, full of news they had not heard from the outside, among which news was that a Major Jonathan Clark had been commended by His Excellency General Washington and promoted to lieutenant colonel, and awarded a medal of honor by the Congress, for his part in Colonel Light Horse Harry Lee's daring attack on Paulus Hook.

This new prisoner, a portly, well-informed, and garrulous fellow, somehow had managed to smuggle a silver flask of brandy aboard, hidden somewhere on his expansive anatomy, and he offered to share it with the other prisoners. It was stretched through tepid water far enough to make a small cup of a sort of grog for each officer in the gun room. Once again Johnny Clark rallied enough to come to the table for a celebration. The captain raised his cup toward Johnny and declared:

"General Washington is alleged to have said that in this dismal year of '79, there were only three bright events: the capture of Stony Point by Anthony Wayne, and of Vincennes and Paulus Hook by two Clark boys of Virginia. I say we raise a cup to the

Clarks of Virginia, but no loud cheering, gentlemen, because we don't want those God-damned Redcoats gaolers upstairs coming down to confiscate our delicious grog before we've drunk it. So, softly, now, for Vincennes, *hip hip.*"

"*Hoorah!*" they all murmured, smiling.

"For Paulus Hook, *hip hip.*"

"*Hoorah!*"

"And for Lieutenant John Clark here, *hip hip.*"

"HOORAH!"

20

CHARLES TOWN,
SOUTH CAROLINA

May 12, 1780

LIEUTENANT EDMUND CLARK STOOD WAITING BEHIND AN earthen breastwork in a street near the Battery at Charles Town and listened to the unaccustomed silence. The men of his company lay at rest against the piled dirt, sweating, some dozing. For weeks the bombardment from the British fleet had prevented anyone from really sleeping, and now in the silence of the truce they were almost asleep on their feet.

Flies buzzed near Edmund's ears. The street behind the breastwork was littered with broken bricks and pieces of glass glinting in the hot, hazy sunlight. Buildings along the street showed broken pillars and smashed roofs. Most of the windows were gaping dark, their glass smashed out, and above some the bricks were sooty, showing where fires had burned.

The rumor was that the truce had been called so that General Lincoln could negotiate a surrender, to save the citizens of Charles Town from the bombardment and from further hardship of shortages. Four years ago General Clinton had failed to take Charles Town, but this time he had got ships and artillery in close enough to seal in its defenders and lay a long, deadly siege upon the city. Day by day the bombshells and cannon shot had crashed and exploded in the town. One by one, officers and men Edmund had come to know had been killed, by shrapnel, by flying splinters, by bursting bricks, by concussion. And the troops could do nothing. They had not fired their rifles. The

352

only fire returned to the British had been by the cannon along the Battery, and it had not been very effective.

Edmund looked toward the headquarters and saw Jonathan coming along the breastwork, his hands behind his back, stopping here and there to speak to some soldiers, answer a question, shake his head. Edmund watched him coming, watched him with a strange, sad affection. Jonathan was almost thirty now; he would be thirty in August: he had been an officer of the Continental Line for nearly five years now, and he looked more like a forty-year-old man. Nine months ago it was that he had been the hero of the Battle of Paulus Hook, and when he had come home on a furlough, he had taken Edmund back to the army with him. Only Billy of all the six sons was still at home now, doing the work of a man to help their father.

Edmund thus far had seen little hope that he would ever get a chance to make such a record for himself as his brothers Jonathan and George had done. Half the period of his enlistment had been spent marching deeper and deeper into the South, and since he had arrived here he had done nothing but watch and hear the British cannonballs smash up the beautiful old city and see the army and the civilians dig out and re-bury their dead. General Lincoln was stubborn and brave and willing to stand the siege forever, but the plight of the civilians was known to be demoralizing him.

Jonathan came to Edmund now, and looked at him with a wistful smile. He put a hand on his shoulder and led him off up the street a little way from the soldiers. Edmund watched him out of the side of his eye. He saw the deep furrows in the pitted cheeks and the sadness in his eyes.

They sat down together now on a stone pedestal where a statue once had been, and Jonathan extracted a clay pipe and a bag of tobacco from his clothing and filled the pipe. He offered the bag to Edmund, and Edmund filled his own pipe. Then Jonathan got out his reading glass and turned until sunlight was focused in the pipe bowl.

The tobacco glowed in white light, and when it began to smoke, Jonathan puffed on it. It smelled good after the harsh odors of brick dust and gunsmoke. He handed the glass to Edmund, who lit his own pipe with it. Jonathan took a deep lungful of smoke and exhaled it with a long sigh.

"Well, Eddie, I think it's a shame that the doubtless best sharpshooter in the whole Grand Army probably won't ever get a chance to shoot at a single Redcoat. Or, maybe it's not a shame.

Maybe it's a good thing. Pa would be glad to have a son, I guess, who's not had to shoot anybody."

Edmund felt heavy inside. "Seems to me what you're saying is that General Lincoln intends to give us up."

"He's heard that Clinton will grant full honors. He's going to surrender. We'll be marching out in a day or two. Prisoners."

"Aw, God." Somehow this did not frighten Edmund; it seemed to him that captivity would be safe and easy compared with waiting day after day for the cannonball destined for himself. But the future looked infinitely gray now that he had heard this, and he almost wished that he had not heard it and that the bombardment would resume. "Prisoners," he muttered after a while, thinking of long-lost Brother Johnny.

"I don't reckon they'll try to keep us long," Jonathan said. "They've caught a whole army of us. Aye. They'll likely parole us on our word. That would mean, for you and me and Bill Croghan, the end of the war."

"For me," said Edmund, "it ends before it started."

THE LONG BLUE RANKS MARCHED SLOWLY OUT FROM BE-hind the breastworks onto the road out of the city, guns unloaded. They trod to the beat of muffled drums with their colors cased, out between the long red ranks of British troops flanking both sides of the road. Jonathan had told Edmund, "March with your head up. We've nothing to be ashamed of."

So Edmund marched with his head up. He glanced aside now and then at the British soldiers. It was the first time he had seen his enemy face to face since he had put on a uniform. Before that he had seen only the detachment of Dunmore's dragoons outside Doncastle's Ordinary, five whole years ago, when he had followed Patrick Henry toward Williamsburg. And he had seen the enemy prisoners George had sent home from the West. Now he was seeing them, all these plain faces—they looked like just anybody, men and boys—as his own enemies for the first time, and he was their prisoner. *B-b-b-bmp, bmp, bmp, b-b-b-bmp, bmp, bmp,* went the muffled drums, and the soldiers' feet shuffled on the dusty dirt of the road, and it was all so calm and sedate that birds were flitting and twittering in the hedges and shrubs along the road. He had not heard any birds all during the bombardment, it seemed to him now as he thought back on it.

Probably it was true what Jonathan had said, that there wasn't anything to be ashamed of.

But a whole army surrendering! Maybe it wasn't shameful, but it was ignominious.

It was nice to hear birds again, but birds or no, it was, Edmund was sure, the most mournful day he probably ever would have.

PIQUA TOWN, OHIO
August 8, 1780

JOE ROGERS, ADOPTED SON OF A FINE, WISE, WHITE-HAIRED Shawnee man and wife, lay face down on the ground inside the shattered palisade and pretended he was dead. He could hear the warriors all around him shouting and running about and firing their muskets out through the gun ports, and he could hear the voices of Cousin George's men whooping and cheering outside, a hundred yards up a slope opposite the stockade. Against his hip he could feel the weight of a Shawnee warrior who did not have to pretend he was dead. The Shawnee's warm blood was running onto and down Joe's hip. Joe's nose was clogged with dust and burned with the smell of gunpowder and he needed to sneeze, but he knew he could not allow himself to sneeze because he was supposed to be dead, although the warriors trapped in here with him probably were too busy and desperate to notice whether one of their dead sneezed. He pressed his nose hard against the dirt to stop the sneeze but could not stop it and it burst from him.

But no one noticed the sneeze because at the same moment another one of the awful cannonballs smashed through the log gate and the cannon boomed and everything and everybody in the fort, alive and dead, twitched and shook once. He heard outcries of more wounded warriors and heard broken wood creaking and rending and then falling with a thud just a few feet away. Then the Americans cheered the shot and Joe Rogers could distinctly hear one voice yelp, "Yow! Gate's down! God damn!" It was a raucous, awful, profane shout, but it sounded like music to Joe: a white man's voice, cursing triumphantly in English. His heart squeezed at the sound of it and although he had been a good, obedient Shawnee son for more than three years, since his capture on Christmas Day of '76, he knew when he heard it that he was not really a Shawnee but a Virginian.

Now through the crashing and howling of battle one of the chieftains was shouting an order for the warriors to gather up their wounded and flee over the back wall of the stockade and try to retreat through the tall corn to the bluff above town. Joe

Rogers gave thanks to the Christian God he had always prayed to secretly, and prayed that when they were gone he would be kept safe and alive long enough to slip out of the wreckage and make a break for the white men's lines. That would be the dangerous part, but he had rehearsed it in his mind all the last night, since he had learned that an army of the Long Knife Chief was coming toward Piqua Town. He had not been able to plan just when or how he would slip from the Shawnee lines, but he had determined that somehow he would find or make a chance during the confusion, and when those Virginians were within hailing distance, he would rise and reveal himself and go toward them with his hands held high, telling them in English that he was one of them.

Joe Rogers was scared of the risk of this, but he had put his faith in God and grown confident that he would somehow manage to be reunited with his people. It seemed in fact so much like God's own design that the man coming to attack Piqua was his own Cousin George, the very man Joe had been serving at the moment of his capture; to Joe Rogers in his state of mind the whole remarkable coincidence had taken on a personal aspect. It was as if George were coming after all these years to rescue Joe from the plight he had put him in, as if that had been George's one obsessive purpose since that Christmas Day. Joe knew better, of course, but nonetheless it had seemed that way to him, and he was so anxious for the imminent reunion that he could scarcely lie still here playing dead. But he had to wait for the right moment. His deliverance was so close at hand now that he knew it would be the worst kind of stupidity to get himself shot in the back by the Shawnees just at the moment when he could cross that desperate line back to his own people.

And so he forced himself to lie still as the fleeing warriors' moccasins beat the earth around him, even as another cannonball smashed through the palisade and shook him and showered dirt upon him. He made himself lie still by listening for George's voice, and by imagining their smiling reunion and the feel of George's strong handshake and hug, and by thinking of all the wondrous things he would be able to tell George—and then his own beloved family!—about life among the Shawnees.

It had been a strangely good life, almost a period of enchantment, of acceptance and belonging and warmth, just as George had used to tell him about his time among the Mingoes. Joe had come to admire the Shawnees, for their good humor and their hardiness and their incredible courage and their complex codes of honor. And his body and soul would never forget the enveloping love of the doelike girl who had been his wife since the springtime of the present year. But he was, he knew, a Virginian. He lay listening to the uproar of rifle fire and shouting and whacking bullets, trying to pick George's commanding voice out of the distant din. Once or twice earlier in the attack he had thought he had heard it, but maybe only because he wanted so to hear it.

He knew it was Cousin George's army. He had been hearing the Shawnees speak with awe about a white leader called the Long Knife Chief for more than a year now, and when the chiefs of other tribes had come back from the great councils with the Long Knife at Cahokia, Joe had learned then that the English name of the terrible white chief was George Rogers Clark. Joe had heard of the capture of the Scalp-Buyer at Vincennes a year ago, and then all through the last winter and spring there had been rumors that the Long Knife might yet come and strike the Shawnees for refusing to council with him. And then this summer Joe had heard time after time of the Long Knife Chief's ominous deeds: He had built forts at the Falls of Ohio and at the mouth of the Ohio. And when the British at Detroit and Michillimackinack had sent a thousand Lakes Indians down the Illinois River to capture Cahokia and St. Louis and Kaskaskia, they had been defeated and routed by the Long Knife Chief, whom they had not even known was there. This seemed to be a chief who never slept, who always knew where his enemies were going, and who was there waiting when they arrived. Already it was said that some tribes would not join the British to go against places where the Long Knife might be. Joe Rogers the Shawnee had shivered with pride at the sounds of these legends when he had heard them, but had known better than to say it was his relative.

And then three days ago the warning had flashed through Piqua Town that the Long Knife Chief was sweeping up through the Shawnee towns, burning them and destroying their crops, to avenge a massacre of a white men's town on the Licking River one moon ago. Piqua had been put in a state of defense, all its women and children and old people sent away deeper into the Shawnee country for safety. It had been determined that the braves would hold Piqua for as long as it was possible, but that if defeat became fully apparent, the hidden route of escape through the bluffs would be used so that the survivors might live to fight another day.

And then this afternoon the Long Knife's army had crossed the Mad River a mile below Piqua Town with their brass cannon, and through the afternoon they had driven the braves back and back through wooded hills and across grain fields and gardens and finally through the town itself and into the shelter of this triangular log stockade. they now were blowing apart. Already perhaps fifty to eighty braves had died, and now there was nothing for the rest to do but retreat through the bluff, and they were doing that now.

Joe Rogers, being a white man by birth and never tested before in battle against the whites, had not been sent to the outer defense. He had been in the village and then the fort all day, listening to the sounds of battle coming closer and closer. And when at last the white army had set up its lines on the slope opposite the stockade and brought forward its cannon, Joe still had not been put in a position of having to aim a gun at them. At the first cannonball's impact, Joe had fallen to the ground with a dozen others, many of whom had not been able to rise again. And Joe had stayed down, playing dead, scarcely breathing, waiting, seeing this as the opportunity he had begun to think would not come.

Now most of the Indians were out of the stockade or going over the far wall into the cornfield; Joe peered out under his arm and saw that the only ones still near him were the dead ones. Slowly he raised his head and saw that there was no one between him and the stove-in palisade to his left. Outside the wall there was low brush and weeds. If he could get out of the stockade through that breach in the wall, he would be on the opposite side of the stockade from the fleeing Shawnees! Then he could make his way under cover close enough to call to the white troops! This was the chance he had prayed for. His Christian God still heeded his prayers.

Joe Rogers gathered his muscles like springs and then leaped into a crouching run and dove out through the hole into the weeds. The whites' fire was still peppering the stockade, but the cannon seemed to have stopped firing. Joe crawled fast on elbows and knees through the weeds until he was well away from the stockade and then stopped and lay, panting, looking all around. Apparently no one had noticed his flight. By raising his head slightly he could now see the rise of ground from which the army had been firing. The forward slope of it was covered with the tawny forms of dead and wounded braves who had been shot during one last rush to repel the white men. And the whites, apparently beginning to realize now that no fire at all was coming from the stockade, were beginning to rise, some coming down the hill to take scalps from the fallen warriors. Now there was no more gunfire from either side, only a lot of triumphant shouting and yodeling from the troops.

And now above those voices Joe heard it, and he knew it was true this time: there was Cousin George's voice!

Joe rose to his knees, heart pounding, looking for George. He saw him then, saw him standing near a great warhorse, swinging a saber back over his shoulder in a summoning motion, bellowing in his deep voice for the scalp-takers to get back in ranks. In the glow after sunset there he stood, now in an indignant rage, roaring, "GET BACK HERE, DAMN YOUR EYES! Cap'ns! Round up those blood-suckin' fools or I'll drag 'em back myself, by their necks! BACK HERE! FALL IN! By damn, no army of mine turns mob on me! That fort could still—"

Joe felt himself swell with happiness at the sight and sound of that great, roaring relative of his, whose voice when he was in a temper could be heard clearly all over a battlefield. It was the happiest moment in Joe's life. After these years his love and admiration of Cousin George Clark swept back into him, whole and entire, George Clark who now was coming down the slope in long strides himself, still bellowing, coming to reform his disorderly Kentuckians. His own cousin, miracle of miracles, now but a hundred yards from him and not a living Indian in sight to prevent their reunion.

Joe leaped up from his hiding place in a mad rush of joy and sprinted toward him, yelling, "COUS-IN! COUSIN! IT'S ME! IT'S ME!" It was wonderful to be yelling words in his own tongue, wonderful to be alive, wonderful to be running full tilt across a meadow slope toward the best friend he had ever had. "GEORGE! IT'S ME! JOE!"

He was too ecstatic to notice the several startled Virginians who stood up near their commander and raised their long rifles to protect him; he was too overjoyed to remember that he was dressed like a savage, and too excited to think of what he had intended to shout. All he could see was George's face frozen before him in astonishment.

The bullets all hit Joe in the chest almost at once.

George shut his eyes and groaned. He had recognized Joe just at the instant the rifles crashed. He opened his eyes and saw his young cousin now tottering backward, face amazed, mouth still working, and groaned again. "That's Joe. God, how—"

When he reached him, Joe was lying on his back, terrified eyes rolling, blood welling from his mouth, freckled bare chest punctured in half a dozen places with ugly, puckered holes.

George knelt beside him and slipped an arm under his shoulders and raised him enough that Joe's dying eyes could look at him. Joe was trying to say something, but whenever he formed the first word he would have to stop and swallow blood. His eyes were glazed, then sharp, then glazed, then sharp. George felt the Rogers blood soaking hot through his sleeve. "Joe," he said, "why didn't you get away from 'em sooner?" He didn't expect an answer. It was a question addressed to fate, not really to Joe. He thought now of the Rogers family, his mother's family, that wonderful family so like his own, and of Johnny Rogers and of Uncle George, of Auntie Frances. Standing behind him and looking over his shoulders were his own men, those who had shot the oncoming figure to protect him, and they saw that the dying youth had copper hair, like their colonel's, and they were exclaiming that it was a white man.

"What, Joe?" George groaned, hot tears running down his cheeks and off his nose as he watched his cousin work his bloody mouth.

"I . . . nnng . . . Vir . . . nng . . . Virginian . . ."

And then the body in George's arms sagged down, and their reunion was over.

21

CAROLINE COUNTY,
VIRGINIA
October 29, 1783

THE WAR WAS OVER AND ALL OF HER HEROES WERE HOME, ALL except Dickie, who was still out West. Ann Rogers Clark came down the stairs slowly, paused in the hallway a moment to take two deep breaths and wipe her eyes with a kerchief, then braced herself and went toward the library, where she could hear the menfolk talking loudly. From the nursery upstairs came a child's yelp, then Annie's voice, and then a baby started crying. Mrs. Clark stopped and looked up. The baby's voice dropped off to little sobs and then was still, and Sarah's voice was softly lullabying, so Mrs. Clark went on down the hall to the library door.

She rapped with her knuckles at the open door and when they turned toward her, she said:

"Johnny's awake now. Ye might go up and tell 'im the news. But don't get 'im overly stirred up. And keep those voices down, if you please; th' house is full o' babies." She compressed her lips, then opened them with a little smacking sound, shaking her head. "Seems this house always is."

They got up, laying down their pipes and brandy glasses, glancing seriously at each other. They knew the meaning of her feigned gruffness. It meant Johnny was worse. Lately she had taken to disguising her anguish this way. John Clark squeezed her hand as he went past her into the hallway. George looked into her red-rimmed eyes as he went by, and frowned. Jonathan put a hand lightly on her shoulder. Edmund murmured something inaudible to her. Bill Croghan remained seated on the edge of a chair near the hearth, and she told him: "You can go up, too. Y're one of 'is brother soldier-boys." He rose to follow them, and for a moment the hallway was filled with broad backs, gold braid and epaulets, tromping boots, and the reek of tobacco smoke and brandy that eddied out of the library after them. "It smells like hellfire and brimstone in here," she called at their backs. And as they went up the stairs she went into the room, fanning her hand before her face, and opened the windows. Then, blinking, holding both hands clasped before her stomach, she went aimlessly around the room for a few seconds, and finally sat down in the chair her husband had occupied. His pipe lay in a brass bowl, still smoking, and his glass of liquor was beside it.

Ann Rogers Clark glanced toward the empty hallway. Then she picked up the glass and the pipe. She had never smoked tobacco, and had never drunk anything but sherry. Now she put the pipe stem in her mouth and drew on it, making a face and squinting her eyes against the pungent fumes. She raised her glass as if to an imaginary roomful of listeners, and said, growling deep in imitation of a man's voice: "By God, *I* won this war." Then she blew out the mouthful of smoke and poured in a mouthful of brandy, and swallowed part of it. Her eyes began pouring tears and her mouth puckered up, and she spat the rest back into the glass. Great Lord in Heaven, she thought. No wonder they can stand wars. If they can stand that! She pitched the dregs into the fire and it flared with a *pouf!*

Oh, Johnny, Johnny, Johnny, she thought. My poor poet romancer, always had Cupid's arrow stuck in your heart. What have they done to you!

And she sat there gazing into the fire with her husband's glass and tobacco pipe in her hands and the cold draft from the window stirring the graying hair at the edges of her dust-bonnet.

THE MEN FILED INTO JOHNNY'S BEDROOM, PRETENDING TO be jolly but keeping their voices down. The room was bright and clean, and several great, white pillows propped Johnny in a sitting position, so he would not strangle or drown in his sleep. His face was almost as white as the pillows. His eyes were sunken deep in bluish sockets. His cheeks were hollow. In his temples the veins were visible, blue lines beneath the thin phthisic skin. His hair was cropped; it had grown an inch since the ringworm and funguses had been cured. Johnny was mostly white-haired now at twenty-six, and cadaverously thin. One servant was kept busy all the days just rinsing, boiling, and drying his bloody kerchiefs.

His death-haunted eyes moved in their sockets as he watched them come in. The grimace on his thin lips they recognized as a smile. He said, in that just-audible murmur of a voice, "Hey, General. Hey, Colonel. Hey, Major. Hey, Cap'n. Hey, Pa."

"You can call me Lieutenant, Son," said John Clark. "I was, remember."

They chuckled, and Johnny grimaced again, the grimace that was his smile.

George came around beside the bed and took Johnny's hand, which was like a bundle of twigs. George had finished his Revolutionary career as a general of State Militia, and though he had resigned his commission, he still wore the blue uniform for lack of other civilian apparel. Jonathan, a lieutenant colonel of the Continental Line, came around to the other side and took his other hand. Then they went and sat down in chairs near the bed while Johnny greeted his father and Edmund and Bill. "We've some items of news for you, Son," said John Clark. "We've been holding it for much o' the day, as those lasses been takin' all your time." Neighborhood girls had been in all morning, going away weeping. Miss Betsy Freeman had been in, and had left looking stricken.

"I'm 'bout too tuckered t' fight 'em off anymore," Johnny murmured, and gave a soft *mmm, mmm* sound that was a chuckle. "Tell me the news, then."

"The treaty was signed in Paris last month," George said. "Great Britain recognizes our independence. About time, say what?"

"Ahhhh," Johnny breathed. "Bravo."

362

"And listen," said John Clark. "All that Northwest land that George took: it was ceded to us, not Canada. D'ye know what that means, Johnny? It means George here all by himself dou-led the lands of our new country."

"God Above," breathed Johnny.

"Not all by myself," George said. "I had help from the Su-reme Director of All Things, as you yourself remind me so ften. And a company o' the best rascals that ever chawed acon."

"More news," Edmund said. "George, tell 'im of the survey, nd about the Indians."

"Well, it's this, old Johnny. Bill and I went down to William nd Mary College, and got us certified. I've got appointed Indian gent for the territory. And also to survey all the bounty lands Virginia's giving her soldiers. And Bill Croghan here's my as-istant."

"Ah! Good!" Johnny's eyes gleamed with tears. "The most . . . most fitten wage for soldiers . . . land in their own country . ." He cleared some mucus from his throat, and it almost but ot quite stirred up a coughing fit. He worked his mouth for a vhile and spat into a kerchief, then said, "Lucy's not goin' to ike ye, George . . . takin' her . . . Bill away . . . just as she's narryin' age."

They all laughed. Bill Croghan whooped, blushing. He was ot calling Lucy "Little Brother" anymore, because at eighteen he had nearly completed her metamorphosis to butterfly, and hough not a beauty, she was a handsome and compelling young voman, of striking coloration and full, strong figure. Only now nd then did the tomboy still slip through. Johnny went on:

"Going t' marry 'er, aren't . . . aren't ye, Bill? . . . Be hon . . hon'able . . . Every girl . . . some man's daughter . . . eh, 'a? And likely someone's . . . sister. . . ." John Clark and Ed-nund looked at each other, then at Johnny. Bill Croghan was eaning forward, head cocked, to hear all this plainly. Suddenly, imid the levity, there was something intensely earnest here; hough Bill did not know the allusions, he sensed that Johnny vas not joshing him.

But then just as suddenly Johnny was, or seemed to be, laugh-ng, a wheezing, wet, horrid sound, dangerously wracking his orry lungs. And when he had recovered from this awful gasping it, he said, "No . . . Wouldn' do . . . that to . . . Bill. No . . . promises at th' . . . at the deathbed . . . I'd never . . . 'Cause I .now . . ."

They watched him and wondered at this. Johnny's face had

taken on a deathly rictus of a smile, and he was now sitting with his head back, trying to take deep, slow breaths. It was perhaps five minutes before he was composed, and at last he said, "What more . . . more news?"

"Something we read in the paper that might int'rest ye quite some," George said. "It's about the *Jersey*. They burnt 'er down and sunk 'er deep."

Johnny was still for a long time, his head tilted, gazing out the window at the red leaves that were being stripped from the high trees by the cold wind, but he was not seeing the leaves. Before his eyes was a red blur in a misty rectangle of light and that red blur became the candle-lantern that had always hung over the table in the gunroom. After a while he said, between gasps:

"She can lay on th' bottom . . . a thousand years . . . 'fore th' sea . . . can wash th' unholy . . . stink off of 'er."

DOWNSTAIRS IN THE LIBRARY, ANN ROGERS CLARK STILL SAT in her husband's chair, the cold pipe and empty glass in her hands, the powerful, rancid tastes of brandy and tobacco still in her mouth but forgotten, and gazed around the room. In her memory's eye she saw a scene of just ten days ago. There on the table in the center of the room, the Rev. Archibald Dick of St. Margaret's Parish had baptized Jonathan's first child, Eleanor Eltinge Clark. The little dark-haired thing had crumpled up her chin as if to cry at the touch of the water, but had not made a sound. Ann Rogers Clark could remember that so vividly. And the others, where they had been around the room, while a cold, wet wind gusted against the windows: The mother, Sarah Hite Clark, sitting beside Jonathan. George there, a tenderness melting his eagle eyes. John and Edmund standing beside him. Lucy and Elizabeth standing there, dark curls and red curls, both absorbed in the novelty of being aunts at such a special event. And Owen Gwathmey and Annie standing here, those two already old hands at this baptism thing. Annie had had no babies in '79, '80, or '81 but then Owen had come home from the war shortly after the Battle of Yorktown, and the very next year she had borne Diana, and now she was gravid with still another. They had just celebrated their tenth anniversary and already she was carrying her fifth. Fruitful as Ann Rogers Clark's own life had been, she had had only four by her tenth year—and John Clark had never left her alone to go to war, either.

The scene of the baptism faded and she found herself staring into the middle of the room, and there stood son Billy, and Owen Gwathmey. They had ridden up to Meadows to get some documents and she had not heard them return. Billy was looking at the pipe in her one hand and the empty brandy glass in the other, his mouth hanging open and his eyes wide. He was thirteen now, tall, with thick, gristly wrists and big feet and hands, and that untameable forelock of flaming red hair. Owen looked equally perplexed. Quickly, Mrs. Clark set down the glass and pipe. She opened her mouth, then decided it would be worse to try to explain it than not.

"Where they all?" Billy asked. He had been hanging around his brothers all day every day, watching and listening, so full of hero worship he was almost dumb. And now that he was back from the Gwathmey place it was of course his first question. She got up and began picking up pipes and glasses, as if she had just been tidying the room. She rolled her eyes toward the ceiling. "Up with Johnny," she said. "Don't go up just now, please. If they haven't wore 'im out by now, I'm sure you would with your starin' and questions. They should be down directly. Owen, what on earth's got *you*?" She realized suddenly that he was looking distressed.

He turned his palms up and looked down at them. Then he looked up at her. "I've just heard some sorry news. Your . . . your brother-in-law Parson Robertson's passed on."

"Oh! Oh, dear Heaven, please not! We'll have to go to Rachel."

Owen had heard the story of it from a neighbor of the Robertsons. The old parson, schoolmaster of George and Jonathan, Edmund, Johnny, and Dickie, and of such prominent Virginia patriots as Hancock Lee and John Edmundson and James Madison, had been brought news of the Treaty of Paris. After the messenger had gone, he had said to Rachel, "Ah! Now! All the principles I've taught my pupils have finally seen fruition. I can rest now at ease." He had gone to bed early, saying he was fully weary. And after an hour of silence in the house, Rachel had gone up to look in on him. He was neatly in bed, hands crossed outside the covers. And he had gone to sleep for good.

Ann Rogers Clark envisioned every bit of it. She saw her sister's face and how it must have looked when she had found her husband dead.

"Things all come at once," she said, starting out of the room, the door indistinct in a blur of tears.

Bootsteps were coming down the stairs. The men were talking low as they came. They stopped halfway down when they saw her standing there, her eyes full.

"John?" she said.

"He's stayed in," George said. "Johnny wanted to talk private to 'im. What's wrong, Ma? What in Heaven's name . . ."

She told him in a low voice, saw the sadness pass through his face, and started to push past him up the stairs. He held her hand and stopped her. "Don't go in and tell 'em just now, please, Ma. It'd fall too heavy on Johnny."

"Aye. Where's Jonathan, then?"

"Stopped in the nursery to see Sarah and the baby. Tell him. He was 'is favorite."

Jonathan was bent like a huge question mark over the cradle by the wall, looking down at his daughter. He was as proud of her as he was of his gold medal of honor, but she was much more mysterious. Children of various ages were everywhere in the room, all of them Annie's. Sarah and Annie were sitting in rocking chairs; Lucy, Elizabeth, and Fanny sat near them. Needlepoint and sewing lay in their laps or at their feet. Elizabeth hopped up. "Oh! Mama and George, to see the baby!" She was mad about Jonathan's baby daughter. She danced across the room to give her mother a spontaneous hug for happiness, then recoiled. "Mama! Y've been *smoking*? And *drinking*!" The others turned in astonishment.

"Hush! No, I haven't. Jonathan. Son, come, there's something I've got to say . . ."

JOHNNY HAD JUST TOLD HIS FATHER, IN HIS MURMURING voice, between painful breaths, about his vow concerning Betsy Freeman, about the death of young Mike Freeman on the *Jersey*. John Clark sat slowly shaking his head. Johnny said:

"It's good . . . about you and . . . Ma. How you . . . How ye be. Would . . . wouldn't it be a . . . sorry life . . . married to a . . . lass ye didn't like!" Then he began coughing, and coughed for a long, hard time. When he could go on, he said:

"But honor's honor . . . as you say. . . . And I told Betsy . . . today . . . that I'll marry 'er . . . soon as I . . . can get up."

He shut his sunken eyes then, and smiled a twisted, drawndown smile, a bitter-looking smile, and took two more long breaths. Then his smile softened.

And he still had that sad poet's smile when John Clark put the pennies on his eyes.

THEY BURIED JOHNNY ON NOVEMBER 2, A CLEAR, COLD day, in the oak grove, dry, brown leaves rustling on the oaks about. Militiamen fired minute guns as his brothers carried his coffin. There were many young misses at the graveside with the family, all with tears in their eyes, but all looking curiously at one another. The Rogers family were there. And Aunt Rachel, still black-garbed from her own recent loss, had come. She held her arm around Ann Rogers Clark as the Reverend Archibald Dick concluded:

". . . accept our prayers on behalf of the soul of thy servant departed, and grant him an entrance into the land of light and joy, in the fellowship of thy saints, through Jesus Christ our Lord. Amen."

As Christmas drew near, George often would sit in the library with his sisters around him before bedtime and talk to them about things he didn't talk to his brothers about in their regular councils. Lucy and Elizabeth had made the mistake of telling him that they had been reading novels, a popular pastime of the day. George, who usually had had several brandies by this hour, would snort.

"Don't! Novels will make ye silly! Life's not like novels! Rowr!" And they would laugh at him and call him an old curmudgeon.

But one night he had drunk more than usual and his eyes were sad, and he had more to say. He gave his usual tirade against novels, but then he went on.

"If my life had been like a novel, it would've ended in the spring o' '79. Those happiest of my days. That's th' way novels end. I've seen a few of 'em, looked at 'em till I flang 'em down in disgust. A novel would've ended me right there: Victory, without one soldier's death on my conscience. All the Indians quiet. Spring a-comin', and me sailin' 'round to the Missipp, to see my good friend the Spanish Governor, and my beauteous sweetheart. Larks and bluebirds singing all about. Sunlight on th' river. Frenchmen serenading at their oars, me looking forward to an easy capture o' Detroit. Aye, that's how a novel would've ended me. But"—He scowled and shook a big forefinger. "Lives don't stop at a nice place like novels do. Lives go muckin' right along till all th' glory's gone. There's always another battle. Friends and brothers and cousins die, and get killed useless-like. Government never sends what ye need. All your allies go in debt and get bitter. Your friend the Spaniard dies, and your poor orphaned sweetheart's sent back to Spain while you're far away chasin' Shawnees."

He paused, his mouth drawn down almost into a pout, his red-veined eyes scowling into the fire. He was quiet for a long time as the girls waited for him to finish what he was saying. Finally, Elizabeth the romantic said:

"George? What *of* your sweetheart?"

"Sweetheart? Oh! Well, maybe that novel would end with him and his sweetheart sittin' on a porch—a big, high porch with white pillars, looking over a river—watching the sun go down over the water."

Lucy was looking at George curiously, shrewdly, sucking the inside of her cheek, but Fanny was laughing.

"No, George! *You're* the one that's silly! *Your* sweetheart, big silly general! The one you said they sent to *Spain!*"

"Silly, am I?" He drew back, looking comically indignant. He wished he hadn't mentioned Teresa, and wondered if he'd spoken her name. "Silly, am I? Well, that proves what I said, for I've been tellin' ye a *novel!*"

LIEUTENANT RICHARD CLARK WAS A DAY'S RIDE OUT OF Louisville on the Old Buffalo Trace going toward Vincennes in a cold drizzle, and he was beginning to wish he had waited a day or two for an escort. George had always told him never to travel between the forts without a squad of men at least, because there were people aplenty, red and white, who would prize a scalp that had come off a Clark's head.

Evening was coming on now and this strange, rolling, dipping, tranquil landscape grew eerie in the misty gloom. Dark shapes seemed to shift just off the eye-corners, and Dickie stopped his horse every few hundred feet to try to sort out something he kept thinking he detected in the margins of his hearing. But when he would stop, it would stop, and he had begun to believe that what he was hearing, if really anything, was the echoes of his own progress.

The Trace, trampled out for hundreds of years by migrating buffalo herds, was an easy road to follow and to ride. It was almost a highway—a wide, grassy, scrubby swath through the hardwood forest. Dickie had traveled it twice with George before the war's end, and several times since with detachments of militiamen. And now this was his first time alone, and he wished he had been more careful. A road like this was always watched, and he felt—he could not shake off the feeling—that whoever the watchers were along here right now, they were watching him. But the watchers, if there really were any, were invisible. He could not tell whether they were following him, or in ambush somewhere ahead of him, or in the gloomy thickets to right or left of the Trace.

He was in the valley where the forks of the Blue River met, and not far ahead of him, though he could not see them through the mist, he knew there lay a range of steep hills full of caves and sinking rivers. George had shown him several caves just off the Trace where a man might come in out of the rain, build a fire, even keep his horse in shelter with him. Dickie was thinking of one of these caves in particular, one whose mouth was protected by a natural parapet of earth and a thicket of trees that would hide from bypassers' eyes the glow of a fire built inside. He wanted to get to that cave tonight if he could because his clothes were wet and he was getting chilled, and if he was going to have to hole up in the vicinity of some unseen Trace-watchers, he wanted it to be in a place where he could defend himself.

So now he spurred his horse into a canter and prayed silently that if there were people stalking him, they were not between him and that cave.

THREE HOURS LATER, DICKIE WAS BEGINNING TO SMILE AT the fears he had been feeling earlier. He lay in his blanket upon a pile of dry leaves on the floor of the cave, stomach full of venison jerky and johnnycake, two swallows of rum from his canteen making his eyelids grow heavy as he gazed at the small flames licking the end of an oak chunk in the coals of his fire. Tethered in the mouth of the cave a few feet away stood his horse. The oak burned with very little smoke, and that smoke rose to the ceiling of the cave and flowed up and out through the cave mouth into the night, as well-draughted as in a flue. Dickie could hear the rain still hissing in the leafless woods outside and snugged down further into the blanket, his pistols by his hip, his head propped on his saddlebags, and he was glad he had come to this cave instead of trying to make a camp in the open somewhere. Compared with those cold, wet woods, this cave was a paradise.

That thought entertained his sleepy mind for a while. He thought of home in Caroline County, the big, snug, handsome stone house he had been born and raised in, the beds with their clean sheets and fluffy goose-down comforters, and wondered what his mother would feel if she knew he was as blissfully grateful for these comforts of a cave as he had ever known to be for those of the house. The thoughts of his home and his mother made him homesick now, gave him a pang of longing for the family.

They're all there but me, he thought. Even George is there. He could remember those years before the war when he himself had always been there and only George had always been missing, always out here on this side of the mountains. He rolled onto his back and watched the dying fire gleam on a trickle of moisture along a contour of the sooty, irregular ceiling of the cave. Farther back in the cave he could hear the tiny, echoing *ploip, ploip* of water dripping from the ceiling into a little pool. He tried not to think of the skeleton he had found back there. A human skeleton with a broken skull. That was one trouble with caves. They were such good places that every Indian and every renegade knew where they were. He tried not to think of this. He thought instead about how good it would be to see old George when he came back, and to hear the news of home. George had gone back for the purpose, among other purposes, of persuading the family to come out to Louisville town and settle on the beautiful lands he'd claimed for them, and Dickie was sure George would persuade them. George was some persuader.

Dickie remembered the night they had talked about making him an officer and about all the things they would have to do to hold the territory, and how true that had been, everything George had said. Dickie had been in several smart battles since he had joined George, and George had won them all, and had kept the territory together—all with virtually no help from the state. And Dickie had indeed become, as George had said he would, the travelingest lieutenant this side of the mountains.

Dickie was thinking these warm thoughts about George and the family when he went to sleep in the cave with rain falling outside in the dark.

He dreamed he heard a horse nicker, and it awakened him, and in the last small flare of the oak-wood fire he saw a devil-face shining above him. His heart slammed once in his chest and a cry mounted to his throat but before he could grab a pistol the face moved quickly and Dickie felt a blade come through the blanket and between his ribs, and he felt it go into the core of his life.

CHRISTMAS CAME. THE CLARKS ALL WALKED OUT TO THE oak grove to put a wreath of pine and holly and mistletoe on Johnny's grave, on the white wooden cross with his name on it. A stone was being carved, but it was not ready yet. Then they went back for their last Christmas feast in the big stone house. George had divided his tracts of land near the Falls of the Ohio and had deeded the ones on the south bank to his father and to Jonathan. John Clark's new farm in the West would be where the spring poured from the ground near a mulberry grove on a hill. Jonathan would set out with George and Bill after Christmas, when they left with their surveying party. He would take a work party of skilled Negroes and they would start next spring to build John and Ann Rogers Clark a fine two-story house of mulberry logs. George showed them a drawing of it that he and Uncle George Rogers had designed. When John Clark sold the Caroline County place here, they would come across the mountains and down the Ohio, and their new home would be waiting for them, on the richest piece of land George had ever seen. "And I've seen a lot of land in my days." There were thousands of people going every year to Kentucky now. And the Clarks would be the foremost family among them.

So now it was almost time to quit Virginia, and John Clark was as eager as a young man to go to the land his son had shown him a dozen years ago. The father was ready to follow in his son's footsteps.

AFTER CHRISTMAS, GEORGE RECEIVED SOME MAIL FROM Richmond. One letter agitated him visibly. His family watched him scowl as he read. The State of Virginia, it said, could not honor his request for payment of the vouchers he had signed out West, because there was no sign anywhere of the itemized accounts he claimed to have sent to the Auditor's Office in 1779. "By Heaven, I *did* send 'em," he hissed. "Dickie was there, he'll swear to it. By George Shannon with a strong guard I sent 'em, seventy packets full, and he brought me back their receipt! Well, we'll see this gets resolved! Many a good patriot out there's ruined, myself first, if some fool's lost those!" He remarked too that the letter ignored his request for his officer's pay for the duration of the war. Billy saw that George's hands were shaking.

The other letter was from Governor Jefferson, and this one restored his good humor. "Well, what o' this! They're talking at the capital about sending a party of exploration up the Missouri, to seek a water way to th' Pacific! Think o' that! And he asks would I like to lead it! Well, if I haven't dreamed o' *that* a thousand nights!" His eyes seemed to look through the walls and afar off. He was remembering a day at the Missouri's mouth, his hand in the swift water. Teresa.

"Pacific! The Western Sea?" Billy breathed, his own eyes full of blue distances. "May . . . Maybe I could go with'ee?"

George winked. "Maybe so, but don't load on your knapsack yetawhile. From what he says here, there's not much hope they

371

can raise a fund for it. It's another o' Tom's great daydreams. Like mine. By time it ever goes, I'll likely be too old and feeble."

"No, ye won't! Not ever! We'll go, George. I just *know* it!"

George squeezed Billy's shoulder with a gruff, fond chuckle. "Ah! Aha! I do believe," he told the family, "we've got us another Westerner here!"

BOOK TWO

1784–1799

22

CAROLINE COUNTY,
VIRGINIA
October 20, 1784

HEY SAT ON TRUNKS IN FRONT OF THE COLD FIREPLACE OF
e library, John Clark and his wife, and looked at each other.
he house echoed with distant footsteps and the voices of girls,
ith knocks and sounds of scooting. The light from the rain-
attered windows was pearl-gray.

He cleared his throat and the sound reverberated in the emp-
ness of the stripped room. "Eh, well, a cheery birthday to ye,
nnie," he said.

"Likewise to you, John. Cheery it is." She took a long breath
rough her nose, then sighed heavily, looking around the room.
le rectangles and ovals on the smoke-dulled walls marked
here pictures had hung for years.

The hair showing under the edge of her bonnet was as much
ver as red-gold now, but still as thick and wavy as that of a girl.
he rims of her eyelids were pink and moist, and the end of her
raight, narrow nose was ruddy. From the hallway now came
e sounds of the girl's voices and footsteps and rustling dresses as
ey went out the front door for the last time, and John Clark
w a great sadness in his wife's face at these sounds. He gave a
uick sigh then, and slapped his big, callused, blunt-fingered
and down on his thigh. "By Heaven, I do mean cheery!"

Her back stiffened slightly. "Aye, John. Cheery it is." But this
me she did smile. "A birthday is the start of a new life, isn't
at so?"

"Surely is in our case." He raised his eyebrows, which were
ick and black, sprinkled with white, and squinted one eye, and
e furrows down his cheeks deepened as he tried to smile, but
e smile went away and his black eyes gazed as if through the
all. His hair was almost white, thinning above his freckled fore-
ead, and a few white hairs had fallen on the shoulders of his
lack frock coat.

John Clark had long anticipated that this day of their depar-

ture for Kentucky would be a joyous and eager day, but th
house seemed full of ghosts. And he could not stop thinkin
about Dickie. And though neither he nor she had said anythin
about him for weeks, except in their private prayers, he was sur
she was thinking about Dickie too.

Door hinges squealed somewhere and footsteps came up th
hallway, hard heels on hardwood. John and Ann Rogers Clar
looked toward the door as if eager for someone to interrupt thi
awkward silence.

Edmund bustled into the room, tall, red-haired, sturdy, an
cheerful. He wore a coat of brown wool and leather legging
flecked with mud to the knees, and carried his three-cornere
hat in his left hand. He saw how morose his parents were. "Eh
No more o' this mopery on your birthdays, you two," h
boomed. "And on th' day you set out for Paradise! Well, every
thing's loaded but what ye be sittin' on. It's time." He extended
hand to his mother and she rose to stand, majestic as a queen
almost as tall as he was. John Clark put his hands on his knee
and stood up too, come to life at last.

"Cupid," he bellowed. The rangy servant appeared in th
doorway, his head tilted. "Give me a hand here, and be lively
We've got a thousand miles to go!" The Negro bent and graspe
one handle of a trunk, and John Clark grasped the other. The
lifted it from the floor and looked into each other's eyes for
moment, and each saw the glint of tears. Cupid had been in thi
house as many years as they had.

Edmund grabbed both handles of another trunk and hoisted i
onto his thighs. "Eddie," his mother said, "get York to help y
with that, ere y' split your gut." He ignored that, and staggere
out with the load, chanting:

"Fare ye well, Virginia, and hullo, Kentuck! Here come som
more Clarks!"

Three loaded wagons, roofed with tarpaulins stretched ove
ashwood hoops, stood in a row on the muddy driveway in fron
of the entrance. From under the canvas came the murmur an
laughter of the girls, who were making their nests amid the bag
gage, sheltering from the sifting cold rain. Saddle horses wer
tied behind the wagons. Mrs. Clark squinted against the rain a
she came out of the house, and passed a gaze around the bi
trees, which were still about half-clothed in autumn colors
Then she looked back at the house with its two rows of white
shuttered windows. "I will say I liked living in a stone house,
she said.

"Aye, Ma," grunted Edmund. He heaved the trunk onto th

ack of the second wagon and came around to help her up onto he front seat. "But there's many a stone house, and I daresay e'll be the rare lady who's got herself a grand house made o' nulberry logs, bright yellow mulberry wood. And it's a fine-built place, too. Jonathan cut no corners. George likes it so well he aid he might come live there with'ee."

"Huh! Fancy *him* settlin' down anyplace!" She was arranged n the hard seat now. York, big, pudgy, now fourteen, was on he seat beside her, importantly posed, holding the reins with ne hand, an umbrella in the other. He gave the umbrella to her nd she held it over her head, looking balefully at the waterdrops alling from its edge. "O' course it *would* rain on this day," she nuttered.

Now the last of the baggage had been lashed on, and most of he voices had fallen to mumbling.

"Well, what are we waitin' on now?" she demanded. John Clark, going forward to take the reins of the lead wagon, an-wered aside:

"For Cupid. Went back for some o' his things."

"Slow as ever," she sighed. She gave a rueful look at York, vho had never seen Mrs. Clark act so crotchety. "What in tarna-ion's he got, anyways, but what 'e can carry on 'is back?" The inswer came when Cupid emerged around the corner of the nouse. He was wearing three coats and apparently several layers of old clothes. Mrs. Clark suddenly laughed. "He *is* carryin' it all n his back!" Swaddled like a mummy, Cupid had some diffi-ulty clambering aboard the wagon, the girls laughing at his ex-rtions.

William suddenly appeared from somewhere, hatless, a shock of wet red hair sticking to his forehead, yelling, "Ready? Ready! 'm set to go to Kentuck!" He grabbed York by his coat and pulled him down off the driver's seat, vaulting into his place and snatching the reins.

"Eh, Master Billy," York whined up from the driveway, "I wan' to drav."

"Soon enough," said William. He was fourteen now, but al-ready taller than his father. "But on a big start-out like this'n, got o be a Clark man drivin' every wagon, don't y'see?"

York made a toad mouth and bulged his eyes. "Thowt I *was* a Clark man." Then he shrugged and went back to hoist himself over the tailgate.

"*Gee-ya!*" came John Clark's voice from the lead wagon, and t began rolling forward.

"*Gee-ya!*" William whooped, flicking the reins, and the second wagon lurched away from the house.

"*Gee-yah!*" Edmund's voice bellowed behind, and the third wagon came along.

The convoy rattled off among the rain-dripping trees, and one by one the Clarks looked back at the big stone house where the family had lived for a quarter of a century.

The creaking wagons were not two hundred yards from the empty house before Ann Rogers Clark called out:

"John, stop here!"

"Ah, sure, Annie. I was stoppin'."

The three wagons came to a halt. Faces began peering out from under the canopies. Mrs. Clark was clutching her skirts and climbing down the wheel to the ground. "Everybody out," she commanded, and made her way onto a graveled path that led among the massive trunks of an oak grove, and in a moment everybody, men, girls, and slaves, had got off the wagons to follow her. John Clark caught up with her and walked beside her with his right hand at the small of her back. Raindrops dribbled off the oak leaves. She led the procession to the small glade where scythed grass lay wet and yellow. In the middle of the glade stood a new, small slab of granite, on which was chiseled:

CAPT. JOHN CLARK IV
15 September 1757–29 October 1783
Died of
Man's Inhumanity to Man

The family and servants formed a semicircle in front of the stone while the fine rain dampened their heads and shoulders. When Mrs. Clark saw that all heads were bowed, she stuck her elbow in her husband's ribs. He cleared his throat.

"Our Almighty Father, look upon us with favor as we make this last visit—like as not it'll be our last visit—with our beloved son and yours, Johnny Clark, who ought to be with us now in the glory of his youth as we set out for the Kentuck."

He paused. Several pairs of eyes peeped at him to see if he had finished already, but he continued.

"We ask Thee also, our Almighty Father and Supreme Director of All Things, to protect his brother Richard, whose whereabouts in that wilderness You only know. But if Ye've already gathered him unto your bosom, where Ye hold this beloved Johnny Clark, then may our two fine sons walk the gilded streets of Thy Kingdom arm in arm, and may they forget the worldly

378

trife that flung 'em untimely to You. And may they remember
us, who remember them every day without exception."

He paused, his breath whistling slightly in his nostrils, then
said, "Amen."

Fanny pulled a branch with oak leaves and acorns from a low
limb and placed the cluster on the grave as they left.

For years during the war they had had to live overshadowed by
the unknown fate of Johnny. Now they knew where Johnny was.
But months ago Dickie had vanished somewhere along the wilderness trace between Vincennes and the fort at the Falls, and
nothing had been heard of him since, and now that mystery
hung over the family, like these heavy gray rainclouds, dampening the joy of their departure to the new land.

THE WHEEL RUTS OF THE ROADS WERE FILLED WITH A SOUP
of red-clay mud. It balled up on the horses' hooves and clogged
the wagon wheels and sucked at the boots of anyone who stepped
down into it to put a shoulder to a mired wagon. The mud was
slick as grease and sticky as glue at the same time. Gobs of it
would slither down the back of a slow-turning wheel and fall
with a *flob, flob* sound back into the ruts, to be picked up again
by the next passing wheel. The horses were caked with muck to
their shoulders, and balls of it clung like berries to the hairs of
their long tails. The men had mud smears up to their lapels,
even on their hat brims, because of their struggles with wheels
and horses and harness.

They made only fifteen miles the first day, slowed by mud,
and by neighbors who came down to the road to say farewell. As
the evening grew gray, they reached a familiar zigzag fence of
split rails and soon turned up the road to the home of George
Rogers. Quarters had already been created for the mud-caked
travelers, in Joe's empty room and the upstairs ballroom, and the
servants were bedded in the old slave quarters where Governor
Hamilton and his fellow prisoners had been kept, so long ago.
Johnny Rogers was here, handsome, and still unmarried, helping his father run the plantation and his building trade.

George Rogers was sixty-two now, totally white-headed but
still ruddy-faced and vigorous. In candlelight at the late meal he
mentioned, in his grace, his nephew Dickie, asking for his
safety, and there was no doubt in anyone's mind that George
Rogers was remembering the years when his son Joseph's fate
had been just such a mystery. Both of them had been lost by
following George's dream, but George Rogers did not say that.
Even after all that had happened, George was still his favorite

nephew. That Joe had died in his arms, reunited at last with his own race, had made that bond of uncle and nephew even more profound.

A celebration of John and Ann Rogers Clark's birthdays was observed at the meal. He was sixty and she was fifty. George Rogers talked wistfully with her for a while about the mischiefs of their childhood, and though the Clark girls were heavy-lidded from the strain of the day's travel, they came very much to life, as children do when treated to anecdotes of a parent's youthful aberrations. "Why!" George Rogers exclaimed in mock astonishment, "d'you mean to say, Sister, that you've never told them that you were a mite shy o' being an angel?"

"I was some'at closer to that ideal than *you* were, Brother George, and I'll remind ye that when you point a finger at another, you're pointing three at yourself. Go on any more and I might be compelled to reveal what I know about a certain blazing barn." And now his own sons and daughters gaped at *him*.

George Rogers puckered his mouth, and after a while he said, "It grieves me to see ye go so far away to live, Sister. But seeing what sland'rous memoirs my sons and daughters might ha' been exposed to, I reckon seven hundred miles might be just about comfortable."

And they embraced each other, laughing with tears in their eyes.

THEY HAD HARNESSED THE WAGON TEAMS AND WERE ON the road by dawn. The rain had continued throughout the night, soaking the countryside. The road now was like a creek of clay soup. The air was chillier; breath condensed visibly.

York drove the second wagon this morning. Young William had saddled his bay and he ranged around like a scout, advising of the condition of the road ahead, which was always bad, and dismounting frequently to help pry a swamped wagon out of a rut or a fast-running ford. He had lost another hat, and his red hair was lank with rain.

They passed through Fredericksburg and crossed the Rappahannock early in the afternoon, stopping for nothing, as they intended to reach Gunston Hall by evening if they could possibly make the distance. They had written ahead to old George Mason about their departure for the West, and he had sent an express back down, inviting them to lay over at Gunston Hall at least one night. He had greetings and messages, he said, for George.

Above Fredericksburg they found the road much improved, some of it having been topped with gravel, some of it with logs.

Late afternoon found them in Prince William County. John Clark hailed his son. "Billy, ride on ahead and announce us to Colonel Mason, so's we'll not surprise the good gent. Here. Take my pistols."

William looked as if nothing could please him more than to run afoul of some highwayman who'd test his mettle. But as he started to gallop ahead, his mother called him. He wheeled and came back. "Billy," she said, "ha' ye not a lick o' sense? Put on a hat, and by heaven, don't you lose this'n."

Momentarily a boy again, he went back among the wagons and emerged with his prize fur cap on his head. It was one he'd made himself from a muskrat he'd trapped.

"All right, then," she said. "I know that's one ye'll not lose. Y're off now, and Godspeed."

He thundered away, his horse's hoofs flinging mud, and vanished into the woods ahead. He was a man again.

THE WAGONS ROLLED UP THE DRIVEWAY OF GUNSTON HALL in twilight, between giant elms and stretches of level, cropped lawn. Here was the field where George had run and jumped and ridden and won wrestling and foot-racing medals in those carefree days before the war. Under each tree lay a carpet of yellow leaves. Light glowed in the downstairs windows. The house was of brick with four tall chimneys, one of the finest mansions on the Potomac. It was cozy with firelight and candles inside. George Mason, portly and round-faced, sat in the embrace of a scarlet, wing-backed Chippendale chair with his foot up on a gout stool. He groaned and his breath wheezed whenever he reached to shake a hand, but he was cheerful and his eyes twinkled as he apologized for being unable to rise. John Clark sat in a black leather armchair across the hearth from Mr. Mason; Edmund sat reverently next to the oak writing table upon which, he knew, Mason had composed the Virginia Declaration of Rights and the Virginia Constitution. Colonel Mason had come to be known as "the pen of the Revolution."

"Your son William," Mason said warmly. "I see George stamped all over him. Such a vigor! An Olympian, that George!"

"Billy's made right on his pattern," agreed John Clark. "A bit more amiable, perhaps, without that temper George had."

"No better a scholar, though," Edmund remarked, winking at William. A chuckle went around the room. William grinned. Any comparison was fine with him.

"Well, there are kinds of scholars," said Mason. "Some who

381

can prove beyond question how a ghost might pass through a needle's eye, others who understand our present world and know how to make things work in it. George was that latter kind. It matters not that he doesn't spell a word twice the same way; he makes words move men, and farther than they've ever moved before, at that." John Clark was beaming at this tribute to his son from the great Virginian.

"But even more," Mason went on, "eloquence by deed. No man I know of, nay, even Washington, ever made a finer example for men to copy." He paused then and looked thoughtfully, rather sadly, at John Clark, but said nothing more for the moment.

After dinner, George Mason made a present to the Clark family of a fine inlaid backgammon board. And, while Mrs. Clark and her children hovered over it and began playing on it against each other, the host got himself and John Clark off into the library for a glass of brandy, pipes, and a few confidential words. John Clark could see that a matter of some delicacy was about to be broached, as Mason was grave and awkward. At last a question came forth.

"Tell me. Does your son George, ah, like liquor?"

At first John Clark presumed that Mason was merely thinking of sending George, perhaps, a keg of good brandy as a gift. "Why," he replied, "I don't know many a Virginian who doesn't. Look at ourselves." He raised his glass and smiled, adding, "And from what I've heard, there are even fewer Kentuckians who don't."

"But I mean to say, sir, is he, ah, temperate?"

"Why, I daresay as temperate as either of us, sir. Why do you ask me that?"

Mason shifted heavily in the chair and gazed into the fire as he replied.

"Sir, as you must know, seats of government are like laundry rooms, for rumor and gossip. And political men are worse than laundresses. If one must absent himself from a room, he may be certain that he will be the subject of calumny from the moment the door closes behind him. Your son George, as you know, is an important man who, being beyond the mountains, is forever out of the room, so to speak."

John Clark flushed with indignation. "By heaven! Who dares? Why, praise is all I hear of 'im!"

"Yes, yes. Yes. But you, sir, do not frequent the seat of government, where every utterance is calculated not to express truth but to advance him who utters it."

John Clark's lips were thin and hard. "Then mayhaps I *should* frequent the seat of government now and then, and grab someone by the scruff when I overhear a lie. Come, now, Dr. Mason. I sh'd like to know who 'tis that says such things." His voice had been rising, and George Mason made a calming motion with one hand, glancing toward the library door, beyond which the Clarks could be heard at their cheerful game.

"Sir, I'd not name names, for I don't like to create enmities. I'll only say this, that the rumor first appeared in the war's last days. You'll recall there were some militia expeditions from eastern Kentucky that were very ill-conducted."

"Blue Licks?"

"Aye, among others. Well, sir, my guess was that certain county officers, wanting to make it seem George's fault—"

"But he was a hundred miles from Blue Licks at the time of that debacle!"

"Nevertheless. Governor Harrison chose to believe certain persons, who insinuated George was incapable because of the habit."

"He has no such habit! And the governor *believed* that?"

"Eventually—belatedly—he investigated and found out it wasn't so."

John Clark was almost grinding his teeth. "George *saved* that country! He shouldn't have an enemy in it!"

"You don't know how small men can become until you give them a political place. Now that the Kentucky land is divided into three counties, there are factions, you know. Lincoln and Fayette counties feel they give more than their due share of men and provision for protecting the country. They resent it that Jefferson County needs more protecting. And George, of course, bases himself in Jefferson County."

"If these be county lieutenants you speak of, then the snake I smell in the brushpile is Arthur Campbell. Long Jaw. I know how he and George are about each other."

Mason shrugged. "As I say, I speak no names. I just hope George understands that he does have jealous enemies. And rumors of that sort are never quite forgotten. I am as solicitous of your son's reputation perhaps as you are. Any time I hear such an allegation, you may be sure, I say what I can to scotch it."

THE MUD OF THE ROAD HAD FROZEN. THE WAGON WHEELS, which had been sinking out of sight at the start of the journey, now banged and creaked and threatened to break as the vehicles lurched through the deep, rock-hard wheel ruts. The girls wailed as trunks and bundles slid and toppled against them, had to be righted, then tumbled again.

The sleet had turned to a fine, stinging snow as they had entered the Allegheny foothills two days ago; it blew in swirls over the new-fallen brown leaves in the mountainside forests, and in one end and out the other of the wagon canopies. The girls were wrapped in blankets like Indians. Noses grew red and feet numb. Cold-stiffened fingers were painfully stove against hard falling objects time and again. "Eddie," called Fanny, "can't we just stop at somebody's house and wait for better weather?"

"Nay, little sister," he called over his shoulder. "Winter won't wait. Got to cross this pass ere it's snowed shut. And get down the Monongahela ere she freezes over. Winter won't wait, sister, even for us!"

The blizzard hit them just as they reached the top of the pass and started easing down the westering road toward the Monongahela. One minute they were looking at the iron-gray, snowless mountains rising into the overcast on either side of them; the next minute everything was blanked by a whirling white veil of driven snow.

"Whoa up!" John Clark roared back to the other wagons, and hauled back on the reins. In a moment William appeared on the ground beside him, squinting. There were snowflakes sticking to his fur hat and his eyelashes.

"Hey, Pa! I like t' drove plumb into th' back o' your wagon! All's I could see o' my own team was their rumps!" He was shouting into the gale. If he was worried, he was hiding it behind a happy mask.

Edmund materialized out of the whiteness. His head was bent forward and he was holding his hat on as he came up. "I doubt we'll outrun this winter, after all!" he shouted.

"Shelter," John Clark yelled. His hat blew off his head and tumbled back into the wagon, where some quick black hand caught it. "Know of any shelter close by?"

"Empty cabin, but it's a good mile down," Edmund yelled. "Can we get there?"

"Grace o' God! Only if these wagons don't slide off th' mountain! Only if we can see it when we reach it!" Edmund sounded very worried. He had been through this pass before, going to and from the frontier, but never before in a snowgale, burdened with his loved ones and all their belongings.

"Dast we stay here?" John Clark shouted into the wind.

"May have no choice," Edmund cried. "But I fear we'd perish sure. I . . . I maybe could go down, look for that cabin, mark a way . . ." He sounded dubious. And his father was faltering, in the face of the two apparently hopeless choices. "It's sure we can't turn around, Lord help us."

John Clark would always get around to bringing in the Lord when things were tight, but not usually so quickly. Young William noticed this. And he noticed that anxious female voices were coming from back in the wagons and the snow was deepening while the two older men hesitated. He was the youngest male Clark and he fully respected his father and brothers. But sometimes, it seemed to him, he saw certainties quicker than most grown men did.

"I say this," he spoke up, wrinkling his freckled nose and trying to blink snowflakes out of his lashes. "I sure wouldn't split up the family in a blind place like this!" They looked at him, as if eager for advice even from a boy. He pointed to the lead horse of his father's team. "I'm good with Flag there. I'll walk and lead. I can keep the road, on foot. And cabins aren't all that hard t' find, either. How say 'ee, we stay in a bunch and go ahead down?"

They had nothing better to advise; the boy found himself in charge. He grasped Flag's bridle and started, straining to see into the whirling whiteness. York drove the second wagon. William let his feet do the ground-seeing that his eyes couldn't. When his one leg or the other would plunge down thigh-deep into the snow, chances were good that he had stepped into one of the wheel ruts and was still on the road. A few seconds' groping would confirm that.

And thus, a cautious and suspenseful yard at a time, with twilight turning the white to gray, voices calling questions or encouragements through the blindness, the three wagons came down from the top of the pass. And before nightfall, William sensed, more than saw, a squarish form off to his left.

They had crept four hours since the blizzard started. But without a mishap, William had brought them to the cabin.

WIND WAILED AROUND THE EAVES. THE WALLS OF THE abandoned cabin had large gaps where chinking had fallen out but these gaps had been stuffed with anything available—extra clothing, shoes and hats, leaves and straw raked up from the cabin floor—and baggage had been stacked around the walls almost to the ceiling, so the cabin was snug. The entire floor was covered by people rolled in blankets and quilts, snoring, sometimes turning over with groans of discomfort. It was some indefinite hour after midnight, and Ann Rogers Clark had been awakened by the aches in her right hip and shoulder. Slowly, to avoid disturbing her husband, she eased herself over onto her left side. John stirred slightly and snorted but did not wake up.

At the end of the cabin, the ceiling was yellow with light from the hearth fire. She could smell woodsmoke and tobacco.

She saw one figure sitting up by the fire. It was William, smoking a pipe, staring into the blaze, his profile limned with yellow light.

Ann Rogers Clark looked at her youngest son and wondered what their plight might have been by now if he had not done what he did in the blizzard.

All froze to death, we'd be, as like as not, she thought. Or rolled down the mountain.

She watched William turn his face away from the fire and look in her direction, at all the sleeping people, the people of his family and their Negroes. She couldn't see his face now that it was turned toward the darkness, but she could see the firelight outlining his red hair, and it could have been George some eighteen years ago when he was that age. William looked into the darkness for a minute or two, not knowing his mother was looking at him and thinking these things about him. Then he bent down and she heard him beating the dottle out of his pipe, and then she saw him stand up. She watched him swing a cloak over his shoulders and put on his fur cap and move silently as an Indian to the door. There was a momentary rise in the noise of the wind, and an eddy of cold air.

She was back to sleep when he came in from checking the horses.

TWO FEET OF SNOW LAY ON THE MOUNTAINSIDES FOR three days after the blizzard had passed, and the Clarks had no choice but to remain in the cabin until a melt. They were well provisioned and wanted nothing but space. There were fifteen people, including the Negroes, and the cabin was no more than twenty feet square. The air was close and odorous and full of "excuse mes" whenever anyone moved. Elizabeth and Fanny and Lucy crowded in a corner, playing backgammon or reading. There were bags of wheat and barley and corn, and a steel grain grinder, so Old Rose could bake fresh bread. There was salt pork from a small keg. There were turnips. On the second day Edmund and William went out in separate directions and each killed a deer. William spent much of his time outdoors, roaming the heights and the steepnesses with York. The young Negro was strong but rotund, and was forever panting and calling after his master to slow down please.

William knew almost every living thing in the wilds and had been trying for years, diligently but without much success, to teach York to identify useful trees and plants.

"Name me that one, York," he'd say, standing in knee-deep snow and pointing.

"Mast' Billy," York would say plaintively, "I can't tell 'em without they leaves, I told you that already."

"Ye can't tell 'em *with* their leaves, either. It's 'cause you don't pay any attention to anything 'cept what's eatable."

York could only grin, because that was true.

"Grin, y' old pork barrel!" William would say, trying not to laugh. "But someday, y'll find youself out someplace where there's *nothin'* eatable 'less you know what it is. Or else with your appetite y'll pick up somethin' poison. And then y'll lay there on the ground a-huggin' that big belly and screaming, and *then* by heaven you'll wish you'd paid attention to me."

York would stick out his lower lip in a pout. "I don't wanta go places where they's nothin' to eat!"

"Well, hey, now, if you want t' be my man, y'll be goin' places y' never even heard of. Y'do wanta be my man, don't ye?"

"Sure do, Mast' Billy."

"Well, I want you to be, too. So now," he'd say, pointing again to the shrub or tree in question, "try t' think, and name me that."

"I just can't tell 'em without they leaves on, Mast' Billy."

And at that, William would yowl with mock fury and jump on York like a panther, and a great, whooping, bone-creaking, snow-flinging wrestling match would ensue, with the quick, sinewy red-head pinning the stronger York deep down in the trampled snow.

A WARMER WIND CAME OUT OF THE SOUTHWEST AND THE snow vanished in hours, allowing the party to leave their cabin in the mountain pass and move on.

The frozen road thawed almost as fast, and the ruts were soon filled with melt water. Again the wagons were hub-deep in mud and brown water, and the men were wading in the icy muck again, hauling at spokes.

At midafternoon, Edmund's feet slid back out from under him as he strained with his shoulder at a wheel, and he fell full-length into a runny stew of muddy water, clods, and soggy leaves. Rising, he had mud over his entire face and body; gobs dribbled from his fists, which were clenched at his sides. He spat muddy water away from his lips and blinked it out of his eyes and lamented loudly:

"This is damn low living for a former captain of the by God Continental Army!"

William gasped with laughter and continued to strain at the back of the wagon. "Hell's fire, Cap'n," he snorted. "This is easy goin' today. All downhill."

After two days of such effort, they reached Fort Cumberland, a shabby and overcrowded little outpost guarding the mountain passes. It was garrisoned by a small force of militiamen and three officers. It was but a token fort now, with no war going on, and stood only as a refuge from Indian raids for settlers in the vicinity. But it seemed more like a warren of drifters and adventurers, of frontiersmen and fur trappers traveling east and land-seekers and speculators going west. The Clark girls were bewildered and even frightened by the near-savage appearance of some of the backwoods dwellers. There were men dressed more like Indians than white men. There were brutish, scarred men missing an eye or an ear, and one whose nose had been bitten off by something or someone; there were louts who reeked of whiskey from morning to night; there were steely-eyed long hunters with greasy hair and skin, wearing clothes so stiff with blood and filth and so smoke-blackened that they looked like iron. There was a huge, crazy-eyed woman, survivor of some Indian raid, whose face from the cheekbones down was flecked with embedded black gunpowder; there were two brassy wenches smelling like dead fish and constantly scratching, who seemed to belong to nobody or anybody in the fort.

Living conditions in the fort were scarcely better than in the little cabin, but the Clarks were treated to every kindness the garrison could afford. Among the raffish sojourners here, it happened that there were several who had served under George, and these tended to grow teary-eyed with nostalgia when they sat and told about the high point of their lives, which had been the wonderful victory over General Hamilton in '79. It was almost impossible to believe that men of such appearance could have been heroes, but anyone who had been a part of that campaign was acknowledged to be one.

Edmund drifted close to a heated discussion near the fort's stables. There were three lean men in buckskins, and a stocky man in a dark green velvet jackcoat standing unheeding of the ankle-deep mud in the compound, all waxing derisive about "the dang Spaniards," and their blockade of commercial traffic on the lower Mississippi. Edmund had heard it much discussed while he had been in Louisville working on his parents' new home. It was said to be strangling Kentucky.

The stout man, Edmund soon learned, was a shipper of lumber, tobacco, flour, and other produce from the burgeoning Kentucky settlements. The other three were trappers.

"I can't eat furs," said one of these. "I can eat what was inside of 'em. But pelts stackin' up with no place to go, why, that's not goin' to buy me no gear. And I tell ye, this is the last time I take the trouble to haul anythin' *up* th' God-damned Ohio River. I want to go *down* the Mississippi. I wonder, do them bright gents in th' government yonder know rivers run easier downstream?"

"They might know," growled the shipper. "But as for carin', why, they don't seem to at all. I went to ever'body I ever heard of, an' talked till my feet sweat, but most I got was a 'Hum, now, that is a pity indeed.' What I ain't sure they know is whether there *be* a Mis'ipp' out there, nemmine whether she runs uphill or down."

"Y'know my feelin's," grumbled another of the fur traders. "A guv'ment that don't know y' exist ain't your guv'ment atall. I say Kentuck ought t' break off an' be its own country, and go down and deal with Spaniards our own way." He raised his clenched fist. "You, sir," he said to Edmund. "Y'seem to have an interest. Pray, what's your stance on it?"

"No stance," replied Edmund, "as I'm from Virginia, not Kentuck. I listen to learn, by y'r leave."

"Hm," the man said, nodding. "Then learn this: my stance as I say is make our own country. Then send General Clark down with an army o' Kentuckians to pluck the tailfeathers out o' that Spaniard governor."

Edmund drew a corner of his mouth back and sucked an eye-tooth. "Clark, y' say?"

"The very man. I went with 'im agin the Shawnees, both in '80 and '82, and he's a man could open New Orleans up real wide. Y'know of 'im, bein' a Virginian, I'd reckon."

"I'll admit," Edmund answered after a moment, "I have heard considerable about the man lately."

WHEN THE CLARKS SET OUT FROM FORT CUMBERLAND for the Red Stone Fort on the Monongahela River the next morning, they had an uninvited escort. Five mounted men, with two packhorses, were waiting at the gate. Their leader apparently was the trader in the green coat. He sat his horse, the early sunlight of a fair, cold day harshly illuminating the stubble and oiliness of his fat jowls and the boils above his collar. The four men with him held long rifles across their pommels. One of them was the man with the bitten-off nose. "Oh Lordy me," Lucy moaned to her mother. "I'd hoped never to have my eyes fall on that pig-snout again. It gives me shivers."

"Rather picked him up than what I did pick up," Mrs. Clark said, discreetly scratching at a part of her lower body.

"You too, Ma?" whispered Elizabeth, whose own fingernails were chasing a newly acquired louse through her armpit.

The trader rode close to Edmund and extended his hand. "Forgive me not knowin' ye yesterday, Cap'n Clark. My name's Greathouse. Ye might like some company down to Red Stone?"

Greathouse, Edmund thought, and he wondered whether this was one of the Greathouses George had spoken of, who had murdered the family of the Mingo chief Logan a decade ago, thus setting off Dunmore's War. "You're welcome to go along with us," he said reluctantly, "though I fear our wagons'll slow ye down some."

It was customary for groups to enforce each other as they entered the Indian country. Still, Edmund whispered to his father and William to keep their eyes open for any sign of treachery.

So they started southwestward down the long valleys toward the Monongahela under a clear November sky. It was their easiest going yet. Greathouse's men tended to ride as a group in the advance, while the trader himself stayed close by.

As for the women, they were glad that the pig-snout man was far ahead and facing the other way.

"Y're going to the Falls of Ohio, then, I presume," said Greathouse, riding alongside the wagon Edmund was driving.

"Ye presume right."

"I might be of service then. I have boats for hire at Red Stone. Roomy and sound. Ask anyone. And not costly, as ye'd be ridin' down with paid freight."

They discussed fares and the Clarks found them reasonable; an agreement was made.

"I've a cousin served with y'r brother," Greathouse said after a while.

"Do ye, now."

"Aye. At the battle of Vincennes. He never stops talkin' of it."

"M-hm." Edmund was beginning to envy those who had been on that campaign, despite their sufferings. It must have been a tidier and more satisfying war than the one he'd been in. He remembered mainly the endless and aimless marching of huge bodies of blue-coated Continentals from place to place, and the helpless burrowing from bombshells at Charleston, and the sadness of defeat.

"Have y'ever heard of a General Wilkinson, sir?" Greathouse asked.

Edmund had; he searched his memory. "Clothier-General, asn't he?" Edmund vaguely remembered some scandal. Dis-iissal for neglect of duty or something.

"Aye. Him," said Greathouse. "Well, he came through here not ong ago. Downriver someplace now, maybe at Louisville."

"Well, that's interesting," Edmund said after a while, "but how oes that concern me, may I ask?"

"In that he's reputed for venality and uncommon ambition, here he goes, folks want to watch out. Especially folks of posi-on."

Edmund studied the trader from the corner of his eye and ondered what ax he had to grind.

"I only hope General Clark will be wary, sir," Greathouse said nally.

Edmund felt a sudden surge of appreciation. He smiled at Great-ouse. "Brother George is the wariest o' men," he said. "And I ankee for y'r good counsel."

With the road so fine and the sky so fair, they made a third of the istance down to the Monongahela before dark. Greathouse's riders ad selected a campsite in a cliff cave and built a fire by the time the vagons arrived. The cave was the size of a ballroom. Its smoky walls lowed it had been long used as a shelter.

The Clarks and the Greathouse party contributed to the dinner ible—though there was no table—and a fine dinner of pone, enison, bean soup, and apple jam was served. The Clark women ied not to look at the noseless man during the meal, as he was a articularly unappetizing sight with his face lit from below by a onfire. For a man who evidently was some extraordinary brawler, lowever, he had a shy and soft-spoken demeanor. And when Greathouse coaxed him to go get his fiddle and start playing reels, e quickly became as pleasant a companion as any man. Great-ouse's men stomped and capered through a pair of jigs, whoop-ng and flapping their elbows with more vigor than grace. When he fiddler changed to reels, the young Clark ladies began getting ip to dance, paired first with their brothers, then with the strang-rs. A dark jug had appeared sometime, from somewhere, and the iddler played "Betsy Kiss My Lips" as it was passed from one man o the next. The Negroes looked on in delight. York eventually eaped up and began capering near the fire, his huge body bend-ng and straightening in motions totally unlike what the others vere dancing, but he was so animated that eventually everyone lse stopped for a while to watch him.

The high point of the evening came when William, flushed vith good spirits—his own and those he had drunk—at last persuaded his mother to get up and take a few turns around the cave with him. She grumbled and protested a great deal at first, saying: "I don't know how t' dance; I been busy havin' you ten babies since I was fifteen!" But she soon was whirling so prettily that old John Clark was stirred into action, and got up and danced her around and around the fire, the two of them looking at each other, eyes alight with long memories.

And Lucy thought she heard her mother say, in the dark after midnight when the cave was full of snores:

"Remember, John. We agreed. Ten's enough."

WHEN THEY SAW THE OLD RED STONE FORT TWO MORNings later, it stood glowing, almost brick color in weak morning sunlight against a backdrop of frost-white, leafless trees. The frozen road sparkled with frost. The morning was stinging cold. A horizontal curtain of woodsmoke from the fort and nearby houses hung a few feet over the low bluff on which the fort was built, next to the mouth of Red Stone Creek. Above the settlement rose a massive silver-blue mountain; below the bluff curved the slate-gray Monongahela, which was to be the start of their long water road down to their new Kentucky home. Along the river there were mooring posts, and two wharfs of plank and pilings, and a windowless row of Ohio Company log warehouses. There seemed to be more boats along the riverbank than houses in the town: blunt-ended flatboats with shanties built on them, featureless barges lying low in the water, scows and skiffs, and one row-galley with a mast and boom. There were windlasses and winches. Bark and wood-chips littered the ground of a boat-building yard.

But there were no vessels coming or going out on the river. Greathouse frowned as he rode, wrapped to the nose in a muffler, and studied the river. It was a still, gray sheet of ice.

"Damnation," Greathouse mumbled. "May have to lay here till a thaw, Mister Clark, sorry t' say."

The Clark convoy started up toward the town to inquire about lodging while Greathouse went down to look his boats over for ice damage and to talk with rivermen about the freeze.

"Hey, Pa," Edmund called. "What say'ee nobody mentions Brother George here? I'm 'bout honored out. All in favor say 'aye'!"

Several voices from within the wagons called "Aye." But Mrs. Clark added:

"'Less we need somethin'."

The early freeze-up of the river had bottled up westward trafc, and the town was full of transients and rivermen. It appeared hat no lodgings would be found, and that the Clarks would have o live in their wagons for as many days as they might be here. Or maybe Mr. Greathouse will let us live aboard a flatboat," ohn Clark said.

"Nonsense," said Mrs. Clark. She threw off the blanket in which she had been wrapped, climbed down from the wagon eat, and went into the public house. There she told the pub- can that she was the mother of George Rogers Clark.

In less than an hour all the Clark party was quartered in the an and in private homes around the town.

"I WAS HERE IN '78," SAID THE INNKEEPER, POINTING HIS ipestem at John Clark across the table, "when that boy o' your'n as here tryin' to recruit his army. And never in my days have I eed Fate so stubborn against a man. Every single day I expected o see that lad just give up and go home." The innkeeper had a reasy-looking head of graying auburn hair and a narrow, stub- ly, undershot chin that canted to the right as if it had been nocked off center. He set the stem back between his teeth with click, puffed, and went on: "But he had a way with people, nd he could get the unlikeliest scoundrels all het up about doin' reat sarvice. I'll say this, things were mighty quiet around here or a while after he'd left, as 'e'd signed on and took with 'im nost every tavern-wreckin', eye-gougin', horse-stealin', bear- apin' outlaw and general ring-tailed roarer from the whole ountryside. I remember tellin' 'im, 'Colonel Clark, sir, y've got 'rself as felonious an army there as ever walked, and they'll fair hew up y'r enemies and spit out their bones, if they don't do th' ame to you first.'"

HAVING BEEN ICE-LOCKED FOR A WEEK IN RED STONE SET- lement with their boats and cargoes, some of the rivermen were estless and unpleasant. At night they could be heard going roar- ng drunk up and down the street of the little town, breaking mptied jugs, kicking dogs, cursing each other with jovial famil- arity or acid belligerence, and sometimes kicking each other if here were no dogs within reach. As a breed, these rivermen eemed to fight more with their feet than with their hands.

"Wonder why that is," John Clark mused to Edmund one fternoon as they sat drinking rum near the door of the public iouse. Outside, two big riverboatmen were trying diligently to crush each other's private parts with spectacular, grunting kicks.

"I reckon," Edmund observed, "it's 'cause they won't la' down their jugs long enough to free up their hands."

That evening, though, in the dining room, a pair of burl' flatboat pilots did show that their feet were not their only weap ons. John Clark and his sons were sitting with Greathouse over a supper of venison stew, when the door leading down the guest room corridor burst inward, torn off its hinges and splintered and with it came the two pilots, locked together in a stamping scuffling, careening embrace and emitting a double-voiced snar that made them look and sound like some two-headed, four footed beast trying simultaneously to tear off its own limbs and dance itself to death.

This apparition reeled across the room until it struck the end of the Clarks' table and fell upon it, smashing crockery and sloshing venison stew in every direction.

And then the diners, sitting aghast and dripping stew, watched one pilot bite off the other's underlip with bloody, seesawing teeth while his victim broke all the fingers of the biter's left hand.

"Of such," said the innkeeper after the brawlers had been clubbed unconscious and repaired with splints and bandages. "was a considerable part of your son's army made, Mister Clark. Less wonder 'e caught th' British, eh?"

John Clark wiped stew off his weskit, gazed at the wrecked, blood-spattered table, and shook his head.

"Or else *more* wonder," he replied.

ANN ROGERS CLARK WAS AWAKENED IN DARKNESS BY DIS tant shouting and running feet. Fanny was snuggling close to her in fright, and Mrs. Clark for a moment could not remember where she was. The bed was musty and the corn shucks of the mattress rustled under her. It had been ages since she had slept on corn shucks, and it seemed as if years had fallen away and she was a young woman back in Albemarle County. Then she re membered: Red Stone.

Under the voices there was a strange, deep, shuddering, grind ing sound, so faint at first that only gradually did she become aware of it.

"I'm scared, Ma. What is it?"

"Maybe just a little earthquake, Fanny girl. Nothing to be scared by." She hugged Fanny and patted her shoulder. If it was an earthquake, it was doing little quaking.

She saw a line of lamplight under the door and heard the board floor creak somewhere. The people of the house were get ting up. Good. "Stay here, darlin'. I'll go see."

She slipped out from under the quilts into the icy air and, shivering, groped with her feet to find her slippers. She drew a woolen robe on over her nightdress, patted her cheeks to give them color, and made her way to the door of the bedchamber and opened it. Mr. and Mrs. Howell, her hosts, were up. He was pulling on a cloak in the lamplight and she was laying new wood in the fireplace. Mr. Howell smiled.

"Good news for ye, Ma'm. Th' ice is a-breakin' up."

THE THAW WAS NOT ALL GOOD NEWS TO GREATHOUSE AND the other boatmen. Slabs of drifting ice during the night had jammed against pilings and moored boats. Dawn's light revealed jagged, shifting mass of pan ice stacking itself three and four feet high among the vessels, grinding and shuddering in the river current. Some of the big flatboats were being tilted up as the ice shoved heavily under them; others lay hull-down in the ice, being slowly squeezed until their seams gaped and popped. Two large freight boats, one of them belonging to Greathouse, were becoming keel-hogged as the ice jam wedged under them and lifted their bows.

Through the morning of a gray-warm November day, scores of boatmen swarmed over the boats and the dangerously slippery ice, wielding axes and pikes, prying and hacking at the blue-green ice, rigging tackle and windlasses with desperate ingenuity to pull boats this way and that, shouting curses and warnings with the same ferocity they had given to their drunken binges in the past week. As if this were but another kind of brawl, the rivermen kept themselves fired up on jugged fuel while they worked, and a few who overvalued their sense of balance had to be fished, blue and gasping and suddenly sobered, out of the icy water.

By twilight the crisis was past. Three large vessels had sunk in the shallows and would have to be raised. Several others would require extensive caulking before they would be serviceable.

"Ask the Lord," Greathouse said to John Clark, "not to freeze up the river again until that's done. I doubt ye want to winter here or at Fort Pitt when y' got a new home a-waitin' in Kentucky."

The Clark family's belongings were loaded onto a repaired flatboat at daybreak two days later. John Clark sold his three wagons on the spot, to a teamster who was hauling hides and furs west. The Spanish squeeze of the lower Mississippi had increased the freight traffic up through Redstone, and wagons were at a premium.

Much of Red Stone's population was down on the riverfront to see off the family and the first flotilla of boats to leave since the freeze. The girls picked their way through the mud of the river-bank and tottered cautiously up the gangplank while the villagers called their names and bade them farewell. Mrs. Clark then marched slowly up the plank, steadied by the noseless man, who reached a long arm to her. "Thankee, Mister Manifee," she said, stepping onto the plank deck.

She stood there blinking in the chill of morning, now and then waving vaguely to the waving figures on the shore. Ropes and pulleys creaked, booms swung overhead, bundles and kegs, crates of chickens, bags of seed, slung in rope nets, were raised from shore and lowered into barges, as boatmen sang out loud, firm directions: "Hold, hold, hold. Easy now, easy now. Off left, off . . . there she be! Lower awayyy."

The boat smelled of fresh pitch, oakum, woodrot, stagnant bilgewater, animal dung, smoke, hemp, tobacco, tannin, and fish, and that singular dank pungency that is simply and un-mistakeably old riverboat.

The Clark men came aboard then, and finally, Greathouse, whooping orders to cast off. Thick ropes were thrown through the air and thumped against wood. Goats bleated, chickens squawked, horses whickered, people yelled. Men on shore leaned on long poles thrust against the boat hulls, and slowly, slowly, shoved them out into the current. The boats began to move silently on the green water, at the river's own pace, and the little fort and town grew smaller, smaller, at the foot of the long gray hill.

John Clark stood close to his wife and they watched the people move on the distant shore, watched the plank rudder at the end of the twenty-foot hickory sweep adjust ponderously left and right in the burbling water to guide the vessel toward midstream. Two barges and a smaller flatboat of Greathouse's fleet lined themselves up astern. A whiff of wood smoke from the chimney of the flatboat shanty whirled down. The girls were leaning with their arms on the gunwales, studying the water below thought-fully. William was already on the roof of the shanty with the noseless Mr. Manifee, who was manning the sweep, talking with him about the river and learning about steering. The Clarks had not seen much of William at Red Stone; he had been schooling himself all day, every day, on boat building, ropes, knots, river navigation, loading cargo, manifests, caulking, and the termi-nology of river shipping.

Greathouse came out of the shanty looking anxiously at the sky, which was bright with a thin, shimmering overcast. The air was bitter cold, full of the hint of snow and more freezing. "When ye so desire," he said, "there's hot water for tea or toddy."

"Thankee," said Mrs. Clark. "Again, Mr. Greathouse, how far to Pittsburgh?"

"Not twenty leagues," said Greathouse. "We'll put in there tomorrow midday, I reckon, barring anything unforeseeable."

"Eh, well," John sighed, gazing back. "Fare thee well, Virginny." He turned to her. "What would'ee have, Annie? Tea, I'd reckon?"

"Nay, John." Her eyes were misty. "Meseems this is the time for a toddy."

"Well said. Two toddies, then, Mister Greathouse."

"Make that three, sir," said William's voice from above.

THE MONONGAHELA WOUND IN GREAT LOOPS THROUGH the grim mountains. At each turn another silvery curve would come into view, smooth as glass, or sometimes boiling over shallows and shoals. Manifee's tutelage of young William went on like an apprenticeship. "Y' can misgauge an outside bend like this all too easy," he would say, "and swing too wide. Be under that bluff afore y' knowed it. Watch this now." He put his chest against the sweep and lunged toward the starboard side, forcing the rudder hard to port. William gasped; there was a rocky shoal just alongside and, thinking Manifee hadn't seen it, he expected them to be aground at once.

But the vessel responded so sluggishly that it was past the shoal before the bow began to come around. And William saw that if Manifee had waited a moment longer to jam the sweep, they would indeed have run under the bluff on the outside curve of the bend.

Manifee handed the sweep over to William that afternoon, telling him to steer according to what he thought he'd learned, but to look lively and be ready to do anything he was told to do whether it looked right or wrong.

As the afternoon wore on, William made no mistakes, and Manifee did not have to shout at him once.

"I do b'lieve y're born to it, lad," said the noseless man.

MOST OF THE MONONGAHELA SHORELINE WAS STEEP WILderness. But on the bottomlands and low bluffs they would see a cabin now and then, a faint pennant of chimney smoke, the yellow-brown stubble of a harvested corn patch dotted with dark tree stumps, a skiff or pirogue drawn up on the shingle, a horse or cow, a man carrying a hunting rifle, a woman carrying a pail. In some of these clearings there stood only chimneys. John Clark now stood at the starboard gunwale with a mug of steaming toddy, watching the landscape slide past and the afternoon deepen. One of the slaves scooped a shovelful of horse dung from the foredeck and pitched it over the side into the river, then another, and another. Its smell was dense and rich in the chilling evening air. The horses stamped hollowly on the thick deck planks as the slave moved among them. Then John Clark felt the sting of snowflakes on the side of his face.

"Damnation!" Greathouse had appeared beside him and was squinting into the snowfall. It was not a blizzard, of the sort that had struck the Clarks in the mountain pass, but it was a nearly opaque cloud of drifting whiteness which obviously was going to make further progress this afternoon impossible. The small, hard snowflakes hissed into the dark water and vanished. "Steersman," he growled, "put us in at the Willow Island."

"I'll take 'er," Manifee said to William. "This next is a bit tricky."

"I'm a-willin' to try," William said.

"Give me it," Manifee said, snatching the sweep and scowling, so suddenly in a changed mood that William was startled, speechless, afraid he had somehow annoyed his new friend and teacher.

John Clark had seen and overheard this and, when William came morosely down from the roof, took him aside.

"It's just something y'll have to learn, Son," John said, putting an arm over his shoulders. "Takin' charge o' things is a delicate business. Sometimes y've just got to stay in the second place."

THEY WERE TIED UP IN THE NARROW BACKWATER BEHIND A long, sandy island that night, all sleeping or sitting in the fetid confines of the overheated deck shanty. What affability Greathouse had exhibited earlier was gone. Now he was unhappy and was making no effort to hide it; here they were halfway between Red Stone and Pittsburgh, blinded by snow and darkness while the river froze around them. The boats might or might not be damaged by this new freeze, but it was a distinct possibility that they would.

The family lay awake a good part of that night, uneasy in this unfamiliar circumstance, hearing water gurgling under them, hearing seams creak, thinking they could hear water trickling in the hull. Greathouse was up at all hours, sighing loud, exasperated sighs, stepping over and on sleepers, clinking a rum bottle every hour or so as he refilled his cup, letting in blasts of icy air every time he opened the shanty door to go out and check the freezing. It was a bad night, which ended just before first light when Greathouse stumbled in, issued a stream of riverman's profanity and announced that they were "froze God-damned fast," heaved himself onto his cot, broke wind loudly three or four times to the embarrassment of the womenfolk, and then passed out.

They made a brief effort to chop the boats out of the ice that morning. The boatmen stood along the gunwales with long, steel-tipped pikes and jabbed at the ice, piercing it and chipping away chunks all around the hulls. But by the time the hulls were floating free, the men were too exhausted to break channels ahead. The Clark men spelled them on the pikes then. But eventually the whole process became too obviously futile. An hour's ice-breaking would move a boat only twenty-five feet. Even in the main channel, the ice was thick enough to support a man's weight. The temperature, in the meantime, was dropping fast. The sky had cleared to a hard, bright blue, and the dry snow blew across the river ice in streamers.

"It's the kind o' cold that stays," said John Clark. "I reckon these boats are here for quite a spell."

"Then that means we are too, Pa," said Edmund.

"Well, it could mean just that. But it needn't."

"What say ye, Pa?"

"Well, I don't intend to make a permanent residence for my wife and daughters on a marooned shantyboat with a drunken fart-bag for its admiral, that's what I mean to say. We've got horses enough aboard here to carry the womenfolk. You boys and me, we could walk and lead 'em, and carry our necessaries on our backs. Pittsburgh's only twenty-five miles." He scratched his jaw and gazed down along the right bank. "Put two girls on a horse, that'll free up a beast or two to carry valuables, victuals, some tools. Furniture and the like, why, we won't need that. Greathouse can float it down to Pittsburgh when he gets his old scows freed up." He sighed and stared downriver, looking resolute. "Maybe I was a fool t' sell the wagons when I done. We were a-doin' just fine till we hitched up with boats and river rats."

Edmund smiled at his father's resolve. "That's true, but we'd no way o' knowin' she'd ice up so early in th' season."

"Well, this boat's no fit place for a family to live. Yep, two ladies to a horse. Old Rose and Venus ought to ride. Rest o' th' Negroes can walk, like us."

"So be it, Pa. Y're the boss."

John Clark chuckled. "Tell that t' your ma," he said. "'Twas her idea we abandon ship."

Greathouse grumbled a bit when John Clark announced his intent. But he agreed to deliver their bulk goods to them at Pittsburgh when the river thawed.

"If we find the Ohio open," John Clark said, "we just may hire small boats to take us on down to Louisville. In that event, ye'd float our baggage on down there when you can come. How sayee?"

"So be it, Mr. Clark. I am sorry to see you set off, but I can't say I blame ye. If I could leave all this and go to Pitt, why, that I would."

"Mind, now, Mister Greathouse, take every care of our belongings. They might not be fancy, but they're family things, most dear."

"My word on't. If my boats get down th' river, so shall y'r household."

THE ICE AROUND THE BOATS WAS STRONG ENOUGH NOW TO support horses. Wide gangplanks were laid over the boat's sides and secured so that they wouldn't slip. William led and coaxed Flag over the precarious walk first, then the other horses followed over willingly. Soon all the Clark horses had been led across the ice to shore, and light baggage, selected carefully, was bundled and strapped onto the backs of two of the beasts. Lucy rode one of the saddle horses, with old Rose—who had never been on horseback in her long life—locked onto her with desperately hugging arms. Elizabeth rode the second saddle horse, with the Negro woman Venus sitting behind her. Mrs. Clark rode the third, mounted saddleless and astride like an Indian, with Fanny behind her. One of the Clark men led each saddle horse and carried his rifle in his free hand. York led the pack horses. The boatmen came down on shore and shook hands, and with the slaves following on foot, the procession started down the east bank of the Monongahela. It was midmorning. The snow was striped light blue with tree-trunk shadows. But the air was snapping cold and the sunlight so weak it could hardly be felt. Edmund led the way. The snow was to his knees. They found fairly level bottomlands for the first five miles.

Within two hours, each of the girls had remembered at least one item she had forgotten to bring with her from the boats. Each of these was an allegedly essential implement or priceless keepsake, without which the young women were certain they could not live out the day. But there was no turning back, and so their laments soon died down. The entourage struggled quietly on through the snow. There was no talk now, as if the frozen grandeur of the rugged valley had intimidated them to silence. There was only the heavy breathing and grunting of the men as they high-stepped through the snow and flung one leg, then another, over some fallen log, the steamy snorting of the horses, the creak of baggage and loaded tack, a cough, now and then a whine of complaint or a sigh from a weary slave in the rear of the column, the occasional crack of a dead branch, sometimes a few notes of a hummed tune.

They came in early afternoon to a place where the river swung westward, cutting into a sheer bluff that rose in their path. Edmund stopped and studied the height, and the rest of the column came to a halt behind him. The rise was steep and thickly overgrown and doubtless was slick with snow and ice. The only passage appeared to be under it, on the river ice. He waved toward the river and led the animal that way. At the river's edge, he handed up the reins and went out to check the ice. He stepped onto it, stamped, walked out farther, and sprang up and down on flexed knees. He brushed aside some snow, knelt, and poked at the ice with the point of his hunting knife. Finally he was satisfied. "It'll hold, I reckon," he said. "I 'spect we could go all the way down to Fort Pitt on this river, just like a highway. But," he paused, "just to be prudent, you get down. While we're on ice, we'll walk the horses without your weight on 'em. Just to be safe and sure, eh, ladies?"

And so the womenfolk all dismounted and the horses were led down the river ice a few feet offshore from the bluff. The pack horses, heavier with their loads, were led over next, and when they had proven the strength of the ice, the women and slaves followed on foot, straggling singly or in pairs, picking their footing gingerly on the slick surface.

They passed three or four miles thus on the ice over the deep water, becoming more familiar and at ease until someone would slip and fall, then would get up and proceed again as if walking on eggs. The river began curving off to the right then, and there was a stretch of bottomland for some distance ahead, so the women mounted to ride again, their legs weary and shaky with the tension of ice-walking. Four miles farther on, the river looped again, under the steep shoulder of a mountain, and the party dismounted to walk for the next two miles. The cold intensified; the air seemed to sear their nostrils as they went along. The mountains on the west side of the river were high and steep, and by midafternoon, the sky still crystalline blue, the sun disappeared behind a ridge, taking its hint of warmth with it.

But as the day grew colder, their faith in the thickness of the ice increased.

"Oh, thunder," Elizabeth exclaimed later in the afternoon, breaking a long period of silent concentration, "I know what I left on the boat: my skates!"

There was a chorus of laughter and wails.

"Me too!"

"Oh, of all things!"

It was true. Every child in the Clark family had been given a pair of ice skates on his or her sixth birthday, skates John Clark had made for them in spare time at his small forge, and everybody in the family was a skillful skater.

"Aye," Mrs. Clark exclaimed with a shivery laugh, "and with the extra pairs, we could've put one or two o' the horses on skates, too."

The whole family roared with laughter at the notion.

"And," Fanny chimed in, "we'd all have been at Fort Pitt by now, we would!"

"Well, I reckon so," exclaimed William. "By heaven, if we ain't a vacant-headed family I never saw one!"

"LORD, THIS IS A MISERY," GROANED ROSE, HUGGING LUCY Clark from behind for warmth and support as their horse clopped monotonously along on the windswept ice.

It was late afternoon, the snow was in violet shadow, the sky was fading. The womenfolk had exhausted themselves mounting and dismounting, and now simply stayed on horseback whether crossing land or ice. Their bones ached with cold; their feet hung numb at the horses' flanks. They had wrapped their faces in shawls. The men, leading the horses, were slump-shouldered with fatigue. Edmund knew of a cave in a bluff within a mile or two. He was pressing to get them to it before nightfall.

The column was long strung out now. Some of the Negroes were as much as a quarter of a mile behind, limping and moaning prayers, sometimes falling on the ice and then just sitting there lamenting, giving up. Cupid had taken the responsibility for the rest of the servants at first, and he frequently had retraced his steps to go back and harangue and haul at these poor souls until he'd gotten them back on their feet. But at last Cupid himself had run out of grit, and now was just stumbling along hugging his own misery to his bosom, ignoring his flagging brethren.

Mrs. Clark was riding the last horse now, with Fanny shivering behind her. William had given his mother the reins and gone up the column to talk with his father.

She turned her head and glanced back at the straggling Negroes. She saw them strung out almost out of sight around the river bend, dark figures on the gray ice in the purpling twilight. She saw small objects lying on the ice near them and knew they had sunk so low in apathy that they were dropping their belongings. She saw Cupid weaving and stumbling along, paying them no heed.

"Got to go back and light some fire under those wretches," she told Fanny. "Elsewise they're just goin' to sit down and perish."

She tried to rein the plodding mare around, but she wouldn't respond.

"C'mon, now," she snapped, yanking the reins harder. The mare started; she began to pivot to the left, but lost her footing. Her hind hoof skidded from under her and she fell sideways onto her hindquarter. Mrs. Clark and her daughter both yelped as they tilted toward the hard ice.

The mare's heavy fall broke the ice. Two cracks angled away toward the riverbank and then a third crack shot between them, and a three-cornered slab of ice tilted down under the struggling horse. Fanny screamed. The floundering mare whinnied and flailed with her forehooves, and more pieces of ice caved in. Mrs. Clark felt herself slide sideways off the animal, back into the frigid dark water, and heard Fanny's scream end in a dreadful gulp. Mrs. Clark was twisting around to clutch a handful of her daughter's clothing when her own head slipped under the shocking-cold water.

The shock was so stunning that she wanted to gasp her lungs full of air. But it would be water. She was almost paralyzed immediately, but her hands were trying to seek her daughter down in the airless current under the ice. Something powerful smashed against her hip and pressed her down; it was the panicked mare thrashing in the water.

Then something tugged down on her arm. She grabbed; it was a piece of cloth. Fanny's dress. She held onto it with numbing fingers. The current was tugging at the weight in it.

Mrs. Clark opened her eyes to gray murkiness, to vague, large, moving shapes. She groped with her free hand for the surface. She could not tell which direction was up or which was down. She wanted to take the fatal inhalation. But she couldn't. If she gave up, Fanny would die.

I didn't expect the whole thing to end this way, she thought: Things shouldn't end when they're just starting . . .

WILLIAM HEARD THEIR OUTCRIES AND THE WHINNYING OF the mare, and as he turned to look back he heard the sudden wails of the Negroes.

He saw the horse floundering, surrounded by breaking ice and churning water; he caught a glimpse of color disappearing into the water; his mother's cloak. He turned to run back to the place but slipped and fell on his side. "Pa!" he was yelling as he scrambled back on his feet. "Hurry!" He was closest to the mishap, but a hundred yards or more from it, and he knew that mere seconds in the water and under the ice would mean the end of his mother and sister. An awful sense of helplessness filled his breast even as he ran; he seemed to be moving with a dreamlike slowness and, as in a dream, could not seem to make himself move faster.

Only the horse's head and neck were out of the water. William threw himself forward when he was ten feet away, and sledded and crawled forward on his belly to the edge of the broken ice. He saw a swirl of cloth a few inches under the water and grabbed for it. He pulled. The weight pulled him. The current was strong. He tried to press the front of his body against the ice for traction, to hold the weighted garment until his father or someone could arrive, but it pulled and he was sliding. He would have to let go, or be pulled into the water.

He held on. If he let go now, he knew, his mother would be carried under the ice and that would be all. Fanny, he presumed, was already lost. He sobbed and held to the cloak, and finally, when he could hold himself in check no longer and slid over the broken edge into the water, he grabbed the horse's bridle with his free hand.

The beast fought frantically against this new weight that was pulling it down. The water churned. William kept his head above water and gasped from the shock of the cold.

Now he could pull. He hauled at the wet cloth, drawing it toward him, lifting. His teeth were chattering and the cold seemed to be sapping all his strength at once, but he kept pulling and lifting, and suddenly his mother's stricken face appeared above the water beside him; she immediately began drawing for breath with desperate rasping sounds. He released her cloak and cupped his hand behind her neck to keep her head up. She was trying to say something.

"Fanny . . . Fanny . . . Here . . ." She was pulling something and William realized then that she had a grip on Fanny's clothing.

He guided his mother's free hand to the horse's bridle, and she clutched at it. He released her neck then and grabbed for the garment she held. He pulled. He groaned and pulled, vaguely aware of his father's voice now nearby.

Little by little the weight came toward him from under the ice. It was dreadfully inert, not struggling at all. He felt he was pulling up a dead body.

There were familiar voices around now. He got Fanny's blank pale face above the surface and simply tried with the last of his strength and consciousness to hold it above water. The horse seemed to be sinking now. William's head was going blank. Now he could not tell whether he was holding anything or not; all was numbness and shuddering. Then there was nothing.

FOR SEVERAL HOURS THAT NIGHT, IT WAS DOUBTFUL THAT Fanny would survive. She had regurgitated water and had kept up a shallow kind of breathing, scarcely perceptible under the violent shuddering. Mrs. Clark and William had come around quickly, though both had suffered severe chill and shock.

After they had been hauled out of the river, all three had been wrapped in blankets and coats and carried with difficulty to the cave. There their limbs had been rubbed and their frozen clothing removed, a huge bonfire had been built, and they had been dosed with whiskey. Pneumonia had seemed likely for all three, but by midnight William was able to sit up before the fire and drink broth, weak but not ill. God, he thought. George was in ice water for days, going to Vincennes. God!

As soon as she was able to move, Mrs. Clark got up, wrapped in blankets, and went to the place beside the fire where Fanny lay. She lay down beside her and drew all the blankets around them so that her body would warm her daughter's. She looked at the delicate features, at the face white as paper; she listened to the slight, gurgling breathing; she held the frail and clammy little body along her flank and willed her own warmth into it. She thought briefly of the gray, icy, churning moments when they had been on the very edges of their lives, and she thought of that hand that had come down to pull her back to life and air. Once again Billy had acted, and they were all still alive.

She lay holding her daughter and thinking about that thin edge over which a life can fall so easily. She thought about how fragile life is but how tenacious it could prove to be as well. Incidents that might kill a body one day can be survived another day.

405

I've seen it so often, she thought, *seen that guts and will are
all we have to protect us from the fateful things.*

So much I've seen in half a century. So much.

*Come now, Fanny. Come, baby girl. Guts and will, that's al.
ye need. And if ye've not enough o' your own, have mine. That'.
what I'm for, my baby.*

23

MONONGAHELA VALLEY
November, 1784

WHEN MORNING CAME, FANNY WAS STILL BREATHING. AND
she had color in her cheeks now, but it was the flush of fever
She could whisper, but talking hurt her throat. She wanted to
know however she would be able to ride. William came up with
an answer. He had once heard Brother George describe a
wooden frame that the Indians used to trail behind a horse to
carry loads, even sick and wounded people.

And so he and Edmund went out into the piercing-cold wood
with axes and ropes, and cut saplings to make a *travois*. The
family and slaves then breakfasted on hot pone and reloaded the
animals, and set off up the bank of the Monongahela for the last
dozen miles to Fort Pitt, with Fanny jouncing along wrapped
like a mummy in blankets and strapped on the *travois*. They
stopped once about noon to make a hot broth for the girl, then
continued on, and by midafternoon they could see the mouth o
the Monongahela and look up at the cabins and stone houses o
Pittsburgh and the long earthworks and palisades of Fort Pitt
and smell woodsmoke of the town.

"Thanks be to heaven," John Clark said. "We'll have care fo
our darlin' inside an hour."

The site of Pittsburgh was imposing and solemn. The winter
stark mountains crouched behind it; the town lay clustered on
prominent wedge of land in the Y formed by the joining of the
Monongahela and the Allegheny rivers, and the fort brooded
above the village like some grim old castle: high earthen re
doubts and salients now snow-covered; earthen walls topped with

ong rows of pointed logs, ditches and dry moats, thick log blockhouses, crenellations with the dark muzzles of cannon sticking
through them to command the rivers and the roads. There was
something terribly lethal about such a structure in the eyes of
Ann Rogers Clark, and even though its walls meant shelter and
security, she did not like the look of a fort. She thought of her
sons who, so recently as soldiers, had had to hurl themselves at
such monstrosities in the course of that long war.

They rode toward the hulking place from the east, and it was
silhouetted by the glare of the setting sun off a wide expanse of
river ice. Edmund pointed. "The Ohio," he called back to the
other riders. "Yonder's our Ohio River!" There it was, the road
to their faraway new home in Kentucky.

They rode on, now through cleared fields with rustling corn-
stubble sticking up through the snow, along rail fences, past
farmhouses and stables and orchards on their right, and wharfs
and rickety piers jutting into the frozen Monongahela on their
left, with flatboats and galleys iced-in fast. A curtain of smoke
hung over the whole area, yellowing the sun, and away to the
westward, down through its hills and bluffs, ran the frozen mirror of the Ohio, out and out into the frontiers. Now they began
to encounter sledges on the road, heaped with firewood, pulled
by steam-snorting oxen. Down by a boatyard on the riverside, a
plank-saw rasped slowly, steadily. Now to the right, almost under
the shoulder of the fort, some outdoor fires billowed blue smoke,
and amid the smoke stood perhaps a dozen cone-shaped tents,
the camp of some visiting Indians. Men on horses came past
now, some dressed as gentlemen, some looking half-soldierly,
others wrapped in skins like savages; these people stared at the
Clark entourage, at the *travois* carrying the swaddled figure, at
the Negroes straggling behind. Some of the men would tip their
hats as they rode by; others would simply stop and gawk, particularly at the pretty faces of Lucy and Elizabeth; still others appraised the handsome Virginia horses they rode, or peered
closely at the men's faces. It was a way men had got about them
since the war, a constant lookout for old comrades.

"Billy," said Edmund, "trot on into the fort by that postern
gate there and find us the whereabouts of a doctor, quick, now."
He turned to his father as William sprinted away across the
snow. "A shame that General Irvine isn't still commandin' the
fort. He was a physician himself. But I'm sure there'll be one
here. And if not, Ma can take care of her here. She knows more
remedies than any doctor, d'ye ask me."

They watched William disappear inside the gate.

And not half a minute later he reappeared, still running at full tilt. "What the devil?" muttered Edmund. "He hardly took time to turn around."

"Lucy!" William was calling. "Lookahere!"

And then they saw another figure come running after him, full tilt out the gate with cape flying. Lucy was craning to see what this was about, and then she recognized the running man; her blue eyes widened and her mouth went into a little O. She threw her right leg over the horse's withers and slid off to the ground in a billowing of skirts, leaving old Rose alone, terrified, on the horse. She ran forward past her father and past Edmund, then past her brother William, all propriety forgotten, and now Bill Croghan was laughing as he ran toward her, and they fairly collided in the road, arms around each other, Bill Croghan swinging her in a circle and then setting her on her feet and holding her and looking into her eyes and smiling still bigger, then blinking and swallowing and finally saying, as the rest rode up exclaiming wonder and greetings, "Lucy girl, Lucy girl, oh my God, oh, you beauty!"

It was clear that his days of calling her "Little Brother" were over.

The Clark entourage was herded into the fort in a hubbub of greetings and questions, requests and commands. George, in preparation for their arrival, had sent Bill Croghan up to Fort Pitt to greet them and escort them down the Ohio. George himself had been unable to come because in his role as Indian Commissioner he was arranging a midwinter council with the Ohio tribes. He and Croghan had been occupying Mulberry Hill, keeping it warm and its pantry stocked, when they were not on the trails surveying or meeting with Indians. "It's a splendid place. George says the first Christmas there will be the best Clark Christmas ever," Croghan reported. "He'll be there for it, he vows."

The most pressing business now, though, was Fanny, and Croghan had good news: Here at the fort this very week was one of the best physicians on the Continent, one of General Washington's own army surgeons, Dr. Jim O'Fallon. "He was at Valley Forge with us," Croghan said, and he sent an orderly running across the parade ground to fetch the doctor from his lodgings.

There would be quarters aplenty for the patient and her family. The fort had barracks and houses enough for several companies, but since the disbanding of the army after the war, only twenty regular soldiers were here, under command of a major

The major was almost frantic in his concern for the Clarks' comfort; he had been a junior officer under Light Horse Harry Lee, and to him Jonathan Clark was no less a hero than George.

The quarters were Spartan but clean: a large room for the Clark men, another for the women, and a small, attached room for Fanny. Dr. O'Fallon arrived at once, a charming Irish fellow who seemed to have great confidence in himself. He was a physician of the leeches-and-garlic school of medicine. Finding her pulse high, he immediately bled her with the repulsive parasites, leaving them on her arm until they were swollen like plums. He then put salt on them to loosen their hold and remove them, and daubed the leech bites with a disinfectant paste of gunpowder and whiskey. Then he made a hot, stinking poultice of mashed garlic for her to breathe through, and prescribed that she must sleep sitting up, wearing a necklace of garlic cloves.

So far he's done just what I'd ha' done, Ann Rogers Clark thought, so he must be a fair proper physician.

It soon became apparent that Dr. O'Fallon would lavish even more attention on his patient than her own mother would have. He came to the quarters a dozen times a day to see how she was. At first everyone presumed that he was simply showing the usual solicitude the Clarks had come to expect from old comrades-in-arms of their famous sons. But Elizabeth was the first to suggest that something else lay at the heart of it. "The poor fool's just gone fond-foolish over 'er," she said.

"Oh, nonsense," scoffed Lucy. "Y're imagining things, like some silly novel reader. She's scarce twelve yet!"

"You'd never notice it yourself 'cause you can't see anything but Bill Croghan," Elizabeth retorted. "But that doctor's gone simple over Fanny."

"You're just green-eyed 'cause ye fancy him yourself," Lucy said.

"That's not so. But mark my word, under all that fever-sweat and garlic-stink, he sees somethin' he likes a whole lot, and she knows it, too. She's not too sick to see what she's a-doin' to him. Why, she asked me not an hour ago if the fever makes her cheeks look pink!"

Bill Croghan pulled his attention away from Lucy long enough to report the news from downriver and dispense advice from George. Dickie had not been found yet, and George was spending all the time he could with an armed squad searching along the Trace for a sign of him. And every hunter and runner and bush-loper who frequented that trail had instructions to keep eyes and ears open and to inquire among the friendly Indians.

Still, nothing. "Well," said John Clark, "we'll just keep right on praying."

"We should go downriver in as large and well-armed a body as we can," Croghan said. "Some bands, Shawnee in particular, have been preying on riverboats this fall. George forewarned me not to bring you down without a sizeable escort. He said too to keep a keen weather eye, and not leave Pitt if an early winter threatens. Unless there's a general melt in the next week, we'd best resign ourselves to stay here till the spring thaw."

"To my mind," Ann Rogers Clark said, "it's Fanny who determines whether we stay or go. Whether she's got the pneumonia."

By the end of a week the rivers had thawed, but Fanny was not well enough to go on.

Greathouse came down the Monongahela two days after the thaw. His boats were leaking badly from the pressures of the ice and had to be unloaded and hauled up for caulking. The Clarks had their belongings near at hand again now, in a rat-infested warehouse by the boatyard. The sky cleared and the temperatures fell, and again the Ohio was frozen hard. Fanny was improving, but still too weak from the bleedings, Dr. O'Fallon said, to travel. "So," said John Clark, "let's make the best of it. We seem to be here for the winter. Edmund, next trip down to the warehouse, fetch that nice backgammon board Colonel Mason gave us. I'll wager, if we practice all winter, we'll be able to play the breeches off George when we get to Kentuck."

But they had less time for backgammon than they might have expected. Pittsburgh did not give them much idle time. The town, raw though it looked, had its little society, and the society knew that the Clarks of Virginia were present, with their illustrious name, with their comely daughters. Pittsburgh society was a mixture of the crude and the genteel. It was a funnel for news, gossip, and rumor pertaining to everything and everyone passing to and from the west. And so it happened that the Clark family spent its Christmas of 1784 in the society not of Louisville, but of Pittsburgh. Their host was a Pennsylvanian, Colonel Neville, who had helped George obtain provisions three years before, during one of his futile efforts to raise an expedition against Detroit. A large and merry entertainment was held in the Colonel's home, and by now Fanny had recovered enough to attend. Dr. O'Fallon was present, and he watched her as closely as if she were still mortally ill. Whenever she was approached by any young buck of the town, or danced with one, the doctor would break away from any conversation he was in to come and see how she was feeling, or to admonish her against exhausting herself.

Late in the evening, Elizabeth and Fanny were filling their cups at the punchbowl. Fanny leaned over the bowl, sniffing, her face rapt. "Come," Elizabeth said.

"Wait," said Fanny. Her eyes were shut and she was breathing deeply. Elizabeth looked at her curiously; she looked as if she were in a trance, swaying, inhaling. Elizabeth got a little alarmed and touched her arm. "Are ye faint? Drunk?" Fanny kept breathing the steam from the bowl, her cheeks flushed.

"Nothing. I'm well!" And when she came away she said, "That dear doctor! He got me so stunk up with garlic, nobody can come near me! Here, Betty, Hon, do I smell better now, like clove and ginger?" She had been trying to perfume herself with the fumes from the punchbowl.

"O Lord, Fanny, ye silly! What you smell like now is an ol' toddy-sot!"

Dr. O'Fallon kept coming to see Fanny every day though she was quite recovered now. He spent New Year's Eve going around with the Clark family to the different homes to which they had been invited, and at Colonel Neville's, when the clock began bonging midnight and the cups were being raised all around, Dr. O'Fallon and Fanny Clark turned their faces to each other, and Dr. O'Fallon planted a kiss upon her ivory forehead. Her deep blue, long-lashed eyes widened so far that the whites showed all the way around the irises, then closed, and her face glowed pink, and she was aware of the New Year's greetings only as a chorus of happy murmurings whirling around outside her head.

"Oh," she gasped to Lucy a few minutes later, after dragging her into the privacy of a vestibule, "oh, Sister, I'm going to marry that James O'Fallon, that's my first thought of the Year of our Lord 1785!" Lucy had to admit to herself that Elizabeth had been right.

"Well, little sister, you might as well make it your resolution," she said. "I've been resolving every year now that I'm going to marry Bill Croghan, and he's only just now coming to believe it himself, I think!"

Dr. O'Fallon had come to be a good friend of the Clark menfolk, too, helping them keep the backgammon board busy in the evenings, riding out in the countryside with them to hunt when the winter confinement gave them cabin fever. One mild January day, which had melted most of the snow in the forest, they

411

came upon a level piece of woodland flanked by ridges. The earth had a strange, bumpy look to it; grass seemed to have grown over a thousand little hummocks. A shoe of William' horse clinked upon something in the grass. William dismounted and picked something up. "Look'ee, Pa, it's from a singletree." He passed the object, a rust-eroded iron ring attached to an iron band, to his father.

"Aye, that's what it looks like." A few feet farther on William' sharp eye found another rusty bit of metal; he pulled at it and an old bayonet ripped out of the roots of grass. A few minutes of turning up old brass spurs and buckles and gorgets and iron barrel hoops and ramrods, and then a broken human skull, and old John Clark suddenly understood. It was an old battlefield, and the irregularities in the ground were all overgrown bits of junk from the battle. Everywhere there were wagon wheels, hubs and bolts, bones, tomahawk heads, bucket handles, shoe buckles. "Look at the trees," William said, pointing. The bark of many of the trees was puckered, the scars of old bullet holes.

"May th' Eternal have mercy," John Clark said, taking off his hat and holding it on his breast. "This'd be Braddock's battle ground." He took a deep breath and his eyes went deep as he remembered. He told them again of the day when the news of the slaughter had swept through Albemarle County. "Near thirty years ago, it was, and I'd never in my life felt so low and black in my soul!"

The young men looked around as if the place were haunted. John Clark went on: "Many a patriot o' the war just past got baptized in blood here. Gen'l Washington. Gen'l Morgan. Dan' Boone. Gen'l Andrew Lewis. Those were some that lived, thank the Lord. Boys, take your hats off, because this ground has been watered with the blood of a thousand brave Englishmen." He paused. "And lest we've forgot," John Clark added sadly, "we were Englishmen then."

Now they took off their hats.

THE RIVER ICE GRUMBLED AND BROKE UP EARLY IN FEBRUary, and though the sky was leaden and rainy, Mister Greathouse felt it in his bones that the river was through freezing, and came up to the fort and told John Clark he was ready to set out next day, and asked him if he and his family wished to throw in with him again and risk a little discomfort to get to their new home by early March. The family discussed it with Bill Croghan, and then John Clark said, "Aye, Mr. Greathouse. Put our furniture aboard. We'll bring some Negroes down to help."

And so they packed their small things that night, and sent notes of thanks to their hosts and friends of Pittsburgh, and were aboard the next morning by daylight. Some of the Pittsburgh people were on the wharf at that early hour to wave them off.

There was another small crowd, too, seeing off another traveler. This was a dapper, handsome young man of about twenty-seven with a hearty personality, mellifluous voice, and courtly grace. "That's General Wilkinson," Greathouse said in a low voice to Edmund's ear. "Y'll recollect we spoke of 'im last fall? He's paid fare as far as the mouth of the Kentucky. Ye'll get a chance to know 'im. But I say, look out." The girls could scarcely keep their eyes off him, not even Fanny, who had been in a profound slump since the departure of Dr. O'Fallon a few days before. "D'you suppose he's a married gent?" Elizabeth murmured to Lucy. On the wharf, the young dandy and his friends were drinking from a silver flask, using its cap as a glass. He was making cheerful toasts whose cleverness seemed to be keeping his friends in a high state of amusement. At last he embraced them all, men and women alike, sprang lightly upon the gangplank with an elegant swirl of his cape, and leaped lightly to the deck. He bowed to the Clark women with sparkling eyes. "Good day, my fellow sojourners!" he burbled. "A word with you, Mister Greathouse, about some arrangements, and then I must meet these distinguished-looking passengers. Excuse us, my dears."

"That," queried Ann Rogers Clark with a pursed smile and raised eyebrows, "is a *general*?"

John Clark smiled and winked, then squinted into the sleet to watch the boatmen cast off. William climbed topside, greeted his old friend Mister Manifee, and at once was hard at work as if earning his berth. He stood on the cabin roof with his feet wide apart, face flushed, gazing in awe at the long, broad, northwesterly curve of the great Ohio, whose flint-gray surface was dimpled and ruffled with sleet, dotted with great hunks of floating ice. As the boat moved past the point of land, he watched the Allegheny pouring in on the right, watched the little people on the wharf stop waving and begin filing up the road toward the town. He watched the gloomy fort grow smaller and smaller astern.

"Well, Master Clark," said the helmsman, "we're under way again, goin' to a new world, eh? And I wonder what it is you're a-thinkin'."

William turned to look at the strange noseless face, which had come to be no more ugly than many another face, and answered, "Thinkin' a lot. About where this river goes. And tryin' to count up how many times my brother George started down this river from here."

"How many I don't know," Manifee said. "But I do remember the one time, that May o' '78, on th' way to Kaskasky. That I'll never forget, m' boy, 'cause I was with 'im."

William's mouth dropped open. He stared at Manifee's deep-socketed eyes, which were squinting into the sleet. Those eyes glanced over and saw William's surprise, and crinkled with a smile.

"Y' never told me that before," William said.

"A man don't tell all 'e knows right off."

"Were you one of 'em as marched to Vincennes?"

"That I was, boy, and it was weather just like t'day. Y'see how cold that water looks? Wal, it feels three times colder."

"I know about cold water," William said, remembering the Monongahela.

"Well, boy, there's a lots of us 'long this ol' river who set out with 'im on that day, and I'll tell y' this: no man ever drug me through so much hell and misery as he did. But I'll tell y' another thang. Does Gen'l Clark ever need me again, I'm set t' go." He swallowed a scraggy Adam's apple and gazed at the high, gray, wooded bluffs along the river. Then he said: "Your family. It's a bad country we're a-goin' to. But I'll tell ye. There's nothin'll happen to 'em that I can help. My word on't."

They were not ten miles down the river, all sitting over tea in the stuffy little cabin of the riverboat, before General James Wilkinson had offered his friendship to the Clarks and told them everything about himself that he thought would impress them. It was really a bit hard to look at the elegant young fellow with his unlined face and believe it was all possible. But likely it was approximately true, as no one, surely, would have the audacity to make up such a history. He had grown up on a Maryland plantation and had studied medicine as a youth; and had been commissioned a brevet brigadier general in the Continental Army and appointed secretary to the Board of War. He said he had been with Benedict Arnold on his march to Quebec and, without actually saying it, managed to give the impression that he was somehow the guiding spirit in the events that later uncovered Arnold's treason. Wilkinson also claimed it was he who had delivered to Congress the news of Burgoyne's surrender at Saratoga in 1777—"That was when I was aide to General Gates," he added casually—and he just happened to have a document on his person that proved the truth of it. "I was invited to address Congress with particulars of that great victory," he said, "and in consequence, that great body generously appointed me a brigadier general." He tilted his head and a modest smile curved his shapely lips. This last account nudged a corner of John Clark's memory, and he raised a finger over the table, and said:

"Yes, yes! I read o' that. Some said Gen'l Dan Morgan of Virginia should have got that promotion, for what he did at Saratoga." He sat back and looked at Wilkinson. The young officer raised his eyebrows at this, which seemed to be a note of contention from his heretofore complacent listener, then quickly adapted himself.

"I myself felt that," he said, "as Daniel Morgan certainly was an able and brave man, aye, one of our true best. But of course I could only accept."

"Of course, of course," said John Clark with a slightly mocking smile. Whatever else Wilkinson might have intended to tell about his illustrious career, he now dropped, perhaps being aware that he was talking to a man of some knowledge, rather than a gullible old gent.

Wilkinson now went on to more current achievements, telling how he had married a daughter of the eminent Philadelphia Biddles after the war—the Clark girls looked at each other and shrugged—how he had been elected to the Pennsylvania Assembly, and now was building a fine home in Lexington, Kentucky, where he was stationed as a partner in an important Philadelphia trading firm. He intended, he said, to use his political capabilities for the advancement of Kentucky's interests. "I become convinced that Kentucky has needs that none of the leaders in Virginia seems to grasp," he said. "As you might know, there's strong sentiment among the Kentuckians to be made a separate state from Virginia."

"Are you, General, of those sentiments?" Bill Croghan asked.

"Why, Sir, I am trying thus far to evaluate the matter. But forgive me!" he exclaimed suddenly, stirring on his bench and smiling around at the semicircle of Clarks. "How can I forget manners so reprehensibly as to engage in political talk in such charming company? I shall never forgive myself if I bore the ladies! So. So, so. You are all the Clarks, and you're going to Kentucky, eh? What part, pray? I should hope Lexington, that we might perhaps see each other . . . ?"

"To Louisville, sir," said John Clark proudly. "We're moving there lock, stock, and barrel, from Virginia. Our sons have made us a new home there, on a fine site."

415

"Splendid! How admirably devoted of them. What line are they in, if I may pursue my curiosity?"

"Soldiers," Ann Rogers Clark interjected in a quick, strong voice. "Surely the general has heard of Colonel Jonathan Clark, hero of the Battle of Paulus Hook, and General George Rogers Clark, conqueror of the Northwest."

"And father of Kentucky," Edmund added just as proudly.

At the names, the young officer's face momentarily froze, then he was instantly more effusive than ever. "By Heaven, you don't say so! Of General Clark himself! Why, why, sir, Madame, may I kiss your hands! Why, ha! ha! Here I have been, going on and on about myself, never suspecting that I spoke to the—well, what? Shall I say, ha, ha, the grandfather and grandmother of Kentucky?"

"That, sir, is not particularly gracious," said Mrs. Clark.

"I jest, forgive me, Madame. Ha, ha! One could not mistake you for a grandmother." Wilkinson now was reaching into the duffel bag that leaned against his bench.

"It would be no mistake," she retorted. "I am one."

It was obvious that the young dandy's charms were being wasted on this grand and handsome lady. He quickly flashed his silver flask over the table, unscrewing its cap. "Cognac," he said, "from LaFayette's own stock. Do have some, against the chill, and of course I should like to drink in honor of your illustrious sons!"

"You're generous with a precious stuff," said John Clark, taking the cap and passing it under his nose.

"An investment well made," Wilkinson replied jovially, "as it's my belief that the way to a man's heart is down his throat. Drink up, Mister Clark. To your great sons and lovely daughters."

GENERAL WILKINSON HAD THE UNUSUAL ABILITY TO BE fawning and overbearing at the same time. And the Clarks, despite their immediate distrust of him, could not but enjoy his company as the keelboat drifted silently down the gray Ohio. His wit and joviality warmed the dank cabin in which they sat with blankets over their laps. He seemed to be able to drink a bit every hour of the day without becoming really intoxicated; his faculties were such that he could win at backgammon even while carrying on a learned and entertaining discourse on the most complex subject, be it medicine, politics, or the foibles of Eastern society. He was a cartographer of masterful skill, as he proved by showing the Clarks a portfolio of battle maps he had made during the recent war; the maps were superior in detail and draftsmanship to any they had ever seen, including Peter Jefferson's. He knew a great deal about Indian affairs, it seemed, about treaties, and he carried on a learned discussion with Bill Croghan about the history of British Indian affairs under Sir William Johnson. He was impressed that Bill Croghan was related to famous Tories but had become a patriot.

Wilkinson could leap from serious discourse to affable banter and back without losing a step. "You, my dear Miss Fanny," he would say with an avuncular smile, "as the youngest member of such an illustrious and handsome family, what do you expect you'll be as the years go by? Will you be a famous beauty of the stage? A governor's wife? If there were a clean, white china cup here to read tea leaves in, I'd tell your fortune. But, ha, ha! to read in these stained and rusty vessels of Captain Greathouse would be like probing the bottom of an old cistern, would it not? And it's plain your future will not be dark like that, nay. What, come now, do you expect for yourself?"

Fanny was by no means backward. "Sir," she replied after a swift glance at her mother, "I expect to marry a doctor, I do, and I sh'll be to him as my mother is to my father: his helpmeet and partner in every way, so that he'll need me and depend upon me."

He clapped his hands together and squeezed them. "Well said, and such a fine tribute to your mother!"

"Fine and true," said John Clark, reaching over and laying his hand on his wife's wrist.

"And you, my dear," he said to Lucy, "what about you?"

"I," she said, tilting her head toward Bill Croghan, "am waiting to see if this gentleman has any plans in that same line." Croghan raised his eyebrows and stuck his tongue in his cheek.

William had come down from topside during this, red-nosed and teary-eyed from the cold, and stood just inside the door looking around in the gloom. "By heaven," Wilkinson exclaimed, turning to look at him over his shoulder, "enter the young scion, glowing with the cold. Master Clark, come sit by me. Would your parents object if I offered you a dram of bottled sunshine?"

"Likely not," William said. "They always dose me with it when I cough. *HOUAGH! HOUAGH!*"

Wilkinson threw his head back and roared, then wiped his eyes and chuckled as he poured a potion in the little silver cap. All the Clarks were laughing with, or at, him. William drew up a stool and sat at the table with his cape still on and laid his pipe

417

and a carrot of tobacco out on the table, and stuck his hunting knife in the tabletop. Then he passed the liquor under his nose. "My, my! I'd say that's good enough to sip." He took a small bit and let it trickle down over his tongue, and it spread a glow down his throat. He evidently had pegged this dandy as someone to be shown off to in a manly way; with men he deeply respected he was quiet. Wilkinson, of course, had no suspicion that he was being taken lightly. "My brother George taught me to tell by a whiff whether something deserves to be sipped or bolted," William explained.

"Ah! A connoisseur, is he?" Wilkinson said.

"I don't know about that," William replied, taking another sip, "but he used to cough a lot."

"Oh, Billy, that's not so!" exclaimed Fanny. Wilkinson seemed to be putting something down in his mental notebook for a moment, then he laughed again and he watched William trim some riffs of tobacco off the end of the twist with his razor-sharp knife and fill his pipe.

"I'm only joking," William said, pulling a candle to him and craning his head over to draw its flame into the pipe, puffing up a fragrant blue cloud.

Wilkinson sniffed it and assumed an expression of bliss. "Mm-mmm! Now, *that's* for connoisseurs!" he exclaimed.

"He grew and cured it himself," John Clark said.

"Really! Is your curing method a family secret, Master Clark?"

"It's like this, sir. I hang it up in a barn."

William's mother quickly put her hand over her mouth to hide a smile. Oh, my, she thought, this lickspittle dandy's sure to make me laugh out unladylike yet, I swear!

WHEN GREATHOUSE'S BOATS STOPPED AT WHEELING, WILLIAM pointed up at the fort and told General Wilkinson, "My brother George built that fort." They all went up for a look at it, and, predictably, Wilkinson raved about the structure. Here at Wheeling, other boats joined Greathouse's, and soon a dozen vessels were floating or rowing along within sight of each other down the widening breast of the Ohio between the ominous, wintry cliffs and bluffs. The numbers were reassuring. Since the war the flow of British goods and weapons into the tribes had diminished some, and tribes living north of the Ohio, angered by the constant flood of white men into the valley, felt justified in taking what they needed from the whites whenever they could catch lone vessels or weak and unguarded parties. Greathouse kept his flotilla out of musket range in midriver, and sentries constantly alert.

Bill Croghan and Lucy Clark spent most of their time wrapped up in each other's company, probably talking marriage, though no one could overhear them because they murmured like doves. William spent most of his time topside with Manifee, sketching and writing in a notebook, inquiring the name of every tributary, learning the navigational hazards. "A good riverman's a prize," Manifee said, obviously including himself. He told William funny stories about George's favorite pilot, the one-eyed Davy Pagan, whose nautical language was so salty he went by the nickname of "the forepoop swabman." "Y'll meet 'im ere long," Manifee said. "'E runs a ferry now 'twixt Louisville and Clarksville. Ha, heee! What an old sea-cock that'n is!" Now he pointed. "Yonder to larboard's Grave Crick."

"Hey," William exclaimed, and called down. "Ma! Pa! Here's where George made his first farm, before the war!"

It was corn stubble and clearings now, the Indian mounds clearly visible.

And later that day Edmund pointed to the place where George had first encountered Chief Logan. "There's where they sat and smoked," he said. They all gazed at it and remembered the story, remembered George's telling of it long ago.

This scene was repeated over and over as they floated down the wintry river: Pipe Creek, where George had first fought Shawnees, with Cresap. Yellow Creek, where Chief Logan's relatives had been massacred; Greathouse was grim and silent as they passed it. The mouth of the Kanawha, where Chief Logan had shown George the French plaque, and where General Andrew Lewis had fought the major battle of Dunmore's War. Days later, Limestone Creek, near where Joe Rogers had been captured on Christmas Day of '76. One morning when they had been on the Ohio for three hundred miles, Manifee pointed to the mouth of the Licking, where George had formed up his armies in '80 and '82 to march against the Shawnee towns. By now the whole family was aware that this wilderness was dominated by George's spirit. Ann Rogers Clark lay that night on the shelf of straw that was her bed in the keelboat's cabin and looked at the little candle-lamp glowing on the table in the middle of the compartment while the water of the Ohio gurgled under the hull, and the sense of all those events was boiling in her mind and soul.

Look at all that's grown out of the head and heart of that boy of ours, she thought. Look at all these boats going down to Kentuck, and he *made* Kentuck. And now here's John and me goin' out like pilgrims a-followin' him on and on west, we who've been Virginia planters for so long, just giving up home and following, 'cause where he goes it seems like everybody rushes in after him.

And when she thought of George, this wonder of a man everybody talked about here on this side of the mountains, she thought of him in the way that only a mother can think of a great man, and she remembered that stormy November day in '52 when he was born, and she remembered the thunder and the lightning and the storm and the chicken-stealing Indians, all those omens, and then his emergence into the world. Thirty-two years ago, she thought, and a world turned upside down since, and yet I can remember it just plain as yesterday.

The womb never forgets, she thought. She thought of all this, and shifted in her blanket, the stale blanket with all the old riverboat smells in it, shifted her weight to snuggle closer to the warmth of good old John, strong, wise, devout, able old John Clark, as good a man as any woman could ever want, who for onto thirty-five years now had lain beside her like this, radiating heat like a stove and making all the nights snug and safe, first out in the wilds of Albemarle, and then in the big house at Caroline, and now in wagons and huts and caves and forts and boats as they migrated west, and soon he'd be warming her in a big mulberry-log house in some wondrous place called Louisville, where they'd likely finish up their days together.

I kind of hope we die together, she thought. I don't think it'd be a fit world for either of us t' live in if the other was gone.

Old John Clark said "Hm" in his sleep and put his arm across her waist, and she went to sleep in his warmth, floating down the river through the wilderness.

FEBRUARY TURNED INTO MARCH AND THERE WAS NO SIGN of spring yet on the silver-gray river bluffs, but great V-shaped flocks of Canada geese, ducks, and brants were flying forever across the valley, honking and barking. The barge was so wide and long that, with its corral of horses and its overlapping communities of slaves, crewmen, and passengers, it was, as Elizabeth expressed it, "like a *place* that moves." At the end of this trip, Greathouse said, it would be dismantled and sold as lumber and plank to make houses in Louisville. There were people there already, he said, who looked down their noses at log houses.

"Son Jonathan wanted to plank over our mulberry house," John Clark said, "but I told him, 'Skip such expense as that. A log house was good enough for you t'be born in.' That's what I told 'im. Jonathan's come to be one who wants things fancy. The newest fancy thing he hears of. I think it's Sarah's makin' him thataway, don't you, Annie?"

"I don't know," she said. "Mought's well blame a woman."

"George means to build a sawmill north of the river," Bill Croghan said. "That'll be where to get plank. He's designed the machinery so it'll run a gristmill, too. And thinks it would be good business to build a still."

"Ah, whiskey," said Greathouse. "A good way t' store corn. till the damnblasted Spaniards open th' Mississippi to trade."

"Aye, so? From what I've heard o' folks at Louisville, ye couldn't store that form o' corn very long," said John Clark.

In such future talk the days and evenings passed, flowing day into day as the keelboat floated on. There was some time for music in the evenings, with Manifee on his fiddle, though the cabin was too crowded for dancing. So the family just listened and sang. They would sing "Barbara Allen" and "The Hog's Heart" and "The Lawyer Outwitted." Manifee sang several pungent variations of "Yankee Doodle," and Captain Helm's old swigging song with its *"glup, spit, patoo!"* He could also make up songs, and one catchy, nonsensical piece of singing and whistling soon became their favorite:

> *Whicky picka chicky*
> *Whicky picky chick a ram*
> *Listen to me whistle*
> *(Wheet a wheet a wheetee!)*
> *A whiskey-pickled chickadee*
> *That's what I am!*

Most often, though, he would play "Katy Cruel," and when he sang O *diddle lully day, O de little lie-o day*, sometimes his grotesque ruin of a face would be tracked with tears.

They would reminisce about the war, particularly about the clever tricks George had done here in the West. General Wilkinson would listen tirelessly to these wondrous tales, saying wistfully that it had been impossible to effect such brilliant strokes in the East because of Washington's "deliberateness." At this, Edmund reminded him of Paulus Hook.

And always there was talk of Indians. Now that Virginia had ceded her Northwest Territory lands to Congress, Indian policy likely would become hopelessly muddled. "If you think the Virginia Government didn't know anything about Indians," said Greathouse, "wait till you see how much Congress don't know!"

"Well, I'll say this for Congress," Edmund offered. "They had enough sense to make George an Indian commissioner. George says he's comin' to see matters more the Indian way than ours.

Well, ye know what he'd always say, about chief Logan and all. But, especially since Gnadenhutten, he says sometimes he's ashamed to be a member o' the white race."

A painful, gloomy silence followed. No white man liked to be reminded of the Gnadenhutten Massacre.

In '82, a company of soldiers from Fort Pitt had tied up a hundred peaceful Christian Indians, Delaware men, women, and children converted by the Moravian missionaries, and systematically crushed all their skulls with cooper's mallets. Even among men who loved to boast about the Indians they had killed, there was seldom a man who would admit to having been at Gnadenhutten.

Eventually this guilt-shadowed recollection led to the mention of the massacre of Chief Logan's family a decade ago by a man named Greathouse.

Suddenly there was an embarrassed silence. The boatmaster had been staring into the lampflame, chewing on a homemade toothpick and saying little, and now he was aware of the silence. Without raising his head, he lifted his eyebrows and glanced all around at everyone and answered the unvoiced question: "That was *Jake* Greathouse done that."

But he did not say whether he was related to Jake Greathouse. And as if to keep anybody from asking, he got up and went out on deck.

"THERE SHE LAYS," SAID JONAS MANIFEE THE NEXT AFTERnoon. "The Kentucky River." He had put the helm over to swing the keelboat toward a gap in the forested south shore of the Ohio. William could see a few cleared acres, some chimneys, a half-collapsed wharf on the near side of the mouth, and on the far side, in a stump-dotted clearing, stood a one-story log house, windowless, very severe and solid, its roof shakes still the yellowish-white of new wood. "'Twas right here," Manifee was saying, "that we put ashore in '78. Hit was rainin' like a tall cow pissin' on a flat rock that day, I 'member."

"Hey, bo'!" someone yelled from one of the other boats. "Redskins yonder!" He was pointing toward the Ohio's north shore a mile away. Now William could hear boots thumping on the plank decks below, and urgent voices.

"There, I see 'em," said Manifee. And now William saw them, too: a long, low canoe, a mere sliver on the water, where the Ohio began a gradual bend toward the northwest. The canoe was going downstream along that shore.

"Big canoe," Manifee mused. "What y'see, Master Clark? Fifteen, twenty people in 'er? My eyes ain't what they used t' was."

"About that," William said, squinting. He could feel his pulse beating in his neck and temples. Greathouse was clambering up the ladder onto the roof now, with Edmund Clark and Bill Croghan following. Below, Wilkinson was looking at the distant vessel with a brass army telescope. Men were everywhere on deck now with their rifles, scanning both banks of the river and looking into the bare, snow-floored forest as far as their eyes could penetrate. The mouth of the Kentucky was yawning wider as they drifted toward it.

"What sayee, Mister Greathouse?" said Manifee. "Do I put in, or no?"

Greathouse was now looking warily at the river mouth, and he said, as if wondering aloud, "Might there be some up th' Kentuck? Wait, Manifee."

"Better say it quick, Mister Greathouse, or I'll overshoot th' point. I cain't back this thang up, y'know."

"Now, just—"

"Put in, Mister Greathouse," General Wilkinson's voice ordered from below. "I'm damned if a pack o' heathens a mile off makes me miss my landing. Have your man put in."

Greathouse's bad teeth showed in a clench-jawed sneer, but he did nod to Manifee, saying, "Aye, then. Bear in. Any other savages in view? Eh? Keep y'r eyes clear, lads! If there's any lurkin' up the Kentuck there, stand ready to pole us off into th' current. All look t' your powder now, we're headin' in."

William watched the long rectangle of the boat swing ponderously inshore, and he had got the feel of it well enough now that he was sure it was going to swing a few yards too wide, because of Greathouse's hesitation, and be nudged back out by the current of the Kentucky. But Manifee yelled down to a man who stood among the horses on the foredeck with a rifle resting across a mare's withers:

"Jaybo! Git on th' bow an' be set to flang a noose on that pilin'! Go, man! Git them 'fraidy bones out from 'hind that horse! Ain't no redskins out there! Ha! He, hee!" The man moved out among the horses, leaned his rifle against a rail, vaulted the rail onto the prow and picked up the end of a coiled rope. It had a slipknot, which he pulled open and held at his side. By now the stern of the keelboat had swung downstream, and the prow was pivoting slowly past the end of the old wharf, a good fifteen feet from it and slipping past. "Rope it, Jaybo!" The man swept his arm out in a curve and the loop settled around the piling. "Yip!" Manifee shouted, and the man smiled, and looped his end of the rope around a cleat-post. The rope straightened, wood creaked, and they were fast. William looked up the Kentucky, between its formidable bluffs, and saw no one. And on the other side of the Ohio, the big Indian canoe was now out of sight beyond the bend. It was interesting to him how much alarm one canoe could cause.

"Here's where we must say adieu," Wilkinson told the Clarks when his baggage had been handed down into a rowboat. "This would have been a dreary voyage for me indeed, but for your company. Pray come and visit me whenever you're in Lexington." He shook hands with John and Edmund Clark and kissed the hands of Mrs. Clark, Lucy, Elizabeth, and Fanny. "I've left gifts for you all in your cabin," he said. Then he turned to William. "Young sir, I feel we'll meet often, as this country grows. Maybe we'll serve together sometime, in some way. I certainly hope so."

"Aye, sir. And, ahm, here's something for you." William fished in his pouch for the twist of his home-grown tobacco, brushed some lint and pone crumbs off of it, and handed it to Wilkinson. The dandy took it, as if delighted, and let himself down into the rowboat. "Godspeed," he called as the four oarsmen dug into the water and the rowboat started up the Kentucky. Most of the other vessels followed; they were en route to Lexington, Harrod's Town, Danville, and Boonesboro, with goods for those Kentucky river towns; the keelboat was the only big vessel going directly on down to Louisville.

The gifts Wilkinson had left were small but elegant. For each of the Clark ladies there was a lace-trimmed handkerchief; for the men he had left a gallon of brandy.

"Well, he is some dilly," said Ann Rogers Clark, touching the fine cloth to her cheek. "Just a bit of everything, isn't he?"

"I reckon," said her husband, "we'll hear more o' him. A man like that surely won't just fade into the countryside."

THE LOG HOUSE ON THE OTHER BANK OF THE KENTUCKY's mouth was, Greathouse said, the dwelling of Captain Bob Elliot and his wife and daughter. "It's Elliot," Greathouse said, "who's clearing land here."

"I should like to go see him," John Clark said. "I promised him I would do." This Captain Elliot had used to shelter at the Clark house in Caroline when he was passing through to Richmond during the war. "Row me over," John Clark said. "It's not so long till night, and he's said we're welcome to his house."

A skiff was untied from the keelboat's side, and the man called Jaybo rowed John Clark across the mouth of the Kentucky. Mr.

Clark wore a find woolen cape and tricorn, and his powdered wig, which he had got out of a box because this was a matter of calling. He looked as fine and dignified as a governor, and no one would have guessed he was still crawling with lice acquired from Red Stone Fort, and some more recent ones from the bunk straw of Greathouse's barge.

Here and there in the clearing around the house lay huge piles of slash and brush and stumps. Some of these had been partially burned. As the skiff came ashore, John Clark saw that the log house was very large and sturdy, almost a fort, with rifle slits instead of windows. Its door was of oaken plank put together with iron straps. This would be a sound house to stay the night in, he thought, his mind turning to that Indian canoe. Elliot's built himself a real fortress here. No wonder, being as he's right across the river from Shawnee country. It's odd, he thought, nobody's come out of the house, what with all our boats over there. I wonder if anybody's home. He stepped up onto the hewn-log stoop and rapped on the door. He thought he could hear footsteps inside, and one querying syllable in a child's voice. A cold swirl of wind from the river brought chimney-smoke to his nostrils. But no one came to the door. He waited. He looked at the gun slits in the walls, feeling that he was being watched through them. He knocked again. "Hallooo, there," he called. "I'm John Clark, from Caroline County, come for to see Captain Elliot! Are ye there, Bob Elliot?"

A latch clacked on the other side of the door, and the heavy door swung slowly inward a few inches. A woman's face, of pretty features, was looking at him out of the gloom, with the wary eyes of a cornered animal. John Clark lifted off his hat and bowed. "Good day, Ma'm. Are you Mary Elliot?" She nodded, and the door opened a bit wider. Now he could see that her comely face was dirty, her hair lank and loose. Her gray linsey-woolsey dress was smudged with ashes and grease. A dirty little girl's face peeped around from behind her hip. "I'm your husband's friend, John Clark of Caroline County," he said again. "Is 'e here, please?"

"Gone a-hunting," she said in a small voice.

"Eh. Well. Say, then. Has the captain ever spoke of me to you? He used to stay with us." She nodded but said nothing. John Clark continued, now beginning to wonder if Elliot had married some sort of a half-wit: "My family's in yon barge. My wife, three girls, and two sons." He paused. At this point, any Virginian would be offering hospitality. But it did not appear that she was going to do so. Instead, she looked more alarmed and wary than ever, even closing the door by a few inches. "D'you expect your husband yet this evening?" he pursued.

"I don't know."

He looked to the left and then right, feeling awkward in the face of this cool and uncouth reception, wondering how Captain Elliot could have bragged as much as he always did about so backward a woman. At last he turned to her again, noting the fright in her eyes, and asked, "Is everything all right here? Is there anything I can do for you?" She put her fingers over her mouth and shook her head, and it looked as if her eyes were going to spurt tears. The little girl still hung back and peered around as if he were an ogre of some sort. Well, by the Eternal, he thought, I can see we're not welcome here. "So, Mrs. Elliot, I'll just say good day, and please tell the captain we came to pay respects. Please tell him that, won't you?" She nodded again. He doffed his hat and bowed once more, trying to keep the annoyance from showing in his face. He thought of offering to pay for lodging, but decided that the poor thing must be so addled that it might not turn out well at all.

He had Jaybo row him back to the keelboat. "Let us be getting on down the river," he said, scowling now. "There's still daylight." And as they moved away from the Kentucky's mouth, he described the strange encounter to his family. They were disappointed, having expected to spend a night on dry land, in a solid cabin with a blazing fire. The girls' imaginations were running wild. "Suppose there was a savage in her house, holding her a hostage?" Fanny asked. "And she was just afraid to speak or let you in?"

"No," John Clark replied, "I asked her if she was all right."

"Tell ye what I think," said Elizabeth, with a sort of smirk. "I think there was a man in there, all right, but her paramour, more likely."

"Shame, Betty, to presume so about a poor strange woman," said Mrs. Clark. "Do those novels make you think thataway?"

The keelboat drifted on down the river in deepening twilight. At one point William thought he saw the Indian canoe along the north bank, but by the time he'd fetched a spyglass there was no sign of it. A few miles farther down, Greathouse pointed out a sandbar at a distance off the south bank where the boat might be anchored offshore for safety.

That night, as the Clarks were getting ready to get into their bunks, John and Edmund and William having a glass of the fine spirits Wilkinson had given them, they looked up suddenly at the sound of feet on the roof above their heads. They could hear

Greathouse up there, exclaiming about something. They threw open their door and climbed the ladder to the roof.

Far up the river, above the trees and bluffs, a dull red light glowed, as if some large fire were reflecting off the underside of the clouds.

"I would reckon it's a bonfire o' those redskins we seen," Greathouse was saying. "Looks to me as it's 'bout a mile up, and on the north bank. 'Bout where we last saw th' canoe."

"T'me," Manifee said, "it looks farther. I gauge it's nigh th' Kentucky's mouth."

Then the man called Jaybo said, "Heck, I know what it is. Ha, ha!" His voice was full of relief. "It's at Cap'n Elliot's place, where he's doin' all that clearing. He's just burnin' slash! You saw it there, Mister Clark."

It seemed a reasonable explanation, but William was not satisfied with it. "We ought to go back and see," he suggested. "And then if that's all 'tis, why, Cap'n Elliot would be home and we'd see 'im after all."

"We can't go back up," Greathouse said. "This barge don't go upriver."

"We could take a few men in the skiff," William said. "Be there inside of an hour."

"Oh, yes, lad? Come now. That boat won't carry but three–four men, and if they got there and found Indians, what could they do but get themselves kilt, I ask? Nay. I'm not riskin' my crew to go look at bonfires in th' night."

"Then Edmund and I and Pa could go up, and Bill Croghan."

Greathouse was silent for a minute, looking at the glow in the distant sky. "I'm the captain o' this here scow, lad, and I'm the owner o' that skiff. Now, aside from that, I am not aimin' to float into Louisville t'morry and meet Gen'l George Clark there and have to tell him, 'Sorry, Gen'l, but I lost your Pa and brothers by puttin' them on a night river in a skiff out amongst redskins.' No, lad. Ye don't have permission t' touch that skiff, d'y' hear me?"

That was that, and it did make sense. But John Clark did not sleep much that night. He kept seeing that frightened, lonely young woman's face in the doorway and the little girl behind her skirt. And while William was atop the cabin taking his turn at guard after midnight, he kept thinking about that glow in the sky, although it was gone by then. Maybe it *was* just burnin' brushpiles, he thought. That does sound likely. And I suppose if there's been Indian trouble, we'd ha' heard a shot or two. But still, I'd like to have gone up and made sure.

427

"Look at it thisaway," Edmund muttered to him when he relieved the post at two in the morning. "If there *was* a raid there, we were lucky that woman *didn't* invite us. Would ye want Ma and the girls to been in such a thing?"

William thought on that. Somewhere on the south bank a barred owl was calling. *Who-who, who-who! Who-who, who-who-aw!*

"No," William agreed. "Sure not, forbid it Heaven!"

"Well, then. If y'd been in the war you'd accept that some lamentable things you can do nothin' about. Go bunk down. And don't bump around. Family's not slept well t'night."

Who-who, who-who! Who-who, who-who-aw! Another owl called farther upstream.

"All right. Say, Eddie. Listen hard at those owls. Do they sound real to you?"

"I'll listen at 'em. You go on down and bunk. 'Night, brother."

About an hour later, Edmund decided the owls weren't real when he heard one of them sneeze and another strike something metallic. They sounded as if they were on the bank opposite the sand bar. The horses on the foredeck were getting nervous, stamping and blowing. Quickly and silently Edmund went down and roused Greathouse from his bunk and whispered to him in the darkness. Greathouse flung off his blankets.

In minutes the whole crew had been silently awakened, and were on deck with their rifles ready, listening to the night, while Jaybo was reaching out like a cat to untie the mooring lines.

And when the rest of the Clark family arose at daybreak they found themselves already ten miles down the Ohio drifting in midstream through a snow flurry with blanket-wrapped riflemen at every corner of the boat and old Jonas Manifee up on the roof manning his steering sweep, breath vapor coming out of his pig-snout. "Mornin', Master Clark," said he. "Reckon we'll be at Louisville 'fore day's end. Will you be glad t' git there as I will? Been a long haul, ain't it? Started last fall. 'Member that shivaree we had in the cave by th' Monongahela, where your Ma and Pa pranced? Gonna miss you folks."

"How comes it we're under way so early, Jonas?" William asked suspiciously.

"Just eager, I reckon. We all like Louisville a lot."

"But . . ."

"Now, come on, Master Clark. I know y' be some real river rat, but Mister Greathouse *can* run his boats without waitin' for you t' wake your sleepy head up. Ha. Ha!"

428

"Now, husband," said Mrs. Clark, "I must ask ye to step out for a spell, and I want you to stay by the door there and keep menfolks out, because I'm going to clean up these daughters o' yours. Bundle up, for this likely will take us a couple o' hours."

"What!" He looked indignant, but he was happy and eager because he would be in Louisville this day and see his new home. "I'm to stand out in the cold and guard a door for ye, just so ladies can primp up?"

"John dear, this will be a sight more than primping. We're going to clean right to the bone, and dress fresh from th' skin out, for I'm not going to take riverboat vermin into our new house, nor am I going to step my daughters ashore in a new city lookin' anything less than the princesses they are. Now, have Cupid come here and stoke up this fire, and send Venus in. I expect we've got to boil ten bushel o'. clothes, ere we get rid of all the creepy crawly creeturs that's joined us on our migration."

John Clark chuckled and went to fetch the servants. And soon the passenger quarters were full of soapy steam, naked, groaning, gasping girls, stewing petticoats, trunks spilling over with clean linen, clothing fragrant with camphor and cachets, and the smells of hot curling irons and scorching hair. Mrs. Clark assigned the girls each to search the other's body hair for anything that moved, and to wash each other's ears without mercy. The men of the Clark party and the crewmen smiled and winced and shook their heads at the chorus music of anguish, smoked their pipes, watched the high, gray bluffs glide by, and yearned for the comforts and pleasures of the town. The snow had turned to a cold rain, which hissed on the green surface of the broad river.

"Ere long now," Edmund was telling his father, "we'll pass an island and the river will bend to the right, and there'll be a few cabins, and looking down that bend ye should be able to see high up on the left just a glimpse of your new house. Just th' roof is all. I hope they get finished with their tortures down there in time that they can come out and see it too."

Suddenly William's voice came down, chilling them: "I see a craft back there, followin' us down. Can ye make it out, Mister Manifee?"

Instantly everyone was peering up the river, remembering the glow in the sky they had seen last night, remembering the noises that had alarmed them and caused them to slip from the mooring before daybreak.

It was a small vessel, just a speck in the sizzly mist of rain on the river. Mr. Greathouse brought up his telescope and told all his crewmen to check their powder and keep their eyes peeled for canoes along the banks. "I'm damned if I let a pack o' Shawnee stop me when I'm this close to Louisville. I come too far. Boys! Heads down when we run the narrows by th' island!" It seemed likely that an ambush might have been set up there, where the barge would be in close range of either riverbank or island, and that the vessel now following would swoop down on the stern just then.

John Clark rapped on the door of the passenger quarters. "Get them dressed quick," he called in. "There's trouble a-brewin'!" Alarmed voices responded from within.

The great boat slid along at the river's ponderous and unhurriable pace. The craft astern was gaining, its mist-blurred shape growing larger. "Odd," Greathouse said after a while with his glass to his eye. "Oars. That's no canoe, it's a skiff. Just one man a-rowin', it looks t'me."

And a little later, as the barge was entering the narrow water to the left of a brushy island, all the men down behind rails with their rifles ready, scanning the close dark shores, a faint voice came down the river. It was from the little boat.

"He's hollerin' for help," William said.

"Mebbe a decoy," Manifee muttered. "They do that. A fool would heave to in the narrows here and wait to help 'em. Looks like they timed it thataway."

"That is a white man," Greathouse said. "Maybe a hostage decoy. Keep mid-channel, Jonas. Watch those shores, laddies! Master Clark, get down ahind of somethin', if you please."

Now Manifee was the only exposed figure on the superstructure, standing there alone and in plain sight in easy musket range of either side. It took guts to stand there, but it was necessary to keep a man on the sweep; to run aground in an ambushed bottleneck would be the worst kind of blunder.

Shivering, blinking rapidly, expecting anything, William crouched behind the siderail with his thumb on the flintlock of his rifle and watched the reddish willow-slips and yellow-brown reeds of the island glide by. The island was long, more than a mile, it appeared, and every drift-log that loomed in the corner of his vision looked like a concealed canoe. From behind the barge now, the white man's voice was more distinct.

"Wait! Help me! Help us."

"By th' Eternal," Greathouse's voice said, "that's Cap'n Elliot, sure as I breathe! Got womenfolk with 'im! Jack! Jaybo! Stand ready to take 'em on when we clear this island."

Elliot! John Clark thought, remembering his old acquaintance, thinking of the poor dingy woman and child in the door of the log house 'yesterday, thinking of the fireglow in the sky. He stood up and started along the deck toward the stern, still holding his pistols in his hands.

"Pa!" Edmund hissed. "Down!"

John Clark bent a little at the waist but went on to the stern. Then he knelt there between two crouching riflemen and watched the little boat, watched it catching up, saw Elliot's desperate but exhausted labors at the oars, watched the other huddled figures in the skiff.

And at last the downstream end of the island slipped astern, and Manifee put the sweep over to swing the big boat a little toward midstream, and the two crewmen at the stern stood up and put down their rifles, and the one called Jaybo picked up a coil of rope to throw to the little boat. "Here, Cap'n," he called. And as the skiff drew close, Manifee's voice muttered low and harsh:

"Oh, God damn. Oh, help them poor . . ."

John Clark and William were standing at the stern now and they winced at the miserable spectacle in the little boat.

In the bow lay a large, curved, fire-blackened lump. By its shape, and by the white teeth showing where cheeks had been burned away, it revealed itself to be the burned body of a man, drawn up in the shape of a stillborn infant. In places where the charred skin had been pulled loose, the cooked meat of muscle tissue showed through red and gray and brown.

Captain Bob Elliot had caught the thrown rope. His face was sooty and blistered; much of his beard and his eyebrows were singed away. The rags on his body were full of burn holes, and wherever skin showed, it was covered with huge blisters. He grimaced, teeth white in his blackened face, each time he hauled at the rope; his hands were like raw meat. The butts of the oars were black with dried blood and shreds of skin from his hands.

In the stern seat, looking at the barge with glassy eyes, were the woman and girl. They were sooty and abraded, hair hanging in wet strands, naked except for torn, burned cotton chemises gray-black with ash and clinging with wet to their bony bodies in the cold rain. The woman and little girl hugged each other for warmth and gaped at the big riverboat with their jaws hanging slack, as if they lacked the strength even to close their mouths.

And as they were being lifted one by one from the rowboat onto the barge, John Clark went, with tears in his eyes, to the shanty door. He went in. His wife and daughters were waiting

431

inside, all dressed in clean clothes, faces pink, worried, wondering what all the commotion was outside.

"Ann," said John Clark, "brace yourselves now. Here come some poor wretches, and we're going to have to make your room a hospital."

Within fifteen minutes, all the Clark girls were working like nurses under the direction of their mother, sweating, their fresh dresses wilting in the hot room and stained with blood, soot, ointments, and tears.

Bob Elliot told the awful story to John Clark while Mrs. Clark was cleaning his burnt limbs and smearing them with one of her homemade salves.

The body in the boat was his brother. This brother, with three Negroes, had been at work behind the hill, clearing brush for spring planting, when Mr. Clark had come. "When he came down, learnt Mary'd turned y'away, he scolded 'er proper. She fixed 'em vittles, then took Sally t' bed. Whilst they were at table, in bust the door. Shawnees. Tommyhocked 'em. Didn't see Mary and Sally inside the bed curtain. Thank Merciful God. They slipped out the back door, hid down by th' riverside. Dark by then. Murderers looted and scalped and set th' house on fire. It was all on a blaze when I come upriver in th' skiff from huntin'. I . . . I had to lay low till they all went screaming away. I was all of a despair, thought Mary and Sally was in there."

He swallowed and blinked, breathed hard, gritted his teeth as Mrs. Clark spread ointment on his face, then went on.

"But thank Merciful God we found each other. Long time it was 'fore th' house fell in, fire burnt out. I dug my brother out, what y' seen there of 'im. Couldn't find th' darkies. Put 'im in the skiff an' rowed since midnight about." He stopped and swallowed several times, groaning in his throat. "Nothin' left, Mr. Clark. No house, tools, furniture. Nothin'."

"Nothing, you say? Your lives y' call nothing? Shut your eyes now and pray thanks, Mister Elliot, for your precious lives."

Elizabeth and Fanny were kneeling beside a bunk, washing and soothing Mrs. Elliot, while Lucy administered to the stunned little girl Sally. These two were not burned badly, as it was Mister Elliot who had dug in the coals for his brother. But Mary Elliot was too much in shock to speak yet, though she was trying to say something. Every time she would clutch Elizabeth's arm and form her lips to say something, she would be so overcome with weeping that she could not say it. Elizabeth soothed her, tucked a blanket closer around her, gave her broth to sip. And when Ann Rogers Clark came to see how she was, Mary

Elliot was calmed enough to speak. She had lost her voice through exposure, but she could whisper.

"Forgi' me. Forgi' me, Ma'm."

"Forgive ye what, poor dear?"

"I turned y' away . . . turned y' away from my door. I knew . . . I knew who your husband was. My Bob spoke so often how grand ye were. How grand your house is. In Virginny. How ye took 'im in, lent him horses. O, forgi' me! I'd not seen grand folk in so long. I, I was backward. 'Shamed o' th' dirt. Hard bread. Spoiled meat. I just got so backward, got confused. 'Shamed. I told Bob's brother I been, and he call't me fool. I'm true sorry, Ma'm."

"Oh, hush now. O' course no man'd understand that. But I do. So you needn't say another word on't. Now rest easy and don't try to talk."

John and Ann Rogers Clark stepped out onto the rain-wet deck a little later. She was sweaty and dishevelled and stained for her arrival at Louisville. But of course that was unimportant now. The body of Captain Elliot's brother lay wrapped in canvas and rope. William was up with Mister Manifee again. Edmund and Bill Croghan were standing at the rail watching the shore. They were quiet and grave. "Next bend o' the river we'll see the fort at Louisville," Edmund told them. "We all forgot to look at the mulberry house back there. How the Elliots?"

"Barrin' pneumonia, pray the Almighty, they'll be all right," said Ann Clark. "John, do I have your permission to take 'em in?"

"Take 'em in?"

"At Mulberry Hill, till they're fit again. There's room, if the house is as grand as all I've heard."

"Oh! Oh, surely. I've already told Mr. Elliot they may." He shook his head and gazed toward the shore. "He explained t' me why she shut th' door. She—"

"Aye. She told me, and begged our pardon."

"Begged our pardon!" John Clark exclaimed, looking high over the bluffs and shaking his head. "Begs our pardon! While if she'd let us in, we'd surely all be dead in the ashes by now, like him!" He glanced down at the lump of canvas, and they looked, paling, just now realizing this. "Don't ever say it to 'er," John Clark added, "but th' poor awkward thing was the salvation of us. Aye, she can stay with us the rest of 'er days, is what I say. Let's bow our heads now and give thanks."

*   *   *

"JUBILATION! WHAT A LAND WE'VE COME INTO!" JOHN Clark exclaimed as the army wagon rolled eastward up the slope from Louisville toward Mulberry Hill.

"Papa," said Elizabeth, "am I just under a spell, or are those trees twice as big as Virginia trees?"

"I'll swear they look it," he said, reaching across in his excitement and squeezing her hand.

The seats in the army wagon were planks parallel with the wagon's sides, so the passengers rode going sideways, facing each other. It was an odd feeling to ride that way. Elizabeth sat opposite her parents and between her sisters. She really did feel as if she were in some kind of an enchantment. It was like living in a novel. This morning there had been that terrible business with the fear of Indians and the rescue of the Elliots, and then they had landed at the wharf in the raw, sawdusty town of Louisville, and there had been that sudden great bustle of people down to greet the family of General Clark, and that princely Major Anderson bringing down the army wagon from the fort to carry them in, and now here they were going up through the gigantic landscape with an honor guard of mounted soldiers, and people running alongside calling happily to them.

But now the big horse pulling the wagon loosed wind again, loudly and richly, and Elizabeth had to bite the inside of her cheek to keep from laughing. She could sense Lucy and Fanny almost bursting with hilarious embarrassment too. Here they were parading along like a royal family, and that big oaf of a dray horse just a-pootin' and a-flutin' as if it meant to keep this all from being too elegant. And that Major Anderson who was driving the wagon, he was trying to look so dignified through it all, tall and fair and fine-featured as a prince he was, but Elizabeth could see that his neck and ears were a flaming red, because of what that horse kept doing so unabashedly. Animals are so . . . so . . . *indifferent*, she thought. Elizabeth loved horses, and she loved this particular one especially now.

The major was from the Hanover County Andersons, practically neighbors back in old Virginia. He had been to the Clark house with Jonathan long ago, but Elizabeth had been just a child then and couldn't remember him. He was probably fifteen or twenty years older than she. Yet there was something about that careful dignity of his, and about the way he had looked at her when he met them at the wharf, something that had made her feel a way she had never felt before: a kind of strange, wild, mischievous impulse to snatch his hat off and put it behind her back until he lost all his dignity and ran after her begging for it, blushing. She had had that impulse to make him blush, but of course she would never have done such a naughty thing, as she was the most proper of John Clark's daughters. But now that awful, wonderful old horse up there was doing it for her, making that princely officer blush.

Well, it was such a funny and unexpected thing, all so light and silly, and Elizabeth found herself so uncommonly amused and titillated by it. Somehow the meeting of this princely officer, here in this rough new town in the magnificent countryside, had cast her into a storybook mood, like something in a novel, in which the most fetching people always appear just at the most exciting times.

"Now here we go up to Mulberry Hill!" announced Edmund, who sat on the driving seat beside Major Anderson. The wagon was turning off the muddy public road onto a side road, an uncommonly pretty side road, rather like an avenue, with a footpath and two rows of young locust trees on each side of the carriage way. A high, handsome wooden gate was visible at the far end. John and Ann Rogers Clark were now craning in their seat, their mouths open. "Oh," she was saying, "it's impressive, and it's Jonathan's doin's, if I know him!" She looked as if she couldn't make up her mind whether she would laugh or cry.

"It's so," said Edmund. "His crowning touch, just before he left. He thinks people should *know* they're comin' someplace uncommon, and by Heaven, they will know it, won't they?"

"Aye, but the *land!*" John Clark exclaimed. "Look at this *land!*" To the right of the avenue were fields already cleared, and on the left was a deep hardwood forest, with poplars and walnut trees and oaks five feet through the trunks. "Stop here, please, Major! We want down."

The wagon stopped and the rest of the caravan stopped behind it—the furniture wagons, the wagon with the servants, the wagon with the poor, bandaged Elliots in it, the horses that William Clark and Bill Croghan were riding. Gaping like a wondering child at the vista of the great river far below, old John Clark climbed down from the wagon and helped his wife and daughters down, and then he walked slowly, softly off the road and into the wet spring grass among the locusts.

"Feel that! Smell that," he exclaimed. "Step on this soil and it breathes up at you!" Beside one of the locust trees he knelt on the ground. With his big hands cupped he scooped up the dark, moist soil, and crumbled it between his thumbs and fingers, murmuring, "Mmmmmmh! Mmmmmmh!" And then he brought it up in his palms and put his face in it and breathed of it.

"Down here," he said. And they all understood him and knelt near him. Elizabeth, imagining that Major Anderson was looking at her from ⁀back at the wagon, now felt the ground-damp soak cold through to her knees. With crumbs of earth still on his face, John Clark said, "O Almighty God, help us to be good custodians of your fruitful soil. Amen." And then he sat back on his heels and exclaimed with a wide-eyed smile, "Looks to me like, after you put a seed in that ground, you'd better jump back! Ha, haaaaa! Now! Let's go up and taste that spring water!"

The spring was likewise to his taste, and now they were within a few yards of the house, and the girls simply broke away and made a run for it. It was an imposing place, so long and steep-roofed that it looked more massive even than their great stone house in Caroline. The yellow-gray logs were two to three feet broad, yet dove-tailed so precisely at the corners that they might have been done by a clockmaker. There were porches front and back, and at each end stood a great stone chimney. The house, springhouse, smokehouse, servants' row, stables, and the stone kitchen house were all enclosed by a white-painted five-plank fence, the only painted fence they had seen either in Louisville or on the ride out. All the windows of the house had glass panes and thick oaken shutters. "Lordy, it could be a fort!" William cried from somewhere.

"Mama, you should be the first in the house!" Elizabeth called from the broad front porch, "as it's to be your domain!" To Elizabeth it had always seemed that way; her father's domain was the land. From here on the porch now, Elizabeth was seeing the vista that George had first seen: the splendid woods and meadows sloping away down into the great broad river valley, the high, dark bluffs opposite, the white water of the Falls downstream.

And up the flagstones of the doorpath came her mother now, tall and important as a queen, though her skirts and sleeves were smudged with soot and ointment and blood. John Clark came walking at her side, in that way of his with his hand at the small of her back so that it seemed he was leading her and at the same time following her. Bill Croghan was coming up the path behind them, and Lucy had run to join him, and, Elizabeth saw, he was walking her in that same protective way. Down at the wagon, Major Anderson was off the wagon and among the honor guard as they dismounted. In her fancy now Elizabeth foresaw herself walking with Major Anderson touching her waist just so—and suddenly felt the heat of a flush on her own face.

Their steps resounded in the wide central hall. "Just like home!" John Clark exclaimed. There was the sideboard halfway down the hall. And though the house was of hewn logs, the doors and banisters were all planed and rabbeted and fluted. It was plain that Louisville had fine craftsmen already.

"Just *like* home?" Ann Rogers Clark retorted. "It *is* home!" They made a quick tour of the three stories. On the top floor were two garret bedrooms with dormer windows. These would be the girls' rooms. Elizabeth stood in a dormer window and looked down at the soldiers near the wagon. Major Anderson was standing in front of the dray horse, stroking its throatlatch, and it looked as if he were talking to the animal. Fanny was sitting in the window seat of another dormer, crying, "Oh, a body can just see all the world from here!" Footsteps were thundering everywhere in the house, and Ann Rogers Clark's voice was saying, ". . . must get the rugs in, just right away."

George's belongings were in one downstairs room, Bill Croghan's in another. Mrs. Clark stood looking in at her son's worldly posessions: a chest, a trunk of books, a cot, an extra pair of boots, one uniform on a clotheshorse, a jug, a writing box, a sheaf of maps on a field desk. It's not much property for the main gent of a territory, she thought. But then he's never had a place to light, always been on the move. George was gone now, had been gone for more than a week, Major Anderson had told them, off on some business of the Indian Commission. John Clark stood beside his wife in the doorway of the spartan room, and said, "It's going to make me very happy to have that boy under our own roof a while again after these dozen years."

IT WAS ANOTHER WEEK, AND ALL THE FURNITURE WAS IN place, when George came riding up the road one rainy day with a squad of hard-looking men-at-arms, all mud-spattered and haggard and unshaven, returning from Vincennes. "Welcome at last to Kentuck, old family," he boomed. He was grinning a grin that looked more like a grimace; there was something pained in his eyes. He wrapped his mother in a teary-eyed bear hug, and held her that way for a long time, patting her back and swaying her from side to side. Then he hugged his father, then William, and with his arms over Edmund's and Bill Croghan's shoulders praised them for getting the family down safe. Lucy kissed his stubbly cheek and then fussed that he was as stickery as a raspberry patch. Elizabeth hugged him and told him he had surely found for them the most perfect homesite in all the country. "Ah, you're more beauteous than ever," he told her, "and kind with your words, which makes ye twice so." Fanny squeezed him around the waist, her eyes squinted tight with the effort of the squeeze, and said:

"I can see from my window, the place where you want *your* house to be, on that dark promontory above the Falls. You should want to live closer to us!"

He laughed, and held her at arms' length. "Promontory!" he exclaimed. "What kind o' language is that for a girl o' twelve? Well, listen, Fanny, I'm too busy to build a house yetawhile, so I'll be livin' as close as ye'll want: I mean right here."

Then they had their old style of a reunion, with toasts at the sideboard. He sent his riders around to the kitchen house to be fed, then he toured through the house with the family, cheerfully acknowledging how they had placed everything to make it a home, carrying a brandy in his hand, asking them how they liked this and that. But his mother could see that he was distracted, that there was something glum underneath; he was behaving as if he were just letting them have their jollity out and trying not to spoil it. At last, having him in a corner somewhere, she asked him if there was something heavy on him.

"Aye, mostly to do with the Indian business, but never you mind it."

Later, though, when he was alone with his parents, he told them.

Coming back from Vincennes, he and his riders had combed the lands along the Buffalo Trace, and they had queried all the friendly Indians in the vicinity.

And then somewhere near the Forks of the Blue River, he said, they had turned up some horse bones, and the remains of a saddle with the initials R.C. branded in it. "Dickie's saddle," he said. His mother closed her eyes, her face paling. His father's jaw muscles clenched. George said:

"It doesn't mean we should stop prayin'. It might mean though that the prayin' won't ever be answered."

24

WILLIAM CLARK STOOD SWEATING, ARMS FOLDED, WATCHING the furious Shawnee and listening to his hissing and snarling and shouting. The tension in the council house was like a finger on a hair-trigger. William eased his hands secretly over the butts of the pistols in his belt, his father's fancy pistols. He was aware that he was in greater danger than he had ever been in before and probably ever would be in the future—as there very well might be no future. William had talked his father into letting him come with George to the council with the Shawnees here at Fort Finney, and now he was almost wishing his father had not let him come.

The large council room smelled of new wood, tobacco, and the body musk of seventy Indians, Delawares and Wyandots as well as Shawnees. Brother George and two other Indian Commissioners, General Butler and Mr. Parsons, sat behind a table at the end of the room, and a dozen white soldiers and officers stood along the side walls, all drawn tight as fiddle strings, their eyes darting over the crowd of seated savages.

The shouting Indian, a tall, sinewy Shawnee chieftain, was standing in front of the treaty table, practically on tiptoe, his nostrils distended and his eyes sparking, holding in one hand a peace belt of white beads and a war belt of red beads. Under a breastplate made of rows of colored quills, his chest was rising and falling rapidly. He was talking so fast and so hatefully that spittle was bubbling in his mouth-corners. The translator was having trouble keeping up with him, but the gist of his tirade was plain enough to William and to everybody: He was telling the Commissioners in effect that they could take the terms of their treaty and go bury them where the dog buries his waste. This outburst was stunning; it was the first breach of ceremony in all the days of the council. The negotiations heretofore had been serious and tough, but amiable. The Delaware and Wyandot chiefs, and the old toothless Moluntha, chief of the Maykujay Shawnees, had listened respectfully to the Indian Commissioners, and had kept the younger hotbloods, such as this one, under control. They had acknowledged that their warriors' raids into Cain-tuck-ee were causing distress not just to the whites, but

439

to their brothers in the peaceable tribes. They had professed a yearning to lay down the tomahawk. They had agreed that many white women and children they held captive were guilty of nothing and should be returned to their families. It had all been amiable, and William had met and learned to respect many of the Indian chiefs and chieftains, and had even joined with braves and squaws in the incredible excitement and abandon of one of the evening entertainments, a kind of copulation dance, in the Indian village near the fort. But just this morning George had cautioned: "It's going too well. They'd be fools to swallow the damned terms we're offering. The old chiefs are doing what they can. It's always the old ones who want peace. But mark my words, the young buckoes are going to raise hell before pen touches paper!"

And now this young chieftain, whose name was Ke-hene-pe-li-tha, was poised over the table, shouting, hissing, snarling at the Commissioners, and the seventy Indians in the room seemed to be rising an inch off the floor they were seated on, while the three Commissioners sat on their chairs with their faces set grim.

Ke-hene-pe-li-tha was saying that the Long Knives had grown too proud after throwing down the King of England. He was saying that the Shawnees would never give up the land east of the Miami River as the treaty said they must. "We do not understand dividing this land, some for you, some for us," he was shouting. "The Great Spirit gave it all to *us*!" William remembered George's story of Logan and the unseen lines on the land.

Ke-hene-pe-li-tha now protested the part of the treaty that said the Shawnees must leave five chiefs as hostages until the white captives were collected and brought here for liberation; he said the Shawnees had never given hostages, that their word was enough. William heard the "*ah-hai-ee, ah-ah-hai-ees*" of approval the excited Indians were murmuring everywhere in the room. He watched George.

George, for some reason, was not looking at the ranting chieftain. His eyes were on old Moluntha, then on the terribly scarred face of chief Buckangehela of the Delawares.

Now Ke-hene-pe-li-tha had put the war and peace belts on the table and was waiting for answer. William heard George say, "Firmly, Mr. Butler."

General Butler, a solid, granite-faced Pennsylvanian, said:

"We will not rely on your word, as we know the Shawnee breaks his word."

A subdued roar of fury filled the room. All the soldiers were fingering their flintlocks. General Butler picked up the white and red beads the chieftain had put on the table and said, "We will

440

not change our terms. And we will not accept these strings because you put them here in anger." And he flipped them carelessly back on the table. The Indians growled at this treatment of their tokens, but still did not move.

And then, to William's horror, George raised his swagger stick and, still staring into the eyes of Moluntha, swept the belts off the table. They whispered into a heap on the floor. William's heart was slamming so hard inside his ribs he thought it would burst out. And he was thinking, George, you gone mad, brother? That's too much!

But George had not finished. He stood up and, his steely blue eyes at last fixed on the bulging eyes of Ke-hene-pe-li-tha, he put his foot on the belts.

It ended the meeting. The Shawnees rose in a furious muttering and stalked out of the building into the cold air, followed hesitantly by the Delawares and Wyandots, who kept looking back dubiously at George. The soldiers eased down the hammers of their guns, which they had cocked when the Indians rose. All the Indians streamed out of the stockade and strode, almost running, toward their camp. "Cap'n Finney," George said, "have every man ready to defend the walls. Don't shut the gate. But be ready to."

William looked wonderingly at his brother from time to time in the next hour as the other commissioners and the interpreter stood near him talking. And then Captain Finney came in. "Sir," he said, "they're back, and they beg another meeting."

"Good," George said, as if this were what he had fully expected.

This time the spokesman was old Chief Moluntha. His speech was short. He held a white belt in his thin, gnarled hand. "This," he said, "is to do away with all our warrior said in heat. We wish your country to have pity on our women and children. We have named three chiefs to go and bring your prisoners. We have named five to stay as hostages until they come."

George nodded and shook old Moluntha's hand, then made a brief speech, thanking the older chiefs for their wisdom. Most of the white men were barely concealing their relief and their sense of triumph as the peace pipes were smoked. But George displayed no delight.

"IT'S A FARCE, BILLY LAD," HE SAID THAT NIGHT AS THEY SAT on their cots and pulled off their boots. "Even old Moluntha will live longer than this treaty."

There were two vertical frown lines above his nose, and William realized that they were always there now.

When the candle was out and they were lying in the cooling dark of the room, the little hearth-fire making a glow among the rafter poles, William heard George turn heavily in his bedding, and then his voice came, as if he were talking to himself.

"On and on. Just one treaty and then another. It's like old Chief Logan told me: it just can't work. This continent's not big enough. Everything that fire-eatin' Shawnee said today is true, about the land, I mean. Sad thing: Old Logan died a drunk, because it's too sorry a thing to bear."

It was quiet for a long time, and then William asked, "What's a body to do about it?"

It was another long time before George's voice came again. "Y' have to be true to your own people. But these savages, they're as right as we are. Damn it. Have y'ever seen a finer people than these Shawnees you've met here?"

"No. Truly."

"Well, someday soon, I fear, you'll be fighting 'em, Billy. And then you'll see how fine they really be. And how terrible. They've been pushed as far as they'll be pushed. Congress expects 'em to believe its promises. Hell's fire, Billy, I can't even believe Congress my own self. I've got such a putrid taste in my mouth and such an empty feeling in my pockets from public service." His voice trailed off. Then after a while he said:

"I'm talking too much."

William had been sleepy, exhausted by the strain of the day, but now his mind was in an uproar. He was only fifteen, but duty and love of country had always been of such importance in his family that one believed in them almost as one believes in the light of the sun. And now to hear his brother George, renowned as the greatest patriot of the family, doubting and speaking bitterly of his government even while risking his life to serve it, caused a strange, disturbing shadow in his mind.

Now George's voice was saying tiredly in the darkness:

"Mark what I say. This is going to stick in the Shawnee's gizzard. He's going to forget this treaty like you forget a dream by breakfast time."

THREE WEEKS AFTER THE SIGNING OF THE TREATY, THE FIVE Shawnee hostages deserted. As they left the vicinity they kidnapped the wife and children of a settler near Fort Finney while the man was absent on a hunting party. The Indian War of 1786—actually the continuation of a war that seemed to have gone on forever—was begun.

George Rogers Clark was totally unaware of it. On his return to Mulberry Hill from the treaty councils, he had fallen into a deep illness. *"Your brother George is with me very sick,"* John Clark wrote to Jonathan in March, *"his complaint being of such a nature as keeps us in doubt."*

ELIZABETH CLARK SAT IN THE PILLOWED ROCKING CHAIR BEside George's bed and looked at his gaunt, craggy face in the light of the single candle, and hoped he would not stir and go into a delirium again. She sat in dread of those, during her watches over him. Some nights he did not have them at all, or had them while Lucy or her mother were sitting up with him. Each of the females of the household sat a three-hour watch over him every night, except Fanny, who was considered not old enough to know what to do if he had a crisis.

And there was always a man up, too, either John Clark or William, or Bob Elliot, armed and going like a sentry through or around the house, because of the Indian raids. There had not been a raid on the Clark house yet, but on two nights there had been sounds of distant shooting and the red glow of fires visible from the upstairs windows. These things had been terribly frightening at first, but, as Elizabeth had learned to tell herself, one can grow accustomed to anything, and the stark fright of these long vigils had settled lately into a deep, edgy dread, only now and then leaping up as real fright when some night-noise in or around the house would make her ears prickle and her heart pound and her mouth dry up.

And so there had not been much sleep in the Clark house at Mulberry Hill for almost a month.

Elizabeth looked at the two points of candlelight, the real one and the one reflected on the window pane, and she thought about Major Anderson of the militia. She remembered detail by detail, emotion by emotion, as she had done a hundred times probably, the moment last Christmas Eve when, flushed from dancing, she had gone down the hallway to stand in the cool mud-room off the back porch. She had been standing there, of all places, in the dark amid the mud-and-wet-wool smells of cloaks and boots, when suddenly she had felt two hands on her shoulders. She had hardly started at the touch, because somehow she had thought, or had prayed, that he would follow her. And he had, silently he had followed her, and had put his hands on her shoulders.

Lord, though, she thought now, if that'd happen now since this Indian trouble, I'd have wet myself!

It's a good thing Papa keeps the shutters shut nights, she

thought, or I'd be afraid to look at that window for fear of seeing Indian faces in it.

George groaned and made a gurgling sound deep in his lungs, and she looked at him. He had to lie propped up with pillows almost in a sitting position so he would not choke or strangle. When he was unconscious it was so much deeper than mere sleep that he could perish without waking himself up. She listened and watched until the sounds stopped, and his breathing was even, then she leaned back in the chair, carefully so it would not creak and frighten her.

Here I sit in a room with the man all the Indians are scared of, she thought, and I'm timid as a lamb in a wolf den.

I wonder whether the Indians know this is the house the Long Knife Chief lives in, she thought.

If they do, they must not know he's dying, or they'd have fallen on us by now.

It's a good thing the shutters are shut, she thought again. If some of them crept up on the porch and could look in and see the Long Knife Chief here in a sleeping spell, or when he's thrashin' around all sweat-soaked or whimpering with chills, or messing his bed . . . Merciful and Almighty God, what would become of Kentucky and us who live here!

It was better to think of Major Anderson, better to look at the two points of candle flame and remember Christmas Eve, than to look at George the way he was and get all shivery with dread, or all poignant with thinking how beloved he was and how awful a loss it would be to everybody, not just the family. She took another quick look at him and wondered how it could be possible that in the same family there could be one person too timid to look behind her rocking chair and another bold enough to throw sacred beads on the floor in a room full of warrior chiefs. William had told the family about that, over and over.

So she thought of Major Anderson's hands on her shoulders, and remembered how in the cool mud-room she had felt his warm breath on her neck and smelled the wassail-bowl smell and how then he had said, "Miss Elizabeth," so softly, and then had put his mouth to her ear and inhaled, a shuddering breath.

She shivered violently, just as she had then.

He had jumped back then, and stammered an apology for startling her—because he had mistaken her shiver for a start of fright.

And that had struck her so funny at the time that she had just burst out laughing, a silly, hiccuping laugh that had utterly disconcerted him. And he had said he was sorry, he felt like a perfect fool.

And then Elizabeth had said such a rash thing; it had just rushed out of her because of some giddy, loving rush of sympathy; she had said—Oh she could remember still exactly the words—she had said:

"Richard Anderson, sir, the very first time I laid eyes on you, I wanted to make you feel like a perfect fool! I wanted to grab your hat off and make you blush!"

Somehow those words had completely flustered him. He had stammered, "I . . . I . . . Wh . . ." and then he had turned and all but fled back to the ballroom, and had not spoken to her the rest of the evening, only blushing red on that princely visage whenever the dancing brought them face to face.

Ah, I handled that in a sorry manner, she thought now. She had seen the major three or four times since. Now that the Indians were ravaging the countryside, the militia were on the roads constantly, and often it was he who came to inquire whether General Clark was well enough to be moved yet, and to urge John Clark to bring his family and George into the safety of Fort Jefferson.

And still he would blush when he saw her, and she felt so sorry for him, and she prayed for a time when they might talk alone together, so that she could explain.

That time will come, she thought. I just know such things as are going to happen someday, and I know that once he's no longer afraid I'm laughing at him, he's going to say what he came out in that silly mud-room to say, and that is, that he loves me.

For a while she had thought that Major Anderson came by the plantation so often because of his unvoiced affection for her. But then one day she had heard him say to her father that everyone wanted George to take the leadership of the state militia again and do something that would put a stop to the Indian activity.

John Clark had flown into a rare state of temper at that.

"Mister Anderson," he had said through tight lips, "my son has ruined his health and lost his fortune in serving this state, and all the reward he's got is being slandered in Assembly! I doubt he'll get up from that bed ever. But if he does, I pray you'll all let him alone a while, and stop trying to thrust the sword of Duty into his hand, for it's his nature to take it, even when he shouldn't! Let him rest!"

Elizabeth looked at George now, at the massive forehead, the red hair, the sunken eyes, the great, long-fingered hands on the counterpane, and wondered whether he would ever get up. It all would depend on whether he wanted to or not. That, no one knew. Now he turned his head to and fro on the pillow. She could hear William trudging up the hall, and upstairs the floor was creaking, her mother getting up to come and assume the vigil. Early birds were cheeping querulously outside. Outside the bullet-proof oaken shutters, she knew, the light of a spring day would be starting to pale the eastern firmament. Another night past and the Indians had not struck, and George had neither improved nor died.

She wondered whether Major Anderson was awake at this hour and whether, if he were, he would be thinking of her.

George gurgled deep inside. One of his hands flew up, then flopped down on the counterpane. And he said something that sounded like:

"Trees."

He dreams of trees so much, she thought.

Why might that be?

I should ask him sometime, she thought.

And then tears welled up, stinging her tired, dry eyelids, when she realized that she might never get a chance to ask him.

ELIZABETH AWOKE TO A BABBLE OF EXCITED VOICES, HER heart pounding. Downstairs there seemed to be a score of voices crying incoherent words, shouting at each other, some wailing, and doors banging and footsteps thundering. They were all female voices, except for York's. He kept yelling, "Oooooooh Yes'm! Oooooh!" Somewhere else, Mary Elliot was screaming like a madwoman.

Elizabeth had come up to sleep a few hours after her watch over George, and had slept deeply. Now her racing heart was trying to pump the somnolent numbness out of her extremities. "Mama!" she cried out. "Mama! What's happening?"

Someone was running up the stairs. The door flew inward and Lucy came running in, carrying George's long, slender fowling gun, her face set with a fighting firmness such as Elizabeth had not seen since Lucy had tried to stop being a tomboy. Lucy ran to the dormer window with the gun. Downstairs now, their mother's voice was commanding, "Pull all those shutters to. Move, York, MOVE!"

"Yes'm! Oooooh!"

"Lucy! What's wrong?" Elizabeth cried, at last getting her feet out of the bedclothes and onto the floor.

Lucy was pulling open a casement of the dormer window. "Indians," she said. "Slaves come a-runnin' in, said they saw a passel of 'em in the woods yonder." Lucy was peering out and down now toward those woods. From the next room came Fanny's voice:

"See any yet?" Apparently she was at her window too.

"Lucy! Betty! Fanny!" Mrs. Clark's voice came up the stairs. "Where are you all?"

"Eeeeeeeee! Eeeeeee!" Mary Elliot was screaming, and then she was sobbing, "God have mercy! Oh, God have mercy!" And her daughter Sally was wailing.

"We're up here, Mama!" Fanny's voice called down.

"Get down here!"

Lucy's lips were drawn back and her white teeth were clenched, and she was peering into the gray-brown woods beyond the white fence, trying to penetrate the delicate screen of new green leaf-buds, the shotgun poking out the open window. "I don't see any."

"We'd better go down," Elizabeth gasped beside her. Her heart was thudding so hard she could scarcely hear her own words.

"Not yet," Lucy said. "Ye can't see a thing from down there, shutters all closed. Better stand back, case I get a shot."

"There!" Fanny's voice shrieked from the next room. "Oh, Heaven save us! It really is! Oh! Oh!"

Elizabeth could scarcely believe this most dreaded of all things was finally happening. It was like something out of George's old stories about Harrod's Town and Boonesboro, and it was just too terribly unthinkable that she herself could be in the midst of real mortal danger. But she could not keep from looking now. It was a bright, clear morning out there. She stood behind Lucy, looking over her shoulders toward the woods. And then she saw them.

Moving between two huge oaks, coming toward the fence in a swift, crouching run, was an Indian with blue paint on his face, and a gun in his hand, and behind him came another, and then there were more. The first one reached the fence, paused, then put his left hand on top of a fence post and one foot up on a plank. At that moment Lucy cocked the hammer of the fowling gun with a *click*. She had never fired a gun in her life, but had watched her brothers do it, and she had drawn a bead on many an imaginary Indian with unloaded guns, back in her pea-shooter days.

The blue-faced Indian was pulling himself to the top of the fence now, his hideous face looking toward the downstairs of the house. Lucy pulled the trigger.

The gun's crashing recoil spun her backward against Elizabeth and they both fell to the floor, the gun on top of them. They had not seen whether she had hit the Indian. Lucy was groaning in pain, her eyes squeezed shut. But Fanny's voice was crying from the next room:

"They're hiding! They're hiding! Shoot again!"

"Oh! I can't! I think my shoulder's broke!" In a tangle of skirts, she and Elizabeth were trying to get up. "Oh! Damnation! I forgot to bring up more powder and—"

Suddenly there were sounds like axes whacking a tree trunk, and gunshots from outside and below. The sounds were of musketballs hitting the mulberry logs. There was a sound of tinkling glass somewhere. "Oh!" Fanny's voice cried. "They're shooting at our house!"

Now they could hear more footsteps mounting the stairs, and their mother's voice calling to them. "Lucy! Fanny! Get down here! Elizabeth Clark! You come down!" Another gunshot reverberated in the house.

They went down with her. Another gun boomed below as they went down the stairs, the four of them, Lucy holding her right shoulder with her left hand while Elizabeth carried the shotgun. She could smell the burnt powder.

The downstairs was full of slave women, lying on the floor praying and moaning. Mary Elliot and her daughter were sitting on a mammy bench outside the library, hugging each other and sobbing. In the library, York, the only male in the house except the unconscious George, was loading a rifle, tamping powder down with a ramrod. Billy had taught him to shoot and he was a fairly good marksman when shooting at game. But now he was trembling so violently that he was spilling powder as he primed the rifle. Now he poked it quickly out through the saucer-sized rifle port in the shutter and pulled the trigger with his eyes closed, then jerked the rifle back in and crouched behind the window sill to reload it.

"Oh, York! You craven!" Lucy screamed at him. "Y' have to *aim*! D'ye think they're scared o' mere *noise*?"

He just crouched there reloading, shaking his head and saying, "Ooooooooh! Oooooh!"

But, as if mere noise had scared the attackers, there was no more shooting from outside now. But far away, down the road, there was yelling, and the sounds of galloping horses.

A few minutes later, John and William Clark rode up from the fields, Bob Elliot and half a dozen armed field hands following them, and up to the gate thundered a squad of militia scouts, who had heard the shooting while passing on the public road below. Major Anderson was not among them, to Elizabeth's disappointment. They rode all over the grounds, but found no trace of the savages, except their footprints on the ground in the woods and outside the yard fence. There were some buckshot pellets in the white fence, and a few small blood spots on the fence post where Lucy had aimed the bird gun.

Maybe the Indians had been expecting a totally undefended house, with a few women easy prey in it, the militiamen speculated. Maybe they had been very edgy about coming to this house anyway, for surely they knew it was where the Long Knife Chief lived, and they had quit at the first sign of a defense. Again the militiamen implored John Clark to bring his family in to the safety of the fort, and this time he said he would think about it.

As for George himself, he had been totally unaware of the attack. All the shooting and screaming had failed to rouse him from his coma.

One thing was certain, something they had learned in a year since they had come to their new home: Kentucky was no paradise.

It looked like one, but it surely wasn't.

"LUCY, IT'S YOUR BEAUUUUUU!" FANNY SANG OUT.

Lucy was outside and off the porch and down to the gate before Bill Croghan reached it. He swung off his horse, laughing, lifted Lucy up and swung her in circles, then set her down and kissed her on the mouth, while Fanny chanted from the dormer window: "Little Brother Lucy has a beau! Little Brother Lucy! Ho, ho, ho!"

Lucy raised a fist at her, then winced.

"Lucy! You hurt?" Bill Croghan exclaimed.

"Just an achy shoulder. I'll tell you later." They were walking up toward the house now, and other members of the family were coming out on the porch to greet him. The leaves of May were full out on the trees now, fresh light green, and the yard was edged with wildflowers transplanted from the woods.

"How about George?" he said.

"I swear you ask o' him 'fore you think o' me!"

"Not so, not so!" he laughed. "I just want 'im to get well so I won't always have to be away from you doing *all* the surveying! I take it then that he's better?"

"Some better. We have to sit on 'im to keep him abed."

"Ha! Good news! Hello! Hello!" He tethered his horse at the post and went up onto the porch, hugging everybody. "So the old Long Knife's getting his edge back, eh?"

"Aye, and raring to talk to you," said John Clark. "We worried so much about you. Did ye hear that four–five hundred savages struck Louisville last month?"

"I heard."

"A band of 'em struck our house," Elizabeth said. "This very house. But Lucy fought them off!"

"Ha, ha! No doubt!"

"No! Really truly! See the bullet holes in the logs?"

Bill Croghan paled. "You're serious, aren't you?"

"Yes. And she really did, too," said William, who had just come out. They embraced and thumped each other on the back. "George's in there bellowin' for you, can y' hear 'im?"

"Hey? What do you say? I can't hear you for that bellowing in there. Ha, ha! Let's go see him. I'm running over with intelligence from upriver, and I'm sure he's got plenty on his mind too. Hey! Pipe down, General! I hear you! I hear you! Ha, ha! Come on, everybody, let's swarm on him!"

"IT SEEMS TO BE A CONFEDERATION OF TRIBES," BILL Croghan said, "mostly of the Wabash area. Weas, Piankeshaws, Miamis. Depending on who's talking, there's fifteen hundred on up to five thousand of them."

George nodded. His face was very pale and thin, but the old keenness was back in his eyes. "That's about what I hear. Their base is Ouiatanon, isn't that so?"

"Ouiatanon. Correct."

"That's awful close to Vincennes. I bet our friends up there are in a state of nerves."

"They well might be," Croghan said. "Do you have a name of their main chief? I've heard a name something like 'Mishy-ginny-something.' Do you know of him?"

"It's Michi-kini-qua. Little Turtle. I remember him, a Miami. A good face. He's something to be reckoned with. I'd say he has more shrewdness and dignity than all of Congress put together. Though that's not saying much, is it? What I hear is, some of the Shawnee are keen to join his confederation. If they do, this country's as forlorn as it was any time in the war."

In the year since William had been in Kentucky with George, he had come to understand that one of his chief advantages was his unofficial network of spies. They were not really spies, but they were a set of friends so diverse and wide-ranging and observant, and so eager to keep him informed, that even here in his sickbed he probably knew more of what prevailed in the territory than any other man. These friends were French bushlopers and merchants, American scouts and Indian fighters, rivermen, mili-

450

tia officers, long hunters, innkeepers, surveyors, county clerks, old comrades-in-arms, explorers, even some of the Indians he had known in the war, both as friends and as enemies. These people brought him news and talk, some of it rumor and some of it gossip and some of it reliable truth. He absorbed it all and assimilated it and fit things together in his mind until he was very certain he had the specific truth about any one thing, and a general picture of how all the little things fit together. William by and by had come to realize that it was knowledge, as well as courage and endurance, that had made his brother the most successful leader in the West. Now as William sat with George and Croghan and listened to them talk by the hour, he understood a little better how it worked. George had a voracious appetite for facts and his attention never flagged. Although he was lying back on pillows, he seemed to lean forward.

". . . some of the savages they killed up at Limestone had new British muskets," Croghan was saying.

"Aye," George replied. "I . . ." He was rubbing his hands together and he looked down at them. "These empty paws o' mine are giving me the jimjams," he said. "I need a pipe in one and a glass in the other when I'm listenin'. Billy, will you go fetch me those? Medicinal," he said with a wink.

And when William came back with them, George was talking about Detroit. "The place is still full o' Tories," he said. "It's ours by the Treaty but it's theirs because they occupy it. If I'd got the help I needed in the war, we'd be there now and there'd be no Hair-Buyers there to keep pumping up the savages. That would be some help. Thank'ee, Billy. Ah. Well, I learned how to run up and butt the mountain. I'm glad I'm not a general anymore. Especially now, by God. Serving Virginia was perplexity enough to put boils on a man's brain, but now a body has to satisfy Congress too, and that's like trying to braid a comet's tail. No, I sure don't want to be anybody's general again."

"They want you to, you know," Croghan said.

George took a sip of his "medicine" and smacked his lips. It made his eyes water. "D'you know, Bill, the first sight to greet my eyes when I gathered my faculties was, in place of the Angels of Heaven, a delegation of gents standin' round the foot o' this bed asking me to go up and thrash the Wabash tribes. Never mind that I resigned my commission three years ago. Never mind that I can't handle a pen yet, let alone a sword. Never mind I still haven't been paid yet for my last war. They told me I was the only one could stop the Wabash Confederation.

"But I've learned a thing or two about people who flatter to get you to do things for 'em. They'll get you to commit your whole body and soul, and then they won't give any help. That's been done to me by every governor Virginia's ever had. And the County Lieutenants are worse at it. No, siree. Those tribes are in Federal lands, but Congress won't bear the expense o' controllin' 'em, so they're free to carry their torches into Kentucky, and now gents gather round my sickbed and beg me, 'Go do what Congress can't.' Ha!"

"Then you won't, I take it."

"I didn't say that. I just say I'd be a fool to. Listen, Here's what I'd be getting myself into: I've studied the Invasion Law. It says a state can wage a campaign against any Indian nation that invades it, but it can't take the militia out o' the state without their consent. That's the Invasion Law, and here's why it worries me: Lincoln and Fayette County don't see this as their war, but as Jefferson County's. To them the only Indians are the Shawnees directly across the river from 'em. I learned long ago they'll raise troops in a hurry to go kill Shawnees, but try to do something worthwhile, like going to Detroit, and they balk. They'll know it's not legal for me to take 'em against Ouiatanon without their consent, and if they get balky, I fail. And I don't mean to fail, Bill. My whole name's what it is because I've never failed. And my name's all I've got."

"Bill," said Lucy's voice from outside the door of George's room, "I'd hoped you and I might take a walk and talk about ourselves."

"Oh! Yes," he said, partly rising from his chair. "Just a wee bit, my dear. Then I'll be along."

They could hear her breathe an exasperated sigh. Then she said, "Are you giving that poor invalid whiskey and tobacco? Oh, damnation! Ye've all got about as much sense as a turtle has hair! Ooooh! Rrrrrr!"

They smiled sheepishly as her footsteps went away down the hall, but George put his glass on the floor out of sight under his bed, just in case his mother should come in. Bill Croghan said then:

"Seems to me you've thought a long way into something you say you'd be a fool to do. I'll ask again: are you going to do it?"

"Probably," George said after a pause. "If they cry loud enough and assure me I can count on 'em, I'll do it. If not, I loaf here at home as I deserve, till we all get killed in our own houses. Billy, I'm feelin' puny. What if you fetched me another medicine? But watch out for Lucy."

*   *   *

So the leaders of Kentucky did cry loud enough and gave him assurances enough, just as he'd said they would, until at last George Rogers Clark agreed to lead the expedition against the Wabash confederacy, and then almost immediately he found many reasons to regret it, most of them exactly the reasons he had expected.

The militia officers came from their three counties with 1200 men, half the number promised. They rendezvoused at Clarksville, across the Ohio from Louisville, and the base camp was no sooner occupied than the officers began quibbling over George's plan of attack.

He wanted to march straight toward Little Turtle's camps on the upper Wabash and strike them at once. He had learned that the Shawnees were getting ready to join the confederacy, and he wanted to attack before they could arrive to reinforce it. George thought these 1200 militiamen could succeed if they moved quickly and attacked without delay. The officers were more cautious. They thought it would be better to wait for another thousand men to be drafted. They did not want to march the 150 miles straight northwestward to the confederacy's gathering place. Instead, they wanted to go to Vincennes first—a hundred miles almost due west—wait there for the new draftees and for large stores of flour and beef to be brought by boat up the Wabash to meet them at Vincennes, and only then march up the Wabash from there.

George argued that such a slow, indirect approach would almost surely make the expedition fail. But the officers knew the law; they knew that he could not lead them out of Kentucky without their consent, and they were not going to consent unless he agreed to do it their way. Their men, they said, would not go without plenty of manpower and plenty of supplies.

At length George hammered out a compromise. He would take them to Vincennes and wait there for the boatloads of supplies. That would take time. But to wait for the new consignment of draftees would allow the Shawnee army plenty of time to join the confederacy.

Instead, he insisted, let Colonel Benjamin Logan of Lincoln County lead the later contingent against the Shawnee towns in Ohio, to divert the Shawnees from joining the confederacy. They would be Fayette and Lincoln County men, and the Shawnee towns were near them, and they always wanted Shawnee blood anyway.

"That's as far as I'll bend to you people," George concluded. "You begged me to lead this shebang, and by heaven I don't aim

453

to go out there and fail at it. So what sayee? Do you bend to meet me on this point, or do I go back into retirement?"

They consented, and at last the column moved out of Clarksville in the dusty heat of mid-September, picking up the Buffalo Trace toward Vincennes, and they marched slowly, sullenly, reflecting the sulkiness of their officers. The land was rolling and beautiful and the Buffalo road was as clear and hard as a highway, but terrifically dusty. The column rattled and clanked along, the troops' canteens and pans and kettles sounding like a mile-long scullery. A herd of beef cattle was being driven along in the rear because of the insistence on plentiful meat, but driving the cattle was unpleasant, dusty duty and no one wanted to do it, and so the column was further slowed by the need to round up strayed animals.

Adding to the discontent were the jealousy and resentment between the militia units of the respective counties. The Jefferson County men were the smallest portion, their county being so thinly populated, and they were firmly attached to George. The Fayette County men were under the command of Colonel Lev Todd, who seemed to have dropped certain old resentments toward George and had vowed to be as useful and cooperative as he could; these Fayette men were in moderately good morale, but tended to mock the enthusiasm of the Jefferson boys. The Lincoln troops, mostly grumbling and ill-disciplined draftees from the most populous county, made up fully a half of the army. And with the reassignment of Colonel Ben Logan, they were left under the command of Colonel Jim Barrett, whose main weakness seemed to be his desire to be liked by his troops, even if it meant echoing their unruly attitudes.

And so the whole noisy, disorderly column, strung out longer than a mile, shuffled westward through the countryside, raising a cloud of dust among the heat-wilted woods and plains, and their pace was half that of a spirited army. It was soon obvious that the three-and-a-half-day march to Vincennes would take a week.

George, still thin and weak from his convalescence, rode ahead with William beside him, and he was glad William had come, because he could say to a brother things he would not have aired with others. "I could have taken Detroit with an army half this size back in '79," he mused sadly. "But I wouldn't have tried it with *twice* this many if they'd been as sulky and negligent as this mob is. Oh, I tell ye, Billy, I'd made those old boys into real Spartans. And could do the same with these, had I a free hand. But look at 'em. God damn!"

It was William's first ride through the Indiana Territory, and

George, despite his preoccupations, had much to teach him about it. "Down yonder," he'd say, pointing down a valley, "down near where the Blue River runs into the Ohio, there's a cave that's likely the biggest cave in the world. Got some rooms in it so big they have whole hills o' broken rock in 'em. The Wyandots say it's dry as a house inside and goes for miles under the ground. Maybe you and I'll explore it when this present trouble's past, Billy."

"God, yes! I can't wait!"

"Now on the other extreme, there's a cave farther along west that's always full o' water, because it's a whole danged underground river. Y'see this plain off to the right? Look how potty and dippy it is. Ever see land that shape? Sinkholes, that's what those are. Where underground water's eat away the stone underneath, it seems. There's thousands of 'em, some you can go down in, others plugged up with debris."

They rode over a rise later, and George paused to point. "See that next range o' hills there? It's a honeycomb o' caves. I've slept in many a cave while passin' through here. Places where 'ere's stone chips from making weapons, tools. And in the river valleys, strange thing: There's huge mounds o' mussel shells. They say a people, God knows how long ago they lived, ate mostly mussels. Those shells would pile up fifteen, twenty feet high, and they'd build their villages atop 'em. One I saw where you could tell there'd been ditches and streets.

"Billy, I want us t' study all that. Come peace, we'll wander over this territory, you and me. Take notes. Just like Tom Jefferson. A little way on, there's a lick where the water smells like bad eggs. The French and the Indians both take it as medicine."

On the next day out, George got to a point he seemed to have been building to in all this talk. "Listen, Billy," he said, "you're most excited about goin' to war, eh? Aye. I remember how that is. Like wanting a woman, that first time is. Your blood runs so high y' think you'll die with being eager. Some people like it so much they want to go at it every year. Well as I see it, brother, there'll be war over this land for a hundred years. You'll be in it, so much you'll be sickened. It's *duty*. But there'll come a time when you'll know as well as I do what a blessing peace is.

"Y've met Indians you liked. At Fort Finney. Well, someday, maybe next week, if we ever get there, you'll be a-facin' the ones you like, over a gunsight. And there'll be times when you admire some o' them more than ye do some of your own.

"When matters are like that, Billy, duty's a curse. I tell you, there's more glory in seeing a new horizon, in finding a new

455

river, or understanding someone else's God, than there is in makin' war. Remember how Pa would use to preach at us on that? Well, he was right. Somehow in his wisdom he's learned the direct way, without havin' blood on his own hands, what a false glory making war is. Y'll see, Billy. God damn it, ye will if you live long enough."

William could remember the exuberant, whooping, happy George who had used to roar into Virginia from the West, and it was plain that much had happened to change him. George now was like those elder chiefs at the treaty council.

"Here," George said, now pointing up a ravine on their left, "is where Dickie's saddle was found. Likely his bones are up in a glade someplace, unburied. But . . ." He reached across and put a hand on William's arm. "Never say that to family. It's no picture we'd want in their minds, hear?"

By the sixth day, the army had come down off the slopes and rolling woodlands onto plains as flat as a tabletop. They were in the Wabash flood plain. "All this," George told William, with a wide sweep of his arm, "it was all ice water up to a man's middle in February of '79. By the Eternal, I still shake to think of it. Past this wood here y'll see Vincennes."

They rode out into a vast clearing then, and there, trembling in heat waves from the sunbaked meadows and grain fields, lay the distant cluster of houses, and beyond, the long palisades and squat blockhouses of the fort on the bank of the Wabash.

William saw the distances and the grim prominence of the fort, and now, even though the season was green and hot, the whole panorama of that bleak, drowned landscape and the desperate drama of the battle, which he had heard told and retold so many times by so many veterans, coalesced at last in his understanding, and became even more marvelous. William looked at the lean, hard, brown profile of his brother, saw him squinting across space and time, this familiar, this blood, of his very own, and his heart squeezed so hard in his breast that it seemed to block his breath.

Now the people of Vincennes were pouring out of their houses and across the commons, racing toward him, waving, yelling their greetings in French and English, joyous at the return of their old friend and protector.

And William wondered, without thinking it in words, whether he could ever, somehow, be a man of such a stature.

The people of Vincennes were cheerful, vivacious, and shabby. They were desperately poor. While the army waited

t Vincennes for the boats to come up the Wabash with flour
nd meat, William met the townspeople, learned of their love
or George, and came to understand the straits they had been
ut in by allying themselves with the Americans in the Revolu-
ion.

Virginia had promised the French *habitants* a strong and pro-
ective government, advantages in trade, and compensation for
he help they had given the Long Knives. None of these prom-
ses had been fulfilled. And then Virginia had ceded their coun-
ry to Congress, and Congress had shown them even less
:oncern. Under the rule of the United States, they complained,
hey had been like abandoned children. Being "Americans"
1ow, they could no longer trade through New Orleans because
of Spain's blockade of the lower Mississippi. Their farming tools
vere worn out, they had little food or powder and shot. Only
Spanish traders came to Vincennes anymore, and they charged
:ruelly high prices. Furthermore, they were believed to be sell-
ng guns and ammunition to Little Turtle's Indians.

And now the Wabash Confederacy with its 1500 warriors
hovered a hundred miles above them on the Wabash, and was
expected to fall upon them any day.

It was no wonder that the people of Vincennes were so delighted to see this army from Kentucky.

And yet, the army's presence here could cause difficulties, of
course, Major LeGras noted apologetically. The *habitants* could
scarcely feed themselves. To try to quarter 1200 soldiers upon
the town would be impossible.

And so, the Army of Kentucky would make its camp across
the river from Vincennes and await its supply boats. And it obviously was going to be a very long wait. The Wabash was so low
that boats would have to be dragged. George took one look at the
river, grumbled a curse, and called a meeting of his officers.

"Now look at that river," he told them. "It will be a week at
the very least before those boats get here, if they can get here at
all. They're bringing five days' provisions. Damn it all, we'll eat
more than that sitting here waiting for 'em! I told you before we
started that it would be a fool's errand to come to Vincennes! If
we'd marched straight for the enemy, we'd have been at his
throat by now. Listen to me, and listen well: we've still got ten
days' rations. We can march on Little Turtle in three days, strike
him, and be back here by the time those bedamned scows arrive.
I say we march *now*. We'd be idiots to sit here and wait ten days
for five days' grub, all the while the Shawnees are joining Little
Turtle. Idiots we'd be! D'you choose to behave like idiots?"

They chose to do so. George was overruled. And so his army sat on the west bank of the Wabash, consuming its flour and cattle, and waiting.

The Indians, of course, knew of Long Knife's arrival at Vincennes, and soon an important Miami chief named Pacane appeared, bringing a message. George arranged to meet him in the fort. Pacane was a richly dressed, lordly chief with finely sculptured features, kindly eyes, and a small, prim mouth. He could have passed for a schoolmaster except for his ornaments: a silver ring in the tip of his nose, long earrings made of ten beaded pendants, silver armbands, and one long, tightly braided queue hanging from the crown of his otherwise shaven head. George knew Pacane, an old friend of the British who still carried as his most cherished possession a silver-mounted knife given him in 1778 by General Hamilton.

Pacane now came to profess that he was not hostile to the Long Knife and wished for peace. "If that is true," George said, looking straight into his sleepy-looking eyes, "you should tell it to your warriors." He then named several of Pacane's chieftains who had been recognized on raiding parties in Kentucky. Pacane's eyes shifted, but he made no explanation or apology. George continued: "I am glad you came to see me. You can tell the tribes on the Wabash, who said that I dared not come into their country, that I am here. If they are men, let them come and fight men, and not be killing our women and children!" He gave Pacane a belt of red beads, saying, "I send these bloody strings that they may accept my challenge."

Pacane nodded his handsome head politely, took the war belt and strode straight for the open gate of the fort, his escort around him. George noted that the log gates were about to collapse. In the seven years since he had captured this stronghold from Hamilton, it had been standing here rotting. He gazed at the open gateway and remembered the day when his troops had carried him through it on their shoulders.

Then he looked at Colonel Todd and Colonel Barrett and the junior officers. They were well fed, well armed, tanned, healthy.

They're ten times as numerous and ten times as robust as my old boys were, he thought. So why in hell should it be that they've got a tenth of their spirit?

"Well, gentlemen," he said. "Let's get back to camp and put those boys to drill. When and if those boats get here, and all our stalling is done, we'd best be well fit to fight."

Pacane came back in a few days. He brought a red belt, but also some strings of white wampum and a peace pipe. He pre-

458

sented a sarcastic letter from Little Turtle, written in the hand of some white man, likely a British agent or officer. It said the confederacy was glad to hear the Long Knife announce his presence, and added that the Indians would be pleased to talk with him before he marched. To George's mind it was nothing more than a feeble ploy to delay the confrontation until the arrival of the Shawnees from Ohio. And so he gave it no reply.

By the time the boats from Kentucky arrived, two weeks had passed. The new provisions on the boats amounted to nothing but five days' worth of flour. The beef had become so spoiled it had had to be thrown overboard. George's quiet fury was like a blue flame.

"Well, gents, y've had your way," he told the officers. "We've fiddled a half a month away, and now we've just got food enough to feed us a week, which should be just enough if we march quick and attack and return—as we should have done in the first case. Now we have no leeway. Either we go *right now*, or we give it up, and leave the savages free to massacre your families. And listen:

"If you fail me now, by Heaven, their blood will be on your hands, NOT MINE!" He glowered around the table at them. Most of them looked sheepish.

"May I speak, sir?" It was Levi Todd. He stood and leaned toward them with his knuckles on the table. Colonel Todd had been a back-stabber in the closing days of the war, and George had no idea what his unexpected speech was going to contain. If Levi Todd talked doubt now, the whole expedition might as well be abandoned. George tried to plumb his eyes, but they revealed nothing except anger.

"Gentlemen," Todd began, "this expedition has been lame from the start. Our boys been knowing the Invasion Law, and their rights by it. I daresay I made sure mine did. So now, seems like what we got us here is not an army o' soldiers, but an army o' lawyers. An *army* of lawyers! And boys, you know how bad *one* is!" Several of the officers laughed. Todd's family was full of lawyers. Todd went on: "Now, do we need reminding, that it was our own selves that begged Gen'l Clark to lead us against the Wabash Indians? Aye! It was! And why did we? Because we know he's the best soldier in Kentucky and always was! In God's name! No wonder he took pause about taking us on! Who in hell would want to lead twelve hundred lawyers? Well, we've put Gen'l Clark in such tight sleeves he just can't hardly move an arm. Well, I've seen the light. As for me, by God, I'll vow that my boys and I are going to follow the best soldier in Kentucky, and"—he banged his fist on the table—"we're going to do whatever he requires!"

George looked down the table at Todd and swallowed. He glanced at William, who seemed scarcely able to contain his emotions.

"Nicely spoken," George said, his voice warm and calm. "That kind o' sentiment overcomes everything. Now, gents, get your boys fixed to march. We'll forget the bad feelings we've had, and head up the Wabash at daybreak, all of one heart, and God willing, we'll be marching back to a safe Kentucky inside o' a week!"

AND SO THEY HAD STARTED OUT, UP THE WEST BANK OF THE Wabash, while the people of Vincennes waved and cheered from across the river.

They had forded to the east bank and gone in good order for two days, with scouts out ahead, and the weather had been mild; the cottonwoods and sycamores along the Wabash had begun to turn yellow; the Jefferson and Fayette troops had sung heartily in the fresh air of early October. William had ridden beside George through the sun-dappled bottomlands, swearing over and over to himself that in the battle he would not flinch or cower, but stay at George's shoulder so that his brother could see him and be proud of him.

And now it was the morning of the third day, and they were opposite the mouth of the Vermillion River, one day's forced march from Little Turtle's camp, which meant they might meet the first lines of resistance within hours. They had breakfasted on mush and jerky and folded their camp and loaded the horses, and were forming for the march. William was honing his saber, a ritual he had observed every morning at breakfast. "Keep grinding that thing down," George joked, "and ye won't have enough steel left for a knitting needle." William grinned, picked up a fibrous stalk of horseweed, and swished the blade through as if it were butter, saying:

"It's sharp enough to shave with."

"Ha, ha! Aye, if y'had anything to sh—"

He rose, suddenly looking down along the column. Someone was yelling:

"Who's for home? Hey! Who's for home?" And in an instant, other voices, many voices, were chorusing, "Who's for home?"

"What's this now?" George muttered, and he grabbed the reins of his big dappled gray from the soldier who held them, swung into the saddle, and thundered off toward the uproar.

William in a flash had his sword sheathed and was mounted and off after him. Captain Morrison, head of a troop of cavalry, galloped up and fell in alongside George. "It's the Lincoln men," he cried. "Th' bloody cowards are turnin' back!"

George and William galloped among the trees, following a wake of dust and loud voices. Off to the left, on a low bluff, stood Colonel Todd's Fayette troop, already in ranks, watching the scene in silence.

In a moment George overtook the tail of the column The soldiers heard him coming and cringed aside as he galloped past, his jaw set in a fury, his young brother at his heels. As he rode toward the head of the file he could hear them shouting, "What use goin' on, nothin' to eat?" "We're for home, Gen'l! Ya-haw!"

At the head of the column rode an officer waving his hat in the air, a Lieutenant Robards. He turned as he heard the hoof-beats coming behind him, and a grin dissolved from his face when he saw that it was General Clark.

George halted and wheeled his horse in front of Robards, grabbing the reins from him and shouting: "Stop right there!" His voice was curdled with rage and contempt. "The enemy's back that way, ye bedamned poltroon!"

Robards' chin was trembling, but he retorted:

"What's the use o' going on, Gen'l? With nothing to eat?"

"Where's Colonel Barrett?" George demanded. The troops were drawing up behind Robards, and fanning out to make a semicircle and watch this confrontation. "I said, where's Barrett? Answer me, pup, or I'll use your guts for garters!"

"I—I don't know, sir."

"Don't know where your colonel is? B'god! Go find him! Want him up here in two minutes answering to me!" He flung the reins into Robards' face and the young man rode away, flushing, eyes full of tears. George and William sat their horses in the path of the Lincoln troops. George's eyes were flashing and his nostrils were distended, white-edged, his clenched jaw muscles working, his hands shaking. The troops were gathering around like an armed mob now to look insolently at the general and his ashen-faced young brother. William could see that George was having one of his legendary struggles with his own volcanic temper. At last George began looking into faces, and their eyes fell before his.

"You, Larkins! You're an old soldier of mine; you're no coward. What's this, turnin' your tail on Indians?"

The man dropped his eyes. "We all voted, sir."

"Voted? Who? Where's your colonel?"

"We don't have to go, Gen'l!" someone yelled from far bac[k], out of sight. Now the others began yelling.

"What use goin' on?"

"Nothin' to eat!"

"We don't have to go! Don't have to! Nothin' to eat!"

George bellowed over them:

"Nothing to eat? Hey, you all sound like you've memorize[d] that song! Listen to me! There's enough and you know it! We take more at the Indian towns! And there's hundreds o' horses, we get that hungry! Where are your officers, I want to know! want to see Barrett!"

Now most of the five hundred Lincoln County militiame[n] were in a gawking, jabbering circle around George and William[.] George turned his horse around, looking for Barrett or his sub[-] alterns. He could not see a one of them, although some of th[e] Fayette officers had ridden down. He could see Captain Mose[s] Boone, and Captain Gaines, and Lieutenant Anthony Crocket[t] and Lieutenant Craig, all of Fayette County, but not one of th[e] Lincoln officers. Robards seemed to have vanished. Now, wit[h] none of the officers to direct his fury at, George took off his ha[t] and stood in his stirrups, and his eyes now looked wet, and h[is] voice quavered a little as he cried out:

"Don't shame yourselves! D'you know what mutiny is? It's a[n] unspeakable shame, that's what it is!" Some of them were listen[-] ing and looking ill at ease, others were laughing at him. Willia[m] watched George, and his heart twisted with pity as he heard hi[m] plead: "Listen, you men! Only promise to go on with me, and [if] I don't give you victory and a mountain o' food in two days, I'[ll] forget and forgive this mutiny, and go back with you! Don[']t make me ashamed of Kentucky men! Don't make Kentuck[y] ashamed of Lincoln County!" He was almost weeping now, an[d] William was so knotted with chagrin, so frustrated for him, h[e] was almost crying himself, and wanted to whip out his sword an[d] slice the rude mockery off the hundreds of faces around hi[m.]

"Come on, boys, let's go home!" someone shouted.

"We know the Invasion Law, Gen'l," someone shouted. "W[e] voted! Ye can't do nothin' to us!"

"Home, people! The general can't starve us on th' trail! Yih[-] ha!" They began drifting on around him, heading down the rive[r] bank toward Vincennes.

George, through eyes now blurred with tears of outrage, feel[-] ing all his power and honor slipping out of him, bellowed onc[e] more: "I want to see Barrett!" Meantime, the Fayette and Jeffe[r-] son officers had ridden down alongside the flanks of the retreat[-]

462

ng mob, and began cursing them as cowards and traitors. A
oldier, cocking his rifle, snarled at Captain Boone: "You ain't
ny officer, Mister! Don't y' yell at me!" The dust and babble of
he retreating mob rose in the glade, the shuffling of feet, clink-
ng of cook-pans and canteens. They milled past the officers,
ullen, insolent, some shame-faced, but most affecting high
heer, and George, slumped in his saddle, watched them flow
y, and William felt as if he were standing in a stream of sewage.
o see his brother's dejection made his heart ache with pity. And
t was more than the personal agony; even in his youthful inex-
erience, William could sense that some awful historical turn
vas happening here, as in stories he had read somewhere, of
ingdoms toppled, of lordly reputations lost.

"Billy, come on," he heard George saying. They spurred their
norses and plunged out of the mob, scattering soldiers out of
heir path. When they burst out, Fayette officers were coming
oward them, their faces contorted. "Gaines!" George yelled.
'Crockett! Where do you stand in this?"

"We're with you, sir! Damn sure!"

"Have you seen Barrett?"

"Not since an hour. Him and Robards, both lookin' guilty as
uck-egg dawgs," Gaines answered.

"Ye think they did have a vote, likely?"

"Surely must have, sir, they're in such accord."

George was blinking hard and trying to keep his mouth firm,
He had never in his life felt so hurt, so betrayed. Except when
Teresa deLeyba had quit the country without leaving him so
nuch as a word. Suddenly he reached over and grabbed Gaines's
arm in a powerful, desperate grip, nearly pulling him off his
norse. "On your word of honor," he demanded. "Did *your* regi-
nent vote?"

The sudden hurt and hauteur in Gaines's face vouched for his
words: "God and my honor, sir, we didn't!"

"Good. Thank you." George released him. "Go tell Colonel
Todd to call assembly. I'll be there in five minutes. No, ten."
Then he started riding away, down toward the riverbank, toward
a shady copse of sycamores and willows, putting the sight and
sound of the stragglers behind him. William followed. George
urned and said, "I don't need you just now, Brother. No offense. I just need to think."

"Aye." William reined in and watched him ride into the
shade. He sat his horse, gave it rein to graze, and tried to quell
the dreadful, confused remorse and anger he felt. He listened to
the horse's teeth ripping grass, heard locust calls spinning

through the sunlight, heard the *cheer, we! cheer, we!* of a blue bird and saw the flash of its indigo wings dart through a sun beam. Somewhere nearby a warbler was saying *whit chew wh chew whit chew whit!* While down the shore, fainter and fainter men's voices were laughing and shouting. And up on the rise, bugle sounded Assembly.

William waited, and suddenly began to have a strange dream about George. Once William had known a young man in Caroline County, a jilted swain who had gone out of sight and killed himself. He, too, had told his friends he needed to think. William jerked his horse's head up and rode toward the sycamore, his heart in his throat.

In the deep, cool shade he could see no sign of George. Then he saw his horse, standing riderless. William rose in his stirrups and peered around in alarm.

Then he saw his brother, silhouetted against the river.

George was on his knees in the grass. His sword was jabbed into the earth in front of him and his hands were clasped over the hilt and his forehead was on his hands. He was all right after all. He was praying. Praying men don't kill themselves.

William turned his horse and walked it silently back out into the sunlight. In a few seconds George rode out. His face was drawn and grim, but more composed now. "Let's go up, Billy." His voice was low, but the tremor was gone out of it. William still could not think of anything proper to say, and his own bewildered dumbness convinced him that he was still a boy, that manliness required more than just the size and strength to swing a sword; it required the wisdom to say right things.

George rode so slowly that William could feel his reluctance to face the rest of the army after this disgrace. The seven hundred militiamen of Fayette and Jefferson counties were in a large ring around a field table. Several captains and majors stood with Todd near the table. Todd saluted as George rode in with William behind him. George saluted and stopped, but did not dismount.

"Colonel," he said, "I want you to put it to all these people whether they're still with me or not."

"Yes, sir." Todd turned and bellowed: "Every man who's still with General Clark step forward and say aye."

The whole circle, to a man, surged inward with a deafening roar.

Todd looked up at George and saw tears running down his cheeks. William, a few yards back, had to bite the insides of his lips to keep from crying.

"Sir," Todd said then. "Some of the men have already begged permission to go after the deserters and force 'em to come back."

That so moved George that he was speechless for several more seconds. Then he smiled through his tears and answered, "That's like music to me, Mr. Todd. But o' course"—he swallowed—"we can't have two Kentucky armies fighting each other in leagues from the enemy. We'd best council on what to do. We're up a creek, frankly. We've got but half an army here. The savages are three to our one now, and defending their own ground, they'd fight like furies." He dismounted. "Let's talk, gentlemen."

ABOUT HALF THE SENTIMENT WAS FOR GOING ON TO ATTACK the Indians, even with the reduced force. But the chances of succeeding in that—even surviving it—were finally deemed too slim, and the vote was to return to Vincennes. And so they rode and marched out of camp at midday, not toward the enemy towns but away from them, following the messy trail of the deserters, every footprint, every gnawed bone, every cast-away bag or keg, every fly-blown turd or scrap of refuse along the trailside a reminder of the morning's disgrace. For the first two hours of the ride, George slumped in his saddle, the unfamiliar weight of failure feeling like a boulder on his back. He looked up and listened only when scouts came in to tell about Indian signs. The Kentuckians were being followed and watched by a few Indians, twenty scouts or so. But there was no large force anywhere near. George thanked them and led on, still thinking of the awful sight that morning of the deserters' backs going down through the trees in their cloud of dust, and the pack horses. He thought of the spectacle as it would look through the eyes of those Indian scouts, and thought of the report, the astonishing report, that they would carry to Little Turtle and Pacane and the other chiefs—the Shawnees too probably were among them by now, after all that delay—the astonishing report that Long Knife's army had come within a day's march of the battlefield and then had turned back. That'll puzzle them for a while, he thought. Worse, forbid it Heaven, they'll learn about the mutiny! *Long Knife,* he thought. He had fought and schemed and suffered for eight years for the Long Knife's reputation. But he knew how fast fame can blow away once a warrior has suffered a defeat or turned from a contest. Again he saw through the Indian scouts' eyes, saw these 1200 Kentuckians going back whence they had come. He tried to imagine Little Turtle receiving this

news. He could remember the chief's candid, intelligent fac
He tried to imagine what the chief's keen wit would make of

Soon George was stroking his jaw thoughtfully. He was n
used to thinking defeated, and knew that if he did give this a
up, the tribes would plunge into Kentucky with magnifi
boldness. While he was here in their territory, surely he cou
do something. He had sent war belts, but then had turned ba
before battle. Incomprehensible! He thought of Pacane takin
the red belts, he remembered Pacane's appeal for peace, whic
he had spurned as insincere.

Suddenly, he sat straighter in his saddle, his brow knit in co
centration. A notion had begun to gleam like a coal in the da
ashes of his despair. He had begun thinking of Pacane, of whit
beaded peace belts. And it was starting to come together in h
mind; the coal of an idea was being fanned into brightness.

"Colonel Todd," he called back, suddenly turning in his sa
dle, "have the troops look sharp! Get up a song." And soon the
were swinging and singing down the bank of the Wabash, loo
ing not at all like a retreating army, teaching each other bawd
verses they knew to "Yankee Doodle."

> "Two and two may go to bed,
> Two and two together
> And if there isn't room enough,
> Lay one atop o't' other!"
> (slap, slap, slap slap slap)
>
> "Dolly Bushel let a fart,
> Jenny Jones she found it,
> Ambrose carried it to mill,
> And there the miller ground it!"
> (slap, slap, slap slap slap)

William kept glancing out of the corner of his eye at h
brother, who, though his face was still pained and solemn, w
concentrating on his thoughts and now and then showed a wr
smile. George was up to *something*.

VINCENNES WAS IN A STATE OF ALARM.
The Kentucky army they thought had come up to scatter th
nearby Indian confederacy had instead come straggling back
half of it, an unruly mob demanding food. Then, learning tha
the general was close behind them, they had headed out in sma

466

roups bound for home. Few of them wanted to be around when
e got there.

George, immediately on his arrival, occupied the old fort,
ummoned Major LeGras and went into a secret council with
im and Levi Todd and a few of the faithful officers. William
tayed by him as his aide and messenger, and at last it became
vident what George had been plotting during the march.
Sometimes, Billy, there's nowt to do but bluff. Now I reckon
've won as many contests that way as I have by force, and it
night work again now."

William listened in amazement as George dictated a message
o be taken to the Wabash tribes.

> "To the chiefs and warriors of the different nations on the
> Wabash:
> "The frequent murders your young men have committed on
> our women and children have obliged us to take up the hatchet,
> and we are determined not to lay it down until the roads are
> perfectly cleared. Our women and children may cry, but the
> more they weep the more we shall seek revenge. We are now in
> your country and will not go far out of it till this be completed.
> "I sent you the other day, by my friend Pacane, a red
> belt to let you know that we are here. You sent back the red
> with some strings of white wampum and a pipe for us to
> smoke. You also prayed to hear from us before I saw you.
> This determined us to return down our road, though we
> were already three days' journey towards you."
> He winked, then went on:
> "To convince you we are not devoid of humanity, I send
> you today some strings of white, and invite you to come to
> a grand council at Clarksville on the twentieth of Novem-
> ber, when we shall endeavor to agree upon terms of peace
> and friendship. . . . If you do not come, I will conclude
> that you are still for war. But you may rest assured, if you
> do continue the war, that we shall adopt measures to take
> possession of your lands and make a conquest of them for-
> ever, without showing you any mercy . . . If you have any
> intention of coming to treat, let me know it without delay,
> and I shall provide everything necessary for your reception.
> Be not afraid; there will be no danger for you in our towns.
> "I am, etcetera."

And then LeGras dictated his own letter to the tribes, a totally
eparate document:

"*I have received the good words you sent me by Pacane. . . . All your brothers the French, having a tender heart, enjoined me to send after Long Knife's army to invite it to return, which, with a great deal of intreaty, we obtained, promising them that you would remain quiet on your lands. Do not make us liars! Had I not stopped the Americans, the birds of prey would eat your women and children and your towns would be confounded with the wilderness.*

"*Hearken therefore to the speech your brothers, the Americans, send you. Though you spill their blood every day, they have pity. Let us all have but one dish. The women and children have long enough slept in fear.*"

So that's it, William thought. They're to believe *this* is wh we turned back!

And now he understood why George had wanted the army return with such a demonstration of spirit.

When the interpreter had left with the messages, George go about the business of establishing a garrison at the fort. He wa able to keep only 140 men; the rest had to return to Kentucky fo harvests. He sent a letter to the governor of Virginia demandin an investigation of the mutiny, and suggested that Todd also ir sist on it. "There's going to be lies and excuses thick as a be swarm when those Lincoln County boys go slinkin' home They'll try to fault me as a bungler and a jug-sucker, as the used to whenever something went wrong in the war."

Word came to Vincennes in a few days that Colonel Logan expedition against the Shawnee towns had been a success—c sorts. With most of their warriors gone to join the Wabash con federacy, the towns had been defenseless against Logan's 79 horseman. One of the militia leaders, a Colonel Kennedy, ha chased down seven fleeing squaws and hacked them to death on by one with his broadsword. The good, ancient chief Moluntha having surrendered and holding the Fort Finney treaty to hi breast, had been tomahawked between the eyes by Captain Hugl McGary.

It had been a disgraceful performance. But Colonel Logan wa boasting of it, as it had destroyed more than 200 of th Shawnees' dwellings and virtually all their winter food supply That would put the Shawnee nation out of the warring busines for the rest of the year. The barbarous acts would further harde the Shawnees' hatred against the Kentuckians. But at least th eastern theater of George's strategy had worked: the Shawne

468

warriors, on hearing of the raids, had turned away from the Wabash confederacy and hurried back to their own ravaged country. That would have disappointed Little Turtle and perhaps would make him a little more susceptible to the audacious bluff that George and LeGras had prepared. "We'll all be on tenterhooks here till their answer comes," George told William. "But we'll be too busy to worry. What we've got to do now is make some way to support this garrison here." Winter was coming on. George appointed a commissary officer. He sent a request to the French in Kaskaskia and Cahokia for flour. He sent a letter to Benjamin Logan asking him to impress food and clothing from the Kentucky counties for the outpost at Vincennes. But he saw little hope of obtaining anything soon, if ever, by those measures. And so he turned to an expedient closer to hand.

Lying at wharf in the low water of the Wabash just below Vincennes was a large Spanish row galley, full of rum, clothing, shoes, ammunition, and merchandise. The cargo had been brought up from New Orleans for a Spanish trader named Bazadone, who had set up business in Vincennes, and who was suspected to be supplying ammunition to the Wabash tribes. Bazadone did not have a passport to trade in this country. Furthermore, his presence was an affront to both the French and the Americans, whose own trade down the Mississippi had been totally blockaded by the Spanish at New Orleans.

Because the Spaniard was trading without authorization, it seemed that the garrison commandant could, by military law, appropriate his cargo. So a court-martial was convened, of four captains who knew the law. Bazadone was questioned under oath, and when he admitted that he was trading without passport, the court ordered his goods confiscated, and put in the commissary store to be issued directly to the troops or auctioned publicly, with proceeds going to the support of the garrison. After studying the ruling and being satisfied that it was not irregular, George signed it. Bazadone, squealing protests through his black beard and yellow teeth, was given a receipt signed by General Clark, relieved of his goods, and advised to leave. "That," George told William, "is how ye may have to support your troops sometimes, when your government is far removed or little concerned. I know it looks somewhat like robbery, but it's legal. I know one thing: it would be morally worse to dissolve the garrison for want of supply and leave this town at the mercy of the tribes. Now, Billy, such proceedings do leave a polecat taste in my mouth, and I'm going to wash it out with a sip o' Spanish taffia, of which we seem to have acquired several hogsheads. Would ye care to join me in my quarters?"

"I sh'd be delighted, Brother Long Knife. This soldierin'—if that's what we're doing—does tend to parch a man out."

George drank and talked cheerfully enough for a while. But after a few drinks of rum, he revealed to William that the day of the mutiny had been the worst day of his life. "When a disgrace like that happens," he said, "y' start losing your name. And by God, my name is the main thing I've got! D'ye know, there's rumors back East that I'm not competent. That I like this stuff too much. For the life o' me, I can't trace the rumors. But my name's shrinking back there."

William was ill at ease with such discouraging talk, which was not Clark-like, and even less like George. Wanting to turn him away from it, he said, "I thought I'd turn over when ye told those fifteen hundred Indians to come down and talk peace or else, and here's us in this ol' rickety coop outnumbered ten to one! You really do be some snorter! They'll come, won't they?"

"I don't know. It depends what's left o' the Long Knife's name. But I'm getting nervous. It's been a week and no answer. Like as not they'll come with their hatchets out. Little Turtle is no fool. He's a better man than anyone here, except you and me. I expect he's waiting to see if we leave. Count on this, though: He won't be goin' off to raid Kentucky as long as we sit this close to his towns."

AND FINALLY, AFTER TEN DAYS OF OMINOUS SILENCE, THE miracle happened.

The chiefs began coming down to Vincennes bringing the white belt, begging peace. First came Tobacco's Son of the Piankeshaws, full of remorse at having turned against his old brothers the Big Knives. Then came Crooked Legs, of the Ouiatenons, then Loon, of the Kickapoos, then others. They wanted a truce until the peace council. They asked that the council be held at Vincennes, a place they knew, instead of the unfamiliar Clarksville. And as they yet had to provide for their women and children for the coming winter, they asked that the truce be extended until the next spring, instead of this November.

The officers could not believe such good fortune. With this one desperate bluff, Long Knife had turned his first failure into a triumph, and had gained Kentucky half a year's reprieve—maybe even a permanent one—from the Indian invasions. And just in time. Their provisions had run out, and they would have to quit the fort and go back to Kentucky. They gathered to celebrate one night in late October after the last chief had left in peace. William's admiration of his brother was wider and deeper even than it had been when he was three years old.

"God in heaven," Levi Todd said. "Gen'l, I think Vincennes is your blessed place! Here you take your longest chances, and here you come out best. Hear, hear!" he cried. "A toast with Spanish rum to Long Knife at Vincennes!" They all roared approval and hoisted their cups.

That night the officers and troops finished the last of Bazadone's rum. William passed out with a smile on his face. George enjoyed the rum very much.

If he could have foreseen the troubles it would soon be causing him, he probably could not have swallowed a drop.

25

MULBERRY HILL

April, 1787

JUDGE HARRY INNES WAS NOT A CLOSE FRIEND OF THE CLARK family, but having been a classmate of George and Jonathan in Rev. Robertson's school, he was a cordial acquaintance of long standing. And so when he came to Mulberry Hill in April of 1787, riding up the road between the budding locust trees through a gentle, misting spring rain, he was greeted warmly by John and Ann Rogers Clark, presented to the daughters, given tea, and shown the premises.

He spoke with the Clarks about mutual acquaintances, dwelling at some length on Elizabeth's beau, Richard Clough Anderson, now a Colonel, and on James Wilkinson, whom he seemed to hold in higher esteem than did the Clarks. "He came here once," George said. "Borrowed some papers of mine."

"Really?" Innes seemed surprised, as if it were unusual for Wilkinson to do something without his knowledge. "Pray, what sort of papers d'you mean?"

"Some reports on the Vincennes expedition, proceedings of the court-martial on the Spaniard's goods. Such things."

Innes was gracious as always, but obviously preoccupied. He had come in his capacity as Attorney General of Kentucky, and had business of a confidential nature with George. Soon, therefore, the rest of the family withdrew and left them the library.

George pulled the big walnut-wood doors shut and decanted an amber liquid into crystal glasses, while Judge Innes watched him minutely and cleared his throat. "Peach brandy," George said. "A new product of Louisville." He was out of uniform, dressed in old-style brown wool frock coat, weskit, and breeches, lately brought out of a storage trunk to give him something to wear as a country gentleman; virtually all his wardrobe was uniforms and buckskins. Innes touched his glass to George's, saying simply, "Health," and studied the sharp, flat planes of the general's face, the high, broad forehead, the new, slightly saddened aspect of the eyes, which now were surrounded by fine squint lines. But the eyes were still keen and piercing, an intimidating deep-water blue—certainly not the eyes of the addled inebriate the rumors in Eastern Virginia had him to be.

If anything, the years of experience seemed to have made him even more attractive than he had been in his youth. Innes could remember that the Tidewater lasses had been mad about young George before he had disappeared beyond the mountains. He wondered now what feminine company George might be keeping, what belle of which family might be in hopes of marrying the famous Kentuckian. Innes was addicted to social gossip, and had strangely heard no such gossip about Kentucky's most illustrious bachelor. All he had heard was that he drank.

The judge observed, though, that George did not take his brandy like a drunkard, but merely sipped and savored it, his mind not on it but on the moment.

"Now, Harry, what brings you? I hope you're here to look into the mutiny. Or that you've brought me some instructions from the Capital on the Indian treaties. They're due, you know."

"George, what I have is from the governor. But it's neither of those matters. You know, I presume, that the Foreign Secretary's trying to negotiate a trade treaty with Spain." He cleared his throat.

"Of course. I daresay every man of sense in Kentucky speaks of it four or five times a day, afeard that they'll barter away forever our right to float down the Mississippi."

"Aye. Well, as y' know, George, the majority of states want that treaty most desperately. They've got goods rotting in the warehouses and ships left half-finished in the yards." Innes cleared his throat still another time, and George wondered why he should be so nervous.

"What's this to do with me, Judge?"

"Why, George, something very direct, I'm afraid. Now, it's not just the governor, George, but his council, and the Congress too." He cleared his throat again. "They've a fear that, ahm, they . . . you see, they've learnt that you seized a Spanish boat at Vincennes."

George's eyes narrowed. He was detecting the drift of this, and he interjected:

"First," he said, "'seized' is hardly the word. I followed lawful proceedings. Second, I wonder how the Executive, who seems to have a deaf ear for anything from Kentucky, should hear o' that obscure event so clearly." He thought for a moment, for some reason, of Wilkinson.

"Well," Innes said, "albeit obscure, it's alarmed them. They're afraid it might lose us the treaty, even provoke war with Spain."

"War? Preposterous! He wasn't even legitimate! He had no passport!"

"They're also alarmed that your garrison at Vincennes could be construed as a hostile move against Spanish interests on the Mississippi."

"What! How could they—By God, Harry! Let's remind 'em, the Executive *authorized* that damned expedition! And Congress condoned it!" In his astonishment, George reached for the decanter and refilled the two glasses while protesting: "That was an expedition to save Kentucky from Indians. It had no connection with Spain whatsoever. And when we impressed those goods, we'd never yet even *heard* of John Jay's precious treaty!" He was pacing like a lion fretting in a cage, and paused only to toss down his brandy. "Besides that, the garrison at Vincennes is long since disbanded. It had nothing to exist on! By God, Harry! Sometimes I swear, government's an ass, and I'm out here pullin' on its blind side!" His voice had been rising with his anger to the kind of volume that can carry through walls, and suddenly he brought it down. Turning to face Innes squarely, he said in a low tone, "Very well, though. I'm used to this. What would they have me do to soothe their troubled little minds, eh? Do they wish me to crawl down and kiss his Catholic Majesty's ring and beg his forgiveness? What?"

Innes cleared his throat still again, held out his glass, and formed his reply as both gulped another dram. "No, Gen'l," he said at last. "They've already apologized to Spain. What they want is . . . for me to prosecute you."

George froze. His eyelids hardened, his nostrils distended. He

473

seemed to become tense as a drawn bow, and for an instan Judge Innes actually felt a fear of physical harm. In the silence the clock in the corner ticked menacing seconds. Innes unbut toned the flap of a coat pocket, took out a folded and seale packet, and held it forth.

Breathing deep with the effort to contain his fury, George snatched it, broke the seal, and shook it open. The first sheet wa a handwritten letter from the governor.

Richmond, March 4th, 1787

Sir: By advice of Council I enclose you an act of our Board, in which you will perceive certain Complaints exhibited against you. The Council conceived themselves bound to issue the enclosed proclamation also.

I am Sir Your Mo. Ob. Serv.

EDMUND RANDOLPH

The second sheet was printed.

By His Excellency Edmund Randolph, Esq.
Governor of the Commonwealth,
A PROCLAMATION!

Whereas it has been represented to the Executive that George Rogers Clark, Esq. after having, under color of an authority wrongfully supposed to be derived from them, re-cruited a number of men for the support of St. Vincent's, had moreover seized the property, of a certain subject of His Catholic Majesty to a considerable amount. In order, therefore, that the honour of this commonwealth may not sustain an injury, from a belief that the act above men-tioned has in any way received the public sanction, I do hereby declare, with the advice of the Council of State, that the said violence was unknown to the Executive until a few days past, and is now disavowed; and that the Attorney-General has been instructed to take every step allowed by law, for bringing to punishment all persons who may be culpable in the premises. Given under my hand and the Seal of the Commonwealth, this twenty-eighth day of Feb-ruary in the year of our Lord One Thousand and Seven Hundred and Eighty-Seven.

EDMUND RANDOLPH

474

When George looked up at Innes, the whites of his eyes showed all around the blue, his teeth were clenched, his face was livid, his whole body was shaking. "This has been *published*?" he demanded. At Innes's timid nod, he flung the papers to the floor and ground them under his heel, shouting: "He says *I* would injure the honor of the Commonwealth? My God! I've given every power and penny I ever possessed, *for* the honor of Virginia! And now he will sacrifice my good name, will he, to mollycoddle a Spanish king and his slimy ministers?" His voice was roaring in the confines of the room now, and there were footsteps in the hall, and creaking stairs, as if his bellowings were causing members of the family to scurry about the house.

Many men had watched George Rogers Clark strain to master his temper during his ten years of command. Now Harry Innes was seeing him vent it, without restraint, at last. George swept his hand to the floor and snatched up the papers, crumpling them in an upraised fist over Judge Innes' head, shouting at him: "You've smirched your hands just *carrying* this paper to me! By God, Innes, if you mean to prosecute me, then you betray as staunch a patriot as this country's ever had! And by all the Powers," he snarled, now shaking the papers under the nose of the cringing judge, "YOU KNOW THAT'S TRUE!"

Innes was so far back in his chair that it nearly tipped backward, but he was waving his hands back and forth in a calming gesture and trying to speak. George's fist looked as hard and heavy as a war club and his eyes were full of violence.

"No," Innes finally gasped, "no, George, I wouldn't do it! I'm not going to! God, no, I'd never *do* it!" George now stood poised over him, still thrusting the papers in his face, perhaps not really hearing him, when the doors of the room suddenly opened and Mrs. Clark stood there glaring in at the two men.

"George," she said. "*George!*"

He turned to look at her, at the admonition in her imperious blue eyes, and slowly collected himself out of his threatening stance. She said simply:

"Mister Innes is our guest."

The judge gathered his composure, bowing his head slightly toward her. And when George blinked and took a deep breath and said, "Yes, that's so," she curtseyed and closed the doors.

Now George stood glaring at Innes, and the judge was clearing his throat repeatedly and soothing down his lapels. Finally Innes said, "I'd never *do* it, George. No, there's technicalities by which I can decline to prosecute."

"Technicalities? Ye should refuse to on *principle*, God damn your little gray lawyer's soul!"

"Aye! Surely! Surely! It's, ah, on principle that I refuse, but by a, ahm, *by* a technicality. I say, I must be stirring, General, I've, ah, got another call in Louisville yet." Innes was still half frightened for his safety, and was, besides, unaccustomed to being cursed; he was scowling and clenching his jaws even while going through the motions of a graceful withdrawal, bowing and offering his hand. George did not take the hand, but instead crammed the crumpled papers into it, demanding now as Innes backed toward the door:

"So ye bring me nowt but this insult? Nothing about the most pressing business at hand? The Indian councils?"

"General, you need not concern yourself about those. You have, ahm,"—he had his hand on the door handle now, and opened the door—"you've been, ah, succeeded as Indian Commissioner."

George's face now paled. "By whom?" he growled between clenched teeth.

"By General Wilkinson."

So saying, Harry Innes darted into the safety of the hallway, where the elder Clarks sat like sentries on a mammy bench. He pulled the door shut just as a mighty bellow of rage reverberated through the room, followed by the shattering crash of glass against the inside of the door.

The corners of Ann Rogers Clark's eyes crinkled momentarily with the chagrin she felt, both as a hostess and as a mother.

Before anyone could speak, the doors were flung open. "Harry, you'd *better* prosecute me," George growled, pointing his finger at him like a pistol. "Let the *facts* come forth. They'll not condemn me without a *trial*!" He started to close the doors, then instead advanced and snatched the papers out of Innes's hand, and stalked back into the library. The last thing he saw before banging the doors together again was his mother's face, full of mortification and pity.

He swallowed three more glasses of brandy in quick succession, while reading the proclamation through a second time, stung to the heart, muttering aloud its incredible words: "'Authority wrongfully supposed'? 'Violence'? 'Punishment'? 'Culpable'?" He thought back over the decade in which he had exerted every cell of mind and body to maintain the defense of Kentucky against impossible odds, against the hostility of British and Indians, against the shortsightedness and indifference of the state's own leaders; he thought of the interminable Indian councils, of his spirited harangues to his troops, of the long, excruciating marches, of the constant shortages of men and money, of the slanders made behind his back in the East, of the allegations of his sottishness, of his economic ruin. All this, he thought, to end up condemned out of hand as a criminal against his beloved state! The governor obviously had taken someone's apocryphal account of the incident and swallowed it whole. *And gave me no chance even to speak the truth!* he thought. *By the Eternal, he was in a hurry to throw me to the wolves!*

He poured down more brandy while he brooded, and he might as well have been pouring it on a chafing dish; it leaped and fluttered like an alcohol flame over his despair and his simmering contempt for Governor Randolph. Now he snatched paper from a desk drawer. As he dipped a quill in ink, he heard his mother's voice querying outside the locked door. "I won't see anyone!" he yelled. "I'm not fit!" And, not hearing the words of her reply through the roaring of his emotions, he scrawled:

His Excellency
Governor Edmund Randolph

Sir: I respect the STATE of Virginia.
The information you have received hath already been stained with the blood of your country! Facts will prove themselves.

I am, Sir, yours,
G.R. CLARK

George was gone from Mulberry Hill. Nobody knew where he had gone, but they all knew the state of mind he was in, and they were very worried about him.

He had stayed in the library alone the rest of that day after Judge Innes had left. One by one the members of the family had rapped on the door and entreated him to come out for something or other, and one by one had been told to leave him at peace. Then, very late, after they all had retired to their rooms, they had heard, through the hiss of April rain, hoofbeats going at a gallop from the stables down the avenue to the public road.

They found the library door open, wads of paper strewn over the floor, these proving to be awkward starts of letters to Thomas Jefferson, addressed to him in Paris, with salutations, then first lines scratched out. All the liquor decanters were empty; the room reeked of whiskey and tobacco smoke, and vomit dribbled from the sill of an open window. The pantry door was ajar and two jugs of liquor were gone. George's room was open; his saddlebags and pistols were gone, as was his old buckskin coat from the Revolution. Cupid came to the back door to report: "Ma George woked me up to saddle his stalyum, nen he rad off s hawd 'e make dust in ne mud!" Prodded, Cupid admitted tha George had looked like the Devil himself, and added, "Seem m he been awful fragment wi' corn spirits, come near fall off th stalyum!"

The next day, John Clark put on a rain cape and rode down t Louisville, ostensibly to inquire about a shipment of seed tha was due, but mainly to inquire, discreetly, whether George ha been seen. As the city's founder and most celebrated citizen George could hardly move in Louisville without half the popula tion knowing he was in the town and where.

John Clark went from the land office to the wharf; from th town hall to the apothecary; from the public house to the for finally he even made unannounced calls at the doctor's offic and the homes of a few merchants. He idled briefly or discusse business matters with them all, but his casual inquiries indicate that George either had not been through Louisville at all, or, i he had, he had gone through by night. There was hardly any place where he could have been in secret.

Except . . . John Clark now sat his horse in the drizzle, gaz ing down the street toward a large riverside house built of flatboa lumber: the one place where gentlemen went in secret. A fairl new establishment in the growing river town it was, with a gen eral downstairs entrance for soldiers and riverboat men, and more elegant and discreet upstairs section, with a hidden en trance, for pillars of the community. John Clark did not go t inquire there. First, because he would not have set foot on th premises; second, because he truly doubted George was there o ever had been. But as it was the one place he had left unex amined, it stayed in the back of his mind to nag him as he rod back up to Mulberry Hill. George had been, after all, in a wors mental and emotional state than anyone had ever seen him in In that condition, might he not have gone there?

For the next three days, John Clark told no one of George' disappearance. It was discussed only within the family. Might h have ridden off toward Harrod's Town, toward Lexington, even God forbid, toward faraway Richmond, the source of his trou bles? Might he have set out alone, in his condition, to go ther and confront the governor in person? It did not seem likely What seemed certain, though, was that if he had left Louisvill alone for anyplace—Vincennes or Boonesboro or simply ou into his old hunting and fossil-digging grounds—he would be in extreme danger. George himself had warned everybody that unless the government called for the great April Indian Council he had arranged, the tribes would feel they had been tricked, and return to the war path. If George was out there alone . . . That thought had haunted the family, and William in particular. William kept remembering the trail to Vincennes, and that spot along the way that George had pointed out, where Dickie's saddle had been found.

William had been unable to get that out of his mind, once he had thought of it. What if some like tragedy should befall George, somewhere out there in that expanse of wilderness, some swift, violent surprise, some treachery, a musketball or arrow from ambush, a knife flashing in firelight.

"I don't think we should lay idle any longer," William argued on the fourth morning. "I think we should get some riders from the fort and go a-lookin'!"

"But we'd have to, well, ah, *explain* things," old John Clark protested. "And then if it turned out he's been right in Louisville the whole time . . ." He was thinking more and more about the brothel. About what a disgrace to the family it would be if a hue and cry went up, and a searching party went out, and then it would be revealed that George, all the time, had been wallowing with whores. Or, even worse, what if he should turn up in some friendly Indian camp, among poxy squaws? John Clark did not, of course, discuss these dreadful possibilities in the family, but he was thinking them, and they troubled his devout Episcopalean soul—and Ann Rogers Clark knew he was thinking them. "No," John Clark said now to William. "I sh'll ride down to town again today. Likely I'll find him right there someplace." His voice trailed off in a sigh.

"Why don't I go?" William said. In his mind he had decided he would have to take this matter into his own hands. "The fields are too wet to work in. I'll ride down to town, Pa. I'll look around. And don't worry, I won't say things."

"I say let Billy go, John," Mrs. Clark declared suddenly. "He can track a butterfly through a whirlycane, and by my faith, I want t' know George is safe! That's foremost! I swear, John Clark, y're so cautious, ye'd ha' been a Tory, if I hadn't prodded at you to set your mind! I say let Billy go look!"

John Clark was, in a way, glad to let William take up the search. He himself had been exceedingly tired and depressed by his day of inquiries.

An hour later William was riding past the house from the

stables when his mother stepped out of the back door and called him. She looked him over with a shrewd eye. "What kind of rig is that for a trip to town?" She asked. William was in leggings, moccasins, and hunting shirt, with full saddlebags and canteen and his rifle on his arm. "Do ye swear to me you're going to Louisville?"

"I swear it," he said, and she could see that he was not lying.

He rode down the avenue through the fresh, damp smells of soil and foliage. Each locust tree was draped with long, creamy-white clusters of blossoms. Somewhere off the road the drumming of a grouse started, a slow putt . . . putt . . . putt in the air speeding up to a quick flutter. William turned onto the public road then, dug in his heels, and tore down toward Louisville at a fast canter, flinging mud behind him.

It was true that he was going to Louisville. But not as his father had. He was going straight to the fort. He was going to get Captain Dalton or Captain Stribling or whoever was on duty and tell them his fears. It wouldn't be necessary to tell about the drinking, just that George had disappeared. These officers had served with George; they would comb the territory for him if they knew he was out there somewhere by himself. Or maybe they would already know where he was. Militiamen were always on the roads between the settlements, and if any had seen George going anywhere, the captain at the fort would know of it.

William passed ox carts and wagons on the road, carrying logs and lumber and bundles and people toward and away from the raw new town. He sped past log houses and stone houses and pole shacks, brush fences and split-rail fences, acres of smoking brush piles, and stumps and girdled trees and plowed ground with fresh green sprouts of corn coming up in rows, and to his right, beyond the trees and thickets, there was the great, rain-swollen, beautiful Ohio, with scows and flatboats coming down bringing new people, just as he and his family had come two years ago. And down there now he saw the ferry coming ashore, the ferry operated by old Davy Pagan of the Illinois Regiment, the ferry to Clarksville and the Vincennes road.

William reined in suddenly. There, by Heaven, was something that could bear looking into. He wheeled the horse and galloped down to the edge of the ferry road, dismounted there, and waited.

Davy Pagan waved at him from the tiller as the Negroes gave the oars a last hard pull. A boy on shore caught ropes thrown from the ferry boat and hitched them around pilings as the prow bumped against the landing.

The old ex-sailor was wizened, but still spry as a monkey, and his good eye twinkled at the sight of a Clark. He scrambled forward among horses and cows, and hopped ashore to squeeze William's hand. "Why," he said, "happy I am t'see ye, m'lad! Goin' over to th' mill, air ye?"

"Why, no. No, Mr. Pagan. Actually, I came down to inquire"—he led Pagan off the road by an arm—"by any chance have y' taken my brother over lately?"

The old salt was halfway between nodding and shaking his head, and obviously was having to ponder what should have been a most simple answer. So William said: "You have, haven't e?"

Pagan glanced at the ground and then scratched his hat, as if a at could itch. "Well, lad," said he, "the gen'l asked me not to ell. But he'd not've had me lie to his own kin, I reckon. Aye. I ook 'im over, 'twas three nights ago. Way late. I'd not make a ight trip for anyone else."

"How was he? Where was he headed, Mister Pagan?"

"How was he? Well, let me see, lad. He was, ahm . . ."

"Intoxicated?"

"Now there's a fine word, milord, an educated word, a genlemanly word, and I like it ye said it y'rself; aye. Pickled like a ig's foot, I might ha' said, but I like your phrase better."

"And did he say where he was going? To Vincennes, maybe?"

"Why, no, sir, he didn't *say*. But his horse, it's up at the mill, n'lad. Aye. At 'is mill." His face suddenly fell, then he looked up and was squinting as if in pain.

"Poor, poor, poor," he seemed to be muttering, but just above a whisper, as if to himself. "I'll be goin' over again afore noon," he said, "if the drayman I'm 'spectin' gets here by then. Would y' like to go? I sure do hope so."

THE MILL STOOD ON A STEEP BANK OF SILVER CREEK, a clear stream that ran down through the Illinois Regiment Grant Lands and fell into the Ohio at Clarksville. A dam had been built upstream from the mill, and a wooden sluice brought water from the reservoir to pour over the huge millwheel. George had designed the machinery inside so that the great driving axle could be meshed to drive either a grinding-stone or a set of gangsaws with only a few minutes' adjustment. But now neither was working. The sluice had been diverted from the wheel, and the only sound was of falling water.

George's horse, in a pole corral, nickered as William rode up. William dismounted and wrapped his reins over a pole, and went up a muddy slope to the plank door in the stone wall, pushed it open, and entered the cool, cavernous mill, which smelled sharply of new wood. It was unusual not to hear the rumbling of the machinery. But the high, gloomy space was not silent. Under the muffled sound of falling water there was a voice, deep, growling, sometimes rising to a shout. William peered about in the half-dark. The voice rose and fell in the patterns of oratory, but the words were indistinct, muffled in their own echoes. Something thumped; there was another shout, another thump, then the sonorous rise and fall of the voice again. William made his way over the oak-beam tracks by which logs were skidded into the sawpit, and put his hand on a ladder that led up to the grain-mill on the next story. As he climbed up he could hear the voice more clearly; it was George's voice, and sounded as if he were in an argument with someone, a violent argument, though there was no voice replying. Glad he had brought his pistol, William hauled himself up the last two rungs of the ladder and peered over the dusty floor at a strange and pitiful spectacle.

On the far side of the room, at a long plank table used for flour sacking, two big men sat in the tiny light of a candle, and one of the men was George. He was carrying on a slurred tirade which rumbled in the vast space. The other man's head was on his arms, as if he were asleep. Bottles and jugs gleamed in the candlelight. Over it all lay a faint silvery pall from one tiny slatted vent high in the gable. On the floor near the grinding wheel lay a large heap of the sacks that usually were on the table; a rumpled blanket was over them, as if they had been used as a bed. Just then some bottles on the table clattered and fell over as George brought his fist down on the tabletop with a shout.

"INGRATES! Hear me, Freeman?" So, the big silent man was Freeman, one of George's old troopers, who now was the mill supervisor. Freeman responded nothing, obviously being unconscious, but George went on: "Ingrates! Ingrates, Mister Freem'! Ingrateful! Wou'na given y' even a hund' acres 'cept hounded hounded HOUNDED!" He banged the table again, then swept his arm sideways and sent jugs flying. They bounced and rolled hollowly on the plank floor. "Ouch. Ruined me, Freeman. RUIN' ME! But f' what th' state owes me . . . I'm no w . . . . not worth a . . . a SPANISH DOLLAR! Spanish. Hey Freeman . . . Know why 'is mill is shut, eh? Know? Eh? 'Caus' o' Span'sh! Bedamn SPAN'SH! Shut up God damn Mississipp' . . . Miss . . . Span'sh treaty. It'd shut up Miss'pi TWENTY FIVE YEARS! Kentuck'd die. DIE! But East' states want .

reaty. Hell with Kentuck. Hell with Illinois! Hunh. Hunh! Indins be ruin us anyway . . . No council wi' th' Indians . . . Fall
n us any day now, Mist' Freem' but but this time, Long Knife
von' help. BY GOD NOT!" He hoisted a cup to his lips and
norted into it and sucked its contents and banged it on the table
vhile reaching for the jug. "Long Knife re . . . retired f'm savin'
ountries, Mist' Freem'. Long Knife likes Indians better'n Long
Knife likes gov'nors. Tell ye that, man. FREEM'!" He reached
cross the table and grabbed Freeman's vest and shook him vio-
ently, yelling, "Pay 'tention God damn Freem'! Y'r com-
nander's talkin!" Freeman, his balance dislodged, sagged
ideways and fell on the floor like a sack of rocks. George sat
linking through the candlelight at the place where he had been
itting then began to laugh. "Ha! ha, ha! Begod, one thing 'bout
ou, ol' Freem'! Ye do know when t' quit! Ha, Ha! Ha, ha,
HAH, HA HA HA HEEE!" The laughter brought on an awful,
acking, wheezing cough then, and finally he said, "But I don'
now when t' quit. But I do now, bejesus. I do now. I quit savin'
ountries. No more . . . Hullo. Hullo, who's 'ere, eh? Who . . .
Dickie? Billy? Billy."

William had climbed up and come around barrels and machinery, and he stood now beside the heap of Freeman's body
and looked at George in the candlelight, and up close now
George looked so horrible that William could only swallow and
move his lips and blink in shock and disbelief.

George's eyes were red-rimmed, bloodshot; his eyelids were
puffy. Reddish stubble darkened his chin and sunken cheeks; his
skin was pasty, and agleam with oil and sweat and smudges.
Dried blood encrusted his forehead and speckled his filthy, torn,
vomit-stained linen shirt. His hair hung lank and greasy down
the sides of his face, part of it snarled with lint and twigs and
sawdust. His big hands, now on the tabletop, were black, as if he
had been digging in ashes. Worse even than the dirt and di-
shevelment, though, was the dullness, the stupidity, in that face
that always had been keen, intense, or merry, throughout William's memory. He had seen George intoxicated before, or,
rather, thought he had; he had seen him flushed and animated
and jovial with liquor a few times, at home on holidays and
furloughs, and had even seen him teary-eyed with sentiment or
snapping mad in arguments, pointing for emphasis with a glass
of sloshing whiskey in his hand. But never had he seen him
stupefied, slack-lipped, wobble-headed, puke-stained, as he was
now, with the bloody abrasion on his forehead, probably from

falling, and the stunned, unfocused eyes making him look like a pole-axed ox.

George was trying to rise now; his hands were clattering among jugs and cups and clay pipes as he tried to lift himself. "Thought saw Dickie, I . . ." And then his eyes began pouring tears. "Bu' he's gone . . . poor green . . ." George was half-standing now, his contorted face lit from under the chin by the candle, a little silver daylight from the high vent limning his shoulders and the crown of his head, and he swayed backward, then forward, and back, then pitched forward face down among the crockery. The candle was snuffed under him.

William went around and dragged him off the table and hauled him to the pile of sacks, struggling with his inert weight, and there he covered him with the blanket. Sobbing, he went down to the creek and wet several sacks and climbed back up and tried to clean George's face with them. Even unconscious, George would not lie serene. He thrashed and flopped and wept and moaned in nightmares, twice calling something that sounded like "trees," pouring sweat until his shirt was sodden. William was afraid to leave him for fear he would move around and fall down the ladderwell to the skids below. Nearby, Freeman snored on in the slumber of an ordinary drunk.

At last, in mid-afternoon, George lay quiet, though still sweating. William put his ear to George's sour, stinking shirt front and listened to his heartbeat. It was thumping like a deep, erratic drum, but nearly drowned out by the volcanic burblings and growlings in his guts and his shallow, sometimes gasping, breathing. William once had heard of a man dying from intoxication, back in Caroline County, and wondered if George could be at such an extreme. It was clear that he had been saturating himself all during his absence. His breath was putrid.

It was raining on the roof. William, feeling empty as a used barrel, left George then and galloped down through the half-built, half-deserted town of Clarksville to the ferry landing. He found Davy Pagan there under an awning on the boat, smoking a pipe and watching the rain sizzle on the gray-green river. He told Pagan what he had on his hands. The old ferryman was not surprised, saying, "'E looked as 'e was headin' f'r a real rum-buzzamaroo." He sniffed, and William realized that he was crying.

Pagan agreed to help William carry the general down to the ferry and take him across, but suggested they wait till evening. "Ain't nobody ever seen our gen'l like this," he said, "and nobody orter."

And so at dusk they led General Clark's horse down with something in a blanket draped over it, which Pagan told his Negro oarsmen was bagged meal, though they knew meal sacks did not groan and retch and wear boots.

And the ferry crossed the broad river in the rain of night, and then from somewhere, in a moment, Pagan conjured a wagon, driven by someone William recognized as another old Illinois veteran. "Pray God th' jug's not got a holt on 'im," Pagan murmured to William in the drizzly darkness. "A true 'ero's got a long way t' fall."

"I'll pray. Thankee, Mister Pagan, and good night now."

Pagan put his forefinger to his lips. "I'm blind and deef. Haven't seen the gen'l for a month, y'see?"

And the wagon went up the public road eastward along the night river toward Mulberry Hill with its cargo in a wet wool blanket, and William rode alongside, heart full of ashes, leading George's stallion, and prayed that the jug had not really got a hold on George in those four awful days, but feared that it had. "A long way to fall," old Pagan had said, and William thought those words over and over as he took George home to his family.

To the Clerk of Jefferson County

Sir

This is to Certifie that I am willing a Licence should Issue out of your Office for the marriage of my Daughter Eliz^th Clark to Col'o Richard C. Anderson

Given under my hand this 1st day of August 1787
JOHN CLARK

"Thank you, Mr. Clark," said Colonel Anderson. He gripped John Clark's hand hard, and both men's eyes reflected that kind of embarrassed bond that exists only between a virgin's father and the man who desires to possess her.

"We'll all be proud to have you in the family, Dick," John Clark said. It crossed his mind that he would again, after four years, have a son named Dick.

"Nothing compared with my pride in being of the Clarks," Anderson said.

"Now I reckon a toast is in order," John Clark said. "Billy, would ye pour for us?" William, who had stood witness to the consent, went to the decanters, which were on a mahogany buffet by the wall. Opposite the wall was George's room. As William poured their drams, he was aware of the room beyond the wall, aware that George was in there, that he had shut himself in upon learning that Anderson was arriving, and said he would come out after he had left. "But Elizabeth's invited him to stay through Sunday," William had told him. "Then I'll be out after Sunday," George had replied. "Look, Billy, lad, I've no grudge against the man. It's just that he'll want to talk Indian affairs. Well, he and James Wilkinson are the Indian Commissioners now, they've replaced me, so I take that to mean my Indian policies are nothing now, so therefore why should he get advice from me? No. Y'll just have to say I'm indisposed. As I will be."

William poured the brandy and felt all too sure that, beyond that wall, George was pouring brandy too.

As Davy Pagan had said, it was a long way to fall. And George had fallen long and hard that first time. It had lasted for weeks, even after William had brought him home from the mill. There had been no controlling him. "If they all believe me to be a jug-sucker," he'd say with a bitter laugh, "I might's well live up to my reputation. Reputation's mighty important, don't I know it!"

Sometimes he would try, and try valiantly, to shake off the hold that liquor was getting on him. Sometimes the family would get him dried out a bit, and he would profess shame, and pray alongside his father and mother, and go to church meetings with the family, and go on long hunting and exploring trips with William, to places where no liquor was.

But sometimes, after he had kept himself sober for a long time, he would come to table all glassy-eyed, enunciating words so carefully that he was incomprehensible, and they would know then that he had been nipping again, in the pantry, in his room, and was trying to seem sober to please the family, for he knew they hurt for him.

What saddened them most to see was how he would feign contempt for public affairs. Public service had ruined him and broken his heart, so he would pretend he was utterly indifferent to it. He had resigned as principal surveyor of the bounty lands, leaving Bill Croghan in that post. When the Indian councils he had arranged for April had gone neglected by the new Indian Commissioners, and the Wabash tribes and Shawnees had resumed their marauding, there had as usual been delegations of people coming to ask him to lead again. To their entreaties he had just smiled in a mocking way and replied, "You'd better not give me an army just now, because if I had one I'd be tempted to lead it against the Capital rather than the tribes." As a private man he found that he could say just about whatever he pleased, and he enjoyed, when he was a little in his cups, the freedom to mock the state government. But they all knew there was a bitter pain behind that mockery, and he was only protecting his own wounds when he talked that way.

Aye, William thought as he capped the decanter and picked up the tray with the filled glasses. He's into it in there again, I'm sure.

And just then he heard through the thick wall the dull *thuds* of a body falling down.

God, George. *Oh, God.*

GEORGE SAT IN HIS ROOM AT HIS PARENTS' HOUSE AT MULberry Hill, a candle burning on his desk, a fire in the hearth nearby, and an unopened jug sitting on he mantel. He was writing. Sometimes he would keep the jug there during his dry spells just as a challenge, to see how long he could keep himself from breaking the wax seal. The longer he managed to do this, the stronger he felt he would become. Sometimes he would look at it and almost grow dizzy at the thought of opening it. But he would resist. When he was sober he was aware how his problem worried his parents and he would resist for their sake. Sometimes he would think that if he were far away from them, he would start opening jugs and never stop until he had found permanent peace six feet under the ground. But most of the time he would try to stay sober, try to think his way out of his problems, try to find a way to resume the ascent he had begun during the war.

It was hard to leave the jug sealed this night. Ben Logan had come to see him, and had left him with the feeling that any hope of being relieved of the war debts was really in vain.

Governor Randolph had asked Logan to get together all the records of the expenditures in the western campaign, so that Virginia's war debts could be settled up with the United States. The governor, aware of what he had done to George, had been afraid to ask George himself, and so had written to Logan, who then had brought the letter to George. Now that his fury toward the governor had cooled, George felt he could write to the governor in a cordial way and explain, once again, the matter of the vouchers. In the years since the war, Virginia had maintained an Accounting Commission, with traveling officials and bookkeepers, to try to determine the liabilities. George wrote, as calmly as he could:

> I can assure you, Sir, that this was delivered eight years ago, as I have told you and the Commission repeatedly, and lodged in the Auditor's office. . . . When I reflect on

487

these accounts, and the great expense that hath already attended the settlement of them, it appears obvious to me that all my support of an active war for seven years, when reduced to Specie, will be found to amount to a less sum than has already been spent on this Accounting Commission since the war, owing to our frugal manner of living and the want of almost every necessary.

He put down the quill, shook his head, poured sand over the ink and then funneled it back into its jar. He looked at what he had written and decided it would be useless to elaborate still again. That was all that could be said about it. Now there remained only to comment once upon the sorry manner in which he had been treated after the Bazadone affair.

I have been obliged to lay aside instructions and act discretionary sometimes. I dared to do this as the salvation of the country was of more importance to me than the rank I bore.

After a while George got up and walked to the window, and stood there with his hands behind his back, gazing at the dark silhouette of himself refected, all wavy and distorted, on the uneven surface of the glass. It looked as if he were dissolving at the edges—which was not unlike the way he felt sometimes. Smiling ruefully at that, he turned and went to the fireplace. He stood with his hand resting on the mantelpiece one tempting inch from the jug. For a long time he stood that way. Then, instead of reaching for the jug, he reached down and got a poker and adjusted the logs. They glowed orange and bathed his hand and face in dry heat. Then he went back and sat down again at the desk and picked up his pen.

After suffering the fatigues that I have undergone—and yet have to pay large sums of money for supplys that the state could not get credit for,—A person might reasonably suppose that of course I must be unhappy. The reverse hath taken place. Conscious of having done everything in the power of a person under my circumstances,—not only for the defense of the country, but to save every expense possible,—I can with pleasure view countries flourishing that I have stained with the blood of its enemies. I am

> Your Excellency's Humble Servt,
> G.R. CLARK

There, he thought. I guess I never need have another word with that man.

He felt cold now, and went to the fireplace again. He kicked the front log with the toe of his boot, his hand again resting on the mantelpiece one tempting inch from the jug.

Fires don't seem to keep me keep warm since that winter of 79, he thought.

Seems only one thing will.

He touched the jug with his fingertips, then the palm of his hand.

He felt warmer already.

But it made him sad, because he knew he was going to open it.

"O ETERNAL GOD, CREATOR AND PRESERVER OF ALL MAN-kind, Giver of all spiritual grace, the Author of everlasting life."

Everlasting life, Elizabeth Clark thought, eyes down but feeling the tall presence of Richard Clough Anderson at her right, and feeling the new heavy circle of gold on her left hand, *Everlasting life. Us together forever. This is the beginning of that.*

"Send thy blessing upon these thy servants, this man and this woman, whom we bless in thy Name; that they, living faithfully together, may surely perform and keep the vows and covenant betwixt them made, and may ever remain in perfect love and peace together, and live according to thy laws; through Jesus Christ our Lord. Amen."

Then the minister reached for Elizabeth's right hand and guided it to Richard's right hand, and Richard seized it with a warm, fervent, damp grip. She had been trembling until now, but at the touch at last of his hand she was not trembling anymore, but her heart was coming up like a sunrise. The minister said, "Those whom God hath joined together, let no man put asunder."

Back among the people she heard someone sniffle, and she was sure it was Fanny. They had become so especially close, so confidential with each other, in the last days before this frightening and glorious day. Elizabeth had professed to Fanny that Dick Anderson made her want to live forever; she would never want to die, never want one of them to have to live on without the other. And she had said to Fanny, "Make a prayer with me, in secret, and we'll never tell Dick or anyone that we made it, for it might go against his ambitions: help me pray he will never ever go away to any war again. Because he's a man and he's a soldier, and they don't know how precious their lives are."

And Fanny had understood her feelings exactly, and had said,

489

"I'll make you a trade deal, that you'll pray the same for Jame
O'Fallon when I marry him, may it be soon." And they had
prayed their secret prayer together.

"I pronounce that they are Man and Wife, in the name of th
Father, and of the Son, and of the Holy Ghost. Amen. Now yo
kneel," the minister said softly. There was the rustling of he
gown and the creak of Dick's shiny boots, and she was terribl
aware of her body again because she had just moved it into thi
new attitude, and she had the curious thought: *Now it's his bod
too. I know he's glad of that.*

". . . bless, preserve and keep you; the Lord mercifully wit
his favour look upon you, and fill you with all Spiritual benedic
tion and Grace, that ye may so live together in this life, that i
the world to come ye may have life everlasting.

"*Amen.*"

Amen, Ann Rogers Clark thought.

And she watched Colonel Dick Anderson bend his blond hea
down to Elizabeth's upturned face.

So there would be still more grandchildren soon. Elizabeth
had all the traits of a fruitful one. Her hipbones were wider; sh
was not so racehorse-narrow as the Rogers women were, s
surely it would be easier for her to bear them. And she was—
well, there was simply a *juiciness* about her; she was like damp
fertile soil, as some women so especially seem to be. Aye. Mor
grandchildren. Annie had just had her sixth and seventh b
Owen Gwathmey: boy and girl twins, just lately learned of by
letter from Virginia. And just last month, Jonathan's third chil
had been born, a boy, named Isaac after Sarah's father. Tha
news had just come by mail from Virginia too. Ten grand
children already, she thought, ten. Lordy.

Ann Rogers Clark now heard a soft *Hm* beside her. It wa
George. He had not touched a drop for a week, by a massive
effort of the will, in order that he would be able to stand here a
Elizabeth's wedding without the reek and the glazed look, be
cause the public did not yet know about George's problem, and
Colonel Richard Clough Anderson did not. And for Elizabeth'
sake, George did not want Anderson to know.

Ann Rogers Clark looked at George's grand profile. On
would never know by a look at him the binges he had been or
for seven months—except by being close enough to see his trem
bling hands.

Ann Rogers Clark felt a sudden hollowness, and she wa
thinking, as the bride and groom concluded their long kiss and
the congregation began to stir and murmur:

490

I don't think he'll ever give me grandchildren, George won't. Forbid it Heaven, but I come to fear he's married to the face in the bottle.

26

To the Clerk of Jefferson County
                                   Mr William Johnston, Clk

Sir
This is to Certifie that I am willing a Licence should issue out of your office for the marriage of my Daughter Lucy Clark to Maj[r]*. William Croghan—*
Given under my hand this 13th July 1789

                                   JOHN CLARK

"So, then," said the clerk, shaking his head and smiling wistfully, "so it's Miss Lucy now! Well, Mister Clark, it pleasures me to give this license, for your daughter's got one o' the best in this fellow. And she'll never want for anything, surely, as he's a prosperin' man!"

That was true. Everything Bill Croghan touched turned to wealth. Besides his surveying fees, he had amassed a wealth of fine land. He had designed and built this very Court House. He was a town trustee, striving to establish a hospital and school for Louisville. He was a trader in hemp and tobacco, pork goods and dairy products, with an establishment near the river front and Dick Anderson as his partner. Bill Croghan was one of the best things that had ever happened to Louisville. He was also one of the best things that had ever happened to the Clark family, as they had known for a long time. Just lately, Jonathan, his old compatriot, who was prospering almost as well, as a merchant back in Spotsylvania County of Virginia, had invested a substantial sum of money in Bill Croghan's Louisville enterprise. It was turning out to be as George had said it would: the Clarks were the first family of Kentucky. John Clark himself was so rich in land now that he could hardly keep track of it. George, in order to keep his own extensive holdings from being attacked by old creditors of the Revolutionary days, had deeded most of them over to his father. George still tried to believe that Virginia or the United States would someday compensate him for all the war bills he had signed, but that hope grew more and more feeble. Among the immigrants to the West there were lawyers, of course, and several of them had built their practices on encouraging George's old allies to sue him. Any penny he made, from his mill or from the sale of his lands, was snapped up by his creditors. And thus, as George would joke bitterly when he was drunk, the Father of Kentucky was now also the Orphan of Kentucky. Once he had even been arrested, to be sent to jail for debt, and only on a technicality had he escaped that ignominy. But the disgrace of it had thrown him into such a slump that he had gone off on another swigging carouse, from which he was recovering only now. All the Clarks and those in their family circle were prospering. All except George.

ELIZABETH CLARK ANDERSON SAT IN THE NURSERY WITH her first baby at her breast, humming, rocking gently. She had pulled her shirtwaist down off one shoulder and whenever a breeze would come in through the open window from among the big maples outside it would feel like angel caresses on her sweat-damp skin. She looked down at the baby's dark, fine hair. His head was just about as large and rounded and delicate as her breast. She could see the faint blue veins under the baby's translucent skin just as she could the veins of her swollen breast. Dick Anderson liked the look of those veins; he would often kneel here before her and talk about how fine and delicate his wife and son were. But the veins disturbed Elizabeth. They reminded her how delicate life is. She and her baby were here by a miracle. The birth had taken hours, excruciating hours, and there had been a question whether the mother would have to be sacrificed for the baby, or the baby would be lost to save the mother, or, at one point, whether either of them would survive.

Elizabeth remembered her secret prayer. It seemed to be coming true. Her husband was not a soldier anymore and it seemed he was so absorbed now in the business of making a fortune that he would never again have a desire to go to war. He had even named their home—this massive stone house, ten miles east of

Louisville—Soldier's Retreat. Elizabeth did not have to worry about him going off to war anymore, and only now and then, when he went away with General Wilkinson on business of the Indian Commission, did she have to fret for his safety at all. The wealthier he became, the more cautious he became.

Now, in fact, the fears she had used to have for him had been all succeeded by those she now had for herself.

She loved Dick Anderson even more than she had loved him when they were just sweethearts. He was a perfect husband. Their life was just right: just enough wealth, just enough position, just enough society and dancing, just enough time for the tendernesses of the home. Elizabeth grew every day to understand better what the bond was between her own father and mother: they were each other's whole worlds, just as she and Dick Anderson were coming to be. Yes, she loved him even more than she had loved him at first, and he seemed to be likewise even more in love with her.

But whenever she would lie with him from now on, because of the horrible danger of the coming of their first baby, she would be holding to him and fearing for her life.

Out somewhere among the sunglided treetops a mourning dove was making its forlorn announcement of the fading of the day. *O-ah, ooo, ooo, ooo. O-ah, ooo, ooo, ooo.* Such a lovely bird, and thought to be good luck. But if that's so, why must they sound so sad, she wondered. Someone had asked that question once, Elizabeth thought while the baby's dear sucking mouth made just-painful twinges of pleasure around her nipple. She thought back.

It was Lucy who had asked that. So long ago! Back in Caroline County, one late afternoon like this in their room upstairs.

Lucy! Oh, yes, Lucy! Elizabeth smiled. At last Bill Croghan's Little Brother Lucy is going to be his Little Wife Lucy! Elizabeth could just barely remember when Lucy had first declared she was going to marry Bill Croghan. Back in . . . '76, I guess it was, when she was the awfulest gawkiest tomboy with that fool's crush on him, and hardly only eleven or twelve at the time. Thirteen years she's been making that come true!

But as they said about the redheaded ones of the family, they'd make up their minds far ahead about something they dreamed of doing, and then, no matter what, those dreams were destined to come true. Just four days from now the wedding would be. With Fanny as the maid of honor. Won't she just be beside herself! That Fanny!

I wonder if George will do as well staying sober for Lucy's

wedding as he did for mine. I must pray for George tonight. I
forgot to last night, more's the shame on me. Make a point to
pray for strength for his soul, and for some turn of fortune in his
favor.

I wish I knew, she thought, whatever happened about that
lady he loved in the war, that he'd tell us about but not really tell
us.

I bet if whatever sad thing it was that happened to them hadn't
happened, he'd be married and happy now, happy as he deserves
to be.

Poor George!

O-ah, ooo, ooo, ooo!

"ALMOST THERE," GEORGE SAID BACK OVER HIS SHOULDER
as he plunged and ducked through the jungle of saplings and
bushes and broad-leafed weeds, shirt-back soaked with sweat, the
long piece of rolled paper in his left hand, his walking stick in
his right. William panted and kept brushing gnats and no-see-
ums away from his eyes so he could see to follow. If he can go
like this now, how did his troops keep up with him when he was
young and healthy? William wondered. Off to their right,
beyond the foliage, the Falls of the Ohio rushed loudly. They
pushed on, and the noise of the water fell behind.

"Now, here we be." George led out onto a rocky, sandy shoal,
sparsely vegetated with willow and shrubs, and stopped in the
sunlight. Almost straight above was the Point of Rock, as George
called it, the place where he hoped to build his house if his
fortunes ever improved. Farther along the shore were the few
little buildings of Clarksville, and the mill. "See where we are?"
George said, sluicing sweat off his brow and chin with thumb
and fingers. He was not even breathing hard. But he did sweat
copiously at these times when he was coming out of a long wet
spell, William had noticed that.

Now George was squatting on a flat rock in the sunshine,
spreading out the piece of paper and looking upstream and
down. He weighted the corners with a chalky seashell or a piece
of fossil, raised each arm to mop his temples with his rolled shirt
sleeves, then signalled for William to squat beside him. William
already knew, as George had taught him, that there were seashells in the rock here because once this threshold of rock that
made the Falls had been the bed of an ancient sea. The discussions they had had about how that could have been, and about
where the sea might have gone, had stretched William's mind
out of shape for weeks. There was no question about it in Wil-

liam's mind: his brother could see more of what lay before his eyes, and then make more fascinating speculations beyond what could be seen, than just about anybody. There were a lot of interesting people around Louisville, but anybody's company, after a spell in the company of George's mind, was pretty ordinary.

On the sheet of paper was George's drawing of his plan for a boat canal around the Falls. His finger tapped a place on the paper. "Here's where we are. Now, y'see, up here the boats would come in. A jetty would run right off there, and they'd come into here 'stead o' going into the rapids. Down there where I showed you the first lock'd be, that gate would be closed and this stretch would fill up with water to the same level as the river above the Falls. Then when the boats got to the gate, th' water would be let out till they were down five feet, and then the gate would be opened, and they could float out to the second lock. And so on. As for boats coming upstream, why, they'd come into the low end o' the canal, the low gate would be shut behind 'em, like I said, that'd fill up with water till they could float up to the next, and so on, till they'd just come out right here at this level and row right out onto the upper river. See how simple it is?"

"It's so simple it's got me amazed. First time I saw those Falls, I didn't reckon there'd ever be a way to get a boat by 'em except pull 'em right up the rapids by tow rope."

"Aye. And that's about ten times as hard and tricky as it looks to be. Here's the point, Billy. On all the miles o' river, from New Orleans up to Pittsburgh, there's only been *one place* where boats had to be unloaded, portaged, or what have you, and that's right here. All the rest is navigable. Now if I build a canal and locks here, I've solved the one obstacle on this whole waterway. What little toll I'd charge would be cheap compared with the labor they hire to unload or portage, but it would pay for the canal in a few years. And it would sooner or later enable me to pay off all those bedamned creditors. Besides that, it would make Clarksville a great port, and all my old boys that's got grant lands up here would benefit from it. As they well deserve, as it was them that won this land. And my mill would have plenty of business, too. You'd see me in charge o' my own destiny once again. For I'll vow, Billy, I *have* to work my way out o' this bind. Since apparently the State's never going to do me justice, I'll have to do it for myself. Well, I'm used to that. I've fought my way out o' worse straits than this!" He set his jaw and looked up and down the Falls.

495

William studied him and felt full of hope. As long as George had a hope and a plan, it seemed, he could resist the bottle. And he seemed to generate his own hopes and plans.

"Y' know, Billy," George said over the rushing of the Falls, "when me and my good boys shot these Falls under an eclipse that June day back in '78, I was so scared I thought I'd wet th' boat and sink it."

"Ha, ha! I'll bet!"

"And I thought then that someday something would have to be done about this obstacle. So that's why I did up this scheme." He pointed down at the drawings. "I'll tell you. Everything I've ever done started out as a night-ponder. Like that night at Harrod's Town during the siege. Yep. Everything worth doin' starts out with one person by himself, scratchin' his head and sayin', 'Hmmm.'"

"I reckon that must be so. Maybe I ought to scratch my own head now and then and say, 'Hmmm.' Ha, ha!"

"Ha, ha! You better! Women, too. Look at Lucy. I bet when she first saw Bill Croghan, she scratched her head and said, 'Hmmm.'"

They laughed and slapped each other's shoulders. "That's exactly how it happened," William whooped. "She tells it so herself!"

ON THE MORNING OF JULY 18, LUCY WAS AWAKENED FROM A profound sleep by a variety of unaccustomed sensations in her lower abdomen and loins, just one of which was a pressing need to answer a call of nature. For one moment, as she rose reluctantly against the languid gravity of sleep, she half-dreamed of a long-ago Christmas morning when she had lain in her younger sisters' body-warmth just like this needing to get up for this same reason, but reluctant to leave her reveries of Bill Croghan . . .

BILL!

Her eyes popped open with the rush of realization.

She was married to Bill Croghan! The memory of their wedding night just past explained her strange feelings down there, and the body lying warm beside her was Bill's! She stared dopily at the ceiling remembering his incredible ardor of the night. It was no wonder she had slept so deeply. That scoundrel had exhausted her. She lay for a moment realizing, from the light in the room, that it was very late in the morning—perhaps it was even afternoon—and recalling with a wild confusion and something like shame the way they had been last night—or, rather, this morning it had been, as the wedding celebration had run into the small hours before they had been spirited off by their guests to this bed. *Merciful Heavens*, she thought, *what came over us! Why, I was like a . . . like a . . . well, never mind like a what, but a redheaded one!*

Bill Croghan had not let the guests get him drunk, and he had been keen and strong and good and clean-mouthed and exciting, and he had laughed once at her and said, "Lucy, darling, understand me that it's been a long wait!"

She smiled a little now, thinking, *Well, if that's what it's like, and we can do it whenever we please, it's hard to imagine we'll be wanting to do much of anything else.*

Oh my. Am I wicked to think like this about it?

I wonder if I'd dare tell Bill what I think of it.

But, well, as Mama says, she's read the Bible three times through and's never found anything forbids a body liking it. Not if you're married.

And I'm glad I am.

Now she looked over at him. He was lying on his back, breathing evenly, eyes closed. She looked at his eyelashes and the shape of his nose, and studied his lips, in ways she had never been able to before because he had always been awake. The bright light in the room showed clearly the smallpox scars under his cheekbones, the little healed craters on his forehead, and her heart compressed with love and pity when she thought of him suffering back then, and she wanted to kiss the little scars.

I wonder if he's awake with his eyes shut, she thought, and she whispered:

"Mister Croghan, dear, are you awake?"

His lips moved into a smile.

"I'm sound asleep, dreaming I'm in Paradise."

Then he stirred suddenly and his arm was over her and his right eye was looking at her right eye, so close it was big and out of focus. "Do you know what a honeymoon comes from?"

"Silly! From getting married." They were not whispering now, but murmuring.

"I mean the custom."

"I could guess: 'cause you're sweet as honey, and you moon over me."

"Hm, hm! All right. But it's this, that long ago, when men had to get wives by capturing them, then they'd have to go hide from her father for a month—a moon—and they would eat honey all that time."

"Get wives by capturing 'em! Well, I'll declare times have changed, then, as here we lay in my father's own house!"

He chuckled and nuzzled her neck, and his hand came up and he pushed his fingertips through her curls. She began to wonder whether he was going to try to do it to her again now, and she began to wonder what she would do about the business of needing to use the chamber pot with this man right here in the room with her. He said, while stroking her hair:

"Soon you'll have the nicest house in all Kentucky." He had shown her the plans he had drawn of it. It was going to be a grand house of brick with four chimneys. In the meantime they would be living in a wooden house in town. But all that was some time off, and right now she had a more urgent consideration and didn't know what to do about it that wouldn't seem too awkward. Her mother had failed to tell her about this absurd little matter, and she hadn't even thought to ask.

If he tries to do it when I'm like this, I'll bust, she thought. Outside the window a mockingbird was making all sorts of ridiculous noises, and it seemed as if it were making fun of her and her secret dilemma.

But just then Bill solved it. He kissed her on the mouth and said, "Excuse me, my darling, but I must leave the room for just a while," and he sat up on the side of the bed and began pulling on clothes.

Ah, she thought, *I do have myself a prince!*

October 22, 1790

IT LOOKED DEAD CERTAIN THAT HIS FIRST INDIAN FIGHT would be his last.

Ensign William Clark lay on his belly in the frosty grass, his mouth dry as corn meal, feeling his heart beat on the ground and looking across the Maumee River toward the low-hanging smoke of a huge Indian war camp. It was daybreak. His feet were sore from the all-night march. Around him in the yellow grass and weeds he could see felt hats and rifle muzzles and tense young faces, and a few yards off in a thicket of hazel bushes he could see the horses of Colonels Hardin and Hall and McMullen. Those bushes were the only cover on the plain, and the colonels were meeting in there with the majors and captains to determine what to do about the problem.

Their problem was that they had expected to find a hundred warriors here, and instead had found a thousand or more. Two days ago, here where the St. Mary's and St. Joseph's Rivers met to form the Maumee, those hundred Indians had killed twenty o

General Harmar's soldiers in an ambush, and in a mad retreat the soldiers had been left unburied on the riverbanks. Colonel Hardin had demanded Harmar's permission to bring 400 Kentucky militiamen back here and bury the corpses and, if possible, find and destroy the Indians. Now they were here, and to their dismay they were facing a major part of Little Turtle's army. Colonel Hardin's scouts had seen Little Turtle himself, and the Shawnee chief Blue Jacket, and Simon Girty, the white renegade, in the camp at first light.

So now it was daybreak, and the Kentuckians were sure to be discovered at any minute. They had only three alternatives, all desperate:

They could form a defensive square here on this unfavorable ground and wait to be attacked. Or, they could begin a retreat, with hopes that some of them would survive long enough to get back to General Harmar's army. But the army was at least twenty-five miles away, and heading in the other direction.

The third alternative was to attack: cross the river swiftly and, by force of surprise, scatter the enemy. In the face of their superior numbers, this would be supremely dangerous. But it would offer probably the only chance of success, and Colonel Hardin being the kind of man he was, it likely would be his choice. Hardin, as the soldiers had come to phrase it, had more guts in his bellybutton than General Harmar had in his whole great boozy paunch.

William lay here now thinking what a contrast this campaign had been to his only other military experience, George's troubled Wabash expedition of '86. Back then it had been the general who had wanted to fight and the troops who had wanted to turn back; now the troops were eager to fight, but General Harmar would only retreat.

It was inexplicable, and Harmar had refused even to try to explain it. He had eleven hundred militiamen, three hundred twenty regulars, three horse-drawn cannon, and a troop of mounted swordsmen, and plenty of beef cattle and grain. Harmar, President Washington's own choice as commandant of the new Army of the United States, had assembled the force in Fort Washington, at the new town of Cincinnati, and two weeks ago had marched them confidently up the Miami River under the proud and approving eye of old General Arthur St. Clair, governor of the new Ohio Territory, to seek and crush the confederacy of Little Turtle at last. This army had advanced far into northwestern Ohio, burning some abandoned Indian towns. But when a captured Indian had revealed that Girty and the chiefs were gathering near the headwaters of the Maumee, Harmar's confidence had dissolved. The general had sent out a few sorties, and then, after the ambush two days ago, had turned his whole army around and started back down the Miami toward Fort Washington, to the dismay of everybody. Last night Hardin had literally demanded that the general let him come back to the Maumee to get the bodies of the ambush victims, and so here they were now, Hardin and his mere four hundred facing the force Harmar had been afraid to meet with fourteen hundred.

William glanced to his right now and saw Major Wyllys, one of the regular officers, coming through the grass at a crouching run, all too visible in his blue coat and gold epaulets. He knelt here and there to talk to militia officers hidden in the grass. At last he knelt beside William, flushed and breathy. "At sunrise, lad," he said, pointing, "on hand signal, no noise, *please*. We cross the river right there. Fountain's horse troop will go straight into their camp, Colonel Hardin and us on their tails. We'll have the sun at our backs; that's good. McMullen will take the right wing;"—he pointed downstream—"Hall the left. Keep your boys tight in; the colonel wants our front no more than a thousand yards from wing to wing, so's to form quick if need be."

"So," William said, feeling a strange, cool resignation, "we do without Gen'l Harmar, eh?"

"Colonel's sent him a rider," Wyllys said. "Might be we'll get reinforced later. All right, Mr. Clark. Sunrise. And do y'r name credit, eh?" He squeezed William's wrist and went whispering away through the grass to the next officer. William looked over his shoulder. The edge of the sky was pearly. The sun would be peeping over in five or ten minutes. Maybe the last sunrise I'll see, he thought. He was twenty. Short career, he thought.

He crawled back to instruct his company. Stubbly jaws, white faces, burning eyes, sorrowful eyes, silent nods, final attention to their priming powder. Then he crawled up to the place where he had been lying in front of them and lay watching the hazel thicket for Colonel Hardin's signal, and he remembered and recited to himself the litany of advice George had given him: *Head a-swivel. Dread nothing; see everything. Keep comrades in the corners of your eyes. Don't hesitate ever. If you're hit don't stop; run on 'im before he can reload or raise an arm. Half a second can make the difference. Yell and be happy; there'll be time later for crying and puking. Let the wolf in ye come out, but by Heaven no Clark better ever stoop to take a scalp.*

William thought of the express rider being sent after Harmar. No hope in that, he thought. Take three or four hours at least for him to get there and bring back cavalry. This kind o' scrap won't last that long.

Somehow he had it set in his mind that combat could only last ten or fifteen minutes. He had never known anyone capable of doing *anything* at full tilt more than ten or fifteen minutes at a stretch, and surely killing must be a full-tilt kind of thing.

He looked at the grassy, brushy ground sloping down to the shallow river and then up to the smoke among the sun-gilded sycamores on the other side and foresaw his route across that distance, his heart beating on the ground and his limbs feeling all twitchy with dreadful eagerness, and then he looked back at the horizon where the top of the rising sun was shining like a spark through distant tree tops, and then he heard something like a sigh all around and looked toward the hazel thicket where Colonel Hardin had just ridden out and was sitting on his war horse, looking lean and hard as an ax, glancing to his right, then to his left, then drawing his saber.

William remembered then to pray, but there was time to say only *Our God help us all* before Colonel Hardin slashed down with the saber and dug in his spurs, and Fountain's cavalry streamed out of the thicket. And then the morning was full of the swishing and thumping of men running downhill through dry grass.

Of course they would have been naive to suppose that the Indians were unaware of their presence. The cavalry were out of the far side of the river and the infantry were splashing thigh-deep through the cold water when William felt something whiff past his temple. At the same instant he saw a cavalryman jerk in his saddle and drop his sword to clutch at an arrow in his throat. Musket fire roared then, and muzzle flashes and smoke erupted from the sycamores just ahead. A soldier fell in the water on either side of William. An arrow cracked against his rifle stock and fell in the water. It had all started. *Now*, he thought, lifting his knees high to run in the water, *now. Yell and be happy!*

His yodel poured throbbing out of his throat and his heart felt as big as a barrel. Hundreds of throats opened up with his, and now he was splashing out of the river among sycamore roots and could see painted faces and brown bodies moving among the tree trunks, and there had been no time for the savages to reload their muskets. Some of them were sprinting back toward their camp, others were standing fast, drawing bowstrings or rushing forth with raised tomahawks. A brave with a very boyish, round face with a stripe of vermillion painted across his nose and under his eyes had just notched an arrow and was pulling his bow ten feet

501

away with William as his target. He was only a boy and except for the painted face looked terribly much like just anybody in a schoolroom, and William didn't want to kill him, but had to, and put his rifle to his shoulder and squeezed the trigger and saw the stripe-painted young face jerk back, one eye blown in through its socket and spouting blood. The arrow went whirling sideways.

And so now William had done one of the big things in life: he had killed a man—a boy, at least. But there was no time to think about it: a warrior was in his path with his tomahawk cocked behind his shoulder and his black eyes on William's and his teeth bared. William raised his empty rifle in front of his chest to parry the blow. The tomahawk whacked so hard his hands stung. *Don't hesitate ever.* He brought his knee up into the Indian's groin and ran over him as he doubled over. *Head a-swivel.* They were through the sycamores now, howling murder, the line still moving forward even though every step forward was a mortal fight for every man. This bank was a narrow level bottom of tall horseweeds and willows on silty ground. It was a chaos now of running and wrestling bodies, powder smoke, gunshots, grunts, shrieks, thuds, curses, neighing horses, cracking of wood on wood, crunch of steel into bone, men sitting or lying dazed and dying, dark blood pouring onto the gray soil. Some yards off to the right Colonel Hardin rode hatless, maneuvering his great wild-eyed stallion with one hand full of reins and the other slashing with a crimson-bladed saber as if he were mowing wheat. Major Wyllys fired a pistol point-blank into the face of a huge Indian, but then dropped to his knees with an arrow in his side. William clubbed a warrior with his rifle butt and then whipped out his sword and slashed his throat as he fell, and his hand was bathed with spurting hot blood. Two yards ahead of him an Indian was pounding in the skull of a fallen militiaman. William ran up and kicked him; when the Indian yelled and spun about, William slashed across with all his might and the Indian's body jerked and flopped, headless, jets of blood pumping from the ghastly stump of meat and gristle while the head rolled the other way like a ball in the dust. This shook William, this that he had done so often to chickens and turkeys for the family table and had now done in a reckless fury to a human being.

The slaughter continued all around him and he stumbled ahead now like a man hacking his way through a thicket. A bullet passed through his clothes with a yank and he felt warm blood from a grazed flank running to his waist. Most of the Indians he saw now were in flight. He stubbed his foot on an iron kettle and realized that they had advanced into the camp. He sheathed his bloody sword and knelt to reload his rifle, head still a-swivel. His hands were sticky with blood, which smeared his powder horn and ramrod as he touched them, and he reloaded, still looking right and left. He remembered the feel of pig blood on his hand, that first slaughter so long ago.

The banging and howling continued around him, and men were falling and powder smoke burned his eyes and nostrils. His heart was thudding fast in his ribs and he had lost count of the men he had killed, and suddenly he was struck with the realization that he had no idea of the *shape* of the battle; he had been too involved in rushing and personal bloodletting to notice how the battle was going—the very *purpose* of all this frenzy had gotten lost somewhere; he had been a wolf, an animal for which there is no design, no future. Men to his right and left were hacking and shooting and stabbing and howling with the same sort of blind impetus, no different from his. But he was supposed to be an officer, responsible for a larger part of this battle than just the radius of his sword's swing. He began looking beyond that distance, standing with his rifle in his left hand and drawing his saber with his right. At his feet a dead Indian lay face down in a still smoldering campfire, his flesh cooking with a smell like venison. A few feet away a saddled gray horse, its neck red with blood, lay on its side twitching, trying to raise its head. The battle roared everywhere, a whirlwind of mortal struggle, but it was impossible to determine what was happening in the large view. Everywhere in sight lay the blue-coated bodies of regular soldiers; they seemed to have been chosen as special targets by the warriors, and William could not see a one alive anywhere. Sunbeams slanted in through dust and the dense smoke of campfires and gunpowder. A horse galloped through the melee a few feet in front of William, its rider, foot in stirrup, being dragged, flopping and bouncing, under it, and William saw that it was Major Fountain, commander of the cavalry detachment.

And now through the acrid curtain of smoke and dust in front of him came a dire howling, war cries from countless throats, and then a wall of dusky bodies materialized through the haze, coming toward him. It was a counterattack, a great wave of savages coming from somewhere, scores of them abreast, brave and disciplined, moving as if with a single will, driving back the militiamen who were still on foot. Arrows and bullets hummed and whispered thick as hail across the battleground and Kentuckians were crumpling to earth everywhere. William began backing up, yelling over the din:

"FALL BACK TO THE RIVER AND FORM A LINE!" He tried to repeat it but his throat was clogged with dust and he could only croak.

But they had heard him, and when their retreat carried them back to the sycamores, they did not plunge back into the river but turned to reload and fight. A brown figure sprinted straight at William, waving a war club. He parried with his sword and the blow of the club wrenched the sword from his blood-slippery hand. As the savage whipped his arm back to deliver the death blow, William punched him between the eyes with his big fist and the Indian caved in.

Some of the troops managed to load and fire here, and a score of Indians tumbled. The rest of the horde dropped into the weeds and behind cover, but kept crawling forward.

"Stand your ground and reload!" William bellowed now. He saw a face coming forward among the weeds, a face with a blue circle painted between the eyebrows. He threw his rifle to his shoulder and put a ball in the blue circle.

He glanced up and down along the river bank while reloading. A few hundred yards upstream, Hall's men were already retreating across the river in a cloud of gunsmoke, and several of them at that moment were crumpling into the water. Downstream, Colonel Hardin suddenly appeared from the trees, and rode out into the middle of the stream. "Fall back!" he was roaring in a mighty voice. "Back 'cross the river and form up!"

In a moment the river was full of splashing, scrambling militiamen trying to get back to the east bank, desperate to put the river between them and the howling horde. William repeated the command to the men around him, and when they were in the river he stepped off into the water himself. He retreated, sidestepping on the mucky bottom, keeping his rifle on the sycamores. He could see motion among the trees as the savages moved to the bank, but could not get a clear shot at any. Then a fusillade of shots erupted. *Chewp! chewp! chewp!* Balls hit the water around him. One flicked the top of his hat; another pinged on the brass of his sword scabbard.

The watersoaked leather of his leggings weighted his legs as he scrambled out on the bank. Hats floated slowly on the current. Hands reached up out of crimson-stained water and then sank. His men—the few of them who remained—were milling or lying on the bank. "Load up!" he roared. "Here they come!" Now the savages were leaping in the water to come after their quarry, high-stepping through spray, a yodeling mass of painted skin, feathers, and quills, weapons in both hands, mad for victory. Hardin was riding back and forth now, trying to rally his men and move them upriver toward Hall's struggling force. "Fish in a barrel, boys!" William yelled, and aimed for an amulet on a brown chest. He squeezed the trigger and was reloading by the time that Indian had sunk. Now his men were doing their business well. Almost every shot found its mark and at least a dozen Indians were slumping or reeling in midriver. Smoke rolled yellow in the sunbeams; ramrods slid down and up; rifle fire roared continuously from the shore, and the river ran blood. The Indians were now stumbling over the floating bodies of their own dead and wounded. Some began to turn and wade back to the west bank. But now Hardin was close by, virtually driving his troops before him. And William could see through the smoke now that the Indians had crossed the river downstream; they were pouring across onto the ground Hardin had vacated. "Up! Up!" Hardin was barking. "Close up with Hall!" His face was strained white, hollow-cheeked as a death's-head; he was frantic.

And now William could see why. The Indians who had crossed the river were fanning up the east bank, up the slope toward the hazel thickets, outflanking the retreating Kentuckians, trying to compress them into the low ground of the river bottom, encircle them, cut them off before they could reach Hall's men. Hardin was right; there was nothing to do but retreat up the river, and they would have to fight every step of the way. An army sergeant trotting past William suddenly cried something that sounded like "HUNG!" and dropped his rifle and went knock-kneed. He fell face-down with an arrow through the X where his shoulder straps crossed his back. There were hardly any of the blue-coats to be seen now. There had been eighty of them on the assault; there were only a half-dozen or so still moving. William herded his own men along now, making them move as rapidly as they could while still loading and firing back.

He kept to the right, picking off any Indian he could see trying to get around their flank. Hardin up on his big stallion now seemed to be the main target for all the Indians, and though he appeared to have a charmed life, it was not good to be near him. Several men were nicked by bullets aimed at him. "Colonel!" William shouted at him as the wild-eyed, frothing stallion danced near. "Where's Colonel McMullen?"

"Decoyed off someplace, the fool son-of-a-bitch!" Hardin snarled. "Left our right flank wide open. HEYAH! HEYAH!" He dug in his spurs, shouting: "HEYAH! Some o' you idle jackasses tote them wounded! HEYAH! Don't leave a livin' soul for those murderers! HEYAH!"

It was a bad-luck day. It looked as if half of the men were walking wounded now. Some, stained with their own blood, were carrying or dragging blood-soaked comrades whose heads wobbled on their necks. William, aiming at a sprinting Indian, heard a gasp beside him and felt a body slump against his leg. He fired; the Indian tumbled; he reloaded, and only then looked down. Lying there by him, propped on an elbow, face chalky, a sinewy runt of a fellow with salt-and-pepper hair was blinking in disbelief at a bloody arrowhead that protruded from under his left collarbone. It was one of George's old campaigners. William knelt beside him amid the shuffling of feet and the roar of gunfire and howling of Indians, and said, "Care to walk with me, old-timer?" and stretched out a hand.

"Just as soon not," the man wheezed. He was not bleeding from the mouth; likely the arrow had missed his vitals.

"Want to lay here then till they come scalp you alive?"

The man reached for William's arm. "No, don't b'leev I do." William got him up and he was able to hitch along with his right arm over William's shoulder, his left hanging, bloodsoaked. His eyes bugged now and then, and William knew he was doing his damnedest not to faint.

The shooting and wailing and cursing went on and it was like being herded along a gauntlet of Hell's own demons. Now the retreating troops were within a hundred yards of Hall's soldiers; the Indians, in a last effort to keep the two groups divided, suddenly came rushing down the slope and up from the rear, and were splashing into the river from the other bank.

It was bewildering how they could swarm and maneuver so effectively, like bees by some common instinct, yet fight singly with such initiative. Even as they came down in this terrible onrush, William had to admire them, and sense the greatness of Little Turtle and Blue Jacket and Black Hoof and such chiefs.

He had to let the wounded man down. He fired one shot and then there was no time to reload because the warriors, all swift, hard muscle and joyous frenzy, had crashed into the mass of Kentuckians from three sides, and now it was just simply a deadly brawl, tomahawks, clubbed rifles, bayonets, swords, knives, fists, teeth, and feet, the awfulest melee one could have dreamed of in a nightmare. William stood and plunged, ducked and swung and skipped, kicked and stabbed, reeled from blows, saw sparks, drew blood, twisted one braceleted arm until it broke, knocked out teeth, squeezed someone breathless and bit off his nose, yanked out a handful of black hair, fell to his knees from a blow on his back but somehow got up again, his vision coming and going until he could see again, and what he saw was a savage straddling the poor old fellow with an arrow through him, ripping open his abdomen with a knife, reaching in, yanking out the still-beating heart and sinking his teeth into it. "Oh, no, God damn you," William roared and, with an infuriated lunge, thrust his hunting knife through the Indian's temple up to the hilt into his brain. The Indian died, blood from the torn heart bathing him; William could not pull his knife out of the skull and so left it there, and resumed the battle with a tomahawk he found lying on the ground. He fought on with a cold, sick efficiency, mostly reflex, unable to forget the sight of the gushing, bitten heart. He knew the Indians believed they could obtain the strength of an enemy by eating his living heart. But what strength had that fainting old man had?

Yell and be happy, George had told him; *there'll be time later for crying and puking.*

So William yelled, his voice curdling with fierce joy and unbearable sadness, and flung himself on the broad bare back of a Shawnee who was trying to scalp a bluecoat soldier.

"YE KNOW SUCH KENTUCKY BOYS BE FAIR HAND-FIGHTERS," William was to tell George and the family back at Mulberry Hill the next month, "so we fit our way to Colonel Hall, and there we formed a square, and drove 'em back to where we could shoot again. Well, we retreated up the river for about a hundred years, bloodyin' every foot of it. Colonel Hardin wouldn't let us break and run all morning, thinkin' Harmar would send reinforcements. But none ever came. Damn, damn! Finally we drove 'em off, or else they got bored killin' us and just up and quit. We hauled our wounded back twenty-five mile till we got to Harmar's army, where he'd just been a-*settin*'! George, listen: our messenger had got to him, all right. But 'stead o' sendin' even a troop o' horse to come help us, he'd ordered that whole damn army—nigh a thousand men, mind you!—to form a square and just *set*!" William's eyes were brimming and his mouth was contorted. George nodded, and William went on.

"And when we'd drug ourselves in, did he set off for the Maumee to strike back? No siree, he didn't. He ordered us all back to Fort Washington, cannon and all. We were *dumbstruck*, George. The men wanted to go back and fight, but the general said give up!

"A hundred and nine men, George. Left for the scalping knife and the buzzards. Meat left to rot, as you used to say, Pa. Not a one with a grave to sleep in." He shook his head and put his palms over his face. The family looked at him in the light from the chandelier, and no one knew what to say. Finally George spoke.

"Well, Brother, ye've had your taste o' war now. And didn't I say, there's a time after for cryin' and pukin'."

"Aye, you were so right, too." William touched his tongue to the little scar just below his lower lip. He had discovered after the battle that he had bitten his lip through. Except for the bullet graze on his flank, it was the only scar he carried from that battle where death had flown so thick and fast.

All the bruises and sprains that had been in every part of his body had left no scars.

George looked at William with a heart-quaking affection and deep respect. In all the combats he had been through himself, he had never been exposed to such an intense or sustained hail of lead and steel as that must have been, and he wondered if he could have borne it the way William had. Survivors of the battle had told George that his brother Ensign William Clark was "brave as Caesar" and "blessed with eyes all the way around his head."

John Clark, sitting here now hearing his youngest son talk, was aware that he had killed so many Indians that he had lost count of them, and this brought the old confused sadness over him, for he still suspected that the Gate of Heaven is closed against those who have taken human lives, even though some passages of the Bible seemed to justify slaying in a right cause. John Clark heard and watched his youngest son now with anxiety for his soul. At least it was good that William did not seem to exult.

And now William said: "I'm sick for the whole miserable United States Army. Its first campaign was a disaster, damn that fool Harmar. I wish you'd been leading 'em, George. It wouldn't ha' turned out so."

"Hear, hear!" exclaimed Dr. James O'Fallon. He was sitting across the room, in a straight chair, Fanny Clark in another chair at his side. He had come down the Ohio at last, after long travels in the South and East, to see the girl he had doctored and then become infatuated with back at Fort Pitt. And he had found her here, now grown into a stunning, sweet-voiced, shapely young woman of seventeen, and here his travels had stopped. He had been here for weeks now as a house guest, occupying William's empty room. And her parents were expecting him at any moment to announce his intentions, which were already quite plain. Fanny was so a-brim with happiness that she could not bear to see William brought to such low spirits.

"Billy," she said, in that same precise language and musically modulated voice that had been her mark since she was three years old, "it certainly was an occasion to be mourned and regretted. But we who love you are thankful for the miracle that you were not among those hundred and nine. We've something to praise the Almighty Lord for, haven't we?"

William looked at her for a moment, at this marvelous creature who had been a part of his life for as long as he could remember, who had never in all those years vexed him in the slightest, even though she had long ago taken from him the privileges of being the baby of the family, and suddenly the gloom passed from his face and he began to smile upon her, his blue eyes full of adoration.

"Fanny," he said, "d'ye know there are times when I'm really glad I pulled you out o' that cold river?"

And amid the family's laughter, she leaped up from her chair, actually leaving Dr. O'Fallon's side for once, and ran across the room to hug her brother Billy around the neck.

27

LOUISVILLE,
KENTUCKY

February 4, 1791

To William Johnston, Esqr
Clerk of Jefferson County

Sir

This is to certifie that I am willing licence should Issue out of your office for the Marriage of my Daughter Fanny

Clark to Doctr James O'Fallon Given under my hand this
4th day of Febry 1791

JOHN CLARK

"This is your last daughter, is't not, Mister Clark?"

"That she is," John Clark replied. "Why, Mister Johnston? Are ye getting weary of issuing us licenses?"

"Ha, ha, ha! Why, no sir! No indeed! These are glad occasions for me, and I'd be delighted to keep on if you had a dozen more! May you and yours increase, sir, as there's no better a people in Kentucky! In truth, were't not for you Clarks, there'd probably be *no* people in Kentucky!" He nodded and winked at George, who had just witnessed the document and was laying down the quill. George nodded at this tribute with a small smile. The clerk was a jolly, inquisitive sort, almost in the nature of a gossip, but he was still a staunch champion of the Clark family. Once, it was said, Johnston had ejected from his office a man he had heard chattering to bystanders about General Clark's weakness for the bottle.

It was true that John Clark's tribe was increasing. By his daughter Annie Clark Gwathmey back in Virginia he was now the grandfather of nine, including a set of twins; by son Jonathan, four more, the latest being a daughter Mary; by daughter Elizabeth, two more, both of whom had nearly killed their mother in coming into the world; and by daughter Lucy a grandson named in his honor, John Croghan. That child's father, Bill Croghan, now stood beside George, looking at him through the corner of his eye, and knowing a secret about him that so far George did not know himself: just last night, in a profoundly tender, intimate moment with Lucy, there had been an enthusiastic consent that if their second child should be a boy, he would be named after George. If a girl, it would be Lucy Ann, they had agreed, but Lucy had expressed an intuitive certainty that it would be a boy, and a red-haired one at that. Lucy had a firm faith in the potency of her mother's Rogers blood.

Lucy's concern over her brother George had been very deep during the years of his crisis with the bottle. She and Bill Croghan both worried about the distress it caused her parents. And Lucy had often been annoyed at having to admit any weakness in a Clark. But lately they were hopeful for him, as George had not gone on a binge for more than a year. According to the reports from their parents at Mulberry Hill, the same sealed whisky jug had sat untouched on the mantel in George's room from one New Year to the next, gathering dust. Doubtless there had been many a night when he had yearned for it, as his financial troubles grew ever more hopeless, but not once had he ever touched it to make fingerprints in the dust on its rounded shoulders. "I'm letting it age, so's it'll be good and mellow," he would joke about it. But to William in confidence he had added: "May it mellow forever, for it'll never be good enough for me again. If I touch that, I'm a lost soul for sure." And so that dusty jug had stood for month after month now as a sign of his determined will to save himself. Even when his cherished plan for building a canal and locks around the Falls had fallen through for lack of financial backing, George had resisted the temptation to turn back to the jug for solace. That, his family believed, had been the turning point in his struggle. The iron will and self-discipline that had made him the conqueror of the Northwest Territory had borne him over the slump of that failure, and now he was keeping himself intoxicated not with liquor but with reading and writing, and with great new schemes and hopeful projects. As in the old days, he was thinking big and thinking all night.

THE GRANDFATHER CLOCK BONGED THE HOUR OF TWO IN A far room, but it awakened Ann Rogers Clark, and she could not go back to sleep because detailed thoughts about Fanny's wedding kept rising up. And after a while she began to sense that somebody else was awake in the house. She slipped out of bed and pulled on a robe and slippers, pausing now and then to be sure her rustlings weren't awakening John. Then she eased out through her bedroom door and went down the hall. A rectangle of light reached out into the hallway from the open door of George's room. She stepped softly up to the door and looked in. A blaze was roaring in his fireplace.

Lamplight was on his left hand, with which he was rubbing his forehead. He was in his linen shirt, sleeves rolled up, and was agleam with sweat. Handwritten papers were adrift all over his desk, and there were rolled sheets leaning against the wall, and papers on the floor covered with sketches of machinery—windlasses, levers, wheels. The unopened jug stood on the mantel. And the hum of night seemed like the hum of his brain's own machinery. Sometimes when he was like this, his mother thought she could hear his brain rumbling and humming like a mill.

She thought now that he was sunk too deep in his cogitations to have noticed her presence. But he still had the senses of a scout, and without looking up he said, "Hey, Ma," and reached his hand out. She went and stood by his chair, and he put his arm around her waist. She patted his shoulder and looked down at the papers that lay immediately before him, covered with the complex hieroglyphics of his night-ponderings.

She put her hand on his left wrist and pulled his hand down, softly admonishing, "What've I told you about a gent keeping his hands away from his face? You're gettin' bald up in front, and it's from all that head-rubbin'."

"Hm, hm." Still without looking up, he asked, "Whatever became o' that book o' your proverbs?"

"I've still got it," she said. She didn't tell him that it still had not one proverb in it. She hoped he wouldn't ask.

And now he said, whether to her or to himself, she didn't know:

"There's nothing a man can't think his way out of, if he can bear the strain o' thinking."

"I'm sure o' that."

"But few can."

"So it seems," she said. "What's this now?" She pointed at a drawing of intermeshing gear wheels.

"An upstream boat."

"An upstream boat? Of all things!"

"I'll tell ye more of it when I've worked it out better. It's so plain to me I suspect there must be something wrong in my reckonings, or else why hasn't some tinker-by-trade invented it already?"

"Well, I'll declare this: Donald Robertson, rest him in peace, if he could see you now, he'd know there'd been something wrong with *his* reckonings!"

GEORGE'S MECHANICAL DEVICE TO DRIVE BIG BOATS UP- stream was soon all laid out in drawings. But he still felt there might have been a flaw somewhere in his reasoning, so he took his plans down to the boatwright, one of his old veterans he could trust, and they began building a dinghy-sized model of it. George knew from his years on the rivers that oars were an ineffi- cient way to propel a boat against a steady current, as they were not working while out of the water between strokes, and they tired rowers so fast. So he had designed a windlass which could be turned by men or a horse, and whose power would be trans- mitted by a set of gear wheels to a large number of oars, half of which would be in the water pulling while the other half were out on the return stroke. The boatwright worked for days making the gear wheels out of maple and fitting them into a small boat. And then one day they hauled it on a covered wagon to a se- cluded part of the river and launched it. Using a two-handled crank to operate the windlass, they pattered steadily upstream for two hours without even breathing hard.

He came home in a rapture. He sent a request away by Dr.

John Brown, a friend of influence, asking that Congress give him exclusive patent rights for fourteen years. He had read up on patent law and naval law, and knew that if he obtained the sole right to make his mechanical boat on the Continent, he would also have a monopoly right for mechanical boats on all the rivers.

After he sent the request, he would grab his mother or Fanny whenever he passed them in the hallway and waltz them around until they gasped for breath. "Look at me!" he would exclaim. "I'm going to be the Admiral of the Upstream Fleets! My troubles are over." And he settled down, murmuring and chuckling, to await Dr. Brown's reply, and to keep himself from fidgeting to death in the meanwhile, he worked on half a dozen other projects. He was drafting for publication a thesis explaining the mysterious disappearance of the ancient mound-building Indian civilization. He was collecting and classifying fossils and giant animal bones from the limestone beds of the Falls and from salt licks upriver.

It was as if he had rediscovered his mental powers, and this was intoxication enough for him. With his brain he was going to make himself independent; he was sure of it. His room was now stacked with manuscripts and books, charts, maps, and mechanical drawings. On his desk were always pencils, straight-edges, compasses, and his well-thumbed Euclid.

Further rekindling his old passion for independence was the news from overseas of the French Revolution. He read every newspaper he could lay hands on, and was the local expert on that distant struggle. "We infected 'em with Liberty," he would expound to any listener, "while they were here as our allies. Our hearts should chime with theirs. They've learnt from us that it's right to throw off a king!"

Another project was now serving to restore his old pride in himself. It was the writing of a memoir of his war years, a memoir begun at the request of his friends James Madison and Tom Jefferson. At first this request had struck him as an unwanted obligation. In his bitterness, he had tried to forget all his deeds that had in the end paid off in ruin and ingratitude. He had even used some of his diary and note pages as scrap paper, so contemptuous had he become about his dashed fame. But the memoir, begun so reluctantly, had grown to be a challenging and surprisingly pleasurable task. Reviewed through the telescope of time, the story had the aura of a bittersweet legend about it—the daring, the outrageously long odds against his mission's success, the great-heartedness of his ragged followers, the laughter and

513

songs and dreams of glory that had enabled them to transcend their sufferings, the pure, childlike trust of his French allies, and those brief and poignant interludes with Teresa and her family. Of course he could not write it as a legend, nor would he have done it if he could have. He fancied himself no man of letters, and had, after all, been asked to write a historical report from a military view. The glorious moments, the moments of hope and heartbreak, the great glowing or moody landscapes, all these were elements he could not even try to capture. But they were there; they pervaded the whole memory, and the challenge was in trying to record the military facts without discoloring them with emotions. Some of the facts and dates and figures were difficult to recollect over the intervening dozen years. And so George had written to George Mason, asking to borrow from him the long, detailed report he had written for him right after the 1779 Vincennes campaign. But Mason was old and very ill and had misplaced it somewhere, so George had to proceed without it. In pursuit of details half-forgotten, George would go visiting many of his old campaigners, some of whom he had not seen in years. Their reunions often produced laughter, tears, a few authentic details, and a vestige of the old indomitable spirit of those heady days before the disillusionment. And many a man told him, "Gen'l, if y' ever go to war again, be it Indians or them besmirched Spaniards, just whistle me up and we'll go do it the way we used t' done it." Then they would look moistly into each other's eyes and see not the wrinkles in each other's faces and the rheumatic hesitancy in each other's movements, but that old magic camaraderie they had felt in those terrible but happily remembered days. George would come away heartened to know that he still had an army.

Thus time had gone by, with a light burning always in the window of George's room at Mulberry Hill, and the same dusty liquor jug sitting on the mantelpiece. John Clark had calculated that George in the last year had burned more lamp oil and candles than the rest of the household combined. And Mrs. Clark had said, "So be it, and let us thank God for every drop he burns, as oil's a far better fuel than alcohol."

"I, FANNY, TAKE THEE, JAMES, TO MY WEDDED HUS-band . . ."
". . . to have and to hold from this day forward . . ."
". . . to have and to hold from this day forward . . ."
". . . for better for worse, for richer for poorer . . ."

514

". . . for better for worse, for richer for poorer . . ."
". . . in sickness and in health . . ."
". . . in sickness and in health . . ."
". . . to love and to cherish, till death us do part."
". . . to love and to cherish, till death us do part."

Till death us do part, Fanny thought, and she remembered the secret prayers she and Elizabeth had exchanged three years ago, that their husbands should live long and safely. Now James O'Fallon, the object of her prayer, was slipping the gold band onto her finger, and he held it there with his cool, healing hand as the church full of people droned with the words while a trickle of perspiration went down her spine and between her nates under the gown and all the petticoats.

"With this ring I thee wed: in the name of the Father, and of the Son, and of the Holy Ghost. Amen."

And Dr. James O'Fallon, holding her hand, felt her shiver.

LATE IN APRIL A STORY CAME DOWN THE RIVER, A HORROR story. When it came to George's ears, it drew his mind back over almost twenty years.

Jacob Greathouse, the man who had killed Chief Logan's family and disemboweled his pregnant sister in 1774, thus sparking Dunmore's War, had just this month been caught by a band of Shawnees on the Ohio near the mouth of the Scioto, in a party of several dozen white settlers. The Shawnees had massacred and mutilated all the party. But they had recognized Greathouse, and remembered, after all these years, and had saved him and his wife for a very elaborate death.

They had stripped them and whipped them to a pulp, from neck to knees. Then they had cut into their abdomens, detached the lower ends of their small intestines and tied them to saplings. Then they had forced them to walk around and around the saplings until all their guts were wound around the trees. Finally they had scalped them and filled their empty torsos with coals.

George remembered Chief Logan as he had last seen him, besotted and bitter. He gritted his teeth and shook his head. Maybe Chief Logan could look down from wherever his afterworld was and know this vengeance had been wrought. "I always wondered," George said, "whether the story o' Greathouse and Logan would ever be finished. I'd say now it's finished."

ALL JOHN CLARK'S MARRIED DAUGHTERS SO FAR HAD BEEN sheltered well by their husbands. Annie Gwathmey and her large brood still lived in Owen's family estate, The Meadows, back in

515

Virginia. Elizabeth Clark Anderson lived in her husband's great stone house, Soldier's Retreat, ten miles from Louisville. And Bill Croghan had just completed a magnificent brick plantation house he called Locust Grove, four miles northeast of Louisville, as the place where he and Lucy would dwell and build their branch of the clan. But it was apparent to everyone that Dr. James O'Fallon was not ready yet, not nearly ready, to provide any such solid seat for his lovely bride Fanny to live in. They made their honeymoon at Mulberry Hill, and it gradually became clear that he was in no hurry to move out. Bit by bit, his belongings came down the river from places he had left them during his travels, and bit by bit they were brought into the Clark house at Mulberry Hill. Bit by bit the new O'Fallon couple began expanding to fill the upstairs rooms that had been left vacant by marriages of the other daughters.

"It's nice to have a doctor in the house should we need one," John Clark would say sometimes to his wife. "But so far, even with no need for one, we seem to have one. Do we not?"

"We'll have a need of 'im along about Thanksgiving time," she told him one day that May, three months after the wedding. "I mean, that is, if a doctor can be of any use delivering his own child."

"Eh! What, now? Are you saying—"

"That our littlest darling's about on the way to giving us a grandchild."

"By Eternal Heaven! Then we'd best not, er, urge them to leave, had we? Say, now! Wouldn't it be an event to have one born here in our own Mulberry Hill!" He clapped his hands once and rubbed the palms together, his eyes full of tender anticipation.

"Seeing as how that news delights ye so, Mister Grandfather Clark," she said, looking at him with one eyebrow raised, "you might turn handsprings to know what else I've learnt this day."

"Eh? What else?"

"That Lucy's in the same condition again."

He gasped. "Noooo!"

"Yesssss. And knowing this family, they'll probably have 'em both the same night, so's that I'll have to be two places at once!"

Lucy Clark Croghan's second son and Fanny Clark O'Fallon's first were not born on the same night, but were so close together that Mrs. Clark scarcely had time to come back from Locust Grove to Mulberry Hill between them. Lucy's red-headed boy, named George, was born on November 15, and

516

anny's dark-haired boy John, named after his grandfather, ame into the world on the night of the 17th. But the doctor ho had been in the house for so long when not needed was not n the house when these events took place. He had departed ome weeks before on a trip of business to the Carolinas and Georgia, where he was involved with many other gentlemen in ome sort of a large and puzzling land speculation. All he had ver explained to the Clarks about it was that he and his fellow ntrepreneurs would one day become rich as kings from it, hough in the meantime most of his personal wealth was tied up n it and that was why he was not in a position just now to build home for Fanny.

And so she had had her child with no knowledge of her hus- and's whereabouts. And lying in bed afterward with the infant t her breast, a wistful smile making her look even more than sual like an angel, she said, "Whatever shall we do, I wonder, Mama, for a nursery?"

"Well, I suppose . . . I suppose ye might have Billy's room for ne while."

For William had gone off to war again, this time as an ensign n the Regular Army. Ohio's Governor General Arthur St. Clair, one of George Washington's old Revolutionary generals, ad been appointed to raise a large army and proceed into the orthern Ohio lands to wipe out once and for all Little Turtle's Vabash Confederacy. They had marched out of Cincinnati ear- er in the fall, heading north, with orders to build a series of orts as they penetrated the Indian country toward the Wabash eadwaters. All Kentucky had been awaiting news of the expedi- ion. General St. Clair was a brave man, and had proven himself ery able during the Revolution. Surely, it was thought, he vould not make the same mistakes General Harmar had made he year before. Surely Little Turtle and his alliance of tribes ould not defeat the Army of the United States two years in a ow.

But just as a matter of custom, the Clark family prayed every ight for the safety of William.

A LETTER CAME FROM DR. JOHN BROWN.

Hands trembling, George opened it. His parents watched.

Alas, it said. The very patent and monopoly that George had een seeking had just recently been awarded to a Maryland gen- leman named James Rumsey, for his model of a pole-driven nechanical boat.

George lowered the paper, and let it fall to the floor. His face

was pale. Without a word, he turned from the library and wer
down the hall to his own room. He locked the door. He went t
his desk and scooped up his stack of boat papers, then went t
the fireplace and heaved them straight into the flames.

"*Pole-driven*," he murmured. "That'll never even work!"

Then he took the dusty jug down from the mantel. H
wrenched the cork out and threw it in after the burning papers

GEORGE WAS STILL ROARING DRUNK TWO DAYS LATER WHE
the news rolled down the valley that the Army of the Unite
States had been all but obliterated by Little Turtle's Con
federacy. Governor General St. Clair had led his army into
battle as disastrous as Braddock's awful defeat thirty-six years be
fore.

On the headwaters of the Wabash River, 632 men and officer
had been killed, 200 camp followers slaughtered, and nearl
every one of the survivors, some 300 of them, had bee
wounded. The retreat had been nothing less than a disgracefu
stampede. Even in the great battles of the Revolution, betwee
armies numbering in tens of thousands, never had so man
American soldiers died in a single engagement.

And of the enemy, Little Turtle's tribes, it appeared that les
than a hundred—perhaps as few as fifty or sixty—had bee
killed!

THE APPALLING NEWS OF THE DISASTER ROLLED THROUGH
the new nation. President Washington had asked for a Congres
sional investigation, in hopes that his old friend General St
Clair might be exonerated. Newspapers were printed with 3
black coffins in rows across the top, each labeled with the nam
of a slain officer. The Clarks' only solace was that William's wa
not among them. He had not been in the battle. He was now a
Fort Washington, serving as an acting lieutenant now that th
army had such a sudden shortage of officers.

John and Ann Rogers Clark now sat alone in the library a
Mulberry Hill, reading from such a newspaper. George was no
here, nor had he been for days. On first news of the disaster, h
had ridden away, tipsy and tight-lipped, into a snow flurry. An
yesterday John Clark, entering the public house on some busi
ness, had heard George's voice issuing loudly on the lack of dis
cipline in the army and the stupidity of Eastern generals
George's voice had sounded so full of drunken inflection tha
John Clark had just turned, flushing, and gone back into th
street.

And now here he sat with his wife, in the library of the big, nearly empty house, in this land they had expected to be such a paradise, reading aloud. Fanny was at home, but she was still upstairs, lying in after her childbirth, and John Clark had not wanted her to be exposed to too much news of the catastrophe.

And so it was just Ann, his wife, by the fire near him, working on needlepoint with her eyes cast down, as he read aloud from the newspaper a long funeral elegy written in verse. His voice quavered with emotion as he neared the end:

> *"If great JEHOVAH takes the shield*
> *And guards us round about*
> *No Indian will his tomax wield,*
> *Nor arrow dare to shoot. . . .*
>
> *"Let's not forget the soldiers brave,*
> *Who fell with Indian ax,.*
> *Who scorned to flinch their lives to save,*
> *Nor on them turn'd their backs. . . ."*

"I thought," Ann Rogers Clark interrupted, not looking up from her needlepoint, "that most of the army threw down their guns and ran."

"Please, Annie, this is an *elegy* for them." And he read on:

> *"Nine hundred hardiest of our Sons,*
> *Some in their early prime,*
> *Have fell a victim to their rage,*
> *And are cut off from time. . . .*
>
> *"Our country calls us far and near,*
> *Columbia's sons awake,*
> *For helmet, buckler and our spear,*
> *Th' LORD's own arm we'll take.*
>
> *"With conq'ring might he will us shield,*
> *And INDIANS all destroy,*
> *He'll help us thus to win the field,*
> *And slay those that annoy!"*

The paper rustled as he laid it in his lap; and he sighed and looked into the licking yellow flames at the gleaming brass andirons. Then he sighed again. "How heavy on the heart this is," he said. "D'ye remember how like this we felt when the news came down o' Braddock's Disaster?"

"I recall it," she said. "That was hard news too. But at leas one didn't have to suffer as well an elegy writ so bad. Why, that' worse than what Johnny, rest his soul, used to write when he wa in love!" She looked up and saw her husband looking at her wit mouth agape.

"Annie," he said, "sometimes meseems I should pray for you irreverent soul."

She was quiet, eyes downcast to her needlework for awhile the fire whispering and fluttering in the hearth. Then she said

"Pray instead, if you're going to pray, that President Washing ton finds someone other than a fool to control the Indians. O soon we'll all be dead." She cleared her throat. "If he had th sense he's said to have, he'd give our George the task."

Nay, John Clark wanted to tell her, remembering with sham the scene of yesterday, *George is fit only to bellow and reek in pub house.*

But of course he could not bear to tell her that.

ON JUNE 1, 1792, A PLEASANT, BALMY FRIDAY, THE JUBILAN news swept through Louisville that Kentucky had been admitte into the Union as the fifteenth State. Guns were fired into th air, cannon boomed at the fort, and people were running an shouting in the streets.

All this uproar barely penetrated into the fuming, whirlin senses of the Father and Protector of Kentucky, where h slumped in a chair in a dark corner of the public house. A burs of gunfire and a chorus of shouting just outside the tavern door stirred him for a moment. He saw men moving across field in front of him, saw powder smoke, saw Indians coming a a run.

"Master Lovell," he muttered. "Lay on that drum. Stan' you groun', boys."

And then his arms slid forward across the table, knockin glasses over, and his head fell forward to rest on his arms. An he whispered against the sour-wet wood of the tabletop:

"Trees."

28

MULBERRY HILL
January, 1793

THE LETTER FROM VIRGINIA WAS IN GEORGE ROGERS' HAND-writing, and Ann Rogers Clark noticed sadly as she broke the seal that her brother's script was shaky, just a bit. He had been hale and solid the last time she had seen him, and she had ever since pictured him that way, but of course some eight years had passed since then and he was beyond seventy now. We're old, she thought.

That whispering undercurrent of mortality was still in her soul when she unfolded the letter and read that her youngest sister, Rachel Rogers Robertson, had passed away late the last year, in the same bed in the old parsonage where Donald had died so peacefully at the end of the war.

John Clark saw the tears in his wife's eyes, saw her figure slump a little, and took her hand.

"Rachel's gone," she said. "Oh, my, John! And she was the baby of the family."

It meant to Ann Rogers Clark that she might expect more such letters now. For once one's gone, the others will begin to go.

John Clark had his arm around her now. She turned her face to him, and though she was blinking and her chin was crumpling, she looked angry, defiant. He understood that she was not angry at him but at the notion of mortality. And she said:

"I warn you, John. Y'd better not go before I do." But then she remembered another thought she had had once about this, sometime long ago: when she had wondered what John would ever do without her if she went first. "I mean," she said. "Oh, I don't know, John. Whatever are we going to do, you and me?"

WILLIAM STOOD OUTSIDE HIS TENT ON THE RISE AND watched the troops being drilled down by the creek. One thing was certain: lack of discipline would never be the big problem in this new army of Mad Anthony Wayne.

A whole battalion of foot troops, companies on line, were rushing across a meadow down toward the creek, at a fast march, almost a trot, bayonets fixed and pointed at an imaginary enemy, their captains bellowing commands at them. At the moment

521

they reached the bank of the creek, a command went along th
line for them to flank to the right, and the whole line shifte
simultaneously and started upstream. Another right flank was o
dered, and now they were charging back up the slope. It wa
marvelous parade-ground precision, like magic to behold, a
those people functioning as if by a common will. How effectiv
it would be against concealed Indians in the woods was anothe
matter, in William's mind, but one thing certain was that the
surely did obey.

William had a dreadful fear that Mad Anthony Wayne, bein
an Eastern field officer, was doomed to make the same mistake
that had ruined Braddock and then Harmar and St. Clair
Wayne believed in the bayonet, the direct charge with cold steel
fully erect and in perfect ranks. Wayne expected his men to be a
brave and tireless and direct as he was, which was a great deal
Though he was old and portly and arthritic, he was still toug
and bristly as briar. He was also a man of gruff good humor, an
showy. He loved elegant uniforms, and insisted that his Legions
even while training and fort-building in the wilderness, look a
if they were on parade. The battalion of blue-clad men charg
ing across that meadow down there in their straight lines migh
be pouring sweat and covered with burrs, but from here the
looked as smart and colorful as an army of toy soldiers on
tabletop.

York came up with a tray and tea service for William, an
stood beside him, watching the lines of blue and white move thi
way and that on the meadow, and he was smiling, working hi
fleshy lips wryly, as if enjoying the sight of so many white me
being ordered around. "They sure purty, eh, Mast' Billy?"

"Sure pretty. Now you watch this, York, what happens next, i
you want a laugh."

Down there another right flank was commanded, then an
other, and once again the battalion was moving swiftly dow
toward the creek with their bayonets flashing. William's tent
mate, an amiable youth named Lieutenant Towles, now came
alongside William and York to watch, shaking his head and grin
ning. He too knew what was next. "There they go," he said.

This time when the line of soldiers reached the bank of the
creek, they were given no command. And so the whole bat
talion, erupting with a roar that was a combination of battle cr
and outburst of chagrin, plunged into the cold, mucky stream
their crisp blue uniforms sinking into brown water.

They splashed and slogged and hollered but stayed on line
And at midstream they were ordered to halt at attention and to

present arms. They stood that way in midstream, looking ridiculous. York's eyes were bugging and his mouth hung slack. Then his great belly began to quake with a voiceless laughter. "Oh, laws," he exclaimed, "tha's *pitiful*!" Probably he was thinking about all those wet clothes and muddy shoes someone would have to clean. "Why they do that faw, Mast' Billy?" It was York's first visit to the camp, and he had never seen such things back in the fort, where he kept William's quarters.

"So they'll do what they're told, no matter what," William said. He turned and took a cup and nodded for Towles to have one. And he said to York, "Maybe I should ha' trained *you* like that. You'd maybe not be so slow and dilatory sometimes. Y'old lazy scallywag."

"Hmhm," York chuckled. "Anything I c'n do faw you gen'men, right this minute?"

"Y'might spoon me some molasses. This tea tastes like tanbark." He winked at York and grinned. Maybe he had always been too easy on him, but he couldn't help it. The rascal was so damned droll and likeable that he was worth it. He seemed to have selected the role of buffoon.

That night William sat in the tent at his field table while Lieutenant Towles slept, and wrote in his diary by the light of a bear's-oil lamp. There was always plenty of bear oil in this army, as General Wayne encouraged his men to spend their spare time hunting bears. He believed it improved their character and whetted the kinds of skills they would need when they met Little Turtle. There was a standing rumor in camp that a bear-hunter would get a double ration of whiskey if his bear was dead of bayonet wounds. So far no one had tested that, and it was suspected of being a joke.

William wrote of such things in his diary, which he was keeping not because he wanted to keep a diary, but because Sister Fanny had asked him to.

"Why?" he had asked with a groan. "I don't like to write diaries."

"Because," she had said, "one day you'll be as great and renowned as George is, and I wouldn't want you to be caught as he is now, with a memoir to write and no diaries to go by."

"Oh, phshhhew!" he had retorted. "That's a crock o' butter if ever there was one!"

"Well, then, Mister Reluctant and Modest Sir," she had said with a saucy toss of her pretty head, "for my amusement, then. Is that reason enough, I being your favorite and most beloved sister?"

"Frankly, no," he had replied, but actually it was, and so he had been keeping the diary for her during his tours of duty, and actually enjoying it sometimes. She would write letters to him gushing about how much she had enjoyed his clear and witty descriptions of so and so, and his anecdotes of this or that, in his latest batch of entries, and how she was keeping them for posterity. And after each such letter, he would try even harder to be witty and wise in his journal. As her husband was always away and William was always in some training bivouac without much to do, their correspondences grew longer and more frequent. And little by little, one of her true intentions was coming true: her unschooled brother, whose education she had secretly taken upon herself, was learning to handle the written language. His handwriting had improved, from a scrawl at first resembling the blood track of a mortally wounded centipede, to a very handsome cursive script. And though he still spelled the same word twice the same way only by coincidence, he was learning to express even abstract ideas and complex emotions by the written word.

The most intricate thing William was called upon to express in his journal-writings was his ambivalent feelings toward his commanding officer, General James Wilkinson.

At first William had hated being near him, remembering all the old suspicions about Wilkinson's rise and George's fall, all those unproven hints that somehow Wilkinson had been the one who had destroyed George's reputation in the Virginia capital. People had used to say, back in those days, that James Wilkinson's ambition could be seen darting through all the shadows. Wilkinson's tenure as Indian Commissioner, after George had been forced out, had produced absolutely nothing of note, but somehow, after St. Clair's defeat, Wilkinson had managed to get himself appointed commander of the Western forts.

But then while serving under Wilkinson's command, William had, little by little, come to like the charming, worldly-wise Marylander, to want *not* to suspect him, and simply to enjoy the benefits of knowing him. After all, Wilkinson was such an able man, a talented man, a brave officer; surely he was not that mean. And if he had actually done so much covert evil to George, why had he befriended William so earnestly and favored him among his subordinates?

It was plain that Wilkinson *was* a masterful underminer. He was always making subtle mockeries of his own commander, General Wayne. He referred to him in private as Mars, or sometimes as Big Turtle, alluding to his ponderous and thoroughgoing methods. Wilkinson liked to ply his officers with good liquor, which he always seemed able to procure from somewhere, and when they were in a merry mood he would cultivate snide jokes about "that

524

umbrous body," General Wayne. William had hated himself for taking part in such merriment, but it was easy to do because he agreed in principle with Wilkinson's criticisms. Wayne really did seem to be set upon a course of orthodox maneuvering that would once again play into the Indians' hands.

And so William, often troubled with a foreboding of some great future disaster but impatient for any kind of decisive action, and feeling faintly disloyal because of his association with the dubious Wilkinson, wrote much in his diary these days, and enjoyed the tart flavor of sarcasm as he wrote it. He was beginning to understand George's bittersweet attitudes about duty.

And Fanny, whose old notions of marital rapture were beginning to sour in the long absences and preoccupations of her husband, was beginning to relish the sniggering tone of William's writings when they came to her in the mail. She felt that only they in this family—and perhaps George, in his different way— were canny enough to see through the unquestioning naiveté of their parents' precepts. From General Wilkinson, by way of William, she was beginning to acquire worldly wisdom.

And so, when George began hatching his desperate scheme to forsake his ungrateful country and become a leader in the French Revolution, Fanny was the only one at Mulberry Hill who felt in the least able to condone it.

REVOLUTIONARY FRANCE WAS AT WAR WITH THE MONARCHIES of Europe, Spain among them. George's mind and soul were caught up in contemplation of his old allies' glorious struggle so far away, and he worked less and less on his memoir these days, and spent more and more time at the public house, drinking and talking. One of the chief topics these days was the French minister.

Citizen Edmond Genet, the revolutionist, recently had come as France's minister to the United States, and he was being feted everywhere in the East. He was already speaking of France and America as allies in France's war against the kings, and word had come downriver to the interested ears of Kentuckians that he was proposing an uprising of Louisiana French against Spanish authority.

Frankfort, on the Kentucky River, had been chosen as the capital of the fledgling State of Kentucky, and one of George's old lieutenants, Isaac Shelby, was the first governor. George and his father rode down to the new capital one day to see the place and get the drift of public sentiments. With them rode Dr. James O'Fallon, home for a while from the Southeast.

Frankfort swarmed with people with big ideas and strong opinions. As a frontier capital it was a rough and rowdy place, full of opportunists and favor-seekers. Quite a few of George's old soldiers were around, some of them now looking prosperous and important, many looking old and broken. But John Clark was moved by the way they greeted his son, and he saw that their greetings were bolstering George's self-esteem.

There was a common refrain in the discussions and arguments they heard in Frankfort. Many men of affairs were saying that since Spain and France were at war, Americans had a clear obligation to go down and help the Mississippi Valley French drive the Spanish rulers out of New Orleans. They kept reminding each other that without French help Washington probably would have lost the war for independence. Many said that if there were an invasion of Spanish Louisiana, they and their friends would join it, and open up the Mississippi to Kentucky commerce at last, while they were about it. Even Governor Shelby had sentiments like that, and furthermore, he hinted, so did such people as Thomas Jefferson and Patrick Henry. And John Clark heard many a man say that his son George should come out of retirement and lead such an invasion himself. George did not tell his father about the notions that were swirling through his mind as they rode back to Louisville a few days later with a group of travelers and a militia escort. But he was beginning to conceive, with that old sense of boldness and long vision and moral righteousness, one last chance to get off his knees.

George found in his own household a ready accomplice. Dr. O'Fallon was already involved in land deals discomfiting the Spaniards in the Southeast. He had traveled much in those parts and was already up to his neck in activities inimical to Spanish interests, and could be trusted to conspire further against them. He could also write and spell most respectably, in an elegant script. And so, in sessions late at night, at George's desk, a new jug of whiskey sitting sealed on the mantel to test George's willpower, an ambitious plan was conceived and drafted, and addressed as a letter from General George Rogers Clark to Citizen Genet.

He began by stating that his desire to help the French Republic in its causes was as strong as it ever had been during his own country's revolution, and then summarized the deeds that he and his American and French followers had done in the West. These same men, he said, at the very least 1,500 of them, would flock to his standard, and in one short season take the whole of the Louisiana Territory for France. Dr. James

526

O'Fallon's scalp prickled as he wrote down the forceful words George dictated.

"Some of the first and best men in this Western country will certainly accompany me. All we immediately want is money to procure provisions and ammunition for the conquest. . . . For our pay and gratifications in land, as we abandon our own here, we shall confide in the justice and generosity of the great nation we shall serve, after our labors are over. To save Congress from a rupture with Spain on our account, we must first expatriate ourselves and become French citizens. This is our intention."

He stalked about the room thinking of his next phrases. Each time he came near the mantel, he would look at the jug and tremble. Never had he done anything so defiant, so final, as this, and it was excruciating to do it sober. He had loved his country more than his life, but now he had come to the point where he was ready to forsake it, and he needed to say why. He pointed to the paper before O'Fallon and continued.

"My country has proved notoriously ungrateful for my services, and so forgetful of those successful and almost unexampled enterprises which gave it the whole of its territory on this side of the great mountains, as in this my very prime of life to have neglected me. Since I relinquished my command over the Western country, Congress has had not one successful campaign in it!" He paused, breathing hard. "All this is *true*, Jim," he hissed. "Ye know that?"

"I do." O'Fallon was sweating, sitting on the edge of the chair as he wrote.

Neither of them noticed the soft tread of Fanny, who had come to the door of George's room looking for her husband. She was standing there when George concluded.

"On receiving a reply from you, I shall instantly have myself expatriated. And as soon as commissions for myself and my officers shall have been received and due provision made for the expedition . . . I shall raise my men and proceed to action. I thirst . . ." He glanced at the jug on the mantel, then turned on his heel away from it. "I thirst for the opportunity!"

And then he saw Fanny's beautiful, pale face in the doorway, suspended like a waning moon in the darkness of her hair, her clothing, the gloom of the unlighted hallway; and for an instant she looked exactly as Terese de Leyba had looked the first time he had seen her face framed in an upstairs window of the Spanish Governor's mansion in St. Louis.

Spanish!

*   *   *

GEORGE WAITED FOR GENET'S ANSWER, BUT HE DID NOT SIT still and wait for it. He rode from town to town in Kentucky and got tentative promises, promises of enlistments, provisions, arms, and services, to be called upon when and if Genet should accept. George approached only the Kentuckians he could trust. Their eagerness to march against Spain under his standard restored his self-esteem bit by bit. He was beginning to feel like a warrior again—even like a patriot, ironically. But it was an anxious time. There was a slight chance that Genet might not like what he would find as he investigated the reputation of this ambitious partisan. Sometimes, late at night, when there was nothing more that could be done until morning, George would sit, stone sober as he had been for months, gaze at the lamp flame and think of the possibility of being rebuffed—or, worse, ignored—by Genet, and he would break out in a cold sweat. And Fanny Clark O'Fallon would look at George and think of the same possibility, and she felt that her brother had climbed hard and boldly to stand once again on a high precipice. If Genet accepted him, he might stay on the high place and be everything he once had been. If not, his fall would be terrible.

DR. JAMES O'FALLON HAD GONE AWAY AGAIN, ON MORE OF his mysterious business. And now, with Fanny watching the post for letters from him as well as from William, she was always at a window. She wanted to know where her husband was so she could write and tell him the news.

She was pregnant again, and she had an awful, intuitive fear that she might well never see her husband again, that he might never see his second son.

George was always watching for the post, too, waiting for some sort of a message from Citizen Genet. He worked at his memoir now and then, trying to concentrate on it; he had completed about a hundred handwritten manuscript pages. He wrote almost every day, also, trying to forestall the creditors and their lawyers who had plagued him for so many years. And he met often every week with old veterans of his who would come to bring or receive intelligence about the Spanish defenses in the Louisiana Territory. He was, through his spy system, learning as much about the Mississippi now as he had before his expedition in 1778. Once again he was playing on a mental chessboard half a continent wide, and this time his unsuspecting opponent was the Spanish Governor in New Orleans. But he could do nothing but plan until Genet's answer came, if it should come, nothing but plan and wait for the post. And so one day in June when a ost rider came trotting up the road between the locust trees, George and Fanny nearly collided in the front door going out to meet him.

The letter was not for either of them, but for the family. It was stunning news, written again this time in the shaky hand of their Uncle George Rogers.

His beloved second son, Captain Johnny Rogers, that brave, good, and enterprising man who had sailed the *Willing* to Vincennes in 1779 for his cousin George, had died in the prime of his life at age thirty-seven, still unmarried, a sudden death believed to have been from pneumonia.

Everyone at Mulberry Hill, but in particular George, went into a profound state of grief that was a long time in lifting.

ONE DAY A FRENCHMAN WITH THE BOLD GRACEFUL DEmeanor of an adventurer and the smudgy, stale, unkempt look of a river boat traveler appeared in a carriage at the door of Mulberry Hill. His name, he said, was Michaux. He was a botanist and explorer. He was soon to be engaged, he said, in a journey of exploration for Thomas Jefferson, across the continent from the Mississippi to the Pacific, but in the meantime he had been diverted here at the behest of the French minister, to deliver a message to General Clark. He gave George a packet. It was from Citizen Genet. It was an officer's commission from the French Republic. It had been filled in to designate George Rogers Clark a Marshall of France, a Major General, and the Commander-in-Chief of a special military unit to be known as "The French Legion of the Mississippi." Michaux saluted. "I am at your service, mon general. I am to serve as your aide." George's parents stood watching, old, gray, shocked.

George stood taller, his head whirling, too confused with his emotions, for a moment, to say anything. His reputation was still something!

But now he would have to do what he had promised. He would have to expatriate himself. He would have to renounce his citizenship in his once-beloved Virginia, in the Kentucky he had founded and protected, in the United States that had so greatly profited by his efforts. George very badly wanted a drink. Instead, he took Michaux's hand. "Good," he said. "Now we can proceed."

Things began to move then. A thousand pounds of pork, four hundred barrels of flour, and a pair of brass cannon were sent over the mountains by Charles DePauw, an entrepreneur who had come to the continent with Lafayette. Major Busseron

529

offered cannon from the artillery of Post Vincennes. George's men began cutting timber from woodlands near Louisville for construction of an armed fleet. Ten tons of buffalo meat and another five tons of pork, several hundred bushels of corn, and a huge quantity of ammunition came on the next shipment from DePauw. George and Michaux rode much of the winter, confirming recruitments. Michaux was extremely impressed with General Clark's influence over this formidable variety of men—county officers, planters, scouts, hunters, tradesmen, teamsters, rivermen. Yes, they were assured: about mid-February, if the rivers had thawed and if the million dollars promised by Genet had been delivered, the word would speed through Kentucky and the Tennessee country and along the Ohio and the Wabash and the Mississippi, and as many as five thousand armed men would come to the rivers and be ready to descend on Spanish Louisiana. Michaux watched George Rogers Clark move among these men and watched them gather around him, their faces wreathed in smiles, and his likewise; he watched men of no rank jump into the general's path with a whoop and a grin, watched him dance them around in a bear hug, and thought, *Oui, vraiment, voici égalité, fraternité.* Michaux was astonished that a man some people called "a helpless sot" could remember so many names and so many details about men's lives.

Here, he thought, is a leader. I would not want to be in the shoes of the Spanish governor of Louisiana.

"BY TH' SWEAT O' THE SAINTS, CAP'N CLARK, IT'S NOT A PLACE I'd chase a scotched bear into," exclaimed Lieutenant Towles.

"Nope," William replied, peering through his spyglass, "but how 'bout a Little Turtle?"

Towles gave a wan smile and a shake of the head, and peered toward the place. It was the awfulest tangle of tree trunks and root boles and dead limbs William had ever seen in his life, where some past tornado had blown down a whole forest on the swampy banks of the Maumee River, and it was full of Indians. In the snarl of gray-weathered trunks and rotting bark within the round of his lens he caught glimpses of half-concealed movement and colors: a dab of vermillion war paint, a flash of honed steel, a patch of red cloth. It was a natural fortress, and now the Indians of Little Turtle's Confederacy—at least a thousand of them, according to the scouts—were forming their defense in it. Beyond the great blowdown stood Fort Miami, the British fort on American soil that had been supplying the Confederacy with

530

uns and ammunition and knives. And it was obvious that here was the place where Mad Anthony Wayne's slow, inexorable two-year advance was going to end in a showdown at last. Wayne had President Washington's authorization to attack the British fort if he deemed it prudent, and to destroy it even though the two countries were not officially at war. His main objective, though, was to crush the tribes that had twice crushed the United States Army.

Wayne had got his 2,500-man army into the heart of their country by avoiding four of the mistakes that had ruined Generals Harmar and St. Clair: he had kept a whole company of scouts out at all times; he had kept his cannons and supply trains up with the troops; he had kept iron discipline over Regulars and volunteers alike; and he had never stopped anywhere even for one night without building fortifications. Wayne had constructed seven forts during his tortoiselike progress into the heart of the Algonquian country, and countless fortified campsites—one at the end of every day's march. In all this time, not once had the tribes been able to catch Wayne off guard. They were calling him The Man Who Never Sleeps. They were also calling him The Long Knife, William had learned, and he had felt a deep, sad bitterness on hearing George's sobriquet applied to a new leader.

But now by good management Wayne was here; he had moved his hardened, polished army through an infinity of the world's deepest woods and prickliest, swampiest landscapes. The reckless courage that had earned him the nickname of Mad Anthony in the Revolution had matured into this Alexandrian thoroughness. He was middle-aged, fleshy, and sat on his mare nearby now, his rheumatic thigh wrapped in layers of flannel; and his legions, their blue uniforms wet from a morning rainshower and the sweat of a three-hour march, were maneuvering into positions for the charge, and surely the Indians swarming in that tangle were licking their lips in anticipation of another hearty draught of blood. Here was Wayne's parading army in blue, lining up for a frontal assault against a concealed hornet swarm in a gigantic brushpile, and to William it seemed that the whole phenomenal progress would prove to have been in vain, that Wayne was going to make the same fatal mistake that the other generals had made.

General Wilkinson came riding along the ranks, looking pink, sleek and nervous, handing down General Wayne's words. "Be set," he told each company as he came along. "After the advance guard decoys them out, listen for the drums. Run over them with bayonets. Don't shoot till they're in full flight!" He reined in near William, leaned down and muttered: "I do be lieve he's mad after all. Look at that pile of jackstraws! I swear we'll all die in there!"

Though this was what William had been thinking himself, Wilkinson's criticisms seemed out of place, here on the brink o battle, and William replied, trying not to show his irritation:

"I reckon this is time not to doubt but to pray." Wilkinson surprised, maybe disappointed, raised his eyebrows, grew pinker and poutier, and rode on to the next company.

The muggy air was thick now with apprehension, as if every man's nerves were giving off atoms of fear that combined with the others to create an invisible miasma of it all over the field All the low voices, all the whispering of hooves and boot through the brush and of cloth on cloth, all the wheel-trundling all the gun-handling and sword-drawing and the thousands o nervous adjustments of gear and clothing, combined to make . rushing sound like waterfalls. Every infantryman now stood with his bayonet gleaming and musket loaded with a ball and three pellets of large shot. Down by the river on their big warhorses sa the helmeted dragoons, with sabers drawn and resting aslant on their shoulders; their duty would be to slash their way around the Indians' left flank, while the mounted Kentuckians of Genera Scott would prevent the Indians' right wing from breaking out o the timber. If I was running this thing, William thought, I'c send Scott clear around 'em to cut off their escape. Wilkinsor had proposed this to Wayne, but the commandant had his own notion, from which he would not depart: a swift, solid front o cold steel, nothing fancy.

The steady murmur of the troops rose now. The advance scouts were in a skirmish line spurring their horses into a tro straight through the weeds toward the distant gray mass of dea tree trunks. William raised his spyglass to watch. On the limb o a sumac tree in the foreground perched a female cardinal, a dul ruddy brown, with rusty crest and brow, tilting her head left and right, her bright orange beak opening for tiny *cheeps* that coul not be heard over. the great murmuring rustle of the moving army. William twisted the eyepiece, and the cardinal dissolve and now the fallen timbers were in focus and he could see the woods crawling with Indians. He slid the brass tube shut and pu it in his pouch and drew his sword.

The advance party rode straight on, closer and closer toward the blowdown, almost like sacrifices to the god of war, their black hats and white crisscrossed belts jogging up and down William's pulse seemed to be jarring his eyeballs as he breathed shallowly and watched them go. Their dangerous role was to draw fire, feign panic, and draw Indians out of the woods in pursuit.

Then the blue-white smoke and the staccato rattle of guns poured out of the woods amid the howling of massed warriors. The vanguard hesitated, some men flinging up their arms and tumbling, others discharging their weapons into the trees; horses wheeled and fell; gunsmoke screened the gray woods from view. And now through the yelling and rattle of gunfire came the chattering beat of the general's drummers, and the officers' shouts: "Arms at ready! Double step! For-ward!" And the whole front of them, shoulder to shoulder, nearly half a mile from wing to wing, swept forward like a wave in that surprisingly swift pace they had practiced and practiced and practiced on the fields at every bivouac.

Now the survivors of the vanguard came thundering back, blood-smeared, wild-eyed, through the thinning smoke, many riderless horses and unhorsed riders among them; and close behind came the howling of the warriors who had sprung from the woods to pursue them. The infantry opened ranks to let the horsemen through and then closed again and swept on, and as they closed on the astonished Indians they began bellowing, a deep, angry chorus in monotone.

A din of clattering and clinking swept along the line now as bayonets and swords and tomahawks clashed. William was where he had been half a dozen times before in his young life: where little bits of death whizzed thick as bees through the air—musketballs, arrows, and blades.

But for once, the clash did not slow the onrush. The line of blue, with its gleaming edge of steel, overran the tawny warriors and rushed on against the jumbled timbers like a wave against a reef, leaving in the weeds behind it a few dozen struggling forms, men trying to pull their bayonets out of flesh, while the warriors trying to flee back into the woods got in the way of those who were still in there trying to shoot.

Now William plunged into the crazy tangle of limbs and roots, hacked across a fleeing red back, laying flesh open to the ribs; and to right and left he could see and hear his soldiers crashing and yelling and thrashing. The Indians had had no time to reload, and their desperate swipes with warclub, knife, and tomahawk were too short; a man with a five-foot musket and a two-foot bayonet had a superior reach. William was suddenly beginning to understand Mad Anthony's faith in this weapon. Indians doubled over, their hands clawing at gun muzzles, as the steel slid between their ribs or punched into their abdomens.

And the very tree trunks and limbs and roots the Indians had chosen for their defense now impeded their retreat, and entrapped them. Some tripped backward and lay squirming under the probing bayonets; some were pinned to tree trunks as they tried to scramble over them; some were impaled as they tried to crash through mats of dead wood. William could hear virtually no gunfire and not much shouting; now it was mostly a crunching and crackling and munching, like a herd of animals rushing through undergrowth, here a gasp, there a groan, now and then a scream of dying or a curse or a command in English, and, somewhere behind, the chattering of drums.

"They're on the run!" William shouted. "Keep on! Don't give 'em a breath! Don't lose each other! Bear hunt! It's a bear hunt." A russet arm, smeared with sweaty ochre war paint and grease, flashed across his vision and then tightened like a hawser around his neck and his breath was cut off and his hat was down over his eyes, and a heavy hard body was on his back. William anticipated the stab of a knife, but before he could struggle, the arm jerked tighter and then released and there was a loud grunt. William turned, his hat falling off, and saw one of his troopers pressing and twisting on his musket, driving the speared warrior to the ground. William croaked through his bruised windpipe: "Thankee, man!" The Indian was on the ground gaping like a fish and twitching, still holding the knife he had not had time to use. It was one of those British-issue scalping knives with a red-painted wooden handle.

The soldier who had saved William's life now pulled his bayonet out of the Indian's side and without a word crouched and went under a log farther into the tangle.

The battle had been won in minutes, and from then on it had been just a matter of climbing and crawling through the fallen forest after the fleeing Indians, finishing off those who had crawled into coverts to hide and die. Halfway through, the companies were halted and reformed, refreshed with a shot of whiskey and words of praise, and then ordered to push on. Now mosquitoes and snakes were the only living enemies in this close, damp, dizzying world of deadwood. The sweating troops began emerging from the other side of the blowdown at about noon, onto a weedy meadow, and there, less than a mile ahead, stood the palisades and block houses of Fort Miami with the British flag, hanging limp atop its flagstaff. Spread far around the fort were Indian dwellings, hundreds of acres of corn and vegetables, and the British trading post. The legion was halted here to form a defensive line in case of a counterattack.

But there would be no counterattack; that was plain. William climbed up a slanting limb of a huge fallen oak, slid out his spyglass, and gazed on a pathetic scene. .

Hundreds of warriors, many limping, some carrying wounded comrades on their backs, were crowding toward the British fort; some were pounding on its gate with their weapons and demanding refuge. But the British officers and soldiers stood above, gazing toward the American Army, and made no move to open the gates and let the Indians in.

"Look'ee, sir," William called to General Wilkinson, extending his spyglass. Wilkinson rode over and took it and studied the scene. William said through clenched teeth: "Some allies, the Redcoats, eh? They hire the savages to war on us, then shut 'em out when they're whipped! By God, but that fort's an insult to all that's human!" he growled. "Pray he'll let us storm it, eh, and cut off the Hydra's last head! We've come too far not to, right, sir?"

Wilkinson handed the telescope back up to William, and there was a cynical half-smile on his mouth. "I don't know, friend Clark," he said. "As y're aware, His Excellency is a cumbrous body, and yon fort might decay before he decides to knock it down."

GENERAL WAYNE DECIDED NOT TO ATTACK THE BRITISH stronghold, but, instead, simply to scorn it out of existence. He encamped his army within plain view of it, building the usual breastworks and setting up his cannon to bear on the fort. He put his troops to work then destroying the British trading post and all the Indian dwellings that lay under its "protection," and to burning all the grainfields and trampling vegetable gardens under hoof. By now all the remnants of the whipped Indian force had vanished. General Wayne, accompanied only by his aide, Lieutenant William Henry Harrison, then rode within a stone's throw of the fort's walls and casually inspected it all around. This action so infuriated the British commander that he sent a messenger out to Wayne under a white flag, demanding to know why an American army had come to stand so insolently close to one of His Majesty's posts, as he knew of no war between the two countries. Wayne sent back a note telling the Englishman to quit his fort and get out of American territory. But he would not attack the fort. He did not think it was worth starting another war with Great Britain.

*   *   *

Two days later, to a dirge of drums and fifes, a funeral ceremony was performed over the graves of the two American officers and twenty-six men who had died in the attack in the fallen timbers. One of these officers was William's tentmate, Lieutenant Towles, who had died somewhere deep in the timbers with a tomahawk in his chest.

The cannon fired three rounds to conclude the ceremony, and then, baggage wagons creaking with the additional burden of a hundred wounded, the army left its camp and began to retrace its route, from fort to fort, back through the Ohio country toward the winter quarters at Fort Greenville. General Anthony Wayne was certain that he had at last completely defeated the Algonquian Confederacy. Most of the officers were not so sure.

Discomfort and hunger set in when the army was back in Fort Greenville; a supply train and herd of beef cattle had been badly delayed. William was exceedingly gloomy in his billet, the empty bunk beside his reminding him of Lieutenant Towles' death. The diet of pan bread and bear's oil, the lack of liquor or tea or coffee, kept his stomach sour and growling. Firewood and clothes and shoes were constantly damp, and half the garrison was sick; every assembly sounded like a coughing chorus. The troops wounded at Fallen Timbers were mending slowly on the poor diet. William thought of the tons of good Indian food that had been destroyed. He filled his off-duty hours by writing in his journal, and grew every day to hate army life ever more. There had been letters from the family awaiting him at Fort Greenville, letters expressing concern over Brother George's expatriate scheme, which saddened them and offended their patriotic sense even though it seemed to be restoring his spirit and keeping him sober for the most part. William's own sympathies were with George; he himself had become disillusioned with everyone else's brand of leadership—with that smugness of Anthony Wayne, with that witty cynicism of General Wilkinson.

These dreary days, when Wayne was dead certain he had defeated the Indians once and for all but most of the officers were certain that he had let real victory slip through his fingers, William thought often of resigning his captain's commission and going to join George's phantom legion, an army with a cause. There was something more noble, more worthy, William thought, in going to war against the corrupt tyrants of Spain than in helping Congress methodically push Indians out of their own

536

lands. It was, after all, this same Congress that had refused year after year to honor George's war debts until it had at last wiped out his great loyalty. In the night hours William struggled feebly to retain the precepts of his parents, their faith in God and Country. His diary pages for Fanny grew still more cynical. Fanny's letters were low and bitter, too. She had a new son, Benjamin, but never saw her husband.

Such doubts and discontents had been gnawing at William's morale in the gray weeks at Fort Greenville when, one day, a joyous shout from the parade ground signaled two cheering arrivals.

The first was expected—long expected. It was that overdue supply train, with its flour, its liquor, its medicines, and, above all, its herd of beef cattle. "Mmm—OOOooo! I'm just *dying* to be beef roast for th' soldier boys!" someone yelled, running alongside the beasts.

The other arrival, unexpected, showed up first as a rap on William's door an hour later. "Come in," he called, turning from his writing box to see who was coming in off the muddy compound.

The stranger, an ensign, stepped into the room so stiffly he appeared to have a ramrod down his back, shut the door with a strange erect pivoting motion, and took his hat off before facing William. He was not tall, but his compact figure gave an immediate impression of hickorylike strength and hardness. He was mud-caked as high as his thick-muscled thighs, and markedly bowlegged; even though his muddy heels were smartly together, his knees gave each other an inch or two of leeway. His face was not really handsome, its mouth being small and severe and his round ears jutting like handles, but the eyes, winter-sea gray and deep-set under a massive forehead, were utterly startling. The lids were long-lashed, heavy-lidded, almost sleepy-looking, but the quick gray eyes themselves had that all-perceiving acuteness in them that William had seen only rarely, in certain scouts. One glance at them and William somehow was aware of the untidiness of his own room and person. They were a bit like old Daniel Boone's eyes, but the face was not relaxed and happy as Boone's was; it seemed instead to have been cut from granite and then polished to a girlish smoothness. The man's hair was thick, auburn, pulled tightly back behind his prominent ears and queued in back. Now this man, this tight bundle of force, gave a formal little bow and said, as William rose from his chair:

"Captain Clark, Sir? I am Meriwether Lewis."

*　　*　　*

THIS STRANGE YOUNG SPECIMEN OF AN ARMY OFFICER, it happened, was to be William's new billet-mate. It was news not immediately to William's liking, as Meriwether Lewis at first glance seemed an odd combination of prig and spartan. He was as orderly as a housemaid; worse, there was as much tension about him as about a drawn bow. William mused on him, wondering if he slept at attention. He watched from the corner of his eye as Ensign Lewis opened a portable bookcase to display a collection of books of sorts that had bewildered William in the years of his own education: Plutarch, Plato, Aeschylus, and the like, giving William to believe that atop all his other miseries, he was to be locked up in a room all winter with a man of inferior rank and superior education. William thought again on the notion of resigning his commission, and wondered how long it would take him to get out.

But soon, to his pleasant surprise, William began to find Meriwether Lewis somewhat interesting. *Quite* interesting, even, and a bit more personable than his initial rigidity had suggested. The first good sign was that when William asked him what name he went by, the answer was "Lewis." Good. It would have been awkward sharing a room with a fellow one had to call "Meriwether," or "Merry," or such a thing. And then it transpired that Ensign Lewis knew a good deal about the Clarks. He had, in fact, been born in Albemarle County, not ten miles from the old Clark farmstead where Jonathan and George had been born. And only five miles or so from Thomas Jefferson's estate. The Lewises were close friends of Jefferson. Lewis had, furthermore, schooled under the Maurys, who had educated Jefferson.

It soon became apparent, too, that Meriwether Lewis was not a prig or a sissy. Though he was of the land-rich and distinguished Warner Hall Lewises and the influential Meriwethers, he was at twenty years of age the protector of his family; his mother Lucy Meriwether Lewis Marks was the widow of first one officer and then a second, and this solid lad had thus been the head of his family since the age of seventeen.

Anecdotes and recollections began to bound back and forth between the two young officers so fast that each had two exciting questions and a story backed up behind his throat while the other was talking. "*Your* father rode against Dunmore over the gunpowder affair? Blast my eyes! So did mine, and my brothers, too!" And so on it went, the excitement building.

"My parents, come to think of it, went to your sister's wedding, just before I was born—or just after, I'm not sure. What year . . ."

They talked about their families, faces alight with fondness and humor, told anecdotes about them, purging themselves of their homesickness. They talked about the army, and Lewis's wholesome concept of duty was so refreshing that William vowed down inside himself to stop being so cynical about it, and felt much better at once. Lewis, just before getting his orders to come here, had been serving under Jonathan's old commander, Light Horse Harry Lee, at Red Stone Fort, part of the force President Washington had sent out to quell the Whiskey Rebellion. William at last got a full and understandable account of that remote and rumored disturbance.

"The duty I've really prayed for," Lewis said, "is one of exploring. From the Mississippi to the Pacific. Mister Jefferson wants to send a French scientist, Michaux. I've asked permission to go, but . . . So far, nothing."

"The Pacific! Aye! He's intended that a long time, I know. Once he asked Brother George to do it. George and I have talked on it a lot."

"I've dreamed of it," said Lewis, "since I was old enough to walk."

"Michaux is with my brother now," William exclaimed. "If y'd come home with me on a furlough, we could see 'im!"

They agreed on it. They would go at Christmastime.

Gone was the prospect of a gloomy winter in Fort Greenville. William was happy as a boy again. It became apparent that Lewis was a woodsman and naturalist of considerable experience, with a hungry fascination with natural science reminiscent of Brother George. Fate had brought to William, when he needed it, a friend to stretch his mind and warm his war-chilled heart.

And a few weeks later, when the chiefs of the Seven Nations came down to talk peace with General Mad Anthony Wayne, and the Indian wars were, truly, concluded for a while, William Clark and Meriwether Lewis knew they would indeed be free to go down to Mulberry Hill for Christmas. They drank to it.

"To a long friendship," said Lewis.

"To a great friendship," said William.

GENERAL GEORGE ROGERS CLARK, COMMANDANT OF THE French Legion of the Mississippi, was in the public house at Louisville with Andre Michaux, outlining details of the Spanish defenses at New Orleans with old comrades who were secretly officers of the Legion, when a messenger leaped off a boat at the wharf and ran up the street. He appeared in the doorway of the pub, looking left and right in the dim light, then slipped in among the rough soldiery and handed a piece of paper to Michaux. The Frenchman perused the sheet, then shut his eyes and, with a sigh, let his chin fall to his chest.

"Yes, what?" George said, and Michaux handed him the paper without looking up.

President Washington, it said, had learned of the plan to invade Louisiana. Enraged at Citizen Genet's plotting right under his own nose, appalled by this violation of American neutrality, the President had outlawed the plot, demanded Genet's recall to France, and ordered General Anthony Wayne to build a fort on the Mississippi to keep the French Legion from going down the river. Michaux, too, would have to go back to France.

George slumped in his chair.

Well, he thought. There goes my last dream o' glory.

He slapped a gold coin down on the table. "Hey, take that over and buy us a jerry-boam o' French brandy. Be sure it's French. I intend for the Legion to go out with a roar."

So THAT LAST GRAND SCHEME HAD FAILED, TOO. BUT NOT entirely. The Spaniards in New Orleans, learning how close they had come to being invaded by an army of angry frontiersmen, decided to lift their restrictions on American shipping. General Clark's army, without even marching, had at last opened up the mouth of the Mississippi. Now all Kentuckians could prosper from the trading down the river.

All, that is, except General Clark.

FOR THE FIRST FEW HOURS THERE HAD BEEN INTERVALS WHEN the pain would ease for a while and Elizabeth had been able to breathe and think a little, and the midwife had cooled her face and neck and shoulders with damp linen, but now there were no intervals, and the enormous pain was not only always there, it was growing worse. She felt as if a hand as big and strong as God's own hand had closed around her waist, trying to pull the lower half of her body off. For a while in the beginning she had felt that the baby inside her was alive, and for a while she had been able to hear Richard's voice out in the hall talking with the doctor. But now she was sure that the mass inside her was not alive, but was a mass of death, like a tombstone or something, and that the death in it was trying to spread out and invade her heart; and as for her beloved Richard, she could not hear him anymore; she could not hear anything except a terrible harsh sound like furniture being scooted across the floor in an empty house, and the room kept getting darker and darker. She wanted her mother to come, bearing a lamp.

Then there seemed to be a cooling wind, a wind the color of silver, and there was no pain anymore. The silver wind seemed to be blowing over the roof of the house, above her bedroom, but yet at the same time she was in the silver wind, or was the silver wind itself. Gray wings caressed the silver wind, and there was a familiar, lovely sound.

Oh-a! Ooo, ooo, ooo.

THE QUESTION BEFORE THE CLARK FAMILY NOW WAS whether they ought to go up and tell Fanny that her sister had died. John and Ann Rogers Clark were still so benumbed by the news from Soldier's Retreat that they could not judge whether she should be told or not. They seemed to want to ponder on that question rather than on Elizabeth's death itself, and discuss softly and politely whether or not she should be told, but they could not really decide; they could only stand there looking gray and confused and saying, "What do you think, my dear?" George was of the opinion that she should be told, but he did not want to be the one to go up and tell her because he had been drinking when the message came from Soldier's Retreat and he knew he was slurring his speech and needed to shave, and he did not want to go up to Fanny in that condition and say, "Fanny, your sister and her baby died."

And so it was left for William to handle the matter, and he knew he could tell her as well as anyone because he was closer to her than anyone, except, perhaps, her mother. So he said, "You all just rest a spell and I'll go up and take care of it." They all seemed very relieved.

So he started up the stairs toward Fanny's room, and he went slowly and reluctantly, choosing his words as he went.

It was going to be a hard thing to tell Fanny this forlorn news, because her husband Dr. Jim O'Fallon had taken sick on his eternal travels and just lately come home to die, leaving Fanny a young widow with two small sons.

"NO LASS O' SUCH BEAUTY'LL STAY ALONE LONG," ANN Rogers Clark said of her widowed young daughter. And she was right. Fanny was scarcely out of mourning black before the amazing Captain Thruston came to Kentucky and found her, and fell helplessly in love with her.

Charles Minn Thruston was a compelling young man with a golden tongue and a sense of his own worth, scarcely older than Fanny herself but well on his way already to becoming a man of real substance. He had entered manhood early; before he wa quite twelve years old he had gone with his father to fight in the Revolution, and had not let loose of the reins of his own destin for a moment since.

It was Charles Thruston's opinion that the town of Louisville had become about all it ever would be, and that the new town o Westport, twenty-five miles upstream from the Falls, showed mor promise of becoming a great city. And so there, with a workin party of Negroes he had brought from Virginia, he built a hand some house and established a store, and in a short while persuade Dr. O'Fallon's young widow to marry him and share these bold nev beginnings with him. Her two sons by James O'Fallon, he said, h would love as if they were his own, because they were of her flesh and he adored her so. If nothing else about the remarkable youn gallant had won her, that would have.

And so, in January of 1796, Fanny was married again, and sh moved to Westport with a purposeful and vigorous young ma who, her mother believed, would provide her the lifetime of do mestic bliss and security that Jim O'Fallon had only promised

"I could be wrong," Ann Rogers Clark said to John Clark "but meseems Charles Thruston is the fellow she should hav waited for at the first."

"He's some'at harsh on his slaves," John Clark mused, "bu young men in a haste sometimes are, and likely he'll outgrow it Outside o' that, there's nowt I can see to fault 'im for, and reckon we'll all be glad he came to Fanny when he did."

And in the spring of that year a letter came from Westpor down to Mulberry Hill with the happy news that Fanny wa again with child. If it was a boy, she said, it would be name Charles. But its middle name would be William, in honor of he closest brother.

IN SUMMER OF 1796, THE BRITISH FORMALLY YIELDED UP TO General Mad Anthony Wayne their stronghold of Detroit, wher they had remained for thirteen years since the end of the wa despite the fact that it was in American territory. Wayne was too sick to participate in the ceremonies himself, but his old enemy Chief Little Turtle of the Miamis, was there. British troops and Loyalist citizens then left the city and moved across to Canada

When the news came to Kentucky, George Rogers Clark rea of it and then sat in a gaze that went far beyond the walls o the public house. He shook his head slowly, muttering. "All th mischief that's come out o' that bedamned place, just because never got the men I needed to take it! God damn them all to

542

Hell, and now it's given up without a battle. All that useless mischief. *Bejesus!*" Somebody else, another general the Indians now called Long Knife, had finished the game of chess he had never been allowed to win. "All that mischief," he muttered again, his lips drawn in a narrow sneer.

In the basement of the British Government House there, the newspaper had reported, 2,000 moldy, dusty, rat-gnawed scalps had been found.

That was the mischief he meant.

A SMALL BUT NOISY CROWD HAD GATHERED ON THE STREET in front of a cobbler shop. It was a cool evening after a heavy summer rain, and the streets of Louisville were ankle-deep in mud. Victor Collot, a retired French general on a tour of the Ohio and Mississippi valleys, had just dined at one of the city's new inns and was walking off the heaviness of the meal when he saw the crowd and heard their laughter and jeers. One voice was shouting angrily amid the merriment. Tucking his sword-cane under his arm, Collot ambled up the street toward the disturbance.

A big man was lying face-down in the mud. He wore good boots and an old-style army coat. "Aye, by God, sure and it's him again," someone was saying. "Ha, ha!" someone else was laughing, "it's the old traitor hisself!"

At this, the man who had been shouting at the crowd roared a furious oath and swung his fist at the man who had said it, but missed. This enraged fellow was middle-aged and gray-haired and his face was contorted. He wore a heavy leather cobbler's apron. Now he was grabbing people by the arms and shoving them away. "Git, damn your eyes! Go on! Move away, ye scum-gut buzzards! GIT!" He shoved someone, was shoved back and taunted. "GIT AWAY!" he screamed, "or I'll drive nails in y'r head!" His voice broke. Now he turned and limped, arms swinging, into the cobbler shop where a lantern burned low over a work bench. He emerged carrying a blanket, forced his way through the crowd, knelt, and spread the blanket over the prostrate figure, muttering and growling like some swarthy troll. Then he stood up, and with upraised fists and curses again tried to drive the onlookers away.

"Come," the Frenchman broke in gently now, gripping someone by the arm. "Enough, no?" He pulled people away. They looked at his large stature and respectable dress, shrugged, and by ones and twos began moving on up the street, laughing and talking, out of the light from the cobbler's window.

"Thank'ee, Gov'nor," said the cobbler. "Now would ye gi' me a hand here?"

They rolled the big man over in the blanket. The cobbler grasped him under the arms; the Frenchman leaned his cane against the building, knelt, and lifted him by the knees. They stumbled into the shop and past the bench and laid him down on a cot near the back. The cobbler's eyes were wet with tears. He was muttering and snuffing as he stooped and wiped mud off the man's face with a corner of the blanket. "There, now," he was saying. "I'll send for Cap'm William. Y'r brother takes good care o' ye, don't 'e, Gen'l." And suddenly the Frenchman guessed.

"*Mon Dieu!* Is this General Clark?"

"Eh, 'tis," muttered the cobbler, now smoothing the blanket upon the broad, muddy chest. "Aw, God. He's forgot for now, what 'e done fer us. But we're obliged not t' fergit. I cover 'im from th' contempt o' people like them scum-guts out 'air, people who never follered 'im to Vincennes, th' way I done. Awwww, God!"

When Collot backed out of the shop and picked up his cane, the cobbler was kneeling beside the cot in the lamplight, soothing with his palm the massive brow of the unconscious man.

29

MULBERRY HILL

Christmas Eve, 1798

"A HAPPY CHRISTMAS TO YE, BILLY. IT GLADDENS ME YOU'RE home."

"A happy Christmas to you, Ma. Uhm, I could light us a candle."

"No! No, don't. I don't want you to look at me. I don't want anybody to see me thisaway. That's why I, I made 'em put up the black drapes. I want everybody to remember me the way I used to look—which some said was uncommon fair."

"By heaven, that's so." William felt awkward saying that, and even more so in saying, "Nobody ever had a more beauteous Mama than us."

"It's not that I'm vain, you know that, son. But I'll be gone from here before long."

He tried to joke. "Oh? Where ye headin'? West?"

"I can tell it, I can. Heh . . . It's about time, I suppose. But I don't want one person, no son or daughter or grandson o' mine—and sure not your father—to think back and recollect me how I look with this accurst, this STUFF all over me. That's why I have it dark in here."

William swallowed hard. Oh, this is bad, he thought. She doesn't deserve it to be like this. Not her.

"Y'see the chair there," she said. "I had Venus sew a white slip on't so's a body can find it in the dark. Y' set yourself down there. We don't need light to talk by, do we? Remember how I'd tell ye stories, all o' you, in the dark o' your room? Don't need light to talk by. Can you understand me all right? Can you?"

"Surely I can, Ma."

"I can think clear as crystal. And I do my tongue and . . . voice just like I always have done. But . . . but my lips are so swole and tender I reckon it makes me mumble . . . like if I was talkin' with a mouthful o' week-old cornbread. Hm, hm! Tell me if I'm not clear."

"You're clear, Ma."

"So, son, set ye there, and let's us talk. Tell me all where you went and all what you did. If y've got anything to read to me, why, just pull my bed curtains to, and light a lamp. Now, talk."

"Well, first off, I got a lot done for George. I finally got that dang suit that Spaniard Bazadone's held over 'im so long, I got that dismissed. Best thing I've ever done! I sold off some o' George's lands, paid off some debts, so much on th' dollar. Put off a few other greedy folk for a while, without havin' to hit anybody. Ha! I feel like a real circuit-ridin' lawyer! Y' know, Ma, I've reckoned up how many miles I've done in the saddle since I took up this business o' his, and I'd ha' been to the Western Sea and back if I'd gone straight, 'stead o' zigzagging all over Kentucky and Virginia. That's no exaggeration. These last few years, I've ridden onto nine, ten thousand miles. I, uhm, I doubt I'll ever get it all done, but I've trimmed a bit off here, stalled a bit there."

"Your Pa says if you'd put all that effort toward yourself, you could ha' built yourself a fortune in all this time."

"Well, I rather do this. Doesn't seem to me there's much justice in this world, so whenever I manage to squeeze a drop out of it for George, well, I feel good."

"Poor George." She worked her tongue around in her mouth and moaned a little as if it hurt. "He's been bad off while you were gone . . . How is he tonight . . ." Her voice was whispery gurgly.

"Just his old self. Hear 'im singin' down there?"

"What's that . . . they're singing? That's no carol."

"Why, no, that's 'The Spoiling o' Katy Morah.' Ha, ha!"

"O! That bawdry! They should . . . be singing carols."

"Ye tired, Ma?"

"Oh, keep on. Ye saw Jonathan? Edmund?"

"Aye, they're rich and sleek, both of 'em. I saw lots o' your grandsons you've yet to see. That—"

"I'll not see 'em."

"Sure you will. Little Billy told me he's named after me. Seems he's gettin' the idea how things are done in this family. The baby, George Washington Clark. Well, talk about a little lard-tub! Roly-round as York is! Ha!" William leaned forward toward the indistinct shape on the high pillows, trying to hear her breathing.

"Talk. I'm still here."

"Jonathan 'spects to be migratin' out here in two more years. Him and Edmund. He's got a joke. Says he and Edmund are just like they were in the war, always a rear guard."

His mother made a noise that sounded something like a laugh. "Oh, what a knee-slapper that is."

"Yay. Heh, heh. But ol' Jonathan, he gets enough chorkles out of his own jokes for everybody."

After a while her voice asked, "Has Edmund got himself a lady yet?"

"Not the right one, I guess. He escorts some dandy ones, but . . . well, don't jump in the air and expect any grandchildren from *him* b'fore you land."

"What o' you, Billy?"

This question had almost the tone of a plea, and he realized she wanted him to answer yes. So he said, "Me? Well, fancy you askin', because it just happens . . ."

She stirred, rustling bedding. "Don't tell me it's so!" For the first time there was a lilt of her old happiness in her voice, or so it sounded to him. "No. *Do* tell me. Who?"

Now he had got himself into a corner. She wanted to know something he himself didn't know yet, but only anticipated.

"Well, Ma, I laid over a while in Fincastle, at the Hancocks'—"

546

"Ah . . . Fincastle? George and Peggy Hancock, that would be?"

"Right you are. Well . . ." William was flushing at the memory of his stay there, and not sure what to say. There had been a houseful of golden daughters there, all fair as sunshine on wheat and periwinkle, and in a couple of whirlwind days, he had actually fallen in love with all of them, and had got the wild notion that he was destined to marry at least one of those Hancock girls. But they had confused him thoroughly. He was plainly not much of a swain. The ones old enough for courtship had toyed with him and left him wondering whether they took him seriously. Only the little one, Judy, had seemed really to adore him. She had told her sisters not to tease him. She had told them that she thought he was handsome, even if they didn't, and she had told him she would marry him when she was old enough. The trouble with Judy was that she was only eight or nine.

And now his mother was asking: "A Hancock girl, then? Which girl, Billy?"

"Uh, Judy," he said weakly, making a fool's-face in the dark. And she said:

"A mere babe she must be. There was no Judy when we knew 'em."

"Well, but . . . It's been fourteen years since we left Virginia, Ma."

"Is she fourteen, then?"

William squirmed. "Well, would I ask her age of a miss? Well, she's young, o' course. But won't always be." Behind his eyes he was seeing peach-colored flesh and an aura of heavenly golden light that had begun to suffuse over the memory of those sisters, so that they were all starting to blur together. All except little Judy. William had not meant to tell his mother that he was going to marry Judy Hancock in particular. But it would have sounded silly to say, "One of the Hancock girls, at least."

The air in the dark sickroom was redolent of the powerful ointments that had been used against his mother's affliction, which was called St. Anthony's Fire, but for a moment William remembered a warm lilac scent that had surrounded all those fetching nymphs, and he was stirred by a vague longing and a deep, miserable confusion.

"Son," came the weak voice from the bed, "how far did ye press on this Miss Hancock?"

He wished the subject had never been mentioned. He was talking of daydream butterflies, but she was demanding that he pin one down.

"Uh," he mumbled, "I talked with her father." That was not exactly a fib. He had chatted generally and awkwardly with Colonel Hancock about wanting to come back and acquaint himself better with the girls. The colonel was a staunch admirer of the Clark name and had seemed to take this as a proper overture to some very acceptable formal proposal yet to come.

"And?"

"He, ah, he said he'd be pleased to talk of it with me in an earnest way after the century turns."

He could hear his mother chuckling. "Billy, Billy! Now didn't that strike ye as a strange reply?"

"Maybe a bit. But it's just another way o' saying wait a year or so. Eighteen hundred is that close. We'll be a-feelin' the century turn, Ma, in a year and a week."

"That's so, isn't it," she said after a while. "But it's true she's young, this Judy?"

"Young." They were all young. Enchantingly, virginally young. William's intimate knowledge of womanflesh had been gained primarily among camp-followers and squaws and inn-wenches, and so to him a virgin was a rather mythical being.

"Have ye been moved to write poetry?"

"Poetry? Oh, no."

"Good. Poor Johnny, rest his beloved soul, was the only one ever got in such a state. Don't y' ever make a fool of yourself . . . Or be made one of . . . You go down now . . . Join family . . . Sing with . . . Gladdens me y're home . . . Listen, Billy. I know you're rare good . . . Marked, as George was . . . I love ye dearly now. Would ye send your Pa up when you go down . . . I must scold 'im for singin' that bawdry, huh . . . Don't kiss me on the face or touch me . . . it hurts. But I'm hugging you, Billy, in my heart . . . just like always. A happy Christmas, dear son."

"Ma, don't make me bawl, now." He was gulping. The sound of her voice in the dark was so sweet and terrible and far, as he could not see her or touch her. He had in a way misled her. And it was plain that she wasn't going to be here long.

"O' course y'll not bawl. Go on down now."

OH, I'M SO DISAPPOINTED IT'S GOT TO BE LIKE THIS, Ann Rogers Clark was thinking as William's boots tromped away down the stairs.

A body thinks on how 'twill be and I always pictured it would be in a bright room with me and John looking at each other, him a-sitting close by the bed holding my hand

And me looking pale and pretty as ary old saint
Young'uns all roundabout the bed
Wonder if George can still do a whippoorwill song
Poor George
I've a feeling I'll not see this Christmas
Not quite
Oh, what time is it I wonder
Midnight yet? I didn't count the chimes last hour
I wonder can a body feel it when a new century comes around
Like something silent turning out among the stars
Mercy I don't know
I never felt new years or birthdays
It's all got to do with clocks and calendars
Years themselves just roll on like a millwheel without beginnings or ends
Reckon centuries do too
Eh well but I do wish I could linger a spell and watch things . . . cotton gins and steam engines and whatnot
But I reckon you can watch from over yonder too
Over across the River
Find things out over yonder too, surely so
Like whatever became o' poor son Dickie
And I'll see Johnny there too all healthy and handsome and rosy-cheeked like he was before the prison boat . . .
I'll see Elizabeth
Ma
Pa
Rachel
I guess I'll be going to see as many as I'm leaving
And the Almighty at last
Oh my what will old John do without me though
Fifty years he's had o' me and I can scarce remember a time before him
Sometimes I feel I was born married to that man
He'll perish without me to look after him
What was the best time of all I wonder
Oh I'd have to say it was that morn in Albemarle John and I rode the ox cart up on the meadow o' spring flowers and he bade me keep my eyes shut till he was ready for me to look and he showed me where our first house would be If there was one best time I'd say that was it
I wonder if the next place I see will be like that meadow that morning
It will be I'll bet Oh I hope so

Come on John ol' Darlin'
I know it takes you a long time to climb a stair

"JOHN? SIT IN THE WHITE CHAIR.
"John. I think the time to go has come. It's really just sort o'
like fainting, is all.
"You aren't cryin' are you? Now listen what I ask: John dear,
keep my coffin shut. Whoever speaks over me have 'im say I was
a patriot too. It's no inconsiderable a thing what a mother does.
"Did I ever tell ye, John, that the first time I laid eyes on you I
knew. I knew it would be you and me right up to the end."
But
This isn't the end at all
It's the beginning
Across the River I'll see ye there
I see the far glory shine like sun on water
Come on when you're ready

ANN ROGERS CLARK DIED CHRISTMAS EVE, 1798, OF
erysipelas. She was buried at Mulberry Hill in a grave at the edge
of the woods. They had to burn the frozen ground to dig a place
for her. Much of Louisville's population stood there in the cold
when she was put down.

Her husband John Clark did not stay long after she was gone.
He became bemused, would not bother to eat, and stood for
hours at a time gazing out the window at her headstone out by
the woods.

In July of 1799, with three witnesses, he dictated his will.

*In the name of God Almighty, I, John Clark of Jefferson
County and State of Kentucky Being at present in a weak
and low state of health But at the same time perfectly in
my senses, and considering the uncertainty of life,*
   I give:

He divided some 8000 acres of land among his sons Jonathan
and Edmund, his three sons-in-law, and his grandsons John and
Benjamin O'Fallon. To William, his youngest son, he gave
Mulberry Hill and all its livestock and furnishings and servants,
including William's bodyservant, York.

To George he could give nothing but the old slaves Cupid and
Venus, because anything else given to George would be subject
to seizure by his creditors.

One night, a week after the will was completed, John Clark

550

went quietly to his bed in the bedroom where he and Ann had slept since 1785. He lay looking at the far wall, and out the window at the stars over her grave, and he remembered one morning half a century ago when he had stood with her in a meadow in Albemarle County and shown her where their first house was going to be.

And then John Clark decided there was nothing else to get up for again.

A few days later, with most of Louisville's people up on Mulberry Hill again so soon, this time in the heat of August, he was buried beside Ann, at the edge of the woods, a long way west of Virginia.

BOOK THREE

1803–1806

30

FALLS OF THE OHIO

July, 1803

GEORGE ROGERS CLARK LOOKED INTO THE AMBER RUM IN the bottom of his glass and smelled its fumes, and for a moment he was without any thought whatsoever. It was unusual: his mind was blank—without a plan, without a word, without a recollection. From inside his log house came the musical voices of Fanny and her children, but they were faint and remote, as if from another world.

It seemed there were two great emptinesses in his soul: one where there had always been a purpose, one where his mother and father had always been. Now those two places were vacuums.

It was surprising how much he missed his parents. He thought much about the embarrassments he had brought upon them in their last years.

I always intended they'd be happy in Kentucky, he would think. It's my fault they weren't. Oh, I guess they were, but not as happy as they might have been. But then, who is?

At least now I can drink without shaming them, he would think.

I mean unless they can see me from where they are.

But I guess if they can see me from there, they can understand me from there too.

He was sitting on the porch of his new log house on the bluff above the Falls, shaded from a hot, late-afternoon sun, caressed by a breeze up from the river. This was his third glass this afternoon, and he was beginning to embrace the likelihood that he would not stop.

There was no reason to stop, really. Up here on Point o' Rock, there was no one it could embarrass. He was away from the society of Louisville, away from Kentucky altogether. It was the Indiana Territory on this side of the river, and no one lived here but his own old veterans and his old French allies, and Indians.

He was living in the first real house he had ever owned, except that little cabin on Grave Creek thirty years ago, and here he sat like an old eagle in its aerie, high above the Falls, looking far. It was no mansion, but it was his, and it was where he had long since dreamed he would have a house. It was a two-story structure of hewn poplar logs, sturdy as a fort, with a large stone fireplace at each end, a kitchen and pantry house attached at the back, and this front porch overlooking the most spectacular stretch of the Ohio. It had been built by brother-in-law Owen Gwathmey, lately arrived in Kentucky with Annie and their great brood of children. Owen had come over with his crew of skilled Negroes and built the place according to George's plan and under his supervision. It was as well built a log house as any he had ever seen, and Uncle George Rogers would have been proud of it, if he had lived to come and see it. But he had died last year, he who had taught George everything he knew about engineering and building, and that too had left a great empty place in George.

Although it was not the pillared white house of his old dream, and although there was no beautiful wife to sit with him and watch the sun go down as in that old dream, it was where he had wanted it, and here he could sit and think, and drink when he damn pleased, and his old comrades and even his old enemies could come here and drink with him, and Louisville's society and America's government could think what they wanted to think of him, or forget him if they chose to forget him, which seemed to be the case. George had quit working on his memoir long ago; indeed, he didn't even know where the manuscript was now.

Anyway, the ones who really counted back in the East had not forgotten him. President Jefferson, Madison, Monroe . . . They still wrote to him now and then. And he was not entirely alone, even out here in this wild place. He had the two old servants, Cupid and Venus, whom his father had willed to him, and who were so old and decrepit that the creditors wouldn't bother to take them from him. And Fanny and her sons were here, to fill these vast hushing silences with their sweet voices.

Fanny was the proper sister to be here with him, because her fortunes had been hard and devastating like his, and she could commiserate and understand. Fanny was a widow again, widowed by a swift, violent tragedy, and this high, lonely place was a retreat for her, too. She was glad to be in hermitage, for a twice-widowed woman of thirty, with small sons by both marriages, was an anomaly at Louisville's balls and fetes where the mating of well-born swains and maids was the paramount purpose, just as it always had been in old Virginia.

And so now, Fanny was the beautiful lady who sometimes sat with George and watched the sunsets in the valley. Not his wife, but his sister. It was always blood family, it seemed, that stayed alongside and helped one fend off the despair. Fanny and William now were his closest soulmates and helpmeets. And neither of them deplored his drinking. They did not encourage it; in fact, they tried to keep his spirits high enough that he would not fall into it. But they weren't embarrassed by it and they understood when he took a slide, as he felt he was about to do now. Jonathan and Edmund, who had finally come West last year and were deeply involved in becoming pillars of Louisville society, were somewhat offended by his drinking—or, rather, his reputation for it—while Lucy and Annie, as matrons of the town, pretended that his problem did not exist. But the youngest ones, William and Fanny, lived with it and understood it and gently tried to loft him over it. William and Fanny.

And now William was coming stronger and stronger into George's mind: good, sturdy, patient, cheerful, selfless William, as fine a Clark man as had ever trod the ground. With the thought of him, the emptinesses in George's soul began to fill up again. He put down his glass on the bench beside his chair, and folded his hands on his lap instead of refilling the glass. He looked down toward the river road, and he had a notion, a notion that came upon him from some unexplainable somewhere, that William would be along any time now.

George straightened in his chair and began to concentrate his attention on Clarksville and the river road below: his old mill, the ferry, the jetty and ditch where his canal around the Falls was to have been, the old boatyard where his mechanical upstream boats would have been built, the half-abandoned town where his great city of Clarksville would have grown.

It was strange. He had not seen or heard anything to tell him William was coming. William was, as far as anyone knew, still away off east somewhere on his travels, advocating George's causes, arguing with lawyers and creditors, perhaps stopping in Fincastle County to court his Miss Hancock. There was no reason to believe he would be coming along soon. Usually when he did come home from his travels, he would stop at his Mulberry Hill place first and send a messenger over to announce his return, and no such messenger had come. And yet, something told George:

Billy's coming.

So he listened, and watched the river road, and didn't touch his glass.

UPSTAIRS IN THE GUEST BEDROOM, FANNY SAT ROCKING, with her right elbow on the arm of the rocking chair and her chin in the palm of her right hand, her index finger laid along her cheek. There were fine little squint lines around her beautiful eyes now and vertical frown lines on her pale brow. She rocked and rocked. In the room across the hall her two sons Johnny and Ben O'Fallon were having a lively discussion about crossing the Alps, a subject planted in their imaginations by their Uncle George. Johnny believed that Hannibal's crossing had been more remarkable, but Ben felt that it would have been easy, using elephants to carry everything, and he favored Napoleon as the greater Alps-crosser. Their discussion was as spirited as if they had been veterans of those respective armies, and their voices rose and fell, erupting sometimes with scornful snorts and jeering laughter.

Standing here by the sunny window in front of Fanny's rocking chair was her son Charles William Thruston, aged five, who somehow seemed a being apart from his older half-brothers, though they were careful never to exclude him. He was a quieter boy than they, and was more interested in dogs and horses than in martial history, and the few times he had been drawn into their arguments about great soldiers he had always brought up his trump card, the only military fact he cared to know: that his father had been a Revolutionary soldier before he was twelve. This would always silence Johnny O'Fallon, who was just now going on twelve and still played with toy Redcoats.

Charles William Thruston in fact seemed to remember his father as a boy soldier instead of a man. It was as if the shock of his father's murder had erased the man, the Westport merchant, from little Charles' mind, leaving only the boy soldier. Fanny sat rocking and looked at Charles and all at once the horrible images came up whole from her memory. Little Charles' third birthday party. The father holding the boy's hand while berating a surly slave man. The Negro beginning to tremble with anger. And then, suddenly, unbelievably, lunging forward with a kitchen knife in his hand. And Captain Thruston, bewildered, gushing blood, sinking to the floor, still grasping the hand of his screaming son.

Fanny groaned now as she always did at the memory of that moment. She tried never to think of it, but it surfaced so often from her memory, suddenly and unexpectedly, as now, making these awful upwellings of grief.

She had gone later to see the Negro hanged, but that had not helped. It had only made it worse somehow, had only given her another horrid set of images: the sudden yank on rope, the *thump* of the sudden weight on the gallows, the Negro's contorted face and grotesquely tilted head, the feces dropping from his pantleg. It had not compensated for the other death, nor had it even seemed to have anything to do with it. Her brother William had taken her arms and guided her away from the spectacle, the body slowly turning, turning, the bulging eyes and craning necks of the crowd of white people.

"I hear a horse," said little Charles, turning from the sunny window to look at his mother.

"You sure, darlin'?" she said after a moment. He was so crazy about horses he was always hearing them. "I don't hear it."

"I do," he said.

Maybe he does, she thought. She got up and went to the window and stood behind him with her hands on his shoulders, looking down over the summery meadow that sloped away from the house to the distant trees by the river road. She saw and heard nothing but the rapids of the river. But there might be a horseman coming along down there. And she thought:

Might be Billy's coming home. Lordy, that would be nice.

And then, having thought it, she somehow felt sure of it. This did after all seem like the kind of a day when William would show up.

"CUPID," GEORGE CALLED INTO THE HOUSE, "FETCH glasses, and that bottle with the red wax on the cork! Here comes Billy!" And at that moment the interior of the house came alive with quick footsteps and excited voices.

He knew the horseman was William even before he saw him, because he had heard the horse jump the rail fence down by the sycamores—William's own shortcut. And now here he came out of the trees onto the meadow at a full gallop, on a big gray George had never seen before, standing in the stirrups and waving his hat. George was standing on the porch laughing already, feeling better a thousandfold. Fanny and her sons poured out of the house, all smiles and cries of welcome. Cupid followed them out with a tray and set it down, beaming all yellow-toothed, then shambled down the porch steps with his hand up, ready to take the bridle.

"By the saints! I knew it was you!" George bellowed as William swung off with a wink and a nod at Cupid.

"Ha, ha! Just can't sneak up on ye, can I?" William dumped his dusty saddlebags on the porch and began catching leaping youngsters in his arms, hugging and patting them. Then he squeezed Fanny almost breathless, she hanging on him and kicking up her heels like a ten-year-old. Then William and George pounded each other on the back, and the red seal on the special brandy was broken. Homecomings in the Clark family were just as good as they had always been.

Later, when the children were out on the meadow playing shuttlecock with the new game set William had brought them, George and Fanny and William seated themselves on the porch in facing chairs. William quickly summarized all the news of friends and relatives back in Virginia, then took a long sip from his glass, sighed, set it on the floor between his feet, and drew a letter from his pocket. "D'you remember my particular friend Lewis?"

Fanny smiled. "The smart one, with the jug-handle ears."

And George said, "The one so bowlegged his horse could walk out from under 'im and he'd not know it was gone till he fell on the ground."

William threw back his head with a laugh and his merry eyes crinkled. "Well, as y' know, two years he's been President Jefferson's secretary. He got those papers we sent for on your claims, George, and here they are, and we'll work on 'em after bit. But also he's writ me a letter that ought to interest you quite some, and I can't wait any longer for you to hear 'bout it, so here." He handed the letter to George and contemplated him as he read it, reaching over to hold Fanny's hand.

George's expression changed often as he held the rustling pages, changed from bright interest to deep thoughtfulness, with now and then a skeptically cocked eyebrow, a nod of approbation, or a shadow of sadness. He glanced up occasionally at William as he read. When he came to the end of it, he murmured, "So. The route to the Pacific." Returning to the beginning then, he reread phrases, lingered over them.

"Well, for heaven's sake, I'm perishing with curiosity," Fanny exclaimed. "Read it out loud! Or let me."

And so George began, his voice deep and deliberate, with the high, carefree shouts of the children in the background, and the tone of the letter was so confident, its scope so grand, that to Fanny it seemed that the words could have been George's own, instead of Meriwether Lewis's.

"'My plan: It is to descend the Ohio in a keeled boat of about ten tons burthen . . . thence up the Mississippi to the mouth of the Missouri, and up that river as far as its navigation is practicable with a boat of this description, there to prepare canoes of ark or rawhides, and proceed to its source, and if practicable ass over to the waters of the Columbia or Oregon River and by escending it reach the Western Ocean.'" George paused, his yes unfocused. He was remembering the Missouri, the wide, nuddy mouth of it, remembering his hand in the water, remembering all those thoughts he had had so often about the veinwork f these very rivers. Then his eyes returned to the words at the nd of his finger, and, moving the finger again, he read on:

"'I feel confident that my passage to the Western Ocean can e effected by the end of next summer or the beginning of autumn. . . . Very sanguine expectations are at this time formed y our government that the whole of that immense country waered by the Mississippi and its tributary streams, Missouri inlusive, will be the property of the United States in less than welve months from this date. . . . You will readily conceive the mportance of an early friendly and intimate acquaintance with he tribes that inhabit that country.'" George tapped the page vith his knuckle. "This is Tom Jefferson talking through your riend Lewis. His notions are stamped all over this. By heaven, his stirs me, Billy!"

"Read her about the scientifics," William urged. "It's the very hings you advised Jefferson clear back when he first wrote you bout such an explorin' trip!"

George looked up from the paper at William. "Ye remember hat, do ye! Remember that day he wrote me about it? Why, hat's twenty years if it's a day!"

"Do I ever remember it! It's been in the edge o' my mind ever ince! Read that part, George." All three were squirming.

"All right, here. 'Other objects of this mission are scienific, . . . ascertaining by celestial observation the geography of he country . . . learning the names of the nations who inhabit t, the extent and limits of their several possessions, their relation vith other tribes and nations, their languages, traditions, their rdinary occupations in fishing, hunting, war, arts, implements . . diseases prevalent among them and the remedies, the articles of commerce they may need, or furnish . . . the soil and ace of the country, its growth and vegetable productions, its animals, the mineral productions of every description, and in hort to collect the best possible information relative to whatever he country may afford as a tribute to general science.'" George aused and blew out a breath, shaking his head, and Fanny interjected:

"Mercy, but that's a tall order! All that, and canoes as well?

561

Does he think he can do all that, that little man? How would he even—"

"Wait, sister," said George, with a tilt of his head and a sly smile. "O' course he can't do any such a thing all by himself and that's why he's writ the following words. Listen:

"'Thus my friend you have a summary view of the plan, the means and the objects of this expedition. If therefore there i anything under those circumstances, in this enterprise, which would induce you to participate with me in its fatigues, its danger and its honors, believe me there is no man on earth with whom I should feel equal pleasure in sharing them as with yourself. The President has authorized me to say that in the event of your accepting this proposition he will grant you a captain's commission.'"

"Oh, my dear Billy!" she cried, jumping up and clapping her hands to his cheeks. "You! Why, if you go with him, he could do all that so easily it would be a lark! Oh, I'm so proud of you. Billy! Oh, haven't I always told you you'd get some chance to make yourself as grand a name as any!"

"Hey! Hey," he laughed, grabbing her wrists and pulling her hands away from his ruddy cheeks. "Hey, I haven't even said yet I'll go! Ha, ha!"

George kept scanning the letter. Then he looked up and said, "So, then. At last Tom Jefferson's going to do it: the route to the Pacific!" He paused. "Will you go?"

"I'm considering it right hard. Thought to get your opinions on it."

"My opinion ye fairly know: do it. I wish I could. Too late for me now, though. You do it, I say. Such a chance, by God, by God!" He shook his head and his eyes were moist and full of westering. "That about the States owning that land inside a year. What d'you reckon they're up to? Buyin' it from Napoleon, or what?" Three years ago Spain had ceded her Louisiana Territory to France, and since then every thinking Westerner had been wondering and worrying what the ambitious Bonaparte might intend to do in the New World.

"Lord knows what they're doing," William said. "By the way, Fanny, Lewis warns me this whole plan o' his is a secret o' the most delicate kind, so we dasn't speak on't outside of ourselves.'

"Good for me!" she exclaimed. "I fancy knowing something no other woman anywhere knows. If other women thought as I do, there would ne'er be gossip."

They laughed with her, then George said, "If we lived by the Shawnee code, there'd be precious little of it. Their punishment for gossip about people is death."

"What a splendid idea!" Fanny exclaimed. "Tho' I doubt it would silence some Louisville women I know."

"Ha, ha! I'll say this, though," William ventured. "We'd have no government. Every man jack'd be on the gallows a week after he took office!"

They laughed so that Fanny's boys stopped their game and looked curiously toward the porch. George gazed upon William and Fanny and for the moment was almost happy. This news of the western exploration had so affected him that he felt as young as they. And it strengthened his old faith in Tom Jefferson. Once, not long ago, in a letter to Jefferson, George had asked him to consider William for appointment to some kind of leadership in the West where his abilities might be used and some honors gained, and he had reminded the President that he had every right to expect such a favor. And now this. It was obvious that Tom Jefferson still held the Clark name in high esteem. That was very gratifying.

William was saying now:

". . . to keep it a secret from the British mostly, I daresay. The President and Lewis are of a mind on that. Neither of 'em trusts Britain as far as a one-arm man can fling an ox."

"I don't either," George said. "And I'd wager this expedition o' theirs is in the nature of a race, to dominate that western space before Britain gets a hold on it. Ever since Mackenzie went cross Canada, I've had a spooky notion that th' Northwest will be full o' Scotch fur traders and Sir Merchants before we ever set foot in it." He pointed his forefinger like a pistol toward William. "Y' better go, and not go slow, that's my thinking. We'll never be peaceful with Britain till they're back on their side o' the sea." He opened the letter again. "Now I would take issue with 'em about this, though: the size of the expedition. Back at the first, I told Tom that four or five gents, of the best caliber, traveling light, would best serve, as so small a number wouldn't alarm the savages. Looks here as how he means to make it a lot bigger party. A ten-ton boat! Jove! Don't they know what it takes to move a ten-ton boat up a fast river? Why, thirty or forty men just to take turns a-rowin'! Or else," he growled, "one o' General Clark's Unpatented Nonexistent Upriver Mechanical Barge-Paddlin' Engines. Mark my word, Billy, every day you'll curse all that weight a thousand times. Here where he asks you to scout up some hardy young men, as he says, 'accustomed to bearing bodily fatigue in a pretty considerable degree.' I'll say this for him, he does foresee the strain o' such a load, but what I wonder is, does he know y'll fair be a crew o' galley slaves goin' up that Missouri? Meseems your friend's been in the White House so

563

long, he desires to take it all with 'im, desks, bureaus, draperies, casements, and all! Ten tons, three thousand miles? B'God, that'd give Hannibal a hernia!"

William rolled his head back and guffawed. He loved to hear George rumble on in such spirit as this. And he knew George was right about the burden. William himself had been to New Orleans and back twice by riverboat, and he well knew that upstream rowing is slave work. "Well," he said, "I'd reckon it's on account of all that science he wants done along the way. And too, from what I've heard by Missouri fur traders I met, the Sioux up the Missouri are mean as pirates. I guess it would take a considerable strong party to push on by such as them."

Fanny's face darkened for an instant with worry. She had been imagining this daydream of a venture as a peaceful trek through a gigantic landscape with nothing more dangerous than perhaps a few bears or oversized serpents. She liked it that there was no war in the land, and had not expected she would have to worry about her beloved brother fighting Indians again. Now George was saying:

"I'll grant you that. But I'll wish luck to anybody who has to do natural science and haul a ship up that bedamned Missouri at the same time. Ha! Well, maybe His Excellency the President figures you'll want a ship to bring 'im back a live mammoth. I remember he doubts there's maybe ancient beasties still roaming in those places. Like those." He tilted his head toward a pile of giant fossil bones just off the porch, specimens he had been collecting in the Falls, and in salt licks of the region, at Jefferson's request. "He expects ye to run onto a Megalonyx, no doubt, or a mammoth at the least. Y' be wary of mammoths, now, hear? Ha, ha!"

"How can you laugh?" Fanny asked George. "What if there are such things, and your own brother meets them?"

"Well, if there are, I'd like to've been the first man to see one. Since I can't, I'm glad it'll be Billy." He winked at William. "I don't worry about Billy, but the Megalonyx better watch out. As for Lewis, well, all he'll have to do is stand his ground, and a charging mammoth would just past right 'twixt his bow-legs. Ha, ha!" George was having a rare good time making light of the dangers, trying to mask his own deep-flowing anxieties. It was not huge beasts that concerned him, but the real dangers he knew attended long marches: Starvation. Cold. Injuries. Bad judgment. Exhaustion. Indians. Recklessness on the part of vainglorious leaders. Disease and demoralization among the men. William would have to follow Lewis. George trusted William's good sense, but Lewis's wisdom was an unknown quantity. And so he said:

"This friend of yours. Ye trust him all the way?"

"With my life," William said immediately, not pausing to ponder it. He drained his glass and reached down for the bottle, and dribbled the remainder into their glasses. George called:

"Cupid! Fetch us that bottle with the green wax on the cork!" The old slave, his poll frosted with white kinks, brought it at once. William took his hand and said. "My boy York asked me to tell you. 'Hey, Cupid.'" The old slave smiled and replied:

"Please to tell him the same, Mast' Billy. Tell me, sir, you goin' take that ol' fat boy Yo'k?"

"Eh? Take 'im where?" William passed George a lighted pipe.

"To where you goin', sir. To th' 'Cific Oshum."

George chuckled at William, then said, "Cupid, ye scoundrel, what've I said about eavesdropping?"

"I wasn't, Gen'l Clark, sir. Clark men just got big voices. I can't fetch you a jug with my fingers poke in my earho's."

William laughed, his ruddy cheeks furrowed with deep smile-lines. "Cupid, you're bad as that York is. Yes, I'll take 'im. What would 'e do with 'imself, without me to pester? Just sit an' turn to lard, is all. Now scat. And not a word o' this to a living soul, y' hear?"

"By what I see," George said through a stream of exhaled smoke, passing back the pipe, "you don't need my opinion. Y're decided on going." Fanny looked at William, biting her lower lip.

"Pert near," William admitted. He saw a momentary shadow go over George's face, and understood what it was. So he said:

"Jonathan can take over your suits and all. He'll prob'ly do a lot better by you than I've done. He's got law in 'is bone marrow."

"Aye. Well," George said. "But he's all wrapped in his own affairs. You've been the best helpmeet a man ever had. I'll . . . I'll miss ye, youngster."

George sat for a while, moist-eyed, gazing westward. He drank half a glass down without saying anything, while Fanny nursed a glass of sherry and watched her sons swat their new shuttlecock to and fro down on the sunny meadow, Ben and Charles against Johnny. William, who was accustomed to his brother's pensive spells, sat silent, gazing eastward, back toward Virginia, whence he had just come, and now the hazy blue distances dissolved and he was beside the bricked-in spring on the hillside where he had last dallied with his Judy Hancock. Another of her picnics.

Picnics were her favorite diversions, and that babbling spring among ferns and dogwood trees, with its little brick terrace and pewter dipper and stone bench, was her favorite place on the whole Hancock estate for picnics. She seemed to be aware that the place surrounded and enhanced her fair beauty as a filigreed frame does a portrait. And there Judy would take William for picnics and allow him to gaze upon her as if she were a picture in a gallery. They would nibble on dainty tidbits her father's chef had prepared and packed in a basket, and she would talk to William of all manner of lovely and exquisite things out of her education: of fables, of music, of Grecian gods and goddesses, of Florentine art. And to William, Judy herself was a goddess-child, work of art, her voice music. It was hard for him to remember sometimes that she was only twelve; he would see her as the lady she was to become. Sometimes he thought he understood now how Bill Croghan had been, waiting for Lucy to come of age. William was surprised that he could spend so many hours in the company of a twelve-year-old and not be bored, but she seemed to know more soul-stirring things about the loftier realms of civilization than anyone. She could write poems that marched along in cadence and rhymed at the ends, poems full of words like Pride, and Charity, Prudence, Vanity, and Forbearance. She knew of an ancient Greek island where some lady poet had run a sort of outdoor girls' school, and William would daydream of dozens of beautiful creatures, like Judy and her sisters, scantily clad in diaphanous shifts, romping through meadows, and every part of his soul and body would be stirred by those reveries. The other Hancock girls had simply faded from William's ken, into courtships and marriages with elegant neighborhood swains, and so it was turning out true, what he had told his mother in her last hour: it *would* be Judy Hancock. Her father had agreed that when she became eighteen, if they both still so desired, he would sign his permission for a marriage license. *Six years to wait!* William had left Fincastle in a daze, wondering how he could endure such an eternity.

But then this letter from Meriwether Lewis had reached him, and now those six years did not seem so much at all. And what a lady Judy would have become by the time William returned from the Western Sea, crowned with an explorer's laurels!

William blinked away these fancies, almost embarrassed, wondering: *What if George knew what's in my mind! He'd think I'm naive. Probably say I'm thinking like a novel-reader.*

And now he was looking at George, at the saddened eyes, the bitter downturn in the corner of his mouth, the little red capillaries in his face, his hands gnarled and big-knuckled from arthritis and his joints stiff with rheumatism. George knew the sorry truth about laurels. William realized suddenly, with an uprushing in his breast, that almost everything he knew, every manly trait and skill he possessed, George had taught him. *No greater a man has walked this land*, he thought.

And now he thought of one more thing he could do for George.

A big thing.

At that moment, like a statue coming to life, George inhaled, sighed, sipped from his glass and spoke:

"I'm glad it's a Clark going. I'm glad it's you. I pushed the frontier to the Mississippi ere I reached the end o' my chain. Now you go the rest of the way. Y' know what I wish?"

"What?"

"That Ma was still here, so we could walk in and tell 'er."

"Aye, Brother," William said. "Wouldn't ye love to see her face!"

"Ha, ha! She'd probably have some proverb on the proper way to greet a Megalonyx!"

Fanny smiled and put her hand over her mouth, but her eyes were suddenly abrim with tears at the thought of her mother.

"Here's to Ma," said George, hoisting his glass, "who gave us the red in our hair and the flint in our soul."

The brothers clicked their glasses and drank, then William hoisted his again. Fanny's children, wearied by their play, were coming up the meadow toward the porch, likely thinking of supper. A smell of roast meat was wafting from the kitchen house.

"And here's to Pa, who gave us kind hearts and steel in our sinew," said William.

"Aye. To Pa."

"To them both. May they rest in peace together."

Fanny rose from her chair, her lip between her teeth, touched each brother on the shoulder, and then moved across the porch to meet her sons and steer them into the house. In this family, it seemed to her, no matter what might have befallen any old dream, there was always a new dream.

George and William sat in the light of the descending sun, drinking, mellow, looking westward, making hmmms in their throats, thinking of rivers. "Tell me," George asked eventually, "just how drunk might ye be willin' to get?"

"Hard to say, Brother, hard to say. But before we find out, let's us go eat, and tell those boys o' Fanny's some tall tales."

Once again, subtly, William was steering George from the bottle.

"By damn, that's a good idea," said George. "They could stand to hear about how I first met Logan the Mingo, couldn't they?"

"And I'll do y' one better," William replied. "I'll tell 'em how I met Indians I've not even met yet!"

"Capital!" George gripped his chair arms to hoist his stiff frame. He grunted. He swayed a little, then limped toward the door. "I think you should tell 'em about the giant Sioux chief who rides to church on a wild mammoth."

William rubbed his eyes and followed George in, chuckling. "To *church*? A Sioux?"

"Well, then, make him a Delaware. It doesn't matter, as long as it's the truth. Hey, I'm going to miss you, Billy. I wish I could be along."

"Hey, George. One thing's sure: with me, you're always along."

31

FALLS OF THE OHIO

October, 1803

EVERYONE STOOD STILL AND WATCHED AS GENERAL GEORGE Rogers Clark clumped stiffly back and forth with his cane and old army boots across the deck and in and out of the cabin of the keelboat that Captain Lewis had had built at Pittsburgh. George would tap the new, fragrant, yellow-gray oaken deck planks and gunwales with his hickory walking-stick and listen to the *clack, clack* with a tilted ear as if he were a musician tuning a fine instrument. The men on deck watched him and said nothing; the only other sounds were the burble of the sparkling Ohio around the hull, the steady rush of the Falls a few hundred yards upstream, the rustle of golden autumn foliage in a cool breeze, and the murmuring voices of the crowd of soldiers and townspeople on the wharf and the shore. Meriwether Lewis, dressed for this occasion in his full army uniform of the new style with parallel rows of buttonhole braid, a cocked bicorn hat on his head, stood with his thick bowlegs wide apart and his hands clasped behind his back, waiting patiently and glancing from one to another of the Clark brothers as the old warrior, in his obsolete, swallow-tailed, buff-and-blue Revolutionary War uniform, appraised the vessel. General Clark's coat was creased and linty and smelled of camphor from its long hibernation in a chest, but he looked grand and grave and dignified. He reminded Lewis of Washington.

William Clark, in a new captain's uniform, hat in hand, strolled alongside his brother, pink-cheeked with pride, merry eyes glinting like new blue buttons through his red lashes, his copper-red forelock now and then stirred by the breeze, and he turned once or twice to wink at young Lewis. Two other Clark brothers stood on the deck, likewise tall and solid. There was Edmund, with his thick red hair, fortyish, a little jowly now; and Jonathan, prosperous-looking, with graying sidewhiskers. Jonathan was thinking that poor Captain Lewis had inherited his father's looks instead of his mother's.

Standing near Lewis's feet was a huge, black, broad-skulled Newfoundland dog, panting with the tip of a pink tongue hanging from his grinning mouth, watching the old general tap about. At length the quiet intensity of the scene made the dog look up at Lewis with quizzical eyes, and a long, squeaking whimper from his throat intruded on the stillness. "Hush, Scannon," Captain Lewis whispered, and the dog flopped down with his chin on his forepaws to continue watching the man with the cane tap on his master's boat.

Finally, George whacked the mast once with his cane and turned to Lewis.

"Well, Captain, she's snug and sturdy enough for your purpose, I'd reckon. And roomy in th' hold. Shows care and skill. Not bad. As I told William, it's a bigger scow than I'd ever want to haul so far up the Missouri. But not bad. Do what I said, like I did on the *Willing*. Have your carpenters make hinged lockers along here, that can be put up as breastwork. M, hm. She's fifty-five feet, y' say? And draws how much?"

"Three feet unloaded," said Lewis. "About four loaded."

"Not bad. The shallower the better, from what I've seen o' the Missouri."

"I'm glad you think she was worth waitin' for," Lewis said, a bit surly. "Those scoundrelly boatwrights took twice as long and charged me twice as much as I expected. Lazy louts, drunkards! They'd get a skinful when ye'd think—" He stopped suddenly, his eyes darting with embarrassment, apparently just remembering General Clark's reputation as a sot.

"Well," George said with a wry smile, "I've noticed that among boatwrights myself."

William looked ashore at the crowd. There was a colorful mob of rivermen, citizens, Negroes, and even Indians on the bank and the wharf, talking in groups and admiring the vessel. Among the onlookers were his sisters Fanny, Ann, and Lucy, with a horde of their children. Sitting on the dock atop William's field desk and trunk was York, red bandanna on his head and a gold ring in his right ear, beaming and nodding importantly, talking to a cluster of river folk and slaves. Since learning that he would be a member of this portentous and mysterious journey for the Government, York had become something of a star in his own eyes and had been making the most of his newfound eminence. Right now he was rubbing his great paunch with his palm and telling his listeners:

"Mast' Billy say he cou'n' go lest I go 'long."

"York." William spoke to him over the side.

"Jessaminit," York advised his audience, then rolled his eyes up and said, "Yes, Mast' Billy?"

"I thought ye had my gear on board long ago."

"Oh, why, no, sir, I surely don't yet."

"Well, then, by heaven, if it won't impose on ye too much, maybe y' could bestir that great bulk o' yours and do it, ere we cast off. What sayee, my man?"

"Why, surely could, surely could, sir," York replied cheerfully, smiling large, and with an apologetic nod to his listeners, he began thrashing like a beached whale to rise.

Jonathan grinned. "There, I think," he said to William, "might prove to be your chiefest load to pull up the Missouri."

"He'll work out," William said. "York, what did I promise I'd do if ye prove dead weight?"

York, standing now and reaching down for the chest, straightened up and rolled his eyes. "Feed me to the Mammus," he said in what may have been either real or mock fright.

"Aye. So now shake a leg there. Mammoths," William explained to Jonathan.

York reached down and grasped one handle of the heavy chest, snatched it up as easily as if it were empty, and guided it onto his shoulder. Then, with his other hand, he hoisted the field desk and held it aloft as if he were bearing a tea service. He started up the gangplank.

"See?" William said to Jonathan. "Even loafin', he can do three men's work. I think we'll be glad we brought 'im."

Some of the soldiers Lewis had drafted on the way down the river were in their shirt sleeves, at work putting aboard kegs and crates. Standing at ease on the shore was a squad of young soldiers whom William had hand-picked from among the Kentucky army posts. Most of them he had known for years. Each private soldier attached to the expedition would get ten dollars a month and food and clothing, and as added inducement had been promised a piece of land. Several sons of local gentry had applied to William for berths in the westerly venture, hoping to achieve some personal glory, but William had discouraged those who were unaccustomed to labor or hardship. He had selected men not only for their qualities of character, but for their skills. Private William Bratton, now standing solemn and thoughtful on the riverbank, a twenty-five-year-old Virginia-born Irishman, taller than six feet and erect as a post, was a superb hunter, blacksmith, and gunsmith, and professed to be "likely the world's only all-sober Irishman." John Shields, at thirty-five the oldest member of the party, was a blacksmith and gunsmith, and also had spent years as a boatbuilder. Even the expedition's youngest member, tall, gray-eyed, eighteen-year-old Private George Shannon, was an accomplished carpenter, as well as a fine hunter and horseman; he also brought to the party a pure tenor voice and a repertory of almost all the songs anyone had ever heard. John Colter, going on thirty, was a tall, blue-eyed, quick-minded huntsman who had already compiled an adventuresome history as a scout and ranger. Sergeants Nathaniel Hale Pryor and Charles Floyd, who were cousins, were both masters of virtually every known skill, from surveying to hide-curing, and were judicious leaders of men besides. William had rounded up a commendable squad of Kentuckians indeed to add to the crew Lewis had been recruiting on his way down the Ohio to Clarksville. And he was getting leads on others. "Remember, now," George was telling him, "at Massac, don't fail to interview George Drouillard and take 'im on for an interpreter if he'll go. He knows the Indian hand-talk and all the foreign tongues as well, and ye'll need 'im, or someone like 'im. He's got a steel nerve, too, just like his pa." Young Drouillard was a son of one of George's old interpreters, Pierre Drouillard.

William nodded. "I'll do it." He had already enlisted as Indian interpreter a private named George Gibson, who was a hunter and fiddle-player as well. But, keeping in mind his mother's old admonition never to put all the eggs in the same basket, William had resolved to have at least two good Indian interpreters before starting up the Missouri, in case something might happen to one of them.

"Gentlemen," Lewis interrupted them now, "while there's fair daylight, we should be taking our leave. General," he said, extending his hand to George and squinting up at him into the afternoon sun, "we're indebted to you for your good counsel. And o' course for all your early deeds that enabled this venture. I pray you'll enjoy some civil justice while we're gone, and I promise I'll watch over your brother—though he's probably a better hand at watching over me. Shall we get the men aboard, Cap'n Clark?"

"Godspeed, then," George said, releasing Lewis's small but iron hand. "Do your best for your country, and I pray she'll reward ye better than she's done me. Youngster," he said now to William, "step ashore 'fore ye cast off, I've something for ye that might be useful. Jonathan, fare thee well and I'll see you soon." Jonathan was going downriver a few miles to visit his daughter Eleanor and her husband Reverend Temple, and see his first granddaughter. He was going to ride down that far on the *Discovery*. He put an arm over George's shoulders, and another over Edmund's, and hugged them firmly in an unusually open display of affection; it was obvious that Jonathan was emotionally stirred by the portents of this day, though he had said little. Then Edmund steadied George down the gangplank to the wharf. William followed them off, and ordered his recruits aboard. Ann and Lucy came forward and hugged him, faces stoical but wet-eyed, and wished him success and safety. Then Fanny gave him a kiss on the cheek and a tearful Godspeed.

The crowd was growing excited now as the departure neared. Several citizens began checking the priming in their pistols and rifles, women began fidgeting and getting their handkerchiefs ready; musicians on shore shifted their drums and fifes and fiddles. Sergeant Floyd ran out the little American flag on the *Discovery*'s stern standard, and crewmen stood to the mooring ropes, others to the oars.

George nodded toward Cupid, who came forward and handed him a long, cloth-wrapped object. Cupid murmured, "Godspeed, Mast' Billy," and then receded into the crowd.

"Here y'are, youngster," George said, handing the object to William.

"Thankee, George," William said, holding the thing and looking at it. "And what might it be?"

"A shade umbrella," George said. "Maybe prevent you from fryin' your brains someday. This opens it. But y'll notice it's also a smoking-pipe tomahawk."

William held the contraption across his chest. "That'll keep me busy," he smiled. "I thankee, George."

"It's precious little compared with what y've given me. But what else I have for you will be more useful," George said, looking deep into William's eyes. "It's advice. Here's a thing y' might need to know, with so far to go. Your friend Lewis is a somber, rainy sort and he might not know this, but listen: men can go in times farther than they think they can—if ye give 'em three things along the way:

"Songs. Jokes. And a dream o' glory." He paused, and William knew he was remembering Vincennes. George concluded:

"I know it, youngster. Those three things will do sometimes in the place o' food and comfort, where the leading o' men is concerned."

LINES WERE CAST OFF A FEW MINUTES LATER AND THE MUSIcians struck up a squeaky, squawky "Johnny Has Gone for a Soldier," as the *Discovery* moved out into the current, heavily sternladen, gunwales less than two feet above the water, the troops standing at attention with their rifles at Present Arms, Sergeant Floyd atop the poop deck leaning on the tiller. There was a rising buzz of voices on shore as the vessel moved away; then, when she was twenty yards out, three cheers went up from the crowd, punctuated by a staccato of skyward gunshots and shouts of "Godspeed! Lord love ye, lads! Hiyo! Hiyo!" At a command from Captain Lewis, a salute was fired into the air by the riflemen aboard the keelboat, and the shots echoed back and forth across the river. York and Cupid gazed at each other across the widening water with tears streaming down their black cheeks, and waved slowly. And likewise, George Rogers Clark and William Clark gazed at each other, each with a hand to his forehead in a soldier's salute, not looking away till distance and the blur of tears had melted their blue-coated images away. The odds were strong, they knew though they never had discussed it, that they would never see each other again.

George watched the *Discovery* grow smaller and smaller on the breast of the Ohio, and his heart felt so swollen that he could not turn away from it and let anyone see his face. He watched it go and remembered that June day almost a quarter of a century ago when he with his own high-spirited boys had set out from this same place under an ominous eclipse of the sun, bound for the Mississippi Country.

Thank God anyway he's going in peace and not to war, he thought. Because he's the best of us all.

William had been the best friend and champion George had ever had, and George had long been aware of that, but within the last month William had done something so generous that

573

George could not even think of it without feeling humbled. A his last piece of business before departing for the West, Willia had sold his whole inheritance, the Mulberry Hill estate, Jonathan for ten thousand dollars.

And then he had applied the entire sum toward paying off few more of George's creditors.

"So BILLY'S GONE WEST," GEORGE MURMURED, GAZIN into the blazing hickory-log fire in the fireplace and sipping o some persimmon brandy that one of his old troopers had create and brought to him. "Gone West to get some glory."

"As he well deserves," Fanny added.

"Leaves me to do my own beggin' again, though, it does. George sighed and reached to the table for his letter-box. Beggin He was going to try it once more. It had long been plain that h country was never going to appropriate any money to reimburs him for those old war expenses. "One thing these United State has a-plenty: land. I know because I got it for them."

He set out ink bottle and paper, took a sip of brandy, an rubbed his forehead while pondering on the words he was goin to write. He could hear Venus and Cupid talking low in th kitchen as they worked, knocking bowls, making dough for to morrow's bread.

Fanny, darning one of Ben's stockings, watched George pre pare to write. She knew it was odious to him, this begging fo what he thought was his rightful reward, but she was glad to se him turn to the task again, after having given it up for so long William's departure for the Far West evidently had inspire George to try once again. Fanny's own soul was expanding wit hope again, with the bittersweet faith that good things could yo happen.

She had even begun to believe that she might marry again something she had vowed never even to think of. Today at th wharf, in the holiday excitement of the expedition's departure Fanny had become aware of the attention of several fine-lookin young gentlemen in the crowd. She had realized that she stil was, despite her misfortunes, as pretty and well-born and accom plished as any of Louisville's younger belles, and certainly not s silly. And so her heart was rich with empathy for George, an with an optimism for renewed efforts. She said, "You're going ask for land?"

He stirred, and turned toward her, his expression earnest. H was pleased to answer her question; he was glad of any excuse t put off such writing.

"Aye, Fanny. A lot of land." He shifted in his chair. "Let me tell you a story you might not remember, so's y'll understand what I'm askin' 'em for. This is a good story. Ma and Pa and the boys used to like it, but I think you were too wee-bitty to've understood it back then."

"Good, a story. How long since you told me a story!" She sounded eager as a young girl. She crumpled her chin and was blinking.

"So, then. It was right after I captured Vincennes, in '79. Most impressed by the happenings was a Piankeshaw chief there, named Sonotabac; Tobacco's Son, we called him."

"I remember his name."

"This chief was so bumfuzzled by what we did that he trailed me around like that black dog o' Cap'n Lewis' does him. He proclaimed himself a Big Knife, my brother, and he tried to give me anything I'd take. He offered me squaws, wanted to get some Long Knife blood in the veins of his people. He offered—"

"Did, did you accept the . . ."

George grinned at her and slapped his thigh. "You and Pa! Ha, ha! That was *his* first question, too! Well, the answer is no. As I told that panderin' Indian, no thankee, I'm already betrothed. And so, next day he . . ." Fanny was about to interrupt to ask him about that betrothal, that old half-secret romantic episode she and her sisters had always wondered about, but George put up his hand to shush her and went on: "Next day that chief came to me and he offered me the deed to a huge, *huge* tract o' land that his tribe controlled. I say huge. About one hundred and fifty thousand acres it amounted to when I surveyed it out. Think o' that!"

"One hundred and fifty thousand!"

"Right. And listen, baby sister: D' ye know where that land is?"

"No."

"You're sittin' on it this minute." Her mouth dropped open. "Aye," he said. "This little parcel this house is built on is one corner of it. The rest of it's up there and over there." He swept his hand north and east. "The Illinois Regiment Grant. My old boys and their families live on it. You know the meetings I go to in Louisville every month? I still administer all that land for all my old troopers. It's the last public service I'll ever do, and I reckon I'll do it long as I can walk and talk. Y' didn't know that was the story o' this land, did you?"

She was shaking her head. "But, but did you *give* it to them, or what?"

"Back to my story, and y'll understand. Y'see, when that

Piankeshaw offered me that land, I doubted I could accept it as a private man. Because then, what I was, all I thought I was was a soldier for Virginia. So I took that deed, and put it in trust for the State of Virginia."

"My heavens! And *could* it have been yours?"

"As well as I can make out the laws, yes. But what happened then was, I gave that deed to Virginia, as this tract fell in their charter lands. Well, then, Sister, when the war was over, and it was time for the State to reward my regiment o' heroes with the land it'd promised 'em, Virginia didn't want to give that land to my boys, because it was on this side of the river. D'you know," he said, now jabbing his forefinger into the palm of his hand, "I had to go to Capitol and all but do corporal harm to those be-damned Assemblymen—*years* it was I fought those snot-snifflin picayunes!—before they'd grant those promised lands to my boys? And it was this land as'd been given to *me!*" She was shaking her head slowly, making silent Os with her mouth. He went on: "Sister, I know you've heard my old tunes of lament so long and so loud you probably try to stop up your ears to 'em by now. But that about this land is just like everything else that's been done me, and compared with the rest it's so niggardly you've never heard me speak of't."

"Oh, George! This I can hardly believe! I've known what-all Billy was fighting for in your cause, but . . . this too!"

"Aye. This too. And so, that's that bedtime story. The share o' this Illinois Regiment Grant I finally got for my pains was some ten thousand acres. Most of it the creditors took from me. I signed a great spread of't over to Pa so those vultures couldn't snatch it, and this little piece we sit on is all I have left me. That's the story, and now here's what I aim to do, baby sister," he said, picking up the quill again and twirling it before her eyes. "Right now—I mean, as soon as I have another tongueload o' persimmon juice to wash the putrid taste o' begging out o' my mouth—I'm going to write me a letter to the Committee on Public Lands at Congress. And I'm going to tell Congress that same bedtime story, and I'm going to ask for a hundred and fifty thousand acres—a same-size tract as I gave Government—somewhere out of the Public Lands. Either in this territory I won 'em, or out in that Western country Tom Jefferson's just bought from Bonaparte. Now, the land-grabbers are already all over this old territory like ants on a bread crust. But that beyond the Mississippi, where Billy's headed now, why, it's next to boundless, I'd say, and I reckon I deserve some parcel o' that before the ants get it. I know that sounds like a big asking, a hundred fifty thou-

576

sand acres. But it only amounts to one five-thousandth part of what I won for this country, and they'd be damned mean to deny me that." He sipped the brandy and savored it on his tongue, and adjusted the paper in just the right position. "Our friend Senator Breckenridge says he'll take the letter to Congress for me," George muttered, "and then I'll sit here and wait and pray there's a shred o' conscience somewhere in Congress."

"If," she said, "if they gave you land out West, would you leave us and go there?"

He looked and saw the woebegone look in her eyes, and chuckled. "Why, no, Fanny, what I'd do is sell it, and if I got a fair price I might pay off the rest o' these damned debt-vultures and pass the rest of my years in peace. Or . . ." Now he paused and got that long look in his eyes again. He was remembering the rich Mississippi bottomlands near St. Louis, the vast spaces beyond. "Or maybe if there was some left over, I might remove there. And then I'd bring the rest of ye there after me. And maybe there we'd all find the peace and plenty I brought you here for, eh? How would you like to pass the rest o' your days in sight of the greatest river of 'em all, eh, Fanny?"

She smiled, and the little dimples appeared in her mouth corners. "I see it's true what I've been thinking just lately: There's just no bounds on what this family can dream, is there?"

"No. A body can dream as far as a star, as Ma would say. Now excuse me, Fanny, as I'm going to tell Congress a bedtime story."

It was an hour later when he had finished recounting the history of the land tract in his letter, and when he looked up from it the fire was low, and Fanny's chair was vacant. The house was still; even the old servants had retired from their noisy duties in the kitchen. George decanted a little more liquor. His brain was rushing with its own familiar night-hum, and from far down the hill came the sound of the rapids. He wrote again, his pen scratching, while the tall clock across the room woodenly ticked the seconds away.

> . . . I engaged in the Revolution with all the Ardour that Youth could possess. My zeal and Ambition rose with my success, determined to save those frontiers which had been the seat of my toil, at the hazard of my life and fortune. At the most gloomy period of the War, when a Ration could not be purchased on Publick Credit, I risked my own, gave my Bonds, Mortgaged my lands for supplys, paid strick attention to evry department, flattered the friendly

and confus^d the hostil tribes . . . and carried my point.

Thus at the end of the War I had the pleasure of seeing my Country secure. But with the loss of my Manual activity, and a prospect of future indigence—Demands of very great amount were not paid, others with depreciated Paper—Suits commenced against me for those sums in Specie

My Military and other lands, earned by my service, as far as they would extend were apropreated for the paym^t of those debts, and demands yet remain to a considerable amount more than the remains of a shatter^d fortune will pay

This is truly my situation—I see no other recorce remaining but to make application to my Country for redress—hoping that they will so far ratify the Grant as to allow to your Memorialist an equal quantity of land now the property of the United States. . . .

There. He had done his begging. And having scraped so low, it was less hard to beg even more abjectly for any bone they might toss him if they wouldn't give him the lands. So he added:

. . . or such other relief as may seem proper.

Then he signed it and thrust it far across the table in disgust. He sat in the ticking stillness now with his glass in his hand and gazed into the coals and thought back to that higher and happier part of the day, when he had attended the start of William's brave new venture. He raised his glass to the level of his eyes and, although he was alone in the room, he said aloud:

"Godspeed ye, youngster, to the Western Sea. Here's to your dream o' sweet glory. And may they never ever curdle yours as they did mine."

32

Proceded on a jentle brease up the Missourie.
        —from the journal of William Clark

The bow cannon bucked on its swivel and belched smoke and its *boom* rolled away over the broad brown Mississippi. The crowd of farmers and hunters on the shore whooped and stamped and fired their guns into the air. Two barefoot boys, frowning with self-importance, freed the mooring lines from the pilings and threw them to the crew. And the *Discovery*, low in the water with her ten-ton cargo, slowly parted from the muddy riverbank where she had lain all winter. With her flag flapping at the stern, she swung out onto the sun-glaring expanse of water. A sergeant's deep voice called a cadence, the oars, eleven on a side, began rising and dipping, swishing and dripping, and sluggishly the boat began to move across the current toward the distant mouth of the Missouri.

God, but she's a ponderous barge of a thing, William thought. He stood on the roof of the poop-deck cabin looking down along the rows of faces of the men on the oars, and thought of the hundreds and hundreds of miles they would have to row this overloaded floating fortress against the Missouri's current, and he felt a wave of pity for them. They would be like galley slaves, as George had said, though right now they all looked as cheerful and eager as a boatload of excursionists on a Sunday outing. Master Sergeant Ordway stood like a slavemaster calling the measure out in a deep, round voice. *"Yo-ooooooo, heyyyyyyy. Yo-ooooooo, heyyyyyyy."* Beside William, Sergeant Charles Floyd stood with the tiller under his arm, squinting past the mast into the afternoon sunlight, and he looked as if he were straining with all his might to keep himself from laughing aloud with joy.

On the deck of the bow fifty feet forward stood the two Missouri Creole river pilots, Cruzatte and Labiche, who had agreed not only to accompany the expedition all the way, but to enlist as privates in the U.S. Army—a remarkable commitment for two independent *voyageurs*. Cruzatte, small and wiry, was an extraordinary creature. Having but one eye, and that near-sighted, he was nevertheless known as the best riverman on the Missouri. He was also a master of sign language and the Omaha Indian tongue, and could play a fiddle to make one's legs twitch. To William he seemed like a combination of the riverman Manifee and George's old one-eyed steersman Davy Pagan, and thus sure to be full of good luck.

In a bright red dugout pirogue ahead of the keelboat were eight more local Frenchmen who had been attached to the party, but these were only temporary. They had been hired to paddle that canoe with its freight only as far up the Missouri as the *Discovery* could navigate, and there they would be transferred to the big boat and help bring it back down to St. Louis. Six American army privates also were on such temporary duty, and at this moment they were rowing a smaller pirogue, painted white, which moved alongside the red one. These two vessels were also heavily laden, carrying supplies and equipment that had overflowed the keelboat. Friend Lewis had thought of an astonishing number of things to bring along, and although every item made sense in terms of the expedition's purpose, William felt almost overwhelmed by the sheer mass and variety of things. Lewis had spent most of the winter across the river in St. Louis, purchasing more supplies and interviewing traders and officials, leaving to William the enormous tasks of training the men and listing and packing all the equipment and provisions.

William took a last look back at Camp Wood, the cluster of cabins that had been the first winter quarters of the Corps of Discovery: the trampled parade ground, the planks and broken barrels and skids, the rifle targets off against the shore, the bare flagpole. Here William had spent the busiest winter of his life, hammering the forty-five boisterous, headstrong, hard-drinking volunteers into a disciplined, spirited crew, weeding out those who weren't quite right for the rigors ahead. Here he had re-designed the keelboat's superstructure according to Brother George's recommendations, adding the hinged, bulletproof lockers, and ridgepoles for a canopy to shade the rowers. And here he had labored for weeks packing and making inventories of the thousands of items of food, tools, and weapons, ammunition, navigational instruments, medicines, liquors, papers, notebooks, ropes, clothes and boots, tin, iron, and blacksmith tools, and a profusion of Indian gifts, enough of every conceivable necessity to last the expedition for at least two years in a vast wilderness which was a complete blank on every map and which might or ight not be hospitable to human life. Lewis had acquired several new inventions, through the War Department and other urces, that he felt might sometime save them in an emergency. The gunpowder was in heavy lead canisters with water-ht screw-on lids; when emptied, the canisters could be melted wn to make rifle balls. He had obtained many big tins of porle soup, dried and fortified with iron, which might feed the orps someday when the hunters could get no game meat. He d bought an airgun, a rifle powered by compressed air in a ass globe. It was an inaccurate and erratic weapon—in fact, ewis had slightly wounded a woman in one of the Ohio River wns with it last fall while demonstrating it for a crowd of spectors—but he imagined that Indians would be impressed by the agic of a gun that shot without smoke or noise. Lewis also had d made at a forge in Harper's Ferry a folding boat frame of on rods—his own invention, which he believed could form the eleton of a large cargo boat if covered with animal skins—just case they might someday need to build a boat where there was o timber. And so its ninety pounds had been added to the huge ad the rowers were pulling. And one of his most remarkable urchases had been a quantity of Dr. Saugrain's chemical atches: small glass tubes that, when broken to expose their connts to air, would create flame. These would certainly amaze e Indians; they had already amazed the troops, who had always ved in a world dependent on flint and steel for fire-starting. ewis's fondness for useful novelties apparently was one result of s long exposure to President Jefferson, and his thoroughness in quipping his expedition likewise reflected the thinking of his entor in the White House. But it had nearly driven William lark out of his wits at Camp Wood, as the endless trickle of ewis's purchases had come over from St. Louis, filling and surassing the available space. He had constantly revised the manest, even while training and indoctrinating the soldiers. It was leriwether Lewis's expedition in name, but as far as the men of e Corps of Discovery were concerned, they were William lark's men.

Even now, at what William considered the true start of the oyage, Lewis was missing. He was still at St. Louis, attending to st details with the Army agent there, and was going to ride verland and join the boat at a village several miles up the Misouri.

Still, William had lost none of his faith in Meriwether Lewis. Villiam would have preferred a smaller, less-burdened party, nd would have trusted their ability to live off the land, to im-

provise things rather than carry everything that could possibly be
needed. But Lewis had explained convincingly his reasons for
every item he had purchased, and certainly had engaged enough
strong-backed soldiers to move it all along. Lewis was thorough,
and thus it was a big expedition. That was just the way it was.
The rowers were strong, and the thirty-two-foot mast was rigged
to carry a large squaresail that would augment their muscle
power. All the same, it *was* going to be an ordeal. William had
been up and down the Mississippi a couple of times on
freightboats, and he knew how that rowing could be. Usually it
was done by Negroes, not white men like these.

Well, give them their whiskey ration every day and I reckon
they'll bear anything, he thought.

He had never seen such a collection of whiskey lovers. Except
for Private Bratton, who drank none, and two or three others
who could live without it, most of these frontier soldiers seemed
to need whiskey more than food. During the tedious months of
winter bivouac, they had drunk as their official army ration
about 180 quarts a month, but that had only been enough to
prime them. A family of bootleggers had moved in near Camp
Wood and, despite orders banning them from the camp, had
continued to infiltrate the garrison and sell their gut-blistering
product all winter long. Most of the breaches of discipline had
been committed by soldiers drunk on duty—especially by those
whose duty it had been to guard the army whiskey from the
others.

Eh, well, William thought. No matter; look at 'em now that
they're sober and have something to do.

They were really as hardy and handy a set of men as ever he'd
seen, and he knew their qualities pretty well. Several who had
volunteered for the expedition last fall had backed out during the
winter when they began to understand the distance and danger
that lay ahead, and now William was sure of the ones he had
left, almost to a man. *Almost.*

He looked hard for a moment at the smirky young face of
Private John Collins, a Marylander recruited from Kaskaskia.
Collins had too quick a tongue sometimes, too quick to retort
and too quick to lie. One of the best hunters, he had been sent
out one winter day to get meat, and had returned with a skinned
haunch that he had tried to pass off as bearmeat. The next day
William had sent around the neighborhood to inquire of local
farmers whose hog it was. Aye, this Collins had the earmarks of
a blackguard. But he had good qualities too, and would have a
chance to prove himself.

The *Discovery* was midstream in the Mississippi now, the wide mouth of the Missouri yawning ahead, and the juncture of the two great rivers afforded an expanse of open water so wide it was like a small sea, with a warm south wind laying over it strong enough to ripple shirts and ruffle hair. The Mississippi's current was bearing the cumbersome vessel sideways downstream faster than the rowers could move it across. William wet a forefinger and held it up. "Mr. Cruzatte," he called forward to the pilot, "would ye approve of trying some sail?" The one-eyed Frenchman nodded with smiling enthusiasm, and a moment later the sheet was hauled up. It filled with a rustle and rumble like small thunder, and began pulling. The rowers cheered. Most of them never had been under a sail before, and seemed delighted with this simple boost from nature.

York, who had been up and down the Mississippi with his master, soon took the opportunity to represent himself to the men as an old hand at sailing, and sat on a locker in the sail's shade making up tall tales about great shipwrecks and capsizings he had survived. After a while, William heard angry voices on deck, and went down. Collins was at the heart of the uproar, and he explained.

"Cap'n, sir, I don't find it fair that twenty-two white men has to pull on oars while a Nayger loafs an' spins yarns." Some soldiers murmured in apparent sympathy; others grumbled derisively at Collins's complaint.

William bit back his temper for a minute. Then he replied: "Collins, hear me now: This man York has plenty to do as cook and orderly. But if it would please you to try to make him take your oar for ye, then you and him may hash that out personal, and I won't interfere."

York grinned and rolled his thick muscles under his body fat. Collins scowled at him, then looked away and kept rowing. The others laughed. William suspected Collins would complain no more about York.

Joining Cruzatte on the bow, William studied the bottomlands at the Missouri's mouth, into which the vessels were now moving. Off to the left now was the bluff where George had first beheld the Missouri, a whole long quarter of a century ago. William had heard that story when he was a boy and had always been able to envision George riding down that bluff, dismounting, wading out into that low water, just about there, probably, and putting his hand into the current of the Missouri while his bodyguards and his Spanish friends had waited atop the bluff.

Now I'm as far west as George ever got, William thought. And after a while, as the *Discovery* nosed up the wide, turbid stream he thought: *Now I'm farther west than George ever got.*

ONE IMAGE GEORGE'S STORY HAD LEFT IN WILLIAM'S MIND was that of the many full-size trees floating like straw on the Missouri's current. And now the *Discovery* was in that current and an alarming number of uprooted trees came barreling along. In no river had William seen these silent boat-wreckers come so thick and so fast. Cruzatte, now wielding a long, iron-tipped pike with which to fend them off, explained: "T'ees God-tamn Missou-*ree*, alway she caving in t'e banks! You see someday, *mon capitaine*, whole forest fall in at one time!" It was the river' constant undermining of her banks and relentless channel-shifting that caused this, he went on, his one eye darting ahead, pike at the ready. Cruzatte had already catalogued enough other navigational hazards peculiar to the Missouri—rolling sandbars, false channels, quicksands—to make himself seem quite indispensable. Suddenly he whistled, and Labiche appeared beside him with another pike-pole. Without a word, the two pointed their poles toward a dark, gnarled, glistening snag that was sweeping straight toward the prow, bobbing in the roiling water. The poles touched it. The two Frenchmen strained and pushed in a single-minded effort; their poles bent slightly; the dark snag veered and rolled over and slid harmlessly by on the starboard side. At once Cruzatte was peering forward again, watching for more. He shook his head. "*Mon capitaine*," he said, "permit me telling, t'ees boat too high in t'e bow. She could run *onto* a tronk." He demonstrated with his hand and the shaft of his pike. "Better she have her nose down, like plow."

William nodded, understanding. It would mean a tedious, strenuous shifting of cargo down in the hold, moving weight forward, re-drawing his sketch that showed where everything was. But he knew that Cruzatte was right. He had seen riverboats run over logs that had stove in their hull planks because they couldn't be got out from under. "We'll do that when we get to St. Charles," he said. It was plain, Cruzatte knew boats.

A LINE OF CLOUD PASSED UNDER THE DESCENDING SUN, and in its shadow came a dank breeze. Soon a heavy rain was falling. The sail grew sodden, and was hauled down, and the men rowed onward, barely moving the vessel against the Missouri's stiff current. William returned to the afterdeck and stood beside Sergeant Floyd, watching the rain pock the vast gray surface of the water. Cruzatte shouted back: "Right rudder, Mistain "loyd!" He was pointing at a V-shaped turbulence dead ahead, ts point upstream.

"Hard right, sergeant," William commanded, and Floyd put he tiller over. The boat swung slowly by the ripple.

"What was it, Cap'n?" Floyd asked, watching it.

"A planter," William said. "Trees that get anchored to bot-om, and sway back and forth just under th' surface. Can't see em, except for that ripple. They've sunk many a flatboat."

Floyd was quiet for a while, squinting ahead in the rain. After a while he said, "I kinder 'preciate that leetle Frenchman, don't ou, Cap'n Clark?"

William nodded. "I do, too."

Cap'n Clark he calls me, William thought. *So little does he know.*

William set his jaw and frowned. He had determined not to dwell on it, or even to think about it. But Floyd's words had put t in his mind, and his stomach churned with bitter anger as he hought of it.

William's commission from Secretary of War Dearborn had come a few days ago. Instead of the captaincy promised him by Lewis and Jefferson, he had received only a lieutenant's rank. It was an insult, and it stung, and it had reminded him of all the insults and injustices his brother George had suffered at the hands of government. For a while William had even thought of quitting the expedition because of it. But Lewis, seeming to be almost as indignant about it as William was himself, had pleaded with him. He had apologized on Jefferson's behalf, explaining that the President could only recommend a rank; it was the Sec-retary's decision. And then he had said: "To the men you're al-ready Captain Clark, as you are to me. None of them, or anyone else, needs to know about the rank. In command with me, you'll remain full equal. And when we're done, I'll see you're compen-sated equal. Please, friend Clark. Who in heaven could I ever find to take your place? If you quit me, it won't show the Secre-tary of War anything. But it'll trouble me and the troops some-thing awful!"

Finally, William had answered. "Two things I'd not want to live with. One's failing you. The other's not seeing the Pacific Ocean. I've got my heart set on that, and I guess I'll go. And I take ye on your word, that I be co-captain in every way. Mark this: *never* remind me I'm but a lieutenant!"

Lewis had gripped his arm and looked intently into his eyes. "When we first met, remember, you were a captain and I was an ensign. You were as fine a captain as ever I saw. That's why I told the President I wanted you. Knowing that, d'you think I'd ever bear rank on you?"

And so William had accepted that, and had resolved to himself that he would be as valuable as Lewis every step of the way to the Western Sea, as he had sworn to do when he'd signed on.

For, he told himself, whether governments keep their word or not, by my God, Clarks *do*.

May 24, 1804

THEY HAD BEEN ON THE RIVER FOR HALF AN HOUR WHEN THE sun came up astern. William was on deck, watching the river's roiling surface change colors with the light: pewter, mustard, brass.

This was the start of the tenth day, and they had been working harder than they had ever worked in their lives, but still they had come only fifty miles up the Missouri.

William had thought he knew plenty about rivers, but this one was teaching him new lessons every hour, and she was a rough and ruthless teacher. Already, a week ago, the convoy had been forced to stop at the French village of St. Charles, to unload and rearrange the keelboat's cargo. Cruzatte had been right: Too heavy astern, the *Discovery* had run onto three floating trees on the second day out. William could still hear and feel those sickening moments: the Frenchmen's nasal shouts, the *thud*, *thud* and the grinding rumble, the splintering of oars, the tilting, the loss of headway, the sight of York falling down and dropping a tea service all over the deck, the dismayed yells of the men and then all the strenuous and tricky effort to get the boat around and the tree out from under, in the swirling, murky water, while boat and tree floated back down over distances so tediously gained; then there had been the frantic inspections for hull damage. Fortunately the *Discovery* had withstood all those collisions, and now, loaded nose-heavy, she was plowing upstream toward the new hazards this day promised to bring. Sometime this morning they were due to reach a notorious stretch of water that Cruzatte called the Devil's Raceground, and it promised to teach still more hard lessons.

Now William paced between the rowers, giving them jokes and cheerful words. They needed all the encouragement they could get. William paused in his pacing to look down at Private Collins's bare, red-welted back. The muscles moved under a coat of grease as he rowed. Collins could not wear a shirt yet since his whipping.

A week ago, during their stopover at St. Charles, Collins had left camp without permission to attend a ball in the town, and on returning, drunk, had made some disrespectful remarks about his commanding officers. Next day he had been found guilty by a court-martial of his peers and sentenced to fifty lashes. The men had administered the punishment at sunset that day, and Collins had taken it without whimpering. He had even chosen to go back on the oars next morning instead of lying sickabed as he could have done. His spirit was admirable.

"That back looks better today, Collins," William said.

"Aye, sir," he replied over his shoulder. "Feelin' much better, thank'ee."

"Good. Y'know what I hope, my lad?"

"What, sir?"

"That those heal up before y' earn yourself any more. Stripes on stripes hurt just about unbearable, I've heard it told." William had hated whippings ever since he had first seen them in Wayne's army, and hoped there would have to be no more in the Corps of Discovery.

"I don't aim to earn any more, sir," Collins said.

"That's good to hear. But then I don't reckon y' aimed to earn those, either, did ye now?"

The nearby rowers laughed, and Collins laughed with them instead of taking it in bad humor. William was so pleased with this that he had an impulse to reach down and pat him on the shoulder and call him a good man. But no, it was too soon to ease up on him.

As William walked back toward the cabin, Lewis limped out its door onto the deck, grimacing. His face and hands were covered with red abrasions. Just yesterday afternoon, while exploring a high stone bluff on the left bank, he had got close to the edge, and the stone had crumbled under him, dropping him down the face of a 300-foot cliff. Alerted by the frantic barking of Scannon, William had looked up to see Lewis hanging like a spider on the face of the cliff. Lewis had stopped his fall only by digging his hunting knife into the cliff, thirty feet down. After going up and rescuing him with a rope, William had lectured him.

"You may be my superior officer, but if ye want me to go on with you, promise me no more such foolhardiness as that. Damned if I'll go back and tell Mister Jefferson, 'Sorry about your Voyage o' Discovery, Mister President, but Cap'n Lewis kilt hisself 'fore we could get fifty miles up th' Missouri.'" Lewis had promised.

Now William and Lewis nodded to each other, and Lewis said, "Hear that water?"

"Aye. Th' Devil's Raceground. Cruzatte says it's right 'round the next bend." Already they could feel the increased velocity of the current and see dirty brown foam drifting by the boat. "We should put in up by those willows and set the towing party on shore."

Twenty minutes later, the boat was creeping into the rushing narrows. Half the crew was on shore now, on the left bank, straining forward on the long tow rope, slogging along and stumbling like slaves through rocks and muck and willow thickets, shirtless, pouring sweat, their shoes and trousers heavy with clinging mud, tormented by mosquitoes and black flies. They had the rope over their shoulders most of the time, but often had to snake it high and low to keep it from snagging in brush and branches. This rope was attached to the bow. On board, the rest of the soldiers were laboring on set-poles, and by these combined exertions the *Discovery* began inching forward through a narrow channel formed by a rocky left bank and a mucky midstream island. The current in this channel was fast and turbulent, and gurgled and hissed loudly against the hull. Above its liquid turmoil William could barely hear the curses and the shouted advice among those laboring onshore.

This turbid channel seemed to extend for about half a mile, and at the rate they were moving it apparently would require an hour to pass through it—provided there were no hidden surprises in the muddy water, provided the tow rope wouldn't break, provided the men's strength wouldn't give out.

Cruzatte stood poised like a panther on the bow, watching the water below and the shoreline ahead, while Labiche listened to his directions and moved the bow oar. The soldiers strained on their poles and the heavy vessel crept, just perceptibly. The morning sun was already blistering.

"So far all right," William said almost an hour later. The troops were gasping, slipping on the sweat-slickened deck. "York, take 'em water." The slave went along with a bucket and dipper. "Now," William said, "take one o' those set-poles, why don't ye, my man, and apply those great muscles o' yours." York looked astonished at this suggestion, but took one and got in line, and Collins whooped once with delight.

The channel was widening now; they had passed the rocks and were abreast of the upper end of the island. "Almost through," William said. Lewis nodded, grim and anxious.

588

But the hard labor wasn't yet over.

Half an hour later they were past the island, above the Devil's raceground, rowing now, but the current was still too powerful for oars alone and the towing crew was still laboring along the wooded bank. William watched them with admiration.

When we get above this, he thought, they'll all merit an extra dram o' whis—

Cruzatte shouted something, and there were cries from the shore, and then that end-of-the-world sound: the muffled roar of riverbanks caving in. A few hundred yards ahead of the towing crew, acres of wooded riverbank were dropping into the water; hundreds of birds were flying up out of the toppling trees.

Cruzatte yelled again and signaled violently for the helmsmen to steer for the right bank.

"Lay on those oars!" William yelled above the uproar.

Where they found new strength he didn't know, but they did, and the vessel began to veer toward midstream, away from the collapsing shore. The shore crew stayed where they were, paying out a little rope while getting ready to run in case the part of the bank they were on should start to give way under them.

The *Discovery* was making headway to the starboard shore now, and William was just beginning to plan a way to bring the towing crew across—we'll ferry 'em over when th' pirogues come up, he was thinking—when the keelboat suddenly shuddered, and listed so far to the right that he almost fell overboard.

Sandbar! he thought, scrambling to his feet on the tilting quarterdeck. "Aground!" he yelled.

Now her bow was wheeling to the right; Cruzatte and Labiche both had poles against the hidden bar and were straining to stop the drift. But she was sideways to the swift current now; the water was thundering broadside against her hull, and she was tilting, tilting against the soft, hidden sand. The men on shore were digging their heels into the ground, pulling the long line to keep the boat steady, and the rope was so taut that water drops were popping out of it. For an awful, wonderful moment, the bow stopped swinging, even nudged a few degrees back into the current.

But then the tow line was snagged by a floating tree, stretched one last unbearable inch, and broke. With a sickening swoop, the bow was driven downstream again; the Frenchmen's poles snapped; the whole long hull was again broadside to the current, and the boat was about to be overset, her starboard rail almost in the water. The men, half by instinct, half by the little river-wisdom they had gained already, were swarming toward the upper rail, Abandoned oars were breaking in the sand or plunging away in the muddy whorl above the invisible sand bar. William bellowed:

"All hands over the larboard rail and bear down!" He swung himself over the quarterdeck rail to show the way.

They did it. Even those who were non-swimmers—a good half of them—and even York, and Captain Lewis himself jumped out on the upper side and hung far over the water on straining arms, their feet and seats in the swift, cold, brown water. Scannon barked once and leaped overboard after his master, plunged into the water, and disappeared.

They hung on; they groaned, they yelled; they waited. Their weight on the upper side had stayed the tilting, but it was merely a hanging balance and there was nothing they could do beyond what they were doing, and it seemed just a matter of time.

But then the current helped them, for a change. The sand gradually washed from under the hull, and the bow began to turn downstream, the boat slowly righting herself as she floated off. The men, sopping wet and whooping in triumph, tried to swarm back aboard.

But now the vessel had wheeled end to end and was again coming broadside to the current, now her starboard side, and was cross-current again when her port side hit the next sandbar. Now she began listing that way, and was about to turn over again, and the men, this time not needing orders, scrambled across the deck and flung themselves over the starboard rail. Again they held her in balance; again the current scoured the sand out from under her; again she wheeled, and her larboard side was athwart the current when she sighed onto the third sandbar, just a short way above the upper end of the island. The men went out over the upper side again and hung there.

But now there were only two places she could go next time the sand washed out: against a great, jagged mountain of bleached driftwood on the upper point of the island, or, if she wheeled the other way, into the churning chute of the Devil's Raceground itself, which now was full of speeding, bobbing trees and root boles from the collapsed riverbank. William was on deck now, glancing around for a recourse. This precious boat had been at the mercy of the Missouri River long enough; the river was going to destroy her. It was time to get her back.

Plunging into the cabin and snatching up a coil of rope, he scrambled back topside and made one end fast to a cleat. "I need strong swimmers!" he yelled.

Among the three or four who clambered toward him were Captain Lewis, Collins, and York, their chests heaving. William

inned at Lewis and shook his head. He passed the free end of
e rope to York and Collins and pointed across the chute. On
e far shore were the men of the towing crew, who had been
nning down through the brush opposite the drifting ship.
Can ye take this to them?" William demanded. York and Col-
ns looked at each other, grinned, and nodded. "Go, then, and
ep it out o' the trees if ye can!"

Holding the new rope, Collins and York leaped off. They were
p to their thighs on sandbar for a moment, then their footing
as swept from under them and they disappeared under the
ater. In a moment York's kinky poll appeared; his scarlet head-
erchief had come off and it went away down the brown water.
hen Collins's head emerged, and they struck out for the far
ore, strong arms slashing into the water, being borne down-
ream much faster than they could go across. Somewhere be-
w, Scannon's deep bark resounded. "Look," William yelled.
he dog was on the island, running back and forth excitedly,
opping now and then to shake out his wet coat, his black ears
nd pink tongue flapping. He was having a marvelous time.
Captain Lewis sighed with relief, then turned to watch York and
Collins anxiously.

Huge trees kept bearing down on them, but they kept out of
e way. Finally, by the time they reached the other bank and
ere hauled ashore by their waiting compatriots, most of the
ebris had already gone down. Now the new rope was carried up
e shore and tied to the broken end of the old one, and the
wing crew, reinforced by York and Collins, set off up the river-
ank once more. The last sandbar dissolved under the hull, and
he *Discovery* nosed upstream once again, eight men now on her
ur unbroken oars, and bit by bit she was rowed and towed up
to the open water.

A camp was made in a bright green wood near the Rivière La
Charrette, where an extra ration of whiskey was doled out to the
hilled, trembling, exhausted, laughing soldiers, and then cook-
ng fires were built. Scannon had been picked up off the island
y one of the pirogues and reunited with his happy master.

While pork and pone were being cooked, the hunters George
Drouillard and Private Alexander Willard emerged from the
/oods with four horses they had been bringing up from St.
Charles.

"God Almighty!" yelped young George Shannon, pointing at
he tow-rope burns on his broad shoulders. "Why didn't ye bring
s them damn nags two hours ago when we needed 'em?"

THE CARPENTERS CUT WOOD AND MADE NEW OARS THA[T]
evening. William stood for a while watching John Shields wor[k]
the new white wood with a drawknife. The work was mesmeriz[-]
ing. Pulled so surely and effortlessly by Shields's powerful hand[s]
the razor-sharp two-handled knife whisked off long, perfect, cur[l-]
ing shavings as if the tough, green ash wood were soft as soap. I[n]
ten minutes Shields could produce one perfect oar and a pile [of]
fragrant shavings a foot deep. Shields drawled, still pulling th[e]
knife tirelessly, "Sir, that man York o' yours, he surely amaze[d]
me what 'e done today. I never knowed a nigger to voluntair f[or]
nothin' afore. 'Specially anything hard or dangerous."

That had amazed William, too, even more than Collins's pe[r-]
formance had. York had always liked to brag big and bold, bu[t]
this was the first time he had ever really put himself on the lin[e]
and William had been wondering whether York finally might b[e,]
after all these years, undergoing an improvement of characte[r.]
He looked over toward the mess fires, where York was suppose[d]
to be fixing supper. His cookfire was untended and smoky, an[d]
he had not even started to fix the food, because he was too bus[y]
telling everyone about his heroic swim.

Nay, William thought. 'Twas but a fluke. He's the same a[s]
ever.

SHOUTS AT DAYBREAK HERALDED THE APPROACH OF A LONG[,]
overloaded dugout with a small crew of Frenchmen. It proved t[o]
be Regis Loisel, a fur trader who had wintered 400 leagues u[p]
the river, in Sioux Indian country. Lewis had heard of him i[n]
St. Louis, and now invited him aboard the *Discovery* to drin[k]
coffee and tell all he knew about that long stretch of river.

Loisel, sturdy, smelly, thickly bewhiskered, was mainly in [a]
mood to curse the Sioux. Numerous, well-armed, and arrogan[t]
and partial to the British traders of the North West Compan[y,]
they often turned back other traders who came up, Loisel sai[d;]
they had bullied him and forced him to sell his goods at suc[h]
low prices that he would have no profit this year. The Sioux ha[d]
come to conceive of all white men as cowards and weakling[s,]
Loisel said. He warned Lewis to be wary especially of a snake [of]
a chieftain called Partizan. Lewis thanked him for the advice[,]
but said:

"I don't expect we'll let ourselves be scared back by a snak[e]
called Partizan. My own Cap'n Clark here, as you can see, is [a]
copperhead."

William smiled politely. Lewis's jokes, he had noticed, were [a]
bit like Brother Jonathan's.

592

But he had a conviction that the Sioux were not going to be a king matter, when the Corps of Discovery reached them.

Twelve hundred miles to their country, he thought, looking at it at the Missouri, which now in this morning light looked like piling mercury. By the time we reach them we might be worn down to our hands and knees by that bedamned river.

FALLS OF THE OHIO

June 15, 1804

GEORGE AND FANNY KNEW BETTER THAN TO EXPECT ANY more letters from William for a long time, but whenever the post rider came up the hill, they thought of him. He had written last letters to them just before setting out up the Missouri last month, and they had no reason to expect any more word from him for a year at least.

Now they sat opening a bundle of mail on the porch as the post rider went away down the hill toward Clarksville, and quickly ascertained that there was nothing from William.

George would always divide his letters, putting those from friends and relatives in one stack and those concerning business or civil matters in another.

Fanny's were all personal. She was looking for one in particular. And here it was: Young Judge Fitzhugh's flamboyant script. It would be the same thing he wrote her every time: a plea for her to move back across the river to Louisville so they could see each other every day. She was weakening on that point, and she knew that one of these days she would likely be having to tell George. She dreaded that; she dreaded the thought of leaving him here alone. And so she kept hoping that his mail would contain some happy news, some great turn of fortune in his favor, so that he would be cheerful about other things and not so likely to plunge into a drinking spell when she left. She felt guilty about the mere thought of leaving his roof. But after all, she was being courted by a truly charming and worthy man, and she was not getting any younger. And her sons, though they doted on their Uncle George and probably learned more from him than they would in any school, really should not grow up little recluses here on this wild and lonely Point o' Rock. So now she opened Dennis Fitzhugh's letter, smoothing back a wayward lock of hair at the edge of her dustbonnet, as if Dennis could look up from the page of his letter and see her. George saw the

tenderness melting her face, and so he delved into his own le
ters.

A shiver ran through his cheeks. There was one from
Breckenridge, in the Senate. The sight of it made his hand trem
ble. He decided he would read it last, knowing that its content
whether good or ill, would so outweigh the others as to distra
his attention from them altogether. Besides, he wanted to hav
just that exact degree of a rum buzz in his head when he opene
that one, and he had not yet had even a sip today. So, whil
Fanny read her love letter, George unstoppered the little jug be
side his chair as unobtrusively as possible, and trickled a dram
into a glass, and sipped this while opening the personal mai
These were the usual things. Inquiries as to his health. Invita
tions to the birthday parties of nieces and nephews and the son
and daughters of old comrades. A note from Diana Gwathmey
his favorite niece, that she would like to come up to Point e
Rock for a few days' visit. Requests to borrow books from h
library. A request for advice on personal conduct from Lucy
son George Croghan, now thirteen. Some questions from
Brother Edmund, now a Louisville Trustee, concerning th
town's earliest surveys. A letter from some stranger askin
whether George thought the recent murder and scalping of Jir
Harrod might somehow be connected to the mysterious counci
being held everywhere by the young Shawnee war chie
Tecumseh. A letter of good wishes from old Francois Vigo, dic
tated by him and signed with his X. George read all these and le
the rum diffuse throughout his body.

Eh, well, he thought. Now for John Breckenridge and new
on my land petition. He poured two fingers of rum into his glass
paused, saw that Fanny was not looking, poured two more
gulped half of it, then broke the letter's seal, ready now for any
thing, though his heart was pumping mightily.

It was a short and apologetic note from the Senator, enclosin
a report from the Committee on Public Lands. George read, h
mouth gradually dropping open, a great heat slowly building i
his breast.

He could hardly believe the course of reasoning that the Com
mittee had followed to decide on his petition: They had twiste
the language of his request around so as to imply that he ha
asked for the original Piankeshaw grant itself. Then they ha
gone on to rule that that piece of land was not available to give
since it had already been divided up among the veterans of th
Illinois Regiment.

George threw the whole contents of his glass down his throa

nd banged a fist on his chair arm. "I didn't ask ye for *that* land, God damn it!" he shouted at the report in his hand. "I made it lain I was asking for a *like* piece!"

Fanny had started up from her love letter and when she saw George scowling red-faced over his letter, the rum glass shaking n his hand, she thought:

Oh, no. Someone's dashed him again, and bad this time.

The report concluded:

> *The Committee therefore, on this ground alone, independent of any arguments drawn from the policy of practise of the federal government, have no hesitation in giving it as their opinion that the prayer of the petitioner ought not be granted.*

He rose from his chair, flung the report to the porch floor, nd stamped on it. "By th' Eternal! Can't senators even *read*?"

"George, what is it?" Fanny asked.

He didn't answer. He sloshed another long ration of rum into is glass, and then as quickly down his throat. He paced back nd forth the length of the porch, teeth bared, eyes blazing, pitting on the report or spurning it under heel each time he assed it. Finally he flung the empty glass down at it; the fragments shot out into the sunlight. "George!" she cried. Cupid's ace appeared at the doorway and then vanished.

George stood scowling down at the soiled report now, chest heaving. He picked up the jug from the bench and took a long ull direct from it. "O' course they can read," he snarled. He wiped his mouth on the back of his hand. "They *pretended* to misread it, for an excuse to say no. Deliberate God-damn ettifoggery's all it is!"

"The Indian's grant?" Fanny queried.

"Aye. Congress didn't like my bedtime story."

"George, oh, I'm so sorry."

Maybe it's because o' the Genet thing, he thought. That had long been in the back of his mind. Some people back East chose to consider him a traitor, though he had never, in writing, actually quite got around to expatriating himself.

"Well, by damn, that's the last time Congress will ever hear from me! Those ingrates shall never have the satisfaction o' turning me down ever again! If they gave me something now, I'd pound it up their nostrils! I've lived broke a quarter century on account o' what I gave this country. I reckon I can keep on living broke. What's it matter? I'm richer than any scoundrel in Congress anyhow, for I've got my honor in me!"

And with that, he sank into his chair, tilted up the jug again, guzzled, then began bellowing the old marching song, the one his boys had sung on the way to Vincennes, while Fanny shrank in her chair, blinking, her love letter clenched in her hand. He sang gruffly, grimacing, waving the jug:

> "When I first came to th' town
> They brought me bot-tles plen-ty.
> But now they have changed their tune,
> And bring me bot-tles emp-ty!
> O diddle lully day!
> O de liddle li-o-day. . . ."

Well, this is no time to leave him, Fanny thought, and she joined in her small voice:

> ". . . O diddle lully day,
> De liddle li-o-dum day!"

33

ABOVE THE MOUTH
OF THE KANSAS RIVER

June 29, 1804

WILLIAM TRIED TO CONCENTRATE ON HIS JOURNAL. BUT IT was hard to write when a whipping was on his mind.

There was always so damned much writing to be done!

William sat at his field desk under an awning with his leather-bound journal open in front of him and wrote laboriously, trying to bring it up to date. It seemed that every spare minute had to be devoted to writing, and there were few spare minutes. Sometimes days would pass before any opportunity presented itself for journal-keeping, and then there would be such a backlog of notes, so much to record, because every day in this new country brought to their eyes new kinds of plants and animals Jefferson wanted to know of. And there were descriptions of the land, the weather, the minerals, the Indians; the health of the party: the ax wounds, the snakebits, the boils, the dysentery, and the treatments thereof; reports on food: the successes of the hunting parties, the amount of flour and meal and salt pork consumed, the new kinds of edible vegetation found along the way. William found himself writing and thinking constantly about food. Food was a preoccupation for a party of forty-five men engaged in endless labor of the heaviest kind and having to live primarily off the land. It was hard to believe how much meat the men required; William had been calculating, and it seemed to average eight to ten pounds of fresh meat a day for each man. Fortunately, game animals were various and abundant, and so tame and inquisitive sometimes as to make killing them seem more like murder than hunting. But the party's appetite was not surprising, considering their exertions. They were up every morning at dawn light, out on the water doing battle with the swift current and obstacles of this demon of a river. In suffocating heat, they rowed, poled, towed, and pushed the fleet upstream. Several times in their six weeks of travel thus far, the boats had been nearly swamped or overturned by encounters with trees and sandbars and rocks. Masts had been broken, pirogues punctured, oars shattered. Three weeks ago the keelboat had been snagged and spun around broadside to a veritable avalanche of floating timber. Only the quickness and strength of the men, leaping overboard to manhandle the huge craft, had saved the vessel. Private Gibson had nearly perished as the keelboat swung over him and ground him against the riverbed. More than once the captains had been moved to praise their soldiers. *"I can say with confidents that our party is not enfereor to aney that ever was in these watters,"* William had written on that day. And five days later, the *Discovery* again had been almost swamped by collapsing riverbanks, and he had written, *"We saved her by som extordenerry exersions of our party who are ever readdy to incounter the fortigues for the promotion of the Enterprise."*

William's affection and admiration for the men, and their appreciation of each other, was unexpectedly becoming one of the best aspects of the adventure. Comradeship kept their morale high even through the fierce, sultry heat, the sudden windstorms, the long downpours of rain, the ceaseless torments of mosquitoes, ticks, flies, and gnats.

Fine as they were, though, they were men, and therefore not perfect, and the imperfections of a couple of them had brought up this gloomy prospect of the whippings.

Collins had disappointed him again.

Three days ago, while several tons of flooded baggage from the *Discovery* were spread on the shore to dry, Private Collins had been assigned to guard the whiskey barrels. Private Hugh Hall, tempted by his usual great thirst, had persuaded Collins to relax his vigilance. They had been caught at it. A five-man court martial had been assembled under Sergeant Pryor, and had sentenced Hall to fifty lashes for stealing whiskey and Collins to one hundred lashes for being negligent on guard duty. The punishments were to be administered this evening by the enlisted men.

That dadblamed Collins, William thought. I hope for his own good that he learns this time. I'd hate to have to give up on a man of such spirit and send 'im back.

He returned to his journal. It was hard to think and write now. A whipping upset his day. It always had. As his mother had often said, "The worst way a body can waste his time is in hurtin' another body."

Brother George had been right about one thing, this journey had proved already: about songs and jokes. The best part of these days for the men had been the evenings, when Cruzatte and Gibson would get out their fiddles and play dancing music around the campfires. Men whom one would have thought too exhausted to move would get up and dance like dervishes, yipping and stamping and cavorting. And they would sing home songs sometimes, and josh each other about things that had happened on the river during the hard, hot days. It was high spirit, not fear of the whip, that made them try so hard.

William sighed and dipped his quill. This is surely the writin'est expedition as ever was, he thought, and we Clarks never were much for talkin' with ink. He and his brothers had kept journals at particular times—usually times when they suspected they were making history and would have to be accountable for their actions. George had kept journals when he could during the Revolution, and William had kept one, mainly for Fanny's pleasure, during his years under General Wayne. Brother Jonathan, methodical as he was, had kept a daily diary since he was twenty, but it wasn't very enlightening. Its usual entries were only a one-word description of the weather and where he had happened to be that day. Once in his childhood, William had snooped in Jonathan's diary, looking for any references to himself, but had abandoned it with a mighty yawn aften ten minutes.

But now here he was trying to keep up this elaborate log of the Voyage of Discovery, with its narratives and descriptions, with its map-sketches and coordinates, its sketches of places and artifacts and animals. And Lewis! Well, Meriwether Lewis was a bona fide writin' fool. He not only told everything that happened and how everything looked, but also how he felt about it. Lewis *really* had the sense that he was making history, and he felt that even whether he had the flux or hard stools was history.

Lewis had also encouraged the men—those who could write—to keep journals, too, so that everything would be recorded even if he or William had forgotten something. Privates Gass and Whitehouse and Frazier were keeping journals. Sergeant Floyd had been seen writing on various days, and Sergeant Ordway kept a little sweat-stained writing book inside his shirt. The journals revealed the patterns of their progress.

William had commanded the boat most of the time, being a better waterman than Lewis. He was also in charge of map-making, and the constant recording of weather, measuring temperatures, wind direction, rainfall.

Lewis was happiest hiking on the riverbank, alone and communing with his field notes, or with Drouillard, hunting for game. He always had a notebook and a pencil with him, and a bag for collecting plant specimens. In one hand he would have his rifle, and in the other an espontoon, an obsolete infantry pike he had picked up at the Harper's Ferry arsenal. He liked to use it as a walking stick, and also had found that it made a fine gun rest. It was a common sight to see Lewis standing on the brow of a distant hill, silhouetted against the blazing sky, the butt of the espontoon firm on the ground in front of his left foot, left hand holding his rifle barrel where it rested on the espontoon, aiming one of those incredibly long shots offered by prairie hunting.

William, as the expedition moved farther and farther toward the plains, hunted ashore more often, too, leaving the vessel under the care of the sergeants. He had lost count of the deer and elk he had killed. He still shot offhand, seldom using a gun rest. Instead of an espontoon, he usually carried the tomahawk-umbrella George had given him, using its shade to keep his fair skin from blistering and his brain from baking in the merciless prairie sun.

In these six weeks they had encountered several trappers' rafts coming down, loaded with hides and peltries and animal fat. From one such trapper they had bought 300 pounds of grease for cooking, but had been using it mostly to coat their bodies as protection against sunburn and insects. Everybody stank of rancid fat; everything was stained with it.

Two days ago they had passed the Kansas River, having labored nearly 400 miles, and a great bend in the Missouri there had changed their course from a predominantly westerly direction to a northerly one. The Missouri's current seemed to grow swifter every day, and some days, even with half the men rowing, the other half towing, and the sails full of a stiff breeze, the *Discovery* could barely make a mile's headway in an hour. The men's energy flagged in the heat, and some had suffered sunstroke. Dysentery weakened most of the party most of the time. William attributed that to the Missouri's muddy water, which, he wrote, had *"half a Common Wine Glass of ooze or mud to every pint."*

But all the miseries and mishaps could not blind them to the beauty and the richness of the land, the fine, thickly timbered bottoms, the rolling plains aswarm with game, and the stupendous skyscapes. "Sunrises like Creation Day," he had heard Sergeant Floyd say, "and storms like Doomsday."

"Aye," William had added, "and the evening sky so big, a whole sunset can get lost in one corner of it."

BUT NOW WHAT HAD TO BE DONE WAS SMALL AND UGLY. The troops were being assembled. Each soldier had been instructed to cut nine green switches, long and limber. Now, armed with these, they were formed into two ranks facing each other at six feet apart. Hall and Collins stood at one end of this gauntlet, shirtless. Each was gray-faced but resolute. Collins's back still showed pink stripes from his first whipping. Offshore, the *Discovery* lay at anchor, glowing in late afternoon sunlight. Beyond her was a sandbar overgrown with lime-green shrubbery, and beyond that flowed the muddy river, with a high, grassy, treeless bluff as background for the whole scene, all overtopped by a sun-gold anvil cloud piled five miles high in the north sky. Sergeant Ordway was indignantly lecturing the two culprits.

"We only got so much whiskey," he was saying. "Now, you steal some, Hall, and that's so much less for y'r friends. So you admit you deserve this, say what?"

Hall nodded.

Ordway went on: "And God damn y'r eyes, Collins, it were your sacred duty to proteck our whiskey from people like yourself, isn't that so?"

"That's so," admitted Collins, and for the first time his defiant look wavered. Being put in these terms, it reached his conscience.

"So be it," said Ordway. "According to th' judgment of a court o' your peers and friends, then, you men will walk—*walk,* mind you—down 'twixt these two ranks, and take your due. Hall, you'll walk through twice. Collins, you'll walk through four times. If you faint or fall down, it won't do y' any good, 'cause you'll have to finish when you get up. Now, then. Ready, gents. Hall, forward, *march!*"

Hall started down the line, head held high, staggering a little under the pain, but with a grin on. Each soldier, as Hall passed, drew back his fistful of nine switches and with righteous fury wrought them whistling down upon Hall's flesh. Hall grimaced; pieces of willow snapped off and littered the ground. When he reached the end of the line, blood was oozing from his back in a dozen places where lashes had crossed each other. He halted. Ordway ordered him to face about and march back, which he did. The grin was gone and his face was white when he was through. "Now go to Cap'n Lewis," Ordway said, "and he'll put some medicine grease on it."

Then Collins made his round trip, blinking rapidly and grinding his teeth, turned about, and once more went down the line, and came back. The bits of switch on the ground were flecked with blood, and the tattered handfuls of willow slips the men still held were crimson.

"Now go to Cap'n Lewis," Ordway said. "Comp'ny, atten-shun! By this example, may we all be more true to our duty and fair to each other. Fall out!"

Captain Lewis's eyes were dark and heavy-lidded as he smeared ointment on Collins's seeping welts. He had nothing to say to this miscreant. But William looked at the soldier's trembling jaw and said:

"Last time ever, Collins?"

"Aye, sir. I sure hope."

OVERLOOKING THE MISSOURI RIVER
August 20, 1804

FORTY MEN STOOD ON THE BROW OF THE HIGHEST BLUFF, hundreds of feet above the broad river, the hot wind over the treeless plains blowing the hair on their uncovered heads, making their clothes flutter around their limbs. They were not looking at the river, or their ship and pirogues tied at its shore, or at the smaller river that flowed into the Missouri half a mile upstream. They were instead looking at the shape wrapped in buffalo hide lying in the bottom of a fresh grave. Captain Lewis was reading over the body of Sergeant Floyd, and his voice said in the whiffing and buffeting of the wind:

". . . grant him an entrance into the land of light and joy, in the fellowship of thy saints, through Jesus Christ our Lord. Amen."

The men looked at the body and listened to the wind. Charles Floyd had died a long way from home. It had started with an ordinary bilious colic almost three weeks ago, and Captain Lewis had doctored him with everything he knew to use, but now Floyd was a dead man at age twenty-two, and this was an awfully lonely place to have to lie for eternity.

The men looked at him lying there. Not a soul of them had ever disliked him for a minute, even though he was a sergeant. Now they would have to leave him here on this high overlook, the highest point they had found, and they would go on still farther from home. William glanced around at the men, and he suspected that this lonely grave would haunt each man as they went on. He knew it was going to haunt him. This was a faraway place to die in. And they were getting closer to the Sioux country.

Floyd on his last day had dictated a letter to his parents, and William had written it down for him. But it might be a year before there would be a way to send the letter back to his parents. In the meantime, they would not know, and he would be lying here, a cedar post for his headstone, covered with rocks to keep wolves from digging him up, and the wind would whistle over him, and the river would flow by below. And maybe the Corps would never be back this way.

Captain Lewis's gray eyes lifted now from the grave and he looked up the Missouri. Somehow, he felt, it was the bad water of the Missouri that had killed this fine young man. He had done everything he knew of, and felt sure that even a doctor back in the States could have done no more. He did not want to lose any more men to this river. They were his men and he was responsible for them. Here he stood with the book of prayer in his hands over Charles Floyd, and it crossed his mind that Thomas Jefferson, for whom they were doing this, did not believe in God. Lewis cleared his throat, and said:

"We'll leave our friend here. And so that it won't be forgot where he lies, we'll name that stream"—he pointed to the unnamed tributary—"the Floyd River in his honor, and that's what it'll be on the maps, from this day on. Now, cover him secure, and let's go on down."

THE FRENCHMEN HAD BEEN TELLING THE CAPTAINS FOR weeks about what they called *"les petits chiens,"* which they surely would be seeing soon here on the high plains. Labiche liked to throw the party into fits of knee-slapping hilarity with his imitations of "the little dogs." He would stand on tiptoe by the campfire, hands hanging limp together at the center of his chest, peer around alertly while puckering his mouth to show his two front teeth, then would suddenly emit a series of high-pitched barking sounds, shrill as the chirpings of a bird. Whenever he did this, Scannon would leap up from his master's side, and respond to the Frenchman with deep-throated barks until told to lie down. The Americans loved this show, and had made it part of their regular evening entertainment every night—partly, it seemed, to dispel the gloom over the loss of Sergeant Floyd.

Now, two days above the mouth of the shallow, sandy Niobrara River, word came back from one of the advance scouts on shore that a city of the little dogs lay ahead. Immediately, three or four men jumped up from their oars and made rodent faces, imitating Labiche's imitation.

The report galvanized Meriwether Lewis into action, as new species always did. Over the last few weeks, the captains had discovered, described, and collected several new species of plants, such as buffaloberries and prairie apples, and had even observed a water snake that roared like a bull. But here would be their first new mammal, and Lewis could scarcely contain himself. He ordered Sergeant Ordway to bring the boats to a safe anchorage, then sprang ashore with his notebook, rifle, spyglass, and espontoon, and raced up the bluffs after the scout, with William at his heels and Scannon following.

"Scannon, no," Lewis called, pointing to the boat. "Go back! He'd go wild if he saw a real one and drive 'im into hiding," he explained. The dog, tail drooping with disappointment, went back to the shore and sat down.

"Doucement," the scout said, putting his forefinger on his lips. They made their way silently through the willows of the river bottom and then ascended some forty or fifty feet up a grassy bluff onto the high plain. They walked swiftly and softly through the thigh-high grass, a great, boundless, rolling meadow spread-

603

ing around them to all the horizons. A herd of buffalo darkened a large knoll two miles away. Everything in the distance trembled through heat waves; the buffalo herd appeared to be floating on air. "Listen," William said.

Above the long, dry rasping of locust songs now they could hear faintly the voice of the colony: those chirping barks.

And then there at their feet lay the "city." An area of several acres spread just before them, dotted with small dirt mounds. Each mound, on close look, appeared to have a hole in the top. These apparently were doorways into burrows. The ground among the burrows was almost denuded of grass, and packed smooth as a street. Over these acres frisked or stood hundreds of creatures that looked like large, fat, yellow-brown squirrels, but with short, black-tipped tails. They stood upright in groups at the doors, their little forepaws hanging in front of their breasts, looking around and chatting like neighborhood gossips. Some hopped down the streets, stopping to visit with others who seemed to be sweeping their doorstoops, using their tails as brooms.

"Bless me," William breathed, "it's just like Louisville!"

Lewis had his spyglass up to his eye, and his hands were trembling with excitement at the sight of this strange, highly developed little society. But at that moment some of the nearest creatures became aware of the human intruders; immediately they scurried for their burrows, but almost every one, just before vanishing into the ground, stopped and barked a few times in those high-pitched chirps. This alarm spread across the colony in seconds, and soon the whole town lay deserted, baking silent in the sunlight.

Lewis turned to look at William, and his eyes were a-glitter. "By heaven! Mister Jefferson must get one o' these!"

"They're a wary tribe," William said. "Maybe they'd come out an' council if we showed the peace pipe."

"I wish they would. I want one o' these alive!"

This proved a tall order. Lewis conferred with the best hunters and trappers. First they crept close and lay in concealment at the edges of the village, and when the creatures would come forth to resume their social life above ground, the men would spring out and try to net them, chase them into the open grass beyond the refuge of their burrows, or any other trick they could think of. But the animals were too alert; their warning system was foolproof. After several hours, Lewis decided it would be necessary to dig them out. Leaving a sentry on each boat, he ordered the entire party up to the village with picks and shovels. Groups of two or three men would spell each other on the shovels while others stood around them in circles, ready to catch any of the little beasts that might be unearthed.

Shovels *chunk*ed in the earth for more than an hour. The men poured sweat, laughed, swore, and clowned. Every few minutes one man or another would put his hands to his chest, make himself look buck-toothed, and cry, "Yip! Yip! Yip! Come out, pup! It's only me, y'r Uncle Ground Dog! Yip! Yip!" At the far side of the village, one or two of the creatures would stand up at the mouth of a burrow and chirp back at the sweating soldiers as if taunting them, then would disappear.

After excavating to a depth of six feet, the men in one group ran a pole down into the burrow. "Lord a mercy," someone exclaimed, "we ain't half there yit!"

"Keep at it," Lewis commanded.

There were several large excavations in the village now. The men were almost faint from the heat, and they were getting tired of this. But Lewis made them keep digging. "Damn him," someone muttered, out of his hearing, "I think his brain's parched. Nobody needs a damn dirt-squirrel this bad."

"We keep a-diggin'," someone drawled, "and we'll strike water sure."

"There's an idea," said Lewis. "We'll fetch water an' flush 'im out."

In a few minutes, a bucket brigade was formed, from the Missouri bank to one of the burrows. Using every available bucket and kettle, the shirtless men passed water up onto the prairie, and it was poured down into the hole. The men in the excavation labored in a grand mess of mud, sending kettle after kettle of water gurgling down the little tunnel.

"Ye wanted one alive?" William exclaimed. "This one isn't goin' to be alive 'less 'e's a fish!" God, he thought, what if George could see what this here fool's army's a-doin'! This blind persistence was a part of Lewis that he didn't like, and he was wondering how he might, without embarrassing him, make him ease off.

But soon, after five or six barrels of muddy Missouri water had gone glugging down the hole, a drenched little head floated up through the ooze, blinking and shaking. "Thar 'e be!" a man yelled, and grabbed the half-drowned little beast by the nape of its neck as it came floating out. Lewis was fairly dancing with triumph. "Shields," he shouted, "quick, go down and build a cage!"

The sun was low over the western prairie by now. The Corps

605

of Discovery traipsed down the bluff to the river, sweaty, exhausted, mud-smeared, laughing, arguing whether the funny creatures were barking squirrels or chirping pups or burrowing beavers. Now that they had succeeded, they were forgetting how disgruntled they had been. They had spent the greater part of a day capturing the doughty little mammal, and most now were feeling it was one of the best days they had ever enjoyed.

After the animal was cleaned and put safely away in a cage with several handfuls of fresh herbiage and some corn, the men kept coming by to look in on it and give it friendly little barks. Scannon, ordered to stay clear of the cage, lay five feet away from it and stared at it, cocking his head and whimpering whenever it moved.

The men bathed and washed their clothes in the river, enjoyed an extra gill of whiskey with their dinner, and went to bed still chuckling about the "damned little pups of the prairie."

Off in the dusk somewhere, William heard the Fields brothers' voices.

"Lordy, Joe, I never been so tired. Heh, heh! But I sure am glad we come along."

"Me likewise."

They were thinking prairie dogs instead of Sioux, and William was pleased.

"Yip, yip!" someone piped up in a far corner of the camp. William listened to the men's chuckles blending with the gurgling of the Missouri, and he went to sleep smiling.

"LORD GOD, THIS'S EVEN BIGGER THAN A MISSOURUH CAT fish!"

"That was Jonah's own fish, in its day, I'll bet it wahr!"

The men thus exclaimed as they dug in stinking, black-sulphur soil at the top of a bluff on the south side of the river, exposing the fossilized bones of what seemed to be a fish without end. When at last they had uncovered the last vertebra, a rope was stretched from one end to the other of the skeleton and measured. "Forty-five feet," William announced. He wrote it down in his notes for September 10, and then the men were put to work gathering up the bones, each labeled and numbered for shipment to Thomas Jefferson.

"D'ye reckon, Cap'n, there's fish like this still in this her river?" The query was from Private Goodrich, the Corps' most dedicated fisherman. William chuckled.

"I doubt you'll catch one this size," he said.

"I sorta hope not. In a way," Goodrich said wistfully.

"When this fish swam," William explained, remembering things George had told him so long ago back at the Falls of the Ohio, "this land we're on likely was under sea."

Goodrich paused and looked at William, uncomprehending, thinking perhaps he was joking. "Anyways," he said then, "I sorta would like to catch one like this."

William smiled. Dreams o' glory, he thought.

34

AT THE MOUTH
OF THE BAD RIVER
September 25, 1804

WILLIAM LAY ON HIS SIDE IN HIS BLANKET ON THE QUARTER-deck watching the sky brighten to gold above the distant bluff, hearing the Missouri trickle and swirl under the hull of the *Discovery*. He had hardly slept all night, thinking about the Sioux. He was tired, but was relieved to see daylight come so that something could be done.

He sat up in his bedding and rubbed the corners of his eyes. Lewis lay nearby, his dog asleep beside him. Down on the main deck, on lockers and on the foredeck, two-thirds of the Corps lay rolled in their blankets, literally covering every available foot of space. It had been decided the night before that because of the nearness of the Sioux, most of the men should sleep aboard the boat, while a detachment of fifteen stood guard on the sandbar beside which the vessel lay anchored. Opposite the sandbar was the clump of willows that marked the mouth of the Bad River. Beyond those willows was the main village of the Teton Sioux, the notorious "pirates of the Missouri." A grand council with the Sioux chiefs had been arranged, and it would be held on this brushy sandbar, beginning about midmorning.

"Ordway, you awake?" William said.

The sergeant sat up nearby. "Aye, Cap'n."

"Let's have reveille and use this light."

The men awoke quickly, those who had slept, apparently remembering their situation at once. Those who had not slept moved about, haggard, bleary-eyed, anxiously peering toward the Bad River. Patrick Gass, who had been elected sergeant to succeed Charles Floyd, rumbled orders.

The men worked until breakfast, setting up the council place on the sandbar. They erected the keelboat's mast as a flagpole. Then they stretched the barge's awning over poles to make a shade canopy. They set up a field table under the canopy, and moved several bundles of Indian presents from the boat to the table. As the sun peeped over the distant bluff, they bathed and shaved on the shore of the sandbar, donned the blue coats, leggings, boots, and top hats of their parade uniforms, and slung the white belts of their bayonets and cartouch boxes over their shoulders. It had been a long time since they had looked so much like soldiers, and though this uniforming felt strangely formal here on a sandbar in a prairie river without a fort or even a tent within a thousand miles, it seemed to brace their morale.

The sun was halfway up the sky, and William was under the awning laying out the Jefferson medals, flags, hats, tobacco, and other gifts, when Lewis touched him on the shoulder and nodded toward the mouth of the river.

William looked and a shiver went down his neck. "Got us a lot outnumbered, haven't they?"

There were hundreds of Indians filling up the shore over there, tiny figures of ruddy skin and tawny deerhides, bristling with spears and guns and decorated poles. Most were afoot, but many were on horseback. Their voices droned above the watery whisper of the Missouri. From somewhere far off came a regular, jingling beat, not distinct, but something rather like a tambourine.

"Well," said Lewis. "Let's go back aboard and get spruced up for the chiefs."

By ELEVEN O'CLOCK, THREE COLORFULLY DRESSED CHIEFS and about two dozen bodyguards had gathered near the flagpole. With them were two bedraggled captive Omaha squaws, through whom Cruzatte could interpret when hand signs were inadequate.

The two captains put on their bicorn hats, climbed down from the keelboat into one of the pirogues, and were rowed to the sandbar. They walked up to where the chiefs stood. The principal chief, in a full headdress of hawk feathers and a long, clean, beaded doehide tunic reaching his knees, stood in front, and the other two stood slightly behind him, to his right and left. Cruzatte, self-conscious and nervous, placed himself at Captain Lewis's right hand. The chiefs' eyes stayed mostly on William, whose stature and fair coloring apparently made them believe he was the leader.

The principal Sioux chief, Cruzatte said, was Un Ton-gar Sar-Bar, meaning Black Buffalo. He was tall, about fifty, with a kindly, broad, deeply lined face and a mashed-looking nose. The second chief was Torto-hon-gar, known as Partizan. The captains glanced to each other. This was the one whom Loisel had described as a snake. His eyes were cold and furtive, his lips thin. The third chief was introduced as Tar Ton-gar Wa-ker, or Buffalo Medicine. The chiefs touched hands with the captains. Each of their bodyguards wore a headdress made of a raven's skin with head, wings, and tail intact, the beak projecting over the warrior's forehead.

William did not like the appearance of these Teton Sioux. They seemed less wholesome and more ill-proportioned than the Kickapoos, Missouris, Otoes, and Yankton Sioux whom the expedition had met downriver. These Teton Sioux looked like chimney sweeps or coal-diggers; their faces and bodies were smeared with matter that appeared to be a mixture of charcoal dust and lard, and they were short-limbed and bug-eyed. Somehow, too, they seemed sullen and reticent, and they either misunderstood, or pretended to misunderstand, Cruzatte's translations.

"Tell them," Lewis said, "that we bring them samples of our food." He pointed to a row of salt pork and flour kegs. There followed some more talk, and two Sioux bodyguards stooped to open a hide bundle, which Cruzatte explained was meat the Sioux had brought to the Americans.

It lay there on the opened skin now, perhaps two hundred pounds of it, not red but dirty, graying, stinking in the sunlight. It was many days beyond freshness, and its pungency made the captains recoil. William asked, "Do they mean this as an insult?"

"Non, *capitaine*," said the Frenchman. "Meat of a rankness is very estimable to them. They favor it."

But the chiefs had already seen the revulsion in the Americans' faces, and they now looked even more sullen.

"Sergeant, parade the men and raise the colors," William said.

The Indians watched with unreadable expressions as a squad of blue-coated soldiers, impressively tall in their black hats, shouldered arms, marched in perfect step, flanked, and wheeled, tramping and swinging their arms in unison as if they shared one spirit. Then the squad halted in a rank and stood at Present Arms

609

while the American flag was hauled up the pole. Then the chief and their bodyguards were invited to settle themselves in the awning's shade. The pipe was lit and passed in silence for a quarter of an hour, while everyone looked everyone over.

The next order of ceremony was Captain Lewis's speech. William sat down on a keg beside the table while Lewis stood before the chiefs, Cruzatte by his side, and began.

"Chiefs of the great nation of the Sioux, hear me." He pointed upward. "Today you have seen the flag of the United States put above this land. Your white father is now the great chief of the United States." He waited while Cruzatte translated this. The Indians looked around, looked up, looked at each other, shrugged. It was obvious that either Cruzatte was not translating well, or the Sioux were insolently pretending not to understand. When a pause came and Cruzatte nodded, Lewis continued.

"Your former fathers the Spaniards have gone across the great water where the sun rises. We have come very far with our flag to tell you this." Again Cruzatte limped along with his hand signals and his limited command of the Sioux tongue. The chiefs seemed to be more interested in his curious appearance and his eyepatch than in what he was saying. They also seemed more interested in the array of gifts than in the words being spoken. During Cruzatte's desperate pauses for word-searching, the whine of flies was loud under the awning. It seemed that a million of them had congregated around the great pile of tainted meat lying out in the sun.

"Your new father cares more for the Sioux, and for all the red men in the land, than your Spanish fathers cared. He wants to see your chiefs, and hear them, and know them, and to trade with all your people. Your new father does not want the Sioux to be hungry in the winters. He wants the Sioux to have many useful things, such as we will show you soon, so that the Sioux may live with more ease."

Cruzatte struggled through this part, which seemed to be more interesting and comprehensible to them; Lewis went on then.

"Your new father does not want the Sioux to waste their time making war on other nations. He does not want your women to cry because their men and their sons die in wars that are not necessary. Your father wants all the red men to be at peace with each other, and with the new flag. When nations are at peace, there is time to do good things. There is time to hunt, and to store food, time to make goods, to trade and grow wealthy. Your women can have things of many beautiful colors, and machines of iron, to grind grain."

Cruzatte was unable to come up with a word for "machines."

"Tell them we will show them later," Lewis said. "Tell them that if they are peaceful with our flag and with other nations, we will sell them good guns, to hunt better." This made their eyes glint. But then:

"Also: Tell them that they must no longer stop traders on the river and frighten them and take their goods. Say our government will send many more soldiers like us to make them obey, if they keep doing this. Say they will grow rich only by being honest and fair and peaceful."

It was plain that the Indians did not care for such admonitions. They were frowning and muttering to each other. So Lewis decided to bring his harangue to a close before the whole ceremony could deteriorate in rudeness.

"Tell them," he said now, "that we have presents to give them, and some implements to show them." He turned and looked darkly at William, obviously very disappointed that the Sioux had taken his President's noble overtures so disrespectfully. In the crowded shade, a sense of trouble seemed to flicker like heat lightning.

William supervised the giving of gifts and Cruzatte translated. Black Buffalo was given a medallion, about three and a half inches across. On one side was stamped an image of President Jefferson. "This," William said, "is your new father, the great chief of the United States." Cruzatte grunted and burbled his Omaha syllables, and the chiefs looked scowling and murmuring at Jefferson's resolute profile, as if to appraise his character from it.

William turned it to show the reverse side, which depicted two hands clasping, with a pipe and a hatchet crossed above them. "These marks," he said, stooping so close to indicate the tiny letters that he could smell the chiefs' strong breath, "these are American words put on the metal. They say, 'Peace and Friendship.' Those we want and expect: Peace and Friendship."

Next he gave Black Buffalo a small American flag on a stick, a cocked hat with a feather in it, and a scarlet uniform coat decorated with lace.

The chief nodded and acquainted himself with his new treasures, rubbing them between his fingers, sniffing them and looking at them minutely. In the meantime, William gave Partizan and Buffalo Medicine each a smaller medallion. These depicted domestic animals, and a farmer sowing grain. Lewis had picked up a large number of these plentiful medals from the War Department; they were left over from George Washington's presidency. He also presented these two chiefs with pairs of red leggings and garters, a knife apiece, and twists of tobacco. Buffalo Medicine seemed pleased, but Partizan looked disdainfully at his small hoard, holding the items in his hands and sneering. William leaned to Lewis.

"Good thing for him my Ma's not here," he said. "She'd whap his hindy end for takin' a gift in such bad manner."

"Tell them," Lewis now said to Cruzatte, "the chiefs are invited to come on our big boat, and we'll show 'em some of our implements."

Each chief summoned two bodyguards, and they all went down to the pirogue at the edge of the sandbar and got in. The chiefs looked quietly at the keelboat as they were rowed out to her, and then climbed aboard over the side. Buffalo Medicine almost leaped back into the pirogue when he came up over the side and got a glimpse of York standing there huge and plumb-black.

"Get below," William told the servant, "and have Ordway pump up the air gun and bring it out." York disappeared into the cabin, followed by the wondering eyes of the chiefs.

Lewis seated the chiefs comfortably on lockers amidships and then began demonstrating, one at a time, his implements. First he showed them the steel corn mill that was bolted to the gunwale, and gave each a handful of corn to put in the top. Sergeant Pryor then turned the handle and Lewis gave each chief a handful of the fine corn meal that came out of the bottom. Then he brought forth a compass. "See this little arrow," he said, stooping near. "Always the arrow aims at the north, whence the winter comes, you see?" He rotated it and they saw that it did indeed always point to the north, no matter how he held it. "A great power makes it point there," Lewis said. "You turn it and see. You cannot make it point south." Black Buffalo manipulated the brass instrument for a while and then agreed that with all his chiefly powers he could not make it point another way.

"Now see me," Lewis said. "I have power to make it point south." He had palmed a magnet, and held it behind the compass, and the chiefs, who had just newly come to accept the truth that a compass arrow always points to the winter quarter, now saw it come vibrating around to point south. The chiefs were hard pressed not to appear as mystified as they really were, and were still apparently thinking about this when Lewis brought forth his next implement of great medicine, a telescope. William tood watching and hoped that they had never seen a spyglass before. If they had, he knew, Meriwether's proud show of adgets would suddenly seem like a transparent display of trickery nstead of great medicine. "See the flag over there," Lewis said. How small it is, so far away. But now aim at it through this tick and it will be close." Black Buffalo held the telescope to his ye, and it took quite a while for him to learn to aim it. In the meantime, Partizan and Buffalo Medicine were growing restive nd their attention was straying. Buffalo Medicine kept looking oward the door of the after-cabin for a glimpse of York, who eemed a bigger magic than any of this. Eventually Black Buffalo ot the enlarged image of the Stars and Stripes, and his mouth ell open.

"Ai!" he murmured.

"The United States will come close to you like that," Lewis aid, and Cruzatte translated. The chief seemed to appreciate his analogy. Then Partizan and Buffalo Medicine took their urns at the eyepiece. And while they were still wondering at it, Ordway brought up the air gun.

The Indians looked at it with wonder. Being one of Lewis's avorite gadgets, it was kept in a fine polish at all times, its brass leaming and its varnished stock rosy; it was an elegant-looking iece compared with the nicked, rusty, ill-made muskets carried y those of the Sioux who had guns. Of greater interest was the pple-sized brass bulb just forward of the trigger guard. This was he pneumatic chamber, which Ordway had just secretly umped full of compressed air with a hand pump below decks.

Lewis took up his espontoon and, standing near the bow of the keelboat, rested the gun barrel on it. "Sure hope this shoots bet-er than last year," he muttered to William, alluding to the lady he had accidentally wounded with the inaccurate gun near Pitts-urgh. "See that tree," he told the chiefs.

Lewis now aimed at a large cottonwood near the crowd on hore and squeezed the trigger.

The gun's soft *pop*, no more than that of a puff of air expelled rom the lips, made the chiefs smirk at each other; they thought he gleaming gun had misfired. Now Lewis dropped another pel-et into the loading-hole above the breach and squeezed the trig-er again. Again the *pop*; again the chiefs looked smug and contemptuous. But then a cry came from shore, followed by an astonished murmur from the crowd; a brave had gone to the distant cottonwood and found the pellet-holes in it. The chiefs vere suddenly attentive again, and watched in amazement as Lewis fired several more smokeless, noiseless shots without seem-

613

ing even to reload. Black Buffalo was watching the tree through the telescope now and he could see bark fly from its trunk every time Lewis pulled the trigger. The chiefs were talking among themselves excitedly now, and Cruzatte said that they were calling this great medicine, a gun that shoots without powder. "He say it is beyond all he have comprehend," Cruzatte said.

But William, who had been closely watching Partizan, saw that this chief was not happy with the proceedings. His mouth was fixed in a sneer. Apparently it did not suit him to have the great chief Black Buffalo responding with such childish wonderment to the gadgetry of the Americans. He seemed embarrassed for him.

The show was over now. "Captain Clark," said Lewis, "now let's serve 'em a dram. But just a small one. I don't want to see that Partizan get uglier than he is already." The chiefs were subdued, almost timid, while York towered over them, pouring from William's favorite crystal decanter into wine glasses. William raised his glass. "To Peace and Friendship," he said, and Cruzatte translated. The chiefs and their bodyguards, and the captains and their translator, drained their glasses.

William felt the rich, hot liquid steal along his tight-strung nerves and hoped everyone would become convivial. But the stuff seemed to dislodge the knot of rascality that Partizan had been containing down inside himself. He muttered something to the other two chiefs and held up his glass for more, and the other chiefs also extended theirs.

"No more," William said. "You see it's empty." Cruzatte translated that piece of disappointing news. Partizan evidently did not like it. He leaned forward, snatched up the fine decanter, which William had received long ago as a present from his parents, upended it, and sucked on its neck. "Careful o' that, ye scoundrel," William muttered. "Break it and I'll break y'r headbone." Partizan released it quickly when York reached for it.

But now the other chiefs had caught Partizan's mood and began frowning and demanding more whiskey. Partizan, as if to mock the little ration he had received, got up and began staggering about the deck like a drunken sailor. Lewis was now grinding his teeth with pent-up fury, and his gray eyes were all but crackling. "Cap'n," he said softly to William, "reckon it's time we put this jackass ashore?"

"Aye, gladly," William replied, getting to his feet. "Mister Cruzatte, kindly tell these gents they've wore out their welcome and we're proceeding on up the river." He cast sharp glances around to the sergeants, alerting them to the possibility of a scuffle. Big Sergeant Gass moved to a position behind one of the Sioux bodyguards; Sergeant Ordway got around close to another. William hoped the chiefs would go peacefully; he was aware of the horde of Sioux a few hundred feet away, and of the other bodyguards on the sandbar who were, according to Loisel, dedicated to protecting their chiefs even at the cost of their lives. William hoped to avoid a scrap, but he remembered what George had told him: that it was a fatal mistake to waver in the face of Indian belligerence.

Cruzette had conveyed the message; the chiefs understood it but did not like it. All trace of friendliness left them now. Black Buffalo began speaking in a loud voice, while Partizan, suddenly acting stone sober again, grunted affirmation and looked hateful. The chief, said Cruzatte, was now telling the captains they could not proceed farther up the river. "Tell him," snapped Lewis, "we didn't come this far to be stopped by the likes of him."

There followed another growling exchange through the interpreter, in which Black Buffalo said that if the party proceeded upriver, one of its pirogues must be loaded with goods and left here. Lewis's reply was:

"Put these beggars off my ship."

William closed a big hand around Partizan's bicep, firmly but not roughly, and propelled him toward the side. One of the bodyguards gathered himself tight as a spring and reached for his knife, but found his wrist immobilized in an iron grip. Sergeant Ordway had him.

A strange, shuffling activity now occupied the deck of the *Discovery*, almost like an awkward dance, as the sergeants and officers tried to urge the chiefs into the pirogue without actually manhandling them or pitching them overboard. On the shore and the sandbar, warriors were beginning to stir, point, trot to and fro.

"York, c'mere," William said. "We need a bit more muscle."

When York moved into the activity like a large black bear, the chiefs stopped resisting and climbed down into the pirogue. They seemed a bit uncertain yet whether he was some kind of a medicine chief among the soldiers or a full-fledged evil spirit. They sat down sullen but obedient among their presents. William climbed over the side into the pirogue with them, summoning Cruzatte and saying to Lewis, "Keep me covered. I'll try to mollify 'em as we go." The soldiers in the boat dipped their oars, and the pirogue moved away toward the sandbar.

"Sorry y're being like this," William said to Black Buffalo. "We all could've had such a good time, if ye'd just been civil."

The chief did not answer. "You'll see," William went on as the pirogue approached the crowded sandbar where many of the bodyguards and warriors stood poised, "we're not like the traders. We can do more good for you. But if your hearts ate bad, ours will be bad."

At the moment the pirogue touched the sandbar, a big Indian wearing a raven headdress jumped onto the prow and hugged the mast. Three other warriors seized the mooring rope. The chiefs gathered their presents and stepped into the calf-deep water and waded ashore. Thirty or forty braves now milled about on the shore. William, with a rifleman on each side of him, followed them onto the sandbar, determined to pacify the chiefs if he could, or at least retrieve the flag and awning.

Partizan, meantime, had dumped his armful of gifts contemptuously on the beach, and now he turned on William, his face distorted with hate. He snarled some words.

"He say you do not give enough presents; you cannot go on," said Cruzatte. William glanced at the four warriors who resolutely held the boat, and he knew they would not let go until ordered to by a chief. Partizan now advanced on William, pointing a finger in his face and spewing out words that seemed to have all the force of curses and the flavor of obscenities. William felt himself growing very heated. His mouth worked, as if it wanted, on its own, to spit into that yammering face. But he held it, remembering: *Clarks don't spit. No matter who at.* He said to Cruzatte:

"Tell them we're not traders, nor squaws, but warriors. Tell them it's our own choice whether we go or stay, not theirs."

Cruzatte conveyed that, then translated Black Buffalo's reply.

"He say, t'ey have warrieurs, too. Many more. He say, if we go on the river, they follow, and take us bit by bit."

And Partizan began yapping again, and with a quick move, lurched forward against William, as if to topple him into the water, then drew back, smirking. The warriors, all along the beach, put arrows to their bows.

Here, William thought, is where he expects me to lose my nerve.

Instead, he reached across his waist to the hilt of his sword. "Ready arms," he said to the two troopers as he pulled the blade out of its scabbard. He heard the hammers of their flintlocks click back. He brought the sword point up to a place inches from Partizan's throat. Everyone, especially Partizan, was silent now. William heard the whispering of the river, the buzz of flies, the breathing of the soldiers, the soft thumping of the Indian ponies'

ooves on the ground. Across the water came Lewis's voice calm
ut clear: "Every man stand to arms. Put grape in that swivel
un. Load the blunderbuss with buckshot. Sergeant, get a squad
eady to go to Mister Clark. Lively, now." William could hear
he faint bustle as the keelboat was put in fighting trim. He heard
he hinges squeak as locker tops were raised to make the vessel
ullet-proof.

Now we'll see, William thought, sweat trickling into his
ollar. They could massacre us, but they know it'll cost 'em
lear.

Now he turned to face Black Buffalo. "Tell him to get his
eople off our boat," he said to Cruzatte. The Frenchman
assed that message, but Black Buffalo did not respond. "Tell
im again," William rumbled.

This time Black Buffalo strode down to the beach and grabbed
he rope from the three warriors, and tossed it aboard. He said
omething to the fourth Indian, who released the mast and
tepped off into the shallows. William realized that, though the
oat was now released, he and the two troopers beside him were
urrounded. He spoke calmly to the men on the oars. "Go get
hat squad." He still held his sword point in front of Partizan's
ace, and was careful not to let it tremble the least bit. "You," he
aid now to Black Buffalo. "Hear what I say. We were sent here
y your new father the grand chief of the United States. Try to
misuse us, sir, and he will send enough soldiers like those to
destroy you all in a moment. By God, your manners are a disgrace! Did someone tell me the Sioux are proud and great? Ha!
I'd say y're nought but a gang o' peevish ruffians. Great men
aren't mean in spirit!"

While he was thus haranguing the chief, the pirogue returned
with its squad of riflemen, bristling with their shiny rifles. The
warriors, perhaps sixty or seventy of them now, and more coming over from the mainland every minute, still held their arrows
pointed at William.

But Black Buffalo evidently could see now that bluster had
failed, and he said through the interpreter:

"I see you are not merchants. You do not have many goods.
But we are sorry to see you leave so soon. We would like our
women and children to visit your great canoe. They have never
seen such a thing." Now they were asking, not demanding. William sent men to get the awning and mast.

"We're going on," William said, now sheathing his sword.
The braves were returning arrows to their quivers. "You will see
that we do what we wish. You will remember it. Now," he said,

617

suddenly breaking into a big smile and holding out his hand "forget what was unpleasant today."

They ignored his extended hand, and turned to go back up on the sandbar. Partizan joined them and the three stood, seemingly having an argument, while the dismantled camp was put aboard the pirogue. William got in the boat and a last soldier shoved it off the sand and hopped on the bow. The boat turned and as the rowers propelled it toward the keelboat, Black Buffalo and Buffalo Medicine turned away from Partizan and came running into the shallows, each with a bodyguard following. To William's astonishment, they begged to spend the night on the big boat. William ran through his mind all the possible subterfuges this might mean; but the look in their faces was so guileless—they seemed like different people without Partizan between them—that William relented. He gave them a hand and they clambered aboard, water pouring out of their moccasins and leggings.

William decided to try to believe them; probably they really did want their families to see the keelboat. But he knew that with these two men and their braves aboard, it would be another wakeful night.

THEY ROWED THE KEELBOAT A MILE UP THE RIVER. IN THE light of sunset, they anchored off an island, which Lewis dubbed Bad-Humored Island in recognition of the way he felt about their first day with the Teton Sioux.

BY DAWN, WILLIAM WAS THINKING THAT THE CHIEFS' ONLY reason for inviting themselves onto the boat had been to keep the Corps from getting any sleep.

Black Buffalo and Buffalo Medicine had wanted to sit up all night in the crowded cabin of the boat, their elbows on the little table, in the warm light of the oil lamp that hung from the ceiling. They had been amiable enough guests, smoking plenty of the good Virginia tobacco, drinking two drams each of whiskey without getting more than a good hum on, and finally sipping something they never had tried before: coffee. Maybe the coffee had been a mistake, William thought now. He loved coffee himself, and it had never kept him awake. But these Indian chiefs, unaccustomed to the stuff, had broken out in a sheen of sweat and sat wide-eyed until far past midnight, wanting to talk. William and Lewis had tried to take the opportunity to learn all they could from them, about the Sioux's sphere of influence, their beliefs, their attitudes, their enemies—all those matters

President Jefferson had asked to know about—but all these two chiefs had seemed to want to talk about was getting the white men to stay for a few days. They had kept insisting that all the Teton Sioux, men, women, and children, should have the opportunity to see this great boat and all its magic objects. Stay, they had pleaded a dozen times. We will give a feast and a dance for you. There will be women for you to lie with. You are brave men and we would like to have your blood in the veins of the Sioux people. In the meantime, the sentries had kept reporting all night that the riverbanks were aswarm with whispering, prowling Indians, apparently trying to stay near their chiefs. The guests finally had lain down to sleep after two in the morning, but no one had slept more than a few winks. The chiefs had kept rising all night to go topside and urinate into the river—another result of coffee—and whenever one had gone up, so had their bodyguards, and the whole boatload of fitful, suspicious Americans had been stirred out of sleep again.

Now William was up with the dawn's first light, dressed in uniform and feeling as dead and gritty as a run-out hourglass, and the first thing he saw on the banks of the gray river beyond Bad-Humored Island was Indians, hundreds of them. "I suspect," Lewis said, joining him at the gunwale, "why they want to keep us here so earnest is so that more warriors have time to gather. Are you o' the same mind?"

"I'd like to trust our honored guests," William replied, "but frankly they don't inspire much confidence, do they?"

"I almost wish that Partizan had come aboard, 'stead o' these two," Lewis mused.

"Aye," William said, scanning the shore for a sight of him. "So's to keep an eye on 'im, eh?"

"Rather, we'd have had a chance to drown 'im last night."

Everybody on deck laughed, and William felt better.

THEY DECIDED TO GET THE BOATS UNDER WAY EARLY, BUT when the chiefs came up, puffy-eyed and scratching themselves, and saw the preparations, they again began begging the captains to stay over for a day of Sioux hospitality and friendship.

"Well, what d' ye say?" William asked.

"I'm heartily tired o' these people," Lewis said. "But I think we inspired some fear in 'em yesterday. And diplomats *is* one thing Mister Jefferson sent us to be," he reminded himself. "Sergeant Ordway, put the men at leisure and let 'em breakfast. We'll not be movin' out yet."

Late in the afternoon, William said, "If they kept us here for their people to look at, they must be done by now. I been looked at so much I feel like I've got blisters from it."

He scanned the high riverbanks which were, as they had been all day, covered with Sioux of both sexes and all ages, sitting, standing, strolling, pointing, and murmuring. The boat deck had come to seem like a stage in a crowded theater, with the audience watching it with minute attention from the sloping high banks above, noting every move the soldiers made. Indeed, the crowd had so enjoyed watching Private Bratton move his bowels over the side that William had ordered a keg set below decks as a latrine lest the Corps of Discovery lose all its dignity.

While waiting for the summons to the feast, William sat at his little desk on the quarterdeck and brought his journal up to date, writing about the incident on the sand bar the day before. Having finished that, he now picked up a telescope to study the Indians and make notes on them. It was amusing to be here watching them watch him. He laid the telescope down from time to time and wrote:

> great numbers of men womin & children on the banks viewing us, these people Shew great anxiety, they appear Spritely, Genrally ill looking & not well made their legs and arms small genrally. they Grese & Black themselves when they dress make use of a hawks feathers about their heads. the men wear a robe & each a polecats Skin, for to hold ther Bawe roley for Smoking, fond of Dress & Show badly armed with fusees, &c. The Squaws are Chearful fine look'g womin not handsom. High Cheeks Dressed in Skins a Peticoat and roab which foldes back over ther sholder, with long wool

There was a commotion on shore now. Six muscular young braves came trotting through the crowd to the river's edge, carrying a rolled hide. They talked for a moment with Cruzatte, who turned and called:

"Sirs, t'ey come for t'e red-hair chief!"

Lewis pursed his small, narrow lips. "That's you, my friend," he said. But as William rose, Lewis, looking suspicious, put a hand on his arm to detain him, and called to Cruzatte:

"Ask them why just one of us!" His eyes came back to William, smoky and alert. "I don't like this; they're dividing us for some reason." Then Cruzatte's voice came back from the shore:

"For that they can carry but one at a time, *mon capitaine!*"

"Carry?" William frowned, donning his hat and buckling on his sword.

He understood when he stepped from the pirogue onto the shore. The six braves unrolled the hide and spread it on the ground. It was a beautiful buffalo robe, its skin side up, finely tanned and painted with colorful hunting scenes and symbols. "T'ey say, please to sit, *mon capitaine.*"

He sat on the robe, crossing his legs, holding his rifle across his lap. The braves, three on a side, stooped, got firm grips on the edges of the hide with both hands, and lifted. The crowd clapped their hands and murmured happily as the men started up the bluff with their burden. William grinned at this amusing conveyance. "If these fellers be pallbearers," he joked to Cruzatte, "I don't aim to lay down dead."

Cruzatte, walking alongside, explained. "You are too honored; your feets are not permit to touch the dirt."

It was several hundred yards to the village, and the braves were sweating and huffing by the time they reached it. William, though rawboned and grown quite lean during the four months coming upriver, still weighed probably two hundred pounds. As this portage continued into the heart of town, many of the spectators from the river followed, the women chattering, boys running with the agility of antelopes through the crowd. William rode as comfortably as he could in this strange mode, hoping he did not look as ludicrous as he felt.

The village was large, nearly a hundred tipis and mound-shaped lodges, all covered with neatly sewn hides decorated with painted symbols. The streets among these dwellings were packed dirt and crushed tan prairie grass. Here and there stood burial scaffolds on tall poles, the mummies covered with wooden latticework to keep off the buzzards and ravens. The village was tidy, pleasant, full of rich food-smells and people-smells, and, in the mellow golden crosslight of the late prairie afternoon, aglow with beautiful colors. The costumes of the men and women were even more brilliant; the Sioux must have spent countless hours dyeing, cutting, and sewing ornaments of quills, feathers, fibers, and beads. Belts, leggings, breechclouts, pouches, and moccasins were thus decorated, and almost every adult wore a necklace of beads, bear claws, or metal bits. Over the hubbub of voices and laughter there were those persistent, rhythmic, rattling, and jingling sounds. Everything has a meaning, too, William thought, and despite his weariness he was stirred by an understanding that the society of these Indians was as rich and complex as that of the white men—perhaps even more so.

621

"Look, *mon capitaine*," Cruzatte said. "Omahas there; prisoned, I t'eenk."

To his left, William saw them. In a corral of poles, under guard, stood and sat about two dozen wretches, squaws and boys, in different garb, some naked, most of them dishevelled, many looking sick or hurt.

That looks like the stuff for a peace lecture, William thought. "Talk to those prisoners today if ye get a chance," he told Cruzatte. "Find out how they got taken. Tell 'em we hope to do something for 'em." Cruzatte was fluent in the Omaha tongue.

The bearers had brought William to the center of the village now, and were carrying him toward the door of a great council house. It was a loaf-shaped structure, not conical like the tipis. It seemed to be forty or forty-five feet in diameter, made of skins sewed together and stretched three-fourths of the way around a circular pole frame to leave the south quadrant open. As he was carried through the entrance, he saw that about seventy finely dressed men were seated on robes in a circle inside. In the part of the circle opposite the door, the three chiefs sat, all in their showy feather headdresses. There was a space vacant between Black Buffalo and Partizan on his right, and another between Black Buffalo and Buffalo Medicine on his left. The eyes of all the men in the lodge were on William as he was carried to the place on the chief's right. Here the bearers stopped and let him step down onto another fine, dressed buffalo hide and take a seat upon it. Then they left. Cruzatte, at a sign from the grand chief, seated himself on another robe behind William.

Nothing was said yet; apparently they were waiting for something. Black Buffalo nodded to William with a pleasant enough visage, then stared ahead. William turned to look at Partizan who kept his profile to him and did not even nod. William had the customary white man's urge to fill this pause with greetings or small talk or something, but restrained himself. They've got all the time in the world, he thought. So he took off his hat and placed it before him, and used the long pause to study his surroundings and the people, just as the gathered Sioux were using it to get acquainted with his looks.

Directly in front of Black Buffalo there rested, in two upright forked sticks, a peace pipe, with a carved and painted wooden stem at least three feet long, decorated with feathers, its bowl already loaded with kinnickinnick. Scattered on the ground under this pipe was a quantity of swan's down. On one side of the pipe stood a small Spanish flag, and on the other, the American flag they had given the chief yesterday. Two other pipes stood ready on each side of this display, and in the center of the room was a large firepit, burning almost smokelessly, and on a spit above it, already nicely broiled, was an animal that, by its size and musculature, he realized could only be a large dog. His stomach, already queasy from sleepless nights and tension, turned over. There were other foods in clay pots in a row before the fire.

William sat thus in the pleasant, rosy half-light of the council lodge, studying the impassive faces of chiefs and warriors around the room, now and them gazing out through the wide door at the sun-gilded panorama of the Indian village, the yellowing willows of the Missouri bottoms beyond, and the rolling, tree-less, blue-shadowed bluffs in the distance. The Indians in turn studied this remarkable-looking white chief who sat among them, a lean-muscled giant in a gold-trimmed coat of a dark blue that was the same color as his eyes, a very dignified and kind-faced chief with a high, broad, white forehead and thick red hair pulled back into a plait at the back of his neck. They all had seen already, or heard, that he could not be shaken.

Among the older Sioux there was a legend about another red-haired chief of the Long Knives, one who had come suddenly to the Father of Rivers to conquer the British, in the long war be-tween England and the Long Knives twenty-five summers ago. That red-haired chief had filled the eastern tribes with admira-tion and fear. Old Sioux had seen that legendary Chief Red Hair in his councils. Others had heard the story, and it had never faded, as such pictures do not fade in the memories of the bearers of legends, and now here was such a red-haired chief of the Long Knives, who seemed that he might be the very same one, except that this one was young and could not then be the red-haired chief in the legend. Some of the Sioux had talked of this during the night and some of them were thinking about it now as they looked upon him and watched his long fine face and proud head glow in the shadows between the dark weathered faces of their chiefs.

William was unaware of their thoughts of George. All he knew was that they stared and stared.

People were hurrying in the street outside the lodge now, and soon William saw the six braves again approaching the lodge, this time with Meriwether Lewis riding their robe, as stately as some poonjab on a carpet, William thought. I hope I didn't look as pompous as that, he thought, though I reckon I must have. Lean, dark George Drouillard walked alongside Lewis; the Fields brothers walked behind, armed with rifles and pistols, as his bodyguards, and all the rest of the troops, except a squad left on the boat as guards, followed, marching sharp with Sergeant Pryor beside them. Lewis looked as rigid as he had that very first day William had ever seen him, back at Fort Greenville.

The troops filed into the lodge and were seated in a semicircle behind their captains and the chiefs, and at last the ceremonies seemed ready to begin.

A very old man, wearing raven headdress and a fine deerskin tunic that hung loose on his frame, rose from a place near the chiefs and delivered a short talk in praise of the white men's peace mission, asked them to be kind to his people, and to forget the anger of the day before; and then on behalf of this village he made them a present of another huge pile of buffalo meat, some three or four hundred pounds of fine-looking cuts, pink and fresh.

He then relinquished the floor to the Grand Chief Black Buffalo, whose speech was equally apologetic and asked for mercy for his poor people. Captain Lewis got up then to reply, and gave in essence the speech he had tried to deliver on the sandbar the day before. This time it was heard much more attentively. Black Buffalo pointed to the little flags in the ground and said he now understood the change in flags from Spanish to American, and that the Sioux were pleased at the thought of being peaceful with neighboring tribes. Now, he said, the Sioux would like to hear the words of the Red-Hair Chief.

"I saw prisoners in your village," he said. "I think they are Omahas. Will the Grand Chief tell me how these people came to be here?"

Black Buffalo seemed proud to explain this. He recounted the details of a battle two weeks earlier in which his Teton Sioux had destroyed forty lodges of the Omahas, killed seventy-five of their warriors, and taken the women and children whom Chief Red Hair had seen. It was a great victory, Black Buffalo said.

"Then," said William, "if you destroyed their lodges, that means you went against them, at their village. This is not the deed of a nation which wants to be peaceable." Black Buffalo chose not to reply to that, and William went on: "If you wish to follow the advice of your new father, as you say you do, then you must become friends with the Omahas. You would commence that friendship by returning those poor, naked prisoners to their people. Will y' do that?"

Black Buffalo was on a spot. Obviously he was not pleased with this demand. Partizan seemed even less so, and his eyes were flashing. But after a brief consideration, Black Buffalo

624

agreed that he would return the captives. William doubted that he really meant to, so he said:

"Good. Your great father will be pleased. Now, we have Frenchmen who will arrange to take the prisoners back to their people. May I have this man, my interpreter, go and speak to the prisoners today and tell them the good news?"

There was no way out for Black Buffalo, if he meant to be a man of honor; he agreed.

William sat down, and as he did he glanced to Captain Lewis, who nodded to him and lowered one eyelid. A wink from Meriwether Lewis was a very, very eloquent expression of approval.

The pipe of peace was taken up then, pointed to the heavens, the four quarters of the globe, then to the earth, and lighted from a bowl of coals, and the captains smoked it with the chiefs.

Once Brother George had told William that there are no two mixtures of kinnickinnick alike, and that the various leaves, barks, and flowers mixed in with the Indian tobacco often had surprising properties, as the Indians knew a great deal about such things. This particular batch, William noted, smelled somewhat like alfalfa, and he had had no more than two puffs on this peace pipe before he was feeling very peaceful indeed. The greatest harmony seemed to reign now between the Corps of Discovery and the Teton Sioux. Words sounded resonant and full of deep meaning; he almost imagined he was understanding the chief's statements even before they were translated. Time seemed to have stopped flowing; the late afternoon sunglow on the tipis outside seemed never to change its angle, but only grew more intense in color. He no longer felt the weariness in his back that he had been suffering after two sleepless nights; indeed, he was hardly aware of his body, and there seemed to be no place where he ended and his surroundings began. He looked over at his friend Captain Lewis a time or two, or perhaps a hundred times, and saw that he was actually smiling, and he felt a great rush of brotherly affection for him. Suddenly he wanted to thank him profusely for inviting him to come on this splendid adventure, but first he would have to wait for Black Buffalo to stop talking, and while he was waiting for that he forgot what he had wanted to say to Lewis. Sometime during this eternal hour, Black Buffalo took in his hand the raw testicles of the dog that was cooking on the spit, held them near the Stars and Stripes, made the statement that they were a sacrifice to the new flag, and then threw them into the coals. It seemed a most appropriate gesture rather than an outrageous one, for some reason which William could not quite explain to himself, and he wanted to thank the

625

Grand Chief for providing this keen revelation of primitive insight, but didn't know how to put it in words, and soon that impulse, too, had passed and was forgotten.

After an imperceptible while William became aware that it was now twilight outside, and the firelit interior of the lodge was brighter than the light from outdoors, and that the dinner was being served up in great wooden platters. His strange, spacious feeling had passed as quickly as it had come.

The food was dished out with the large curved horn of a mountain sheep, made into a scoop that held about two quarts. The courses were pemmican, a mixture of pounded buffalo jerky and grease, broiled dog, and a root.

"What d'ye think?" William asked Lewis. He could barely be heard over the grunting and lip-smacking of threescore Sioux gourmands.

"Good," Lewis said. "Pretty tasteless, this root, but I'll wager Mister Jefferson's chefs could use 'em well in place o' truffles. Aye, they'd do well." He was happily talking around a mouthful of meat.

"Ye rather fancy th' dog, too, don't you?" asked William, who had not yet been able to make himself take a bite of it, even though it obviously was a favorite delicacy of the Sioux.

"Jove, yes! It's quite good!" Lewis exclaimed, smiling around the lump in his cheek at William's squeamishness. "Come, now, Clark. Try it!"

William picked up a well-seared piece from his platter, turned it to and fro, looking at it sadly. Then he said, before sinking his teeth into it:

"Well, I'm sure glad pore Scannon's not here to watch us." The smile vanished from Lewis's face.

THE NEXT SMOKE DID NOT AFFECT WILLIAM AS MUCH AS the first had, and that was just as well, as the ensuing ceremonies were awesome enough even to a sober mind. When the remains of the feast had been taken away by squaws, the cooking fire was loaded high with dry willow chunks, and the interior of the lodge was full of flickering fireglow and huge man-shadows. A dozen musicians came in and encircled the group, carrying tambourines made of skin stretched on hoops, jingling and rattling instruments made by tying deer hooves and metal scraps on poles, and other ingeniously devised noisemakers. When they started an anarchic beating and jingling, two columns of gaudily dressed warriors entered, each on one side of the fire. They shuffled toward each other, dragging behind them skunk-pelts that

626

vere tied to the heels of their moccasins, while the musicians
hanted. When the two ranks of warriors met in the center of the
odge, some of them practically in the bonfire, they shouted and
umped high into the air, shaking rattlesnake tails and other de-
ices that gave off chattering sounds. Then they retreated while
he drums and tambourines thumped, and repeated their ap-
roaches. Their shadows on the skin walls of the lodge were
igantic and shaggy and grotesque, leaping and stretching and
eceding. They began to sweat profusely as the dance warmed
p, and the firelight gleamed on their shining dark skin; their
eaddresses bobbed and shook. Now and then one brave or anther would separate himself from the others, leap high, shout-
ng for attention, then come forward and begin reciting in a loud
oice. Cruzatte translated into William's ear, well enough to let
im understand that the performances were, for the most part,
ewd jokes. The singers then would pick up the vilest phrases and
epeat them in screechy voices. Meanwhile, the advancing and
etreating, the shuffling and drumming continued, and the shad-
ws leaped in the flickering firelight, until the entire place
eemed to be pulsating and trembling. The drums, hard beat,
ght beat, hard beat, light, were like an agitated heartbeat.
hough the dance had a general direction and flow to it, it was
lmost chaotic. It was, William thought, like battle. Now and
hen William would find his pulse beating in his temples as fast
s the drums, and to keep his mind orderly he leaned over to
oke with Lewis. "We should 'a' brought York up; he can dance
vorse'n this."

"That would be bad manners," Lewis called back, "to scare
hem to death while they're trying to scare us to death!"

When all the dancing warriors and their noise had begun to
ive William a headache, they retired into the night and their
laces were immediately filled with a company of women bril-
iantly garbed and decorated, their eyes bright with excitement,
arrying poles with scalplocks attached, and various weapons.

These women, Black Buffalo explained, were to continue the
var dance. The scalps and weapons were trophies of war taken
y their fathers and husbands. Brandishing these trophies
roudly, the women danced, their voices shrilling, their body
notions becoming more voluptuous and obscene than warlike,
until almost midnight. William looked over his shoulder and
aw that the men were being reduced to a bad state of morale.
Ie knew they were as tired as he was, but could see in their
aces that their baser natures were becoming aroused by the
bandon of the dancing women. Lewis was watching this effect

627

too, and now he said to William: "Look at the men. They're tired and randy. They wouldn't be much use in an emergency, d'ye think?"

William nodded. "Another hour and they'll forget they're soldiers."

And so Lewis proposed to the chiefs that the ceremonies be concluded so that the Americans could return to their ship.

The chiefs seemed a bit put out by this proposal. "No. Look," said Black Buffalo, extending a hand toward the women, "you can stay and sleep in their lodges. They wish you to do this."

The thought was both enticing and alarming to William, and he did not like the way he felt about it. To lie down in a bed of skins with one of these tawny girls, to relieve that long pent-up yearning, then to fall asleep in comfort and satiation, would seem like Paradise to any one of these lonely, weary men, himself included. But likely every man would be throat-cut before dawnlight, he suspected. Or poxed, he thought.

And so, to erase the visions of oiled thighs and shapely, dusky arms and long black hair from his mind as the troops were marched in darkness back to the vessel, William conjured up the radiant, virginal face of his fiancée Judy Hancock, whose peach-blush cheeks and wondrous blue eyes, her golden halo of curls, hung before him in his vision like the image of a distant angel. Against her image the Sioux women seemed more and more repellent. His mind and spirit had been on a long, deep visit into a pagan purgatory this long evening, but now with Judy Hancock in his heart and a clean prairie wind blowing across the Missouri to cool his sweaty face, he felt he had been delivered back up to a brighter place more worthy of a Clark's soul.

THE CHIEFS HAD AGAIN INSISTED ON SLEEPING ABOARD THE boat—apparently fearful lest the Americans pull up anchor and vanish up the river—and so it was another fitful night. In the margins of the sleep of utter fatigue, William lay feeling the constant rub of the river under the boat's hull and smelled the bodies and breaths of the chiefs, heard the little exchanges outside among the poor exhausted sentries, saw occasional flickers of torchlight on the riverbanks, and felt as much a prisoner of the Sioux as those poor Omahas he had seen corralled in the village. They're going to swallow us up somehow yet, he thought, depressed by that desperate, impotent feeling that comes in the small hours when there is nothing one can do but lie listening to one's heartbeat and imagining the worst. Cruzatte, during the festivities, had left the lodge to talk briefly with the Omaha prisoners, and they had warned him that the Sioux intended to stop the Americans from continuing up the river. William could not keep from thinking about that, and thus he was glad to have the chiefs aboard as, in effect, voluntary hostages, even though their presence made sleep all but impossible.

He came unrested out of a short, deep snooze just at dawn, rising to find the chiefs already up and the riverbanks as usual lined with spectators. The Corps of Discovery was beginning to seem like a traveling circus among these gawking Indians, and it was difficult to keep smiling. Captain Lewis, never a jolly sort to begin with, was having difficulty staying civil in the face of the Sioux chiefs' tireless demands, entreaties, and dubious declarations of friendship.

Now the chiefs were pleading with Lewis to lay over yet another day, as a large part of their nation was coming in from another village to see the Americans and get to know them. Lewis and William conferred on this. The greater the numbers of Sioux warriors, Lewis noted, the more willing the chiefs might be to storm the Corps and massacre them all. And yet, the two captains agreed, there were still so many of President Jefferson's wishes that could be carried out. If the Sioux's trading ties could be swung away from the British-Canadian companies and into the American sphere, it would be worth a week of such exhausting diplomacy. So they agreed to stay over another day, even though their sense of security was screaming against it.

With three sleepless nights now behind him, William went through the obligations of the day almost in a trance. He visited a succession of big lodges belonging to principal men of the village, including Partizan, talking with them on all the matters of importance to the expedition, describing the size and power of the United States, giving presents, and declining their offers of feminine companionship. In late afternoon he visited the lodge of Black Buffalo, giving some gifts to the chief's wife, and there was informed that another banquet and dance was planned for the evening. The Sioux from the other village had not yet arrived, the chief apologized. William, sure that he and Lewis were being duped again, gritted his teeth and replied with all the tact he could muster that he was looking forward to another such wonderful ceremony.

During his tour of the village, he saw several sights that impressed upon him the severity of Sioux life. He saw a brave who sat with arrows stuck through his biceps and forearms, his face expressionless. A good friend of this brave had died, it was explained, and the arrows were testimony to his grief.

There were several men who bore deep, puckered scars on their chests, near their nipples. These, he learned, were the results of a self-torture practiced when a warrior was initiated into a special society. Wooden skewers were stuck through the flesh above the nipples. These skewers were tied to long ropes attached to the tops of saplings. The brave then would pull backward against those ropes until the saplings were bent toward him or the skewers were torn out of his flesh. The members of this special society, William learned, were the bodyguards to the chiefs, and also acted as village police. William saw one of these warriors strip and whip two squaws who had been quarreling with each other, and he noticed that women and children always cringed at the warriors' approach.

Another duty of the village police sept, William learned, was to walk through the village at night like town criers, singing the occurrences of the evening—in particular, who had been punished and for what. By heaven, he thought, what a myth is that of the freedom of savage life! No privacy, and they're controlled as strict as the ants in an ant hill.

THE BANQUET AND DANCE WERE SO EXACT A REPETITION OF those of the night before that William now and then was not sure which day he was in. Everything he heard had already been said, and everything he said the Indians had already heard. Time here did not seem to move forward with the hands of a watch, but stayed still, everything repeating and repeating itself. Even without the kinnickinnick, he felt, Indian village life must have this sameness. He almost thought "roundness." Aye, he thought: the round of horizons, the round of days and nights, the round of seasons, the round of generations; even their symbols and their lodges are round. No corners, no straight lines, no lines leading beyond horizons; nothing pulling them in a *direction* like the pull on a compass needle, nothing like this westward pull on my people.

Aye, round, he thought. For them even time is round.

AND NOW HERE THEY WERE AGAIN, JUST LIKE LAST NIGHT, returning to the keelboat, having ended the festivities earlier than the chiefs would have done, and again the chiefs had invited themselves aboard to spend the night. The only difference was that this time the grand chief was staying in his village and Partizan was coming to stay on the boat. The pirogue moved across

630

the dark fast water toward the speck of torchlight that marked the location of the *Discovery*, lying at anchor a hundred yards offshore. The oars groaned and bumped and dribbled. The rowers breathed hard. Partizan and Buffalo Medicine sat forward in the boat, the dim glow of the pirogue's lantern lighting their ruddy faces from below. Captain Lewis and his guards were still on shore, waiting for the pirogue to return and ferry them out. Suddenly William sat up straight.

"Oh, oh, helmsman," he said as they drew near the keelboat. "Y're too far up. Hey, watch—" His blood rushed.

The strong current was bearing the pirogue broadside toward the looming dark bow of the *Discovery*. Suddenly the pirogue lurched and tilted for an instant as it skidded against the keelboat's anchor cable. The cable, taut as a bowstring because of the strong current, parted with a *thunk.*

"Hey, on board!" he yelled, so suddenly and loudly that the two chiefs nearly fell off their seat, "y're adrift! Man the oars!" From the deck above came a sudden scurry and bustle and bumping and shouting as the soldiers comprehended the warning and rushed for their places.

The two chiefs in the pirogue, meantime, not understanding a word of the shouting, and probably thinking all manner of terrorized thoughts, began bellowing alarms. Onshore, then, other Indian voices took up the alarm, and William could hear them relaying the panic toward the village, shout after shout echoing off into the night.

"Calm down, God damn ye," William snapped to Partizan, and of course the chief did not understand. The next few minutes were blind chaos. William was shouting to Ordway, Ordway to the rowers; from shore came the querying voice of Lewis, the shouting of countless unseen Indians, the running of feet and rattling of weapons. It sounded as if the whole Sioux nation were charging toward the river. Partizan continued to yell at the top of his lungs, and Cruzatte was trying in a high, fast voice to explain something to him.

"*Mon capitaine,*" Cruzatte cried, "he tells them the Omahas are attacking him!" William saw red, and felt like throwing Partizan into the river, but he was too busy. He had taken the tiller from the unlucky helmsman and was steering toward the drifting keelboat.

Ordway had the *Discovery* under control in two minutes, and William directed him to head for the starboard bank and find a mooring place.

Within a half an hour the *Discovery* was tied to willow trees on the east side of the river, under a high and badly undermined bank, and Lewis and his guards had been ferried over. Lewis was ashen-faced with cold anger, his eyes shooting darts at Partizan. "The minute that villain yelled, Black Buffalo was at the river with two hundred warriors fully armed," he hissed to William. "If that doesn't prove me their rascally intentions, I'm a dunce! By God, my friend, come daylight we're going on up the river if we have to cut through a thousand black-hearted Sioux to do it!" Scannon, unsettled by his master's fury, whimpered for attention.

They lay tied under the riverbank the rest of the night, half the troops on guard in a defensive perimeter, expecting the shore to cave in, expecting the Sioux to cross to this side of the river and attack, expecting anything. Partizan and Buffalo Medicine were afraid to talk to the infuriated captains, and got into their blankets.

The captains stayed up. It was their fourth sleepless night.

William got crews out in the pirogues at dawn to search the river bottom for the lost anchor, under the eyes of some two hundred Sioux warriors on the banks armed with guns, spears, bows and metal-tipped arrows. The pirogues were rowed up to the place where the *Discovery* had been anchored, then passed back and forth over the spot for an hour. The men probed the bottom with boat hooks and long poles. When that failed, they devised a rope drag, weighted with rocks, suspended it between the two pirogues, and dragged the bottom for another three hours as the sun mounted the sky, flashing blindingly off the river surface, and grew fiercely hot. Sand blew in clouds off the sandbar. William watched the keelboat apprehensively, expecting the horde of warriors to start descending on it at any moment. Even at this distance he could see that Captain Lewis was all but ignoring the chiefs on board.

"Let's go back," he said at about midmorning. "That anchor's sure buried under a ton of ooze."

Soon the pirogues were manned by their regular crews, and the *Discovery* was ready to be untied and cast off.

"Now," Lewis said, turning to face the chiefs directly for the first time all morning, "we're done with you. Are you going to get off my ship?"

The chiefs seemed incredulous, unable to believe the last minute actually had come. Partizan began issuing statements through Cruzatte: "You are welcome to stay with the Sioux. Or

632

you may go back to the Father of Waters from which you came. But you may not continue up this river."

Lewis stepped past him, lips bitten white. "Every man to your place. Collins, go ashore and untie us."

William felt a chill at this moment. He saw that all the warriors were moving down the shore, closing in on the keelboat. He saw Partizan twitch his eyes toward someone on shore, and saw four of the bodyguard warriors move quickly to the tree where the mooring line was tied. Collins was off the gangplank by now and on the beach, and he saw the warriors at the tree. He glanced back with a question in his eyes.

"Go ahead," William said. "Untie us." Collins squeezed between two of the warriors and untied the rope. Suddenly one of the warriors snatched the end of the rope from his hand and retied it. Collins stood there, his fists balling in anger, his breathing heavy.

"By God, that does it," Lewis hissed, and spun on Partizan. "Get off. Now! Help 'em off, boys."

Before the chiefs could move, they found themselves gripped on the arms by half a dozen soldiers and thrust out onto the gangplank.

Unwilling to stand on that precarious place and argue, they sidestepped down and stood on the beach. Now Black Buffalo came down near them and said, "We are sorry to see you go. But give us one piece of tobacco and we will not stop you from going." Lewis stepped to a keg, got out a twist of tobacco, and threw it at the grand chief. It fell at his feet, and a warrior picked it up. Collins still stood on the beach among Indians, and William nodded to him. Collins started for the willow tree again, but the warriors got another signal from Partizan and closed against him. Lewis's eyes were blazing. He drew his sword and stepped to the gunwale, apparently meaning to cut the cable. But the grand chief was speaking again. Cruzatte interpreted.

"He say t'ose men are warrieurs, and you must give them tobacco or t'ey will not release."

"Tell him," William said through clenched teeth, "we'll not be trifled with anymore." He glanced up and saw that most of the two hundred braves were within spitting distance of the boat, all their weapons at the ready. "Give me that," he said to the gunner, and took from him the buckshot-loaded blunderbuss. He raised it and pointed it at the grand chief. All the warriors at once seemed to take a breath and tense up like snakes. William spoke directly to the chief.

"You have told us you're a great man with power. Show us

633

your power by making those men untie that rope. I mean it. I'm damn mad!"

This was translated, and the chief replied: "Black Buffalo is mad, too, to see the Red Hair Chief be so hard over one piece of tobacco."

William put his thumb over the hammer of the blunderbuss and when he cocked it in the silence, everyone could hear it.

Black Buffalo, looking stricken, whether with shame or fright or regret, moved down to the willow tree. He handed the warriors his own twist of tobacco and untied the rope. He took the rope from the braves and handed it to Collins, who came up the gangplank with it. The gangplank was pulled in, the oars dipped, and the *Discovery* moved out from under the guns and arrows of the Sioux army, the pirogues following nearby like goslings swimming after a goose. Sails were unfurled.

William eased down the hammer of the blunderbuss and handed it back to the gunner. The eyes of all the rowers moved back and forth between him and the Sioux, who stood unmoving, their faces grim with disappointment and uncertainty, growing smaller and smaller. The breeze was favorable, so the vessel could move at a stately pace away from them. William wanted to sit down.

THEY GATHERED LARGE STONES FROM THE SHORE A LEAGUE farther up, fashioned a makeshift anchor from them, and anchored off a sand bar in midstream early in the afternoon, determined not to camp ashore until they were well past the Sioux nation. William and Lewis wrote in their journals for a while as meals were cooked. William, his hands now shaking, concluded the day's account:

I am verry unwell for want of Sleep
Deturmined to Sleep to night if possible

He looked up and saw Collins sitting amidships on a locker, eating stew from a bowl, and nodded at him. Collins nodded back. William thought:

I'll never doubt him again.

And Collins after a while said to someone beside him:

"I don't care how drunk I git. I'll never trouble Mister Clark again."

35

AN ARIKARA TOWN,
1600 MILES UP THE MISSOURI

October 15, 1804

YORK STOOD LIKE A COAL-BLACK COLOSSUS IN THE CENTER OF the main lodge of the Arikara village, stripped to the waist, feet wide apart. On each side of him stood an Arikara brave. York's arms were outstretched, and each brave was gripping one of York's fists in both hands.

"Now," York said to himself.

His huge biceps and chest and shoulder muscles swelled and rippled in the ray of skylight from the smokehole above. A murmur of astonishment ran among the crowd of warriors and chiefs in the lodge as the braves were raised from the floor and hung there at the end of his upraised arms, their feet dangling above the dirt floor.

He stood there holding up the braves, whose combined weights totaled more than three hundred pounds, until the murmurs of admiration had risen to a loud babble, then his scowl suddenly melted into a grin, and he set them down.

William smiled at Lewis, and Lewis shook his head and smiled back. York was turning out to be an even greater showpiece than the air gun, the compass, and the corn mill combined. He was getting to be known along the Missouri as great medicine, and he missed no opportunity to exhibit himself and be the center of attention. In each village he would stand in the council lodge with his shirt off, while the Indians examined him from top to toe, exclaiming over the thick, tightly curled hair, trying to rub his blackness off with moistened fingers or even lick it off with their tongues. In some of the exhibitions, the Indians would remain unconvinced unless they could see him fully naked. York had no false modesty, and he would oblige. In those gatherings where squaws were permitted, his awareness of their scrutiny sometimes would cause his great purple pendulum of a sex organ to raise its head, at which sight the squaws would coo and giggle behind their hands and stare in frank admiration, while the men would joke in the ribald way of the social Indian and josh the women about their carryings-on.

Most often, York's exhibitions were for the chiefs and men only. For them he would dance to Cruzatte's fiddle, and they would be astonished that a man so large could be so agile; or he would demonstrate his muscular strength in one way or another. Once he had taken a whole buffalo carcass, put its forelegs over his shoulders, and raised himself by the strength of his oak-trunk thighs to stand with its full weight of some nine hundred pounds supported on his back. Egod, William had thought that time, to imagine I used to trounce him in rassling.

Something seemed to be happening to York lately. He had little by little become less a lazy oaf and more a man aware of his own worth. The rigors of the 1600-mile struggle up the Missouri had melted away that great laughable paunch of his, and he looked like a statue of Hercules carved in ebony. Collins and all the others had treated him like a full comrade since that day in the Devil's Raceground, and he was learning to live up to their respect. The impossible seemed to be happening: York, once the whining, indolent buffoon, was achieving dignity.

But not entirely. He was still a natural show-off. He sensed his peculiar value to the expedition, and enjoyed being Great Medicine. Each time the convoy hove to near another riparian Indian village, it found that the legend of the Black Giant had preceded it, and the shores would be lined with anxious spectators, waiting for a sight of this dark monster.

But York was not the only legend. Other news had raced up the Missouri ahead of the vessels, and this was news of what the Teton Sioux had learned: that here on this great lodge-canoe was a red-haired chief who could not be trifled with or bullied. All the Indians they had met since that confrontation had been friendly and respectful. Even these Arikaras, who had their own reputation as river pirates, had shown the explorers only hospitality and generosity.

Now it was time for more pipe-smoking and serious speeches in the Arikara lodge, so York dressed and went out, followed by the wondering gaze of the Indians. As soon as he stepped out into the cold October air, there arose outside the lodge an uproar of women's and children's voices, all overridden by York's own booming laughter and his imitation of a roaring monster, and then more childish screams.

"I'm a turrible robustious bad devil-man," he was bellowing. "Befo' the Red Hair Chief ketch me and tame me, I used to eat a dozen child'n for breakfast! Rowr! An' *two* dozen at supper! Rowr! ROWWWRR!" And the screams grew louder. The braves and chiefs in the lodge were beginning to look alarmed by all the commotion. William rose to his feet.

"Tell the chiefs to excuse me a minute," he said to Lewis. "Looks like I'm going to have to tame him some more."

Outside, he found York stomping and slobbering around in the street, arms outstretched and hands hooked like claws, while scores of squaws and children, half amused, half terrified, milled round him in a circle, near enough to see him well but far enough to keep out of his clutches. "ROWR!" he went on, while Drouillard played the game and translated for the people, "I'm hungry! Big Devil Man wants a dozen fat babies *rat now*! I want nat one, she look all tender and—"

"*York!*"

He stopped and turned and looked at William. "Sah?"

The women and children stood with eyes wide and mouths gape. William said:

"Don't make yourself *too* turrible. We don't want a panic."

"Oh, indeed, sah."

"All right. Use your good judgment, y' hear?"

"Aye, sah."

The Indians now were looking with awe at the Red Hair Chief as he turned back toward the lodge. The great black giant was powerful medicine; this Red Hair Chief with eyes like the summer sky must have greater medicine. With nothing more than soft words he could tame the monster!

"Eh, York," Drouillard said now, a smirk on his keen hawk's face, "I heard a squaw there say she bet you don't eat babies at all."

York raised himself tall and spread his arms wide, crossed his eyes and made his mouth into a pucker. "Hey, then," he said, "you tell that lady she bes' keep her babies close by!" The Frenchman conveyed that, and nervous but good-natured laughter swept among the women. One cried something.

"She say," Drouillard translated, "that she have no baby."

A repartee was building up, a rare public repartee with these strange brave men from the big canoe, and the Arikara squaws were warming to it. And so was York.

"No baby!" he exclaimed. "Well, nen, ask 'er, Mist' Drooyah, o she want one!"

The answer was a dubious but excited yes, which seemed to delight the whole crowd.

"Oh, my, oh, my," York said in a thick voice. "I think I like Rickyrahs away way better'n them Siouxs!"

ANOTHER WHIPPING. WILLIAM SET HIS TEETH AND WATCHED John Newman, a powerfully built private, go through the gauntlet three times and take his seventy-five lashes. Newman had talked mutiny. He had told Captain Lewis that no free man should have to labor as these had. He had been court-martialed

by his peers and found guilty. In addition to his whipping, h[e]
had been disbarred from the permanent party. He was to be sen[t]
back to St. Louis next spring when the *Discovery* sailed back[.]

An Arikara chief wept when he watched the punishment. I[t]
had been explained to him, and he understood, and agreed tha[t]
a man who had said such things should be punished. But th[e]
Arikaras, he said, never whip their people, even the children. I[f]
this man had been an Arikara, the chief said, he would hav[e]
been killed for his crime, but not whipped. The Arikara chie[f]
wept as he said this.

Newman wept, too, but not because of the whipping. He wep[t]
because he realized that his outburst had made him an outcas[t.]

"Please, sir," he pleaded as William doctored his back, "[I]
really want to stay with you all. I'll do anything, sir. I'll be th[e]
best man y've got, sir. I'll atone for what I said. D' you thin[k]
Cap'n Lewis will take me back?"

"I don't know, Newman. Y' know he's a strict man. But we'v[e]
got all winter to fort up at the Mandan villages. That's a lot [of]
time. Do your best, that's all I can advise."

"I want t' go to the Western Ocean," Newman sobbed. H[is]
heart hurt worse than his flayed back.

ONE OF THE ARIKARA CHIEFS, WHOSE NAME WAS POCASSE[,]
came to Lewis and announced that he had made an importan[t]
decision. He had come to like and trust the American captain[s]
so much that he would, as they had invited him to do, go an[d]
visit their Great Father the President of the United Fires. Whe[n]
the Big Canoe came down next spring from the Mandan Coun[-]
try, he would be ready to get on it. He wanted to see the civiliza[-]
tion they had come from and to meet the great Red Hair whos[e]
face was made in metal on his medallion, and to hear h[is]
wisdom. Yes, he was eager. If Pocasse went past the Father [of]
Waters and on to the White Lodge of Chief named Jefferson, h[e]
himself would become a legend among his own people. H[e]
would wait eagerly for the Big Canoe to come back down th[e]
river next spring, and he would be ready to go.

The acquisition of this promise seemed to please Lewis [as]
much as had the acquisition of the prairie dog. Here was anoth[er]
live specimen from the far country for his mentor and com[-]
mander-in-chief to see.

They had reached a very northerly latitude. Winter wou[ld]
come soon and the Missouri would freeze. Not far ahead, whe[re]
the Missouri made a great bend to the west, lay the large, peace[-]
ful civilization of the Mandans, vaguely rumored to be th[e]

638

mythical Welsh Indians. They lived at the farthest place where traders had gone from St. Louis. But there were British traders among them. Near the Mandan towns the Corps of Discovery would build a fort, its winter quarters, and there cultivate the Mandans, learn what lay farther west, and wait for the Missouri to thaw in the spring. They had come 1600 miles against the force of the great river in five months and it had tempered their sinews like steel and made them feel they were a special, glory-bound people.

But the wind of the High Plains and the water of the river were more icy every day, and it would be good for even such a special people to have a warm place to hibernate and rest, because the harder part of their journey still lay ahead.

"Imagine after all this time," Sergeant Ordway said longingly, "how it'll feel t' sleep under a *roof!*"

Fort Mandan, Dakota Country
November 6, 1804

WILLIAM CAME OUT OF SLEEP TO THE SOUND OF KNOCKING. An eerie dream of gray-eyed Indians faded as he woke. A cold draft through the unchinked logs of the unfinished hut had made his neck so stiff it hurt to move.

"Who's there?" Lewis said in the dark.

"Sergeant o' the Guard, sir," came an excited voice through the door. "There's something in the sky!"

Something in the sky. It was an awesome thing to hear. In the blackness of the room the captains could hear each other moving quickly, groping for moccasins. William called out:

"*What's* in the sky?"

But the sergeant did not reply; apparently he was gone. Lewis got to the door first and opened it. The air was so cold it seared the nostrils. It was past midnight, and there was no moon, but there was a strange, soft, reddish glow above the roofs of the row of huts, and William first thought it was another of those stupendous prairie fires the Indian hunters sometimes set to drive buffalo herds.

Several soldiers were standing on the trodden, frosty parade ground looking toward the north and talking softly. William looked up and a shiver of awe went down his arms.

"Egod! What is it?"

Above the leafless cottonwoods, something vast, ghostly, and luminous was moving, rippling across the cold northern sky. At the moment William first saw it, it looked like a rippling curtain of moonlit gauze, mostly silvery, but tinged with blues, oranges, and yellows. In the next instant it had changed, transforming itself into vertical streaks that reminded him of fluted Grecian columns, white as marble but transparent, weightless, afloat against the black velvet sky. And then those columns were closing together, then drawing apart; then they dissolved, leaving only a shimmering, shapeless radiance, which in its turn assumed the form of gossamer draperies, billowing in languid motion.

At last, Lewis's voice intruded on the eerie quiet:

"The Northern Lights! That, by heaven, is it!"

William looked for a moment at Lewis's profile, at the breath condensing under his nose; then he turned his eyes back to the immense, delicate display and watched it tremble, drift, furl, like stardust or moonfilm, silent, yet creating in his mind's ear an almost audible tinkling, like diamond-sand sifting through Eternity's hourglass.

Far away, from the Mandan Indian villages across the Missouri, he could hear voices, coming faintly across that great distance, through the windless dry cold air of the prairie night, voices so small they seemed the vocal chorus to that imaginary star music. Mandans are out, too, he thought, standing among their houses looking up at this same heavenly show. And I wonder what they're making of it in their superstitious fancies.

He turned to look westward, up and over the gray ribbon of the river, and could just see the nearest, and largest, Mandan town, Matoonha, on its fine bluff overlooking the river.

It was a strange and mysterious place, that Mandan nation. The Mandans were Indians, right enough, yet they were unlike Indians in some strange and subtle ways. For Indians, they were stable, not nomadic, and prosperous and peaceable. Their lodges were spacious, earth-covered domes, laid out in a town surrounded by an earthen wall with a dry moat outside it in the manner of ancient Old World cities William had read about. Since the arrival of the Corps here more than a week ago, the Mandans had shown generosity and peaceful intentions, and a willingness to accept the Americans as their neighbors for the winter. They had brought many gifts of corn, squash, beans, and meat. They had accepted the Americans' meager gifts gracefully and had responded with unbridled delight to the white men' fiddle music and dancing—particularly when the French engage Rivet had danced upside down, on his hands.

The Mandan women were boldly affectionate toward the white men, and their husbands complaisant, even encouraging, in that matter, and William knew that a few of the soldiers already were establishing diplomatic connections with their new Indian neighbors, in that most intimate of ways. "I tell ye it's so," Sergeant Ordway had exclaimed one day, "it hung down 'twixt her legs like a night-crawler, long as my cock! Well, almost as long." Some of the Mandan women, it seemed, stretched the clitoris, for ornament.

"And how d'ye know it was that long?" William had asked. "Did you make comparisons?"

"Well, yes, sir," Ordway had replied, "I did."

MOST INTRIGUING OF ALL TO THE CAPTAINS, THOUGH, WERE some of the myths of origin they had heard from the Mandan elders. They told of a flood over all the earth, and of a great canoe in which men and animals had been saved from drowning, and a dove sent to find land. They told of a son of the Great Spirit, who had come to live on the earth, and had been killed, and had become alive again. No one remembered his name.

Some of the Mandans had gray eyes and auburn hair, and from all this evidence Lewis had come to suspect they were descended from the fabled white Indians about whom Jefferson often had speculated. Some legends had it that the white Indians had come from Wales in a fleet of long ships, nearly a thousand years ago, and had been forced deeper and deeper into the heart of the continent by native Indians, gradually becoming less Welsh and more Indian and forgetting how to read or speak their Celtic tongue, forgetting the name and the nature of their Christian God.

This was an eerie legend to ponder, and William had dreamed of the white Indians two nights. William was a practical sort of man, not fanciful, not often spooked by mysteries. But this of the Mandans had troubled his sleep, and to think of such things now, to think of such great spaces and ages while standing under this cold light-show in the firmament, sixteen hundred miles from white civilization, this could make him shudder, as ghost stories had when he was a boy back in Caroline County.

Imagine it, he thought, standing here half a continent away from home, looking at cold flames in the northern sky.

Imagine a people ever forgetting who they were. Imagine a people ever forgetting who their God was.

November 11, 1804

THIS SQUAW WAS A CHILD HERSELF, BUT SHE WAS BIG WITH child.

William put his pencil down on the map he was making, and stood up behind his desk to look at her. "*This* is the Snake Woman?" he asked.

She was so spare and small that the swollen belly made her look like a snake that has swallowed an egg. On her shoulders she bore a huge bundle of tanned hides, which must have outweighed her.

"*Oui, capitaine,*" grunted the flamboyant French Canadian who was her husband. "Yes," he corrected himself, his swarthy brow knit in embarrassment; he was trying to hire on as an interpreter for these Americans and already had replied in a wrong tongue.

"Tell her to put that load down," William said. The man grunted something and she lowered it to the floor.

William looked at the little squaw-girl and at her rancid, grizzled oaf of a husband, who was probably three times her age, three times her size. His name was Touissaint Charbonneau, and even his big sturdy body hardly seemed big enough to contain all his self-importance. He had three Indian wives, he had boasted; this pregnant waif, of the Snake, or Shoshoni, tribe, was his youngest. The Shoshonis lived far west in the high mountains, and thus this wife was of great interest to the red-haired captain.

William had seldom seen such big, intense eyes as hers; he could almost feel them staring at him. "What d'ye call her?" William asked.

"Sa-ca-ja-we-ah," said the Frenchman. "Ees Hidatsa, mean 'bird.' Good name, ha! She eat little, chatter much!"

William repeated that in his mind, to make it stay. Still another Indian name to remember, among the scores he had learned since the arrival in the Mandan country. *Sa-ca-ja-we-ah.* Outside the hut, a constant din of ax-blows and saw-groans went on, the sounds of the Corps building its winter quarters. The scent of new-cut willow wood was everywhere. Now and then a harsh, barking noise would pass overhead, another southbound flock of geese.

He looked at the girl and said:

"Shoshoni?"

Her eyes widened at this word. She nodded her head.

"Tell me," he said, "how you come here."

Her face took on a look of despair as her husband translated this request into the Minnetaree tongue, with oathlike bursts and peremptory gestures, the gruff and contemptuous manner of a big man trying to impress other big men with his bigness.

The squaw-girl mumbled a few protesting words, which provoked a sneer and another snarling outburst from Charbonneau. He turned and shrugged to William.

"Slowly, *M'sieu le Capitaine*. She say she may not talk of the dead. But I will make her tell." He tensed his lower lip and turned on her. His face was shining with sweat and greasiness. He looked impatient, and resentful that the American captain was more interested in his squaw's knowledge than in his own.

William smiled and went back behind his own desk, motioning toward one of the crates that were stacked everywhere in the room. "Have her sit and take her time. I want to hear."

"Capitaine, she is but a stupid woman. Anything she know, I know ten times over. She talk too much already, and should not be encouraged."

"Mister Charbonneau, you talk too much yourself. I already know your history, and an interesting one it is, too, but now I want to hear hers."

It came slowly, dredged up through a memory turbid with five years of slavery, terror, and drastic change, and translated through the exasperating interruptions and abuses of Charbonneau. She had been the daughter of a great Shoshoni chief. Her people had lived in the Shining Mountains. They had come down from the mountains to hunt buffalo every year in a plain where three rivers came together to start this great river. Minnetarees had attacked their camp one spring, caught her running, killed many of her people, probably her father among them.

Then, starving and often beaten nearly to death, she and her fellow captives, all women, had been brought down the great river. One woman had vanished on the trail, perhaps escaped. Sacajawea had been brought here to the Knife River towns and grown up a slave. She had been passed among families, and finally a few seasons ago she had been won by Charbonneau in a game of hands. This, Charbonneau said, concluded her story. "I am most skilled in such games, and it is her good fortune," he boasted. "I bring my women good gifts from trade. They are happy to be the women of Charbonneau, to bear me sons. This," he growled with a yellow-toothed grin showing through his greasy beard, "will be the second son that I claim." He pointed with a dirty-nailed thumb at the girl's abdomen. "Ha, haaah!"

"Now ask her this," William said. "Does she remember the land of her people? Would she know the way back? Does she know where their towns are?"

Charbonneau rolled his eyes. "She war only eight, nine year old then," he protested.

"Ask 'er, please," William said. "It's important to us." William and Captain Lewis had been here at the Mandan nation for two weeks now, and during their stay they had questioned many chiefs of the Mandans, Minnetarees, and Anahaways who coexisted in this area, to learn whatever they might know about the Upper Missouri and a passage through the Shining Mountains. It appeared now that only the Shoshonis would know of a way through the mountains. Too, the Shoshonis were known for their large herds of fine horses, and horses would be needed to carry the Corps and its baggage across the mountains where boats could not go. If this squaw-child knew how to find her people and could talk with them, it could mean the difference between getting to the far Columbia and not getting to it. It had become necessary to plan hundreds of miles ahead, seasons ahead. It would be next summer or fall before they would reach those mountains—if they ever reached them—but they would have to be ready for them when they got there.

The girl-squaw had gone far back behind her eyes, and now she was talking. Charbonneau said:

"She remember this: where three rivers come together, in a wide valley in mountains. There is a great rock which look like beaver head. Here it is that her people were killed and she was caught. Above that place her people live different places in the mountains and would be hard to find. She was very young then."

William had taken up a pencil and was writing down this about the landmarks. It did not seem like much, but it proved to him that her memory was remarkably good. Other Indians had spoken of the three forks. Many of the Minnetaree men had been there as hunters, and also to raid the Shoshoni horse herds. From their descriptions of the Upper Missouri, William had been sketching crude maps of the route they would take next spring—filling in, with informed guesses, that vast blank space that existed on any map of the continent, between these Mandan villages and the Pacific shore some 1500 miles away. He knew that somewhere about two hundred miles upriver from the Mandan towns, a great river the French called *Roche Jaune* emptied into the Missouri from the southwest. The next great landmark, some 350 miles beyond that Yellow Stone river, would be a tremendous Missouri River waterfall whose noise could be heard for miles across the high plains. Less than a hundred miles above those falls lay the first range of the Rocky Mountains, which the idians called the Shining Mountains. The Missouri River, as e now could picture it, would meander through broad valleys mong three ranges of the Rocky Mountains, navigable by small oats, and there would be the three forks and the Shoshoni unting grounds. The northernmost of those three forks would tch up against the fourth and last range. Somewhere there was pass over that range, and with the help of Shoshoni guides and hoshoni horses the Corps would be able to cross over the pass find the headwaters of a westward-flowing river full of the rge Pacific fish called salmon. From there of course he could resume that it would be an easy downstream boat ride to the acific. Downstream! he thought. How good that sounded after e five months of rowing, poling, and towing that had brought em from St. Louis to this wintering-place!

As for the mountains they would have to cross, the Indians' escriptions made him believe they were not like the Alle-henies, as Jefferson believed, but probably much higher. Still, e had been led to believe they should be no harder to cross than e Alleghenies, thanks to rivers. If the forked Missouri wound mong those mountains as the Potomac and Shenandoah and Ionongahela rivers wound through the Alleghenies, the ranges ould be no great obstacle. But the traverse apparently would :quire the cooperation of the Shoshonis, and that was why Wil-am Clark now was having this unorthodox notion of taking a irl squaw along as a member of a military expedition. Her hus-and Charbonneau was a man of no observable merit except his bility to speak in the Minnetaree tongue. But he was strong and ilderness-wise and would not be a burden if he had to be taken long as a condition of obtaining his squaw's services. William ad made up his mind to hire the couple, come next spring, and ould broach the idea to Lewis this very afternoon. At the mo-ent, Lewis was in another of the huts, doctoring two soldiers ho had cut themselves with axes while hewing logs for the fort.

Charbonneau now was opening and displaying, on the floor, e huge bundle of skins he had made his squaw carry over.

At this moment, the door of the hut was opened. The little idian girl gasped, then yelped. William glanced up. She was etrified, both palms over her mouth, and he saw what she was aring at.

Lewis had come in, so blinded by afternoon sunlight that he ad almost stepped upon the girl, and the front of his clothing as drenched with the blood of surgery. It was he whose appear-nce had made her gasp. And behind him loomed the horror at had made her cry out:

York, hulking, scowling, his clothes also spattered with crim
son.

"Tell her," William said quickly to Charbonneau, "that th
black one will not hurt her. Better tell her he's human, too," h
added. Then he looked to Lewis, who was just taking in the sigh
of the visitors. His face was still tense from the strain of surgery

"Had to fix a cut artery," he said to William, setting down h
medicine chest. "Whew! A bloody blood bath. Hm. What hav
we here?"

At that moment the girl started again; another large, blac
apparition had appeared in the doorway, following York. It wa
Scannon, pink tongue hanging between white fangs, tail wag
ging. He went straight to her and licked her hands, which wer
still clasped over her face. She cringed, squinting. Her husban
was laughing at her and telling her what William had said. Yor
was looking at her with a kindly smile.

"These are our new interpreters, with your permission," Wil
liam told Lewis. "He talks Minnetaree and she's a Shoshoni."

"Interpreters? You mean, take a woman along?" Lewi
growled. "Y're daft."

"We'll talk about it," William said. He knew he could con
vince him.

And he looked around the room at the strange scene: th
surly, blood-soaked Lewis, the beaming black York, the rancid
looking *voyageur* and his pregnant wife-child, whom Scannon
was soothing with great slurps. This roomful of unlikely charac
ters would be the nucleus of an army expedition into an unmap
ped land. He couldn't help it: he started chuckling.

Lordy, he thought, if Brother George could see *this* menag
erie!

PRIVATE JOHN NEWMAN HAD BEEN TRYING HARD TO ATON
for his crime. He sat in Captain Lewis's quarters now, stooped
far over, his hands and feet in a pan of tepid water. Trying to d
his best on a hunting trip, he had run into the river's edge to pul
out a wounded antelope that had plunged through the ice. Now
Newman was being treated for frostbite.

"Cap'n Lewis, sir?"

"Aye, Newman?"

"Have you reconsidered, sir? About me going back?"

Lewis said after a pause:

"You've been an exemplary soldier, Newman, and in ou
minds you stand forgiven. But you can see that I'd weaken ou
temper if I changed the sentence, can't you?"

"Will you not bend at all, sir? I really want to stay with the Corps, truly I do, sir."

"I appreciate that sentiment, Newman. But let's not talk about it any more just now."

December 16, 1804

"WE KNOW," CAPTAIN LEWIS TOLD THE THREE VISITING traders, "that your interpreter La France has been spreading bad word about us in the villages. This must stop, or else. We learn also, Mister Larocque, that you intend to give British flags and medals to the Indians here, and that your North West Company has a notion of building a fort at the Minnetaree village. Let me advise you very strongly about such notions." The other two traders, George Henderson and George Bunch, looked out of the sides of their eyes at Larocque, then sullenly stared at Lewis, whose contempt for them was scarcely masked. William watched these proceedings, and remembered Anthony Wayne, a decade ago, ordering the British to vacate their Fort Miami, which they had so audaciously built on American territory. Some things, it seemed, never changed. "It's plain," Lewis went on, "that your visit with us is to learn why we're here. I'll answer that: because this is American land. Now. While you're visiting here, we'll do anything in our power to make you comfortable, and to prepare you for a safe return to Canada. But mark my words well: Your company and its sharp practices have no place in this territory. Understood! Now. Let's eat."

36

FORT MANDAN,
DAKOTA COUNTRY
December 25, 1804

WILLIAM WAS JOLTED AWAKE IN HIS SLEEPING ROBE BY THE sounds of a gun battle, the crashing of many rifles, right outside. He flung off the musty buffalo robe and reached in the dark for his rifle in its place on the wall above his bed, his heart slamming. The air in the room was bitter cold, though the smoke-scent from last night's fire still rankled and there were still coals glowing orange. Lewis was thrashing about with equal urgency in the darkness on his side of the room, and from the interpreter's room next door Charbonneau could be heard calling *"Mon Dieu! Mon Dieu!"* while the voices of his wives keened fearful queries. William and Lewis bumped into each other as they rushed for the door—and at that moment, William remembered something and noticed something. He grasped Lewis's arm and whispered, "Wait."

There was no battle-sound going on out there now, no yelling; it was dead quiet.

A smile spread on William's face. He whispered something to Lewis, unlatched the door stealthily, and flung it wide, and they shouted into the compound:

"Happy Christmas, boys!"

Forty men were standing there crowding the little parade ground in the predawn halflight, wreathed with gunsmoke, their rifles still pointing toward the fading stars.

"Happy Christmas, Cap'n Lewis! Happy Christmas, Cap'n Clark!" they roared back, then filled the compound with three boisterous cheers and an uproar of laughter.

York limped out of the orderly room carrying a torch, and came to stand beside William. "Merry Christmas, Mast' Billy."

"Merry Christmas, my man." They had spent every Christmas they could remember together.

The torch cast a warm flickering light around the snowy compound. York looked even more enormous than usual; he had taken to wearing two entire suits of underclothes and two suits of deerskins, since that subzero day two weeks ago when his feet and his penis had been frostbitten. His frostbite had become a grand joke among the men. It had suspended York's performance as a Great Medicine Stud among the Mandan women.

The men were awaiting the first speeches of the day from their captains. They knew they had better be brief, because it was cold as the Arctic pole here on the Upper Missouri. There had been nights of forty degrees below zero. It was not quite that cold now, but it felt like zero to William.

Lewis began.

"Thank you, gentlemen, for your good cheer. And not just on this day of our Lord's birth, but your good cheer every day of this arduous year. Well, we're a long way from the comforts and the affections of our homes and families—just think how far!—but I

648

should like to wager that there's few families closer knit than we've all come to be, eh, what?"

They all murmured their assent, nudging each other affectionately and some of them gripping hands; it was as true a thing as they'd ever heard. He went on then.

"This is to be our own day. I've asked the chiefs to keep themselves and their people at home, because this is our Great Medicine Day, so we won't have the usual parade of savages through here." The men laughed and feigned relief; the chiefs, curious about everything and always wanting to sleep in the fort, had become a daily annoyance. "There'll be no female companionship for any of us today"—this was acknowledged by a collective moan of mock disappointment—"as the only women permitted among us this day are those in the seraglio of our interpreter." The men looked amusedly at Charbonneau, who now stood in the doorway of his hut. Lewis went on: "Cannon will be fired at the raising of the colors. Controlled amounts— *controlled amounts*, mind you—of brandy will be dispensed during the day." More cheers. "Thanks to our hunters, we've choice meat, which York is preparing for the banquet. You've all been issued sugar, pepper, dried apples, and the like, so you can try your hands at making Christmas delicacies at your own hearths—and if anyone should concoct anything he deems really superb, why, bring me some, and I'll be happy to judge it." They laughed, and he nodded. "The orderly room's being cleared for dancing, fiddle music courtesy of Private Gibson and Saint Peter." Saint Peter had become Cruzatte's nickname. "As we've no chaplain in this army, every man who wants prayers will pray for himself, and Cap'n Clark and myself shall pray for all of you. That's all I have to say now, except Merry Christmas, which I wish you from the very core of my heart. Cap'n Clark, anything to add?"

The men were visibly moved by this unusual warmth and humor from their chief.

William waited for their happy murmuring to subside, then he said, "Only this: there's good news for the Mandan ladies up the river: York's frostbite is healing up, and"—he turned with a wry smile to the big black man—"we won't have to amputate." York capered with glee, and the men roared.

"Now, boys," William said, "I know y're old hands at entertaining yourselves, so have at it. A merry Christmas day to you all, and God bless every man of you!"

They truly were good at entertaining themselves, and from the moment at sunrise when the swivel cannon saluted the hoisted colors, the new fort began to ring with exuberant shooting, laughter, fervent conversations, songs—some holy, some bawdy—Creole and Kentucky fiddling, the bleating of tin horns, the dashing of tambourines, the nasal-sounding twanging of jew's harps, the thudding feet of men who danced with the grace of drunken bears.

The fort was fragrant with the odor of roasting buffalo and baking sugar-cakes. York had been working since midnight basting and seasoning the buffalo sides, baking a sourdough bread laced with currants and cinnamon, and cooking a succotash of ground potato, pulverized corn, suet and seasonings. The men enjoyed the freedom of going to eat whenever they were hungry, whatever the time of day, and the pattern set itself early. They danced till they were famished, ate till they were stuffed and wheezing, rested and digested until they could dance again, then danced until they were famished again.

William was drawn into the dancing room in early afternoon by a particularly catchy new kind of rhythm he had never heard before—an infectious tempo of snapping and slapping—and found Charbonneau at the center of the room performing hilarious light-footed antics astonishing for someone of his bulk and his surly appearance: a French-Canadian dance involving the snapping of fingers and slapping of thighs. He was teaching it to the Americans, and was thus redeeming himself a bit in the eyes of the troops. Most of them had envied him his harem and considered him a buffoon.

His squaws, in compliance with the orders of the day, were allowed to look on but not participate in the white men's dancing. They were obviously intimidated and bewildered by the merry mayhem in the room, by the high, squalling, squeaking, jiggling noise of the fiddles, which they surely had never heard before. The three women watched, open-mouthed, sometimes wincing at the shrill notes or the thundering voices, and they watched their own man Charbonneau with particular interest; obviously they had never seen him cavort in this manner before, and they seemed uncertain whether to admire him or make mockery among themselves about him. They kept turning to catch each other's eyes, to smile or make round mouths, to cover their mouths with their palms or make hand signs.

Charbonneau's women all were comely. The oldest was not yet twenty, and had a face round as the full moon, and very full lips and huge breasts. The second was fine-featured and big-bodied, but her eyes were dull and she gave an impression of being slow-witted. She held a two-year-old boy, Charbonneau's son, in her lap. She too was a Shoshoni, William had learned, but she seemed to have neither the intelligence nor the accuracy of memory to be any use to the expedition.

The slight and big-eyed one, though—Bird Woman, or Sacajawea—was of a different caliber, and William had become even more impressed by her. For some reason—perhaps because she had been a chief's daughter—she was not timid in the presence of men, and would speak up when something needed saying. William had even heard this child-woman contradict her husband at times when he was being untruthful or making an ass of himself. But for all that courage, she was not brazen, not a shrew. She was, in fact, demure, and capable of a childish wonderment yet. She reminded William of a doe more than a bird, with those great, soft eyes. York favored her, hanging around and being avuncular, and Scannon seemed to have designated himself her protector; he stayed by her nearly as much as by his master now, lying near her, looking up at her now and then and thumping his tail on the floor. Just now, while Charbonneau was teaching the men to dance, Sacajawea was rubbing Scannon's head, scratching under the black, silky flaps of his ears, causing him to close his eyes and tilt his head in utter bliss. Ordinarily Scannon would flee from fiddle music, because the high notes sometimes made him need to howl. But apparently he now had rather be near the Shoshoni girl than away from the music. William watched them for a while, then turned to watch Charbonneau. Suddenly he seemed to feel eyes on him; intensely he felt it, and he glanced over to see the girl studying him. She was studying him with such absorption that she failed to drop her eyes, and for a moment, through several bars of the music, they were looking straight into each other's eyes.

When she realized that he was smiling at her, her eyebrows raised and she returned his smile—just for an instant, then dropped her gaze to Scannon and moved her brown fingers to caress under his jaw.

Back in his cabin, William sat down near the fire and wrapped a flannel shawl around his neck. The rheumatism was fierce, and he could hardly turn his head. Lewis looked up at him from his writings and, without saying anything, got up and put a kettle of water near the fire. Then he took a large section of flannel cloth, fashioned it into an oblong pad, and returned to his notes. When the water was steaming from the kettle spout he poured it into a bowl, steeped the flannel in it, and said:

"Open your collar, and take off that shawl." He applied the wet pad, almost too hot to bear, around William's neck, and then refilled the kettle to heat more water. "We'll keep this up off and on during the day," he said.

"Thankee. Feels relieved some already."

"Heat," said Lewis. "Amazing what it'll do for bones and sinews." He poured a brandy for William and one for himself from William's decanter. William raised his glass and they touched their drams with a *clink*.

"Amazing what brandy makes ye *think* it does," William said, "It's heat, too, though, isn't it? Merry Christmas, my friend."

"The same, my friend. Now I've something to say to you." He squinted, as he seemed to need to do before declaring something from his heart, and said: "All my life, it seems, it's been the darling project of my life to make this crossing to the Pacific. I've wanted the doing of it. I've wanted to be the first white man to see the head of the Missouri. I've wanted to be the first to peek over the Great Divide, and the first to reach the Pacific Ocean overland. I've wanted the first doing of it, and I've wanted the repute of it. I wanted men to say, 'Meriwether Lewis made the crossing, it was he.'"

"And so it shall be, my—"

"No, listen. I've not told ye this, and I might not be moved to say it again; I'm no humble man, as you know. But I'm not obtuse, Clark, and I see it clear, that you've carried more than your half of this command. I . . ."

He paused, and William could see that this was costing him something, this heartfelt talk. Then Lewis went on.

"I just want y' to know that I'm not blind to it. And I intend to make Mister Jefferson know, when God willing we get back, that you're every bit my equal in whatever credit comes to us." His eyes were misty, and he set his jaw to keep his sentiments from showing too clearly. "That," he said, "is what I wanted to say." He added, "Clark."

William put out his hand and they gripped. "God bless ye for sayin' it."

Both turned their eyes into the fire now, and cleared their throats. After a while, Lewis said, "Guess this is as good a time as any to give you this." He reached into his duffel kit and brought forth a small object wrapped in doeskin. William held up his finger, then bent to pull a long package from under his cot.

"Not much out here in the way of shops," he said, "but here's this, and a Merry Christmas."

"And Merry Christmas to you."

A whoop and a new outburst of fiddle music came through the wall as they sat unwrapping their gifts.

"By God, that's choice!" William exclaimed, holding up the

silver pocket flask Lewis had given him. "Just like yours, the one I've coveted! And it's full, too!"

"Got it in St. Louis," said Lewis. "And hey!" he exclaimed, lifting from a long box an Indian belt of the most delicate bead-work, depicting mounted hunters in pursuit of buffalo. "Thank God," he laughed. "I saw that long parcel and feared you were tryin' to give me that blamed umbrella of yours!"

William laughed. "No. Brother George would put it up me from behind and open it if I tried to give it away! Ha, ha! No, I got that belt from that Arikara chieftain who was so anxious to give us his wife. Remember? I told him, 'No, but I will trade y' a pretty for her belt.' And so that's what we did."

Chuckling, they drained their brandy, and William refilled their glasses with drams from the new flask. "Cognac," Lewis said. "The best in St. Louis."

It diffused like sweet fire in their mouths. "Furthermore," William said, "probably the best anywhere *west* of St. Louis!"

THE TROOPS OF COURSE HAD HAD NO OPPORTUNITY TO shop in St. Louis that winter that now seemed so long ago and otherworldly. But no matter. Today they dug into their duffel kits and came forth with an astonishing variety of gifts for their captains, their sergeants, and each other: sheephorns, Indian ar-tifacts, samples of beadwork, pieces of scrimshawed bone and antler, beaver skulls, eagle-feather pens, handmade belts, bear's claws and wolf fangs, snake rattles, quill toothpicks, awls, to-bacco pouches, even maple-sugar chunks they had been hus-banding since last spring at Camp Wood. Somehow they had managed, even during those long strenuous days ascending 1600 miles of river, to find minutes here and there, now and then, to make things and collect things. And they had accumulated these things, even though every item added to the enormous weight they had to haul against the Missouri's swift current. And now they gave their little treasures away, because it was Christmas and they were with the only family they knew now.

The frolicking, eating, dancing, singing, and gift-giving went on all day and into the evening, when sentiments and home-sicknesses began running wide and deep. Several men made it a point to visit the cage of the captive prairie dog, to bark at him and give him morsels of grain or dried fruit. And Scannon dined like a king's pet on handouts.

William stayed indoors most of the afternoon, near the fire with the hot rag on his neck to ease the rheumatism, but did put on boots and coat and a lynx-fur cap to go for a walk in the snow

down to the river and watch the sunset. He had to get away b
himself, because a medley of carols now echoing through th
fort had suddenly made him so homesick for Mulberry Hill an
his family that he almost strangled on the lump in his throat

There was a crust of ice on the snow, and it crushed so loudl
under his boots that it nearly drowned the voices and music fron
the fort. When he would stand still, the Yule sounds would win
out to him over the dry, blue snow. There was no wind this day
but he could see where the wind had been; he could see it in th
carved, curved, crested snowdrifts, where the constant blast fron
across the unmeasured prairie had scoured out sinuous depres
sions. What a blessing is any rare day, like this, when that mu
derous wind stops, he thought. But it hardly ever stopped
Summer and winter it blew, whistling and moaning, sandblast
ing the sunburned skin or slicing through clothing like a razor c
ice, sculpturing and polishing stone, turning up the fur of an
mals, riving trees, turning prairie fires into infernos, whippin
the river into whitecaps. But today there was no wind.

Above the chalky blue of the snow, the sun lay like a sma
blood-hued ball in the ruddy layer of smoke and haze that hun
over the Mandan villages to the west.

Now William stood on the bank of the frozen Missouri an
looked toward the sunset. The keelboat lay, unrigged, locked i
the river ice with snow drifted up against her windward side an
more snow covering her main deck. Far up the river he coul
see Indians walking on the frozen Missouri.

William watched the Mandans walking on the ice now an
thought about the various chiefs who were forever visiting th
fort, and of the Mandan men, who were so eager to trade, and c
the Mandan women, who were so eager to breed with the whit
men. Generally the Mandan husbands encouraged their wome
to lie with the Americans, and except for one early unpleasantry
in which an Indian had beaten his squaw for fornicating wit
Sergeant Ordway, everybody seemed quite happy with this forr
of diplomacy. Its only apparent drawback so far had been a fe
cases of venereal disease that lately the captains had begun trea
ing along with the troops' other maladies. York's penis may hav
been the only one frostbitten, but it was not the only one in fo
consultation.

William sighed, desperately lonely for his family. *Back hom
the sun's already set and it's deep dusk, I'll wager*. He turned i
gaze back eastward, where the sky was darkening already, when
the faraway willows in the afterglow looked as fine and red as fc
fur, and he tried to remember how his favorite overlook on Mu

654

erry Hill looked at dusk in the Yule season. Imagine a land so
broad, he thought, that it can be daylight at one end and night
n another! He had never had that thought before, and wondered
f anyone ever had. Only Mister Jefferson, if anybody, he
hought. Perhaps friend Lewis, though surely if he'd thought it
I'd have heard him say it.

It might be the first time ever a man's had that very thought,
he told himself. Now wouldn't that be something, to be the first
soul on earth to have a particular thought! It's privilege enough
to be the first man to *do* a thing, he thought; though that can be
done easy enough, so long as there's frontiers.

But to be the first to have a thought!

His head almost reeled at the notion.

You can know and prove, of course, if you're first to *do* a
thing. Like crossing the Great Divide. Reaching the Pacific
Ocean. But a first *thought*: Why, no, there's just no way o'
knowing.

I must speak of this with Lewis, he thought; it's a notion worthy of such a Christmas Day as this. I wish I could tell it to
Brother George, and see if he's ever thought it too.

He started back up toward the fort with his thought, eager to
share it. The sun was under the horizon now, and the triangular
fort, with its spiked pickets and double gate of fresh willow logs
and puncheons, and a pair of elk antlers above the gate, looked
shadowy and insubstantial now, like a figure of geometry set
down in a rolling infinity of snow where geometry did not belong.

But no, it was not a mere shape; it was a *home*—the singing
and the woodsmoke and fiddle music spilling from it proved
that—and it was the home where all the people lived who were
his family now. Friend Lewis had said that well.

> "... *The holly bears a blossom*
> *As white as lily flow'r;*
> *And Mary bore sweet Jesu*
> *To be our Sa-vi-our,*
> *To be our Sa-vi-our. ..."*

Jonathan Clark stood beaming with pride, because the carolers
sang beautifully and they were his four youngest children. Isaac
was seventeen, Ann was twelve now, and Billy was nine, and
they were old hands at this caroling business. But this was the
first recital for the youngest boy, George Washington Clark; he
was only six and this was the first time he had been entrusted to

655

carry a tune at a family gathering. He was singing with all his force until his face was red. Every listener in the ballroom was watching him intently, mouthing the words mutely as if this assistance would keep him from forgetting the words, and so far he had not missed a syllable or bent a note. His Uncle George was leaning on his cane with one hand and keeping time with his punchglass with the other, and now, craning toward the proud father of the choir, he whispered in his ear: "I do believe he's going to make a perfect performance, unless 'e explodes first!" Jonathan nodded, grinning.

> ". . . *The holly bears a berry*
> *As red as any blood,*
> *And Mary bore sweet Je-su*
> *To do poor sinners good.*
> *To do poor sinners good. . . ."*

In the big fireplace at the end of the ballroom the Yule log was blazing, a great chunk of walnut. The room was lighted by three dozen candles in wall sconces, and more candles, on the sideboards, flanked the big old family wassail bowl that John and Ann Rogers Clark had brought with them from Caroline County. At the other end of the room stood a fir tree in a tub, its branches studded with small candles and festooned with ribbon and homemade decorations dating as far back as Jonathan' childhood in old Albermarle.

> ". . . *The holly bears a prickle*
> *As sharp as any thorn;*
> *And Mary bore sweet Je-su,*
> *On Christmas Day in the morn,*
> *On Christmas Day in the morn!"*

"Hooray! Bravo! Fine, fine!" the audience cried, clapping and laughing. The room was full of Clarks, old and young. Jonathan was the eldest Clark now, a sturdy fifty-four years old, slower moving but still not sedentary. His wife Sarah was forty-six and now a grandmother, but still retained the youthful, firm handsomeness that was a trait of the Hite family. Here too were Owen and Ann Gwathmey with their children. And Bill and Lucy Croghan with theirs, and vivacious Fanny, who, though now twice a widow at thirty-two, looked radiant and coy as a bride-to-be, because she was, in fact, once again a bride-to-be. Judge Dennis Fitzhugh, her fiancé, was making himself as much a

656

part of this tight-bonded clan as he could, being careful not to say anything that might sound foolish to her elder brothers. They were an intimidating lot, those three Clark brothers standing there together near the fireplace. They were hearty, civil, approachable gentlemen all, but there was something around them, something which could only be defined as their *Clarkness*, which made them seem like a sort of an exclusive society.

The carolers were retreating from the ballroom now, singing, as they went, their parting "God Rest Ye Merry Gentlemen" to the clapping and laughter of the crowd.

"A fine entertainment," Edmund said to Jonathan. "Nearly makes me yearn for children of my own. But not, ah, not quite, not quite." There was a little bit of wistfulness in this regular joke of his; Edmund was beginning to feel he was missing something important. He was forty-two, and certainly was prosperous enough to support a family, but it looked as if he never would. Edmund was neither planter nor businessman at heart. He brooded sometimes over the chances he had missed to prove himself a great soldier, a leader, another Clark on a heroic scale. Instead, he had become a trustee of the town of Louisville, and had slid gradually into the role of town record-keeper and historian. That was a dry, dusty, and solitary preoccupation that year by year was making him less and less fit for the role of suitor. He kept company with this and that lady, but clearly was not sweeping them off their feet.

"Well, you two bachelors," Jonathan said now, laying his arms over their shoulders, "what sayee to a deep breath o' brandy and cupful o' fresh air?" That was one of his favorite jokes.

THE NIGHT WAS MILD, JUST COLD ENOUGH TO KEEP THE snow from melting off. Candlelight from the brightly lit house made soft-edged rectangles on the snow under the windows. The great leafless oaks and elms and mulberry trees reached for the starpoints. Voices and songs came faintly from the servants' quarters behind the house; in the stables a horse blew and a hoof woodenly bumped.

Sleighbells jingled below on the public road. "Hear that," Jonathan said, pausing, his cup in one hand. "Who has a sleigh in Louisville, d'ye know?" Edmund blew out a mouthful of tobacco smoke and replied:

"Well, if anybody does have, and it's not y'rself, something'll have to be done about that, eh?" Jonathan was as wealthy as anyone in these parts, and if there was something to be had in the territory, he felt it was his natural prerogative to have the first one.

"Aye," he said. "Jove, wouldn't the youngsters enjoy a sleigh ride on a Christmas night like this, though! I'll wager if I sent up an order to Philadelphia now, there could be a nice manufactory sleigh delivered by *next* Christmas. One with bentwood runners and a leather dash. Egod, I *do* love a sleigh! Aye, I'll start inquiring right after the New Year. Hm. Hm."

This was strange to George, all this sending away for things, store things, luxury things, to be sent to a town that had not even existed a quarter of a century ago when he had first come here into the Kentucky wilderness with his boisterous little band of volunteers. He remembered the first time he had stood here.

He looked down from the high ground where they were walking, looked westward along the Bear Grass Creek toward Louisville, that little line of street lamps down by the river, that town he himself had surveyed and laid out so many years ago. The rows of houses and warehouses were dim dark shapes in the snowy bottomland, still just visible in the faint, lingering afterlight of evening.

Civilization, he thought. Everything I did, I did to bring on civilization, and now look how it's swallowed me up and gone on past.

He remembered the visions he had used to have of white stone cities, neat and clean and peaceful like the pictures of old Athens, on these stately bluffs above the Ohio. Well, Louisville was surely not that kind of a picture now. Perhaps it could be a great stone city someday, but now it was a dirty, disorderly, shabbily built collection of unpainted plank and log and stone buildings, their fronts usually spattered waist-high with mud from the miry streets, a town of pigs foraging in the streets, of mills and tanneries whose stinking wastes ran right off into the Ohio, of jerry-built wharves piled with kegs and bales and overrun with rats and brawling flatboaters and drunken Indians. Someday, he hoped, as the town grew richer maybe it could become more beautiful. Sometimes he would hope he would live to see that; other times he did not care what Louisville should become, or whether he lived to see anything. Sometimes he thought it would be a pleasure to sit on his porch across the river at Clarksville and watch a flood come along and wash the whole reeky mess of Louisville over the Falls. Sometimes Louisville affected him that way; it was so often a bitter reminder that everyone but himself, its founder, profited from it, and that anyone seemed all too ready to believe he was only its town drunk.

658

They stood on the brow of the high ground now, at the place they called their Overlook, gazing down and away at the wide river, the Falls, the hills of the Indiana lands on the other side. George's bones were starting to ache as they did whenever he was in the cold air, but he ignored the ache.

The three Clark men stood in the snow and puffed their pipes, and thought. They thought of their father and mother in their graves side by side at the Mulberry Hill house.

They thought of Johnny, of his secluded grave back at old Caroline.

They thought of Dickie, who had no grave.

And they thought of William, of William, who might well by now be lying in some shallow grave on a wind-swept prairie or frozen stiff in a riverbottom or buried under a mountain avalanche; and their minds turned up the far Missouri. They all had prepared themselves to accept that he might be dead or lost, as no word had come for many months; they all realized that they likely were by now the three surviving sons of John and Ann Rogers Clark. But none of them ever had said that to any of the others.

George looked down the familiar river and his thoughts went with its flow, and he blinked and swallowed, because the face of Teresa had just risen for an instant in his mind and then vanished. Then he thought on up the unknown Missouri far, far beyond St. Louis, where the sun would just now be setting, and said:

"A toast, hey?"

They raised their cups and touched them, and then George raised his and held it toward the northwest, and they did likewise.

"A Merry Christmas to Brother Billy," he said.

"A Merry Christmas," said Edmund.

"Merry Christmas, William," Jonathan added.

And they drank their brandy and turned away from the river and went back toward the house with the lighted windows.

37

YORK WAS PUTTING TEA BEFORE CAPTAIN LEWIS, TRYING TO
find a place for it on the table among the stacks of blotting paper,
the pressed flowers, the vials of seeds, the tin boxes, the labeled
insects, mouse skeletons, rattlesnake skulls, and bits of paper,
when a shuddering groan of pain came through the walls and
caused them both to turn their heads. Scannon raised his muzzle off his forepaws and cocked his ears, with a small, squeaking
whimper. Lewis shook his head with sad resignation, and said:

"I thought it was supposed to be easy for Indian women.
Haven't you heard that, York?"

"Yas, Cap'm."

"And for your women, too, I've heard."

"White folk do say that, Cap'm."

"Isn't it so?"

"Sah, any wommin hurt the same, an' I thank the Lo'd I
never have to hurt like that, but the diff'ns be, Cap'm, how
much do they holler."

Lewis looked at the wall and thought of this, then he said,
"This one hasn't yelled once. But she's been groaning and panting like that for a long time. It's her first baby."

"Yas, Cap'm." York knew more about Sacajawea than anyone
else did. York, and Scannon, had become deeply attached to the
pregnant child, and protective of her. Lewis could tell by the
anguish in their eyes that both were suffering with her.

Charbonneau's other wives had moved back to the village, so
they were not here to serve as midwives. Charbonneau himself
was out hunting.

Lewis had tried to help her several times today; he had examined Sacajawea and as far as he could tell there was nothing
awry, nothing turned wrong or anything; she was just little and
narrow in the pelvis and the baby was big, that was all. Though
Lewis considered himself a competent lay physician, births had
always rattled him. So he had left Sacajawea in the care of an
Indian woman who was the wife of René Jessaume, an interpreter, and had come back into his own room here to work on
the plant and animal specimens for President Jefferson.

It was an enormous job. In the crates and boxes and tins and bundles stored about this crowded little outpost, in the stacks of notes and sketches and maps that Clark had done, was contained more knowledge about the territory west of the Mississippi than had ever been recorded—surely a hundred times more knowledge. William's maps, prepared from surveys and celestial sightings and interviews with scores of Indians and trappers, without a doubt would instantly render every other map of the West obsolete. And its value was enhanced by reams of information about weather patterns, navigational hazards, soil and minerals, food and fur game, and the histories, languages, dispositions, enmities and alliances, numbers and living modes of all the Indian tribes the Corps of Discovery had thus far encountered. Furthermore, the data did not even stop here at Fort Mandan; Clark had even made a projected map of the Upper Missouri to the Rocky Mountains, based on more interviews with wide-ranging Indians.

The storehouse of the little fort was stacked to the ceiling with crates full of specimens and artifacts of the sort Mr. Jefferson had ordered: the skins and skeletons and horns of animals unknown to science: mountain rams, antelopes, mule deer, burrowing squirrels, badgers, red foxes, gray hares, even a skin of the ferocious yellow bear, terror of the far plains; the expedition had not encountered such a bear yet, but had obtained a hide from the Indians, along with dire warnings of the beast's strength and ferocity. There were Indian weapons and articles of their clothing and handiwork; there were hides upon which Indian artists had painted representations of historical battles; there were plants reputed to be remedies for the bites of rattlesnakes and mad dogs. And in addition to all these inert specimens, there were the cages in which magpies, prairie hens, and the beloved prairie dog had been kept alive for these many months. As for plants, Lewis had thus far preserved more than a hundred new specimens, pressed in purple blotting paper, with detailed notes on when and where they had been discovered, as well as any nutritive or medicinal values they had.

No, Mister Jefferson was not going to be disappointed. The Corps of Discovery was hardly halfway to the Pacific, but already had collected enough specimens to open and stock a museum, and it was invaluable.

It was such a lot of worry, though. Sometimes Lewis felt he would go mad from it. The crates and bags and portfolios and notes, the papers and specimens had to be put in comprehensible order by spring thaw, had to be protected from mold and vermin and deterioration. In the spring this treasure would have to be loaded on the keelboat, entrusted to Corporal Warfington, and put on its hazardous way back down the wild Missouri, past the Sioux, to St. Louis, and thence over or around the other side of the Continent to Washington.

To add to Lewis's worries now there was the keelboat itself. It was so locked in layers of river ice that parties working for days with axes and heated water had thus far been unable to free it. The keelboat would have to be released before the great spring ice-breaking, lest it be smashed to splinters.

Then there was all this worry about the British traders from the North West Company. These accursed British agents were consumed with curiosity about the expedition, and were forever visiting Fort Mandan, and pumping the neighboring Indians for information.

Lewis was certain now that his Corps of Discovery was in an unannounced race to the Pacific with the British concern, and this added to his anxieties. Jefferson had made it clear that a key objective of the journey was to thwart England's designs on the control of trade in the Northwest; now the British seemed to suspect that the race was on and that this little American Army unit was its vanguard.

A few of the Indian chiefs had refused to become friends of the Corps. One important hold-out was the head chief of the Minnetarees, Le Borgne, the One-Eyed. He was reported to be very suspicious of the Americans and had thus far refused to come down from his town on the Knife River and smoke the pipe. His loyalty to the British traders could someday prove troublesome, and Lewis worried every day about him.

Most of the Indians in the vicinity had, however, been completely won over by the Americans. Both captains spent hours of every day treating the Indians for everything from rheumatism and infections to frostbite and snow-blindness; and Private Shields, that extraordinary blacksmith, had probably done as much for the cause of diplomacy by mending their tools and weapons, as York had done by infusing Strong Blood into the tribes' unborn generations.

Now another heartbreaking groan came through the wall from the interpreters' quarters, and Lewis winced over his tea.

Lord but I wish Clark was here, Lewis thought. The girl's come to trust him like an uncle. If he was here I'll wager she'd settle back and loosen up and yield that babe slick as pawpaw pulp, just to please 'im.

But William was not here. He had gone downriver a week ago, leading a hunting party of eighteen men. The stocks of meat put by in November and December had been nearly depleted, and game was scarce within fifty miles of this cluster of Indian towns. So the hunters had set out across the blinding and featureless desert of ice and snow, leading three pack horses and pulling two handmade wooden sleds, determined to go as much as a hundred miles to find game if they had to. Their peril, out there in the deep snow and subzero prairie gales, had added to Lewis's anxieties, as had the resultant undermanning of the fort.

And now on top of all those concerns, there was that nerve-wracking labor going on in the next room. If it were merely the suffering of a nameless and inconsequential squaw, the pity of it would have been distracting enough. But this girl, whose short life had already been an unremitting series of tragedies, was no mere squaw now. It grew ever more apparent that she would be a critically important figure when the expedition reached her people in the mountains. Lewis was growing alarmed at the possibility that she might die in childbirth.

He sipped at the edge of his teacup, then set it down with a sigh when another awful whimper came from Sacajawea's quarters. That one had almost surfaced as a scream. He put the cup down. "Come," he said to York. "Let's see if we can do *something*."

They met René Jessaume going in. Jessaume was in character somewhat like Charbonneau, perhaps even outweighing him in self-importance. When they entered, they found Jessaume's squaw sitting useless and apparently unconcerned with the sufferings of Sacajawea. This woman was older, something of a harlot, and Jessaume customarily rented her out to anyone who wanted to partake of her sluttishness. Jessaume threw her a few contemptuous Mandan words as they entered the room, and she rose sullenly and climbed the ladder into the sleeping loft above the room. Then Jessaume turned to look at Sacajawea, who lay on a pallet close to the fireplace. She was naked, covered with a sheen of sweat, having thrown the buffalo robe off the upper part of her body. Her hair was lank with sweat and bear grease. She was so small-chested and looked so stricken that she seemed more like a child with her belly swollen with illness than a mother in labor. She tried to smile at her friend York, though her little rib cage was heaving with the exertions of her breathing.

"*Merde!*" Jessaume swore, stomping snow off his boots. "Who put this creature in the way of my fire?"

York swelled up and looked like the ferocious beast he was reputed to be. "I did," he growled.

"Eh," Jessaume said with a false smile. "That is good for her comfort." He shrugged off his blanket-coat, looking down at her. "Jesu," he growled. "How long does she do thees?"

"Since this morning," said Lewis. It was now late afternoon.

"*Eheu,*" he muttered with a shrug. "Ees pity this be the cold season."

"Eh? Why say so?"

"Could catch the rattlesnake, and use its rattle."

"What's this?" Lewis said. "I have a snake's rattle. If I can find it."

"Eh! Get it, *mon capitaine.* Jessaume will show you how the Arikaras hurry a stubborn *enfant.*"

Lewis hurried into his room and rummaged among boxes for the rattles he had kept as a specimen when one of the men had killed a western rattler in the plains last summer.

He found the specimen and took it in to Jessaume. The Frenchman separated a segment of the rattle. York watched distrustfully from the bedside, where he knelt gently sponging the girl's face and neck with a wet cotton cloth. To York, a rattlesnake was nothing good, and from what he had seen, a French Canadian was no better, so he was fearful for his suffering young friend. "Seem to me," he ventured, "if a crittur's p'ison at one end he be p'ison at the other."

"No," said Lewis. "Let's just try it. Anything!"

Jessaume was now breaking the rattle into a tin cup with his strong, dirty thumbs; it looked rather like pie dough being crumbled. Then, whistling tunelessly through the gap between his yellow teeth, he lifted a kettle off the fire and poured hot water into the cup, then picked up a dirty spoon and stirred it, looking as insouciant as if he were merely fixing himself a cup of sweet tea.

"Now," he said, squatting close to the pallet, "one must tell the woman what it do." He clucked and gurgled a statement in the Minnetaree tongue, and she stopped groaning and lay panting through an open mouth, listening to what he said. Apparently it was convincing; the girl reached out to touch the cup as Jessaume lifted her and brought it toward her lips. She sipped at the cup's edge.

Lewis watched. He saw the skinny brown squaw child lying swollen in the musty buffalo robe, her eyes sunken, hair uncombed, watched her drink the disgusting potion; he smelled the body smells and old woodsmoke and the tangy rough-hewn raw wood of the hut walls, saw the smoke-and-grease-blackened leather leggings stretched over the thick thighs of the squatting

Jessaume, saw Jessaume scratching lice or fleas under his arm with his free hand, saw his black-bearded uncivilized face, heard Jessaume's wife break wind loudly up in the loft, heard the prairie wind howl around the eaves of the hut; and he suddenly felt a profound depression over the squalor of this little Indian girl's life, her pained struggle to deliver an ignominious life into the world, all as a result of the apparently insatiable lust of that arrogant pig of a man Charbonneau; it was all so totally and unexpectedly sordid, so savage, so lacking in meaning or human hope or dignity, that Lewis despaired over the absence of glory in most human lives. He had always had his own dream of glory, this great exploration of the Northwest, and somehow now, this wretched scene, the genesis of a savage life, was like a profanation of his dream. Dear God, he thought, would it were in a man's power somehow to ease the human condition!

Now the girl had swallowed the concoction; Jessaume had put the cup on the dirt floor and gotten up and was hanging up his gun and powder horn, apparently through with his ministration and unconcerned with its results. Sacajawea lay back on the robe now, and did indeed seem to be going tranquil. Either it's just a placebo, Lewis thought, or she's lying back to die. He felt her pulse, that regular little blood-beat under sweaty skin next to the small wrist bones. It was fine. He laid his hand on her forehead; she was not overly feverish. Jessaume's potion had not done her any harm that he could perceive. She was still conscious; she was still laboring; she was still hurting and bewildered; he could see all that in her face. But now at least she did not seem to be dying of it. Lewis looked at Jessaume and said, "What does it do? How does it work?"

The Frenchman shrugged. "Jessaume he is no doctor. Only I know the *enfant* will be here soon."

"York," Lewis said, rising, "watch after her. I'll be next door if ye need me."

Back at his desk, he sat with a piece of the purple blotting paper in his hands, looking at the showy pink flower pressed on it, a new flower discovered last summer near the mouth of the Platte River; he sat looking at the flower and trying to shake off that odd pall of despair, sometimes thinking of his friend Clark, wishing he could hear the shout of his return at the gate.

But the shouts he heard then were not William's. York's joyful whoop rolled through the wall, followed immediately by Jessaume's throaty laughter and then the glorious angry wail of a newborn baby.

"Yo! Cap'm Lewis!" York's voice thundered. "We got us 'nother man for our army! He, he!"

Lewis heard the sentry and several other soldiers beyond the walls laugh and cheer. He rose from the bench, a smile spreading over his narrow mouth, the gloom suddenly blown off his soul, and headed for the door.

"Well, well," he was saying to himself. "Well, well. Damn me, wait till Mister Jefferson hears o' this! Everybody'll want a rattlesnake!"

LOCUST GROVE PLANTATION, KENTUCKY
MARCH 1, 1805

"NOW, NICKY, CHARLIE," LUCY SAID TO THE TWO RED-HAIRED toddlers whom the nursery mammy had led into the parlor, "would you say how d'ye to your Auntie Fanny?"

Both little round identical faces broke into elfin, nose-wrinkling grins. Both of the twins had always liked Fanny, even before they had known her name. And now as she bent forward in her chair and tilted her head and spread her arms toward them, they both at once let loose of the servant's hands and hurried toward her, their eyes fastened on her smiling mouth. Males of every age were entranced by Fanny's lovely white smile, even age two. They came into her embrace, one in each arm, murmuring, "Huwwo" and other words less comprehensible. She kissed one on the cheek and asked:

"And who are you?"

"Jaws," Charles pronounced his name.

And she kissed the other one and said, "And who are you, sir?"

"Neckwuss," Nicholas said.

She laughed her plangent laugh and held them at arm's length to look at them, one hand on each of their identical white yoke collars. "Well, I don't know how you know which of you is which," she said. "Did anyone ever tell you you look as like as two buttons on a shirt?"

"I biggo," said Charles. He was a little stockier. This was Lucy's second son named Charles. Her first Charles had lived only ten months.

The twins were Lucy's seventh and eighth children. Now forty, she was still strong and erect, regal and red-haired as her mother had been, with the same fair, sensitive skin now showing the tiny squint-wrinkles. But she was not a beautiful woman, as her mother had been at this age. She looked, rather, with her long Clark nose and thin, firm mouth, more like her brothers than her sisters. It was as if the tomboy of old had passed through her two decades as a vivacious belle and then emerged looking like a handsome, not very effete, good fellow. To Bill Croghan, though, she was still beauteous. And to those who knew her well, she was still vivacious. To outsiders, who usually saw her only in the back of Colonel Croghan's gleaming black carriage, or in the family church pew, or passing in and out of shops, she was only the matronly sister of General Clark, sharp-eyed, impassive, confident of herself and her position, looking rather like him.

Her face reflected displeasure in the same way as his: a flashing of the dark blue eyes, a visible clenching of the jaw muscles. And that expression hardened her visage now. Something was displeasing her at this moment, just as the twins were being led out of the panelled room. It was George's voice, loud and arrogant and liquory in its inflections, coming across the hall from the drawing room, where he was smoking and drinking with William Croghan and Judge Fitzhugh, Fanny's fiancé.

". . . bedamned Webster didn't know what he was talking of! *Dam-NATION!* Any one o' those mounds would've taken De-Soto *ten years* to build, and he was only in these parts for—"

The door shut, and George's words became indistinct, but the rumble of his voice went on. Lucy's lips were in a thin line. With an exasperated hiss of a sigh, she asked:

"What in heaven's name is he ranting about now? And why must he be so *profane* in my house?"

Fanny knew from the few words what his topic was. She had heard him go on about it many times while she was living at Point o' Rock. "It's that about the Indian mounds," she said. George had written a treatise debunking the prevailing theories about the mounds: that they had been built by a great Indian race like the Incas, now extinct, or that they had been built by the Spanish explorer DeSoto. George's own research into the mounds and interviews with Indian chiefs had convinced him that the great network of mounds had been built by none other than the ancestors of tribes still inhabiting the Mississippi watershed. And now, in the room across the hall, he was pontificating on his old theory for a new set of ears, those of Dennis Fitzhugh.

"That again?" Lucy snapped. "I swear I don't know how a man can stay so riled over a lot of Indians that's been dead a thousand years! I mean so riled as to *cuss.* Why, when my boys Georgie and Johnny go visit him, it takes me a month and ten balls o' soap apiece to wash th' stain of impiety out o' their mouths!" She was tapping her foot angrily and shaking her head.

"They worship him," Fanny explained. "They just try to be like him. Surely you know that, Lucy dear."

"Don't I know it, though! Especially Georgie. Why, d'you know what that scamp was doing this week? He was a-ridin' lickety-cut up the road and tryin' to yank Johnny up onto the saddle behind of 'im, just like George used to do brother Johnny, rest his soul. Both my young fools like t' *killed* 'emselves, fallin' off, and draggin' in the road." Georgie, now a sinewy, tireless, reckless bump-around of thirteen, coppery-haired and good-looking, seemed determined to pattern himself after his namesake uncle, and Lucy was beginning to see the hazards of having a darling son emulate someone whose past was such a wild legend. "And the worst on't is," she continued, "a body can't tell him anything. He thinks he's always right, just as yon bellowing brother does. Just like this o' the mound Indians! I swear, Fanny! Aren't you afraid sometimes to bring that beau o' yours around, for fear he'll drive 'im off?"

Fanny's mouth had dropped open, and a pink flush had tinged her ivory face. Now she faced her sister and said calmly:

"Lucy, Lucy, how you've changed."

"What? I?"

"Yes. You. You act *ashamed* of George! Well, let me tell you, a body could do worse than try to be like him. Look what it made of Brother Billy. You, Lucy! Will you sit there in front of me who knows better, and pretend you yourself never tried to ride like Brother George, and fight like him? Why, the stories in this family about you and your slingshots, and your make-believe armies! General Lucy! Why, you're more like George than he is himself, but you choose to pretend not!"

Lucy, the matron of Louisville society, was blinking and gaping at this harangue from her mild and sweet youngest sister. And though she worked her mouth and stared indignantly at Fanny for several seconds, all she could produce in reply was:

"*I* don't drink and fall in the streets."

"Nor did he, till he'd been treated in the spirit you're in now. What would Mama have made of what you just said, Lucy?"

Lucy's angry stare suddenly faltered, dropped. She looked at her hands for a moment. Fanny's words had gone straight in and struck her at the heart. And it was such a revelation of herself to herself that she did not retort or deny.

And Fanny was saying now, in that rich, gentle voice of hers:

"Of course he goes on and on about being right when others e wrong. It's because he always was, you know. And knowing *at* is all he's got left."

FORT MANDAN
March 9, 1805

HE WIND WHISTLED FROM THE NORTH. IT SCOURED THE lains, and blown snow all but blanked the features of the land-cape. William Clark, Toussaint Charbonneau, and the two sol-iers with them leaned into the wind, squinted, and trudged into e gale, high-stepping in the deep snow, their faces muffled to revent frostbite.

"Look, *capitaine*." Charbonneau pointed ahead. Five Indian orsemen, appearing and vanishing like ghosts in the shifting hiteness, were riding slowly toward them.

"Look to your pieces, boys," William said. They checked the riming in their rifles while William plowed a few yards ahead nd then stopped to wait with his right hand raised in salute. he Indians had seen them now and rode forward, ominous lhouettes in the flapping buffalo robes in which they were hrouded.

"By gah," Charbonneau said, "that one is Le Borgne!"

"Eh? One-Eye? Y' sure?"

"He is big man of my village."

Well, well, thought William. Is the great bogey man finally eakening? Looks like he's headed for the fort. The Min-etarees' head chief, reputed to be a bloodthirsty tyrant and trongly partial to the British trading companies, had refused all vinter to visit the Americans. There were several reasons why ewis and Clark wanted to talk with him; the most important ne was to try to persuade him to stop his annual spring raids on he Shoshonis in the Rocky Mountains.

One-Eye had halted his horse twenty feet away now, and a ood look at his face satisfied William that this chief was as ugly n the outside as he was said to be on the inside. His empty yesocket was black and scarred and hideous; it looked as if a ole had been punched in his face by a burning stake. His good ye, as if straining to do the work of two, bulged like a fish's eye. le had tossed back the cowl of his robe to show himself at his nost formidable. His long hair was tied in a knot at the top of is head, revealing a strong neck and long-lobed ears hung with brass rings. His mouth was his cruelest feature: thin-lipped, hard-bitten, surrounded by deep, black, downturned scars and creases. I'd say this one's maybe even meaner than Partizan, William thought.

The chief's eye passed over Charbonneau as if the Frenchman were not there, then fell on William, who gave the chief a friendly smile and said aside to Charbonneau:

"Well, Big Tess, introduce us, and ask if I can be o' service."

Charbonneau talked volubly, waving his big mittened hands around like bear paws. The chief kept looking at William's eyes and spoke short, throaty syllables in a voice that gurgled in its own depths.

"Le Borgne say thees: that he go to the fort only for one cause; his people talk of a man all black. He say he is tired hearing the lie from people who are fooled, and go to see."

William was amused by this transparent excuse, but managed not to laugh. "Tell him I agree a man should see things with his own eyes—er, eye—and that the black man will be happy to prove himself. Tell him our chief, Captain Lewis, will give him gifts and smoke with him. Tell him my boat-makers up yonder are expecting me, so I can't go down with him. But say I might be back to the fort before he leaves. Got all that? And listen, you're our Minnetaree talker, so you go to the fort with 'im. They'll need ye there more than I will here."

THE WIND WAS LESS FIERCE AMONG THE COTTONWOODS and the boat-builders were hard at work in the trampled, sooty, bark-littered snow. From large bonfires they were transferring shovelfuls of coals into the hewn-down cottonwood trunks, to burn the wood and make it easier to hollow the logs. A canoe would be burning inside one end while a man, black as a chimneysweep, would be swinging an adze in the other, routing out the charred heartwood. One of these laborers looked up, bloodshot white eyes in a black face. William smiled, and said, "That you, York?" The man grinned, and answered:

"No, sah, Massa! I's Collins!"

Sergeant Gass came over, laughing. The barrel-chested Pennsylvania Irishman was in charge of the canoe detail. A blast of wind shook the woods, and Gass flinched as hot coals and ash swirled around him. He unreeled a string of colorful epithets.

"How goes it?" William asked.

"Well, Cap'n, well enough, considerin' what we got to work with. The goddamn trees up here's growed up so windshook an stunty and cankerous, y' might's well whistle a jig to a milestone as look for a good tree. Lookee there at that cockled-up eel's turd of a log, f'r instance. Look at that grain, would ye? Crapy as nigger hair, and carvin' 'er's like tryin' to chaw gristle without no teeth. And when she dries, she opens up like a squaw's cunt."

Gass went on and on in his campfire eloquence; obviously he had been rehearsing his complaints and storing them up for the captain's visit.

"Aye, Sergeant, I'd give a pretty for half a dozen nice down-home tulip poplars, wouldn't you? Eh, well. Shields has got plenty o' tin to cover up splits. It'll have t'do. Now, listen. Here's what I came to say: we took inventory of what we have to carry, and we're going to need two more canoes. So start a couple more."

Gass looked stricken for a moment, then seemed to be having a tantrum deep in his innards, but finally just nodded.

"Well," William said for pleasantry, "how 'bout Indians? Ye had many visitors?"

"All day every day," Gass growled. "They hunker in our hutch an' eat our jerky an' supervise like a gang o' grand vi-zeers. Be glad when th' river thaws so they can't walk over here."

William cocked an eyebrow. "But then how would you get over to the village evenings, to y'r sweethearts?"

Gass winked and popped his cheek. "We're boat-builders," he said.

Gass and his party were close to Black Cat's village and also to the town of the Hidatsas, and, being detached from the fort, had an unusually free rein to fraternize with the squaws in this vicinity. Between the sleepless nights and the constant smoke, they were all getting the most spectacular red eyeballs. But they liked the duty. Strenuous as it was, it was easier than being at the fort. Down there, everyone was always working like a beaver from dawn to dark, making crates and rope and parfleche bags, calking and repairing boats, smoking meat, making leather clothes and moccasins, and cutting and splitting wood for the charcoal that fueled the smithy's forge. Bad as this boat yard was, it was easy compared with the fort.

"Here, Sergeant," William said now, "I brought up your ration o' spirits. I'm going over to smoke with Black Cat 'fore I go back down."

"Ah! Have a good, ah, *smoke*, sir." Gass nodded toward the distant town. "My compliments to the ladies." He winked again, a lewd, face-twisting exaggeration of a wink. Gass wondered whether the captains partook of the squaws' favors. There was speculation that Captain Clark had bedded some of the towns'

671

handsomest maidens—even chiefs' wives—as many of the women spoke of the great beauty of the Red Hair Chief. So far none of the men had gotten any first-hand knowledge of any such liaisons, but they were happy to believe it. As for William, he let them wonder. Some things an officer and a gentleman did not discuss.

Anyway, what the troops envisioned with the greatest amusement was the brusque, rigid Captain Lewis with squaws. "He don't need a hard-on," Private Colter had joked, "he *is* one."

WILLIAM EMERGED FROM HIS LONG, SHUDDERING SPASM OF pleasure, growing aware of the murmur of voices outside the lodge, of moans in his ear, fingers on his back, the smell of woodsmoke and oiled hair and musky flesh, and as the intense tickle ebbed from his loins, he opened his eyes and saw her delicate red-brown ear and neck and open mouth and trembling eyelashes. She was still convulsing, her pelvis surging against him, and her moans were turning up at the ends, becoming little cries. Outside, the voices rose into laughter and cheers: "Hai-ee! Hai-ee-ee!" The Mandans had been listening outside and now were happy because he had satisfied the girl. William doubted that he would ever get used to this, to being publicly applauded for such a private act. But he understood. They were happy enough that the blood of the Red Hair Chief was coming into their tribe; they were even happier that he was pleasing her, too, as she was a select maid. He did not really know *how* she had been selected for this, but she was a pleasing choice indeed, comely and smooth, clean, and a very cheerful and passionate giver. He had supposed, when she first entered the lodge wrapped in a blue blanket and stood looking at him, that she was the daughter of a chieftain. She had taken the blanket off then to reveal her whole self, making his throat feel engorged, and she had acted neither brazen nor coy, but had smiled, as if at calm inner thoughts, gone around him and lain down on the pallet, all russet-brown on the black buffalo robe, and watched him undress with glinting dark eyes.

Now she was descending into languor under him, happy, nameless, her fingers caressing his hard, freckled shoulders, her breathing deep and full, the gleam of oil on her face and bosom moving as she breathed, and William looked at her with simple gratitude and admiration, trying not to think of Judy Hancock. Judy Hancock had nothing to do with this; it was a matter of *this* world, not the safe and elegant world in which she moved.

But now he *was* thinking of Judy Hancock, and telling himself hat this did not affect his love for her. This was a thing of the flesh only; his love for Judy was a matter of the soul. She was a far away dream-picture, golden like summer sunlight, scented like lilac and camphor, not smoke and bear-oil; he was a Clark and would marry a virgin Hancock of Virginia; it was as unthinkable that he could have real affection for this dusky flesh-woman under him as that he could have affection for a slave woman.

That, at least, he thought, I've never done.

Almost every Virginian gentry-man he knew had lain with slave women; even Jefferson had a slave mistress; indeed, it was said that he loved her. But William had never done that, never lain with a slave woman, and was fairly certain none of his brothers ever had.

But this with an Indian girl, he thought, now easing himself off her to lie beside her on the buffalo robe and stroke her and return her wordless smile and look at her anonymous eyes and fine thick eyebrows, how natural a thing this is, yet how odd. Here we've crossed all the boundaries of flesh and nerves, but can never cross those of our souls because of who we are. Maybe she'll have a red-haired baby someday and will have that baby all her life out here on the plains to remind her of the day she did this for her tribe, but we can't love. A red woman and a white man can't really love, can they? Do Charbonneau and Sacajawea really love? I don't see much sign of it. He just *owns* her.

He was looking at the face and body of this nameless maid on a buffalo robe, feeling all languid in his loins, and was seeing Sacajawea in her buffalo robe with the little dark-haired baby boy at her breast, and he was thinking of her, and was thinking of her with a true affection, he realized, and that was confusing.

But this of a man out of his own world doing the body act with a maid in her own world at the request of a Mandan chief—this, he thought, it's only diplomacy, and, o' course—he smiled at the little *moues* she was making with her mouth—it's a fairer duty than some we've got to do.

As William plowed through snow returning to Fort Mandan in a twilight of driving snow, the scene of morning repeated itself. Once again five horsemen materialized in the swirling snow dust; once more they proved to be Le Borgne and his escort. This time Le Borgne was smiling, though it looked more like a death-rictus than an expression of pleasure. William saluted him.

Charbonneau was not present now to interpret, so there was a moment of awkwardness. But Le Borgne opened the front of his robe. He was wearing a scarlet shirt from the expedition's stores, a shiny metal gorget, and a Jefferson medal. On his arm an American flag was draped. William nodded, and made hand signs meaning "good" and "I am glad."

Then Le Borgne inhaled and drew up to make himself seem huge. He made a wavy motion over his head with his fingers. He licked his forefinger and rubbed it on his chest. Then he reached down and cupped his hand before his groin and waggled it up and down as if hefting a gigantic penis, looking down with an expression of astonishment.

William smiled and nodded. He understood. York had once again proven that he was real. William made another hand sign, one that meant:

"What I told you is true."

A FEW DAYS LATER WILLIAM RETURNED TO THE FORT FROM another visit to the canoe factory. The parade ground of the fort was full of working men. Some were stretching and coiling hide ropes, some were shelling corn, others were moving crates about, still others were carrying charcoal to the forge, where Shields's, Bratton's, and Willard's hammers clanged tirelessly. In addition to the Corps' own blacksmithing work, they were making axes and tools to trade to the Indians for corn, tallow, and jerky. William had been hearing the hammers from two miles up the river. The good smell of smoking meat hung thick in the compound, but so did the stench of urine and animal brains used in the curing of hides.

"Problem. Big problem," Lewis announced gloomily as he came in.

"Eh? What now?" He stamped snow off his boots and laved his hands over the fire.

"That Charbonneau. I suspect the damned Britishers corrupted him, or maybe the One-Eye did. Anyway, he made demands today. Says if he goes with us he won't work or stand guard like the ordinary men. Wants to be free to turn back if 'e gets miffed with anybody, and bring away any provisions he wants to carry."

William made a chirp with the corner of his mouth. "What a bloat-head. Ye sent 'im packin', I reckon?"

"Aye. He's moved out, takin' his squaws. But I told 'im to think on it. I said we'd forgive and sign 'im on if he got those grandiose notions out of his head."

William unbelted and peeled off his leather coat and hung it on a peg. "The problem's not him but Sacajawea, o' course.

"O' course. We'd be better off without him, that's my opinion. But we'll need her."

William paced, lit a pipe, and paced some more, in the little walking space remaining among the scientific cargo. He stopped. 'Reckon we could take her regardless of him?"

"He'd call it kidnap. The British could make a hue and cry of it, and would." Lewis shook his head. "Shame, isn't it, we find a Shoshoni just by a good hap, and by ill hap she belongs to that bumptious cock-a-hoop."

William sucked his pipe stem and gazed into the fire. He knew that the Shoshoni girl was almost a-quiver with eagerness to make the journey back to her people. She'd never be the same if that French fartbag ruined it for 'er, he thought. The poor thing would never dare hope again. "What let's do," he suggested, "let Charbonneau think we might hire Gravelin or Le Page or Jessaume in his place. How long d'ye think he'd swell up over that before bustin'?"

Lewis tapped his temple with three fingers and his face brightened a bit. "I wager he might change his tune in a week at most. Give him time for his pride to deflate a bit."

"I'd say five days. Now, why don't we fetch Gravelin, in such a way as Charbonneau will know of it?"

IN THE NEXT FOUR DAYS THERE WAS ENOUGH SUNSHINE TO permit the Corps to spread clothing, bedding, collections, and parched corn out to dry. Joseph Gravelin came to the fort, walking right past the tepee Charbonneau had erected outside the pickets. Charbonneau saw Gravelin move his gear into the fort.

And on the fifth day, Charbonneau sent word by his colleague Le Page that he was sorry for his foolishness. He asked to be forgiven for his simplicity.

They called him in and signed him up on their original terms, and he was so elated he even boasted that he could cook for them the best Creole food they'd ever taste.

PRIVATE NEWMAN STOOD BEFORE CAPTAIN LEWIS AMONG THE piles of baggage. He had been called in, and he was full of hope.

"I want you to know, Newman, that I'm writing a report on you that will stand you in good stead at your next post. In our minds you stand acquitted by your behavior."

Newman began to glow.

"We are sorry to lose you, but I can't rescind my judgment. You'll . . ." Newman's gaze stayed on Lewis's face, but he seemed to shrink half a foot. "You'll pack your gear to go on the keelboat party back to St. Louis."

"That, that's final, sir?"

"It is. That's all, Newman. Regrets."

"Didn't I say so?" Colter remarked later when he heard of it. "The man's a walkin' hard-on."

38

FORT MANDAN
April 7, 1805

THE BOW GUN BOOMED, AND ITS SMOKE ROLLED AMONG THE hundreds of yelling and chattering Mandans on the shore. The keelboat turned on the flint-gray water and began slipping downstream, her small crew under Corporal Warfington waving back.

A reply was fired from a swivel gun in the white pirogue, which was still moored at the bank, and the *huzzah*s of the soldiers on shore were, for a moment, louder than the droning voices of the Indian crowd. William had to shout into Lewis's ear to make himself heard, pointing at the *Discovery*.

"I wish she had come up as easy as she goes down!"

Lewis nodded, then shook his head. They both were remembering the half-year of perilous toil expended to bring up the great boat, which now would return to the Mississippi, without such toil but in twice as much peril, bearing its priceless cargo of knowledge. Its downriver pilot was Joseph Gravelin, the least dishonest Frenchman they had encountered on the Upper Missouri and reputedly an excellent waterman; therefore it was not so much the river itself, but the return voyage past the belligerent Teton Sioux, which posed danger for Warfington's crew.

The Indians on the shore were as melancholy and excited as the Americans. These white men who were leaving this day, going both up the river and down, leaving behind a willow-log fort full of smoke-smells and life-smells and the ghosts of laughter and music, had changed the world for them. They had given them a new way to think. They had caused tribes to declare peace with each other. They had cured many diseases and injuries for the Mandans and their neighbors. They had left much strong new blood in the Mandan nation; many squaws, no one knew how many, were carrying within themselves babies they expected would have gray eyes or blue eyes, red or yellow hair, and fair skin. Also there were many of these squaws who could expect their babies to have black skin and hair like wool and the strength of bears. Several of the soldiers, in return for what they were leaving in the Mandan women, were bringing with them the burning, itching, seeping symptoms of venereal disease.

Many of the soldiers, now gathered near their pirogues and canoes on the trampled shore, stared good-byes into the eyes of certain squaws who drifted down near them, and a few small gifts and remembrances were passed between white hands and brown hands.

William's heart was full of happiness and sadness as he watched the farewells. He saw Sacajawea, in a spotless fringed tunic and calf-high moccasins, her greased hair immaculately combed, parted and bound into two braids, her baby in a cradleboard on her back, standing amid a cluster of other squaws. Some of them were embracing her and giving her gifts, or folding their wrists over their bosoms in the sign of love, tears on their faces—and yet there was something bad, something alien and sullen in the faces of several of them. The other two wives of Charbonneau hung back from her, their eyes full of plain hatred, and William could understand that; it was simple jealously. But the strange reserve of the others dawned on him slowly. Of course: she was even less a one of them now than she had been as a Shoshoni slave of their people, or as a Frenchman's squaw. She was a woman now leaving The Nation, one Indian woman in the company of many white warriors, going with them into distant lands where they would and could never dream of going. Thus she was lost to them, different from them, very bad medicine.

William looked at her. She was certainly not gloating about her special status. In her face, that unusually delicate and guileless face whose expressions he was learning to read, were both the sadness of partings and the pain of rejection. It's all right, girl, he wanted to go and tell her. In three or four months, God willing, we'll have you among your own blood people.

Captain Lewis, in full uniform, now was standing face to face with Shahaka, known as "Big White," major chief of the Mandans. Each gripped the other's shoulder with his right hand, and they clasped their left hands underneath. The crowd grew still around them, to hear their words, for they loved their old chief;

and the quiet spread through the throng like a ripple on water until there were no more human voices, only the whiff of the cool, spring-scented wind, the barking of dogs, the rush of the river.

Chief Shahaka spoke first. He wore a Jefferson medal on a necklace, proudly displayed on his chest. It had become his most important piece of ornamentation. Now he began, in a voice that could be heard all along the riverbank.

"My people have shared food and kindness with you. You have made my sick people well, and you have been fair in all matters. We weep to see you go. You and Chief Red Hair have taught us to turn our backs on old wars, and to look east to your nation for protection and for trade. I, Shahaka, and all my people trust you. We will always watch up the great river for your return. But even if you do not come back this way, we will remember you, and our sons and grandsons will hear of the winter when you lived among us and made us glad. This I say for my people: you have made friends of us forever." The crowd murmured in approval; some voices keened, "Aii-eee! Aii-eee!"

Lewis blinked and swallowed as this was translated. Then, still holding the chief's left hand, he responded:

"We have been secure and happy as your neighbors, and we will miss our brothers the Mandans. When we return from beyond the Shining Mountains, we will embrace you again.

"You see our ship going down the river. The talking leaves we put on that ship will tell our Great Father about your goodness and your brotherhood. And when I see our Great Father face to face, I will tell him the same in my own voice, and he will look kindly on you. He will send men to bring goods to sell you at fair prices, as I have promised. The friendship of my nation and yours started when we came here before the winter, and it will never end."

The tumult of affection and farewell grew loud again as Lewis and the chief embraced. Then the chief hugged William; the sergeants bawled orders, and twenty-seven white men, one black man, one Shoshoni girl-squaw, one two-month-old papoose, and one black Newfoundland dog the size of a pony, arrayed themselves in the pirogues and canoes. Captain Lewis, armed with his rifle and espontoon, accompanied by George Drouillard, waved them off and started hiking northward along the shore. The small canoes, hacked out of poor, wind-twisted willow trunks a few weeks earlier, were sorry-looking vessels, patched with tin to cover and hold the splits and faults in their grain, but they were riverworthy nevertheless, and even though heavy-laden, they were light as feathers compared with the old keelboat *Discovery*, to the delight of the men on the oars and paddles. The water was fast and gray, even now dotted with cakes of rotten ice. William put a hand over the side into the river and it ached with cold.

"Careful, boys," he called. "No one wants to find himself swimming in *that* by an accident! Now, put your minds off those dusky sweethearts o' your'n, and blow th' lodge smoke out o' your lungs. Stroke water, boys! It's a long haul to th' western sea!"

From the Journal of Meriwether Lewis:

> *Fort Mandan April 7th, 1805*
>
> *Having on this day at 4. P.M. completed every arrangement necessary for our departure, we dismissed the barge and crew with orders to return without loss of time to St. Louis. . . . We gave Richard Warfington, a discharged Corpl., the charge of the barge and crew, and confided to his care likewise our dispatches to the government, letters to our private friends and a number of articles to the President of the United States. . . .*
>
> *At the same moment that the Barge departed from Fort Mandan, Capt. Clark embarked with our party and proceeded up the River. As I had used no exercise for several weeks, I determined to walk on Shore as far as our encampment of this evening.*
>
> *Our vessels consisted of six small canoes, and two large perogues. This little fleet altho' not quite so rispectable as those of Columbus or Capt. Cook, were still viewed by us with as much pleasure as those deservedly famed explorers ever beheld Theirs; and I dare say with quite as much anxiety for their safety and preservation. We were now about to penetrate a country at least two thousand miles in width, on which the foot of civilized man had never trodden; The good or evil it had in store for us was for experiment yet to determine, and these little vessells contained every article by which we were to expect to subsist or defend ourselves. however, as the state of mind in which we are, generally gives the colouring to events, when the immagination is suffered to wander into futurity, the picture which now presented itself to me was a most pleasing one. entertaing as I do, the most confident hope of succeeding in a voyage which had formed a darling project of mine for the last ten*

years, I could but esteem this moment of my departure as among the most happy of my life. The party are in excellent health and spirits, zealously attached to the enterprise, and anxious to proceed; not a whisper of murmur or discontent to be heard among them, but all act in unison, And with the most perfict harmony.

May 9, 1805

THEY HAD BEEN COMING ALONG AND COMING ALONG, SINGing, shouting, cursing, laughing, groaning, under the vast, indifferent prairie sky.

They had toiled up the Missouri more than a hundred miles a week since the sendoff from Fort Mandan. They were in high plains no white man had ever seen now, lands of overwhelming spaciousness, where immense storms cruised through distant quadrants of sky, or sometimes came over and struck the boats squarely with frightening force; where gigantic prairie fires crawled orange and black along distant horizons, and coal-seams smoked and stank as if hell were leaking; where mineral-water runoff stained the bluffs and the river the color of lye and made the water taste like medical salts; where hundreds of bison, drowned in the breaking ice of late winter, lay flyblown and rotting with a stench that made men gag.

They had watched spring appear, then recede, then reappear, in this wondrous landscape. They saw it coming in the air, where uncountable flocks of geese and brant etched their northering arrow-formations, and where the first mosquito of the season appeared one day early in April, forerunner to millions. They saw spring on the land, in the cautious green buds of elm and cottonwood and arrowwood, then in the pale new grassblades amid the dry yellow-gray of last year's buffalo grass, in the tiny color-flashes of strawberry flowers and primrose, trillium, violet, and plum-bush blossoming in sunny meadows. And these delicate advances then would be buried when the wind backed into the northwest and brought down surprise snowfalls, and blew so cold it formed ice on the oars or whipped the river to froth and chased the boats into leeward shelters. One such gust, coming on a mid-April day on a mile-wide expanse of the Missouri, had nearly overturned the white pirogue, which had been spanking along under a squaresail and a spritsail with the excitable Charbonneau as its helmsman. Charbonneau had dropped to his knees, releasing the tiller to pray to the Mother of God. That had been a near catastrophe, as the vessel carried most of the expedition's instruments, papers, medicines, and Indian presents. That the pirogue had not sunk seemed to indicate that even Charbonneau's prayers were heard.

The boats had continued to meet all the Missouri's old familiar hazards—falling banks, sandbars, and mudflats, submerged logs, blind channels, wind-squalls, and blowing sand—and now the explorers had jokingly added Charbonneau to their list of navigational perils.

But they had been coming along and coming along, rowing and sailing and poling and towing the boats, often jumping into the numbing-cold river to lift and shove the floundering vessels out of drift logs and off sandbars. Men on the tow ropes often had to clamber through huge mats and mounds of tangled driftwood, much of it carved by the deft chisel-marks of beavers' teeth. The captains had exercised their medical skills on rheumatism, dysentery, boils, abscesses, felons, lacerations, sprains, and on coughs and sore eyes caused by blown dust; but these afflictions only irritated the hardy troops, and put none of them out of action for even an hour. Captain Lewis had brought vials of kine pox vaccine, and used a rest stop to inoculate those of the men who had never had the smallpox. In general the troops all remained in robust health and good spirits, with appetites which devoured elk, buffalo, fowl, goats, and beaver almost as fast as the hunters could dress them out.

The men had been coming along and coming along, seemingly as enchanted and excited by the new world as their captains were; there had been not one breach of discipline since Fort Mandan; they enjoyed a deepening sense of harmony, as if their special brotherly bond were growing tighter with every league they went into the unknown. The only thing even resembling a quarrel occurred one evening when one unfortunate beaver got itself caught in two traps, and Colter and Drouillard had had a hot, bellowing debate over whose beaver it was. William had divided the beaver.

They had come along and come along through landscapes as strange to them as the moon. They had seen an infinity of lime-green treeless plains, dark-blue cloud-shadows racing over them, and far to the south a range of low mountains, still snowy in their shady slopes, had been visible for several days. They had camped in the shadows of long, flat-topped mesas with flanks as steep and regular as castle walls. They had passed rivers whose waters emptied white as milk into the dark, muddy flow of the Missouri; they had seen tortuous arid canyons eroded by those rivers, canyons with steep walls white as chalk and striped with veins of clay in a hundred subtle shades of red and pink, yellow and gray-blue. Late in April they had entered the wide, lush valley where the Yellowstone River flowed in from their left, its bed nearly a thousand yards wide at the mouth, most of that an enormous sandbar bright green with cane and young willow and aswarm with geese, gulls, and ducks. The fertile bottomlands and the plains above had been covered with herds of buffalo, elk, and antelope, so tame and curious that they actually followed the men, trying to determine what they were. This place, grassy and well-timbered, seemed such a paradise that the party celebrated its arrival with a dram of whiskey and a dance to Cruzatte's lively fiddle.

They had come along and come along then beyond the great Yellowstone, feeding on the plentiful elk and buffalo and beaver shot by Drouillard or the Fields brothers, or by the captains themselves, and on geese and rabbits, and even a small antelope that Scannon killed and dragged into camp; they had seen the amazing, nimble big-horned sheep springing along the faces of perpendicular cliffs. And here above the Yellowstone they also had had their first encounters with the formidable grizzly bears of which the Indians had warned them. In late April, Lewis and a hunter had shot a young male of the species, weighing about three hundred pounds, and deduced that the legendary beasts perhaps were not so formidable or dangerous as they had been represented. But that appraisal had gradually begun to change as the party met more and more, bigger and bigger ones. On May 5, William had entered in his journal:

> in the evening we saw a Brown or Grisley beare on a sand beech, I went out with one man Geo Drewyer & killed the bear, which was verry large and a turrible looking animal, which we found verry hard to kill we Shot ten Balls into him before we killed him, & 5 of those Balls through his lights

The beast had measured eight feet seven and a half inches long, and its heart was as large as that of an ox. And Lewis, after another encounter, had written:

> I find that the curiossity of our party is pretty well satisfyed with rispect to this anamal, the formidable appearance of

the male bear killed on the 5th added to the difficulty with which they die even when shot through the vital parts, has staggered the resolution of several of them, others however seem keen for action with the bear; I expect these gentlemen will give us some amusement shotly as they (the bears) soon begin to coppolate.

Burping happily after one of the best dinners he had ever eaten, Lewis sat chuckling and writing in his journal an entry that he believed would entertain thoroughly Thomas Jefferson the gourmet:

> *Thursday May 9th 1805*
> *Capt. C killed 2 bucks and 2 buffaloe, I also killed one buffaloe which proved to be the best meat it was in tolerable order; we saved the best of the meat and from the cow I killed we saved the necessary materials for making what our wrighthand cook Charbono calls the boudin (poudingue) blanc, and immediately set him about preparing them for supper; this white pudding we all esteem one of the greatest delacies of the forrest; it may not be amiss therefore to give it a place.*
> *About 6 feet of the lower extremity of the large gut of the Buffaloe is the first mosel that the cook makes love to, this he holds fast at one end with the right hand, while with the forefinger and thumb of the left he gently compresses it, and discharges what he says is not good to eat, but of which in the sequel we get a moderate portion; the mustle lying underneath the shoulder blade next to the back, and fillets are next saught, these are needed up very fine with a good portion of kidney suet; to this composition is then added a just proportion of pepper and salt and a small quantity of flour; thus far advanced, our skilfull opporater C———o seizes his recepticle, which has never once touched the water, for that would intirely distroy the regular order of the whole procedure . . . and tying it fast at one end turns it inward and begins now with repeated evolutions of the hand and arm, and a brisk motion of the finger and thumb to put in what he says is bon pour manger; thus by stuffing and compressing he soon distends the recepticle to the utmost limmits of it's power of expansion, and in the course of it's longitudinal progress it drives from the other end of the recepticle a much larger portion of*

*the————than was prevously discharged by the finger and
thumb of the left hand in a former part of the operation;
thus when the sides of the recepticle are skilfully exchanged
the outer for the iner, and all is compleatly filled with
something good to eat, it is tyed at the other end, but not
any cut off, for that would make the pattern too scant; it is
then baptised in the Missouri with two dips and a flirt,
and bobbed into the kettle; from whence, after it be well
boiled it is taken and fryed with bears oil untill it becomes
brown, when it is ready to esswage the pangs of a keen
appetite of such as travelers in the wilderness are seldom at
a loss for.*

William was amused by the sight of his friend grinning over
his notebook. Lewis, who oftimes had been uncomfortably intense or gloomy during the winter, was happier now than William had ever seen him.

Lewis looked up from his notebook, his eyes twinkling in the
firelight, to say:

"We should send Charbonneau back to Washington, as chef
for Mr. Jefferson's kitchen, eh? Can't you imagine him in the
Executive household, this great rancid goat? Ha, ha!"

Over by the big bonfire, the fiddle was squeaking happily and
the men were cavorting and laughing over their evening dram.
The wind boomed against the skin tent where Sacajawea sat
tending to her son Pomp; the river hissed in the darkness beyond.
William gazed in wonder at Lewis, at his dishevelled hair, his
torn buckskins, his stained, dusty tricorn, his face tanned dark as
oiled leather and glinting with chin-stubble.

"My friend," William said, "it's all I can do to imagine *you* in
the White House!" Yet, strange though it was, this gristly little
frontiersman here beside him—this bodacious, dog-eating, cliff-
hanging, grizzly-bear hunter, squatting here by a wind-whipped
campfire twenty-three hundred miles from civilization digesting
a meal of buffalo guts—actually had lived in the White House!
Fate, William thought, plays curious games!

May 14, 1805

BOTH CAPTAINS WERE WALKING ON SHORE THIS EVENING.
That was unusual. But the land was interesting, and they had
things to discuss, so they walked along the shore together, now
and then glancing out toward the white pirogue, which was

coming along under sail in midstream. Charbonneau was visible at the helm, his red wool cap marking him. Sacajawea sat under the awning amidships with her baby in her arms. Three oarsmen, one of them Cruzatte, were working against the stiff current while another man held the brace of the squaresail, and the boat was making the pace of a walking man. Following were the red pirogue and the dugout canoes, in a ragged single file. The weather had been changeable all day; the riverbanks down-river were softly illuminated now by a setting sun, but across the river a drift of black clouds came flying low, its lower edge sweeping along like a tattered skirt. The waves on the river were building up and beginning to break into whitecaps.

"Hey, now," William said to Lewis, "I wish it wasn't Charbonneau on that tiller." He was remembering the last time.

Lewis opened his mouth to reply, but paused at the sound of rifle fire far behind. Four shots, faint over the wind, in close sequence. They peered down along the river, counting sails. Five. One of the canoes was either still around the bend or had put ashore. "What d'you reckon?" said Lewis. "They gone ashore to hunt?"

"A salvo like that, I'll wager they're makin' war on a grizzly," William said.

They walked a bit farther, the wind from across the river whipping at their clothing, and Lewis looked worried, glancing first at the choppy waters and then back down the river.

Two more rifle shots sounded. And after a while four more at close intervals. "Damnation," William said, stopping and turning around, "s'pose they've got attacked by Indians?"

"Oh, oh!" Lewis cried just then, staring out into the wind. William looked. The white pirogue was heeling and turning under a blast of wind from the squall line; William saw the wind come shivering across the water, blowing tops off the waves, and felt it beat cold around his face, and just then Lewis cried into the gale at the top of his lungs:

"PUT HER BEFORE THE WIND! HEY! YOU FOOL! PUT HER BEFORE THE WIND!"

But Charbonneau was responding dead wrong, just as he had the last time. He threw the tiller to the left and the pirogue luffed into the wind. The squaresail immediately began whipping and fluttering violently, so violently it tore the brace out of the soldier's hand, and the vessel went onto her side as if shoved over by a giant unseen hand.

"Godalmighty!" Lewis screamed into the wind, watching the vessel with all its valuable cargo—almost everything needed to complete the journey—laying over in the pounding waves, shipping water fast, only the resistance of the awning against the water so far keeping her from turning turtle. Lewis and William both were shouting now, but the wind across the water virtually blew their voices back into their mouths, and the tiny figures aboard the boat kept moving with an infinite slowness, doing nothing effectual. Lewis fired his rifle into the air to attract their attention; William fired his; but the little figures continued their slow, confused movements, unheeding. William, his heart sinking with a sense of tragic helplessness, watched Charbonneau drop the tiller and fall to his knees in the bilges, wringing his hands; he saw Scannon slide and fall overboard into the icy water; he saw Cruzatte hanging onto the bow for his life while the soldiers clawed the gunwale for a grip. They could hear Charbonneau's screaming prayer come across the wind: *"Mon Dieu! Mon Dieu, aidez-moi!"* Cruzatte's voice came, too; he was yelling in rage at Charbonneau. Sacajawea, now to her waist in water, seemed to be grabbing for items as they floated over the side. And far downstream, as if to add to the confusion, another rifle banged.

"CUT THE HALYARDS! HAUL IN THE SAIL!" William roared through cupped hands. He heard something hit the ground beside him. It was Lewis's rifle. Then his shot pouch and espontoon fell beside it, and William turned to see Lewis unbuttoning his coat and running toward the water's edge.

"No!" William yelled, and sprinted after him. He caught his wrist in an iron grip just as Lewis flung off his coat.

"Let me go! I'm—"

"You can't swim in that! You'd perish in two minutes!" He hung onto Lewis's straining arm and turned to shout again: "HAUL IN THE SAIL! Look," he cried, "they're doing it!" The men were gathering in the sail, desperately, with great difficulty. William prayed silently for them; he knew that two of them could not swim, and neither could Charbonneau. And this water was too cold for even a vigorous swimmer.

Lewis was watching, no longer pulling toward the water, perhaps beginning to realize that the high waves and frigid water would be fatal. "God!" he groaned, "if that boat goes under, I'm as well off dead!"

"Swallow such talk," William snapped. "Look! She's righting!" The mast was a little more vertical now, as the sail came in. But the hull was almost submerged, full to the gunwales with icy water, waves breaking over her windward side. The woman remained kneeling in water amidships, babe in one arm, snatching up floating objects with her free hand. Charbonneau was still bellowing supplications to his God, utterly ignoring the swinging tiller, and the boat was in danger of getting swamped by a wave broadside. But now Cruzatte was roaring at Charbonneau; he had drawn his pistol and was pointing it at Charbonneau in the far end of the pirogue. *"Tirez! Tirez!"* His voice came on the wind now: "Take the helm, or I shoot!"

William stood, still holding Lewis's wrist, and watched the desperate little crisis act itself out among the tiny figures, so remotely distant, but so detail-clear in the glorious cross-light of a prairie sunset. The red pirogue and the following canoes were having their own battle with the gusting winds, but were not in any trouble. "Never do I give that buffoon the tiller again," Lewis hissed through clenched teeth. "He's surely the most timid waterman in all the world!"

"Aye! That woman of his, though. Look!" She was still working swiftly, holding her baby while capturing drifting articles in the sloshing water.

"There! He's come to. He's got the helm now!" Cruzatte's threat had at last moved Charbonneau out of his paralysis, and he was at the tiller. The sail was in now, and Cruzatte had organized the crew. Two men were bailing with kettles, while Cruzatte and another were on oars, pulling the pirogue and its great load of water toward the shore, slipping fast downstream on the current. The vessel was so low in the water, so fully swamped, that the high waves broke over her, refilling her as fast as the bailers could pour. But, little by little, she was coming across the distance. Scannon, his head a dark spot on the river, apparently tired of swimming around and just then decided to climb back aboard; one big forepaw reached over the gunwale. Oh, no, William thought, that great beast'll overset her again.

Cruzatte was yelling at the dog, now threatening him with an oar.

"SCANNON!" Lewis yelled. "SCANNON! COME!"

The dog, fortunately, heard, and turned away from the boat to come swimming strongly toward his master.

Scannon came floundering out of the river's edge a few minutes later, shook himself mightily, and then ran up and down the bank, barking in his deep voice at the oncoming pirogue. The other vessels had turned toward the bank now. William and Lewis waded out into the numbing water to their waists to meet the vessel and help haul her in. The danger past, Cruzatte and Charbonneau were yelling at each other in French, Cruzatte damning, Charbonneau whining in his own defense. Despite their exertions, the people in the pirogue were shaking with cold. As they hopped out and pulled with their last energies to get the vessel onshore, William looked in dismay at the pathetic mess floating or sunk everywhere in the hull: notebooks, charts, lists, specimens, medicine boxes, navigational instruments, pans, parfleche bags, decanters, strips of jerky, flour kegs, powder horns and canisters, hats, moccasins, beads, medallions, and trinkets meant to be used as Indian gifts. God knows what's lost in the river or spoiled, he thought.

THEY MADE CAMP ON THE SPOT. A LARGE BONFIRE WAS built to warm and dry the occupants of the pirogue. The men stripped to the skin and rubbed the fire's heat into their bodies, then hung their sodden buckskins on poles and bushes to steam in the fire's heat. Sacajawea was trembling violently, but was tending first to her baby, kneeling near the fire, drying him. William got a dry blanket and draped it over her shoulders, and she looked up at him with eyes eloquent in gratitude. He made a hand sign which meant "good," and then returned to the shore, where a desperate effort was being made to salvage the articles. William's own wet leggings and breeches were chilling him through, making his old winter rheumatism ache, but there was much to do and little light left. The sky was blown nearly clean of clouds now; it seemed there would be no rain in the night. That was a boon. Everything from the canoe was lifted out, dribbling, and carried up and laid out on the bank to drain. Papers were spread on the ground and stones set on their corners to keep them from blowing away. As this process was continued in the twilight, it became apparent that although everything was soaked, hardly anything was missing except a few iron cooking utensils, which had sunk, and one notebook containing Captain Lewis's journal for the first year of the voyage.

"God bless that girl," Lewis exclaimed. "She's saved us, I'll vow!"

"Doesn't it beat all!" William breathed. "I mean, most squaws wouldn't ha' conceived how this stuff was important. That one's got a head on her shoulders, she has."

He went up by the fire to thank her for what she had done. Her baby was snug now in his cradleboard, packed in dry cottonwood down, and Sacajawea had stripped her own sodden tunic off and hung it on a pole close to the fire. For an instant her naked little figure glowed ruddy-gold in the firelight before she wrapped herself in the blanket.

There were a few words of English the girl had learned. William knelt beside her and reached toward the fire. "Janey," he said, "thank you." It was the nickname York had given her. William made signs as he talked. "What you did was a great thing. Our hearts are yours." She smiled, the biggest, fullest, white-toothed smile he had ever yet seen shine through her reserve. By God, he thought. We'll give her some kind o' reward. She deserves more than we heap on those chiefs everywhere we go.

There were shouts down by the river. In the gathering darkness, the last canoe was coming ashore. The men were whooping and yelling something about a great bear.

They emerged into the firelight. Two were soaking wet, and stripped to wrap themselves in blankets.

"Lookee here!" someone yelled, and two men held up an enormous grizzly-bear hide, a thick, fine-haired yellow-brown. It was riddled with bloody bullet holes.

"Sergeant!" Lewis called to Ordway. "A gill o' spirits for every man, and let's hear a tall tale!" He was relieved and happy; the losses from the boating accident likely were going to prove minimal after all.

"A tall tale, aye, sir," explained Collins, "tall but true! And here's the monster's coat to prove it!"

"Hear, hear!"

"Aye, Johnny, tell us how it happened!"

"Well, boys, we seen 'im a-loafin' on open ground about three hundred paces from the river, so we put ashore and all six of us creept up, and by stayin' downwind and ahind of a little rise, we got within forty paces of 'im, an' he had no idea, just layin' there wallowing on th' grass. Hugh and me, we held our fire, like ye've advised, Cap'n, and t' other four all shot at once for his heart. Well, God damn me, not one of us missed, but that roarer just jumped onto his feet and came at us with 'is mouth open as big as a cave. Hugh and me, cool as y' please, shot right at 'is face. He staggered, with a broke shoulder, I think, but he come on like he was a racehorse and we was the finish line."

The men around the fire were spellbound. Some of them had been thus engaged with grizzly bears already and the others had spent a lot of time imagining it and expecting it. Collins continued:

"There was just six of us, but we hied off in a hundred directions. I personally all by myself went ten directions at once, all of 'em toward the river." The soldiers laughed. "No time to reload, just run," Collins went on. "He was closin' on us. I could feel his feet shakin' the ground, and I bet I got blisters on my butt from them flames he was blowin'.

"Well, John and Dick, bein' the two scaredest, they dove in the canoe. Rest of us, we scattered inter th' willer brush and reloaded, while ol' monster-bear crushed around roarin' and lookin' us up. We all took another shot at 'im, damn nigh point blank, an' every time a ball hit him he turned and come for the man who'd shot it. Lordy, if I'd a had five loaded guns, I could a kilt him five times!

"Well, he flushed Hugh and George out an' chased 'em, and—he, he!—they flang away their guns and run right off a cliff, till about ten paces over the river in midair, they saw they wasn't no ground under 'em, and then they dropped twenty feet straight into the river—that's how they got all wet, y' see."

The two nodded in their blankets; Collins wasn't lying.

"Wal, then," Collins went on, eyes ablaze, "ol' bear he jumped in the river right after 'em, an' made a splash high as th' treetops, an' almost sunk George, he was that close. Dick an' I run out atop that cliff then, a-loadin' our pieces, and we saw Hugh an' George swimmin' so fast upriver they was leavin' a backwarsh, an' ol' bear swimmin' after 'em, makin' the river red from all them bullet holes he was a-leakin' out of. So anyways I got down on a knee an' got a good steady bead on that bear's head down there, an' by God, with that one I kilt 'im, the last time, didn't I, boys?"

They nodded and grinned at him admiringly. It was he who had stopped the bear, and so he could tell it just as he liked.

"Wal, that's th' story," Collins concluded. "Drug him ashore and butchered 'im, and found eight balls'd gone through 'im in different directions. One as I say'd broke 'is shoulder, and th' rest gone through parts such as would ha' stopped a bull! Now I say this:"—his eyes fell on York, who was just now breaking cottonwood limbs over his knee for the bonfire—"next time I go hunt a yaller bear, I'm a-gonna do it th' easy way, an' take my nigger friend here t' *rassle* 'im to death! Eh, York?"

York understood this was a compliment, and broke into a big smile. "Shoo will, Mist' Collins. I mean, lest I be too busy otherways!"

So the rest of the evening was taken up with eating, and with tales and retellings, and warming by the big fire, and the cleaning of weapons and repair of moccasins, some of the men lying back holding steaming poultice-rags on their boils. The regular ration of whiskey seemed to affect most of the men twice as much as usual, perhaps because of the altitude, or because of the infrequency of its use recently, and everyone was having a hilarious time, except Charbonneau, whose poor seamanship and frantic Catholic prayers were the butt of some pretty severe josh-ing. He glowered and hung back out of the firelight as much as he could, and made a few feeble excuses. He had enough sense not to get angry, because the good humor of the men was only thinly masking their contempt, and there were several—little Cruzatte foremost among them—who would have enjoyed thrashing him. *"Mon Dieu! Mon Dieu! Aidey-moi, Jesu L'En-fant!"* Cruzatte mimicked him in a whining voice, then added: "God hears you not, eh, Big Tess? Maybe is because he don' recognize your voice in a prayer, eh, *sauvage*? Oh, but God tells *me*: 'Pierre Cruzatte, put thy gun on that maniac's head and give him some wisdom!'"

The troops roared.

"Merde!" growled Charbonneau. "I think you are so brave for you think you could *walk* across the river, eh?"

"Caution," Cruzatte said softly. "I could shoot you yet."

Deciding that all this had gone far enough, Lewis stood up and raised his cup. The men fell quiet until there was no noise over the crackling bonfire and the wind on the river.

"Listen," he said. "I address your attention to the wife of Char bonneau. She has enough gumption for their whole family. I salute her, gents. Three cheers for the squaw! Hip, hip . . ."

"Hooray!"

"Hip, hip . . ."

"Hooray!"

"Hip, hip . . ."

"Hooray!"

And Sacajawea, looking up quizzically into this uproar and seeing that these great strong white men were all beaming on her, grew so flustered that she turned to bury her face in the nearest refuge. It might at another time have been the bosom of another squaw; it might even have been a wall. As it happened now, it was the shoulder of the person nearest her, someone she trusted and admired in the extreme, the kindest man she had ever seen: Chief Red Hair. William felt the face pressing against him, and was delighted, yet full of pity for her embarrassment, and he was suddenly so suffused with affection that he put his arm around her shoulders and squeezed her to his side. "Here's to 'er!" he exclaimed, raising his cup, and three more cheers erupted.

A few days later the captains dubbed a small river Sacajawea's Creek in her honor, and everyone approved.

Except Charbonneau, who remembered Chief Red Hair's arm

around his squaw, and who imagined that this was why all the *Americains* smirked at him.

39

Sunday, May 26, 1805

AND THEN THEY HAD COME ON AND ON THROUGH LATE MAY, through days of scorching sun and eye-scouring dust and nights when water froze in the canoe bilges and camp kettles, through thick morning fogs and high, bright blue afternoons that brought the rattlesnakes out to sun on the rocks wherever men might step. The hills and mesas above the river valley were rugged, treeless, and almost grassless; the main vegetation now was prickly pear, whose needles pierced right through the soles of moccasins. The ground had been imprinted when wet with millions of buffalo hoofprints, which had dried in the sun into a ridged, jagged, ankle-twisting, moccasin-tearing plaster. Dry stream beds broached onto the river, proof that the land was generally as arid as it seemed in this season. Nearly every day one man or another had an encounter with a grizzly bear, till Lewis issued an order that hunters or anyone else leaving the camp must not go alone but in pairs or groups. *"These bear being so hard to die reather intimedates us all,"* Lewis wrote in his journal. *"I had reather fight two Indians than one bear."*

Buffalo were not so numerous as they had been, but the hunters provided elk, deer, bighorn sheep. Every night the horizons echoed with distant wolf calls.

Scannon, cornering a wounded beaver one Sunday afternoon, had been bitten on a foreleg by the desperate animal, and its chisel-sharp yellow teeth laid the flesh open so badly that the dog nearly bled to death.

The evening encampments these days were great gab-fests. Every evening there was some new spill or close call to talk about, as the rapidity of the current now was continually breaking their elkskin tow ropes and endangering the canoes.

Twanging Kentucky accents rose high in the valley as the men tried to express their wonderment at the beasts and plants and landscapes that were beyond anything they had seen in their lifetimes as hunters and rangers and woodsmen back in the green forests of the Ohio watershed. They were enchanted in particular with the bighorn sheep, which stood ghostly gray on the jagged faces of nearly perpendicular bluffs, looking down curiously with their big, wide-set eyes at the struggling boatmen, or sprang with incredible sureness from crag to crag. Their huge, graceful backward-curling horns were prized; every man yearned to have a pair as a souvenir. The head and horns of a male that Drouillard killed one day weighed twenty-seven pounds. "I still want some," remarked John Colter, who sat by a campfire pulling prickly pear thorns out of his bloody feet, "but damned if I'll carry anything that big on up this unmarciful river. I'll wait 'n' get some on the way home."

The men were mad for bighorn meat and beaver tails, which they proclaimed the finest foods they had ever tasted and which were made a hundred times more savory by their work-whetted appetites. They were entranced by the vast, flaming, purpling evening skyscapes, the orange sunsets blazing off the river, the vivid rainbows arching over rainwashed gray-blue cottonwoods and brick-and-lime colored willow thickets, the bald, fissured hills on both sides of the river turning violet and then black in the twilight, the moon rising the size and color of a pumpkin over the river behind them. They comprehended that they were in the vanguard of civilization; many of them by now had creeks named after them, and they wore the knowledge of those namesakes with quiet pride, like medals. And thus most of them now seemed to consider themselves the most fortunate men who had ever walked—even though walking was now a wincing agony and their feet were sprained and bruised and punctured by riverbed stones and prickly pear. They gazed dreamily into the light of pungent buffalo-chip-and-willow-wood campfires; they fed themselves with their right hands while wiping mosquitoes off their faces and blowflies off their meat with their left hands. And they were usually so fatigued that they would fall asleep with their poultices still on, and would dream of snow-topped mountains.

AND NOW THIS SUNDAY MORNING THE MEN WOKE UP groaning with their pains and stiffnesses, and William knew just how they felt because he felt the same. He had to wince to bend his neck far enough to put on his moccasins and leggings. As he struggled with aching fingers to tie thongs, he heard George Gibson groaning. Gibson had dislocated a shoulder the day before while trying to climb a cliff. Several men had pulled and twisted his arm for what had seemed like an eternity until it was back in its socket. "How is it this morning, Gibson?" William called over.

"Sir," came the man's voice, "th' onliest part o' me that could hurt worse would be th' soles o' my feet, so I thank the Lord I don't have any soles o' my feet left."

William smiled grimly. It was the kind of joke a hurting man thinks up when he hurts too much to sleep, but it was a joke nonetheless, and it meant Gibson was still game.

But that about the soles of the feet was not much of an exaggeration. The mere touch of moccasin leather to his own feet made William tremble with pain inside, and he had not yet even stood up to put weight on them this morning.

Now he clenched his teeth and got up as quickly as he could. It was best to get it over with—if it didn't make you faint. And the instant his weight was upon those bruised, twisted, stove-up, lacerated, needle-punctured feet, they felt as if he had just stepped on an exploding powder keg. His heart quailed and a hundred suns floated around behind his eyeballs for a moment.

"Where to so early, Clark?" Captain Lewis's voice came through the whirlwind of pain.

"Why," he panted, "I aim to climb that cliff o' Gibson's and get out o' this canyon for a look-around. Sunday mornin's a body should see the world from a lofty station, as my Ma used t' say, rest her soul."

IT TOOK HIM AN HOUR, A WHEEZING, SCRABBLING, GROANING, panting hour, climbing on steep slopes of loose, sharp-edged, parched, cactus-and-rattlesnake-infested rock, on wind-scoured cliff faces, to reach the upland hills. Here he turned and looked back down. A mile below and behind, the little string of canoes and pirogues was inching along the edge of the rushing gray river, the men onshore and in the water, looking tiny and industrious as ants. Now and then he would hear a snatch of voice from down there. He watched them come along now, as they had been doing foot by laborious foot for more than two thousand miles, and for a moment he had the feeling that here is what an Indian, or a mule deer, or a bighorn sheep, or an eagle, would be seeing and hearing as the first white men penetrated into their country.

Then he had a curious, chilling sensation that something or someone was behind him, likewise looking down at the oncoming Corps—for an instant he remembered the image of Chief Logan the Mingo standing behind George in that old story—and he turned, his thumb on the hammer of his rifle.

No one was there. Just the thirsty, eroded, scrubby, yellow-green and gray, rock-studded hills rolling away treeless into a hazy blue infinity.

But no!

His mouth dropped open and he shaded his eyes with his hand and stared at something just above the shimmering horizon. It shone like the white crest of a wave.

His heart beat fast, as he turned, scanning the horizons up beyond the westering rivercourse. There were more of them, more of those shining crests.

William climbed for a while farther along the summits of the river hills, entranced, limping but hardly aware of the pains that made him limp, his gaze fastened on those distant masses of white, perhaps twenty, perhaps fifty, miles ahead. And at last he stopped and turned back to go down and tell friend Lewis what he had seen.

What he had been the first to see.

From the Journal of Meriwether Lewis

Sunday May 26th 1805
Capt. Clark walked on shore this morning and ascended to the summit of the river hills he informed me on his return that he had seen mountains on both sides of the river running nearly parrallel with it and at no great distance; also an irregular range of mountains on larboard about 50 Mls distant. . . .

In the after part of the day I also walked out and ascended the river hills which I found sufficiently for-tieguieng. On arriving to the summit of one of the highest points in the neighborhood I thought myself well repaid for my labour; as from this point I beheld the Rocky Mountains for the first time, I could only discover a few of the most elivated points above the horizon, the most remarkable of which by my pocket compass I found bore N. 65 degrees W. . . . these points of the Rocky Mountains were covered with snow and the sun shone on it in such manner to give me the most plain and satisfactory view. While I viewed these mountains I felt a secret pleasure in finding myself so near the head of the heretofore conceived boundless Missouri; but when I reflected on the difficulties which this snowy barrier would most probably throw in my way to the Pacific, and the sufferings and hardships of myself and party in thim, it in some measure counterballanced the joy I had felt in the first moments in which I gazed on them; but as I have always held it a crime to anticipate evils I will believe it a good comfortable road untill I am compelled to believe differently.

Wednesday, May 29, 1805

ONE MOMENT THE DARKNESS WAS SILENT, ABSOLUTELY STILL but for the liquid music of the Missouri nearby; the next it was full of uproar: splintering wood, thumpings, shouts, earth-shaking hoofbeats, a gunshot, the chesty breathing of some great creature, still more shouts, and then the explosive barking and snarling of Scannon.

Jerking upright with his hair on end and his heart in his mouth, William felt Scannon scramble out of the tent in a frenzy. The hoofbeats, the heavy panting, rushed toward the shelter, as if a mammoth were running into the camp. A great, heavy force shook the tent. Lewis's voice, Charbonneau's, Sacajawea's, her baby's, all erupted at once, adding to the chorus of confused shouts from the troops nearby, but above it all was Scannon's mad outburst and then a desperate bellowing, mere inches away, and another gunshot.

When the hoofbeats and barking had receded away down the river and torches were lighted, the shaky captains and nervous sentries were able to study tracks and piece together the near-catastrophe.

A huge bull buffalo apparently had swum the river from the far side, and in landing had clambered over the white pirogue, upsetting it, stumbling in it, breaking York's rifle and a blunderbuss that had been left in it. Then, thoroughly panicked, the bull had galloped headlong up the rows of sleeping men, its sharp hooves missing their heads by inches, straight toward the officers' shelter, while sentries fired blindly into the air. Only Scannon, charging into the face of the onrushing buffalo, had caused it to veer past the shelter, sideswiping it as it thundered away with the Newfoundland at its heels.

Lewis kept fondling the dog, laughing weakly, shaking his

head, looking as if he wanted to kiss the shiny black nose. Scannon sat panting, favoring the foreleg that was still bandaged from its beaver wound, and soaked up the praise, tail beating happily. Sacajawea, who was just beginning to understand through her imperfect hearing of the white men's language that her friend the black dog had probably saved several lives, was very happy, and she held her baby and leaned unthinking back against the good Red Hair Chief. And it was so natural, under these circumstances, that William was hardly aware of it until he saw Charbonneau glaring balefully at her. So William moved around to kneel close by the dog and run his hand over the silky black hair of its shapely head. Lewis was saying:

"I'd never have thought of bringing a dog on this journey, but that I read of Mackenzie's dog, that crossed Canada with 'im. Somehow that just appealed to me, I guess, and that's why I bought this beastie. Ha, ha! Well, that's *one* good idea I'll have to admit I got from an Englishman!" He shook his head, chuckling. "But I ask you, Clark, have y' ever seen so sagacious an animal in all your days? Good dog! Gooooood Scannon!"

LATER THAT DAY, THE MEN STILL WADING TO PULL AND PUSH the canoes, the party came to the mouth of a crystalline river that poured into the muddy Missouri from the south. Because of the purity of its waters, William proposed to call it the Judith River, in honor of his Judy Hancock of Fincastle. He made a point of praising that fair golden maiden within the hearing of Charbonneau. William had always tried to treat Sacajawea with detachment, even though his affection and respect for her increased day by day. She, on the other hand, did not have enough guile to try to conceal her admiration of the Red Hair Chief, and so Charbonneau seethed and grew sulkier. Thus William wanted the Frenchman to know he already had a woman— a woman far away, certainly, but a woman of his own kind. And then William put the whole matter out of mind.

Sacajawea had been hard at work making double soles of raw buffalo hide for the men's moccasins, to turn the prickly pear needles, but these helped only on overland walks, and the men still had to wince along barefoot when they were on the riverbank or in the water, which was most of the time. A pair of moccasins lasted about two days on this terrain. The Corps had gone through hundreds of pairs.

The men had every reason to trust that their leaders had worked out in advance every step of their way to the Pacific, and there were a hundred proofs already behind them that both captains were possessed of an uncanny sense of direction and terrain. They had always arrived where and when they had said they would; they never got bewildered, even when hunting and exploring parties split off; even in the treeless, monotonous plains they had always come and gone, departed and rejoined, with an unerring certainty. Shannon and other hunters had got lost for days, but never the captains. All the evidence was that Captains Lewis and Clark were infallible guides, perfectly oriented; there simply was never a reason to doubt their direction. Until Sunday, June 2, when the Corps of Discovery came upon a fork in the river where none was supposed to be: two rivers of apparently equal size, either of which could be the Missouri. The party paused and made camp in a cottonwood grove while the captains consulted their projected maps and wondered aloud why the Minnetarees at Fort Mandan had never spoken of this fork.

It was June now, a week since they had first seen the distant Rocky Mountains, and to go up the wrong river and butt up against the mountains far from the headwaters of the western river would cost them the rest of their traveling season; then there would not be time to cross the Rocky Mountains before the snows made them impassable. The only way to know would be to learn which fork had the Great Falls, the high waterfalls the Minnetarees had described on the Missouri.

Evening fell, cool and damp.

The captains had no answer. The Indian girl could not remember this fork in the river. Sacajawea had caught a cold and looked weak and dishevelled and confused. Charbonneau seemed scornful, indignant that they would even consult her about such a question.

She stood and sniffed the air, turning slowly, like a doe, expressionless, and at last pointed up the river that came from the left, from the southwest. Some of the men snickered. This was nothing to go on, they were thinking. That river was clear. The one coming in from the north was muddy and gray-brown, just as the Missouri had been for twenty-five hundred miles. They all felt that it was the Missouri. They were surprised that their captains, who always knew the way, were even hesitating.

Monday, June 3, 1805

THEY MOVED THE CAMP NEXT MORNING ACROSS THE CLEAR-running river and set up on the point made by the junction of the two rivers, and in this camp Captain Lewis set the men to work dressing elk skins, to make new double-sole moccasins and clothing, and also for a hide covering for the collapsible iron-frame boat he had brought all the way from Harper's Ferry. He looked lovingly at the bundle of iron tubes that, according to his plan, would be fitted together to its thirty-six-foot length and covered with elk hides, thus making a vessel much lighter than a pirogue but capable of carrying five tons of load. He was very fond of this invention of his, and had high expectations for it.

Now it was time to make the decision about which fork of the river to take. Though every man in the party believed that the muddy one coming in from the north was the true Missouri, the captains were inclined to believe it was the clear one coming up from the southwest. In order to make an informed choice rather than a merely intuitive one, they sent a canoe up each stream, with three good woodsmen in each canoe, to learn the widths, depths, currents, and waters of both streams, as far as they could push up the two streams and safely return by evening. Sergeant Gass took the party up the southerly fork; Sergeant Pryor took the one up the north. They also sent several small parties afoot with instructions to climb the heights along the way and see the distant bearings of the rivers.

"Now, friend Clark, let's us climb the height up yonder ourselves and see what we can see," Lewis said.

"I'm with you."

The morning was pleasant and fair. They hiked up the greening slopes out of the valley, Lewis using his espontoon as a walking staff, William shading his eyes under the tomahawk-umbrella George had given him. For a time as they went up they could see the scouting canoes crawling slowly up the divergent rivers; then those were lost to sight in the willows and below the brow of the bluff. They were limping soon; some of the prickly pear thorns pierced even the parfleche outersoles of their moccasins. But they were accustomed to that, and went on to the top.

They stood now, the wind fresh on their sweaty faces, and looked over a vast plain, evenly covered with pale new grasses and wildflowers, blackened here and there by distant herds of buffalo, thousands of them, attended by tiny wolves like shepherds. There were smaller herds of elk, and scattered antelope grazing with their young beside them. To the south lay a range of high mountains, partially covered with snow, and at a great distance beyond them lay a loftier range, entirely white with snow. It was not possible to discern the directions of the rivers very far, as their channels soon simply blended into the surface of the immense plain.

"Now we've seen it, let's sit and smoke on it," Lewis said.

"Let's find a bench, though. Prickly pears're bad enough in the *feet*."

They sat on a flat rock and lit a bowlful of tobacco in William's versatile umbrella. Finally Lewis asked:

"What d' you say, Clark?"

William blew smoke and, squinting across the plain, through the heat waves that made the distant animals and mountains tremble, replied:

"I think Janey's right. This river"—he nodded toward the southerly branch—"looks like a mountain river to me. Clear, a stony bottom. I feel it's come to us from those mountains."

"Go on."

"T' other fork boils and rolls all muddy like the Missouri we know. So I don't think it comes through mountains, lest it be away, way north."

"Like from Saskashawan."

"Aye. From there, or from thereabouts. But I think it rises this side o' th' mountains, not in 'em."

"Thus it's turbid here, eh?"

"Aye. And ye recall, the Minnetarees said the Missouri veers southwest before the mountains, and that you have to go that way to reach the falls."

Lewis puffed and nodded. "Let me play Devil's advocate, though," he said. "Suppose we're putting too much faith in what the Minnetarees told us. Didn't you ever feel they were sometimes makin' things up when they weren't sure?"

William thought on this unsettling question. He had had that notion sometimes himself. But now he said: "I think their facts petered out *beyond* the Snake tribe country, true, and after that they just cheerful-like obliged us with whatever they thought we'd want to hear. But everything they told us up to this place proved out well-nigh exact, didn't it?"

"Everything *seems* to, let's say. But this big river from the north, that they never mentioned, that does give me pause as to their veracity. Say what?"

"Not me, Lewis. Maybe we miscomprehended something they meant, but I think I can judge when an Indian's at least a-*tryin'* to tell the truth. Now, I would take that south river without a pause, if it was just me. But this is a bigger consequence and we have to be sure. So let's study on what our boys find out."

"I think like you," Lewis said. "The south fork is our river. But we have to be dead sure. Now let's go down and look to our footsore boys."

THE MEN IN CAMP WERE WORKING HARD, BUT THEY WERE doing as much as they could sitting down, trying to keep their weight off their feet. York was doing most of the standing work, hauling in firewood, cutting boughs for beds, cooking, making tea, and delivering it around the camp in steaming kettles. He limped and grimaced, but kept up such cheerful talk that his grimace could have been mistaken for a grin. He also hovered around Sacajawea a great deal; she was listless and dull-eyed, hardly even caring for her baby. Since almost everyone in the camp was suffering and had fallen off in vigor and appetite, the Indian girl's condition caught no one's attention particularly. But York was ever solicitous of her well-being. There was a special bond between these two; even though they knew scarcely twoscore words in common, they seemed to understand each other fully. York was teaching her some English and she was teaching him some hand signs. They were sensitive to each other and, with her baby and the invalid Scannon, they seemed to have formed a little society unto themselves. In camp, the four of them were almost always near each other. York coddled and tended the baby in much of his spare time, and could make it laugh with such frantic glee that its piping voice would carry throughout the camp. York, Sacajawea, Scannon, and little Pompey: they were the only members of the expedition who in one way or another were not white, male, adult humans. And, though each had his or her attachments to the military party itself, they were as well their own community, a community of slaves, mascots, and tagalongs, most unlikely in a military expedition—though they were so familiar to it by now that no one thought them odd anymore.

When the scouting parties came in that evening, a conference was held under the cottonwoods around a smoky bonfire, the two dubious rivers flowing together before them with their relentless liquid rushings. The scouts had found the north fork slower and more navigable, but nothing else conclusive had come of their sorties. To a man, with due respect to their captains, they all still believed even more firmly that the north fork was the way. "To us all, it's plain as poop in a pan," said Sergeant Ordway, "though o' course, sirs, whatever way y' choose, we're happy to go. But there's not a one of us here puts a bit o' faith in what a squaw-girl smells in th' air, even though she be a good soldier by what we seen, no, not even 'er own husband does. Eh, Big Tess?"

"She knows nothing, *mes capitaines*," said Charbonneau with a shrug.

"It's not just Janey's nose we're judgin' by," said William. "It' other things we know."

Lewis stood up now, and looked around the circle of firel: faces.

"You all know it's not our mode to go off half-minded. S Captain Clark and I have decided to satisfy ourselves before w lead on. Pryor, Drouillard, Shields, Windsor, Cruzatte, and L Page, you men be prepared to walk out with me tomorrow early and we'll go up the north fork till we have no doubts about i Cap'n?"

"Going with me," William announced, "I want Joe and Rub Fields, Pat Gass, Shannon, and York. We'll ascend the sout fork. Sergeant Ordway, you'll be in charge of th' camp here which I expect will be in th' main a hospital for bunged-up fee Y' can all sit around and make clothes, just like a sewin' be back home." Laughter passed around the campfire. "So be it, he finished. "Those ordered, be ready to go at eight in the morn ing with marching kit. And now, it's time for our nightcap."

"AAAAAAAA!"

Joe Fields's scream in the willow thicket jerked up everyone head. William could hear him running toward the camp b could not see him yet. The voice came again:

"Grizzlies! Help! Oh God, help!" William, Sergeant Gass Reuben Fields, Shannon, and York grabbed their rifles up from the bundles and bags and raised them to their shoulders. Wi liam's heart raced as he pulled back the flintlock. The rifle w: rain-wet and he could only hope it would fire. Joe Fields ha strolled back into the willows to dump his bowels and now h was coming out in desperate haste. He burst from the edge of th willows, fifty feet away, more hopping than running, holding h pants up around his thighs with one hand and lugging his rif with the other. The moment he appeared, two of the gre: yellow bears materialized from the switch-willows and came lo ing after him onto the beach, one slightly ahead of the other an almost on Joe's back now. Joe's hobbling breeches now topple him and he fell on his face. William put his sights as well as h could on the motion-blurred head of the leading bear an squeezed the trigger. Three other rifles crashed beside him; acr powder smoke drifted. The first bear had fallen on its side, a most on top of Joe Fields, but it was not hurt badly and w: thrashing to get back on its limbs. The other bear had skidded a halt in the face of this volley and now reared on its hind fee standing seven feet tall, its tiny sharp dark eyes glittering, its teeth and four-inch talons gleaming as it seemed to try to make up its malevolent mind whether to charge or retreat. This instant of terrible suspense seemed to be forever, then the bear began to roar.

There was no time for anyone to reload. Someone had not fired yet; that meant there was only one bullet in reserve. William dropped his rifle and grabbed up an espontoon, and out of the corner of his eye he saw young Shannon, fair, gray-eyed, and graceful, getting a bead on the standing monster, aiming right into its huge red mouth. The other bear was up on its front legs now and its attention was on Joe Fields, who was trying to roll away from it.

William waited an instant until Shannon's piece crashed; the standing grizzly's roar broke off and its head twitched, and now was the time. William howled the woods Indian battle cry and ran forward with the espontoon. Beside him, York was bounding forward with his smoking rifle held like a club, bellowing in a voice that filled the valley, and on his other hand Rube Fields was sprinting with his hunting knife out toward the bear that hovered over his brother. Sergeant Gass was reloading.

It was reckless, desperate. But it worked. Both bears, bleeding and stung by bullets, confronted by these howling, roaring, charging creatures, abandoned the beach and fled, snuffling and growling, back into the willows.

The men reloaded their guns while Joe Fields, pale as snow and shaking, got his breeches up and tied the waist string. "Goddamn gun wouldn't shoot." His voice quaked. "Wet." He cleaned out the flash pan, and by the time he had it recharged, his hand was steady.

"Let's go in and finish 'em," William said. He didn't want wounded grizzlies dogging them as they went on up the rocky river.

The willow switches, thousands of them, all slim and vertical, were dizzying to pass through. The men pushed among them, parting the saplings with the muzzles of their rifles, penetrating the dense thicket ahead with their sight and hearing. William glanced over at York on his left, saw the red handkerchief, the gold earring, the yellow eyes in plum-black skin, the Herculean physique in rain-wet elk skins, slinking tense as a black panther through the thicket, and for an instant he was utterly amazed. A year ago William would never have dreamed he would one day see that craven lard-bag chasing grizzly bears.

By Heaven, he thought, feeling a new kind of respectful love leap across the space between them. By Heaven!

They found the two wounded bears, which had been joined by another, staggering through a sloping meadow, far enough away that they could shoot at them and reload with relative safety until all three were dead. They took meat from the youngest and tenderest of them, and proceeded on up the river in high and confident spirits.

By this second day they had come nearly forty miles up this clear river, and were laboring along the bottoms through clouds of mosquitoes and gnats. Their nostrils and mouths were full of gnats. Across the river, to the southeast, lay a range of mountains covered with snow. A ridge of those mountains came across and approached the river, forming cliffs of dark stone. William led the men through the cold river and up the steep flank of the ridge. At last, panting, chilled now by the wind on their soaked clothes, they flung themselves down on the ridge crest to rest while William moved out onto a precipice and took in the lay of the land.

For as far as he could see, the river valley ran southwest, the water deep and fast. Now there was no doubt in his mind. This river rose in those mountains, as the Minnetarees had said it did. Somewhere out of sight up there the Great Falls would lie; he knew that without question even though he could hear no sound and see no sight of them. And further up, in the valleys between those distant snowy ranges, they would reach the place where three rivers joined to make the headwaters of the Missouri, and thereabout they would somehow find the people of Sacajawea with their great fine herds of horses.

He remembered now how she had sniffed the air and pointed this way, and he thought: Somehow she is as certain of it as I am, and yet, how could either of us know?

With her it could be the instinct that birds have, he thought, because that was her home and she's pulled toward it the way pigeons are, and geese that know which way to go. I don't know if you can trust that instinct in a human as you can in a bird, he thought. But some Indians have it very strong, along with their way of seeing things and remembering them. Sacajawea means Bird Woman, so maybe you can trust it in her.

But I've never been there and so it can't be a homing intuition with me, he thought. But yet I can feel it and I trust what I feel. But why?

I think I feel it in the tilt of things, he thought. I feel it in my feet, even though my feet are so bunged-up right now I can't feel

nything but sparks and aches, yet I can still feel the way the
and tilts.

He remembered how he and Brother George had stood on
nillsides and river banks and meadows a hundred times in those
ears after the war and had talked about the watersheds of the
continent, and he remembered what George had said about that
palancing instinct that tells you which way a perfectly flat horizon is actually inclining, and how if you have that, you can even
pe walking up the east slope of an Ohio Valley hill and still sense
hat west is downhill until you're in the Missipp.

So he thought about George for a while and came to feel that
George was inside him looking out through his eyes with him for
a long time up this valley, such a valley as George had never
een and never would, yet would understand it and, just like
nim, just like Sacajawea, would say, "That's the way West."

On a tree he carved, "Wᴹ CLARK JUNE 5 1805." Then he
ed his men back down toward the base camp in the forks of the
iver to let Lewis know what he had decided.

40

CLARKSVILLE,
INDIANA TERRITORY
JUNE, 1805

"THEY'RE HERE! GEN'L! BOAT FROM MISSOURI!" THE SHOUTS
came up across the meadow ahead of the rider, who was standing in his stirrups and approaching at a full gallop over the sunny
grass, laying the whip back and forth over both sides of the
horse's withers.

George smiled. He had told the boys down at the landing not
to waste any time getting the word to him when the boat showed
up, and they were not wasting any time. George was rising
slowly from his hickory chair, lifting with his arms to ease the
pain in his hips and knees, and his heartbeat was quickening.

News of Billy! By the Lord God, now at last we'll see how fares
that long-gone whippersnapper! he thought. As the messenger
brought his steed to a sit-down halt in a cloud of dust by the
porch, George shouted into the cabin door, "Cupid, saddle up

ol' Blackleg! I'm goin' down to th' river! Hey, Thad," he said to the youth who was swinging out of the saddle, "I'll wager you're thirsty."

"Usually am, 'specially now."

"I heard the gun," George said. He tipped the heavy jug over a glass, bracing himself with a palm on the back of his hip as he poured. "Who's with 'em, could y' tell?"

"Nup, Gen'l. I didn't wait for 'em to land. But it is one o Mister Gratiot's Saint Looy boats, about a dozen folks on board—thankee, to y'r health, sir."

"To yours, likewise."

"And there be Indians on board, and I seen your brother Edmund, and two-three army regulars." The messenger's sweaty dark horse was drinking noisily from the hollowed-log water trough under the hitchrail, and the messenger himself was slurping as noisily over the edge of his glass. George's legs hurt terribly, but he was too excited and impatient to go to sit back down The *chirr* of a locust stretched down toward the watery rush of the Falls.

There were hoofsteps, and old Cupid came around the corner of the cabin now leading the horse.

"Good," said George, putting on his old black hat and setting his glass on the porch. "Drain up, Thad, and we'll ride. Cupid. I'll have guests up for dinner, I reckon. Maybe a dozen, so get ready to feed maybe twenty." Now, he thought, let's see can this ol' carcass still get itself aboard a horse.

"Twenty?" Cupid whispered to himself and shook his head, but without losing his smile. "Gen'l, sir, it will be ready."

I wish I could cheat a little and mount from the porch George thought. But don't want people to think I'm goin' feeble He gritted his teeth and gripped the saddle with his left hand full of reins, and with a supreme effort that made bolts of pain in his knee and hip, he bent his leg and got his foot into the stirrup. Then he hauled himself upward mostly by his arms, swallowing a wheezing groan, and flung his right leg over. Sparks were floating around in his vision from the hip pains and the effort Lordy, he thought. Then he turned to the young man, who had just vaulted aboard his own horse without even using the stirrup, just as George had so easily used to do, back in the old days, and he said, "All righty, Thad, m' boy. I'll race ye down to the dock!"

GEORGE SMELLED THE MUSTY LEATHER AND THE STRANGE, mildewy, smoky scents from the willow-wood crates and the parfleche bags, and could not keep himself from reaching a hand out and running it over the heaps of bundles in the gloomy hold of Gratiot's boat. His fingers trailed over stiff rawhide and sawn wood, over woven willow lath and elk hair. He sniffed familiar smells and strange ones: buffalo skin and beaver castoreum, pine pitch, damp rag-paper, fox fur, sage, bear oil, musk, herbs, sulphur, the cloying odor of dead flowers, the dense putridity of old skeletons and sinews. William's hand was evident everywhere in the packing: the bindings, those tight pairs of half-hitches George had taught him to tie twenty years ago, the labels addressing this to the President's House, that to the War Department. George smelled the smells and felt the textures under his fingers, and for a moment now he was seeing not these carefully packed and stored bits of western wilderness, stacked in a stinking riverboat hold, but the distance—the long, winding river, the forests, the treeless plains—as if he had actually witnessed them himself. There was not room enough in this riverboat hold to stand up straight or take a full pace in any direction; and yet for the moment there was an expanse of two thousand miles.

And by now he's likely gone a thousand more, he thought. George turned to Edmund, who was beside him fingering a beaver pelt, the pale light from the hatch shining in his red hair and softly outlining his fleshy cheeks. "What ye thinking, Brother?" George murmured.

Edmund shook his head, looking melancholy. In his businessman's dark frock, Edmund looked tame, somber, hardly like a Clark boy at all. His blue eyes in pouches of well-fed flesh looked wistful. It was the look of a man who had not become what he would have chosen to become.

"I wish," Edmund said, "I wish I was yonder, 'stead o' here."

George understood everything those words meant. He put an arm over Edmund's shoulders and wished he could make him feel better. "Why, hell, Eddie, what for? He's probably got it so tamed out there by now it wouldn't be any fun."

THE ARIKARA POCASSE COULD NOT SEEM TO TAKE HIS EYES off George that evening. He studied him in the candlelight over the table almost constantly, and whenever George would turn to find himself being so studied, the Indian's broad, pleasant face would suffuse into a smile like a sunrise.

Gravelin explained.

"He now sees the man called 'Long Knife,' of whom he has heard legends since he was a very young man. It is a great joy to him to be in parley with you, General Clark, in your lodge."

707

George nodded and smiled at the chief. "Tell him Long Knife remembers. In the treaty at Cahokia there was an emissary from the Arikaras, who came with a body of the Sioux. The name of that Arikara was, I remember, Horn Bow."

Gravelin was astonished at General Clark's power of memory; the Arikara perhaps was a little less so, because he would have expected the white leader to remember an Arikara who had gone so far to see a treaty; nonetheless, he was impressed, because that had been long ago. George said now:

"Tell him Long Knife is pleased with the Arikara, who were friendly with my people when they went up the Missouri, and especially with my young brother, the one he calls Chief Red Hair."

Gravelin translated that, and the chief talked long in reply, beaming.

"He says," Gravelin interpreted, "that he has seen many great things since the Americans come to his village last year, but the greatest thing he has seen is two red hair chiefs who are both brave men, and great fathers to the tribes, and brothers to each other."

George smiled and nodded. He ran his hand up his forehead and onto his balding dome, then tugged at the silvering red hair at his temple. "Things being as they are on my crown," he said, "that gentleman is some flatterer." Edmund and Jonathan and most of the others at the table chuckled. "But you can tell him, M'sieu Gravelin, that he will see in Washington City the chiefest red hair chief of 'em all. What say to a toast, friends and honored guests, to that man who's got us all into whatever situations we're in: Tom Jefferson."

"Hear, hear!"

They were having a merry time. They had talked for hours, about the powerful and capricious Missouri, and about Fort Mandan, about the British traders, about William's cool defiance of the Teton Sioux; they had speculated long and deep about the legend of the Welsh Indians. They had mused about gloomy Captain Lewis and his sagacious dog Scannon, and about the Shoshoni girl-squaw and her papoose; they had laughed about the capture of the waterlogged prairie dog; they had talked about the amazing half-blind Cruzatte, and about Drouillard. They had gone solemn in talking of the untimely death of Sergeant Floyd; and then to cheer themselves up they had swung over to the topic of York the black monster and Great Medicine Stud, and had slapped their knees over the account of his frostbite. "Last winter is known among the Mandans," Gravelin had squealed with laughter, "as The-Year-the-Black-Man-Froze-His-Man-Part!" George had looked up then—the clock by the wall was striking two A.M. at the moment—and seen old Cupid lounging in the kitchen doorway listening, shaking his head and beaming.

"Dat Yawk," Cupid murmured, wagging his head on his long wrinkled neck. "Sayin' he eat chillums! Gaw, I never seen such a boy!"

It was a fine night. George felt as if William sat here at his elbow. Everyone was getting a fine, sentimental hum in his head.

But there was one face in the room that sometimes looked melancholy. When the grand spirit and goal of the expedition were being extolled and toasted, that one rugged, pugnacious face would look utterly abject. Edmund Clark perceived it, and so he turned to John Newman. "Soldier," he said, "you're a quiet one."

"Sir, there's two generals here, and an Indian chief, and you a cap'n, and various civilians of substance. I do feel some 'at over-ranked, Sir."

"I do myself," Edmund said. "I understand you're on your way home to a furlough, in Pennsylvania, eh?"

"Aye, sir. But I wish I was goin' t' other way, sir."

"With them, you mean."

"Aye, sir. Up that bedamned Missouri. It's cold, it's wicked, it's a hard go, sir. I got sick of it. But by the Eternal, Cap'n, I ought to be with them boys, and I hate what I done." He was pouring it out, now that he had found an ear for it. Gravelin was now listening obliquely, too. "I done all I could to right myself," Newman went on, his voice breaking. "I took my stripes without cryin', though it broke my heart to feel how hard they whipped me, my own friends. That's what'll surprise ye, sir. You expect your own messmates, at least, to flog easy, but they swing meaner than th' rest. I didn't understand that at th' moment, but I did, soon as I'd thought on 't. Anyhow, I tried to make myself right. After that, I made myself worth two men."

"This is true," said Gravelin. "Many times this man saves the barge coming down, by strong arm and heart."

"Cap'n Lewis himself told me I was worth two," Newman went on, "but said sorry as he was, he couldn't take me back. He's a stiff man, he is. Now sir, I 'spect if it had been left to Cap'n Clark, he'd have took me back on. Your brother is a for-givin' man, sir, most fair, most fair." He sighed now and shook his head. "Well, I'm a marked man, I am. But it's my own fault, I reckon. Me and my temper."

Edmund poured more brandy in Newman's glass. "Well, soldier," he said, trying to console, "ye'll make it all up somewhere else along the way. Don't be too severe with yourself, that's all I'll say."

"Right y' are, Cap'n. Sure. But a man don't get many special chances like that in his life. Oh, Cap'n! To be 'mongst them people! Bone tired, by a big fire, a gut full o' buffalo hump, St. Peter playin' his fiddle, everybody joshin' an' singin', and a million miles o' black space around ye, and tomorrow just one big question! An' I've thought, why, I'd cheerfully take a beating every day if I could be where they are now."

Edmund nodded emphatically and took a sip from his glass. "I hear ye, soldier. Oh, I do hear ye!"

JONATHAN AND EDMUND SAT ON THE PORCH THE NEXT morning after Gravelin's party had left, and drank strong coffee with George in the fresh morning light before starting down for the river and their homes. They were all thoughtful, less talkative than usual. Their minds and souls had been stretched by what they had seen and heard and felt, and words sounded feeble in their new inner spaciousness. They gazed down over the meadow and the locust trees and cottonwoods at the Falls and watched boats move on the wide gray-green surface below, and remembered, each in his own way, their impressions of yesterday and last night.

Jonathan at the moment was considering what the new Western Territory would mean in terms of trade along the Ohio if the expedition did indeed find a water route to the Pacific. Much of the China trade that now went around Cape Horn likely would come right through Louisville. He thought of something he had been wanting to get for Sarah: a carved elephant of jade. Think of all the fine things that would pass through Louisville on their way east, he thought. Then he looked at George, and wished the Clarksville Canal and the upstream boat patent had materialized for him. With just one such commercial advantage, he thought, he could turn his fortunes around and gain something of what he deserves in this country.

Edmund was still remembering Private Newman's sad story and ingesting it into his own discontent.

And George was thinking of William, remembering their long walks and rides and talks together, remembering their long-ago surveying and hunting and exploring trips together back when

George could ride, remembering the day when William had ridden up here with his letter from Meriwether Lewis and asked for advice; George remembered that day, and remembered how he and William and Fanny had stayed up the whole night long, talking, and then how they had sat out here the next morning— a morning so much like this, it had been—drinking the coffee that William so loved, the strong, strong coffee, black as ink, with blackstrap molasses and chicory in it, and had foreplanned the greater part of the Voyage of Discovery between them, right here on this same porch on just such a morning as this. George shook his head, remembering this. It was a fine memory. He filled a pipe and lit it.

"I wonder me," said Edmund now, "when we'll hear next from Billy."

George answered. "His letter to me said a party o' men will be detached and sent back in a canoe when they've found th' Great Falls of the Missouri. They place those falls some six hundred miles upriver from Fort Mandan; it wouldn't surprise me if they've got there by now. And so, God willing, we might hear from 'im again in another two months or thereabouts." He puffed and then pointed down at the Falls of the Ohio with his pipestem. "Think of it," he said. "Here we sit at this falls, the only one blocking the Ohio. And Billy likely at the Falls o' the Missouri, nigh three thousand water-miles out yonder. And all the way 'twixt these falls and those, it's all boating water, nay, not one solitary portage. That is a marvel to think on, is it not?"

"Time for me to saddle up and go home," Jonathan said, rising, putting a hand on George's shoulder. "All this distance is stretchin' my head all out o' shape. Either that, or I drank intemperate last night."

"I seem to remember you did," Edmund said. "I'll ride out with you. I want to stop in town and tell the newlyweds the news. As it is, we're prob'ly all in deep trouble for not fetching Fanny up here for last night's confabulation!"

41

AT THE FORK
OF THE MISSOURI
Sunday, June 9, 1805

"HERE'S WHAT I'VE BEEN THINKING," LEWIS SAID, HOLDING A morsel of roasted elk on his knife point to cool before putting it in his mouth. "If indeed this south fork is our river—as only you and I and the squaw seem to believe—the boys'll be convinced only when they see the Great Falls. So I'll take a party ahead to find the Falls and you follow on with the boats. Now, we don't know what we're in for above the Falls. If we do manage to find the Shoshonis, we can't be sure they'll treat us friendly, since they've never seen a white man before. And we don't know what kind o' muscle will be required to cross the mountains. So what I'm getting at is this . . ."

He put the meat in his mouth now and chewed it, his eyes reflecting long thoughts. William swallowed his own mouthful of elk roast and waited, feeling fireglow on his face and night chill on his damnable rheumatic neck. Lewis went on.

"I don't think we can spare—" He winced and killed a mosquito on his temple. "I thought these pests couldn't fly when it was cold. Anyway, I don't think we can spare any men to take news back to the States, as we'd intended from here."

William raised his eyebrows in surprise and considered this. "I see your point, but . . ."

"Since we hadn't told the boys we'd intended to anyways, nobody'll be let down."

"*They* won't, that's true. But Mister Jefferson and everybody back east will be. We wrote 'em to expect more maps and more news by this fall."

"I know we did. But it seems to me we'll just have to disappoint 'em. We can't spare anyone, I really believe that."

"When no word comes as promised, y'know, they're goin' to take us for dead."

Lewis chewed on another bite of elk and his eyes were deep. "Aye," he said after a while, "likely they will. But I reckon it's better to be *thought* dead than to *be* dead, eh? And meseems that having those few boys with us could make it so or not."

"It could," William admitted. He could see that, and he could see that his friend had his priorities straight. But William could remember how it had been at home during the war when nobody had known for a year at a stretch whether George was alive or dead, or Jonathan, or Edmund, or Johnny, and how they had never really learned it for sure about Dickie but over the years had just had to let the hope die and the emptiness become permanent. He wouldn't want his brothers and sisters to have to go through that kind of thing over himself, but it appeared they would have to.

Lewis was studying him now, and he said, "Y' look so wistful, my friend. Oh, I know! You're afeared that pretty Judy Hancock o' yours might marry up somebody else if she doesn't hear from you." He laughed, and William laughed weakly.

"Wrong," he said. "I hadn't thought that at all."

But he was thinking it now, and knew he would be from now on.

AND SO THEY DECIDED TO DEPOSIT HERE THE RED PIROGUE and all the heavy baggage they could afford to leave behind, and proceed up the south fork. Lewis named the north fork Maria's River, in honor of a fair cousin, Maria Wood, and took sightings to mark the location for their return trip. Some of the men were put to work under Cruzatte's direction digging a cache of the sort used by the French *coureurs de bois*. It was a sort of cellar dug in dry ground, wider at the bottom than at the top, floored with boughs and hides, its narrow mouth to be sealed with its original piece of sod so that an Indian might stand nearly upon it without seeing it. Dirt from the hole was thrown onto hides to be carried away, and thus show no signs of digging.

Into this cache were to be put some provisions, salt, some tools, gunpowder, and lead, Captain Lewis's writing desk, tinware, beaver traps, most of the botanical specimens collected since Fort Mandan, and William's revised map. As the blacksmith's bellows and some of his tools were to be secured here too, Shields was first put to work repairing any damaged weapons, including the air gun, whose mainspring had been broken.

Now that the load was lightened, the red pirogue could be left behind. She was drawn up on a small island in Maria's River, tied to trees, and covered with bushes. Captain Lewis then named Drouillard, Gibson, Joseph Fields, and Private Goodrich to accompany him on his search for the Falls. William was to bring the canoes, the white pirogue, and the remaining tons of baggage up the swift rocky river, which they still presumed to call the Missouri.

Sacajawea's cold had evolved into something more serious.

She was moaning and had at last driven Charbonneau into a fury. He was disgusted and impatient with her and went to sit with the other Frenchmen at the bonfire, scowling, wishing he could have left her at the Minnetaree Village. William, hearing her four-month-old baby crying, came into the hide shelter late in the afternoon to find the squaw, naked, rolled into a ball on a buffalo robe with her fists jammed into her crotch, her face sweat-slick and contorted with pain, ignoring the squalling baby in its cradleboard. "York," he called. Lord have pity, she must be *bad* sick if she can't tend to that papoose, he thought.

He put York in charge of the infant, then conferred with Lewis about medication. "She needs a dose o' salts," Lewis said. "She's got what I had on the river t' other day, just intestinal cramps." He went to his medicine chest and came back with a dose of the bitter salts in a cup. William had wrapped the naked shuddering girl in a woolen blanket and was squatting beside her, sponging her forehead with a wet cloth. She simply stared wild-eyed at Lewis and shook her head. "Here, Clark, you give it to 'er. She trusts you."

She drank the bitter concoction when William held it for her, then, helpless and wordless, lay back in the blanket and shut her eyes and went into silent battle with her pain. Her black hair was a small dark blur in the evening gloom within the shelter. "If she's no better tomorrow," Lewis suggested, "better bleed her." He was too busy now, getting his party outfitted for an early-morning departure, to hover over her. Outside, York sat by the fire with the tiny swaddled baby encircled in one arm. "Don't you eat *that* child, cannibal monster," Lewis joked at him.

York rolled his eyes the way he had when frightening the Mandan and Arikara children, then opened his mouth wide as if he were going to gulp the baby down whole. "This 'd be a sweet un, he would." York grinned then, and began rocking it, looking for all the world, in his red headkerchief and gold earring, like some gigantic, muscular mammy. He rocked the baby and hummed while Cruzatte's fiddle began squeaking at the big bonfire, and the laughter came over the river-hush, and the singing started, those big, raspy, resonant or leather-lunged voices, filling this timbered place in a fork of rivers, echoing a way along the bluffs, then vanishing in the cold air of the immense wilderness night.

WILLIAM RAN THE RAZOR-SHARP BLADE OF HIS PEN-KNIFE through the smokeless flame of his alcohol lamp, then knelt beside Sacajawea's pallet. "Now, the basin, York, if y' please."

714

Raindrops pelted the skin cover of the lodge, and the girl looked, frightened but trusting, too sick to protest, at the big, red-headed captain, then at his knife, then at his face. She had seen bleedings done and knew it was a part of the white men's medicine, so she was resigned to it and believed it would make her well. She winced with another great spasm of pain and then waited, her brown-nippled little breasts barely rising and falling with her shallow breathing.

William placed the basin under her left elbow and told York to tighten a thong high on her arm. "Squeeze your hand tight, Janey," he said, and, not knowing whether she knew the word "squeeze," he showed her by making a fist. She balled her hand and clenched it till the knuckles whitened. Soon the veins on the inside of her forearm stood in relief. "Now, here we go, Janey."

And with a swift, clean motion he made a slit through the brown skin and along the bluish vein and pulled back on the skin from the other side of her forearm so that the slit vein stood open and the dark blood welled out and began dripping, then running steadily, into the pan under her elbow. York loosened the thong and knelt looking thoughtfully at the shiny blood spreading over the pan's tin bottom. The girl had shut her eyes and her head lay back and she seemed to be getting smaller as the blood ran out, smaller and more frail. God let this do it, William thought. Suddenly this little creature had come to be of supreme importance, her survival a hinge on which everything else hung.

If we hadn't come along, William thought, her life would've been as inconsequential and anonymous as that of a doe in the thicket. But we need 'er.

He bent over and put his ear to her chest, and listened to the tiny bumpings of her heart. A life's so fragile, he thought. He breathed the musky smell of her body, the gamey smoke-and-sweat smell of the sleeping robe with a trace of the Indian baby's urine in it. *Bump*-bump. *Bump*-bump. *Bump*-bump. When he raised his head off her bare breast, he saw Charbonneau looming in the entrance. The Frenchman's eyes were flashing and he was breathing hard.

Oh oh, William thought. He doesn't like something, and I think I know what it is. "Ye want something?" he said, pulling the robe up to her shoulder. Charbonneau stood simmering for a moment, then said in a voice pinched by fury. "A word wees you, Capitaine."

"Stand out of my light, Charbonneau. I'll see you when I'm through here."

715

He bound the little wound when the pan was full of blood, and had York carry the pan away. "Now," he said, rising to stand under the low shelter, before the puffed-up Frenchman. "What is it?"

Charbonneau was almost in a fighting crouch and his fingers were like claws. His lips were drawn thin across his yellow teeth, and William had a sudden premonition that he would whip out his skinning knife. William put his hand unobtrusively alongside his own sheath. "What, Charbonneau?" he demanded again.

The Frenchman thumped himself on the chest. "Charbonneau have decide: he will take his woman and go back. Char—"

"Stop right there!" snapped William. "So help me, I won't hear it."

"Charbonneau will take his woman—"

"Now hear this: Y're contracted, remember?"

"Charbonneau does not like thees arrangement." The Frenchman's eyelids were hardened.

"What you like doesn't weigh much with me right now. God damn it, I have to doctor your squaw; York has to coddle your baby. I'm damned if I'll coddle you! If you weren't stuffed as full of yourself as one o' your own gut sausages, your family would fare just fine, and y' might be happy enough with your arrangement. Now get out."

Charbonneau crouched lower. His face was twisted with hatred; he was on the edge of his soul. William saw his hand moving back toward the antler handle of his knife, and so, conspicuously, put his hand on his own, and Charbonneau saw it.

"Try to cut me," William said, "and I'll have you fileted, even before York can get in here to mash your skull."

The Frenchman froze, considering this even in his passion. And suddenly he seemed to crumble inside. His hands came around in front of him, palms up; his scowling thick eyebrows rose and his eyes brimmed.

"Please, *mon capitaine*! If you understood—"

"Cap'n Clark, sir!" It was Ordway's voice outside.

"Aye, Sergeant?"

"Need your judgment on a matter, Sir."

"I'm comin'. Now," he said to Charbonneau. "I'd have you flogged for mutiny if you were a soldier. But if you'll straighten y'rself up, and act a man, and pull your load like the rest of us, I'll forget this tantrum. Is that a deal?"

Charbonneau nodded, slump-shouldered.

Later that day, William got Baptiste Le Page aside while the boats were being loaded for the next morning's departure. "Do you know," he asked, "what goes on inside Charbonneau's head?"

"*Un peu.*" Le Page shrugged. "Can anyone know?"

"He's sore as a boil. Any idea why? Trust me; this is in confidence. Only to keep the peace."

Le Page's eyes grew furtive. He looked around, pursed his lips and popped them with his index finger. Then he sighed. "Great delicacy, *mon capitaine*. I say this only because you ask. You yourself are a matter." He rolled his eyes. "Oh, great delicacy."

"How am I a matter?" William thought he knew.

"Charbonneau. You know him. His pride is here." Le Page stroked his groin. "Ees a hard time for heem now. He no can . . . Ahm, ees the custom he no can make the *la la, la la* weeth hees squaw while the enfant ats her mammel. So . . ."

"But what—"

"You, *mon capitaine*, have make him *jalouse.*"

"I give him no cause."

"The squaw, M'sieu, not what *you* do. But the squaw: she see you highly; she see Charbonneau a fool. Oh, *mais non*, she not *ay* thees to heem, but he, ah, *feel* it."

Aye, William thought, remembering how Charbonneau had looked when he found him auditing her heartbeat. Le Page added:

"He see these merry mens laugh. *Alors* . . ." Le Page put his forefingers up beside his temples like horns and waggled them. "Een his brain." Now Le Page grabbed his crotch, to show where Charbonneau's brain was, and said, "Een his brain they laugh at heem."

"Now I see. It is, as ye say, delicate. Then listen, Baptiste: if ve can—I mean, delicately—assure him it's all in his head."

"I do that, *mon capitaine*. Already I do."

"Thankee. It *is* all in his head, ye know."

Le Page tilted his head and closed his eyes, then turned with a half-skip and sauntered back toward the pirogue.

I'm not sure even *he* believes me, William thought. Now I'll be damned. If this isn't a silly brew o' things.

He thought of the squaw-girl, of her little heart bumping against his ear, of her little brown breasts, of the musty, musky smells in the buffalo robe. Then he remembered other brown bosoms, other dense-smelling buffalo robes.

Then he brought Judy Hancock's peach-colored face up behind his eyelids, and followed Le Page down to the shore.

*   *   *

717

"Reckon I know why the cap'ns picked this river," groaned Private Windsor, up to his knees in mud, the pirogue tow rope rubbing his shoulder raw. " 'Cause the other'n looke too easy!"

"I heard that, Windsor!" William's voice came unexpected from the bluff just above. "And y're absolutely right, lad. seemed to us this little voyage's been too much a lark, and tim you boys earned y'r pay!"

Windsor cringed, looked up into the smiling face above th willows, and replied:

"Right y' are, sir! And we're much obliged, as we all been pinin' for some exercise!"

Laughter rippled along the line of gasping, straining, stum bling, fly-bitten laborers.

"*Sacré du diable*," muttered Charbonneau. "Laugh and laugh *Toujours le comédie*."

Lewis and his scouts had been gone for three day now. For William and the rest of the following party, the ha up the river had become a hell of toil and pain. The curre grew more and more swift and turbulent as they ascended th south fork. Poling, rowing, or sailing were useless now; the me could move the boats only with tow ropes, stumbling along th muddy, rocky banks, which squirmed with rattlesnakes, or, those long reaches where there were no banks at all, by flounde ing in the frigid river, twisting their ankles on slippery roun stones or gashing their feet on sharp-edged rocks. Every minu or so one man or another would fall and go under completel then rise, spitting and gasping, to resume his place on the tov line. Now and then the whole line of men on a tow rope woul drag each other down, and the canoe they were pulling woul lurch and ship water, get away, or grate against rock so violent that it would have to be hauled out and patched.

Sacajawea was gravely ill. She had been declining steadil and in her sleepless sufferings had made sleep impossible f William and for York and Charbonneau. She was listless an feverish, attacked by violent pains in her abdomen and groi and was incoherent much of the time, lying in the shade und the awning of the pirogue, unable to tend to little Pompey. Yo was becoming almost sick with worry. "Get well, Janey," he to her, stooping over her pathetic, wasting little figure one evenin "Now, I love this yea 'poose o' yours, but I ain' made to be perm'nent mammy." He was beginning to realize that such w a distinct possibility.

Collins joked that evening, trying to ease the worried look on York's face: "I don't blame ye, boy. I can see why ye wouldn't want t' be th' mammy of a child that Charbonneau was th' daddy of!" York frowned at Collins for a moment and then laughed for the first time in two days.

William had come to consider himself as good a stomach doctor as any layman could be. But the remedies that worked unfailingly on the men had no effect on her. Lord God, he thought suddenly this evening, what if this is no gut matter, but the female region?

"York," he said, "will you kindly take th' papoose outside and sit with 'im, and all I want ye t' do is make sure that hysterical husband o' hers doesn't walk in. I mean, make *damn* sure."

If that blamed jealous fool knew I was a-doin' this, William thought, I'd have to fight 'im a duel sure. "Janey," he said softly, peeling the robe down off her skinny, naked body, "I must look at your woman-part now. Do ye say yes?"

She opened her legs listlessly, uncaring, thinking only how strange that he should ask. Neither Charbonneau nor any of the Indian men who had owned her before Charbonneau would have bothered to ask.

William reached down into the dark place, hesitant, uncertain, self-conscious. How'm I going to know what I do find? he thought as his finger spread the labia and a strong, disagreeable odor came up. I don't know anything about the womanly region.

No, reckon not, he replied to himself. But I've dealt with enough infection lately t' know corruption when I see it, no matter where I find it, he thought.

She lay still and let him look and feel and probe. She knew that Chief Red Hair was the best of medicine men and that he was as gentle as one's own mother. She believed that he could make her well if anyone could do it, and she had reached the place in her soul where all was equal, and if she could not be made well now, she would choose to die and go beyond this misery.

For a moment as he looked into the glistening pinkness he thought this surely was the strangest moment in his eventful life. Here he was three thousand miles from civilization, down on his knees and elbows in a tepee on a riverbank, looking into the bottom end of a dying Indian girl, while his black man sat outside crooning lullabies to a papoose and stood sentinel against her husband. But there was no time to dwell on the absurdity of it. He palpated the inner labia and then slipped his forefinger up into the snug vagina, to find, he presumed, lesions or pus or some other clue to her disorder. He withdrew his finger and there was nothing. He inserted his finger again and touched gently around the mouth of the uterus, pressing harder then against the gristly firmness of it and now watching her face for signs of pain. Suddenly she had a spasm and he saw the flash of white as she bared her teeth in a grimace.

"Hurt?" he said.

She groaned and nodded. He pressed again, at a different angle. "Hurt?" he said again. No. "Now? Hurt?" No. Then again and she jerked.

Well. It told him little; it told him only that likely there was something in her reproductive organs that hurt. And if the trouble was there, he did not have any idea what to prescribe or do about it, and he was sure that even if Meriwether Lewis were there, he would not know what to do about it either.

We both know well enough how to stop and start the bowel and lance pustules and treat felons and set broken bones and cure clap and clean infections and sew up gashes and pull teeth and amputate frosted extremities, he thought, because our boys have had a steady round of those things.

But none o' them has anything like this, he thought. How can we be prepared for something like this?

HE GAVE HER A DOSE OF LAUDANUM TO EASE THE PAIN so that she could sleep. Possibly the cold she had has got her infected someplace down there in her menses, he thought. He remembered how his touch in her had made her wince.

But it could be that the press of my finger just bothered some inflamed place in her intestines, he thought.

He realized that he was having wishful thinking; that if it really was intestinal he might still be able to do something for it. So just in case, he gave her a dose of Jesuits' bark, cinchona. She was almost too listless to drink, and just trustingly let him trickle the fluid into her mouth, and she swallowed it. He then soaked a wad of gauze in it and inserted it into her vagina, packing it in next to the uterus.

I wish Lewis was here, William thought. He's the doctor when it comes to real bad cases.

Many of the men this evening were in pain with swellings, swellings in their joints, swellings in their groins, painful hot swellings in their armpits, all of which seemed to be aggravated by the constant cold water and the bruisings they were taking in the river. Many had horrendous boils and carbuncles in those places where their flesh sweated in elkhide and rubbed constantly

ith their movements: in their crotches, under their arms, inside
eir knees. William himself had a swelling on his ankle that
d started, if he remembered correctly, when a prickly pear
ine had broken off in the tendon and had been rubbed con-
antly by the edge of his moccasin. It was hard like a grape
der the skin and he could feel that it was achingly distended
ith pus, but he could not take time to sit down with poultices
d draw it to a head; he was too busy with running the con-
gent and doctoring the others. In exhaustion this evening, he
d to do a job he particularly hated: a tooth extraction, on
atton.

The soldier sat on a log before him, his left cheek big as an
ple.

"Well, now, Bratton," William joked. "I don't know how I'm
osed to work in your mouth if y' don't spit out that quid first."
atton, one of the few men of the whole Corps not addicted to
bacco, grinned lopsidedly and drooled. With his hands
enched between his thighs to control his fright, and that dis-
rted grimace on his face, the big Virginia Irishman looked like
perfect imbecile, and some of the soldiers in the sick line were
errily telling him so.

"Y' don't drink, either, do ye, Bratton?" William noted. Brat-
n shook his head. "That's a pity," William said. "You know
ere's a dram o' whiskey for a tooth-pull. T' ease the hurt. Want
urs? No? All righty, then. Open up here."

"I'll drink his whiskey for 'im, suh," said Collins.

William stood with his pliers ready, and said, "Y' know, I
nce had you wrong, Collins; I thought ye were a shirker. But
ow y' just volunteer for things so eager-like!"

The men laughed.

"Sense o' duty, suh," Collins said, bowing like a courtier. "I'll
rink his whiskey gladly."

"But Collins, you don't have a toothache."

"I can git one, suh."

And while everyone was laughing at that, William reached in
ith the pliers and yanked out Bratton's decayed yellow molar.
atton sat there stunned with surprise and pain, drooling blood,
yes bulging and pouring tears. "Now, Bratton, here's your
am. Y' can do what ye like with it, even give it to Collins
ere."

Bratton held the glass, looked for a moment at the angelically
niling Collins—and then tossed it down his own throat.

"Horrors," groaned Collins. "Another saintly soul lost t' th'
orn Devil!"

"THIS IS A TRULY SORRY STATE," ORDWAY WAS LAMENTIN
to William the next afternoon. "Not countin' the pint or
Cap'n Lewis is carryin', we're down to one gallon of ardent sp
its."

William tried to make light of this depressing report. "We
we knew it couldn't last forever, didn't we? Not with a crew li
this 'n."

"Hi! Hi! Cap'n! I see Joe Fields a-comin!" cried a voice ov
the roaring water.

William clapped Ordway on the shoulder. "Don't they s
good news always follers bad?"

They could see him now, high on the distant bluff, half-lo
ing and half-limping, rifle in one hand, the other hand wavi
in great sweeps as he came toward them. Now they could fain
hear his voice. "What's 'e sayin', Cap'n, can y' make it ou

A smile was spreading over William's face. "Unless it's ju
wishful hearin', Sarge, I think he says they found th' Gre
Falls."

The men had heard this now, and they knew at once it mea
that their captains had been right all along and every one
them had been wrong, but they all stopped where they sto
now, in the cold, rushing water, on the banks, all turned to gr
at William now, and as if on a signal, they all began to che
him. He gave them a big wave, then jumped off the riverbar
and waded to the white pirogue, clambered dripping over th
side and knelt by Sacajawea. She had raised her head slightly
the sounds of shouting and she looked at him, her face gray ar
slick with sweat, eyes sunken, hair hanging in damp strings.

"Janey," he exclaimed, grasping her hand. "Janey, liste
They found the falling water! Soon now, very soon, Janey, we
be in the land of your people! D' ye hear me, child? *Your pe*
ple." A trace of a smile began to show on her wasted visag
"Aye, Janey," he said, "we're a-goin' to need ye then, so ye
start gettin' well right now, y' hear?"

She nodded, a weak, weak motion, then her head fell bac
His smile wavered.

He knew it might be weeks yet before they could find h
nomadic tribe.

And in truth, she did not look as if she would last another da

FIELDS GAVE HIS REPORT WHILE SITTING ON A ROCK GE
ting prickly pear needles tweezed out of his feet. William l
tened and pulled the needles and asked questions.

722

"Thursday morning," said Fields, "that's when we first heard the waterfalls. Goodrich heard 'em first whilst we was a-movin' over high ground, and he hollered. We went to look. We seen a cloud of mist 'fore we got to the Falls. Then we seen 'em. Cap'n; 's the damndest most stupefyin' sight ever fell on my eyes, I swear t' God! Eighty feet high if they's an inch, and th' whole damed Missouri comes over white as snow. And roars? Ye have t holler to talk over it. Cap'n Lewis he went out on a buttment f rocks just below the middle of the Falls, midst all that white ater, an' sat there I don' know, an hour, two hours, three, just -writin' notes. I swear, Cap'n, th' ground itself seems t' shake. Vell, sir, as if that wasn't enough, next day we went on up and ound four more falls, all in less'n ten mile, I bet." The men, et, mud-smeared, were standing around listening eagerly to all ais.

"Ten mile, ye say," William commented. "Y'd make the por-ige then to be about ten mile?"

"Mebbe more like twenty, Cap'n. See, there's a bad rapid naybe three—four miles this side o' the Falls, that we didn't see n the way up, but I found it today comin' down 'cause I hung loser by the river. Ouch!" His foot jerked as William found nother thorn. "An' then," he went on, "they's some horr'ble eep ravines openin' through the cliffs into th' river; those would ave t' be gone 'round, sir; add mebbe four—five mile. But these guesses, Cap'n. A survey'll show some better."

"What's th' overland like?"

"Flat to rollin', sir. Hard stony ground an' prickly pear, not a lessed tree anywhere, 'cept a few in the bottoms—and there's carce any bottoms at that. It's hot as a griddle on them plains up nere, too, when th' sun's out. More buffalo'n I ever seen in one lace, an' elk galore. Goodrich been catchin' a trout a minute, oo, so th' eatin's real good. But hit's goin' be a tough haul, sir, o way t' make it easy, I'm afear'd."

William had already arrived at that conclusion. Twenty miles n summer heat over stones and prickly pears, toting all these anoes and baggage. That'd kill ordinary folk, he thought.

But we can't let on, he thought. "Doesn't sound too bad, does , boys?" he suggested. They all hooted and laughed. They ardly seemed to be thinking about the hardship of it; they were ust glad they were on the right river.

"As for me," said George Shannon's clear, young voice, "I'll e happy to git out o' water for a spell anyways."

William smiled and nodded. These aren't ordinary folk, he hought.

CAPTAIN LEWIS CAME DOWN WITH HIS SCOUTS AND MET TH
main party at the foot of the big rapids, and made straight for th
shelter where Sacajawea lay near death. She had been refusin
to take medicine, and seemed to have prepared herself to die. H
knelt hatless by her pallet and gazed down at her, daylight shir
ing on his sun-bleached hair, and studied her while taking h
pulse with a very grave face. His face had been sun-and-winc
burned to a color darker than hers. She was in fact more gra
than brown now.

"Fetch me my pouch there," he said. "I got some chokeber
root bark in there last week up the river. I was likin' to die on
day with a seized-up gut, and that bark cured me entire by bec
time. Have York boil a black tea of it. Meantime, let's try to ge
some opium in her. Got to strengthen that pulse ere she ju:
slips away."

"The boys found a sulphur spring t'day," William said, knee
ing near the girl and unconsciously stroking her forehead wit
his palm. "Reckon what that might do?"

"We better try it, too. Aye."

"I had 'em bring back several gallon of it for us all. There's a
plenty."

When the Indian girl was full of every remedy they coul
think of, the captains spent two minutes congratulating eac
other on their good judgment about the river fork and the find
ing of the Falls, then set about planning the portage. "God ble:
us," Lewis exclaimed. "Wait till you see those cascades! I've see
many a grand spectacle, but never a thing like 'em!"

They decided to leave the heavy white pirogue rather tha
portage it. They would dig another cache to lighten the loa
further, and begin making a skin covering for the iron-fram
boat, which would be considerably lighter. Lewis unpacked
and found every piece for its assembly—except one screw
Somewhere along the tortuous way in the two years of this jou
ney, a single screw had been lost. One essential screw. "Damna
ion!" Lewis cursed. This boat was his pet.

John Shields bent down near him, and looked at the hol
where the screw was supposed to go. "Heck fire, Cap'n," he saic
"Don't y' fret about that. I'll make y' one just like 'er in 'bout
half an hour."

"Shields," Lewis said, "if I was a general, I'd make you a colc
nel."

They decided to stay here until the squaw either got better or died. They would not try to move her in her present condition. William sent Private Frazier, a fair map-maker with a keen land sense, out with another man to examine and sketch the land on the south bank of the river. Lewis had decided already that the terrain on the north side of the river was too broken for portage.

"Now, friend," Lewis said, casting his gaze over the canoes and bundles and tools, kegs, bags, weapons, powder canisters, ropes, sails, hides, and instruments, "if you had to transport all that baggage over a long stretch—as ye do—how would you go about it?"

"Why, I'd just load 'em up on oxcarts and wagons, and I'd tell the teamsters, 'All right, boys, I'll meet ye at the other end.' That's how I'd do it if I had my choice." He smiled wistfully.

"Aye, me too. But so much for that. Havin' no oxen or wagons, as we don't, how would you do it then?"

"Well, I'd dread to try it without wagons. The men could carry it all over on their backs, then carry the canoes. But that would take a lot of trips. Like ants. And over prickly pear. But say . . ."

"Are you thinking what I am, maybe?"

"I'm thinkin' we can't make oxen or even horses. But I'd reckon a people who can manufacture an iron screw in a place like this could make a wooden wagon. As for beasts o' burden, our boys already shown us they're that."

"Aye. And we've leather aplenty for harnesses. Let me get a notebook here, and we'll design us a wagon or two, say what?"

"PULSE REGULAR," LEWIS SAID WITH SATISFACTION. SINCE the dosage of sulphur water, she had been improving steadily. But then it could have been the cataplasms applied to her uterus, too. Whichever it had been, intestines or female organs, they were getting better. By the third and fourth days she was eating broiled buffalo and broth, sitting up for long spells, and, finally, walking. By Thursday, as the carpenters were finishing the two frail wagons, the girl was able to walk to the river and go fishing.

Throughout the chasm of the Great Falls there hung a stench of rot. It came from countless dead and decaying buffalo. The beasts, immense herds of them crowding down narrow, steep trails to the river to drink, were forever pushing each other off into the swift river, and many were carried over the Falls and killed. Their carcasses, in every state of decomposition, were heaped in the shallows and bottoms, where they attracted buzzards, wolves, grizzly bears, and clouds of flies. The stench was nauseating in the extreme, but it was just something to get accustomed to. The presence of so many bears made it necessary to go armed and in pairs everywhere. Scannon barked all night at the scent of prowling bears, probably keeping them out of the camp but definitely costing everyone much needed sleep.

And so the carpenters worked in the heat and the stink, black with flies, and the men moved the canoes up a creek where the banks were sloped gently enough to permit them to carry them up onto the plain. The men had found only one tree in the neighborhood big enough and sound enough to make wheels of: it was a cottonwood twenty-two inches through at the base of the trunk. From this they had cross-sawed two sets of four wheels, and a few spares. These would be brittle wheels, they were sure of that, so they cut still more spares until there was no wood left. There seemed not to be a straight enough piece of wood in the valley for axletrees, so it became necessary to cut up the mast of the pirogue.

The little four-wheel carts were then outfitted with tongues, and the men made harnesses for themselves, with all the predictable jokes about who was dumb as an ox or stubborn as a mule. The white pirogue was lashed down in a brushy covert, and a few more expendable items interred in a second cache. Moccasins were patched and double soled. Charbonneau was bawled out roundly for suggesting again that he wanted to take his squaw and go home. William surveyed the portage route in detail, finding that there were several gullies that could not be avoided, and that there was one big hill of gradual slope, and one steep hill, that would have to be climbed. William also measured all the Falls by instrument, pausing now and then to sit down and just marvel at the hissing, thundering, flashing, steaming, foaming, rainbow-catching beauty of it.

What a poem Johnny could have written about this vision, he thought. The steep, high, striated rock cliffs, through which this boiling water-chute had carved its way, were massive—two and three hundred feet, and nearly perpendicular—and yet seemed to tremble frail as silk in the mist beyond the thundering cascades, as if all this rock might yet simply dissolve and be washed away in a moment. After a while William realized that his equilibrium, even his whole sense of real being, was being altered by this constant rushing motion, by these great translucent sheets and opaque waves that were never still and never the same, yet never changed their shapes; and so he returned to get his surveying instruments, then went to the portage trail, gradually recovering as if from a trance.

726

He and his surveyors drove stakes to mark the way, and the sweat in their eyes and the prickly pear spines in their feet brought them, little by little, back to the painful reality of the task ahead. As if the spines were not sufficient torture, the clayey ground itself—trampled when wet by hundreds of thousands of buffalo hooves and then baked hard as brick by the sun—twisted ankles mercilessly and tore moccasins to shreds. Every step was a jolt of pain now. And they would have to cross and recross this route, he estimated, for two or three weeks before the portage was done.

Finally, Meriwether Lewis took his small advance party, laden with the ninety pounds of iron boat-frame, and set out for the head of the Falls, where they would set up an advance camp, and assemble and cover the vessel. And by the night of the twenty-first of June, all was ready.

The ordeal would begin at sunrise.

EACH WAGON HAD FOUR OF THE WILLOW-DISK WHEELS. Each wheel stood about as high as a man's knee, had been sawn about six inches thick so it would not be apt to split easily under the weight and the jouncing, and had a round hole in the center cut to fit the shaved end of an axletree. The wheel and axletree were lubricated with tallow. A peg, fitted snugly through an auger-hole at each end of the axletree, secured the wheel to keep it from wobbling or working its way off. Two sets of axles and wheels were set parallel on the ground about ten feet apart, then across them two long sapling-trunks were laid and strapped tight with wet rawhide. When a canoe was set down on these saplings with its round bottom between them and then lashed in place with more rawhide, it made a capacious wagon bed, which was filled with baggage. Elkhide ropes were passed through auger-holes in a tongue forward of the front axle, and to these ropes each man's leather shoulder-harness was attached. Thus each wagon could be pulled by a team of as many as ten men. The first two canoes had thus been converted into wagons the night before, and loaded, and were standing on the plain silhouetted by the dawn light this morning when the men awoke.

In anticipation of their labors, the troops were fed all they could eat of hoe-cake, elk, and buffalo. They were a happy lot this morning. They chewed, and sipped tea, and gazed proudly at the wagons. "Not too sorry, considerin', eh what, Joe?" one would say. "Fancy that," another would exclaim. "*Wheels*! I never thought t' see a wheel agin, did you?"

Sergeant Ordway was to be left in charge of the goods here at the base camp, with Charbonneau, York, Goodrich, Sacajawea, and the papoose. Lewis, Sergeant Pat Gass, Joe Fields, and Shields the smithy had already carried their loads of iron and tools up to make a camp on an island at the far end of the portage, where they would assemble the iron-frame boat. That left Nathaniel Pryor to be the sergeant in charge of the wagons, and he was soon swaggering around calling himself the "muleskinner" and saying, "Now, whar'd I put my whip?"

The sun was still behind the purple eastern mountains when the harnessed men hitched themselves up to the wagons, laughing, snorting, stamping the ground, and braying, "Heee, haw, hee haw!" William slipped his shoulders into a knapsack containing about seventy pounds of meat, a notebook, and some instruments and medicines, laid his rifle across his shoulder and put his umbrella-tomahawk in his belt, squinted ahead over the lilac-gray prairie, looked back at York and Sacajawea, who stood marveling at this, then he yelled out, "All set, Sarge, move 'em out!"

"GEE-YAP!" Pryor bellowed, swinging his arm around his head as if snapping a twenty-foot bullwhip.

The men leaned forward into their harnesses; leather creaked; the hide ropes stretched; the men leaned farther, and the wheels began to turn. Slowly, grinding and squeaking and rattling, the wheeled canoes began trundling over the stucco-like ground. The men arched their backs and pushed with their brawny legs and the vehicles came along, lurching and jolting, their bare masts swaying. "Son of a bitch," groaned Private Proctor, sweat breaking out on his face before he had taken twenty steps, "this lunker is *heavy*!"

"Nice and easy, boys," William sang out. "Plenty o' time! No racing!" The men laughed between gasps.

"*Comédie*," Charbonneau muttered, watching them go. "Always the beeg jokings." He was full of bitterness. His squaw, under his questioning, had told him how the Red Hair Chief had examined her in that part. He had nearly burst with jealous rage. And when he had demanded to take Sacajawea back to the Mandans, he had been tongue-lashed! Charbonneau in that moment had come within an inch of sticking his knife in the red-haired *capitaine*. He turned and looked at his squaw. She was standing there laughing and smiling and waving at them and the men all were laughing at the words of the *capitaine*. "*Tu*," he muttered. "You ought to died."

The novelty of being human mules was soon gone, and the laughter was replaced by groans, the rasp and gasp of desperate breathing, by quick curses and long, involuntary moans. Under the best of circumstances it had been impossible for a walking man to avoid all the prickly pears; now, confined in their traces, they could hardly sidestep any. Even the rawhide outersoles of their moccasins could not deflect all the spines, and soon every man's feet were viciously sore in a dozen places. Every puncture was magnified by the pressure of the pulling. William knew what the weight was doing to their feet; the weight of his pack seemed to drive every spine an inch deeper into the flesh of his feet, and twist his ankles that much more sharply whenever he stepped into the cement-hard track of a buffalo's hoof. The carbuncle on his ankle burned and throbbed steadily, as if a brand were being held on it.

From the moment the sun came over the mountains, it had been scorching, and at once all were pouring sweat and wishing they were back in that cold river from which they had just escaped so gratefully.

At midmorning they came to the first hill. They started up. It was one of those long, long prairie inclines that look minor because of the surrounding vastness, but come to seem endless as their horizons keep receding. On this slope the weight of the canoe-wagons seemed to triple. The men soon were straining so far forward in their harnesses they appeared to be crawling. William looked back once and saw them coming along this way, literally on all fours now, clutching at knobs and stones and tufts of grass for one more ounce of pulling power. They really did look like beasts of burden now, four-limbed little creatures struggling across an enormous, shimmering, yellow-brown desertscape, billows of white dust drifting off their little wheel tracks, the blue mountains looking on indifferently from three sides, while a now-forgotten river thundered down giant stairsteps in its sheer-walled canyon two miles to their right.

THEY HAD COVERED EIGHT MILES BY NOON, AND IT HAD begun to seem that they might reach the upper end of the portage by nightfall. But now the awful roughness of the ground had started taking its toll on the rickety wagons. Coming down into a shallow ditch that formed the head of a deep ravine, the first wagon lurched into a depression with a crunching jolt that snapped its front axletree. While the men assigned as wagonwrights knelt in the suffocating ditch to attach a new one, the others shrugged out of their harnesses, gulped water from a keg, then slumped down on the bare ground in the blazing sunlight

729

and gasped themselves to sleep. When the wagon was fixed they got up, into harness, and pulled.

WILLIAM WENT ON AHEAD. FOR A WHILE HE COULD HEAR them behind him, their voices coming faintly across the treeless space, now and then a laugh—for, amazingly, some of them were still merry—and sometimes that low, wooden trundling of the wagons. He limped on under the heavy pack, sweat gushing from every pore. The sky was hot, naked pearl, and the sun burned straight down on the top of his head. When he thought his brain was going to broil, he remembered the tomahawk umbrella and raised it. He stood in its shade a moment, resting, looking back, and saw the wagons, mere specks now, move down a gentle slope and disappear behind the shoulder of a rise. He turned and limped on, heading toward the next route stake. He kept looking for places where he might restake the route to shorten it. He had had to put in a few zigzags to keep it on level ground around hills and gullies, and there might be places where it could be improved. Any mile I can save them they'll bless me for, he thought. Damnation, but they've got to be the best men ever walked, he thought. They're like those people George had going to Vincennes. He remembered how George's eyes would always fill up when he talked of the Illinois Regiment, and now he understood.

William was going on ahead because he wanted to improve the trail if possible and also because he wanted to deposit this meat at the upriver campsite and then come back and be of a little more help with the wagons. Now that noon had come and gone and the earth was baking in the afternoon sun, the plain had become like an anvil, the sun like a hammer. After that first long hill, some of the men had fainted, and he knew that more would be fainting all afternoon. I might do the same right now if I didn't have this bumbershoot over me, he thought. Wish there was some way to keep a canopy over the men who's pullin'.

But how could that be done? he thought.

It couldn't, he answered himself. They'll just have to bear it.

He slogged on, his tortured feet sending up sparks of pain with each step, his sweat-sodden elkskins rubbing him raw between the thighs, his neck and shoulders burning with the load of the pack. The plain crept under his feet; the far hills shimmered; the faraway Rockies trembled white with their snowcaps.

How can there be snow in this hell of a world, he wondered. Ouch. God, I don't know if I can take another step.

But then he remembered what George had told him once

about pain. You know what you can do, even if your body says quit. It's only pain.

It's only pain, he thought, hearing George's voice and seeing his eagle-face. If anyone would know, George would, he thought.

And truly, he thought, it's the most useful one thing a body can know.

HE LEFT THE PACK OF MEAT AT A CAMPSITE HE HAD SE-lected near the head of the Falls. There were no trees to hang it in, so he piled rocks around it. Nothing should be able to get in there before we come back, he thought. He pulled off his moc-casins and removed the spines from his feet. They were hard to see because of the sweat that ran stinging into his eyes and the gnats and flies that swarmed around his face, but soon he had extracted all he could find. The carbuncle on his ankle was the size and color of a half-ripe plum now. He got up, wincing, and went down the bank for a drink of cold water. He held it in his mouth to warm it so its coldness would not cramp his stomach in the overheated state he was in. Then he started back. Despite the pains in his feet, he felt as light as a gazelle now for a while, without the weight of the pack. He could have run.

Here at the upper falls, the river was nearly on a level with the plain, and in places off to his left he could see the surface of the river, blue under reflected sky, white where rapids ran. A distance to the north and northeast of him, though the river descended out of sight into its deepening canyon, he could see plumes of mist marking two of the cascades, and he could hear the deep, steady thunder-roll of their fall. A shadow passed over the blazing yellow ground in front of him; he squinted up and saw an eagle coasting past the sun and down toward one of the columns of mist.

The one that lives by the Falls, he thought. They had seen her nest the other day, high in a cottonwood tree on a tiny island amid the churning froth below one of the high cascades, a soli-tary and spectacular homesite, completely protected from any kind of predator that walks, and usually overarched by a misty rainbow. Safe, surely, William thought, but imagine being born and growing up in such a thundering eyrie, those eaglets. Like growing up next to a battlefield it must be.

Maybe it's that, growin' up next door to space and tumult, he thought, that makes eagles what they be.

He stopped there and paused to think of that, as the eagle glided down into the mist, and it seemed to be something he and

George had talked about there on the porch of George's cabin—
nay, his eyrie—on Point of Rock above the Falls of the Ohio

And for a moment he was there again, his brother George
there beside him.

Then he shook his head and went on.

WHEN HE GOT BACK TO THE WAGONS, IT WAS LATE AFTER
noon. They were still several miles from the upper camp, and
were good and stalled by a broken tongue, which the carpenter
were trying to mend with a soft, brittle, crooked piece of cotton
wood—the only piece of lumber they still had. The men were in
pitiful condition, now scarcely able to hobble. "Lots of 'em been
a-faintin' on me," said Sergeant Pryor. "Thank God that sun'
goin' down!"

"All set t' go, sir," called Bratton.

And so they labored and strained and stumbled and rumbled
on for two more hours, the setting sun blazing straight into their
eyes until it dropped below the peaks of the great range. In the
twilight they heard the melodious trill of some sort of lark in the
grass near the trail, heartrendingly sweet. They went on through
the dusk, past great herds of buffalo, whose sentinel bulls trotted
out toward the wagons, closer and closer until their caution over-
came their curiosity and they retreated.

When night fell the wagons were among the dry rills that ran
down into the second great ravine, and these were too tricky to
negotiate in darkness.

"Nothing for it then but t' leave 'em here till morning," William said. "We'll back-tote all th' precious goods we can carry
up, have a nice dinner and a deep sleep. Come morning we'l
haul up the rest o' the baggage and then trundle the empty wagons back to lower camp for another load, eh?"

The hike was agony. They could not see the prickly pears in
the dark.

They dragged themselves into the upper campsite before midnight. A scurrying and growling in the darkness warned William
that something was trying to get into the meat he had cached. It
did not sound like bears, but he cocked his rifle and yelled. Now
he could see them scrambling, some staying, some running, and
their low shapes under the starlight revealed them to be wolves.

He fired a shot into their midst, the powder flashing yellow-
orange; one yelped and they all fled.

"Sorry, boys, little fresh meat tonight," he said. The wolves
had managed to tear down the rocks and had shredded the pack
and eaten most of the meat.

He wrote briefly in his journal that night, hardly able to keep his eyes open. Never had he hurt so badly as he did now everywhere below his knees. Most of the men were already deep in slumber. The pages swam in the firelight as he wrote.

> . . . *the men has to haul with all their strength wate & art maney limping from the soreness of their feet   some become faint for a fiew moments, but no man complains all go chearfully on. to state the fatigues of this party would take up more of the journal than other notes which I find scarcely time to set down.*

"Now, Cap'n, sir." It was Sergeant Pryor's voice coming in through the red blaze of pain. "They's no reason for you to cripple yourself permanent, is there?"

William turned, gasping, and looked at him. Pryor had come forward from the wagons. "Y've walked five times what we've done," Pryor went on. "Nobody'd take it ill if you was to go back to camp and doctor them trail-beaters o' your'n. Fact, it's makin' us all hurt to see you a-hobblin' so. With respect, sir, if you fall down, my boys got enough to carry without you added on the load."

"I'll grant y' that," William said. "All right, Sergeant. I think I will go back." It was true. He had traversed this portage route at least a dozen times in the last six days. By replacing stakes he had managed to shorten the road nearly a mile for the wagon-haulers, but he had limped countless miles over prickly pears and jagged hard ground to do it, and he knew his feet were nearly ruined. He stood with his pack on his back and watched the wagons creep along. He waited for them to go out of sight because he didn't want them to see him turning back, even though they knew he was. He leaned on his gun, and nodded and waved at them as they went on. A strong breeze was rising out of the southeast, and it cooled his face.

It was four miles back to the lower camp. *I can make that, I reckon,* he thought. *Don't know as I could've made it fourteen miles to the upper camp, though.*

Up to a point it had been as George had said—only pain. But it was beyond that now. From here on he would be damaging himself. *And that,* he thought, *is a fool's business.*

But even knowing that, it was almost as hard to turn back as to go on. And he couldn't bear to have them see him do it. So he

733

stood and watched and waited. The wagons grew smaller and smaller. At last he turned and started back, the breeze in his face, limping and stumbling. Soon he turned for a last look after the distant vehicles.

They were stopped. Something had stopped them there on the level ground. The men were moving around them, doing something. William turned to follow them and see what was the matter.

He saw something white on one of the canoes, then on the other. What the devil? he thought.

And then he understood; he saw what they had done: Someone had thought to raise the sails on the canoes. The white rectangles filled; the men in harness pulled; the canoe-wagons were now moving at a brisker pace.

"Well, I'll be damned!" he exclaimed. "Sailboats on dry land, as I live and breathe!" For a long time he watched them creep away over the prairie, then turned and went happily limping toward the lower camp. During his walk back he stopped to make some corrections on his sketch-maps of the river. The same wind that had propelled the sailing wagons whipped several of the sketches out over the prairie. Damn, he thought. Have to do those over another trip. He was too lame to chase them across the prairie.

SERGEANT PRYOR WAS BEAMING WHEN THE MEN CAME trundling the empty wagons into the lower camp.

"Pretty smart, those sails," William said. William had been sick all day, his bowels loose, and had pampered himself by drinking some of their precious coffee, the first he had had since winter.

"My own idea," Pryor said. "Gave us as much go as four more men in harness, those sails did."

"Might be you do better without a captain along."

"Wal, I wouldn't say that, sir," Pryor replied. "Seein' as how we'd be a-goin' up the wrong river!"

THERE WAS STILL A LITTLE DAYLIGHT, AND PRYOR'S MEN used it to carry two more canoes up the bluff from the lower camp to the prairie above, so they would be ready for an early departure next morning. While they did this, William wrote in his journal, looking up now and then in admiration at the men toiling up the steep path with the canoes. York was helping them now, and this was much to their advantage. Sacajawea sat bare-chested, nursing Pompey near the fire, busy as usual sorting and packing what York called her "mouse foods"—the various roots and bulbs and seeds she was always gathering—and now and then looking across the flames at William's face, looking at him with such open warmth and affection in her eyes that it made him squirm sometimes. It was disturbing to be in such fond, wordless communication with a young woman who was by any standard desirable and was growing even more so in this woman-less place.

"Janey, I will write that you are all well now. Is it true?"

"Yes. Have not hurt in any part now, thank you so."

He remembered how she had looked only two weeks ago, how near death she had been.

"Your good health makes me happy," he said. The sentiment in the words made his voice thick and tremulous, and she heard the tone; he could see in her eyes that she heard it, and for a moment then there glowed in her face such naked, unguarded adoration that he wanted to step around the campfire and kneel by her and put his head against her bosom. He wanted to hear her heartbeat now; he could feel his own and he wanted to hear that hers was racing too.

They sat like this for an indeterminate time, their eyes on each other's mouths and eyes, until gradually the sounds of the camp came back into William's consciousness and he glanced about to see if anybody was watching. Cruzatte arrived just then, asking what should go in the new cache he had been assigned to build here, and the strange enchantment of the moment was broken. William was both annoyed and relieved.

A moment later he felt something give way in the dense pain under the hot poultice on his ankle, and when he lifted away the steaming linen he saw that at last the accursed carbuncle had headed up and opened, and the pus was welling out, thick and yellow and blood-streaked; it looked as if a cupful were discharging from the center, while the swollen red flesh around it itched and tingled and softened. He watched it with grim fascination as it seeped into the linen.

There, he thought, there's that bedamned thorn! "Janey," he said, "fetch me that rag from the kettle, and wring this'n out, if ye please."

She did, and then watched as he blotted more and more of the corruption out with the steaming compress. "You be well also," she said, putting a brown hand on his blond-haired wrist and smiling at him, her face but a few inches from his. He could smell the clean musk of her breath, the milk at the baby's mouth.

735

"Aye! I'll be a-walkin' again t'morrow, I will!"

"Good," she murmured. "Good. I am joy." And she stroked the hair on the back of his hand.

"Might be we'll walk together up on the prairie one day soon, eh?" he said. "And see all the fallin' water? And the eagle in the treetop?" It would be a chance to redraw the map sketches that had blown away. Then he added quickly: "And old Charbonneau, too. I bet he's tired o' bein' camp cook all day long." I'm glad she has a husband, he thought. It was a strange thought, and he did not want to examine it.

"York too!" she cried. She was suddenly almost as if dancing, even while kneeling still before him. "York come with!" She was like Judy Hancock, getting all wound up with enthusiasm for an outing, her eagerness just like a white girl's.

William laughed. "Say, we'll have a proper picnic, like!" And then he had to explain to her what a picnic was, and as he talked about it—about packing a lunch and eating it out of doors, close to nature—the puzzlement on her face stopped him, and he laughed and said: "Lordy, by this definition, every meal we've eaten in five months been a picnic!"

IT WAS DARK WHEN THE CANOE CARRIERS CAME BACK DOWN. Sergeant Pryor led them back into camp and then collapsed by William's campfire as they went for the fragrant meal Charbonneau had cooked. His face was gray. "Feared I've took sick, Cap'n. Sorry." William dispensed some salts for him and then kept him long enough to get the news from the upper camp. Shields had Captain Lewis's iron boat frame assembled, and the hunters were out getting more elk hides to cover it. Young George Shannon had got lost again, but had turned up after being gone two days.

William shook his head. "One of these days," he said, "that boy's going to get lost for good. Let's hope it isn't till we get back to St. Louis."

"St. Louis!" exclaimed Pryor. "Lord-a-God, I'd almost forgot there be such a place!"

A little later, the sounds of Cruzatte's fiddle started up, and dancers cavorted in silhouette against the big bonfire. York came to the table, chuckling and wagging his head. "Them white boys, Mast' Billy! They haul wagons thutty-five mile all day, 'n 'en carry canoes up to th' prairie. 'N 'en a fiddle play, an' they all git up an' shake a leg!" He kept wagging his head. "Just don't know when to lay down an' die!"

But ten minutes later York himself was in their midst, dancing with the energy of several demons.

         *   *   *

WILLIAM STOOD WITH CRUZATTE BY THE CACHE NEXT
morning and made notes on its exact location.

Cruzatte closed the cache, and William watched as he erased
all traces of it from the ground. In it were some of Lewis's books,
more of his plant specimens collected since Fort Mandan, some
of the men's personal articles they had finally tired of carrying
upstream, two blunderbusses, and a few kegs containing extra
food and ammunition for the return trip.

Well, he thought. There's the stuff would have gone back to
civilization this fall, could we have spared the men. There's the
stuff would have told our families and government that we're still
alive so far. When that doesn't show up as promised, they're
going to think us dead, sure.

NOW THEY HAD CARRIED THE LAST CANOE AND THE REST OF
the baggage up to the prairie, and were rolling the wagons along, in
high spirits because this would be the last of these torturous trips
around the Great Falls. At the upper camp, they knew, was an
enormous supply of good meat that Captain Lewis's hunters had
been killing and putting by for days. Soon they would be back in the
Missouri, headed those last few miles into the great mountains that
had been looming on their horizon for a month. The miseries of
traveling the riverbed had not been forgotten, but they seemed
minor in comparison with the agonies of this overland toil. And it
would be light going, too, they reckoned, because that accursed big
white pirogue, which in their memories weighed heavy as lead,
would have been replaced by Captain Lewis's collapsible boat—a
mere ninety pounds of iron covered by a passel of elk hides. In their
imaginations it floated light as cattail fluff.

WILLIAM'S ANKLE WAS STILL SORE WITH A SHARP, WET,
stinging pain, but having drained that carbuncle at last, with its
huge throbbing pain, he hardly minded it. The sting of it almost
felt good because it said the thing was healing.

He felt a rising of wind, but it came out of the southwest and
would not work for using the canoe's sail. The wind had a rain-
smell to it, and a chilly edge, and it came from a mountain of
dense purple-black clouds mounting on the western horizon,
flickering with lightning and grumbling with thunder. It was astonishing to see how rapidly it grew. God, I hope this one by-
passes us, William thought. It's going to be a hard blow, up here
with no shelter.

There was a chance that it might go by. Out here on the high prairies, William had noticed often, the sky was so immense that a storm might be filling a quadrant of it with thunder and violence while in another a serene sunset was on display.

Another blast of icy wind now rocked the canoe on its truck hats went flying, and whirlwinds of dust and sand, debris and prickly pear blossoms spun through the air. William ducked his head and squinted as driven particles began stinging his face like bee stings. He had to brace himself, leaning into the wind, to keep from being blown over backward. A blaze of lightning blanked out all shadows; a crack of thunder nearly deafened him, then the wind rose in a catamount's wail.

"GET LOOSE OF THE WAGONS!" he yelled. The wind whipped his words away unheard, but the men were already shrugging out of their harnesses, crouching to keep their footing in the windblast. If the wind sent the wagons tumbling, he thought, they would drag these boys to death.

Suddenly something struck William's thighs and shoulder with bullet force, and he was knocked to his knees. With an incredible rattling, hissing din, egg-size hailstones were pelting the hard ground, hitting it at a shallow angle, some bursting to bits, most rebounding ten feet high before rolling to a halt thirty feet farther on. They struck with bruising force, and there was no place to hide from them. William staggered toward the wagons, feeling like some poor biblical sinner being stoned to death. Through the gray slanting veil of hailstones and, now, ice-cold rain, he could see the dark shapes of the wagons, the men crouching and stumbling, their arms crossed over their heads, some down, some getting up and being struck down again. He heard howls amid the drumming and rattling of the ice, whether the men's voices or the gale he could not tell. Now the ground was white with ice and ricocheting hailstones, sometimes glaring blindingly in lightning flashes. A blow on the top of his hat staggered William as he struggled toward the wagons, and he knew that if he had been bareheaded it might have fractured his skull.

Now most of the men were huddled under the lee side of the canoe, and William got in among them. Collins grimaced and yelled something, but his voice was inaudible under the wooden drumming and crashing of ice against the boat hull.

When everyone was at least partially sheltered, they settled to wait out the bombardment. Lightning bolts like great dazzling spider-legs stalked across the prairie, shaking the ground sometimes within thirty yards of the huddling men. William waited fatalistically, his heart in his mouth, for a bolt to strike the wagons and kill everybody. Some of the men were moving their mouths, evidently praying.

Another barrage of huge hailstones thundered on the wagon. William was soaking wet now, and the wind was like a knife of ice. His teeth chattered.

He started praying, but it was an angry prayer. *God*, he prayed, *All I know is You won't find better people than these even in your churches and your monasteries. So don't hurt them!*

After twenty minutes the storm passed and the hot sun blazed down. The ice, two inches thick all over the prairie, quickly melted and turned the ground into a glue of mud. William examined the men, most of whom were severely bruised, but found no fractures or concussions.

They stood in a line, up to their ankles in the clinging mud, as the storm thumped away eastward and a meadowlark sang and they jabbered in relief, while William doled out whiskey to chase away their aches and chills.

"Thank the Lord," said Private Tom P. Howard, one of the Corps' most dedicated whiskey-drinkers, draining the cup.

"Thank him hearty," William said. "We're nigh out o' this stuff, I'm afraid. You're soon going to have to learn to drink water."

"Water?" Howard said, handing back the empty cup. "Y' mean that terrible stuff that flows in th' Missouri?"

THEY HAD CONSUMED ALL THE WATER FROM THEIR CANteens during the ovenlike morning, before the hailstorm, and so lay down and drank eagerly from puddles to chase their whiskey. They refilled their canteens and got back into harness. But they had not gone fifty feet before the wagon wheels were so clogged with mud, and mired to the axles in it, that William told them to stop the vehicles and make a few hours of leisure until the ground could harden.

"As for me," he said, "this gives me a chance to take the river way, and remake those sketches the wind blew away. Mr. Charbonneau, you bring Janey and Little Pomp, and we'll have us that picnic I been promisin'. York, what sayee pack us a lunch, and come along?"

York was delighted. He had been too long confined below the cliffs in the lower camp. He capered around Sacajawea laughing, his feet sucking in the mud, and she laughed with equal exuberance and tried to dance with him, flashing her white smile, pirouetting in the ooze, the baby in its carriage-board on her back cooing happily. Charbonneau looked sullen, disapproving, until William gave him a friendly punch on the shoulder, smiled disarmingly at him and exclaimed, "Eh, Big Tess? For once, ye won't have to cook!" A big, yellow-tusked smile finally spread reluctantly through the Frenchman's matted whiskers. You're not such a bad sort as y' seem, William thought expansively. I reckon I could make a real friend of you if I had twenty-four hours a day to work on it.

And so they had come along this spectacular high stone bluff, stopping at every bend to look down into the thundering, seething river two hundred feet below them, while William sat down now and then to sketch and take readings on the large compass. They were a carefree and colorful and curious crew now, William with his tomahawk-umbrella over his head, Charbonneau stripped to the waist, the soiled scarlet sash around his waist matching the scarlet wool stocking-cap, whose tasseled crown hung jauntily over his left ear, his girl-squaw in her quill-decorated tunic walking along, pigeon-toed, singing, the papoose on her back, while York fairly strutted along in the rear with his rifle in the crook of his arm and his gold earring glinting in the sun. They stopped to examine formations of eroding lavender-pink shale, which could be pried apart into flakes almost as thin as paper. They saw huge rocks, square as quarry blocks and big as houses, that had fallen into the river below. They saw perpendicular cliffs on the opposite side, honeycombed with round holes and subtly colored by orange, bluish-green, white, and yellow lichens. They watched the spare, yellow-green grass wave in the wind, the shrubbery shudder, the prickly pear mask its treachery in delicate blossoms. They looked down at the green, lush little islands and bottomlands that lay in the river far below, seeing on some of them the remains of old Indian lodges. Sacajawea studied those old sites, raising her fingers toward her mouth, growing tense and vibrant like a pointing dog. "My people those," she said softly. "Ai, Shoshoni." William looked at her profile, at the straight, grease-shining black hair pulled into bound braids, at the round, brown face of the raven-haired baby on her back, then down at the river in the abyss far below, and he felt space and time without measure; he sensed her instincts, her yearnings, her yearning love for those wild nomadic people of hers. Savages or no, he thought, family's family.

"The eagle goes home," Charbonneau said nearby, pointing to the west, and they watched the great lonely bird circle down into the chasm by the hissing, rumbling waterfall and alight on its nest in the cottonwood on the island, where it raised and lowered its wings and settled itself. Sacajawea watched it with particular fascination, perhaps herself thinking about returning home, and she turned to look at William with a glow of pure joy in her face.

York came running up now, full of excitement about something, pointing to a dark mass on a grassy knoll a mile from the river. "I surely would like to slay us a buff'lo calf to cook for our picnic, Mast' Billy, with you p'mission. Look." There were some calves in the edge of the little herd.

"Aye," William said, "veal would be a nice change. Now mind, though, York, keep us in view. And if ye see any bear sign, don't get bold. Keep your gun loaded."

"Heyo, Big Tess," York cried, "come 'long with me, we get us some veal!"

But Charbonneau was not disposed to leave his squaw and baby alone with the Red Hair Capitaine.

"*Non*," he said. "I stay."

York shrugged and took off at a lope toward the herd. "Don't stray too far," William called after him. "Y've got our brandy!" York waved his hand in acknowledgment without looking back.

For an hour then William and Charbonneau and the squaw moved up the south bank of the bluff, almost breathless from the view of the mighty river and the stupendous skyscape above. They were about a quarter of a mile above the great cascade when another towering, silver-edged black cloud cast its shadow over them and hit them with a blast of cold wind that had that same feel and smell to it as the recent hailstorm. William was instantly alarmed. He glanced at the Indian girl and saw the keen edge of fright in her face, too; she had taken the papoose's carrying-board off her back and was carrying it in her arms and she was sniffing and watching the lowering sky. The wind suddenly came whipping across the plain toward them, flattening the brush and grass as if it were a giant invisible hand passing over it, and when it hit them, it nearly knocked them down. Yellow tumbleweeds came bounding across the plain, scarcely touching the ground, and sailed down into the wide canyon.

We've got to find shelter, he thought, or we'll be blowed right off this cliff. Or beaten to death with hail. "Come on," he yelled over the whistle of the rising wind. "The ravine!" God, but it comes up so quick, he thought. They leaned into the wind and tried to run for the ravine that lay across their path a few hundred yards ahead. He remembered that there were shelving rocks in that ravine under which they could hide from hail. It was simply the only place within miles that could shelter them.

They struggled onward into the cold, howling gale, squinting against the wind-driven debris—grasses, seed pods, flower petals, uprooted scrub and prickly pear, sand, and buffalo chips—that stung and beat their faces.

The first icy drops of rain were pelting them when they reached the lip of the ravine and scrambled down a steep defile between the rock-shelves. The floor of the ravine was full of boulders and rock detritus and animal bones and dead scrub. "There!" William pointed toward a ledge made by strata of flinty rock, and they ducked under the ledge. They pressed themselves under the stone, against the dirt, panting, and watched the rain darken the earth all around them. Everything was in motion now, dirt swirling, rain steaming, sticks and particles streaking across the sky above the ravine; the wind was screeching and whistling now like a hurricane. It was the strongest wind William had ever seen, and he knew that if they had stayed up on the prairie they surely would have been blown off into the chasm by now. He and Charbonneau leaned their guns against the rocks, and William set the compass down in a niche where its glass would be protected from harm. He lay his shot pouch and powder horn and the tomahawk-umbrella next to it and tried to arrange himself a little in front of Sacajawea and the baby, to shield them against flying debris. He hoped York had found something to get under. If he had killed a calf by now, he could have crawled under it. The men on the portage trail of course had learned by now to get under the wagons, so he was not so worried about them.

Everything was a strange dull blue now and smelled of wet earth, and William could hear water rushing. A hundred yards down, the ravine opened into the canyon, and he could see a few feet of fast river, and beyond it the far side of the canyon, a somber brown beyond a swirling veil of rain. Sacajawea had taken her baby out of the cradleboard, preparing to put him inside the blanket with her where he would be warmer; she had lain the baby on the ground for a moment. He was naked, kicking and crying, his little high voice audible for just a moment before everything blazed white with lightning and the skies opened up again with a crash. William saw Charbonneau squinting up, mouthing what probably were Hail Marys, and now the rain came in such a deluge that it was like being under the Great Falls themselves. William had never seen so much water come down at once, and it was mixed with hailstones the size of cannonballs. Thank God we're out o' that, he thought. But then he felt a frantic clawing at his sleeve. Charbonneau was wild-eyed, gesturing up the ravine, and when William looked, what he saw made his heart seize up.

A flash flood of brown water was coming down the bed of the gully, tearing everything before it, boiling with rocks and mud and tumbling boulders. Mud was dribbling down off the shelf above them. It would be only instants before the gully they were in would be a torrent of muddy water. They were in danger of being washed down the ravine into the deep canyon and over the great waterfalls below.

"OUT! OUT!" William bellowed into the din of the storm. He grabbed Charbonneau's arm and gestured violently up the slope. The Frenchman came to life, ducked out from under the ledge and clawed his way up the muddy side of the gully toward the plain above. "Janey!" William roared. He grabbed the baby from the ground, and with his free hand gripped Sacajawea's arm and shoved her out after her husband. William turned then to snatch up his rifle and shot pouch. To his horror he saw that the roaring brown water had risen to his knees, and already it was pulling him, as if to carry him and the infant down into the river. He lunged with all his strength and got out from under the ledge and onto the slope, which now was slimy mud. The water in the ravine was rising so fast now that it was climbing faster than he climbed. With each step he took upward the brown torrent rose a yard. Sacajawea had stopped right in front of him, unable to gain a purchase on the muddy slope; he put a shoulder under her rump and shoved upward, yelling:

"Tess! Tess, damn ye! Give your woman a hand!" Charbonneau might have heard, but he was too intent on getting to high ground to turn and reach down for her.

She began singing, in a keening, mournful voice; it was her death song. We're like to die here, William thought, it's true.

But he did not have a death song. All he could do was keep pushing as long as he could move a muscle.

At last she found a handhold, and moved up a few inches. When William looked up he was hit square on the forehead by a hailstone that made a yellow flash behind his eyes. The water was to his waist now, gurgling, gulping, pulling at him. There was a handhold of firm rock within reach; if he let loose of the baby he might reach it and at least save himself. Instead, he dropped his rifle to free his left hand, and grabbed the rock.

He hung now by his left hand on the slippery rock of the ledge, the baby in his right arm. The water had reached his ribs by now and its force lifted his feet off the ground and turned him so that he was facing down the torrent, his wrist twisting and fingers slipping. It looked as if this would be the end of it.

Sacajawea's death song had stopped. William craned his head backward for a last look at her. Hope surged in him. She was reaching down for her baby with her right hand; Charbonneau, lying flat on the ledge above, at last had got the courage or sense to reach down for her and grab her left hand.

She got the baby by its tiny wrist and lifted it. Now William had both hands free, and he hauled himself out of the tugging water. The squaw and her baby now were disappearing above the ledge and his way was clear. He sank his finger-ends into the steep wall of dissolving mud and with a final surge of energy managed to swarm up onto the high ground.

Now the three huddled on the open plain, kneeling inward over the baby, and for a few more minutes they were pounded by hailstones, drenched, shivering, cold, while the wind tore at them. The ravine was full to its brim now, twenty feet of roaring muddy water where, five minutes earlier, it had been a dry gully.

As quickly as it had come, then, the storm left, thundering and hissing away eastward. But the baby was naked and slick with icy mud, its blanket lost down the flood, and Sacajawea, just recovered from a mortal illness, was soaked through. Sure she'll have a relapse, William thought, 'less we get dry clothes.

"Up and run," he cried, hauling them to their feet and grabbing up the baby. They started at a trot over the muddy plain, splashing through puddles, heading for the wagons, desperately trying to keep warm with running. They heard a deep-voiced shout. York was galloping toward them, mud-smeared up to his neck, his face a grimace.

"Thank the good Lord!" he panted. "I thought y'all be dead sure!"

William gripped his shoulder with desperate affection.

"You're a sight to see! Quick, man, give me that canteen so I can get some brandy in these people. D'ye get pounded much by the hail?"

"'Bout a hundred," York replied, "but I wa'n't hurt, for they all hit me on my head."

They all took brandy, which rekindled their inner fires, and then trotted on through the sucking mud toward the wagons, William carrying the baby inside his shirt next to his skin for warmth. The baby's cries of terror and upset had settled to a long, ceaseless whining. Sacajawea trotted along beside William, staying close to her infant, often staggering.

They were shocked by the bloody, battered condition of the soldiers. Caught in the open some distance from their mired wagons, most of them hatless and clad only in breechclouts, they

ad been severely bruised and cut by the hailstones. Dried blood
tained their heads and faces. One man had been knocked un-
onscious three times. Most were limping and chilled to the
one. William rationed out another grog made from the nearly
pent liquor supply.

It had been a costly adventure. William had lost a fine gun,
mmunition pouches, moccasins, the Corps' only large com-
ass, and that precious tomahawk-umbrella George had given
im. Sacajawea had lost the baby's cradleboard and all his
lothes and bedding. Still, there was much cause for gratitude.
No one had been killed. And when the ravine dried out, they
ound the compass in the mud.

When they limped into the upper camp, they learned that
Captain Lewis and his party had been protected from the hail-
torm by the willow trees, and to celebrate their deliverance from
hat bombardment, Lewis had mixed them a large kettle of grog.

And to make it more refreshing, he had iced it with hail-
tones.

MOST OF THE NEWS IN THE UPPER CAMP WAS ABOUT
rizzly bears, with which that area was infested. Joseph Fields
ad survived his second grizzly attack—three bears at once—but
ad escaped with only a cut hand and knee by dropping over a
liff and hiding on a ledge. Drouillard had been chased a hun-
lred yards by a bear he had already shot through the heart.
icannon had been awake almost all night every night barking at
ears. Because they so dominated the place, the upper camp had
een named White Bear Island.

Here, in the shade of the willows, the two captains touched
he rims of their glasses and drank to Independence Day. Nearby
tood the provisions and equipment, under tied-down hides, and
he canoes' sails had been stretched between willows to make
wnings for the camp.

"Two years ago this day," Lewis said, "Mister Jefferson and I
ouched glasses like this to celebrate the purchase of the Loui-
iana Territory. It's hard to believe that was but two years ago,
ecause I'll swear it seems like I've been in this same bedamned
Louisiana Territory since I was born."

"Likewise," said William with a wink. "And, say, wouldn't it
e a fine joke on us if he'd got tired of it and sold it back to 'em
vhile we been out here?"

Lewis threw his head back and laughed. He was in an un-
isually good state of mind. His iron boat—which the men had
lubbed *Experiment*—finally had been sheathed with shaved elk

skins and singed buffalo hides, submerged in the river and the
placed on racks over smouldering fires to shrink the skins tigh
and he was immensely pleased with the look of her. Eight me
could carry her easily despite her length, and she would accom
modate, he estimated, five to eight tons. He still had not devise
a satisfactory way to seal the seams, but was sure that ingenui
would arrive with something. He had scoured the valley for pi
driftwood, which had been put in a homemade kiln to cook o
pitch, but that thus far had been in vain; it had yielded non
"Never mind that," he said. "Bees wax, buffalo tallow, and cha
coal will make 'er tight enough to float till we get up in th
mountains, and there we'll find pine gum enough to cork
navy. But I'm very anxious to go. The season's wasting."

"Aye. Three months since we left Fort Mandan, and we'
still not into the mountains. We've had two Independence Da
on this river, and I hope to have my next in Kentucky."

Lewis looked at him for a long time. "Well," he said, "dor
bank on it."

Up on the plains they could hear the mating bellows of bu
buffalo; it sounded like hundreds of them were roaring at onc
Lewis slapped himself on both sides of the neck, killing sever
mosquitoes that were feasting on him there. "As for now," h
said, "let's us go make our speeches to the men, and then have
the feast." He sniffed the air. The aromas of bacon, bean
dumplings, and buffalo tongue came from the camp.

Several of the men pretended to weep—or perhaps real
did—as the last ounce of the Corps' whiskey was poured th
evening after the feast. But they got suitably merry on it, an
danced to Cruzatte's fiddle until a rainshower at nine o'cloc
drove them in under the sail awnings, and there they sat an
sang and told jokes and tall tales until the middle of the nigh

"Oh, God, Cap'n," Sergeant Ordway asked William in a lugu
brious tone, "why did you gentlemen only bring enough arde
sperrits for two years?" Everyone in the shelter nodded.

William put a hand on Ordway's shoulder and replied with
wistful smile, "Reckon we just didn't know you fellers we
enough. We thought we'd brought enough for *five* years."

LEWIS COULD NOT EVEN WAIT TO GET DRESSED THE NEX
morning. He clambered out of his bedding and darted down
the *Experiment* in only his breeches. William saw him run dow
the shore to the place where the vessel lay bottom up on its rac
over the coals, silhouetted against the glittering morning-lit rive
Then he saw him running his fingers over the hull. Then he sa

746

aim turn and swing his fist downward as if flinging an imaginary hat to the ground.

"Oh, oh," William murmured, and he got out of his blanket and, barefooted on the cold, dewy ground, went down.

Lewis was scowling; his eyes were puffy from sleep but watering with tears of frustration. "Look. Damn it. God damn this place!" The suit of skins had dried snug on the boat frame, as they should have, but the stitch holes gaped; through virtually every one, a speck of light could be seen. "Damnation, what a corking job that's goin' to be, and not a drop o' pitch to be had. Well. Well somehow, we'll make do."

William said nothing. But when the hunters went out for meat, he quietly told them to keep a lookout for trees big enough to make a few more dugout canoes—just in case the *Experiment* might prove a failure altogether.

IT DID.

By July 9, Lewis had covered the entire hull with the bees wax compound, so that it looked not like a skin boat but a smooth black hull molded all in a piece, and for a few hours of that day he had the joy of seeing the long vessel floating like a duck. Then a sudden windstorm swamped the *Experiment* and all the canoes, wetting most of the provisions, and when the storm had subsided, most of the composition had peeled off the skins, and the vessel was as seaworthy as a sieve.

Lewis stood in the river, water to his knees, hands on hips, and stared down at the sunken boat, nibbling his lips, while everyone stood away, afraid to say anything.

"Lookee there," he said. "The stuff stayed on the buffalo hides, 'cause we left hair on 'em. If we hadn't shaved the elkskins, she'd likely be afloat yet. Well. Live and learn. No time to start over. We've got to move on. Sergeant Gass, knock 'er down and fold 'er up and bury 'er. Save the hides for our tailors."

And he said not another word about his beloved invention.

William's party of boat-hewers labored for four days in a mosquito-infested cottonwood grove up the river where they had found two large but windshaken trees. Much of the time was spent in replacing tool handles, fourteen of which broke the first day. "God," Shields groaned once. "What I wouldn't give for a nice piece of ash."

By carving to clear the cracks and twists of the cottonwood, the woodsmen finally completed two deformed but serviceable dugouts to carry most of what would have been borne in the

Experiment. The main party, meanwhile, had buried the boa
frame, some more baggage, William's map of the Great Falls
and the wagon wheels that had carried all this freight around th
falls.

It was July 15. The portage around that great obstacle ha
required almost a whole month. The little dugouts were s
loaded with meat, grease, baggage, and Indian trade goods tha
everyone but the oarsmen would have to walk. Some twent
miles ahead stood the snow-topped first range of the great Rock
Mountains. Somewhere about two hundred miles up within th
maze of mountains they expected to find the next landmark th
Indians at Fort Mandan had told them about: the high, wide
fertile valley where three mountain rivers flowed together t
make the headwaters of the Missouri. By their reckonings, the
had labored twenty-three hundred miles up this mighty and trou
blesome river; the Missouri had come to be their very lives.

They rowed the canoes up the river now, a river one hundre
yards wide and flanked with sand banks, through a land ablaze
with blossoms: prickly pear, great, nodding yellow sunflowers
narrowdock, salmonberry, and lambsquarters. On the plain
above them the bull buffaloes roared and mated; behind them
the thunder of waterfalls, which had been in their ears for a
month, began to fade.

Just ahead lay the Rocky Mountains, gigantic, unknown, ye
to be crossed, and they were running out of summertime. To
morrow was a great question mark.

42

FALLS OF THE OHIO

July, 1805

"GENERAL CLARK, SIR!"

George heard the voice above the rush and trickle of the
water, and looked up from the work of his fossil-diggers to see
Freeman the mill-hand riding toward him across the shallows of
the Ohio. George squinted against the blazing white stone and

bright yellow mud of the fossil bed exposed by the low stage of the river.

George waved, signaling the man to come on, then turned back to his helpers. *Tick, tick, tick, tick,* went their picks and hammers, and their shovels grated as they scraped away marl fragments and mud. Here on this flat, the muck of the riverbed dried into dizzying patterns of rectangular cracks, and it was across this that the messenger was now riding. George brushed flies away from his face. The sun burned through the linen shirt on his shoulders and broiled the bald part of his scalp. "Finesse, now, Hez," he warned. "That's the biggest and best cockleshell ever, and I don't want it broke."

"Here's another one o' them putrified buffalo pats, Gen'l," said one of the shovelers, prying up the edge of a turban-shaped rock with the end of his shovel.

"'Petrified' is the word, Jack. Put it over yonder with those." Now the rider was close, and George turned to greet him. He hoped it would not be a real interruption. The river seldom got low enough to uncover this shelf, and whenever it did, he spent most of his daylight hours here. He had found many fine specimens here, from mammoth bones to coral and many-legged seabottom creatures perfectly imprinted chalk-gray on the surface of darker stones. When he worked here his mind was submerged in the slow coagulation of eons, and the problems and disappointments of the present seemed to matter not at all.

"Sir," Freeman said, "they say it's the Vice President come to see you, sir!"

"Eh? Aaron Burr is here?"

"They say that, Gen'l." The messenger's eyes were alive with curiosity.

George instructed the diggers to bring up on mules the specimens they were working on, and reluctantly mounted his horse.

"Is this Mister Burr really the same what kilt Alexander Hamilton?" Freeman asked as they splashed across the shallows. The items of Eastern news were read from newspapers by those who could read, and then circulated by word of mouth among those who couldn't, so the people in Kentucky, like this fellow, knew the news, but vaguely.

"Aye, it is," George replied, now urging his mount up through a leaf-strewn gully out of the riverbank, "shot him in a duel, they say. I gather he's a ruined man back east, on account o' that."

George had been annoyed at this intrusion. But now the many intriguing things he had read and heard about Burr came crawling into his mind, and his curiosity began to wax. It was not unusual for fugitives from failure and scandal back east to drift westward through these parts, often on new schemes. And as George had learned through his encounters with James Wilkinson, it was good for a guardian of the back country to know as much as he could about the intentions of any heroes or scoundrels who came through.

Wilkinson, he thought now, riding up through the baked-earth streets of Clarksville. I wonder does this visit have anything to do with Wilkinson. Wilkinson had got himself appointed governor of the new Louisiana Territory, with his capital at St. Louis.

If Mr. Burr tells me he's on his way to St. Louis, George thought, I'll wager it's him and Wilkinson up to something.

IT WAS A GOOD VISIT FROM THE START. BURR WAS CHEERFUL and charming; he seemed not in the least bitter or dispirited about his fall from grace. He brought more news, and insights into the events of the news, than a dozen newspapers. But he was a voracious listener and a probing inquirer as well, and seemed to have a hundred questions about the West. He was a dandy on the surface, as graceful as a dancing-master, hair silky-black and curly above a high, pale promontory of a forehead, brown eyes alert and quick under satanic eyebrows, a handsome, sensuous, sometimes mocking mouth set in a strong but fine-boned face. He was three years younger than George but looked twenty years younger. George noticed that he only *seemed* to be drinking, as if to guard his words. It was this that first caused George to feel that Burr was up to something covert; his demeanor was so reminiscent of Wilkinson's.

They talked for a long time about the French Revolution, about Napoleon, about the Louisiana Purchase, about the Voyage of Discovery, about Meriwether Lewis.

They went down off the porch once to examine some of the fossils and great bones. Burr sat on the huge bone George sometimes used as a bench and touched it with his hand. "I shouldn't want to have lived when this did," he said. "A fellow of my stature would make hardly a bite for it. Ha, ha! Now, you, General, would make two bites."

"Likely it would never have eat either of us," George said, "'less we'd happened to be up in a tree it was dining on at the time. My opinion is, the beast was arborivorous, notwithstanding what inferences they've made at the academies. Come look at this tooth on the porch and I'll show you what I mean." George showed him that a tooth of the great beast was not the tooth of a meat-eater.

"I'd no idea you were a naturalist," said Burr. "One hears back east only of your generalship, your accomplishments in the Revolution."

"My thirst," George growled. Then he wished he had not said that. Even to a trusted man, it was not good to reveal one's bitterness. But the liquor had made him a little hot-brained. "Anyway, if they remember that service at any time, they forget it when it's time to vote me any relief."

"I know of your disaffection with the government," Burr said now, as if he had been waiting for some cue to bring forth a particular subject. "I was most interested, sir, in your part in the Genet matter. I should have given my whole approval to those moves, had I been in a position to have done. Ahm . . ." He paused here, and George made a business of pouring liquor so as not to seem too intently curious about where Burr was going to go with this line of discussion. "I think Washington was too indulgent to the arrogant Spaniards."

"Eh. Well. That's past. Just another of those things, as my Ma would use to say, that turn out one way rather than the other. And p'r'aps better this way, as Louisiana's ours now and no blood shed for it either. That makes it better, to my mind."

"An unusual sentiment from a celebrated warrior, if I may say it, sir."

"My kind of war, Mister President, was to gain as much as possible with as little blood wasted as possible. I lost not a man in my Illinois campaign."

Burr sat with a forefinger laid in the hollow of his cheek and studied George, and looked as if he were pondering whether to say something. At last he ventured: "You are, I gather, still disaffected with your country."

"With my country's *government*," George corrected him.

"Your government, then. Would you now, ten years later, still be of a spirit to do such a thing?"

"That's an odd sort of question, sir. I should have to have a grievance against someone besides my own government in order to go against that someone. And Louisiana is ours now; there is no Spanish block anymore, so I am indifferent to Spain, if that 'someone' you're alluding to is Spain. I am, in fact, indifferent to the whole business of government squabbling. Still interested as a student of war and power, of course, but indifferent. Another way of saying it, sir, is that I have since the activities of Citizen Genet considered myself retired from the public life, and right glad of it too."

"A naturalist." Burr seemed deflated, disappointed. George said:

"Aye, sir. I am hard to provoke anymore. Maybe I'm a fossil, like those." He smiled, with just a shade of wistfulness, and inclined his head toward his boneyard. Then he said: "If I may inquire, to what do we owe the honor of having you tour among us?"

"Oh, ahm." Burr straightened suddenly in his chair and brought his hand down from his cheek. "I am most interested in the West, General. But I know as little about it as you know much. Since the affair at Weehawken—Secretary Hamilton, I mean, rest his soul—I've felt a need for open space. The West." He gazed out over Kentucky.

"The West is out there, now," George said, pointing down the Ohio toward the setting sun. "This isn't the West anymore."

"I'm on my way to St. Louis," Burr said.

So, George thought, Wilkinson *is* in this, whatever it is. I wouldn't go near it. But what are they up to, I'd like to know. "Allow me to tell you a story," George said. "This is one I've hardly even told my family, as it doesn't much illuminate the better side o' man . . ." He leaned forward. Sometimes if one gave a confidence, he would get one in return, and this was an old harmless one, not much to give out. Burr leaned forward eagerly to hear it. "As you may remember," George said, "I once was in opposition to a man named Hamilton, too. Governor *Henry* Hamilton."

"Ah, indeed!"

"Well, in my case, the vanquished fared better than the victor. He was freed in an exchange o' prisoners, and went back to Canada to govern again. Then to Bermuda. Anyways, when he returned to resume his mischief in Canada, he sent me a secret emissary here. 'Twas near the end of the war. He offered me great wealth and position if I'd switch sides."

He stopped there, sat back, sipped. After a pause, Burr half-smiled, and said: "Invitation is the sincerest flattery!" Then he chuckled at his own wit.

"I dispatched him without much ceremony," George concluded. "But I will say, encounters o' that sort do make a body wonder where the honor is that gentlemen profess."

For a while then the talk circled around and about the word honor, and then Burr asked: "Have, ahm, have you ever stood on the field of honor, sir?"

George's eyes bored into Burr's, and it was a while before he said: "If you mean the dueling ground, no. For some reason, nobody's ever flung a glove in my face. Rather, they turn knives in my back."

THE VICE PRESIDENT STOOD LATER ON THE FERRY LANDING at Louisville and gazed back across the river toward Point o' Rock. He was very disappointed that General Clark was no longer interested in adventures of conquest against the Spaniards. He had been led by some back East to believe the old conqueror might be available.

Still, it had been a most pleasant day, and that evening in his guest lodgings in Louisville, Burr wrote:

I never met a man of greater intelligence and natural capacity than Gen'l Clark.

On the other side of the river, George sat gazing over a solitary dinner grown cold on the plate, the corners of his mouth downturned, unconsciously rubbing his thumb back and forth along his index finger. The Vice President's mysterious visit had been a delight, but now it left George with a vaguely unsavory aftertaste. Burr had revealed nothing, really, of what he and Wilkinson were up to, but George had a feeling that President Jefferson should be keeping an eye on them. And George was glad he had made it clear he was not going to get embroiled in it. Even if there might have been a fortune in it. With those two involved, it surely was no *little* scheme.

If I were to guess what they're aiming at, I'd guess they mean to overset the Spaniards in the Southwest somehow, and make themselves emperors or something. They've both got that air about them of would-be emperors, he thought.

They still come to me, he thought. They still come looking for someone to lead a Western army.

But now they're looking for one they think might betray his country one little way or another.

I'd rather they'd just forget me altogether.

Anyways, it's Billy carries the point for this family nowadays.

753

43

NOW DOWN IN THEIR SOULS THERE WAS AN UNRELENTING
sense of urgency. They awoke in the darkness to the sounds of
Scannon barking at bears, of coyote-howls, of mountain lion
coughing and yowling, of the gurgling, murmuring Missouri
they awoke with mosquitoes at their ears or rain-damp on the
cheeks, and lay thinking about time and distance and chance
and they would be unable to go back to sleep for thinking about
it: that they were racing against time but had no way to go faster.

It was late summer now, and they were in the canyons among
the Rocky Mountains, and still they had not seen one Shoshoni
Indian. They had found old Shoshoni lodges; they had found
little sun-screening booths made of willow bushes; they had
found Indian roads; they had found horse tracks four or five days
old; they had not seen, however, one Indian. They had come
through gloomy, rugged canyons with steep crags of purplish
brown volcanic stone; they had found, too late now, forests of
pine that would have provided pitch for the iron boat. They had
poled the boats between perpendicular cliffs of flint and solid
rock sixteen hundred feet straight up, so sheer and forbidding
that they had named them the Gates of the Rocky Mountains.
The captains had taken turns leading advance parties to search
for the Shoshonis, pushing ahead through the towering landscapes until they could scarcely walk from fatigue and tortured
feet, leaving pieces of paper, ribbon, and linen on bushes along
the trail as signs that they were coming as friends; still they had
not seen an Indian.

This search for a sight of the elusive Shoshoni would have
been frustrating enough if there simply were no Shoshonis
around. But there were. The captains were certain they had
been seen by Shoshonis, or at least that their hunters' guns had
been heard. On July 20, upriver from the Gates of the Mountains, they had seen clouds of smoke in the sky to the southwest,
as if the whole countryside had been set afire. That was the sign
among tribes that an enemy was approaching. "Hard fortune for
us," William had groaned. "Now we'll have to try to find 'em

754

where they hide. And even if we do that, we'll have to convince 'em we're friendly." Sacajawea had gazed at the yellow-white smoke with her forefinger on her lips and a speechless appeal in her eyes. It was as if she were trying to send her thoughts ahead to her people, to make them wait, to make them stay and see that these were not enemies.

THIS FEAR, THAT THE SHOSHONIS WITH THEIR WONDERFUL horses would fade further and further into the mountains, drove William like an obsession. Leaving Lewis to bring the main party and the canoes along, he took Private Frazier, the Fields brothers, and Charbonneau, and they set off ahead, carrying in their knapsacks a few light gifts for Indians.

They went twenty-five miles over an Indian road through the mountains the first day. The prickly pear was worse than ever, as if making the men pay in blood for the beauty of its blossoms. By nightfall William's feet were blistering and lacerated and swollen, and the old carbuncle on his ankle was swollen again.

They covered a like distance on the second day, all limping now. The country was opening out now, onto a wide and fertile plain. William drew Frazier up beside him on a rise, and pointed. "There," he said, "mark my word, will be the three forks."

Frazier stood, panting, pinched sweat out of his eyes and said, "The end o' the Missouri, Cap'n? Truly?"

William nodded. "There's God knows how many miles of river above it, but no name for it. Aye, Frazier. Th' end of the Missouri."

"Praise the Lord!"

AND IT WAS. THEY FOLLOWED THE FAST, DEEP, CLEAN MIS-souri between steep, crumbling gray bluffs about three hundred feet high, bluffs layered with well-defined strata of uptilting stone, topped with juniper and pine; they crashed through cottonwood and willow thickets, refreshing themselves with gooseberries and serviceberries and currants, and watched the valley spread out before them as they plodded toward the southwestern end of the canyon.

"Lookee there. She forks once." William pointed. Just beyond the funnel made by the canyon, a small river led in from the opposite shore. The party stayed on the right bank of the larger stream, going ahead in the stifling heat, tormented by flies and mosquitoes. That was just *two* forks, William thought. Lord help us if we've got bad facts from the Minnetarees. "Wait here." He

went to the bluff, hobbling through rock debris at its base, an
began climbing.

Chchchhhhrrr!

He jerked his hand back and waited for the rattlesnake to un
coil and slither away, then pulled himself up farther, until h
was above the tops of the thickets. He pressed himself against th
rock and looked down the valley, and the sight he saw made
smile spread on his face.

There, a mile or so ahead, through a maze of islands an
meanderings, came another river, pouring in from the right
Beyond it the valley lay shimmering in the sun, fresh green, fu
of grasslands and marshes, cattails and willows. Geese and duck
and smaller birds by the hundreds rose and settled and wheele
everywhere. On every side of the valley stood distant dark blu
mountains, their angular peaks and long saddles gleaming wit
snow.

That river on the right, he thought. That one's our way, I'
wager on it. It came curving into the valley from the southwest
apparently from somewhere in the gigantic mountain range tha
lay to the west of the forks. The middle stream came fron
straight south; the left branch had come from almost due east
Aye, he thought, remembering all that the Minnetarees had tol
him. It'll take some checking out, but I'll wager that's our way t
the Divide, that on the right.

He fairly bounded down the cliff to the river. "Hey, boys! Th
end o' the Missouri! We've done it!" They started to their feet
cheering. Of course they knew there would be many more mile
of smaller, swifter tributaries to ascend, and the way, if change
at all, was going to be even harder. But they had come tw
thousand five hundred miles up that cruel and tricky Missour
for sixteen months they had lived and struggled in it and on i
and along it, and now, even if it was only a term of language t
call this the end of it, they were overjoyed to be able to call i
that.

WILLIAM LEFT A NOTE ON A BRANCH, TELLING LEWIS THA
he was going on up the right fork toward the mountains, and le
the men off again.

This stream was full of beaver and otter. It was shallow an
swift and cold, its course confused by islands. William led th
limping party on for another thirty-five miles. Charbonneau'
ankles were collapsing, and Joseph Fields's feet were so swolle
he groaned aloud at every step.

They came to a cliff and were forced to cross the river, wadin

756

hest-deep in the fast current. Halfway across, a rock turned under Charbonneau's failing ankles, and the pain made him yelp and he fell sideways into the current. Not being a swimmer, he panicked when the water closed over his head. He was close behind William when it happened, and the other men were far behind, yelling. William turned and saw Charbonneau's arm grasp upward, then his open-mouthed face emerge and go under again, and saw that the Frenchman was unable to get on his feet and was being borne downstream into deeper water. There was nothing to do but go into the deep water after him, and so William flung his rifle onto the riverbank and went. He could barely swim himself with his knapsack and shooting-gear on. He went stroking down toward the last place he had seen Charbonneau, and when he got there, there was no sight of him. He tried to stand up, but there was no bottom to be felt. He dog-paddled a moment, drifting, turning, and trying to see; and then there was a swirl on the water fifteen feet downstream, a glimpse of a wet sleeve, and he stroked with all his might toward it. His hand hit something in the cold water, something soft, and he grabbed it and pulled upward, and Charbonneau's wide-eyed face and gasping mouth broke the surface. When he saw William he grabbed him and they both went under, William struggling in the cold current to get out of Charbonneau's arms.

He broke the surface behind Charbonneau, gulped air, and grabbed the long hair at the back of his head, and lifted him; then, holding him thrashing at arm's length, stroked with one arm and his last strength toward the nearest shore. He was lucky now; his feet found gravel just at the moment when he thought he could not manage another stroke. Charbonneau was as inert now and as heavy as a waterlogged flour keg. William had to wait for Reuben Fields to come down the bank and wade in to help carry him ashore.

But he was alive. They squeezed the water out of him. He coughed for a long time and then started praying. While the sun warmed their sodden elkhide clothes, William checked his rifle and found it muddy but undamaged. Reuben Fields was stalking around with his lips bitten white. Once he stopped over Charbonneau and spat at his feet. William took him aside. "What is it, Reuben?"

Fields hissed: "Listen to that reeky poltroon of a Frenchman, prayin' to the virgin Mother o' Jesus who woulda been no virgin five minutes if he'd 'a' been there!"

"Never mind," William said, putting a hand on Fields's shoulder.

"If you'd drownded y'self over that wuthless polecat, Cap'n, I'd 'a' wrang 'is neck till he was dead ten times!" It sounded like a scolding.

William understood the sentiments Fields was expressing so violently, and he blinked and swallowed. "Listen," he said. "Whatever a man's soul is worth, if he's a member o' this Corps, we do what we can for 'im. Y'know that. And by Heaven, Reuben, you're guilty o' the same sin I am; *you* saved him from a grizzly once, remember?"

TWENTY-FIVE MILES UP THIS FORK, JOSEPH FIELDS'S FEET and Charbonneau's ankles gave out, and William left them on the stream bank to make a camp and doctor themselves. "Careful Big Tess don't try to bugger you," Reuben warned his brother with a mean leer.

On the western side of the wide valley was a small mountain, and the fork seemed to bear to the right around it. William pointed to a ridge that ran out from its south end. "From up yonder, I don't doubt we can see to our satisfaction where this stream comes from. And maybe find some spoor o' the Shoshonis, too. Feel fit for a climb, boys?" Rube Fields and Bob Frazier looked at each other, then at William's feet. His moccasins were bloodsoaked and there was a yellow stain of pus from his suppurating ankle.

"Do you, Cap'n?"

"What I feel most like," he said, "is lying down in the shade and drinking one bucket o' whiskey while I soaked my feet in another bucket. But since we don't have any whiskey, and since we need to raise us some Indians, why, let's climb."

They started up. The mountain was stark, jagged rock, hot as an oven, its fissures choked with thornbrush and scraggly juniper and prickly pear. William felt weak and feverish. He had felt somehow broken inside since his rescue of Charbonneau in the river. But he could still go. He had to find the Shoshonis. This was their hunting ground, where Sacajawea had been kidnaped and her people massacred. This was the place, here at the three forks, where the Shoshonis summered, and he knew they were near, and there was precious little time left to find them.

The hour of climbing was lost in a feverish blur, now marked by the scampering of a jackrabbit, now by the chilling chatter of a snake's rattle, now by a swoop of faintness. But it proved worth the effort. From the top of the ridge he could see how the stream curved on up into the great blue western mountains, just as the Minnetarees had said it would. And to the south he could see

758

the middle fork winding its way through the lush plain, full of beaver dams.

"Look at that place!" he breathed to Frazier, pointing with a pencil. He was trying to make a sketch in his notebook. "Can't ye just picture a good, solid log trading post right there where the rivers meet? Here, give me a sheet from your notebook. Mine's soaked and won't take a pencil."

He sketched and made compass readings and notes on elevations, terrain, and vegetation for as far up the stream as he could see, but the page swam before his eyes and the sun seemed to scorch his scalp. He would break out in a sweat, then shudder with chills. His lower bowel felt as distended as one of Charbonneau's buffalo-gut sausages.

They were parched coming back down the mountain, and drank heartily at an ice-cold mountain stream. Within ten minutes William was almost doubled over with stomach cramps; he had drunk the cold water too fast. That evening he was too sick to eat the fresh fish Joe had caught and Charbonneau had cooked. He sat sweating with a fever in the cool evening air and pulled thorns out of his feet. Lately they had come into still another species of foot-destroyer, this one a kind of needle-grass much like a bearded porcupine quill, which went through moccasins and leggings and stuck in flesh like a barb.

The Fields brothers both came to him, and told him they hoped he would lie here and wait for Captain Lewis and the main party.

"You two been talking to each other," he said. "No, boys. It'll be two or three days 'fore the boats catch up with us. We'll use that time to go a ways up the middle fork. Maybe somewhere up it we'll find Shoshonis. We'll move out early and get some headway 'fore the sun gets too hot." They shook their heads and frowned. But they knew better than to question his judgment.

Frazier played a jew's harp. And for a while as the night turned cool and stars shone diamond-blue above the fire, they sang a ditty they had composed for the occasion:

> Yankee Doodle lookin' hard
> To find him a Shoshoni.
> Yankee Doodle's feet so tar'd,
> He needs to ride a pony!

He was awake much of the night with chills and throbbing feet and aching bones, but got the men up when the first stains of pale yellow were silhouetting the mountains on the east side of the valley. "How are ye this mornin', Cap'n?"

"Pretty bilious. But fit to travel, I think."

They limped and hobbled all day along the middle fork, a handsome, swift, clean little river, with enough beaver in every mile to make a man a fortune, but to their great disappointment saw no fresh Indian sign at all. They tied more colored rope and cloth on branches whenever they found Indian paths.

When they returned to the headwaters of the Missouri that evening, William knew he had overdone it. His fever was alarmingly high. He groped through his little medicine bag with shaky hands, hoping that the emetic pills, known as "Dr. Rush's Thunderbolts," had not been ruined by dampness. They were intact, and he took five of them, then lay down in his blanket to wait.

He dreamed that night of a great log fort surrounded by blue mountains. In the fort he and Brother Jonathan had a store, and the store was full of tomahawk-umbrellas. Thousands of Shoshoni Indians, an endless parade of them, all looking like Sacajawea, rode in from the mountains on magnificent mares and stallions, which they traded for umbrellas, and another endless file of Shoshonis walked back up into the mountains, each shaded by an umbrella. William woke himself laughing, and as soon as he was awake he had to get up in the dark, because Dr. Rush's Thunderbolts had lived up to their name.

From the Journal of Meriwether Lewis

Saturday July 27th 1805

We set out at an early hour and proceeded on but slowly the current still so rapid that the men are in a continual state of their utmost exertion to get on, and they begin to weaken fast. . . . at 9. A.M. at the junction of the S.E. fork of the Missouri and the country opens suddenly to extensive and beautiful plains and meadows which appear to be surrounded in every direction with distant and lofty mountains; supposing this to be the three forks of the Missouri I halted the party on the Lard. shore for breakfast. . . .

at the junction of the S.W. and middle forks I found a note which had been left by Capt. Clark informing me . . . he would rejoin me at this place provided he did not fall in with any fresh sighn of Indians, in which case he intended to pursue untill he overtook them. . . .

at 3 P.M. *Capt Clark arrived very sick with a high fever on him and much fatigued and exhausted.*

we begin to feel considerable anxiety with rispect to the Snake Indians if we do not find them or some other nation that have horses I fear the successfull issue of our voyage will be very doubtfull or at all events much more difficult in it's accomplishment, we are now several hundred miles within the bosom of this wild and mountanous country, where game may rationally be expected shortly to become scarce and subsistence precarious without any information with rispect to the country not knowing how far these mountains continue, or wher to direct our course to pass them to advantage or intersept a navigable branch of the Columbia, or even were we on such an one the probability is that we should not find any timber within these mountains large enough for canoes. . . .

however I still hope for the best and intend taking a tramp myself . . . to find these yellow gentlemen if possible

My two principal consolations are that from our present position it is impossible that the S.W. fork can head with the waters of any other river but the Columbia, and that if any Indians can subsist in the form of a nation in these mountains with the means they have of acquiring food we can also subsist.

A bower of bushes, like the Shoshoni sunscreens they had been finding, had been built for William to lie in while he recuperated. Here the captains brought their journals and maps up to date while William reclined with his feet in a kettle of heated water. They named the east fork the Gallatin, after the Secretary of the Treasury, the middle the Madison, after the Secretary of State, and the western stream, which they would be following in their search for the Continental Divide, the Jefferson. "In honor of that illustrious personage," said Lewis, raising an empty hand as if toasting with it, "who is the author of our enterprise."

"To him," William toasted grandly, hoisting his cup of emetic salts.

Sacajawea sat outside the bower, her tunic pulled down to her waist, the fat, dark-haired baby pulling at her nipple, and with the help of Charbonneau she told them the story of her capture here by the Minnetarees five years earlier. She pointed to the plain where her father the chief and his buffalo hunters, armed only with bows and arrows, had been shot at by the guns of the Minnetarees, and a shoaly place in the river where she had been crossing to make her escape when she was struck unconscious from behind and captured. She told it with scarcely a sign of emotion, which Lewis found eerie. A little later, while she was bent over Scannon, crooning to him and picking the needle-grass barbs out of his shiny black coat, Lewis said, "She's got no emotions. I swear, give her enough to eat, and a few trinkets to wear, and she'd be content anywhere."

William looked at her, at the greased, smooth black hair, the brown, slender back, the fine profile of a shaded face, the yellow-green grass blowing beyond her and the blue and white mountains ringing the distant horizons. She and Charbonneau were talking together in Minnetaree. She was in her homeland again, and it was true she seemed totally unaffected. "Still," William said, "we don't know what's in 'er heart just now."

"You, Husband," she was saying just then to Charbonneau. "The Red Hair Chief swam in danger to keep you alive. I ask, would a man do this if he wanted your squaw as you say he does?"

"Woman," he growled. "You know nothing of why men do what they do. Nor do you even know of women, that they are meant to be still and not cross the words of a man! When we find your people they will ask me, why do you not thrash this bird woman who chatters always at you?"

She bit her lips, stroked Scannon's broad, silky, sun-heated head, and gazed at the bower where the Red Hair Chief lay with his writing books, looking toward her with his sky eyes. She thought of him drowning, as he might well have done, and she thought what a sad thing it would have been if that worthy man had died to rescue this man of hers. At the thought of Red Hair in death, her heart squeezed with frightful sadness; then she gave thanks that he was alive, and such a thankfulness sang in her that it was like the voice of a meadowlark. And she thought about what must happen when they would find her people. She would be returned to The People. There might be some of her family still alive, or tribe members who might remember her, but perhaps they all had been killed by the Minnetarees. There was the one woman who had been captured with her, then had vanished one day. Had she died, or had she escaped and gone back to The People?

And if Sacajawea came back to The People, and if she interpreted the language for the white men and helped them buy horses, then what? Would they be done with her there? Would they leave her with The People? Or would Charbonneau take her back to the Mandans?

Whatever happened, she would surely have to say farewell to the Red Hair Chief and let him go on toward the setting sun, as he was bound to do, while she would have to go another way. This thought she could hardly bear. All she needed was to be near the Red Hair Chief, and she would be content anywhere.

She remembered the day when she had been at the opening of the cave of death and the Red Hair Chief had put his ear on her heart and then had made her want to live and she had lived.

She looked at Charbonneau, who was digging in his nostril with a stiff finger.

The Red Hair Chief had made her live. He had made her husband live. In the storm at the Falling Waters he had made her baby live. There were many of these funny and brave and gentle white men here who were alive because of the Red Hair Chief, *Clark*, his name was, and there were many Mandans and Minnetarees and Hidatsas back in the old place who were alive because of this *Clark* man with his sky eyes and his medicine and his steady strength, this man who made people live; and she wished she could go to him and put her ear on his heart and make him well.

What would happen? He would go on and she would stay or go another way and the most important person in her heart, ever, would be gone.

She thought all this as she had been thinking it for weeks, and the world hummed with rich sadness.

But on her Indian face nothing showed.

"To my friend Captain Clark on his thirty-fifth birth-day, and with gratitude for having lived to reach it," Lewis said on the morning of August 1, raising a cup of tea. And then he prepared to set out up the Jefferson River with Drouillard, Gass, and Shields, intending to scout ahead of the main party until he found Indians. William was reluctant to yield the forerunner role to him, but was still too weak from his illness to go on himself.

Sacajawea had counseled Captain Lewis with suggestions for winning the trust of her people should he find them. The Shoshoni lived hidden in the mountains, mostly on roots, berries, and fish, because they had no guns and were at the mercy of the Plains Indians—the Blackfeet and the Minnetarees—when they came down in the fall to hunt buffalo. Thus the Shoshonis distrusted all strangers, and would flee at the sight of anyone who came carrying "firesticks." Therefore, she said, one must show at once that he was a white man. Most of her people had never seen a white man, she said, and they might be fearful, but at least they would know a white man was not a Blackfoot. As you approach the Shoshoni, she advised, say, "Tab-ba-bone, tab-ba-bone," meaning, "I am a white man."

Other winning ways she suggested. Vermillion was a sign of peace and friendship to her people. And they were mad about blue beads. A sign of friendship was to wave a blanket by its corners and then spread it on the ground. And, she added, smoking was done barefooted, signifying that if one should go back on his declaration of peace, he should have to walk barefoot in this prickly and flinty land. Those were all the hints she could give from her memory of girlhood among The People.

Lewis set out with his three men. William, barely able to walk, began leading the main party up the river soon after. Setting poles and ropes were necessary to move the boats.

The river was twisting, narrow and fast, and in many places so shallow that the heavy dugouts had to be dragged over stretches of rock-bottom. The troops all felt like slaves. There never was a breeze, it seemed, in the rivercourse, and they felt themselves suffocating and broiling even while mountaintops clothed in snow and ice towered over them. The river had become a worse ordeal even than the portage around the Great Falls three weeks earlier. They struggled in swift water through a mountain canyon ten miles long between perpendicular cliffs of black granite. Daily now, canoes were swamped or turned over by the force of water over rocky shallows; men suffered severe sprains, dislocated joints, and strained backs; and bit by bit the cargoes—parched meal, gunpowder, medicine, Indian presents—were drenched and damaged by these dangerous and exasperating spills. At one point the party labored for some distance up a wrong branch of the Jefferson. Lewis had written a note directing them to take a channel that he had explored, and had hung the note on a green willow stick. But a beaver then had devoured the green stick and the directions were lost. The canoes then had had to be brought back down and turned up the correct branch. In the meantime, young George Shannon had gotten lost again. Another tumor had risen on the inner side of William's ankle and he could scarcely walk. Private Whitehouse had fallen in the way of an out-of-control canoe and his leg had been ground between the hull and a rock as the heavy vessel passed over him, leaving him bruised and scarcely able to move.

And as the battered, exhausted party stopped to spread articles onshore to dry, Lewis returned with the depressing news that he had still found no trace of the Shoshoni tribe.

There was not a smile to be seen anywhere.

"Even the Capitaine Clark has no jokes thees day," mused Charbonneau. And he realized that this frightened him.

"THIS TIME," WILLIAM SAID, "YE BETTER FIND INDIANS, OR else catch some grizzlies and train 'em to carry packs. We're about to run out of river, it looks like t' me."

Lewis chuckled at the thought. "Pack bears! There's an idea! Hear that, Drouillard?" He was trying to be cheerful.

The hunter swung his knapsack onto his back and his brown face split into a brilliant smile. "I will breeng you bears, *mon capitaine*. But *you* train them!"

Lewis laughed. He loaded a few small American flags and some awls, beads, looking-glasses, and vermillion paint in the top of his knapsack, swung the weight onto his shoulders, and took William's hand. "I won't come back without Indians this time." He looked down at William's ankle. A linen compress bound around it was yellow and red with pus and blood. "Take care o' that," he said, "lest it poison your blood." Then he fondled Scannon's silky black ears for a moment, told him "Stay," and, hitching his shoulders under the weight of his knapsack, said, "Come on as best ye can."

"Godspeed!"

They moved out then, Lewis, Drouillard, Shields, and Hugh McNeal, carrying a few days' rations of flour and meal and pork in case game should prove scarce. William stood with York and Sacajawea and Sergeant Ordway and watched them go out of sight over the brow of a low, treeless hill, their shoulders and heads outlined for a moment against the snowy crest of a mountain. The top of that range, William was certain, would be the Continental Divide. Sacajawea had recognized a hill shaped like a beaver's head and told them that up beyond it was the place where her people were accustomed to cross the mountains to their home of safety. "There you will find our road," she had said, pointing. "There you will find The People, unless they have seen us and gone to hide."

The captains had faith in her remarkable memory. They had learned that it was always at least as reliable as the directions the Minnetarees had given them. "Maybe if we'd send her out to hunt with Shannon," William joked, "he wouldn't be forever getting lost." He could make such a joke today because Shannon had showed up this morning at breakfast after three days' absence, sheepish but greatly relieved.

William looked back to the loaded canoes. There was one les now. So much cargo had been spoiled by water that they had decided to stash here one of the dugouts they had made with such labor back above the Great Falls less than a month ago

"All right, gents!" he called. "Let's see if it's possible to sai clear up to the rooftop of the continent!"

44

Near the
Continental Divide

August 9, 1805

Lewis and his scouts ascended sixteen miles along th river on their first day out. On the second day, they found freshly traveled Indian path and followed it westward to a plac where the river emerged from a line of hills. They passed unde a high rock wall whose base was alive with rattlesnakes. Fiv leagues farther along the trail they entered a pleasant level valle where the river divided into two small branches. Lewis examine both narrow rocky streams, then came back to where the me sat, and grimly tore a sheet of paper from a notebook. "No cano can go up either of 'em," he said to Shields. He wrote a note t William, telling him to halt the boats here and await his return that he was going up the left-hand fork and would return. H put the note on a willow branch—a dry one this time, one th beavers would not find so succulent. "This is the end of it for ou navy," he said to his scouts. "Now, gents, we must find us som cavalry."

But a mile and a half up this fork Lewis decided it was th wrong one; there was not a sign of Indian travel. So he returne wrote a second note to tell William he had changed his min and was going up the right-hand fork instead, and hung it wit the first note.

By the next morning they were far up this right-hand fork an had lost the Indian path. Lewis sent Drouillard out on his rig flank and Shields on his left to search for the path. If eith found it, he was to signal by raising his hat on the muzzle of his rifle.

Lewis was sweeping the valley with his pocket telescope when into its little circle of view moved an apparition that made him feel as if his hat would leap off his head.

There, coming directly toward him across the plain, was an Indian with a shield and bow, riding on as fine-looking a horse as Lewis had ever seen.

"McNeal! Look!" He handed the glass to the soldier, and almost trembling with joy, he began walking toward the Indian at a quick but easy pace, untying the thongs that bound his blanket roll as he went. The Indian kept coming. When the Indian was less than a mile from him, he reined in his horse and sat watching. Lewis stopped, shook out his blanket, raised it overhead by two corners, then made the motion of spreading it on the ground. He repeated this signal of friendship three times, hoping the Indian was seeing it. "Come, red brother," he wished out loud. "Come and join us."

The Indian did not come. He had caught sight of Drouillard and Shields, who were advancing as if to flank him, and he was watching them suspiciously.

"Damn you two, stop," Lewis pleaded in a low voice only McNeal could hear. "Stop, ere y' spook him away!" He would have yelled at them but they were too far away to hear. He would have fired his rifle to get their attention but was sure the Shoshoni fear of gun-carrying tribes would send him fleeing.

Drouillard and Shields kept advancing, and the Indian was alert, turning his horse this way and that. "God," Lewis hissed, "if they scare 'im off, I'll have their hides." Almost frantic, he shrugged off his knapsack and drew out a bundle of trinkets. He gave his gun to McNeal and began advancing toward the Indian. The brave remained where he was, and seemed to be willing to wait, but he kept turning and watching the two distant men advancing on the flanks of the valley with their firesticks across their arms. Lewis kept trying to signal them to stop, but they seemed intent on the Indian. Surely, Lewis thought, his heartbeat speeding up as he drew closer, surely those two have enough sense not to close on him when I'm trying to parley with him!

When he was within two hundred paces, the Indian turned his horse and slowly began to move off. Lewis's heart hammered. He cupped his hand beside his mouth and, remembering as best he could the words for "white man" that Sacajawea had taught him, he bellowed:

"Tab-ba-bone! TAB-BA-BONE!"

His voice rolled in the valley. Drouillard turned and looked, and Lewis made a hand signal. Drouillard saw it and stopped, and put his gun on the ground. But Shields was still moving forward.

The Indian stopped his horse and turned it sideways and again seemed to be waiting. Lewis, coming within one hundred fifty paces of him now, rolled his shirt sleeve up to show the whiteness of his forearm—his face was so sunbronzed he might have looked like an Indian—and again yelled, *"Ta-ba-bone! Ta-ba-bone!"* Then he held a handful of the trinkets overhead, shaking them to make them jingle and flash in the hazy sunlight.

Maybe he'll stay, Lewis thought. *Maybe he sees my white skin. Maybe . . .* He glanced to his left. *Damn you, Shields, stop! God, make that fool stand still.*

Lewis was now a mere hundred yards from the Indian, who watched with keen interest but was wary as a wolf.

"Tab-ba-bone! Tab—"

With a slash of the quirt, the Indian started his horse into flight, leaped the creek, and vanished like a jackrabbit into the willow brush. Lewis exploded then. He flung his trinkets on the ground and howled in a fury:

"Shields! Drouillard! Come here, you God-damn fools! COME HERE!"

And while he waited for them to lope down, he watched the distant willow brush move with the Indian's flight, and tears of mortification blurred his vision.

Shields tried to defend himself by insisting that he had not seen the captain's signals. But that was a feeble excuse, he realized; Lewis let him know, with a sarcasm as abrasive as prickly pear on bare skin, that anyone but the sorriest greenhorn should not even have needed a signal to know to stop. "By God, man, if we've lost this critical chance and can't recoup it, I'll have to hold you responsible for the failure of our whole venture!"

It was the most painful reprimand Shields had ever received in his life. He had always felt himself one of the most favored and amply rewarded members of the expedition because of all he had done at the anvil; now a whole year's praise was swept from him in a single sentence, and he could not look anyone in the eye for a while.

WILLIAM WAS GOING THROUGH SCRUB, IN A SUN-BAKING gulch, with his head down, following the fresh hoofprints of a small deer. He had come a long way following it, and had not caught a glimpse of it yet, but was determined to get it because the men had had no fresh meat for two days, other than a few trout and some beaver. They needed huge quantities of food because they were straining and exhausting themselves hour upon hour with the heavy dugouts in the fast, cold water, and in these days on pan bread and fish they had been weakening noticeably, and were covered with boils and hives.

Leaving the one canoe behind had freed several more men for hunting. But game was scarce in these bald and rocky hills. To find fresh deer tracks was cause for great and hopeful excitement. He who brought in meat these days for the famished and aching boat-pullers was the hero of the hour.

Chhhrrrr! William froze in midstep.

It was a large rattlesnake coiled directly in his path, tail vibrating, head tensing back to strike the oncoming foot.

With a grunt, William struck down with the end of his espontoon, mashing the snake's head against the hard ground. Its body flailed and flopped and lashed, and at that moment something large and tawny crashed and moved in the corner of William's eye. It was his deer, startled by the grunt and thud, and it sprang out of the scrub, twenty feet away, up the bare, eroding side of the gulch. William dropped the espontoon, jerked his rifle to his shoulder, the rattlesnake instantly forgotten; he cocked the flintlock as he made a hasty sighting far forward on the animal's shoulder, and even as he squeezed off what he knew was a desperate and nearly impossible shot he felt the thrashing snake hit his right legging a few inches above his infected ankle. For an instant as the gunshot echoed and smoke billowed in the gulch he had an awful sense of loss and confusion, a sense that he had surely both missed his deer and been bitten by the deadly rattler, a sense that he had somehow in that flurry mismanaged the whole thing.

But no! The deer was clambering ungracefully, slipping and stumbling up above; surely he had winged it, at least, after all. He looked down and saw the rattlesnake still writhing, and its head was mashed and torn. He grabbed up the espontoon and hacked the snake once more quickly and it lay almost still, merely rippling a bit along its length; then he examined the elkhide legging at the place where he had felt the blow. There was no mark there. Obviously the snake had merely hit him with its body in its death throes and had not got fangs into him. If that poor snake had bit *that* ankle, William thought, it would be *him* that died o' poisoning.

Now he stepped over the serpent and limped through the

scrub after the sound of the deer, which was out of sight now. Bloodspecks led up the draw. It was incredible but that wild shot had found a living mark. William ran, reaching for his powder horn to reload, following the red drops and hoof-scuffed earth around an outcropping of yellowish flintlike rock.

And there was his deer. It was a doe, and her hind legs were collapsed; likely his shot had hit her spine. She was making a desperate, wild attempt to run, scrabbling with her forelegs, her eyes terrorized, not understanding this hurt and this help-lessness. Now she was sliding sideways in the dust and rock-trash, her neck strained forward, her hind legs twitching, her mouth open and tongue protruding.

William had advised the hunters not to waste shots, both to conserve powder and to keep from alarming the Shoshonis un-duly. William did not like to see a deer in this awful twitching pathetic state, and he wanted to dispatch her with a shot through the head. But he remembered his own policy about shooting, so he just advanced on her, those last few intimate yards, his heart beating hard, until he stood directly beside her. Then, keeping his eye on the sharp hooves, he put his gun on the ground, moved in with the steel-tipped espontoon, and with a thrust powered by both arms he drove the weapon through her heaving ribs and into her heart. He stood back panting as blood poured out of her mouth and soaked into the parched ground, and she died, the wild terror fading from her brown eyes until they be-came dead and dull as bottleglass.

Well, there was more meat for the boys. But he hoped he would never have to kill a deer that way again, close enough to watch the life die in the eyes.

He had killed deer and elk and buffalo beyond count, but the only thing he was glad to kill was a rattlesnake.

LEWIS HAD PUT YESTERDAY'S DISAPPOINTMENT BEHIND HIM, and now he and Drouillard and Shields were moving forward in the same wide line as before, searching for fresh Indian tracks, looking for a well-traveled path, while McNeal followed with an American flag on a long willow pole which, it was hoped, would be interpreted as a sign of peace by any Indians who might be watching from the high meadows.

An hour ago they had found some of the sunshade bowers at a place where Indians had been digging for roots. The diggings were fresh, less than two days old. Now they were on a well-beaten Indian road that ran in and out of ravines, parallel to the streambed. Lewis's hopes were waxing again; he was sure that these traces would lead within a few more miles to some Shoshoni village. But he could only hope that the Indian who had fled on horseback yesterday had not alarmed them all to the point of flight.

And now the stream they had been following had dwindled to a mere brook. "Cap'n, sir!" McNeal called. Lewis turned around.

There stood the grinning young private with one foot on each side of the water, waving his flag, and yelling now.

"Praised be th' Lord, I've lived t' straddle this here thought t' be endless Missouri! Yeeeeeee HAAAAAA!"

Two more miles up the twisting valley they came to the base of a ridge that made a saddle between two mountains. From the base of the ridge issued a rivulet of ice cold water. Lewis waved Drouillard and Shields in and the four men sat to rest. Lewis seemed almost rapturous. He said:

"Gentlemen, this is a moment my mind's been fixed on for many a year. I'll have a drink now from the extremest fountainhead of the mighty Missouri. And you have spent so many toilsome days and restless nights with me to reach it, you'll drink with me!"

He lay down to drink first, his heart beating against the ground, and kissed the surface of the fresh, crystalline water, inhaling the scent of wet rock, and drew in a mouthful of water so cold it made his palate ache, and swallowed it, and a teardrop fell off the end of his nose into the water. Then the other men drank. "Now," he said, his eyes glittering, and pointed up to a saddle of land between two mountains straight ahead. "See where the trail goes over that pass? That I'll swear is the Great Divide! What'll y' wager before nightfall we'll be on th' yonder side tastin' a sip from a like fountainhead of the Columbia?" Now they all had teary eyes, and were impatient to get back on their feet.

The ascent was gentle, and they walked in a close group up that last half mile. "Bejeesus," Shields exclaimed as they slogged upward between two barren, windy peaks. "Y' mean it's all downhill from there on?"

They went on, each wondering in his own manner of thinking what the western side would look like. Perhaps a descending rank of foothills, hills maybe like the Alleghenies, dropping away and away, lower and lower, with the blue and peaceful ocean lying out there somewhere on the horizon? McNeal, who had seldom heard his captains talk about the geography, probably was envi-

771

sioning it that way. Drouillard and Shields had been around the captains more and probably had a less simple foreview of it, but in their souls they, too, were starting to think downhill, downstream, westerly. Captain Lewis himself knew there were probably more mountain ranges, but he knew that the waters leading down that western watershed would wind among them probably to the Columbia—or some other, as yet unknown—river, and that to the Pacific. He knew that in descending from this divide back down to the Gulf of Mexico, the easterly waters dropped gradually, some three thousand miles down the Jefferson and Missouri and another thousand down the Mississippi. He knew also from coordinates that the Pacific likely was no more than five hundred miles due west of this divide. Thus the westering rivers must make a comparatively short, steep rush down to sea level, or else twist and wind through an incredible maze of mountain ranges. All these long-held expectations were coloring his thoughts as he climbed the Indian trail to the top of the ridge. But still he was not prepared for what he saw.

Range after range of immense, purple-sided, snow-capped mountains stretched away to the west until they were lost in each other. Many of the peaks seemed to stand much higher even than this ridge upon which the four white men now stood. Over and through those incredible gleaming towers and dark valleys moved the shadows of clouds, and a silence so deep it seemed to make the ears ring from within.

It was a long time before anyone spoke, and it was Shields, who said:

"God have mercy on us! That sure don't look downhill t' me!"

THIS WESTERN SLOPE OF THE RIDGE WAS STEEPER. LEWIS tried to hearten the men as they made their way down the Indian trail. He reminded them that they enjoyed the honor of being the first Americans to cross the Divide, and assured them: "You have indeed passed over the rooftop of the land, doubt me not."

"I'm not a-doubtin' you 'bout that rooftop, sir," Shields ventured to joke, emboldened now by Lewis's apparent high spirits, "but them out there's surely the most turrible lot o' *gables* I ever seen!"

And then, three-fourths of a mile down the slope, the Indian path veered along the bank of a bold, leaping little creek of cold water. Here again Lewis stopped to lie down and drink. He stood up, grinning, bright-eyed. "Help yourselves, boys. By my soul, this is our first taste of the great Columbia, and I swear she's the best stuff I ever drank, except whiskey."

772

"Please don't say that word, sir," McNeal pleaded. "Ye'll make e cry."

THEY CAMPED THAT NIGHT AT A SPRING BESIDE THE INDIAN ad where there was willow-brush for a fire, and ate the last of eir pork. As they had done the night before, they hung awls d pewter looking-glasses on a pole near the campfire, but as far they knew, no one came to see them.

The next morning they were still following the Indian road d had come about ten miles, and were moving down a rolling ain within a valley when Drouillard whooped once and inted toward a rise about a mile ahead. Lewis looked up and s heart skipped.

On the brow of the height stood three Indians—a man and o women—and several dogs.

Lewis was elated. This time there would be no stupidity like at before. Shields and Drouillard would not risk that kind of ngue-lashing again. And this time the Indians were on foot, d thus less likely to flee so quickly. In fact, they seemed to ow no alarm at all yet, but were watching, immobile as states. The two women sat down as if to wait for their approach.

When Lewis was within a half mile of the group, he directed e men to stop. He put down his pack and rifle and took the g from McNeal, unfurled it, and began walking slowly up the pe toward them, one hand full of trinkets. *Stay*, he thought, if trying to project his thoughts across the distance to them.

But suddenly the two women rose and disappeared over the ll. The man still stood, watching. Lewis stripped up his sleeve d called, "Tab-ba-bone! *Tab-ba-bone!*" Two of the dogs began ging down the slope toward him, their wolfish faces alert and ary.

But the man at the top of the hill turned and vanished.

Damnation! Lewis ran toward the top of the hill, but when he rived where they had stood, there was not a sight of them. nly the dogs remained, circling him warily at a few yards dis-
nce, or sitting down to scratch at fleas with their hind legs. It as incredible how quickly and completely the savages had dis-
peared. Lewis waved back for the men to come on.

Then he had an idea. Perhaps if he could tie a few trinkets on dog's neck with a handkerchief, the animal would carry these kens of friendship to its masters. This would be a precedent in plomatic envoys, he thought, feeling a sense of the absurd. He elt and began snapping his fingers, whistling, and cajoling em with crooned entreaties. "Come! Come, fellow! Come on!

773

Good beastie!" A couple of them were cringing near. "Tab-ba
bone," he added, and made himself laugh. The laughter, or th
bared teeth of his smile, somehow struck the dogs wrong, an
they all moved several yards out of his reach, their hackles rising
"Come, now, good boys," he said sweetly, trying to keep th
desperation out of his voice. They looked at him with their yel
lowish, half-vulpine eyes, but would not come forward. "You'r
sure sorry-mannered beasts compared with my Scannon," he fe.
compelled to tell them, but he said it nicely.

Now the dogs' ears pricked up on the arrival of McNeal an
Drouillard, who were coming over the brow of the hill. The me
looked at each other in puzzlement at the sight of their captain'
posture. One dog wagged its tail. "Help me lure these mang
coyotes," he said. "Come, boy, come!" And soon Shields arrived
too, and for five more minutes the four explorers, the advanc
scouts of white civilization, were kneeling, whistling, cooing on
hilltop in a valley surrounded by gigantic mountains, trying t
entice a half-dozen scrawny brutes into their service. "Shame we e
our pork last night," Shields said. "Chunk o' that would fetch 'em.

But at length the pack apparently tired of this surfeit of atten
tion; two of them turned and trotted down the Indian trail, the
the rest lost interest in the white men and ran off after them
Lewis stood up with a morose sigh and put his fists on his hip
and watched them disappear.

"Eh, well. Let's get on, boys." He really looked gloomy now
"Chirk up, Cap'n," McNeal offered. "It can't be far to town.
"So. But I'm worried th' town'll be alarmed and gone. C
worse: up in arms. Set to attack us without asking any questions
We've got to look peaceable, lads, but be set for anything."

They were descending the trail into the narrowing valley, a
four close together now moving alongside the tortuous creek
scanning the terrain for signs of the elusive Shoshonis, whor
they were now beginning to imagine as wraiths, will-o'-the
wisps, forever vanishing, luring them deeper and deeper into
towering, mythical landscape.

And then there before them, so close Lewis almost fell back
ward, were three female figures, looking up with an astonish
ment as complete as his own: an old Indian woman, a youn
one, and a thin girl, who had been so engrossed in foraging tha
they had not heard the white men coming around the creek
bend. All were in ragged, undecorated, almost colorless elkhid
tunics, kneeling on fresh-dug earth, and before them was a wide
shallow woven-grass basket partially filled with serviceberries
chokeberries, and roots.

The young woman leaped to her feet quick as a deer and fled, flashing of bare brown legs, into a thicket down the stream, but the elderly woman, and the girl, who appeared to be ten or twelve years old, remained where they knelt, their faces transfixed in terror. When Lewis laid down his gun and advanced on them, they lowered their heads and shut their eyes as if ready to be struck dead.

Lewis walked up and stood over the old woman, who was so patiently awaiting her fate; her unbound hair was grizzled and hung down to hide her face entirely; he could see her bony shoulders move with her quick breathing. The girl sat likewise; she was trembling; there were rashes and scabs on her arms, as from scratching poison ivy.

Lewis reached down gently for the old woman's right hand, a gnarled bundle of frail bones in dry, brown, skin covered with dirt from the root-digging. He pried her fist open with his thumb and put into her palm a short string of blue beads. While she was looking at this, he took the right hand of the girl and put a small pewter looking-glass in it. Then he stood back. The men had come abreast of him now and were all standing close, watching the abjectly bent heads, the dirty brown hands examining the bright and unexpected gifts. Somewhere up the valley a crow was cawing.

The old woman's head began to rise, and her red-rimmed eyes in their baggy folds of skin traveled up Captain Lewis's dusty leggings, up to his hunting shirt, the pistol and tomahawk in his belt, then to his hard brown face, and the three-cornered hat on his head. Her age-puckered mouth was open and she had no teeth.

Remembering then, Lewis stripped up his shirt sleeve to point at his untanned forearm. "Tab-ba-bone," he said. "Drouillard, come here and try to hand-talk to 'em. See if you can make her call back that squaw, ere she goes and alarms her town."

The old woman and the child were so nearly overcome by everything—their delivery from death, the gifts, their first sight of white skin—that it seemed they would never respond to the Indian gestures Drouillard was making. Or maybe, Lewis thought, these signs don't mean a thing to these people anyway.

But at last the old woman seemed to come to her senses, and she got to her feet, smiling a rapturous, even beautiful, old smile, her face full of fine creases, tears glimmering in her eyes. She was dreadfully hunchbacked, yet so full of excitement that she shuffled in a feeble dance of joy. The girl jumped to her feet and stood there turning, looking at her eyes in the little mirror. It was, Lewis thought, probably the only time she had seen herself, except reflected in water; and he thought for a moment of all the young white women he had known in the East, and how essential their mirrors were to them, and this notion enhanced his sense of moment.

By now Drouillard had conveyed his message, and the old woman turned her face down the valley and screeched a syllable, then again. And in a minute the young woman came running back up the path, her breasts bobbling in her tunic. She came up panting, wild-eyed, still frightened until the other two showed her what they had received. Then she bounced up and down a couple of times on her heels, in a gesture poignantly reminiscent of feminine delight such as Lewis had seen a thousand times in his own race without really noticing it. He gave her a moccasin awl. Then he told McNeal to find the jar of vermillion in his knapsack and open it.

Now Lewis dipped his fingers in the yellow-red pigment and painted the women's russet cheeks with it, and everybody was smiling and laughing. The young woman went to McNeal and rubbed a dab of the color off her cheek and thumbed it onto his, and he laughed and smeared her own paint from her cheeks down to her chin, in the meantime getting as close to her as possible, rubbing her large breasts as if by chance, and she laughed and pressed against him. Shields watched this and grinned. "Been a long time, ain't it, Hugh?" he said. And McNeal answered:

"Oh has it ever! I'm a-gettin' me a cockstand already, old Johnny!"

"Well, save that," Lewis warned. "She might belong to somebody."

Soon Drouillard had expressed by hand signals that they wanted to be taken to the chiefs and warriors. The girl picked up the forage-basket and the two women cheerfully beckoned and started on down the trail.

They had gone about two miles this way, following the squaws, and had emerged into a narrow, treeless valley, the women ambling happily several yards ahead on the dusty, well-worn trail, when Drouillard raised his head and hissed, "Listen!"

Lewis heard it now: a thundering of hooves. And then immediately, over a sloping rise, riding straight at them at full gallop, came a horde of armed warriors mounted on excellent horses, raising a cloud of dust, shaking bows and spears above their heads. Lewis felt a thrill of fright, and in the corners of his eyes saw his men instinctively raise their rifles. There were sixty or seventy warriors in the band.

"No," Lewis snapped. "McNeal, give me the flag!"

The horsemen, at a shouted command, wheeled their mounts to a whinnying, dust-swirling halt a hundred yards away. At once three horsemen separated themselves from the band and came trotting their steeds forward to meet the three females. Good, Lewis thought, and he put down his gun and pack. "Stay here," he told the men, and began walking forward holding the flag at his shoulder. His heart was practically fluttering, but he was determined to show no fear.

The women and girl were now capering around the three advance horsemen, showing them their gifts and chattering like birds. Lewis advanced resolutely toward them. Now the three leading horsemen came riding slowly toward him through the grass, and he could feel the soft heavy tread of their horses' unshod hooves on the ground and hear their slobbery blowing, that beloved horse-sound he had not heard for so long, and he could hear the slight jingling whisper of ornamental quills and claw-necklaces and shells and horn. The men were agleam with oil and their faces were garish with paint. Feathers in their hair and in their horses' manes and on their bows and lances swiveled and bobbed. And now they were close enough for him to smell: horse-sweat, smoke, bear-oil, body-musk. The man in the center was gaunt, sunken-cheeked; every fiber of his long muscles, every vein in his arms stood in relief. He wore a bonnet made of a hawk's skin with feathers and head intact, and a necklace of claws. He was bare to the waist and carried a two-foot painted shield strapped on his upper left arm; in his right hand was a long, iron-tipped lance whose entire shank was decorated with a comb of eagle feathers. His dark, deep-set eyes were drilling into Lewis's face. Lewis met them with his own intense stare for a moment, then smiled and turned back his sleeve to show his white forearm.

Now the three riders had reined in their fine horses around Lewis. The chief's stallion was all white; an ochre handprint had been made on the side of its brawny neck. The other two men, apparently subchiefs, now sat on their horses flanking Lewis, and he noticed that each held a long war club covered with rawhide. He could hear them breathing, and he had a notion that it all might well end right here for him with his temple bashed in with a stone-headed club.

"*Ah-hi-ee,*" the chief said in a breathy voice.

"Ah-hi-ee. Ah-hi-ee," said the other two. And then all three moved suddenly and slipped off their horses, landing lightly on their feet around Lewis. The chief in the hawk-skin bonnet stood

so close Lewis could smell his breath. Then his teeth bare
white; he put his greasy left arm across Lewis's shoulders, grip
ping him in a sinewy hug, and rubbed his painted cheek o
Lewis's cheek. Then he released Lewis and let the other chief
hug and caress him. Everyone was smiling and exclaiming, "A*
hi-ee,*" which he knew was their exclamation of joy, and the firs
chief summoned the warriors forward, and Lewis called to Drou
illard and Shields and McNeal, and then for the next fifteen c
twenty minutes everyone hugged and patted everyone else unt
Lewis, even though almost overwhelmed by relief and gratitude
was altogether besmeared with paint and grease and heartily tire
of the national hug. All the Indians were scrawny as dogs; a
were armed only with clubs and bows and spears, except three h
noticed who held poorly made light muskets of the kind trade
by the North West Company. There was hardly a piece of meta
to be seen among all these warriors; even their knives were c
flint. Yet, for all their gauntness and poor equipment, they wer
unusually fine-looking warriors, much more handsome and lith
than the Sioux or Mandans, certainly. And there was no doub
that they were a good-hearted, cheerful people, childishly extrav
agant in their affections. Lewis thought of Sacajawea. Thes
were the people from whom she had sprung.

"Gawd!" McNeal was saying. "If their squaws are this lovey
let's git on t' town!"

THE CHIEF SAID HIS NAME WAS CA-ME-AH-WAIT. THROUGH
Drouillard's hand language, Lewis was able to convey that h
came in peace, that he had been seeking the Shoshonis for
long time, that he had small gifts for them, and that a large
party of white men was coming along with boats several day
behind, that these boats contained more articles which h
wished to trade for horses, and that a woman of their nation wa
with the boats. All of this seemed agreeable to Ca-me-ah-wait
Lewis brought out a pipe and tobacco. The Indians seated them
selves in a circle around the four white men and removed thei
moccasins, and the white men removed theirs. The chiefs note
the swollen, cut and blistered condition of their feet, but sai
nothing.

It was a strange parley, here in the sun-baked meadow with n
lodges or water nearby. Lewis gave the Indians some small gifts
of which the best received were blue beads and vermillion paint
"Tell them now," Lewis said to Drouillard, "that we want to g
to their camp and tell them our whole story."

*　　*　　*

THE SHOSHONI ENCAMPMENT WAS REACHED AFTER A MARCH of about four miles. It was in a fertile, level plain through which ran a fast, clear stream about forty yards wide and three feet deep. There were perhaps a hundred Indians but only two poor lodges, one made of willow brush and another of leather, and a scattering of small brush shelters. Ca-me-ah-wait explained that his people had been attacked in the spring by Indians from the plains, who had killed and captured about twenty of his people and had stolen many of their horses and all of their leather lodges. He took off his hawk-feather bonnet to show that he had cut off his hair in mourning for his murdered relatives.

THE OLD UNHURRIED CEREMONY OF THE PEACE PIPES RE-sumed then in the lodge, in pleasant shade, with everyone seated on antelope skins spread over green boughs, moccasins off, all the elegant and solemn ritual in which the chief presented the pipestem to the heaven and center of the earth and the four quadrants of the horizon, and then the long and heartfelt pream-bles to longer and more heartfelt speeches. It was late afternoon now and Lewis and his men had not eaten a bite of food since the night before, and their empty stomachs gurgled and growled, and the native mixture in the pipes made their heads buzz. The business took about ten times longer even than usual, for want of interpreters, and much of it surely was lost because sign language could convey only so much. I wish Sacajawea was here, Lewis thought over and over. The sun was going down.

Then it was his turn, and he stood and told of the large party he had back over the mountain, and how they were going to the great lake where the sun sets, and would find a route by which tools and hunting guns and other fine things from his nation could be brought to the Shoshonis to make their life easier and richer, and how the Great Chief in the east would protect them and enrich them if they would be peaceful and helpful now. Ca-me-ah-wait was rapt as Drouillard signaled all this to him; it was obvious that the lot of the Shoshonis was particularly hard, and these promises made him feel that good things were to come during his time as the head of the tribe, and that he would be remembered for them. While Lewis talked, scores of women and children stared into the shelter at these men with white feet and light-colored hair, the first such men they had ever seen. Then Ca-me-ah-wait harangued his people for another long spell, and told them they should help these new friends in any way they could. He told Lewis that they were on their way down to the plains to join their friends the Flatheads and hunt buffalo for their winter's meat, but that they would help before they went if the white man would tell them what they needed. He explained that he had come out against them as a war party because the Indians who had seen them approaching that morning had come and alarmed the village, and he had feared that these strangers were allies of the Blackfeet. Lewis learned only now that *tab-ba-bone* meant "alien," that there was no Shoshoni word for "white man."

Lewis told them now what he needed. He would like some people of the tribe, and about thirty horses, to go back beyond the great ridge and meet the rest of his people, and help carry his party's goods across to this place. He would like guides to show them a route for boats to the great river that flowed to the western lake. He would like their help in finding large trees for making canoes to float down that river. And if it should be necessary to cross mountains to reach such a route for boats, he would want to buy enough horses from the Shoshonis to carry the party's baggage to that route. All of this Ca-me-ah-wait found reasonable, but he warned that this little river, and a larger river it flowed into, a day's march below, were too full of rocks and foam for passage by boats. He said too that there was little more timber on that lower river than here, and that the other river wound between unclimbable mountains.

Lewis glanced at his men, and saw their faces looking grim. This was bad news, but perhaps, he thought, the chief exaggerates.

"But now," Lewis said, "our needs are simpler. We have eaten nothing today."

To his astonishment, the chief replied that there was not a bite of meat in the village that he knew of, as his hunters had had no fortune for many days. All the Shoshonis had to eat were a few cakes of sun-dried berries. Lewis looked around at the gaunt natives and understood. But, Ca-me-ah-wait said, the people would share what they had.

It was almost night when the parley broke up. The chief had his people bring dried serviceberries, and the white men were fed. "I promise you," Lewis told him, "tomorrow my two hunters here," he indicated Drouillard and Shields, "will take their fine firesticks and will hunt meat for your people."

That sounded good to Ca-me-ah-wait and he announced it to his people, who responded joyfully. A bonfire was kindled in the twilight, and a merry dance ensued. The music and the manner of dancing were similar to those of the Missouri tribes, and the soldiers were quickly absorbed in the eager and affectionate society of the tribespeople. It was still going strong at midnight when Lewis grew too sleepy to stay up. He was taken to a small bower, where he put up his mosquito net and retired. He was awakened several times during the night by the exuberant yelling of the men and Indians, but was too weary to stay awake long. The decision to hunt meat for the Indians was a good one, he knew; it would further strengthen this bond that had begun so well, and he suspected, too, that William and the main party would need another day at least to reach the forks where he had left instructions for them to halt.

Aye, he thought, dozing with the beat of drums in his head, things seem to be going well.

Maybe too well, he thought.

No, he told himself. Expect the best.

DURING THE VOYAGE, DROUILLARD HAD KILLED SEVERAL pronghorn antelope even while hunting afoot, and so Lewis was certain that he would be able to kill some of those fleet beasts while mounted on a fine Shoshoni horse. Lewis was proud of Drouillard, and when a herd of a dozen pronghorns was spotted in the valley next morning, Lewis told Ca-me-ah-wait there would be meat soon.

Drouillard and Shields were quickly mounted on fast horses, and, accompanied by some twenty young Indian men, set out to pursue the herd.

The chase swept hither and yon through the sunny valley for about two hours, most of the time within view of the village, and it was a good entertainment. But, perhaps because of their carousing the night before, Drouillard and Shields were not up to their usual level of skill. The Shoshoni hunters were unable to get within bow range of the antelope, which moved more like birds than earthbound beasts, and early in the afternoon the hunters rode in empty-handed on their sweat-lathered horses and there was no meat for the village after all. So Lewis gave Drouillard one sullen look and then ignored him for a while; the Indians ate berries again, and the white men ate berries cooked in a little flour paste.

That afternoon Lewis continued his conferences with Ca-me-ah-wait and made observations on the living mode of the Shoshonis. He noted that they were almost as flighty and wary as antelope themselves, that each warrior kept at least one horse staked near his lodge day and night, and that the whole male population could be mounted and armed within seconds. They were all superb horsemen, so much a part of their mounts that they seemed like centaurs, and gave the impression of being awk ward, incomplete, half-creatures when afoot. The horses them selves were fine. "Indeed," he wrote in his journal, "many o them would make a figure on the South side of the James River or the land of fine horses." Drouillard made a count of th horses, both tied and grazing loose, and said they numbere about four hundred. The Indians also had a few mules, whic they said had been obtained by other Shoshoni tribes far to th south, from some source Lewis had a hard time understandin until he saw a bridle bit of Spanish manufacture. Yes, Spanish Ca-me-ah-wait said; that was their name. But the Spanish woul not sell guns to the Shoshonis because they appeared to fear th thought of Indians with guns. Ca-me-ah-wait's own tribe ha never been to the Spaniards.

It was agreed that Indians and horses would go with Lewi next day toward the creek fork back on the other side of th divide, and meet there his friend the Red Hair Chief with th boats. This settled, the hungry Shoshonis and their hungr guests launched into another evening's entertainment, and th dancing and carousing lasted late.

Once, shortly before midnight, McNeal came staggerin blissfully out of a brush hut, sat down by a happy-faced Shield near the bonfire, sighed, and said, "Stud York better get her soon. We a-goin' need some reinforcements."

From the journal of Meriwether Lewis

Thursday August 15th 1805

This morning I arrose very early and as hungary as a wolf. I had eat nothing except one scant meal of the flour and berries. . . . we had only about two pounds of flour remaining. This I directed to McNeal to divide and to cook the one half this morning in a kind of pudding with the berries. . . .on this new fashoned pudding four of us breakfasted, giving a pretty good allowance to the Chief who declared it the best thing he had taisted for a long time

I hurried the departure of the Indians. the Chief addressed them several times before they would move they seemed very reluctant to accompany me. I at length asked the reason and he told me that some foolish persons among them had suggested the idea we were in leaugue with the pahkees and had come on in order to decoy them into an ambuscade . . . but that for his part he did not believe it. I readily perceived that our situation was not enterely free from danger as the transicion from suspicion to the confermation of the fact would not be very difficult in the minds of these ignorant people who have been accustomed from their infancy to view every stranger as an enimy.

I told Cameahwait that I was sorry to find that they had put so little confidence in us, that I knew they were not acquainted with whitemen and could forgive them, that among whitemen it was considered disgraceful to lye or entrap an enimy by falsehood. I told him that if they continued to think thus meanly of us that . . . no whitemen would ever come to trade with them or bring them arms and ammunition . . . and that I still hoped there were some among them that were not afraid to die, that were men and would go with me and convince themselves of the truth of what I had asscerted. that there was a party of whitemen waiting my return either at the forks of Jefferson's river or a little below coming on to that place in canoes loaded with provisions and merchandize. he told me for his own part he was determined to go, that he was not affraid to die. I soon found that I had touched him on the right string; to doubt the bravery of a savage is at once to put him on his metal. he now mounted his horse and haranged his village a third time . . . that he hoped that there were some of them who heard him were not affraid to die with him and if there was to let him see them mount their horses. . . . he was joined by six or eight only and with these I smoked a pipe . . . determined to set out with them while I had them in the humour. at half after 12 we set out, several of the old women were crying and imploring the great sperit to protect their warriors as if they were going to inevitable distruction.

we had not proceeded far before our party was augmented by ten or twelve more, and before we reached the Creek which we had passed in the morning of the 13th it appeared to me that we had all the men of the village and a number of women with us. this will serve in some measure to ilustrate the capricious disposition of those people. . . . they were now very cheerfull and gay, and two hours ago they looked as sirly as so many imps of satturn.

*   *   *

AGAIN TODAY WILLIAM HAD BEEN STRUCK AT BY A RAT
tlesnake; then, later, while fishing in the evening in the late sur
at the foot of a steep bluff, he had looked down from a drows
daydream to find a rattler coiled between his feet. He had sa
quietly waiting until it unwound itself and slithered away. Ther
on returning to camp he saw Sacajawea, gathering cottonwoo
down for Little Pompey's cradleboard, leap backward sudden
with a little outcry. He ran to her, his string of trout floppin,
beside him, and saw the scaly pattern of a big rattler's bac
streaming into the brush. She had not been hit.

The place was infested.

The party had made fourteen miles along the twisting rive
this day, but it was only about six miles in direct distance. Th
men had been almost constantly in the cold water, and the
ached in all their joints. William yearned for whiskey to alla
their miseries. Fortunately the Fields brothers had fared well i
their hunting, and there was meat from five deer and an ante
lope, as well as plenty of trout, to stoke their inner fires, and the
were jolly enough tonight, though they all moved like old mer
around the camp.

Maybe it was because of the rattlesnakes, but William felt
particularly tender kinship with the Indian girl tonight.
seemed marvelous that she and her little fat baby were alive, an
that the playfulness of fate had put their vulnerable lives into hi
care. It was a remarkable situation to which everybody had be
come entirely accustomed, and yet sometimes in the evening
like this, by the campfire, it would all come over him again s
poignantly, the *domesticity* of it. That was what it felt like, do
mesticity: food by firelight, writing by the light of a little lamp
York humming in his baritone as he sand-scoured a kettle, Scan
non lying nearby with his muzzle on his paws, probably dream
ing of his master, Sacajawea sewing something for the baby c
mending something for William. And he would have that feel
ing which was so natural until he would think the words for i
the words were that he felt *married* to this squaw-girl, this Janey
and he felt as if the little fat baby boy with his alert eyes an
ready giggle was *his* boy. And he would pick him up in his bi
hands, and hold him while the baby's strong little legs kicked
and laugh and call him "my little dancing boy Pomp," an
would look into those perfect obsidian baby-eyes with fireglint
in them and would feel a miniature hand close around hi

humb, and the little red mouth would form a perfect leer of a nansmile and the voice would chortle and coo, and William hen would glance up at Sacajawea and find her beaming at him vith pure intimate sharing in her eyes. William would have that trange and wonderful notion then, as incredible as it was natural, that no man and wife could be more truly akin to each other han this.

Charbonneau in those moments would seem not to exist, and t was largely his own fault, because he preferred the company of is old compatriot Le Page, and would nearly every evening go o sit and talk French with him and Cruzatte, bragging about his eputation as a sharp trader and a drinker of taffia and a steely-nerved gambler and a famous *paillard* among Indian maidens rom Canada to the Missouri. That was what he was doing at his moment, when across the camp came a clucking sound like hat of a galloping horse: the sound of *Le Capitaine Clark* making tongue-noises to the baby on his knee, calling him Dancing 3oy, and the little high hoot of glee the baby made in response, and a laughing syllable in Sacajawea's voice. Le Page and Cruzatte smirked at each other, and Charbonneau saw them do t, and they might as well have made cuckold-horns at him, because he was quite aware of that domestic scene over by the captain's fire; he had been watching it out of the back of his head ill evening. His eyes went dark and murderous and he glared at his countrymen in a way that meant *this is beyond joking*, so hey lowered their eyes to the willow-wood fire and began discussing the best recipes for beaver-trap bait.

But Charbonneau had been stung to a rage by the sight of that knowing smirk and the cheerful sounds from his wife and baby. He stood up and wandered slowly among the campfires and the blanket-wrapped sleepers and the low-talkers still sitting up, and went down to the water's edge, and stood there with his breeches open making his contribution to the source waters of the great Missouri. He mumbled to the sentry who stood, a dark shape, by he canoes, then went a little way up the shore until he was in he shadows near the captain's fire. He had no real notion of what he might do, but he was full of a sense of outraged honor, and he squatted in the dark fingering his skinning-knife and having a fantasy in which *Le Capitaine Clark* would come down to he water's edge to relieve his bladder and suddenly there would be a knife through it and a hand over his mouth and then he would be dead in the river and no one would ever know what had happened to him. Charbonneau had dispatched an Indian that way one night long ago after a rum-soaked dispute near a British trading post, and had never been found out.

He squatted here by the liquid whisperings of the little river, where the captain most likely would come down at least once before bedding down; he was not really planning anything, but his hands and body and nerves were enacting and reenacting certain swift moves, each time giving him a kind of grim satisfaction, each time healing his wounded pride a little bit.

And suddenly there were moccasins patting the earth close by him and a walking figure coming toward him in the darkness, silhouetted briefly against the glow of the captain's campfire; it stopped three feet from him and there was a pause, then the sound of water being made on the ground, and the smell of urine in the cold air—and then a gasp: he had been seen. He stood up quickly, not sure what he was going to do, and then the figure before him said, "Who ess?" and it was Sacajawea's voice. The sound of it at that moment made his seething rancor explode in him, and with a growling curse he rose to his feet and struck with his fist full of knife handle straight at the place from where her voice had come.

The blow was loud and hard and wet-sounding and she cried out in pain and her body crashed in the brush as she staggered and fell backward.

WILLIAM HEARD THE SOUND OF HER VOICE, AND THE BLOW, and her outcry and the rustle of brush, and leaped to his feet, crying, "Janey?" York was holding the baby now, his yellow eyes bulging toward the darkness. William snatched up the little alcohol writing lamp and ran into the brush. Other voices were making queries in the darkening camp.

Five strides down the bank his lampglow picked out the scene: Charbonneau standing half-crouched, half-ready to flee, his bearded face surly as a devil's; Sacajawea sprawled in the scrub, trying to rise, one hand over her mouth. The little lampglow did not reveal Charbonneau's right hand behind him with the knife in it.

William was furious. He glared at Charbonneau while reaching down to help the girl up. She rose, whimpering a little, and William pulled her hand down; there was a trickle of blood coming from the corner of her mouth.

William's hand lashed out and snatched the front of Charbonneau's blouse. And the half-dressed soldiers who had come running to investigate the commotion found them there, a strange little tableau in the light of the lamp: the little squaw-girl working her tongue in her bloody mouth; Captain Clark holding Charbonneau's bulk practically off the ground, with the lamp right under his nose, telling him in the most steely voice they had ever heard their affable captain use:

"By the blood of Jesus, Charbonneau, I swear I won't stand a man beating his woman! I've a mind to bat you around just as you've done her!" He shook him back and forth till his head bobbled. "By God, you greasy craven, d' you hear me? Once more you put a hard hand on that girl and I'll have you makin' a sausage of your *own* guts!"

"She ees my squaw, *Capitaine*," Charbonneau wheezed. "We have dispute."

"Your squaw, aye, but she's worth five o' you! Now you may give me your word, man, or I'll throw you in that river and hold you under, instead o' fishin' you out: you don't ever put a hard hand on her again!"

There were so many people standing around now, Charbonneau moved his hand in the darkness behind him and slipped his knife back into its sheath.

"*Eh bien*," he breathed. "On my word, *alors*."

"I wonder me," Sergeant Pryor muttered, just loudly enough for anyone to hear, "how much that's worth."

"KILL SOME MEAT, FOR GOD'S SAKE," LEWIS hissed. "IF WE and all these Shoshonis starve to death, we'll never live it down." When he realized what he had said, a rueful grin broke through his dark intensity. Aside from a small wad of watered flour the four white men and Ca-me-ah-wait had shared at the end of yesterday's march, no one had eaten since the previous morning, and everyone looked gaunt and lethargic.

Lewis asked Ca-me-ah-wait to keep his young men close by, lest they frighten off any game before Drouillard and Shields could shoot it. But the request seemed to unsettle the Shoshoni chief. He and his principal men had a frantic, buzzing, private huddle. And when the two hunters rode out up the valley, two small bands of mounted Indians set out, one on each side of the valley, to follow and watch them. Lewis put his fists on his hips and scowled at the chief, who looked back at him blank.

Eh, well, Lewis thought. They're still suspicious we might be a decoy for their enemies. If I protest, they'll only get more dubious.

Much of the tribe was faltering anyway. Despite a harangue by the chief, most of the villagers turned to go back to their town. Now only twenty-eight men and three women elected to continue with their chief on this fearful mission with the white men. Ca-me-ah-wait himself looked as if he would like to go back with them, but he had given his word. And so now the brave ones set out, following the hunters up the valley, with the laments of the others droning after them.

Because Drouillard and Shields each had borrowed a horse, the owners of those horses had to double up; one rode behind Lewis on his tired horse and the other behind McNeal. It made for a hot, uncomfortable, jostling ride.

Now riding up the narrowest part of the valley, with Ca-me-ah-wait beside him, Lewis saw an Indian racing back down the valley toward them, whipping his horse furiously. Lewis saw a look of alarm on Ca-me-ah-wait's profile, and his own heartbeat raced. What if by some awful chance some of their Blackfeet or Pahkee enemies actually *had* shown up just now?

The messenger, one of those sent to spy on the white hunters, now wheeled across in front of his chief, shouting and making signs, then raced away in the direction from which he had come. A cry burst from the Indians' throats and they lashed their horses into a headlong gallop. The Indian riding behind Lewis was whipping the horse unmercifully, but with its two riders it was being left behind; the Indian only lashed it harder.

Being without stirrups, Lewis was jouncing painfully on the horse's back; he felt as if his molars were crashing together with each step. "Stop it, damn your eyes!" he yelled back over his shoulder after about a mile of this, but the Indian did not understand and only whipped the beast harder. All right, then, Lewis thought, clenching his teeth, and he suddenly reined in the horse, which stopped abruptly despite the whip. The other horses were a good three hundred yards ahead, a cloud of dust going up the rolling valley. Now Lewis turned to try to forbid the Indian from using the whip, but the Indian was no longer on the horse. Lewis saw him hit the ground on the balls of his feet and sprint ahead like a jackrabbit. McNeal's horse was far ahead now, too, with McNeal and his Indian pounding ahead lickety-cut, the Indian howling in McNeal's ear. Lewis had no idea what the riders were in such frantic pursuit of, but knew he had better be there for whatever it was. He dug in his heels and soon was thundering after the dust cloud. He overtook the running Indian who had been sharing his horse with him, rode alongside him briefly, giving him a bemused look. But the Indian was pelting along at the pace of a good track horse and seemed to be getting where he wanted to go, so Lewis urged the horse onward and left him in the dust.

And then, soaring over a rise and down into a defilade, he saw in the low ground a few hundred yards ahead what the pell-mell rush was about.

Drouillard was there, dismounted, kneeling, butchering a deer. He had thrown the guts out, and half a dozen Indians were off their horses scrambling for them. The rest of the party was just now converging on the scene. Lewis saw them dismount even before their horses had quite stopped, and run tumbling in over each other like a pack of starved wolves for the offal. An Indian would snatch up a piece of liver, a kidney or spleen, and tear at it with his teeth, blood running from the corners of his mouth. Those who had got pieces of the paunch or lengths of intestine gnawed with equal frenzy at their slimy yields, but what exuded from their lips was of a different color and consistency. Lewis had to tighten his throat against a rush of nausea. Though his Corps of Discovery had been like a moving abbatoir and the sight of animal guts was as ordinary as the sight of leaves on trees, and though he himself had watched intestines being cooked into table delicacies for his own pleasure, he had never seen human beings brought down so close to the nature of wolves. He watched Ca-me-ah-wait then; the chief was trembling with hunger and salivating, but he stood back and let his people feed, took nothing himself, and forbade them to throw themselves on the carcass of the deer, which McNeal was now skinning and butchering, as that was the white men's meat, which they had killed. And in that sight of Ca-me-ah-wait, Lewis found something so admirable that his nausea turned to pity for a people whose life could be so hard. So he told Drouillard to save but a quarter of the deer, and gave the rest to Ca-me-ah-wait to divide among his people. They fell on it with knives and devoured the whole of it raw. And while they were thus polishing the bones, Drouillard and Shields mounted their horses and rode off to continue their hunt. Again Ca-me-ah-wait sent a party of watchers out after them. Soon thereafter, as the whole party was moving down toward the stream, a rifle shot echoed down the valley. Drouillard had killed another deer. Virtually the same scene was reenacted, but Lewis here found rush for a fire to cook his men's share of the venison. Some of the Indians now were patient enough at least to scorch their venison over the fire. And while the Shoshonis were devouring every shred of flesh on this deer, even the soft parts of the hooves, Drouillard's rifle cracked again in the distance, and in a few minutes he came trotting down to the fireside with another small deer strapped over his horse's rump. Lewis kept a quarter of this one and gave the rest of it to the Indians. When this one had been devoured, and the Indians seemed at last to have compensated for their long hunger for meat and were in a good humor, and the horses had been permitted to graze, Lewis encouraged Ca-me-ah-wait to continue on with him.

Now Ca-me-ah-wait insisted on a little ceremony. He put over Lewis's shoulders a beautiful mantle made of ermine skins—it appeared to be fifty skins or more—similar to those some of the leading men wore, and gave similar garments to Drouillard and Shields and McNeal. Now, sunburned as they were, the white men looked like Indians themselves. Lewis responded by putting his hat on Ca-me-ah-wait's head, and urged him to bring his people along to the forks where he expected to meet the Red-Hair Chief. He gave the American flag to an Indian to carry, so that they might be more readily recognized by the other white men. And at last, toward evening, they all descended to a place from which they could see the creek forks two miles below. Lewis's heart sank.

The place was as vacant as when he had first seen it. There was not a sign of Captain Clark's party. There were the small streams joining; there were the clumps of brush. But there was no one in sight.

Ca-me-ah-wait halted his horse, studying the distant place with a face full of distrust, and all the other Indians began a sinister murmuring. This was the place where the white man had said his people would be waiting with a Shoshoni woman and boats full of good things to trade for horses. But if there were people down there, they must be hidden—in that ambush of which the old women had warned. Lewis was sure Ca-me-ah-wait was thinking this; somehow he had to restore the chief's tenuous confidence and detain him or lure him on until William arrived. From the looks of Ca-me-ah-wait and his people, they were ready to gallop back into the mountains, where surely they would vanish for good. "Drouillard, come here," Lewis said. "Tell the chief this and make it clear to him: To prove we're not tricking him, I'm going to give him our guns. Tell him—'

Drouillard gave him an oblique glance. "My gun too?"

"Aye, yours too. Tell him that if he believes his enemies are in those thickets down there, he can defend himself with our guns, and he's welcome to shoot me as a liar as well."

This gesture seemed to inspire a little confidence, and the party now moved warily down toward the forks. Lewis now was as nervous as the Indians, but for his own reasons, and all sorts of awful possibilities passed through his head. What if the river

ad proved so impassable that William had halted to wait somewhere far down? What if these nervous Indians persuaded them-
elves that they were indeed being tricked, and decided to kill
him and his three unarmed men with their own weapons? If they
didn't come upon the main party soon, that might well happen.

Now they were within a mile of the forks, the scouts moving
ahead, looking as taut as their own bowstrings, ready to fight or
flee. Other warriors were riding near Ca-me-ah-wait, mumbling
into his ear words that Lewis was sure would further undermine
his trust in the white men.

I've got to do something else to assure him, he thought, but
what? I've done about all I can. Now it's all up to Ca-me-ah-wait
and his courage and his concept of honor.

Then he remembered something, something that might
stretch this filament of trust out a little further, and it was, ironically, a deception: he remembered the notes he had left on a
willow stick at the forks. "Drouillard," he said, "come do some
more talking for me." They halted. "Tell him we have a way of
speaking on white leaves. Explain as well as you can what a note
is, understand? Then tell him I left such a message—tell him
just *one* —down there on a stick for our friends. Then I'm going
to send you down there, with a scout as witness, to get that
note."

"There are *two* notes there, *Capitaine*," Drouillard reminded
him.

"Exactly. And I want you to act surprised when you pick up
the second note. Then you'll bring 'em back to me and I'll play
it from there."

Ca-me-ah-wait seemed dubious as Drouillard tried to explain
what writing was. But he was patient. He seemed to welcome
any excuse to delay going down that last ominous mile.

Drouillard then galloped down to the forks in the twilight with
one brave alongside, and he returned with paper in his hand.
Lewis took the notes, looked at one, then with greater interest at
the other, and then showed them to Ca-me-ah-wait, who looked
at the markings with keen curiosity; then Lewis had Drouillard
translate to the chief in hand language:

"This white leaf is a message I left six days ago for my brother
chief, the Red Hair. This other leaf is a message Red Hair put
here today for me. It says the canoes are heavy and the water is
shallow and it is harder to bring them up than we expected, but
they are just below the mountains and are coming up slowly. It
says I should wait until they bring the canoes to this place."

Lewis smiled. "This is good, eh? They are so close, and we will probably meet them tomorrow if you stay here with me."

Drouillard, even while translating, looked at Lewis with admiration for this piece of lying. Ca-me-ah-wait seemed about half-willing to believe all this, but his advisers seemed to be trying to talk him out of it. So Lewis continued:

"If you do not believe me, I have a way of proving my word. It is almost night now, and this is a good place for us to make a camp. Before the sun tomorrow I will send my hunter here down to meet the Red Hair Chief and tell him we are here waiting. One of your men may go with him; in fact I will pay him gifts to do this. I and my other two men will stay here with you, and you have our guns. If you will not desert me now or tomorrow, your brave will come back and tell you that he has seen my people and that they are as I have told you. You will meet them soon, and they will have many beautiful things to trade you for horses. But if you leave me and do not meet my brother chief, and go to hide in the mountains instead of helping us, then our great father in the east will forget you when we come back in later seasons with guns and provisions, and you will remain poor and hungry as I have seen you to be."

Ca-me-ah-wait agreed, but it was apparent that he less than half believed in the safety of it. In the light of a small campfire of willow brush Lewis wrote a note for Drouillard to take to Captain Clark in the morning, urging him to come on with all possible haste as there was not a moment to spare.

The chief now, with six of his closest advisers, bedded down close to Lewis's mosquito net, while most of the braves went out to camp hidden in the willow thickets where they might be safer if the camp were attacked during the night.

Lewis was exhausted, but had little expectation of sleeping well this night. The fate of the expedition, which he had long held to be more important than his own life, seemed now to depend on the caprices of these few fickle and flighty savages, who he expected might well kill him or vanish in the night.

Lewis had barely begun to doze when he became aware of excited whisperings around him. He lifted the edge of his mosquito netting and saw by the starlight and the glow of Drouillard's nearby campfire that Ca-me-ah-wait was sitting up, listening to some of his men who had come to crouch beside him and hiss in his ear. Lewis suspected this might be the moment he had dreaded, and stealthily he slipped his knife out of its sheath.

Then he heard Drouillard chuckling, and called to him, "What goes?" The half-breed's deep, soft voice came back:

"Eh, *mon capitaine*! I am tell these Shoshoni there ees our man of black skeen and hair like burned prairie grass! They scoff, but I theenk they stay weeth us to see thees monster eef nothing else!"

Lewis sighed and relaxed in his bedding. "Drouillard, God bless ye, you're a genius! Why didn't I think o' that?"

IT WAS SEVEN IN THE MORNING, AND THE CANOES WERE loaded and the men were taking their places on the tow ropes to begin their daily suffering. It was a fair but cold morning, with the rising sun slanting through mist, and the men were slow to begin because they knew from experience that the water would be shockingly cold and their bones would be aching from the start. They had been saying often lately that they wished they could leave these accursed heavy canoes and the burden of goods and just walk the rest of the way to the ocean. They had said it in jesting tones so they would not sound like real complainers, but the sentiment was heartfelt, and William had no trouble understanding it. He had done enough of the poling and rope-pulling himself up the Missouri and Jefferson and Beaverhead rivers and now up this shallow, stony, twisting creek that he felt he could say truthfully that this Voyage of Discovery had deteriorated into what was probably the longest and most strenuous and most painful ordeal of labor any group of soldiers ever had suffered. It didn't take Hannibal this long to cross the Alps, William thought, and he had elephants to carry his canoes if he had canoes.

This morning, as was the custom, the hunters would be out on the flanks and he himself would walk ahead scouting the route and watching for signs of the Shoshonis and for Captain Lewis, whose absence, now in its eighth day, troubled William so much he had scarcely slept. This morning, as usual, he would have Sacajawea up ahead with him so that she would be ready to interpret in case the expedition got lucky and met her people. And, suspecting that Charbonneau had struck Sacajawea the other evening over that old jealousy business, William had excused Charbonneau from work on the boats and let him come along in the advance to see for himself that his squaw and William were not hopping into the thickets to cuckold him.

Now they had come about a mile this morning and William had dropped a few yards behind the couple to try to get a good look at a new kind of crow-sized bird he had spotted up on the

bluff, a pale grayish-brown sort of bird with dark wings. But
had kept darting over rocks up the bluff and he had not bee
able to get a good image of it, so now he was moving ahead
catch up with them. Charbonneau was hulking along with h
red cap bobbing with every step and the girl-squaw was walking
few paces behind him in her bright scarlet blanket with its wid
blue stripe running down the back, with that hump-backed loo
caused by the papoose on her back, and suddenly that steady
graceful, pigeon-toed stride of hers faltered. She was doing some
thing odd, and William squinted in the sunlight to see what wa
happening. He thought first that she had come up against an
other rattlesnake.

The girl was dancing. She was hopping from foot to foot an
turning in circles around Charbonneau. She was uttering sma
cries like a bird. William trotted forward to investigate. Wit
each turn she would point up the valley, and when Willia
looked he saw them.

Several Indians on horseback were trotting toward them dow
the streamside path. One of them was slightly ahead of the oth
ers, riding with his right hand held high. A thrilling shiver, o
pleasure but also of apprehension, buzzed through William'
scalp down his neck and spine. He caught up with the pirouet
ting Sacajawea now, and as she whirled around he saw shinin
in her face the purest joy he had ever seen. Her laughter was lik
a shower of silver; her teeth flashed in her brown face. Even h
baby was infected by her joy, and was laugh-gurgling as h
swayed in the cradleboard with her gyrations. Now the squa
would lean forward toward the distant horsemen, makin
mmmm, mmmm sounds in her throat while sucking her fingers
This sign William knew: it was that she had eaten with them
they were her native people; they were Shoshonis!

William was so swept with happiness that despite the presenc
of Charbonneau he grabbed her hands and whirled with he
twice, then held her face in his hands and kissed the end of he
nose. Charbonneau was too transfixed by the sight of the ap
proaching riders to notice. "Come along!" William cried, an
they began striding briskly toward the Indians, William holdin
high his right hand.

Now the first rider kicked his horse and loped ahead of th
others, and as he came closer that white flash of a smile looke
familiar. "By heaven!" William whooped. "Drouillard!"

Sacajawea had broken out in a trilling song-chant now, an
it was taken up by the voices of some of the oncoming riders.
was as keen and full of longing as a meadowlark's song, and th

sound of it made William's throat ache and his eyes blur. It was a song of homecoming. *Home!* he thought, and his heart clamped. Drouillard's horse was among them now, blowing, hooves thudding in the dewy grass, and Drouillard, his cheeks smeared with vermillion, was off its back with his arms thrown around William's brawny shoulders, kissing him on this cheek, then the other, in the most extravagant emotional release the half-breed had ever shown. William pounded him on the back of his white ermine shawl, and yelled in his ear over all the noise of greetings: "*Cap'n Lewis?*" Drouillard nodded his head vigorously.

"Yes, *mon capitaine!*" He pointed up the stream. "Not far! *Tout va bien!* He has a chief!" William felt a flood of relief.

Now Cruzatte came running up from the main party to investigate the tumult, and skidded to a halt at the sight of horses and Indians. William yelled at him: "Bring 'em on, bring 'em on! We've met the Snakes!" Cruzatte peered myopically into the milling group, leaped three feet off the ground, crossed himself when he landed, then spun and darted back down around the bend shouting the news. Within half a minute a roar of deep voices rolled up the valley to blend in the chorus of greeting.

NOW WILLIAM AND SACAJAWEA AND CHARBONNEAU STRODE ahead briskly up toward the end of the valley, Drouillard leading them toward the forks, while the warriors rode alongside still singing their greeting song with the greatest appearance of delight. Sacajawea stumbled along nearby, chewing her smile, tears streaming down her face. As they went, Drouillard told William the tale of the week past: of their first glimpse of the Shoshoni, of their first tenuous meeting, of the poor starving village, of the ceremonies, and the dances and the horses, of the Shoshonis' timidity, of Captain Lewis's desperate ruse of the notes. Even above all this hubbub, singing and talking, William could now and then hear some leather-lunged huzzah come echoing from down the valley, where, he was sure, his stalwart boys were pulling the boats on with a renewed vigor, in the knowledge that they might not have to pull them another day beyond today. Likely, too, they were thinking of Indian maidens.

William could hardly bear to look at Sacajawea now; her transported visage made his throat knot up with caring. She was so close to her people now, and, being so far from his, he could understand the terrible poignancy of her longings, as if foresee-

ing his own homecoming, sometime in the far future, his own
homecoming from a far place and a long time.

45

August 17, 1805

THEY WALKED OUT FROM BETWEEN THE BLUFFS AND ONTO
the yellow-brown grass of the plain where the creek forked.
Above the fork they could see smoke rising from a copse of
willows, and a skin tent stretched over a clump of willows for a
shelter; at this distance it looked like a handkerchief dropped on
grass. Twenty or thirty people were coming across the plain from
that place, running and riding; they had heard the homing song
and were coming. Most were young men; there were a few
women. William felt a shiver as he saw them coming; they were
colorful and full of eager motion, and they were an entirely new
people, and if Sacajawea was representative, they were a fine
people, a primitive, uncorrupted highland people who lived on
the roof of the continent. They came hurrying over the meadow,
hooves and moccasins. Part of the meadow was in the shadow of
a high, fast-moving cloud, and the edge of the shadow ran silently off the field to leave it all glowing fresh and gold in the
morning sunlight. Around the plain there were ridges with blue
cloud-shadows running up their flanks, and above and beyond
them in the blue were streaks of white, the snowy tops of mountains. Behind the running crowd of Indians there were three
men who walked together and they all looked like stately chiefs,
with their wild headdresses and vermillion-painted faces, but one
of them was bowlegged and there was no mistaking his walk; it
was Meriwether Lewis.

The air was still cold and fresh, and as the people came close
William smelled them, the wood smoke in their clothes, rancid
grease, fish, and something like wet tea leaves. It was much like
that nearly forgotten earthy smell of the Mandans, but cleaner
and sharper.

The Indians stopped a few yards away, and William and his

party stopped, and they all stood looking at each other for a moment. The singing braves fell silent and reined in their horses to watch.

William stood with his feet widespread, his fine rifle cradled in his left arm, the leather bill of his lynx-fur cap shading his eyes. Charbonneau stood posing with his thick chinwhiskers thrust out.

The Shoshonis were as colorful as a field of flowers, the yellow-orange painted on their faces, their leather clothes and shields decorated with patterns of quills and shells and dyed grasses, colored feathers shaking in the morning wind, claw necklaces, collars and tippets of small-animal fur, headdresses of bird skins and buffalo horns, lances festooned with down and scalplocks.

Sacajawea stood stockstill in this hush, in her red blanket with the baby slung on her back, and her glinting dark eyes searched theirs, all those pairs of piercing eyes in bony faces. And then suddenly one of the women slipped out from between two horses, came out staring at Sacajawea, mouth agape, slowly raising her hand to her face as she came, and then her eyebrows rose and her face crumpled as if she were going to cry, and she began making the *mmm* sounds and sucking her fingers. Sacajawea's gaze now fixed upon that young woman, and her eyebrows flickered the same way, and then the two spoke some syllables to each other with their arms reaching. They came together and wrapped their arms around each other, and with their faces buried in each other's necks they softly began crying, "A-hi-ee! A-hi-ee!" and patting each other, and William gulped down a groan and blinked rapidly.

Charbonneau listened to their soft exclamations, seeming, for once, to be at least somewhat moved by his squaw's emotions, and he turned to William, and said, "Thees I bleef was woman name Otter, capture weeth her but escape. She has tell me of thees sometime!" He seemed genuinely affected, perhaps a little awed, perhaps for the first time aware that she, his third and least-favored squaw, was a person whose heart had come from someplace before she had become his.

William felt his own heart aching with a bittersweetness. There was something about this affectionate meeting of the two alien peoples here in this beautiful little valley on the top of the world—the end of the long, desperate search, the plaintive greeting song, the sight of his compatriot Lewis, the reunion of the two young squaws—that was making him feel so delicate in his heart that he could hardly stand it. *God Bless ye, Janey,* he thought as the Shoshoni squaw led her gently into the crowd, holding her wrist with one hand and stroking her cheek with the other.

And now Lewis came through the crowd straight to William. They saluted, smiling, then Lewis gripped his hand and slipped an arm over his shoulder, saying, "Begod, Clark, but you're a balm for these eyes o' mine!"

"And you!"

The Indians were murmuring and patting their hands together as the captains met. The chief was standing nearby holding his hands together in front of his chest with the two upraised fore-fingers laid alongside each other, and his cadaverous yet hand-some face was aglow with a smile as tender as a woman's.

"I've a thousand things to tell, but first must present you to their chief. He's Ca-me-ah-wait, and he's as lovable a savage as I've met."

As if to prove it, Ca-me-ah-wait swarmed over William with the Shoshoni hug, smearing his cheeks with the paint from his own, and that was the signal for everyone else to dismount or run forward and do the same, and everyone was chorusing, "A-hi-ee! A-hi-ee!"

"Godalmighty!" William wheezed to Lewis over the shoulder of some mighty brave who was hugging the breath out of him, "ye've sure seduced *these* folks!"

THE BOATS REACHED THE FORKS AT NOON, AND THE HUG-ging took all of an hour, there being so many white men to greet, and the cries of joy and amazement never let up. The Shoshonis were astonished by everything as the men arranged the baggage onshore, by all the tools and instruments and goods. And they were captivated by the black giant York, and by the sagacity of Scannon, who put on a perfect show of cheerful grinning obedience as Lewis put him through his tricks. The hunters had killed four deer and an antelope, which they shared with the Indians in a high-hearted banquet. Lewis demonstrated the air gun, which Ca-me-ah-wait declared to be surely the greatest medicine of all the great medicines these wonderful strangers had brought, and for several hours the little camp was as festive as a country fair. Sacajawea sat in a willow arbor with the three other Shoshoni women and was queried about her place in a tribe of remarkable white strangers such as these, which she tried to explain with her imperfect recollection of her native tongue. Often she was overcome with happy weeping and could not explain.

The three women could not keep their hands off of little Pompey. They saw that he was as fat and strong and beautiful a baby as they had ever seen, and they learned that his father was the thick white man with thick face-hair and the red hat who had walked here with her. It seemed to the women therefore that if a Shoshoni woman coupled with a man of white skin, good blood would result and the baby of such blood must be fat and strong and beautiful like this one. This was a point of keen interest to the three Shoshoni women who were here in the arbor with Sacajawea, even the old one who was so bent that she had to walk with a stick. And so when Collins and McNeal paused outside the arbor, and Collins asked McNeal, "Eh, Hugh, is this all the women this tribe's got?" and McNeal answered, "Heck, no, they's a passel of 'em over t' their main camp," the women looked out at Collins and McNeal with fat babies in their eyes, even though they had not understood what the men had said. And the soldiers grinned and bowed to the women and were very polite.

The white men had very rosy memories of the villages around Fort Mandan, and it had been a long time since Fort Mandan, and judging by the appearance of the two young women with Sacajawea, these Snake women were far handsomer than the Mandan women had been.

DOWN BY THE CREEK BANK WHERE THE DUGOUTS HAD BEEN unloaded, the Indian men strolled and looked with admiration at the fine articles that had been arrayed. The captains had ordered the goods laid out to dry, but they were aware too that the Indians were looking at these things like shoppers in a bazaar, and that their desires for these articles would grow, and this would be advantageous when it came time to bargain for horses. Ca-me-ah-wait had told the captains that his people did not steal, and it soon became apparent that this was absolutely true. Even when no one seemed to be watching, a Shoshoni who picked up a kettle or a knife, a tool or a string of beads or a hat to examine it, would always put it back. The white men and the Shoshonis were growing ever more pleased with each other.

The troops fully understood now that this, after three thousand miles, was the end of their uphill canoeing, and if there had been a tub of grog available it could not have made them more jolly than this knowledge.

"What I've heard so far about the westering rivers isn't very promising," Lewis told William during one of the few times they could sit down and talk together. "I know the creeks over by their main camp lead to the Columbia. One thing, a man gave me a piece of fresh fish to eat, and by Heaven it was salmon. But from what they say, those waters race down through steep canyons so fast that they're beat into a perfect foam on the rocks, for miles at a stretch. Unless they're exaggerating that, well, we'll likely have to cross some mountains before we reach a navigable branch of the Columbia." Nearby, a scrawny yellow dog of wolfish ancestry was trying to sniff up an acquaintance with Scannon, who, with an expression of injured dignity, kept turning around to try to confront him face to face. Lewis picked up a pebble and tossed it at the mongrel, which leaped up with a pained look and then ran off with its tail between its legs.

"And what of the mountains?" William asked.

Lewis looked westward, frowning. "I recollect when Mister Jefferson and I would sit there at his desk and plan this little voyage. He would say to me, 'From all that's known of them, the Western mountains oughtn't be more obstacle than the Alleghenies—a day's crossing at the most.' I wish it would be so, but, well, I saw 'em from up there on the divide, and they like to made me timid."

"Formidable, ye say."

"Formidable. What we've come through thus far looks to be but a start of 'em."

William almost shuddered. "Reckon there's time to get over before winter?"

Lewis pulled back a corner of his mouth. "I'll want your judgment o' that. What I want you to do is take a party—with boatmaking tools, just in case—go over the divide to the main Shoshoni camp and proceed downriver from there to see if it's navigable, and where. I'll stay here and arrange to get the baggage over the divide. Lord knows," he said, "you deserve a chance to rest and languish with these folk. But we have to push on, as you well know."

That was fine with William. Lewis had had his turn at being out in front, and he had done fine things with it, but now he felt it was his turn to be out in front.

BY LATE AFTERNOON, WHEN YORK WAS COMPLAINING THAT his skin had been rubbed raw by the fingers of the Shoshonis trying to get the soot off of him, it was time to hold a council.

Under the awning in the willows, the two captains were seated on white robes, with Drouillard and Charbonneau next to them. A dozen of the Shoshoni men sat in a facing semicircle, moccasins were removed, and the chief bent down and tied six small, pearly seashells in William's hair, while the councilors smiled and hummed their approval. William was aware that these likely were seashells from the Pacific, acquired probably by trade with Columbia River tribes, and so the significance of them was as real to him as it must have been to the chief. Then the pipe was presented to the earth and sky and the four winds and was smoked by the captains and the chief, then passed among the councilors.

"Now tell them," Lewis said to Drouillard, "that in order to speak better with them, we want their permission to bring a woman into this council—the Shoshoni woman we brought here with us, the wife of Charbonneau."

This was a shocking request, and was met with all the expected frowns and indignant protestations. Charbonneau seemed almost pleased; it looked as if his squaw, for once, might have to keep her place. But the captains insisted. The woman had been brought all this way as an official member of the party, they said, for this purpose. Some things could be said by hand language, they argued, but now there were things to be told and arranged that would require the completeness and exactness of spoken language.

Ca-me-ah-wait soon agreed that there was wisdom in this, and told his councilors that it would be so. "Go get Janey," William told Charbonneau.

She came into the shade, for once without Pompey on her back. She had left him with the women. Charbonneau had warned her that the chiefs were not pleased by this and had told her to remember that she was a squaw, not an American *capitaine*. When she entered, she felt the resentment of the Indian men and kept her eyes down. Ca-me-ah-wait was obviously a little embarrassed at having permitted this, so he did not look at her.

"Sit there, Janey," William said, pointing to a place between Drouillard and himself. Sacajawea did not look around at the men; rather, she took on the proper aspect of an interpreter and looked at William. Ca-me-ah-wait, too, looked at William, as if the squaw did not exist, and sat attentive now, ready to hear the whole business like a statesman.

"First, say this," William began. "Tell them we come to bring trade and peace to the Shoshoni people. Tell them that for the sake of peace we have already made the Minnetarees promise they will no more come and attack the Shoshoni people." This seemed to William a very reassuring and favorable piece of news with which to bring the smiles back onto the faces of the Indian men. He waited, looking at Ca-me-ah-wait, for these words to be translated: first by Drouillard in French to Charbonneau, then in Minnetaree by Charbonneau to Sacajawea, then by her in Shoshoni to the chief.

He heard Sacajawea utter a few syllables, and then there was a strange break in her voice, followed by a deep silence. No more words came. *Come on, Janey,* he thought. He had put faith in her intelligence and made an issue of getting her into the council, and it would be a huge embarrassment now if she could not do the job.

The silence continued, and people were beginning to stir. *Come ON, Ja—*

A small, strangled sound came from her throat. William saw Ca-me-ah-wait's eyes flicker toward her, and he himself glanced at her. And what he saw was bewildering.

She was staring glassy-eyed at the chief, her mouth gaping like a fish's mouth, and she was starting to rise. Her hands were clawing open the blanket she wore.

Then, before the astonished faces of the whole council, she fairly leaped across the distance between herself and the chief, flung herself on her knees before him, crying and gasping words, whipped her arms and blanket around him, and, looking in his eyes for an instant, began weeping and sobbing. Everyone in the tent was dumbstruck for an instant; some braves had started up as if to defend the chief; but now Ca-me-ah-wait was returning her embrace and his craggy face was softening, crumbling.

It was Charbonneau who first caught the sense of this. His mouth falling open, and eyes bulging, he rose to his knees pointing at them and exclaimed:

"*Sa frére! Mon Dieu,* thees her *brother!*"

"Brother?" Lewis exclaimed.

"Oh, great Heavenly God," William groaned, and then he could only kneel there watching the pair of them, the red blanket shaking with their sobs and outcries of "*ah-hi-ee, ah-hi-ee,*" and when he tried to swallow so that he could speak, it was like trying to swallow a horse.

It was quite a while before the councilors could get over this wondrous revelation. The Indian men were trying to be stoical as warriors should be, and the white men were trying to be stoical as soldiers should be. But the men of each race could see how those of the other were affected; it obviously was another part of the great medicine of this day, and it was not necessary or even good to hide one's feelings in moments of great medicine, and soon tears were eroding the vermillion of friendship on the cheeks of all the men in the shelter and all the braves were patting their palms together and crooning, "*Ah-hi-ee, ah-hi-ee!*" I rejoice, I rejoice!

The brother and sister held a choking, sniffling conversation for a while still, and then Sacajawea returned to her place by William, who put his hand on her arm and gazed encouragement into her stricken face until he thought she had recovered enough to go on. But after a few words her voice caved in and she poured tears, and at last it was decided to continue without her for now, and they let her go back to the women and her baby. They would try again when she was able.

What had overcome her, no doubt, Ca-me-ah-wait explained in hand language, was what she had learned today about the rest of her family, what she had never known in the five summers she had been gone: that the Minnetarees had killed her father the chief, and her mother, and her older sister. "I am alive, whom she thought dead; and our brother is alive, living now at another place, and this gave her joy. But we three are the only ones of our family now, and knowing this for the first time surely is why she could not continue to exchange words for us. Forgive my sister's weakness, she is only a girl. Perhaps she will be able to speak tomorrow."

Forgive her weakness, she is only a girl, William thought several times as the council droned into the evening, and plans were made, and medals were given to the leading men, and useful things like knives and tobacco were given to the others. *She is only a girl.* And he wished he could go to the willow bower where she was, and hold her and comfort her, and dandle her baby, his little Dancing Boy, on his knee to make her laugh. But of course he could not because there was all this man's business to be done for President Jefferson.

August 18, 1805

Now Clark was gone, heading up over the Great Divide with his men and their tools and baggage, and Charbonneau and Sacajawea were gone with him, and Ca-me-ah-wait and most of his band; and Meriwether Lewis had stayed here with the troops to make packsaddles, and to sink the canoes in a nearby pond so they would not be damaged by wind or grass fires before—or if—they should be needed again.

It had been a warm morning but at noon a misty rain had started, bringing with it a chill that felt like winter. It would be days yet before Clark could determine a route through the Western Mountains, and before Ca-me-ah-wait could bring his people and extra horses back, and Lewis had an awful foreboding, a gloomy half-certainty that winter would close the mountains before the Corps of Discovery could go through. If it did, they would be forced to spend the winter here in these gameless valleys with the half-starved Shoshonis. If that happened it would be unlikely that the expedition could continue next spring, because surely they would have used up everything they had by then, or starved, or become fully demoralized, and would have to return down the Missouri to civilization, a failure even after two years of trying. If the voyage was not to fail, it would have to get over the mountains in what was left of this year. And that chill in the air told him there was very little of this year left.

And so now without his friend Clark to talk his spirits up, Lewis turned to the only other outlet for his personal thoughts, and he wrote in his journal for Sunday, August 18th, 1805:

> This day I completed my thirty first year, and conceived that I had in all human probability now existed about half the period which I am to remain in this sublunary world. I reflected that I had as yet done but little, very little, indeed, to further the happiness of the human race or to advance the information of the succeeding generation. I viewed with regret the many hours I have spent in indolence, and now soarly felt the want of that information which those hours would have given me had they been judiciously expended. but since they are past and cannot be recalled, I dash from me the gloomy thought, and resolved in future, to redouble my exertions and at least indeavor to promote those two primary objects of human existence, by giving them the aid of that portion of talents which nature and fortune have bestoed in me; or in future, to live for MANKIND, as I have heretofore lived FOR MYSELF.

46

In the Bitterroot Range

T WAS September now and in the evenings and mornings
was so cold that the ink would freeze in their pens when they
ied to write. The pitch pines and the jagged granite cliffs on
ither side of the river were dark with dampness from the rain or
iist, and the mountaintops close above them were almost al-
·ays invisible in the clouds that hung over them sifting wet
iow. They had had to leave the warm but spare comforts of the
hoshoni nation all too soon, and were high in the Rocky
Iountains now, west of the Great Divide, seeking the way down
irough the maze of ranges to a navigable tributary of the Co-
imbia. The captains could not keep an exact daily record of the
imperatures anymore, because their last thermometer had been
roken. It had happened during a heart-stopping, awful moment
hen a pack horse had slipped on a loose rock and gone whinny-
ig and rolling and sliding down a mountainside steep as a roof,
i a clattery, rattling avalanche of stones and deadwood and bun-
les and bags and pieces of packsaddle, while the men had stood
bove grimacing and shouting. Whenever this happened, as it
id all too often, the men would have to pick their way down to
herever the horse lay struggling, sometimes in the river itself,
ther times jammed against a tree halfway down the slope. It was
n awful feeling to see something as precious and as big as a
orse tumble like a pebble down a rocky mountainside, and the
ien climbing down after it would take their guns, expecting to
ave to shoot it.

It was amazing that so far they had not had to shoot a single
illen horse, and not a one had been hurt badly. They had hide
:raped off and gashes cut in their shoulders or flanks, and they
ould struggle white-eyed, flailing their hooves, trying to get off
ieir backs or sides and out of the stone rubble, and it would be
while after they were on their feet before the men could tell
hether they would have to be shot or not. But as they had no
roken legs, the men would soothe them, reload them, and then
art the slow, lunging, sliding, clacking, steep climb back up to
ie trail, leading those wonderful, pitiful, bleeding beasts and
icouraging them until they were back in the pack train again.
he horses were fine and lovely and no one wanted ever to have

805

to shoot them, but there was a little edge of secret disappointment in it sometimes, because if a horse had been truly crippled and it had been necessary to shoot it, there would have been meat to eat. As it was, there was no meat. These mountains were as empty of game as the Shoshonis had warned they would be.

The Shoshonis were but a memory now. They had kept their word and helped Captain Lewis and his men carry the baggage over the divide and, after some hard bargaining, had sold twenty-nine horses to the white men, and finally had said farewell to these rich white men, and had gone on down to the plains of the Missouri for their fall buffalo hunt. They had gone down, taking with them memories of strange new foods and sugar cubes and fiddle music and a black man, taking with them promises that white men someday would bring them guns and good steel tools and iron kettles.

And the white men had gone in the other direction, toward the pass through the mountains, to find the westerly rivers that would lead them to the legendary Stinking Lake, where the Shoshonis had never gone.

Sacajawea was still with the white men. Something had happened to her among her people, after her miraculous and joyous return to them, something that had made her decide not to stay with them after all, but to continue with the white men even though she had served her intended role as interpreter among her people. The Shoshoni women, after a few days of hovering around her and her baby and caressing them weepily and wonderingly, had begun looking at her with puzzlement and envy, scolding her for joining men in councils, even for having a husband who cooked.

She did not fit anymore within the ring of protective mountains and the narrow concerns of the Shoshoni women. She had been over too many horizons and heard too many tongues. Her husband thought the Shoshonis too poor and wanted to go back eventually, to the Mandans. And Red Hair was going on toward the setting sun.

And so now Sacajawea, with her papoose bundled in the red blanket on her back, rode on a horse of her own near the head of the column, hanging on grimly as the animal picked its way along precipitous paths more suitable for mountain goats. She was quiet, her heart doubtless wrung out by her bittersweet sojourn of a mere fortnight among her long-lost people. As the column snaked its way over vast screes of rock trash and around rocky monoliths or fallen pines scattered like jackstraws on the slopes, sometimes almost doubling back on itself, William, at its head, would find himself across from Sacajawea, above or below, going up while she went down or down as she went up, and he would look over at her little fine dark face set against whatever she was feeling inside. He would try to imagine what it would be like to return to his family after this voyage and then have to leave them immediately with no certainty of ever seeing them again, and he knew that whatever she had just come through, it was at least as bad as that would be.

Usually her eyes would be on the trail just under her horse's forefeet or on the steep depths below. But much of the time, she would be looking forward at the Red Hair Chief, at his broad back, at the long, swaying fringes of elkskin on the yoke of his coat, at the queue of red hair hanging over his collar from under the lynx-fur cap.

It had been hard for her to choose to leave her people, and she would have felt colder and emptier and bleaker than winter if she could not have looked ahead now and then to see the Red Hair Chief.

It seemed to her that if she could keep following within sight of him it did not matter where she went.

THERE WAS NOW ANOTHER INDIAN WITH THE CORPS OF DIScovery, and he rode or walked always in front.

He was a wiry little old man with an unpronounceable name that the captains had shortened and anglicized to Toby.

Toby was so dark and wrinkled and skinny that Sergeant Gass had described him as "a raisin with bones," and although he had been recruited from among the Shoshonis he was not a Shoshoni. He was a displaced member of the Nez Percé, or Pierced-Nose, nation who lived to the northwest of the Shoshonis, over on the western side of the great mountain range which now lay on their left as they rode northward.

The captains had named this range the Bitterroot Mountains, after a new plant they had discovered there, a hardy little needle-leafed flower with a thick, bitter-fleshed, dark-skinned root. Despite their urgency, the captains were still complying with Thomas Jefferson's instructions, still collecting, classifying, and describing the new forms of life they found in this strange land. The bitterroot was a food of the hungry Shoshonis.

Toby himself, as a member of a newly found tribe, was a new and unheard-of life form for the captains. He had a few yellow teeth in the front of his mouth only, and through the cartilage between his nostrils he wore what appeared at first to be a sliver of white bone the size of a short pencil, but was actually a tu-

807

bular seashell. His people on the Columbia River, he said, traded for these with the Indians who lived down on the coast of the Great Stinking Water. Toby seemed to value this ornament more than anything he had, except his new nickname.

William had met many remarkable Indians, great chiefs all across the continent, but was coming to believe that this wizened, insignificant runt Toby was perhaps more remarkable than any of them. There was no explanation why Toby should have been living among the Shoshonis, who had all but ignored him for many years, but it was as if he had been placed in their village by Providence so that he would be available to guide the Corps of Discovery when it should arrive there. None of the Shoshonis, not even Chief Ca-me-ah-wait himself, had known of a passable route to the waters of the Columbia River.

The river that flowed by their main village, the Lemhi, did run into a greater river called the River of No Return, which then roared many days, white and foaming, down between nearly vertical canyon walls into a larger river, known as the Snake, which in turn flowed into the great river that went to the sea. This was the traditional knowledge among the Shoshonis, though none living had ever tried to go down that River of No Return. But, Ca-me-ah-wait had said, there is an old man of the Pierced-Nose nation here, who is said to know a way through the mountains farther north used by his people when they cross to go down to the plains for buffalo, for there are no buffalo west of the mountains. And thus by the narrowest luck William had found old Toby with the shell through his nose, who was probably the only man living on this side of the mountains who could show them a passable way through these Bitterroot Mountains to a river where canoes would not be smashed to splinters. With Sacajawea's help, William had interviewed Toby.

Toby was cheerful and agile. He looked like a man of seventy years, and might have been fifty or sixty. But he was as springy and quick-minded and far-seeing as a man of thirty, and he had immediately taken a great liking to the Red Hair Chief and said, yes, he would be very happy to go and show the northern pass where his people crossed the mountains. William had told him he would be well paid for this, and so old Toby had thrown in his lot with the Red Hair Chief. Late last month, while waiting for the main party to make its carry over the divide, William and his party, with Toby, had ridden forty miles down the Lemhi to look at the River of No Return and see if it was as bad as the Indians had said.

It had proved to be that bad, or worse. William had explored several miles down its terrible canyon, whose walls were too steep for even the sure-footed Shoshoni horses to walk, and where the water had swirled and roared so loudly it had been necessary to shout a conversation. William had done his best trying to plan a means of moving canoes down that river, but finally had determined that it would not have been possible even to ease them down through the maelstrom on the ends of ropes; for even to attempt that risky technique would have required cutting a road through the solid rock of the cliffs for miles and miles. No. It had been true, all that had been said about that river.

And so now, with all the party together again and its faith placed in old Toby's memory and the patient strength of twenty-nine horses, they were making their way a hundred miles northward, through land only a little less precipitous, to the Nez Percé crossing place that Toby with his strange, throaty, toothless way of speaking called Lolo. They were passing between two parallel ranges so high that the sun rose late in the morning and set early in the evening. They calculated that they were nearly a mile above sea level now, and their rare clear-day sightings on the snow-covered Bitterroot peaks to their left had showed some of them standing a mile higher. This barrier of grim gray stone and deep snow seemed to stretch forever northward barring their way to the west, and they could only hang onto their trust in the sinewy old man with a shell in his nose, and follow him to where he said the Lolo Pass was.

One of the discouraging thoughts that preoccupied the captains, now that they were traveling northward again, was that their celestial sightings showed they were only about a hundred miles due west of the Gates of the Rocky Mountains, through which they had passed a month and a half earlier. They had labored almost three hundred miles out of their way in order to obey Jefferson's instructions and go to the headwaters of the Missouri. In accomplishing that objective they had expended more than a month of precious summertime. But they had been obeying Jefferson's directives, so there was no point in moping about that easier way they might have come. And they had accomplished plenty in those extra fifty days.

"One of us might split off a party of horse on the way back east next year and explore out that route," Lewis said one evening in camp, gazing eastward. "The other could bring the main party back the way we came, and rejoin at the Falls."

It was good to hear Lewis talking a year ahead; he had been very gloomy since their disappointment of the River of No Return. This expedition, William suspected, was more of a strain on Lewis's soul than he would ever admit. It was the biggest thing in his life; it was his obsession; and not many of his fore-plans had to go awry to sink him into a lowering funk.

Lewis was not as confident about old Toby as William was, and did not like to rely entirely on the memory of one old man for a safe passage down the western watershed. Sometimes Lewis would sit by the fire staring balefully across at the merry old fellow as if he took him for a complete fraud. The increasing severity of the weather, the closing in of winter, the scarcity of game to feed his men, further depressed Lewis. The camps now were usually huddled among howling pines, peppered by sleet, and sometimes the whole diet consisted of roots and seeds from Sacajawea's long and patiently accumulated hoard—what York liked to call her "mouse food."

And so it was good now to hear Lewis talking about next year, about the return trip, and to keep things in that vein, William said:

"If we do divide the party on the way back, tell y' what I'd love to do, and that is, find the head of the Yellowstone and return by it. See what kind o' country it runs through!"

Lewis looked at him for a long time, then said, "You never see too much country, do you?"

And at last he smiled.

THE RIVER THAT RAN NORTHWARD THROUGH THIS VALLEY was wide and swift and gravel-bottomed but it had no salmon in it, which convinced William that it must have high waterfalls somewhere farther down. Toby did not know about the lower part of this river because it ran far to the north and was not the way his people came through the mountains.

They named this the Clark River, as William had been the first white man to see it. The trail was easier now, on the gently sloping meadows above the banks. On September 9, as they came up the valley of this river, the sun at last came out. The last shreds of cloud dragged their shadows up over the snowy mountains to the east, and the sky was clear.

For a few minutes this cheered everyone. They felt the sun on their chilled and aching limbs and faces, and began taking off their damp, stinking coats and shirts to let them hang and dry and to let the sunlight caress their skin. They led the horses along, beaming, basking, for a little while. But then the sun also warmed up the flies, which had been waiting out the chill, and they came by millions from wherever they had been, and began

810

feeding on the men and horses, clustering around eyes and nostrils, gathering behind ears and in folds of skin and on sweaty backs to drill for blood. Soon everyone was cursing and slapping at the bold sharp bites, and spotted and stained with blood, and the horses were jumpy, swishing their tails madly and twitching their ears. The soldiers got to the keg of animal grease as soon as there was a rest stop, and slathered the stuff all over the exposed parts of their bodies.

The hunters kept coming back empty-handed. "I don't understand it," growled Collins, "why there ain't a single meat-bearin' animal in this whole God-blamed valley."

Sergeant Ordway slapped the side of his neck, killing a dozen flies at one blow. "I do," he said. "These flies et 'em all up, cracked their bones, an' sucked the marrow. Then they picked their teeth with the bones, an' crawled down t' hide an' wait in ambush for us to come along."

By afternoon the hunters had managed to kill nothing but three geese, which provided about one bite of meat and a cupful of broth for each of the famished men. There was no flour left.

In the evening Toby rode ahead over the meadow to look at the mouth of a large creek that came down from the mountains in the west. He came galloping back with his face crinkled in pleasure. He reined up in front of the captains and pointed to the creek.

"Lolo," he gurgled.

They brought Sacajawea up to talk to him in Shoshoni and find out if he was sure of it. He swore he was. How was he so sure? Taste, he said, making a cupped hand gesture under his mouth. There were hot medicine springs near the top of the pass, where his people would sometimes drink and bathe, and one could taste a trace of the minerals even here at the bottom of Lolo.

They rode over to a pleasant, brushy bottom at the mouth of the creek. The captains tasted the clear, icy water. It tasted like pure snowmelt.

"You taste any minerals?" Lewis asked.

"Not a bit," William said. They looked curiously at Toby, and had Sacajawea tell him they could not taste it. He looked a bit indignant at that. Then he talked rapidly to her.

"I to drink," she said, dismounting. "He say, whitemen all time tobacco-mouth, not can taste." She knelt at the edge and drank. She stood up, and nodded. "Medicine spring," she said, pointing up the rugged valley. William looked at Lewis and shrugged.

"Well, old friend Tobacco-Mouth," he said. "Looks like this is where we start to climb over the Bitterroots."

THEY NAMED THE PLACE TRAVELER'S REST, AND MADE A day's camp here to allow the horses to graze and rest up for the big climb. The place was black with flies but otherwise comfortable. The hunters were sent out all the next day in hopes that they might get in a store of meat for the climb. They had no luck.

There was nothing to eat but some half-spoiled dried fish.

During the halt at Traveler's Rest, three men of the Flathead tribe, armed only with bows and arrows, were led warily into camp by John Colter, who had been hunting up in Lolo valley. Colter had encountered them several miles up the creek, and had scared them half out of their minds by his strange appearance, but then had convinced them of his friendliness by laying down his rifle and making sign language.

Toby conversed with them and learned that they were trying to track a pair of Shoshonis who recently had stolen horses from them. They confirmed that this was the way to the big river that led to the sea. They said the crossing of the mountains required five sleeps, but would take longer if there should be snowstorms up there. In their opinion, the snowstorms were a certainty.

The soldiers were fascinated by the language of these Indians, which sounded like a gurgling in the throat with an impediment on the tongue. "Y' ever hear a Welshman talk, Cap'n?" Private Whitehouse asked.

"Aye," William said.

"I have too, and if that ain't Welsh brogue, I'm deaf. Y' ask me, these sound more Welsh than the Mandans did."

That revived the old haunting legend of the lost Welsh clan, which seemed even more eerie now in these towering mountains than it had a thousand miles back on the plains around Fort Mandan. And so Lewis took time to write down a selected vocabulary of their words, in hopes that Mr. Jefferson might someday find out whether the words seemed Welsh in origin.

That evening the hunters came in with four deer, a beaver, and a grouse. They made for a very welcome meal, and a little left over for breakfast.

THE HORSES HAD STRAYED TO GRAZE AND NEEDED TO BE rounded up in the morning, then loaded, so it was three o'clock in a hot afternoon before the column waded through the stream and started up the right bank of the creek along the old Nez

Percé hunting road. It was a narrow and steep valley, but the trail had been sensibly laid down and was relatively easy to follow. But as the climb continued, the mountainsides around every bend looked steeper and rougher and more forbidding. The creek itself, clear as windowglass and ruffled with white where it tore around boulders, zigzagged crazily down the winding valley through thick undergrowth and under fallen pines, sending its liquid music up the slopes to the trail. It was a constant background tone under the clatter of rocks, blowing of horses, the shouts and sometimes snatches of song as the column climbed.

But it was hard to sing much on an empty stomach when the last cheerful light of the sun was fading off the snowy mountaintops on the far side of the valley to leave the canyon a cold, stark gray, when the ragged little junipers were beginning to look like hunching dwarfs and the dead pines like gaunt ghosts, and soon there was no singing and little talk. Despite the effort of walking, the men were quickly chilled in the twilight. The flies had gone with the sunlight, and that was good, but the climbing had made the men hungry as wolves, and they had not heard a single gunshot roll down the valley. The hunters up there evidently had found nothing all day, and it would be too dark soon for them to get anything.

They had come seven miles up the steep pass when they reached a place level enough to make a crowded camp. It was an old Indian lodging ground. The old lodgepoles lying around were brittle or rotting, and grass grew amid the charred wood of campfires that had been extinguished for two or three years. These old black chunks were thrown onto the new deadwood the soldiers dragged into camp.

The next morning they awoke covered with frost. Everything was white with frost: the evergreens, the grasses in the little meadow, the baggage. The hunters went out early, up through the sparkling landscape. By the time the pack horses were loaded, the frost was gone with all its beauty, and the climbing valley ahead looked gray and dark and flinty.

They started up. The timber became thicker, the valley narrowed, and the mountainsides became steeper. Soon they were again moving up and around such steepnesses that the horses were in danger of tumbling. They crossed several small, roaring, ice-cold creeks.

"Lookee there, Cap'n." Sergeant Ordway pointed to a large patch of pine trees whose bark had been peeled. "What d' you reckon 'bout *that*?"

William asked Sacajawea to ask Toby, and his reply was that

813

his people sometimes would have to eat the inner bark on these particular pines by the time they had come this far from the west.

"By th' Eternal, I hope we never git *that* hongry," muttered Ordway. As if in response, the bang of a hunter's gun reverberated down the valley. Several more shots were heard during the afternoon as the pack train traveled along a ridge. Then the trail led back down to the creek, and here the troops were delighted to find their hunters skinning out four small deer. After these had been entirely consumed, a more cheerful caravan resumed the march, going across two more creeks and then turning away from the gorge at a place where the trail started up the ridge of a high mountain. This was a very rough and rocky ascent, through thick timber, and sometimes the only sign of the Nez Percé road was the worn-off bark of trees, where horses and their packs had rubbed against them in narrow passing-places.

Evening was coming and the descending sun now flashed off the creek below. Up here now there was no water at all, and they plodded on into the dusk, men and beasts gasping through parched throats. The road now turned back down toward the creek. In the fading light the descent became even more frightening, but there was no place on the mountainside level enough to stop. Almost in darkness now, they crashed and rattled and grunted down through the woods, the horses sometimes almost on their rumps.

Somehow, though, they reached the creek without a mishap. It was ten o'clock at night and they could scarcely see where to take the horses to drink. It was a bad place to have stopped; it was in the woods still and there was almost no grass for the horses. They were unloaded and hobbled. The slope was so steep that there was not a level place to lay down a blanket. The men had to sleep jammed against tree roots and rocks and baggage to keep from sliding or rolling into the creek.

The next morning everyone arose in the half-light, aching from their awkward sleep, and went out limping through the chilly forest to round up the horses. They recovered all but one horse and a colt. There was not a sign of them.

"Well, we can't hold up the whole army for 'em," Lewis said. "We'll send the hunters back to look for 'em maybe, but my guess is they fell in the creek and couldn't get out."

They climbed two miles along the creek under a cloudy sky. The air was tangy with the smell of wet evergreens, but soon another odor began to creep under that sharpness; a thick smell like that of bad eggs. And then through a break in the trees they saw what appeared to be wisps of smoke rising through dark woods at the base of a large bluff of weather-rounded mossy boulders. "There, I'll wager, is the hot spring Toby spoke of," William said.

They walked out into a pleasant, humid little field of bright green grass, crisscrossed with deer paths and Indian trails. William went up toward the steaming bluff, sniffing the moist, warm odor. Hot water spouted from fissures in the dark wall of rock. He knelt and put his forefinger into a steaming rivulet and snatched it out again; the water was nearly boiling. A few feet down, Indians had built a small stone dam to contain the hot water and make a bathing pool. Here in the pool the water was quite hot, but not unbearably hot.

He put his hand in up to the wrist and watched the hand grow pink and felt the old cold-morning aches go out of it, and sighed with pleasure. He sipped a handful and tasted the good, strong mineral flavor. It was surprising that anything smelling so fetid could taste so refreshing.

THE MEN WERE LETTING THE HORSES GRAZE OFF THE RICH grass, and were themselves wandering around the springs exclaiming about the strange beauty of the place, stooping to dip up handfuls of the mineral water. "Oh, Cap'n, oh Cap'n, oh Cap'n," moaned Shields—William could not see him through the steam, but realized just then that he knew every man's voice—"oh, Cap'n, I'd give up a week's rations to be 'lowed a whole day here, just to lallygag in that there pool till all th' rheumatiz an' all the sprains and strains be gone out o' my old carcass."

"Well, my man," Lewis's voice came up, "if we'd come on this place at the after end o' the day instead of early morn like this, why, here's where we'd camp and soak. But you know as well as I do, we can't dawdle anywhere. Ordway! Pryor! Gass!" He told the three sergeants to let the men drink from the hot springs, that it probably would be good for their innards. "Let 'em wash up in it," he said, "and soak their feet a bit if they like, but in half an hour we move on." There was a chorus of groans and grumbles, but it quickly turned into a cheerful uproar as the men enjoyed what they were allowed to of the luxury.

Lewis appeared through the steam and sat down beside William and took off his moccasins and wool stockings and eased his feet into the water. William did the same. "I'd love nothing more myself than to lie in that and soak like some caesar at

Pompeii," Lewis said, "but give men a luxury this time o' day and it'll turn their resolve to a mush. We'd never get 'em moving again."

"Aye," William said. He knew that was true on the march. "But speakin' of Pompeii, look at that."

Little Pompey, naked, was being laid down on a blanket on the edge of the hot pond by his mother. He squirmed and cooed at the sensations of warmth and dampness. And Sacajawea herself, oblivious to the presence of a dozen soldiers who were lounging around the pool with their feet or arms in the hot water, sat and took off her calf-high moccasins, then stood and pulled her tunic over her head. She stood naked, slim and tawny as a doe, for a moment, while the men got strange, faraway looks in their eyes. Then she picked up the infant and stepped carefully down into the water. Lewis's face clouded with outrage and he opened his mouth, but William laid a hand on his arm. "She didn't understand your order," he said. "Look, neither did Toby." The old guide, a rack of bone and sinew covered by a map of veins, had cast off his clothes and was stepping into the water on another side of the pool.

And in a moment the squaw was modestly immersed to her ribs in the water, bathing her child in such a natural and delightful and motherly a way that, if there were any desires stirred in the men by the sight of her, they were only the old, good desires for loving kindness, for comfort, for tenderness.

A FEW HOURS LATER, WILLIAM FOLLOWED TOBY ONTO A treeless saddle ridge that connected two wooded peaks. William stopped on the ridge, squinting against a damp, chill wind that seemed to rush up over the saddle like draft up a flue, and, clamping his hand over his hat to keep it from sailing off, clenched his teeth and groaned at the sight that spread before him.

Stretching off to the west, as far as he could see, was a maze of dark, wind-scoured ranges, jagged and long, their steep sides black with tamarack and larch, fir and pine and enormous cedars, with snowy peaks poking up white here and there along the ridges like backbones jutting through an animal's hide. Down alongside the nearest spur and off westward among the ridges tore a creek wilder and faster and more tortuous than the Lolo. Beyond each shaggy ridge was another ridge, and beyond that, another, each fading a little grayer, away and away; they appeared to be an infinity of mountains, eventually fading into the clouds and hazes and snows of a wintry sky.

816

Toby did not stop, but headed down the other side of the ridge.

Lewis came up beside William, tying his hat on his head by passing a bandanna over it and under his chin. He looked stricken. "I wasn't expecting this," he said. "D' you suppose that Toby really knows a way?"

"Shhh," William warned. The men were coming up onto the ridge with them now, and every man had that same stunned look. "Don't seem to doubt, or they'll lose heart for certain."

No one knew how far these mountains went. The Flatheads at the foot of the pass had said passage would require five days if there was no snow. Old Toby had not forewarned them of this awful spectacle from the top of the Lolo Pass.

Lewis was looking dubiously down the slope now at the tiny figure of the old Indian, who was standing in a gray-brown meadow, gazing now toward the ranked mountains, now back up to the ridge where the white men stood in the path of the wind. *Come on*, the attitude of his fragile-looking little body seemed to say. *Come on.*

Lewis said again, softly so the men would not hear him doubting: "D' you really think he knows, or is he lost?"

William gritted his teeth, suddenly annoyed by this question. It was William who had found the old man and judged him capable and hired him on, and now Lewis was implying that it might have been bad judgment. It was not that William was being blamed for this doubt, not yet anyway, but if Toby did get the expedition lost, William would be held accountable for it in Lewis's mind, even if Lewis did not, as he probably would not, say anything about it.

"Just ye look at 'im," William said in Lewis's ear. "Does he look like a man who doesn't know where he's a-goin'?"

William himself, looking out over the infinity of hostile mountains, was now something a little short of confident. But he turned to the men, who stood huddling in the lee of the pack horses, and put on his most reassuring Clark grin, and yelled, "Come on, boys! It's all downhill from here!"

He was astonished to hear someone—he thought it was Private Potts, but in this wind could not be sure—yell:

"We heard that before!"

William gritted his teeth, glanced at Lewis's angry face, then chose to make it all sound like jest.

"Aye," he yelled back, "and ye'll hear it again till ye know it's true!" He pointed at the gray sky. "That's up!" Then he pointed toward the little figure of Toby below. "That's down! Come on, boys, down we go!"

THEY DESCENDED FROM THE RIDGE, AND WITHIN A FEW hundred yards found a spring gushing icy water that leaped down this westerly slope and down through a glade that opened onto a large meadow before disappearing into the dense forest. Far below, in a v-shaped chasm whose steep walls were almost black with evergreens, short chutes of the stream could be seen dashing white and tiny down its narrow bed. Bald eagles and ospreys rode the wind above the treetops. The captains named this Glade Creek, and made a camp at the lower end of the meadow. Next morning they ate the rest of the meat, loaded the horses, and started up a steep, high mountain spur.

On this side of the windy ridge, the forest was so different it was like still another world. This was a wet forest, and it was dense and lush and tangled. Now as well as the familiar pine, tamarack, spruce, and fir, there were tall, delicately shaped larch, enormous cedars a hundred and fifty feet tall, their deep-fissured, gray-barked trunks as much as six feet thick, and giant hemlocks with their bent-over crowns. The trees were like thousands of black-green spires. The earth was damp, grassy in the glades, decorated with huge ferns in the woods. But little of the ground could be seen in these forests; almost every foot of forest floor was crisscrossed with the gigantic, mossy carcasses of fallen cedars and firs, the older ones half-rotted into the soil, the newer ones in lesser states of decay, the most recent ones often shattered and split by having fallen on the others, or upon boulders; great bare splinters sometimes slanted thirty or forty feet through the ferns. The creek was fed by mossy springs every few feet, thick with beaver-gnawed saplings. The springs and brooklets trilled down through steep gullies, parting and rejoining, sand- and rock-bottomed, bridged by the huge trees that had fallen over them. The Indian trail wound ingeniously among these steepnesses and huge tangles, but every few yards there would be a new tree trunk, split and twisted by the violence of its fall, and these recent obstacles had to be climbed over, walked around, or, sometimes, cut through by axmen. As they labored in these confines, the choppers began to notice an effect of yesterday's visit at the mineral springs. Their bowels were active and full of gas. They broke wind at each other like bugles, then wheezed with laughter at the sulphurous odors they produced.

After some four miles of such tortuous labor and climbing,

818

the caravan found itself traveling southwestward along a rocky ridge crest, through stunted and wind-blasted trees, looking far down at one creek on their right and another on their left. Now William, having been in the tangled, choked valleys, could understand why much of the Nez Percé trail seemed to seek ridges. Maybe the wind was as cold and sharp as a knife and the sun seared one's face without even warming it and there was no water to drink, but there was some open space here to travel through.

This ridge gave them a roof-top view of the world for a while, but soon the snow-topped mountainous labyrinth ahead grew vague and gray as clouds closed in, and a cold, penetrating rain, mixed with hail, began to pelt them and sting their faces. They bent their heads and went onward, concentrating on the mud and slippery rocks of the ridgetop. The slopes now fell away on both sides for a few hundred feet until they faded into invisibility. The ridge now was like a narrow island in a sea of cold, dank gray with no horizons and no foundations.

The ridge ran out, and they came sliding and crashing down out of the clouds in a winding, four-mile descent into the valley. Here the creeks they had seen on their left and right converged. They crossed the left fork and immediately began to climb another ridge. "Koos-Koos-Kee," Toby said, pointing down at the stream.

It was another four-mile ascent over and around fallen timber, and put them eventually upon another cloud-cloaked ridge. Now they could hear the Koos-Koos-Kee rushing through the gray oblivion far below them on their right. They picked their way along the ridge for another five miles until it began to descend, and again they scrabbled down out of the misty clouds and into the rain-blackened forest, emerging in a marshy valley where two more fast streams converged, now swollen almost to the size of rivers. And now something seemed to be wrong with old Toby. He was as agile as ever, but he was hesitating.

Lewis came up and put a hand on William's arm. "Your man," he said, "is confused."

WILLIAM COULD NOT DENY IT NOW. THE OLD INDIAN seemed perplexed by the sight of this second fork. Yet they had not left the Indian trail. The path could be seen; there were still rubbed places on the bark of the trees in narrow passageways. "We're on an Indian trail," William murmured feebly. "But is it the right one?"

Toby squatted on the rocky bank of the stream that poured in from the left. He tasted a palmful of water and looked up and down. There was a steep, black mountainside rising almost directly from the far side of the valley below the fork, and another climbing ridge on this side. The streams were crystalline, running fast over a bed of jumbled, water-rounded rocks, bluish-green, rust-brown, white-veined, as small as fists and as big as horses.

Toby got up now and clambered among the boulders, then gave a shout, barely heard over the rush of water. The captains ordered the troop to stay, and took Sacajawea and Charbonneau down to follow him.

He was pointing at the remains of a lattice of woven willow that lay at a place where rocks had been moved to make a chain of step-stones all the way across the stream. He talked rapidly, often making arching motions with his right hand and touching his lips. After a while Sacajawea and Charbonneau were able to translate. It was a place where Toby's people came down to catch much salmon in the springtime, he said. That was why there was a trail down to it.

"And where, pray tell, is the main trail?" Lewis demanded to know. It was getting darker and darker in the gorge.

Toby looked sad and sheepish. He pointed across the river to the long, high, gloomy wall of mountainside on the right side of the valley, and talked.

"On up," Charbonneau interpreted through his squaw.

"Damnation!" Lewis snapped.

It had been a bad error. It eventually became clear what had happened. Coming down off that first ridge to the first fork, Toby had come onto several converging trails, two of which led up the spurs onto ridges. In the mist he had taken the left trail instead of the right and had brought them onto the wrong mountain. He had not begun to suspect his error until the unexpected descent to this fork. Lewis's mouth was bitten pale, a mean slash amid the dark stubble of his whiskers. He looked as if he wanted to kill Toby.

"It's a bother," William soothed him, "but not a hard mistake to comprehend. He doesn't come through here every day, y' know."

The error would cost them at least another day, they reckoned. They would have to cross the river here, just above its confluence, and then go along the other bank until they found a place where they could climb that dark mountainside and regain the trail on the ridge.

"At least," William said, putting a firm hand on Lewis's shoulder, "we're not lost." Lewis seemed less sure of that.

They forded the icy, roaring north fork in half-light, getting wet to the waist, and fought their way through darkening, dripping woods, among enormous trees, for two miles before they found a place open enough to camp on. They were famished and almost too fatigued to stand up. The hunters had had no luck; they had only two grouse. These would not have fed two men, as spent and cold as these were.

"Well, then," Lewis said, brightening a little, "I reckon it's time we got into that portable soup we've been carryin' three thousand miles for just such an occasion." It was another of his prized purchases, and he was as eager to try it as he had been to assemble his iron boat. Water was fetched from the roaring river and kettles were hung on poles over fires. Tins of the stuff—lackluster dried vegetables fortified with iron sulfate—were opened and dumped in, along with the two grouse. The men waited, both eager and dubious, as the stuff softened and clouded the water. Then it was served out into the men's cups. The first reaction made it clear that it was as poor an experiment as the iron boat had been. Sergeant Gass spat into the fire.

"By the guts o' God!" he roared. "It's puke! It's portable puke, that's all it is!"

Most agreed. "Quick," someone shouted between gagging sounds, "fish out them grouses afore they git spoilt!"

There seemed to be as much iron in the soup as there had been in the collapsible boat, and it felt as if it were scouring all the enamel off their teeth. Lewis sat bravely forcing down one spoonful after another, listening to the exaggerated sounds of retching and moaning. William grinned at Lewis, a strange, half-nauseated grin. "Y' could court-martial 'em for disrespect of army rations, if they weren't so many in agreement."

"Beggin' your pardon, Captain," said Ordway, coming around the fire, "the men say this stuff—er, good as it might be—won't do, chilled an' tuckered as we all are. They request permission, sir, to butcher a horse."

"You know, Ordway, we've just enough horses left to carry baggage. We can't be killing 'em."

"Then one o' the colts, sir. That's what we brought colts fer."

The captains themselves could feel their bodies clamoring for meat. This ghastly vegetable brew might keep them from starving, but would not give them the strength or inner fire they needed in their condition.

"Permission granted," Lewis said.

A wolf was howling down the valley. In the pause between its quavering wild notes, William heard, in the trees just outside the firelight, the ax-blow between the blindfolded eyes, the thud

821

of the falling body as the long-legged colt crumpled to the ground.

The meat, as Ordway wrote in his journal that night, "eat verry well at this time." And the creek they had crossed above the camp they named Colt Killed Creek.

WILLIAM AWOKE IN GRAY LIGHT WITH THE SOUND OF THE river constant in his ears. He saw York moving along the shore, his breath condensing against the dark backdrop of the wooded mountain across the stream, then saw him stooping to gather wood for the morning fire. The route of yesterday's march was nagging at William's mind, so he extracted note paper and a pencil from his clothing and made sketches of the way they had come and the way they should have come.

The party set out after a breakfast of colt meat and picked its way with great difficulty over steep stone spurs and through enormous tangles for about four miles, through groves of great cedars, past several old Indian campsites, until they arrived at a more elaborate salmon-fishing site, where there were remains of many of the willow weirs. Here a much-worn trail turned to the right and led toward the long mountain. The riverbank looking even more impassable ahead, they decided to ascend the mountainside here and regain the main trail along the mountain ridge. They asked Toby about it, and, seeming glad that they still valued his guidance, he said it was the course they should take.

The trail wormed up a steep, rock-strewn rise about a hundred feet, then the slope became gentler, and on this slope the brush was jungle-thick—willows, alders, little maples, chokeberry honeysuckle and huckleberry and great ferns—on a spongy yielding, water-squishy soil almost like peat, mostly of rotting plant fibers. The men and horses were wet constantly by droplet shaken off leaves; their moccasins and the horses' hooves were stained with black muck. They snaked around fallen cedars and firs and pines for ten minutes, sloshing through springs that ran everywhere; then suddenly found themselves at the base of a wall of boulders, spruce trees, lodgepole pines and larches: the mountainside itself.

It was the steepest incline they had encountered anywhere. The Indian trail, probably used only for access to the salmon fishery, could not climb straight up such a grade. Instead, it was a switchback trail, a foot or two wide; it would ascend laterally across the face of the mountain, then double back for twenty to fifty yards, then redouble. At any moment the head of the car avan was looking down onto the hats of a line of men going left below it, farther down, the hats of a line going right, then another going left. Other times the leaders could not see anyone below because of the density of the evergreen foliage.

The voice of Sergeant Gass, who was bringing up the rear, roared up the trail once: "Potts, ye blaggard! Watch out up there! Your horse just beshit the top o' my hat!" It got a laugh all up the line, but it was a reminder that if a horse fell here it might well fall on two or three horses or men below.

The trail was muddy and slippery; sometimes it was blocked by tree trunks that had to be climbed over, by wind-felled pines that had to be ducked under. As horses are not ducking and crawling animals, these latter obstacles created the worst problems. Such trees had to circumvented by wild scrambles almost straight up, to the next level of the path above. Or, if that were simply too steep, the axes would come out and the trunk would be cut through while the whole caravan waited. Sometimes these trunks were three feet thick, and would have required hours to chop or saw through, and when such a one blocked a path, there was nothing to do but cut a shorter zigzag path through the undergrowth and rejoin the Indian path farther up.

By noon they had traversed back and forth more than a hundred times, climbing five miles by William's estimate, and still were but halfway up the mountain. He paused at a switchback, sweat steaming in the cold air, and looked down at the tops of trees, at the hats of men, at the packsaddles on horses' backs, at the thick-timbered spurs and mountainsides and ridges enclosing them in every direction, and saw snow falling on mountains to the west, and for an awful moment had a feeling that they were trapped, finally and inescapably trapped, in these endless, gloomy, hungry mountains. Above him now there was little living timber. The whole mountainside from here nearly to the summit was mostly a dead forest, killed by forest fires and mowed down by windstorms, looking like one huge logjam of dead spruces and lodgepoles, scattered like straw, studded with charred fir trunks still standing thirty to fifty feet tall amid the gray debris, softened only by new green pine growth and scrub a few feet tall. It was as bad a tangle as Fallen Timbers, and on a steep slope to boot.

"Eee yah! No!" "Whoa!" And then that awful thumping and crashing and whinnying. William looked down to see a white-and-brown piebald mare below him rolling down the slope, crushing the baggage it carried, including William's own field desk. The horse tumbled through two lines of climbers, miraculously missing everybody, until it was brought to a halt by a sturdy juniper tree forty yards down. Papers and notebooks and pieces of desk lay scattered all the way down. The whole party was halted for an hour, getting the horse back on its feet, checking it over, gathering and repacking the strewn materials, reloading. The pieces of desk were tied in a bundle and put back on the mare, in the wan hope that Shields might be able to repair it. The desk was important, as both captains had been using it as their outdoor office ever since Lewis's desk had been cached.

By midafternoon several more horses had slipped and rolled backward, two of them hurt badly but able to continue because no bones were broken. Up here in the devastated part of the forest, it was lighter but windier. Heavy clouds swept the mountaintop, sometimes hiding it, and the wind moaned. A bald eagle materialized from the underside of a cloud, screamed as if astonished at the sight of these ground creatures intruding in its lofty domain, then soared off eastward and out of sight over a ridge.

By late afternoon, the climbers had reached live timber again, the alpine fir and whitebark pine of the very high country, and the clouds blew open enough to show them the ridge a few hundred feet above. Here there was old snow behind the north sides of boulders and under lightning-blasted trees. All of the horses that had fallen were still coming up, but two other horses had simply given out; they had gone to their knees and then keeled over on their sides to lie on the slope, unable to rise, slobbering, sides heaving, necks stretched. Their loads had been distributed among the other horses, and those two defeated creatures had been left behind. It was no use to kill them for meat; they were too gaunt and poor; there wasn't time to butcher them; and every man and horse was too heavily burdened and exhausted to add even a pound of bad horseflesh to his load.

William's legs were twitching with a fatigue that had become like a pain of burning; his chest felt as if it would break open with its efforts to expand and extract some oxygen from the thin mountain air, his throat was parched and raw from gasping, and his shoulders were aching and raw from the pull and chafing of his knapsack. He reckoned they had climbed eight or ten miles on the zigzag path to reach this ridge. Below, in the dismal gorge, the fast river was invisible and too distant to be heard under the moan and whistle of the wind.

Scannon had long since given up his desire to move; he wanted to lie down and lick his bloody paws or sleep, and now York had made a leash for him from a rawhide strap and kept yanking it to make him come along, bellowing now and then: "Come 'long, you lazy black scound'l!" This, and the collapse of the two horses, redoubled William's admiration for his men.

They're stronger than horses and dogs, he thought.

They were on the ridge at last. There was the main Indian road again, that beaten footpath around rocks and along the crest, leading westward on this long, long ridge. And down on the other side of the mountain was another river gorge, probably the north fork of the Koos Koos Kee, William presumed, a thread of water winding below still another distant ridge, beyond which he could see peaks of snow, faint through the mist.

Now it was deep dusk, and the chill wind whipped the warmth of climbing out of sweat-drenched clothes immediately, and every man was trembling and twitching with cold and hunger and pain. Only Sacajawea and her papoose were riding. Everyone else walked and led a laden horse. William looked at her. Her blanket was pulled over her head and she held it closed over her mouth, her eyes half shut, caught up in destiny, again going away and away from her people. The horses limped along the ridge as the caravan moved on in the howling, blue-gray dusk, the distant mountains growing dimmer and then being swallowed by darkness. They went on, over knobs bare of trees, along saddles of ridgeline where the bent trees shuddered in the windblast; they went on, looking for a level place to camp. They would have to stop soon. They could hardly see the road.

Toby yelled. He had found water.

A small spring gushed from rocks a little way below the ridge. It was not a level enough place to camp, and there was no grass for the horses, but in the lee of a boulder, a hasty fire was built and a ration of the portable soup was heated. This time the men drank it without complaint. Then the fire was stamped out and the caravan continued along the ridge. Toby assured them there was a place not far ahead where they could stop.

There was old snow underfoot now, and they could see a vague grayness before them, but below everything was black and howling.

At last they were on a wide, rounded eminence. It was the bare, treeless promontory of a mountaintop, and in its center a scarp of stone stood like an old castle wall. The baggage was unloaded and piled near it to make a windbreak. Enough deadwood was found to make a small fire and melt snow for more of the portable soup. The horses were hobbled and let out to forage on the sparse ground cover.

It was all that could be done. No journal-keeping tonight, no washing, no undressing. The flames and sparks of the campfire were whipped by the wind, and soon all the firewood was gone.

The Corps of Discovery rolled, clothes, moccasins, and all, into their blankets and lay down on the trampled snow in utter darkness, on the backbone of a mountain range, pulled their heads inside to muffle the woeful dirge of the wind, some perhaps thinking for a moment of their dismal and Godforsaken circumstances, but were all, except the sentry, plummeting into the numb sleep of exhaustion within ten minutes.

Only the sentry saw the snow begin to fall.

"LORD-A-GOD, WE'RE IN FOR IT NOW!"
Sergeant Ordway's shout, in the whistling wind, made William sit upright in his blanket. He saw a whirling blankness, with shapeless gray lumps here and there where the men were sitting up in their blankets to peer around. Farther out were the ghostly shapes of horses. William shook his blanket, and snow fell off of it. On the ground around him the snow was two or three inches deep. The packsaddles and baggage bundles were almost hidden by drifted snow. He could see as the snowflakes drove across the face of the stony escarpment that they were large flakes. It was no mere flurry. It looked like the kind of a snow that goes on all day.

William's feet and legs and shoulders ached so fiercely that he could hardly move. He thought with heavy dread of the weight of his pack and the walking and climbing that would have to be done today, with the snow making it still harder and more dangerous. But this snow meant more than just hard going: it meant that the Nez Percé trail likely would be obliterated. And it meant that if there were any game animals around, they would be invisible at a hundred yards.

"We'd best make what distance we can early," Lewis said, "while we can still see where the trail is."

"Got a good excuse for skipping breakfast, anyway," William said. "No food." There was nothing left but a few pounds of the dried soup.

Few of the men had stockings anymore. They spent a few minutes wrapping their feet in rags, then mending their moccasins. Sewing the leather was excruciating and clumsy with their cold-stiffened fingers. Men sat huddled over this work, shuddering, their noses running. When they were done, they pulled the repaired moccasins on over the rags on their feet and then rose painfully to go out and round up the horses for loading. But even in the midst of this misery, there was laughter. Some of the men were warming themselves up with a snowball fight. Scannon, who apparently had slept off his fatigue rolled in a ball with his tail over his muzzle, was now among them, leaping to try to catch snowballs in flight.

Sacajawea knelt, her blanket draped tentlike over her, cleaning Pompey's cradleboard and repacking it with new down. She smiled up at William as she administered to the baby. She put the child to her breast, keeping him, as always, close to her skin's warmth and sheltered from the snowy wind. "At least one of our boys is a-gettin' some breakfast today," Sergeant Gass remarked.

THE SNOW WAS TWO INCHES DEEPER BY THE TIME THE PACK train was underway. Parts of the trail were so drifted over it could be found only by watching for worn places on the bark of trees. William and old Toby moved ahead searching for this faint trail. As the drifting snow filled in their footprints almost at once, William had to blaze trees with his tomahawk, chipping away bark at eye level, to leave a way the pack train could see.

You wouldn't think it could be so hard to keep to a trail that runs along a ridge, he thought. And yet he and the old Indian had to backtrack repeatedly; often their progress would lead them to cul-de-sacs or the edges of cliffs, even places where it would be impossible to turn horses around. So these places had to be followed to their dead ends before William could go back, find the true way, and only then make his marks on the trees.

They groped along this ridgetop for hours in this manner. The snow kept falling and the clouds they were in curtained everything beyond one or two hundred yards. The trail went along wooded saddles and over treeless knobs where the wind blew so strong that it was necessary to lean into it. The knobs were blank fields with grass-heads whipping wildly in the wind above waving currents of blowing snow. Far below there would be barely visible treetops, and below them, snow, mist and cloud. Some of these bald ridges seemed as narrow and steep as roof peaks. William, and even old sure-footed Toby, slipped and fell on their sides often on these slippery snowy edges, and William could see this was going to be exceedingly dangerous for the horses, topheavy as they were with their loads. A horse tumbling from here might go down like a sled for hundreds of yards before crashing into a tree or sailing off some invisible cliff down there and would be almost impossible to bring back up, even if unhurt.

The same for a man with a pack, he thought.

Toby ranged here and there tirelessly, cowled like a monk in the buffalo robe wrapped around him, the feathers on his bow twirling in the wind. William remembered how scrawny he had looked naked, how fragile he looked compared with the brawny soldiers, and wondered from where he drew his strength and endurance. When the old guide would turn around to look at him, William would see that dark raisin of a face with the white shell through the nostrils, the hooded eyes darting and searching. The old face never looked worried. That helped William a great deal.

The snow was six to ten inches deep in the open now, and in drift places it was to the thighs. William's moccasins and socks and leggings were soaked through and caked with snow. In the falls he had taken, his elk-hide tunic and mittens had gotten snow-packed and wet. He was as cold and wet all over as he had ever been in his life.

Got to consider, he thought, that my feet could freeze. They well might, even if I keep moving.

One wind-smoothed slope of snow proved to have nothing under it, and he fell through and began sliding down through a cold cascade of snow-clods. He felt a tree limb as he went down and grabbed it. He got to his feet on the slope, heart slamming violently. Toby's face appeared over the crest above him, then broke into a relieved grin. William floundered back up onto the ridge. He stood shivering and brushed snow off his rifle, out of the muzzle and the crevices of the flintlock and the steel frizzen. He took off his mittens so he could work. He cleaned out the powder and recharged it, tilting the small end of the powder horn down into it. While he was doing this he felt a tug at his sleeve.

Toby was pointing forward and down the slope. A few yards below the place where William had fallen, a gray animal was moving, half obscured by blowing snow. William saw its black tail-tuft and the long ears, saw it spring once like a goat from the chest-deep snow onto a ledge, then turn to look curiously up toward the ridge.

A mule deer! It was within easy range, not more than twenty yards below. It was small, but would give the troops at least one mess of venison which they sorely needed.

William raised the rifle to get a bead, and saw as he did so that Toby was notching an arrow on his bowstring.

William squeezed the trigger. The hammer snapped. *Damnation!* He thumbed the hammer back again and squeezed the trigger and again it snapped. He knew the primer was dry; he had just changed it. He cocked the rifle again. Now the animal was starting to move away. It turned and began winding down through a cleft in the ledge, passing for a moment behind a shrub. William heard the *thung!* of Toby's bowstring at the same time he squeezed the trigger. The arrow touched a twig of the shrub and went awry just as William's flintlock snapped for the third time. He clenched his teeth, cocked it and heard it snap again, and watched the deer, moving away slowly into the snow curtain, unhurried, unaware of its absurd good fortune so far. Toby notched another arrow and let it fly, while William examined his rifle again, but the deer was far down now. It apparently heard or saw the arrow pass by, spraddled and leaped a few more steps, then faded into the white whirl as William snapped three more times with the accursed rifle.

He felt even colder now that the excitement of the hunter's chance had drained out of him. He shook his head sadly, and old Toby nodded with sympathy. William saw the trouble now: the flint was loose, apparently dislodged in his fall. He adjusted it and tightened the thumbscrew down—or thought he did, as he could not tell whether his benumbed fingers were giving it any pressure at all. Then he searched in the snow until he found his mitten. He pulled it on and worked his fingers vigorously inside it, but the mitten was soaked and cold. A great shudder shook him down the length of his body. He pointed his rifle down the trail, and Toby nodded and they proceeded on along the howling ridgeline.

At midday they went back two miles and found the pack train coming along. Lewis said several horses had fallen but had been returned to the trail with difficulty. Several men also had taken tumbles down the snowy slopes, but no one had been hurt. "You're showing frostbite on your cheeks there," Lewis said. "When we stop for soup, better get some grease and rub 'em."

"There's grass for the beasts about two hundred yards up yonder," William said.

William looked anxiously around at the men as they huddled in the snow around a bonfire sipping the steaming brew. They were wasting, losing flesh. The horses were pulling at sparse grass in a steeply sloping little meadow where the scouring wind had kept the snow from getting deep.

"I hate to keep going in this snowstorm," William murmured "but I haven't seen a place yet to make a camp."

Lewis nodded. "Just have to keep 'em going," he said. "Got t work our way over this blamed range before the snow gets ov our heads."

William rose, the hot soup eating like acid in the pit of h stomach. "We'll go on ahead," he said. "We'll find a place, swear it."

"Take Colter with you. He hunted all morning and didn't fin so much as a sparrow. His luck's due to change."

William did not mention the mule deer and the failure of h rifle. The party did not need to hear that kind of a hard-luc story just now.

COLTER'S LUCK DID NOT CHANGE. THREE MORE DEER WER seen during the rest of the long and torturous and chilling afte noon, but they vanished into the snow veil like ghosts before sight could be put on them. The clouds stayed on the ridge an the snow kept falling. It took the rest of the afternoon to go s more miles along the crest, the trail growing more and mo faint as snow began sticking to the tree trunks.

THE SNOW WAS GRAYING WITH DUSK WHEN WILLIAM AN Colter found a heavily wooded cove with a running spring, just few yards down the north slope from the ridge. There was not real any level ground, but there was the water and there was a little gras and there was a wealth of fallen deadwood. "This is as good a hom as we're going to find this night," William said. "Best thing we ca do till they catch up is fix up bonfires." Shivering, soaked, the dragged up wood and made high piles of it. "I hear 'em a-comin, now," Colter said when it was almost dark.

"Good. Fire up those piles and I'll walk back and lead 'em in

When William met the head of the column, Lewis was loo ing wild-eyed with anxiety. Then he saw the flames glimmeri through the trees and managed a smile. "No game," Willia said, "but we can warm up their outsides anyway."

"Might have to let 'em kill another colt," Lewis pante "They've got to have some meat. Got to."

York came alongside William as he led them along to t ridge toward the firelight. He had a scarf wrapped around h face up to his eyes. "Know what this night mind me of, Ma Billy?" he said in a muffled voice. "'Memmer when we was crossin' the Allegheny bringin' you Ma an' Pa an' sisters, an' yo led us through th' snow to that cabin?"

William's mind leaped back across two decades and a continent, and he remembered. "Yes, by heaven, I do. Ha! Just like the old days, York, say what?"

"Just like," York said.

"But I know one difference. I'm not fool enough to rassle you in any snowbank anymore. Y've outgrown me, old friend." Tears suddenly smarted in William's eyes as he said this. He didn't remember ever having called his slave "old friend" before.

He's no slave anymore anyhow, William thought. *He's a man like all the rest of us.*

And that night as the men stood around in their steaming elkskins as close to the roaring bonfires as they could get without singeing their whiskers, almost giddy with the aroma of roasting colt meat, William took a long, loving look at York and made a decision.

I won't tell 'im yet, he thought. *But when we get back to Louisville, I'm going to sign that man free.*

ONE COLT OF COURSE MADE ONLY ONE MEAL, AND A SCANT one, for three dozen men accustomed to eating eight or ten pounds of meat a day per man. And although they now were consuming their meat in the Indian manner—organs, brains, tongue, guts, suet, and marrow as well as the red flesh—their famished bodies, doing superhuman work in the cold, burned up the nourishment even as they slept, and so there would be nothing else to eat unless the hunters should have better luck today.

It was the seventeenth of September, and this morning it was clear to everybody that winter in these altitudes had arrived. What they had dreaded had happened. They were caught by winter in the Bitterroot ranges. This morning the snow had stopped, but it lay a foot deep in most places. The clouds overhead looked pregnant with more snow, but they had lifted enough to permit several miles' visibility. And in a way this was bad; yesterday it had been possible to hope that beyond the next misty mile lay the end of the mountains. Today they could see high, jagged, snow-covered peaks towering around them in every direction, and every man had to rid himself of any hope that the ordeal of the mountains was nearly over. The men looked at those frightful ranges repeating themselves off into the purple distance, and their stomachs growled and their bones ached; their extremities stung with freezing and thawing, their faces were raw and flaking and suppurating; they shuddered uncontrollably with cold and hunger and, for the first time after nearly two years of eager and faithful following, they began talking dis-

couragement among themselves outside their captains' hearing
The horses had foraged far through the snowy woods during th
night, and most of the morning was spent in stumbling throug
the snow and catching them all. Every hour thus spent mean
another hour's delay in these mountains. Sergeant Ordwa
brought back to the captains those first murmurings of despai
that he had been overhearing.

"Some are a-sayin' these mountains are a trap without an exit,
he said. "I heerd 'em talkin' about the wolves howlin'. I hear
Bratton say, 'I don't like them wolves, they're a bad sign.' I told him
'Bratton,' I said, 'if a wolf tries t' eat you, eat him.' Well, sir, h
laughed then, but others are a-talkin' low-spirited too."

"Thankee, Sarge," said Lewis.

"Welcome, sir. I thought y' oughter know what they're a
sayin'." He shivered and looked westward, and shook his head
"I'll say this, sir. These are sure the most turrible mountains
ever beheld."

Because of the delay caused by the strayed horses, there wa
little hope of making more than ten or twelve miles this day
William and Colter and Toby went out ahead again, and me
who could be spared from the pack train to hunt went down int
the woods on both slopes of the mountain. William heard a fe
gunshots during the afternoon and prayed that they would yiel
something.

The afternoon was a repetition of the day before, but in som
ways worse. Branches of the evergreens were loaded with snow
and this was forever sliding off onto heads and shoulders, slidin
down collars, wetting clothes and mittens and gun locks. Th
temperature came up near the freezing point during the afte
noon, and the snow grew slick as grease. William fell countles
times, and Colter fell, and even Toby fell, and William wa
almost sick imagining what it must be like back there in the pac
train. He imagined, over and over, Sacajawea's horse rollin
down the snowy mountainside, crushing her and little Pomp un
der it, and somehow this was the worst possible mishap he coul
imagine. She had to ride, of course; she could not be expected t
wade through this snowy wilderness carrying a baby. But unde
these circumstances the privilege of riding was surely no privileg
at all.

As he expected, darkness was on them before they had pro
gressed more than ten miles. He found a meadow on the moun
tainside near a gushing brook with a round deep sinkhole full c
water nearby, and here again had a bonfire going by the time th
rest of the party came creeping along the trail. The hunters ha

shot only a few grouse, not enough even for a good mouthful of fowl for each man. One hunter had chased a bear "all over the blag-dagged mountain," as he reported it, but had been unable to get a clear shot at it. And so this night the third and last of the colts was butchered. The men devoured its boiled flesh and guzzled the broth ravenously but without their usual delight. "They usually eat like happy pigs," Ordway commented, watching them. "Now they mind me more o' wolves, like."

The men knew there were no more colts and they knew the captains would not let them kill the pack horses for food. This night there had been only enough firewood around to cook the colt, and so the men could not have the luxury of basking near a blaze and drying out their clothes. All they could do now was get into their blankets with all their damp clothing and moccasins on and hope to generate enough body heat to keep from freezing. William and Lewis separately toured among the squads giving medicine and treating chilblains and sprains and boils, and tried to talk encouragement and to gauge the real morale of the soldiers.

"They scare me now," Lewis said. "Every one of 'em looks like 'e's lost twenty pound o' flesh. We've got dysentery and rheumatism and skin rot and windburn on near every man. But what bothers me most is how quiet and sullen they be."

"Aye," said William. "I got th' sense from one or two that they'd as soon gnaw a chunk off me or you as off a horse's haunch."

"I'll say this. Drouillard hasn't shot more than a grouse all these days, and when *he* gets nothing, that means there *is* nothing." He paused. A wolf's eerie, lonely, hungry plaint wound along the horizon. He looked up at the sky. "Stars," he said.

William looked up. The clouds were thinning and shredding overhead. "Going to be mighty cold up here by midnight," he said.

"I think our main threat," said Lewis, speaking very low, almost whispering now, "is loss of spirit. I don't want to eat any pack animals, because we need everything we've got and can't drop off another pound o' baggage. But if it comes to that, we will. What these boys need most, though, is to know there's a way out o' these mountains. Drouillard told me the men don't believe in Toby anymore. They keep talking about how he got us lost back yonder. And they don't believe in us believing in him either. They think he led us in here and doesn't know a way out."

William clenched his back teeth. He knew that his faith in the guide—and thus his own judgment—was on trial. And now Lewis continued in a surprising new vein on the same subject.

"Somebody, in fact, has said that Toby's brought us in here to perish so his tribe can come up and get all our guns and goods."

William frowned in the feeble glow of the coals. "Empty guts," he said, "make full imaginations." It was one of George's sayings. "Anyways, you're right what they need: To know that these mountains *do* end. Well," he said, "here's what I propose. Tomorrow I could set out early with a small party, no baggage. We could travel twice as fast as the main body. I'm sure from what Toby's said that we're more than halfway across the range. I believe right well I can reach the far side o' the range in two fast days like that. Get down where there's game, or find the Nez Percés and buy some from them, send it back up to you. I don't only think it's a good idea, I think it's an outright necessity. Without a cheerful report from ahead, these boys won't hold together another week." He remembered something, vaguely, something echoing in his memory that made him believe even more strongly in his proposal than he had when he had first suggested it. Yes. It was the ruse that Brother George had used on the way to Vincennes, when he had sent his scouts ahead across the flood and told them to bring back a favorable report no matter what they found. That had worked for George, that of having someone go far ahead and send back good word. "Aye," he said now to Lewis, "they don't believe there's an end to the mountains because there's nought but Toby's word on it. That's why they think him sinister, too. But they'll take heart if I prove there is. Do I have your agreement?"

"How can I not? We've nothing to lose."

"I'll want our best hunters. And, ah, I'm goin' to leave Toby with you."

"Eh? Why that? How d' you expect to find the way without the one man you say knows it?"

"Lewis, listen: I can find it, because Toby's told me it so clear I've got it mapped on my eyeballs: that wild river down below us is the Koos Koos Kee. Just beyond these mountains a clear water river runs into it from the north. On down the Koos Koos Kee beyond that is level land. And game. And Indians. And now the reason I don't take Toby is what ye just now said: They don't believe in him."

"All right. All right, man, I do see your point. So do it. Go early. And I'll try to keep their body and soul together and bring 'em along."

"Godspeed, Clark."

They shook hands in the dawn light, the milk-pale light silhouetting the mountains behind them, the mountains they had been creeping over for more than a week. It was bitterly cold under the cloudless sky. In the blue above there was a faint segment of moon looking like a skim of ice taken from a water-pail and flung up there. The breath of the horses steamed white and crystallized. William looked back over the camp by the frozen sinkhole. The troops were getting out of their blankets and moving stiffly and slowly as walking corpses, reluctantly setting out through the crunching blue snow to round up the rest of the horses. Their loads would have to be repacked and redistributed this morning to assimilate the load the scouts' horses had been carrying. It had been decided that William and his advance party would go on horseback for the sake of speed. Sacajawea sat huddled in her blanket nursing Pomp and looking sad-eyed at William. The baby had cried much of the night; his mother's milk was failing because she was starving like everybody else. Scannon's bark echoed among the peaks. He had by some instinct become a herder, and these last two mornings he had been helping the men round up the horses. It was going to be a brilliant, clear day. The mountainsides sloped down and down snow-shadowy blue and pine-forest black to the little twisting rivers in the bottom of the gorges, and it was so windlessly quiet that the rushing of their waters could be heard all the way up here on the crest. The ridge twisted on and on ahead like some gigantic reptilian backbone, from peak to peak to peak until it seemed to terminate in a bald, white monolith some twenty or thirty miles ahead. William clucked, put his heels into the flanks of his black-spotted mount, and moved out, his rifle cradled in his arm, and his hunters fell in behind him: Drouillard, looking every inch a Shawnee, then blue-eyed, calm-faced John Colter, then John Shields and the Fields brothers, Reuben and Joseph, and Private John Collins.

The cold was intense; it rankled in the nostrils, and benumbed the cheeks and hands and feet. It was colder riding than walking. The world was crisp and blue, and William imagined that the poles of the earth must have this kind of stark, stinging stillness. William led along the crest of the ridge, and when they could, Drouillard and Colter rode flanking, one down each side of the ridge a way, searching the woods below for game or tracks.

As they rode the sun came over the mountains behind them and made all the peaks on either side gleam pale orange with alpenlight, and as the sky brightened, the moon dissolved.

Hooves crushed in the crusty snow, the rivers whispered far below, and now and then some cold-bitten tree would crack like a shot. "Wish that noise was my gun," said Collins, "shootin' a fat deer."

They went over a bare spine and then down through the dark fir woods on an intervening saddle, then veered slightly left with it and climbed onto another of the treeless promontories. William reined in his horse here to look backward and forward. Shields and the Fields brothers rode on by him, muffled to their noses in rags and scarves, eagle feathers drooping from their fur hats, draped in shaggy elkskin coats with foot-long fringes, parfleche saddlebags behind them, looking for all the world like members of some tribe of Arctic savages, or like, perhaps, the Mongols of the old Khans. Incredible it was to look at the brothers and know they sprang from a fine family of Virginia's Culpepper County, and were grandsons of a Byrd just as he was himself grandson of another Byrd; incredible to look at Shields and know he was a blacksmith and artificer of genius with family roots sunk deep in Augusta County, well married with a wife named Nancy and a daughter named Janette, both of whom likely had given him up for dead by now. They rode past William, who shaded his eyes with his mitten and gazed back over the way they had come. He was only doing what he always did, looking back to memorize the look of the land over which they might have to return next year, if there was no ship on the Pacific Coast to take them home; he was only memorizing the way home, and not expecting to see what he saw now, and was not even sure for a moment whether he was really seeing it. But yes, there they were, maybe three or four miles back there, an infinitesimally tiny line of specks on the vast snowy mound of a mountaintop amid a universe of mountaintops like a line of ants crossing a many-gabled roof: two dozen men and a squaw and a papoose, with Indian horses carrying trading goods and guns and ammunition and tools and notebooks and clothes and pelts and medicines and flags and medallions—everything, he thought, but food—coming along and coming along as they had for two years and three thousand miles now, like a line of ants but much smaller from here, mere specks, yet he had come to know every one of them as intimately and caringly as he knew his own relatives. Lewis, in fact—likely that first dot in the line?—was as much his brother as anyone could be without being a Clark; and Sacajawea . . . Yes, what about her? She was not a sister, but she was closer to him than Fanny; she was not a lover, but he loved her even more than he loved Judy Hancock. He had never

d this to himself before, but he knew in his soul that it was
ae.

Better not to fathom this, he thought now, and tore his mind
vay from the little line of specks so far behind, and from his
her loved ones a thousand times that far behind, and he told
imself: *You're farther ahead than anyone has ever been.*

He wheeled his horse and trotted through the snow, passing
ields and the Fields boys and their frost-snorting horses, and
de up to the brow of this summit, and now he stopped his
ount again and looked westward along the mountain spine to-
ird that final white peak like a skull at its end, now perhaps
teen miles ahead. There were other mountains beyond it, of
urse, but from the looks of the land, that knob was the end of
is ridge, and beyond it, if his faith in Toby was justified, would
the place where the river far down on his left and the river far
wn on his right would meet, and there they would be able to
irt down out of the mountains and find food to send back and
irt looking for wood to build canoes again.

Canoes, he thought. Imagine sitting in a nice fresh-hewn ca-
e and just floating down the river easy as a lord, just dipping a
iddle in now and then to stay ahead o' the current, guts full o'
lmon and elk, singin' in the sunshine like a lord goin' down to
ew Orleans, but goin' not to the Gulf of Mexico this time,
here all too many a riverman has gone already, but to the great
ue Pacific, by a way no white man's ever gone, *farther ahead*
an anyone has ever been!

Oh, he knew from experience by now that it probably
ouldn't be all that easy; it never was as easy as you'd expected; it
ever had been as easy as expected in more than three thousand
iles; nonetheless he could already taste the salmon and the elk
id he could already feel the autumn afternoon sunshine on his
ce—it'll still be autumn when we get down out of these moun-
ins, he thought—and he could already smell the fresh-hewn
ood of the new canoe, and he could even hear already the
appy quick squeaking of Cruzatte's fiddle, which hadn't been
eard since about a month ago back in the Shoshoni town.

And these thoughts were all rolling and tumbling through his
unger-intoxicated brain as he rode his horse here squinting to-
ard a sunlit mountaintop fifteen miles ahead, his feet and
ands numb with cold, his ruddy cheeks whitening with frost-
te.

BY MID-AFTERNOON THEY WERE ALMOST BLIND FROM THE
are of sunlight on snow. Their faces were scarlet with sunburn,

and where the sunburn had scorched their frostbite they we
leprous-looking with huge blisters. And they were almost fai
with hunger. They had not seen one animal of any kind. W
liam had been pulling leather thrums off the sleeve of his co
and chewing them until they were soft enough to swallow.

But now they were at last struggling the last mile through tl
snowdrifts toward that bald, white mountain they had been loo
ing at all day. The sun glared off the snowcrust so brightly it w
like looking straight up into the sun itself, and they had to ho
their mittens over their eyes most of the time or they would l
permanently blinded, he was sure. The peak they were ascen
ing was as rounded and barren and white as a skull, and for tl
moment there was nothing beyond and above it but that blue s
and that eye-burning, ray-shot, shimmering sun, so intense
white that it looked blue and sometimes black within its aureo
of rays. They rode into this brain-searing glare for an eternity,
seemed, before they reached the top of the mountain, and the
they had to stop their horses and press their mittens over the
eyes for a few seconds to rest them so they could look out and s
what was beyond.

William pulled his cap-brim down as far as he could to sha
his eyes from the sun above and put his forearm in front of I
face to block the reflected glare from the snow below, and no
he could see what was in the distance.

"Oh, God! Oh, God, Lookee yonder! Tell me if it's true wh
I'm seein' or is it a mirage?"

"Yeeeeee-ahhhh-HOOOO! YOW-HOO!" The Fields bo
were whooping, startling their exhausted horses into brief sta
of bucking and turning. "That there is a *plain*, Cap'n Clark! I
a green *plain*, and I'll swear t' God hit's summertime dow
there!" Collins was looking at William and beaming.

It might have been thirty or forty or fifty miles away, for a
they could tell, but it was level ground; it was green, it was l
God the land beyond the mountains, and they could see it, ar
anything they could see they knew they could reach. Tears ra
down over the sunburned frostbite-blisters on their faces and the
howled in triumph, howls broken by sobs, because they ha
crossed the Bitterroots, that last and most rugged range of tl
Rocky Mountains, and their captain, that God-danged, goo
hearted, red-headed, blue-eyed wonder who never made a mi
take no matter how it might look at any hard and awful give
minute, had been right as usual. There *was* a way out of tl
mountains, and he had brought them to it.

AND SO THEY RODE DOWN OFF THE END OF THE RIDGE TO the river and found a place on a creek to camp before dark, and although they hadn't found a thing to shoot for dinner, it didn't matter. They went to bed without having had anything to eat for twenty-four hours, and so they gave the creek the name of Hungry Creek.

On the next day, as they rode the descending valleys, still crossing and detouring fallen logs, they saw before them seventy yards away a brown horse standing on a knoll looking toward them. Drouillard glanced at William and William nodded and Drouillard killed it instantly with one shot through the heart. They noticed as they were skinning it that it had a sort of brand on its rump and thus it was an Indian's horse, so they knew they were near Indians, the Nez Percés, no doubt. They ate nearly a quarter of the horse, and hung the rest in a tree to keep it from wolves till the rest of the party should come down, and then they rode on down through a precipitous gorge until they came to a village of Nez Percé Indians, who were at first scared and suspicious, but who, after comprehending Drouillard's sign language, proved to be a fine and hospitable people, even more cheerful and generous than the Shoshonis, and gave the white men a horse-back load of heavy cakes made of camass root flour, some berry-cakes and two huge dried salmon. William immediately sent Reuben Fields back toward Lewis's party with that load, and went on down to the main Nez Percé village where the main chief, Twisted Hair, lived, and began building a friendship with him.

WHEN FIELDS REACHED THE MAIN PARTY, HE FOUND THEM tired and sick nearly unto perishing. They had made a supper of a quart of old bear's oil and twenty pounds of candles, then two miles later had found the horse carcass William had left for them, and had dined sumptuously on it. They had caught and devoured crayfish from Hungry Creek, a couple of grouse, and one coyote that had wandered close to the camp on the scent of the cooking grouse.

WHEN THE PARTY CAUGHT UP WITH WILLIAM AT TWISTED Hair's village, he had already scouted the Koos Koos Kee River, found tall ponderosa pines for canoes, and sent his men out to hunt. Almost everyone was sick with gas-bloated bowels because of the starvation followed by the roots, and some of the men lay for hours along the trailside before they could get up and follow. Lewis himself was so sick he could scarcely stay on his horse.

William bombarded the men's intestines with Dr. Rush's Thunderbolts.

They were about as sorry a passel of human animals as William had ever seen, after their eleven-day ordeal in the Bitterroots, their faces raw as ground meat, running sores in their whiskers, but they were alive and glad of it.

And Captain Lewis wrote in his journal:

> The pleasure I now felt in having tryumphed over the rocky Mountains and descending once more to a level and fertile country where there was every rational hope of finding a comfortable subsistence for myself and party can be more readily conceived than expressed, nor was the flattering prospect of the final success of the expedition less pleasing.

He looked over at William, who was just now throwing a barrage of Thunderbolts down his own throat while farting camass root gas like a horse, and he said after a while:

"Clark, I think I really picked the right partner."

"Yes, you did. And I think y'll admit, I picked the right Indian."

"Yes, you did."

47

ON THE

KOOS KOOS KEE RIVER

October, 1805

IT REALLY WAS ALL DOWNHILL FROM HERE. THEY WERE ON a swift, cold river in four large new dugout canoes and a small one, all trim and symmetrical, burned and hewed out of wonderful straight ponderosa pines, and were tearing through glassy green rapids down among the high, rugged, pine-dark hills, their route to the Columbia having been drawn on an elk hide for them by the good Nez Percé chief, Twisted Hair. They had branded their trailworn horses with Lewis's name and left them in the chief's care, and now they were once again in canoes, and for the first time in two years they were not struggling upstream. It was all downhill, and it was exhilarating.

A few times it had been almost too exhilarating. A canoe with Sergeant Gass at the helm had got sideways in the rapids, nearly turning over, a hole stove in her side, and had sunk in the rapids with all the Indian merchandise and several men aboard who could not swim. Rescue and repair had delayed them for a day, and they had had to set a guard over the merchandise where it was laid out to dry, because the Indians of these riverside tribes had a way of making unguarded items disappear.

It was exhilarating several times every day, because the river kept rushing down over bad rapids. On one day the boats had slithered and plunged down fifteen stretches of roaring white-water, providing so much exhilaration that old Toby the guide deserted the moment he got ashore. He was seen running up over a hill, having not announced his departure or even collected the pay he had been promised for his service as guide over the mountains. Everyone was puzzled and astonished and sorry he had left, because he had proved himself a fine Indian after all, the cheerful old rascal, and they were all sorry for having doubted him, and they all wished that he had stayed for his pay; it left them all somehow with a sense of unfairness that he had not claimed his reward. William suggested borrowing a horse from one of the Nez Percé villages and going after him. But no, a Nez Percé chief advised; whatever he was paid would only be taken away from him by the Indians on this side of the mountains. An old man like that.

And so it was October now, and the dugouts were plunging down the wild rivers between canyons of evergreen and fern, with their haggard crews on the paddles, the parfleche bags and bundles and kegs and canisters loading them down so heavily that they were almost awash; and now in every boat along with the cargoes and crews there were tied ten or fifteen new passengers: dogs.

They were the big, rangy Indian dogs, gray and dun, rough-haired, looking more like wolves than dogs. They were snarly and unpleasant, and their presence made Scannon very disdainful, but they had been deemed a necessity. They had been bought from the Indians as livestock. They were the only fresh meat available. There were no buffalo on this side of the Rocky Mountains. There were moose and elk and deer and bighorn sheep, but they were far up in the mountains. Here in the river valleys they had been long since hunted out by a dense Indian population, and even Drouillard and Collins and the Fields brothers, with all their skills as hunters, could seldom bring in so much as a deer in three days' hunting. And of course there could be no three-day hunts now, or even one-day hunts, because it was October and the days were growing short, and there were still four or five hundred miles to go to the Pacific, and the boats were moving too fast to permit the dispatching of hunting parties. So now the hunters were in the boats manning paddles like everyone else. Now the expedition bought most of its food from the Indians in the villages along the river, trading beads and bits of ribbon for dried salmon and cakes of camass root. The salmon was extremely oily, and gave everyone stomach cramps and severe diarrhea; the cooked camass roots were sweet and palatable, but also caused stomach pains and sometimes swelled the guts up so that it was difficult to breathe for hours after eating them. And so almost every man of the party had been sick almost every day since emerging half-starved from the mountains, and it had appeared that on this new diet everyone would remain sick indefinitely. Until one day when Le Page and Cruzatte and Labiche, with the resourcefulness of truly hungry Frenchmen, had bought some Indian dogs and cooked them for fresh meat. Immediately they had recovered from their stomach disorders, and so now dog meat had become the most desired provision, and the party had bought all the dogs it could obtain at every village along the way.

Virtually everybody in the expedition soon developed a liking for dogflesh. Lewis simply loved it, and swore that he was healthier and stronger on dogmeat than he ever had been on any other diet. But William could not eat it. "I'd rather have diarrhea," he would say, watching distastefully as Lewis gnawed on a well-roasted piece of dog haunch. "How can ye look Scannon in the eye with dog-grease on your lips?" "It's different," Lewis would say. "Scannon has a soul; these don't." Then Lewis would finish the morsel and give Scannon the bone. "How can you say he's got a soul?" William would persist. "Lookee, he's a shameless cannibal."

The Indians here, Nez Percé and Cho-pun-nish, were well built and handsome and friendly and helpful, and the captains befriended many chiefs, despite their haste. The Indians were very fond of ornament, decorating their elkhide and goatskin clothes with white beads, seashells and bits of mother-of-pearl and braided grasses stained with natural pigments. Some of them wore jewelry made of bits of brass bought from tribes living farther down the Columbia. It was the first evidence of Indian trade with the sailing ships that came to the Pacific coast. These Nez Percés had never seen a white man, but knew they existed be-

842

cause they had heard of them from the coastal tribes below. Lewis and Clark smoked tobacco and showed off York and the air gun and gave out medals and bells and mirrors from their dwindling supply of merchandise during their brief stops with these Indians, but the aid they got in return for these little attentions was invaluable. The Indians helped them pilot rapids, gave them food, and often helped them retrieve lost goods and paddles after spills in the rapids. Sometimes the stops were extended while the captains doctored sick Indians, many of whom were victims of eye irritations and venereal diseases. And even though the canoes sped down the boiling rapids faster than a horse could run, somehow their fame as white medicine men preceded them down the steep-sided, pine-covered gorge; there were crowds of Indians on the shores every few miles, watching them and cheering them through the turbulent waterchutes. There was tribe after new tribe never heard of before, and little time to study their customs, but the captains made their notes on them as well as they could, and wrote down vocabularies of their words. Numerous as the Indians were, they never seemed threatening. William wrote:

> *The preasence of Sah-ca-gar-we-ah we find reconsiles all the Indians as to our friendly intentions   a woman with a party of men is a token of peace.*

AFTER SIXTY MILES ON THE RIVER, THE FLOTILLA ON October 10 came out of the mouth of the clear river onto a wide greenish river that flowed through barren hills from their left side. The Indians here called it the Kimoo-en-im. "I'm sure what this is," William said. "We've just come into the Snake. Remember that wild river we couldn't take when we left Ca-me-ah-wait's town? 'The River of No Return,' they called it? This is it. If Toby was still with us he'd tell us so. This is where he said we'd get on it. Aye, by damn, this water's from that same watershed we were on two months ago. Think how quick we'd have been here if only we could a' rid it down!"

"Well," said Sergeant Pryor, "I don't believe how it could be any more mean than this 'n we're on right now." Another dugout this very morning had run onto a rock and hung on it, getting a split hull.

"You didn't see the No Return like we did," retorted Sergeant Gass. Pat Gass was shaking as with ague from the last dashing ride through the rapids, but he said, "This we're on is a smooth leetle canal compared with that other one, ain't that so, Cap'n?

And if we'd 'a come down it, we'd be strowed on th' banks her stinkin' like them hundred million dead salmon."

The river banks along here were silvery and putrid with th countless salmon that had spawned upstream and then died.

"BEJEEZUS, CAP'N, I JUST CAIN'T KEEP UP WITH THE COUN tryside," said Private Frazier. Frazier was working on his own journal and map, and had come up to go over some points with William. "I mean, two days ago, there we were 'mongst we green mountains with pines two hundred feet high if they's foot, and now I'm blind if this don't look just like the deser roundabout the Great Falls o' th' Missouri, don't it, though? No a tree anywhere, and Lord help us, prickly pear agin!"

It was a barren, rolling, ochre-yellow land, broken with gullies, the eroded stone river bluffs looking like old fortress wall stacked one above the other.

"It does, Frazier, for a fact. And I wouldn't mind the view on mite, if only it had the buffalo like that did."

Frazier rolled his eyes and licked his lips. "Oh," he groaned clutching his stomach, "oh, yes, for a nice fat hump o' buffale just now! No more scrawny dawg! Oh, my!"

Now, according to what old Toby and the Nez Percé chief had told them, they would be on the Snake River about a week and then it would fall into the Columbia itself. Lewis seemed to strain forward like a hunting dog in his impatience to be upon that long-sought river to the sea.

The week passed swiftly on the water of the Snake. There were so many spills and wrecks on the rapids that the cap tains worked out a policy for negotiating the most formidabl rapids: Men who could not swim would be put ashore to carr indispensable gear, such as rifles and papers and instruments The captains would walk down the shore then and study the rapids for the most feasible channels. Sometimes, Indians from the vicinity would get into the small dugout and pilot then through. Then two of the big canoes at a time, with the bes steersmen and paddlers manning them, would head down through the thundering channels, and usually all would get through right side up. But nearly every day one canoe or anothe would be swamped or turned over or struck hard enough to star leaking. Then there would be the frantic salvaging of wet spille bedding, food, and bundles of merchandise. A camp would be made below the rapids and articles would be dried and repacked and split hulls repaired and recaulked. Then above the nex rapids, the process would be repeated. At every stop the part

844

would buy salmon, more camass root, more dogs, and firewood for cooking. In these treeless regions there was no fuel but what driftwood the Indians had collected, not even buffalo chips; thus many trade goods were expended on firewood. The only game the hunters could get were ducks and prairie-cocks and other birds that, to the astonishment of the Indians, they were able to shoot out of the air.

AND SO IT WENT, INTO MID-OCTOBER. IT WAS DANGEROUS and hard, but compared with the ascent of the Missouri and the ordeal in the mountains, it was a lark. On October 16, after shooting six bad rapids in the morning, the party at noon reached the place where the Snake River flowed into the great Columbia.

Captain Lewis and Captain Clark looked at each other with weary eyes. They had come thirty-seven hundred miles, in seventeen months of strenuous, hazardous travel, to reach this place. As if to commemorate their arrival at this landmark, many Indians came down from their villages on the surrounding plains, at least two hundred men and women on foot, chanting and beating on drums and clacking sticks. They parted to form a semicircle around the white men and boats, then stood there singing, until their chiefs came forth to smoke. Through Drouillard's signs, the message of peace and commerce was conveyed, and medals, handkerchiefs, and shirts were given to the chiefs. In return, one of the chiefs made a good map of the upper Columbia, showing where different tribes lived along its banks.

These Indians, called Wanapams and Yakimas, were a strange people. Their language was very different from that of the mountain tribes. Many of the women were fat, and some of them had strange, broad, sloping foreheads. Papooses were seen strapped in cradleboards with slabs of bark attached at angles to compress their foreheads and impart this slope-skull profile, a straight line from the end of the nose to the crown of the head, evidently as an attempt at beautification. Bad eyesight and bad teeth were evident in a large proportion of the people; many were blind or partially blind, which the captains presumed to be a result of fishing for salmon much of the year on the sun-flashing river and from the unrelieved snowglare of the treeless plains in winter. The Indians' teeth were worn down to the gums, presumably by the grit in their stone-pounded fish and roots. But they were a cheerful and friendly people, childishly delighted by such wonders as the air gun, the compass, York, and Scannon,

and they were crazed with glee when Pierre Cruzatte tuned
his old fiddle and began to play.

But the troops themselves were almost that gleeful to hear t
fiddle again, and they whooped and cavorted, swinging partne
flapping elbows, rolling their eyes, and popping their chee
until the Indians were almost helpless with laughter.

LEWIS TOOK CELESTIAL SIGHTINGS AND PLOTTED THE GE
graphical coordinates of the confluence, and then on down t
river they went. The Columbia was wide and fast, and so cle
that salmon could be seen three fathoms down. Now the sm
of salmon was everywhere. They lay rotting on the riverbanks
the millions; they hung on frames drying in the sun at eve
Indian encampment, tons of them. Dried salmon hung in t
Indian lodges thick as tobacco leaves in a Virginia curing she
and everyone's clothes reeked of salmon, everyone's skin felt sli
with salmon oil and everyone's nostrils cloyed with it.

Then, as the little fleet bounded down the Columbia, anoth
odor began to insinuate itself, a vaguely familiar, sourish odor
first, noticeable near one of the big canoes. It was a while befo
someone identified it, and that someone was Private Howar
"By th' great god Gambrinus!" he yelled suddenly one eveni
"that's beer I smell!"

And then the secret was out: Private Collins, starting with
mass of camass-root bread that had gotten wet and soured as t
result of a boat-wreck, had been adding to it and nurturing
There were only a few gallons, but it was a good beer and
strong one, and when Collins wistfully shared it that eveni
with thirty men, he was a more popular fellow than he h
intended to be. "You an' yer damn nose," he muttered
Howard once during the evening.

"Well, look at it thisaway," Howard replied. "If you'd 'a kep'
and drunk it all yourself, either it would'a kilt ye, or we 'u
would."

IT WAS A DIFFERENT WORLD THROUGH WHICH THEY WE
passing so swiftly now, a world entirely unlike either the M
souri plains or the great mountains, and their facility as journa
keepers was tested by phenomena never before put in writt
language. The landscape, the river, the plants, the natives, we
so unlike anything known to exist in North America that th
might as well have found themselves on a continent on the oth
side of the world.

As their canoes plunged down through hissing, gushi

846

rapids, they saw magnificent salmon leaping past them at eye level, flashing in the sunlight, desperately flinging themselves up over the foaming cascades. If the men had not been just as desperately fighting the water with their paddles, they could have reached out and caught the fish in their hands.

The dark-walled gorge of the Columbia cut through a vast, tawny land of sage and cactus and dunes, through sheer, thousand-foot walls of fluted lava-rock marked with vertical striations as straight as if cut by an engraver's stylus. Rock islands with perpendicular sides a hundred feet high jutted out of the river bed like old black temple ruins. The only vegetation along the river was willow and lily, hackberry and rushes, yet at every rapid and shallow there were elaborately built wooden scaffolds and racks and weirs. On these scaffolds naked men and boys stood with long-handled gigs or huge baskets, harpooning or scooping up the great fish below the rocks and tossing them onto huge piles ashore, where women split them for drying. Salmon everywhere, the stench of spoiled salmon everywhere. William marveled at the incredible abundance of food that Providence had placed here for these people, even somehow more awfully, wastefully prodigious than the countless buffalo on the Missouri side. At least the buffalo, he thought, you had to go find and kill at some risk; here you just stand in a place and grab it and lift it as it streams by! He saw in one tiny village an estimated ten thousand pounds of dried, pounded salmon, stored in three-foot baskets lined with salmon skins. He looked at the chunky men and corpulent women, and remembered the gaunt Shoshonis who ate maybe three times a week, who had scrambled over Drouillard's deer like dogs for, as McNeal had put it, "a mouthful of guts and arseholes."

Where animal hides had been the fabric of rugs and shelters for all the Indian cultures heretofore, now everything seemed to be made of tightly woven rushes and grasses. Mats and baskets, even the awnings and walls of dwellings, were made of bear-grass fibers so tightly woven they were impermeable. William saw baskets so well made that they could be filled with boiling water in which fresh fish were cooked. On islands in the river they found elaborate Indian burial grounds where beautiful grass weavings and splendidly carved canoes, as much as sixty feet long, had been left with the dead. "I swear," William groaned one evening as he wrote by the light of an oily fish burning like a candle. "This country's so wondrous, it's wearin' out my writing hand!"

ONE DAY THE CAPTAINS STOOD ON A CLIFF WHILE THE CA-noes were piloted down through the rapids below, and saw above

the western horizon, probably more than a hundred miles di
tant, a great, snowy mountain, visible down the long notch
the Columbia gorge. They stared at it and thought of all the o
maps and journals of the Northwest coast that they had studie
before the start of their trek.

"That," William said, "surely that's Mount St. Helens, e
The one Cap'n Vancouver saw from his ship in '92, when he la
off the mouth of the Columbia?"

"Praise God and hurrah!" Lewis said. "We're surely not mu
more than two hundred mile from the Pacific now! And unle
we smash ourselves to death on waterfalls, we'll be there in
couple o' weeks!"

NOW, IRONICALLY, IT WAS THE VERY SPEED OF THE COLUM
bia that was slowing them down. Every few miles in descendi
the gorge they would be confronted by the roar and foam
another stretch of rapids and agitated narrows, and would have
go ashore to study this newest gauntlet and decide whether
would need to be portaged or could be ridden through, an
whether the nonswimmers and precious cargoes would need
be sent overland, whether all the goods would have to be carrie
and the dugouts eased through by ropes.

William found himself bearing the major share of th
effort, it seemed. Lewis had been different since the orde
of the Bitterroots, or at least since his sick spell after the mou
tains. It was hard to define the difference, because he st
functioned extremely well in most of those things he did. He w
working hard to gather as much scientific information as the
haste would allow, and was taking vocabularies of the stran
new tribes, and analyzing their salmon economy and the pec
liarities of their health and their physical traits. But he was n
keeping a journal, and he was not really commanding. He ha
been moody and anxious, curt, often gazing downstream wi
an almost desperate look in his eyes, leaving more and mo
details of commanding and scouting and record-keeping to W
liam.

He's got so many danged talents, William thought, we do
really appreciate what-all he does until he neglects on one thi
or another. Lewis was physically recovered from his digesti
troubles, but something seemed to have broken or gone slack
him; it was the way it had been once when one string
Cruzatte's fiddle had snapped during one of those slow, groa
pieces he occasionally played. The whole instrument was still f
but the sound was different. York had noticed the change

Lewis, too, and he murmured his observation to William one day.

"It's like you Ma used to say: 'He on 'is feet but he off his bed.'"

A CRANE WAS FLYING HIGH OVER A CLUSTER OF INDIAN huts, flying with slow beats of its huge wings. It would be a long shot, but fowl would be a welcome break from the diet of oily, gritty, pungent salmon, so William took a bead on it, then a short lead, and squeezed the trigger. The rifle crashed, and the crane twitched against the gray sky and its wings bent askew and it began to fall. The three men standing on the plain behind William whooped in amazement. "Let's go get 'im," he said, reloading. As they walked toward the village, they saw two or three Indian men running as fast as they could go toward the huts. The huge bird had fallen between the hunters and the village. They picked it up and then went on to look at the place and do the usual diplomatic smoking and hand-talking.

"Wonder where everybody go," said Drouillard. The village seemed deserted; the usual crowds of curious savages did not come forth. Nothing stirred except a few slinking dogs. The lodges were made of mats, and their doors, of the same material, were closed. William gave his rifle to a soldier and walked toward the nearest lodge with his peace pipe across his arm. It was eerie. There were small fires smoldering under racks of fish. If the village had been deserted, it had been within the past few minutes. Yet there was nobody visible on the plains around.

He knelt, scalp prickling with apprehension, and lifted a corner of the door-flap. There was a strong smell of fish and people. He heard noises inside: rustling, a whimper, a short high note suddenly stooped as if a hand had been put over a baby's mouth. "Cover me," he said to the men. Then he stooped and peered in.

He could see in the dim light that the building was full of people. As his eyes adjusted, he made out two or three dozen men, women, and children, all cowering, and as he stepped in among them their murmurings turned to wailings. Some were wringing their hands, others were burying their heads in their arms.

He offered his hand, offered the pipe, and pressed little gifts, thimbles and beads, into their hands, eventually soothing their agitations a little. He sent Drouillard and the Fields boys into the other lodges to do the same. Then he came out and sat on a rock in the center of the village with his pipe, waiting for the men to

come out and smoke with him. Not a soul emerged. Now an
then he would see the bottom of a wall mat move up an inch o
so and a frightened eye peer out under it. "Somethin's skeere
th' bejabbers out of 'em," said Joe Fields. "Reckon they neve
heard a gun before?"

It was not until Lewis and the rest of the party came down
and the Indians saw Sacajawea among them, that they began t
come out of hiding, creeping out a few at a time. They s;
around trembling but acquiescent and smoked with the captair
then, and by and by through sign language the cause of thei
terror was revealed. They had heard a crash, then had see
something fall from the sky, and then from the place where
had fallen they had seen these four come toward the village
They had believed these were not men but creatures that ha
jumped down from the clouds on a thunderbolt.

By the time the Corps had dined and gone on down the rive
the people of this village were no longer afraid, but they seeme
still not entirely convinced that their visitors had been human

THE NEXT DAY THE PARTY SAW PELICANS FLYING, AND COR
morants. But there was still a mountain range between them an
the ocean; it loomed higher and higher ahead on either side o
the westering canyon. Straight ahead now not more than forty o
fifty miles, visible sometimes even from the canoes, was a perfec
snow-covered cone of a mountain that appeared to be at leas
two miles high.

Firewood could be obtained only from the Indians, who sol
it so dear that the expedition's stock of trade goods dwindled fast
The Indians themselves hoarded driftwood jealously because
was so scarce in this arid and treeless country. At one place Wil
liam found huge quantities of prickly pears and spoiled fis
spread in the sun, and was informed that the tribes used thes
unpleasant materials as fuels in the winter, just as the Indians o
the Missouri tribes had used dried buffalo dung. It's amazing
William thought, how folks can get by. "I would surely hate t
have to sit by a fire of these stinking fish in a close room," Lewi
said.

"Aye," William agreed. "But I could take some satisfaction i
seeing prickly pears a-blazing, after all the hurt they've don
me."

COMING TO REST ON AN ISLAND AT THE FOOT OF A DIFF
cult rapid, the explorers were startled by the cry of a soldier wh
had gone behind a heap of rocks to relieve himself. "Bones

850

thousands o' people bones!" he yelped, hopping into view clutching at his belt.

A wooden vault, six feet tall and sixty feet long, had been formed of boards and pieces of dugout canoes propped against a ridgepole. Inside it at one end were twenty-one skulls arranged in a circle on rotting mats. Elsewhere through the vault there were hundreds of human skeletons and parts of skeletons in disarray, and at the other end lay corpses and skeletons more recently placed. These lay in rows on wide boards, wrapped in leather robes and covered with mats, and over them hung baskets, wooden bowls, fishing nets, and trinkets of all kinds. The bones of humans and horses lay scattered all around the vault. It was a depository for the dead.

William examined the mausoleum minutely and wrote descriptive notes. "Our great white father in Washington would do handsprings if he saw this place," he commented, "the way he is about Indian bones."

Lewis looked as if he thought the remark was a little disrespectful. But he said nothing, because he knew how true it was.

"TREES! HEAVENLY LORD, I NEVER THOUGHT I'D BE SO happy to see *trees*," William exclaimed, pointing up toward a scattering of pines on a distant hill. He could also see more brush growing in the gullies. Evidently there was a little more rainfall here as they approached the mountain chain.

"It'll probably prove like the Bitterroots," Lewis said. He was sitting near William in the bow of one of the big canoes, writing in his field notes. "Likely the west side of the mountains get most of the moisture from the Pacific." The sea captains who had visited the mouth of the Columbia had written that it was wet country indeed.

"Alls I know is, I'll be glad to 'scape from this dang desert," said Ordway.

"Where there's trees, there's meat on th' hoof," Joe Fields chanted cheerily, thrusting his paddle in the water.

"Not allus, Brother, not in them Bitterroots there wasn't," Reuben reminded him.

"Listen," said William. They could hear it ahead, that familiar, dreaded rush of rapids and cascades. "Listen to the tone o' that. Waterfalls, or I'm a deaf man. Make for the starboard shore," he called back. "I think we're about on the Great Falls o' the Columbia."

His heartbeat was accelerating. The chiefs had been telling

them about the great waterfalls and the miles of terrible rapids below it, which they would meet here where the Columbia had forced its narrow passage through the mountain range. As far as they had been able to understand, these cascades would pose the last natural hazard in their descent to the ocean. But they would be a considerable hazard. The chiefs had said men could pass the falls and the narrows only on foot. Not even the best canoe steersmen of the Columbia tribes ventured into those terrible swirling waters in the narrows, they had warned. They said coastal tribes brought their large carved and painted log canoes up as far as the foot of those rapids to trade sea shells and wappatoo roots and ocean fish and items from white men's ships; tribes from the upper Columbia brought down bear grass and camass roots and mountain-sheep horn to the top of the falls, and here great trading fairs took place in the summer, with thousands of Indians. But the canoes of the coast Indians had never been above the falls, and those of the upper Columbia never went below the falls, except now and then by a fatal accident. The E-nee-shur tribes that lived at the falls were, so to speak, the middlemen of this annual bazaar.

It was past the season of the barter-market; only a few hundred people of the E-nee-shur tribe were still present when the Corps of Discovery beached its five dugouts and came ashore to study the falls.

A few of these people were enough. The troops looked dubiously at the E-nee-shur standard of feminine beauty and generally decided that it was just as well they were in too much of a hurry to dally. These women displayed most of their bodies, being dressed only in short shoulder-capes, which left their pendulous dugs bare, and narrow leather belts and loin-straps that, worn tight as tourniquets, were almost invisible in the overlapping rolls of fat. Their coarse black hair was braided and worn without ornaments. Many of them had flattened foreheads and the resultant fish-like pop-eyes, which made them seem less than human creatures to some of the soldiers. But far worse even than their gross and alien unattractiveness was the profusion of fleas that lived on and around them. Every Indian and every lodge was leaping with fleas. William stood looking at a pile of baskets sealed with sewn-on fish-skins—baskets full of thousands of pounds of dried salmon—and the baskets were so aswarm with fleas they appeared to be vibrating. The soldiers had not been in this village for ten minutes before every man was twitching and scratching.

On a promontory of dark lava stone he and Lewis stood and

studied the frothy, rumbling, hissing torrent below. "Well, it's a mere dribble compared to the Falls o' Missouri, thank the Lord," William yelled, "but it's twenty-foot pitch if it's an inch! Reckon we best map us a portage!"

Lewis nodded, but continued to stare at the huge cascade, and then he shouted: "How in the world do you suppose the salmon get upstream o' this? You don't imagine they can leap twenty feet, do you?" William looked for a minute, then shouted back:

"It doesn't seem possible, but they must. Look!" He pointed. Near the middle of the stream, several salmon were leaping from the froth at the foot of the falls, flinging themselves at the descending wall of water and being swept back down out of sight. The best of them were reaching heights of ten or twelve feet, but even these spectacular leaps were only half enough.

THEY WORKED OUT A COMPLICATED PORTAGE PLAN. ON THE north bank of the river was a narrow path on a steep slope, by which all the baggage could be back-packed around the falls, a distance of about twelve hundred yards. The path was partly over bare rock, partly over a steep sand dune, and the men stumbled through it with great difficulty. At the lower end of the route, a camp was made at an old fish-drying site. On the south bank of the river was a shorter path by which the canoes could be taken just around the falls, then put into the water in a furious but navigable channel about a hundred yards wide, which would discharge them into calm water just across from the camp. This part of the portage was begun the next morning, after a night made almost sleepless by fleas.

Lewis stayed with a small party to guard the goods at the camp while William and the main body went back up the portage route to the emtpy canoes, paddled them across to the south shore, and began the excruciating process of hauling the four-hundred-pound vessels out of the water, up the steep bank. The more they sweated, the more the fleas nipped at them. Private Shannon let out a yelp of desperate fury, and skinned out of his clothes. He stood there stark naked, hundreds of bites looking like a rash all over him, brushing fleas off his body.

William looked at Sergeant Ordway. "It's a good idea," he said, and quickly began stripping off his own clothes.

Soon everybody was in the cold water, washing off fleas and holding their clothes under to drown or wash the pests out of them. They made the rest of the canoe portage naked and much happier, then came back and got their clothes and put them on wet. By the time they had run the fast channel and recrossed the river to the camp, they were more or less rid of fleas. But when they landed, the fleas covering the campsite immediately leaped upon them and infested their clothes as thickly as before.

THEY WERE STILL NOT THROUGH WITH THE GREAT FALLS. A mile below, the river roared over another huge, jagged, rock-studded sill. This one was eight feet high, so the captains decided that the canoes could be unloaded on the narrow, rocky shore and then let down over the falls by ropes. It was a strenuous job, and somehow the very appearance of the place—the towering walls of the gorge, the huge, black volcanic rocks and pillars dividing the river into several thundering chutes—was so intimidating that the men looked wild-eyed, terrified, as they worked, and clung to footholds and handholds with the tenacity of climbing vines. It was mid-afternoon when this was completed.

As the fleet moved swiftly down the gloomy lava chasm below the falls, Ordway pointed to some rounded shapes moving lively on the dark glassy surface of the river. They looked like the head of swimming beaver. But on closer approach they proved too large. They're maybe sea otters, William thought. He raised his rifle and fired at the nearest one. With a swirl it disappeared. By the time the canoe reached the place, the animal had sunk too far to be retrieved.

Lewis had been busy during the day onshore. He had measured the falls, taken a latitude on the place, bought several fat dogs for supper, and made a canoe-trading deal that both beautified his little navy and made it more seaworthy. By throwing a good steel tomahawk and a few trinkets into the bargain, he had been able to trade the Corps' smallest dugout for an Indian log canoe of the lower Columbia sort: a wide-waisted, deep-draughted vessel tapering gracefully at both ends, its high prow and stern carved handsomely to represent some fanciful sort of serpents with ears. He was pleased with his new flagship, which seemed somehow to compensate for the failure of his iron boat, but he was not all good cheer.

"They warned me," he told William, "that the E-che-lute down at the narrows are planning to kill us. Now, I don't give that a full credence, but have all hands look to their guns and powder, and we'll put on a double guard tonight."

WILLIAM LAY IN HIS BLANKET AT THREE IN THE MORNING scratching assiduously at his groin and waist, watching stars glitter above the black canyon walls, listening to the muttering of the Columbia and of the troops.

Sure no Indians will catch us asleep this night, he thought. The fleas are making sure o' that.

THE NIGHT PASSED WITHOUT A SIGN OF TROUBLE, AND after a breakfast of roast dog, the Corps had the canoes loaded by nine A.M. and launched on the smooth, swift breast of the river. But within minutes they were hearing again the ominous rumble of powerful torrents. William stood up in the bow of the new log canoe and looked over the ears of its figurehead to see what sort of obstacle was being put in their way this time.

He had never seen such a thing in all his years on all kinds of rivers. The river, which had been about four hundred yards wide, seemed to come up short against a tremendous wall of black lava-rock; a huge basin of river water was backed up behind it. On the right shore of this basin, high on a cliff, stood five Indian lodges with all the usual fish-racks and scaffolds. For a minute William could not comprehend where the river could go from here. The dark wall was like a towering dam across the canyon. But the deep water here behind it was not still. It roiled and whirled in confused currents, and the boats seemed to be drifting toward the left side of the canyon.

"God!" He saw it now: a gap of perhaps forty or fifty yards in the steep black wall. From this gap issued the roaring-water sound he had been hearing. "Hard at those paddles!" He pointed. "Cruzatte, steer for the lodges! These must be the Narrows!"

They put in on a small beach, got out of the vessels, and approached the lodges. If these were the Indians who had been planning to attack them the night before, they showed no sign. They smoked and were friendly. One of the elders then climbed with William and Lewis and Cruzatte to the top of the jutting rock, out onto a precipice above the funnel. They were looking almost straight down on it. Lewis pressed his lips in a whistle, which was inaudible over the hollow thundering of the water.

Here, several hundred feet below, the whole great Columbia River was compressed between somber volcanic rock walls no more than forty-five yards apart. Here the mighty river in its yearning for the sea had forced its way through some weak place in a thick lava bed, and scoured out a narrow funnel through which its countless tons of water churned and eddied, dimpled with whirlpools and boiling like milk in a kettle. This funnel ran about a quarter of a mile, then the river widened to about two hundred yards. About two miles downstream it appeared to run into a similar funnel.

Cruzatte was peering studiously down at the turbulence. Lewis was gazing in awe at the valley below. In places, the lava walls rose two or three thousand feet above the valley. "All this lava must've flowed down from those mountains!" he yelled. These narrows evidently were the Columbia's channel through the snow-topped mountain range they had been glimpsing every day since they had been on the river. William nodded and scanned the cliffs of the funnel itself. Indians were beginning to appear everywhere along the cliffs, tiny figures, looking on curiously. It was as if they sensed that these strange men were going to attempt some desperate foolishness here, and they were going to watch it.

"There's no way to portage over that, not that I can see!" William shouted. He touched Cruzatte's elbow. "What say'ee about that water?"

Cruzatte thought. Then he held up a finger.

"One theeng good: It ees *deep*."

William nodded. Unlike the rapids, it would not be forever bashing and splitting the hulls of the dugouts. It would be a wild, heart-in-the-throat kind of a ride through horrid, swollen waters, but unless some vortex sucked a boat under, or hurled one against the dark rock wall, there was a chance.

WILLIAM SAT IN THE BOW OF THE CARVED CANOE, PALMS sweating, and felt the current sucking the vessel faster and faster toward the funnel. As the canyon walls closed slowly on each side, he could see lichens on the lava up high, and watermarks up as far as seventy or eighty feet. The dread was making his vision terribly sharp and his thinking clear. Now he understood how the salmon could get over the falls upriver: in times of high water, so much would back up behind this funnel that the falls those few miles upstream likely would be inundated, no obstacle at all for the ascending fish.

The roaring of water grew louder, more soul-shaking, and William wondered if that sudden understanding might have been the sort of clarity one has in the last moments of living. The canoe was slipping faster and faster into the middle of the great, sloping chute of water. Cruzatte, on the stern oar, was keeping it well aimed. William winked at him. Behind, in the distance, two other canoes were back-paddling, held in wait. Lewis was watching from the cliffs above. It had been their policy not to have both captains in jeopardy at once—not putting both eggs in the same basket, as they would joke sometimes.

All right. Begging your kind intervention once again, Sweet Lord, as "Here . . . we . . . GO!" He looked to heaven and saw brown people, thick as pigeons on an eave, jumping up and down, pointing. And then a glimpse of Meriwether Lewis, foreshortened, silhouetted against blue sky, waving, a pelican soaring above him.

And then with a hand gripping each gunwale, heart pounding, William faced the chute, felt the vessel slip and plunge, dip and slither, felt the stomach-lifting rises and the cushioned jolts of dropping, saw the black walls blurring backward, saw the sucking whirlpools slip under the hull, saw foam, swells, bubbles, bits of flotsam grass being swept along just as carelessly, just as helplessly, smelled fish and moss and wet rock, heard swishing, hissing, gurgling, rumbling, thundering, heard faint yells, felt a high, happy, hilarious expansion in his throat, and then the space around him grew bright and open, and the water was calm, and he was laughing, laughing, surely as happy as he had ever been; and when he turned and looked back at the men in the canoe, some of them were gray under their sunburns, others were flushed and whooping with joy; York's head was lolling on his black bull-neck as he sang something with his eyes shut tight, and Sacajawea was just raising her face out of a bundle of gray blankets, looking at him with a peculiar, wondering smile, as if wondering whether she should be laughing too, be laughing in this mad and happy way. And a half an hour later, when the five canoes had all come through, leaving the E-che-lute Indians dumbstruck on the cliffs as if they had just seen some supernatural spirit pass by, all the men on board were laughing that most exhilarated kind of laughter, the laughter of deliverance, and William called to Lewis as he came floating by in the last canoe, pop-eyed and green-faced:

"Oh, such a ride that was, it even made me forget I had fleas!"

It was a stretch of unrelieved turbulence, here where the Columbia had battered its way through the mountain range. All day every day was spent in shooting rapids or portaging around cascades, climbing with bundles and tools and weapons and kegs up and down narrow paths over the crumbling volcanic rock, easing the dugouts down around foam-beaten boulders by ropes from the shore, unloading, reloading. "I been learning things on this trip I'd never 'a' knowed," Nat Pryor drawled one evening, sitting by a brushfire kneading strained muscles and pulling prickly pear needles out of his feet. "For one, that downhill can be as hard as uphill."

"Y' think this downhill is hard?" retorted Sergeant Ordway, making a face as he burped up some essence of salmon. "Wait till next spring when we git to come back up it!"

"Don't even speak of it," growled Pat Gass. "I rather have it that when we git down to the Pacific Ocean, there 'll be a big ship there, and a dandy officer in gold braid a-sayin', 'Howdoo, ye heroes! President Jefferson sent me out t' fetch ye home, by way of Cathay and Singapoo and such elegant places, a day here and a day there to dally with yeller princesses and dancin' ladies, and then put in at Philadelphia where a parade will be held in your honor.' And I'll tell 'im, 'Thankee kindly, Skipper, and now first show me to my berth, an' I'll have me a three-day snooze on a velvet bed if ye please.'"

Pryor had got a faraway look in his eyes and he said softly, "I wonder if there will be a ship there?"

NOW THEY WERE SEEING EVIDENCE THAT SHIPS *HAD* BEEN there. In the strange Indian villages here and there they had been seeing, stacked among baskets of dried fish and piles of filberts and acorns, certain treasures that could only have come from ships: a brass tea kettle, a cutlass, a British musket. They had seen one savage strutting in a British sailor's jacket and a round hat, his hair in a queue, and had heard another one repeating like a parrot: "Son of a bitch! Son of a bitch! Son of a bitch!" The men had laughed, slapped their knees, egged him on, and listened to the phrase as if it were music. And then they had taught him to say, "Kiss my arse, King George!"

And now within two brief days, the climate and the very look of the world made another dramatic change, a total reversal. They left the brown, harsh, treeless desert behind them; suddenly their eyes were soothed by green foliage, their parched skin was softened by damp air and fog; suddenly there was firewood without limit, there were waterfowl so thick that one could hardly fire a gun in any direction without killing some, there were more of the otter-like creatures, swimming in such numbers that the river was crowded with them. Now the mountainsides along the river were dark green with forests of noble firs, spruces and cedars, taller and straighter and thicker than any trees they had ever seen, greater even than the magnificent elms and poplars of their own Kentucky homelands, and there were also oaks here, and some delicate new species of maple. "Glory be! Maples!" William exclaimed. "What pleasure to see a maple tree!" The cliffs were steep, brown lava cliffs towering above basalt cliffs, colored with a profusion of delicate mosses, ferns, lichens. The distant hills ranged from purple to black, their tops lost in rain-clouds; the river was crowded with perfect, steep-sided little islands cloaked in flowering shrubs, wind-gnarled evergreens, hemlock, and larch. Along the huge, mossy cliffs on the south shore of the river, waterfalls, several hundred feet high and a yard wide, dropped like lacy white ribbons straight from the brinks of pine-covered cliffs into fern-rimmed pools. Sea gulls mewed and wheeled in the misty air above the river. Most of the days were rainy and foggy now, and often the boatmen could see neither side of the wide river. Now and then some of the great log canoes would appear out of the fog, canoes whose high prows were carved and painted as bears' heads. The Indians in these vessels had flattened foreheads and wore colorful clothing of woven grass, and spectacular straw hats. Some of them spoke of great boats full of white men down on the ocean, and showed red and blue blankets, brass armbands and other goods they had purchased from those white men.

These Indians lived in wooden houses, the first board houses the men had seen in almost two years. They were not sawn boards, but had been split, wide and thin and long, from soft timber of perfectly straight grain. But for all their wooden houses and their fine canoes and colorful clothes, they were a dirty and flea-bitten people.

Many of them were arrogant and thievish, and followed the explorers doggedly. William could see that they were plainly getting on Lewis's nerves, but his study of their language and modes of living went on. Sometimes, to get a little relief from the noisome presence of Indians, the party would camp on islands instead of the densely populated shores. At a marshy campsite one night, the party was kept awake all night by a ceaseless cold rain and by the overpowering squawking and honking of thousands of geese, swans, and ducks.

These few days out of the desert, so welcome and beautiful at first, had quickly soured. The rain and fog and chill remained day after day; the men's leather clothes were rotting on their bodies, and every time they stopped at an Indian village or were visited by Indians, they acquired more fleas. They sat by a smoky campfire one night, cold water dribbling off boughs and down their necks.

Sergeant Gass was probing inside his clothes. He held up his hand in the firelight, squinting at his pinched thumb and forefinger. "This here is a flea of the E-nee-shur tribe," he said with an air of pedantic gravity, then crushed it and flipped it into the fire. He reached into an armpit and squinted at the new find. "This one is an E-che-lute." He reached in and found one at his waist. Lewis was watching him with a wry look on his face. "This here little buggerbug is a Chilluckitte-quaw, I can tell by its slopey skull and straw codpiece." He flipped it into the flames and dug in his other armpit. He looked at this flea, then held it up to his ear. "What's that ye say, little feller?" Then he squeaked in a high little voice, "'Son of a bitch! Son of a bitch!' Oho! Such language! Ye must be a Chinook!" He pinched it between his nails and flipped it at the bonfire, saying, "Kiss my arse, King George!"

And on the other side of the fire, York was making his own flea circus. He had taken off his shirt and was picking the insects out of the seams; with scowling brows then he would place each one on a boulder by his elbow and with mock ferocity would smash it with a rock as big as his head.

Sacajawea sat nearby, watching the two while she picked fleas off of her baby son. She could not understand Gass's soliloquy, but York's pantomime was plain and very funny to her. She would open her mouth round and yip with triumph each time he brought the rock down. Then she got in on the act herself, taking Pompey's fleas and placing them on the boulder for York to execute. Lewis shook his head and grinned in spite of himself.

I wonder, William thought, as he lay wet in his damp, stinking blanket that night listening to the rain hiss in the coals, what our Indian neighbors must think when they hear our laughter and fiddle music a-comin' through th' mist.

"CAP'N CLARK! COME QUICK, SIR!" IT WAS WINDSOR, THE boat watch. "Our canoes got in th' water!" William rose in the morning fog.

The dugouts had been pulled up on shore the night before, but now they were afloat, nuzzling each other in their little breakwater among fallen cedars. The men waded in and pulled them ashore.

"The water's riz," Windsor exclaimed, "that's what's happened. Riz three foot, I'll bet!"

And by the time the Corps had finished breakfast, the water was down by a foot. William smoked his pipe and nodded with satisfaction as the boats were being loaded. "Tide," he said. "We're in tidewater at last. 'Twon't be long now!"

The river was wide and open now, sometimes more than a

mile, sometimes so wide that both shores were invisible in fog. The little fleet had passed many islands, some of them several leagues long, and one pillar of black rock eight hundred feet tall standing in the stream, so conspicuous they called it Beacon Rock. There would be no more rapids to fight; they knew that; they were on deep, wide tidewaters, making thirty and forty miles a day now that the endless portaging was over, and the only thing that slowed them down now was the wind on those days when it came roaring chilly and wet up the valley, building the wide river surface into high, choppy, white-topped waves of grayish green, seething waves that would break over the pitching bows of the shallow dugouts, drenching everyone and everything, making some of the men seasick, finally forcing them to put in to shore at some waterfront village of mossy plank shacks, muddy streets, and shrewd-bargaining savages with flattened foreheads and shells through their noses. The Indian women here were almost naked, but as McNeal said with a sigh, "I wish they'd put on some clothes, so I could bear to look at 'em." They were almost all fat, with thick, soft, shapeless legs, and wore tight bindings around their ankles that seemed to cut off circulation, make their feet swell, and add to the gross deterioration of their legs. Many had thick, gnarled knock-knees, caused perhaps by their constant mode of squatting rather than sitting. Something in their diet, perhaps the starchy white arrow root that they ate in great quantities, made them uncommonly flatulent, and they added to their general unattractiveness by farting unabashedly as they squatted at their chores. Shields came into camp shaking his head, swearing that three toothless squaws had had a trumpeting contest for his benefit, grinning proudly at him after their best crepitations. "I 'spect I'll have to be here a lonnn-nnng time afore any of these start a-lookin' good t' me," lamented Ordway. More of the men in these villages wore sailors' clothes, and some carried pistols and tin powder-flasks. The captains found them arrogant and surly, but tried to smoke and be civil with them regardless, and for their pains one day were robbed of the very pipe tomahawk they had shared in the ceremony.

A little farther down they met two canoes full of Indians who spoke a few words of English, most of them profanities. As the vessels lay alongside each other on the rain-spattered gray water of the wide river, a conversation was conducted in sign language and English, by which the captains learned that these Indians were going down to the coast with things to trade with

861

the white sea captains who stopped sometimes at the river
mouth.

Their favorite, they said, was a Mister Haley—that seemed
be the name—who gave more presents than any other trade
The head man pointed to an enormous woman in his cano
saying that Mis-tah Hay-lee was fond of her and always liked
have her brought to his ship.

William gazed at the woman's unkempt mop of hair and h
huge, pendulous udders. "At last," he said to Lewis, "ye can t
Mister President that y've seen a mammoth."

THEY HAD BEEN COLD AND WET FOR FIVE DAYS, AND ITCH
with flea-bites, when on a foggy, rainy November 7 th
emerged through a range of small mountains to find a b
crowded with low islands almost covered by high tide. Th
stayed close to the bold, rocky starboard shore, paddling ha
against great, bashing waves that swashed and seethed whi
against the rocks of the shore. William could smell now in tl
wet air a faint, briny stink, vaguely like medicine, and when l
dipped a handful of water, it tasted brackish.

He squinted into the wet and sticky wind, heart beating fast
and faster, looking out over the rising, falling, rising, fa
ing carved-wood figurehead of the canoe, trying to penetra
the haze of fog and rain for some unmistakable sight of the F
cific.

They rowed on and on, mile after mile of the rocky sho
crawling backward at almost imperceptible pace, the men par
ing, some pausing to retch over the side, as the daylight fade
William looked back and saw the line of river canoes followin
four long, low troughs of pine they had made with their ov
adzes, so long ago, it seemed, on the Koos Koos Kee Rive
They were having a hard time of it. The waves repeatedly bro
over their low, spoon-shaped prows, and finally he realized th
they were running out of daylight, and that the swells were gro
ing higher, and that some shelf of land would have to be four
within minutes, because there was not going to be any sand
gentle ocean beach for a campsite on this evening. By the sm
and taste of it, they were very near the Pacific Ocean, but th
were still struggling against the strange and mighty Columb
River, probably in or near its estuary. The mountains nearby
the right shore and far away on the left were probably the ran
of coastal mountains that Captain Gray had seen from the se
ward side fourteen years before.

"Cap'n, sir, is that a ship?" someone yelled.

862

Something dark and tall stood offshore ahead, looming through the mist. *Oh, Lord above, let it be a ship!* William prayed, suddenly longing so keenly for a dry berth, dry clothes, order, furniture, oaken walls, biscuits, salt, coffee, brandy— *brandy!*—that he did not care whether it was a British ship or French, Portagee or Chinee; it had been so long since he and his fine hardy fellows had been under roof and on wooden floors that for a moment now the thought of setting foot on a ship was as important as setting foot on the edge of the long-sought Pacific Ocean. "Pull, pull, boys!" he shouted at the paddlers.

It was a rock, not a ship. It was a pillar of dark stone fifty feet high and twenty thick, streaked with sea-fowl droppings, standing half a mile off the rocky shore. Eh, well, he thought, luxury later. First then let's us find that ocean.

He could hear something now, or thought he could, under the plashing of the waves against the prow: a deep, regular rush on the air, like the breathing of some immense leviathan beyond the haze.

"Listen! Y' hear it? That's the sound of the ocean, I'll swear it! We'll see the ocean now or tomorrow, I swear we will!" They found a shelf of boulder-strewn land under a high cliff, a niche where a spring poured down, just opposite the ship-shaped rock. By moving some wet-glistening stones, they were able to make enough space above the high-tide mark to pull the five dugouts up and secure them, and lay down their sleeping mats on the stones. There was no wood for a fire.

They huddled in the rain under the glossy dark cliff face and watched the water swirl and seethe just below their feet, in a hissing, howling world the colors of slate, putty and coal, with the stark pillar of rock fading in the fog, watching huge floating trees rise and fall on the swells, visited only by ghostly gulls hanging in the wind with their catlike calls. But William stood facing the west, and whenever someone would come by him he would say, "I swear sometimes I can see the rollers out yonder."

"I can't," Lewis said, "and you can't either. You're just wanting to, as I am."

But the men were convinced that they could see it too, or sense it, the great, salty expanse out there, and there was no doubt that they were hearing it, and they were happy, very happy, despite their misery.

And William wrote in his notebook that evening, hunching over to keep the rain from washing away the ink:

Ocian in view! O! the joy!

*Great joy in camp we are in view of the OCIAN, this
great Pacific Octean which we been so long anxious to See
and the roreing or noise made by the waves brakeing on the
rockey Shores (as I suppose) may be heard distictly.*

But morning showed that he had supposed wrongly. The
could see farther to the westward now, and could discern mo
spits and headlands beyond the surging waters. They were still i
the estuary of the Columbia. So they launched the canoes aga
at nine o'clock and paddled westward through the rain, whic
continued off and on throughout the day. Evening found the
searching for a landing place on another rocky point, most of th
men seasick from the rising and falling and rolling of the canoe
everybody wet to the skin and disagreeable. And they still we
not on the Pacific.

The wind had increased all day, and the waves were so hig
now that there was desperate danger of being dashed against th
steep cliffs. At last they found an indentation in the cliffs,
small, rocky shelf where high tides had thrown perhaps
hundred huge drift logs—gigantic wet gray trees, bigger than ar
trees anyone had seen before. In a pelting rain and howling win
they made a perilous landing, unloaded the tossing canoes, an
drew them up onto the shelf amid the tangle of driftwood.

It was a wretched place for a camp. Their backs were against
stone cliff too steep to climb, and there was not enough lev
ground clear of the tide to lie on or place the baggage. There wa
no source of fresh water. The men had to find places to sit or l
down on and among the pile of logs, and there was not enoug
small wood or dry wood to fabricate shelters or make a satisfa
tory fire. "This is no camp," moaned Pryor, "it ain't hardly
seagull perch!" But there was nothing to be done about it. Th
waves now were pounding against the rocks, bursting into gra
foam, so powerfully that it was impossible to escape from th
rugged niche.

"Pray we don't have to stay here long," William shouted
Lewis over the roaring of the waves as the last gray light fade
"It was a flood tide put these logs here where we sit, and I do
relish being here when the tide's in next!"

But it seemed they had no choice. A winter storm was buil
ing on the coast they had come so far to reach, and they cou
neither go on to the coast nor retreat inland. The immedia

48

IN THE MOUTH
OF THE COLUMBIA RIVER
November 9, 1805

THE NEXT MORNING THE CANOES WERE FOUND ENTANGLED among the drift logs and filled with water by the last high tide, and they groaned and rubbed against the logs, the strain threatening to crush or split them. The men worked much of the morning in water to their shoulders, prying and moving them to keep them safe until the tide receded. That was only the start of the day. William wrote in the damp pages of his battered journal:

November 9th Saturday 1805

Wind hard from the South, and rained hard all the fore part of the day, at 2 oClock P M the flood tide came in accompanied with emence waves and heavy winds, floated the trees and Drift on which we Camped and tossed them about in such a manner as to endanger the canoes verry much, with every exertion and the Strictest attention by every individual of the party was scercely sufficient to Save our Canoes from being crushed by those monsterous trees maney of them nearly 200 feet long and from 4 to 7 feet through. our camp entirely under water dureing the hight of the tide, every man as wet as water could make them all the last night and to day all day, at 4 oClock P M the wind Shifted about to the S. W. and blew with great violence imediately from the Ocean for about two hours, notwithstanding the disagreeable Situation of our party all wet and cold (and one which they have experienced for Several days past) they are chearfull and anxious to See further

*into the Ocian, The Water of the river being too Salt to use
we are obliged to make use of rain water*

*At this dismal point we must Spend another night as the
wind & waves are too high to proceed.*

November 10th Sunday 1805

*rained verry hard the greater part of the last night &
continues this morning. . . .The logs on which we lie is all
on flote every high tide. The rain continues all day we are
all wet also our bedding and maney other articles. . . . .nothing to eate but Pounded fish.*

November 11th Monday 1805

*A hard rain all the last night, dureing the last tide the
logs on which we lay was all on float, Sent out Jo Fields to
hunt, he Soon returned and informed us that the hills was
So. high & Steep, & thick with undergroth and fallen Timber that he could not get out*

*the wind verry high from the S.W. with most tremen-
dious waves brakeing with great violence against the
Shores, rain falling in torrents, we are all wet as usial—
and our Situation is truly a disagreeable one; the great
quantities of rain has loosened the Stones on the hill Sides:
and the Small stones fall down upon us, our canoes at one
place at the mercy of the waves, our baggage in another;
and our selves and party Scattered on floating logs and
Such dry Spots as can be found on the hill sides, and cri-
vicies of the rocks.*

White light. A crash like cannon.

Heart thumping, William started out of his stupor. The spra
from the pounding waves was still soaking his blanket; the win
was howling louder than ever; the huge logs were still grindin
and groaning. Lightning illuminated the swollen water and th
whitecaps offshore, then another thunderclap rolled over th
water and was swallowed by the pulse of the surf. Somethin
hard was clattering against the cliff above him and the log o
which he lay: *Hailstones! Damnation! What next?*

He could hear men's voices in the thundering darkness. H
pulled his watch from his pocket and waited for another ligh
ning flash. *Three in the morning.* He put the watch away an
shielded his face with his arm to fend off the hailstones an
waited for another lightning bolt to show him how the boa

were. They were still there; the boat watch sat precariously on a gigantic root bole, blanket over his head, watching them, hailstones beating on him. William wanted to get up and do something, *something*, but in this blackness it was dangerous for anyone to move. Another flash of lightning showed the men stirring, shifting their wrapped bodies on their hard beds of log and boulder. William knew they were all as wet and shivery-cold as he was. Sleep was impossible now. There was nothing to do but hang on till daylight and look the situation over by lightning flash.

At six o'clock, the hail was still pounding. He thought he could hear little Pompey crying, a shrill wisp of human voice in the shrieking, booming, hissing, rumbling tumult. Outside his blanket now the darkness was graying; all was motion: a gray, marching, swelling turbulence, the waves higher than ever. A violent shudder shook him and left him feeling hollow, soulless, and he admitted to himself for the first time that he and these people of his were utterly, irrevocably at the mercy of the elements now, in deadly danger, and that for once there was not a thing that he or Meriwether Lewis could do to lessen that danger.

I reckon they're all praying now, he thought. *Lord in Heaven, we've come four thousand mile in peace to look at that ocean and to add to the knowledge and prosperity of men. We've not hurt a one of thy native children, and we've kept the best of brotherhood amongst ourselves. There's no set of souls I've ever seen that's better than these. Now, if in thy Divine wrath some souls has got to be destroyed, let them be some crew o' heathen sea-pirates out of Algier, or, or those treacherous Teton Sioux back at Bad River, or . . . or . . . If nothing else, the Spaniard king and all his blaggard ministers. But not these of ours—as fine a people as ever did walk in thy garden. And not my particular friend Lewis! Not such a rare head and heart as his! Nor Janey. Oh, she's a heathen, I know, but no gentler or braver a woman have I ever seen!*

Spare us, O Lord, and I'll serve you well all the days of my life. My man York I'll make free, as any brave man ought to be. And that little innocent boy Pomp. Lord, I'll take him back and raise him an educated Christian so's his life won't be wasted. Heavenly Father, we have walked through thy great garden peaceable and sober—generally—with proper respect and wonder. We've writ a million words to tell all men of your wonders we've seen. Deliver us safe Lord and this wilderness will flourish under the care of an industrious Christian people. I swear it, Our Father. You have my word on it as a Clark!

THE SKY LIGHTENED, THE HAIL STOPPED, AND THE CAPTAINS could make their way amid the drift to look after all their people, who were wretched and soaked and hungry and fatigued, but all still alive and safe. Then from the southwest a huge, low, black cloud came running, bringing darkness and sheets of rain. The rain fell and blew in blinding sheets all morning, and the southwesterly wind coming straight up the estuary from the sea piled the waves higher and higher. These gray hills of water roared onto the shelf and over the bobbing canoes, burst foam-white against the rocks and among the drift logs, sending spray twenty feet high, driving everyone into a huddle against the very base of the cliff, where they set their jaw muscles and hung onto each other and their baggage and watched the giant logs shudder and lurch on the force of the surf, and waited.

They waited until about noon, when the tide was out. "Now," Lewis shouted, "we've got to get off this point and into the lee somewhere! Colter, make your way along there and see if there's a cove of some kind! Rest of you, come with me!"

He led them over the logs and down to the boats. They lifted large rocks into the canoes to sink them, to stop the lurching and bobbing that threatened to break them into splinters. Colter returned in fifteen minutes; he had found a small brook-mouth, a quarter of a mile back, choked with brush and driftwood and no bigger than their present niche, but at least out of the direct road of the wind and waves.

Now they all took up their sodden, rotting bedding, some tools, and their last bag of molding fish, and, taking advantage of the low tide, waded around the base of the cliff to the new camp.

Late that day Privates Bratton, Gibson, and Willard volunteered to take the Indian canoe and try to go around the point and look for a safe harbor. But the waves tossed them so violently that they could not make any headway, and they put in at the cove, panting and puking and glad to be alive.

That evening William forced his way through briars and brush a few yards up the brook, where he speared three salmon trout. It was the first fresh food in five days.

THE NEXT MORNING, WILLIAM CLIMBED THE STEEP RAVINE along the tumbling brook, climbing three miles through dense thickets of pine and thorn bushes, often pulling himself up by his hands. He reached the top of the spur of the mountain fatigued, bleeding from thorn-scratches, and stood on the ridge in the rain trying to make out the ocean or a safe harbor. But he could see only the treetops below him, and curtains of rain beyond them, and clouds. Even through the hush of rain and whiff of wet wind in his ears, he could hear the measured thunder of the waves on the cliffs below.

By the time he had returned to the camp, both sleeves of his rotted elkhide hunting shirt had fallen off through his exertions, and the back had split from collar to waist.

November 14th Thursday 1805

rained all the last night without intermission, and this morning. wind blows verry hard, but our situation is Such that we cannot tell from what point it comes. one of our canoes is much broken by the waves dashing it against the rocks.

The rain &c. which has continued without a longer intermition than 2 hours at a time for ten days past has distroyed the robes and rotted one half of the fiew clothes the party has, perticularley the leather clothes if we have cold weather before we can kill & Dress Skins for clothing the bulk of the party will Suffer verry much.

Colter, Willard, and Shannon had been sent out in the carved canoe the day before, disappearing every three or four seconds in the troughs of huge waves, finally vanishing altogether. They had not come back, and the party had spent the night praying for them, with little hope. Now, suddenly, a shout went up:

"There's Colter! Up yonder!"

HE CAME FROM ABOVE, SLIDING DOWN THE RAVINE, HALF-naked, grinning, his white skin stained with rain-washed blood from briar cuts.

His news gave them heart. Not far around the embattered point, he said, he had found a good sand beach and a good harbor in the mouth of a creek near two Indian lodges. Willard and Shannon had stayed there and he had come back overland, being unable to bring the canoe back around. Now everyone was excited, hopeful; they might escape from here yet.

Capt. Lewis concluded to proceed on by land & find if possible the white people the Indians say is below and ex-

amine if a Bay is Situated near the mouth of this river as laid down by Vancouver in which we expect if there is white traders to find them &c. at 3 oClock he Set out with 4 men Drewyer Jos. & Ru. Fields & R. Frasure, in one of our large canoes and 5 men to set them around the point on the Sand Beech. this canoe returned nearly filled with water at Dark which it received by the waves dashing into it on its return, haveing landed Capt. Lewis & his party Safe on the Sand beech.

The next afternoon the wind diminished, and William shouted the troops into action. They went around to the windward camp, raised the sunken canoes, and loaded them within minutes, piled in, and with a cheer quit the tiny shelf on which they had spent the most miserable and frustrating week of their lives. They paddled out around the blustery point, slammed through the pitching waves, stomachs soaring and swooping; they paddled with arms weakened by hunger and cold and cramping but rejuvenated by this hopeful work; they beat slowly westward around the dark mountain of the coast, and then veered northwestward as did the shoreline. Two large wooded islands and a peninsula lay a few miles to the westward, and beyond that peninsula, surely, was the ocean.

And then as a swell lifted the canoe high, William saw due north of him the sandy beach and the Indian houses. Cruzatte kept the lead canoe quartering into the waves until almost straight offshore from the beach, then swung her about to put the seas on the stern quarter. The other canoes followed without rolling over, and now with a shout they dug with their paddles and raced for the pale sand.

They hit the sloping beach in a froth of surf, men leaping out shouting to haul them up before they could be somersaulted by a following breaker, and the first thing they saw was young George Shannon running down the beach toward them with five Indian men alongside. He laughed and shook hands with William, congratulated him on the safe landing, and brought him up to date on the news.

These Indians were real rogues, he said; they had stolen his and Willard's guns right out from under their heads while they slept, but Captain Lewis had arrived immediately thereafter and frightened them into returning the rifles. Now Captain Lewis and his scouts had gone on; they were following the bay around and would try to cross the peninsula to the ocean, Shannon said, pointing toward that rugged headland. They were to return here tomorrow. From what he had seen and from what the natives said, there were no ships in the vicinity now, but maybe Captain Lewis would learn otherwise.

The Indian town was deserted, but its houses were so heavily populated by fleas that they could not be occupied. So the party appropriated some boards, scrubbed them in sea water, and built a camp above the beach, gathered firewood, sent hunters out for fowl and deer, and with a few hasty prayers of thanks for their safety, prepared to enjoy its first warm, dry camp in nearly two weeks.

November 15th Friday 1805

I informed those Indians all of which understood some English that if they stole our guns &c the men would certainly shute them, I treated them with great distance, & the sentinal which was over our Baggage allarmed them verry much, they all Promised not to take any things, and if any thing was taken by the squars & bad boys to return them &c.   the waves became verry high   Evening fare & pleasant, our men all comfortable in the camps they have made of the boards they found at the town above

Captain Lewis walked into the camp at midmorning the next day with his men, and he was smiling, smiling, but with a peculiar sadness in his face and a faraway look in his eyes. He put his arms around William and hugged him hard, and he said, "I saw it. I saw the Pacific."

When he stood back, there were tears in his eyes.

WILLIAM DIRECTED ALL THE MEN WHO WISHED TO SEE THE ocean to prepare themselves to set out early the next morning, and they started up the beach after breakfast. The sea was too high for canoes, so they would walk the way Captain Lewis had gone. It was a curving route of about fifteen miles around the bay, and they came along under the cloudy sky in a single file, Sergeants Ordway and Pryor, the Fields brothers, George Shannon, William Bratton, John Colter, Peter Weiser, Labiche—and Charbonneau, who had ordered Sacajawea to remain in camp and "keep my son warm."

They went around the bay where the Indians had said ships usually anchored, and there were no ships here. Above the bay they found *Meriwether Lewis* carved in a tree trunk, and William smiled. He and his men carved their names under it. And then they went on along the rough trail, passing high, rocky hills, and streams and ponds. Gulls flew everywhere in the gray sky. In the afternoon, as the marchers neared the peninsula, Reuben Fields suddenly raised his rifle and fired skyward; everyone turned in time to see something bigger than a man fall out of the sky. It was a condor. The men stretched out the wings of the huge, buzzard-like creature and they measured nine and a half feet from tip to tip.

In the late afternoon they climbed through thick timber toward the ridge of the peninsula. As they climbed, William could hear the pounding of a heavier surf beyond the ridge, and he could smell the seaweed, and his heartbeat sped up.

The tops of the pine trees above were bent and waving in the wind, waving hard in that wind off the western ocean. William swallowed and blinked as he climbed, and the men following him had stopped talking and laughing now. Behind and two hundred feet below was the bay, and now just in front of him was the crest of the hill, and just below the crest the trees ended, and coarse, blowing grass waved against the sky, and the roar of the surf was very loud now.

Four thousand miles, William thought, *and now five more paces*.

And then he was on top with the salt wind blowing in his face; he was on top looking down a steep, open expanse of rippling brown grass falling away below him to meet an infinity of silvery-gray water coming in ranks of spume-topped waves from some invisible horizon lost in winter mist, waves marching and marching in to explode roaring and white upon the huge dark brown boulders at the foot of the long slope.

The ten men had come onto the brow of the hill beside him, and nobody passed in front of him. They stood with their mouths open, their chests heaving, each silent and wrapped in his own thoughts.

They stood there for a long time, speechless, looking down past the white-churning shallows of the Columbia's mouth to the rugged gray mountains fading down the coast toward the south, and they turned and looked at the jagged dark mountains vanishing into the mist to the north of them, and then back down at the raging, pewter-and-white infinity of water in front of them, and for once, not one of them had the boldness to make the first joke or utter the first oath. Some of them sat down in the grass after a while with their forearms locked around their knees, and they sat there and watched as William started walking down the long steep hill through the blowing grass toward the shore with his rifle cradled in his left arm. They watched him grow smaller and smaller, his tattered elkskin flapping around him, his freckled arms bare, and no one followed him yet. They saw him reach up with his right hand and take off his fur hat, and the last thing they saw before he disappeared under the grassy brow of the hill was his red hair.

WILLIAM SAT DOWN IN THE LAST MARGIN OF GRASS AT THE bottom of the hill and watched the great brown rocks in the ocean's edge appear and disappear, appear and disappear in the white froth, and he tasted the salt water that sprayed on his face, and felt the ground tremble under him, this very margin of a continent that he had crossed on foot. He could feel all that land behind him, those thousands of miles of land, mountains, plains, deserts, forests, more mountains and fields, all the way back to St. Louis, to Louisville, to Albermarle, to Caroline, to Williamsburg on the James River, all the way back to the beginning, when the first Clark had come ashore.

He sat here now in a tumult of noise, all alone, and thought of Brother George sitting on his porch at Clarksville. And then he thought of Lewis sitting here alone probably just like this two days before, his life's goal accomplished.

He licked some salt from the stubbled corner of his lip. He wished Charbonneau had let Sacajawea come to see this. He wondered what Judy Hancock was doing at this moment. He wondered whether his mother and father, from where they were, could see him here.

One sunbeam through the clouds silvered the sea far out.

It's all done, he thought. *This is the end of the land.* His eyes smarted. He sniffed.

He remembered the hug Lewis had given him, and he understood why there had been tears in his eyes.

I wish Cruzatte was here, he thought. *With his fiddle.*

They camped there that night, and the sea-sound put them to sleep. The next day, to go just a little farther than Lewis had, William walked above a long sandy coast that curved northwestward toward a high, bold, lonely point of land jutting into the Pacific twenty miles away.

That evening, November 19th, he wrote in his journal:

> this point I have taken the Liberty of Calling after my particular friend Lewis
>
> I proceeded on the sandy coast and marked my name on a Small pine, the Day of the month & year. &c. and returned to the foot of the hill

873

Epilogue

LOCUST GROVE,

KENTUCKY

Christmas, 1806

WILLIAM CLARK, THE YOUNGEST SON, SAT AT THE HEAD OF
the table in the dining room of the Croghan mansion, basking in
the light of forty candles and the warmth of his family. He put
down his napkin and leaned back, wheezing, to let Lucy's servants take away his plates.

He sighed. He looked to his right, where George sat gazing at
him with something like worship in his eyes, then to his left,
where Jonathan and Edmund sat smiling at him and fingering
their glasses of port, then on down the long table at his sisters
and their husbands: Annie and Owen Gwathmey, Lucy and Bill
Croghan, Fanny and Dennis Fitzhugh.

Now Bill Croghan, the host, stood up at the far end of the
table, glass in hand.

"Dear ones, I propose we drink a toast to our celebrated young
brother," he said, "before we adjourn to the ballroom for those
wonders up there." All the others scooted their chairs back, murmuring approval, stood and raised their glasses. Bill Croghan
looked around at them all, and then at William, and said:

"To our Billy, who made an odyssey to the land's end and
then came back to us."

"Hear, hear!"

"To Billy!"

They drank. Then George raised his glass again.

"To Billy," he said, "who's giving me the happiest days I've
had since '79."

They nodded, and drank again.

"To Billy," said Jonathan, "who was too young for our war,
but found glory in peacetime."

"Hear! Hear!"

"Yes! Great! Great, great!"

Again they drank.

"One more," cried Edmund. He was blinking. His chin was

874

crumpled. He held his glass toward William and, looking straight at him, said:

"To our brother Billy, who's supposed to be feasting at the White House now with Cap'n Lewis and the President and Cabinet, but who, God Bless his great heart, knew it's more important—" his voice caught— "to be with his family on this Day of Our Lord."

"Bravo!"

"Hey!"

"Merry Christmas to us all!"

And so they all drank, with brimming eyes, and then remained standing, waiting for him to reply.

In the hallway outside the dining room many footsteps were shuffling: that horde of his nephews and nieces, great-nephews and great-nieces, who had finished their Christmas feast in another room and now were lining up to go upstairs and see the promised wonders awaiting them there. Lucy had arranged the whole occasion as if it were an affair of state.

William stood, tall, uniformed in blue wool and gold braid, leathery-faced, eyes full of distance, and cleared his throat.

"I'm, I'm about to bust, and I don't know whether it's because my belly's so full, or my heart."

"Ahhhh," said Fanny, softly.

"I can't help thinking o' my *last* Christmas," William went on, "because o' the contrast. Christmas Day of '05, in that little fort we'd built out there, on the coast of the Pacific. Built in three weeks o' ceaseless rain, it was. And there we had last Christmas, all covered with mildew and fleas. Eat scrawny elk and moldy fish and wappatoo roots, without a gram or dram of . . . of flour, or salt, or sugar, or even *liquor*. Imagine a Christmas with none o' *those*! But we made a celebration of it, all the same. Those boys, those God-blessed boys of ours, they sang us carols in the rain, gave us little gifts o' this and that. Lewis and I, all we had to give them was near th' last of the tobacco. But they deemed that plenty, and were merry the whole day long." He paused and glanced at George, who was alternately nodding and shaking his head, eyes moist and focused only on the far past. "It's just like ye told me, George," William said to him. "Give 'em a joke, and a song, and a dream o' glory."

George and William stood looking at each other now and nodding, and they were both thinking about a kind of camaraderie that the others could only try to imagine.

And then William turned back to Lucy and Bill Croghan, raised his glass to them, and said:

"That Christmas I dreamed all day of a Christmas Day and a family feast like this. My host and hostess, this is the best one ever. But," he added, putting the glass on the table, "I reckon I'll always remember that one, fleas and all, as a good second best. Now, by Heaven!" He clapped his hands together loudly. "All follow me up to the ballroom! I've something up there for you all to see, and a thousand tales to tell!"

THEY GASPED AND MURMURED, ADULTS AND CHILDREN alike, when William swung open the big ballroom doors. Into the second-floor hallway poured a flood of candlelight and a profusion of musky odors.

The ballroom was lit by fifty candles and a Yule log fire. All William's trophies from the voyage had been laid out like a museum exhibit, all manner of things such as no one had ever seen. There were antelope horns, and hides covered with Indian paintings. There were poggamoggan war clubs and bone-bows, shields and stone-tipped spears; there were weasel-fur tippets and intricate baskets and waterproof Clatsop straw hats; there were curled horns of mountain goats, and stuffed birds of strange plumage, and mountain-lion skins, and Indian jewelry made from bear claws and teeth and colored quills and stones and bones and seashells and dyed feathers and glazed ceramic beads; there were snake rattles and rodent skulls. There were seal-skins and otter-pelt robes, the finest fur anyone had ever touched. There were grizzly bear skins as big as ox-hides. And with every one of these articles from the great Western wilderness, there was a tale of how it was got. For hours, till almost midnight, the family prowled among the exotic articles and listened in wonderment to William's tales.

"This I got from an island in the Columbia when we started back last March. Named it Fanny's Island, I did, and ye may guess in whose honor.

"I've set up a company in St. Louis, Jonathan. The Missouri Fur Company is its name. Some of my old boys are involved. I know you're disappointed there's no waterway to the Western Sea, but listen: furs from out there will make us rich, and trade will open up in that space just like it did here after George won the war.

"Here, look at this sea-otter robe. We spent half a day barterin' for that. By then, though, we hardly had anything left to barter with but brass buttons off our uniforms. I swear those Clatsops

876

wouldn't ha' given up this robe ever, till Janey our squaw took off her precious belt o' blue beads—the one we'd give 'er after she saved all our cargo in that capsize I spoke of—and let us offer 'em that. That dear lady! She prized that belt over everything she owned! We tried to compensate 'er for it, gave her a blue coat, and she took it and tried to smile, but she cried days for the loss o' that belt. That girl, I swear, would do just anything for me—for us." He paused. "Hand me that passel o' white furs yonder with the black tail-tips. Thank'ee. This is what Janey gave me as my gift that Christmas. Ever felt anything so perfectly soft?"

They looked at him curiously and wondered just what that squaw-girl might have meant to him. It was true he was going to go on to Fincastle after the holidays and ask for Judy Hancock's hand again, but they had all heard that something in his voice and seen that something in his eyes. George looked at him most keenly, and thought for a moment of his black-haired Teresa, who had loved him without hope in the midst of his own great adventure, a quarter of a century ago.

William told of the Corps' eventful six-month return voyage, during which he had doctored hundreds of sick Indians in return for food and assistance, and had split off with a party to explore the length of the Yellowstone River, while the proud and moody Lewis suffered the pain and indignity of being shot through the buttocks by the near-sighted, one-eyed Cruzatte, who mistook him for an elk. He told how they had gathered a large contingent of Mandan and Arikara and Osage chiefs on the way back down the Missouri, chiefs eager to go to Washington and meet the President. And he told of their triumphant, gun-popping return to St. Louis in September, long after they had been generally given up for dead. The family crooned with joy at the telling of this, and for the hundredth time smothered him with hugs. Because they, too, had almost come to believe he was dead.

But what the family could not hear enough about was the ferocious grizzly, its temper, its toughness. They kept returning to the huge silvery-yellow hides, stroking them, responding with shivery laughter to his tales of the expedition's wild bear-shoots and pursuits.

"Just giant bears, then," George chuckled. "No mammoths, eh?"

"No mammoths," William replied. "And if there had a-been, there might not be now, as our boys could've eat a whole one at every meal!

"Now," he exclaimed, turning to the family, "let's divide up this booty amongst ourselves!"

Then, late in the night, when only the grown-ups remained in the ballroom, George found William standing at a window, gazing westward into the black of night outside. He clumped over to him on his cane and put a hand on his shoulder. Their silhouettes were on the reflecting window-glass, the two of them, tall and big. George said nothing, but William answered the question that was in his mind.

"I was thinking o' Ma and Pa lyin' over there at Mulberry Hill, thinking how they would have liked this Christmas. And, thinkin' o' them made me think o' poor Sergeant Floyd, in his grave out there on a bluff above the river, with nothin' but the wolves howlin' for a Christmas song."

"Eh, well. At least ye can't blame yourself for that. I like what Jonathan said. You got glory, and no man o' yours died for it on your account. I had that same satisfaction after Vincennes, and I'll say this, Billy: You and I been uncommon lucky. Not many soldiers get to come out with their honor good *and* no ghosts on their conscience." They stood there thinking about that, and then George said, "I'm so proud o' you, Billy, I could . . ." He blinked and shook his head instead of trying to find words emphatic enough.

After a while William said, "D'ye remember the days when *you'd* come home from th' West and tell *me* all the stories?"

They grunted then to clear their throats, and stood there together looking westward into the night beyond the window panes, while Fanny and Edmund stood behind them counting the bullet holes in a grizzly bear's hide, and the clock began striking midnight.

AND, SO:

That's how they did what they did, all my sons. My sons and John's, I should say.

A family story never ends, as ye know, but a body's got to stop tellin' it at such-such a place. My story goes on, sure, and I could tell you how my children's children and my children's grandchildren and my grandchildren's grandchildren came to fill up this country from sea to shining sea. I could tell you who they are and what they've done and where they live, and how the blood of the Rogerses and the Clarks has come to run in people's veins in every corner of this country. I could tell you all that, but any old woman who was young when this country was young can tell you the same about her blood, so I shan't go on with that. I could brag about all my offshoots, about who became governors and who became heroes, who became judges, and who went to Congress, and who founded towns, about who became authors and who became actors. I could tell you of some who got rich but in soul were no-account, and I could tell you of some known as ne'er-do-wells who were grand as lords in their hearts. And, I could tell ye of some who were just ordinary folk; there's some o' those in every family line.

But any old woman can tell you the same, so I shan't. No, I simply chose to tell only of those that I myself carried and nursed, for they are the ones whom I made what they were.

John and I did, I should say.

Well, they've all come back to us now, leaving their mortal bones in the soil of this continent that they had walked, run, climbed, crawled, waded, swum, paddled, and rode across, always out in front. And there lie those bones: Johnny's, back in old Caroline County in Virginia, where he was born. Dickie's, buried probably in the silt of a river bottom in Indiana. Jonathan's and Edmund's and George's, side by side on a slope on the Kentucky side of the Ohio, and William's, on a bluff overlooking the Mississippi, where he'd said he wanted to lie.

And here I end my family's story. I pray ye, think on it, for there's no family ever did more to shape this land. And when you see a Clarksville or a Clarksburgh, or a Clark County or a Clark River or park or National Forest anywhere across this land, as y' will, all across, from sea to shining sea, you'll know what Clarks they're speakin' of: my sons.

Mine and John's, I should say.

ABOUT THE AUTHOR

James Alexander Thom lives in the southern Indiana hill country, near Bloomington, in an antique log cabin.

Jim Thom has been a U.S. Marine, a newspaper and magazine editor, a freelance writer, and a member of the Indiana University Journalism School faculty. He now devotes all his time to writing.

Jim Thom researches his American historical novels meticulously, traveling, tracking down primary sources, and even walking in the footsteps of his characters. To convey the experiences of the frontier soldiers in *Long Knife,* he mastered the use of 18th century tools and weapons, and waded the icy flood waters of the Wabash. He walked, climbed, and camped along much of the New River gorge in preparation for writing *Follow the River.* And he traveled the entire route of the Lewis and Clark Expedition while writing *From Sea to Shining Sea.*